BAAL'S HEART - BOX SET VOL. I

BY BEY DECKARD

CONTAINING:

CAGED: LOVE AND TREACHERY ON THE HIGH SEAS #1

SACRIFICED: HEART BEYOND THE SPIRES #2

FATED: BLOOD AND REDEMPTION #3

CAREENED: WINTER SOLSTICE IN MADIERUS #3.5

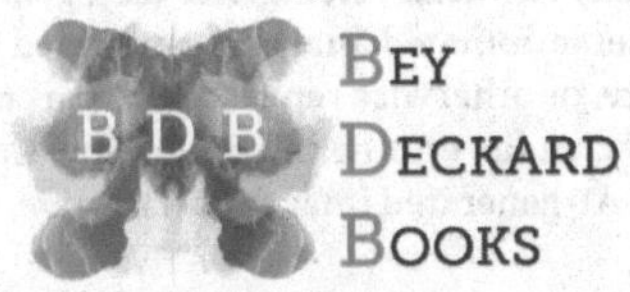

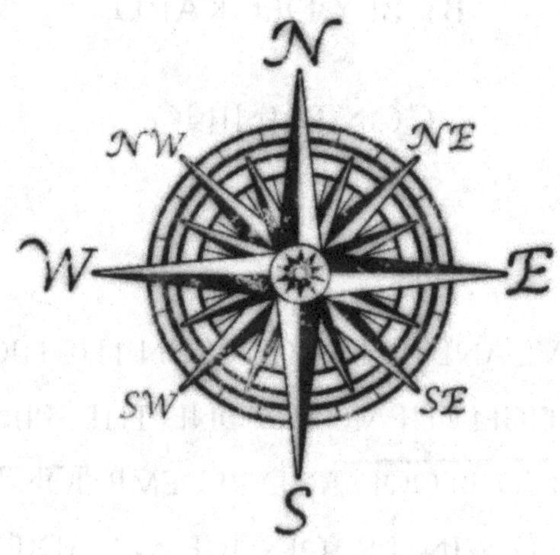

Copyright 2014, 2015, 2016, 2022 Bey Deckard
Published by Bey Deckard
Edited by Quiethouse Editing
All rights reserved

ISBN: 978-1-989250-17-4

This book is sold subject to the condition that it shall not, by way of trade or otherwise, be lent, resold, hired out or otherwise circulated without the publisher's prior consent in any form of binding or cover other than that in which it is published and without a similar condition including this condition being imposed on the subsequent purchaser.

The author does not consent to any Artificial Intelligence (AI), generative AI, large language model, machine learning, chatbot, or other automated analysis, generative process, or replication program to reproduce, mimic, remix, summarize, or otherwise replicate any part of this creative work, via any means: print, graphic, sculpture, multimedia, audio, or other medium. No part of this book has been created using AI-generated images or narrative.

CONTENTS

CAGED: LOVE AND TREACHERY ON THE HIGH SEAS

SACRIFICED: HEART BEYOND THE SPIRES

PART ONE

PART TWO

FATED: BLOOD AND REDEMPTION

CAREENED: WINTER SOLSTICE IN MADIERUS

AUDIOBOOKS & SOUNDTRACKS

AUDIOBOOKS

Baal's Heart is now available for the first time ever in audiobook format. Relive the adventures of Jon, Tom, and Baltsaros, now exquisitely narrated by the talented Michael Ferraiuolo. Find them here: https://geni.us/beysbooks

SOUNDTRACKS

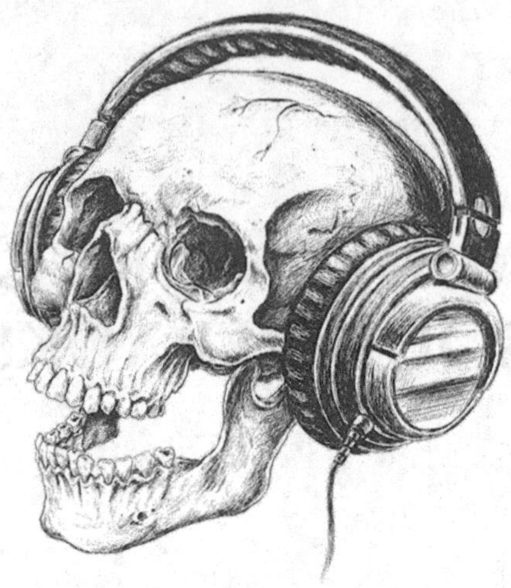

Find the soundtracks for the *Baal's Heart* books here: https://geni.us/soundtracks

BEY DECKARD

Gaged

Love and Treachery on the High Seas
Baal's Heart I

CHAPTER I

PORTSMOUTH

The cure for anything is salt water: sweat, tears or the sea.

— ISAK DINESEN

Jon stood in the shadow of the short wall, hands on hips, looking down over the steeply piled rocks of the harbour to the grey-green waters beyond. There weren't many boats out there, just a few navy frigates near the mouth, some fishing vessels, and what looked like a small corvette just entering the harbour.

He frowned; squinting and shading his blue eyes with a pale hand, Jon saw that the ship wasn't flying a flag.

That's weird.

The wind blew at his dark-brown hair, making the curls dance around his head as he rubbed his eyes to take a better look. He narrowed his gaze against the bright, late-afternoon sun; the black and red corvette was a gorgeous, sleek, three-masted ship. Jon could see the crew, like scurrying ants, running across the deck preparing to anchor down. Jon wished again that he had brought one of the long-sights with him today. He enjoyed watching the boats come in even though the thought of being on one horrified him.

So many people in such a confined space...

The crew of this ship looked to be no more than thirty men, but that was still more than Jon thought he would be able to stomach. As his eyes scanned the approaching vessel, he spotted a lone man standing on the quarterdeck. The tall figure had his arms crossed over his chest; the tails of his long, black coat flapped in the wind behind him as he stood stock-still, supervising the flurry of activity on the deck below.

The captain.

As Jon watched, the man slowly raised his head and looked up at the hill high above the harbour. Though Jon couldn't clearly see the captain's face, he suddenly had the uncomfortable feeling that the man was looking directly at him. Jon's skin prickled with the uneasy thought, and he rubbed his hands over his arms.

He stood with his back to the ancient, crumbling stone wall—dubbed the "first wall" for its dubious role as the first line of defence—and should have been hidden from sight at that distance; there was no way that the man on the ship below could see him.

It isn't possible. You're just imagining things again.

Jon ran a shaky hand through his hair and thought it best to get out of the sun; his head was already starting to pound, and he was beginning to get strange ideas. With a last look over his shoulder at the corvette and the tall, dark man, Jon made his way back up the hill towards the crumbling castle he called home.

The door of the stable banged shut behind him. Jon leaned against one of the stalls with a hand on his head, his eyes closed. *The headaches are getting worse,* he thought desperately; the debilitating pain was becoming an almost daily thing. Jon coughed into his hand, a sudden shiver taking him. Taking a few deep breaths and clenching his jaw, he forced himself to stand straight. He had to get back to his room before the brunt of the agony hit him or else his stepfather would find him collapsed in the hallway again; it was not an experience he wanted to repeat.

Just as he was taking an unsteady step, something came hurtling out of the darkness. With a great bound, the brown and black shape flew through the air and crashed into Jon, knocking him flat on his back to the dirty, straw-strewn floor. He yelled out in surprise and pain. Fending off sharp teeth, he struggled against the creature that was attacking him. A large, pink tongue left a wet trail along the side of his face, and he smiled slightly despite the pain in his head.

"All right, all right, Brutus. You got me. Now… enough. Stop it! Arggghh!" He grimaced and shoved at the giant mastiff's chest, trying to dislodge him.

The dog stopped trying to drown Jon in saliva and sat back on its haunches with an almost-human look of concern on its face and let out a low whine.

Jon groaned and rubbed his temple with a trembling hand; the dog's enthusiastic greeting had torn new holes in the decaying fabric of his composure. These surprise attacks were a habit of Brutus's that Jon had been trying to break him of, with little success, since the night he found the huge dog wandering loose on the high road. He sat up slowly and ran his hand over Brutus's coarse brown and black-spotted fur.

"Shh. You're hurting my head," he whispered, wincing.

The dog stopped whining, and its mouth hung open, pink tongue lolling as he stared lovingly at his master.

Jon sighed and shook his head as he used the dog's sturdy frame to help him to his feet. Standing at nearly four and a half feet tall when on all fours, Brutus was one of the largest mastiffs that Jon had ever seen. His colouring was incredibly unusual too;

unlike the dark-brown or black mastiffs that were raised at the castle, Brutus was a light caramel brown with strange, dark patches. He was a gorgeous animal and Jon's closest companion.

After patting the stable dust from his fawn-coloured leather pants, man and dog walked slowly past the empty stalls to the small castle entrance used by the stable master and climbed the stairs to the apartment Jon shared with the head of the castle guard.

The rooms of the small apartment were sparsely furnished, and the walls were barren except for the family crest on an old, moth-eaten tapestry that hung over the small breakfast table.

He shuffled through the empty front room to his tiny bedroom in the back, which was barely bigger than the cot shoved against the wall. Just as he was finally laying his head down on the pillow, he heard the door open and the heavy footfalls of his stepfather enter the room beyond.

"Jon?" The gruff voice was heavy with irritation. The old soldier's fuse was shorter than ever these days. Despite Jon having no control over his strange malady, he was constantly admonished for shirking his duties.

"I'm here, Reginald," he said, trying to raise his voice.

Brutus lifted his head from his great paws and turned his gaze towards the door just as the portly man crossed the threshold.

When he saw Jon lying on his bed, sickly pale and swallowing against his rising nausea, Reginald let out an exasperated sigh. His dark brows came down over his eyes, and he crossed his arms over his chest.

"You went out when you were supposed to be resting, didn't you? Goddammit, Jon, you're no good to me when you're like this," he said angrily.

Jon pressed his knuckles against his closed eyes, making strange, red and white shapes dance in his vision.

"I thought the sea air would help. It *used* to help. I'm sorry, Reginald. I'll be all right for tomorrow," he said softly, without an ounce of conviction. With a headache this bad, there was little sleep in store for Jon. Without sleeping powders, he would toss and turn, drenched in sweat, and be trapped in nightmares until morning. He wished that he'd thought to go to the old man who mixed medicines for the castle. There was no way he could send his stepfather on his behalf.

The old soldier stared hard at Jon a moment longer.

"What you do *saves lives*, Jon. Don't you ever forget that. I need you to be able to do this," Reginald's deep voice rasped. He frowned when the younger man made no move to answer. Spinning on his heel, the captain of the guard left Jon alone to suffer in misery.

~

Jon stood on the deck of a ship. The wood beneath his soles felt smooth from years of constantly being polished under leatherlike, bare feet. He looked up. It was night. The moon was almost full above his head, and the stars were a shimmering net across the sky. Jon could hear creaking and the soft splashing of water against the hull. He smiled to himself and stroked his hand over the beautiful wood railing in front of him. When he felt something sticky, Jon raised his hand to his face. His palm was marked with something dark. Something that spiked the cool nighttime air with a metallic tang. Jon recoiled in horror and took a step back as a pale hand came up over the railing. The face that emerged out of the gloom was misshapen... The eyes were milky and the jaw hung open unnaturally. Jon took another step back. He recognized the decaying figure as the man he had most recently interrogated: a dockworker accused of rape and murder. The dead man hissed at him as it climbed up onto the deck. Jon tripped on something behind him and landed with a hard thump on the wet wood. Looking down, he realized he was sitting in a large puddle of blood. The shambling figure came closer as Jon crawled backwards into the pool of cold, viscous liquid. The deck felt like it was at an angle. His terror and nausea came to a head when he realized that the blood was pouring thickly over the side and the ship was being dragged down into a stinking sea of red.

Jon woke up and gasped; his breath caught in his throat, and he began to cough loudly, pawing at the phantoms that still lurked in his vision. Brutus was nudging at his arm, whining softly, as Jon tried to clear the bloody images out of his brain. He sat up slowly, his head still screaming in agony. Jon was soaked through; the old linen shirt and shorts he wore to sleep were sodden with sweat. He grimaced, teeth clenched, as a shiver took him. Jon was beginning to fear that something was horribly wrong with him. Another shudder shook his slight frame, and he nearly gagged with a coughing fit that overtook him.

When it finally seemed that the worst had passed, Jon struggled to pull the wet shirt over his head and then threw it in the corner of the room. He lay down and dragged the worn quilt up over his shoulder with a trembling hand.

Brutus kept his chin on the edge of the bed, watching with liquid-dark eyes as Jon struggled through layers of fevered consciousness and tried desperately to reclaim sleep.

Morning came too early. The gulls that flew in circles over the harbour all day were screaming to each other. Though there was no window in Jon's tiny, cell-like room, he could hear them as loudly as if they were right above his head. He groaned and turned onto his back.

The sleep that had finally descended upon him had been fitful at best. Jon was sore in both mind and body as he lay in the murky gloom, trying to find the motivation to get out of bed. Thankfully, it seemed that the worst of the headache was over; maybe his words yesterday hadn't made a liar out of him. Jon thought that maybe after some strong coffee he would be able to make his way to the dungeons. Sighing, he slowly sat up and reached out to pat Brutus's bony head.

Another long day in the dark dungeons interrogating prisoners for all sorts of terrible crimes.

Jon had been very young when his beautiful mother was claimed by the weeping plague. His father had died in a fall when he was still nothing but a squalling, pink thing at his mother's breast and as such had no memories of the man that everyone said he resembled. However, he remembered clearly how his mother had smelled of the mint-and-rosewater she bathed in. Her dark-brown hair, the same colour as his own, had been very long and so very soft, tickling his cheeks as they sat in the summer gardens singing childish songs together.

She had been his whole world; even when she was courted and had eventually married the gruff, heavy-set captain of the guards, she had spent all of her spare time with the strange, small, dark-haired boy. The other castle children shunned him for reasons Jon never comprehended, and his new stepfather understood nothing of sensitive souls; so, when she fell ill and quickly passed, Jon was left completely on his own. Out of loneliness, he had taken to standing silently in the corners of rooms just to watch people interact—a soft-fingered touch on an arm, a brow wrinkled in confusion—nothing escaped his eyes.

One time, the frail, pale-skinned boy had been locked in a room overnight because no one had seen him lurking in the shadows. Jon remembered how he had cried but kept from banging on the door for fear that Reginald would think it was all his fault.

The room soon grew pitch-black as night fell, and Jon, utterly terrified, had felt his way across the tiled floor in search of some sort of shelter in the big, echoing space. In the end, he had curled up like a puppy on a hard horsehair chair. He wrapped his thin arms around himself to ward off the cold. This was the only comfort he had. Quietly sobbing, Jon had played his "what if" game to try to lull himself to sleep. The game was simple; it consisted of running through scenarios in his mind and predicting all possible outcomes based on the people he placed in them.

Over the years the game had taken on a life of its own inside Jon's clever brain. It had turned into a keen empathy, and Jon gained a seemingly magical ability to both predict and recreate the behaviour of others; more and more Jon began to feel that he was having visions and not simply using his imagination.

Nearly five years ago, after it became evident that he didn't have the temperament to follow in his stepfather's footsteps, Reginald secured him a spot with the executioners' guild. The head of the guild had already heard of his strange talent, and when Jon arrived in the dungeons that first day, the man had him sit and interrogate each of the thirty-two prisoners that had been locked up that week.

It had been a gruelling exercise to stare into the hollow eyes of prisoners already broken by torture and decide who was guilty and who was simply unlucky. In the end, the head executioner had agreed with his analyses and had let a few souls free. Though Jon's almost uncanny ability to take the perspective of others served him well as an interrogator, he slowly began to feel like he was losing little parts of himself to the horrific task.

Then the nightmares started.

Jon poured a small amount of clean water from the chipped ewer to the mismatched basin and proceeded to splash the cold liquid on his face. He could hear his stepfather in the next room rummaging around; Jon would wait until Reginald had departed before making his way through the common space they shared.

Brutus, a veritable stomach on legs, bumped Jon's elbow with his nose. There would be coffee, bread, and cheese waiting for Jon in the castle kitchen as well as offal and scraps for the dog; if he was lucky, he might even be able to beg an apple from the cook.

Feeling surprisingly well, Jon took the steps down two at a time. Maybe if he finished his tasks early enough, he'd be able to steal away a bit early to take a closer look at that sleek warship and allow himself to daydream for just a little while about leaving all this dreariness behind.

As Jon walked down the steep, narrow steps to the dungeons, one hand sliding along the damp stone wall, he was dismayed to hear Reginald's voice rising up through the dank air from the large open room below. He sighed, straightened his shoulders, and swallowed down the last of the warm, nutty-tasting bread.

This didn't bode well for him.

Reginald usually shunned the dungeons although they (and the executioners' guild in general) were part of his jurisdiction. Jon thought that perhaps his stoic stepfather stayed away because he was a tiny bit afraid of the men who worked so far underground; he smiled to himself despite the apprehension he felt.

When Jon rounded the last bend, he was greeted by the sight of Reginald's broad back. His dark hands were clasped behind him, as he spoke brusquely to the fat torturer everyone called "Flayer." Jon stepped forward lightly and cleared his throat as his gaze darted to the side to avoid accidental eye contact.

"Reginald?" he said quietly.

The head of the castle guard turned towards him with a broad, gap-toothed smile on his round face.

"Son," he said.

Son? What in hells?

"I need you to follow me. I've told, uh... Flayer to advise the rest of your colleagues that you'll be working up top with me for the rest of the week," said Reginald with a smile.

Interesting.

It wasn't often that Reginald called in a favour. The old soldier was most likely stuck in a bind that only Jon's expertise and talent could get him out of.

Reginald patted Jon on the shoulder somewhat awkwardly before turning to the spiralling staircase. He looked back, his expression fading quickly from fatherly to annoyed, as he waited for his stepson to follow him.

Jon sighed.

The sun was blinding him again. He held a hand up over his eyes and frowned at Reginald's words.

"You want me to what?" he asked, surprised.

"I want you to visit the *Rose Garden* and observe," the older man said gruffly, looking somewhere over Jon's left shoulder as he fidgeted with the cuff of his shirt.

"You want me to go to a brothel and observe? What am I observing, Reginald?" Jon's voice came out a little louder than he had aimed for.

The old soldier glanced at his stepson with a scowl on his face.

"There's always the odd murder of a working girl in that neighbourhood. Usually, they're badly bruised, cut up, and dumped in the river. However, this morning they found one with just her heart missing. She was... displayed in one of the rooms. I have a bad feeling about this. I want you to get a sense of the customers. Take a look around. I want to nip this in the bud. Do you understand?" Reginald growled his words.

Jon hitched his shoulders slightly.

Brothels were crowded. There were naked women. He groaned inwardly.

"Why can't you do this yourself?" he asked and looked down at his clenched fists.

"Because I am asking *you* to do it." The older man flared his nostrils and looked piercingly at Jon as if daring him to refuse. "Now get over there. Use your magic. Do whatever you do... but find *something*. I'm counting on you." With that, Reginald frowned, nodded once to dismiss Jon, and turned to leave.

Jon watched with dismay as Reginald walked heavily away. A slow, burning pit of anxiety was already churning in his stomach.

"How long do I stay?" he yelled out to the back of Reginald's head, but the wind grabbed his words and whipped them away. He stood there awkwardly for a few moments longer and then pulled his grey jacket close around him before slowly making his way down the narrow road to town.

Jon stood looking up at the painted, wooden sign for nearly ten minutes. It featured a crudely drawn, naked woman on all fours with a rose growing out of her rear.

Charming.

He could see that the sign had been repainted a few times; the brothel was one of the oldest in the small town of Portsmouth. Steeling himself, he rehearsed the prepared words under his breath, "Hello, my name is Jon. I am here on behalf of the City Guard. I have come about a murder." He took a step up onto the dilapidated porch just as the front door burst open with a loud bang.

A giggling, half-naked woman ran out and crashed into Jon, knocking him into one of the beams that held up the second-floor balcony. She paused, round-eyed, and gasped.

"Oh, I am sorry!" she said, her voice high and girlish. It seemed like she would reach out to help steady Jon when a bearlike man wearing only a pair of stained shorts ran out the door and quickly smacked the girl loudly on her behind. She squealed in surprise and laughed. Running away swiftly on nimble feet, she went back in through the front door with the staggering, hairy man following close behind.

Jon was left alone on the porch again in a daze, a tiny pulse of pain starting right behind his eyes.

Great.

Jon took another deep breath of air redolent of fish, rotting vegetables, and salt, as he stepped through the threshold to the world of debauchery and vice beyond.

CHAPTER 2
THE ROSE GARDEN

The first thing Jon noticed was just how warm it was in the brothel. The air was moist like a hot, perfumed breath. Jon felt slightly ill from the sudden change in temperature and began sweating under his layers.

He looked up and blinked in alarm at the dimly lit scene before him; it seemed everywhere he rested his eyes, breasts peeped back at him. Women of various ages and states of undress leaned suggestively against walls, reclined in plush chairs, or sat on the knees of pawing patrons. From the room to his left, he could hear laughter punctuated by soft moans of pleasure.

Jon ducked his head and coughed into a fist, unsure of how he'd be able to put one foot in front of the other; he felt frozen in place by red-faced embarrassment. He hitched his shoulders and risked another look around; the decor was frilly and tawdry and *oh god what is he doing to her to make her make those sounds?* He was on the verge of panic and was about to retreat back out to the porch when a pair of large breasts, bound tightly in a red, satin bodice, appeared before him; a gentle hand grasped his arm.

"First time, son?" asked a voice roughened by age and vice.

He pulled his eyes away from the long line of the woman's cleavage and looked up into the heavily painted face of the brothel's madam. She was looking at him kindly, a motherly smile on her rouged mouth; the woman was so close that he could see where the stain was escaping the contours of her lips, little streaks of red in the fjords of her wrinkles.

He licked his own lips nervously and nodded.

"Yes. Wait... no. I'm not here for that. I'm here about murdering a girl," he spluttered, aghast at the words that were coming out of his mouth.

The madam frowned at him, her hand dropping to her side.

"No! Not that... sorry. What I meant was... I'm here about the murder. This morning. Of a girl," he sighed, shrugging his shoulders.

The madam smiled a little sadly.

"You're Reginald's boy, aren't you?" she asked softly.

Jon's brows came down over his storm-blue eyes.

"He's my stepfather," he said, sounding more defensive than he liked.

She reached out again and patted his shoulder.

"Well, I thank you for coming. Your name is Jon, isn't it? You can call me Madam Bellarta," she said kindly.

He smiled crookedly and stared at the tiny mole on the skin of her cheek.

"I would like to see where she was... found," he said, his voice sounding strangely high to his ears. "Was she found here?"

Madam Bellarta frowned slightly but nodded.

"You want to see the room? Why?" she asked.

Jon lifted his shoulders in a tiny shrug.

"To get a sense of what the killer saw. Or his intentions. I'm not sure. It just seems right to go there first. I'm sorry... I don't do this very often. I'm used to interrogating the living, not the dead, but Reginald finds my insight useful. Is that a problem?" he asked, making eye contact for the first time. Jon was instantly transported back to a time when the lipstick she wore had no wrinkles to invade, when her hair was dark without dyes, when her limbs were lithe, before the loose-skinned heaviness of age and misuse. Her catlike eyes, sparkling like emeralds, held his for a moment. He smiled softly at her, and she shook her head.

"Not at all, dear Jon. Follow me," she said and led him towards the wide staircase.

Jon kept his head down, watching his boots and avoiding the curious eyes around him. He could feel the sweat dripping down his spine and wished he had taken off his jacket earlier. Now if he took it off, everyone would see how nervous he was. He trudged up the stairs behind the madam and tried to feel less conspicuous.

Madam Bellarta opened the door to a small bedroom at the back of the house. There was a young, blond woman crouched over a basin of water near the foot of the bed, scrubbing at her crotch with a grey rag.

Jon's head swivelled away, and he closed his eyes. His jaw worked convulsively as he swallowed back his unease, blood hot in his face. He could smell the scent of her sex in the air; the thought brought out a small reaction in the front of his pants. Jon shifted uncomfortably and held his breath while he tried to clear his mind.

"Dee... Can you please do that in another room?" asked Madam Bellarta quietly.

Jon heard shuffling sounds and felt the rush of air and warmth as someone passed him in the doorway. He waited a moment before opening his eyes. Looking around, Jon saw the madam standing a few paces inside the garishly decorated bedroom; he let go of the breath he'd been holding and took the few steps to join her.

"It's been cleaned," he said, turning around slowly, frowning.

Madam Bellarta nodded.

"Of course! We need all the space we can get. I can't afford to have a room not in use," she said simply.

Jon nodded once and rubbed the bridge of his nose; the headache was unfurling like a dark flower of pain inside his head.

"Who found her?" he asked after a moment. He couldn't help but notice the giant wooden phallus on the night table; Jon averted his eyes and concentrated again on Madam Bellarta's mole.

"One of the girls did... But she came to get me right away. I saw it all," said the older woman, face thoughtful. "You know, Sofia wasn't even supposed to be working last night. There was no reason for her to be here... The girls don't sleep in these rooms. They sleep in the dormitory in the back of the house. I just... don't understand it. Why was she here?" The madam looked around, gesturing to the room with a large-knuckled hand.

Jon walked forwards a few steps and turned around. He pointed to the bed.

"She was found here?" he asked. When the madam nodded, he turned back and ran his eyes carefully over the chipped headboard and the coverlet.

"There was a lot of blood? Reginald said she was missing her heart. Was there anything else? Where is she now?" Jon asked, his questions coming more easily and his tone becoming more businesslike. Gleaning information was what he did for a living, after all.

"Yes... She was lying in a huge puddle of blood. There was so much... Those sheets will have to be dyed black to hide the stains," she replied. "And... She's where all the dead bodies wind up, love. She had no family or friends. She's probably already burned up."

Jon grimaced. He'd hoped to take a look at the body before it went to the crematorium.

"What else can you tell me? Was her heart cut out with a knife? Like, were the cuts straight?" he asked, making slicing motions over the palm of his hand.

The madam put a hand to her own breast, a subconscious gesture.

"Yes. It looked very... clean? Like the way a butcher would cut. Yes, just like that! Like she was butchered." She exhaled hard and then, surprisingly, let out a small laugh. "Although I don't know why anyone would want *that* girl's heart. It would be so hard and bitter." She walked to the side of the bed and smoothed the duvet with a wrinkled hand.

Jon frowned.

"She wasn't liked?" he asked.

Madam Bellarta laughed again and shook her head, her neck wattles swaying with the motion.

"No. Not since I bought her nearly a year ago. She was a foreigner... a mainlander. Never got along with any of the girls here. I had her beat, what... not two weeks ago, for being rude to a customer." She sighed. "A bad investment, though she did come cheap. But no one should ever have to die the way she did."

Jon's dark brows came together, a furrow creasing the skin above his nose.

"You think she was still alive when her heart was cut out?" he asked.

The older woman nodded slowly and twined her fingers together.

"She was on her back, not a mark on her except for the big hole in her chest. Her eyes were so wide... It looked like she was seeing the devil himself. Her hands were gripping the blankets so hard." Madam Bellarta suddenly looked pale underneath the mask of rouge she wore. "We had to... break her fingers to get her off the bed."

Jon felt nauseous. He looked up and saw that there were brownish-red dots on the ceiling.

Probably from the knife? The struggle?

The older woman followed his gaze up and made a harsh sound in the back of her throat.

"Now that's no good for a john to see while lying on his back, is it? One more thing to clean." She turned to Jon, her hands clasped in front of her. "I'm not sure how much help I've been, but I really do have to get back downstairs."

She pursed her lips and stared piercingly at Jon.

"Reginald said you would probably stay a while, and that's fine with me, but don't go bothering the customers. I do have a business to run here," she said, smiling.

Jon nodded quickly. With the pain mounting in his head, he doubted how much longer he'd be able to stay.

The older woman turned to leave but paused, hand on the doorknob. She turned back to Jon and looked appraisingly at him.

"For your troubles... Can I offer you a girl for a half hour?" she asked.

Jon felt his heart skip a beat, and he swallowed hard. He moved his hands, subtly he hoped, over the crotch of his worn, brown pants.

"No. No, thank you. That won't be necessary," he answered stiffly.

"How old are you, Jon?" she asked, her green eyes scrutinizing him.

"Twenty-two," he said and rubbed a hand through his dark curls. "Almost twenty-three."

Madam Bellarta chuckled softly.

"That's awfully old never to have dipped your wick before," she said, shaking her head. When she saw that her comment had frozen Jon to the spot, his eyes staring hard at nothing and his jaw clenched tight, she pressed her lips together and nodded. After a moment, Madam Bellarta patted his arm kindly again.

"Take your time, Jon. I'll be downstairs if you need me," she said quietly.

With a rustling of stiff chiffon and satin, the old madam exited the room, leaving him standing alone with his burning thoughts.

Nearly an hour later, Jon stood with his head against the tattered striped wallpaper of the hallway. He had questioned a few more girls, all with the same result: no one liked Sofia, no one cared that she was gone, and no one knew why she had been at the brothel after hours. His head was pounding in time to his heartbeat; it was time to give up, damn what Reginald would say.

He felt slightly dizzy as he pushed himself away from the wall and made his way to the staircase. From below he could hear the strange sibilant accent of the northern isles; it seemed that a new crop of clients had arrived. A few girls that were not already occupied pushed past Jon on the stairs, and he had to clutch at the railing to keep his balance.

Jon's vision swam for a moment as he hung limply against the worn wood; at this rate, he would be lucky if he made it back to his bed before collapsing. Shakily making his way down the stairs, Jon looked around for the madam. He was about to step into the hallway when suddenly his eyes were captured by the sight of a man sitting in a high wingback chair across the room.

The imposing stranger was wearing black leather pants and a crimson brocade vest over a white shirt, which was undone to the navel. A half-naked girl leaned over him, whispering in his ear while stroking the thatch of hair on his broad, deeply tanned chest. The man's booted feet were planted far apart as he reclined in the chair, staring intently at Jon with eyes hooded by a stark brow. Jon's heart thumped hard in his chest; he felt rooted to the spot by the man's brazen stare. The richly dressed stranger looked to be older than Jon and had an exotic handsomeness; he had high, razor-sharp cheekbones and a thin, well-shaped nose sitting above lips that curved like a gull's wings. His face seemed carved of sandalwood, all angles and stillness, as he held Jon locked in his gaze.

A sudden hand on Jon's shoulder startled him, and he turned, finally able to break eye contact with the intimidating stranger. Madam Bellarta stood next to him, a worried expression on her worn face as she peered into Jon's eyes.

"Are you all right, Jon? You don't look very well," she said with concern.

Jon glanced back at the man in the chair, but the spell had broken; a charming smile now bowed his lips, transforming the calculating look into one of amusement. As Jon watched, the man laughed throatily at something the girl said. His eyes, crinkling at the corners, looked at Jon a moment longer before completely dismissing him.

Jon shook his head and swallowed hard.

"I'm... I just need to lie down," he said weakly.

"Come with me. You can use my bed. You poor boy, you're shaking like a leaf!" said the older woman, gripping Jon by the arm.

He looked over his shoulder as he was led away by Madam Bellarta, but the chair across the room was now empty.

Jon lifted his head and blinked sleepily. The room was blessedly dark and smelled like flowers. Jon felt groggy; it took a few panicked moments before he remembered where he was.

The brothel.

Jon's head still throbbed, but he no longer felt sick to his stomach.

How long have I been sleeping?

He sat up and rubbed his face, clearing away the remnants of a deep sleep unbroken by nightmares. Madam Bellarta had kindly mixed a tincture for him before he lay down, and Jon couldn't remember the last time he had slept so soundly. He stretched out his arms, and his shoulders groaned in protest; being so anxious all the time was wreaking further havoc on his health. He smiled sadly to himself and ran a hand through his unruly hair; loneliness and isolation made for terrible mistresses.

Jon could hear footsteps and muffled voices coming from outside the door, and he stood, grabbing his jacket from the foot of the bed. It was time to go; he would find Madam Bellarta and thank her before he left.

After opening the door and stepping into the hallway, Jon came face-to-face with a young man about his age. Naked to the waist, he had his muscular arms draped over the shoulders of a girl to each side of him. The stranger winked at the startled Jon; he was boyishly handsome with smiling eyes the colour of the sea and a sly grin on his full lips. Looking quickly down, Jon saw in shock that the man was rolling one girl's nipple between his finger and thumb; he swallowed and cleared his throat.

"I'm sorry, I was... I'm going this way," Jon stammered and glanced back up.

The young man's face had creased into a wide smile, and he chuckled; Jon frowned.

With his eyes focused on something over Jon's shoulder, the stranger nodded and said a few words in a strange language. Before Jon had a chance to turn, something dark and suffocating came down over his head. Strong arms came around him, and Jon felt his wrists being seized by huge, rough hands. The man holding him seemed a giant; Jon struggled against him, hoping to work himself free of the vicelike grip, but the bag over his head was robbing him of breath. His heart hammered against his ribs as he choked, dizzy with panic, and panted into the material.

A voice that could only belong to the grinning stranger spoke close to his ear, "Aye, mate, if ye stop wigglin', it'll go a lot easier." He spoke the common language accented with the broad vowels and glottal stops of a mainlander. "If ye don't, I'll have to knock ye about a bit. And lovey... We don't want that, do we?"

Jon sagged against the tree trunk that was holding him and nodded weakly. He was feeling lightheaded from the lack of oxygen.

"Please... I can't breathe," he rasped. He heard the man in front of him chuckle as the bag was adjusted at his neck. Cool air touched his lips, and he took in a gulping breath. The giant behind him took a step; Jon was being propelled forwards, his feet clumsy as he stepped awkwardly in the pitch dark.

"Where are you taking me?" he asked, the bag muffling his voice.

"Hush now, poppet. It ain't for me to answer questions," said the mainlander from a few steps ahead.

Jon heard him say something unintelligible, and the girls giggled; the sound of them faded in the distance as he was led around a corner and then down some hard steps. A door creaked, and Jon felt chilled with the sudden wind; they were outside.

As he tried to quell his mounting panic, Jon struggled to understand what was happening to him. His mind reeled, trying to find an answer. Was he being led to his death? Why would anyone want to kidnap him? Their island was a poor one; there was no treasure, no wealth. It just didn't make any sense. Their lord was constantly absent; Jon had seen him only a handful of times in his life, even though he lived in the castle. He had no connection to Lord Barton. Yes, Reginald was the head of the guards, that was true... but that meant nothing in such an insignificant corner of the kingdom.

I'm the son of no one, he thought miserably.

After a few more steps, he said, "I don't have any money!" but there was no response.

As they descended a hill, he tripped and stumbled over rocks in his path, twice nearly twisting his ankle. He could taste the briny, wet smell of the sea at the back of his throat, even through the heavy material. Soon they stopped, and Jon was lifted into what felt like a wooden boat. He was pushed down onto a hard seat and released. His hands flew up to the hood covering his head.

"I wouldn't do that," said the mainlander, sounding very close; though his words were spoken in the same friendly tone he'd been using all along, there was the promise of violence in them.

Jon froze. He then hunched his shoulders in despair and dropped his hands to his lap.

The other man laughed cheerfully.

"Good choice! Now sit pretty, my dove," said Jon's kidnapper.

Jon rocked forward as the boat was pushed off the rocky beach, and he clutched at the splintery bench beneath him. He could hear oars splashing; a gull cried out above them. Jon suddenly felt like he would hyperventilate; it was too much. The motion of the boat was making him nauseous; sour spit pooled in his mouth, and he felt himself suffocating again. In terror, his hands took on a life of their own and grabbed desperately at the bag over his head, pulling it off.

He sucked in the night air and coughed.

"Now why would ye go and do that, lovey?"

Jon whipped his head around. He caught a glimpse of the curved hull of the black and red corvette before something cracked against his skull, making the world flash bright as lightning before Jon felt nothing at all.

CHAPTER 3
CAGED

When a sinister person means to be your enemy, they always start by trying to become your friend.

— WILLIAM BLAKE

It was dark. Jon felt himself jostled, his head hanging down. Were his eyes open? There was a sickening pain in his left temple. A taste of blood.

Where am I?

Jon tried to hold onto consciousness but slowly sank beneath black water.

[...]

It was still dark. There was something soft beneath Jon's cheek... Yes, he was lying on something soft. The pain in his head was making his stomach churn, and he felt as if he were swaying back and forth. Jon could hear voices.

"—hit him so hard in the head? I recall telling you that he is suffering from a brain ailment."

"Aye, ye did, but he wasn't mindin' me, Da."

Jon listened to the two men speak, one with the rounded accent of the mainlands, and the other with the strange shushing sounds of the islands to the far north. He lifted a hand to his head, and it came away sticky with what could only be blood. The pain was immense, and the swaying feeling was a mounting tide of nausea; when he tried to turn, his head the world spun in darkness.

Suddenly his guts clenched, and he felt the vomit leave his mouth in a burning splash. He coughed weakly and tried to sit up but felt hands on him, holding him in place.

"Shit," said a voice above him.

A wet cloth was roughly swiped across Jon's face. He felt his lips being pried open, and he tried to shake his head.

"Stop movin', silly duck. I'm goin' to get this into ye one way or another."

Callused, dirty fingers breached his mouth, and he gagged. A bitter liquid was poured over his tongue; Jon choked, gasping for breath. He realized that he could see now; he had indeed had his eyes closed. The winking mainlander that had accosted him in the brothel hallway was leaning over Jon with a look of exasperation on his youthful face.

Jon blinked, his vision fuzzy. The man holding him down curled his lip in annoyance and tilted the bottle of liquid to Jon's mouth again.

"Drink, ye bloody arse. I'm tryin' to help ye," said the rough young man.

Jon frowned, but something told him that the words rang with truth; there would be time later to struggle. He opened his mouth and meekly drank down the rest of the bitter potion.

"There ye go, lovey. Ol' Tom will make it all right."

Aren't you the one who hit me?

Jon blinked sleepily; a warm, tingly feeling was spreading through his body. He felt a hand pat his chest. His eyes were closed again.

[...]

The next time he awoke, it wasn't as dark. He squinted across the room at the pinpoint of brightness with its yellow halo; a candle on a table was casting a flickering light. Jon's mouth was dry and sour, and his eyes felt gritty in their sockets.

When he reached up to touch his temple, his fingers encountered something that felt like a bandage wrapped around his head. He turned onto his back on the narrow cot, steeling himself against the pain, but he was surprised; though his head still hurt, it was a numbed, distant throbbing. Jon took a deep breath and sat up slowly, looking around at his surroundings.

It seemed that Jon was in a sort of cage that was bolted to the wall. It was about three long paces to each side and was made of flat, wide bars in black metal. Looking up, Jon saw that the bars bent over his head close enough that if he reached up when standing he could touch them. The only furnishings in the cage were the narrow cot he was sitting on, a closed chamber pot in the corner, and a small wooden barrel that served as a table; on the table was a big metal cup, beads of perspiration trickling down its sides.

Jon reached out with a hand and took the cold cup in a shaky grip. He saw that it was clear liquid and sniffed it, but it didn't have a scent. Hoping that it was what it seemed, he carefully brought it up to his lips and took a small sip.

Water.

He was thirsty, but since he didn't know whether he'd get more, Jon only took a few mouthfuls before setting it down again on the barrel. The cold water felt good in his mouth and on his lips, but a small fever-shiver took him.

Jon looked down at himself and saw that someone had stripped him of his pants, boots, vest, and jacket, leaving him only wearing his worn cotton shirt and the linen shorts he wore as underthings.

Slowly standing up, he stepped forward to hold onto the bars; he was amazed to see a large, richly decorated room beyond his small prison. The wooden walls shone golden brown in the wavering light of the candle. The floor was covered in beautiful rugs, the likes of which he had never seen before; they were a riot of dark colours and forms, abstract repeating shapes and flowers twining together to make strange patterns that made his head hurt. In the middle of the room, there was a heavy wooden table surrounded by chairs; they were all glossy and dark with gracefully curved legs, and the chair cushions were made of something dark red and velvety looking.

Jon's eyes rested curiously for a moment on the glass-doored shelves filled with more leather-bound books than he had ever seen; his gaze then swept the walls where heavy-framed paintings hung. He could see what looked like a large map covering most of the wall to the left of him; above the map was a large crest with the black silhouette of a roaring lion resting on a field of red.

Suddenly the floor rocked under his feet, startling him, and understanding dawned.

I'm on a ship.

Memories of the sleek black and red corvette came flooding back to him.

Only when Jon heard a small whispering sound, like paper sliding against something, did he realize he wasn't alone. He narrowed his eyes against the candlelight and saw that the dark shape on the other side of the table was a large, low bed; on it, a figure was reclined, reading a book.

Jon's heart faltered at the unexpected sight, and he tightened his grasp on the bars, unsure of what he should do. In numb panic, he moved quietly to sit back down on the cot; it creaked under his weight, and he anxiously held his breath. The figure on the bed turned another page in the book.

After a moment he heard a man's voice, which was flavoured with the softly sibilant accent of the north.

"Go back to sleep, Jon. We have much to converse about in the morning."

Jon sat still, his heart hammering in his chest. He heard another page turn across the room and pressed his lips in a hard line. There would be no answers tonight.

Frowning, he rubbed his head, mindful of the bandage. He doubted he would be able to sleep, but something in that low voice compelled him to try. He lay back down, noticing for the first time that the covers on his small cot were made of bright, rich fabrics. He pulled the sheet over his slight frame and stared hard at the bars in the dim light. The man beyond couldn't be anyone but the captain of the ship, judging by the size of the room and the sumptuous decor.

What does he want with me?

Surprisingly, Jon soon felt his lids grow heavy despite the nervousness and confusion he felt; as he slipped softly between the folds of slumber, his last thoughts were on the dark-eyed man from the brothel.

~

The forest was black and silver, the trees in it very narrow and tall. Jon looked about in confusion, unsure which way the path to home lay. There was the crackling, snapping sound of something moving towards him, and he turned around just as a massive, black shape emerged out of the woods. It stared at him impassively with glossy, dark eyes. From behind the great lion came a hot wind, ripe with the smell of carrion...

~

Jon was hot, and the sunlight was very bright on his eyelids. With his eyes closed tight, he buried his head against the pillow; Reginald would be up by now. He reached out a hand to touch Brutus's head, never far from his bedside. When his fingers encountered nothing, he frowned to himself. The cot suddenly rocked under him, and there was a small splashing sound from beyond the wall; Jon's eyes snapped open.

The ship.

He lifted his head and narrowed his gaze against the sunlight pouring through the round window above him.

"Well, lookee! The sleepin' princess awakens at long last!" said someone in the room.

He recognized the voice as belonging to the aggressively cheerful youth that had knocked him unconscious the night before; Jon clenched his jaw and turned to look at him.

The muscular young man, stripped to the waist and barefoot, was lounging indolently in one of the dark wooden chairs and noisily eating a wedge of apple off the end of a sharp knife. When he saw Jon looking at him, he curled his pink lips into a smile.

"Yer a noisy sleeper aint'cha, lovey?" he said, carving another slice out of the red-cheeked fruit he held in his rough-knuckled hand.

Jon frowned at him and pulled himself into a sitting position; his shoulders came up as he sat hunched on the bed, staring at the stranger for a few moments.

"Where are my clothes?" he asked softly, his voice hoarse with sleep.

The shirtless man laughed.

"We burned 'em, mate. They couldn't be saved!" he said cheerfully and munched on his apple. "Ye know I was up half the night cleanin' the sick off ye? Bloody awful business."

Jon swallowed and opened his mouth to say something.

Why should I apologize?

"Jon, you should learn right now to take a grain of salt with anything Tom says," said another voice.

Jon turned his head as someone entered the room. His breath caught in his throat as the man who had so brazenly stared at him from across the brothel sitting room walked through the open doorway. He was still wearing the dark-crimson vest over a white shirt, but both were buttoned up and covered with a long black coat with bell cuffs and brass buttons. His light-brown hair was tied back out of his face; when the man turned to look at Tom, Jon saw that his ponytail was held in place with a black velvet ribbon.

"That's unkind, Da," said the shirtless man at the table, smiling up with sea-green eyes at the imposing stranger.

The older man's lips made a little moue of disgust as he shook his head. After turning back to Jon, he dipped his head a fraction of an inch and smiled charmingly.

"I am Captain Baltsaros. This absurdly brash young man is Tom, my first mate," he said in his exotic accent.

Jon realized his mouth was still open; he closed it quickly and felt blood heat up his cheeks.

Baltsaros's brow lifted, and he scrutinized Jon for a moment with dark-brown eyes. When Jon didn't respond, he finished the introductions for him.

"And you are Jon of Portsmouth. It is a pleasure to meet you, Jon," Baltsaros said lightly.

The older man's eyes crinkled at the corners, and he sketched a shallow bow with a large, tanned hand held to his chest. The man breathed elegance into the room with his words and manner, and Jon found himself sitting up a little straighter on the cot.

"We did not burn your clothes; ignore Tom. However, you might be more comfortable in something less... shabby," said the captain, smiling.

The corners of Jon's mouth turned down, his sudden shame swiftly followed by anger. He averted his gaze.

"I like my clothes just fine. I thank you to return them to me. And to release me." Jon's words were spoken through clenched teeth. He looked down to where his hands were clutching the bedsheet tightly; his heart was beating fast and the blood sang in his ears. In dismay, he realized that there was a pounding in his head that was quickly gaining momentum; he swallowed hard, fearing the pain that he knew would soon overpower him.

"You heard our friend, Tom. Please fetch his clothing. It is my desire for Jon to feel comfortable during his stay with us. Whatever he asks for, you shall provide. Do you understand?" asked Baltsaros.

There was a long pause. Jon looked back up and was alarmed to see that Tom was staring at him intently with a new emotion in his blue-green eyes.

Jealousy.

"Includin' lettin' the puppy out of his cage?" the muscular first mate asked as he stood, rubbing the side of his callused thumb on the stubble of his jaw.

Baltsaros shook his head slowly.

"No, I'm afraid our guest will have to stay in his cage for now," he responded, sitting down on the chair that Tom had vacated. He leaned forward and placed his forearms on his knees, hands clasped loosely in front of him. Baltsaros peered curiously at his prisoner and smiled.

Jon's eyes followed Tom's departure.

"Welcome to my ship, Jon. I was being genuine when I said that I would like you to be comfortable; please know that," the captain said, his tone both friendly and apologetic.

Jon turned his eyes to Baltsaros's and was surprised by the warmth he found there. Despite the outrageous situation, he nodded once.

"Why am I here?" he asked quietly.

Pondering the question, Baltsaros sat back in his chair and rubbed a hand on the black leather covering his knee.

Jon's temple throbbed in time to his heart, adding to the mounting discomfort in his head. He reached out unsteadily and grabbed the metal cup, the water in it now tepid. He took a small sip and tried to ignore the pain that shadowed his every move.

"I learned of your unique talent and had to see it for myself," said Baltsaros finally. "I like interesting things; and you, Jon, are interesting to me."

Jon frowned and coughed into his fist; his skin prickled with another fever-shiver. He drank down the rest of the water and started turning the cup around in his hands nervously.

"I'm to be kept in a cage? Like an animal on display? Are you going to make me perform?" asked Jon, his voice sounding harsh.

The handsome face of the captain creased into a wide grin, and he laughed, his eyes twinkling with merriment.

"No, no, no! You misunderstand. You're not to be a pet, Jon." Baltsaros stood and walked to a strange metal cupboard. He opened it and took out a pitcher; motioning to Jon to hold his cup through the bars, he then poured water from it.

Jon was amazed to feel that the water was so cold; the cup started sweating immediately in the heat that had settled in the captain's quarters.

"How... is this so cold?" Jon asked, taking a small sip.

Baltsaros smiled and went to replace the pitcher.

"Ice," he said simply, pointing to the large block of it at the top of the cabinet.

The captain's face became serious as he closed the door and turned back to the man in the cage.

"I can show you many more interesting things, Jon, if you decide to join us."

Jon laughed, though there was no humour in it.

"So if I'm not to be a pet, what will I be? Are you offering me employment? If so... Why all this? Why not just ask me?" he asked. His teeth were starting to chatter, and his words sounded strange to his ears.

"Because you are the son of an honourable man, a lawman, Jon. My ship and its crew... We kneel to no man, no laws. I couldn't be sure where your loyalties lie," said Baltsaros, one shoulder coming up in a small, graceful shrug.

Jon shivered; the pain and fever were starting to take over. He closed his eyes and licked his lips with a suddenly dry tongue.

"And what if I say no?" he asked quietly, lifting his gaze to the man who stood above him.

It could have been a trick of the eye, but the captain's face seemed momentarily to go blank of expression. It was as if something completely inhuman was looking at him through the older man's dark stare.

Jon felt a strange numbness in his body, and his vision seemed to pitch forward. He felt simultaneously hot and cold. All motion suddenly slowed. Before the world went black, his eyes saw a dark hand reach for him.

Then there was nothing.

~

Baltsaros knelt next to Jon's twitching body, a deep frown on his face. He smelled burnt tobacco and realized that Tom was back in the room. The handsome boy walked on cat's feet; without his keen sense of smell, Baltsaros would have had a hard time tracking his motions, and the lad was as dangerous as he was beautiful.

"What's the matter with him, Da?" Tom asked, leaning against the bars of the cage, Jon's clothing tucked under one muscular arm.

Baltsaros touched the stricken man's face; it was burning. He shook his head at the provincial nature of these small towns; without proper medical care, Jon would not have lasted the month.

"He has a brain infection. Your manhandling of him did not help matters, Tom." With a mildly reproachful frown, Baltsaros looked over at his first mate.

Tom chewed on the side of his thumb; he shrugged at Baltsaros. The boy was invariably unapologetic when it came to his violence.

"So he's broken, eh? Are ye goin' to fix him? What do we want with this broken puppy anyway? He's got hands like a girl," said the first mate, curling his lip in amusement. "Maybe I'll get him to use his girl hands on m—"

"You'll do no such thing, Tom. Obey me in this," Baltsaros hissed quietly.

The younger man's sea-green eyes widened, his pupils dilating, and he swallowed.

"Aye, aye, captain sir," he said, his tone only slightly mocking.

Baltsaros nodded once and turned his attention back to the man lying on the floor of the cage. Jon had stopped twitching, but his breath was uneven and a sheen of sweat covered his sickly pale face. Broken puppy, indeed. Baltsaros sighed; he could fix him, but what if Jon refused to join his crew? What point would there be to cure him of his ailment, only to kill him for turning down his generous offer? With a thoughtful expression on his rugged face, Baltsaros slid his strong arms underneath Jon's limp body and lifted him back onto the cot; he would simply wait for Jon's answer before mixing the medicines that would save the boy's life.

He picked the cup up off the floor and placed it back on the small rum barrel before exiting the cage and locking the door. Looking at Tom sternly, he pointed to Jon.

"You're to be the guard dog for this 'puppy,' Tom. I will be up on deck. If there is any change, you must come to me immediately."

He looked back at the stricken man on the narrow cot and frowned. After a moment, Baltsaros picked a shiny, red apple out of the bowl on the table and reached through the bars of Jon's cage to place it next to the empty cup. What was it about this boy that seemed to call to something long buried inside of him? He shook his head slightly.

After narrowing his dark eyes at the first mate again, Baltsaros turned and left the heavy heat of the stateroom for the crisp, blue world of sunshine above deck.

CHAPTER 4

PIRATES

Jon woke up nearly an hour later, groggy and disoriented. The pain in his head was sharp, and he felt terribly weak. Completely miserable, Jon covered his face with his hands; he wanted nothing more than to be in his own bed, Brutus at his side. Hell, he would even welcome Reginald's temper if it meant an end to the raw fear and pain that hounded him. Overwhelmed, he felt shameful tears well up and started weeping quietly to himself.

"Hey, mate... Mate, don't go cryin' now! Shit," said Tom from somewhere close by. Jon heard movement but made no move to acknowledge him. "Now, when did cryin' do anyone a lick o' good? Pssh... cryin'... Listen, lovey: all the tears in the world ain't goin' to get'cha out of that cage, so stop that now."

With his hands hard against his eyes, Jon let out a shuddering breath.

"My head... The pain is like a lightning storm. I can't..." he said hoarsely. The words sounded ridiculous as soon as he had uttered them.

Tom chuckled softly; Jon rubbed his face and cracked his eyes open, shielding them from the light with his fingers. The muscular first mate had pulled a chair up to the bars and was sitting there staring down at Jon with a wry grin on his face.

"No worries! My da will give ye somethin' for that. Soon, soon, lovey," he said, smiling. Tom placed his hands on his knees and leaned forward to get a better look at Jon.

The first mate's chest was broad and tanned, the muscles well defined under his sun-darkened skin. Jon could see streaks of grime where Tom had obviously wiped his hand, the dirt and sweat having made stripes under the man's curling chest hair. Again Jon noticed that he was incredibly handsome; the scar above his eye, the coarse stubble, and the sardonic grin lent his otherwise cherubic face a roguish quality. Tom seemed so very full of good humour, though something told Jon that the handsome youth could murder him as cheerfully as he spoke.

Jon coughed into his hand, startled by how deep it sounded in his chest. Holding his head, he sat up stiffly on the bed and pulled a blanket around himself.

"So the captain is your father?" he asked after a moment. He could smell Tom from where he was sitting: tobacco smoke, sweat, sunshine, and liquor.

The big man nodded, a glint of something in his blue-green eyes.

"Aye, he is!" he said, smiling wide.

Was that pride?

Jon frowned.

"Why do you sound so different then?" he asked. They also looked nothing alike.

Tom laughed and shook his head.

"My mum raised me, ducky. A pirate's got no time for a wee babe. Yer a daft thing, aint'cha?"

Jon's heart pounded. *Pirates.* Despite everything, he felt a small thrill. A distant relative of his had been a pirate. When he was little, his mother had told him stories of this Captain Black, and Jon remembered hanging on every word; it had seemed like such a gloriously dangerous existence.

"So you're pirates, then?" he asked.

Nodding, Tom sat back in his chair.

"Aye. We're pirates. Does that scare ye, dear Jonny?" He pulled his long knife out from somewhere behind him and started cleaning his nails with it. "Or do ye have man-size balls in those shorts somewhere? Da said ye were some sort of torturer. What I think is if I yell 'boo' at'cha, ye'd die of fright."

Jon closed his eyes and pinched the bridge of his nose. Even though the first mate's tone was mocking, he *seemed* honestly friendly; something in his manner was steadily chipping away at Jon's defences. For the first time in a long while, he was completely unable to read someone's intentions. Jon opened his eyes and blinked.

Make that two someones.

The captain was as unreadable as his first mate. Maybe it was just his illness... He looked into Tom's smiling eyes.

"I was just an interrogator. My only tools were my words," he said, pulling his shoulders up closer to his ears. "And sometimes a teacher... I taught others how to read body language."

Tom's brows came down; he looked somewhat disappointed by Jon's words.

"So no torture then? Pah! No wonder yer like a snail without a shell," he said and started to flip the sharp knife into the air, catching it confidently in a rough hand. "I was supposed to get Da when ye woke up. Ye won't tell him I dawdled, aye?" Tom grinned wolfishly and winked. When Jon shook his head hesitantly, Tom stood up and turned to leave, his knife disappearing into a sheath behind him that was buckled into his belt. Jon noticed for the first time that the first mate's large back was a mass of scars under the sweat and tanned skin. He frowned.

"Tom?"

The big pirate turned back towards the cage. "Aye, lovey?" he asked.

Jon groped for his words.

"If I... don't want to join you... Will your father let me go? Alive, I mean?" he asked, his voice faltering.

Tom threw his head back and laughed, the sound booming out of his broad chest. After a moment he looked down at Jon, his face crinkling in amusement.

"Now I don't know why ye'd choose that shithole town over the open sea, mate. Could be I punched ye too hard, eh?" He stopped chuckling when he saw that Jon's face was drawn with worry. "Ahh, Jonny. Just look at those big blue eyes... Ye'll make the captain sad; we came an awful long way to poach yer scrawny arse. Ha ha... but my Da's a good man, heart o' gold, I swear! If ye say no, I'm sure he'll let ye off."

With those words, Tom winked again and disappeared through the open door. Dread descended on Jon like a sheet of cold water; he didn't believe a single word.

~

Baltsaros ducked his head and stepped into the stateroom, his sight momentarily impaired by the change in light. However, he could hear what his eyes could not have told him: Jon's infection had spread to his lungs.

Or maybe it had started there, hidden? Something to think about later.

He heard the crunch of teeth breaking the skin of the apple; the scent of the fresh fruit rose up through the air, mingling with the bitter tang of nervous sweat that emanated from the young man in the cage. Baltsaros walked farther into the room, his vision slowly adjusting to the darker space, and set a covered plate down on the large table. When he turned towards his prisoner, the captain saw that Jon was watching him warily, his grey-blue eyes filled with so much emotion that Baltsaros felt an unexpected tingle of sympathy. He curled his lip into a smile.

"Hello, Jon. I'm relieved to see you up," he said, approaching the cage. "I see you're indeed hungry?" He motioned to the half-eaten apple that Jon mutely clutched in one hand. Baltsaros saw with dismay that the hand was trembling slightly and the younger man's skin had taken on a greyish cast.

After he stepped up to the cage, Baltsaros undid the lock and opened the door. The tall man smoothly lowered himself to one knee in front of Jon and peered into his captive's face.

"How do you feel?" he asked, his stark brow wrinkling in concern.

Jon's eyes slid away from the captain's face.

"I've felt better," he replied softly and tugged the coverlet tighter around him. Baltsaros nodded.

"When did these headaches start, Jon?" he asked. This close, the captain could tell that the infection was progressing far faster than he had earlier thought. Jon's face was drawn and gaunt, sickness marring his graceful beauty. Not for the first time, Baltsaros felt curiously drawn to the sensitive young man. He watched closely as Jon swallowed, his Adam's apple bobbing in his thin neck.

"About a month ago, I think. Maybe less," came the reply; Jon's voice was rough and his breath whistled in his chest. Baltsaros reached out towards Jon's head but stopped short.

"May I?" he asked softly. The younger man stared hard at him a second before nodding once. Holding the back of Jon's head, he gently put a hand to the sick man's forehead; he felt the astonishing heat of the fever in him, as well as the tiny shudders that shook his slight frame. Baltsaros slid his large hand down the side of Jon's face, feeling his jaw clench, and down his throat, finally placing his palm over the sick man's chest; he didn't have to put an ear against him to know that he had fluid in his lungs.

As he looked into Jon's eyes, he was astonished to see that the dark-haired man appeared to be on the verge of tears and not, he believed, from pain. Baltsaros wondered to himself how long it had been since someone had touched Jon with anything resembling affection. He dropped his hands and stood, noting the sudden look of meek humiliation that flashed across Jon's fine-boned face before it settled back into fearful distrust.

"You're very sick, Jon," the captain said simply. "Here, I've brought you something a little more substantial to eat." He turned and exited the cage, leaving the door wide open behind him.

With his back to his captive, Baltsaros pulled the cover off the plate; he smiled to himself when he heard a shuffling step approach. Baltsaros walked across the room and opened the wooden box atop the teak dresser; he pulled out some beautiful, heavy silverware and turned back to Jon. He was wrapped in the sheet, one hand clutching the material to his chest, as he peered down curiously at the food on the fine white plate. Jon looked up at Baltsaros as he approached.

"What is it?" he asked, his storm-blue eyes narrow with distrust.

"An omelette," replied Baltsaros, smiling. "Some vegetables and meat covered with cheese and cooked in an egg. Roughly."

Jon turned back to the dish and licked his bottom lip. Baltsaros could see that the younger man was hungry.

"Sit."

He pulled out the chair and slid it behind Jon, bumping it against the back of his knees. Jon slowly sat, and Baltsaros pushed the chair a little farther before rounding the table to sit across from him.

"Eat," he said, pointing to the plate.

Jon frowned at Baltsaros and let go of the sheet to pick up the fork, turning it around in his hand. He glanced up at his captor, making no move to comply.

Baltsaros laughed in amusement, startling Jon whose eyes widened at the outburst.

"Jon, eat. Please. I would not poison your food. See?" He leaned over the table and plucked the fork from Jon's grasp; he cut a piece from the still-warm omelette and brought it to his mouth. He chewed and swallowed, smiling at Jon before placing the fork back on the plate.

The look of distrust lessened, replaced partially by naked hunger, as Jon picked up the fork again and took a bite of the egg for himself. His eyebrows lifted in surprise, and he took another mouthful, handling the fork awkwardly; it was obviously not an implement he was used to.

Baltsaros waited until the younger man had taken a few more bites before he broached the subject of Jon's future. He leaned back in his seat, elbows on the chair arms, and steepled his hands in front of him.

"Have you given any thought to my offer, Jon?"

Bolstered by the warm meal, Jon looked directly at the captain.

"I'm still not sure exactly what you're offering," he said, his voice stronger than before. "But I don't know that I'm willing to take up with pirates."

Baltsaros dipped his head thoughtfully, acknowledging Jon's words. It was true; the captain had not given Jon anything that would make him feel otherwise. So far this endeavour had been less than ideal; Tom would have to be taught another lesson in obedience.

Baltsaros lowered his hands to the table, palm up.

"Jon, I am offering you a place on my ship. I believe your talents would come in handy with our type of... work. You can see things that others do not, and I think that it would be an incredible boon to us, and to me. Your gifts were being squandered in that dank dungeon, Jon. Here, you will be a free man. Respected. An equal. My crew is varied and loyal, and everyone shares in the wealth. The choice is yours, and you're free to go if that's what you'd like, but... Was I wrong in thinking that you are a man who is extremely dissatisfied with the cards dealt to him by fate?"

Baltsaros widened his eyes at Jon, who had laughed sharply at the word "fate."

"Fate. What is fate, Captain? Is it my fate to be here, sitting at your table, wondering if I will ever get out of this alive? Is it my fate to have been so bereft of choices in my life that when faced with one all I feel is paralyzing confusion? *Fate*," Jon said with disgust and shook his head, taking the last mouthful of egg.

Baltsaros's eyes swept over the man's face; there was an interesting strength behind the high walls that Jon had erected to keep others at a distance. The captain felt that an important corner had been turned. As he leaned towards Jon, Baltsaros smiled grimly.

"How's this: you're dying. Does that change matters for you?"

Jon blinked slowly, and after a moment he nodded; the news didn't seem to shock him. After pushing the empty plate away with one hand, Jon turned his head, looking at the blue sky visible outside the porthole. After a long pause, he spoke in a strained voice.

"Sometimes, at night, I leave my room to stand on the hill over the harbour. It's dark, but I can see lights in the boats or hear a snippet of song, a laugh, and other... things." Jon reddened slightly. Baltsaros tilted his head, listening to the friendless, young man speak of things he had obviously never shared with anyone. "And I'd think to myself, *You could be out there!*" He laughed, the sound ugly, and turned his stormy eyes back to Baltsaros. "But the truth is that I can't. I... am not good in situations where there are people. I'm caged by my own pathetic fear. *Next year*, I think, *next year I will leave the dank dungeon*, as you so aptly put it, *I'll be free!* and now you tell me that I am dying?" Jon's mouth turned down at the corners, and his eyes shimmered. "What a sad, sad little life," he said angrily.

Baltsaros slowly reached out with one hand and placed it gently on the younger man's arm. He felt a twitch as Jon forced himself to accept the touch; a deep crease wrinkled his brow as he stared at the captain's large, sun-darkened hand on his forearm.

"Tomorrow," Jon said faintly. "Let me give you my answer tomorrow."

Baltsaros looked down at Jon, sleeping under the power of the heavy painkillers the captain had mixed for him. After twisting paper around a second dose, he placed it next to the cup of water. Perhaps Jon would find the answer in his dreams. Feeling strangely drained by his conversation with the deathly ill younger man, Baltsaros stripped off his shirt and vest and lay down on his own bed; the captain stared up at the wooden ceiling, thinking hard about the strangely entwined concepts of fate and loyalty.

~

A small whimper woke Jon up.

Sleepily opening his eyes, he saw that it was night. When Jon had woken up earlier in the afternoon and stood to piss in the chamber pot, it had appeared that he was, for once, alone in the room. When he had reached for the metal cup, Jon had found the twist of paper containing the pain-numbing powder the captain had given him. Gratefully pouring it into his water, he had swallowed it down quickly.

It wasn't that he had been in any real pain upon waking; he had simply wanted to be free of thoughts of his death. At least that's what he had tried to tell himself. It wasn't that Captain Baltsaros's touch had brought out an unexpected reaction in Jon that had eclipsed any fear he felt and that he'd wanted to hide from the truth in the dreamless sleep that the drug afforded him.

There was another whimper, a little louder this time. Jon slowly lifted his head and looked around, freezing when he saw movement on the bed across the room.

"Please... Da..." said a voice that was unmistakably Tom's; it was filled with pain. Jon was aghast when he heard Baltsaros's low laughter. There was a hiss of pain and then a groan of pleasure. In shock, Jon pressed the heel of his hand against his mouth; he quickly closed his eyes and put his head back to the pillow.

"You'll obey me, Tom," Jon heard the captain's voice say, rough with desire. There was a low moan that ended in a whimper; it was followed by a gasp.

"Yes... yes, Da. Please... Please fuck me. Fuck me and I'll ob—" Tom yelped as Baltsaros did... something to him.

Oh god... oh god.

Jon's face burned as Tom started murmuring terribly scandalous things, the sound of skin smacking against bare skin punctuating his words. In dismay, Jon felt himself growing hard in response, and he shifted on the bed, trying not to encourage his treasonous erection. Pressing the coverlet hard over his ear, Jon tried to slow his breathing as he prayed for an end to the wanton depravity across the room.

It was a long time before his prayers were answered, and an even longer time before he managed to convince himself the feeling he felt was disgust and not something closer to desire.

CHAPTER 5
THE SHIP

Captain Baltsaros had his hand on Jon's head, feeling for a fever. He moved it down the side of Jon's face and neck, just like he had done the previous day; but, instead of stopping at his chest, it continued farther down. Jon gasped in shock and tensed as the captain's fingers slid warmly under the waist of his shorts, curling around the molten flesh below. His cock grew hard in the captain's firm grip, and Jon clenched his jaw, a tremor of desire running through him at Baltsaros's skilled touch. He was unable to move... or simply unwilling? He moaned softly as Baltsaros's long arm slid around him to pull him closer. He heard the sound of someone laughing. Jon reddened with embarrassment when he saw that Tom was standing there watching the captain fondle him. He watched, horrified, as Tom pulled out his knife. It flashed quickly through the air and slid through the skin of Jon's throat. A torrent of red arced out of him and ran down his chest. He didn't feel any pain, only incredible pleasure, as the captain smiled down at him, his hand spreading the gore over Jon's rigid cock.

~

When he woke, Jon was immediately and uncomfortably aware of his erection pressing hard into the thin mattress. He couldn't remember all the details of the dream, but what he could remember brought blood to his face.

A soft noise, as of something being moved, turned Jon's head; Tom was approaching from the far side of the room. Jon quickly closed his eyes and deepened his breathing to mimic sleep. He wasn't awake enough to deal with Tom's cheerfully menacing banter; besides, the stiffness between his legs had yet to go down, and the first mate was the last person in the world he wanted to see *that*.

As Tom muttered something about chambermaids under his breath, he replaced the chamber pot and refilled Jon's cup. Jon cracked one eye open a slit and saw that Tom was in his usual half-naked state. While wondering wryly whether the first mate actually owned a shirt, Jon noticed with dismay the bruised bite mark plain on Tom's muscular shoulder. The events of the previous night flooded through him, burning his mind anew.

He clenched his eyes shut and tried to still his breathing until he was sure Tom had left. After a few minutes of silence, he risked another look; the room appeared empty. Jon sat up, his head throbbing. Sick to his stomach from the pain and fever, he groaned out loud, tears gathering in the corners of his eyes.

On top of his sickness, Jon felt terrible shame over his body's reaction to the captain and his first mate... his son... being... (*the way he grunted like a beast when he finally came*) lovers. Jon gritted his teeth against the memory and clenched his fists tight in his lap, rocking forward, a tear running down his nose and falling from the tip.

Lovers? There was no love in that.

Jon heard the heels of the captain's boots on the wooden floor, and before he had a chance to resume his possum act on the cot, the older man had entered the stateroom. After wiping his eyes and crossing his arms across his chest to try to keep from shivering, Jon sat mutely on the narrow bed, staring down at the floor between his bare feet. He listened as Baltsaros stepped across the colourful rugs to the front of the cage.

"Good morning, Jon. Are you hungry?" asked the captain, a smile distinct in his voice. When Jon didn't look up or answer Baltsaros after a long silence, he heard the lock on his cage being released and the hinges of the door creak quietly. A hand reached for his shoulder, and Jon recoiled violently.

"Don't you fucking touch me!" he yelled, his throat raw. Jon's eyes were wide as he stared at the startled captain, his teeth bared in a grimace.

Baltsaros's expression went completely flat before confusion slowly etched lines across his brow.

"What happened, Jon?" asked the captain, his voice soft with concern.

The younger man stared at him, trying to find the words. After a moment he replied.

"Last night..." He had a deep pain in his chest that was getting worse with each breath.

Baltsaros frowned for a moment, but his rugged face quickly creased into a wry smile. He held his hands up as if trying not to startle a small, frightened animal and looked kindly down at Jon.

"I'm sorry if Tom and I woke you. This is the downside to keeping you in—"

"He is your *son!*" Jon hissed through clenched teeth and glared at the older man in disgust, though his fever was starting to dull his vision again.

Baltsaros started shaking his head; his lips curled into a subdued smile, and he dropped his hands.

"Tom is not my son, Jon. Did he tell you that?" he asked. When Jon nodded tightly, the captain sighed. "Ah, Tom, always in need of a game to play. Jon... Tom is an ex-slave that I bought a few years ago."

Jon let the words sink in. He frowned at Baltsaros in confusion.

The captain pressed his gracefully curved lips together as he looked down at the dark-haired man on the narrow cot.

"May I sit?" he asked, motioning to the space next to Jon. The younger man sagged back against the bars, and he dipped his chin, feeling utterly drained. Baltsaros sat down slowly on the bed, arranging his hands in his lap.

Jon ran his fingers through his dirty hair, suddenly aware of how long it had been since he'd washed himself or changed his clothing; he could smell his own stink. Embarrassed, he leaned further away from the older man.

The captain continued.

"Tom was a slave. He was slated for a horrendous fate... He had managed to escape from the mines where he was being worked to death. He then murdered his owner and the man's family in their home before he was caught."

Jon swallowed hard.

"He said his mother raised him..."

Baltsaros shook his head.

"He lied. He's never known a mother." The captain let out a low laugh with little humour in it. "Sometimes I believe that the hells simply opened up and a demon pushed Tom out. He's a ruthless killer, Jon, completely without remorse, smiling Death himself. In fact, he was the reason I built this to begin with," said the captain, motioning to the bars surrounding them. "Tom had been put in stocks in the town centre to be punished by the townspeople in whichever way they wanted... and punish him they did; Tom's owner had been well-liked, and his death was seen as a horrible tragedy. By the time I found Tom, he could barely walk. He had been brutally abused by the men in town... I will spare you the details, but it was a long time before he was completely healed."

"And you bought him *why*?" Jon asked, aghast.

"He's very useful in our line of work. I took an interest in his history and purchased him, though now he is as free as anyone in my crew. He spent the first five months locked in this cage... a wild animal. I still haven't *quite* tamed him, but at least my sleep is no longer as disrupted." Baltsaros smiled wide. "I am sorry for all the trouble he has caused, Jon. He calls me Father out of some misplaced affection. I... oblige him. I find him alluring." He chuckled softly. "I did attempt to break him of the habit, but as you might have gathered by now, beating him is largely counterproductive. He enjoys it far too much." The captain grinned; the lines on his face showed a man that smiled often and easily. "Besides... How old do you think I am to have fathered a son Tom's age?"

Jon looked down at his hands. It was true. Tom had to be close to his age, and the captain could be no more than ten or so years older; though the realization didn't alleviate his discomfort over the two men, or any men, sharing a bed, Jon felt suddenly sheepish. He raised his grey-blue eyes back up to Baltsaros and shrugged, forcing himself to smile.

The captain, narrowing his eyes at Jon, went darkly serious.

"If you join us, you will have to thicken your skin, Jon. You'll see far worse than what you assumed you saw, I can guarantee that." Baltsaros leaned towards Jon, a calculating look on his face. "I believe you are stronger than you let on and much more suited to this life than you think you are. I need your decision, Jon. I would like us to become friends. And"—he laughed, all sternness leaving his face—"I crave a little more privacy." His eyes crinkled at the corners.

Jon frowned at the non sequitur until he realized Baltsaros meant that with his enlistment, he would have to move into the crew quarters. The thought sent a sudden pang of anxiety through him, but it was strangely brief; he realized then that Captain Baltsaros had a strong calming effect on him.

Jon stared hard at the man sitting on the low cot, and something inside him suddenly gave. Baltsaros's words came back to him... *free as anyone in my crew*. Jon wanted to believe the captain's words and that this near stranger had more faith in him than his own stepfather.

Freedom.

It was something he'd been wishing for his whole life, and it was right here in front of him. Jon looked searchingly into the captain's friendly brown eyes; taking a deep, shaky breath, and feeling like he was stepping off a high cliff, Jon spoke the words that already seemed written in the air between them.

"Yes. Yes, I will join you."

~

With Jon's words Baltsaros felt a strange sense of relief. He almost frowned, momentarily unbalanced by the sensation, but instead smiled into blue eyes wide with the need for his approval. He nodded and held out his hand; Jon looked confused for a moment before sliding his own hand into Baltsaros's grip. They shook on it, securing Jon's spot on the crew.

The younger man's hand was alarmingly hot; Baltsaros saw immediately that Jon's eyes were glassy, one pupil more dilated than the other. The sounds of his fluid-filled lungs were filling the cabin with a harsh wheezing.

As if reacting to the captain's scrutiny, Jon suddenly went still, his eyes rolling in his head as he fell back.

Baltsaros's hand shot out and caught Jon before he crashed into the hard metal bars; as he laid Jon down on the cot, he looked down at him, a thoughtful expression on his face. Something needed to be done, and quickly.

Baltsaros stood and walked to the teak dresser. After pulling out a few drawers, he selected the ingredients necessary to make the infection-fighting medicine. As he ground them with mortar and pestle, Baltsaros prodded at the surprising feelings he had towards the young man.

When he had brought his crew to Portsmouth looking for the boy with the gift of empathy, it had just been simple curiosity. He hadn't known what to expect. Besides, killing the girl to lure Jon had felt good. Killing always felt good to Baltsaros; it restored the peace in his mind and shored up his self-control. However, when he had seen the boy at the foot of the staircase, hunched as if afraid of being hit, pale and sickly with bright spots in his cheeks, something inside Baltsaros had whispered to him. Like a sculptor who could see the forms in marble just waiting to be released, Baltsaros had seen the potential in Jon.

He frowned as he expertly mixed the ingredients into a paste. Baltsaros had never felt relief at *not* having to kill someone before. It was... noteworthy. The captain pressed most of the paste into a small mould and heated it over a candle. In a few hours, he would be able to remove the tablets and coat them in oil so that Jon could swallow them down. For now, he could just mix the paste with some boiled water to get it down the younger man's throat.

Baltsaros turned with the cup in his hand and saw that Jon was once more awake, watching him with eyes that sparkled with fever. His dark hair was plastered to his forehead, and Baltsaros could see he was shivering. Idly, he wondered whether the brain-swell had caused any permanent damage as he walked back to the sick man on the cot, sitting down next to him.

"I won't be alive long enough to be any use to you," said Jon, his voice quiet. Baltsaros was surprised to hear neither bitterness nor sadness in it. He shook his head and smiled down at the young man on the bed. With one hand behind Jon's head to tilt it up, he placed the cup against his lips.

"Drink. It will taste terrible, but drink all the same," he said.

Jon took a sip and grimaced but drank all the bitter liquid down without complaint. Baltsaros lowered Jon's head back onto the pillow and sat back. The slight dark-haired young man on the bed brought a shaky hand up to wipe his lips. The medicine would work to fight the infection as well as make Jon sleep deeply while he healed.

Baltsaros stood to leave, and Jon's eyes opened a crack, a slight frown on his drawn face.

"You're healing me," he said simply. The captain nodded once, pleased that Jon had deduced as much. "Why didn't you tell me you could heal me before I made my decision?" Jon asked, confused.

Because I didn't want to waste my medicines on someone who was stupid enough to refuse my offer.

Suddenly, Baltsaros wondered if that was the truth. He curled his lips into a gentle smile.

"Because I didn't want you to base your decision on it," he answered. "I would have healed you regardless," Baltsaros added, lying.

Jon smiled softly and nodded against the pillow.

I wanted you to come with me because you chose to, not because I bought you.

The words barely touched Baltsaros's mind before he dismissed them, feeling almost angry. His dark eyes watched as Jon's eyes fluttered closed again before he finally left the cage.

Hours later, Jon woke up with a hollow pit in his stomach and bladder crying out for release. As he sat up shakily, he was surprised to see that the door to his cage had been left open.

So I am, indeed, free.

Jon lurched to the chamber pot and pissed into it, relief so great he almost moaned out loud. His clothes were still sitting in a neat pile on the floor of the cage where Tom had left them, but Jon just frowned; they were the clothes of a stable boy... not a pirate.

He grinned to himself, real excitement bubbling up inside him for the first time. His head still ached and his lungs hurt, but he trusted that the captain wouldn't lie to him; he would be made well. Jon shook his head a little and pulled a sheet off the bed. After wrapping himself up against the cool night air that came in through the open door of the stateroom, Jon took a step outside his cage.

The rugs were soft under his bare feet, and he smiled to himself. The captain's tastes were certainly refined. He saw that there was a covered plate next to a cup on the big mahogany table and hoped that there would be some more of that delicious egg dish for him.

He raised the cover and saw a simple meal of bread and cheese; Jon tried not to let the disappointment get to him. Next to the staples he'd eaten his whole life were things that looked like dried fruit, but nothing he recognized. He lifted the round, yellow shape to his mouth and bit down. The pink-brown meat of the fruit was surprisingly sweet and filled with little seeds that crunched in his teeth; Jon grinned and ate a few more in quick succession. He was delighted when the cheese turned out to be richer and sharper than any he'd ever eaten before, and the bread, darker brown than he was used to, was savoury and flavoured with exotic spices. The cup, he realized in surprise, contained sweet cider instead of plain water. His earlier disappointment extinguished, Jon dug into his meal with relish.

When there was nothing left on the plate but a few crumbs, Jon decided to look around. He could hear the occasional thump of someone walking overhead, and twice he thought he could make out Tom's voice calling to someone, but otherwise, the night was quiet and cool. It seemed like the sea was quiet too as the floor barely moved beneath his feet.

The captain's bed was empty. With a glance to the open door, Jon approached the scene of last night's debauchery with some curiosity. It was a low, wide bed that curved against the inside of the wall. At the head was a wooden board with something carved into it, but it was too dark to see in the candlelight. Jon reached out and touched the scarlet coverlet, running one finger against the soft, silky material. There were beads and embroidery sewn into it to make a strange circular pattern; Jon thought it was the most beautiful thing he had ever seen.

He heard a noise and snatched his hand away, looking over his shoulder in surprise, but there was nothing there. Jon's heart pounded in his chest, and he laughed to himself; what was he doing messing around with the captain's bedclothes in the dark?

Imagine it on your bare skin.

The unexpected thought made his heart leap in his chest, and he backed away, crashing into the corner of the table with his hip. Smarting both in body and mind, Jon stood in the near dark trying to decide whether he should go back to his cage when he heard the splash of water outside.

With breathless curiosity, Jon approached the door and peered out, remaining hidden in the shadows. He gasped as the scene before him rendered his situation finally, and completely, real.

He was standing at the rear of the ship (*the stern*, he reminded himself) looking down the polished wooden deck. There were men lounging on crates and talking softly as they fixed some netting not far from where he stood; the smoke from their pipes and rolled tobacco curled into the air, disappearing into low clouds backlit by a nearly full moon overhead. Jon spotted movement to his right and was amazed as he watched a lithe, dark shape climb up some rigging. The wind rustled Jon's hair, and he could hear the little chuckling sounds of water hitting the hull; there was a steady, soft creak as the ship slid over waves, and the cool night breeze was flavoured with salt. He heaved a long sigh: clean, fresh air. Jon felt his chest tighten.

A fresh start.

He suddenly thought his heart would burst in his chest.

Jon turned to go back inside and saw with a start that Tom was perched on the rail of the quarterdeck; the first mate was staring down at him with eyes glinting in the lantern hanging above Jon's head. He gasped; for a moment the muscular youth resembled nothing so much as the animal he was named for, a malevolent feline shape in the dark. There was a flash in Tom's hands, and Jon saw with disquiet that the man in the shadows had his knife out. Jon suddenly felt genuine fear as the first mate's face curled into a wicked grin.

As he passed through the doorway, he heard Tom's cheerful voice call after him.

"Nighty night, Jonny boy. Sweet dreams."

CHAPTER 6
ALL AT SEA

all at sea • *naval slang (18th century)* in a state of confusion and disorder.

Baltsaros studied Jon's face over breakfast. He was thin to the point of gauntness with patchy, dark stubble covering the fine lines of his jaw. The angle of his nose was slightly crooked, and there were deep shadows beneath eyes that constantly shifted from sky-blue to storm-grey. *His hair is a disaster,* thought Baltsaros with a small smile. It was seal brown, the curls matted from being slept on, and Jon's nervous habit of rubbing a hand through it when he was thinking had caused it to stick up almost comically in whorls and cowlicks. Overall, he made for a charming waif, all big eyes, messy hair, and bird bones.

After taking another bite of his food, Baltsaros sat back, amused. At the speed with which Jon was devouring the meal of egg scramble and sausage, it wouldn't be long before he filled out some, and work on the ship would pile more weight in the form of muscle onto that slight frame. Baltsaros frowned, his nostrils flaring delicately; Jon was a work in progress with one unfortunate trait that could readily be fixed.

He caught the captain's eye and stopped midchew.

"What's wrong?" Jon asked, his voice tinged with a little nervousness.

"You need a bath," said Baltsaros with a wry grin.

Jon's face reddened, and chewing furiously, he stared down at his plate. Baltsaros laughed, adding to his discomfiture. After he took a sip of the strong black coffee, Jon surprised the captain by replying in a sardonic tone.

"*You* try smelling like a rose when you're sleeping and sweating your days away," he said, tearing off another hunk of sourdough from the loaf in the middle of the table.

Baltsaros nodded once, and his graceful lips parted in a wide smile to show sharp white teeth. Jon was obviously feeling better; there was strong metal buried within that frail shape.

The captain rose from his seat and walked to the open door. He put his fingers between lips and whistled a short, shrill blast. In a few moments, Tom came loping down the deck to see what Baltsaros wanted.

The burly young man was sporting a new large bruise across one cheek and a split lip; it had been days since they had last shared a bed, and it seemed Tom was relieving his tension in other ways. Baltsaros wondered who had been on the receiving end of Tom's hard fists and whether there was someone with torn skin in need of stitching.

The look on Tom's face as he approached Baltsaros was both hopeful and resentful at once; his first mate was not dealing well with being ousted from his usual spot in Baltsaros's bed. Jon would have time later to come to terms with the captain's proclivities, but for the moment Baltsaros didn't want to unduly stress him. The captain had decided that as long as Jon was recuperating, he himself would sleep alone. He thought a gentle hand would work best with Jon; it was a pleasant change from the strong touch that Tom constantly required to keep him in line.

"What is it, sir?" asked his first mate, blue-green eyes sliding away from the captain's scrutiny.

Sir...

Baltsaros sighed and reached out a large hand to cup the back of the first mate's neck. He drew Tom into a quick embrace, pressing his lips to the bruise on the man's cheek; Baltsaros hoped that was enough to mollify Tom for the time being.

"Start heating some water, and bring a tub to my quarters, Tom," he said, releasing him.

The muscles in Tom's strong jaw moved under his tanned skin a moment before he nodded somewhat curtly.

"Aye, Da," he said and turned to leave. As he ran down the deck, Tom began bellowing for ship hands to start hauling the nonpotable water out of the large tank at the front of the ship.

Baltsaros shook his head in amusement as the crew scrambled to obey Tom's orders. If nothing else, the ex-slave made for an effective taskmaster; half the crew was terrified of him.

After he stepped back through the door, the captain saw that Jon stood in front of the large map, the sheet he had taken to winding around himself discarded on the chair where he had been sitting a moment ago.

Baltsaros walked up to him.

"It's a map of the known world," he explained.

Jon's brow furrowed as he looked at the large drawing mounted on the wall.

"Where are we now?" he asked, turning his blue eyes to Baltsaros. The captain reached out with a sure hand to trace the curve of the islands they were currently sailing past and then tapped his finger on a spot near the mainland.

"Here. Roughly," said Baltsaros, smiling at Jon.

The younger man frowned again at the map.

"I'm not understanding the scale, I think. Where is Portsmouth? How far have we come?" he asked, curious.

Baltsaros slid his finger along the course they had taken, about three inches across the shaded waters.

Jon's eyes widened, and he stepped back.

"We've only gone that far in five days? Is the world so big?" he asked, his eyes darting over the whole map. Baltsaros chuckled.

"Well... We aren't going full speed; but, yes, the world is big. Bigger than this map shows, even. This is all that we have discovered. There may be far more." He crossed his arms over his broad chest and watched Jon as he absorbed the information. Jon nodded then looked back at Baltsaros.

"Where are you from?" he asked, somewhat shyly.

Baltsaros felt a small pang in his chest, strangely touched by the fact Jon wanted to know more about him. He reached out again and slid his finger far north, nearly to the top of the map.

"This is where I was born," he replied. "In my mother tongue it's called 'Heaven's Gate,' but it's really just a lot of snow and darkness." He smiled. "It's not such a terrible place, but I prefer the warmth in the south."

Jon smiled back at him.

Baltsaros leaned once more towards the map and pointed to a spot about three feet south-east of their position. His dark hand rested on the map a moment, his mind suddenly full of the smell of fresh figs and ripe oranges.

"This is where my home is," he said softly. "It's called Madierus." When he turned to look at Jon, the young man had a sad expression on his face; was he missing his own home? He was about to ask the question when a loud crash sounded behind them.

Startled, Baltsaros saw that Tom had dropped the metal tub on the wooden floor. In dismay, he saw that Jon and his first mate locked eyes for a tense moment before Tom turned to the captain with a broad grin on his face. Baltsaros was not happy with the hostility that Tom was showing towards their newest recruit.

"The water'll be here in a jiff, Da," said his first mate. Jon's shoulders came up in an awkward hunch; he was obviously made uncomfortable by Tom's presence. To make matters worse, the muscular youth winked sassily at Jon.

"Don't worry, love! Yer majesty will get her bath!" he said with a short bark of laughter. Tom, seeing the dark look on Baltsaros's face, just grinned wider and strolled out of the room, the handle of his knife peeping above the belt at his narrow waist.

Watching Tom walk away, the muscles moving fluidly under the scarred skin of his sun-darkened back and the saucy way his hips moved as he padded silently on bare feet, Baltsaros felt a sudden pulse of desire. The dangerous young man was indeed a beautiful specimen.

He turned his head back to Jon who was staring at him with an expression bordering on horror. Jon quickly settled his face back into a neutral expression, but Baltsaros felt uncomfortably like he had taken a peek inside his mind.

Interesting.

The discomfort gave way quickly to curiosity. He wondered what else Jon could see; was he just reading expressions or could he predict intentions? From what he had heard, Jon could read someone's future simply in the way they drank their coffee, but Baltsaros dismissed that as ignorant hyperbole. Regardless, the boy's talent was certainly intriguing. The captain couldn't wait to put it to the test.

They watched in silence as deckhands poured bucket after bucket of hot water into the large metal tub. When it was three-quarters of the way full, Baltsaros dismissed them.

Tom stepped lithely back into the stateroom and smiled; he crossed his arms over his tanned chest, his large forearms scarred and muscular, and leaned against the wall. Baltsaros frowned at Tom, who pulled the sliver of wood he was chewing on from between his teeth.

"What? I wanted to watch," said the first mate, shrugging; his sea-green eyes were narrow, challenging the captain.

Baltsaros closed the space between them in a few steps and stared down hard at the shorter man.

"Don't be cheeky, Tom. Leave us be," he growled.

Tom glared up at the captain for a few seconds, then, turned on his heel, slamming the door behind him. Baltsaros closed his eyes a moment, purging from his mind the image of his hands around Tom's throat and the sudden surge of lust it brought.

He turned back to Jon, who was just standing still, looking down at the water-filled tub. In amazement, he watched as Jon pulled the soiled shirt up over his head, dropping it to the ground next to him.

He had expected Jon to ask him to leave.

Baltsaros felt his pulse accelerate at the sight of Jon's pale skin, ribs clearly visible next to the starkly defined muscles of his sides.

Not so weak, then.

Baltsaros realized he was staring when Jon stopped moving, his hands at the waist of his shorts, and his eyes fixed on the captain's face. The older man smiled and dipped his head, turning around to give Jon some privacy while he undressed.

When Baltsaros heard Jon settling into the hot water with a gasp, he walked to the chest near the foot of his bed and pulled out a few things. After crossing the room to pull up a chair next to the metal tub, Baltsaros handed a small block of sandalwood-scented soap and a rough towel to Jon as he sat down.

Jon let out a pleased groan as he reclined in the tub. He looked up at the captain and smiled.

"I haven't had a bath like this in ages," he said. He brought the soap to his nose. "This smells great. Thank you, Captain."

Baltsaros watched in amusement as Jon began lathering himself, the dam that had held back his words suddenly broken.

"Reginald didn't believe in hot baths; he said it made a man weak. I took cold baths from the time I was four, when my mother died, until I was able to go to the baths in town on my days off. That was only a little over a year ago. I think I may have actually wept the first time I sank into a bathtub full of hot water. Such a luxury." He laughed and smelled the soap again. "And, never with soap that smelled this good. Can all your men afford these things, or is it only because you're captain?" he asked, looking up at Baltsaros.

The captain smiled and shook his head. "We can all afford these luxuries, Jon. My cut of our... earnings, if you'd like, is only marginally higher, and that is only to defray costs like maintaining the ship or docking in specific harbours. I may be captain, but we are all more-or-less equal on this ship," Baltsaros replied, skimming around the fact that he was the one who meted punishment and could veto all crew decisions.

Jon nodded thoughtfully.

"What will be my work here?" he asked after a moment.

Baltsaros's eyes watched as suds followed the curve of the young man's shoulder and rubbed his palm against his knee before closing his hand into a fist. Jon was definitely having an effect on Baltsaros. He shifted his gaze away from the man's naked skin.

"Not much at first, I'm afraid. Initially, you will work at learning your way around the ship; with that will be a lot of cleaning and putting up with mediocre or odious tasks, but that's because you are new. It's not glamorous, but it's necessary. If you accept it all with grace and patience, you'll earn the respect of the crew." He smiled kindly at the disappointment in Jon's face. "You'll also act as an advisor when I deal with other ships. That is where your unique talent will shine. I plan on using you tomorrow when we unload our current cargo," he added, and almost laughed at the excitement and terror that suddenly widened Jon's eyes.

His gaze narrowed thoughtfully for a moment, and Baltsaros started rolling up his sleeves. Suddenly on guard, Jon's dark brows came down. There was a new tack the captain wanted to try. Baltsaros leaned towards the tub.

"Here, I'll wash your back," he said, keeping his voice light. He had no idea whether Jon would let himself be touched. Jon had willingly put himself into Baltsaros's hands when it came to having his fever taken, but this was a different matter entirely.

Jon's cheeks, already rosy from the heat of the bath, darkened to a deeper shade of red, and he looked like he was about to refuse Baltsaros's help.

"Pass me the soap," said the captain, his tone commanding, and Jon moved to obey him, a strange expression in his stormy-blue eyes.

He really does not know what he wants.

Baltsaros was attempting to ease the young man's anxiety with a human touch, but he realized in dismay that his motives had little to do with how useful that would make him to the crew; the truth was that Baltsaros foolishly wanted to win Jon over, both mentally and physically, for himself.

To what end?

He rubbed the soap onto the cloth and reached out to scrub Jon's bent back. The cloth slid smoothly across his slippery ribs and bumped over the ridges of his spine. The angle was slightly awkward, and when Baltsaros shifted his grasp it brought his thumb into contact with Jon's supple skin, he felt his chest tighten with sudden longing. Baltsaros felt Jon tremble slightly under his touch as he stroked his thumb slowly across his back, following the path of his lithe muscles.

Baltsaros felt suddenly weak and strangely like he was losing control of the situation. Standing quickly, he dropped the towel into the tub, then turned to leave. He looked back over his shoulder at the startled Jon and made his excuse.

"I'm sorry, you'll have to finish bathing yourself. I have pressing things to attend to," Baltsaros said and left through the door, his mouth dry. Where a solid wall once stood in his mind, keeping the messy, howling beast of his humanity under strict control, there was a breach. It was tiny, but it was troubling.

~

Jon watched in shock as the captain left the stateroom, an obvious lie on his lips. He lay back in the tub, a chorus of conflicting emotions in his mind. Over the past few days, he'd felt himself growing bolder in the captain's presence, gaining admiration for the elegantly handsome man. Baltsaros was intelligent and inquisitive; Jon never felt like he was boring the captain with his questions or annoying him with his insecurities. On the contrary, it seemed like he was genuinely interested in him. Jon began to notice the captain looking at him in a way no one else had: like he was worthy of attention. While Jon couldn't admit to himself yet that what he was feeling was attraction to the enigmatic captain, he found his confidence buoyed by it.

Earlier, when Baltsaros had shooed Tom from the room, he had expected the captain to follow him out. When he hadn't, a shocking recklessness had taken over Jon; he had stood there, amazed at himself, stripping his clothing off in front of the other man.

It was only a lifetime of insecurity that had finally stilled his hands as they were about to render him completely naked before the captain's eyes. Baltsaros had just stared, face sombre and eyes dark with something that pulled at Jon.

Then later, the ridiculousness of being washed by a pirate captain. Jon sighed to himself and soaped his shoulders again.

Was it really ridiculous?

He closed his eyes and leaned back. Why had the captain left so abruptly? Had Baltsaros seen something of Jon that displeased him? That small touch, the surprising sensation of skin sliding against wet skin... Jon moved his soapy hand down his chest.

Or had he seen something that pleased him too much?

The thought sent Jon's heart careening, and he laughed softly. The idea of wanting a man to... desire him. It was simply staggering. Jon frowned and thought of the shocking dreams he'd begun having nightly; his cock responded by moving again in the warm water to resume the stiffening that had started with the captain's touch.

The last dream in particular... Baltsaros had been moving over Jon, using him face-up like a man used a woman. Jon clenched his eyelids tighter, the images in his mind filling him with a hot sensation that made the bath feel cool in comparison. His hand slid below the water, down his belly to the dark hair curled around the base of the rigid staff that bobbed stiffly in the water. What was it about the dark-eyed man that made him feel like this?

With equal parts shame and desire, Jon finally closed his hand around his cock. He imagined that instead of his own slim fingers, Baltsaros's long, sun-darkened ones were stroking him. With a low whimper in his throat, Jon began to slide his fist over his shaft in the warm water.

Yes, it was Baltsaros's hand on him. Now his mouth, hot and wet, around his cock. Jon shuddered with pleasure, feeling a little wicked for even forming the word "cock" in his head. He slid further down in the water until his chin was immersed. He spread his knees, imagining the captain's head bobbing between his thighs. With all thoughts to shame out of mind, Jon stroked his shaft, pulling at the sensitive head with thumb and finger, imagining them to be Baltsaros's lips. Nearly panting with the force of his desire, Jon felt the climax start deep within himself. He groaned out loud and clamped the washcloth over the head of his cock as his lust finally crested in hot waves, spilling seed into his covered hand.

For a few moments, Jon could hear nothing but his breathing and the rushing blood in his ears. Thighs trembling, he eventually pulled the cloth out of the water and stared down at it with dismay.

~

Baltsaros had Tom up against the back wall of the galley. Tom's hands were clasped behind his head, tied there by the belt around his throat. The captain was thrusting himself into his first mate in a fury, driving his cock into Tom's ass so forcefully that Baltsaros heard the man's collarbones knock hard against the wooden slats.

Tom had stopped struggling and now whimpered or moaned as he pushed back into every thrust. Baltsaros didn't need to reach around to know that the first mate's cock would be rigid and wet with his own pleasure; the captain gritted his teeth and grunted as he ploughed faster into the younger man. When orgasm quickly burst out of him in a hot torrent, he wrapped his hand around Tom's shaft for the last few thrusts and felt the other's cum hot against his palm almost immediately.

Panting hard, Tom let out a sobbing cry and sagged in the captain's grasp.

Baltsaros, chest heaving, pressed his forehead against Tom's shoulder for a moment before stepping back and releasing him.

The first mate slid, almost bonelessly, down the wall. Baltsaros shoved his softening cock almost angrily back into his pants; he felt strangely unsatisfied and frustrated. Tom looked up at the captain with wet, red eyes as Baltsaros undid the belt that was looped around him.

What was it about Jon that had him so wound up?

He frowned into Tom's upturned face for a moment. Feeling only annoyance at the man on the floor, Baltsaros lashed out, backhanding his first mate as hard as he could. Tom let out a yell and collapsed on his side. Baltsaros crossed the room to the door, leaving Tom bleeding on the floor, and heard the man begin to laugh behind him.

CHAPTER 7

CLOSE QUARTERS

When he heard footfalls behind him, Jon quickly closed the book he was holding. He turned and saw that the captain had entered the stateroom, a plate in each hand, just like he had the past three evenings.

Baltsaros raised his stark brows, looking at the younger man in curiosity.

"You can read?" he asked, sounding amazed.

Jon's guilt at having taken the book was replaced by embarrassment.

"Yes. Of course, I can read. I'm not stupid," he said, hating the fact that he sounded so defensive. Baltsaros placed the plates on the table and shook his head slightly.

"Jon, you'll have to stop assuming that everything I say is meant to wound you in some way," he said in a soft voice, smiling at him. Though Baltsaros had been terse when leaving so abruptly earlier that day, it seemed that he was once more his affable self.

Jon took a deep breath and nodded, his lips pressed into a hard line. He placed the book, a lexicon of mythical sea creatures, back on the shelf and closed the glass-fronted cabinet door. As he approached the table, the captain looked at him appraisingly.

"You look better, Jon," he said. "And the change of clothes suits you."

Jon looked down and smoothed the front of the shirt Tom had given him, feeling a little bit at a loss.

~

Shortly after his bath, Tom appeared with a bundle of clothing for Jon. The muscular first mate, sporting yet another bruise on his handsome face, seemed strangely passive as he set the pile down on the table. With a preoccupied expression, the unusually silent Tom just stood there sizing Jon up before picking out a light-brown, loose linen shirt and dark-grey trousers that could be rolled and tied at the knee. Then, after a thought, Tom also pulled a clean pair of unbleached, knee-length linen undershorts out of the pile.

Jon felt a little suspicious at Tom's placid nature as he took the clothing from him. When the first mate saw his distrust, he just shook his head and tutted.

"Lovey, just try these on, ok? Captain's orders." A hint of his usual brash cheerfulness faintly touched the smile on his face. "I'll even turn around so ye don't have to show me yer willy, Jonny," he added, his grin widening.

Jon frowned at Tom. Earlier, loath to put his soiled clothing back on over clean skin, he had opted instead for the marginally cleaner sheet; he had hoped the captain would come back to lend him some clothing.

Disconcerted, Jon stood holding the sheet around him as he watched Tom turn around, granting him some unexpected privacy.

What happened to you today, Tom? he wondered as he quickly pulled on the shirt and fastened the pants at his hips. To his chagrin, Jon saw that they were too big at the waist. He cleared his throat, and Tom turned around to look at him.

"Yer a skinny thing, aint'cha, lovey," he said, shaking his head. He turned and walked out of the stateroom without another word, leaving Jon clutching miserably at the waistband of the ill-fitting trousers.

However, after only a few moments Tom strolled back into the room, a roll of narrow hemp rope looped over his shoulder. Jon watched as the first mate slid a few feet of the rope through his big, scarred hands, cutting it off with his knife when there were a few parallel lengths. He passed the ends of the pieces through a metal ring and doubled the rope up.

"Be a dove and hold this," he said to Jon, passing him the ring.

As Jon looked on in amazement, Tom's surprisingly nimble hands swiftly braided the lengths of rope together to make a corded belt. When he was done, and the ends were knotted off, he took the ring out of Jon's hand and leaned forward.

Jon flinched and felt his pulse start to race when Tom's muscular arms came around him. Tom's laugh rumbled deep in his broad chest.

"I ain't goin' to kiss ye, poppet. Just keep still like a good little lad," he said, his tone amused. Jon noticed that Tom had fresh abrasions down the side of his neck, and the skin around his right collarbone was mottled and bruised.

He had to close his eyes as Tom fiddled with the belt at his waist; the bigger man was so near that he was completely overwhelming Jon's senses. In dismay, he felt his body responding to Tom's proximity; Jon could feel the heat coming off the first mate, the other man's lusty masculinity making him feel incredibly flustered.

What am I becoming? he thought miserably.

Jon gasped when he suddenly felt Tom's hands stroke down his hips and grasp his buttocks as the first mate pressed him against his hard body for an instant before pulling away with a sly grin. Jon reeled in shock at Tom's temerity, and he tried to quash the steady pulse of desire the bigger man's actions had wrung out of him.

Tom stepped back a pace and cocked his head at Jon, his brash good-nature revived as he winked at the stunned man.

"There. That'll do ye until we dock somewhere's ye can buy yerself something in good leather," he said, his white teeth flashing in his tanned face.

Jon looked down at the belt knotted expertly at his waist, trying to hide the fact that he felt more than a little breathless. When he raised his head Tom had gone, silent as a cat. Jon closed his eyes.

Tom is dangerous, he reminded himself. *He means you no good.* Jon knew he had to keep that thought in mind; anything else was pure folly.

~

As he stood looking down at his shirt, Jon thought he could still smell Tom on him: clean sweat and smoke, and something of the sea. Jon pulled back the chair and sat down across from the captain, forcing his face into what he hoped was a pleasant smile.

It felt uncomfortably like a lie not to tell the captain of Tom's brazen advances, made solely of mischief though they might be. On the other hand, if he did complain, Baltsaros might perceive him as someone who couldn't handle his own problems. So, in the end, he decided to say nothing at all.

The captain lifted the cover off the plate in front of Jon; the smell that wafted up from the meat dish was divine. He smiled as Baltsaros sat down and uncovered his own dish.

"What are we having tonight?" he asked.

"It's called *Cormarye*. Basically a pork roast with caraway, coriander, red wine, and loads of garlic," Baltsaros answered before pulling the meat off his fork with sharp teeth. Jon picked up his own utensils, handling them with increasing skill, and took a mouthful. It was, like everything else he'd eaten while on board the ship, delicious. The captain, seeing the appreciation plain on Jon's face, smiled wide.

Jon chewed happily, his problems momentarily forgotten.

"You have one hell of a cook, Captain," he said, cutting one of the tender, young potatoes in half and spearing it with his fork.

Baltsaros laughed, a glint in his dark eyes. "My cook is very good, yes. However, I make my own meals," he said, smiling at the stunned look on Jon's face. "Cooking is a hobby of mine."

"Well. It's amazing. As always," Jon stuttered, desperately wishing he had half the poise of the older man. The captain grinned and bowed his head, a graceful acknowledgment of Jon's compliment.

Jon watched as Baltsaros looked down at his plate, carving another bite from the juicy meat; his face was all planes and angles, eyes darkly shadowed by his alpine brow. Jon saw that the short stubble on the captain's jaw was lightly dusted with white hairs, but his skin remained smooth and unlined; he found himself wondering what it would be like to run his thumb along those sharp cheekbones down to the rough curve of his jaw.

Baltsaros looked up, his dark eyes widening slightly when he saw himself being observed so closely; Jon's cheeks burned, and he smiled awkwardly. When he reached for his cup, he was happy to see that it was filled with red wine, barely watered. He took a long swallow.

It seemed that the air was thick with a strange tension; the darkened room made a cocoon around the nimbus of candlelight, trapping the men in a warm, glowing space that was increasingly intimate with every glance they shared. Though the meal was one of the best in his life, Jon was beginning to have a hard time swallowing it down.

Desperate to break the long silence, he chose the only subject he could think of.

"Uh. So I can read, yes. Reginald thought it important that I know my letters," he said in a rush. The captain just nodded, the smile on his face now subdued and his brown eyes impassive. Jon longed to know what was going on in Baltsaros's head. Was he making a fool of himself? Was that desire he saw in the other man's eyes? He took another swallow of wine; he was a blind man feeling for pitfalls in a dangerous cave.

Alarmed, he realized the captain was now staring hard at him; Baltsaros tapped his finger lightly against the side of his cup, an oddly nervous gesture for the normally imperturbable man.

Jon was astonished; it was suddenly crystal clear to him that the man across the table was fighting to get himself under control, as though the captain were desperately closing storm windows against a howling tempest within. Only the slightest hint of the struggle showed on Baltsaros's enigmatic face, but Jon's strange talent had honed in on it. Before he had a chance to say anything, he saw the captain's brow crease for a moment, his large hands curling into fists on the table before sliding flat, palms down on the warm wood.

Captain Baltsaros looked at Jon, all expression wiped from his face.

"You'll be moving to the crew bunks tomorrow. Good night, Jon," he said and stood.

Jon watched in dismay as the captain turned his back and walked out into the darkness, the plate of food he left behind barely touched.

Jon felt terribly alone.

High up on the quarterdeck, Baltsaros was lost in thought. He knew that below his feet, Jon would most likely be trying to find sleep on the narrow cot in his cage.

Not his. Mine.

As he drank deeply from the bottle of wine he held in one large hand, the dark-eyed man stared off over waves glittering with the moon's reflection; the night sky was clear and cool, and the stars twinkled like cold embers in a field of deepest blue. However, the man in the long black coat saw none of the beauty as he stood there, the wind blowing against his face.

He took another swig of wine and frowned. Why was he acting this way? It should be nothing to take the boy to his bed—to kiss the dark shadows under his eyes, to bewitch him with pleasure, to show him the secrets of exquisite pain.

The captain gritted his teeth; Jon was like a poisoned well, and Baltsaros was dying of thirst. While something deep inside him reached out with grasping claws, desperate to pull the younger man tight against him, something else screamed *danger* every time he contemplated it... and for good reason: more small cracks were beginning to show in Baltsaros's composure.

He took another long pull from the bottle before whipping his arm out and launching it high into the air to fall unseen into black waters beyond. He closed his eyes and took a deep breath.

"Tom. You're not needed. Go away," he said to the man on the stairs below; Baltsaros had caught the scent of the first mate's cheroot in the breeze. Dismayed at the note of rough emotion in his voice, Baltsaros opened his eyes and turned. When he saw that Tom hadn't yet moved from his perch, he called out. "Bring me some more red. The one in the darker green bottles. Bring it to me, my tomcat, and then leave me be," he said wearily.

The captain watched as Tom's shadow moved stealthy away on silent feet before he turned back to the sea; as dangerous as the ex-slave was, Jon was turning out to be more so. He had seen desire in the young man's face, and it had *rattled him*... And earlier, Jon in the bath... He swallowed hard, and licked his lips; Baltsaros had to keep away from Jon until he regained his inner calm. That night would be the last time they shared a room; things would be better once Jon went to stay with the rest of the crew.

Better? Or worse?

Tom startled Baltsaros from his thoughts by handing him a bottle of the rich red wine he had brought from home. He dismissed the first mate and watched him slink back into the shadows with an expression of misplaced worry on his battered face. He realized then that Tom had never seen his captain drink alone in the dark like this. Baltsaros nearly laughed as he pulled the cork from the bottle with his teeth and spat it out overboard.

The sky was starting to pinken when Jon heard the captain finally return to his quarters. Blearily opening his eyes, he watched as Baltsaros walked heavily to the other side of the room and lowered himself onto the bed. The older man pulled off his boots and threw them to the floor before lying back on top of the coverlet. After a moment, Jon thought he had gone to sleep; however, when he lifted his head he saw that Baltsaros's eyes were open, staring in Jon's direction. Their gazes locked for a moment, Baltsaros's expression nearly inscrutable, before he turned over. Disturbed, Jon laid his head back on the pillow; he had seen something in the other man's eyes he had never expected: a touch of fear.

CHAPTER 8

NELSON'S FOLLY

Nelson's folly • *naval slang (19th century) rum.*

Jon stood uneasily on the deck just outside the captain's quarters, blinking into the bright sun. Tom gave him another nudge from behind, and Jon took a second reluctant step forward. He heard the larger man laugh, and Jon winced; this was not going to be easy. Coming around to sit on a small crate near the stairs to the quarterdeck, Tom looked up at him, brows furrowed in confusion; in the morning light, the first mate's face was a mess of yellows, greens, and purples.

"If yer goin' to be part of this crew... yer goin' to have to, y'know, be part of the crew," he said to Jon, rubbing his thumb against the stubble on his chin. "Now what's the bloody problem, ducky?"

Jon stood barefoot on the wooden planks, staring in near panic at the men on deck who, for the most part, were completely ignoring him.

Stupid. Stupid, why did I think I could do this?

"I... have problems with people. I'm not good with them. I just sort of shut down," he stammered, bringing up his hands to clutch at his biceps. Tom let out a whoop of laughter and slapped his knees.

"Fuckin' hells!" he said, chortling. "Fuckin' bloody fuckin' hells." He shook his head and stood up, forcefully draping one of his muscular arms around Jon's shoulders. Because Tom wasn't much taller than him, Jon was stooped slightly under the larger man's weight as he tried to lean away from his bare side.

Tom started dragging Jon along as he pointed out parts of the ship with a callused, tobacco-stained finger.

"That's a mast. That's a crate... We're startin' real simple here, lovey. That's Old Ben, passed out like usual. Don't let him fool ye though... He's a good one once the hangover wears off," he said, kicking the sleeping man's boot. To one side of the ship, a man who must have been near seven feet tall was pulling a rope through a pulley. Jon suspected he was the giant who had held his wrists at the brothel.

"That's Beard. Well... His name ain't really *Beard*; he just has an unpronounceable name in his shitty northern language. Dont'cha, Beard?" he yelled up at the incongruously clean-shaven man. The huge, burly brute just frowned down at Tom before sending a jet of spit overboard. Tom laughed.

"Can't speak a word of anything else," he said, shaking his head. Jon gingerly put one hand against Tom's warm side to try to pull his head out of the bigger man's hold, but to no avail; Tom just shifted his grip and steered him in another direction. Jon could feel the hard muscles flexing over Tom's ribs and pulled his hand back; the contact had sent his heart racing.

"That is the capstan," Tom continued, pointing to a large spoked wheel. "Ye'll be helpin' to turn that later today if ye don't fall overboard and drown first." The first mate chuckled to himself and then stopped. "Ye *can* swim, right?" he asked, looking down, sea-green eyes crinkled in amusement. Jon nodded quickly, and Tom patted him hard on the head with his free hand. "Good, good," he said and then pointed up, resuming the above-deck portion of his tour.

"Yardarms, ratlines, quarterdeck, mizzen mast... and... uh, the captain." Tom's voice trailed off at the last, the wind blown out of his sails at the sight of the man in the long, dark coat. Jon used Tom's momentary distraction to extract himself from the heavy arm over his shoulders. He stood next to the first mate, looking up at the captain's back, high above them.

When Jon had awoken that morning, the older man was nowhere to be seen, even though it couldn't have been more than a few hours since he'd lain down.

Baltsaros seemed to be watching the wake behind them, standing eerily still, a black silhouette against the bright cerulean sky. The muscles worked in Tom's broad jaw as he watched the captain a moment longer. When he finally turned his head back to his newest recruit, Jon thought he could see apprehension in Tom's blue-green eyes.

What is going on?

The first mate's face swiftly creased into a broad grin, discarding the solemnness that had settled for only a moment; he curled his big hand around Jon's bicep, turning the shorter man around again. Jon had to keep his mouth from dropping open when he saw the woman who was approaching them.

There are women on the ship? he thought with alarm.

She was slim and walked with a confidence that nearly turned her long strides into a swagger. As she came closer, Jon could see that she had dark, almond-shaped eyes and ebony hair in a long braid over one shoulder. She was dressed in a sleeveless, dark-brown leather jerkin and black trousers that came down just past her knees with brown leather lacing down each side. In wonder, Jon saw that she wore two gun belts crossed and slung low over her hips, the beautiful, silver-chased, hardwood handles of the pistols resting against her thighs. Jon was happy to see that, unlike the captain and his first mate, she was an open book. Here was someone who was honestly friendly and, Jon realized, mildly concerned that he was in Tom's care.

The first mate laughed low in his chest.

"Jon, this exotic bit of skirt is Katherine. Don't piss her off or she'll make some new holes in that curly, black head of yers. Wont'cha, lovey?" he said, addressing the last to the woman.

Her lips slid into a wry smile, dismissing Tom completely as she turned her dark-brown eyes to Jon; he could easily feel the deep animosity that existed between the two pirates.

"Kat, if you'd like," she said, smiling. Jon swallowed and nodded, nearly choking when Tom clapped a large hand to his chest.

"Kat, my darlin', meet our new little Jonny. Isn't he a dove? Lived under a rock, so's I can tell from his complexion. Completely mute. Hung like a bloody mule," said the first mate loudly. Jon felt his face grow hot. Tom leaned in close to his ear.

"Ex-whore, this one. Sewed her cunny up tight, I hear to tell, when she took up with the crew. A total man-eater. She's got a string of cocks above her bunk that she stirs her coffee with," he said in a stage whisper.

Jon had to smile when Katherine rolled her eyes at him.

She turned and frowned at Tom.

"I see you fell down another flight of stairs, Tommy. You're so hard on that pretty face of yours," she said; her voice was girlish despite the cocksure way she held herself. Tom shook his head slowly; the smile on his face was almost menacing.

Jon took a deep breath.

"I'm not mute... I can talk," he said, somewhat lamely. Tom's big hand slid up his back and squeezed his shoulder.

"Course ye can, lovey. Course ye can," said Tom, his face filled with mock pity.

The air was suddenly split with a shrill whistle, and Tom's head jerked around quickly. He released Jon and pointed at Katherine.

"Show him the bunks; get him working on deck. He's needed this afternoon for the exchange," he said and took off at a jog towards the rear of the ship. Katherine shook her head.

"Off to see his master," she said, her smile crooked. "It's a pleasure to meet you, Jon. Welcome aboard." She crossed her arms across her midriff and gave him an appraising look. "First time at sea?" she asked.

Jon ducked his head and ran a hand through his dark curls.

"That obvious, huh?" he said. At her laugh, he looked up with a frown. However, there was no malice on her face, only gentle amusement; Jon found himself smiling back at her.

"So," said Katherine, her hands on her hips. "What do you want to know?"

Jon brought up one shoulder in a shrug.

"I suppose everything you're willing to tell me," he said truthfully. Tom's lessons, so far, had been largely unhelpful. He started and then, cringed as a big, black-bearded man pushed past them. Katherine's eyes widened at Jon's reaction.

"Not a fan of people?" asked the woman with the guns, looking at him curiously.

Jon shook his head.

"Not really."

Katherine nodded and pressed her lips together.

"Not to sound unkind, but are you sure you're in the right place?" she asked softly. Jon swallowed hard and shrugged again. Katherine nodded her head once in understanding and swiftly launched into the ship rules. Grateful for her tact, Jon found himself quickly absorbed by her words.

"—and basically, we vote for anything that affects us. You really don't want to go to the eastern seas? We all vote. You're not happy with what Cook's been making? We all vote. Etcetera. It's pretty easy. We're really a skeleton crew on the ship... She could take twice our number, but we're all hard workers and it actually isn't so bad. It also makes us richer," she laughed. "The captain's got the final word on everything, but he's generally happy as long as we're happy."

Jon's eyes turned to the quarterdeck, but Baltsaros and Tom were nowhere to be seen.

"Don't steal. Don't fuck over your mates. Those are the two big ones. We're to be loyal to each other. If you've got a problem with someone, you can resolve it privately. However, if you want to make it the business of the whole crew, the usual punishment for the guilty party is time in the brig," Katherine said. "It might not sound like much, but ask Tom about it some day; he's done three long stretches down there just this year."

Jon felt the corners of his mouth turn down, his impression of the roguish first mate not improved by this news. Also, as the morning wore on, he was becoming increasingly aware of how ill-suited he was for this. Though Katherine was nice enough, he wished that the captain would... Would what? Talk to him? Let him stay locked away in his quarters? When Jon remembered the fear in Baltsaros's eyes he swiftly clamped down on the tumult rising up inside before he lost his nerve.

Just don't think about it. You don't know what it means.

At a touch on his arm, he looked up. Katherine was looking into his eyes, worry plain on her face.

"Are you ok?" she asked.

Everyone is always asking.

As he took a deep breath, Jon straightened his shoulders and stood a little taller.

"I... I can do this," he said, more to himself than to the woman who stood before him.

Katherine tilted her head slightly as she crossed her arms again. After a moment, a slow smile crept across her face.

"So, are you really hung like a mule?" she asked. Jon started to blush but then realized that she was only teasing him. Smiling crookedly, Jon blinked in amazement as he heard himself quip back.

"I'll show you if you get us out of this blasted sun."

~

Baltsaros stood on deck, watching the other ship's approach with his binoculars. Behind him, he could hear Tom barking orders to the deckhands.

"C'mon, ye bunch of lounging fucking strumpets! Put yer backs into it. I want to see them all on deck before we heave to! Shake a leg… Oh, I *am* sorry, lovey! Did I wake the lady from her nap? I'll keelhaul the bloody lot of ye if ye don't put them kegs up smart-like!" The mainlander's rolling accent, amplified by his loud running commentary, brought a small smile to Baltsaros's face—the first of the day.

He sighed and pinched the bridge of his nose. As he turned his gaze up deck towards the bow, he saw that Jon was helping to lower the anchor; on the next spoke of the capstan was Katherine. Baltsaros nodded to himself. Jon would do well by befriending her. She was the best shot in his crew and a fair hand with a sword; their newest recruit could certainly learn a few things from her.

The fact that Jon was out dropping anchor in the hot sun, however, brought a frown to the captain's rugged face; he had explicitly told Tom not to put Jon to work just yet. The younger man was on the mend but in no state to be doing hard physical labour. Annoyed, he looked back to his burly first mate, but Tom had gone belowdecks again. Though the ex-slave was at most times desperately loyal, his interpretations of the captain's orders left something to be desired. With Jon aboard, the problem seemed only to have worsened.

Baltsaros lifted the binoculars to his eyes again and saw that Magrette's ship, the *Nelson's Folly,* had anchored; a jolly boat was slowly being lowered down her side. It was soon time to see whether their newest recruit would prove his worth.

If not…

The captain furrowed his brow and turned his gaze back to the dark-haired young man. After last night's drinking binge, Baltsaros felt less than stellar; however, it seemed to have brought some calm to the storm created by his attraction to Jon. Baltsaros knew they would be working side by side later, but since the captain had taken a step back, he felt that he was again in total control. Or at least he hoped he was. If Jon failed to dazzle, he would simply drop him off at the nearest port.

Why not just kill him?

Baltsaros passed his hand over his face and grimaced.

Why not, indeed… came the whisper from within.

~

"—two small barrels of pepper, and a crate of nutmeg," listed out the first mate. The scrawny, black-haired man then turned to his captain and nodded. "It's all there," he said.

Earlier, Baltsaros had explained that they had recently overtaken a huge merchant ship and were trading off the plundered foodstuff and spices. In return, the other captain, someone they dealt with occasionally, was giving them gold. Jon's job was to make sure that there was no swindle involved; Baltsaros had reason to believe that this Captain Magrette could no longer be trusted.

Trying his best to appear aloof and confident, Jon stood to the left of the captain. In reality, he was so nervous and distracted by Captain Baltsaros's presence that he feared his talents would prove to be useless.

Tom stood to the captain's other side, thick arms crossed over his broad chest, his bare feet planted wide apart on the wooden deck. The first mate slyly glanced over to where Jon stood and winked. After shaking his head at Tom, Jon turned back to the dealings. He watched carefully as the men pulled three small chests up from the boat below. When the third chest was hefted, Jon noticed that the pirates lifted it easier than the other two, and he frowned. Their movements were exaggerated, as if in a pantomime. The men shared a quick glance with their captain before setting the lighter chest down, and Jon's eyes slid from the gold to the pale-skinned man with the large hat. There was definitely something amiss. *Why would they want us to notice that one chest was light?*

The captain of the other ship was nothing like Baltsaros. Where the northerner was all planes and angles, Magrette was doughy lumps and curves. The man wasn't hugely fat; he was just not as slim as his straining clothes would have liked.

Jon narrowed his eyes at the other captain and caught something in the man's demeanour that reinforced his feeling of unease. Swinging his eyes back to the chests that now sat open on the wooden planks, Jon's clever mind presented to him a scenario where a lighter chest would somehow benefit someone trying to hustle them. It reminded him of the way merchants would present an item and "prove" its quality before selling identical-looking wares of an inferior worth. He smiled.

Baltsaros turned to him, his eyes dark and impassive.

"What do you see, Jon?" he asked. Jon felt himself blanch; no one had told him he would have to speak in front of everyone. Foolishly, he had imagined a private conversation with the captain. The silence stretched on, all eyes turning to him. Feeling like he was going to burn his way through the hull, Jon took a deep breath and finally spoke.

"They're short-changing us, Captain," he said in a voice that wavered. The other ship's skinny first mate looked askance at his own captain; Jon could tell that he had not been told of the deceit. When Captain Magrette opened his mouth to dismiss his pronouncement, Jon felt suddenly bold with indignation.

"The third chest, the one on the left, is lighter than the other two. Not by much, but enough. They gambled on you noticing it was slightly lighter and counting the gold in it right away to make sure the amount is right... and it will be. They're trying to make us think that we're coming out ahead of the deal; but, it's only when the other two were emptied that you'd notice that it was the chests *themselves* that were heavier. False bottoms with something heavy like lead inside, I think. Crude and stupid," he finished, looking up at the older man by his side.

Captain Magrette had started to sputter, but the sound of gold rolling across the deck, and Tom's long string of expletives, confirmed Jon's theory. Baltsaros turned to look down at Jon; he was astonished and reassured by the depth of amusement (*and... relief?*) in the captain's brown eyes. Jon smiled.

Baltsaros smiled back; with his eyes still on his newest recruit, he gave the command.

"Tom. Take them," he said, his voice deadly quiet. There was an incredibly short struggle as Tom and the gathered deckhands disarmed the would-be thieves. The scrawny first mate spoke up.

"I ain't never was a part o' this, Cap'n sir," he said, his voice nasal and sharp. Baltsaros raised an eyebrow at Jon and tilted his head slightly. Jon understood this as an invitation.

"He speaks the truth, Captain. He might be a complete worm, but he wasn't a part of this. If you let him go, he'll warn others about what happens when thieves cross us," he said, his breath short in his chest as the captain continued to hold his gaze.

"Katherine?" said the captain, his graceful lips curling further into a pleased grin. There was a splash and yelling from below; Jon gathered that the skinny first mate had been pushed overboard.

Baltsaros nodded once.

"Good job," he said simply and finally turned away. Jon nearly staggered, his heart careening in his chest; however, for the first time in his life, he felt incredibly in control... confident.

He looked on as the captain stalked slowly towards the doughy Magrette. The two men shared quiet words; Jon was unable to hear what they were saying, but it was clear that the fat captain was pleading for his life.

In strange detachment, the captain's new advisor watched as a river of red began to flow down the deck.

~

Jon tripped and ended up sprawled on the floor. He rolled over onto his back and started laughing, his hands clutching his stomach as he fought for breath. Tom's face appeared above him; the first mate's ocean-green eyes were narrow with amusement, and his pink lips were stretched in a wide smile.

"Aye, lovey... Yer a bit of a lightweight, aint'cha?" said Tom, holding out a hand to help Jon back to his feet. The world spun a little, so Jon leaned against the bigger man's side. Tom chuckled as his arm came up behind Jon. Jon laughed again and held out his hand for the bottle of rum they were sharing.

The golden lights of the lanterns made streaks in his vision, and for some reason, that made him giddy with joy. He narrowed his eyes, head nodding, at the men who were dancing and shouting. It was a celebration. He was a pirate! Doing pirate things! Jon grinned wide and wiped at his mouth.

Tom's hand was warm against his side as the first mate took the brown bottle back from him. Jon felt fantastic. He could see Katherine standing on the capstan, a fiddle in her hands as she whipped the men into a frenzy with music birthed from wild emotions. For a moment, he thought he saw the captain's silhouette... Jon fell back against Tom's shoulder and looked up at the endless stars. Tom wasn't such a bad guy.

"You're not such a bad guy," he yelled. He felt Tom's hand squeeze him, and it sent a sudden thrill through his body.

No... this is wrong. Isn't it?

He laughed and shook his head, making himself a little dizzy in the process.

Jon had never been to a celebration before. Not really. There were the times when their lord came back to the castle, and Cook would make something nice for the occasion. Sometimes Reginald's men would gather in the courtyard, and there would be dancing with the maids. But... nothing like this.

The captain was pleased with him! It was because of him that they were drinking and dancing under the stars. On the sea. The calm sea. He was at sea!

He went to take the bottle from Tom's hand but the first mate held it out of reach. Jon grabbed at it, grinning like a fool. Tom pulled the slighter man against him. Only for a moment, Jon felt Tom's scratchy stubble against the bottom of his jaw, and then the muscular pirate poured rum into his mouth.

"I want to show ye something, lovey," said Tom, his handsome face serious... handsome!

Dangerous.

Jon realized that one of his hands had looped around the muscular back of the first mate. He was being led away from the music. They were in the captain's quarters. He managed to stumble over the edge of a rug, and he was down again. Giggling. When had he ever giggled before? Muffled voices. Oh, the captain was here.

Tom leaned down and scooped him up. The boy was so strong. Felt so smooth for being so rough. He shook his head, trying to clear it as he was held upright by the first mate. He smiled at the captain who was reclining on his bed, shirtless and with a book in one hand.

"Hi," he said, feeling suddenly shy. Tom's hands were wandering into strange territory, and Jon pushed at them halfheartedly.

Baltsaros put his book down beside him, his expression frustratingly unreadable. Tom pushed Jon down onto the bed and he rose up unsteadily on his knees on the soft mattress.

"He's drunk," said the captain, or so that's what it sounded like. Jon missed what Tom was saying because Baltsaros's hand came out to steady him. To pull him back. Jon was leaning back against the captain's bare chest. Large, steady, warm hands stroked down his arms, and he felt himself shiver. His mind was reeling; he was leaning against the captain... against him on his bed and *oh god, he's...* Jon groaned when Baltsaros slid a hand into the open collar of his shirt, moving slowly to tease his nipple; an incredible pulse of desire went through Jon.

"You did well today, lad," said the captain softly into his ear. Baltsaros's other hand was doing something at Jon's waist. Jon watched wide-eyed as fingers not his own unfastened his pants.

Sudden panic began to well up inside him when the captain's hand started tugging down on the waistband of his undershorts. Jon's breath was coming fast, and he heard himself moan as Tom's nimble fingers quickly helped to divest him of cover.

Time felt sped up. He felt cool air on his exposed cock and gasped as Baltsaros's hands slid up to Jon's shoulders, holding him gently against his chest. This was too much. He shuddered as Tom stroked the skin of his stomach, of his hips. Just as the first mate's hand came into contact with Jon's growing erection, he heard the captain's voice.

"Use your mouth, Tom," said Baltsaros, his words an order.

Jon's breathless reaction to the shocking command forced blood to surge faster into his cock, making it throb. He felt as if balanced on the edge of a precipice. Was this really happening? His head was foggy from the rum, but when Tom's tongue slid wetly up the underside of his hardening shaft, Jon's senses came alive.

He whimpered, his cock bobbing of its own accord in reaction to the contact. He looked down into Tom's sea-green eyes and held his breath; the first mate's mouth curled into a wicked grin before his lips parted over the head of Jon's cock, completely engulfing the sensitive skin.

The foreign sensation was pleasure that was rendered so exquisitely raw that it pulled a cry from deep within Jon's chest. Tom's mouth was so wet and unbelievably hot. Jon strained against the captain, tilting his head up and back against Baltsaros's strong shoulder, his eyes closed tight.

Tom began swallowing him down, and Jon moved his hips up in response, astonished by his eagerness. Baltsaros's hands stroked the taut muscles of his stomach and chest through his shirt; whisper-light, tender touches that only worked to enhance the rougher treatment Tom was giving him in contrast. Nearly his entire length slid down the red, wet tunnel of the first mate's throat, and Jon groaned.

Tom's hard hands grabbed him around the hips as he forced himself down further, his wide-open lips making contact with the very base of Jon's shaft. Then Tom began to move, and Jon's cock began sliding in and out of the first mate's mouth. Baltsaros's large hand played at his throat, clasping it slowly in time to Tom's motions.

Jon bucked his hips in abandon, hot lust unfurling inside, opening him up. He felt Baltsaros's mouth against the side of his neck, and he let out a shuddering breath. Jon opened his eyes and turned his head, desperately seeking out those graceful, cruel lips with his own.

When their mouths met, Jon let out a soft sob, a fresh surge of desire searing through him. He opened his mouth to Baltsaros's tongue and wantonly quested out with his own; feeling the captain grow hard against the small of his back as their mouths moved together, Jon gasped and brought up his hand, Baltsaros's sharp stubble rasping against the skin of his palm. The tide of pleasure inside him was climbing steeply, and he moaned into the kiss.

Tom steadily increased his pace; Jon had to break away from the captain in alarm, pushing at the first mate's head.

"Don't! Oh god... don't... I'm going to..." he gasped. He couldn't say the words. *I'm going to cum.*

The thought of ejaculating into Tom's open mouth was what tipped the balance, and he tensed as his senses narrowed down to a white-hot spear of ecstasy, the cum rising through him and surging out of his throbbing, hard cock in thick pulses. Jon moaned as his body strained up with the force of his orgasm, his shaft completely engulfed by Tom's talented mouth.

When he finally went limp, shaken and almost weeping, Tom released him. The first mate's lips were red and shiny with spit and cum as he looked down at Jon.

"Ye going to survive?" he asked, wiping his mouth with a smile. With his shirt soaked through with sweat, Jon lay panting against the captain; he nodded, closing his eyes. Baltsaros stroked a hand down Jon's side softly before gently pushing him off.

The young man curled up on his side on the red coverlet, helpless tears leaking from his eyes to darken the bright satin. He felt loose limbed and relaxed... though keenly emotional at the same time; finally catching his breath, Jon wondered drowsily how he would feel about this later.

Across the bed, the captain pulled his first mate into his arms, kissing him deeply. Jon watched, slightly confused. A little bit hurt.

I'm the interloper.

He closed his eyes.

Not so special.

Now that the rush of adrenaline had ebbed, the effects of his overindulgence came creeping back, making his body heavy.

He forced his eyes open again to see Tom working the fastenings loose on Baltsaros's pants. He blinked, and when his vision cleared, the captain was up on his knees, long fingers clasped behind Tom's head as he fucked the first mate's mouth.

Jon's lids were drooping shut as he felt himself being pulled away by sleep. He tried once more to keep them open and saw that the captain was looking down at him. The kiss came back, clear in his mind... and then Jon was gone.

~

Baltsaros watched Jon's eyes close, and he shut his own; Tom's skilled mouth had him skirting the edges of oblivion, but it brought with it none of the blazing, exquisite heat that had clenched like a fist inside Baltsaros at the touch of Jon's lips to his.

CHAPTER 9
A FORTNIGHT

Stand upright, speak thy thoughts, declare The truth thou hast, that all may share; Be bold, proclaim it everywhere: They only live who dare

—VOLTAIRE

Jon rubbed a forearm across his forehead, wiping the sweat away. The sun was beating down on his back, but he was quickly getting used to that. He looked down at the brush he was holding and flexed the cramped fingers of the other hand; he was getting used to this too. After dipping the brush in the water, Jon leaned back down and scrubbed at the wooden planks. Even though the chore was unbelievably monotonous, it felt remarkably good to be useful.

Every night, Jon went to bed exhausted, barely able to keep his eyes open for the evening meal, and woke up stiff and sore in the morning. As he felt the muscles of his arms harden and the blisters on his hands turn to calluses, he also began to perceive other changes. Though he was never going to be completely comfortable in a crowd, being forced out in the open, surrounded by so many people, was teaching him to cope with his anxiety.

Jon smiled to himself as he wet the brush again and crawled slowly backwards to start scrubbing a new spot. The past couple of weeks had been eye-opening to say the least; he now knew how to braid rope and fix a net, gut a fish and clean crab, load and fire a pistol, oil and maintain a block and tackle, as well as the simplest of tasks that he'd never had to learn before, like how to peel a potato.

Jon looked up at the quarterdeck where the first mate was perched on the railing, staring down at him. He'd also learned very quickly to avoid dark corners when Tom was around.

Jon woke up and groaned. The brutal pain in his head sent waves of nausea through him. Was his sickness returning? This felt awfully familiar. However, when he swallowed he realized that there was a horrible taste in his mouth, and his stomach roiled.

He could hear people talking.

Jon's eyes flew open at the sound, and he was immediately and completely disoriented. Above his head was the sagging, corded bottom of a bed with a stained mattress bulging through the supports. He closed his eyes for a moment, but when he reopened them, the scene was the same. As he turned his head, the pain rolling through him with the motion, Jon saw that he was in a bottom bunk in the larger of the two crew quarters. He closed his eyes tight against the light coming in through the small portholes, but his head spun. He groaned again and pressed his fingers to his eyelids.

"Here. You'll probably be sick," said a soft voice nearby. Jon blearily cracked open his eyes and saw Katherine walking towards the bed, holding a wooden bucket in one hand. The dark-haired woman smiled grimly at him as she placed it on the floor next to the bunk.

"What... happened?" asked Jon, his tongue dry and coated. He reached out for the cup of water she was holding.

Katherine laughed and shook her head as she rose to her feet.

"You don't remember getting blind drunk last night?" she asked.

Jon coughed on the tiny sip of water he took. *Drunk. The rum.*

"You got awfully chummy with Tom," she said, frowning. "I... it's none of my business what you do, Jon... but I didn't figure on you cozying up to the likes of him. You do realize that he's more than a little unhinged, right?"

Tom. Oh god... Tom's mouth.

Bits and pieces of last night's debacle were rising up in his mind like pieces of meat in a soup. Jon leaned over the bed and vomited a thin, burning stream into the bucket. He heard Katherine take a quick step back. Jon retched hard, his stomach hitching, and he puked again.

Tears ran down his face and off the end of his nose as he hung over the bucket for a long time, a string of saliva swinging from his upper lip. When it seemed that his stomach would stay put, he wiped his mouth on his sleeve and rolled onto his back.

Katherine picked up the cup he had dropped and walked to refill it from the barrel against the far wall. Jon swallowed, his throat raw. The shame and embarrassment that he felt was threatening to choke him, and not only from what he could remember; what he couldn't recall was what scared him the most.

"How did I get here?" he asked quietly.

Katherine handed the cup back to him and sat down on the edge of the bed. Jon moved his legs to make room for her, sitting up slowly against the back wall. Katherine shrugged.

"I don't know. Maybe you walked?" she said. "I was asleep."

"Tom carried 'im in like a sack o' potatoes," said a rough voice across the room with a dry, raspy laugh.

Jon squinted and saw a dark-skinned older man sitting on the edge of his bunk, rolling up the bottom of his pants. When he grinned at Jon, he could see that though his teeth were pearly white against his black skin, the man was missing a front tooth.

"Ye was loaded to the gunwalls, mate. Near dead," he said and stood. Jon felt like crying. Katherine patted his knee gently.

"Drink the water, Jon. It'll make you feel better... eventually, anyway. Next time, don't drink so much if you're not used to it," she said, smiling wryly. "I just hope you didn't get yourself into any trouble."

Trouble? More like disaster.

Jon took another small sip and grimaced. Katherine touched his knee again—the sister he never had.

"I have to go. Get some more sleep... The captain wants you to report to Cook later this afternoon, but that's hours from now. And here, take this," she said, handing him a small metal flask.

He took it and pulled the plug out. Jon nearly gagged from the smell.

Oh god, no more rum.

"No, thank you," he said, trying to hand it back to her.

Katherine shook her head.

"Trust me. When you feel a little better, drink some. It'll help," she stood, tugging down the bottom of her jerkin and adjusting the gun belts at her slim hips. "I'll come around later to check on you if I can," she said and left.

Jon looked around. The other man had departed too, leaving him alone in the bunkroom with his shame. He slid back down and pulled the thin blanket over his head. If only he could go back in time and refuse that first drink. Slow tears leaked out of his closed eyes from both the pain and the crushing humiliation he felt. That he'd let Tom... do... that to him was bad enough without remembering with horror how he had shamelessly kissed the captain. How was he ever going to face him again?

A short while later, waking up briefly from a dream of Baltsaros's warm mouth moving slowly over his, Jon thought he saw a muscular silhouette leaning against the door jamb.

When he blinked, the man had gone.

~

Jon stared up at Tom for a moment longer and then bent his head to his task once more. It had felt like forever before Jon was able to get out of his bunk that morning, shaking and pale but desperate for something to distract his mind from the previous night.

Cook had turned out to be a tall, bald man covered in lewd tattoos. Jon's first job had been to peel what seemed like an endless pile of potatoes.

Jon smiled and scrubbed the deck harder; his hands had been so raw and full of small nicks by the end of the day that Cook had laughed at him and given him an extra helping of the fluffy, garlicky mashed potatoes with his supper.

The last to leave after the meal, Jon had been putting his dishes away in the back of the galley when strong hands had come up around his hips and slid up his chest; in shock, Jon had let his plate fall clattering to the floor.

Jon frowned, sitting back on his heels; his heart beat a little faster at the memory.

~

"What do we have here?" purred the voice in his ear.

Jon pulled out of Tom's grasp and turned to press his back against the wall. The first mate pushed himself up against Jon and looked down at him, his blue-green eyes half-lidded. Jon could smell the spirits on Tom's breath, and his heart lurched in his chest.

"Tom. Don't," he said and gasped as Tom leaned in to slide his lips against the underside of his jaw.

"And why not, love? Ye seemed happy enough to have me suck yer cock last night," said Tom, his voice husky against the side of Jon's neck.

Through his fear, Jon was dismayed to feel himself stirring in response to the first mate's touch. In a panic, he pushed hard on Tom's shoulders.

"Please, Tom. I was drunk. I'm sorry, but please don't," he said and was amazed when the first mate released him after a moment, taking a step back.

There was a dark frown on Tom's rugged face, his eyes narrowed in confusion.

"Yer feelin' poorly. I get'cha, darlin'," he said, nodding. He reached out and touched Jon's bottom lip with a wide thumb. When the first mate swayed slightly, Jon realized just how drunk Tom really was.

Turning to leave, the burly young man said "I'll see ye, Jonny. When ye feel better."

Jon watched in relief as Tom staggered across the room and up the stairs.

~

That had been only the first of a half-dozen similar encounters. It seemed like almost every time Jon found himself alone in a secluded part of the ship, Tom was there with rough kisses and groping hands. Thankfully, Jon had thus far been able to free himself from the first mate's amorous advances; however, he was both terrified and shamefully excited to think of what would happen if Tom cornered him when the first mate was feeling less tractable.

Word around the ship was that the first mate had somewhat fallen out of the captain's good graces, and Jon suspected that the drunken night in the captain's quarters had something to do with it.

The first time Jon had spoken to the captain since that evening, he thought he would melt into the deck with shame. However, the older man had been so businesslike and dispassionate towards him that Jon began doubting his memory. Only once in the last two weeks did Baltsaros give any hint of acknowledgment of what had happened between them.

They had been going over the plans for yet another exchange of goods when he realized that Baltsaros was staring hard at him as he talked, his dark eyes on Jon's mouth and the tip of his tongue against his own bottom lip. The younger man had felt heat in his cheeks and an incredible tightness in his chest.

Noticing Jon's reaction, Baltsaros had suddenly straightened his shoulders and walked away without another word. Jon stung with the memory. He wished he could do something to repair some of the damage his foolishness had done to the already crumbling relationship he had with the captain. While they had worked side by side on numerous occasions since, Baltsaros and Jon were never alone together.

Jon stood and swung the wooden bucket so that the water poured over the planks and sluiced through the drains that dotted the gunwales of the ship. He turned his head back to the quarterdeck, but Tom was nowhere to be seen. He frowned, wondering where the first mate had gone, when he noticed Captain Baltsaros standing in the doorway to his quarters, quietly watching him.

~

Baltsaros was pleased with the changes in Jon. Nearly gone were the stooped shoulders and the furtive glances; instead, the young man walked with a slight spring in his step, and he was often seen with an easy smile. The peeling sunburn that had plagued him for the entirety of his first week had given way to a light tan that made his blue eyes stand out attractively in his fine-boned, sun-kissed face.

The captain felt a strange pain in his chest as he watched Jon scrubbing the deck. The way that Jon had sought out his lips was burned into him. A fortnight had not been enough to diminish the feeling, and Baltsaros had finally admitted to himself that he did not want to see it diminish at all. He had felt keenly alive with Jon in his arms; the kiss, so fraught with inexperienced desire, had left him completely breathless. Feeling strangely hollow since, his mind had begun obsessively returning to the memory again and again, trying to recapture the feeling.

~

Baltsaros was furious; Jon's unexpected kiss had disarmed him completely, and he was fighting to get himself under control. It was as if there was a terrible, shattering cry echoing down a dark well as he pushed away the unexplainable feelings that Jon had wrenched out of him.

Lust. Bury it in lust.

With a grunt Baltsaros came hard, his cock bumping the back of Tom's throat as he thrust himself into his orgasm. He clenched his fist tight, a handful of Tom's dirty-blond hair tangled through his fingers as he held his first mate still until he was finished. Tom started choking, and Baltsaros pushed him away hard. The first mate fell back against the pillows, his fist moving fast over his own shaft.

"No!" said Baltsaros, his voice rough. "You do *not* get to enjoy this, Tom." His first mate's hand ceased its motions immediately at the command in his captain's voice; but, instead of the usual excitement that blazed in his eyes at being forced to submit to Baltsaros's will, his face was drawn with apprehension.

Tom raised himself up on his elbows, his rigid cock resting against the bulging, hard muscles of his stomach. He stared at the captain, panting slightly.

"What the fuck did I do, Da?" he asked; though his voice was coloured by resentment, Baltsaros heard guilt. He pointed to the young man passed out not far from them.

"You got him drunk, Tom. You shouldn't have brought him here," he said, his voice quiet and stripped of the turmoil he felt roiling inside him.

Tom's eyes slid away from Baltsaros's for a moment; when he looked back his gaze was fierce.

"I didn't see ye complainin' a few minutes ago when ye bloody reached out and pulled him against ye... when... when ye kissed him..." Tom said, his voice breaking unexpectedly.

Baltsaros frowned as he watched the younger man's composure crumble. Tom was right, and the thought unnerved him. Baltsaros shook his head slowly.

"Then why, Tom? Why would you bring him to me if you didn't want me to touch him?" he asked, genuinely bewildered. This was beyond comprehension for the captain. Though he spent his life mimicking the emotions and reactions of others, there were things he could not account for. "Why, Tom?"

"I seen the way ye look at him, Da. Ye never, not once, looked at me the way ye look at that broken boy. Ye want him. I know ye do. I ain't stupid. I just thought..." he said, his voice raw with emotion. Tom's face was red with anger and grief.

As he spoke, Baltsaros finally thought he understood. Like a cat who traps a mouse and brings it to its owner, Tom had brought Jon to him as a gift... His first mate knew he couldn't compete with the effect that Jon had on Baltsaros and had tried instead to win his esteem by bringing him something he knew the man wanted.

Was it so blatant? the captain thought, alarmed.

Baltsaros swallowed hard and sat back on the bed, suddenly feeling terribly weary.

"Oh, my tomcat," he said; his voice was sad though he truthfully felt absolutely nothing for the handsome and brutal young man. Things would never be the same between them, and they both knew it. After a long silence, Baltsaros nodded to himself.

"Tom, please take Jon to the crew bunks. And... find yourself somewhere else to sleep tonight. I would like an evening to myself," he said softly. He watched as Tom paled slightly under his sun-darkened skin, but the muscular youth obeyed, quickly tying up his pants before sliding off the bed. With ease, he lifted Jon over one shoulder.

"Yes, Da," Tom said, his voice ragged and quiet as he turned to leave. The captain watched his first mate depart, closing the door behind him.

As he lay back against his pillows, Baltsaros frowned up at the ceiling. It was incredibly stupid and unwise of him to have let it all happen. He could have simply said no and sent the two away.

Could I have?

~

When Jon saw him staring, Baltsaros smiled. He took the few steps needed to close the distance between them. The younger man's eyes widened for a moment, looking apprehensive.

"Jon. I think we should talk," said the captain quietly. The dark-haired youth looked down at the scrub brush in his hands. In a small voice, he said, "I'm not done with—"

Baltsaros let out a sudden laugh.

"Boy, I am the captain. And when the captain says he wants to speak with you, you say 'yes, sir.' Do I make myself clear?" he said, his tone light and teasing.

Jon looked up, his brows furrowing slightly before a smile creased his face.

"Yes, sir," he said and dropped the brush into the bucket.

Baltsaros felt his breath come up a little short in his chest when he saw the bead of sweat run from the corner of Jon's strong jaw and follow the lines of his throat to the collarbone visible through the open neck of his linen shirt.

"Why don't you come out of the sun. Have a drink with me," he said and motioned to the open door of the stateroom. Jon's eyes flashed in suspicion when Baltsaros said the word "drink", but he turned to follow the captain anyway.

~

Jon ducked through the door of the stateroom feeling bizarrely like he was coming home. Without a word, he walked to the cage and looked in. The cot was bare now, no longer needed. As he touched the black bars with one finger, Jon smiled softly. He'd come far in two weeks.

All that fear and misery...

Jon laughed inwardly. There was still plenty of fear and misery, though now he was in a different sort of cage. It was one of his own design, and Jon was weary of the guilt, shame, and uncertainty he had locked himself into.

He turned and saw that Baltsaros was sitting at his usual spot at the heavy table, an earthenware mug in front of him. Jon slid into his old seat across from the captain and picked up his own mug. When he saw what was in it, Jon grinned and closed his eyes as he brought the mug to his lips, breathing deeply.

Bliss.

He took a sip of the hot, black liquid and sighed.

"Cook's coffee might be good, but yours is exceptional. I've really missed... this," he said and lifted his blue eyes to Baltsaros. He knew immediately that the captain had picked up on his meaning. Though the man's brown eyes were alive with curiosity, his handsome face was entirely devoid of emotion.

"Jon. I should have never let things go the way they did," he said quietly. It wasn't an apology, nor was it an admission of regret. It was something altogether different; it was an offer. Jon watched in amazement as the other man went through herculean efforts to appear calm and collected; to his strange talent, it was clear as day that something was different in the captain. A door had been opened.

"What do you see when you look at me?" asked Baltsaros suddenly, sitting back in his chair, a small smile on his captivating lips.

Jon felt his heart beat hard once before it settled into a swift rhythm. He looked at Baltsaros and took a deep breath. Everything went still inside his head as he spoke the truth laid out before his eyes.

"What do I see? I see a man who has higher and thicker walls than I will ever have. I see a terrifying beast enveloped and hidden by a cleverly fashioned mask. I see tears that will never fall. I see blood and death. I see a heart that devours itself. I see the promise of pain and deceit. I see a lot of things, Baltsaros. Many of them frightening," Jon said, his voice low; the need for titles between them had passed.

Baltsaros showed no surprise over Jon's words. Instead, he leaned towards him, intrigued.

"And you're not afraid," he said. It was a statement.

Jon shook his head.

"I'm not afraid. I should be," he admitted. "But I'm not. I see a man who is so lonely that he's willing to sacrifice himself to the secrets holding him together. I see a man who fears me for what I can see, yet who asks me to look."

Baltsaros's head nodded slowly. He had the distinct impression that the older man felt relieved.

"But... Baltsaros, I'm not your puppet... I won't be your plaything," added Jon when the captain remained silent. "You already have my respect and my loyalty." He laughed timidly as he pushed a hand through his dark curls. "What I *am* scared of is what else you want from me."

The burst of confidence that had caused his words to flow so easily had left him, and Jon was at odds once more. Baltsaros started laughing; Jon saw that the captain was charmed by his words, and he couldn't help but grin despite how self-conscious he felt.

"We will do as you like, Jon," said Baltsaros. "But it would seem that you want the same things, no?"

Jon felt the heat in his face and took a sip of the rich, black coffee to hide his sudden awkwardness; the memory of Baltsaros breathing into the kiss and the man's blatant arousal was making him feel lightheaded. He looked down at the tabletop and tried to find words.

There was the sound of movement from across the table and almost-silent footfalls approaching on the thick carpet. Jon turned his head and leaned it against Baltsaros's shirt, the captain's hard stomach against his forehead. He felt Baltsaros's hand come down and stroke his hair, a simple comforting gesture that, nevertheless, gave Jon goosebumps.

After Jon got the tears that were threatening to fall under control, he leaned back and looked up into Baltsaros's sombre face.

"You have to do something about Tom," he said, his voice thick. He watched as Baltsaros's stark brows came down over eyes that glinted like black glass. Feeling the restrained fury that came boiling out of Baltsaros, Jon recoiled slightly.

"Tell me, Jon. What has Tom done?"

CHAPTER 10

TO RIGHT A WRONG

Baltsaros was unprepared for the rage that had welled up inside him at Jon's words. His initial reaction had been a staggering, almost uncontrollable urge to find Tom and beat him to death with his bare hands, to dig into his flesh like a wild beast and tear him asunder.

When he realized in annoyance that he was pacing, he stopped at the side of his bed and made himself sit down. Baltsaros clenched his jaw as he forced open the tight fists his hands had curled into.

Where was this was coming from? What did he care if Tom was making advances at Jon? Jon was terribly inexperienced; a few rounds with Tom and his talents would do him some good... *wouldn't it?*

Baltsaros swallowed down hard on the anger that spiked hotly in his gut with that thought; looking up, he caught his reflection in the small mirror above the teak dresser and was startled to see the naked emotion on his face. Baltsaros smoothed out his features and groped inside himself for the well of calm that was always within reach.

Before Jon had left, promising to come back to dine with the captain later that evening, Baltsaros had sworn he would take care of Tom.

But... how?

What exactly was the threat? He lay back on the bed, brow once again furrowed. It was midday, and he should have been above on the quarterdeck by now, but his head was still somewhere strange.

Baltsaros's thoughts were again on the reeling, drunken boy that had been so warm against him in the dark cabin. Jon's eyes had been full of stars, and the rum had put colour in his wan cheeks. Baltsaros had been powerless not to touch him; he remembered how smooth Jon's chest was, and how the sensitive pink nipple had hardened alluringly under the captain's fingertips.

He groaned softly at the memory.

Baltsaros pressed his fingers against his eyelids, his other hand tugging at the loose white shirt he wore tucked into his pants. He worked his hand under the waistband and cupped the hardening mound there with his palm, bearing down on himself roughly in response to his tension.

It was only when Tom's mouth had closed over Jon that Baltsaros had realized *just how innocent* the boy really was. Having had his first mate milk the lust out of the beguiling young man now felt like an incredible blunder.

Baltsaros opened his eyes, keenly aware that he was lying on the very site of Jon's ravishment. The thought of anyone else touching him brought a hot, dull ache to the captain's chest.

Never again, he thought angrily. What was Tom even thinking, approaching Jon?

Why shouldn't he? We've shared our conquests so often in the past...

He knew the answer, however: Tom wanted Jon because Baltsaros wanted Jon. He gritted his teeth—those callused fingers running over Jon's soft skin, Tom's rough kisses bruising Jon's lips.

Growling deep in his chest, Baltsaros realized he was working himself into a rage. His cock was rock hard in his hand, responding treacherously to the thoughts of Jon's defilement that ran through his mind.

No. Never again. No one was to touch the dark-haired young man.

However, he couldn't just kill his first mate outright.

He threw open the door to his quarters and looked out; Tom was sitting nearby on an upturned keg sharpening his knife against a small whetstone. When the door banged against the wall, he looked up, blue-green eyes wide; there was that worry in Tom's rugged face again.

Baltsaros frowned at him and cocked his head before retreating back inside, leaving the door ajar behind him. Turning to watch Tom step through the doorway, he breathed deep.

"Close the door, Tom," he said quietly. The first mate moved to obey, darkening the room.

Taking the few steps to reach him, Baltsaros grabbed Tom by the throat and rammed him hard against the wall. Tom let out a grunt as his head cracked against the wood, his hands reaching up to grab the captain's wrist.

Baltsaros brought his face close to Tom's.

"You are not to go anywhere near Jon. *Do I make myself clear?*" he said through clenched teeth.

Tom's eyes went steely as he stared up into his captain's face.

"And why the fuck not, Da?" he asked, venom in his voice. "It's not as if yer fuckin' him yet, are ye? I just thought I'd break him in for ye since yer so keen on the fuckin' brat."

Baltsaros bared his teeth and tightened his hold on the first mate's neck, quickly dashing him again on the hard wood. Tom's face grew red, his fingers scrabbling at the captain's hand trying to loosen his hold.

Baltsaros frowned and eased up slightly.

"I mean it, Tom. Don't touch him. Not ever. And if I find out that you have, *I will take my whip to you.*"

The first mate stopped struggling, going completely still in Baltsaros's grasp. The captain saw the deep hurt in Tom's eyes and pressed his lips together.

"Da... but... ye promised me. Ye promised that I'd never feel another bloody fuckin' lash... never again," said Tom, his breathing hoarse.

Baltsaros felt Tom's pulse racing against his fingers, and his face softened. It was true; the first thing the captain had said, over and over, to the wild, angry young man in the cage was that he would never again feel a whip tear into his flesh.

"Just... leave him alone, Tom," he said softly, memories washing over his anger and smoothing it out like an ocean wave over dimpled sand.

Tom stared hard at Baltsaros, his gorgeous sea-green eyes completely unreadable; after a moment, he closed them and dropped his hands to the captain's waist, deft fingers working quickly to unlace him.

Surprised, Baltsaros made a small noise in his throat. He frowned at Tom as he felt the first mate's rough, warm hands skilfully free his cock from his pants. When he pressed his thumb up into the sensitive nerve cluster under Tom's jaw, Baltsaros smiled at the grunt of pain that burst out of his first mate; however, Tom's hands had not paused for second.

This was Tom's greatest talent; Baltsaros could drown him in pain, and the beautifully muscled youth wouldn't back down. With a low groan, the captain felt his need completely grab hold of him. For the first time in a long time, his mind was completely on the boy in his grasp.

With his free hand, Baltsaros stroked the side of Tom's face. The young man opened his eyes, a silent plea trapped in them, and moved his head so that his lips could brush Baltsaros's palm.

The captain smiled softly, his body reacting to the guileless charm of the younger man. This was Tom, after all. They had done the same dance so many times that the boy's body felt like a second skin. He let go of Tom's throat, and the other immediately sank down to his knees in front of Baltsaros, quickly swallowing the captain's cock down to the root.

Baltsaros rested an arm against the wood panels and pressed his forehead to it, the other hand reaching down to stroke Tom's hair. The captain groaned loud and began rocking in time to his first mate's movements.

~

Jon dipped his brush in the paint and moved to the next curving spindle of the railing running around the quarterdeck. The fumes were making him feel slightly ill, and his hands were covered in red splotches. This was his least favourite chore so far. It had never occurred to him just how much upkeep a vessel of this size required.

From a distance the black and red of the sleek corvette appeared pristine, but it was far from the truth. Damage from the sun and saltwater marred the paint, causing it to curl up and fade. To keep her looking her best, the old paint had to be scraped away and a new coat applied at least once a season. Jon, being the newest on board, was automatically put on the work crew this time around.

Jon leaned down to dab at his first coat, but his attention was caught by what he saw below; Tom suddenly stood up from his perch where he had been watching Jon paint and walked to the door of the captain's quarters.

Frowning, Jon concentrated on his work. The paint was drying strangely in the hot sun, causing it to bubble up when he applied it too thickly.

Baltsaros will be telling Tom not to come to me, he thought.

It would certainly not make the relationship between him and the first mate any easier, but Jon was tired of looking over his shoulder. Strangely, he felt a touch of regret and pushed it away in disgust. Tom was just trouble. A loose cannon. Never mind that his eyes were sly and his smile wicked, or that his tongue knew exactly where to—

Jon's mouth opened slowly in shock. From below him came an unmistakable groan of pleasure. He stood still for a moment, not believing his ears. When another sound of passion came up from the open porthole in the captain's room, he placed the brush down on the edge of the bucket of paint and sat down heavily on the deck; it hadn't even occurred to him that the captain would maintain his... *dalliances* with the first mate. He had foolishly assumed that he and the captain would... *would what?* he thought, feeling perturbed and strangely betrayed.

Staring down at the paint-spattered hands he had folded in his lap, Jon quickly tried to banish the emotions that were ricocheting through his head; he didn't hear the soft footsteps until they were right next to him.

When he looked up, Jon was relieved to see Katherine's concerned face gazing down at him. She gracefully lowered herself to the deck beside him; her hand, confident in a way that Jon's never seemed to be, came up and rested on his shoulder. He felt ridiculous tears rise up hot in his eyes and lifted a hand to wipe them away.

"Jon, what's the matter?" asked Katherine.

Jon shook his head, looking over her shoulder at the clear blue sky. He felt the heat in his face when there was a sharp cry from below.

"Ahh," he heard Katherine say, and he turned his eyes to hers. "This is what they do," Katherine said softly to him, motioning to the captain's quarters below them. "You shouldn't be hurt by it. It's just the way things are."

Nodding, Jon picked at the red on his hands, embarrassed by his reaction.

"It's so completely absurd," he admitted, even though his heart was beating hard, and his mouth was dry. "I just thought he and I..." he said, trailing off. The thought that kept echoing through Jon was simply: *how could he?*

Katherine leaned against his side, a warm pillar of strength. She played with the leather cord at her calf with long, slender fingers; Jon could sense that she was trying to find her words. Finally, she broke the long silence.

"He belongs to the captain, you know," she said, her brown eyes kind.

Jon frowned at her.

"Tom? You think I'm crying over *Tom?*" he asked, incredulous.

Katherine's eyes narrowed at him, and Jon chuckled low, shaking his head at her. Katherine pulled her hand away slowly and looked at him with an expression of disbelief on her pretty face.

"Oh Jon, please don't tell me you're pining for the captain? You know he's..." she began and stopped suddenly. She shook her head, and Jon felt his stomach knot.

"He's what?" he asked.

Katherine grimaced and shook her head again.

"He's... complicated, Jon," she said, "And... he's the captain." she ended lamely, lifting one shoulder up in a shrug.

Jon scowled at her for a moment and then sighed. He looked over the side of the railing and saw that Tom had emerged from the stateroom below; the first mate stood still, looking up at them with a dark expression on his face. Jon almost gasped at the amount of animosity that he saw in the other man's eyes... and then it was gone.

Tom's lips stretched into a wide smile, and he winked before turning away to swagger down the deck.

Jon hadn't managed to get all the paint off his hands, the red having completely stained his skin in some places. He grimaced, feeling self-conscious as he rapped his knuckle against the wooden door.

"Come," was the reply from within.

When he pulled the door open, Jon was bombarded with an incredible, mouth-watering smell. He closed his eyes and took a deep breath. At Baltsaros's chuckle from across the room, Jon smiled and looked at the captain. The older man was leaning over the table, putting down the heavy silverware to each side of the plates.

The sight of him loosened something in Jon; Baltsaros was wearing a long-sleeved, dark-red shirt tucked into his black leather pants. The laces at the neck were partially undone, and Jon could see the captain's broad, tanned chest, covered in curling dark hairs. The man's light-brown hair looked damp as if he had bathed recently; it was combed back and tied with a leather thong, falling in a messy tail over his shoulder.

He took a few steps forward, utterly captivated by the handsome captain as he straightened up at Jon's approach, smiling charmingly. Baltsaros's brown eyes crinkled at the corners.

"Hello, Jon," he said, his accent, as always, lending an exotic flavour to even these simple words.

"Hello, Baltsaros," he replied, grinning ruefully.

Jon had spent the afternoon wrestling with his demons and had come to the conclusion that he was being utterly foolish; he pushed the feelings of resentment and confusion aside, wishing only to be pleasant and not cast a dark shadow over the meal. He was also incredibly curious about what Katherine had refused to say.

Did I know that Baltsaros was what? Dangerous?

76

Jon sat down in his chair and glanced up at the captain who had turned to get something else. As he watched the older man, Jon noticed once again how fluid and precise his motions were. Baltsaros was indeed a dangerous animal, and that was a large part of what drew Jon to him.

He raked back his dark curls with one hand and lifted his eyebrows when the captain set a domed ceramic dish in the middle of the table.

"Lamb *tagine*," said Baltsaros, pulling off the cover and revealing something that looked like a thick stew. "With couscous."

Jon took a sip of the chilled, dark beer and looked on as Baltsaros ladled some of the stew onto the strange yellowish mound on his plate.

It smelled absolutely wonderful.

He scooped some up with his fork and took a bite, acutely aware of Baltsaros's eyes on him. Smiling, he chewed the tender meat and carrot. It was savoury and strangely sweet at the same time, mildly spicy on his tongue. He nodded happily at the captain, who was sitting back in his chair watching the younger man eat, and took a bigger bite.

Baltsaros laughed out loud, the smile creasing his enigmatic face.

How strange is it that a man with such a darkness inside him can laugh so easily and so often? thought Jon as he swallowed.

"I have to admit, Jon... I derive extreme pleasure from feeding you. Every meal is an adventure. I will have to find new dishes to make once I've exhausted my repertoire, just to see that precise look on your face," said the captain, taking a bite of his own.

Jon felt a small thrill at the words. "Oh? You mean to keep me for so long?" he said, amazed at the easy, bantering tone he had taken.

Jon watched as Baltsaros's eyes darkened, and he suddenly sensed the depth of the man's strange isolation. He cleared his throat and looked down at his plate, concentrating on the food in front of him. The long silence made him uncomfortable, but the lump in his throat was preventing him from speaking.

"It's still going well with Calum?" asked Baltsaros, his voice light.

Jon frowned and nodded, glancing up briefly.

"He's a lot stronger than he looks. I still haven't managed to pin him," he replied, smiling slightly.

It was true; the much older man regularly threw Jon down to the deck during his fighting lessons. He was nearly useless when it came to straight boxing, but there was something about learning holds that intrigued him. Jon knew he was fast, and his slight frame came in handy when trying to worm his way out of Calum's grasp, but he was nowhere close to being skilled at anything yet. He rubbed the bruise visible on his forearm and had to laugh.

"I'll get the hang of it eventually," he said, looking up again at the captain.

Baltsaros nodded, the corners of his lips lifted in a small smile.

"I do not doubt it," he said and paused for a moment, putting his fork down. "Jon, I don't know if you've already heard, but it's nearing the end of the season, and we must start our way south soon. We'll be stopping for supplies before we go; the journey is a long one and we need to stock up," he said, narrowing his eyes at Jon. "You will be able to go ashore with the men... if that is what you would like."

Though feeling a little giddy at the news, Jon held his tongue. There was something else the captain wasn't saying. Baltsaros stood and walked to the ice chest, pulling out a pitcher that Jon assumed contained more beer. Refilling the younger man's mug, the captain spoke.

"We'll be near Portsmouth," he said at last, sitting down.

Jon frowned.

"I don't want to go home, if that's what you're so worried about," he said.

Baltsaros took a sip of beer and smiled.

"No, I know that. I just want you to be careful. Your stepfather may be looking for you," he said, his eyes pensive.

Jon laughed, a small, ugly sound.

"Reginald? Looking for *me?* I doubt it very much. The man was most likely glad to be rid of me," he said.

The captain dipped his head slightly.

"It could be so. However... I just wanted to warn you. Sometimes men hide their affections in strange ways," he said, his face serious.

Jon nearly burst out laughing at the irony. Instead, he shook his head and scraped his fork against the plate, trapping the last morsels of the delicious meal between its tines.

"He couldn't fool me," Jon said, *and neither can you,* he added silently.

As he sat there thinking of his former home, Jon was suddenly struck with an idea. Since coming on board, he had been plagued by a reoccurring nightmare and the monstrous guilt that it caused him. He looked into Baltsaros's eyes, bolstered by the affection he saw there, and grinned.

"Something tells me you're not going to like this," Jon said softly.

The man slowly raised his stark brow and waited for Jon to speak.

This was his chance to right a wrong.

"I want to go get Brutus," he said, watching the captain's face.

"Brutus? Who is Brutus?" asked Baltsaros, his brow furrowed in confusion.

"My dog," said Jon.

CHAPTER II
SAFE HARBOUR

Love is whatever you can still betray. Betrayal can only happen if you love.

—JOHN LE CARRÉ

Baltsaros stared at Jon for a moment, incredulous.

"You wish to bring a dog aboard my ship?" he asked, his eyes wide.

Jon grinned and slowly nodded his head, obviously excited to start piecing together the rescue plan.

The captain leaned back in his chair and just stared at the dark-haired young man. Baltsaros's initial reaction was to flat-out refuse Jon's request. However, as he watched the smile fade from the face of the handsome dark-haired man across the table, he realized just how much this might mean to Jon. There had never been a dog on board before. Some cats in the distant past, and once a monkey, but never a dog.

Baltsaros frowned; he didn't quite understand the allure of companion animals. While pets provided their owners with unconditional affection, it was a crude stand-in for human love. At least that's what it seemed like to Baltsaros; he had no need for something to stare up at him with mindless, wordless devotion to make him feel better. Not when there were much more satisfying creatures to tame, like Tom and the slender, sensitive young man that was staring at him with eyes like a storm-heavy sky. Jon's words came back to him suddenly.

I won't be your plaything.

Baltsaros pressed his lips together.

"A ship is no place for a dog, Jon," he said, attempting to use reason to dissuade him. He was completely taken aback when Jon narrowed his eyes in anger at him.

"What? *You* get to have a pet but not me?" he said, mirroring Baltsaros's earlier thoughts. The astonishing outburst revealed the outrage that Jon had been suppressing thus far. Obviously, Jon had overheard the captain and his first mate earlier that afternoon and was not happy about it.

And why should he be?

The captain looked flatly at Jon, concerned by his vitriol but not wanting to appear touched by it. Baltsaros licked his bottom lip, choosing his words carefully.

"Tom is none of your concern," he said slowly. "Please do not mistake my interest in you for permission to openly criticize me."

Jon's dark brows came down over his eyes, and he placed his hands on the table, pushing himself up out of his chair. As he leaned forward over the table, Jon stared hard at Baltsaros.

"Do you want me to lick your boots, Baltsaros? Cower every time you raise your hand? Is that what you want from me?" he asked, his voice quiet and angry.

Tilting his head slightly, Baltsaros scrutinized the fierce young man. There was definitely steel buried in Jon, steel and darkness enough to compete with the same inside Baltsaros. He sighed softly and motioned to the chair behind Jon.

"Sit," he said grimly.

Jon waited a moment before resuming his place at the table, all the while looking distrustfully at the captain.

"It *is* my ship, Jon. I am the captain. My word is the only law here," he said.

Anger flashed quickly again in Jon's blue eyes.

"If your word is law, then why not just *order* me to get down on my knees in front of you and... and..." he stammered, having come to the very edge of a thought that stymied the flow of his words.

Baltsaros stood and walked around the end of the table. Jon watched him with a touch of fear on his face; eyes widening, he turned in his chair to face the man as he approached. Baltsaros leaned against the edge of the table and crossed his arms over his chest.

"Are you quite done with your tantrum?" he asked.

Jon frowned at Baltsaros; the muscles worked in his jaw as his nostrils flared slightly. Jon nodded sharply once, his eyes sliding away from Baltsaros's face.

"Now, before your sudden descent into madness, I was trying to explain something to you," the captain said, his eyes tracing Jon's profile. The younger man wouldn't look at him... out of anger or embarrassment? "There are things you do not understand, Jon. Believe me when I say that I am a man unused to having his authority challenged; I simply will not let you come into my life to suddenly claim superior knowledge of how to run my crew or my personal affairs."

Jon shook his head and laughed harshly.

Baltsaros reached out with a hand and grabbed Jon's jaw, turning the other man's head towards him. Jon gasped at the sudden contact. Baltsaros smiled ruefully, dropping his hand.

"I do not want you to chastise me for things that you only have the faintest notion about. You're not stupid, Jon. Rash reactions like yours just now, based solely on emotion and assumptions, will get you killed in a world like mine," he said. "Like *ours.*"

He looked down at the colourful arabesques in the rug below his booted feet. When he raised his eyes again, Jon was looking at him curiously, almost all resentment gone from his youthful face.

"I took care of Tom *like you requested*, didn't I? He shouldn't bother you again. I threatened him with something... well... something I shouldn't have." He waved at the air with one hand, pushing the thought away. "Tom has been my companion for nearly four years. He's an excellent first mate when you get past all of his audacious chaff... he keeps everyone in line and makes my job that much easier. I trust him—" Baltsaros raised a hand when Jon started shaking his head. "I do. I have to. After all, I spend a good portion of the night unconscious next to him," he said, chuckling.

Jon looked uncomfortable.

"I'm sorry. I know. It's probably difficult for you to understand. However... as inexperienced and as... conventional as you are, you have to realize that you're not a blushing maiden, and I'm not an evil pirate king here to sweep you off your feet and force you to resign your body to me." Baltsaros ran a hand through his hair, pushing the long strands away from his face. "So... do not criticize me. However, I will accept, and cherish, your *informed* opinions. You matter to me, Jon. But you'll have to get past this jejune notion of what that means," he said, his voice kind. "I don't want you to submit to me. Nor lick my boots," he said, grinning. "Unless that's something you like doing, of course." He shrugged and was pleased to see a bit of humour come back to Jon's face.

Jon shook his head, the smallest of smiles turning up the corners of his mouth. Baltsaros was suddenly breathless with the memory of those lips capturing his own. He reached forward and grabbed the front of Jon's shirt.

Jon was so startled that he didn't even try to fight as Baltsaros pulled him out of his chair. Still leaning against the table, the captain moved his feet to either side of Jon's as he drew the captivating young man against him. When Jon started to resist as his hips came into contact with Baltsaros's inner thighs, the captain let go of him, holding his hands up to either side in a gesture of surrender. Jon was so close that Baltsaros could easily see the rapid pulse in his slender neck; his eyes were so utterly conflicted that it made the captain's breath catch in his throat.

Don't hurt me, they said.

Baltsaros lowered his arms slowly; wrapping them around Jon, he was glad to see that he was not going to pull away. Instead, Jon moved into Baltsaros's embrace like a ship finding safe harbour after a long storm. The captain sighed and held tight to the slender body in his arms, Jon's face buried in the crook of his neck. So much pain. So much confusion. If Jon wasn't careful he would rattle himself to pieces.

Or would he?

Baltsaros leaned his cheek against the mess of brown curls.

"I'm a hypocrite, Jon," he murmured. "I ask you to accept my arrangements, yet I can't bear the thought of you in another's arms... I would kill them for touching you."

Jon let out a small groan, almost a whimper, and turned his head so his lips rested against the side of Baltsaros's neck. The captain felt his heart hammering fast against his ribs, a rapturous, warm surge rising up through him at Jon's tentative touch. Baltsaros bit the corner of his lip, and looked up at the ceiling, trying to find restraint inside of himself. He desired nothing more than to do what he just said he wouldn't: sweep Jon off his feet and take from him what he wasn't yet prepared to give.

Baltsaros shuddered slightly when Jon started to kiss his neck and was astonished when he felt his teeth graze him softly. Maybe the young man was more prepared than he thought. However, when he lowered his hands to grab Jon firmly by his backside to pull him tightly against him, the other froze.

Sensing that he was already pushing Jon's limits, Baltsaros sighed again and kissed the side of his head.

"You can have your dog," he said into Jon's hair and was charmed when he felt the younger man's lips curl into a smile against him. "But keep him out of the way. He's your responsibility."

~

Baltsaros smiled at the memory as he stood on the dock, arms crossed in front of him. That had been two days ago. It was maddening that he had yet to kiss Jon, never mind strip him bare and drive him mad with passion. Jon was proving to be a difficult code to crack. Baltsaros would be lying to himself if that didn't make him more enticing.

He lowered a hand to the front of his pants and adjusted himself; lately, his cock felt like it was constantly semi-hard. He was beginning to hurt.

"Where do ye want them?" asked Tom, rolling the barrel of fresh water up the dock to where the captain stood.

Baltsaros frowned and did a few calculations in his head.

"Put half in the storage behind the crew quarters and lash the rest up on deck like we did last year," he replied. "There should be enough room for the extra barrels."

"Aye, Da," said Tom, and grunted as he started pushing the barrel up the gangplank.

Baltsaros turned his head, watching the muscles of the first mate bulge with his efforts.

"Tom. You were gone quite a long time. Did you have any trouble?" he asked.

Tom frowned and shook his head as he heaved the barrel onto the deck and then stood panting, one tanned forearm coming up to dash the sweat out of his eyebrows.

"No trouble, Da. Just stopped for a pint is all," he said, not even having the decency to look guilty for having delayed his work in the name of a drink.

Baltsaros scowled at him and shook his head. Tom winked in return, leaning down against the barrel once more.

The captain saw that Jon, dressed in borrowed long-clothes that included a cloak with a hood, was coming down the deck towards the gangplank. Tom stopped rolling the barrel to watch the dark-haired man walk by; taking an exaggerated step backwards out of Jon's path, he looked at the captain and smiled.

Tom and his games, Baltsaros thought. The young brute was incapable of taking anything seriously for very long.

Jon made his way down the planks and looked at Baltsaros. He seemed both excited and extremely nervous. The captain reached into his pocket and pulled out a small bag of silver.

"This will be enough to hire a horse. You should be able to make it to Portsmouth by sundown," he said, handing the money to Jon. "I know you said that your stepfather was glad to be rid of you, but I'd be cautious. He lost quite an asset in you."

Jon looked down at the leather purse in his hands, fingers pulling restlessly at the string that held it closed.

"Thank you," he said.

Baltsaros reached out to clasp the back of Jon's neck, drawing him against his shoulder.

"I wish you would take someone with you," the captain said quietly.

Jon shook his head and looked up into Baltsaros's eyes.

"It'll be fine. I'll be back before you have a chance to miss me," he said with a grin.

Baltsaros smiled grimly.

"Nevertheless..." he said. "Come back to me, Jon. That's all I ask."

Jon's face went serious, and he nodded. He leaned forward to press himself against the captain quickly before he spun on his heel, trotting down the wide dock towards the small fishing town where they were anchored.

Baltsaros watched him go with a faint worry tightening his chest. He turned his head to look at Tom, who had also stopped to watch Jon depart. When he saw the captain's eyes on him, Tom grinned and started to whistle a jaunty tune as he continued to roll the barrel down the deck.

CHAPTER 12
THE BLACK BRIGAND

J on squeezed his knees against the sides of the grey mare as he looked down at
the town of Portsmouth. It was nearly dark, and some of the larger buildings, like
the taverns and whorehouses, had already lit their lanterns against the falling
dusk.

The horse *whuffed* softly beneath him, and Jon reached down to pat her side as
they came to a stop.

"I know, I know. I'm a terrible rider," he said, smiling ruefully. The mare bobbed
her head as if she understood, pawing impatiently at the ground with a hoof.

Jon wanted to wait until it was fully dark before making his way through town and
up the hill to the ancient, mouldy castle where he hoped to find Brutus.

As restless as his steed, the young man fiddled with the hilt of the long knife at his
hip, wishing suddenly that he had taken the captain's advice and brought someone
along; at least then he'd have another person to talk to while waiting for the sun to
sink down across the water.

He frowned, pulling out the captain's short double spyglass—something Baltsaros
had called *binoculars*—to focus on the crumbling ruin that had been his home for so
long. Part of him felt foolish for how incredibly furtive this all was; for all that he
knew, Reginald thought Jon had simply run away and was glad for it.

"I suppose I *did* run away, though," he said, and the mare's ear flicked back to
listen to him.

It had been nearly a month since that night in the brothel; even if Reginald *had* been looking for him, the old soldier must have presumed by now that Jon wasn't going to return. And, so what if Jon was spotted by Reginald? What's the worst that could happen? Reginald would ask him to stay? Though the captain voiced concern about Reginald's reaction to the loss of his charge, Jon couldn't believe for a moment that his stepfather could make him stay. There was nothing for him in Portsmouth; his future lay in much stranger places.

As if bored by his musings, the mare leaned her head down to nibble on some grass. Jon sighed and put the binoculars back in his bag, deciding he had waited long enough.

Now or never.

After pulling the hood of his cloak up, he clucked his tongue at the horse, coaxing her forward and down towards the softly glowing lights of the harbour town.

Baltsaros was sitting up behind the ship's wheel, drinking strong coffee and rum from a tin cup. The nights were starting to get cold, and he was anxious to get sailing across the wide ocean towards home.

Home.

He laughed. Strange to think that a place where he spent so little time could be considered "home." He took a sip of the warmly soothing black drink and narrowed his eyes at the activity below him.

From the sutler in town, they had purchased almost everything needed to make the long journey, and he expected the shipwright in the morning to replace the rotten boards that plagued the aging ship. Everything was coming together for the trip.

From where he was sitting, Baltsaros couldn't see Tom, but he could hear the first mate barking orders to the ship's hands somewhere below.

"—shake a leg, or so help me gods, ye'll kiss the gunner's daughter! Don't be daft... Here, who taught ye to tie a bloody rope? Fuckin' hell, love... This is more twisted than a demon's cock..." laughed the lusty, young mainlander.

Baltsaros chuckled to himself. The captain was starting to think that maybe he could find a balance between the two young men who fanned his desires so disparately.

After more cursing and shouting, Tom finally appeared at the foot of the stairs leading to the upper deck; heedless of the chill in the air, the first mate was shirtless as usual. Tom's skin shone slightly in the yellow light of the lantern, a thin sheen of sweat covering his muscled torso; lugging heavy supplies on board was backbreaking work, and the first mate never hesitated to help out with even the toughest of tasks.

Smiling up at the captain, the first mate pulled a dark cheroot from behind his ear and stuck it in the corner of his mouth. A match flared in his hand; in the brief light, the captain could see that Tom was covered in streaks of grime. As the smoke wafted out of his nostrils, Tom picked a bit of tobacco off his bottom lip and narrowed his eyes roguishly at Baltsaros.

"Permission to come up, Captain," he said, a cheeky grin dimpling his face.

Baltsaros laughed.

"Permission granted," he replied. He watched as the younger man took the steps two at a time, coming up to sit next to him. As he leaned back against the wide seat, Tom looked up at the bright stars and breathed deeply, obviously glad for the moment of rest.

The captain plucked the burning cheroot from between the first mate's callused fingers and put it to his own lips. He inhaled and blew out a plume of smoke, watching it rise up into the night sky.

"If everythin' fits where it should, we'll be ready to leave by tomorrow evenin', Da," said Tom, reclaiming the slender cigar.

Baltsaros frowned. Never mind that weighing anchor at night was impractical; it was premature.

"We'll sail when all hands are back on deck, Tom," he said to the young man lounging catlike by his side and watched as his first mate sucked in another lungful of smoke. "That includes Jon."

~

When Jon saw the poster tacked to the high gates that stood at the edge of town, he knew something was wrong. Under the rough sketch of a gaunt man with black curls, read the words: *Wanted for murder most foule, Jon "The Black Brigand." Rewarde for capture.*

Jon nearly choked on the surprised laughter that burst out of him.

The Black Brigand?

He stared at the poster, not believing his eyes. After a moment, he frowned; the paper was not yet faded by the sun or rain, which meant it couldn't have been there for more than a day.

What the hells?

Though there was no doubt in his mind that it was meant to be a drawing of him, Jon squinted again at the picture, wondering whether anyone could possibly recognize him in it.

Nevertheless, he tugged on his hood to cast more shadow on his face and nudged his horse forward.

Murder? he thought anxiously; this did not bode well. All thoughts of a relatively peaceful encounter with Reginald, should the two cross paths, were now dashed. The faster he was able to leave, the better.

Thankfully, the route through the small harbour town was not long. Jon spotted a few more of the posters up on storefronts, but the main thoroughfare was mostly empty; the few who walked down the packed-dirt road did not even look in his direction.

When Jon reached the far side of town, he had the mare climb as high as the First Wall. He looped the horse's reins around an old metal support that probably used to hold up the gates, back before they were taken away... or stolen to melt down. Jon would go the rest of the way up on foot, better able to hide in the shadows on the barren hillside alone than atop a horse.

He began picking his way over the rocks and mounds along the roadside, trying not to stumble or twist an ankle in the dark. While he had taken this path many times, he couldn't remember ever having done it on a night so black.

After a while, Jon heard a bark of laughter up ahead and stopped in his tracks, listening. He heard the soft rattle of chain mail and the creak of leather as someone further up the path moved about.

"—you're not fucking serious," said a deep male voice, chuckling quietly. There was the sound of metal on metal and another tinkle of chain mail.

A reedy voice replied.

"I swear it! She stood right there next to him while he was at the bank teller. Said she needed to feel the money in her hand before she'd fuck—*Who goes there?*"

Jon had accidentally kicked a small stone while trying to circumvent the two men; it rolled down the steep slope, clattering against the rocks that dotted the hillside.

Before Jon could react, one of the men pulled open a covered lantern and shone it down the path. Jon lifted a hand against the sudden, blinding brightness. Utterly exposed, he stammered.

"I'm no one. I just got lost. Please, I'll be on my way," he said, taking a step backwards; there were spots in his vision as he stumbled over the uneven terrain. In dismay, Jon heard a shout from one of the men and then grunted as his arm was nearly wrenched from its socket.

As he struggled against the large man, Jon tried desperately to remember his fighting lessons with Calum. He kicked a leg forward into the other man's knee and used the soldier's own body weight to pull him down over his shoulder. When he successfully executed the simple manoeuvre, and his attacker landed with a thump, Jon thought he might actually have a chance to escape. However, he was almost immediately surrounded by more soldiers as they came running at the shouted alarm.

Jon held his arms out to either side, ready to try fighting his way out of the ambush, knowing full well that it was incredibly foolish; there was little hope that he would emerge from this a free man. The worst part, thought Jon, was that he *knew* these men; he had grown up with them. There was no way they would mistake him for anyone else.

As if reading his thoughts, a tall, hawk-faced man wearing an iron helmet (*Christopher? Christian? What was the man's name...*) peered at him, holding a lantern aloft in his lobstered mitt. The man smiled.

"Hello, Jon," he said, his voice oddly deep for a man so gaunt.

He nodded to someone over Jon's shoulder, and the younger man felt cold metal clamped around his wrist.

Baltsaros turned the page of the book resting against his bare stomach and put his arm back behind his head. He was reading a first-hand account of the early history of the large landmass to the far south. Though fascinating, the vocabulary was so archaic that Baltsaros was starting to lose the thread of the narrative.

Suddenly detecting the scent of sandalwood soap and a hint of tobacco smoke, he looked up and saw that Tom was leaning in the doorway to the stateroom, watching him with arms folded across his wide chest.

The captain frowned.

"What is it, Tom?" he asked.

The first mate smiled and pulled himself away from the doorjamb, walking on silent feet across the thick rugs towards him.

Baltsaros shut his book and sat up. He watched the first mate walk towards him with the grace of a panther. It was immediately obvious that Tom had taken a bath; though that in itself wasn't unusual, the fact that his first mate had actually put on a shirt for once was odd.

"What do you want, Tom?" asked Baltsaros, curiosity wiping away any irritation at being disturbed.

Tom just smiled and kneeled down on the edge of the bed. Slowly leaning forward, he lowered his head and softly kissed the instep of the captain's bare foot.

Baltsaros almost gasped at the astonishingly intimate touch. He shook his head as the first mate's hands slid up the leg of his pants, kneading the captain's calf muscle as he pressed his lips to Baltsaros's naked ankle.

"Tom, what in the world has gotten into you?" Baltsaros asked, slightly breathless and charmed by Tom's strangely tender advance. He watched as Tom crawled up towards him, pushing the captain's legs apart and bending his head down to Baltsaros's bare stomach.

Groaning as Tom's warm mouth slid wetly against his skin, Baltsaros pressed his head back on the pillow. Tom's hands came up to stroke the captain's chest as he kissed along his ribs, his tongue leaving wet trails on Baltsaros' skin.

As the staggering passion rose up in hot, pulsing waves in Baltsaros, so did too a tiny thorn of suspicion.

He opened his eyes, chest heaving as he watched Tom seduce him softly and with more care than Baltsaros had ever seen from the rough youth. Tom's lips closed over one of the captain's nipples, and he flicked it gently with his tongue.

Shifting his hips at the growing discomfort in the front of his pants, Baltsaros sighed, a slight frown on his face.

Something felt incredibly wrong.

With more than a little regret he finally pushed Tom up and away with a large, sun-darkened hand against his shoulder.

"Tom, I asked you a question," he said, trying to control his breathing and ignoring the fact that one of Tom's hands was stroking the inside of his thigh through the black leather of his pants.

The first mate smiled softly at him and shrugged.

"Nothin', Da. Just thought ye might want some company now that Jon is gone. I thought ye might like it if I was like this," he said and went to lean back in to resume his caresses.

Baltsaros's sense of wrongness intensified. While Tom was incredibly thorough when it came to his physical relationship with the captain, it had always been pure, glorious, brutal *fucking*. Not this... lovemaking.

With a tight grip on Tom's shoulder, Baltsaros continued to hold him back. He saw anger flash quickly in Tom's blue-green eyes.

"What, Da?" he asked, the corners of his mouth turning down as he clenched his jaw.

"You speak as if Jon is gone for good," Baltsaros said softly, watching Tom carefully; and, there it was: a sliver of guilt in the first mate's eyes.

"Well, what if he doesn't come back?" asked Tom, shrugging again. "He might not, ye know. Maybe he's run off... found himself missin' his old man. Maybe he fell off his horse and broke his neck."

The captain felt a pang of alarm; this was more than wishful thinking on Tom's part.

"Tom, what did you do?" he asked slowly, digging his fingers into his first mate's broad shoulder. The momentary look of uncertainty on Tom's face was replaced with defiance; smart enough to know that he was caught, Tom shoved Baltsaros's hand away and sat up.

"I had to, Da. He was makin' ye strange! Ye don't see it, but I do—" He choked when the captain's hard fist slammed into his throat.

Tom fell backwards off the bed and landed hard on the floor, writhing and fighting for breath. His tearing eyes went wide when Baltsaros planted a foot on his chest, standing above him with his teeth bared in an expression of savage fury.

"Tell me," said the captain, his voice deadly calm. "Tell me all of it."

CHAPTER 13
HOMECOMING

Jon rubbed at his wrists. The iron shackles that bound him were cold and thick, leaching the heat from his blood without ever growing warm themselves. They'd taken his cloak and his boots and left him to shiver alone in the dark cell; Jon sat hunched on a dirty pile of hay, avoiding the damp walls of the dungeon.

Home, sweet home.

The rotten-meat odour of old blood and the acrid scent of heated metal sat thick under the trapped-human smells of piss, shit, and vomit. Even having worked for so long in the castle's dungeon, the odiferous cocktail of misery and pain that bombarded his senses was making Jon feel ill. He had no idea how long he'd been there; it felt like hours, but for all he knew it had been less than one.

Where is Reginald? he thought.

Someone had to come by sooner or later and let him talk to his stepfather. As he shuddered and pulled his knees up, Jon's brain ran wild. Why was he wanted for murder?

Jon stood on the shore of a black sea with water so calm it looked like glass. The rocks beneath his bare feet hurt him, but he couldn't move. He stood rooted there, watching as the ship sailed away from him. The wake it left behind was churning up the water blood-red. Looking down when he felt a sickening tug, Jon realized in horror that there was a dripping, tendon-like rope coming out of his chest. He could feel himself unravelling from the inside, the rope pulling out everything he was, bit by bit, in a long, swaying line across the water. The other end of the strand was tangled in the claws of a giant black lion that stood on the quarterdeck, watching him with sombre eyes.

Jon startled awake at the loud bang on the metal bars. For a half second he forgot where he was; memories of a different cage flooded his mind until he realized he was cold and damp, something he had never been in Baltsaros's care. He lifted his head and peered blearily through the thick bars of his cell at the dark, stony face of the captain of the guards.

"Hi, Reginald," he said quietly.

His stepfather's brow was low over eyes narrow with suspicion.

"Jon," Reginald said.

It wasn't much of a greeting. Jon had the uncomfortable feeling that his stepfather was livid. He got slowly and painfully to his feet, the cold having cramped up his muscles during the long wait. It was well after midnight; he had already heard the changing of the guards some time earlier. Holding onto the iron bars, he looked out at the man who had raised him on a diet of duty and disappointment.

"Reginald, I didn't kill anyone. I don't know what's going on," Jon said. "You've got to believe me."

Reginald pressed his lips together a moment before answering.

"Where the hell have you been for the last month?" he asked, his voice harsh.

Jon frowned. He had been kidnapped and then recruited by pirates; no matter how he worded it, the answer would guarantee him a spot in a gibbet, feeding the crows with his flesh. Pirates were a scourge, according to Reginald, and deserved no better. Jon knew the captain of the guards wouldn't make an exception for him, regardless of their relationship.

Reginald slowly crossed his arms across his barrel chest while Jon tried to put together a plausible story in his head.

"I just... took up work on a fishing boat. I'm sorry but it was very... sudden," he said, wincing inwardly at how ridiculous he sounded.

The old soldier's eyebrows lifted, and he nodded slightly.

"After you spent all that silver, I take it?" asked Reginald.

Jon blinked.

"What silver?" he asked, confused.

His stepfather tapped a finger to the side of his wide, grizzled jaw.

"The silver you stole from the *Rose Garden*," replied Reginald drily.

"What? I have no idea what you're talking about." Jon backed away from the bars, feeling a little lightheaded.

Reginald stood glowering at him for a moment.

"I suppose you're going to tell me that you didn't kill those girls either?" he asked, his head tilting slightly.

"Reginald, for fuck's sake, tell me what the hell is going on?" said Jon, a note of panic creeping into his voice. "What girls? What silver?"

His stepfather took a deep breath, scrutinizing Jon.

"The day you disappeared from the brothel, a large quantity of silver disappeared along with you. I really couldn't believe you would have done something so incredibly stupid." Reginald paused, his dark-brown eyes locked on his stepson's face. "We searched for you, but you had disappeared without a trace. Do you have any idea how it feels to be the head of the city guards and have everyone think your son is a petty thief?" He paused, scowling at Jon. "Not good at all."

Jon kept shaking his head slowly at Reginald's words. One of his crewmates had to have stolen from the brothel that night; it was the only explanation.

Reginald leaned forward and wrapped his hands around the bars.

"I really thought you'd run off for good or gotten yourself killed. Then, this morning, two women were found down by the pier, their throats cut. I had to send a few men down to the inn to keep the peace. Someone had whipped the crowd there into a frenzy with stories of this 'Black Brigand' who was going from town to town, raping and killing women over the last month. One sailor swore up and down that he had seen the murderer with his own eyes and that he matched your description perfectly. He also said that this killer's real name was 'Jon' and that he was the son of a lawman. Keller at the print house made up those posters with your face on it. You can imagine what kind of mayhem that caused. Jon, I nearly had a riot on my hands," said the gruff, old soldier, his face grim. "Everyone thinks you're the murderer."

Reginald let go of the bars and began to pace back and forth in front of Jon's cell.

"You've always been a strange one... I've always thought there was something wrong with you. And then the headaches started, the confusion... your constant refusal to do your job. Was it all just a sham?" He stopped and glared hard at the man in the cage again. "Now you're standing there telling me you just, what, decided to change jobs and didn't bother to *tell anyone?* I... don't think so."

Jon's eyes had narrowed at the mention of the sailor.

"Reginald, was this sailor from the mainlands? Built like an ox?" asked Jon and then pointed to his face. "Scar through his right eyebrow?"

Tom...

"I am asking the questions!" yelled Reginald through the bars, his spittle spraying the man in the cage. "Jon, tell me where the fuck you've been and why I shouldn't have one of your old colleagues work you over for a while?"

Jon closed his eyes and swallowed hard. He had to get out. He had to get word to Baltsaros. Jon felt helpless. He opened his eyes and stared hard at the man on the other side of the bars.

"Reginald, I'm innocent. I told you, I was working on a boat. Maybe I didn't say anything because I thought you didn't give a damn whether I was alive or dead unless I was doing your job for you. I didn't steal any silver, and I sure as hells didn't kill any girls."

Reginald frowned but nodded slowly after a while.

"I'd like to believe you, Jon, but you're not giving me much to go on. The husbands of those two women are calling for you to be hanged. Tomorrow. Be glad my men caught you before someone else did." Reginald looked suddenly a little sad and looked away for a moment. "If Eleana was alive to see you behind bars..."

The corners of Jon's mouth turned down; he felt a little pain in his chest at the mention of his mother.

Reginald sighed and turned back to Jon.

"All right. Give me the name of this boat, and I'll see if I can get someone to corroborate your story."

Jon felt his heart sink to his stomach.

"It... It doesn't have a name," he said quietly.

~

"What do you mean it doesn't have a name?" asked Jon, sitting across the table from Baltsaros for the morning meal. "What kind of pirate ship doesn't have a name?"

The handsome older man took a bite of bread and lifted one shoulder up in an easy shrug.

"My ship, I suppose," he said and smiled, his gracefully curved lips stretching wide in amusement.

Jon frowned and shook his head.

"I thought it was illegal to go into port without a name. Or a flag... which you don't fly either," he said, remembering the first time he had seen the small, sleek warship in the harbour.

Baltsaros nodded.

"No flag, no name: no docking. But silver and gold buy many privileges," he replied. When he saw that Jon was dissatisfied with his answer, he laughed. "She's a ship... just a tool, Jon. Would you name your hammer? Your eating knife?" he asked, his eyes merry.

Jon shook his head.

"But I also don't call my knife *she* either," he replied.

While Baltsaros's smile didn't leave his face, his eyes went strangely flat for the span of a heartbeat.

"The ship used to have a name. Now it doesn't," he said simply and took a sip of coffee.

Jon nodded and looked back down at his food, feeling uncomfortable. Though he wanted to ask more, he felt his questions were touching the edge of a strange pain inside the captain; it was obvious that he didn't want to talk about it further.

Later, Jon asked Katherine about the ship's lack of name. They had been practicing with wooden swords, and the lithe woman was slightly breathless when she answered.

"Did you ask the captain?" she asked, wiping the sweat from her neck with a handkerchief.

Jon grimaced slightly. He sat down on a crate and rubbed at the red marks that Katherine's stick had left all over his arm. She was fast and vicious with her attacks;

even though he had the longer reach she somehow managed to disarm him over and over again.

"I tried that. He wasn't very forthcoming," he admitted.

Katherine sat down on the gunwale and looked hard at Jon. After a moment, she spoke in a low voice.

"Well, it's a sort of mystery. The captain's never really given anyone a straight answer." She laughed suddenly. "You're going to come to the realization very quickly that he's rather... unconventional. But he makes us rich, so we don't ask too many questions." She pulled off the leather thong tying her braid and raked her fingers through her raven-black hair. "I'll tell you the only thing I know for sure. Baltsaros is the second captain to hold this ship. The one before was his uncle and... There was a mutiny led by Baltsaros. It was successful, obviously," she said.

Jon frowned.

"What happened to his uncle?" he asked.

Katherine shrugged offhandedly.

"Captain Baltsaros killed him."

~

Jon had given up trying to force the pin out of his shackle by tapping it against the wall when the guard, a man he didn't know, came and threw water over him at the sound of metal against stone. Shivering so hard his teeth were chattering, the soaking wet young man was still trying to come up with a credible story. However, the look Reginald had given him when he had said the ship had no name was enough for him to believe his efforts were in vain. Reginald was caving to public pressure; Jon would most likely be hanged the next day.

He laughed to himself, a small, sad sound echoing in the darkness. He'd only just started to really feel alive. As he turned over on his side, awkwardly trying to wrap his arms around himself despite the short-chained manacles, Jon felt tears threatening to fall. Tom had to be responsible.

Fucking Tom. If Jon got out of this alive, he would kill Tom.

But... Maybe they'd already left without him.

Closing his eyes tight, Jon took a deep breath and finally let himself think about the captain. When he grit his teeth against the hopelessness that washed over him, Jon realized that touching his feelings for Baltsaros was like tearing open a wound.

Why am I so foolish? he thought.

The sanctuary that lay in the captain's arms was intoxicating. His dreams were constantly filled with what *could* happen... Yet when given the chance, Jon had instead gone on a mission to save a dog.

As he sat shuddering in the cold darkness, Jon knew he was a coward. The desires that Baltsaros brought out in him were intimidating; he felt completely stripped of armour in the captain's presence, and it scared him just how much *he liked it*. A soft sigh escaped from his throat as he remembered how gently the captain had held him in his strong arms. Baltsaros had lowered some of his walls, and in return, Jon had run away. There was no denying that the intriguing man left Jon breathless and aching, staring miserably at the stained mattress above his head in the crew quarters as he imagined the captain and his first mate falling into each other's arms, night after night.

Tears ran down over the bridge of Jon's nose and down his cheek onto the matted straw beneath him. Why couldn't he just... give in?

It was too late now.

Jon was muttering softly to himself hours later in the gloom of early morning when he heard quiet footfalls approaching. Startled, he looked up as a dark figure crept towards the bars. There was a gasp.

"Oh, my god. Jon, you're alive!" said a familiar voice.

He lurched quickly to his feet and pressed himself to the bars. The relief that flooded through him made Jon feel wildly giddy, his heart careening in his chest.

"Kat! You have to get me out of here!" he said quickly, his voice hoarse. Jon could see her eyes darting all over his face as if in shock to see him.

"What's wrong?" he asked.

She just shook her head and squeezed his cold fingers through the bars.

"Later," she whispered. "I have to find the keys."

Jon nodded and pointed up the dark hallway.

"The guards play cards and drink down that way. It's the only place in this hell that isn't damp and cold. There will be at least two," he said hurriedly. He heard the rasp of metal as she pulled her short sword from her belt, a dangerous glint in her brown eyes. "Be careful, Kat," he said, but she had already turned and was running fleet-footed down the dark passageway.

Soon Jon heard a muffled yell but no shouts of alarm. It seemed like only minutes before Katherine was back at the front of his cage, her face creased in a wide smile.

She quickly undid the lock and opened the door, pulling him into a tight embrace. Jon, his hands still shackled together in front of him, could only lean his head down onto her shoulder in return. Katherine pulled away and frowned into his face.

"I don't have time to get these off of you," she said, one hand on the manacle on his wrist. "Are you all right? Can you run?"

Jon nodded, and they made their way swiftly down the dungeon hallway to the winding stone stairs. With Katherine's hand on his elbow, they ran up the staircase and emerged into the courtyard in little time. The sky had only just lost the deep black of night; Jon could easily see the silhouette of the mouldering castle when he looked up.

Katherine tugged at him to move faster, and Jon gasped in pain as a sharp rock cut into the bottom of his foot. Thoughts of the dream came back to him as he lurched forward, crossing the rocky ground to the stables; they hadn't left him after all.

When Jon saw where they were going, he pulled back on Katherine's arm.

"There aren't any horses!" he whispered but was amazed when he heard a snort and whickering sounds from the other side of the slatted wall.

"Well, there are now. Quick!" said Katherine, and yanked open the door.

When he frowned into the dark space, Jon could see that almost every stall was full.

What is going on? he thought as he stepped gingerly over the uneven ground.

The wind was knocked out of him an instant later when he landed on his back on the stable floor. At the sound of Katherine's sword leaving its scabbard again, he struggled in panic against the weight of the dog on his chest, trying to get his breath back. Finally, he sucked in a shuddering lungful.

"Stop! Stop!" he said hoarsely. "Katherine, no, it's ok... Stop! Aaagh, Brutus! Down boy. Get off of me." He strained against the mastiff's huge neck as the dog drooled into his face.

Eventually, Brutus rolled off Jon and sat, wiggling like a puppy, tongue licking his lips and whimpering as he waited for his long-lost master to reach out to him.

Jon saw that the massive dog was dirty, and his fur was matted. As he stroked a hand slowly down Brutus's shivering sides he felt the dog's ribs sticking up through his thin skin.

"Oh, I'm so sorry, buddy. I'm so sorry I left you." His chest felt tight as he crooned softly at the huge dog that leaned into his touch. Jon felt tears come to his eyes.

"Jon, we really have to go. Now. Someone will notice soon that the castle is short a few guards at the gate. Get up! Now!" The slim woman hauled Jon to his feet and pushed him towards the large tan destrier in the stall ahead.

He watched as she swiftly saddled the horse, her motions practiced and sure. Getting him up on the huge horse with his hands still bound proved to be awkward, but soon they were on their way.

Jon bounced uncomfortably behind Kat, his arms looped around her to keep him steady. He saw with dismay that the sun was nearly up; if they didn't hurry, the morning guards would discover them.

At that moment he noticed the pennants flying above the walls; Lord Barton was in the castle.

"Kat..." he said. "I think we're stealing the lord's horse."

The pirate turned her head to the side to look at him. She had a wide grin on her face.

"Good!" she said, laughing.

However, a loud horn blast from above split the air, and Jon heard Katherine curse. They were spotted.

"Hyaaahh!" yelled Katherine, and the destrier leapt forward, almost knocking Jon loose.

As he clutched the narrow waist of the woman in front of him, Jon fought for balance as the giant horse raced out of the courtyard towards the castle gates.

"Hyaah!"

With the woman's cries, the horse went even faster, careening down the steep hill.

Right before Jon closed his eyes in terror at their breakneck speed, he saw the bodies of the guards at the gate, their blood pooling in the thick mud.

It was a crazy ride, every moment feeling like he was going to slip off the horse and drag Katherine down with him. Jon's breath lurched in his chest each time the horse's hooves struck the ground, and he was rigid with panic.

Soon, however, the destrier began to slow as they left the town of Portsmouth behind. Finally, they went down to an easy trot when they reached the crossing of the highroads. Even though the horse was carrying two, it seemed they had been swift enough to leave their pursuers behind.

When he saw that Brutus was keeping up with them, Jon smiled; he could breathe again. After a moment, Katherine's words in the dungeon came back to him.

"Why did you seem so surprised to see me if you were coming to rescue me?" he asked her.

She shook her head.

Jon wished he could see her face.

"It wasn't a rescue attempt," she replied over her shoulder. "It was a fool's errand, really."

Jon frowned.

"What do you mean?" he asked, confused.

"Tom told the captain you were dead," she said, her tone grim.

~

"He's dead. He's fuckin' gone. Ye can forget about him, Da," said Tom through swollen lips.

Tom's words had opened a great, yawning pit inside of Baltsaros. With his jaw clenched tight, he smashed his fist into his first mate's face again.

"How?" he asked, his voice a deadly calm. Jon couldn't be gone. Not yet. Not this way. When his first mate didn't reply right away, he grabbed the younger man around the throat and dashed his head hard against the floor.

"I... I paid a man," sputtered Tom, his left eye almost swollen shut. "I paid him to kill that little shit the second he got to town. And he did it! He killed—uhff!" His head rocked back against the hard wood planks as Baltsaros's fist connected again with his jaw. Tom moaned, but a slow grin soon spread his split lips.

The captain growled. Wrestling for self-control, he slowly stood up, backing away before he could end Tom's life.

"Yer cabin boy's feedin' the fish, Da. He's fuckin' dead!" yelled Tom from the floor. The first mate started to laugh but ended up choking as he coughed up blood. After he wiped his mouth, Tom finally closed his eyes and lay there breathing heavily; tears ran freely down his cheeks.

Baltsaros stared down at his first mate a moment longer before walking to the door. He looked out and saw Katherine nearby.

"Katherine, could you please bring two strong men to my quarters?" he asked in a low voice when she came towards him.

The tall woman nodded, her eyes widening almost imperceptibly at the blood on the captain's shirt.

Baltsaros turned back to the room and stepped over the man on the floor, sitting down in one of the dark wooden chairs.

Jon. Dead.

The words echoed in his head, devoid of sense. It was a... shame. He swallowed hard. When the woman returned with two deckhands, Baltsaros pointed to Tom.

"Take that to the brig," he said and watched as they lifted the unresisting Tom off the floor. He held up a hand as Katherine turned to go. "A minute, please?" he asked.

"Aye, Captain," she replied, crossing the room to stand in front of Baltsaros.

"Tom had Jon killed," he said quietly. He felt so strange.

Katherine's hand came up to her mouth.

"What? How?" she asked in shock.

Baltsaros looked down at the swollen knuckles of his right hand.

"He says he paid someone. I wish I didn't believe him," he replied, shaking his head.

Dead.

Baltsaros realized that he was sitting in the chair that Jon normally took, and he pressed his lips together hard. Why should he care? He felt a light touch on his arm and glanced back up at Katherine. She was looking at him with sadness in her eyes. No... It was more than that... There was sympathy there too.

"I'm sorry, Captain," she said softly.

Baltsaros frowned. Sorry for what? He felt pain in his hand, and strangely, in his chest.

"Tom's a pathological liar," she said. "Do you really have any proof that Jon's actually dead?"

Baltsaros shook his head.

"When have you known Tom to lie about killing someone?" he asked softly.

~

Jon breathed quickly in astonishment as he listened to Katherine recount what had happened.

"You've certainly made an impression on the captain," said the woman in front of him. "He's not the kind of man to waste resources on a gamble."

Closing his eyes, he leaned his forehead on the leather of Katherine's vest. He heard her chuckle softly.

"And... I know he's made quite an impression on you," she added.

Jon felt like telling her to make the horse go faster. He needed to see Baltsaros. To... thank him. His heart lurched in his chest.

"Jon, just be careful, ok?" Katherine said after a few minutes.

He lifted his head and frowned.

"You've said that before. Why? What's wrong with the captain?" he asked.

"He's not like other men," she said after a long pause. "I've never met anyone who was so completely untouched by the violence they did. Hells, even Tom gets drunk after killing someone. But not the captain. He just goes on."

"I know he's dangerous," replied Jon.

"Yes, he is. But that's not quite what I mean. He's just... completely indifferent to people. They interest him like bugs interest little boys. Do you understand what I mean?" she asked.

Jon chewed on the inside of his lip. He had seen the strange flatness in Baltsaros's eyes many times; occasionally Jon felt as if the captain were a large, curious predator just sizing him up for a meal.

"Yeah. I think I do. But, I've seen something else in him," he said, remembering the emotion in Baltsaros's words.

Come back to me, Jon.

"Just be careful, ok? I've sort of grown fond of you, you know," she said and squeezed his arm.

Jon was about to reply when he saw that they had reached the port town where the ship was docked for supplies and repairs; when he saw the familiar shape of it out in the small harbour, Jon felt slightly breathless.

~

Baltsaros grunted as he pulled the new rope through the pulley, lifting the heavy sailcloth. The sun was warm on his bare back, and the physical work made him feel good. After yanking down hard one more time, he finally tied the hemp rope in a looping knot around the metal cleat.

The shipwright had found less damage than Baltsaros had thought he would, and with the captain pitching in with the labour, the crew had been able to finish up the preparations early; at this pace they would be ready to sail well before the sun set. He straightened and wiped a hand across his eyes, looking towards the road into town for what felt like the hundredth time. He had told Katherine to search along the road for signs that Jon was simply late, to only as far as Portsmouth before turning back.

If Tom was telling the truth, Jon would have died in town. If he wasn't, and Jon had stayed of his own volition, Baltsaros didn't care to hear of it.

She should have been back by now.

As he forced his eyes away, he stooped to pick up the rest of the rope that was tied in a wide bundle and heave it up onto his shoulder. He crossed the deck and dropped his load on the extra supplies that would be stored below deck.

Stretching his shoulders, Baltsaros smiled wryly to himself; he was going to be sore tomorrow. He had been spending far too much time in sedentary pursuits since Tom had taken over as first mate. However, that time was now over. He could no longer trust the spiteful creature locked in the brig; but, as much as he wanted to kill him, Baltsaros couldn't.

The captain realized that his gaze had turned again to the road, and he saw that there were figures on the pier now, coming towards the ship. When Baltsaros picked out the huge dog with them, his heart thumped hard once in his chest; he shaded his eyes and watched as Katherine and Jon approached.

Jon...

The captain stepped up onto the gunwale to quickly get by the milling sailors and ran a few steps along the edge to jump down onto the wide gangplank. He walked down onto the pier and stood there, eyes glued on the dark-haired young man.

Jon was in manacles.

All the fury and fear that Baltsaros had locked away seared through him then; it was as if he were a howl of rage trapped in human form.

However, when he saw the raw emotion in Jon's wide blue eyes, staring desperately into his own, dizzying relief suddenly extinguished all of Baltsaros's burning anger, leaving him strangely weak. He staggered slightly, taking a step forward.

Jon was not dead.

Jon had come back to him.

Baltsaros closed the distance with only a few long strides; but, when he was near enough to reach out and touch Jon, he faltered. It was daunting to make that final move across the small space; it was stepping into the unknown.

Jon stole the breath from Baltsaros when he suddenly bridged the gap and captured the captain's mouth with his own. Baltsaros gasped into the kiss and bent his head to it, his hands on Jon's face, in his hair, down his back, grasping at him tightly to pull him closer still.

Mouth open to Baltsaros, Jon took him in; when their tongues moved together they were lost souls found once more.

There was nothing else but Jon, this broken puppy, this dangerous wolf pup, in his arms. Baltsaros wanted to devour him with his kiss and protect him forever.

This was the very heart of madness.

Baltsaros gladly let himself be pulled down into it, unexpectedly made whole with this homecoming, this birth of something previously untasted. Baltsaros groaned and bit softly at Jon's lips; the younger man whimpered, pressing himself hard into the captain's fierce embrace.

When he finally broke the kiss, Baltsaros looked down at the boy in his arms. Jon's eyes were filled with new awareness, pupils wide with desire. After a moment, his chest tight with strange emotion, Baltsaros rested his bruised lips against Jon's forehead and whispered into his skin.

"Never leave my side again."

CHAPTER 14
NO QUARTER GIVEN

J on winced as Beard tried to use the mallet to remove the metal spikes from his manacles. The skin around his wrists was sensitive from being rubbed for hours, and though the big man was trying to be gentle, it was still somewhat painful. Chewing on the strange bread that Beard had given him, meat and cheese baked directly into it, Jon turned his head towards the quarterdeck to watch Katherine and the captain discussing ship matters.

Baltsaros.

Jon blushed slightly, thinking about all the eyes that had been on them kissing out in the open; he still couldn't believe his own recklessness or the captain's reaction.

Smiling, he turned his head back to the giant working to free him. Jon was filthy, starving, and in pain, yet filled with a steady pulse of giddying emotion; it was hard to do anything but grin like an idiot.

The first few minutes on board had been a whirlwind.

After making sure that Jon was in no immediate danger of collapse, Baltsaros had ushered him up the gangplank, a strong arm around his waist. Completely dispelling any fear that Jon had overstepped his bounds by kissing him, the captain had embraced him again briefly in full sight of the crew. Sitting Jon down on a crate, Baltsaros had murmured a quick apology before running off and yelling to the deckhands to weigh anchor.

There had been an incredible flurry of activity as all hands on deck had worked to get the ship away from the dock and out to sea. In amazement he had watched as the captain himself helped hoist the lines to square the sail for their departure, muscles

"

bulging and straining in Baltsaros's arms and broad back as he bent himself to the lowly shiphand's task.

Metal clanged down to the wooden planks, Jon's wrists finally free. He gasped in relief and rubbed at the redness around one arm, smiling at Beard.

"Thank you," Jon said.

The giant man sat there looking at him appraisingly for a moment; Jon was almost startled when the craggy face finally split wide in a smile of large, yellowed teeth.

"Welcome," came the rumbled reply. The giant then stood up and clapped Jon on the shoulder, causing the younger man to cough in surprise, before taking off at a lumbering run down the deck.

Brutus, fast asleep in the sun, was curled up like a giant cat on the deck; he would be ravenous when he recovered from their arduous flight.

Jon looked up and saw that Katherine was now behind the wheel. Earlier, with zero ceremony, the captain had promoted her to first mate, and the astonishment was still plain on her face. Jon pressed his lips together. His mind kept leading him back to Tom, but he was not ready to think about the treachery just yet.

Soon they were underway, leaving behind the piled rocks of the harbour and cruising through open water. However, Jon saw that instead of sailing away from the island, they were tacking to circumnavigate it.

He frowned, finding it curious, but was startled out of his thoughts at a light touch on his shoulder. Looking up, Jon was rendered breathless by the man standing above him.

Baltsaros's hair was windblown; dark-blond wisps of it had escaped the leather tie at his nape and were whipped up by the strong sea wind. Indoors, the captain's eyes had always seemed a deep brown, nearly black, but in the bright afternoon sun, Jon could see that there was more amber in them than he had thought. The corners of Baltsaros's eyes were crinkled as he stared down at Jon, a wide smile on his bowed lips.

"Come with me," he said simply, helping Jon to his feet.

The change of lighting between the deck and the captain's quarters was jarring; Jon felt blind for a few moments and stumbled against one of the chairs in the middle of the room.

Baltsaros's arms came up quickly around him.

It was a visceral shock, this sudden, warm, bronze skin enveloping him so protectively. Jon's heart crashed against his ribs. Now that his hands were free, they came up and grasped the older man around his smooth, muscled waist. He suddenly felt shy as his vision focused and saw that Baltsaros was looking into his eyes with unmistakable desire.

Slowly, as if afraid he would pull away, the captain brought his mouth down to Jon's in a soft, open-mouthed kiss, Baltsaros's tongue questing out to touch the tip of his in a way that was so tender it made him shiver. Baltsaros pulled away.

"Are you all right?" he asked, his eyes darting over Jon's face in worry.

Jon felt a tightness in his chest.

"Yes... I am. I am now. Your touch just makes me..." He swallowed. "Makes me *want*." He felt his words were awkward, but he was amazed when the captain's eyes went dark with emotion, and the man bent again to his lips.

This kiss was fuelled by frantic passion.

Baltsaros twined his fingers in the dark curls at the base of Jon's neck as he savaged his lips.

Jon groaned into the kiss, all his uncertainty being devoured by the fire that burned inside him at the captain's rougher handling. Jon felt crazy with desire, fingers digging into Baltsaros's skin as if he could press himself further into the other man's flesh. In a frenzy to feel Baltsaros's skin against his, Jon began pulling the soiled linen shirt out of the waist of his trousers.

The captain broke the kiss and took a step back to watch Jon strip his torso bare. There was the barest flash of anger in Baltsaros's face when he saw the mottled bruising that covered Jon's gracefully muscled chest; the castle guards had not been kind to him. After taking the shirt from Jon and tossing it aside, Baltsaros bent low and started kissing the dark marks on his skin, his tongue licking at the bruises as if to wash them away with his spit.

The sound that came out of Jon's mouth at the exquisite, unfamiliar sensation was part whimper, part sigh.

Suddenly, it was all too much for him; he felt himself start to shake, and in dismay Jon realized hot tears were slowly running down his cheeks. He quickly pushed Baltsaros's head away from his chest, his fingers snagging awkwardly in the captain's hair and sending the leather tie to the floor.

Baltsaros's eyes widened when he saw the distress that his touch had caused in Jon, and he straightened, his long, dark-blond hair hanging loose around his angular face. Frowning thoughtfully, he drew Jon against his chest to cradle his head in the crook of his neck, hands stroking slowly but firmly down his back.

Jon felt utterly foolish and lightheaded, and there was a deep ache in the pit of his chest; he felt that he was letting the captain down by acting so ridiculous. Jon was so naïve to think that he could just be that brazen and confident...

A shuddering sob erupted out of him, and then he couldn't stop. Jon cried hard against the shoulder of the man who had torn him from his home, who had forced freedom on him when he was too scared to take it himself.

All the while Baltsaros held him tight, his hands caressing Jon's shaking body. The man was silent; Jon was so caught up in his own misery that he couldn't tell what the captain was thinking, and that piled more pressure on his already overloaded emotions.

In alarm, Jon realized that Baltsaros was pulling him back towards the bed; he panicked, fighting weakly against the powerfully built captain.

"Stop it, Jon. Hush. You're having an anxiety attack. Come... I won't hurt you," said the captain, holding firm onto the struggling young man.

Jon felt Baltsaros's calm voice slide like a wedge into the tightening confines of his fear. Slowly, Jon let himself be led to the bed. The sheer terror he felt must have been clear on his face when Baltsaros bade him to lie down; the captain's own had gone serious in concern.

Jon closed his eyes and lay back on the soft bed, his heart beating high and fast in his chest; it was as if the air in the room was too thin to breathe.

When Baltsaros crawled up next to him, Jon took another shuddering breath and held it. Baltsaros stroked a hand slowly across Jon's body as he moved closer still, pulling the unresisting young man onto his side until Jon's cheek rested against his chest. Jon could hear the rumble of Baltsaros's voice and the slow, regular thud of his heart right against his ear.

"Jon... Just breathe. There is nothing I want from you that I cannot wait for. You are safe here. My dear boy, you've been through a terrible ordeal, and you haven't slept in over a day. Everything will be all right. Just breathe. Listen to my voice..."

Between the captain's low voice and the soothing sounds of his calm heartbeat, Jon began to feel himself relax. Baltsaros was right. He had been beaten, thrown in jail, accused of murder, and had faced the looming possibility of his death by hanging... all on little sleep and absolutely no food or water. However, he felt it didn't excuse how he was acting.

Jon opened his eyes and moved his head away from Baltsaros, looking up into the man's enigmatic face.

"I'm sorry," he said softly.

~

Baltsaros frowned at the boy in his bed and shook his head.

"You haven't done anything wrong, Jon," he said.

After a moment, when he felt that Jon was calmer, Baltsaros placed his open hand on his flat stomach and stroked the skin there with his thumb. Jon's breath hissed out between clenched teeth, and the captain felt the muscles tense under his palm.

"This. This is what I do not understand," Baltsaros said softly, curiosity colouring his words. "Has *no one* ever touched you?"

Jon pressed his lips together, and he shook his head.

Baltsaros propped himself up on one elbow to better look at Jon's face.

"I don't just mean sexually. I mean... at all? Has no one touched you in friendship? In compassion?" he asked, fearing he knew the answer. Still, he was dismayed when Jon closed his eyes and shook his head again.

From lips thin with grief, Jon whispered the truth.

"Not since my mother..." he said. There was deep shame in his voice.

Baltsaros felt a terrible anger well up inside him for this beautiful, broken creature that lay against him, shivering at his touch. Jon had told him that his mother had died when he was a small thing, a boy of four. Baltsaros would see Reginald pay for this.

Even he, cruel life that he'd had under his uncle's care, had known warmth among the crew.

"But, what about everyone else in the castle?" he asked, his eyes watching the crease between Jon's brows deepen.

Jon shrugged slightly and opened his eyes. The captain was amazed at the depth of pain that lay trapped inside his gaze. Had no one loved this boy?

"Some of it is Reginald's fault. Some of it is my fault," said Jon, shaking his head again. "It really doesn't matter."

Baltsaros laughed harshly, and Jon frowned up at him. The grieving boy with no one to turn to had grown into a man with incredible empathy and no ability to control his own emotions; someone who craved being touched like a man craved water in the desert without even recognizing it. Jon was so drawn in on himself that it was a wonder he had made it as far as he had in this life. Baltsaros licked his bottom lip, thinking.

There is that steel within him.

Jon watched Baltsaros with wide grey-blue eyes.

"I think it matters," the captain said quietly. "And, I think you matter very much to me."

When he saw that tears threatened to spill again from the boy's stormy eyes, he pushed away the fury that was burning inside him and leaned down to touch his lips softly to Jon's.

The young man eagerly lifted his head to the kiss, tensing only slightly when Baltsaros resumed stroking the skin of Jon's stomach. Soon the kiss deepened, and the passion of earlier was slowly reignited.

Jon started moaning softly as Baltsaros's skilled fingers became bolder in their caresses, and the captain felt himself stir as the boy beneath him gasped in pleasure when his nipples were pinched gently, and then harder.

Baltsaros moved his mouth down to Jon's throat and bit down softly there, curious to see what his reaction would be; he was charmed when he felt Jon shudder and dig his fingers into his lower back. He had been surprised on that drunken night to realize that Jon was a virgin, but hadn't truly grasped how deep the boy's lack of experience went. There was a thrill running through him as he realized he would be the one to initiate Jon to these new sensations, this dizzying world of pleasure.

With Jon groaning and straining up against Baltsaros's body, the captain decided to go further. The captain slid his hand softly down Jon's smooth chest as he pulled his head back, resting up on his elbow again to watch Jon's face as he surrendered to Baltsaros's touch.

The captain's hand slowly made its way down past Jon's navel to the lines where his pelvis dipped alluringly beneath the grey trousers. As he slid a finger under the waistband of Jon's pants, Baltsaros leaned down once more and shared the young man's breath for a moment until Jon's body relaxed anew. More fingers slid under the coarse material at Jon's waist.

The dark-haired youth had his eyes shut tight and his lips slightly open; Baltsaros could see his tongue moving against his teeth in time to the older man's motions.

Finally, the tips of Baltsaros's fingers made contact with the smooth, rounded head of Jon's erect cock. He had expected him to shrink at his touch but was amazed when Jon moved his hips up, pressing firmly into the contact.

Jon's teeth were worrying at his bottom lip softly, and Baltsaros brought his face down so he could bite at the corner of his mouth.

Groaning, Jon opened to Baltsaros and kissed him deeply. However, when the captain's fingers slid further down Jon's shaft, the dark-haired youth hissed a sharp breath and stopped Baltsaros with his hand.

Baltsaros pulled his head back and frowned. Jon was almost panting, his face and neck flushed with desire, but still he held onto Baltsaros's wrist. *Please*, said his storm-grey eyes.

"Do you want me to stop?" Baltsaros asked quietly.

"Yes. No. I don't know," said Jon honestly. More colour mounted in his cheeks. "I don't know how to be," he confessed.

Baltsaros nearly laughed, but he knew it would be misunderstood by the vulnerable youth. Instead, he shook his head.

"Just *be*, Jon," he said.

After a moment and with obvious hesitation, Jon's hand came up to brush the long lock of the captain's hair back over his shoulder; he pulled Baltsaros back down to his mouth. Their tongues moved together, and Jon's stubble scratched at Baltsaros's lips.

Jon suddenly turned his head slightly.

"I... won't last long," he whispered hoarsely.

Baltsaros could almost feel the young man's embarrassment in his hot skin, but it was permission. He buried his face in Jon's neck, almost dizzy with his own desire. However, this was for Jon. There would be time later for other things... Right now he needed to concentrate on the shuddering body against his.

He slowly withdrew his fingers and proceeded to unbutton the waist of Jon's pants; pulling back the flaps, he pushed down on the linen garment underneath.

Jon let out a small whimper and wrapped his arm around Baltsaros. Sighing softly at the nakedness under his palm, Baltsaros slowly curled his hand around the hardened length that had come free from the confines of Jon's clothing. Jon's erection was slimmer than his own but of a similar length, and he groaned surprisingly loudly as Baltsaros began to run his hand along its length. With Jon's rapid pulse against his lips, he quickly stroked the young man's cock.

"That's it," he whispered against the skin of Jon's neck when he began thrusting his hips in time to Baltsaros's moving hand. "That's a good boy."

Jon's breath was hoarse and loud in the darkened room; his sigh turned into a sob at Baltsaros's words. In next to no time, he felt Jon's body strain hard, falling out of rhythm suddenly as his hands grasped desperately at Baltsaros's shoulders, nails scratching at the captain's skin. There was a surging in the hard shaft that Baltsaros held, and he felt Jon's seed spill over hot and slick onto his fist, sliding in wetly between his hand and Jon's twitching cock.

Jon moaned loud, a completely uninhibited sound that lasted on and on as he continued to thrust into Baltsaros's hand, his body rocking in time to inner pulses as he came hard against his captain's body.

Baltsaros kissed Jon softly and deeply until he started to relax and his breathing slowed. When he raised his head to look at Jon, he saw that there was a sheen of sweat that covered the young man's smooth skin and made dark curls stick to his forehead.

Jon opened his eyes, his pupils large as he looked at the captain. A slight frown furrowed his brow as he licked his lips.

"Do you want me to..." he asked, sounding uncertain and once again shy.

Baltsaros felt a pulse in the half-hard mound in the front of own his pants but shook his head and laughed.

"No, no. You are completely exhausted. You'll sleep now. I have things to do above deck," he said smiling.

Jon's face was soft with drowsiness as he watched the captain get up and cross the room. He gasped slightly when Baltsaros returned with a wet cloth and wiped Jon's chest and stomach, being gentle over his spent cock. Jon's soft fingers, not yet rough with hard labour, grasped gratefully at the captain's hand.

With half-lidded eyes, Jon looked into Baltsaros's and smiled sheepishly. Swallowing hard, Baltsaros was confounded by the fierce devotion he felt towards this dark-haired creature of sadness and want. Never before had he felt this need to... cherish.

Smiling, he squeezed Jon's hand, and the young man let go, closing his eyes. Baltsaros pulled the quilt on top of Jon and, without a thought, kissed him lightly before turning to go.

~

Jon, wake up. I have something to show you.

Jon's eyes fluttered open. It was dark in the room, a single candle burning in the middle of the mahogany table. He was brought back to the first night he had spent in these quarters; squinting, he could just see the cage across the room. There was a noise to his right, and he smiled, remembering. Jon reached out his hand and rested it on Brutus's big blocky head.

"Hey, boy," he said softly. The dog snuffled at his hand.

Frowning, he wondered whether he had dreamt the captain's voice. He sat up slowly and saw that the door to the stateroom was open. After swinging his feet over the edge, he stood somewhat shakily, using the dog as leverage. When he realized his pants were still unfastened, Jon felt the strangest combination of emotions: embarrassment, elation, confusion, and something that brought a swiftness to his heart that he couldn't put a name to.

He chuckled and rubbed a hand over his hair.

"Brutus, what have I got myself into?" he asked, and scratched the dog's soft ears.

Fastening his pants, he saw the captain's long black coat was draped over the edge of the table, obviously meant for him. Jon put it on. It was slightly too big, the captain being broader and taller than he was, and smelled like the commanding man who wore it: sun, salt, and something spiced and exotic.

He pulled the coat around him tight and went out into the night.

"Jon, come up," called Baltsaros.

Jon lifted his head and saw that the captain was up on the quarterdeck. He walked to the stairs and climbed up, his bare feet cold on the wooden stairs. Baltsaros met him at the top and embraced him tightly. The autumn air was brisk up on the high deck, and Jon was glad for the coat. He saw that the captain wore a long-sleeved, red leather doublet over a black open-necked shirt.

"Come see," said Baltsaros, a strange urgency in his voice. He pointed to lights off the starboard.

Jon frowned.

"What is it?" he asked, confused.

The captain laughed.

"I suppose you've never seen it from this angle," he said. He passed Jon the telescope he held in one hand, and Jon felt a momentary pang of guilt for the captain's lost binoculars.

He lifted the eyepiece and saw that he was looking at a small harbour town beneath a high hill. At first he didn't understand, but when he saw the barely visible silhouette of the castle up above the town, he realized he was looking at Portsmouth. Jon's mouth went dry.

"What are we doing here?" he asked in dismay, a half-dozen strange scenarios coming to mind at once. Was the captain handing him back to his stepfather? He looked at Baltsaros. Was this all some kind of cruel joke?

When the captain saw the utter confusion in Jon's eyes, he laughed abruptly, shaking his head, taking him into his arms again.

"So quick to mistrust, Jon?" Baltsaros asked softly, pressing his lips against the young man's temple. "Just watch..."

Jon kept his eyes on the town, seeing nothing but darkness and twinkling lights. He frowned. What was he supposed to see?

Then the night exploded.

Eye-wateringly bright streaks split the castle walls; balls of fire, like giant orange blossoms, erupted from the burning ruins. Jon could see the giant clouds of black smoke, blotting out the skies, the sounds of the explosions reaching his ears a second after they happened. He blinked, and there were bright spots behind his eyelids.

The castle is on fire.

He looked away, back to the captain's face. The older man was staring at the conflagration with a grim look on his face, the flames reflected in his dark eyes. Jon turned again to the burning castle in awe. It was beyond comprehension.

"Did you do this?" he asked in a hushed voice.

Without looking at Jon, Baltsaros nodded. A moment later he tore his gaze away from the fires across the water; his eyes were narrow in amusement.

"Well, not me personally. You have Billy and Jim to thank for the show," he said smiling, his teeth white against his dark face. The twin brothers worked the 32-pounder carronades at the front of the ship, and it seemed that they also knew something about explosives.

"Baltsaros," said Jon quietly. "There were women and children in the castle too."

The captain shrugged.

"My men made sure that there were no innocents within," he said and looked back to the burning ruins.

He is lying.

That, or he didn't believe any of them to be innocent. It was as clear as day to Jon: the captain had just murdered a castle full of people and didn't care in the least.

Jon turned and watched the flames lick the sky. Baltsaros had done this out of revenge. Searching inside himself for the horror and sadness that should have been there, Jon was astounded to find nothing.

The captain had done this *for him.*

And it felt glorious.

CHAPTER 15
ROPE'S END

Destruction, hence, like creation, is one of Nature's mandates.

— MARQUIS DE SADE

J on woke up from dreams of Reginald burning.

He sat up slowly and rubbed his face. The self-assurance that he had gone to sleep with the night before had become slightly smudged with trepidation.

A dangerous man indeed.

However, looking over at the captain lying next to him, Jon had to smile.

After the fire had started to burn low, the two of them had nearly tumbled down the stairs in their haste to get to the privacy of the stateroom. There, Baltsaros had once again coaxed Jon's desire to the very edge; however, this time he had delayed Jon's final plunge by releasing him and instead, kissing him roughly on his mouth, chest, and neck until the keen edge of pleasure's knife was dulled. Then he would start up again, hand stroking Jon's cock skilfully, building up his ecstasy until he reached the very cusp only to stop once more.

Jon had been frantic with need, his lips whispering *please* over and over against Baltsaros's neck, each breath a sob. Finally, when it felt like he could take no more, the captain had pushed him down flat and moved down his body to close his mouth over the end of Jon's cock, sliding his lips over the sensitive head and down his hard shaft. Jon's hands had taken on a life of their own as he pressed the captain's head down against him, fingers snarled in the man's long hair. It had been a mind-shattering release when Jon had cum hard into Baltsaros's mouth, each thrust a rough-edged, liquid pulse of pleasure.

Afterwards, he had lain there breathless, watching Baltsaros as he sat back on his heels between Jon's legs. Being with Baltsaros was like dying and being reborn; there was no other way he could describe it.

When he saw that the captain's eyes were darkly shadowed, and his face was taut with blatant hunger, it occurred to him then that Baltsaros was stronger than he was; he could take whatever he wanted from the younger man. At the shocking thought, Jon had felt a finger of fear touch him, and... It had excited him. However, the captain just smiled down at Jon before crawling up next to him and pulling the covers over the two of them. Sleep had found both men quickly.

Jon stood quietly, not wanting to rouse the captain. After only a slight hesitation, and with a small smile, he pulled the captain's black shirt over his head and tucked it into his own grey trousers. On quiet feet, Jon left the captain's quarters, Brutus at his side, and headed below deck.

With a plate of food in one hand, Jon stood in front of the metal cage deep in the belly of the ship. The man in the back of it was crouched with knees to chin. When Jon stepped closer, a pair of fierce green-blue eyes looked him up and down.

"Have ye come to kill me, little man?" asked Tom, his voice hoarse from disuse. Jon walked right up to the front of the cage and placed the plate on the floor, sliding it through the opening at the base of the bars.

"No. Just to bring you your breakfast." Jon took a step back and sat down cross-legged on the floor. "And to get some answers."

Tom laughed harshly.

"Ye can keep yer fuckin' breakfast, love. I ain't hungry."

However, the way Tom's eyes had followed the food belied his words.

"Don't be a martyr, Tom. It's unattractive," said Jon, glibly.

The beaten pirate raised his head and grinned.

Jon gasped at the extent of the burly young man's injuries. Half of Tom's face was a mess of dark bruising, his left eye had a burst of dark red in it, and his lips had a deep split on one side. Jon could see that what he had assumed was grime was actually flaking dried blood that covered Tom from his matted dirty-blond hair to where his torso disappeared behind his bent knees.

When Tom finally uncurled and reached forward for the plate of breakfast, he did it with a grunt of pain; it wasn't only Tom's face that had taken a beating. Taking some egg up with his fingers, Tom began wolfing down the food.

Jon sat quietly just watching Tom eat.

The muscular young man's ocean eyes kept flicking back up to Jon's face in curiosity as he devoured his breakfast quickly. He was soon done and slid the metal plate back across the floor where it clanged against the bars. Tom sat back, his elbows resting on his knees as he looked at Jon. The ex–first mate burped and then smiled.

"So what can I do for you, dear Jonny? Ye've come to gloat? Did ye poison my food?" he asked, finishing the piece of bread in his hand in one bite.

Jon pressed his lips together and frowned at Tom.

"I just want to know *why* you told the captain you had me killed. Why not just tell him the truth?" he asked.

Tom looked away. After a long pause, Jon saw the man's broad shoulder come up in a minute shrug.

"Tom, why not just kill me? From what I've heard, it's something you do well... Why the roundabout way of getting me captured? Why bother?" he asked; the question had burned in him from the moment that Katherine had told Jon of Tom's assassination claims.

Tom looked back to Jon and grinned.

"Aw, Jonny, so did ye wind up in the slammer?" he asked.

Jon leaned forward.

"I did. I would have also swung at the end of a rope if Katherine had not come to rescue me."

At this Tom's eyes went wide, his astonishment real.

"I thought yer da was the lawman?" he said slowly. "He'd a let ye hang?"

Jon nodded.

"The man's a coward. And he's not my father... He's only the man who married my mother."

Tom frowned and looked down at the floor.

"So he's a real cunt, aye?" he said after a long pause. He raised his eyes back to Jon's. "That's somethin' we have in common, isn't it? Our da's can't stand us." An odd look passed over Tom's face. "Listen, love. It wasn't my intention to have ye killed. Truly. I thought yer da would never believe ye killed those skirts. I figured ye'd wind up in a cage somewhere... just long enough to get ye out of my life." The words were spoken in complete truth.

Jon was about to respond when he heard boots behind him on the stairs. He turned his head and saw that Baltsaros, his face completely expressionless, was standing at the door.

"Jon, come away from there," he said quietly.

Jon got to his feet, his brows drawn in confusion.

"That's it, dog. Obey yer master," laughed Tom from his cage.

Baltsaros narrowed his eyes at his former first mate.

"Take him out of there," he growled.

Two deckhands came forward, jostling Jon out of the way to open the cage. With some difficulty, they managed to pull the big man out.

Jon leaned against the wall, his eyes on Tom; he almost gasped when he saw an incredible change go through the muscular brute. Tom had gone rigid with fear, his breath sounding loud in the small space. Following Tom's line of sight, Jon was aghast to see a heavy leather whip looped in the captain's hand.

Dragging Tom behind them, the two deckhands pushed past Jon again and followed Baltsaros up the stairs to the upper deck. Jon went with them, swallowing hard.

Tom struggled frantically as they tied him to the mast, arms spread wide to either side. He kept up a steady repeating plea that made Jon ache with the sound of it:

"—*please Da please don't I didn't touch him Da please please don't oh god Da please please I didn't touch him please...*"

"Tom just said I'd been killed so you'd leave me behind! He didn't figure on Reginald wanting to hang me. Please... Don't do this, Baltsaros... He didn't touch me. He didn't think I'd be killed," Jon said, a hand on the captain's arm.

Baltsaros looked down at him, his eyes cold.

Jon tightened his grasp and tried to find the loving, tender man he had shared a bed with last night in the terrifyingly glacial creature that stood before him.

"The result would have been the same, Jon. He would have been responsible for your death," said the captain, pushing the younger man back a few paces. "Now get out of my way." Baltsaros nodded to Old Calum who came and began pulling Jon away from the captain.

"He's absolutely terrified," Jon said, his voice harsh, and it was true. Tom was trembling and pale as he stood waiting for the captain to mete out his punishment, still whimpering his pleas over and over.

Baltsaros shook Jon off and took a few steps towards the man at the mast.

Defeated, Jon yanked his arm out of Calum's hands and went to stand next to Katherine.

An imposing black-clad figure in the bright morning sun, Baltsaros stood a good five paces away from Tom. He dropped the looped length to the deck with a thud, holding the heavy handle of the whip in his gloved hand. His arm came around in a wide circle above his head, and then the whip cracked out, a red line appearing on Tom's broad back as if by magic. The scream that rent the air was born of pure terror and pain.

Jon felt the blood freeze in his veins.

Crack!

Crack!

Crack!

The whip kept coming, over and over again. Tom's back was a mess of dripping red lines as the captain skilfully changed his grip and approach not to have the braided leather come down in the same place twice. Tom's shrieks became cries and then groans as more lines appeared; Baltsaros began grunting with exertion as his arm came up for the next stroke and the next.

Jon looked around and saw that most of the audience had trickled away. Those who had stayed seemed glued to the spot by horrified fascination. Behind him, Jon heard Katherine let out a soft cry.

Tom had suddenly sagged in his restraints, and his body no longer twitched when the leather continued cutting into him. The captain's face had taken on a look of soft ecstasy as if he were caressing Tom instead of whipping him to death.

Jon felt ill. He took a few steps forward.

"That's enough, Captain," he said loudly. "Stop it." His voice seemed to break through to Baltsaros, and the man blinked and staggered slightly, dropping the whip to the deck in a seeming daze; he looked at Jon, eyes wild. Then, without a word, the captain walked past him and made his way slowly to his quarters, closing the door behind him. The crew stood in silence a moment longer, rife with uncertainty.

Katherine was the first to step forward when Jon's legs refused to move. She went up to Tom and felt at his neck for a pulse.

"He's alive," she said, looking up at Jon with brown eyes wide with horror. It seemed that her dislike for the cheerful brute did not extend to torture.

The breath that Jon had been holding whooshed out of his lungs and time resumed. Everyone scattered to their various jobs, two of the younger cabin boys already coming forward with bucket and brush to scrub away Tom's blood.

Gingerly, Jon tried to undo the knots holding the big man to the mast, but the weight of him had pulled everything taut. He pulled the knife out of his belt and sawed at one of the ropes, thankful to see that Katherine was working at the other. When they had Tom down on the deck, Jon looked around for someone to help. No one would meet his eyes. However, a large, friendly hand soon grasped his shoulder; Beard leaned down and picked up the insensate Tom in his arms like he was lifting a child, carrying him towards the stairs.

When Jon saw they were going back to the brig, he pulled on Beard's arm.

"No... somewhere soft," he said. Tom had paid his dues.

The huge man looked at him in confusion and shrugged, not understanding. Katherine said a few words in another language, and Beard shrugged again, shaking his head. His voice rumbled out a reply, and Jon saw Katherine press her lips into a hard line.

"He's right, Jon," said the woman. "Tom stays in the brig until the captain says he's free."

~

Baltsaros lay on his back on his soft bed, his eyes closed. First the loss of control at Jon's return... That he would kiss another man, with obvious passion, in front of the crew was out of character, but now this? He would have kept whipping Tom until the man died.

As he took a deep breath, he tried to clear his mind. His feelings for Jon were beginning to take a toll on him, his composure full of cracks and his self-control... He grimaced and pressed the heels of his hands against his eyelids. Baltsaros needed to sort out the mess his mind was becoming. A balance would have to be found, but giving up what he had found with Jon was not an option.

Baltsaros heard the door open, and he almost groaned out loud. Jon's soft footfalls came up to the side of the bed and stopped.

"You almost killed him," Jon said softly.

In another man it would have been an accusation, but Jon was just stating a fact. Baltsaros didn't say anything for a long time, hoping the young man would just go away. After an interminable silence, he finally moved his hands and turned his head. Jon stood next to the bed, a deep crease between his dark brows.

Baltsaros sighed.

"I know," he said. When Jon's face didn't change, he looked away. "Jon, because of his lie, *I thought you had died*. He had to be punished."

"Don't say that like you didn't have a choice," said Jon. "Sitting in the brig would have been enough. You must have known how the whip would affect Tom."

Baltsaros nodded.

"It's the only thing he's afraid of," he said softly. "I broke a promise today."

The word *promise* had never meant much, just a means of getting others to do things for him. The captain thought back to his uncle; the man had not left a single mark on Baltsaros's skin, but the terror had been the same. He sat up and reached out for Jon. The young man let himself be pulled into Baltsaros's arms. The captain had done damage today, both to Tom and to Jon, but he didn't think it was irreversible.

"Please, Jon," he said simply.

~

Jon frowned at Baltsaros. The man was obviously in distress, but it stemmed from confusion rather than regret. With a deep breath, Jon lifted his hand and touched the side of Baltsaros's face. He saw no remorse, no guilt in his captain's brown eyes; yet, there lay a deep tide of emotion in them. A complicated man. Part monster, part gentleman.

When Baltsaros's hand started sliding up Jon's back, he closed his eyes, giving in to the caress.

His lover.

"Fix this," Jon said, opening his eyes. He tangled his fingers in Baltsaros's hair and stared hard at him. "If you can find it in yourself to forgive Tom, it would be a great gift to me."

Baltsaros frowned.

"Tom can't be trusted," he said.

Jon smiled at the irony.

"Well, neither can you," he said. Jon watched Baltsaros take in his words with a look of consternation.

After a moment, the captain nodded. The troubled look had left his face. He then spoke quietly.

"Do you trust me, Jon?" he asked.

The younger man ran a hand through his dark curls, thinking. Did he trust Baltsaros? The man lied. He killed people. All while wearing a mask of affable charm. No... He didn't trust Baltsaros, but it didn't change how he felt.

"Yes," said Jon, lying; he realized that, strangely, his answer mattered to Baltsaros.

The captain's face softened, and he pulled Jon down to his mouth. Jon kissed Baltsaros hard, bending the older man's head back. He felt the captain's surprise at his rough handling and smiled against Baltsaros's lips. Jon was changing. But, for the better? He did not know.

Tom.

Jon pulled away from Baltsaros.

"I'm going to go see if Tom is conscious," he said, not waiting for the captain's permission.

Baltsaros stood.

"Hold a moment. I'll give you something for his back," he said, walking to the cabinet. The captain handed him a bundle of dried leaves with the instruction to get a container and hot water from Cook. Jon was to wash the wounds, apply a thick salve, and then plaster over the area with the rehydrated leaves.

"Why don't you come with me?" Jon asked.

Baltsaros frowned.

"No, Jon. I'm still... angry."

Jon stepped down the stairs, carefully carrying the metal container with the leaves in it. He set it down next to the cage and unlocked the door with the key Baltsaros had given him. Picking the container back up, he walked to where Tom was lying on his stomach on the hard cot with his head towards the wall and knelt down. With a cautious hand, he reached out to touch the prone man's shoulder.

"Tom?" he asked in a whisper.

"Go away, love. Just... Go the fuck away," said Tom.

Jon realized that Tom was crying, and he felt something in his heart twist at the bigger man's pain. After putting down the bucket of warm water and the container with the leaves, Jon pulled the small pot of salve out of the pouch at his waist. Without another word, he began to softly clean the torn skin of Tom's back.

CHAPTER 16

UNCHARTED TERRITORY

Things quickly fell into routine for Jon. He would wake up, sore from work on the ship and somewhat tender from Baltsaros's caresses, and make his way to the galley. After grabbing breakfast for Tom and himself, he would head down to the brig and eat, cross-legged on the floor of the cage.

Tom wouldn't touch his food while Jon was there; in fact the man on the cot hadn't turned his head to look at Jon the entire time he had been taking care of him. However, when Jon returned in the evening with another meal, the morning plate was always empty. After Jon had eaten, he would open the pot of salve and gingerly apply more on the prone man's wounds.

The muscular young man was healing quickly; Tom was a hale and hearty brute... at least in body. How Tom's mind fared was what worried Jon the most; apart from telling him to go away that first day, Tom hadn't spoken a word to him, or to anyone else.

Afterwards, Jon would get to work. Sometimes it was in the kitchen with Cook, but most of the time it was above deck for general upkeep. Once that was done there would be target or sword practice with Katherine, and later, hand-to-hand fighting lessons with Old Calum. Then it was a quick trip to the galley to pick up Tom's supper and back to the brig to drop it off, checking on the state of the silent man's wounds again while he was there.

However, his nights belonged entirely to Baltsaros.

Jon would clean up and meet the captain in his quarters for the shared evening meal. There they would talk at length over supper, Baltsaros obviously pleased with Jon's healthy appetite and quick mind. The topics varied: ship matters, geography, politics, history, literature... But eventually, the conversation would inevitably wind down as a different kind of hunger grew in the two men.

. . .

Jon looked down into his glass of wine and frowned. The captain and he were discussing the history of the midland isles where Jon grew up, something that usually fascinated him. However, the way that Baltsaros kept looking at his lips when he talked was distracting him; he couldn't stop thinking about what Baltsaros would do if he suddenly leaned across the table to kiss him.

Jon nodded, not actually hearing the captain's last words, and suddenly realized that the other man had stopped speaking. Jon glanced up.

"Am I boring you, Jon?" asked Baltsaros. Though the captain's face was serious, his eyes were lively with amusement.

Jon shook his head, smiling.

"You could never bore me," he said.

The man stood slowly and held out his hand to Jon.

"Come to me," he said softly.

No matter that Jon had shared Baltsaros's bed for over a week now, the man's sheer confidence and graceful masculinity still made him strangely shy. Heart hammering in his chest and limbs awkward, Jon got up and walked self-consciously towards the man who had captured him, body and soul.

When Baltsaros's strong arms came around him, however, Jon's shyness dissipated like fog in the bright morning sun; he reached up and cupped the older man's face in his hands, bringing his mouth close to Baltsaros's and teasing it with light brushes of his lips. Jon loved the way the corners of Baltsaros's jaw fit in the palms of his hands, his thumbs against those sharp cheekbones as he nudged the captain's mouth open. Baltsaros closed his eyes and sighed into the kiss, his fingers quickly pulling up the bottom of Jon's shirt to run possessive hands over his soft skin.

Any time they were together during the day, no matter how brief, the captain peppered him with small touches: a hand on his shoulder, a light tap of his fingers on Jon's tanned forearm, his hip pausing briefly against Jon's in the course of their shared labour.

You are mine, said these touches. *You are mine, and no one else's.*

In the sombre light of the captain's quarters, those words repeated themselves loud and clear in the way Baltsaros gently withdrew from Jon's grasp and slowly undressed him with deft fingers until he stood naked. The first time Baltsaros had done this, Jon had felt he would die from embarrassment; he was a skinny, pale thing compared to the captain. However, reluctantly raising his eyes to Baltsaros's when he was asked to, Jon had been astounded by what he saw there: *Baltsaros found him beautiful.*

The rush of emotion that had coursed through Jon with that realization had brought hot tears to his eyes. Baltsaros had quickly stepped forward and kissed him hard, taking his breath and tears away.

As then, the roughness of the captain's leather pants and stiff brocade vest against Jon's skin made him acutely aware of his nakedness, and this vulnerability excited him. Jon shivered as the captain's warm hands slid down his back to his buttocks, pressing him firmly against the black leather and the prominent hardness beneath. It was intensely erotic, and it brought out a shamelessness in Jon.

He pushed himself into Baltsaros, his own stiffening length rubbing against the unyielding folds of the captain's pants. Taking one of Baltsaros's hands, Jon slid it between their bodies and pressed the captain's palm hard against his erection, biting softly at those curved lips that constantly drove him to distraction.

Baltsaros began stroking him slowly, his own excitement obvious in the pulse that hammered against Jon's tongue as he ran his open mouth down the side of the captain's neck. When Baltsaros's hand became slippery with the pearls of desire beading at the tip of Jon's cock, he growled low in his throat and started working his own fastenings loose with the other hand.

However, Jon pulled out of Baltsaros's grasp and dropped to his knees on the colourful rug, quickly unlacing the captain with nimble fingers. Looking up into Baltsaros's face, Jon was bolstered by the surprise he saw there and smiled.

Eyes dark, Baltsaros unbuttoned his vest, pulling it and his shirt over his head as Jon began kissing his exposed skin. The curly patch of hair that covered the captain's chest and stomach was surprisingly soft, and Jon ran his hands over it, feeling the hard muscles underneath Baltsaros's skin. The captain's hand came down to cup the back of his head as Jon's mouth moved lower down, his lips and tongue against the curved lines of Baltsaros's groin.

Jon started to falter, but Baltsaros's fingers pushed at him gently; before he could lose his nerve, Jon started tugging down the leather at Baltsaros's hips, finally freeing the captain's cock. It bobbed out at him, hard and thick with a wide head. Jon's hands had been on it many times, stroking it until the captain gasped and moaned in his grasp, but never his mouth. This was uncharted territory.

Hesitantly, Jon leaned forward and kissed the root of it, licking softly at its underside as he lifted it up with a hand. Above him, Jon heard the captain sigh as his fingers began running through his dark curls. Jon slid his tongue along its length and pressed his lips against the ridge where the bottom of its swollen head met hard shaft; after lapping at it gently, Jon finally opened his mouth and slid his lips over the head of Baltsaros's cock, sucking it down.

Jon looked up and felt a surge of desire when he saw the captain's flushed face and half-lidded eyes. Baltsaros's tongue licked at his bottom lip, teeth grazing the soft skin there as he watched Jon take in more of his cock. Shuddering, the captain threw his head back with a hard gasp as the young man swallowed the hard length down, only to pull back and tease at Baltsaros's cockhead with tongue and gentle teeth.

As he held the root of Baltsaros's shaft in one hand, Jon began sliding his grasp along it tightly in time to his mouth's movements, building up a steady rhythm. He used his tongue to add pressure and friction to the head of it on every pass, and Baltsaros moaned softly, broken words coming from him between hard breaths.

"Jon… Gods, where did you… oh, like that… that… yes…" Baltsaros's hand began pushing insistently at Jon's head, snagging in his hair, as his hips rocked with every deepening plunge of his cock down the other man's throat.

Jon gagged at the onslaught, pulling his mouth away more than once, only to return and try to force the captain's cock further.

Baltsaros's other hand came around to clasp Jon's head, and he finally lost control over the situation as the captain's lust made him rough.

Suddenly Jon couldn't breathe, and tears came to his eyes. He began to panic...

I'm going to suffocate... I can't do this...

But then something happened: Jon decided to let go and surrender himself completely.

Throat wide open to Baltsaros's cock, Jon again felt vulnerable... *Baltsaros was fucking his mouth.* Jon shuddered and moaned; incredibly, an overwhelming desire surged through him as his fist closed over his own hard cock bobbing between his thighs. Stroking quickly in time to Baltsaros's thrusts, Jon found himself soon nearing the edge. He lifted his eyes to the man abusing his throat and felt the balance tip within as he saw the bestial look on Baltsaros's face.

Jon came *hard.*

The exquisite pulsing pressure mounting in his groin spread like a crackling fire through him as the first thick spurts of cum pumped out of his cock. Not able to cry out or suck in a deep breath as the pleasure coursed through him in hot waves, he felt giddy and crazed as he stroked himself quickly, not even caring that the captain's thrusts were hard and the hold on his head painful.

All at once, Baltsaros was cumming too. With a deep grunt, the captain abruptly slowed his motions, matching the pulses from his jerking cock as he spilled his seed into Jon's throat. The thick, yolky bitterness filled the younger man's mouth, and he almost gagged again, but instead swallowed the cum down, once... twice.

Finally, the captain sagged back against the edge of the table, his hands going soft in Jon's hair as he panted, eyes closed.

Jon let Baltsaros's spent cock slide out of his mouth, moving to lean his head against the captain's twitching thigh for a moment. Jon was breathless and filled with a warm ecstasy that buzzed slowly through his limbs. When his heart had begun to slow, he sat back on his heels and looked slowly up at Baltsaros in a daze.

The older man was smiling down at him.

"You made a mess on my rug it seems," he said.

Jon looked down with alarm, but the captain just laughed.

"It's all right," said Baltsaros, reaching down to pull Jon to his feet. With the captain leaning on the table, they were the same height. Baltsaros's hand came up, and he ran his thumb along the edge of Jon's tender lower lip.

Jon stared wide-eyed into Baltsaros's brown eyes, and he brought his hands up to the man's waist, feeling the cooling wetness of the captain's soft cock against his.

Baltsaros leaned forward and kissed Jon gently.

"Did I hurt you?" he asked.

Jon shook his head; he felt strange and wanted to tell Baltsaros, but didn't know how to express it. It was like he felt... *free*... But that made no sense to him.

The captain frowned slightly.

"Why are you looking at me this way?" he asked slowly, his accent making the words hiss softly.

Jon shook his head again. There was peace inside him. He lifted his hand to Baltsaros's face and touched the captain's lips with his fingers before bringing his own lips against them once more. Baltsaros held him tight, his open mouth warm against Jon's as their tongues slid against each other. Jon felt like crying or laughing; he couldn't tell which.

Baltsaros grinned and pulled back.

"You're shaking, and your pulse is erratic... Are you quite sure you're all right?" he asked.

Jon had to smile. He shrugged. This time the captain laughed out loud.

"You look drunk," he said and pushed away from the table. After taking the disoriented man by the arm, Baltsaros steered him towards the bed where they ended up sprawled on the soft coverlet with Jon's head against the captain's chest.

Finally his mind was starting to feel more normal as he lay there, Baltsaros's fingers idly stroking his shoulder and back.

"You are definitely something," said the captain, his voice rumbling against Jon's ear. "That was... exceedingly pleasant."

Jon pulled at Baltsaros's chest hair and smiled.

"Yes," he said.

⁓

Baltsaros looked over at Jon sleeping next to him in the wide bed and frowned. What was it about the slender, dark-haired, young man that *pulled* at him so? Part of it had to be that Jon could be a wide-eyed innocent one moment, and the very next, a wanton, naked sylph with the skills of a consummate lover.

For a strange moment earlier, when his cock was being so expertly handled, the captain had been sure that looking down, he would see Tom's sea-green eyes staring back at him instead of Jon's.

It was utterly fascinating; Jon spent so much time trying to "read" people and situations that he began to mimic his subjects. Baltsaros was convinced that Jon wasn't even aware of it.

Baltsaros slid off the bed and padded to the door to open it. The moon was a bright sliver in the night sky, but he couldn't see many stars. Cold air blew against his bare skin, and he breathed deep.

Was that it? Was he so deeply enchanted by the serious young man simply because Jon, unlike others, could actually *see* him? And could, perhaps, become more like Baltsaros?

The idea had merit.

It would be interesting to see what happened as time went on, and Baltsaros wondered if there was anything he could do to increase the effect.

When he glanced over his shoulder at the slumbering boy in his bed, Baltsaros's face softened. No, there was more to it. At the very least, the captain felt extremely protective of this fascinating creature in his bed. Something about Jon made the captain ache... And as painful as it was, Baltsaros craved it night and day.

Baltsaros smiled to himself; the way Jon had stared at him afterwards, like he had been nearly driven mad with passion, made the captain eager to have the young man on his knees again soon.

Keeping the door open a crack to air out the stuffy room, Baltsaros then made his way back to bed, pausing only to pinch the flame from the candle between thumb and forefinger. He crawled up beside Jon and curled himself against his side, pulling the coverlet up to shield them from the cool night air.

~

Jon, balancing two plates and a mug of beer while he descended the dark stairs the next morning, was astounded to see Tom watching him from where he sat on the cot.

The muscular pirate stood and approached the bars, reaching out to hold the plates while Jon forced the iron key into the stiff lock.

Jon smiled, and Tom raised an eyebrow at him, shaking his head, but a small grin curved to one side of his mouth. Jon sat on the floor and Tom sat on the cot, both men immediately digging into the food on the metal plates. Not knowing how to break the silence, Jon just chewed his bread and took a swig of beer before passing the metal mug to Tom.

The big man took a long pull, swishing the beer in his mouth before swallowing it down. As he leaned forward with a large, scarred hand on his knee, Tom looked at Jon appraisingly.

"The least ye could fuckin' do, lovey, is not come in here reekin' like ye've been fuckin' all night long. It's enough to put a man off his feed," he said.

Jon felt the heat in his cheeks; but, before he could stammer a response, Tom just slapped his leg and started laughing, his blue-green eyes twinkling in merriment.

CHAPTER 17

STAUNCHING THE WOUND

"Love is, after all, a selfish thing; and it throws a black shadow on anything between which and the light it stands."

— BRAM STOKER, THE JEWEL OF SEVEN STARS

It was obvious, at least to Jon's eyes, that all was not right with Tom. On his release from the brig the previous day, Tom had been full of his usual bluff good humour, but Jon immediately saw it for what it was: an act.

Sitting atop a stack of crates as he fixed some netting, Jon frowned to himself. He could see the muscular young man from his perch—now just a regular deckhand—laughing with someone near the front of the ship. It looked strangely off to Jon, even from this distance. Getting close to Tom since he'd been freed was difficult, as the man seemed to be giving both him and the captain a wide berth; however, he had seen enough in the last day to know that though the burly man still swaggered and joked, his blue-green eyes had gone dull, and his shoulders tensed at even the smallest sound. Just yesterday, when a board fell over with a loud crack, Jon had seen Tom freeze in his tracks, hands going to white-knuckled fists at his sides. It was as if the lusty fire that had burned bright in Tom had been extinguished.

Jon's eyes kept being drawn to Tom as he worked.

Out of worry or out of sheer curiosity? he wondered idly.

Suddenly the knife Jon was using to cut into a tangle slipped and sliced through the meat of his palm; dropping the net and knife to the ground, he sucked on the bleeding cut and winced. To be fair, not everything was right with him either if the dream from this morning was any indication.

The castle was burning. Jon coughed into the crook of his arm as he tried to see through the thick smoke. He could hear screaming, but he couldn't tell where it was coming from. Walking forward he was almost hit by a burning ceiling beam. He had to find Reginald. More screaming. There was a whoosh, and the old, threadbare tapestries turned into sheets of flame. Maybe Reginald was in the tower. Jon made his way to the stairs leading up and was dismayed to see that there were piles of charred bones in the way. Picking his way over them, he saw the skull of a child. Many children. All the bones were small and fragile, crumbling to black dust as he walked over them in his bare feet. Strangely, though the bones were still smouldering, they didn't hurt him. He climbed up and up, much higher than he thought the tower went. There was a low sound, like the beating of a giant heart coming from the other side of the large wooden door.

"Reginald?" he called. "Reginald, are you there?"

He thought he could hear his stepfather's voice. He put his shoulder to the door and pushed against it hard. Slowly the door opened, but it was as if he were pushing at something through treacle. Finally, it gave way, and Jon stumbled forward. He saw that he was in an unfamiliar, bare room... not the one he had been expecting. The captain of the guards stood in the corner, facing the wall.

"Reginald?" he called loudly. "Is that you?"

His stepfather didn't move. Something behind Jon nudged him, and he realized the great black lion had followed him here. He took a step forward.

"Yes, yes, just this last one and then we can go, right?" he asked.

The nose of the giant lion nuzzled the back of his neck softly as Jon struck the match in his hand, throwing it at the man standing in the corner. As if Reginald were made of dry straw, the older man burst into bright flames.

Jon woke up, choking and drenched in sweat, the phantom smell of burning flesh still thick in his nose. Breathing hard, he clawed at the blankets and sat up, Baltsaros's arms coming around him quickly in the dark; as always he was grateful for the man's instantly calming presence. The dream, incredibly vivid just a moment ago, had already started to fade as he took a shuddering breath, shaking his head to try to clear it. Jon hadn't seen Reginald's face.

Was he the burning man?

He brought a hand up to clasp Baltsaros's strong forearm and leaned back, the captain a solid comfort behind him. When Baltsaros brought his lips to the side of Jon's neck, something nagged at him for a second, but then it was gone. All that was left was the uneasy sense that he should feel *something* about Reginald's death, and of those that perished with him in the fire; however, Baltsaros's warm breath against his skin gave him shivers, distracting him from his dark thoughts.

"It was only a dream, Jon," said the captain's enchanting voice in his ear. "Come, lie down... You're safe here with me."

Jon let himself be pulled back down into the soft mattress, Baltsaros's hard body against him. Questing out with a hand, he felt for the other man's face and ran his fingers along his stubbled jaw before shifting forward to bring his mouth into contact with Baltsaros's. It was hours yet until morning, and Jon wanted nothing more than to forget the dream completely.

～

Jon stared in dismay at the cut on his hand. It wouldn't stop bleeding. After climbing down off his perch, Jon went in search of something to staunch it. Perhaps Baltsaros had something in that cabinet of his.

However, on entering the captain's quarters, Jon was suddenly uneasy; even though he was essentially sharing the room with Baltsaros, Jon still felt very much a visitor here.

Squaring his shoulders as he took a few steps forward, he tried to push away the feeling that he was trespassing. As usual, the large room was sombrely lit and Jon, eyes sliding over the curved walls of the captain's quarters, thought again about how peculiar that was.

By his reckoning, the room had to be about twenty feet at its widest and at least eighteen feet deep, and the whole was poorly lit by two small portholes to either side; even the room where the gunpowder was stored had better lighting than the captain's room.

He frowned. Jon walked slowly around the table and stared at the top of the far wall. Standing on his toes, Jon narrowed his eyes; he had noticed before that there was a decorative cornice above the map and the crest, but from this close, it could almost pass for a window ledge.

With his undamaged hand, Jon dragged one of the heavy chairs over and stepped up onto the wine-coloured cushion. When he peered at the space above the cornice, he saw immediately that the wood was of a different type than the walls. Recalling that ships like this often had a row of windows at the back of the forecastle, Jon lifted a hand up and touched the wood paneling above the ledge. He pushed and it gave a little. It wouldn't take much to pull the thin sheet of wood away.

I wonder why it's cov—

"Jon, what are you doing?" came the captain's voice from behind him.

Jon started; he'd been so focused on what he was doing that he hadn't heard Baltsaros's boots at the door. Jon felt the heat mount in his cheeks, his heart beating a little faster. When he turned to look at the captain, he felt both embarrassed and a little fearful.

Baltsaros's face was grim, and the lines at the sides of his mouth deepened as the muscles moved in his jaw. His eyes, usually warm when he looked at Jon, were flinty and suspicious.

Jon shook his head.

"I'm sorry. I just... It's so dark in here all the time. I wanted to see why..." he said, his voice sounding a little high in his ears as he scrambled down off the chair. In dismay he saw he had left a dusty footprint right in the middle of the velvet cushion.

Baltsaros's eyes travelled over the dirty cushion, up over the soiled knees of his grey pants, past the grime and blood on his linen shirt, and stopped at Jon's face, his brown eyes narrow.

Jon swallowed. One didn't need to be particularly empathic to see that the captain was not pleased with him.

"I'm sorry," he said quietly and dropped his eyes to the floor, not sure what else to say. He heard Baltsaros sigh and was gratified when the man's hand came up after a moment to cup Jon's chin, lifting his face back up to meet his eyes.

"You're a mess," The captain said simply.

Jon felt like a small, dirty child, and the thought rankled him.

"You don't need to climb all over my furniture like a monkey. Why not just ask me why I've covered the window?" asked Baltsaros, the grip on Jon's face tightening slightly.

After swatting the captain's hand away, Jon's brows came down dark over his eyes.

"Because asking you questions is a study in frustration," he said. "Besides, I'm here nearly as much as you are. I figured I have some right to climb on the furniture if I have a reason to."

Baltsaros stared at him for a moment and abruptly started laughing, his eyes warm once more as he clasped Jon's shoulder.

"Yes. Yes, I suppose you do. I've invited you to climb into my bed... Why not on the chairs too?" he said, smiling.

Jon shook his head in disbelief.

Cold and hot.

Though he tried, he could never quite predict the captain's reactions. Then, Jon saw the captain frown and followed his gaze down, grimacing when he saw what Baltsaros was looking at.

"My dear boy, you do have a penchant for getting bodily fluids on the rugs," he said, his brow furrowed but his tone light. "Why in gods' names are you bleeding?"

Jon, having gone red from the memory of being on his knees in front of the captain that first time, laughed awkwardly and held up his palm. The cut was deep and still dripped blood slowly.

"I cut myself," he said lamely.

Baltsaros nodded.

"I can see that. Sit down, I'll need to put a few stitches in or else it won't close properly," he said, pushing Jon towards the chair he had dirtied.

He blanched at the captain's words.

"Stitches? Is that really necessary?" Jon asked, staring down at his wound.

Baltsaros laughed as he rummaged through a drawer in the teak cabinet. After pulling out a little box with brass trimmings, the captain dragged a chair close to Jon.

He placed the box on the table and opened it; inside were a variety of metal instruments, bits of fabric, and what looked like thread.

Jon watched as Baltsaros walked away to pour out a healthy amount of dark rum into an earthenware mug from the bottle atop the cabinet before coming back to sit down.

The captain held out the mug.

"Drink," he said.

Jon's stomach fluttered uneasily at the smell rising up from the dark liquid; since that drunken night with Tom, Jon hadn't been able to drink rum without feeling ill. He took the tiniest sip and shivered, but Baltsaros reached a hand out and pushed the mug back up to Jon's lips.

"Drink it all, you foolish thing. This is going to hurt," said the captain.

With his eyes closed, Jon drank the rest of the burning liquid down in a gulp, his insides roiling in response. Soon, however, a warm, syrupy feeling began to spread out from his chest. What had Tom called him? A lightweight? Jon opened his eyes; he already felt flushed.

Baltsaros was watching him with a curious expression on his face, and his brown eyes held a small note of desire in them. Baltsaros reached for the cup and stood to refill it, bringing the bottle to the table on his return. However, before passing it back to Jon, he wrapped his large hand around the younger man's wrist, quickly tilting the mug over the wound and splashing some of the liquid directly into the cut.

"Ahhhh! Fucking hell!" yelled Jon, jerking in his chair; the wound in his hand was on fire. "Oh gods, that hurts! You could have warned me, you sadist."

Baltsaros grinned and let out a short chuckle. The older man then leaned down, and Jon watched wide-eyed as the captain's tongue slid warmly over his fingers, tasting the runoff of rum and blood that dripped from them. It felt both bizarre and strangely arousing knowing the captain was tasting his blood, and Jon closed his eyes at the sudden hard pulse of lust in his groin. It amazed him that Baltsaros could effortlessly make such a thing so erotic.

"Is that better?" asked the captain, his voice amused.

Jon opened his eyes and quickly nodded his head, feeling a little dizzy from the rum and Baltsaros's soft, mobile tongue.

The captain sat up, a distracted smile on his face as he started rummaging in the small box. The young man watched him, a little breathless but no longer scared. Baltsaros's stark brow furrowed as he seemed to vacillate between two different hooked needles, both appearing alarmingly thick to Jon.

Nervous, he drank deeply from the mug, enjoying the warm glow of courage that the rum brought with it.

The captain's gracefully bowed lips, the top one jutting out a little further than the bottom, curled slightly when he noticed how intently Jon was watching him. Clasping Jon's arm softly, he smiled, showing his sharp teeth.

"Don't worry. It'll be over quickly," he said, pulling a thread, presumably catgut, through the small hole in the needle. "Now ask me."

Jon frowned.

"Ask you what?" he replied, confused.

Baltsaros laughed.

"Anything you'd like. I didn't realize that I was such a frustrating person to question," he said.

Jon's breath hissed between his teeth as the needle hooked through the skin of his palm. He had to look away.

"All right... Why is the window covered up?" Jon asked, his voice unsteady as Baltsaros pulled the needle through the other side of the cut.

The captain laughed.

"The short answer is that there *is* no window. Hasn't been for a long time," he answered, knotting the thread and cutting it with small scissors.

Jon turned back to look at the captain and frowned.

"What do you mean? What happened to it?" he asked.

"Ah. Well, that is the long answer," said Baltsaros, a small, somewhat sombre smile on his enigmatic face. "I broke it. Well, *them*, rather. Originally, there were five panels of stained glass depicting scenes from an old religious text." He leaned forward and poked Jon again with the needle.

The young man was so intrigued that the pain seemed dulled.

Or maybe it's the rum?

He frowned. But what would make Baltsaros break windows? It seemed like a childish thing.

Baltsaros nodded.

"Strange for me to break windows? That's what you are thinking, is it not?" The captain chuckled again. "Jon, there's no bizarre mystery. Simply put, once the ship became mine, I intended to destroy it... out of revenge. You might say that I decided to start with things that reminded me of the man who held the ship before me—"

"Your uncle?" interjected Jon.

Baltsaros pressed his lips together and nodded, glancing up at Jon with dark eyes before returning to his work.

"I see that little birds have been filling your ears... Yes, my uncle. The man was loathsome. Religious. Fanatical. Twisted and depraved. Filthy. I could go on..." Baltsaros shook his head. "My parents died when I was a boy of seven. I lived in an orphanage until the age of nine. I found solace in helping the nurses with the sick and had lofty aspirations of becoming a doctor. Then, this man appeared at the orphanage gates one day: my uncle. Were it not for the fact that he was the very image of my departed father, I would not have believed him to be family, so different was his disposition. He took me away from the simple life that I was living and brought me here."

Finished with his stitches, Baltsaros sat back in his chair and gestured to the walls around him.

"Thus began my life at sea. I was... exceedingly angry, and for a very long time. My uncle tried to find ways of terrorizing me into complete obedience but consistently

128

failed. I had no respect for the man; his crew was slovenly and the ship was disorderly. Calum could tell you of that time... He was there. Finally, I took the ship from him on my sixteenth birthday." Baltsaros's gaze shifted to the boarded up windows. "It was fully my intention to burn the ship or take her apart board by board... But then time passed. I found myself thinking of ways to improve the way the ship was run. I... removed the crew that I deemed disloyal or problematic..."

Jon swallowed at the word *removed*, knowing full well that their bones probably rested at the bottom of the sea as a result of Baltsaros's culling.

"And went to work cleaning her up. I thought that once I had a good crew and a well-maintained ship I could sell her off and return home to pursue my earlier dreams of becoming a doctor." Baltsaros pursed his lips, eyes focused on nothing for a moment. He then reached out to close the small wooden box of surgical tools and stood, holding it in his hands. "But here I am still," he said quietly.

"You're a better doctor than the one we had back home," Jon said.

A man now dead, he remembered.

Baltsaros started to laugh and went to put away his instruments.

"That is most definitely not a compliment, Jon. The man probably still used dung and rusted knives..." he said. Baltsaros took the mug from Jon's outstretched hand and poured some more rum into it, taking a deep swallow himself before returning it to his dark-haired patient. "Everything I know, I taught myself through books and experience," said the captain. "But I could have been more. Instead, I've been holding onto my role as captain, year after year, getting older and more mired as time goes by." A few seconds passed in silence.

"It's because you enjoy it. Immensely. I see it all the time. You're good at it, and it suits you perfectly," Jon said softly, his words made plain by the rum in his blood. "I think it's past time that you fixed the windows and gave this ship a name. Cut your ties with its history."

He watched as Baltsaros's eyes went flat for a moment, his features smooth. Jon shook his head, understanding the crux of the problem.

"You're not trapped, Baltsaros. This is not your prison... This is your home."

~

Baltsaros looked at Jon appraisingly.

His home.

The boy was right. This old ship was much more of a home to him than where they were sailing to; and, it had been so for almost three decades. Baltsaros could leave at any time... But he *chose* not to.

He sighed and reached forward to take Jon into his arms, a comforting gesture for both of them. He rested his lips against Jon's high forehead and frowned.

"You're completely right," he said softly. The anger that he had kept stoked for the man who had mistreated him so long ago wasn't even real anymore, just old habit. At this point, the ship had been his for far longer than his uncle had held it.

Baltsaros smiled and ran his hands down Jon's back, fingers bumping over his ribs.

"Your home too. I haven't been fair to you, have I? My quarters are yours... if you're to be my consort," he said.

Jon pulled away and looked at Baltsaros, dark brows low over his blue eyes.

"*Consort?* Is that what you call it?" he said. "Is that what Tom was to you?" Baltsaros saw the anger and the outrage that Jon kept tamped down and hidden suddenly rise closer to the surface.

"Don't, Jon," he said, lifting his hands to Jon's shoulders.

The younger man struggled out of his grasp, stumbling awkwardly against the chair and slamming the wrong hand down on the table to steady himself. Jon let out a cry and cradled his arm to his chest, furious eyes staring at Baltsaros as though he were the source of his pain.

Irritated at Jon's mercurial nature, the captain clenched his jaw and swallowed down the urge to dash his head against the table. He saw Jon's eyes go round suddenly, wide with disbelief. He realized in amazement that the young man had caught the barest glimpse of his thought.

"Why are you angry with *me*, Baltsaros? Don't I have the right to be fucking furious at *you*? You're the one who just neatly slid another peg into the hole left behind by Tom. You want me to play house with you? I had to watch you lose control and nearly kill Tom. He's... not well, Baltsaros. Neither are you. Gods... What the fuck am I doing here?" Jon's words were followed by a strangled moan, and he rubbed at his face.

Baltsaros felt a little offended.

Out of control?

True. However, Jon was the source of Baltsaros's lapses. He sighed inwardly.

"Jon, sit down. I think you've had a little too much rum," he said.

Jon stared at him, fury distorting his face.

"I'm not drunk," he growled, taking a step forward. When he swayed slightly, the anger in Jon's eyes faltered. "Ok. Maybe a little tipsy... But that doesn't change the fact that I'm not dealing well with your treatment of Tom. Tom, who I am not even *allowed* to talk about, correct?" Jon sat heavily in the chair, the passion behind his outbursts winding down as a sadness came over his features.

The captain knew well enough that whipping Tom had been excessive, but what was done was done. Earlier that day he had tried to have a few words with his former first mate, but the muscular youth shied and cringed away, sea-green eyes wide with fear and pain. Maybe Tom would come around, maybe not. Only time would tell. He hadn't figured on Jon becoming strangely attached to the dangerous ex-slave.

Baltsaros walked around Jon, coming up behind him to put his hands on his shoulders. Jon stiffened but didn't pull away.

"I feel strange. Like I'm losing myself, Baltsaros," said Jon quietly. "I'm all right as long as I don't think about anything too deeply. If I do, it's as if a giant hand is squeezing my heart. I'm overwhelmed... And all I see ahead is more tragedy. More death. One minute I... I can't think of anything but how you make me feel. Inside." The back of Jon's neck was flushed, and Baltsaros felt strangely touched by his words. "At that moment, everything is rosy... Life is wonderful, and my heart swells with happiness. But if I lift the edge of those feelings, there is nothing but a blackened, rotting sea underneath."

Jon's shoulders shuddered slightly under Baltsaros's palms, and the captain stroked the muscles under his thumbs, brow furrowed in concern.

"I'm afraid of being pulled down into it. Am I a fool?" asked Jon, almost to himself.

Baltsaros ran a hand up the side of the young man's neck, and Jon leaned the side of his face into it. There were no answers that Baltsaros could give him; he was glad that Jon couldn't see the confusion that the captain knew was plain on his face.

"I'm... sorry," Baltsaros said softly, the words as sincere as he could make them.

Jon shrugged and let out a shaky breath. After pulling Baltsaros's hand away from his face, he moved it to the open neck of his shirt and slid it between the material and his skin.

Curious, Baltsaros stroked the soft skin of Jon's chest, fingers closing over the puckered nipple as he felt the young man's heartbeat quicken under his palm.

Jon sighed softly and bent his head back, looking up at the man above him.

"Baltsaros, I'll be your consort. Really, whatever you want from me. Just... Help me forget these dark thoughts for now," he said.

Looking down at Jon's stormy-blue eyes that were filled with sadness and resolution, Baltsaros wished again that he could just pluck out the pain that plagued him.

As he leaned down to place a soft kiss on Jon's lips, Baltsaros thought of a perfect distraction, one where he would have the opportunity to expose the inexperienced young man to new pleasures. When he broke the kiss, the captain rounded the chair and got down on one knee in front of Jon.

Jon frowned at him, obviously suspicious of Baltsaros's sudden smile. The captain raised his wounded hand to his lips and pressed a kiss onto the cut gingerly. The younger man winced but didn't pull away.

"There is one place where I would like to take you, Jon. It won't make everything better, but I believe it could help," Baltsaros said, the change in course already being plotted in his head as he spoke.

"Where's that?" asked Jon, curiously.

"The whorehouse at the edge of the world," replied Baltsaros, his grin wide.

CHAPTER 18
THE JEWEL

Jon pulled down on the sleeve of his dark-blue shirt and then ran a hand through his hair, shifting his weight in the new boots Baltsaros had given him.

"Jon, it's a whorehouse, not the cave of a fire-breathing dragon," said Katherine, laughing at his nervousness. "Just relax."

He looked up at her and frowned.

"Easy for you to say. I've never been to one," he replied, rubbing the skin of his freshly shaven jaw. *And I've never wanted to... especially now,* he added silently.

Katherine leaned a hip against the side of the cannon and crossed her arms over her chest.

"That's not entirely true, you know. Didn't we *find* your scrawny ass in a whorehouse?" she asked, a mocking smile on her lips.

Jon grinned despite how tense he felt. "Scrawny?" he asked, arching an eyebrow at the first mate. "I was working. Not... uh... being with a lady." He coloured slightly.

Katherine grinned wide.

"Ha! 'Being with a lady'? That's rich. And yeah... sure you were working... spreading those little cheeks of yours for cock and earning good coin, I hear?" she said, teasing Jon.

The blood was hot in his face, and he threw a mock punch at her arm. He hated the fact that no matter how long he stayed in the company of rough men (*and women,* he thought), he was still so easily made awkward by a crass remark; Katherine in particular loved that she could make him blush so effortlessly.

"What are *you* going to a whorehouse for, anyway?" he asked, eyeing her outfit.

Katherine was still wearing her tightly laced black pants but had put on a dark-green shirt with a drawstring neck and wide sleeves. Sliding alluringly off one shoulder, it showed off her smooth, tanned skin. It was her turn to raise an eyebrow at Jon.

"What do you mean?" she asked.

Jon blinked. Sticking his foot in his mouth was an oft-used talent of his.

"I, uh... didn't realize you... liked... uh..." he stammered.

Katherine's brows came down over her almond eyes.

"You didn't realize I liked *what* exactly?" she asked, her tone challenging.

Jon shook his head, confused.

"Wait... Are there boy whores?" he asked meekly.

"O' will ye stop teasin' the boy, missy," said Calum, his gapped smile bright against his dark skin, "or 'e's like to faint away dead o' shame."

The old man was dressed in a garish orange shirt and had shaved and oiled his head. Jon watched as Calum touched the money pouch at his belted waist with the tips of his fingers before turning to make another circuit of the boat; he wasn't the only one who was anxious about the visit to the whorehouse. However, the current that ran through the crew was excitement rather than the dread that Jon felt. He started when Katherine clasped the back of his neck, shaking him slightly.

Her eyes were narrow in merriment as she smiled somewhat crookedly at him.

"I'm sorry, Jon. I'd love to 'be with a lady' as you so charmingly put it, but my lady back home would have my hide. Lying is not one of my strong suits... And besides, I don't want to lie to her. I'm just going for drinks and a massage... And maybe a game of dice, if the mood strikes," she said, releasing him.

Jon furrowed his brow.

"I thought you said you were married to the owner of a tavern... ohhh..." he said. He squeezed his eyes shut when understanding dawned, and then looked at her with a flustered grin. "I'm sorry. I'm a backwards peasant. I assumed your... uh... wife was a man. Women just don't normally own anything but brothels where I come from," he finished lamely.

Katherine winked at him.

"And most are lucky to own even those, I take it? Ah... Thus is the plight of the lowly woman in most of the world, Jon," she replied.

"Lowly," repeated Jon, shaking his head. "I'd hate to see the state of the next man who calls you 'lowly'." He laughed.

A piercing whistle split the air, and Katherine turned her head aft, looking for the captain.

"I've got to go," she said. After spotting Baltsaros's tall, dark figure, she started walking with long strides towards the rear of the ship.

Tom was perched on the gunwale a few yards away, separate from the rest of the men, with one leg through the ratlines that stretched up to the yardarm. Because he was in direct line of sight, Jon had seen how the ex–first mate's head had snapped up at Baltsaros's whistled call. A little sadness had tugged at him when Tom had blinked his green-blue eyes and frowned before shaking his head to resume cleaning his nails with his long knife, shoulders bent.

Jon's lips were set in a hard line as he watched him; he was utterly confused when it came to Tom. While truly wanting to help him, Jon knew that the only way to do so would be to heal the rift between Tom and Baltsaros.

As he looked down, Jon frowned and picked at the scab on his healing, itchy palm. Even if he *could* somehow make things better between the two men, he wouldn't. It would mean having to share Baltsaros. Jon clenched his jaw, a raw feeling in the pit of his stomach. *Like he would have to share Baltsaros tonight.*

Miserable and tense, Jon watched as the tip of the peninsula came into view. Baltsaros had explained that the whorehouse wasn't literally at the edge of the world (because there wasn't one, according to the captain) but was simply at the most southerly point of the continent; it was the last stop before the wide expanse of deep ocean.

Jon shifted awkwardly again in his new boots; the *Jewel*, as the brothel was actually called, was a much fancier affair than the *Rose Garden*, and the crew was decked out in their finest clothing. Brutus nudged at his hand, and Jon scratched his ears distractedly.

"Poor Brutus. You get to miss out on all the *fun*," he said, his voice tight.

At a roar of laughter, Jon looked over his shoulder; someone had broken out the rum, and a few of his shipmates were miming what they hoped to accomplish that evening. Sighing, Jon turned back and clung onto the ropes, watching the twinkling lights over the still water as he stroked the dog's soft head.

The town was a large one, easily five times the size of Portsmouth; and, sitting right at the edge of the harbour was a large, well-lit building that was fashioned to look like an elegant castle with high towers and smooth stone walls. Hearing a quiet step behind him, Jon knew before the hand came to rest on his lower back that it was the captain.

"That's the *Jewel*. The harbour is too narrow and shallow for us to anchor there, so we'll be going out in the jolly boats. Try to look as though you're not being led to your doom, please," Baltsaros said, his accented voice near Jon's ear.

Shrugging, he fought the urge to lean into the captain; he didn't want to give Baltsaros any satisfaction. He was thoroughly unhappy that the decision had been made for him.

~

"A whorehouse?" asked Jon, his eyes wide. "You want to bring me to a *whorehouse*?"

Baltsaros leaned back at Jon's vehemence, his eyes going stony and dark, two chips of obsidian in his angular face.

"Yes. And it's not up for discussion," replied the captain.

Jon gaped.

"Wh-why? How is going to a brothel going to help anything? No, Baltsaros. It's out of the question," he said, incredulous.

The captain stood, and looked down at Jon. After a moment he reached out with a hand and stroked his cheek, his face still and serious.

Jon tensed slightly at the touch; however, the warmth had already returned to the captain's eyes.

"Jon, you just said you would give me anything I wanted. I want this," Baltsaros said, smiling softly. "Besides! It'll do the men some good!" he added and abruptly turned away from Jon before he could argue.

As he strode quickly out of the room, Baltsaros was already calling out the course change to Katherine, leaving Jon, pale and distraught, behind in his quarters.

~

Jon watched the ship recede in the distance, Brutus's shaggy head peering sadly over the top of the quarterdeck railing. At that moment Jon decided to come back in the next life as a dog, if he had any choice in the matter. Brutus might be sad to see his master go, but at least he didn't have to be subjected to the whims of a madman.

As if sensing his thoughts, Baltsaros's arm snaked around his waist, and he leaned in to start murmuring against Jon's neck. It was some odd bit of history about the town they were nearing, but he couldn't pay attention. Oscillating between hope and fear, Jon was driving himself to distraction.

Maybe we're here, as Katherine said, to game and drink? Maybe a massage? A massage is nothing to be afraid of. But what if Baltsaros meant we're going to... What if he wants me to... do something with a whore? What if I have to watch him? Watch him touching someone else...

Jon groaned out loud and lowered his face to his hands.

Baltsaros just chuckled and patted Jon on the back lightly, making him angrier by the fact that the captain seemed to be enjoying his distress.

Soon the boat bumped up against the floating wooden dock, and the men disembarked. Jon, the last to get off the boat, almost stumbled as he stared up at the building. From this close he could see that the entire castle was faced with an almost pearlescent, veined white stone, and that every window was glazed; it was absolutely beautiful.

Baltsaros took Jon's arm and steadied him, pulling him forward after the rest of the crew. As they approached the colossal wooden doors, men in costumes resembling elaborate guard uniforms bowed and pulled them open.

Jon knew his mouth was agape, but he couldn't help it; they had just walked into a scene out of a dream. The space was *huge*. Rising up on either side of the room were immense, curving staircases with crowds of people going up and down or simply standing there watching the action below. The rest of the open area was an eye-dazzling array of candlelit tables on tiered platforms with an immensely long bar in the back, the coloured bottles of liquor behind it somehow brightly backlit. Above it all hung the biggest chandelier that Jon had ever seen, with dozens upon dozens of candles in it.

Everything was reflected a hundredfold in the mirrors that were found everywhere the eye rested. And the women... There were so many! All of them were in elegant garb that somehow managed to be extremely revealing while only hinting at what was hidden underneath.

When he felt the captain's fingers tighten around his upper arm, Jon turned to him. He must have looked like a fool because the captain started laughing and shaking his head, leaning forward to press a kiss against Jon's temple.

A tall figure draped in layers of diaphanous fabric suddenly appeared before them, pale face covered up to the eyes. Jon couldn't tell if it was a man or a woman; the voice of the graceful figure was melodious and completely asexual. The captain nodded his head in response to words Jon couldn't understand, and then the figure glided away. He watched it go, trying to see curves beneath the flowing material but failing; it was disconcerting not to know what was beneath those robes.

Looking over at the men and women sitting at the tiered tables, Jon spotted Tom. The muscular young man was sitting alone, drinking. As he watched, Tom lifted his sea-green eyes to Jon over the edge of his cup, his eyebrows lifting slowly as he swallowed down his drink. Tom lowered the cup and tilted his head slightly at Jon, his eyes questioning.

Jon realized that he probably looked terrified. He furrowed his brow at the other man and hunched his shoulders; across the wide space, it felt like Tom had grasped his plight. The other man, a small smile curling only to one side of his mouth, shook his head and shrugged before looking back down at his cup. However, Jon could see that he was frowning, thinking about something.

When he raised his head again, Tom pointed to his eye and then to Jon.

I will watch out for you.

Jon felt a small pain in his chest, a twist of poignant emotion towards the other man at this simple gesture. He gave a tiny nod, swallowing hard. Baltsaros then tugged at his arm again; the draped figure had reappeared, and they were being led towards one of the colossal staircases.

Jon turned his head quickly back to Tom and locked eyes. The burly young man smirked, though his eyes were sad, and pushed his chin up with a callused finger before he patted at his broad chest, miming taking a deep breath.

Chin up and breathe, Jon.

Jon sucked in a lungful of air, and Tom was gone, blocked from view by the giant columns that flanked the wide stairs as they ascended.

Baltsaros and Jon were brought to a large room on the second floor. The walls were covered in dark, embossed paper, somewhere between black and purple. There were large windows along one wall, surrounded in wide, ornamental white frames. The carpeting, a dizzying pattern of vines, red on black and purple, was incredibly thick underfoot. To one side of the room, there was a strange, bench-like chair with no back, one side of it raised higher than the other, and it was to here that the two men were led.

Jon sat awkwardly in the middle of the plush red satin and clutched his hands between his knees. Baltsaros, however, reclined against the higher end of the chair, one leg bent off the side of it, knee resting against Jon's, with the other leg stretched out behind him.

After a moment, a door opened to one side of the room, and a beautiful, buxom woman approached them on mincing steps, her hair an extraordinary shade of red.

"Captain Baltsaros! It is always such an incredible pleasure to have you here with us! It has been far too long," she said in a lilting accent that Jon did not recognize. Jon smelled an intoxicating blend of spices and flowers as she leaned forward to clasp Baltsaros's outstretched hand with her long-nailed fingers. Her gaze flicked to Jon, momentarily confused, but she covered it with a gracious smile.

Where is Tom? asked her eyes.

"My name is Fresia," she said, lowering her eyelashes demurely.

Before Jon had a chance to stammer out an awkward reply, Baltsaros rescued him.

"This, my darling, is Jon. He will be joining me tonight," he said, his voice amused.

Jon swallowed and tried to bend his mouth into a smile that seemed sincere.

Fresia straightened and laughed throatily.

"A pretty thing you are, Jon. My girls will fight over you!" she said. She turned her head and motioned to a servant standing against the far wall. The tall, fair-skinned youth, wearing only a loincloth, came forward holding a silver platter in his hands.

"An appetizer, my dears? To whet your passions?" asked Fresia, her hand plucking the lid off a high ceramic jar. There were things that looked like Tom's black cheroots in it but narrower and papered in red.

"Of course," said Baltsaros, and he picked a few out of the jar.

Fresia smiled and bowed low, her cleavage shown to good advantage by the cut of her black dress.

"I will be back with the girls in a moment. Please, enjoy yourselves," she said and left the room in a swirl of perfume.

Jon, frowning at the strange cigars, watched as the captain slid two into the breast pocket of his black vest and put the third to his lips; the young servant came forward again quickly to put a flame to the end of it.

Baltsaros drew smoke into his lungs and closed his eyes, his hand waving the boy away. Nervously, Jon watched as Baltsaros took in another lungful of the smoke and blew out a plume; the smell of the burning herb was sweet and tangy at once and made Jon's nose itch. Curious, he watched a strange softness come over the captain's face.

What is this?

"Here, Jon," said Baltsaros, offering the red cheroot to him.

Jon shook his head, though he was intrigued by the change in the captain. It was as if all the tension had gone out of the older man's limbs, and he exuded a sense of deeply relaxed contentment.

"Please, Jon. Don't say no without trying it. At least once," said Baltsaros, sitting up slowly, a soft smile on his face.

Biting at the corner of his lip, Jon took the small burning thing between his fingers and looked at Baltsaros uncertainly. The captain, his eyes crinkling in good humour, watched as Jon put it to his lips and inhaled. Instantly, he was overcome with a coughing fit, tears springing to his eyes as his lungs burned. A glass was pressed into Jon's hand by the lithe servant boy, and he drank down the sweet juice within, Baltsaros's large hand stroking his back.

"I'm sorry," Jon said in embarrassment, his head spinning a little.

In response Baltsaros narrowed his eyes and leaned forward for a kiss.

Eyes darting to the servant, Jon tensed... and felt instantly foolish. Why would anyone care in this sort of establishment? When he opened his mouth to Baltsaros, he felt a strange tingling in the back of his mind and a soft heaviness in his limbs.

Baltsaros pulled away, his eyes lingering on Jon's mouth a long moment before he looked back up.

He was mesmerized by how big the captain's pupils were as he stared at him. Feeling odd but strangely good, Jon smiled at Baltsaros; maybe this would be ok after all.

After licking his lips, Baltsaros lifted the cheroot, inhaling deeply again; however, instead of blowing the smoke out into the air, he clasped the back of Jon's head and pulled him in for another kiss, exhaling slowly into his mouth.

Jon breathed in the smoke; this time it was less harsh, having been softened by Baltsaros's lungs. He tasted cinnamon, cloves, and something reminiscent of pine. Almost instantly, Jon's head began swimming, and he clutched at Baltsaros in a panic. He heard the captain laugh, and his strong hands pulled him close so that Jon was lying with his head on Baltsaros's chest.

Thu-thump, thu-thump, thu-thump.

He could hear the captain's heart beat loud in his ear, yet somehow it was far away. He felt cold and then incredibly hot. Licking his lips, Jon started to get a little nauseous. The carpet was moving slowly in his vision, the red vines crawling across the floor. He shivered.

"Jon... don't fight it. Just breathe," came Baltsaros's voice from somewhere.

Breathe, said Tom.

Jon narrowed his eyes; there was a ringing in his ears and then a sickening feeling of falling. Jerking his limbs out to catch himself, Jon realized he hadn't moved. Then Baltsaros's hands were in his hair, down his back... pulling the blue shirt out of his pants and stroking his skin, pressing into the muscles that always seemed sore from ship work. He closed his eyes and realized that the falling feeling had settled into a gentle rocking sensation; he was light as a feather and felt great.

When he opened his eyes again, he pushed himself up and away from Baltsaros; he was startled to see a row of girls standing in front of them, all bare-breasted and absolutely beautiful.

When did that happen? he thought in wonder; he had only closed his eyes for a few seconds.

Baltsaros reached for Jon again and slowly lifted the shirt over his head as if he were a child.

Jon shuddered a little as the material left cool trails on his skin, the drug in his system amplifying all his sensations. Frowning slightly, he looked over at Baltsaros, but the man was eyeing the row of girls. Jon turned his gaze to them again. No two were alike, and he found himself wondering how many variations there were to beauty.

Gasping when Baltsaros's mouth touched the side of his neck, Jon felt the captain's tongue come out to taste his flesh, and he shivered again. A flash of disgust crossed the pale face of a blond-haired girl for a split second, and Jon reddened. However, she quickly hid her feelings and smiled coyly when she saw Jon's blue eyes on her.

Baltsaros nipped the skin of Jon's neck gently with his sharp teeth before murmuring softly to him.

"Which one would you like, my love?" asked Baltsaros.

My love.

Jon's heart sped up at the words. Though he knew that to the captain it was probably a meaningless affectation, it made Jon feel a little weak. His breath hitched in his chest as Baltsaros stroked his stomach, and pinched his nipples. Jon watched in amazement as the cheeks of a dusky-skinned beauty with dark-blue eyes became suffused with a pretty pink blush.

"The girl in blue," he said reverently. She found them alluring and wanted to see them kiss... and more. Were he and Baltsaros so enchanting in their caresses?

In wonder, Jon found that his cock had started to harden, and the outline of it was clearly visible through his pant leg. Baltsaros's fingers had discovered it and were stroking him slowly through the thin fabric. When he looked up, Jon saw they were alone with the girl, and she was smiling.

"Come, beautiful men. Come," she said, the motions of her hands fluid in the air, like birds.

Baltsaros untangled his limbs from Jon's and rose, pulling the young man to his feet. They followed the girl through a hidden door in the wall to a room with a large bed and plush armchairs. This room was papered and carpeted entirely in red, the furniture made of a pale wood and upholstered in pure white.

Upon reaching the centre of the room, the girl turned around and slowly unknotted the blue silk at her waist, letting the thin material slide down her tawny thighs.

Jon felt Baltsaros's hands come around him from behind; sliding down his ribs and meeting at his belt, the captain's quick fingers made short work of the knot, followed by the buttons of his pants. Shockingly, Jon was rendered naked in front of the girl and he gasped, his bare cock standing out stiffly from the dark thatch of hair between his thighs.

Baltsaros kissed down Jon's spine, making him step out of his pants and boots before coming back up and wrapping his large hand around Jon's shaft, stroking him. Jon could feel the captain's chest soft against his back and wondered suddenly when Baltsaros had taken off his shirt; time was passing in strange fits and starts.

Watching them with large eyes, the girl touched her tongue against her top lip as the captain ran his hand over Jon's length, his hard grip making the head of the younger man's cock swell. Jon shuddered as Baltsaros moved against him, the captain's mouth sucking and licking at the sensitive skin of Jon's neck; his senses felt completely bombarded.

He was almost panting with desire when the girl came forward to sink to her knees in front of him, her tongue coming out to lap at the head of his cock. Hand clutching the root of Jon's shaft, Baltsaros fed it into the girl's open mouth.

Jon whimpered and clutched both at the girl's head and Baltsaros's thigh, firm against the back of his own. This was so outrageous and delicious, Jon thought as he began to thrust himself wantonly into the girl's mouth, held there by Baltsaros's strong hand.

The build-up of pleasure went on and on, and Jon was moaning between loud huffs of breath, the sweat running down his skin.

"It's the drug, Jon," murmured Baltsaros, when he realized Jon was becoming frantic. "It sharpens the appetite but staves off climax so that pleasure can be drawn out."

Jon nodded but closed his eyes; he wasn't sure how much more he could stand.

As if sensing that Jon needed respite, Baltsaros pulled him away from the girl and led him to a big armchair next to the bed. After pushing Jon down into it and leaning down to kiss him, Baltsaros then turned towards the girl. His long fingers quickly undid the laces at his crotch as he walked, kicking off his boots and then the pants that had fallen from his hips.

The dark-skinned beauty, her lips red and wet from pleasuring Jon, rose smoothly to her feet and submitted readily to Baltsaros's rough kisses.

Jon gasped, a strange mixture of desire and jealousy gripping at him as he watched Baltsaros thrust his tongue into the girl's open mouth; the captain's hands slid under her buttocks to lift her up against his pelvis where Jon could see Baltsaros's hard length slide against the skin of her belly. As one they collapsed on the bed and the older man groaned as he angled himself between the girl's legs and pushed his thick cock swiftly into her wetness.

Glued to his seat, Jon watched with wide eyes as the captain began fucking the girl with smooth, fluid motions of his hips. Jon breathed heavily, his hand on his cock; the agony in his chest was blossoming anew at the horror and beauty of it.

Baltsaros was powerful and graceful, his muscles moving rhythmically and sinuously under tanned skin slick with sweat. The girl began moaning, the sound completely sincere when the captain brought a hand forward to do something between her legs as he plunged his hard length into her.

Jon gritted his teeth and stood unsteadily, his cock throbbing in his grasp. He walked to the bed and slid a hand down Baltsaros's hot flank, lust sinking its teeth hard into Jon as he felt the captain move under his hand. Furious and ecstatic at once, Jon grabbed at Baltsaros's jaw and turned the man towards him, savagely capturing the captain's bowed lips in a frenzy.

The girl beneath Baltsaros let out a shuddering cry, and Jon felt her tense through the man's body.

This was insane. Baltsaros pulled away from Jon and stood, his stiff cock wet and shiny from fucking the girl. On her back atop the white duvet, the lovely whore lay panting and flushed.

Jon watched her for a moment and then clenched his jaw, knowing what Baltsaros wanted from him. He slid a hand under the girl's back as he climbed on top of her, Jon's hand guiding his cock into the wetness that Baltsaros had so recently plundered. Shuddering and gasping, Jon thrust himself into the girl hard, her smooth, wet insides squeezing at his cock as it moved within her.

But... this was wrong. It was the wrong body beneath him.

He turned his head and saw that Baltsaros was lying beside him on his stomach, his arms folded under his head as he watched Jon fuck the whore. The captain's eyes were dark, pupils huge... But his mouth was set in a hard line, and Jon understood that Baltsaros was no longer enjoying this. All Jon could see was confusion in the other man's face.

Immediately pulling away from the whore, Jon stood back, panting hard. Propping herself up on her elbows, the girl frowned at him as he caught his breath, worried that she had done something wrong. Quickly, Jon walked to the clothing discarded on the deep-pile carpet and fished around in the coin pouch that was tied to his belt. He came back to the girl and placed three large gold coins on her curved belly.

"Please. Leave us," he said quietly.

The whore's eyes went huge; it was an incredibly large sum, and she moved swiftly to obey though there was a touch of disappointment on her face as she left.

Jon turned to Baltsaros.

Watching him quietly from the bed, Baltsaros frowned but stayed where he was.

The drug was still coursing strong through Jon, and he wanted nothing more than to run his hands over the man's bronze skin to wipe away all traces of the girl's touch. He walked towards Baltsaros and slid a hand up his muscular calf, feeling the captain tense slightly under his palm; in dismay he realized that his fingers felt rough against Baltsaros's skin now that the sweat of his exertions was drying.

Frowning, Jon looked around, an idea taking shape in his head. When he spied a small, stoppered bottle of liquid on a dainty table next to the bed, he scooped it up in one hand and peered at it curiously. When Jon opened it and saw that it was filled with softly scented oil, he smiled. After climbing up onto the bed, he moved to straddle the captain.

"What are you doing, Jon?" asked Baltsaros, his voice sounding strangely unsure. However, the man didn't move as Jon settled himself down just behind Baltsaros's hips.

"I have no idea," said Jon, truthfully; he just wanted to feel the captain's strong body under his hands. Pouring a little of the oil into his palms, he rubbed them together to warm it before laying his hands flat against Baltsaros's broad back. Jon slid his hands up and over the hard muscles, marvelling at how smooth the captain's tanned skin was. He pushed his thumbs into Baltsaros's back, following the natural curves beneath his hands and was gratified when the captain let out a deep groan.

"Gods, Jon. That's lovely," said Baltsaros, closing his eyes and smiling.

Pleased with himself, Jon kneaded and pressed at the captain's muscles, eliciting moans of pleasure from the man beneath him. However, there was something dreadful gnawing at Jon, poisoning him and casting a shadow over his mind.

Baltsaros seemed to sense Jon's darkness and spoke softly.

"What is it?" he asked.

Jon started shaking his head but then stopped; he realized he was fed-up of being constantly kept off-balance. Breathing deep, he spoke in a quiet voice that belied the emotions that threatened to choke him.

"I don't know what you were trying to accomplish here, but I'm not your whore. I'm yours... but not like that." He pressed hard into Baltsaros's back with a knuckle at a pressure point Calum had shown him, and the man beneath him let out a grunt of pain. His own words, finally spoken aloud, fed into the anger he had been holding back. "I mean it, Baltsaros. I don't want to be with anyone but you. Don't you *ever* make me fuck someone else for your pleasure again. Never."

Baltsaros reached back with one hand and tried to free himself from the painful pressure Jon was exerting, but the young man grabbed his wrist and wrenched it up, his angle giving him the advantage over the other's superior strength.

"Also... I may be yours but understand here and now that *you are mine*. Learn to keep your cock in your fucking pants or *I will end this*." Jon finished, his heart hammering in his chest.

A few seconds passed, sickeningly empty of Baltsaros's response, and Jon began to feel his courage crumble; he was completely devoted to the man but couldn't bear the thought of having to live through this perversion again...

Then, Baltsaros nodded.

It was such a simple thing, this up-and-down movement of the head, but it brought with it a relief so intense that it made Jon's eyes sting with tears. The older man was frowning, his eyes closed and his breathing strangely hoarse. Jon released Baltsaros's arm and resumed his caresses after a moment with a sureness to his hands that hadn't been there before.

Baltsaros's brow smoothed out and he sighed; eventually relaxing under the younger man's palms, he groaned softly at Jon's efforts.

As Jon slowed his movements, the massage became increasingly erotic. Pouring more oil onto the man's lower back and buttocks, Jon found himself becoming incredibly aroused by the fact that Baltsaros was pinned beneath him; in response to these thoughts, his cock stirred from the softness it had settled into. Jon watched as the blood surged into it, his cock sliding along the cleft of Baltsaros's buttocks and getting slippery with oil as it lengthened.

This honestly hadn't been his intention when he started to massage the older man, and Baltsaros tensed underneath him. However, he became almost dizzy with desire when he felt Baltsaros shift his hips ever so slightly so that Jon's cock rested unambiguously between the cheeks of his ass. With no small amount of trepidation, Jon experimentally pressed his shaft into the warm, oiled furrow and was rewarded with a tiny movement of the other man's hips; Jon gasped, and his cock twitched from the sensation. Kneading the flesh of Baltsaros's buttocks with fingers and palms, Jon began to thrust himself slowly against the man, his cock sliding easily over the oiled crevice.

It was divine... And Jon wanted more.

As if reading Jon's thoughts, Baltsaros began rocking his hips and moving himself against the young man with more vigour until finally raising himself high enough that Jon's cockhead began rubbing at his puckered opening.

Was this permission to... Jon couldn't finish the thought; it was too much. His mind took a tumble, and lust claimed him completely.

After raising himself up, Jon quickly parted Baltsaros's thighs with his knee and placed himself between the older man's legs. Jon felt a shiver go through the man beneath him as he caressed Baltsaros for a moment with a thumb slick with oil. Baltsaros lifted himself up on his knees in response, and Jon swallowed hard. With his cock in one hand, he pushed the swollen head of it hard against the rough mouth of Baltsaros's narrow passage and gasped as the exquisite tightness stretched open and engulfed him. He slid slowly inside Baltsaros's body as the other breathed unsteadily beneath him; feeling the hot, slick muscles envelop him completely, Jon groaned and began moving within.

~

Baltsaros shuddered as Jon's cock battered into him, thrusts coming harder as the younger man climbed the steep slope of his mounting pleasure. Jon's words and hands had opened up a raw weakness within him... And he clutched at it.

Baltsaros now belonged to this lithe, dark-haired creature that fucked him with an urgency and passion born of staggering emotion. He himself could never attain it... This depth of feeling that came so readily to Jon. However, he could hold onto this strange ache, this rift inside his deformed soul that belonged to Jon *and only to Jon.* And thus he thrust himself back against the assault. In attempting to possess Jon, he himself had become completely and totally ensnared.

He gasped when Jon suddenly pulled away. However, it was only to coax Baltsaros onto his back so that Jon could enter him anew while kissing him deep, tongue questing for the possibility of shared rapture.

When Jon reached between their bodies to grasp Baltsaros's cock, the captain felt a slow pulse of pleasure start to course through him. He was made aware of a sensitive point inside him as Jon's length continued to slide steadily over it while the younger man's strong hand stroked him to hardness. Soon Baltsaros was moaning into Jon's open mouth, pulling the breath from the other man's lungs as he shuddered with his own advancing climax.

Jon suddenly cried out, his body going rigid as his cock twitched deep inside

Baltsaros. The thought of Jon spilling his seed within him sent Baltsaros careening over the edge of his own orgasm, his muscles tensing as the hot fluid gushed out of his cock in thick bursts, coating Jon's hand and his own chest as he cried out with the sweetly agonizing pulses of release.

Jon's breath sobbed out of his chest, and he soon collapsed on top of Baltsaros, spent and trembling.

Baltsaros felt a keen joy, an incredible lightness within him, and started chuckling as he ran his hands softly over Jon's slick back. The young man raised his head blearily and looked at Baltsaros with a curious lift of his dark brows. The captain clasped Jon's face with his palms and kissed him softly.

"See... didn't coming here help?" he said, teasingly. Jon tried to frown but instead just bit the captain's lip with a wry smile; a moment later he exhaled hard as his softening cock slipped wetly out of Baltsaros, and he shuddered, putting his head back down against the older man's neck.

For a long time, the two men just lay there entwined, bodies cooling as the sweat dried on their skin. Today had definitely not gone how Baltsaros planned. Sharing a woman with Tom had always been a lusty affair that returned them to a fixed point in their relationship, and Baltsaros had mistakenly thought that the same would happen with Jon. He had not been prepared for what had happened instead.

As he frowned up at the ceiling, Baltsaros realized that this somewhat botched attempt at reconciliation had in fact changed everything. Baltsaros smiled. Though the path leading to it had been unexpected, the end result had brought the two men closer together. It was intriguing.

After a while Baltsaros could tell that Jon was falling asleep by the slowness of his heart and a slight twitching of his limbs. In contrast, he felt completely electrified; Baltsaros slowly shifted Jon off of him and onto the soft bed.

"Jon..." he said softly, and the young man's eyes opened a crack.

"Mmhmm?" Jon replied.

"Did any of the girls seem put off by me touching you?" Baltsaros asked, curious.

Jon's face took on a sleepy frown as he thought.

"Mmm yeah. The busty blond. The one in uh... pink," he replied, his eyes closing again. There was a line between his brows, but Jon was so close to sleep that he didn't question Baltsaros.

The captain nodded and smiled, stroking Jon's hair away from his high forehead.

"I have to obtain something, but you can rest here for a while... Can you make your own way back to the boat?" he asked.

Jon nodded, his features relaxing into slumber.

After flicking the edge of the comforter over Jon, Baltsaros slid off the bed and went in search of his clothes.

It had been some time since Baltsaros had obtained a fresh heart, and the particular brand of excitement reserved for the hunt slowly began to build inside him.

CHAPTER 19

BAAL'S HEART

It is not the strongest of the species that survives, nor the most intelligent that survives. It is the one that is the most adaptable to change.

— CHARLES DARWIN

Through the hazy veil of half-sleep, Jon heard the sound of someone clearing their throat and realized that he wasn't alone. He lifted his head and blinked sleepily as the memory of where he was coalesced in his mind. At another soft sound of movement, Jon looked towards the foot of the bed.

Lounging in one of the plush white armchairs, with a wry expression on his handsome face, was Tom. Jon sat up slowly and frowned, rubbing his eyes as he held the white duvet against his nakedness.

"What are you doing here?" he asked hoarsely.

Tom's eyebrows went up.

"I said I'd watch out for ye, didn't I?" answered the burly pirate, his smile crooked. "Was beginnin' to think ye'd sleep all night." He slapped his hands together and then made beckoning motions. "C'mon, lovey. Let's getcha out of bed and back on the ol' tub before *he* thinks ye've run off, shall we?" Tom said with a feigned cheerfulness. He was pale with fatigue, and Jon sensed that Tom had spent the evening drinking alone, though he seemed far from drunk.

Jon felt a pang of shame wash over him and shook it off.

He coughed into his fist, realizing that the herb he'd smoked earlier had made his lungs rough, and he felt a little lightheaded. He watched curiously as Tom suddenly slid out of his chair, striding quickly across the thick carpet to a stand holding a crystal ewer.

After pouring some water into a glass, Tom returned to Jon with it, holding it out in one large, scarred hand.

"Here, pup... Ye'll feel a little bit poorly for a while. Smokin' *char* for the first time ain't all fun 'n games," said Tom with a sardonic grin.

Jon ducked his head in embarrassment and took the cup, drinking down the water gratefully; it was cool as it ran down his throat, and he felt immediately better for it.

"Thanks," he said quietly, deciding that he was glad for the bigger man's presence. "What time is it?" It felt like days had passed since he had crossed into this room with Baltsaros and the girl when it could only have been a few hours. He swallowed hard as sudden, vivid memories of Baltsaros gasping and moaning beneath him brought heat to his face. Jon clutched at the duvet; had he really...?

"It's late," said Tom, interrupting his thoughts. "Past the time ye should'a been back on board. Now up, young Jonny."

Jon nodded and tried to get off the bed while holding the heavy comforter around him.

"Where are my clothes?" he asked weakly, not seeing them on the floor. He stumbled forward, and the material jerked out of his hand, stripping him suddenly bare in front of Tom.

The ex–first mate let out a long, low whistle, and Jon blushed furiously.

"Here," said the other man.

When he glanced up, Jon saw that Tom had his clothes in one fist and was holding them out to him. Desperately trying to seem unconcerned by his nakedness, Jon took a step forward and pulled his clothing out of Tom's grasp.

"Yer lookin' good, lad," said Tom, his voice soft.

Jon turned to scowl at the bigger man as he was shoving a foot into his pant leg, but he saw nothing but frank admiration on Tom's rugged face. He looked down at himself.

It was true; the demanding physical labour required of him aboard the ship had packed hard muscle onto Jon's slight frame. His shoulders were wider than they once were, and his arms bulged with definition; though Jon would never be the powerhouse that Tom was, nor as broad and sculpted as the captain, he was a far cry from the pale, weak thing that had first joined the crew.

"Uh, thanks," he said self-consciously, though he realized he was sincerely pleased with the compliment. He tugged up his pants and buttoned them at his hips before pulling the shirt over his tanned chest.

Tom stood up and Jon, still fumbling to tie his belt, followed him through the hidden door.

As the two men made their way down the broad staircase, Jon saw that the first floor of the brothel was still busy even though dawn was reaching out to pull away the cover of night. Near the tall wooden doors, Jon caught a glimpse of the dark-haired girl that had knelt before him on the soft carpet.

Feeling strangely cocky, he winked at her and was rewarded with a shy smile. He turned his head and saw that Tom had stopped to watch him, a thoughtful look on his face.

The big man set his jaw and motioned to the exit with an impatient tilt of his head; Jon quickly left after him through the high doors and out onto the wide, cobbled street that led to the wharf.

"Ye've changed, Jon," said Tom gruffly, looking askance at him as he caught up.

Jon glanced at Tom in surprise, but the muscular deckhand continued down to the floating dock where the ship's small rowboat was waiting for them. Jon climbed in and sat on the wooden bench, a small smile on his face; the last time he'd been in this boat with Tom, he'd been terrified with a bag over his head.

After pushing them away from the dock, Tom settled down between the oars. His countenance was serious as he took them up in his hands, his large shoulders bulging with the strain as he began pulling the oars through the dark water.

"You've changed too," said Jon softly after a while. "I don't think you've ever called me just 'Jon' before."

Tom frowned and nodded, not meeting Jon's eye. Apart from grunting occasionally with the effort of rowing, Tom was mute.

Jon sat watching him, a troubled look on his face.

"Tom, are you all right?" asked Jon after a few minutes.

Tom's sea-green eyes flicked up to Jon's face, and he was astounded by the hurt he saw there.

"I'm fine, love. I'm fine," said Tom, his words a blatant lie. "And, if ye don't fuckin' mind, yer the last fuckin' person I want to discuss my bloody problems with."

His words were an admonishment, and Jon clenched his jaw, conceding with a tight nod of his head. The rest of the short trip back to the ship passed in complete silence.

~

Baltsaros felt Jon wake when he slid his arm around his warm body in the dusky light of early morning, his own skin slightly cool from being outdoors.

"Mmmm," Jon sighed and pushed back against him, lithe and soft skinned. "Where were you?" he asked sleepily.

Baltsaros pressed his lips against Jon's shoulder.

"It's a surprise," said the captain, smiling as he traced his fingers along the other's side.

Jon laughed softly.

"Oh good. It better be something nice," he mumbled.

Baltsaros expected Jon to fall back asleep but was surprised when he slid his fingers around Baltsaros's hand instead, pulling it down his stomach to where his cock was slowly beginning to unfold itself.

"I was wondering if I could be excused from duty today, Captain," Jon said with a jesting coyness that Baltsaros had never heard from him before. The young man pressed the captain's hand hard against the stiffness in his groin. "I think I'm coming down with some sort of illness." Jon continued with exaggerated worry in his voice. "Feel this... Does this feel healthy to you? Am I dying?"

Baltsaros laughed out loud at the silliness. His fingers encircled Jon's cock, and he stroked down against the hardening flesh, eliciting a pleased groan from the younger man. As he kissed Jon's neck, he touched the tip of his tongue against his warm skin. Jon had never been playful before—eager, yes, but not with this mischievous forwardness. Baltsaros was intrigued. After sitting up and rolling Jon over onto his back, the captain frowned down at him.

"I'm not sure," he said, playing along with Jon. "Does this hurt?" He stroked Jon's gracefully curved cock a few times and then stopped to run his thumb back and forth over the head of it softly when a wetness beaded at the tip; Jon shuddered and let out what was nearly a yelp.

Baltsaros grinned and licked his thumb. He pulled the rest of the coverlet away from Jon's naked body. Gone was the shyness that had plagued the serious young man before; a lusty confidence was in its place as he lay there, unashamed beneath Baltsaros's appreciative gaze.

Jon reached out with impatient hands for Baltsaros and pulled the man on top of him, his legs trapping the captain against his body, his cock hard against his stomach.

"I suppose we can stay in bed a while," Baltsaros said against the underside of Jon's jaw. The young man laughed throatily in response as he clutched at Baltsaros's hips, moving slowly beneath him.

～

Jon glanced over at Baltsaros, sprawled out on his stomach on the wide bed. Grinning, he rubbed at the bite mark on his shoulder and shook his head. Baltsaros was always enthusiastic in his lovemaking, but this time he had left Jon feeling exceptionally loose limbed, albeit a touch sore in a few places; Jon's instigation had certainly brought something out in the captain.

He was still astounded by his own behaviour; Jon couldn't remember a time in his life when he'd been so bold. His growing confidence was making him increasingly aware of a strength of character that years of isolation had hidden from sight... as well as a deep appreciation for the more carnal aspects of life.

Staring down at the gorgeous naked man that he had claimed as his own, Jon debated climbing back into bed to wake him for another round, but the grumbling in his stomach was getting ridiculous. Besides, the captain was exhausted and probably appreciated the chance to sleep; the man had been out all night.

Doing what?

Jon pushed the nagging thought aside and groped around on the floor for his discarded pants, pulling them on quickly once he found them. When he spotted a black shirt of Baltsaros's that he coveted, Jon pulled it from the back of the chair where it was hanging.

Frowning, he was dismayed to find it stiff with something. When he rubbed at the hardened patches, Jon's fingers came away peppered with tiny brown flakes; there was a shiny quality to them that he instantly recognized and, lifting the shirt to his nose, he smelled a meaty, coppery tang mixed with the captain's scent.

Jon turned to look at Baltsaros again; the man had no injuries, where had all this blood come from? Slightly discomfited, Jon draped the shirt back over the chair. He would ask the captain later; surely there was a logical answer.

Shaking his head, Jon dismissed the worry that threatened his good mood. When he found his own grey shirt crumpled on the floor, he pulled it over his head and went in search of something to eat in the galley, thoughts of whorehouses and murders scratching faintly at the back of his mind.

Tom was once again avoiding him.

Jon sat in the shade, pressing down with the handle of his knife on the caulked rope between the wooden boards, mending the deck's weatherproofing as he watched Tom.

The muscular deckhand, a heavy roll of sailcloth on his wide shoulder, climbed nimbly up the ratlines to the leeward spar to replace the upper topsail. It was really a two-person job, but Tom was somehow able to manage it on his own.

Baltsaros was right: Tom was an incredible asset to the ship. He was strong and agile, and, having spent the bulk of his adolescence as a slave in the mines, not afraid of hard work. The mostly friendly, competitive nature of the crew often saw others trying to match Tom's herculean efforts, something that greatly benefited the ship as more work got done as a result.

Jon flipped the knife in his fingers a few times and sat back, staring up at Tom high above. He watched as the other man skilfully attached the sailcloth to the buntlines while standing balanced in the foot loops. It was a dangerous job, yet Tom did it fearlessly. Jon smiled and shook his head; his own worth on the ship would never extend to something so perilous.

Jon laughed when he heard the clatter of nails on wood and watched as Brutus raced down the deck towards Beard. Having found some old saddlebags on board, the huge man had somehow shortened them to fit the mastiff. Jon looked on as Beard pulled two metal flasks from the dog's saddlebags and gave him a piece of dried fish in return. Brutus sat on his haunches and chewed the salty treat happily. The intelligent dog had quickly learned to deliver messages and items from one side of the ship to the other, and his courier service had proven to be an amusing diversion for the crew. Jon smiled and watched the dog turn and make the return trip before bending himself to his task once more.

. . .

About an hour later, while putting more caulk between the boards, Jon noticed Baltsaros at his usual spot at the rear of the ship. For a moment he thought about joining him up on the quarterdeck; however, unless work took him there, Jon had no business being in a place reserved for higher-ranking crew. That he was Baltsaros's lover—his *consort*—didn't change anything. It was bad enough that his shipmates alternated between plying him with small gifts to win favour and teasing him about being Baltsaros's cabin boy; Jon didn't want to call more attention to himself by going where he didn't belong.

He stood and dusted off his pants. The captain's room, on the other hand, was fair game since Jon had moved all of his belongings there. As he walked aft towards their shared quarters, Jon spotted a small boat approaching from town and assumed some shipmates had paid another visit to the brothel while they were still in the vicinity.

He stepped over Old Ben, who was sleeping against a rigging chest, and made his way to the rounded door between the staircases going up to the raised quarterdeck. It was dark inside the large room as usual, and Jon was glad for it; though nights were getting increasingly cold as winter approached, days still tended towards high heat around this time.

When his eyes adjusted, he saw that the captain's quarters were as fastidiously tidy as usual; there was no sign of the bloodied shirt. Jon crossed the room to the ice chest, craving some of the cold, fresh water Baltsaros stored there; his lungs still felt a tad raw.

When he pulled the pitcher out, he saw a lumpy package of something wrapped in paper on the lower shelf. Jon smiled. Perhaps this was the surprise? Baltsaros certainly lived up to his promise of feeding Jon every exotic thing he could come up with.

After replacing the water, he closed the door and walked to the bed, drinking down his mug of water. His head still felt fuzzy from lack of sleep; surely he could lie down for just a few minutes...

A loud crash woke Jon.

He gasped and sat up, looking around in alarm. There was a banging and another crash from above. He glanced up and saw that the room was strangely bright, the boards having been pulled away from the broken windows. Two strange men stood on wooden cases, hammers in hand.

Crash.

Another piece of wood went flying, and Jon slid off the bed, taking a few steps back.

What in gods?

He heard a laugh from behind him, and turned, startled to see the captain standing there with a smug smile on his angular face.

"Serves you right, sleeping on the job," said the captain dryly.

Jon was mortified, wondering how long he had been out. Tom hadn't exaggerated when he said that the aftereffects of the drug were long lasting; he could have slept all afternoon and only woken at morning. He ran his fingers through his curls, though his hair had gotten long enough that it no longer stood up at all angles from the habit.

"Sorry," Jon said quietly.

Baltsaros frowned and shook his head.

"I should put you over my knee for such laziness," he said softly, his eyes glinting with mischief.

Jon swallowed hard, his blue eyes wide. The thought of Baltsaros punishing him, especially in a way so intimate, had instantly elevated his heart rate. He almost groaned out loud; it was all Jon could do not to reach for the captain right there and pull his body against him. Lust was like a constant burning ember waiting only for the tiniest breath to fan it into flame; Jon had a hard time remembering what it was like before he was a slave to this perpetual, demanding hunger.

Baltsaros narrowed his eyes at Jon, sharp teeth visible in his wide smile.

"I see," he said simply, obviously gratified by Jon's breathless reaction.

Jon had to look away before he made things worse.

"What's going on?" he said in an unsteady voice, gesturing towards the men.

Looking pleased with himself, Baltsaros turned his eyes towards the workers.

"This is the surprise... I took your advice. These clear panes are only a temporary measure," he said as he watched one of the men hold up a greenish pane of thick glass to the empty window frame. "When we arrive in Madierus I will have some new stained-glass windows made up by the men who crafted the ones for my home there, but in the meantime I thought you'd be pleased with the change nonetheless," Baltsaros continued and lifted a hand to grasp the back of Jon's neck, his thumb lightly stroking the soft skin behind his ear.

Jon shivered slightly with the touch, his skin breaking out in gooseflesh.

"That's not all, however. Come and see the rest," said Baltsaros, smiling.

As he stared at the captain, Jon felt like he was seeing glimpses of a younger man through Baltsaros's uncharacteristic excitement; it was like a heaviness that Jon hadn't even realized was there had been lifted from the man.

Baltsaros led Jon out of the room and up the stairs to the very back of the ship. Below them, hanging on the wooden bench the men used for painting the sides of the ship, was another worker that Jon did not recognize. The man was painting words in red on the black of the ship's hull, and Jon could see that it would read *Baal's Heart* once the letters had been completely filled in.

He frowned in confusion and looked up into Baltsaros's clear brown eyes.

"What does it mean?" he asked.

The older man's tanned face creased in amusement.

"It is the root of my name, Jon. It means 'lord' or 'god' in an ancient language. And, as you pointed out, this is my home and thus my heart. I thought it was fitting, don't you?" Baltsaros said, looking up.

Jon followed his gaze and was amazed to see a flag flying from the post above them. On it was the same black silhouette of a roaring lion on a red field found on the crest within the captain's quarters, but here it was superimposed on a compass rose. Jon grinned wide.

"Lord, indeed," he said, raising his eyebrows. He laughed. "Yes... yes, definitely. I think it's fitting," he agreed. "It's a noble name and completely worthy of this ship."

This time he didn't hold back, forcefully drawing the captain in for a passionate kiss.

CHAPTER 20
BLOW THE MAN DOWN

Baltsaros pulled away after only a moment, strangely tense. As he held Jon away from him distractedly, the captain studied the horizon with a furrowed brow.

Jon frowned and looked out at the clear water, not seeing anything amiss. Then he noticed that Tom was standing on the gunwale below them, his body also straight and tense as he stared in the same direction as Baltsaros.

"What's wrong?" asked Jon, worried.

The captain licked his lips and glanced down at Tom. The two men shared a look and Baltsaros nodded.

"What is it?" repeated Jon, the fact that captain and his ex–first mate were suddenly acknowledging each other's presence striking a nervous chord in him.

The captain looked at him, but it was a half second before his eyes focused on Jon's face.

"It might be nothing. It might be a storm," he said.

Jon tried to shrug nonchalantly.

"We've been through storms before…" he said but stopped at the concern on Baltsaros's face.

"Not a storm like this, Jon," replied the captain, his fingers digging into Jon's bicep. "Go below. Make the rounds and see that everything is secured. I don't want loose crates and barrels on deck if this is what I think it is."

Jon tried not to be hurt at being dismissed so hastily but moved to obey the captain's orders. Tom met him at the foot of the stairs and pointed to starboard.

"Tie anythin' that rolls or slides, lovey. We're in for one hell of a wild ride if the wind doesn't shift," he said, his brow creased over his ocean eyes.

Fear was beginning to take hold of Jon; what kind of storm could rattle the two stalwart men like this? He nodded and watched as Tom took off at a sprint in search of

Katherine. When he squinted his eyes at the line where sea met sky, he still couldn't see any indication of a storm. However, he had to trust the pirates' instincts. They knew the sea, after all. He jogged along the side of the boat, pausing to secure loose lines and to tie down crates.

Jon was soon satisfied that at least one side of the ship was tidy and secure. Turning aft, he saw the workmen leaving in the small boat he had seen earlier. At the bow, deckhands were already turning the capstan to weigh anchor. Were they going to try to outrun the storm?

Katherine stood close by, hands on her hips as she frowned at the horizon.

"I don't see it," Jon said, walking up to her.

She turned her head and smiled.

"Neither do I, to be honest, but I've learned that if both Tom and the captain say there's a storm coming, you can bet your soul that there will be a storm," she said, her face serious. "I want you out of the way when this thing hits, Jon. The last thing I want anyone to worry about is you getting washed overboard." She reached out and grabbed his shoulder. "I know I normally tell you not to look so afraid, but this might be bad. Just heed me, ok? Keep to your quarters."

"Why are we lifting anchor? Isn't it safer here?" he asked, confused.

Katherine shook her head slowly.

"It would be safer if we could actually get into the harbour, but we're too big for that. If we stay here, all that will happen is the chain will snap or get pulled through the hull of the ship as we get buffeted around like a leaf in a windstorm. And then we'll get dashed against those rocks. No—it's better to face a hurricane on the open sea. For now, can you head to the galley while things are still calm? Help Cook secure things down there. The last time we got hit badly we ate shitty rations for a week because no one had time to lock everything up tight," Katherine said, smiling though Jon could see how worried she was.

"Yes, sir!" he said and squeezed the hand on his shoulder before leaving her to continue her watch on the horizon.

Jon was rolling the last barrel into the big locker beneath the kitchen when the room got ominously dark. The portholes, showing blue skies only a moment ago, were now a deep grey, almost black.

Cook shoved him aside and quickly jammed the door closed, passing a loop of rope through the handle a few times before tying it tight. When he turned to look back at Jon, his eyes were wide.

"Go, Jon. Find somewhere to hole up and pray," he said, pushing him towards the door.

Jon's heart beat hard in his chest as he ran out of the dark room.

. . .

When the first gale hit the ship, Jon was struck with the gut-wrenching terror of being at sea during a storm. There was a high wailing noise that shrieked through the corridor as he frantically climbed the stairs to the upper deck; the ship was shuddering and swaying, making it hard to keep to his feet. Panting with the exertion, Jon just couldn't believe how sudden it all was.

When he reached up and pushed at the door, Jon was certain that someone or something was on it; however, after yelling with no response, Jon realized it was just the force of the wind holding it closed. When he finally got it open, he was instantly soaked as a blast of rain smacked hard into him, thrown by the furious winds. Jon coughed and wiped the stinging water from his eyes, terrified and unsure of which direction he was facing. He struggled onto the wooden planks and then stumbled as the ship pitched hard to starboard.

On his knees in the pouring rain, he gaped at the scene in front of him.

It was dark. Not night dark, but a howling, living darkness made up of swirling rains and black shapes.

There was a bright flash of lightning, and Jon made out the colossal wave just before it hit the ship. Frigid salt water crashed down on top of him, and he struggled to find something to hold. His hands closed on nothing and he panicked, his mouth full of water as he choked and groped around him.

The water receded, and they tilted precariously back, riding another huge wave high into the air. The ship creaked and groaned, shimmying slightly before she dropped suddenly out of the air, smacking down hard onto the water beneath. The wind was knocked out of Jon, and he writhed on the wet deck, trying to take in a breath. Finally his lungs expanded, and he drew in a shuddering breath.

Why in gods did I leave the galley? he thought in horror.

When the next lightning bolt flashed, he realized he was facing aft. He heard someone yelling behind him, and a loud crash. The ship rode up yet another wave, and Jon braced himself, ready for the next impact. There was a high squeal of something sliding against metal, and the ship yawed suddenly backwards.

Jon was utterly petrified, but he knew that he had to make his way to the captain's quarters; the door to belowdecks was lost somewhere behind him. On hands and knees, he crawled across the slippery wood. Where was Baltsaros in all this? Surely the captain knew what he was doing, having been through this before, but Jon was scared nonetheless.

The ship shivered under his palms, and Jon realized they had gone sideways again as yet another wave crashed down over the ship. Jon cried out as he was swept backwards, and for one sickening moment, he was free falling before he hit the deck.

Jon knew he was turned around, but with no lightning and most of the lanterns knocked out by saltwater, he had no way of figuring out which way to crawl. Thankfully, his hand made contact with something a moment later, and he breathed a sigh of relief. However, his reprieve was cut short when he realized that he was against the side of the ship and that there was nothing between him and the raging sea except for the low gunwale. He felt around for rope or a hand-hold but again found nothing. Sobbing in desperation, Jon tried to cling to the slick wood.

Up went the ship, and down again with a hard impact. Jarred momentarily from his spot, Jon slid against the deck. Raising his head, he thought he could see the outline of the quarterdeck right in front of him and decided to make a run for it. He lurched to his feet and took a few steps forward before he realized that the ship was tilting to starboard again. The wave crashed down hard, and Jon felt himself being lifted up into the air with the force of it. He windmilled his arms, trying to find something to hold onto, but it was too late; Jon was dashed against the side of the ship and swept upwards. All he could see below him was the churning, frothing maw of a sea gone mad. Feeling himself slide over the edge with nothing to hold onto, Jon realized he was going to die. He hung, terrified, on the edge of the yawning blackness for a half second before he began to fall...

...only to be pulled backwards by something hard around his waist. He choked and clung to the arm that was holding him as he was dragged across the deck. A few times he and his rescuer were blown down to the planks, but Jon was picked up, over and over again until they reached a sheltered corner.

When he wiped the water out of his eyes, Jon realized that the man holding onto him, one strong arm looped around his waist while the other held onto the stair railings of the quarterdeck, was Tom.

The ship creaked and groaned again, but this time when she landed, Tom was supporting him.

"It's goin' to be ok, mate!" shouted Tom over the wind. "She's already startin' to lose steam."

By "she" Jon assumed that Tom meant the storm. Jon felt limp against Tom, his heart careening wildly in his chest. If Tom had not reached out when he did, Jon would have been sucked down into the cold, black depths, surely to drown in the indifferent embrace of a mindless sea.

The ship went up and down, side to side. Sometimes Jon wondered how she hadn't capsized yet. Through it all was Tom, a wide hand on Jon's lower back as he held them steady in the small shelter of the staircase.

Strangely, the ship's wild movements seemed to take on a regularity, and Jon started to climb out of his terror. The lantern that hung swinging from the wall above hadn't yet been doused by water, and Jon could see Tom's face in the meagre, swaying light. The big man's eyes were narrowed against the water that dripped from his hair as he stared off to the side, watching the patterns of wind and rain with a keenness born of experience; the muscles worked in his broad jaw, and Jon saw that his lips were pressed in a tight line.

When Jon shivered hard he suddenly noticed that Tom, bare chested as usual, was still radiating warmth even though completely soaked with cold seawater. Tom was the very essence of summer at sea, with his blue-green eyes, and the sun's heat coming off his bronzed skin. Just like the sea, he was callous and dangerous... yet...

Shivering slightly, Jon lifted a hand and placed it flat against the bigger man's chest.

Tom's eyes swung to Jon's, wide with surprise.

Jon couldn't tell if it was the storm making him crazy or if he was just reacting to being saved, but he didn't care. Tom's skin was so warm under his palm, the hard muscles moving under his touch as the broad-chested man shifted his stance. Tom was just staring down at him with a frown, his eyes searching Jon's with distrust and confusion. The storm receded in the distance as he felt his heart ache at the look on Tom's face. Jon lifted his other hand to place it against Tom's stubbled cheek and felt him recoil.

Frowning, Jon tried again, reaching this time for the back of Tom's head, his fingers sliding through the short, wet hair at his nape. He watched as Tom blinked at him, his heart beating hard against Jon's palm.

Tom wrenched his head out of Jon's grasp and yelled something, but it was swallowed by the wind.

Jon shook his head, not understanding.

Tom stared hard at him, his forehead creased in seeming helplessness. When he finally leaned forward to Jon's ear, Tom looked as if he was stepping into the path of a loaded gun.

"Are ye *tryin'* to get me killed, love?" he shouted at Jon.

He caught the slight catch in Tom's voice and realized in astonishment that the powerful young man holding him was afraid. However, despite his words and fear, Jon felt Tom slide his thumb slowly against his lower back as he pulled back to look at him.

Jon's world imploded.

Tom was the last man on earth that he should be touching, yet Jon's desire became a living thing; pierced through with a dreadful emotion, it was shoving him headlong to where promises were broken and trust thrown away. He shivered as he stared into Tom's gaze, captivated by ocean-coloured eyes that were utterly heartbreaking. The man was almost terrified, but as he leaned into Jon's touch, Jon knew that Tom was caught up in the same fever that gripped him.

It was utter madness.

Wanting to laugh and cry at the same time, Jon knew he was at the very epicentre of a storm that was stronger than himself; there was something in this that was so agonizingly important that he was completely powerless to stop himself. Jon felt like weeping as he reached up and pulled Tom's mouth to his own.

Tom went rigid for a moment, and Jon felt his shock. However, Tom's fingers began clawing at Jon as he pulled him closer, leaning hard into the kiss.

Jon was breathless as Tom savaged his mouth, his kisses rougher and more frenzied than Baltsaros's. Jon's hands slid around the man's broad back, and he held on as Tom fed all the hurt and misery of his heart into the passion of his embrace. Tom's mouth tasted of anise and saltwater; his rough stubble burned Jon's lips, but he didn't care.

Tom released his hold on the stairs and wrapped Jon in arms that felt like steel, pushing him hard against the wall and tonguing deep into his mouth. This was sin and redemption at once. There was a savagery to Tom that Jon suddenly understood; he'd dismissed Tom as being an unfeeling brute when in fact it was nearly the opposite.

Jon thought his heart would shatter as he felt the layers of Tom's pain come away, wishing this kiss could heal the deep wounds that were nearly crippling the big man. Still Tom came at him hard, the heat of his body melting into Jon's cold skin, driving the passion of their kiss into a dizzying pinnacle of want and desperation.

With an audible groan, Tom pushed Jon away slightly, his chest heaving. The handsome brute shook his head, his eyes dark with desire and a hint of his old waggish smile on his lips. He cupped Jon's face with surprising gentleness in his big, callused hands and brought his mouth again to Jon's ear.

"Bloody hell, Jon," he said, his voice husky and deep. "He'll strip the skin from my bones, ye daft thing."

Jon shuddered; Tom's breath was warm against his neck. He turned his head and placed his lips next Tom's ear.

"I'm sorry, Tom. Oh gods, I am so sorry... for everything," he said and pressed his mouth against the skin of Tom's neck. Jon felt the bigger man's groan against his lips as Tom's strong arms tightened around him again, pressing their bodies together in their small sanctuary away from the storm.

Tom's voice was once more in Jon's ear, rough with emotion.

"Yer a bloody fool, love. It's not yer fault that the man has no heart. I just wish—"

There was a shout and a crash.

Tom's head swung away, and Jon felt the man's body tense.

Jon thought he could hear someone screaming. Tom looked back at Jon, his eyes wide with concern. He noticed then that the rigging chest, and the crates that were normally stacked next to it, had slid across the deck and were leaning against the door to the captain's quarters; there was no way he could get to safety.

Tom's hands tightened around Jon's hips, and the first mate's brow creased as he thought hard for a moment. Quickly, Tom reached for his own belt, untying it and passing it behind Jon.

Jon held onto Tom's shoulders as he felt the man's fingers slide one end of the belt through his own. Tom pushed him back and did something with the ends of the leather before stepping back, a wide grin on his face.

Jon frowned and looked behind him; Tom had secured him to the railing so that he wouldn't be swept away. He laughed, turning his eyes back to Tom.

The burly deckhand's handsome face went serious once more, and he leaned forward to press his lips to Jon's for an instant before jogging away to investigate the yelling. Tom turned after a few steps and pointed to Jon, grinning impishly. He mouthed one word: "Stay!" and winked, taking off towards the stern as the storm's winds lashed against him.

Jon caught movement out of the corner of his eye and saw the silhouette of someone turning away above him on the quarterdeck; however, his thoughts were instantly swept up by the storm as another huge wave crashed over the side of the ship, Jon struggling to keep to his feet as water swirled around him.

The night was long and terrifying. Again and again Jon heard shouts in the distance, and once he was sure that the ship would rattle herself to pieces, so loud was the creaking and popping sounds coming from the deck. However, he stayed well secured in his place, thanks to Tom's belt through the railing behind him.

Finally, the wind seemed to lose interest in the ship, and the waves became gentle. The sky was lightening, and Jon realized that the clouds were fading away, leaving twinkling stars behind. The storm was over.

Jon was shaky and his ears were ringing in the comparative silence that descended over the ship. Jon fumbled behind him and worked loose the knot in Tom's leather belt. It came away, and Jon saw that Tom's long knife was still within its sheath.

He was suddenly filled with a mixture of excitement and dread when he thought of the stolen moment beneath the stairs. However, now was not the time to worry about it; Jon saw in dismay that the deck was a mess of broken crates and scattered detritus. From the looks of it, some rigging had fallen from the foremast and one of the carronades had burst loose from its moorings before rolling down the deck. It was against the base of the mainmast and, in mounting horror, Jon realized that the pile of cloth that was crushed between the heavy cast-iron and wood was actually a body.

He quickly ran forward to see if the man was still alive.

When it finally came up over the battered *Baal's Heart*, the sun shone down on a sadly diminished crew. Three men were dead from injuries sustained aboard, and another five were missing.

Tom was numbered among those presumed swept overboard by the fury of the storm.

CHAPTER 21
BREATHE

Jon paced back and forth across the colourful rugs, his hands holding his head as if it were about to fly apart. With his mind reeling and his heart full of jagged cuts, Jon let out a low, frustrated growl between clenched teeth. He stopped and turned to the man sitting at the table; Baltsaros was watching him, eyes untouched by emotion and arms crossed over his chest. There was nothing human in that face. Jon felt tears dampen the neck of his shirt.

"Don't you fucking feel *anything*, Baltsaros?" he asked harshly, his voice breaking on the captain's name. He laboured against the sharp pain in his chest, a burning tightness that threatened to break into hard sobs. Tom's last words kept playing in his mind:

The man has no heart.

Those words had never been so true as they were in that moment when Jon stared at the glacial creature watching his torture with an air of staid curiosity. Jon shuddered and resumed his pacing, overwhelmed with fury and anguish.

"Jon. I don't understand why you're acting this way," said the captain quietly. "Tom wanted you out of his way and would have done everything in his power to achieve that... eventually. He would not be carrying on about your loss were your positions reversed."

He swallowed hard, remembering the way Tom had held him so tight and the slight tremor in those massive arms when Jon had groaned into his open mouth... The way they had clutched at each other in the swaying light of the lantern; days later, Jon could still feel the heat of Tom beneath his skin. He closed his eyes, and the floor beneath him rocked, not from the ocean's swell, but from the deep exhaustion and hunger that hounded him.

Lightheaded, Jon quickly opened his eyes only to see the floor rushing towards him. Before he hit the carpet, Baltsaros's arms came up around him, catching him, and Jon leaned his face against the soft, dark material of the captain's shirt, gritting his teeth. He was burning with an inner turmoil that threatened to choke him.

Jon hadn't slept in two days, not really... not since the storm.

When it had become clear that Tom was amongst the missing, Jon had fought against it at first, denying the truth; it was more than he could bear. He had then spent hours with his eyes sweeping back and forth, searching the choppy waters for any sign of the lost man. It was only after jerking awake on the wooden planks of the deck earlier that day, after exhaustion momentarily claimed him, that Jon had remembered something that froze him to the very marrow of his bones.

He'd just had a fleeting dream of a giant lion looming over him, its shadow spreading like oil across the deck; he recalled then that someone had been standing above as Tom and he clutched at each other in the shelter of the staircase.

Had Baltsaros seen them?

A fist of ice had opened up inside Jon at the thought, its fingers sharp and long. Had strong, surefooted Tom, a seasoned sailor, simply fallen into the water?

Jon swallowed against the bitter bile that rose up in him at the horrifying alternative that was churning in his mind... that Tom had been pushed. As he shuddered, Jon clutched at the strong arms of the man holding him gently.

Did Baltsaros know?

Jon already knew what the captain was capable of.

Don't think.

When Baltsaros's hand touched his head, brushing his hair back softly, Jon wanted to scream. Lying in Baltsaros's arms, all Jon could think about was Tom...

The man already tried to kill Tom once.

...lying in a murderer's arms...

Don't think.

He couldn't confront Baltsaros without revealing his trespasses; Jon's lungs were on fire.

Breathe, said Tom.

Jon opened his eyes wide, new bricks sliding into the walls around his soul, and looked up into Baltsaros's face. The captain was gazing down at him with concern as he ran his fingers through Jon's rough brown curls.

"It is a terrible thing when the sea claims someone," said Baltsaros quietly.

He could tell that the man was trying to understand the source of the anguish that threatened to drown Jon; he looked desperately for any sign that Baltsaros was hiding a terrible deed.

Would I know if he was? thought Jon miserably. He let himself be pulled to his feet and felt as Baltsaros began tugging his shirt out of his pants, the captain's warm hands stroking up his sides as the material was lifted up. Obligingly, Jon raised his arms, and Baltsaros pulled the shirt completely off.

Wordlessly, Baltsaros unbuttoned Jon's pants and undressed him, frowning at the young man's complete lack of reaction. The captain pushed Jon towards the bed, and he lay down on the sheets, his eyes staring at nothing. Quickly ridding himself of his own clothing, Baltsaros climbed up onto the bed and pulled Jon against him.

Jon closed his eyes and breathed deep. The captain's body was strong and warm around him; the thatch of soft hair on Baltsaros's chest felt nice against his torso, and the captain smelled alluringly of wind, musk, and sandalwood.

Baltsaros's fingers stroked Jon from thigh to shoulder and along his arm with gentle touches that were feather soft.

Breathe in, breathe out.

Jon felt like he was breathing for the drowned Tom, lost somewhere beneath the ocean's waves just as a new flame had started burning within him.

Baltsaros's mouth was hot against Jon's neck as he slid his tongue softly up to trace the lines of his jaw.

He frowned; sex was the captain's solution to everything.

Breathe in, breathe out.

Tom's hands on his face.

Baltsaros's hands on his skin.

Jon felt himself drifting on the sensation of Baltsaros's hands ghosted by Tom's as he counted his breaths. When the captain pushed Jon onto his back and began kissing down his chest, he felt the slow burn of desire begin to warm his loins. He didn't want it.

Tom and his tragic blue-green eyes at the bottom of a blue-green ocean.

Jon gasped and was brought back to the present when Baltsaros's wet tongue slipped between his legs; lapping upwards, the captain licked the wrinkled skin of Jon's sensitive sack, tongue broad and firm as his mouth manipulated the round forms within.

Measured breaths became quickly forgotten as Jon shamefully surrendered, tangling his fingers in Baltsaros's hair and arching his back off the bed as he pushed the older man's head firmly against him.

Tom began slipping beneath the waves and out of his grasp as Jon sighed the captain's name.

"Oh gods, Baltsaros... more... please..." he said in a whimper.

Baltsaros continued to lick slowly, his tongue leaving wet trails on the insides of Jon's thighs, along the lines of his pelvis, teasing so close to his cock and returning to tongue his scrotum; gently nudging Jon's legs further apart, he then pulled his mouth away from the younger man to wet his finger with spit.

Jon raised his head and frowned, his chest heaving. When he guessed Baltsaros's intention, Jon felt a pang of fear-laced excitement. With his eyes locked on Baltsaros's,

Jon pressed his lips together and nodded; Baltsaros smiled as he slid the finger inside him, and Jon breathed a long moan, trying not to tense.

Slightly shaky from the foreign sensation, Jon watched as Baltsaros trailed his tongue along the bottom of his cock to the underside of its head, the long finger stroking gently around a tingling, pulsing point of pleasure deep within.

"Fuck... oh gods," Jon gasped, his chest heaving. This was ecstasy bordering on agony. The finger inside him, slowly starting to move directly over this unfamiliar sensitive centre, added a keen-edged intensity to what Baltsaros was doing with his tongue. He panted and pushed back hard on the captain.

"St-stop. It's too much," Jon groaned.

Baltsaros lifted his head, his dark eyes curious. Heedless of Jon's words, he pressed a second finger to his puckered entrance, stretching him open further. Jon gasped and dug his fingers into the sheets beneath him, a shudder running through his body as his head fell back on the bed; his hips moved automatically with the slow motion of the captain's long digits probing inside him.

Jon gritted his teeth. His cock was rock hard and throbbed in a way that was almost painful, a long string of clear fluid stretching out between its tip and the base of his stomach as the shaft bobbed up in response to Baltsaros's inner caress. He squeezed his eyes shut, a low groan rasping out of his chest with every long stroke of Baltsaros's fingers.

He suddenly realized just how heavily Baltsaros was breathing and raised his head, looking helplessly at him. The captain was flushed, his pupils huge with desire; he gazed wonderingly at Jon.

"I could make you peak just like this, couldn't I?" Baltsaros said, sounding amazed.

Jon swallowed reflexively, words failing him as the pleasure mounted and spread, only to fold back on itself and surge forward again. He licked his lips and gasped again as another rush of pleasure sluiced through him; he reared back on the pillow and groaned loud.

"You're unusually receptive," said the captain, a note of surprise in his low voice.

Jon shuddered when he felt Baltsaros lean forward again to touch his warm tongue to his stretched opening, sliding softly beside and between the two fingers moving languidly inside him, slickening them anew with spit. Jon's breath sobbed out of him, and he reached for his cock, frantically wanting release; however, Baltsaros's hand stopped him.

"No. I want to see how far I can take you," said the captain softly. Jon moaned in desperation, but his breath caught in his throat as a third finger started to pierce him. Jon whimpered and clutched hard at the hand Baltsaros had placed on his chest to hold him down. This hurt... He felt like crying out as the tightness strained over Baltsaros's knuckles... And then it didn't, his passion taking over, loosening his muscles.

As Baltsaros fucked him smoothly with his fingers, Jon felt the pressure mount in his testicles, each little slap of his cock against his taut stomach a little explosion of sensation. Jon felt himself open up; flush with lust and ripe with desire, he held his breath a moment and clutched at Baltsaros.

"Baltsaros, I can't anymore... please... I-I want you inside me," Jon said, his words made plain by the hunger that tormented him; the idea had been building in his head since that night in the brothel.

Jon heard Baltsaros exhale hard before pulling away. He opened his eyes and lifted his head in dismay, wondering why he'd been abandoned and saw that Baltsaros had just retreated as far as the cabinet to fetch something; the captain was back on the bed in a moment.

The older man poured out a small amount of oil into his hand and smoothed it over the head of the thick cock jutting out stiff and veiny from the curled hair between his legs. His other hand stroked Jon's thigh and glided up his leg to grasp his hip, his thumb rubbing against the skin there in a distracted way as he passed his hand over his own length. When Baltsaros's shaft was shiny with oil, he thumbed some into the crevice of Jon's ass, pressing him open to smooth some within.

Jon whimpered and obligingly lifted his knees up, grasping the backs of his thighs. He was terrified of the prospect of Baltsaros's wide cock inside him, yet there was nothing in the world he wanted more.

Tom...

Jon gritted his teeth and growled out a hard breath, wanting to drown the emotions that kept seeping through the walls he had erected.

After shoving one arm under his waist, Baltsaros grunted as he lifted Jon's hips up and pulled a pillow beneath his buttocks, raising him up and opening him further by pressing back on his thighs.

Jon closed his eyes, his heart thudding hard against his ribs, as he waited for the final assault.

Baltsaros's fingers were on him again, pushing into him, spreading the oil, readying him. When the head of Baltsaros's thick cock finally touched him and started to force his way into Jon's body, he cried out softly.

However, while there was pain, it was quickly overshadowed by the pleasure of feeling full of Baltsaros's hard length. The captain pushed his greased cock to the very hilt into Jon's body and groaned.

With hungry hands, Jon pulled Baltsaros down onto his chest to feel the man's weight above him as the cock inside him started gliding back only to slowly stretch him wide again.

With his own oversensitive length trapped between their bodies, rubbing and sliding through the slick trail it left on their skin, Jon was soon crying out, a single, open-voweled syllable repeating over and over out of his raw throat as he quickly came hard; he spilled over onto his stomach with hot pulses as his passion hit a frantic peak, dissolving him with a searing, shattering explosion of sensation and release.

Baltsaros gasped in response, thrusting himself hard, his brows furrowed and his mouth open as his cock was enveloped and milked by the tight throbbing of Jon's orgasm. Baltsaros grunted like a beast, his pounding gone wild as he came deep inside Jon.

Jon pressed his mouth against Baltsaros's neck and tasted sweat on his lips. He was almost uncomfortably sore and incredibly tired, but his mind wouldn't stop its relentless churning. Caught directly between his feelings about the loss of Tom and the suspicion that Baltsaros had played a part in it was this profound emotion he felt towards the man at his side.

Baltsaros sighed happily and ran his fingers down Jon's back, scratching gently at his skin.

"Jon, do you realize how very unique you are?" the captain murmured sleepily.

Despite how perturbed he felt, Jon had to smile; this was the way he liked Baltsaros the best: sated and gentled... It made him seem more human.

After a long pause, Baltsaros spoke again.

"I'm sorry that Tom's death causes you so much pain, Jon. And... I'm sorry that saving you is a debt I can never repay to him," he said, his voice soft.

Jon closed his eyes and pressed his forehead against the side of Baltsaros's stubbled jaw, feeling torn and weary. Jon knew the captain didn't understand, and that the words *I'm sorry* meant next to nothing. However, that Baltsaros was even volunteering them was enough for Jon to clutch to.

He stroked his hand over Baltsaros's broad chest and nodded, his lips pressed together and his brow furrowed. Tom was gone; he had to think more rationally...

Maybe it's for the best.

Instantly Jon felt sick to his stomach with the thought, but it was true.

～

Baltsaros woke when his outstretched arm failed to make contact with another warm body. He opened his eyes and lifted his head. When he saw that the room was empty and the door closed, he frowned. Brutus was also not at his place on the folded blanket next to the bed.

He sat up and stretched his back, spine popping with his movements. Baltsaros then dragged one of the blankets over his wide shoulders as he stood. Reaching down to touch himself, he smiled; his cock had a delicious soreness to it. Jon had definitely surprised him tonight.

After padding across the floor in his bare feet, Baltsaros opened the door to his quarters and looked out. He knew it was too early to feel the difference, but it already seemed that the night air was getting warmer as they headed south.

Curious, he climbed the stairs to the quarterdeck above and saw that Jon was asleep, huddled on the floor fully clothed next to his oversized dog.

Brutus raised his head slowly and looked at the captain sedately with eyes that reflected the light of the moon.

Baltsaros rubbed his jaw and stared at Jon for a moment. Now that Tom was gone, maybe Jon would stop worrying about the former first mate. As he shook his head slightly, he walked forward and pulled the blanket off his shoulders, leaning over to place it over the curled body of his young lover.

When Baltsaros turned and looked at the seemingly endless stretch of water behind them, he found that his own mind had turned to Tom.

CHAPTER 22
FIRE IN THE BLOOD

The captain pulled the lumpy package out of the icebox and placed it on the table, laying it on the thick wooden slab he used to protect the table's surface. Jon, stinking of rum and tobacco, watched him bleary-eyed from the bed.

Three days had passed since the storm, and Jon was still in the throes of his mysterious bereavement. This morning Baltsaros had found him slumped over some crates after a long night of gambling and drinking. It was completely out of character for him, and it baffled Baltsaros; Jon seemed bent on mimicking the man he was mourning.

Baltsaros eyed the pale, sickly looking Jon and wondered if he should make up a tonic for his hangover or just let him suffer.

"What's that?" asked Jon.

Baltsaros looked back down at the package and began pulling apart the twine that held it together.

It's almost a waste, he thought. After pushing open the paper, he held up the contents of the package to Jon.

"It's a heart," he said.

Baltsaros turned it over once in his hands, remembering how warm it had been when he plucked it from his quarry's chest. It was so cold now, and it was too late to eat it raw; the storm had ruined that opportunity.

Jon sat up slowly, his mouth drawn down in a grimace.

"Why do you have a heart in your ice chest?" he asked, his voice hoarse. "What kind of heart is it?"

"Deer," lied Baltsaros smoothly, smiling at Jon.

Jon slid off the bed, his bare feet silent on the thick rug as he came to Baltsaros's side. The odour of liquor was a miasma around him, and he smelled of sour sweat.

"Where did you get it?" Jon asked. The young man was looking down at the heart curiously.

Baltsaros had a sudden vision of Jon covered in heart's blood, and it brought with it a little pang of desire. He ran his hand up Jon's side, smiling when he saw the goosebumps his touch caused.

"I went hunting the other night," said Baltsaros.

The blond woman's legs flashed white as she ran away from him, stumbling over branches and slipping on leaves. The blood pounded hot inside his chest.

Jon leaned into Baltsaros, and the captain could feel little tremors going through his body.

"Oh, I wondered where all that blood on your shirt came from," replied Jon. "But... Where's the rest of the deer?"

Baltsaros chuckled. The body would have been disposed of as per the arrangement with Fresia; the management at the Jewel catered to almost every proclivity of their vast and varied clientele.

"I only needed the heart. It is a custom among my people to eat fresh heart raw at the beginning of a long journey. It brings good luck," said Baltsaros. "But this one isn't fresh anymore. I suppose I could make sausage with it."

Jon looked at him askance.

"I didn't take you for the superstitious type," he said, his dark brows high.

Baltsaros reached up and touched the tips of his fingers to Jon's stubbled cheek.

"Call it... tradition, then," he said softly.

Jon's eyes were bright blue in his pale face this morning. Baltsaros was glad once again that he had convinced him to repair the windows in his quarters; the added light was a welcome change.

Charmed by Jon's unselfconscious nakedness and the way he licked his lips when Baltsaros touched him, the captain felt lust sink her claws into him. He pushed the heart and cutting board aside and pulled Jon around so that he was against the table, facing him.

Jon frowned, and Baltsaros felt a touch irritated; the same look of suspicion had crossed his face often over the last few days, and it was beginning to wear on the captain.

He grazed his fingers over the solid muscles of Jon's chest and down his hard abs, stopping to tug softly at the line of dark hair that led to the thatch around the younger man's cock. Baltsaros was pleased to see that Jon was starting to harden at his touch.

When he looked back up, he saw that Jon's suspicion had been replaced by half-lidded desire. Gently pushing his legs apart with his knee, Baltsaros stepped closer and leaned into him, kissing his neck and grinding his pelvis hard into Jon's stiffening cock. Jon groaned softly, his hands clutching Baltsaros's buttocks to pull him in harder.

Obviously, whatever was bothering Jon wasn't enough to make him refuse the captain's advances.

168

Baltsaros ran his hand up Jon's back and tangled his fingers in the brown curls that now fell to his shoulders. He pulled a handful of it into his fist and tugged hard.

"Ow... You're hurting me," Jon said, wincing.

Tom would have never complained at such treatment unless the captain wanted him to. Frowning, Baltsaros pushed away the thought and looked piercingly at the young man.

"Jon, I want you to stop your nonsense. You have not slept in my bed in three nights. Whatever it is that is going on in that pretty head of yours, put it to rest. Now," he said, his voice intentionally harsh.

Jon closed his eyes, a deep line forming between his brows.

"If you fall apart every time we lose a man, you will be less than useless to me," Baltsaros continued. He slid the thumb of his free hand along the line of Jon's jaw, down to his throat and felt him swallow twice. "And... I do not like to share you with ghosts," he said.

Jon's eyes opened, and he looked startled.

Guilt?

Baltsaros could smell desperation on Jon's skin and a little fear.

"Put away your demons, my love. They serve you badly."

Jon stared at him, an inner struggle trapped in his wide eyes. Then Baltsaros watched a shift take place. It was as if Jon had come to some decision; the lines in his face smoothed out, and his whole countenance changed like a man putting on a different mask. Baltsaros wondered idly what it cost Jon to bury his emotions every time he surrendered to his captain's wishes.

"As you wish," Jon said softly.

Baltsaros smiled and leaned in to kiss Jon. After a heartbeat's hesitation, Jon kissed him back, his tongue questing into Baltsaros's open mouth. The captain released his hold on Jon's hair and savaged him with the heat of his mounting passion, eliciting groans of pleasure as he pressed himself hard against his lover's body. His constant desire for Jon was like fire in his blood.

There was a loud knock at the door.

Baltsaros pulled away from Jon with a groan.

"Come in!" he yelled.

Jon's eyes were wide, his body having gone rigid against Baltsaros.

"Wait... I'm..." he started.

The captain chuckled.

"Katherine has seen her share of naked men, Jon," Baltsaros said as he watched his first mate open the door and step inside.

The lithe woman took in the scene with raised eyebrows, eyes pausing for a brief second on the heart, but made no comment. Tom would have said something completely inappropriate. He also would not have knocked before entering.

Baltsaros frowned to himself. Why was he thinking of Tom again?

"Yes, my dear?" he asked.

Katherine's face was solemn.

"Jim's hanged himself," she said simply.

Baltsaros nodded. He had been expecting something like it; the young gunner had lost his brother Billy in the storm, and the twins had been close.

"Thank you. Can you take care of it? I'm sure you can think of a few things to say to the men," he said, dismissing her.

She frowned and nodded before leaving the room.

When he looked back at Jon, the young man was staring at him, expressionless.

If you fall apart every time we lose a man, you will be less than useless to me.

"I guess that's just one less mouth to feed," said this new version of Jon as he reached for Baltsaros to pull him back into a fierce kiss.

~

Jon cried out as Baltsaros bit him hard on the shoulder. He was trapped under the bigger man, his arms pinned beneath his chest as Baltsaros rubbed his thick cock along the furrow of Jon's ass.

It was maddening.

He thrust his hips up and back against the captain's hard length and whimpered.

"Please," he begged. "Just fuck me already." His cock ached to be touched, but he couldn't move his hands, and Baltsaros would only tease his ass slowly. Jon shivered and groaned, getting what little stimulation he could from the bed beneath him.

Again Baltsaros bit down on his flesh, his sharp teeth closing on the back of his neck. Jon yelped and shuddered.

"Please," he repeated. He had seen male cats bite females on the back of the neck as they mated, and the thought aroused him even more. Baltsaros's cock slipped past his sensitive, puckered opening again, and Jon gritted his teeth.

Baltsaros had been keeping at him steadily, pushing him close to orgasm only to back away, for what had to be over an hour; Jon was starting to lose his mind.

"Please, Baltsaros. Please. I can't," he panted into the coverlet.

Baltsaros remained silent and slowly tongued the spot he had bitten, continuing to slide his cock in the greased cleft of Jon's ass.

"Please fuck me," Jon whimpered again. He clenched his eyes shut, the word *please* starting to flow like a mantra out of a throat dry from panting.

Chuckling softly above him, Baltsaros shifted his hips slightly and moved his hand away from Jon's shoulder. The coolness that came from the sudden loss of contact there made Jon aware that both he and the captain were covered in a sheen of sweat. When Baltsaros shuddered slightly, it dawned on Jon that he had been teasing himself just as mercilessly.

After working his hand beneath Jon's stomach and down to where his erection pressed hard into the bed, Baltsaros took him in hand. Jon moaned at the contact and continued his plea. Another shift of Baltsaros's hips brought the wide head of his cock into contact with Jon's asshole, and Jon gasped, his begging coming to a strangled end.

When Baltsaros started to push into him, widening his narrow passage, Jon almost cried out in relief.

Thank the gods, no more teasing.

He clenched his jaw against the pain; Baltsaros was so big. However, as before, when the head of Baltsaros's cock rubbed against the hard, sensitive spot within him, a keen pleasure started to radiate out of his loins like warm molasses. With Baltsaros's hand firmly around Jon's cock, he let his body go limp as the hard length of the captain's shaft opened him up; but, once his cock was buried deep inside Jon, Baltsaros stopped moving.

Jon groaned.

"Please, no. Baltsaros," he gasped in dismay, "Please, please, no more. Gods, no more..."

"Hush," said the captain, his voice low.

Jon tried to shift his hips to force movement within him, but the man held him still. Jon thought he would start to cry.

Thus began another extended stretch of teasing, the pleasure mounting and receding agonizingly slow as Baltsaros moved his hips in tiny, staggered motions, his cock gliding minutely inside of Jon.

It was a long time before Jon was finally allowed to cum.

When he did, his whole body shook with the force of it as he sobbed loud, the ecstasy crashing through him hot and sweet. His cock throbbed and pulsed, again and again, sending thick gouts of cum onto the bed beneath him, Baltsaros's hand stroking and squeezing with the same rhythms of his orgasm.

The relief was so intense that Jon felt like he ceased to exist for a moment; his awareness shrunk down to a knife's edge, becoming the cock that twitched and jumped in Baltsaros's grasp.

The captain had gone rigid, his groan of pleasure long and low, as he spilled his seed into the younger man. Face pressed hard into the crook of Jon's neck, Baltsaros urgently moved his hips as he rode the tide of his own orgasm, and Jon could feel the man's heart hammer against his back. Finally, the only movement was the heaving of their chests, and only the sound of breathing broke the stillness in the air.

Jon felt almost delirious, and he ached to clutch Baltsaros to him. As if hearing Jon's thoughts, Baltsaros slowly pulled out and lay down next to him with a sigh, his arms reaching out. Jon turned on his side and curled against the broad chest, his forehead resting against the base of Baltsaros's neck.

"Thank you," Jon said quietly.

There were tears in his eyes and they soaked into the sheet beneath him. Baltsaros's hands stroked his back, and he felt the man nod.

"That was gorgeous," said Baltsaros, sounding somewhat dazed. A floodgate of raw emotions opened inside Jon, and he shivered and wept against the captain. He had been conquered and then set free. The word love was right at his lips.

"Jon... Don't cry," Baltsaros said softly, his fingers stroking the back of Jon's neck.

"Why are you crying?" The captain seemed suddenly younger to Jon somehow, a note of awe in his voice.

"Because… I need you," whispered Jon after a moment. "I needed this. I needed you. You came for me. You claimed me. No one has ever made me feel these… things you make me feel. I don't ever want it to stop." As he spoke, Jon realized that no matter what Baltsaros did, he would stay by his side; though he would lose his soul, piece by piece, by the things he would be forced to endure, this is where he belonged.

When Baltsaros next broke the silence, Jon felt his heart skip a beat.

"Jon, I would walk through fire just to hear you speak my name," murmured Baltsaros. "And although I don't understand it, I would be a lesser man without you here with me."

CHAPTER 23

DEAD IN THE WATER

Absence diminishes mediocre passions and increases great ones, as the wind extinguishes candles and fans fires.

— FRANÇOIS DE LA ROCHEFOUCAULD

Jon frowned and looked down at the potato he was peeling. He and Calum were on kitchen duty for the day, and they were going through what seemed like the very bottom of the barrel. The potato in his hand was slightly soft, and it had black spots on its wrinkled skin. They had been sailing southwest for nearly a month, and their provisions were running dangerously low.

Though the storm had robbed them of supplies, they hadn't restocked before leaving for Madierus. Baltsaros had done the calculations and had pointed out coldly that the missing or dead men could not eat; what food and water they had once the storm cleared was ample for the reduced crew.

The captain had not counted on the long weeks with no wind.

Grimacing, Jon cut another rotten piece out of the potato, flicking away in disgust the little white worm he had uncovered.

Calum laughed, and Jon looked up.

"What?" he asked.

The old man shook his head and pointed to the wriggling thing on the floor with the end of his knife.

"Soon ye won't be throwin' away good meat like that, son," joked Calum, chuckling to himself.

Jon's stomach roiled at the thought.

From what he could tell, they were still a few weeks out from the island of Madierus. However, every time he pressed the captain for exactly how far they were, Baltsaros's eyes flashed to anger, and he went stonily silent.

Jon knew that the captain would be sitting up on the quarterdeck right now, just staring out at the still water, his face drawn and eyes hooded.

When he looked over at Calum, who was cutting up the rest of the carrots, he remembered that the old pirate had been on this ship longer than Baltsaros had.

"Has this happened before?" he asked, curious.

Calum sucked at his bottom lip a moment and then nodded.

"Aye. A few times. The worst was when yun' Baltsaros had just come aboard," he said. "We was sailin' to the north and got caught in open water, nary a breeze for the cloth. Dark times."

Jon's hands slowly continued their work as he listened to Calum's story.

Many years before, when Calum was in the prime of his life and newly widowed, he had joined the crew of the *God's Hammer*—as it had been known in those days—to escape prosecution.

Before becoming a pirate, Calum had been part of the standing army for the mainland kingdom. His job had been to train new recruits in different hand-to-hand fighting techniques, something he had learned from his father, a man of dubious employment.

Calum's wife, on her way to visit a sick friend one evening with fresh-made bread and soup, fell prey to a man who mistook her for a prostitute. The man, a well-known aggressor of women, simply slammed her head against the wall when she refused his advances, and the woman died shortly after from her injuries. It was not hard for Calum to track down the murderer, a small lord, and beat him to death with his bare hands.

On the run and with a warrant on his head, there were few choices to him that appealed as much as becoming a pirate.

Calum had been on board working as a simple deckhand for a little over two years when Captain Romas went to retrieve his brother's orphaned boy. It was that summer, a few months after the nine-year-old Baltsaros first came aboard, that Romas had decided in a moment of fanaticism to sail from the midland isles to the lowest tip of the northern continent.

The last-minute course change was fuelled by a rumour that barbarian tribes were threatening villages along the coast and converting them to heathen ways. Romas, being a man who considered himself on God's *one true path*, was incensed by the rumours. He put both his ship and crew in the path of pure folly by sailing them north through a barren sea with few provisions during a time of year that was known for fickle winds.

Calum had watched in dismay as the sails held less and less wind in them every day until they finally went flat and listless. Soon the crew began running out of provisions, and things became strained on the ship.

Since Baltsaros's arrival, Calum had been watching the frail, fine-boned boy with the dark eyes and high cheekbones; Captain Romas, though couching his adoption of Baltsaros as familial duty, seemed hell-bent on breaking him. Romas was under the impression that the boy was somehow tainted and in need of saving, a theme that the religious man was obsessed with.

Night and day, young Baltsaros was set to backbreaking labour; the tasks were often extremely taxing on the boy's health, and he would be frequently found pale and listless at the end of his shifts. However, the captain would shove him awake with a boot only a few hours later and set him on some new, more onerous task. Hard work, said the captain, would save the boy from the devils within.

Baltsaros always bent his head to his work without complaint; the only sign of outrage towards his treatment was a dark fire that burned in his eyes. When Baltsaros wasn't working or sleeping, he was found on his knees in the small chapel; more than once Calum had seen the boy kneeling through the open door as his uncle exited, his hands re-buttoning the front of his pants.

Calum felt pity for the boy and wanted to help, so he waited until the next time the captain went ashore to approach Baltsaros. His offer of fighting lessons had been met with a long, hard stare, one that was strangely calculating for one so young. In the end, Baltsaros had nodded his head curtly and extended his hand to the older man.

Thus began their longstanding alliance.

At first Calum worried that the lessons, in addition to Baltsaros's duties and the meagre sleep he was afforded, would begin to take their toll on the fragile-seeming lad. However, the graceful young boy took to the lessons like a fish to water, and they seemed to give him energy rather than sap it; a new fire burned within Baltsaros.

It was during this windless drifting in the barren northern sea that Baltsaros first used his new skills against the captain.

A fight had broken out between the men in the lower deck, a squabble about the size or quality of rations, and the galley was trashed as a result.

Captain Romas put the three men responsible into the brig; he then dragged young Baltsaros by his neck to the galley and shoved him down to the floor, wanting him to clean up the mess.

At least that's what the captain had intended.

Instead, as Romas went to fling the boy down, he was flipped over into the air, landing hard on his back in the mess. Calum had been there to see the older man staring up in shock at the boy who stood above, a fierce grin on his elfin face.

That afternoon, Baltsaros was sealed in one of the big rain barrels with a few cannonballs and thrown overboard. The barrel was dragged slowly behind the ship by a rope tied around it for nearly two hours. When it was finally hoisted back on board, Baltsaros was unconscious and lifelessly cold from the frigid northern waters.

Calum had been surprised that the boy had recovered. This was to be only the first of many, many times that Baltsaros was lowered into the cold water over the course of Romas's captainship.

As the horror faded from Baltsaros's eyes that first time, Calum noticed something new about him; where Baltsaros had been sober and quiet before, he was now curious and driven. The secret lessons between Calum and the fine-boned lad also took on a different aspect; while Baltsaros worked to hone his physical skills, he asked countless questions of the older man about the ship, the captain, the crew, and the world in general.

He became a more charming version of himself with the other men, winning small friendships onboard. Calum asked Baltsaros what had changed, but the boy wouldn't say.

A week after the incident, the captain dragged the three men from the brig and set them kneeling, side by side, on the deck in front of the crew. There was no longer enough food to feed all of them, and, in a misplaced attempt to further terrorize Baltsaros, Captain Romas was making the young boy choose which sailor was to walk the plank.

Calum had stood quietly in the back of the crowd, watching Baltsaros's face grow cold as he stared into his uncle's eyes. Without a word, the boy pulled the knife from his belt and quickly slashed the throats of all three men before Captain Romas had a chance to stop him. The instant the last body fell limp to the wooden planks, a great gust of wind was felt. It soon filled the sails, and the ship was quickly on its way again; a great cheer had gone up among the crew despite the ruthless killing of the men.

That was the last time Captain Romas publicly tormented the boy.

Baltsaros's workload increased ever more, and his punishments became more frequent, but the first nail in Captain Romas's coffin had been forged that day. The wind, while coincidental, had elevated the boy in the superstitious minds of the crew; their growing admiration and loyalty for Baltsaros was what had made the mutiny possible seven years later.

Jon licked his lips and swallowed.

"So Baltsaros was not always this... ruthless? You think his uncle pushed him to it?" he asked Calum when the story was done.

The old man frowned at Jon.

"I wouldn'a say that, lad. The cap'n... 'E's always been different. I think whatever 'e seen in the deeps just freed what 'e already was. Though I known 'im for near thirty years, I wouldn'a call 'im a friend, see?" The dark-skinned man peered thoughtfully at Jon a moment. "But... I never seen 'im treat a man the way 'e treats ye, Jon. It's none of me business what ye two get up to behind closed doors but outside of 'em... Well, I'd call what ye have friendship."

Jon grimaced. The relationship between him and the captain had become strained as the long weeks passed. Baltsaros had started acting strange; he did nothing but drink and stare out at the water all day long. Aching with worry, Jon desperately wanted to break through the captain's isolation.

"Calum. I... uh... do you..." he started, unsure about how to word the question that still haunted him.

The old man just looked back down at the carrot he was peeling and waited patiently for Jon to form his question.

"Do you think the captain could have killed Tom if he saw him doing something he was forbidden to do?" he asked quietly.

Calum's eyes flicked up to Jon's face with interest. However, the old man was canny, and Jon saw that he wouldn't be pressed for more information. After chewing his lip for a moment, Calum spoke.

"The cap'n wouldn'a kill the boy, no. There's reasons, but it ain't my place to say," he said, his rough voice equally low.

"He would have killed him that day with the whip," Jon pointed out.

The old pirate shook his head right away.

"Aye, perhaps; ye did stop 'im, but I'm likin' to think he'd a stopped hisself. That boy Tom was angrier than a bag full o' cats when 'e come aboard, and it was the cap'n who gentled 'im. No, lad. The cap'n wouldn'a kill Tom," he repeated firmly, looking back down at his hands.

Jon knew that the old man believed his words.

The younger man flipped the potato back in the bin, and Calum glanced back up quizzically as Jon stood.

"I... need to... I'll be back," he said quickly. He strode through the big doors to the galley and rinsed his knife in the basin of standing water that Cook kept there for that reason. He held the long blade flat in his hands and looked down at it.

Tom's knife.

He ran his fingers down the bone hilt, over the markings there, wondering as always what they meant. With his eyes closed, Jon pictured the big brute in his head, the impish grin and the rough hands that had held his face so gently. Jon would never be able to ask him. For all he knew, the big man was rolling in his watery grave knowing that Jon had claimed the knife as his own. Jon smiled sadly at the thought but put his feelings for the dead man away for later.

He needed to see the captain.

~

Baltsaros frowned at the cloudless blue sky and took another sip of the rum and cold coffee from the cup he held in one hand. The wind had to blow soon... But did it even matter now? The sun beat down hard on the captain; he had changed from his customary leather pants to the black linen ones he favoured when sailing to the summer lands, but he was still hot. His torso was bare and his chest hair was dark with sweat. He ground his teeth in frustration.

Why is there no wind?

He turned his head when he heard the soft steps approaching. Jon padded up the stairs and came to stand in front of Baltsaros.

"What do you want, Jon?" he asked, his voice weary and annoyed.

"Come. The ocean can wait," Jon said.

The captain's stark brow raised slowly. He drank down the rest of the liquid in the cup and stared at Jon.

"Not now," he said and turned back to the water and the lack of wind. When Jon's hand curled around his bicep, he wasn't prepared for the anger that crashed through him. He flung his arm out to push the other away... but found himself suddenly flat on his back on the wooden boards.

Jon stood above him, a frown on his face.

"I said come," he repeated.

Baltsaros bared his teeth and sat up.

What is this?

In amazement, he watched Jon simply turn his back and walk down the stairs. Despite the outrage he felt, the captain decided to follow.

When Baltsaros entered his quarters, Jon was standing in the middle of the room, his arms crossed over his chest. He'd taken to wearing a sun-bleached pair of green pants that were cut off just below the knee and, like most of the crew, went shirtless in the tropical heat.

Baltsaros noticed for the first time that Jon was now wearing his hair tied back in a short tail, the dark-brown curls falling softly down the back of his neck.

"Do you know how frustrating you are?" Jon asked when Baltsaros stopped, his face unreadable.

Baltsaros frowned; he didn't have the patience for Jon's ridiculous complaints. The gracefully muscled young man just continued to stare hard at Baltsaros and, after a long minute, the captain's eyes widened.

"You want me to admit that I'm frustrating?" he asked, confused.

He watched the muscles move in Jon's jaw and realized that the man was furious. Baltsaros reached up and rubbed the shoulder that had hit the deck when he'd been unexpectedly thrown down by Jon.

"Jon, I don't have time for this," Baltsaros said and turned to go.

"The wind won't start to blow just by you staring at it. You have plenty of time," said Jon, his voice low and angry.

Baltsaros turned back to the young man in astonishment.

"You think we're going to die, don't you?" Jon asked.

They stood a long time, staring at each other in the sun-dappled room. Finally, Baltsaros clenched his jaw and nodded. It felt strangely good to be admitting it.

"Why?" asked Jon, taking a step forward.

"Even if the wind were to start blowing right now, we would not have enough food or water to last us until we reached Madierus. There is still a great, empty expanse of ocean between us and the island," Baltsaros said softly.

What had made the island so appealing was also its downfall. It was hard to get to because of the paucity of surrounding islands; getting to the small tropical island was no easy task, even for the most seasoned sailor. That it was just a tiny green dot in a wide sea of blue, so very easy to miss, was something that Baltsaros counted on when it came to his enemies; *Baal's Heart* had unfortunately fallen prey to the same dangerous isolation.

"Was that so hard?" Jon's blue-grey eyes searched his face.

"I don't understand," Baltsaros replied slowly. What was Jon trying to accomplish?

"You tell me *nothing*. Do you realize that? Almost everything I know about you comes from talking to other people. I know how you like to have your cock sucked," Jon's face coloured slightly. "But I know next to nothing about what goes on in your head. I've been asking you for days whether we were close to our destination—a place I know nothing about, I might add—and you wouldn't say. Am I not worth answering? Am I not asking the right questions? *What's wrong with you?*" asked Jon angrily.

Baltsaros felt the heaviness in his chest press at him.

"There is nothing wrong with me," he replied curtly.

"That is utter bullshit. For one thing, you haven't come near me in over a week. That in *itself* is cause to worry... And I *am* worried," said Jon, re-crossing his arms.

Baltsaros opened his mouth to refute the claim but realized that it was true; apart from sharing a bed for sleep, the men had not spent any time together. With his lips pressed together Baltsaros scowled at Jon.

"I've been preoccupied with the fact that we will never reach Madierus. The death of an entire crew is not something to be taken lightly," he said, speaking slowly to stress his irritation.

"And yet you could," said Jon, pointing at him. "Do you want to make me believe that you would actually care if everyone died around you, including me?"

At this Baltsaros started shaking his head; Jon spoke the truth but for one thing.

"I would care very much if you died, Jon," he said softly, but Jon narrowed his eyes at the captain.

"I wonder if you would," Jon said, his voice flat with restrained emotion.

Baltsaros pressed his lips together and sighed softly.

"That's not what I care about at the moment," Jon continued. "You're angry. I can feel it. I can see it. You're *furious*. And do you know why? *Because you're not in control.* There is nothing you can do to make this ship move any faster."

Again, it was the truth. Baltsaros felt his jaw tighten.

"I'm not an idiot," said Jon. "You brought me on board to use my powers of observation... And this is me observing a captain that is so caught up in a battle against nature and his own past that he's driven himself half-mad. Do you know that you've called me Tom three times in the past few days?" Baltsaros frowned. "You've barely eaten, you haven't bathed, and you've been treating me like I'm just a bedwarmer. This is not your uncle's ship; this is not the northern sea. There are plenty of fish in the water... We'll make do. We're not going to starve to death."

Baltsaros shook his head.

"We don't have enough fresh water... It's impossible."

Is it?

"Then why not kill off some of the crew?" asked Jon, his eyes suddenly shrewd. "That would save some water."

Baltsaros's eyes went wide. Was Jon serious?

"You know why you won't? *You're not your uncle.* You haven't failed anyone. You may not actually care about anyone on board, but you'll do your best to keep them alive, won't you? Because that's what you do." The young man fell silent again.

Baltsaros's head was starting to hurt, and he looked down. What did Jon know? The frustration and anger of the past few days felt like they were bleaching Baltsaros's bones; he wanted to kill something.

"Baltsaros... Why did I have to learn from Calum that you were horrifically abused? Why not just tell me these things?" Jon's voice had softened when he spoke up again.

The heavy, burning sensation in Baltsaros's chest rose to his throat, the blood singing in his ears.

"The man is dead. What does it matter?" he growled.

"It matters because you've spent your entire adult life trying to prove to yourself that you're not your uncle," Jon retorted. "And that you don't need anyone but yourself."

Baltsaros lifted his head and stared at Jon. When had he ever needed anyone else?

You need Jon.

The boy was the source of his weakness.

Is he?

Baltsaros felt strangely dizzy.

"It occurred to me for the first time today that you might not actually know when you're suffering. You're so fucking damaged that you can't even tell when you're acting strange. Calum said something earlier that I found interesting. He thinks you've always been this self-possessed, unfeeling creature, but that you saw something in the cold depths that brought out a new strength in you. Is he right? What did you see, Baltsaros?"

Baltsaros was back in the barrel again, staring wide-eyed into the solid blackness that surrounded him and shaking so hard that his teeth felt like they would break against each other. Blinking hard to clear the vision, Baltsaros walked unsteadily to the bed and sat down on the edge.

"I saw myself," Baltsaros said quietly. "And it scared me."

Jon took a step towards Baltsaros, and the older man held up a hand.

"Don't," he said. "I'm not well. You're absolutely right."

As he shook his head and frowned, Jon continued to approach.

"I'm not afraid of you," he said.

Baltsaros grimaced.

"You should be. I'm not a good man," he muttered. "I might hurt you. The urge exists within me." However, he leaned his head gratefully against Jon's smooth side when the younger man reached him.

"Listen to me, Baltsaros. You once told me that you would cherish my informed opinions. Well, this is an informed opinion: you have made the best out of what you were granted at birth. I know it's proof that there's something deeply fucked up about me, but I wouldn't have you any other way. Fate has thrown us together for some reason... Now can we please proceed to the stage in this partnership where you start actually sharing with me?" Jon's fingers rubbed the base of the captain's skull, exactly where the tension was the worst.

Baltsaros closed his eyes. *Partnership.* It meant an equality between two individuals.

"I... will try," he said slowly, testing out the idea. He heard Jon exhale hard.

"Good," Jon said.

Baltsaros turned his head so that his cheek rested against the taut muscles of Jon's midriff. The idea that he could need someone was still very foreign to him, but Jon's words rang with truth, and he felt it in the pit of his stomach. They stayed this way for a long time, Baltsaros leaning against Jon's side while the other stroked his hair. Though he still felt on edge, Jon's presence was soothing. The boy was right.

"Did you kill Tom?" asked Jon suddenly.

Startled, Baltsaros's eyes opened, and his brow furrowed. He pulled his head away from Jon and stared up at him in confusion.

"Why would I kill Tom?" he asked, bewildered.

Jon fiddled with the leather thong in Baltsaros's hair, his storm-grey eyes troubled.

"We embraced," he said, his voice barely above a whisper.

Baltsaros felt a sharp pang of something in his chest but shoved it away.

"And you think I killed Tom because I knew about it? *This* is what's been bothering you?" Baltsaros asked, astounded. He sighed when Jon nodded and pulled his hands out of his hair, opening them up against his lips to kiss his palms.

"No. I did not kill Tom. Nor would I kill him now, were he alive at this confession," he said quietly. With a feeling like he was venturing out into strange waters, he offered up something else.

Why not?

"I... miss Tom," Baltsaros said.

It was true. Since Tom's death, his mind kept turning over and over again to his former first mate, no matter how he tried to still his thoughts. It was honestly no surprise to him that he had called Jon by the other man's name. He missed the easy connection he had with Tom, the way that they were almost constantly in sync, working together like two pieces of the same machine aboard the ship.

He missed Tom's rough hands, his unquenchable desire, his love of pain. His feelings for the muscular youth did not run nearly as deep or even in the same direction as they did with Jon, but they were there.

When he looked up, Baltsaros saw that Jon's eyes had gone glassy with tears; he stood and wrapped his arms around the young man. Strangely, the captain felt like he had just sacrificed a small part of himself with that concession. The thought shook him.

Jon suddenly tensed, and Baltsaros pulled away, eyes darting over the young man's face with worry. Had he said too much? Was Jon about to launch into another angry tirade against him?

"What is it?" he asked. Baltsaros watched in amazement as Jon's face split into a wide grin.

"Can't you feel it?" he asked, his voice high with excitement.

Baltsaros started to shake his head but stopped.

From the open door came a strong, cool gust. The wind had started to blow.

CHAPTER 24
LANDWARD HO!

Jon pulled himself out of Baltsaros's arms and ran out the door, feeling ridiculously excited. When he got amidship, Jon was amused to see that the rest of the crew had stopped what they were doing and were standing quietly on deck, just feeling the breeze.

The ship was moving again.

Seemingly at once, everyone started jostling against each other, running to stations that had long been unmanned because of the lack of wind. Then all heads turned to the quarterdeck, and they waited in a hush.

Baltsaros stood a long time holding his sextant, facing the sun hanging above the horizon. When he pulled it away from his eye, the captain's smile was wide.

"All right boys, helm's a-lee! We need to tack some to the south. But... We are on our way home!" yelled Baltsaros, laughing.

Katherine grinned and then turned to the crew.

"You heard him, you lazy curs! Let's get this tub turned due south. Square the sails! Bring a spring on her cable!" she shouted.

Jon ran to the gunwale and started to climb the shrouds. Turning his head as he ascended, he caught the captain's eye. Jon could tell that the man was still worried about supplies running out before they made land, but at least he was smiling, something that he hadn't seen in what felt like a long time.

Baltsaros winked at Jon, his face creased in a sharp-toothed grin. For the first time in weeks, Jon didn't feel anxious or lost; instead, he was filled with hope.

"And... hells... Splice the mainbrace! I think we all deserve it!" yelled the captain, calling for rum to be distributed to the sailors. A great cheer went up through the crew, Jon hollering with them.

. . . .

On the captain's bench, up on the quarterdeck, Jon lay with his head in Baltsaros's lap. He gazed up at the stars and was, as always, filled with wonder at their astonishing number. He knew there were no more stars above the ocean than there had been above his small harbour town, but something about them seemed more awe-inspiring from the deck of a beautiful ship.

A moving ship.

He turned his head and saw that Baltsaros was watching him, his dark eyes catching the light of the hanging lanterns. The captain seemed quietly amused.

Jon smiled.

"What?" he asked.

The corners of Baltsaros's eyes crinkled with his sudden grin.

"I'm happy," said the captain, a tiny shrug lifting his shoulder.

Jon nodded.

"Good. More rum please," he said.

Baltsaros chuckled and tilted the flask carefully, pouring a trickle of the dark amber liquid into Jon's mouth.

After swallowing it down, Jon turned to look at the stars again; he was feeling similarly loose limbed and happy, a state enhanced by the spiced rum they were sharing.

"The wind is strong. At this rate, we may make it home before we have to eat Brutus." said Baltsaros.

Jon looked to the captain and gasped in mock horror.

"Don't even joke about that, you savage," he said. Jon knew there was a good chance that they would be miserable and hungry for the last few days of the trip; however, that was later. Tonight, everything was perfect.

"Tell me about Madierus," Jon asked.

Baltsaros lifted his head and looked at the stars. His long, light-brown hair hung loose over his shoulders, and his relief at their progress had stripped years off his sharp features.

"It's a beautiful little emerald of an island," the captain said softly, his accent exotic like the land he described. "The harbour is actually a naturally deep lagoon. When the ship is anchored there, no one can see her from the waters beyond; it's a perfect hiding place for us. The water is so blue and so warm that it will literally make your heart ache with its perfection and the sand so white that you will think you have gone blind to colour. The island itself is an old, dead volcano; it's incredibly lush, lots of coconut and palm trees. We planned the town further back from the harbour and built it up to mimic organic shapes so that the buildings don't take away from the natural splendour. It's really quite something. Everyone has their own gardens, but there is a plethora of fruit everywhere growing wild. The figs are especially good."

Jon smiled, his eyes closed trying to picture this paradise; it was strange to think that he hadn't known what a fig was half a year ago.

"Where do you live?" he asked. "Though I suppose I should be asking where do *we* live since I'm to join you in this fantasy. Describe it."

When Baltsaros didn't respond, Jon opened his eyes. There were deep lines in the captain's forehead as his eyes searched the dark waters; he seemed to be struggling with the answer.

After a long minute, Jon slowly sat up and looked at the captain, a feeling of dread coming over him.

"What are you not telling me?" he asked.

Baltsaros's mouth twitched, and he rubbed his hand over the short stubble of his chin. When he looked over at Jon, his eyes held a desire for forgiveness in them.

Jon's heart sank. His entire relationship with Baltsaros seemed doomed to be one long strand of misunderstandings, lies, and personal struggles linked together by small jewel-like moments of clarity. Was it ever going to get easier to love the unpredictable captain?

Love? asked Tom's voice in his head. *That's unwise, ducky.*

Jon frowned at the phantom in his mind; perhaps he'd had too much rum already.

"Baltsaros? What is it?" he asked, disturbed by the man's apprehension.

"It's going to sound far worse than it is, Jon. Believe me when I say this," Baltsaros said and took a long pull from the flask he held, the chased silver flashing with reflected light.

Jon waited silently, his hands curled into fists in his lap.

"There's a beautiful castle built into the mountainside. It has high stained-glass windows and graceful arches covered in colourful mosaics; the inner courtyard is one of the most breathtaking things you will ever see, with its reflecting pools, fountains, and orange trees. The smell alone..." He stopped, a small smile on his face. "That's where I live. Where *we* shall live."

Jon frowned and shook his head.

"So you're really an evil pirate king after all?" he asked, his tone artificially light. He didn't understand why Baltsaros was treating this information with such trepidation; Jon had grown up in a castle, albeit an old decrepit one. Being a king or a lord was a good thing, no?

As he laughed a little harshly, Baltsaros nodded his head.

"Yes, I am indeed king. Of a very, very small kingdom. It's a ridiculous affectation... and not one that I would have chosen myself. I like to think of the island as being the same as my ship... all men and women equal..."

"Baltsaros," Jon whispered. What was the man working up to?

"I never desired to be king..." Baltsaros said finally, looking desperately into Jon's eyes. "...but my wife desired to be queen."

Up on his feet before he realized it, Jon stared down hard at Baltsaros.

Told you so, said Tom, chuckling.

"Wife? When the hell were you going to tell me you were married?" he choked out.

Baltsaros's hands were up in supplication. Jon could see he was saying something, but he was so caught up in the shock of the confession that he couldn't understand the man. It had never crossed his mind that the captain might have a wife.

Baltsaros rose and grabbed at Jon to pull him into his embrace. Jon struggled against him, the other man's more powerful arms trapping him tight.

"Please, Jon. Listen to me. This changes *nothing*. You must understand me," said Baltsaros, his mouth right near Jon's ear.

Jon brought up his knee hard in the captain's groin and gasped in relief as the man released him. He reeled back against the railing, his eyes wide.

Baltsaros groaned; he was bent over and clutching his pearls in his hand. Breathing hard, the captain croaked out a few words.

"That was uncalled for," Baltsaros said, his voice hoarse. When he glanced up at Jon, his face was drawn with pain. "I should have you keelhauled," he joked weakly.

Jon shook his head, the immediate shock of the news beginning to recede.

"When were you planning on telling me?" he asked, furious.

After a moment, the captain scooped up the fallen flask and sat back heavily on the bench, rubbing at his crotch.

"Honestly? If I could have gone our entire lives without ever telling you, I would have. However, I was planning on simply introducing her to you when we arrived," he said, wincing as he shifted slightly on the hard bench. After taking a sip of rum, he held the flask out to Jon.

He just stared at the captain's hand for a moment and then sighed, crossing the planks back towards Baltsaros. Pulling the rum from the older man's grasp, he drained the rest of it in one long gulp. The spicy liquid burned his throat going down, and Jon welcomed the feeling.

"Why would you do that to me?" he asked, his voice harsh.

Baltsaros's eyes went flat for an instant; his habit of dropping all expression when he was attempting to speak plainly was one that Jon had begun to recognize. From his experience it either meant the captain had something worse to say or that he wanted to make sure that Jon understood him fully.

Thankfully, in this case it was the latter.

"You will see when you meet her. It's a marriage of convenience. A political and financial partnership... nothing more. There was no point in telling you ahead of time. I wanted you to see with your own eyes that she holds me in contempt," said Baltsaros quietly. "Especially with your gift, it should be obvious that there is no love lost between us. And, as I said, it changes nothing between you and me."

Jon eyed him a moment; it was about as genuine as Baltsaros got. He turned around and sat back down on the bench, resting his elbows on his knees as he leaned forward, trying to absorb the information.

"Still. Baltsaros... You should have said something. Sometimes I think you have only the vaguest notion of what it means to be honest. Are there no words for honesty or truth in your language?" he said. He heard Baltsaros sigh before the man's warm hand touched his back.

"I'm sorry," said the captain.

No, he's not, said Tom.

Hush. Go away, Jon thought hard at the ghost in his head. He could have sworn that he heard Tom's laughter faintly in the night air. Definitely too much rum.

Baltsaros was looking at him curiously, and Jon just shook his head.

"I'm going to bed," he said. "I'm tired, and I'm trying not to be angry at you." Jon lurched to his feet and took a few steps towards the stairs. He stopped with his hand on the railing.

"Are you coming? I demand restitution for the wrongs you have committed against me," Jon said solemnly.

He was gratified when, a moment later, Baltsaros's quiet steps followed him down.

Katherine cracked the wooden sword hard against Jon's ribs, and he yelped, falling over.

"Gods, woman! You don't have to be so damn rough with me," he said, rubbing the welt on his skin that he knew would soon be a bruise.

Katherine swung the practice sword a few times at him, barely missing his head.

"You think that's rough, young man? Can you picture the mess that a real sword would make of you? Get your guard up. Jon, seriously... You're sloppy," she said, her expression one of amusement.

Jon groaned and pressed his fists against the boards before getting his feet under him. Before she had a chance to react, he sprang forward from his crouch and had her pinned to the deck in an instant, her practice sword spiralling overboard to sink below the choppy green waters. He grinned down at her, but Jon was soon in great pain as she managed to snap her wrist free and jab her stiff fingers at his throat.

He coughed and writhed on the deck as she laughed.

"What? You don't think I learned under Calum as well? I know your tricks, pup. The next time you try to pin me like that, you'll be following that wooden sword overboard," she said, pushing at him with a long-toed bare foot playfully.

When Jon managed to suck enough air into his lungs he started to laugh.

"I hate you," he said, smiling. "You're a terrible excuse for a woman."

Katherine kicked him hard in the side and then sat down on an empty crate, wiping the sweat from her face.

Jon joined her after a moment, thankfully accepting the small bladder of water that she offered. There was not much fresh water left on the ship; every drop counted, and hoarding was met with stiff punishment. Jon looked up to where the captain was watching them with obvious amusement and scowled.

Baltsaros smiled and looked away.

Chuckling softly, Katherine shook her head.

"Goddess, you two are pathetic," she said, smiling.

Jon felt his face get hot. He sat awkwardly for a few moments, frowning down at his hands.

"He told me about his wife," he said and lifted his eyes to watch her face.

Katherine's eyebrows shot up, and she pursed her lips.

"He did? Well, scupper that," the woman said, her gaze flicking up to Baltsaros for a second before her dark-brown eyes settled back on Jon.

He felt himself tense.

"You knew? Gods, of course you knew... Why the hell didn't you tell me? You all know, don't you? Have you all just been laughing at the poor naïve boy this whole time?" he asked, his tone peevish.

Katherine reached over and squeezed his arm.

"Nah... I wasn't laughing. I'm actually surprised he told you already," she said.

"You are?" Jon replied. "Isn't it the kind of thing that you should mention when you're... uh... fucking someone?" he said, feeling uncomfortably crass.

Katherine laughed and leaned her shoulder against his, a friendly touch.

"You are doing way more than just fucking, my dear," she said, her grin sly. "But yes... I would have waited until you met the ice queen herself before telling you I was hitched to a cunt colder than the northern sea. Seeing in person how much they loathe each other would have dulled the shock of the news somewhat, I think. Now you just get to dwell and go all miserable, creating scenarios in your head."

Jon huffed out a short, bitter laugh; the image of Baltsaros and his wife in the marriage bed had already started plaguing his dreams. However, with Katherine backing up what the captain had already claimed, Jon felt slightly better. Maybe Baltsaros was right. Maybe it didn't change anything.

He sighed.

They would be there in a fortnight if the wind and weather held, though the fresh water would only last another week at best. Jon shoved the thought from his mind and stood, flexing his shoulders.

"Find me another sword, woman." he said and ducked when the lithe woman levelled a punch at his head.

Jon was taking a caulk on deck when he heard the first shout. Opening his eyes blearily, Jon looked around, wondering what it was that had awoken him. When he heard nothing further, Jon crossed his arms more firmly over his chest, nudging his head back against the gunnysacks that he had piled in the shade of the sails. No sooner had Jon closed his eyes than he heard another shout. It sounded like one of the cabin boys was yelling.

Jon sat up, blinking sleepily. There it was again; this time Jon heard the words clear as day:

"Ship! Ship off starboard! Sail ho! Sail ho!"

Jon rose to his feet and padded towards the side of the ship to squint at the horizon. True enough, there was a dark smudge in the distance.

A small thrill of excitement shivered through him as it always did when they approached another ship. The crew was down to the barest of rations; the "us or them" mentality that came with attacking other ships would be magnified due to their current vulnerability. There was a good chance that the other ship would be in the same dire straits; perhaps their supplies would be just as low.

Jon glanced up at the captain. Baltsaros stood with the spyglass to his eye, assessing the other ship. After a moment he lowered it, his face serious as he rubbed his jaw in thought. With their reduced crew, dead front gunners, and out-of-commission front starboard carronade, the captain was being cautious.

However, after a moment Jon saw Baltsaros nod at Katherine. The captain's eyes then swept the deck, settling on Jon. With a beckoning hand, Baltsaros called him up to talk over plans.

Baltsaros stared hard at his men. After a long silence, he spoke, his voice ringing out over the assembled crowd.

"We are down to the last of our rations," he said, his dark eyes running over the crew. "This means we go hungry very soon, and we still have over a week to go before we make land. However, there is a ship, a large galleon, just at the horizon. Catching up to her will cost us time... And she may actually have nothing to offer us. Could be that she's in worse shape than we are. So... I leave it to you. What say you, men? Do we take the chance and try our luck with plunder, or do we sail home and tighten our belts?"

Though the captain was unquestionably in charge, it always astonished Jon when he asked his crew to pick their fate. This was the closest thing to equality that Jon had ever seen, and it amazed him that it happened at the behest of a man devoid of a natural moral compass, who only pretended to have an interest in the lives of his men.

After some muttering and nodding, the crowd settled down. Beard was the first to raise his hand. In the tense silence, they all heard the giant speak one word in his booming voice:

"Attack!"

Getting to the other ship actually proved to be somewhat difficult. They lost nearly a day tacking back and forth against the strong headwind. Jon spent the time reviewing again and again the role he would play in the initial attack. Since their numbers were so low, they would all have to play multiple parts. Jon, his worth deemed unusually high by the biased captain, would hang back as the crew boarded the ship; he was to man the two remaining carronades along the starboard side.

Powder, pound, ball, light, and duck were the instructions given to him by his fellow gunners. He felt a little ill.

Finally, the other ship was close enough to hail. She was a huge, multi-tiered thing, four masts and an aft castle that towered high above the quarterdeck on their own ship. The ship was heavy in the water and unwieldy; it boasted of a cargo hull full of something.

"Ahoy!" yelled Katherine when the two ships were close enough. There were no men on deck, and the ship was strangely quiet. Katherine waited a moment before repeating her cry. The second time brought about some movement in the stern of the ship, and they spotted a man scurrying for cover behind barrels.

"Go away!" was the shouted reply.

Jon frowned. Something felt off. Katherine was facing the captain, discussing the use of grappling hooks, when Jon spotted someone else on board the heavy ship. The figure ducked back belowdecks but not before Jon had seen the bright red, weeping rash on the man's cheeks. He swallowed hard, his heart sinking.

"Captain," he said loudly.

Baltsaros turned to look at him, his stark brows high.

"We have to get away from that ship," continued Jon nervously.

Frowning, the captain closed the gap between them, coming to stand next to Jon.

"What do you see, Jon?" he asked, looking out at the galleon.

"I think the men on board are infected," he replied. "It looks like the weeping plague."

Baltsaros closed his eyes, the disappointment plain on his face. It was all for naught; they would only bring death to the *Baal's Heart* if they boarded the other ship.

He was startled a moment later when Baltsaros's eyes snapped open, his hands coming down on Jon's shoulders.

"Your mother died of the weeping plague, didn't she?" he asked Jon, his fingers digging into the younger man.

Jon nodded.

"Did you contract it?" Baltsaros asked, staring at him intently.

Jon frowned.

"Yes. But a mild form. Why?" he replied.

With a laugh, Baltsaros dragged him forward and kissed his forehead.

"You're immune," he said happily.

Jon tied the rowboat to the end of the rope ladder and heaved the heavy bag over his shoulder. He made his way carefully up the side of the hull and dropped down over the high gunwale.

A few feet away were the two men they had been communicating with. Covered in horrible, weeping sores and obviously skeptical about Jon's immunity to the disease, they kept their distance. The younger of the two, a swarthy man with dark curling hair and a deep frown on his high brow spoke first.

"I'm Malik," he said hoarsely, his thin lips blistered from the disease. He pointed to his companion, a middle-aged man with ashen hair and a slightly amused look on his face, one brow raised in curiosity. "This is Nathaniel."

The older man sketched a quick bow.

"Welcome aboard the *Maiden's Bounty*," said Nathaniel, a touch sardonically. "We would have rolled out the red carpet for you, but, as you can see, we're feeling rather poorly at the moment."

The man had friendly hazel eyes and a slight gap between his front teeth. Jon found himself smiling back; the man was immediately likeable. With a grunt, Jon dumped the burlap sack down on the boards.

"Well, I'll have you mended in no time," he said. The sack was full of ointments and tinned poultices that the captain had made up. Jon hoped it was enough. "In return for some supplies," he added.

Malik crossed his arms.

"You can have anything you want. We won't need it soon enough," he said, fatalistically.

Jon frowned and looked around.

"Where is the rest of the crew?" he asked. A vessel of this size would have a crew upwards of two hundred men.

Nathaniel laughed harshly.

"You're looking at it," he said.

Jon's eyebrows shot up, and his heart thudded hard in his chest. All of a sudden Baltsaros's insistence that he was immune to the horrible plague was a slim comfort. What if the captain was wrong? As he attempted to still his fear, Jon looked from one man to the other.

"All right. Let's see what you got."

A few hours later, Jon yanked off his gloves and waved to Beard across the water. The huge man started pulling the rope that was tied to the stern of the small rowboat, now piled high with supplies enough to last the crew for the rest of the journey home.

When he turned back to the two men, Jon was dismayed to see that Malik was slumped against the mast, obviously suffering greatly. Baltsaros had explained that the disease was transmitted by tiny, invisible creatures in the fluid that oozed out of the red sores. Once a person was infected, the disease progressed rapidly, normally killing within five days though often sooner.

Malik and Nathaniel had been sick for four days so far; Jon hoped it was not too late to save them. The fact that they were still alive seemed to point to the men being resistant to the disease; perhaps they were part of the small percentage, like Jon, that wouldn't be carried off by the plague.

Nearly a week passed. Thankfully, the captain had been right about Jon's immunity because he didn't fall ill himself as he nursed the two men back to health. Malik, being sicker, had a close brush with death, but he soon recovered.

When Jon ushered them aboard the *Baal's Heart*, he wasn't prepared for the thunderous cheering and applause that met him as he stepped up and over the side of the ship.

As Katherine explained with a dimpled smile, not only had he saved the lives of Baltsaros's men, he had made two valuable additions: Nathaniel was an experienced cartographer, and Malik had just finished his apprenticeship as shipwright.

Blushing, Jon accepted the tankard of dark beer and grinned sheepishly. When he looked up he saw Baltsaros atop a large crate, his arms crossed over his chest and a proud smile on his face. The captain nodded.

Good job.

Jon felt warm all over, and he blinked hard a few times to dry the tears that had sprung up in his eyes at the unexpected and hearty welcome. As he held his cup aloft, Jon looked over the crowd and smiled wide.

"May the wind fill our sails, and the calm waters spur us on quickly!" he yelled. "Landward ho!" He drank down a great gulp of beer, some of it running down his chest. The voices of all the men rose up as one.

"Landward ho!"

CHAPTER 25
THE TIES THAT BIND

The main difference between a cat and a lie is that a cat only has nine lives.

— MARK TWAIN

Jon looked down at himself and sighed.

"Is this really necessary?" he asked. "I feel ridiculous." He lifted up the corner of the sleeveless blue tunic, its long hem decorated with strange abstract black and gold shapes.

Baltsaros frowned at him and straightened the collar over the loose, gathered white shirt underneath.

"Yes," he said simply and began to tie a silken black sash around the younger man's waist.

Jon obligingly moved his arms out of the way and watched the captain's face as he dressed him in the strange outfit. Ever since the island of Madierus had come into view the previous evening, Baltsaros had been acting preoccupied. While everyone else aboard seemed to be in a near-frenzy of excitement, the captain just seemed weary and distracted.

Jon chewed the inside of his lip.

"I never thought I would say this... But I'd rather be naked," he said, smiling.

While it was said in an attempt to lighten the captain's mood, it was largely true. After so much time spent wearing nothing but a pair of thin trousers, Jon felt hot and uncomfortable in so many layers. However, he was pleased that his jest made Baltsaros look up and grin, an easy humour glinting in his dark-brown eyes.

Jon loved the captain's face. One minute, it was a stark, almost cruel landscape; the next, it was creased into a charmingly guileless smile. The corners of Baltsaros's eyes crinkled attractively when he was amused, the lines accentuated by a long life of squinting against the bright sun while at sea. Jon could see that Baltsaros had shaved close; the skin of his chin would be soft if Jon were to reach out and touch it now. Jon knew that later today it would be rough like sandpaper and leave red marks on his neck when Baltsaros kissed him there, and he *would* kiss him. The captain had reiterated this morning that nothing would change between them, that their relationship was sacrosanct as far as he was concerned. Jon held on to that promise like a man with a purpose; he would be damned if he would stand for anything else.

"I doubt very much that you would like to appear in the nude in front of my court. Are you so proud of the stripes you have earned?" Baltsaros said, roughly grabbing Jon's backside with a large hand and squeezing.

With a gasp, Jon leaned into Baltsaros to try to escape the pain; it had been two days since his "punishment", and he was still incredibly tender. Jon felt a shudder of desire go through him with the sensation, and he heard the captain laugh softly against him. Eyes closed, Jon replayed in his mind the lesson he had learned.

~

Jon frowned.

"You don't think you deserve to be punished for dropping one of my books overboard?" asked Baltsaros, his teeth sharp and eyes dark. "That one in particular will be especially hard to replace."

Jon was confused because his senses were telling him that the captain was exaggerating the book's worth in an attempt to justify punishing him. Baltsaros's face was angry, but there was the barest hint of humour in his hooded glare.

Nervous, Jon licked his lips and shook his head.

What are you up to?

"I already said I was sorry. It was an accident," he said calmly.

While the captain had playfully penalised him in the past for what he had deemed were minor infractions, the punishments meted out were always in the form of long drawn-out sessions of almost torturous sex where Jon was held on the brink of orgasm, leaving him a shuddering, sobbing wreck in the aftermath.

This was different.

Baltsaros had something else in mind, and it both terrified and excited Jon. He was willing to submit to Baltsaros but only within reason. The problem was that he and the captain had different ideas of what was considered reasonable.

"I disagree, my love," said Baltsaros. Jon immediately felt a little helpless. *My love.* The words always took away part of his resolve, though meaningless they were; the captain knew this and took full advantage of it. "You disobeyed me in that you brought the book outside to begin with. I told you that the pages were fragile."

Jon shook his head.

"How am I supposed to keep track of all your ridiculous rules?" he asked, his dark brows high.

Immediately he regretted using those words. Baltsaros's face took on the cast of real anger for a split second. Knowing how talented he was at digging his own grave, Jon pressed his lips together and waited silently. Though the mischievous glint returned to Baltsaros's eyes a heartbeat later, Jon grew incredibly wary of what the unpredictable man had in mind.

After taking a step back, Baltsaros crossed his arms.

"Strip," the captain said, his voice quietly authoritative.

With his head tilted slightly at Baltsaros, Jon fumbled at his belt; starting to feel some anticipation break through his reservations, he stepped out of his pants and started to approach the captain. However, Baltsaros held up a hand and stopped him.

"*Kneel.*" It was a hissed order. The captain's face was set in dangerous lines.

Jon's breath hitched in his throat, and he dropped immediately to his knees on the soft rug. A little relieved when the captain smiled, Jon was confused when he didn't come any closer.

Instead, Baltsaros walked to the chest at the foot of the bed and opened it up, looking for something; Jon watched him curiously, heart beating swiftly in his chest. Finally, Baltsaros straightened and came towards Jon with something in his hands. It looked like the captain was holding a few bundles of something red and a piece of dark material.

Though he began to turn around in place on his knees as Baltsaros stepped behind him, Jon stopped when the captain made a sharp, discouraging sound.

What is this? thought Jon, excitement and trepidation making his pulse race further.

He shivered slightly when he felt Baltsaros's hand on his shoulder and was surprised when he heard the other man sink to his knees behind him.

"It's time for a lesson in obedience," purred the captain in Jon's ear.

His throat went dry, and he felt his body react as strongly to the words as if Baltsaros's hands were on his cock instead of just painting shapes with his fingertips on Jon's back. Surprised at his own breathless desire, he nodded quickly.

"Good boy," said Baltsaros and kissed Jon lightly on the side of his neck, right where his pulse was jumping under his skin.

The captain slowly stroked his hands down Jon's arms, and then forcibly bent them behind his back. Jon's first instinct was to struggle, but he quashed it, curious to see what Baltsaros intended.

Good boy.

The words had caused a warm sensation in his loins, and he realized that yes, he wanted to be a good boy. The thought was strangely thrilling.

Behind Jon's back, Baltsaros positioned his arms and hands so that his forearms were parallel to each other, his fingers clasped around his elbows. Jon then felt Baltsaros move one hand away to start looping something around his left wrist.

Jon gasped; the captain was tying him up. A bit of panic was added to the symphony of emotions playing inside him, and Jon cleared his throat.

"W-what are you doing?" he asked timidly. Baltsaros didn't answer but passed the rope around again. Jon felt the bundle of it brush against his back softly, and he shivered again. Baltsaros slid the rope up over his shoulder, the length tickling him gently; it was a sharp contrast to how it bound his arms tightly, biting into his skin.

Working in silence, the captain brought the rope up over his other shoulder, beside his neck, and back down again. Slowly twisting and knotting as he went, Baltsaros's strong hands stroked Jon's skin each time before he slid the rope into place.

Jon found himself holding his breath and releasing it in time to Baltsaros's short caresses. The red hempen rope became a knotted net that covered him from shoulder to hip, binding him tight. The panic he had felt earlier started to diminish as Baltsaros's hands lulled him with their steady, rhythmic movements. However, when Baltsaros paused to tie the soft, dark strip of material over Jon's eyes, fear robbed him of breath for a moment.

"Baltsaros, no! This isn't ok. I'm not ok with this. Untie me. I can't breathe. Please!" he panted, a kind of hysteria gripping him as he started to struggle.

Baltsaros's hands came around him quickly, holding him still. Jon could feel the captain's broad chest against his back and his warm breath on his neck. Robbed of his sight, he had an increased awareness of Baltsaros's hands on his skin; in the warm, dark silence, Jon trembled as the tension slowly leached out of his body, held there by the man who knew exactly how to defeat him with pleasure.

When Jon felt calmer, the captain gently released him, returning to the patterns of rope he was creating. No longer fighting his bonds, Jon felt a curious peace settle over him; Baltsaros was showing him yet another way to surrender.

With his head bowed, Jon breathed a shuddering breath; the experience was pushing his emotions to the surface. He felt vulnerable, subjugated—completely under the control of a powerful man for a single purpose: Jon knew he existed in this moment only to please Baltsaros. He was at the mercy of the captain's whims... And it was intensely arousing.

Jon moaned softly when Baltsaros's hands began passing between his legs, pushing them further apart to wrap his thighs in lengths of rope. Aching for the captain's touch, Jon trembled when Baltsaros finally reached around him to softly stroke the stiffening cock hanging between his legs.

The captain soon had him coaxed to full hardness, and Jon began to thrust his hips, pushing himself with eagerness through Baltsaros's fingers. However, Jon whimpered when the captain stopped his efforts short.

"Baltsaros..." he started but then tensed as he felt a length of rope being passed behind his testicles and around the base of his cock. He held his breath as Baltsaros pulled it tight and looped it around once more, tying it off.

With a gasp at the sensation, Jon felt his cock, held ramrod stiff by the rope constricting the blood flow, begin to throb in time to his heartbeat. When a long time seemed to go by with no further contact from Baltsaros, Jon began to worry anew. The only thing he could hear of the other man was his slow, measured breathing. What was he doing?

Jon panted hard and leaned forward, frustrated. Was Baltsaros just staring at Jon? The ropes binding Jon were unyielding and the silence echoed on. Was this the punishment? When he rocked back on his hips, his bonds tightened around his thighs and chest and he gritted his teeth.

Baltsaros's hand was suddenly on him, pushing him forward.

Losing his balance, Jon landed on his chest and cheek with a grunt. He raised his hips slightly to adjust his cock beneath him, and the carpet scratched at the engorged head, causing him to groan from the sensation.

"Please, Baltsaros," he said softly. He heard the captain chuckle quietly.

Baltsaros spread Jon's legs wide on the carpet, and he held his breath in tense anticipation; but, when something cold and hard touched his skin, sliding up the back of his thigh and tapping his left buttock gently, Jon's eyes flew open in shock behind the blindfold.

"Please, *my lord*," said the captain, correcting him quietly, a natural edge of command in his voice.

"You want me to call you lord?" asked Jon quickly, confused. It seemed a ridiculous request, but whatever it was that Baltsaros held in his hand struck his skin a second later; the pain was intense, and the bound man cried out in surprise and fear. He coughed and panted hard, squirming on the carpeted floor.

"Well?" asked Baltsaros.

Jon swallowed and stammered.

"Is that it? You're my lord? Please, I don't underst—" His words were cut off when the cold thing cracked hard against the sensitive back of his thigh. Jon yelled loud; the place where he was hit was a thin line of agony, like he had been cut with a knife. It dawned on him suddenly what he was supposed to say.

Aye, that's it. Don't think, lovey. Just obey, came the voice of the phantom in Jon's head.

He pressed his lips together to hold back the sob that threatened to spill from his throat. Jon shook off the pain and whispered hoarsely:

"Please... my lord."

In response, Baltsaros laughed and stroked the switch down the curve of Jon's spine giving him a moment's respite, and tapped again at the meat of his backside, as if testing the target for resilience.

Jon whimpered.

"You were disobedient," said Baltsaros. "You were disrespectful of my belongings."

CRACK! CRACK!

Jon choked on his scream, pressing his face hard into the carpet. His skin was on fire. The captain hit him again hard on the buttocks and the backs of his thighs, and Jon felt frantic from the pain.

"Please, my lord!" he yelled. "Please!" What else could he say?

The switch slid into the cleft of Jon's ass, gliding coldly against his perineum before tracing the bottom edge of his buttock. The flesh there felt inflamed.

"Please, my lord," he said softly, panting. The weapon left his skin and he groaned in relief.

The heat from his welts and the adrenaline pumping through him were stimulating him in a strange way. He had feared the initial pain when the switch came down, but when it faded, Jon began to anticipate the next strike. He found himself wondering how much he could take and whether Baltsaros would test his limits. Jon felt a thrill go through him at the thought. He swallowed hard a moment later when he heard the captain drop back down to his knees.

"Please, my lord," he repeated, his voice weak.

His ankle was grasped hard in a big hand, and Baltsaros bent it back to secure it to the bindings around Jon's thigh, doing the same with Jon's right leg. Jon shifted on the rug; he was almost completely immobilized, legs splayed open on the floor.

He tensed, waiting for the captain to do something, anything to him... But nothing happened. Grinding his teeth in frustration, Jon turned his head, questing blindly behind him. All he could hear at first was that Baltsaros's breathing had gotten heavier. When a moment later he realized that he could now detect the shushing noise of skin passing over skin, Jon's eyebrows rose, and his heart skipped over itself in his chest.

Baltsaros was pleasuring himself.

The realization was both shocking and intoxicating, and Jon's cock surged harder in reaction. With his legs spread wide, he was perfectly exposed. The captain would be looking down at him, at the opening between his legs and at the markings that would be livid against the pale skin of his thighs and buttocks.

Jon closed his eyes and tilted his hips back a tiny bit, imagining Baltsaros's dark eyes focused on him. Not knowing whether Baltsaros was going to fuck him was driving Jon crazy. All pain was forgotten. He pictured the captain's thick cock and the man's hand sliding over it. The head would be purplish and stretched full, shiny with the pearls of fluid that would be beading at the tip.

Jon groaned and shuddered. The sound of Baltsaros stroking his cock got louder and faster, and Jon could feel the presence of the man near his skin. When he shifted his hips up again, presenting himself to the captain, Jon licked his lips and waited.

Baltsaros let out a low growl, and Jon felt something hot hit his skin and run down the cleft of his buttocks, getting cooler as it dripped onto his testicles. Jon gasped when he realized what was happening. Another spurt of hot fluid landed on his flesh. Then another.

Baltsaros was breathing fast and hard as he spilled his seed onto Jon's spread ass.

Jon moaned; it was incredible that something that should have been a degrading act was instantly and agonizingly erotic to him. With a deep grunt, Baltsaros shot a last jet of cum directly against Jon's puckered opening and collapsed forward, his chest landing on the younger man's bound ankles.

Jon panted against the pain of Baltsaros's weight on his stretched limbs, but the delicious contact of the captain's cock on him was keenly pleasurable as the man stroked the head of it through the cooling mess between his legs for a moment, spreading it over his skin.

Too soon, Baltsaros pushed away though not to leave Jon cold on the floor. Instead, the captain's hands swiftly began unravelling the pattern of knots, and Jon gasped as his twisted limbs were quickly released. He felt shaky and confused, aroused yet distraught. The blindfold was pulled away from his eyes, and he looked in despair at Baltsaros.

The man's face was slightly flushed as he pulled Jon back up to his knees to undo the ropes binding his chest and finally his arms. Jon felt like a rag doll, limbs tingling and weak.

Baltsaros's dark eyes met his, and Jon felt a little breathless at the emotion that flitted there: a deeply possessive adoration.

Jon's heart ached.

"You enjoyed punishing me?" he asked quietly, reaching out to touch the captain's cheek.

Baltsaros leaned into his hand, smiling.

"Oh Jon, very much so. You were exquisite," he said, his voice affectionate. Baltsaros slid his fingers over the dented, red markings on Jon's chest, left behind by the tight bindings. "You were perfect," he said, his voice soft.

Jon felt curiously proud.

When Baltsaros's hand finally closed over Jon's hypersensitive cock, still bound tight with rope, he hissed between his teeth at the contact. Arching his back, Jon gratefully submitted to Baltsaros's ministrations. The captain curled around behind him and pulled Jon back against his chest, stroking him swiftly and firmly.

"You're a good boy," Baltsaros murmured into Jon's ear, and he was swept up into the waves of his own shattering pleasure.

~

After a quick kiss and a promise to look for each other in the coming days, Jon parted company with Katherine and ran after Baltsaros once they had made it to shore. The heels of his boots sounded loud on the smooth boards of the pier rising above the beach, and Jon longed to remove his uncomfortable footwear to feel the white sand between his toes.

The island was every bit as beautiful as Baltsaros had described, and Jon was already in love.

However, there was no time to explore. Baltsaros's wife, having been notified of their arrival, had sent a carriage to retrieve them, and it stood waiting in the shade of two giant fan palms. The carriage had already been loaded up with the chest containing their belongings, and the white horses nickered softly to each other as Jon approached.

The captain, with an air of strained civility, held the door open for Jon and then followed in after him. The inside of the carriage was stuffy and smelled of wood that had been left out in the damp too long. Jon raised his eyebrows at Baltsaros, but the older man just squinted out the window.

"Welcome to my city, Jon," he said softly.

Jon followed his gaze and gasped in amazement as they passed under a tunnel of greenery, emerging into a scene from a fairy tale.

It didn't resemble any city he had ever seen. The houses and shops were set far back from the wide, cobbled street, some almost invisible beneath the foliage. What he *could* see made his eyes widen; the low buildings had smoothly curved wooden walls, not unlike the hulls of boats. Windows were round, and the doors were painted in the same colours as the flowers that seemed to burst out from every corner.

"That is the *Grog Blossom* tavern," said Baltsaros, pointing a long finger at a squat, wide building with a flower mosaic around the entrance. "You'll find Katherine there if you ever need her. Her wife serves a wonderfully brewed white beer of her own design. I hope that she has some yet." Baltsaros smiled.

Jon could see through the tavern windows that it was a large, airy space; the entire back of the building seemed to be an open, covered patio, strung with what looked like colourful lanterns.

Baltsaros kept pointing out shops and houses, once even opening the door to lean out and shout a greeting to someone. When the captain sat back down, he was smiling wide; some of the tension that had been weighing him down seemed to have melted away as he was reunited with the beautiful island. However, as they approached the graceful castle at the foot of the volcano, Baltsaros's eyes once more turned cold.

Jon was filled with dread and not knowing what to expect had him feeling on edge.

The carriage stopped at a beautiful arched portico, and Baltsaros looked at Jon thoughtfully. The captain opened his mouth to say something but decided otherwise and instead just cupped the back of Jon's head, pulling him in for a soft kiss. When he broke away, Baltsaros stared hard into Jon's eyes, his gaze flicking back and forth as if testing his resolve.

"Jon. Don't worry. Please. This is my home, and I want it to be yours too," he said gently, his fingers squeezing Jon's neck warmly.

Unfortunately, Baltsaros's words just compounded Jon's fear. He had the sinking feeling that his relationship with the captain would be tested shortly. Wanting to appear confident, Jon nodded quickly and took a deep breath.

A moment later, they were standing in the middle of a beautiful courtyard.

Baltsaros had not been exaggerating; it was a small paradise in itself with its perfumed orange trees and bubbling fountains. The columns surrounding it were so high and light with their peaked arches that they seemed terribly fragile, like lace. Small circular patterns like the one on the coverlet in their quarters aboard *Baal's Heart* were picked out in blue and gold mosaics everywhere.

Jon was enthralled when he saw the big gold and red fish swimming under flat green leaves in a star-shaped shallow pool in the middle of the courtyard. He stopped to watch them a moment; however, with a hand on Jon's arm, Baltsaros tugged him forward as he took in the breathtaking sights.

Jon couldn't understand why anyone would ever want to leave this place.

They crossed the courtyard and came to a long, wide flight of white marble steps and entered the castle through high, narrow peaked doors with stained-glass starbursts in yellows and blues high above their heads.

"The woman does have taste," said Baltsaros, looking at Jon's round eyes with a wry grin. "I will allow her that much."

As he turned his head every which way, Jon somehow managed in his distraction to miss the fact that they were walking towards a dais at the far end of the great hall. When he felt Baltsaros shake him slightly, Jon faced forward and gasped at the sight before him.

Atop the low platform, flanked by sculptures of curved dolphins, was a woman and a young girl standing in front of two elaborate thrones.

The woman was beautiful.

Though obviously older than Baltsaros, her lovely, pale skin retained the smoothness of youth. Softly waved blond hair fell below her shoulders and framed a heart-shaped face; her full lips, the colour of raspberries, were turned up in a serene smile. Standing with a graceful elegance, hands clasped in front of her, she silently watched the two men approach and stop at the foot of the stairs.

Jon turned his gaze to the girl standing next to her. She was the prettiest child Jon had ever seen, a petite, shy-looking creature of five or six with long dark hair and huge blue eyes. Her expression was timid as she stared back at Jon, her small white teeth biting softly at her pouting bottom lip.

Can ye see? asked Tom.

Jon frowned. His eyes slid back to the woman.

"Hello, husband," she said, her blue-green eyes cold as she looked down at the captain.

"Hello, wife," replied Baltsaros, his voice expressionless.

Jon felt a little strange suddenly, like a cold wind was blowing against his neck, raising goosebumps on his arms.

What do ye see? repeated the ghost in his head.

Jon stared at the woman. She was looking over their shoulders, searching for something.

For someone.

"Where is he?" the woman asked, her nostrils flaring slightly with what Jon read as trepidation. There was something about the curve of her jaw and the height of her brow that reminded him of something.

"Abetha, Eloise... I'm terribly sorry," said Baltsaros softly. "Tom was lost at sea."

Jon's vision began to swim. He watched as Abetha put a graceful hand to her mouth, her blue-green eyes wide and startled. Her eyes. Eyes that Jon had looked into a thousand times, eyes that had often winked and narrowed in amusement at him. Eyes that had looked deep into Jon's with an emotion that tore him apart. Tom's eyes.

See?

Jon slowly turned his head to the captain, his mouth dry; his mind was staggering over itself in a hurry to make sense of it. Baltsaros was watching him, his face devoid of expression.

As he blinked back furious tears, Jon stared back at the man for a moment longer before turning on his heel and walking quickly out of the castle.

~

Baltsaros watched Jon's departure and turned back to his wife.

She stared at him with narrowed eyes.

"You were to keep him safe," she said, her voice strangely calm despite the fury in her eyes.

Baltsaros frowned and dismissed her by going down on one knee and opening his arms, his gaze fond as he looked at Eloise. The girl smiled and ran down the stairs, her little shoes clattering on the stairs. She threw herself into Baltsaros's arms and hugged him tight. He knew that the news of her brother's death wouldn't greatly affect her; Tom had been a near stranger to her, a brother in concept only.

"How's my little wildflower?" he asked; though his affection for the girl was real enough, he found it useful that Eloise's love for him rankled Abetha. It was such a petty thing but important if he wished to turn the girl against her mother in the future.

"You've gotten so tall!" he exclaimed, hugging her back.

She giggled against him, this exciting and charming father figure she only saw for three months out of the year.

He looked up into Abetha's angry eyes and patted Eloise's back softly.

"Why don't you go on and play in the nursery, my darling. We shall see each other at supper, yes?" he said in a cheerful voice.

The little girl pulled away and looked at him lovingly with her big blue eyes before obediently running off.

Baltsaros stood, dusting off the knee of his soft black pants.

"He was a grown man, Abetha," he said as he watched the woman he called his wife sit down on her gaudy throne.

She frowned at him.

"How do I know you're not lying, Baltsaros?" She asked, "We both know how fond you are of bending the truth. Tell me, did he truly die at sea, or did he perish at your hands?" She turned her head to the left and gestured to the servant standing there. A moment later, another servant quickly stepped into the throne room with two goblets on a tray.

Baltsaros accepted his with a nod and slowly ascended the stairs.

"I promised you that no harm would come to him. That is my only failure: making a promise I couldn't possibly keep. Tom fell overboard during a storm. That is all," he said. Baltsaros took a sip of the rich red wine in his cup and stared down at Abetha.

She looked piercingly at him, turning her own cup in her hands before drinking some down. She then turned her head towards the great doors.

"I take it that this boy you brought into my home is a replacement for my son?" she asked, her quiet voice contrasting with the bitterness of her words. "He didn't know Tom was your stepson, did he? How thoughtful of you to present the information to him thusly. Tell me, Baltsaros... Does your young lover know you are a monster?"

Baltsaros frowned as he looked towards the doors.

"Yes, wife," he said. "He does."

CHAPTER 26
IN ALL HONESTY

Baltsaros walked slowly down the steps and crossed the paving stones to the pond in the middle of the sunny courtyard. He eyed the boots discarded on the ground before sitting down on the wide stone ledge surrounding the water.

Baltsaros reached his hand out and placed it on the side of Jon's head, stroking the soft brown curls. Jon was lying prone on the edge of the raised pond, his blue eyes tracking the motion of the koi swimming under the lily pads. At Baltsaros's touch, he closed his eyes, and a furrow appeared between his brows.

With a sigh Baltsaros felt something he rarely encountered: shame. How could he explain to Jon that he had kept up the lie because he, unaccountably, had found himself unable to speak of Tom? That he had left it this long only because he knew that he would be *forced* to reveal the truth? Initially the lie had simply been used to keep the sheltered young man from bolting... But he had kept it up. Why? Had he not wanted Jon to think less of him?

He frowned and bowed his head. Baltsaros felt off-balance. Jon's words came back to him:

You might not actually know when you're suffering. You're so fucking damaged...

His hand was trembling slightly. He closed his eyes and breathed deep, reaching for that calm place that was always within reach and found that it was smaller and further away than it had ever been. When he opened his eyes again, he saw that Jon was watching him.

"Do you want to see our room?" asked Baltsaros quietly after a moment. Baltsaros saw that there was recrimination in Jon's eyes as he stared at the captain, but it was eclipsed by a profound weariness.

Finally looking away, Jon pushed himself up off the ledge, stooping to retrieve his boots before motioning to Baltsaros to lead the way.

Baltsaros stood and walked swiftly to the groin-vaulted, covered walkway on the left of the main entrance. Not wishing to subject Jon to Abetha's venom, he took a different route that circumvented the throne room, leading him to what he considered his wing of the castle.

With the silent Jon padding along behind him, Baltsaros made his way to the spiral staircase and climbed two floors. When they reached the landing, Baltsaros pulled open the heavy red door and saw with a frown that his wife had not wasted any resources airing or sweeping the long hallway. He guessed that his chambers had not even been readied for his arrival.

Petty witch, he thought.

Jon followed him down the hallway to the big doors on the right. After opening them, he saw that his suspicions were confirmed. The sitting room that fronted his bedchambers was stale and dusty. The only saving grace was that everything was covered in white sheets.

Jon passed him and looked around curiously, dropping his boots to the ground.

Baltsaros reached for the bell-pull to summon a servant and then walked to the large windows, yanking back the thick red velvet curtain. Sunlight streamed into the room, bringing the air alive with floating dust motes.

Raising his eyebrows at Baltsaros, Jon finally spoke.

"That woman really despises you," he said.

Nodding, Baltsaros crossed the room and threw open the doors to his bedchamber. He opened the curtains and started pulling the white dustsheets off the huge four-poster feather bed. Hearing Jon enter the room, Baltsaros turned to watch his reaction.

His eyes wide, Jon walked towards the bed. He reached out and touched the carvings on the tall posts. There were hundreds of fanciful and grotesque figures carved into the hardwood: mermaids, centaurs, giants, skeletons, and other fanciful creatures, all rendered in exquisite detail. Jon looked back at Baltsaros.

"This is... amazing. Who carved it?" he asked in awe.

"I did," said Baltsaros. "I started it the year I claimed this island as my own."

Jon frowned and turned away, stroking his finger down the flank of a tree nymph. After a moment, he spoke softly.

"You said he had no mother," he said, dropping his hand. His accusation was coloured by melancholy. The captain could hear the meaning underneath: *why do you enjoy lying to me?*

Baltsaros wanted to pull Jon into his embrace, to kill the pain with his kisses, but he knew if he tried he would be rebuffed. He looked towards the door when he heard footsteps and excused himself.

After telling the maids to take care of airing and cleaning the sitting room, he walked back to the bedroom and shut the doors behind him. Jon was at the window, gazing down at the gardens below.

"When I said that the devil pushed him out, it was… an exaggeration of what I consider the truth. Abetha has never been a mother to those children, Jon; and, she barely knew Tom. It wasn't a complete lie," he said, hoping his answer would mollify the younger man.

Jon turned to look at Baltsaros, his face twisted in scorn.

"Not a complete lie?" he said, taking a step towards Baltsaros. "Not a *complete* lie? What part of 'don't fucking lie to me' do you *not understand?*" The last words were a strangled shout.

Jon's hands were at the black sash around his waist, untying it as he took another step towards the older man.

Baltsaros tilted his head and frowned. Suddenly Jon came at him, his leg sweeping Baltsaros's feet from under him before he had a chance to step back. When he landed hard on the floor on his back, Baltsaros grunted and then coughed out his breath as Jon fell on top of him.

The two men struggled against each other, but Jon somehow had the advantage; Calum had taught the boy well. Baltsaros soon found himself lying on the handwoven rug on his stomach, his hands tied tightly behind him with the silk sash.

In all honesty, he hadn't fought very hard.

Jon yanked off one of the captain's boots and then the other, and Baltsaros gasped when what felt like Jon's knife slid coldly against his ankle.

Tom's knife.

He lifted his head and tried to see behind him. In dismay he realized that Jon was cutting through his pant leg. It was completely outrageous, and in just a few minutes, Jon had cut most of Baltsaros's clothing off, slicing the captain's skin a few times in the process.

Baltsaros closed his eyes and waited for what he knew would follow.

However, when he heard the bed creak, he frowned. He lifted his head, turning to face it, and saw that Jon was lying on his side watching Baltsaros over the edge of the mattress as he tapped the side of the blade against his cheek.

The young man's eyes were steely grey as he glared down at Baltsaros.

"Jon?" asked Baltsaros, confused. He'd expected Jon to take his anger out on his body, a mock rape to pay the captain back for his lies.

"So you really were fucking your son," Jon said simply.

Baltsaros groaned and closed his eyes, pressing his forehead down on the rug.

"Stepson, Jon. Not of my loins," he replied. "He was as much my son as Reginald was your father." When he looked up again at Jon, he was nodding thoughtfully.

"Why?" he asked, his tone challenging.

"Why what, Jon? Why was I fucking Tom?" he asked, starting to feel annoyed. He hated saying that name now; it brought with it the thrum of a surprising hurt found deep within him, one that brought up questions he didn't wish to think of. "It's... complicated. What was initially an attempt by Tom to wound his mother turned into something else entirely," he finally replied.

Something good.

Jon laughed.

"You want me to believe that Tom seduced *you?*" he asked, incredulous.

Baltsaros shrugged as well as he could.

Jon narrowed his eyes.

"Can you please untie me? I feel foolish speaking to you from the floor," asked Baltsaros, flexing his arms to test the silk binding his hands.

Jon shook his head.

"I like you right where you are," he replied, dancing the blade's tip over the side of the wooden box holding the thick mattress. "Why should I believe *anything* you say?" he asked, but Baltsaros could see that Jon's anger was starting to peter out.

"You shouldn't," replied Baltsaros truthfully. "I've given you no cause to trust me."

Jon laughed again, an ugly little sound.

"But... This is the last of the lies," Baltsaros added quietly.

Jon pushed himself up and sat with his legs crossed, looking down at Baltsaros with a thoughtful expression.

"Tell me, my love... Am I lying? What are your canny senses telling you?" asked Baltsaros. He put his head back down on the scratchy rug, his neck sore from looking up at Jon on the bed.

"Absolutely nothing," said Jon, candidly. "Baltsaros, was Tom even a slave?" he asked after a moment.

"Yes. Now untie me. Please," said Baltsaros and waited silently. He heard a sigh and was gratified when Jon climbed down off the bed. With a quick slice of the knife, Baltsaros was free. He sat up and rubbed his wrists. "Thank you," he said, and Jon nodded.

The captain stood, pulling the remains of his clothing off. As he looked down sadly at the shredded material, he shook his head.

"I really wish you hadn't felt the destruction of my clothes necessary," he said with a sigh and turned to Jon.

The young man had returned to his place on the bed, and after a moment Baltsaros climbed onto the mattress to join him. He was astounded when Jon laid his head against his shoulder. He drew his arm around him, and a warm feeling spread through Baltsaros's chest.

As if sensing the captain's relief, Jon shook his head.

"I haven't forgiven you," he muttered.

Baltsaros smiled. He ran his fingers over Jon's arm, tracing the shape of his muscles through the thin cotton of the white shirt.

"Yes," Baltsaros continued, wishing to dispel his misgivings. "Tom was most definitely a slave. An unknown party kidnapped him when he was seven years old and held him for ransom, but unfortunately, there was no money to free him. Tom's father was a lord, but only in title; the money had long been spent. The kidnappers, disappointed with the failure of their plans, then sold Tom in the slave markets; no one knew what happened to the young boy afterwards. Tom's father took to drinking, eventually hanging himself after a number of years," said Baltsaros, his voice grim. He stroked Jon's side slowly and continued.

"The rest of Tom's history with me you basically know, and it is the truth. He was seventeen when I found him, and it took almost half a year for him to tell me of his parentage. He believed his parents had abandoned the search for him... And in truth, they had. However, I decided to find them for myself. I have to admit that the reasons were selfish; I'd hoped that in the years that had passed, their finances would have improved. They had not, and the reunion with his mother was not a happy one... Ten years of being a slave had changed Tom. She was thoroughly horrified to see what he had become, and Tom felt it keenly. He was no longer a pampered little lordling; he was a man with the rough appetites and experiences of one much older." Baltsaros let out a low chuckle.

"In the end, he chose to stay on with me as a deckhand. We already had a certain rapport, though nothing yet had taken place between Tom and me that first year. But... I continued to visit his mother. She had a title, and I had money. It made sense at the time to ask her hand in marriage. Truthfully, I thought that it would go better than it did. Abetha is extremely intelligent and, as you saw, very beautiful. We have many things in common... But she very quickly turned against me. Taking on her son as a lover was the final nail in that coffin." Baltsaros closed his eyes and leaned his head back on the headboard.

"As intelligent as I think I am, I've made more bad decisions than I'd like to admit. I don't regret Tom, but I do his mother. This winter will be our five-year wedding anniversary. A complete farce." During Baltsaros's monologue, Jon's hand had crept up to the older man's stomach, and he played with the coarse, slightly greying hair there.

"Why not just leave her?" asked Jon.

Baltsaros sighed and pinched the bridge of his nose.

"Abetha has managed to make some powerful allies. Leaving her would be, ah... *unwise*," he replied. "I can't just kill her either; though, gods, would I enjoy that." Jon's hand stopped moving but resumed after a second. "She has 'contingency' plans, as she likes to put it," explained Baltsaros.

"I don't understand why she would want to stay married to you if she despises you so," Jon said.

Baltsaros shrugged.

"Money? Status? She covets my island? I honestly have no answer for you there."

"Eloise... she yours?" asked Jon after a moment.

Baltsaros shook his head.

"No." He felt Jon nod against his shoulder.

"And that's it?" asked the younger man.

Baltsaros squeezed Jon's shoulder.

"That's it," he replied. *For now.*

Jon pulled away suddenly and sat up; Baltsaros thought for a moment that the other had somehow heard him.

However, Jon just looked at him, his grey-blue eyes calm.

"You know, I wasn't going to fuck you just now," he said casually, and started flipping the knife in his hand the same way that Baltsaros had seen Tom do a thousand times.

The captain raised his eyebrows, surprised.

"No?" he asked.

"No. I was going to slit your lying throat," replied Jon softly, his face serene. Baltsaros's heart hammered a double beat that quickened his pulse. His mind started walking a thin line between alarm and desire.

"What made you change your mind?" asked Baltsaros, his voice barely a whisper.

Dangerous wolf pup.

Jon brought up a shoulder in a slow shrug.

"I remembered who I was. Maybe next time... I won't."

~

When he saw that Baltsaros believed his lie, Jon felt some of his confidence return.

A lie? asked Tom. *Are ye sure about that, love?*

Jon saw again the sharp blade in his hand as he knelt over the prone captain. One deep cut to Baltsaros's neck would be enough. No more waiting for the next twisted falsehood to reveal itself. It would be so easy... But the truth was that he would just as soon cut his own throat.

What is it like to be dead? he asked Tom, but the ghost was silent for once.

Jon blinked, clearing the visions away, and saw that Baltsaros was looking at him with desire plain in his face. Jon shook his head and had to smile; it was just like the captain to take a death threat as an invitation to fuck.

~

Baltsaros lay in a daze on his stomach on the bed.

Jon had forced him onto his hands and knees and taken him roughly from behind, sparing the captain no quarter as he pounded into him. In the end Jon had pulled out and ejaculated onto Baltsaros's back with a panting moan, the cum mingling with the blood from the myriad nicks inflicted on him as his clothing had been cut off.

Now lying flat, Baltsaros could see the stains on the white sheets and feel Jon's seed pooling in the crook of his back and running down his side.

As soon as his breathing slowed, Jon hopped off the bed and buttoned up his trousers, leaving Baltsaros to watch him exit the room without a backwards glance.

He lifted his head when he heard Jon address the startled maids.

"Once you've finished in here, please change the bed linens and air out the king's bedchamber. Also, I would like someone to run His Majesty a bath immediately," said the young man, his tone comfortably commanding.

Grinning, Baltsaros put his head back down on the bed.

Jon would forgive him again.

CHAPTER 27

MADIERUS

Love is composed of a single soul inhabiting two bodies.

—ARISTOTLE

Jon picked at his food, his appetite gone; the interminable silence of the meal was making him ill. He glanced up and saw that Abetha was staring at him with a small, polite curve to her lips; Jon smiled weakly at her.

He looked over at Baltsaros, but the man was just staring into his wine cup, the lines of his face hard. The captain looked older, tired.

He turned his eyes to Eloise and winked at the wan child. She blinked her huge, blue eyes at him and smiled shyly back.

"Eat your food, Eloise," said Abetha suddenly.

The child started as if poked from behind and quickly lifted a forkful of the roast duck to her mouth.

Jon sighed and went back to scowling down into his own plate of food. He couldn't understand the woman's insistence that he join them for the shared evening meal. More so, he didn't know why Baltsaros hadn't let him refuse; though, if all mealtimes were so bleak and oppressive, Jon could see why the captain would want an ally present.

He took a sip of the wine, barely tasting it, and looked again at the queen.

She had narrowed her eyes and was watching him over the rim of her cup. Smiling serenely as she put it down, Abetha finally addressed Jon.

"So, Jonathan is it? You've been here a week now... Tell me, how do you like our little island, Jonathan?" she asked.

Jon took a bite of bread, made bland by his nerves, and shook his head.

"It's just Jon, please, Your Majesty," he said tensely. "I think Madierus is very beautiful, Your Majesty."

Eyebrows raised, Abetha looked over at her husband.

"He's a polite little thing, isn't he?" she said, her voice low and smooth as silk.

Baltsaros raised his head slowly and looked at her in confusion; his mind was obviously elsewhere.

Abetha's expression was haughty when she turned her green-blue eyes back to Jon, and he suddenly saw again the resemblance to Tom; he felt like he was being stared down by a giant, malevolent cat.

"Are you enjoying your stay here?" she purred at him.

Eyes flicking quickly to Baltsaros and seeing that he was watching his wife with no emotion on his angular face, Jon nodded slowly. She continued to ask him questions about his upbringing, his education, his taste in books and music. Jon answered all of her queries as straightforwardly as he could. Slowly becoming more at ease, Jon was completely unprepared for the question that followed.

"And... How are you enjoying my husband's cock? You know he used to fuck my son with it, don't you? Do you find it to your liking?" she said, her voice conversational. However, her eyes were now glinting with malice.

Jon gaped and pushed his chair back, scrambling to his feet. He looked helplessly at Baltsaros, his face hot with embarrassment and outrage.

"I... can't do this," he said, his voice choked. Jon took a step backwards and then turned to run; he had to get away from the pure animosity radiating from the queen. As he ran down the hallway he heard Baltsaros raise his voice in anger behind him.

"Abetha!"

Winded from the run and soaked from the summer downpour, Jon pulled the tavern door open. The place was half-full, most of the patrons sitting in the covered patio at the back taking advantage of the cooler wind that the rain had brought; the lanterns swayed in the welcome breeze, making the light dance to the rhythm of the raindrops.

Jon climbed into his usual high stool, putting his forehead down on the glossy wood of the bar. A soft hand ruffled his hair.

"Tough night, Jon?" asked Maya, her voice kind. Jon closed his eyes and nodded without lifting his head. "Beer or whiskey?"

The *Grog Blossom* was an interesting establishment that boasted quite a number of exotic choices; however, the beautiful proprietress had been quick to realize that Jon was a man of simple tastes.

"Both," he muttered, almost to himself. He heard Maya laugh a little sadly and pull her hand away to get him his drinks. Jon lifted his head when she placed a mug of her good brown beer and a tumbler of golden whiskey in front of him, and he sighed.

"Thanks," he said, grateful. He lifted the beer and took a sip, smiling at Maya.

She stood in front of him, wiping out a small bowl that he knew she would fill shortly with the little crunchy, salted dried fish that he'd grown fond of. Maya had her long brown hair in the messy knot at the back of her head that she wore when tending bar; her big blue eyes were friendly, and she smiled softly at him.

Jon smiled back; he had taken to her the moment they'd been introduced.

"Where's Katherine tonight?" he asked, looking around for the first mate.

Maya shrugged.

"Out with the boys," she said, referring to Malik and Nathaniel. "Though she should be back any time now."

The captain had the first mate working with Malik on modifications to the ship, and Nathaniel often just tagged along for company; Jon had a feeling that the two men still felt a little out of place among the tight-knit crew and their families on Madierus.

"So what did the witch do tonight?" asked Maya, putting her elbows on the bar as she leaned towards Jon.

Jon felt himself relax a little; where Katherine was high-spirited and had a dry humour, her wife was gentle, inquisitive, and very sweet. Jon found that they made an interesting couple; he couldn't imagine them arguing half as much as he and Baltsaros did.

"Aren't you afraid of what she might do if she hears you calling her a witch?" asked Jon, licking the foam off his upper lip.

Maya laughed and shrugged, her blue eyes mischievous.

"She's not well-liked, Jon. She might have a few staunch supporters, but the people are loyal to the captain," she said, taking a sip of her own beer. "You can't let her get to you. She's a harpy in a cage of her own devising."

Jon nodded. He still found it strange that no one outside the castle referred to Baltsaros as king, only captain. After knocking back his whiskey, Jon held out the glass for more.

At this Maya frowned slightly but turned to grab the brown bottle, pouring another few fingers into his glass.

"I was 'invited' to sup with her and her *husband* tonight. It didn't go well... And her *husband* did nothing about it," he said, bitterly. It irked him that Baltsaros seemed so dismissive of her rancour towards Jon. The captain kept telling him to just ignore the woman. In fact, that was the advice he had been given by everyone so far.

However, what people didn't grasp was the fact that the whole situation was hurting Jon. Regardless that Baltsaros was not sharing his wife's bed, he was still married to her, and it rankled Jon. He was being forced to endure the spite of a woman who absolutely hated him... merely to keep up appearances.

Even though almost everyone on the island knew and accepted the truth.

Jaw clenched, Jon blinked hard a few times, trying to dry his eyes before the shameful tears fell. Maya, ever observant, quickly reached out a hand and squeezed his arm.

He quickly told Maya what had happened over supper.

"You really love him, don't you?" she said quietly.

Jon felt his insides twist.

"Is it love? I don't know," he said truthfully. "Sometimes I think I'm just addicted to him. Or that he's cast some kind of horrible curse on me where I'm to follow him for the rest of my life, doomed to fall for his lies over and over again." He laughed sourly and drank his whiskey, exhaling hard as the liquid burned like fire down his throat.

This time Maya refilled his glass before he had a chance to ask for more. With a sad look, she tilted her head.

"His lies... Were they about really terrible things?" she asked.

Jon opened his mouth but nothing came out.

"I mean, I'm not condoning his lying, but... It seems to me that he lied to keep you from leaving him, correct?" Maya asked, her blue eyes guileless.

Jon closed his mouth and frowned.

"Didn't you lie to him about Tom? Aren't you *still* keeping from him the full truth of what happened?" she asked gently, her thumb stroking the skin of his forearm.

Her touch and the mention of his infidelity with Tom made him suddenly very uncomfortable. He pulled his arm away and wiped his damp palm on the knee of his trousers.

"Don't make me regret telling you about that," he said defensively. "Aren't you supposed to be trying to make me feel better not worse?"

On his second day on the island, when Katherine had first introduced Jon to her beautiful and incredibly savvy wife, the trio had gotten very, very drunk on Maya's newest brew.

Over the course of the evening, the truth about Jon's indiscretion with Tom had come out. As it turned out, during the storm, the person above them on the quarterdeck had been Katherine. However, she only saw Tom walking away and hadn't thought anything of it. When Jon finally admitted that they had kissed and that it had brought with it a breathless, frantic emotion, Katherine had looked at him like he was crazy.

It was Maya who had stroked his hair that night as he lay with his head on his arms in the dark of the patio, weeping over Tom's death and asking over and over whether it was possible to love two people at once.

The memory still made him blush furiously.

Maya bit the corner of her lip, her dark lashes coming down over her big eyes. She looked away.

"I'm sorry, Jon. I am just laying out the facts," she said, walking to the side of the bar so she could lift the panel to get out.

Jon watched her come towards him, and he swallowed; he found himself unable to move as she put her arms around him in a hug. Maya smelled of spring flowers, and she was all curves and softness. He leaned his forehead against her shoulder and tried to keep his composure.

"I'm sorry things are so complicated for you, Jon. I wish I could do something to help," she murmured.

"Unhand my woman, boy," came Katherine's voice from behind him, and Jon started.

He pulled himself away, feeling strangely guilty. When he turned, Jon saw that the tall woman was grinning at him, her eyes narrow in merriment.

She walked forward and punched him hard on the arm before wrapping herself around Maya, dipping her low for an affectionate kiss. When Katherine released her, Maya laughed and swatted her wife with the back of her hand.

With the realization that all the tension had suddenly vanished from the room, Jon felt could breathe easy again. He glanced over his shoulder and saw that Malik and Nathaniel had accompanied Katherine back to the tavern and were arguing about something. Maya needed Katherine to help her with a barrel in the back, so Jon grabbed his beer and walked a little unsteadily to the table where the two men were arguing.

"I'm telling you. It can be done," Nathaniel was saying, pointing to a scrap of paper with a few notes and lines scribbled on it.

"Not sure it can, my friend. There would be an awful lot of pressure put on the hull by the ice. It might crack up before you got to the other side... And then what do you get? Stranded in an ice field—Oh hi, Jon. Care to join us?" asked Malik, kicking a chair back from the table.

Jon sank down into the seat gratefully and took a long pull from his mug.

"What are you guys arguing about? What ice field?" he asked, looking curiously at the paper in front of Nathaniel.

The older man, his hazel eyes narrow, pointed a finger to a series of small, joined circles arranged in a curve to one side of the writing.

"I think, if a ship was well stocked and modified to withstand continuous, small impacts on her hull, it could make its way through the passage in the Devil's Isles," he said, sliding his finger to the bottom of the drawing where there was a bigger gap between the circles.

Jon shook his head.

"I don't understand. What are the Devil's Isles?" he asked, confused.

Malik grinned and drank from his mug, sitting comfortably back in his chair.

"They're not really islands... more like a mountain range. They're spires that rise up high in the sky like the teeth of a giant sea creature," said Malik, gesturing up with his hands and twisting his face into a grimace.

Nathaniel laughed.

Jon could tell that there was probably more drinking than work done on *Baal's Heart* earlier this evening.

"So... No one has ever been past them. Or at least no one who has come back to tell of it," said Nathaniel, jumping back into the story. "However, there is a gap here that can accommodate a large vessel. The only problem is that the water that far south is completely frozen for most of the year."

Malik nodded. "A narrow gap of time for a narrow gap of water," he said, grinning at his own words.

Jon frowned at the drawing, scratching at the stubble on his cheek.

"Why not put a layer of beaten metal on the front of the ship?" he asked, looking up at the shipwright. "Where I'm from, it gets cold enough to freeze the water outside the harbour. We have ships called icebreakers that go around and crack up the ice, pushing it away to let boats in. They all have this... sharply bent layer of metal on the front," Jon said, putting the tips of his fingers together but holding his palms apart. "Like armour for the ship."

Nathaniel's head swivelled to Malik, his eyebrows high. However, Malik was shaking his head.

"I already thought of that. What do you take me for? It just can't be done! Not on the *Heart*. It will unbalance her way too much. Besides... Where would we get that much steel here?" he said.

Jon shrugged and then frowned.

"Wait... The captain is thinking of taking us there?" he asked, surprised. Baltsaros had made no mention of the trip.

Malik and Nathaniel shook their heads in unison.

"Are they going on about the Devil's Isles modifications again?" asked Katherine, walking up to them. She turned a chair backwards and straddled it, folding her arms along the top.

"Nathaniel, your crazy idea is a death wish. Seriously. Just drop it will you?" said the first mate, turning to Jon. "Don't listen to them... And don't mention it to the captain."

Jon furrowed his brow.

"Why?" he asked, curious. Katherine grabbed Jon's mug out of his hand and downed the rest in one swallow.

"It's just the kind of outrageous thing that the captain would want to try, given enough encouragement. And... I don't know about you, but I kinda like being warm and alive, no?" she said and grinned before calling to Maya for another round.

~

Baltsaros opened his eyes when he heard Jon's step outside the door. He had been lounging in the big comfortable chair in his sitting room reading a book of newly translated poetry while he waited for Jon to come home. At some point he had obviously drifted off and, as Jon opened the door, Baltsaros wondered how late it really was.

The captain cleared his throat to alert Jon of his presence and watched as the young man swayed into the room. He was noticeably drunk.

"Hi," said his wayward lover as he leaned into the door to close it. "I'm uh... Sorry it's so late. You waited up?"

Baltsaros watched him stumble slightly over the edge of the rug as he came towards the captain. He was surprised when Jon came to straddle him in the wide wingback chair and plant a sloppy kiss on his lips.

Baltsaros moved the book from his lap and fumbled to place it on the dainty side table before wrapping his arms around Jon's waist, pulling him closer. Jon tasted of beer and whiskey as Baltsaros nudged open his mouth, breathing in his warm breath. Pulling away from Jon after a few long minutes, he looked fondly at the inebriated boy in his lap.

"I'm the one who's sorry, Jon," he said, running his hand up the front of the young man's shirt to place it against Jon's heart; it beat quick and strong under his palm. "I dragged you into this. I should be doing more to protect you from her." He laughed a little contritely. "You'd think after all this time I would have learned to be more suspicious of her nature."

Earlier that day, when Abetha had asked him to invite Jon to the evening meal, he had thought nothing of it. Granted, he had been distracted; they were nearly three weeks late getting to the island, and he still hadn't finished working through the expense books. The pile of correspondence alone was daunting.

Jon's brows came down, a line forming between them as he looked at Baltsaros.

"She's very angry with you," said Jon, his face soft with drink. "She used to love you."

Startled by Jon's words, Baltsaros looked at him curiously. Abetha had loved him? To Baltsaros it had always been an arrangement that suited the both of them; that Abetha had felt something more had never crossed his mind... She was such a reserved woman.

"Why do you say that?" he asked.

Jon leaned forward and rested himself against Baltsaros, his cheek against the captain's shoulder.

"Mmm... the way she looks at you. Like she lost something. I guess she realized too late that you're incapable of love. Hmmm... misplaced punishment for her mistake. Something..."

Baltsaros felt Jon's body twitch slightly, and he realized that the young man was falling asleep.

"You think I'm incapable of love?" Baltsaros asked softly. When Jon didn't respond, the captain nudged him gently.

Jon sighed and nuzzled against Baltsaros's neck.

"I love you too," he said drowsily.

Baltsaros sat in the chair and watched the candle burn down as he held Jon against him. There was a tenderness inside him, one that could contain tears and laughter at the same time. It was lovely but also painful, the way that a limb waking up from lack of blood flow prickled and stung; Baltsaros cherished the feeling. As he stroked Jon's hair as he slept, Baltsaros thought of love and fate, the future and the past.

The morning sun found the two men entwined on the great bed where Baltsaros had carried Jon when the candle finally died; the captain's arm held the younger man against him tight, both protective and possessive, as if afraid of ever letting him go.

CHAPTER 28
A REVELATION

The only thing that should surprise us is that there are still some things that can surprise us.

— FRANÇOIS DE LA ROCHEFOUCAULD

Jon stood at the window watching Eloise and Brutus play a game of chase. The giant mastiff leapt and trotted around the little girl, and Eloise's spindly legs pumped quickly as she ran and skipped down the garden path.

Though the panes of glass were thick, Jon could swear he could hear her excited peals of laughter; he had a feeling that Eloise did not laugh very often. Grinning wide, Jon watched as Brutus let himself be caught, throwing himself almost dramatically to the ground so that Eloise could crawl over his side: the conquering hero slayed the evil beast.

Baltsaros's hand gripped his shoulder in passing as he walked heavily to the big wooden desk across the room. At the sound of an exasperated sigh, he turned to look at Baltsaros and saw that the captain stood with his back to Jon as he leaned hard on his knuckles over the pile of papers and letters that littered the desk.

"Why don't you have someone to do that for you?" Jon asked, approaching Baltsaros from behind. He put his arms around the other man's chest, resting the side of his head down on the captain's broad back. One of Baltsaros's hands came up to clasp his, and Jon heard the low groan of frustration directly against his ear.

"I don't know. I should. It will be at least the end of the week before I get through this. The worst are Abetha's records; the woman is so vague that every page I read requires an audience with Her Highness just to understand what I'm dealing with," said Baltsaros. "I need a break."

He straightened suddenly and pulled out of Jon's arms, turning around to look fondly at him, his brown eyes warm.

"How would you like to come for a hike with me? There is something I would love to show you," Baltsaros asked with a smile.

Jon had planned on asking Katherine if she needed help clearing more land at the back of her property. Turning farmer on her return home, the first mate now wanted to plant the seeds Jon had found in the cargo hold of the *Maiden's Bounty*; however, a hike with Baltsaros sounded leagues more enjoyable.

Jon's arm was weary from swinging the blade over and over again to clear the path. It would soon be Baltsaros's turn to break through the foliage, and he was thankful for it. He hadn't realized that a hike would mean hot, tiring work as they struggled through what felt like virgin jungle.

Jon paused and lifted the waterskin hanging from his side, pulling the cork and taking a long swallow of the tepid water. With a glance behind him, he saw that the captain was looking curiously at a flat green leaf in his hands, turning it over and rubbing it with the back of his nail. Baltsaros was sweaty and bare chested like Jon but, unlike the younger man, seemed perfectly happy to hack and slash his way through the dense wilds of Madierus. Jon watched as Baltsaros folded the leaf to put it in the bag at his hip, a new "specimen."

When he realized he was being watched, Baltsaros looked up and smiled, the corners of his eyes crinkling.

"Tired?" he asked Jon cheerfully. "I can take over now if you'd like. We're almost there."

The captain had yet to tell him where "there" was, preferring to keep it a secret. Jon hoped it wasn't just an interesting rock formation or a rare medicinal plant. He flipped the long, flat blade in his hand and passed it to Baltsaros handle-first in response.

Jon stepped out of the way to let the captain pass him and took another mouthful of water, following the older man through the narrow swath he cut out of the jungle.

Before too much longer, Jon thought he could detect a thinning of the foliage. The sun started peeking out between the green leaves, and soon Jon could see blue skies. Panting from the long climb, Jon frowned; he could hear something like a rumbling roar coming from ahead.

"What's that?" he yelled at Baltsaros. The tireless man had outpaced Jon by a good distance; at Jon's shout he stopped and wiped his forehead, putting his hands on his hips as he waited for Jon to catch up. Despite his weariness, Baltsaros's sharp-toothed grin was infectious, and he found himself smiling back.

"It's just up over this ridge," said the captain, his eyes bright with excitement. As soon as Jon was close, Baltsaros turned and resumed slashing at the vines though now it was barely necessary.

The rumble grew louder until finally the source of it came into view through the tall, skinny trees ahead.

As he stepped past the grinning captain, Jon's eyes went wide. He pushed through the last of the greenery and stepped out into a breathtaking scene.

In front of them was a waterfall, something Jon had only read about in books. It fell from a gap in the high lip of the volcanic crater above into a wide pool of water surrounded by smooth, sunken boulders and flowering plants; a pair of colourful birds flew by overhead, calling to each other as they eyed the intruders. Mouth agape, Jon stared up at the falling water. He realized that they had come around the west side of the volcano, climbing its slope as they went along.

"Where is the water coming from?" he asked, enthralled. The waterfall made a mist in the air around its base, and Jon could see pieces of a rainbow shimmering there.

Baltsaros wrapped his arms around Jon and sighed happily, looking up.

"I'm not exactly sure. There is a big freshwater lake in the crater, but it cannot possibly be replenished solely by rain. My theory is that there is an underground river that flows beneath the island and is somehow being forced up through the old lava tubes. Perhaps this is why the volcano stopped erupting many, many years ago? It is beautiful, is it not?" Baltsaros said, sliding his hands down Jon's torso. The captain's nimble fingers began tugging at the buttoned fly of Jon's trousers, and he gasped at the sudden contact when Baltsaros slipped his hand between material and skin to cup him firmly. Soon the captain had Jon stripped down to his bare skin, pulling his own boots and pants off in a hurry.

Having expected more in the way of caresses, Jon squawked in surprise when Baltsaros just shoved him hard. He flung out his arms but lost his balance, falling into the surprisingly deep and cold water of the pond. Coughing and spluttering as he reached the surface, he quickly ducked out of the way when he saw Baltsaros take a flying leap towards him.

The man resurfaced, his face creased in a wide, delighted smile.

Jon treaded water and grinned, bringing up his hand suddenly to splash the captain who, in turn, roared in mock fury.

It quickly escalated, the men cavorting and splashing in the pool, laughing and trying to drown each other in its chilly depths. There was no age difference between them, no dead lover, no bitter queen, no stack of responsibilities... No, they were just two boys playing in the warm summer sun of their own tropical paradise.

Jon, in trying to flee from Baltsaros, swam around to the side of the waterfall and found that there was an underwater ledge where he could stand. Panting from exertion, Jon grinned when Baltsaros suddenly popped out of the water beside him; the captain seemed part fish, able to swim for long distances underwater without breathing.

Laughing, Jon pulled the older man towards him and, buoyed by the water, he wrapped his legs around the captain's hips. Instantly their play took on the sharpened edge of lust. Jon looked searchingly into Baltsaros's dark-brown eyes, clasping the back of the man's neck.

The captain's face had gone serious, his mouth slightly open as he looked at Jon. There was suddenly a tiny comma, as if from pain, etched between Baltsaros's brows as he licked his lips.

Despite the loud splashing of the waterfall, Jon thought he could hear Baltsaros breathing.

Large hands coming up to hold his waist, Baltsaros leaned forward and brought his mouth to Jon's, hesitating for an instant before making contact. Though Baltsaros's lips were cold from the water, his tongue was warm as it touched Jon's; the contrast was intoxicating, and Jon moaned softly as he kissed Baltsaros.

There was a subtle difference in this embrace, a new poignancy that had not been there before, and Jon wondered what had changed. Clinging to the captain's body, Jon felt almost frantic with desire, and he shuddered when Baltsaros moved his hand to his cock, squeezing the hardening shaft.

However, despite the fervour of their embrace, Jon realized he was getting cold. He pulled away from Baltsaros and, with a backwards glance, swam to the sun-heated rocks on the far side.

Baltsaros followed him and climbed up to lie next to Jon on the warm boulders. The abrupt change in location had brought with it a slowing of their passion, and Baltsaros started just running his fingers slowly up and down Jon's body as the sun dried their skin.

The line appeared between the captain's stark brows again, and Jon frowned.

"What's wrong?" he asked. "You look like something's bothering you." Jon hoped desperately that it wasn't yet another lie to sour the relationship with.

Baltsaros shook his head.

"There's nothing wrong, Jon. You just..." He trailed off and closed his mouth, his lips pressing together hard for a second before he continued. "The other night when you came back from the tavern... You said you loved me," Baltsaros finished in a strange voice.

Jon brought himself up on his elbows and grimaced.

"Oh gods... I did?" he asked, aghast, and Baltsaros's eyes quickly slid away from Jon's face at his words.

When the captain looked back at him, his expression was distant.

Jon grasped the misunderstanding right away and sat up. He reached for Baltsaros and cupped his lover's head between his hands, fingers tangled in the captain's wet hair.

"No! It's not that! Baltsaros, *yes*. Yes, I meant it! Of course I meant it... I just hate that it had to come out when I was three sheets to the wind. I... love you. I do. Oh gods, how I love you," he said fervently, his heart in his throat as he spoke the foreign words.

The coldness in Baltsaros's eyes had melted away at his confession, and slowly he nodded, letting out a long exhale.

The captain suddenly leaned in to kiss him, pushing Jon back onto the smooth rock.

Jon gasped at the urgency that spurred Baltsaros's desire; the man reached up and slid a hand around Jon's jaw, leaning into his kiss as he pressed himself hard against his body. Baltsaros was demanding and rough, and Jon gave himself up completely to the captain.

When Baltsaros's hand worked its way between their bodies to clasp their cocks together and stroke them as one, Jon felt dizzy with desire. His breath panted out of his lungs and into Baltsaros's as the kiss went on and on, a confirmation of Jon's words.

When Baltsaros finally released him, it was to push apart Jon's legs and kneel between them. Baltsaros leaned forward and reached over Jon's head; when he sat back down on his heels, in his hand was the broken off end of a thick plant-stem that ended in a point.

After a momentary panic, Jon was relieved when Baltsaros just pressed his thumbs into the plant, splitting the skin and scooping a clear gel into his palm. Jon was confused. Was it a drug? His question was answered almost immediately.

"I need you. Now," said the captain hoarsely, eyes wide and desperate with his naked lust.

Jon nodded quickly and raised his knees, watching breathlessly as Baltsaros smeared the plant's juice over his thick cock. Without another word, the captain grasped Jon's hips and rapidly slid his lubricated cock in the furrow of the young man's ass a few times before angling himself with a hurried hand for the final plunge.

Jon yelled loud and arched his back in shock as the captain's cock drove hard into him; however, he swiftly started succumbing to Baltsaros's long strokes and groaned in response.

Jon's cock bobbed up from his stomach and he breathed hard. He grunted at the force with which Baltsaros ploughed into him and realized that his pleasure was climbing swiftly in reaction to the furious pace of the captain's fucking. He could already feel the pressure mounting for the final release in his testicles, and he started to moan and pant with Baltsaros's thrusts. He realized he was going to cum even though his cock was untouched, and he whimpered, pushing himself up on his heels to match Baltsaros's movements.

Fingers scrabbling at the smooth rock to either side of him, Jon felt the captain's thick length carry him over the edge of his climax, sending shocks through him as he cried out again and again.

"Oh gods, Jon," moaned Baltsaros, watching the younger man's cock gush out strings of pearly cum over his own taut stomach. Baltsaros's head snapped back, and he dug his fingers hard into Jon's hips as he was toppled by his own orgasm, the cries of his pleasure loud and unbridled in the green summer air of the jungle oasis.

. . .

The sun was setting when the two men finally came within sight of the small village, and the lights twinkling from the buildings reminded Jon of the fireflies he used to watch as a boy. His hand was curled around Baltsaros's forearm as the captain led him out of the jungle.

Something had happened today that had made a mark on him, and he wouldn't soon forget this excursion. When Baltsaros looked back at him, Jon felt gratified and comforted by his warm smile. Now that his declaration of love was out in the open, Jon was both more confident and hopeful of the coming times. Though the captain hadn't responded in kind, the way he had reacted to Jon's words made him feel weak inside. Jon was filled with a joy that lightened his heart.

He and Baltsaros quickly ran through the castle gardens and, stopping to catch their breaths, they kissed and stifled their laughter when they saw the queen walk by, hiding from the woman they both wanted to avoid.

Suddenly the sky opened up with a heavy, tropical rain, and the men, now boys again, raced each other to the end of the covered walkway, pushing each other out of the way to gain access to the castle. Jon beat Baltsaros to the top of the stairs and wouldn't grant the captain entry to his rooms unless he pledged his undying loyalty to him.

Breathless and silly, the two men finally embraced in the sitting room when a draw had been called, the room lit only by the full moon shining in through the tall windows.

Baltsaros was the first to pull away, decrying the insistence of his bladder.

When the captain had gone, Jon walked to the bell-pull and yanked on it once; the captain's liquor cabinet was bare, and they were in need of some lighting. Before Baltsaros had returned, a spare boy of indeterminate age had already put a flame to the candles in Baltsaros's quarters, excusing himself to fetch a bottle of wine from the cellar.

When the captain walked into the room, he groaned.

"Why, Jon? Now I can see the infernal pile of rubbish that mocks me with its urgency," said Baltsaros, crossing to his desk. "It's bad enough that I get the correspondence for half of my crew; the fact that I get complete gibberish is just taxing."

The captain lifted up an envelope and held it near the flame of the wax candle burning on his desk.

"Take this one for instance... Its label reads 'The Black Brigand.' What does that even mean?" The captain scowled down at the letter and shook his head.

Jon's blood froze in his veins. He swallowed hard and took a step towards Baltsaros.

"Can I... Baltsaros, please can I see that?" he said, his voice unsteady.

The Black Brigand.

He couldn't remember if he had told Baltsaros what Tom had called him in the lies the jealous first mate had spread in Portsmouth. Katherine knew but... Jon broke the seal at the back and pulled out the single, folded sheet. The message was written in a blockish, unadorned hand:

Dear Jonny,

I thought you might like to know that a navy fleet passed this way. The man leading them was a dark-skinned fella with burn scars on his face and hands... I think you might know who that is? Turns out that killing a small lord in the shit-soaked, ass-end of a kingdom is enough to grant you a visit from the navy? Who knew? Bad news though, love: they know exactly where you are. Tortured it right out of Fresia, the fuckers. I'd get everyone ready for a small war, if you know what I mean.

Regards,

— T.

Jon's heart beat fast as he looked up into Baltsaros's eyes.

"Tom's alive," he said quietly.

CHAPTER 29

ENEMIES AND ALLIES

Baltsaros read the words again and frowned.

Gods be damned, Tom! he thought angrily.

A fleet? What did Tom mean by a fleet? Three ships? Five? The letter wasn't even dated; how in the blasted hells was he to know what to expect and when? The mail came but once a month from the nearest island, and there was no way a reply would reach Tom in time. Baltsaros assumed the "this way" in Tom's letter referred to the *Jewel*, given his mention of Fresia.

He rubbed his thumb over the initial at the bottom, picturing in his mind the way Tom's tongue poked from the corner of his mouth when performing the rare act of putting pen to paper.

Why address it only to Jon?

Baltsaros frowned and took another swallow of wine, looking over at the naked young man curled in slumber next to him. Baltsaros hadn't liked the way that Jon's blue eyes lit up at Tom's miraculous resurrection.

He scanned the message in his hand again. Why did he feel so... vexed by Tom's refusal to acknowledge him in his missive? After drinking down more wine, Baltsaros leaned his head back on the pillow and stared up at the colourful silks draped above his head. He had felt a keen, almost painful relief when Jon spoke his hushed words: *Tom's alive.* Jaw clenched, Baltsaros passed a hand over his tired eyes. Why had it turned so quickly to anger?

Unable or unwilling to go to sleep, Baltsaros slipped off the high bed and went to stand at the window; looking out at the pinkening sky, the captain attempted to turn his mind from thoughts of a hunt to soothe his rage to preparations for the possible battle to come.

Jon drank down the beer in his mug and grinned eagerly.

With her lips slightly pursed, Maya frowned at him, her blue eyes softly reproving. She shook her head.

"I'm glad the man isn't dead, Jon... but aren't you being a little ah... openly optimistic about Tom?" she asked. "I'm really not seeing a reunion in your future, given what I know of your relationship with the captain. Please tell me you aren't seriously thinking of suggesting that you go find him." She wiped down the bar with her rag and watched sympathetically as his expression teetered on the edge of disappointment.

"Yes, Maya. I am. If Baltsaros sees Tom... maybe..." he said, his conviction faltering. If Baltsaros sees Tom... what? They all live happily ever after? He swallowed and looked down into his empty mug, blinking hard.

"Jon," said the soft-spoken woman, leaning across the bar to pat his hand. "I know you think you saw something in Tom; maybe it was real... Maybe it was just a fleeting thing. I only knew him briefly, but I honestly don't see anything good coming of wanting him back in your life. While I'll admit that he was handsome in a roguish sort of way, he was a known troublemaker with violent tendencies. Why not just be glad that he sent us warning when he did and let the rest go? You just said you had a good thing with the captain, why stir up old wounds?"

Somewhat chastened, Jon frowned and nodded.

Maya pulled the mug out of Jon's grasp and turned to fill it anew. When she slid it back in front of him, her eyes were narrowed with worry.

"Now... Tell me again the part about the navy," she said, sitting down.

That evening Jon found Baltsaros high up in one of the towers. The captain was at the window with his arms crossed, staring out over the water. At the sound of Jon's footfalls, he turned.

"Oh hello, Jon. You got my note," said Baltsaros, looking pleased to see him.

Jon crossed the room, gazing around him. The walls were covered in maps of all kinds. Some seemed to be reproductions or earlier versions of the one aboard *Baal's Heart*; others were details of the midland isles or the coastline of the northern continent. Jon assumed that many of them had been drawn by the captain himself though he spotted a few that were yellowed with obvious great age, the landmasses on them unrecognizable.

Jon stepped up to the heavy oval table in the middle of the room and saw that its surface was covered in sheets of paper with half-finished drawings of buildings and figures. Curious, Jon began to flip through them and was startled to come upon a sketch of his likeness. It was an image of him looking off to one side, his brows low over his eyes, his lips slightly parted as if deep in thought. Jon felt suddenly shy; the drawing was beautifully rendered.

When he lifted his eyes, he saw that Baltsaros was watching him curiously. He felt almost breathless with the sudden tightness in his chest; it always amazed him how his love for the captain came in bursts of blinding intensity that caught Jon unawares. He looked away quickly and cleared his throat, trying to ignore the lump that had formed there.

"So this is what you do when I wake up in the middle of the night and you're nowhere to be found?" he asked, trying to make his voice light. With a glance back up at Baltsaros, he saw the older man nod.

The captain crossed to the table and gazed down at his drawings.

"I've been at sea for so long that I have problems sleeping when I'm ashore. It's too quiet, too still," explained Baltsaros with a small smile.

Jon tapped the drawing of him with his fingertips.

"Do I always look so grave?" he asked, curious.

Baltsaros's eyes narrowed appraisingly at him, and he shook his head.

"Not as often as you used to, no. However, while I dearly cherish your smile... It's the sober, pensive Jon that sticks in my mind when I have charcoal in my hand," Baltsaros replied quietly. "Perhaps it's just the medium that lends itself to solemnness."

Sighing, the captain looked again at the open window after a moment, his mind obviously occupied.

"I wish I knew how much time we had before Reginald arrives, if he comes at all," he muttered distractedly, walking back towards his post. The high vantage point meant the captain could see ships approaching long before they arrived, but the lack of time frame made for a frustrating wait.

The toe of Jon's boot brushed against something; looking down, he frowned at what he saw.

"Come with me; I would like to pick your brain about your stepfather, but I desperately require some sustenance. Shall we see what I can make for us in the kitchen?" said Baltsaros from behind him.

Jon looked up quickly and nodded. As he followed the captain out of the room, he threw another backwards glance at the paper in the shadows under the heavy table, Tom's smiling eyes peeking up at him from its crumpled surface.

Baltsaros leaned over the table in the great hall and pointed to the map.

"There are some old cannons that we can place up high... here in the rock face," he said, circling with a finger a spot slightly east from the castle. "I assume that the fleet will be approaching us from the north; however, if they decide to come around and land on the south side of the island, dragging those cannons up to the ridge will have been for naught."

Katherine folded her arms and frowned down at the map.

"You think they could come from the south?" she asked.

"The element of surprise. The man in charge was a soldier for a long time and a gifted tactician. I wouldn't put it past him to try to catch us off guard. They might also split the fleet and try for both. It will be hard to defend on all fronts if that's the case. While the letter we received did not outline the navy's intention, the fact that they tortured someone for the location of Madierus suggests that they are coming here with destruction and violence in mind. It could be that they are solely looking for me... But the man leading the fleet would see every pirate and their kin hanged. There are a lot of lives to protect," replied the captain, straightening. "They would have been here by now if the letter was written shortly after the storm, which isn't the case. However, it couldn't have been that much later, given that the letter arrived here with the last ship."

He sighed and pinched the bridge of his nose. He was feeling uncomfortably tense. Jon was completely right about his control issues; he had zero patience for unknown variables, and there were too many on his mind, his actions to blame for all of them. Not for the first time, he thought about how blowing up the castle at Portsmouth had been a terribly rash decision on his part.

To be fair though, how could he have known that killing such a small-town nobleman would spur an attack backed by the crown? Baltsaros had a feeling that Reginald's obstinacy was part of it. From what Jon had told him, the man had a streak of vengeance in him that rivalled Baltsaros's.

And then there was Tom.

Two men he thought dead suddenly resurrected in one fell swoop.

Quickly pushing away a sudden, sharp image of Tom from his mind, he clenched his jaw and swallowed as he lifted his gaze to Jon; he saw that the younger man was looking at him from across the table with sympathy in his grey-blue eyes. Baltsaros watched as Jon's face went pensive for a moment.

"How many people are on the island?" Jon asked, looking around.

"About two hundred and thirty at the moment, why?" Baltsaros asked.

Jon looked down, nodding thoughtfully. When he raised his head, Baltsaros could see that he had an idea.

"What if we sent everyone who is unable to fight onto *Baal's Heart* and out of the way? That way we can concentrate on the attack rather than worrying about kin," suggested Jon. "We'll have plenty of notice of the navy's arrival if someone keeps constant watch from on high, right? Enough time to load everyone onto the ship and take her out of harm's way?"

Baltsaros nodded.

"Yes, Jon. However, we need those guns. The ship is our biggest line of defence," he replied.

Jon pointed to the mouth of the harbour on the map.

"Let's say it's a fleet of four or five ships maximum, right? Probably being frigates or sloops, they'll be bigger and almost definitely outgun *Baal's Heart*. So why fight them on the water when they have the advantage? How many of them will be able to fit into the harbour? Two? At most? The rest will be out of range. What can they do then? Let's make them bring the fight to us," he said, smiling.

Baltsaros tilted his head slightly at Jon; the idea of removing the vulnerable from the equation certainly had merit. Seeing that the rest of the assembled group were all looking at him waiting for his response, Baltsaros nodded slowly.

The bulk of the population of Madierus was made up of the crew's family; of those, a good third were capable fighters. With the weak, young, and infirm out of the way and safe aboard the ship, the rest of them could certainly hold their own on the island. At the very least it meant that his men's loyalties wouldn't be divided.

"They'll still have two ships within firing range in our own harbour," Baltsaros pointed out.

Jon shrugged.

"I don't think there's any avoiding that. There will be damage, yes, but I think it's worth it in terms of lives saved," he said.

And that is what is important, said Jon's solemn grey-blue eyes.

Baltsaros smiled softly at his younger lover. Yes, that was indeed important. Jon was right that though Baltsaros largely felt indifferent to his crew, he had made a pledge dedicating himself to their well-being.

Baltsaros was not his uncle.

"What if we made it so that there were *no* ships able to enter the harbour," said a voice from the back.

Baltsaros frowned and shifted to see who was speaking. Nathaniel stepped through the gap that formed in the crowd, and Baltsaros looked at the cartographer with interest.

"How so?" asked the captain.

Nathaniel stood next to Jon and turned the map slightly, frowning down at it.

"At the narrow point here," he said, gesturing to the mouth of the harbour as had Jon. "Why don't we drop big rocks or boulders overboard at intervals with long ropes attached. Float some wood and plants at the ends of the tethers. See... We would make it look like there's a narrow land bridge closing off the lagoon—no way to enter. It'll only look real if the water is calm enough though," said Nathaniel, crossing his arms and furrowing his brow.

The captain grinned wide, picturing the result in his head. He clapped his hands once.

"Bravo! Good work. I think this could work. We'll keep *Baal's Heart* outside the harbour while this happens. The jolly boats could load everyone on board and drop the last boulder when done. They will still come through in the end; all it will take is one boat trying to disembark on this 'land bridge' to see through the ruse, but I believe it will be enough to keep the ships out of the harbour," he said, pleased with the plan.

"If they choose to come from another direction, they'll have to come up on foot anyway. There's no way their guns could do any damage from the south or west. From the east, it wouldn't be much. But... Why not set up the old cannons on the beach instead of the rock face? It would be far easier, no? We could just hit them as they're coming at us?" said Katherine with a smile.

Jon's brows came down low over his eyes as he stood looking at the map.

"We still have to find a way to destroy the ships. Sink them. That way they won't return," he said, his voice thoughtful.

Malik, standing next to Jon, nodded and raked his hair back. He looked up at the captain, his dark brows high.

"I might be able to come up with something interesting if I can have a few men and the use of a small rowboat during the attack," said the shipwright. "I know more than a few ways to sink a ship... The trick is to get them to go down while on the run and not cluttering the harbour."

Baltsaros nodded and smiled. He was pleased.

"Good good. Katherine, can you please start organizing everyone? We will destroy these invaders!" he said loudly, and the crowd hooted and hollered. The captain slid his eyes fondly to Jon.

As the assembled group filed out of the room with purpose, Baltsaros leaned his hip on the table, watching Jon as he circled around to come stand in front of the captain.

"Do you think it will work?" Baltsaros asked.

Jon shrugged and reached for Baltsaros's waist, pulling himself flush against the captain.

"I'd say it's a fair bit of labour to prepare for something that might not even happen," Jon replied. "But yes, it's worth a shot."

Baltsaros closed his eyes as Jon placed his lips against his neck, warm tongue sliding up behind his earlobe.

"Yes; and, the idea of a land bridge is a good one. I think perhaps when this is over, we could look to making a permanent version... something with a false opening to let in the *Heart* but to dissuade others from trying," Baltsaros said and moved his hands down to grab Jon's buttocks, pressing himself against him. "We may start to get more unwanted visitors; there's no telling who else Reginald has told of our location."

At this Jon pulled his head back.

Baltsaros opened his eyes and saw that he was looking at him with narrowed storm-blue eyes.

"Why does Fresia know where Madierus is anyway?" asked Jon, confused.

Baltsaros shook his head at the young man's expression, grinning.

"We were an island full of men for a long time, and while that's fine for some," he said, pushing his pelvis playfully against Jon, "most were a touch lonely. Let's just say I imported some 'wives'."

His eyes went wide, and Baltsaros could tell Jon was running through the list of women he had met on the island.

"No," Baltsaros said laughing. "Ha! They weren't all whores, Jon—and they weren't all women! They came of their own free will; lots of the folks who immigrated were just tired of tyranny or repression. Now... Stop talking and go back to what you were doing just now."

~

Jon felt a little rush of adrenaline as he swiftly unlaced Baltsaros's pants in the great hall. Despite the captain's assurance that the queen rarely ventured out of her rooms at this time, Jon still felt terribly exposed down on his knees on the hard marble floors.

Baltsaros's cock was a long outline under the tight black fabric, and Jon mouthed it, blowing his hot breath through the material. Baltsaros's hands were in his hair, pushing the back of Jon's head a little insistently as he was teased. He nudged at the flaps of material with his nose, pressing his mouth up at the soft mound between the man's legs.

Above him Baltsaros groaned quietly, spreading his legs a little further apart.

"Stop tormenting me, boy," said the captain, his voice rough with lust. Jon smiled and continued to kiss Baltsaros's cock through his pants; however, when the man shifted his hips, the unlaced flaps came apart, and Baltsaros's cock freed itself.

Baltsaros's fingers pulled hard suddenly in Jon's hair; he winced and looked up past the thick cock to the captain. Jon saw that, though Baltsaros was looking down, his eyes were distant, and his face was set in a fierce sneer.

Jon's heart quickened, and he slipped a hand down the front of his own trousers, aroused by the bestial look on Baltsaros's face. He placed his mouth under the purple head of the captain's stiff, naked cock and tongued the bottom ridge of it. The shaft bobbed up in response and Baltsaros let out a small, frustrated sigh.

"Open your mouth," said the captain, moving one of his hands to Jon's jaw. Baltsaros's thumb stroked the side of his neck. "Now."

Jon moved his hand over his own cock. Aroused by the captain's commanding tone, Jon kept teasing him with small licks and brushes of his lips over the sensitive head.

Finally, Baltsaros growled and curled his fingers around Jon's chin, forcing his mouth open.

Jon panted out an excited breath and tilted his head back, letting Baltsaros feed him his thick cock. As he shifted his knees on the hard floor, Jon struggled to grasp himself better in the tight confines of his pants. With Baltsaros thrusting himself into his mouth, Jon tugged at the front of his trousers, and a button went flying in his hurry to free his erection.

However, his desire became confused as Baltsaros began fucking Jon's throat with a punishing pace, moving to trap Jon's head between his large hands. With a firm grasp on Jon, Baltsaros grunted and slowed suddenly, forcing his length as far down as he could.

Jon gagged and tried to pull back, but Baltsaros held him in place, making him crane his neck further up. Unable to breathe, Jon grabbed Baltsaros's wrists, and there were tears in his eyes as he started to panic.

Baltsaros stared down at him, his face brutal and angry, and then started to thrust harder, bruising Jon's throat muscles as he gagged and fought desperately to free himself. There were spots in Jon's vision as he pleaded with his eyes at Baltsaros, his nails digging in and raking the skin of the captain's hands.

In response to the sudden pain, Baltsaros started as if coming out of a trance, releasing Jon and stepping back to stumble against the table.

Jon coughed and choked on his hands and knees, his head close to the floor; a string of saliva dropped from his lips to the marble tiles.

"What the fuck, Baltsaros?" Jon said hoarsely, when he had caught his breath. He looked up and saw that the captain was breathing hard, staring down at Jon with a confused expression.

Jon's throat burned and his jaw felt strained.

"What the hell was that?" Baltsaros liked being rough with Jon but never to a point so far past his limits.

Baltsaros's eyes went flat, and the muscles twitched under the skin of his stubbled jaw.

Jon wiped at his mouth with the back of his hand and pulled his pants back together, all desire flown with Baltsaros's excessive handling of him. He stood shakily and glared at the captain.

"What's *wrong* with you?" Jon said angrily, his voice rough.

"I... am sorry, Jon. I'm not sure what came over me," said Baltsaros, his accent slurring his words slightly in his daze.

Jon bit back another retort and took a deep breath. Something was seriously bothering the captain; there was a strange vagueness in his eyes that Jon had never seen before. At the memory of the crumpled drawing in the map room, Jon's face softened.

"It's Tom, isn't it?" he murmured, watching Baltsaros's expression closely.

The older man's brows came down as he tilted his head to the side like a large, bewildered creature, but Jon saw the minute crease appear and disappear almost instantly on Baltsaros's high brow.

That was it.

He dismissed the anger at his treatment, as well as the tiny pang of jealousy he felt at the former first mate's ability to affect Baltsaros from leagues away, and pressed on.

"Did you just... mistake me for Tom?" he asked, the idea coalescing in his head. "Baltsaros, I know Tom is alive, but—"

"Tom is alive?"

Jon blinked and swivelled his head in shock when he heard the voice come from across the room.

The queen, her eyes crackling with wildfire, stood haughtily in the open doorway.

Baltsaros snapped out of his stupor, pushing his cock back into his pants at the woman's startling presence.

"Abetha, what are you doing here?" the captain asked, his brow creased.

Jon blushed furiously realizing that the woman could have been here the whole time and he wouldn't have noticed.

"When were you planning on telling me?" she asked coldly, ignoring Baltsaros's question.

The captain grimaced and looked at Jon.

"Could you please excuse us?" he said, turning back to the queen.

Jon gritted his teeth at the summary dismissal.

"I'll be at the *Blossom*," he muttered, turning on his heel.

However, as Jon walked out of the room his mind was spinning. Baltsaros had once confessed that he simply missed Tom. Jon now realized that it was much more than that.

~

Baltsaros frowned at the icy queen staring him down in the echoing great hall.

"I only just found out," he said, angrily.

"Baltsaros, don't you think the first person you should have told was his *mother*?" she asked, her voice low and measured as always.

Baltsaros looked down and started relacing his pants, his mind still on what had happened between him and Jon. For a moment... For a worryingly long moment, the boy kneeling at his feet had been Tom. He licked his lips, feeling off-balanced by the conflict of emotions that suddenly swelled up inside him. Then, just as quickly, they were gone again, leaving him barren and cold. All he wanted to be was alone with his thoughts.

"Don't pretend you are the least bit affected by Tom's life or death," Baltsaros said wearily, lifting his head. He saw that at his words, Abetha had raised her chin higher, a glimmer of wetness in her beautiful ocean-coloured eyes. Remembering Jon's assessment of the queen's feelings, Baltsaros realized in dismay that he may have indeed been wrong about the seemingly dispassionate woman.

"And what would a creature like you know of things like a mother's love," Abetha asked, her nostrils flaring slightly and her cheeks flushed.

"Or a wife's love?" Baltsaros asked quietly.

Abetha's brows came down quickly, and her lips thinned. As she turned to leave, Baltsaros called out as he walked towards her.

"Wait. Abetha," he said hurriedly. "Queen Bee."

She turned to him, a startled look on her face.

"You haven't called me that since those early days, Baltsaros," she said, her expression one of suspicion.

"Why didn't you tell me that this was more than an arrangement for you?" he asked, looking down at her.

She lifted a pale hand to her blond hair and brushed it aside, glancing away briefly with a deep line between her brows.

"Oh it wasn't, Baltsaros. I never intended it to be more. What kind of doting wife wants to pine for her husband for eight or nine months of the year?" she smiled, but it didn't reach her eyes.

Baltsaros frowned.

"Then why this animosity?" he asked. "Jon thinks you loved me." Abetha's eyes flicked away from his face, and he saw they were shimmering again with tears that would never fall.

She laughed softly.

"He's an observant one, isn't he?" Abetha said, her smile genuine when she looked back at Baltsaros. She sighed. "I will admit that I fell for your charms... And that I was imprudent with my thoughts of you during that first long absence. I don't know what I expected... But I certainly did not think that you would come here, to my home, to blatantly paw at my son before my very eyes."

Baltsaros thought of Tom, and he closed his eyes; the boy had stolen into his bed like a sylph and gifted him with pleasure in return for pain.

The great hall had gone suddenly airless.

"I did not 'paw' your son in front of you, Abetha," he said, his voice barely a whisper, trying to bring himself back to the present. "But my indiscretion was an unforgivable lack of respect. I do see that now... And it seems that I wounded you." Baltsaros opened his eyes and looked at his wife. "That you had an attachment to me beyond friendship never once entered into my mind."

At this, Abetha shook her head sadly.

"Baltsaros, we were never friends. Partners, yes. Friendly? Once, definitely. But never friends." She smiled again, and Baltsaros nodded, realizing the truth of it.

In light of this new knowledge, Baltsaros felt oddly driven to confide in the woman who had loathed him for so long; perhaps if her detachment could extend to his relationship with her son, she could help him to see...

To see what?

His expression was open and honest as he looked down at her.

"Tom is indeed alive. He sent a letter to Jon, and we found it only yesterday. Abetha, Tom and I had a falling out, and it was entirely due to my mishandling of my relationship with Jon. I was... excessive in my reaction towards Tom's misconduct," Baltsaros said hesitantly. "I am greatly relieved that he is alive," he continued, shaking his head. "But, I believe there is some troubling connection between Tom and Jon. And... I am having problems reconciling my... emotions." Baltsaros's voice sounded weak to his ears, and he felt strangely lightheaded as if he needed to sit down. Nonetheless, it was good to speak the words out loud.

Abetha's eyebrows had risen in astonishment during his confession. When he stopped speaking, she narrowed her eyes at her husband and looked searchingly into his face.

"How very uncharacteristic of you, Baltsaros. It seems that perhaps I misunderstood something about you as well," she said quietly. After a moment, Abetha tilted her head and appraised him thoughtfully. When she finally spoke, Baltsaros immediately noticed the change in the intelligent woman's tone.

"Would you care to join me in the gardens? I could have some of the white summerwine you love so much brought out. We should speak further. I think you and I need to start again if we're meant to be allies," she said, with a reserved smile on her full lips.

Allies? thought Baltsaros with surprise.

"That would be incredibly gracious of you, my dear," he said and with no small amount of relief, followed her out of the room.

CHAPTER 30
THE BLOOD NEEDS

Life is a battle between faith and reason in which each feeds upon the other, drawing sustenance from it and destroying it.

— REINHOLD NIEBUHR

The night was dark, the woods deep. At the edge of it, Jon stood watching a big tawny cat prowl back and forth at the shore of a black sea, like it was desperate to enter the water but afraid. Taking a step forward, Jon realized that he was covered in blood and lifted his hands, trying to see if the blood was his. He looked up and saw that Tom was there, an amused look on his face.

"When I said he had no heart, I didn't mean for ye to give him yours, lovey," said the big man.

Jon frowned and Tom pointed to his chest. Jon looked down and saw that there was a huge hole cut out of his chest. Alarmed, he put his hand over it, attempting to staunch the blood flow.

Tom laughed, shaking his head, and Jon saw that the young brute had a matching hole. There was a flash of lightning, and the wind started to blow.

"Come!" yelled Jon.

Tom shook his head slowly and pointed to the edge of the water. In the tide were red objects, moving and flopping in the currents against the night beach. Jon saw that they were excised hearts and knew that his and Tom's had to be among them.

"No!" shouted Tom. "Ours are safe."

They were on the ship, and the giant black lion stood on the deck, eyeing them. From its bared fangs dripped blood, and Jon saw that the boat was littered with the dead. He turned

~

Jon groaned and pulled the covers over his head, but he could still hear Baltsaros arguing with Maya outside the door.

"He still doesn't want to see you, Baltsaros," said the proprietress of the tavern.

"I think we should leave that up to Jon, no?" asked the captain, his voice low and annoyed.

With a sigh, Jon sat up. He'd been hiding out in Maya and Katherine's spare room above the tavern for the last two days, avoiding Baltsaros. He still felt shaken and angry about the way that the captain had treated him. And the queen... Her eyes had been so violent.

Jon wasn't sure he could ever return to the castle.

He'd asked Maya to keep Baltsaros away so that he could sort out his thoughts; however, all he'd managed to do was work himself into a worse state thinking about Tom.

Tom and Baltsaros. Baltsaros and Tom.

He rubbed his eyes and stood up a bit unsteadily. The whiskey bottle that Maya had brought up for him was nearly empty on the chair next to the bed. He stumbled over his boot and pitched head first into the door, managing to catch himself at the last second before his face slammed into the wood. As he pressed his forehead against the jamb, Jon took a few deep breaths and unlocked the door, opening it a crack.

Maya held out a hand, her big blue eyes startled.

"It's ok, Jon. The captain was just leaving," she said. Her face was taut with anger as she glared at Baltsaros.

Jon shook his head tiredly.

"Let him in," he said softly. "It's fine. Really."

Baltsaros had turned to look at Jon through the opening, and he could see the effect his state had on the captain. Jon was shirtless, his hair tangled, his face probably pale and haggard. It had been a long two days, and he was certain he reeked of liquor and sweat.

The captain was staring at him with his stark brow raised, the surprise and worry looking out of place on the man's sharp-featured face.

Jon opened the door wide, nodding once to Maya to convey his gratitude before swinging it closed and bolting it shut again. He walked around Baltsaros, who stood like a statue in the middle of the room, and picked up the whiskey, collapsing onto the bed with it.

"Well?" Jon asked and took a swallow direct from the neck of the bottle.

Baltsaros looked down at his hands, a crease appearing between his brows. Taking a step forward, he went down on one knee in front of Jon, his head bowed.

"Jon, forgive me," said the captain, his voice quiet.

Jon goggled at Baltsaros for a moment before breaking into harsh laughter.

"For what? Being a sadistic prick?" he asked, shoving at Baltsaros's shoulder with a bare foot.

The older man fell to his rear on the wood floor but didn't look up.

Jon frowned and took another sip of whiskey before sitting up and setting the bottle down.

What the hell? he thought drunkenly as he stood.

"Forgive me," repeated Baltsaros. When the man raised his eyes to Jon's, he saw that they were wet.

Anger boiled up hot in Jon.

"No!" he said pointing at the captain. "Don't you *dare* do that!" Jon shouted and levelled an awkward kick at Baltsaros's side.

With a grunt from the impact of Jon's foot meeting his ribs, the man just frowned and held his ground.

"I need you," Baltsaros said simply.

Jon rubbed his jaw and circled around the man sitting on the floor. When Baltsaros made no other move to speak, Jon dropped onto the floor next to Baltsaros with a sigh and looked at him in exasperation.

"You're a fucking manipulative bastard. I don't believe those tears for a second," Jon said, shaking his head. He looked down and gritted his teeth, scratching at a dirty spot on his trousers with a fingernail. With a long sigh, he lifted his eyes back to the captain's. "Gods, don't you *ever* be that rough with me again. That was a really shitty thing to do. You're lucky I didn't bite you." He frowned at Baltsaros. "Is that how you treated Tom? No wonder he was afraid of you."

Baltsaros's expression went flat for a moment before he tilted his head quizzically.

"Afraid?" he asked, his voice confused. The captain's eyes went distant like he was remembering something. Incongruously, he chuckled suddenly.

Jon frowned.

"Can you believe that he used to beg me to use him that roughly?" murmured Baltsaros, his eyes refocusing on Jon's face. "He used to make me angry on purpose so that I would be violent with him. Jon, he loves to submit. I can hurt him and hurt him *and he takes it*... and loves every damn minute of it. No, Jon... Tom was only afraid of the whip. Not of me. Never of me."

Jon swallowed hard at the captain's words and thought back to the first time he heard Baltsaros and Tom from across the darkened room.

Baltsaros's eyes were warm and brown as he looked at Jon.

"Tom is beautiful and broken, Jon. He knows it and accepts it for what it is... And *there is nothing wrong with that.* Hells, he's better at coping than you or me," said Baltsaros, rubbing the spot where Jon had kicked him. "He soothed the beast inside me with his submission for so long that I didn't understand what was happening when he was gone."

As Jon listened, he shook his head; the night of the storm showed him a side of Tom that was rough-edged but desperate in its desire for love. Jon wasn't able to reconcile that with the picture that Baltsaros was painting of the muscular brute.

Jon's eyes went wide as he suddenly realized something through his haze: the captain was actually talking about Tom with what seemed like true affection.

"Baltsaros? What happened?" he said slowly, the whiskey in his blood making it hard to think straight. The captain's eyes were hooded and his face strangely bleak as he looked at Jon, and, for the first time, he felt honestly concerned for Baltsaros.

"I think I owe Tom an apology," said the captain quietly.

Jon frowned and stretched an arm out, grabbing the bottle to offer it to Baltsaros.

The captain accepted it with a laugh and drank down some of the amber liquid, grimacing.

"She could have at least given you something decent," Baltsaros said, smiling wryly.

Jon shrugged and ran his fingers through his dark hair, trying to untangle it while he thought. As he stared up at the rough-hewn undersides of the ceiling boards and beams, Jon tried to find the words that had eluded him for the past two days.

"Yes... You do need to apologize to Tom." He nodded. "Will we go find him?" he asked after a moment.

The captain licked his lips and took another swallow of whiskey.

"He may not accept my apology," said Baltsaros, looking sidelong at Jon.

Jon just lifted his shoulders.

"I think he will once he realizes you mean it," he responded. "And for once I really think you do." Jon took a deep breath and took the plunge, deciding to be painfully straightforward.

"I need Tom," he said.

～

Baltsaros closed his eyes.

I need Tom.

Three simple words, similar to the words he had spoken to Abetha in the gardens a few days prior: *I need Tom back.*

It had taken time for him to come around to that understanding. He had forgiven Tom a long time ago for the part he had played in Jon's arrest, but it was only sitting in the beautiful castle gardens, laying his words out to a newfound ally, that he had finally and truly understood:

Baltsaros was angry at *himself.* For his treatment of the sinfully gorgeous youth that had bent and finally broken at his hands. For the fact that he had dismissed Tom's

240

affections so quickly. For the fact that he was utterly crippled when it came to understanding his own needs.

In the shade of the orange trees, Baltsaros had turned the idea around in his head and realized that he had truly wronged his former first mate. Abetha had looked sad when he had said as much. While speaking of her son in such a way had obviously made her uncomfortable, when the queen had seen how earnest he was, Abetha had sighed.

Then go to him, she had said.

Was it really that easy? Baltsaros put the empty bottle down. Jon made him crazy; this was something that he had come to accept. Baltsaros literally wanted to lock the young man in a cage sometimes, away from everyone else. It was an insane impulse and based on next to nothing, an urge that had stripped him of reason, time and time again.

He had *never* felt this way about Tom. In fact, one of his favourite things to do when in port was to throw women and men at Tom to see how well they could use the talented, submissive young man. It was all in good fun.

However, the fact that his former first mate was still alive had become something that was slowly burning him from the inside, rendering him nearly as crazy as Jon made him.

Tom was alive, yes. But was he well? Did he truly hate Baltsaros? It seemed that he would not be satisfied until he saw the young man with his own eyes. The realization that he needed Tom had been hard to swallow for Baltsaros; however, now that it was out in the open, he felt he could think straight again.

He frowned at the dark-haired youth who sagged against his side, made soft and vague by far too much whiskey.

Tom and Jon.

Once, he had hoped exactly for that. They were day and night, summer and winter; yet they weren't exactly opposites. Baltsaros frowned: could he accept that which he had forbidden? As he turned to look into Jon's half-lidded eyes, Baltsaros realized that he would have to try. Baltsaros hadn't enjoyed watching Jon fuck the prostitute like he thought he would; could he deal with watching Tom touch Jon? Watching Tom *fuck* Jon?

He was playing back that first drunken night with the two boys in his mind when he heard his young lover's voice break through his thoughts.

"Tom loves you," whispered Jon.

Baltsaros pressed his face against Jon's dirty, tangled hair. He nodded.

"Yes. I realize that now," he said softly. Such a blind spot for love. Did he love? Did he just obsess? What was this need that called to him? Blue-green eyes... storm-grey eyes. Bodies that moved beneath his hands, minds and hearts that somehow *meant* something to him. Baltsaros felt the impromptu urge to gift something to Jon.

"My marriage will be dissolved," he said. He felt Jon stiffen and watched him sit up sleepily.

Jon looked at him, confused.

"Won't she send more people after you?" he asked. Jon's eyes were large in his pale face, his skin slick from too much drink and not enough sleep. However, his seal-brown curls framed his face attractively and brushed the hollows of his collarbones in a charming way.

Smiling, the captain shook his head.

"No... Abetha and I have come to an understanding. One that should have come a lot sooner. She will stay on as queen. It is I who abdicates the crown," he said. "Abetha will continue to rule here... I honestly don't care. She's done it for the last five years during my absences and, as I have found out in the last day, does a rather spectacular job of it." He ran his hand up Jon's side, smiling. "I'll build us a hut on the beach for next year," Baltsaros said jokingly.

"But... her records?" asked Jon, pulling slightly out of the other man's grasp.

"Just a means of rankling me," replied the captain, grinning a little self-consciously. He reached out and placed his palm against Jon's cheek, his hand somewhat hesitant.

"We'll go find Tom when this is over. I promise you," he said.

Jon, brow knitted, looked at Baltsaros.

"Why?" he asked, his eyes hopeful.

"Because I need him too," he said and leaned in to kiss Jon's lips.

Baltsaros lifted his head off the pillow and frowned. Something had woken him up, but he couldn't hear anything. The bed was narrower and harder than he was used to, but the warm, sleeping body pressed tight against him made it more appealing than the softest feather bed.

Baltsaros smoothed Jon's stray hair out of his face, and he laid his head back down, curling protectively against the younger man. Baltsaros's arm ached slightly from the cut Jon had inflicted on him, and he smiled.

~

"It's a pact," said Jon, his eyes manic with the whiskey coursing through his veins. They were sitting on the floor in the dark, wrapped in the intense embrace of a hot, drunken night, the kind that fuelled desire and wrung promises from even the hardest of hearts.

Baltsaros frowned and looked down at the knife in Jon's hand; the young man was clutching his wrist with the other, intending on slicing through the flesh of his forearm.

"A pact?" asked Baltsaros, intrigued.

Jon nodded slowly.

"Yes... Soldiers would often do this back home to show their loyalty; it was a kind of pledge to always protect each other," he said with a rough emotion in his voice. "They would mingle their blood and be forever part of the other's life."

Baltsaros felt a strange sentiment rise up in him at Jon's words.

Forever is a long time.

He looked thoughtfully at Jon and then dipped his chin in permission.

The knife slid through the skin of his arm, a red, wet line that began weeping a moment after it appeared. The pain was nothing.

Baltsaros felt a strange excitement at sharing his blood with another man. When Jon quickly cut into his own arm, Baltsaros became keenly aroused. It was such an incredibly intimate gesture. Pressing his arm to Jon's, Baltsaros closed his eyes, imagining their blood mingling in each other's veins.

With a strangled moan, Baltsaros opened his eyes and crushed himself against Jon. Jon responded with equal passion, his mouth capturing the captain's in a savage kiss. They soon found themselves entwined on the bed, fumbling with buttons and laces, groping at sensitive skin, wet with spit and blood.

However, in the end their lovemaking was gentle and drawn out; curled into each other like spoons, Baltsaros had stroked Jon slowly to orgasm while buried deep within him from behind. Feeling soft and strangely fragile, Baltsaros's own climax had brought with it a resurgence of the tears that had glistened in his eyes earlier. He didn't understand but didn't question it, simply burying his face in the back of Jon's neck and breathing deep.

~

Jon's eyes opened when he felt Baltsaros lift his head again.

"What is it?" he asked, his voice rough. The inside of his mouth was coated, and his head ached. Baltsaros raised himself up on an elbow behind him, his hand resting on Jon's side, thumb stroking the skin over his ribs. When he blinked his eyes shut again, Jon heard it this time, and his heart beat double.

It was the alarm bell.

Reginald was here.

CHAPTER 31

DARKNESS FALLS

Baltsaros stood in the tower window squinting into the long telescope he had set up. There they were: three dots on the horizon.

Thank the gods it's not more, he thought grimly.

He swivelled the instrument to the mouth of the harbour where the last of the jolly boats was strewing long pieces of wood tied with vines and foliage among the anchored pieces of the false land bridge. Since they hadn't had time to complete the work, the captain hoped that the quickly cobbled-together solution would be enough to sustain the illusion. *Baal's Heart* would be leaving within the hour; Baltsaros was amazed and somewhat proud of the fact that everyone was so organized. Again he thanked whatever forces there were that they had found the letter when they did; the timing couldn't have been any closer.

Baltsaros smiled ruefully at his own inadequate preparations, having wasted the last two days on incredibly selfish pursuits.

Though, was that time really wasted? he wondered. He had successfully navigated the confused courses of his own mind to forge an alliance with a worthy collaborator.

After pulling his eye away from the sights below, Baltsaros turned his head to the handsome, dark-haired young man who sat cross-legged on the floor next to him, trying to kill his hangover with strong, black coffee. Baltsaros had also managed to pull Jon closer to him with the promise of a sacrifice that excited him with curiosity. While he might not survive to see the fruits of what was sown these past few days, he was glad for what had happened.

Jon groaned and leaned his head back on the stone wall. When he turned back to the window, Baltsaros's grin faded, and he clenched his jaw. He felt no fear or worry for the coming battle, only a sense of deep outrage that a man such as Reginald could presume to trespass on Baltsaros's domain.

The captain would personally hasten the old man into the arms of death this time.

〜

Jon swung the blade a few times, testing the heft of it in his hand. It was much better balanced than the practice swords that he and Katherine had spent months using aboard the ship, and he was pleased with how well it moved in his grasp.

Katherine, watching him with her arms crossed, nodded once.

"That'll have to do," she said.

Frowning, he made as if to poke her with the curved tip of the sword.

"Hey! I thought that was pretty damned good, considering whom I had as a teacher," he teased, trying to lighten her mood.

Katherine's lips were pressed together in a hard line, and there was a twitching tightness to her jaw that exposed her worry. She just frowned at him and nodded again distractedly.

"Yes, sure. Now go deliver the rest, Jon," she said and turned to give orders to the next man.

Jon, trying not to let the dread of the coming battle get to him, ran off with the armload of freshly sharpened swords. As he jogged down the wide, cobbled street that ran through the small village, Jon could see through the gaps in the foliage that the three ships were now visible to the naked eye.

The fleet, consisting of a galleon and two smaller frigates, were still a few hours away, but the sight of them made Jon's blood run cold. He could just imagine Reginald, fuelled by zealous revenge, standing high on the aft castle of the galleon staring at the small island through his spyglass.

Picking up the pace, he rounded the corner and descended the old coral-rock stairs that were a shortcut to the beach. As he ran down the uneven steps, he scared the small green lizards that were baking themselves in the hot noontime sun on the low wall. Jon breathed in deep the scent of pink frangipani flowers that bordered the narrow path down, wondering if he would live to smell them this night when they were at their most fragrant.

Caught up in his gloomy thoughts, Jon nearly stumbled when his foot sunk into the soft sand at the base of the stairs. As he looked around at the men working to position the six cannons, Jon spotted Calum.

The old man was sitting on a boulder, a dark hand the colour of walnut shading his eyes as he watched the coming fleet.

After dumping the swords beside Calum, Jon breathed heavily. He was still labouring under the effects of his overindulgence. Earlier, when Baltsaros had pressed him to sleep some more, Jon had been unable to relax enough to do so. Bent over with his hands on his knees, he looked over at Old Calum.

"Shouldn't you be aboard *Baal's Heart* with the rest of the old and infirm?" he asked jokingly. By attempting to make everyone else smile, Jon knew that he was just trying to make himself feel less afraid.

Calum cracked a wide smile, his missing tooth like a broken fencepost in the straight, white grin.

"Should'n'ye be there too, lad? Bein' a wee nipper like yerself... Yer bound ta get crushed underboot, nay?" laughed the old man.

Jon smiled and let himself fall backwards into the soft sand. If anyone could take a coming battle lightly, it was Old Calum. Jon lay looking up at the leaves of the coconut tree overhead and tried to clear his mind of worry.

Calum kicked his leg, and Jon lifted his head. The old man was holding a flask out to Jon, and he tried not to notice how Calum's hand shook; though it was from age and not from fear, it underscored the fact that they were facing an enemy with a scant, motley group of their own.

Jon took the flask from Calum, hoping it was anything but whiskey, and put it to his lips; he was thankful when the liquid that touched his tongue was sweet, spiced rum.

With *Baal's Heart* crammed to the gunwales and making the two-day journey to the next island over, Madierus's population now numbered one hundred and thirty-four men and women.

Jon was glad he had missed all the tearful goodbyes earlier; between the hangover and the fear, he would have been a wreck. It was better this way; he had managed to keep his head thus far.

One hundred thirty-four against how many? Four hundred? Five? he thought. It didn't seem fair that now that his life was filled with love and hope, it should be cut so short.

He took another mouthful of rum and passed the flask back to Calum. Jon laid his head back down in the sand and closed his eyes.

It was almost dusk when the three ships loomed large just past the narrow mouth of the harbour. The captain stood on the roof of the *Grog Blossom* looking across the bay, his face stony and solemn.

The rest of the assembled group was quiet as they watched the three navy ships lower boat after boat over their sides, and Jon rubbed a hand over his face, the fear of the coming battle rearing its ugly head to bite hard at his guts.

Baltsaros, seeing the young man's terror, reached out and pulled Jon against him, a strong arm across his back. As he shuddered slightly in the captain's embrace, Jon tried to get ahold of himself. As always, Baltsaros's heart beat slow and strong in his chest; this time, however, it served only to highlight just how fast Jon's pulse was racing.

"Hush, my love," murmured Baltsaros, stroking Jon's dark curls against the back of his neck. "Don't be afraid."

Jon closed his eyes tight, wishing he had the captain's effortless confidence. They could hear the sound of horns in the distance, heralding the coming battle. Jon took a few deep breaths and leaned hard against Baltsaros.

The captain slid his hand down the younger man's back.

"If you assume that you will die today, you drag death to you as a cold, unforgiving stranger. Instead, embrace death like an old friend, for you will fight side by side with her; and, if death decides to choose you as her champion, you may yet live to fight, and love, another day," said the captain softly into Jon's ear.

After a few minutes, Jon slowly opened his eyes and realized he was calm. He lifted his head from the captain's shoulder and met Baltsaros's fierce gaze with his own. Jon felt ready, almost impatient, for the fight to start.

Baltsaros cupped the side of his face and ran his thumb over Jon's cheek before he leaned in to kiss him, maybe for the last time. The thought made Jon's heart pound harder, and he put all of his love into the kiss, without a care to those watching. Baltsaros's lips were insistent; the force of his ardour was an almost bruising embrace as he leaned in hard, breathing in Jon's breath as his own.

The false strip of land worked well to stall the coming boats; though the illusion was broken when the first boat to reach it tried to disembark onto it, two uniformed navy men sank immediately below the water. Only one man was pulled back into the safety of the boat, and the pirates amassed on the beach let out a roar. They had claimed their first casualty.

With the men on the boats trying to quickly untangle the floating mass of wood and vegetation to get past it, Baltsaros gave the order to start firing. The oldest of the cannons proved to be useless right away when her casing cracked, but the remaining five quickly started sending men to their watery deaths.

BOOM!

BOOM!

Jon thought he would go deaf from the noise, every volley a punch in the chest. After a few minutes, he was surprised when he could hear a strange whistling sound above the racket of the aged cannons and turned his head to Katherine to see if she could hear it too...

...only to see that her arm suddenly ended at the elbow as the small black ball bounced past them on the beach. Stunned into incomprehension by what he had witnessed, Jon watched the blood arc into the air as someone else was nearly cut in half.

Katherine fell to her knees, her face an almost comical mask of shock as she touched the bleeding end of her stump, and Jon looked on as she toppled over onto her side in the muddied red sands. He turned around and looked out over the water and saw a flash come from the side of the lead ship, then another.

The air was rent with screams, and Jon suddenly understood what was happening: they had underestimated the range of the galleon's guns.

"Get back! Get back!" roared Baltsaros from somewhere to his left. Shaken, Jon looked around and saw that the captain had picked up Katherine over his shoulder, motioning for him to follow. The air was filled with whistling as the small cannonballs bounced up the beach, throwing up sand and blood and wreaking destruction wherever they hit.

Jon snapped out of his daze and ran for the low wall; pulling himself up onto it, he reached down for the unconscious woman. Baltsaros handed Katherine up, and Jon hefted her onto his back as he struggled up the slope between the trees. The captain was beside him, lending a hand whenever Jon stumbled.

Soon they were at the tavern, but Baltsaros hastened them on. When they were far enough, the captain stopped him with a hand and helped lay Katherine down on the cobblestones.

From behind him, Jon heard Maya's strangled cry; he stood and turned to take her in his arms as she struggled against him. Stroking her hair, Jon watched as Baltsaros pulled his shirt over his head and cut into it with the short sword at his hip.

After tearing it into strips, Baltsaros twisted them together and passed the loop around the end of Katherine's bleeding stump. There was a pool of blood under her, and the woman was pale.

"A stick!" yelled the captain, and Jon let go of Maya, scooping up a thick twig from the side of the wide throughway. The captain pulled it from Jon's grasp with bloodied hands and passed it through the end of the loop, twisting it round and round to tighten the tourniquet around Katherine's arm, finally tying it in place when the blood had stopped flowing.

The woman's eyelids fluttered as Maya wept and stroked the side of her face.

Baltsaros lifted his eyes to Jon.

"Bring her to the castle. Abetha should have set up a space for the wounded by now. Maya... Maya—listen to me!" said Baltsaros loudly.

She turned to look at the captain, her eyes huge and scared.

"Maya, you have to get water into her when she wakes. She's lost a lot of blood. Nod if you understand me." Maya slowly nodded, and Baltsaros turned back to Jon.

The captain squeezed his arm and smiled tightly.

"Come find me after," said Baltsaros, his face set in hard lines.

Jon nodded and picked up the stricken woman again. As he made his way up to the castle with Maya, he heard the continued booming of the cannons on the beach; Jon sent a little prayer to the brave men and women who were manning them, out in the open and at the mercy of the naval guns.

The sounds of fighting reached his ears as he made his way through the dense foliage. The sun was starting to set, and the coming twilight would make it hard for them to see. To his left, Jon could hear what could only be a death rattle, and he hoped that it was coming from the throat of a navy man and not a friend's.

The big guns on both the galleon and on the beach had been silent for the last little while; there was nothing else to fire upon on the blood-strewn beach, and all the boats had made their way to land, disgorging men along the shore.

Jon, never a good swordsman and not much of a marksman, was put to work helping to haul the wounded to the castle. Every trip there and back was a harrowing experience for him; he hated leaving Baltsaros's side. It was as if keeping the captain within his sights would guarantee that the other man would live.

As he ducked beneath the long, spiny leaves of a huge aloe plant, Jon picked his way to where the captain was watching the fighting from a vantage point above the town square. Baltsaros was stripped to the waist, having sacrificed his shirt to Katherine's arm, and was covered in sweat and blood.

Jon could see that there was a long cut across the captain's chest, but it was only weeping blood slowly and didn't seem to be deep.

When Baltsaros spotted Jon, he jumped down from the low roof of the shed. The captain's eyes were wide and worried as he looked over Jon, and he felt both ashamed and touched that his well-being was the only thing that seemed to break Baltsaros's composure.

"Beard's dead," Jon said sadly when the captain reached him, and Baltsaros nodded. The giant man had taken a lead ball to the temple and somehow lived long enough to take down another three men before he had succumbed to his injuries.

While the odds were definitely in the navy's favour, the pirates of Madierus had managed to cut the invaders' numbers by over half. That still had them outnumbered at least two-to-one, but the battle wasn't over yet. Losing Beard was a terrible blow; however, the man had single-handedly killed a good thirty men on his own.

The great hall of the castle was filling up slowly with the wounded, and Abetha was running a tight ship with the attending servants. Almost all animosity between him and the intimidatingly self-possessed queen had gone away in light of the alliance forged between her and the captain, and the rest of it had dissipated over the course of the past few hours.

Jon saw how incredibly dedicated Abetha was to her subjects and how composed and undaunted she was by the horrors taking place. Jon had a feeling that the population's opinion of the queen would be changed greatly by her actions this day... if any of them survived.

"Abetha says that Katherine is trying to get back out to fight," said Jon, a grin on his face despite everything.

Baltsaros's face creased into a smile, and he laughed loud.

"She would," he said, shaking his head.

Just then the sounds of fighting got closer and Baltsaros's head turned, his eyes like chips of obsidian, flashing in the light of the setting sun.

Baltsaros was torn between running into the fray and keeping back to protect Jon. This was the problem with attachments: they made you weak. Growling under his breath from frustration, he swung his head back to Jon and pointed up to the castle.

"I want you to remain with Abetha," he said, his words a command. Jon's face fell, and Baltsaros cursed under his breath. How to explain to him that to fight, Baltsaros needed to know that Jon was safe?

"Jon, please. Do as I say. Go to her. Protect her," he said, making his voice soft. Baltsaros didn't want to think about Jon being in trouble... Even now, an image of the young man pierced through by a sword was making his heart hammer fast in his chest.

Jon's mouth came down at the corners, and he shook his head.

"I won't leave you! I can fight!" he pleaded.

"For the love of the gods! Jon... Go. Obey me!" growled Baltsaros. "You'll be no good to me dead." When he just stood staring at Baltsaros, the captain lifted his sword and placed the point of it against Jon's right shoulder.

"So help me gods, I will cripple you myself to keep you safe." Baltsaros felt ill saying it, but it was true; he couldn't bear the thought of Jon dying. The sword trembled in his hand. "Please..." he said, his voice hoarse. He swallowed hard. "Please, I don't want to die knowing the pain of your death."

Tears coursed down Jon's face in reaction to the captain's words; he pushed the blade aside and stepped towards Baltsaros. However, he stopped when a group of navy men suddenly burst out from the alley beside the tavern, running towards them.

"Go!" shouted Baltsaros and was gratified when Jon finally spun on his heel to sprint up the road. A cold fury descended on Baltsaros as he watched his lover run before turning to meet his attackers' blades with his own, an ear-rending roar bursting from his throat as he submerged himself in the lust of battle.

Jon stopped to watch a moment, his eyes stinging from tears and sweat.

Baltsaros let out a war cry and turned to the five men who had moved to surround him. The captain was a blur of motion as he hacked and parried with the long, straight sword he held in his right hand, while his left hand darted in like a snake to stab into his attackers with a short, pointed blade.

Jon cried out when he saw the captain take a cut to his thigh but forced himself to look away. He just couldn't watch his lover die.

He won't fall. He won't fall. He won't fall.

The words were a rapid-fire mantra coursing through Jon's head as he ran as fast as he could towards the castle, feeling like he was leaving his heart behind. He sobbed as he ran, the ache in his chest almost too much to bear.

However, when he reached the covered portico, Jon quickly ducked behind a column in alarm. Standing on the wide marble steps were two naval men holding long-guns.

How did they get through the line of defence? he wondered breathlessly.

At first Jon was rigid with panic, unable to move. However, when he heard Maya's scream, his body reacted by hurtling him through the courtyard like a madman, his blade swinging.

Through sheer blunder, Jon managed to knock one of the men backwards down the stairs while attempting to cleave into the second. His blade went wide, but the other man's gun went off as it landed on the marble, sending a lead ball straight up through the bottom of the standing man's jaw. Jon quickly spun around and slashed at the other man's throat, thankful when he saw that it was a killing blow.

After stumbling up the rest of the stairs, Jon ran through the entranceway and pressed himself against the wall next to the open door of a sitting room; he had heard Katherine's voice raised in anger and, a moment later, the low, growling tones of a man that Jon had hoped never to see again. There was the smack of flesh hitting flesh and another loud cry from Maya.

As he gritted his teeth, Jon tried to think of a plan. However, when his mind came up blank, he just took a deep breath and simply stepped over the threshold. Maya was on the ground, and Katherine was on her knees beside her, breathing heavily, a sword held up awkwardly in her remaining hand. She was glaring up at a man who had obviously struck Maya, but made no move to attack.

Jon guessed that the blood loss and the fact that the sword was held in her off-hand stayed her; the woman was probably expending all her reserves just holding the heavy blade aloft.

Abetha and her servants were nowhere to be seen.

With a shiver of revulsion Jon saw that standing in the middle of the room, with a mantle covering his head, was the man he had refused to call "father." He took another step forward.

At Jon's entrance, one of the navy men let out a sharp bark of surprise, and all heads turned to look at the intruder. Even from across the room, Jon could see that the entire left side of Reginald's face was a mass of burn scars, and the sight of it made him sick to his stomach; the old soldier resembled nothing so much as a melted candle.

"There you are, Jon," said Reginald pleasantly. "I'm glad you could join us!" The older man motioned for him to step forward.

Instantly, Jon was taken from behind by two of Reginald's men, his sword wrenched out of his hand. They pushed him further into the room, and Jon struggled in their grasp.

"I was just asking your collaborator here whether she knew of your whereabouts. She was unwilling to help at first so we decided to give her a little incentive," growled Reginald with a crooked smile.

Jon's eyes flicked to Maya's prone form and was glad to see that though the woman was unconscious, she seemed to be breathing easily. He moved his gaze to Katherine's face and saw that the wounded pirate was staring at him in anguish. Jon could see that she had broken out in a sweat; it wouldn't be long before she was too faint to hold herself upright.

"I take it by your lack of surprise that you were somehow alerted to our coming," Reginald said, shaking his head as he pulled at the edge of the hood he wore. "Now, I've been given to understand that you've taken up with the man who is wanted on a few dozen charges, not the least of which is the death of Lord Barton," said the old soldier-turned-privateer.

At this, Jon scowled. He cleared his throat and spoke up.

"I can't understand why the king would authorize such an incredibly stupid enterprise! Barton was a small lord. It seems completely blown out of proportion—"

Reginald suddenly lashed out and kicked a small table. It slid across the floor and crashed to its side, one of the delicate legs breaking off in the process.

"I'm sorry? Jon? What did you say?" asked Reginald, his scarred face bland as he tilted his head towards his stepson.

Jon blinked and frowned. Reginald's mind had obviously taken a beating along with his body.

"Let them go, Reginald. Just... Let them go. You want me... Don't hurt them," he said, lifting his hands.

Reginald's one eyebrow raised in his forehead.

"You?" the scarred man said, his face splitting into a grotesque grin. "No, Jon. I don't care about you. I'm looking for Captain Baltsaros. I'm to bring him back to the king for public execution. The rest of you... Well, I suppose we'll take care of you here once the prisoner is secured. Now," said Reginald, leaning into Jon's face. "Where is he?"

Jon recoiled from the madness trapped in Reginald's single, dark-brown eye and swallowed. Knifing through his fear was a brittle sadness that made his chest ache. He shook his head.

"He's dead," Jon said softly.

He must be. He willed himself not to break down.

"Your men attacked him in the town square."

He heard Katherine's sword clatter to the floor behind him, and Reginald bared his teeth at Jon.

"He can't be dead! I won't allow it!" the man shouted, his spittle hitting Jon in the face. "They're supposed to take him alive, dammit!" The barrel-chested man started walking back and forth in front of Jon.

The younger man heard the sound of another sword falling in the next room and frowned, but Reginald was too caught up in his fury to notice. As he allowed himself to feel a pulse of hope, Jon turned his head, straining to hear more.

The next few minutes were a confusing blur for Jon as he was suddenly dropped by the two navy men holding him, their hands quickly drawing their swords as they turned to face whatever it was that had startled them. Jon stumbled but did not fall, and he swivelled in time to see Calum and a few deckhands burst into the room.

Reginald stood as if frozen in stone for a moment, watching his men fight the pirates.

Jon fumbled at his belt; sliding Tom's long knife out of its sheath, he held it up to Reginald.

The older man turned, honest surprise on his burned face.

"Jon? What are you doing?" he said, putting his hands up.

Jon could see that the fingers of Reginald's left hand had fused into a shiny fist of scar tissue from the fire. "Oh, we weren't going to execute you! You're my son! Jon...

Put the knife down." Reginald stopped mid-step when Jon's knuckles whitened on the bone hilt of the blade.

"Your son? Your witch hunt took the life of the only man who ever believed in me," he growled through his teeth. The sounds of fighting grew quiet around him as he stared down the old soldier.

Reginald's eye had gone wide at Jon's words.

"Believed in you? What was there to believe in? Just come home..." said Reginald and suddenly stepped forward, tackling Jon.

The two men struggled; Reginald had the advantage in size but, being crippled, wasn't quite able to grasp Jon to restrain him.

Gnashing his teeth, Jon let out a grunt and threw all of his weight against his stepfather; Reginald and Jon fell to the ground, grappling at each other. Jon's knife cut into Reginald again and again, but the man seemed immune to the pain.

Blood dripped down onto Jon's face when Reginald was finally able to pin him on his back. Jon bucked his hips but wasn't able to dislodge the heavy-set man who straddled him. After wresting his arm free from Reginald's good hand, he managed to push the man off his other arm to bring his knife up again.

Jon slashed at Reginald's neck, but the man grabbed his wrist, stopping it mid-arc. When Reginald squeezed, Jon felt small bones grind together, and he panted hard in pain and fear; he realized that the old soldier was far stronger than he was.

With an almost lazy movement of his hand, Reginald succeeded in turning the point of the blade towards the man beneath him and, without further struggle, buried it up to the hilt in Jon's chest.

Jon gasped and let out a soft moan.

Reginald glared down at him, breathing hard.

Jon thought it weird that he felt no pain, but the edges of his vision started to go a strange grey. Jon licked his lips and tasted blood, coughing weakly.

"No!" came a strangled cry from above.

Jon lifted his eyes, confused. It sounded like Baltsaros. If the priests were right, he would be seeing the captain again soon on the other side.

A moment later a hooked sword appeared to one side of Reginald's neck, and Jon watched in a haze as another blade passed cleanly through the stem of the ex-soldier's thick neck. Hot blood gushed over him like a red wave, and he turned his head away. Jon could only see a narrow tunnel when he opened his eyes again, and he imagined that he saw the face of Baltsaros above him, brown eyes wide with worry.

Jon smiled.

I'll see you soon, my love. His eyes slipped closed in the dark...

...and then Jon knew nothing else.

CHAPTER 32
ENTR'ACTE

"Come!" yelled Tom. "Come back! You're out of the woods, love. Just sail to me..."

~

His cheek was warm, and the light beyond his eyelids made the world bright red for a moment before he opened his eyes.

He looked up and blinked.

Above his head were the familiar sails of colourful silk draped over the high, carved posts of Baltsaros's bed. When he turned his head slowly, he saw that the curtain was pulled back from the open window, and the bright sun shone down on him; he could smell the orange trees and the sea air.

Shifting his shoulders slightly, he let out a groan; his chest was a tight, burning mass of pain. At the sound of his voice, he heard someone move beside him, and he turned his head the other way. Baltsaros was lying on his side, eyes closed in sleep.

Jon gasped and reached out a tentative hand, afraid to believe in what he saw. However, when the tips of his fingers made contact with the older man's brow, his heart leapt in his chest.

Baltsaros's eyes slowly opened, and Jon's vision swam with sudden tears.

Alive!

He watched Baltsaros's gracefully curved lips stretch into a relieved smile.

"Hello, my love," said the captain, his voice hushed.

Jon tried to move closer to Baltsaros, and he gasped again in pain.

Baltsaros quickly sat up and pressed down gently on Jon's shoulder.

"Don't move... You're badly hurt."

With a confused frown, Jon stared up at Baltsaros.

"Reginald?" he asked, startled by how hoarse he sounded. Images of the fight came flooding back to him. Hesitantly, he touched his chest, and his fingers encountered a thick bandage; he remembered how sickeningly easy the blade had slid into him.

"You're lucky to be alive," murmured Baltsaros, taking Jon's hand into his own and pressing his fingertips to his lips.

"How are *you* alive?" rasped Jon.

Baltsaros's brows came down in a startled frown.

"Me? Why wouldn't I be?" he asked, smiling.

Jon's eyes slid down Baltsaros's body, seeing for the first time all the bandages and bruises that covered the captain's tanned skin.

"I saw you get cut—" Jon started to cough, every spasm a fist of pain pummelling him hard.

Baltsaros quickly slid a hand beneath Jon's head and held a cup of water to his lips when the coughing subsided.

Jon drank the cool liquid down thankfully, washing away the slight taste of blood in his mouth.

Baltsaros lowered him back down on the pillow, and Jon realized he was famished. As if reacting to his thoughts, Jon's stomach growled loudly, and Baltsaros chuckled.

"Hungry?" he asked.

Jon nodded.

"I'm not surprised. We've been feeding you only broth while you were out. I think you might soon be ready for something a little more substantial," said Baltsaros, his face creased in a grin.

Jon closed his eyes and swallowed. He felt so groggy.

"How long was I sleeping?" he asked, looking up at the captain.

"Twelve long days," said Baltsaros, his eyes large and serious. "I thought I was going to lose you." Baltsaros's voice was rough with emotion as he looked down at Jon.

Twelve days? Jon felt himself tremble, and his breath hitched in his chest.

"Reginald managed to miss your heart and only just nicked your left lung. I had to keep you sedated so you wouldn't cough and open the bleeding wound in your lung further. Then a fever settled in on the fourth day, but amazingly you started recovering. There were a few times when I thought you were awake; however, you were ranting and raving about Tom, and hearts, and how we had to go to the Devil's Isles. You didn't even know I was holding you," said Baltsaros, his hand stroking Jon's hair softly back.

As he blinked sleepily, Jon turned his head and captured Baltsaros's hand, pressing it against his cheek.

"I love you," he said softly and promptly fell back to sleep.

~

Baltsaros watched Jon's eyes flutter closed and smiled. He felt more confident about the young man's recovery. Baltsaros decided then not to tell Jon exactly how close it had been.

When he placed his palm on Jon's forehead to check his temperature, Baltsaros was brought back to the first time he had touched the young man; it felt like a lifetime ago.

Jon frowned in his sleep and his mouth twitched.

Baltsaros pulled his hand back quickly; Jon was cool, and sleep was what he needed the most. He stretched out on his stomach beside Jon and laid his head down on his folded arms to keep vigil while the young man healed.

～

The sword sliced into his thigh, but Baltsaros knew instinctively that the cut was not deep. He simply spun in place, neatly shearing off the sailor's arm. It had been a long time since he had taken part in combat, and Baltsaros's muscles sang with pain and fatigue. However, he kept on, knowing that Jon would be safe in the castle as long as their line of defence held.

Grunting as he pulled the long blade out of one man's chest, he dipped low and slid his short sword through the back of another's ankle, crippling him. Baltsaros breathed heavily, the world narrowing down to the reach of his swords. Slash, duck, spin, stab; it was a graceful, deadly dance. Again a sword bit into him; this time it was his bicep. Shrugging off the pain, Baltsaros turned again.

Slash, duck, spin, stab.

More men came at him. Baltsaros fought for freedom, but it was more than that... He fought for friendship. He fought for love.

Jon...

The hilts of his swords became slippery and then sticky with the blood of his dance partners. As he turned and swept low with the long sword, Baltsaros pivoted on the ball of his foot, felling the men who came at him until finally... He stood alone.

Panting in the gloom of the open town square, Baltsaros wiped the sweat from his eyes; in a daze he stared at all the bodies around him. Blinking slowly, he raised his head and looked around, realizing there was a voice calling to him.

Jon?

However, the dark-haired man running towards him from the direction of the beach was Malik.

"Captain!" yelled the shipwright. "All three ships are being crippled as we speak, but someone spotted a boat docked far to the east. There's a path beaten through the brush... Nathaniel thinks there may be trouble at the castle—" Malik hadn't finished speaking before Baltsaros turned on his heel and ran full tilt up the cobbled road.

Jon.

On the way up to the castle, Baltsaros caught up to Calum leading a small group of ship hands in the same direction.

"Defences breached?" asked Baltsaros breathlessly as he slowed his pace.

"Aye, Cap'n. Queenie sent a runner down," said Calum, his voice low. The old man's left eye was swollen shut, and he walked with a slight limp, but he radiated a powerful ferocity. Beneath the lined skin and grey hair, Baltsaros saw once again the intense young man that had taken him under his wing on the *God's Hammer*.

The captain ground his teeth and nodded sharply, momentarily rendered speechless with worry.

Calum frowned and reached out to Baltsaros, his gnarled fingers digging into the captain's shoulder.

"Jon?" he asked, his face hard.

Baltsaros nodded again once.

"Well, Cap'n, let's go give 'em hell," growled Calum and took off again at a steady jog.

The captain pushed back on the fear tightening his chest and took off after the old man.

~

"The rest of it happened pretty quickly," said Baltsaros, watching Jon take another huge bite of the freshly baked bread. "Apart from the men in the room we found you in, there was a scattering of other sailors. However, Abetha, clever woman, had managed to poison over half of them by sending her servants to sprinkle dried moonberries in all the water jugs. Crude but effective. I have a feeling that Reginald's fleet may have been running out of fresh water by the time they reached us, given how quickly his sailors drank everything in sight," he said, chuckling.

"Calum and his men dispatched everyone quickly. I had no idea where you were; in our haste we passed right by the sitting room where Reginald was holding you. I backtracked when I heard Katherine's sword fall but was beset by a few of Reginald's men. I... thought the worst when I saw Reginald stab you. I was sure you were dead." Baltsaros rubbed his jaw, remembering for a moment the anguish that had coursed through him. "I cut off the head of that human wastrel, and... Then you moved."

Jon's fingers slid over Baltsaros's forearm, stroking the skin while he listened, as if unable to break contact even for a moment.

"The rest of the navy men?" Jon asked, chewing.

Baltsaros smiled.

"What rest? With their ships crippled and set ablaze, drifting out to sea... I don't think there are any more to speak of." The captain's face got serious. "We lost nearly a third of our number. The funerals are still going on. It's going to take a while to rebuild."

Jon nodded, his face sombre.

Katherine was recovering slowly, but it would be a long time before she would be able to fight again. Maya was fine, her broken nose mending nicely.

As a man who was not given to religious flights of fancy, Baltsaros was trying not to attribute their incredible victory to anything other than pure luck. However, he was having a hard time of it. He slid his arm under Jon's fingers to grasp his hand firmly. It truly felt like something had been looking down on them with favour.

Jon smiled softly and squeezed Baltsaros back. The younger man was pale and weak as he sat back against the pillows, devouring a meal of bread and thick soup, but he was gaining strength daily.

Feeling his heart swell in his chest, Baltsaros looked fiercely at Jon, and the dark-haired man frowned at him.

"What is it?" asked Jon, his voice alarmed.

Baltsaros licked his lips and swallowed.

"I'm just so very glad you're alive, Jon. So very glad," he said softly. "You are my everything."

～

Jon walked slowly down the wide cobbled street. While his deep wound had healed well, he was taking his time as he was still prone to dizzy spells. Baltsaros assured him it was from having spent so much time in bed and not from anything permanent; Jon hoped the captain was right.

As he looked out at the harbour through the gaps in the tall palms by the side of the thoroughfare, Jon could make out the mizzenmast of the galleon sticking up from the water just past the mouth of the lagoon. While the frigates had burned a long time, drifting out into deeper waters, the bigger ship had succumbed quickly and went down within sight. Since it wasn't actually in the way, Baltsaros had decided to leave the mast where it was to serve as a warning to other ships that might come their way.

After all, Reginald had died without disclosing whether he had told anyone else of the island's existence or coordinates.

Jon pulled open the door of the *Grog Blossom* and winced as the motion stretched the scar tissue that graced his chest. Baltsaros had said that would pass too.

As he stepped into the large room, Jon smiled to see Baltsaros leaning over a large map, arguing good-naturedly with Nathaniel and Malik over the modifications that were taking place on the ship.

"It'll be harder to make her come about with all that extra width!" said the captain, lifting the mug of beer to his lips to take a deep swallow. "I like my ship sleek. You're making her into a fat sow!"

Malik laughed and shook his head.

"What? You prefer we get stuck in the ice? Your fat sow will be able to navigate the growlers and bergy bits!" he said, grinning at Baltsaros. "I'm sure of it." Malik spotted Jon approaching and smiled wide.

Baltsaros lifted his brow curiously at the shipwright and turned to look over his shoulder. The absolute pleasure that came over the captain's starkly defined face at seeing Jon made him feel weak. Quickly coming to Jon's side when Baltsaros saw him falter, the captain helped him down into a chair.

"Jon? Are you all right? What's the matter? You suddenly looked like you were going to fall," said Baltsaros, his eyes darting over Jon's face and chest.

Chuckling, Jon just wrapped his fingers around the back of Baltsaros's neck and pulled him close, capturing the captain's lips with his own.

"When you look at me like that..." he said softly after a moment, his blue eyes wide. "It feels like I'm home."

The captain's pupils dilated, and his eyes got dark with emotion.

Jon felt a pang of desire; the last month had brought a tenderness to their lovemaking that wasn't solely based on having to be careful of Jon's injuries. Jon craved Baltsaros's hands on his body day and night.

Baltsaros, sensing the shift in Jon's mood, opened his mouth over the younger man's again.

"Gods, you two are bound and determined to make me ill," drawled Katherine as she kicked Jon's chair in passing.

The captain frowned, lifting his head, and Jon had to laugh.

It was as if the battle had smoothed away all icy formalities between the crew and their captain. The mood was now, more often than not, warmly amicable, the men and women less afraid of lightly teasing the captain.

Jon smiled ruefully. Baltsaros seemed the better for it; it was nice to see him taken off the pedestal from time to time.

Katherine deposited one of the mugs in her hand on the table beside Jon before she sat down in another chair, crossing an ankle over her knee. She still held her amputated arm awkwardly against her chest as if afraid to bump it, but the coordination of her left hand had greatly improved.

"I can't believe you guys are actually going to go through with it. You're out of your heads... You all have a bloody death wish," she said, shaking her head. Katherine wouldn't be coming with them. Not only was her wound still on the mend, but Katherine had claimed that a quieter life helping to rebuild Madierus was more to her tastes.

However, Jon knew from Maya that the ex-pirate often woke up screaming in the middle of the night; the fight had been cut out of Katherine.

"Death wish! Please. We're only just going to attempt navigating through a narrow, dangerous pass in the Devil's Isles to reach goddess-knows-what on the other side!" said Nathaniel, smiling wide as his hazel eyes twinkled in merriment.

"If that's not a death wish, I don't know what is," replied Katherine, holding up her mug in salute.

Baltsaros had stood to turn back to the map and was flipping through the sheaf of papers that was stacked on it. The captain and Malik had collaborated to create detailed drawings of all the modifications that needed to take place for the dangerous journey.

"I'm still not convinced about this..." Baltsaros continued where the conversation had left off.

Katherine narrowed her eyes at Jon.

"What happens if Tom says no?" she asked quietly.

Jon took a swallow of beer before replying. Without Katherine as first mate, and the only other feasible candidates killed during the fighting, Baltsaros had astounded him by saying they would sail north to the *Jewel* to start their hunt for Tom as soon as Jon was able to travel. For such a dangerous voyage to the unknown, rationalized the captain, no one else would do.

Jon shrugged slightly, the motion causing him some pain.

"Tom won't say no," he said simply.

He can't, Jon wanted to say. *There is something incredibly important that isn't finished between us.*

However, he kept his words to himself. Katherine already thought him crazy for his affections towards the cheerful brute; he didn't want to make it worse by telling her that Tom was now calling to him nightly in his dreams. When he had confessed as much to Baltsaros, the man had just nodded, his expression guarded. It remained to be seen what would happen to their relationship when they found Tom.

Jon drained his beer and turned his thoughts away from his worries. Grinning, he held out his mug to Katherine.

"Barkeep, I believe I'll have another."

CHAPTER 33

THREE-SIDED TAPESTRY

If you are not too long, I will wait here for you all my life.

— OSCAR WILDE

They left at the end of the month.

The hardest part for Jon was saying goodbye to Katherine and Maya; he would miss them terribly, and there was no way to know whether he would ever make it back to Madierus given the danger of the trip they were undertaking.

Katherine reiterated again and again that it was a fool's errand to attempt the journey past the Devil's Isles, but both Jon and Baltsaros were resolute.

The goodbyes were heartfelt and tearful; Jon wouldn't soon forget the friendships he had made.

In the end, he decided to leave Brutus behind with Eloise; the huge dog had become the lonely little girl's best friend, and Jon wouldn't think of separating them.

Abetha was gracious and reserved at their parting, but when the ship made its way out of the harbour, Jon looked back and saw that the queen was flying a banner of Baltsaros's modified family crest above the castle.

That first evening out, Cook made an astonishing discovery: in the big storage area below the galley were three huge casks of Maya's excellent wheat beer. While the crew drank and celebrated the start of the journey, Baltsaros kissed away Jon's tears before coaxing soft moans and sighs out of him in the dark of the quarterdeck above.

The first stop on their long journey was to the neighbouring island to resupply and take on some new deckhands. They were short on so many posts, but there would be plenty of opportunity to learn duties and become a cohesive crew during the six-week-long trip to find Tom.

Baltsaros had sent word ahead so that little time would be wasted since they had such a narrow window of opportunity. If the weather held up, Baltsaros and Jon would have less than a week to search for Tom; any longer and they would miss their chance at making the crossing between the high spikes of the Devil's Isles while the water remained largely unfrozen.

If they were unable to locate the estranged mainlander, the crew would take a vote to see if they were willing to chance it without Tom's expertise or wait another season. After all, they might have found a worthy replacement among the new crew by that time, as unlikely as that was.

As if something wished to hasten their journey north, the wind blew steady and strong, and the trip was uneventful. Jon made some new friends aboard, but mainly kept to himself, the worry of finding Tom making him tense and quiet.

What if he was wrong?

Jon stood up on the crates lashed to the mainmast, watching the peninsula come into sight nearly a week early. The sun was just over the yardarm, and the blue sky was dotted with clouds like fat, fluffy sheep. However, though it was warm, it lacked the open-mouth kiss of the southern islands' humidity.

His knuckles white as he held onto the rope above his head, Jon rubbed the healed scar on his chest and frowned. The letter that Tom wrote was months old now; there was no guarantee that the man was here.

But, where else could he be? Where else can we start? he thought.

This was a busy port town, making it unlikely that Tom was still here; he could have taken a ship to anywhere in the known world from this harbour. Tom was an expert sailor and powerfully built; finding employment aboard another vessel would be terribly easy for the burly, surefooted mainlander.

As he leaned against the mast, Jon tried not to let his thoughts spiral out of control again. The question that sat heavy in his heart had made his doubt an almost crippling thing:

Why hadn't Tom come to their aid?

Why had he simply warned them? There were so many reasons Jon could think of and most of them were negative. Every time he let his mind wander down that path, Jon found himself feeling raw and frantic by the end of the day; only Baltsaros's strong arms and mobile mouth were able to soothe the unease that trembled through him then.

Jon jumped down from the crate and ran to help turn the capstan so they could anchor outside of the harbour. The mood aboard *Baal's Heart* was one of nearly giddy excitement; while the goal of the trip north, before turning south again, was to find Tom, the captain had promised the crew a little fun.

However, since the sailors earned no wages, sharing equally in plunder instead, some of the newer ship hands were looking a little forlornly at the beautiful building at the edge of the harbour; *Baal's Heart* had yet to pillage another ship or take part in smuggling this season, so there was no plunder to be shared.

Jon grinned a little crookedly as he walked to his quarters, thinking about splitting up some of his own money to cover the cost of some drinks for them at the very least.

Jon opened the door to the stateroom and smiled at the sun streaming in from the stained-glass windows behind the captain. The five panels that showed the silhouette of a roaring lion in red standing above a mound of ivory skulls was somewhat morbid, but it was based on Jon's dreams, so he loved it. It made Jon feel like the ship contained a small part of his soul... like he truly belonged there.

Jon saw that Baltsaros had dressed in a dark-red shirt and his black leather pants. The older man stood straight, buttoning a charcoal grey vest over his shirt as he watched Jon cross the room.

Jon gazed in awe at his tall, handsome lover.

The captain had a way of making the act of dressing as sensual as the reverse; his agile fingers slipped the glass buttons through the slits in his vest in a way that made Jon feel like he was watching something terribly intimate. Walking up to Baltsaros, Jon pulled one of his hands away from their work and kissed the deeply lined palm.

Baltsaros reached up and caressed the side of Jon's face.

"Ready?" asked the captain, his expression unreadable. They were taking the first of the jolly boats across the harbour to start asking about Tom, and Jon had the impression that though Baltsaros was his usual stoic self, he was feeling nervous.

Jon swallowed hard and nodded.

The captain lowered his hand and started towards the door.

"Don't worry. We'll find him."

Awkwardly standing beside Baltsaros as he angrily questioned the figure wearing the long silks, Jon looked around.

The *Jewel* looked the same as it had so many months before, but this time he was seeing it with more experienced eyes. Not able to understand the language the captain was speaking nor the strange body language of the draped figure, Jon's talent was proving to be useless in this endeavour; he couldn't tell if there was information being kept from them.

However, as his eyes scanned the tiered tables, his gaze came to rest on a familiar figure: the brunette that had entertained him and Baltsaros the last time they were here.

She caught his eye and smiled; Jon blushed slightly and smiled back, thinking she remembered him.

A moment later, however, the pretty girl's eyes widened and she looked quickly away; Jon had the distinct feeling that she had just made some sort of connection and was nervous about it. When he recalled that she had previously seen Tom and him together as they were leaving, Jon felt the thrill of hope. Slipping away from the captain's side, Jon navigated the staggered platforms, making his way quickly towards the girl.

Looking at him in surprise when he deliberately placed a coin on the table in front of her, the girl's eyes darted to a door to one side of the bar before meeting his gaze again with a bland, lustful look on her face.

"Hello, pretty man," she said in her accented voice, leaning forward to run a finger down his chest. "I make you feel some love?"

Jon leaned forward and stared into her dark-blue eyes.

The girl looked down shyly, pulling her hand away from his chest to finger the watered silk at her cleavage.

"Where is he?" asked Jon softly.

The girl's full lips, dark like blood in her dusky face, pressed against each other as she swallowed. When she turned back to him, there was a worried look in her eyes.

Jon shook his head and pressed on.

"It's ok. I'm not going to tell anyone you told me. You know where Tom is, don't you?" he asked gently. "I need to find him."

The girl's gaze went pointedly to the door again and back to Jon.

He nodded and placed another gold coin on top of the first before walking swiftly to the door. No one was watching him as he opened it a crack and peered inside. On the other side was a long, dark corridor.

With a glance back at the captain who was still speaking with the host or hostess, Jon slipped through the door and walked quietly down the hallway. There were doors to the left and right, but when Jon tried the handles they were all locked. His heart high in his throat, he continued along the passageway, fearing that someone would come upon him trespassing.

I'll just say I got lost, thought Jon, trying yet another handle.

This one turned easily in his hand, and he started to open it, sunlight streaming into the dark hallway from beyond. However, Jon froze when he heard the familiar cadence of a mainlander accent coming from the other side. Though Jon couldn't hear what he was saying, the laugh that burst out of the man a moment later was unmistakably Tom's.

All thoughts of caution evaporated as Jon pushed the door open the rest of the way. He realized he was standing at the rear of the building in some kind of loading dock; stacked around him were rough-hewn, open crates of bottles and other supplies intended for the bar.

As he squinted against the light of the midday sun, Jon could see a group of men talking and laughing as they unloaded a cart full of fresh produce. Jon heard Tom's chuckle again, and his eyes snapped towards the man in the centre.

He felt a little faint.

The broad, muscular shoulders that tapered down to a narrow waist were heartbreakingly familiar. However, where before there had only been scars on the large expanse of tanned skin, now were intricate, black lines that curved and meandered down the left side of the burly man's torso, disappearing beneath the waistband of a pair of dark-green pants that were rolled up at the calf.

Jon took a step forward. He could see more tattoos peeking above the low-riding waistband on the right side too, curling around the defined lines of the man's hip. The matching scrolling, black designs on either side were exactly where Jon would put his hands if he were to—he swallowed.

As Jon watched, the massively built man shook his head and smacked the shoulder of the worker next to him with a large, scarred hand. Rooted to the spot and speechless, Jon felt his heart thrumming hard against his ribs. One of the workers, a case of wine high up on his shoulder, scowled at Jon and growled at him in passing.

"Ye could a' least help instead o' standin' there like a bloody post, son," he said, his voice rough.

The tattooed man's back went rigid, and he turned around slowly. The black lines that graced the man's back also curled around the left side of his chest, and Jon could see he had a metal ring through that nipple. The sight was alarming and terribly beguiling.

The thing that made Jon finally speak was the intense cascade of emotion that widened the man's beautiful sea-green eyes: shock, relief, and breathless elation.

"Tom," said Jon, his unsteady voice rendering that simple syllable into a near-croak. He took a step forward.

Tom's mouth was half-open as he stared across the space at Jon. A mere second later it was as if a metal door had closed in Tom's eyes, shearing off the emotions that had set them alight.

Jon heard the captain's soft step behind him.

"Well, well. What the fuck do we have here?" asked Tom, his face going taut with resentment.

"Hello, Tom," said the captain quietly, placing a hand on Jon's shoulder.

The muscles bulged in Tom's jaw, and he shot an accusing look at the dark-haired youth. When Jon shook his head gently, Tom's composure thawed slightly.

"What do ye want?" Tom asked, his eyebrows tilting up as he looked at them with suspicion on his rugged face.

"Just to talk," said Baltsaros. Though his voice was smooth and unhindered by the emotions running through Jon, the younger man thought he could feel a slight tremor in the captain's hand.

Tom stared at them for an uncomfortably long time, his face wavering between indignation and despair.

Finally, he nodded.

Tom turned to the men who were watching the strange spectacle and gave orders to square up with someone at the bar before motioning with his chin for Jon and Baltsaros to follow him.

Wordlessly, they went back down the corridor and up a set of spiralling stairs that Jon had missed. When they reached a flat panel in the wall, Tom looked back at Jon; he could have sworn he saw the tiniest hint of guarded emotion in Tom's otherwise grim face. The reason why was clear when they pushed through the hidden door to emerge into the same room where Tom had found Jon that fateful morning; the day Tom had been lost.

Jon's breath sounded loud to him as he stood, uncomfortable, watching the captain and his ex–first mate size each other up.

Tom began pacing back and forth across the thick red carpet, glancing up at Baltsaros with every pass, and Jon frowned.

The captain stood straight and tall, not a hint of emotion in his hooded eyes. Then, as if some decision had been reached in his mind, Baltsaros extended his arms to either side.

Tom stopped his pacing and let out a sharp bark of a laugh, shaking his head.

"Ye think it's that easy, *Captain?*" he spat, his hands balled at his sides.

Baltsaros made no move as he stared hard at Tom with his arms out.

The muscular young man looked down, bringing a hand up to rub the side of his thumb against the coarse, dark-blond stubble of his cheek. Tom laughed harshly again; however, when he looked back up, Jon was astounded to see that his blue-green eyes were wet and wide with anguish.

"Ye *promised*, Da," Tom said hoarsely. "And still ye whipped me like a bloody fuckin' cur." Unable to stand still, Tom renewed his pacing; it was a frantic motion, like an animal trapped in a cage.

There was a lump in Jon's throat, and he shifted on his feet, feeling like he was an interloper.

Baltsaros just nodded slowly and beckoned with his hands.

With a hitch in his breath, Tom surprised Jon by suddenly stepping forward into Baltsaros's embrace, trembling visibly.

Jon stared on in misery, unable to look away.

As he wrapped his strong arms around Tom, Baltsaros leaned down and murmured something in the big man's ear, words that were not meant for anyone else to hear.

Tom nodded and whispered something back.

His face burning, Jon stared down at his feet. This was not how he had imagined their reunion would be; no, this was suddenly a horrible, gut-twisting mistake. Why in the blasted hells had he thought himself capable of... of... this. He ground his teeth and blinked hard to clear his eyes of the tears that were threatening to fall.

There was no competing with the relationship between Baltsaros and Tom.

Completely overwhelmed and forgotten, Jon was debating whether he should leave when he heard Baltsaros's voice.

"Jon?" said the captain softly. Jon looked up and saw that Baltsaros was staring at him over Tom's shoulder, his brown eyes warm and kind. "Come."

It wasn't a command. It was an invitation.

Jon saw that the tension that had held Tom so rigid had melted away; he literally sagged against the captain.

"Come," repeated Baltsaros, his face gentle.

With a deep breath, Jon walked a few steps forward.

Baltsaros held out his hand and took Jon's in his own, pulling him the rest of the way. He felt breathless and nervous, utterly confused by the situation... And then Baltsaros placed Jon's palm flat against Tom's back. He felt Tom stiffen with a gasp under his hand, the hard muscles sliding under his touch.

Baltsaros stroked the back of Tom's neck with his long fingers, watching Jon with what his innate talent read as gratitude. The captain slid Jon's hand up Tom's warm side, and he felt the big man exhale with a small vibration against Jon's palm. Strong, unexpected desire began burning its way through his misgivings, and he brought his other hand up to grasp Tom's waist; this time the soft moan that came from Tom was audible.

Under Baltsaros's curious and inviting gaze, Jon traced the edges of Tom's tattoos with his fingertips, his heart beating swiftly in his chest as he watched his touch raise goosebumps on the bigger man's skin. Then, Jon leaned forward and did the unthinkable; he pressed his lips against Tom's broad shoulder, opening his mouth to touch his tongue to the man's salty skin.

The big man smelled of sunshine, whiskey, and tobacco, a familiar scent that made Jon warm with longing.

Tom's breath hissed out of him, and Jon looked up to see that Baltsaros had sunk his teeth hard into the other side of big man's neck. With a groan, Jon pressed his chest against Tom's broad back and slid his hands down over the other man's hips to press Tom back against him, kissing the hard muscles of his shoulder. Tom moved his pelvis to grind against Jon, and he nearly cried out at the hard surge of lust that shook him.

Breathless, Jon knew he had to step back, had to let go. His heart was careening in his chest, and he was growing uncomfortably hard in the front of his pants.

Tom turned at Jon's sudden departure, and he registered confusion and dismay on the handsome brute's rugged face.

"I... don't know what I'm doing," was all that Jon could say. His chest was tight, and he felt lightheaded; Jon wanted this more than anything in the world, but he couldn't wrap his head around it. It was too staggering.

Baltsaros pulled away from Tom and stepped back, a thoughtful expression on his face. He then turned and took the few steps to the bed, climbing up and leaning back against the pillows, his hands folded in his lap with his legs stretched out, ankles crossed. With a small smile, he pointed at Jon.

"Tomcat," he said. "Help Jon out of his clothing."

Jon's heart hit a new peak rate as he watched Tom turn around and look at him intently.

He was absolutely gorgeous, and terribly intimidating; the tattoos on his bronze skin outlined and enhanced Tom's musculature, making him seem even more brawny than he was, while his green-blue eyes recalled the warm waters of the tropics. Though Tom was staring at him with open desire, there was also the hint of how completely astounded and still somewhat skeptical of the situation he was.

Jon wanted to recapture those stolen moments during the storm, but with the captain present, how were they supposed to...

"Tom?" repeated Baltsaros from the bed.

Tom stepped forward as if pushed, and he grinned despite the tension in the room. Ducking his head, he reached for the front of Jon's grey shirt and undid the laces holding the neck closed. When he saw the terrible scar on Jon's chest, Tom's eyes flicked up to his in concern; Jon just shook his head and smiled grimly.

Later.

Tom's brows came down, and he suddenly leaned forward to capture Jon's mouth with his own, urgent and protective. The bigger man's hands came around him as he savaged Jon's lips and yanked his shirt free of his pants; Tom released him only long enough to pull it over his head before pressing himself hard against Jon again.

Jon was flooded with relief.

He had not been wrong about Tom's feelings for him.

He opened his eyes and saw that Baltsaros was staring intently at them, unmoving. What was the captain feeling about all of this?

Tom's hands had snaked down to the front of Jon's pants, and all thought left his head as he felt the buttons come loose. After a moment, Tom dropped to his knees in front of Jon; he then gently, almost reverently, peeled Jon's pants down, looking up at him with naked hunger as he did so.

"Good boy," said Baltsaros. The captain's eyes were dark and unreadable, but the hand curled over the front of his pants betrayed the desire he was feeling.

Jon's breath heaved in his chest, and he stepped out of his boots as Tom tugged at them. He was now stark naked in front of Tom who remained on his knees, gazing up at him. Jon could see the bigger man's pulse jumping in the veins at his neck, but he frowned in confusion when Tom made no other move. He realized with a start that Tom was waiting for Baltsaros's next command.

Jon reached out and touched the top of Tom's head, running his fingers softly through the short, sandy-blond strands.

"Do you want him to suck your cock?" asked Baltsaros, almost conversationally.

The question made Jon feel like he had just stepped off a cliff. He gulped and closed his eyes, nodding quickly.

"Tom, please use that talented mouth on Jon. However, let's not let him peak too soon, shall we?" said Baltsaros.

Despite the light tone Baltsaros was using, Jon could hear that the captain was breathing heavily, and it sharpened his arousal.

When Tom's hot mouth slid over the sensitive head of his cock, Jon let out a full-throated moan. He was so turned on that he didn't think he would last very long. His cock slid slowly down the back of Tom's tongue, impossibly far, the muscles of the kneeling man's throat enveloping him as his lips tightened to reverse the thrust.

With a gasp, he pushed on the back of Tom's head, wanting to feel the long, smooth plunge again once more before he had to pull away, lest he climax.

When he heard the creak of the bed, he opened his eyes and saw that Baltsaros was coming towards him. There was a familiar smell in the air, and when the captain pressed his mouth to his, Jon breathed in a lungful of the drug *char*.

Tom had stopped moving, realizing how far Jon had already come in his pleasure.

As the drug started swirling through his veins, Baltsaros nodded, and Tom resumed gorging himself on Jon's cock.

Baltsaros and Tom. Tom and Baltsaros.

They worked effortlessly as a team, even in this. The drug would work to offset Jon's climax while enhancing his pleasure; this time, however, Jon didn't feel as dazed as the first time, and he was glad for it.

Experimentally, he pushed on the back of Tom's head when his cock was in the bigger man's throat and held him there. Tom obediently stayed put, unable to breathe and shuddering slightly as Jon rocked his hips minutely to feel the head of his cock sliding down the back of the bigger man's throat. He threw his head back and Baltsaros put his arms around him, pinching his nipples and slowly kissing the side of his neck.

When Jon finally released Tom, the other man collapsed back on the carpet, coughing and wiping his mouth; however, there was a smile on the big man's face, and his eyes were wide with desire as he came back up onto his knees.

"You weren't kidding," Jon said to Baltsaros, amazed at Tom's eagerness.

The captain chuckled and slid his hands down to Jon's stiff, wet cock to stroke him.

"I don't 'kid' about much, my love," said the captain in his ear. "You know what I would really like to see? I want to watch you fuck him."

Jon closed his eyes and gave himself over to Baltsaros's hands for a moment. Tom had come forward again and licked softly at the cock in Baltsaros's grasp.

"You're really ok with this?" Jon asked softly.

"Yes," said Baltsaros.

Jon thought he could hear some hesitation in the captain's response, but it didn't worry him. The realization that this was not about competing with Tom and Baltsaros's relationship was beginning to hit him.

Something to think about later, he thought.

For the moment, Baltsaros's last suggestion was ricocheting through his mind. As if reading his thoughts, the captain released Jon and went to Tom.

"Up," he said, and Tom lurched to his feet. Baltsaros's hands stroked down the sculpted muscles of Tom's chest, lingering at the small silver ring in his nipple. The captain's brows went up as he tugged at it lightly, obviously pleased with the addition. Sliding his fingers over Tom's taut stomach, he eased his fingers under the waistband of the first mate's green pants and tugged forward. Baltsaros kissed Tom roughly as he undid the front of his pants and pushed them down when they were loose enough.

Jon watched as Baltsaros grabbed Tom hard by the throat and pushed his gracefully curved lips against the big man's jaw, just beside his ear.

"On your stomach on the bed," hissed Baltsaros loud enough that Jon could hear.

Tom's cock bobbed in response to the words; its thick length was already a hard curve pointing up toward his stomach.

Jon watched in fascination as the muscular young man obediently lay down on his chest on the bed and closed his eyes. Baltsaros knelt beside him and slid two pillows under Tom's hips and then spat into his hand. Roughly pushing Tom's legs apart, he smeared the saliva over his puckered opening; Jon watched in a hot daze as Baltsaros slid two fingers inside Tom, readying him, and he realized he was breathing hard from the sight.

When Jon finally, impatiently, took his place between Tom's legs, he felt like a wanton beast. His hands closed exactly over the tattoos that curled over Tom's hips, like they were guides. He groaned and slid his whole length smoothly in one motion inside Tom.

Under him, Tom moaned and shuddered, pushing back on Jon. Unlike the last time he shared a lover with Baltsaros, this body was the right one beneath him.

When he turned to look at the captain, Jon saw that the man's eyes were half-lidded with lust, his top lip curled on one side in a wicked sneer of desire as he stroked himself while watching Jon and Tom. Bolstered by the captain's reaction, Jon started thrusting hard into Tom, his breath heaving and groaning out of him from the glorious sensation of the man's slick muscles enveloping and sliding over his cock.

Tom met every plunge with a low moan, one hand frantically twisting the coverlet in his fist while the other worked his own hard shaft beneath him. The sound of Jon's pelvis slamming hard against Tom's muscular ass competed with the bestial sounds coming from the two men's throats.

Wanting to see Tom's face as he fucked him, Jon tugged at his thigh; the perfectly submissive brute below him obliged immediately when the man fucking him simply murmured: "On your back."

Tom looked up at Jon, his eyes narrow and forehead creasing in a look of almost agonized desire with every thrust, his lips parted to moan out his passion.

"Fuck... Jon, oh gods," Tom repeated over and over, his fist moving fast over his cock as Jon pounded into him.

Suddenly the mattress sank on either side of Jon's knees, and he felt the captain grab his hips and slow him. With a grunt of surprise, Jon stopped moving and gasped with shock as he felt the captain's fingers, slick with oil, slide into him. Almost dizzy with lust, Jon realized what Baltsaros aimed to do.

As he stroked deep inside him, the captain pressed and rubbed against the spot within him that triggered the waves of intensity that sent shocks through his body, enhancing all his sensations. Whimpering when Baltsaros's fingers left him, Jon moved forward when the captain brought Tom's legs up, almost losing his balance.

Low down over Tom's chest, Jon saw that the muscular rogue was smiling up at him.

"Breathe, Jon," said Tom, and Jon almost burst out laughing.

However, when Baltsaros's thick cock pushed slow and hard into his body, Jon captured Tom's mouth with his own, forcing himself to relax into the sensation of being stretched wide. He groaned loud, and Tom twisted his fingers into Jon's dark curls, kissing him with frantic, rough passion.

Baltsaros began fucking Jon with long strokes that drove him hard into Tom's body. It was perfect and exquisite, this feeling of fucking and being fucked.

Soon Jon was crying out loud with every thrust, the tempo becoming brutal and fast until it finally sent him toppling over into the throes of his ecstasy, a long low moan of pure pleasure bursting out of his open throat as he rode the staggering peaks of his orgasm, cumming hard and thick into Tom. With the last pulse, Jon pushed himself up onto his hands, elbows locked and head bowed as he panted hard over Tom.

He saw that the man beneath him was flushed, nearing his own culmination.

Baltsaros pulled out of Jon with a groan and crawled to Tom, his dark hand pumping the thick cock in its grasp, the purple head of it swelling with every hard stroke.

In a daze, Jon watched as a clear drop fell from its tip onto Tom's collarbone a second before the captain growled low in his chest, sending jets of pearly white cum over Tom's chest and stomach. Jon felt Tom's ass clench over his cock, and the man beneath him arched his back up suddenly, letting out a hard yell and sending hot jets of his own seed to mingle with Baltsaros's.

Jon collapsed onto Tom, heedless of the mess, completely spent. His thighs were shaking and his heart felt like it was going to crash through his ribs.

After a moment, Tom wrapped his arms around Jon, turning them onto their sides facing each other, and Baltsaros stretched out behind Jon.

The older man brought up a hand to start stroking Jon's side, gliding his fingers up over the hard muscles of Tom's arm and back down again to Jon's hip. Now that their passions were slaked, the room felt cool, and Jon was glad for Tom's constant heat. He nuzzled up under the big man's jaw.

I missed you, he wanted to say, among other things, but he didn't want to push his luck with the captain here.

Sex was one thing, emotions were another, and Jon was curious to see how things would settle in the end. He couldn't tell if it was the effects of the drug or the mind-blowing sex, but he thought he could sense strands pulling the three of them together. It was as if their talents, strengths, desires, and weaknesses were woven into a three-sided tapestry.

His fingers traced the rounded muscles that covered Tom's sides, and thought of the analogy. Meanwhile, Baltsaros's hand had slowed its motion and finally stopped, twitching once.

Tom lifted his head to look over at the captain and then put his finger to his lips, grinning: Baltsaros had fallen asleep.

After pulling away from Jon and sliding off the bed, Tom twitched the side of the duvet up and over the captain before walking to the closet to take out another thick, white blanket and a towel. Draping the blanket around his shoulders and wiping his chest with the towel before throwing it on the floor, he cocked his head at Jon and motioned with his chin for the dark-haired man to follow him.

Intrigued, Jon gently pried himself out of Baltsaros's grasp and padded after the big man to the far side of the room where there was a low, wide couch.

Tom turned around and sat down, the blanket spread out behind him and up over his arms.

When Jon saw that Tom meant for him to sit next to him, he stifled a laugh. It seemed silly at first, but when he sat down tight against Tom's side, the bigger man lowered his arms, wrapping them in the soft blanket, making Jon feel wonderfully safe. He leaned comfortably back on Tom's broad shoulder and saw that the man was looking at him with affectionate blue-green eyes; he felt warm, happy, and protected.

Tom leaned in to kiss Jon, deep and gentle and tasting like the ghost of tears shed.

"I've been wantin' to do that for a long time, lad," he said gruffly when he broke away.

Jon nodded. There were so many things he wanted to say but couldn't think of a single thing to start with.

The silence was finally broken when Tom started laughing to himself.

"Talk, my ass," he said, chuckling.

Jon looked up, confused, but Tom shook his head in amusement.

"When I asked Da what ye wanted. He said 'just to talk' didn't he?" asked Tom, grinning. "Aye... Fuck talk, I guess."

Jon shrugged with a small sigh. He desperately wanted to know what Baltsaros had said to Tom, but he knew it wasn't his place to ask; but, whatever it was, it had made things better between the two men.

Tom made a low, pleased sound in his chest and tightened his arms around Jon before leaning down to kiss him again. This time when Tom pulled away, Jon was smiling wide. The big man was so warm and effortlessly cheerful; it was soothing, reassuring, and incredibly addictive.

While they sat huddled in their comfortable embrace wrapped in the warm blanket, Jon then told Tom everything that had happened since they had parted ways.

Tom stared at Jon as he spoke, shaking his head at the news of Katherine's arm and the death of the others. When it came to his mother, Tom pressed his lips together and looked dismayed, though he honestly looked happy to hear of Eloise and Brutus.

Jon assured him that things would be different with Abetha should he decide to go "home", and Tom's eyes darted to his at the use of the word, but he didn't say anything.

When Jon told Tom about the final fight with Reginald and how he had nearly died, he saw Tom's eyes go glassy with tears. Tom pulled back the blanket and leaned forward to kiss the tight scar on Jon's chest.

After a moment, the big man settled back to tell his own tale.

• • •

272

Tom had latched onto a floating barrel after having fallen off (*Of course I fell, don't be daft, boy. Who would'a pushed me?*) and was carried back towards the peninsula where he was picked up by a fishing boat by pure luck. (*You should stop calling me 'lad' and 'boy', Tom. As it turns out I'm over a year older than you, said Jon. Tom laughed. All right, old man, he replied with a kiss. Now, hush... I'm telling my story.*)

It was about six weeks later that Reginald and the fleet arrived. Tom had done everything in his power to dissuade them, including telling Reginald that the whole crew had died in the storm, but the crazed ex-soldier wasn't satisfied with Tom's answers.

Instead, he had put poor Fresia in irons and tortured her for a day and a half before she caved. She had since recovered but had chosen to leave town with a wealthy man who offered to put her up in a house of her own, and Tom didn't blame her.

Tom had sent the letter as soon as he could, hoping that it would reach Jon in time. (*Why didn't you come? asked Jon with a frown. How? With my own boat? Ye think I got rich floatin' in the ocean? Listen, love... I would have come. I would have. I prayed for ye every night, replied Tom.*)

When Jon saw the pain in Tom's eyes, he believed his words. Tom had also wanted to distance himself from Jon and the captain so as to remove temptation that would earn him some more stripes. (*Are you still afraid of the whip, Tom? asked Jon. Aye, love. Now and always, answered the big man.*)

Tom had taken up work at the *Jewel* doing maintenance and repairs and had recently been promoted to warehouse manager, a position that Tom thought suited him well. (*Well... mostly liftin' boxes and yellin' at folks, answered Tom truthfully to Jon's question. Same as on board, really.*)

Tom had given strict instructions to everyone he knew not to let Baltsaros know of his whereabouts.

"Because I was so angry, lad. So bloody fuckin' angry," said Tom, his face deadly serious.

"Because you love him," said Jon to Tom, his words plain.

"Aye, I love the shite out of that asshole, ducky. He's strong, smart, and fucks like a bloody madman. What's not to love?" responded Tom with a rueful twist to his lips.

"The fact that he had no heart," said Jon, looking curiously at Tom. "That's what you said to me that last night. Before you disappeared."

The big man nodded slowly to himself. Tom then frowned and looked sidelong at Jon.

"He been good to you, love?" asked Tom. "Da seems... different."

Jon nodded.

"I think whatever it was that was broken inside him has finally started to mend," he said softly. It was a hope not yet made fact, but it was something he liked to think was truth.

"All's it took was thinkin' ye died?" said Tom, his eyes suddenly bland in an attempt to hide his jealousy.

"Thinking that *we* died, Tom. Don't be such a fucking martyr. Your 'death' was the catalyst," said Jon, smiling. "Let's stop talking about death... I liked the subject of love." He still felt loose limbed and sentimental from the combination of *char* and fucking.

Tom grinned wide.

"Aye... love," said Tom. "Ye know, the difference between ye both is ye do have a heart. Ye might make my cock hard, but ye soften this." Tom tapped two rough fingers against the spot over his heart.

Jon had to laugh.

"Gods, Tom... That was almost poetic," he said, stroking his hand down Tom's chest and tugging playfully at the big man's chest hair. "Listen... The captain can beat the fuck out of you, and when you're done, you can come to me, and I will kiss you better," said Jon.

Tom's lips parted in response, and he stared at Jon with eyes suddenly darkened by desire and turbulent emotion. Tom's arms tightened around Jon again, and when he licked his lips, his breathing had a shaky quality to it.

"Gods, love," was all the big man said, and Jon had to laugh.

"You'd like that?" he asked, realizing the strange mastery over the powerful creature that held him.

"Aye," responded Tom, his voice barely a whisper.

Jon's heart beat double. They kissed again, only coming up for air when Jon had to beg off to relieve his bladder. When he came back and Tom lifted his arm again, Jon frowned, noticing something he hadn't before.

He sat down on Tom's left and peered curiously at the black lines that curled and swooped along his thickly muscled side. Tom watched curiously as Jon traced his fingers along the path they took over the bigger man's ribs.

"Ye like it?" asked Tom. Jon's fingers tapped a spot right under Tom's pectoral. There... That looked like something he recognized.

"Jon?"

As he looked up into Tom's eyes, he smiled.

"Sorry... Yes, they are extremely fucking sexy if you must know," he said, scarcely believing the words coming out of his mouth. It was simply the truth; somehow the markings enhanced the muscular young man's beauty in a way that made Jon feel hot inside. "But... What do they mean? Do you know?" he asked.

Tom looked down at himself and shrugged.

"The lot of it could be pure fancy, love. But... the man who did it, he told me that this here"—Tom put his fingers over Jon's—"is a map of the Devil's Isles and beyond. Somethin' about lost knowledge."

Jon's breath caught in his throat and he looked at Tom, alarmed.

"Gods, Tom. Now you won't believe me when I tell you what we're planning," he said in a hush.

Tom was quiet for a long time after Jon told him of their plans and of the captain's intention to ask him to be first mate again.

Jon rested against Tom's wide shoulder, waiting for the big man to say something. When Tom finally spoke, it was a rumble against Jon's ear.

"If ye don't mind, love, I'd like a day to think about it before I give ye my answer. Can ye grant me that, lad?" asked Tom, his rough hand coming up to rest against Jon's bare chest.

Jon nodded his head and closed his eyes.

"You're going to wear a groove in the boards and make Calum throw you overboard if you don't stop your pacing, Jon," said Baltsaros, looking down at Jon.

Jon laughed, but he felt completely frantic with worry. Tom had said that he would come give them their answer early this morning, but it was now noon, and there was no sign of him.

"It's not like we have to leave immediately, Jon," said the captain. "If Tom's not ready today, maybe he'll be ready tomorrow. He can be extremely proud, like his mother. I did him wrong, Jon... And an afternoon spent playing on bedsheets won't make it all better. We can afford to wait a day or two."

Jon nodded. He hoped it was the case. He'd already made two trips back to the mainland to see if he could find Tom on his own, with no avail. They could also put off the trip for this season if Tom was unwilling to join them. Jon was sure he could convince—

"Bloody fuckin' hells, Da! What in gods have ye done to my fuckin' boat?"

Jon started and looked over his shoulder.

The ocean-eyed, burly youth swung himself up over the edge of the raised gunwale like nothing was amiss and landed on silent feet on the deck next to Jon. After dropping his bag with a thump and ruffling Jon's hair affectionately as he passed by him, Tom swaggered to the stairs of the quarterdeck and looked up, feet splayed and hands on his hips.

The captain, his relief and amusement obvious for a mere second, brought his stark brows down in a fierce scowl.

"*Your* boat?" the captain repeated loudly. "She'll be yours over my dead body." Baltsaros allowed himself a small smile, and Tom grinned wide. "Whip these boys into shape, if you remember how," said Baltsaros as he lifted his head to look over the gathering crowd.

"First mate on deck!" shouted the captain.

Some of the old-timers reached out to pat Tom's shoulder as he made his way down the deck while the newer shipmates just peered curiously at the tattooed sailor that was built like an ox. However, when Tom started bellowing, everyone jumped quickly to obey.

"All right ye lot o' bleedin' twats, move yer asses. Shore up that fuckin' clutter and tighten those lines, ye bilge rat. Aye! I'll drown ye meself if ye don't heed, boy..."

Jon grinned, listening to the first mate yell out orders in his nonstop, rolling mainland accent that was thickly peppered with cursing and laughter.

He looked out over the calm water and took a deep breath. Jon knew there would be trying times in the coming months, both from inside the ship and from without, but at this precise moment in time, he felt he could face anything.

Jon picked up the bag that Tom had dumped unceremoniously beside him and trotted to the captain's quarters to throw it inside. With a glance up at the tall, dark man above him on the quarterdeck, Jon smiled.

There was nowhere he would rather be.

～

END OF BOOK I

EPILOGUE

While it was bitterly cold outside, the two men in the stateroom glistened with sweat. Tom, his arms bound behind him and his ankles tied to the legs of the table, grunted and hissed as another stream of hot wax landed on his bare skin. Jon groaned in response; he loved the way Tom's muscles tightened over his cock with the sudden pain. He thrust himself into Tom's body a few times, his hands sliding over the tattooed skin of the bound man's side.

The candlelight made Tom's skin pure gold, and Jon thought it was beautiful.

The door banged open behind them, and Jon turned his head. The captain stepped in amidst a swirl of snowflakes and quickly shut the door against the wind.

His cheeks were red with the cold, and the collar of his greatcoat was pulled high over his ears. He yanked his gloves off, sighing happily from the heat in the room, and nodded at Jon to continue.

Jon turned back to Tom and spilled some more burning wax on him, moving within his body. With the captain's eyes on him, Jon felt his pleasure mount quickly, and soon he was pounding into Tom, a harsh growl bursting out of his chest as he pulled his cock out to rain his seed down on the bound man's back.

Breath heaving fast in his chest, Jon began untwisting the hempen ropes that were binding Tom. He looked curiously at the captain. Baltsaros's face had darkened with lust at the display; he loved to watch the boys "play", as he put it. However, he made no move to join them as he usually did.

Tom straightened and flexed his wrists, his head cocked curiously at Baltsaros.

"What is it, Da?" he asked, still using the ridiculous title though the two were no longer related through marriage.

Baltsaros smiled wide.

"I thought you boys would like to know that we've arrived within sight of the Devil's Isles," he said.

Jon and Tom looked at each other in excitement. It had taken nearly two months to reach them; finally it was the time to see what it was they were up against.

BEY DECKARD

Sacrificed

Heart Beyond the Spires
Baal's Heart II

PART ONE

JON

Every day is a journey, and the journey itself is home.

— MATSUO BASHŌ

"You're going to wear a groove in the boards and make Calum throw you overboard if you don't stop your pacing, Jon," said Baltsaros, looking down at Jon.

Jon laughed, but he felt completely frantic with worry. Tom had said that he would come give them their answer early this morning, but it was now noon, and there was no sign of him.

"It's not like we have to leave immediately, Jon," said the captain. "If Tom's not ready today, maybe he'll be ready tomorrow. He can be extremely proud, like his mother. I did him wrong, Jon... and an afternoon spent playing on bedsheets won't make it all better. We can afford to wait a day or two."

Jon nodded. He hoped it was the case. He'd already made two trips back to the mainland to see if he could find Tom on his own, with no avail. They could also put off the trip for this season if Tom was unwilling to join them. Jon was sure he could convince—

"Bloody fuckin' hells, Da! What in gods have ye done to my fuckin' boat?"

Jon started and looked over his shoulder.

The ocean-eyed, burly youth swung himself up over the edge of the raised gunwale like nothing was amiss and landed on silent feet on the deck next to Jon. After dropping his bag with a thump and ruffling Jon's hair affectionately as he passed by him, Tom swaggered to the stairs of the quarterdeck and looked up, feet splayed and hands on his hips.

The captain, his relief and amusement obvious for a mere second, brought his stark brows down in a fierce scowl.

"*Your* boat?" the captain repeated loudly. "She'll be yours over my dead body." Baltsaros allowed himself a small smile, and Tom grinned wide. "Whip these boys into shape, if you remember how," said Baltsaros as he lifted his head to look over the gathering crowd.

"First mate on deck!" shouted the captain.

Some of the old-timers reached out to pat Tom's shoulder as he made his way down the deck while the newer shipmates just peered curiously at the tattooed sailor that was built like an ox. However, when Tom started bellowing, everyone jumped quickly to obey.

"All right ye lot o' bleedin' twats, move yer asses. Shore up that fuckin' clutter and tighten those lines, ye bilge rat. Aye! I'll drown ye meself if ye don't heed, boy..."

Jon grinned, listening to the first mate yell out orders in his non-stop, rolling mainland accent that was thickly peppered with cursing and laughter.

He looked out over the calm water and took a deep breath. Jon knew there would be trying times in the coming months, both from inside the ship and from without, but at this precise moment in time, he felt he could face anything.

Jon picked up the bag that Tom had dumped unceremoniously beside him and trotted to the captain's quarters to throw it inside. With a glance up at the tall, dark man above him on the quarterdeck, Jon smiled.

There was nowhere he would rather be.

~

PRESENT DAY

Jon pulled the woollen cloak tighter around himself and shivered. His fingers ached from the cold; damp from saltwater spray, his gloves were scant protection from the frigid weather. He'd give his soul just to be back in Baltsaros's bed, warm and far from all this fucking snow and ice. Miserable, he tried once more to undo the ropes tying the crate of supplies to the mast.

"Fucking hells!" Jon yelled into the icy wind when his numb fingers refused to close around the knot. He clenched his teeth and kicked hard at the wooden crate, his shoulders tense and hunched.

"What's wrong, love?" asked a deep voice from behind him.

Jon let out an exasperated groan and rubbed his face, leaning wearily into Tom's side as the first mate put an arm around his shoulders.

"I am so tired of this weather," he said, embarrassed by how peevish he sounded.

"I can't get anything done. I'm just so fucking cold. Tom, I can't even feel my hands." Jon flexed his fingers, and tried to form a fist but failed. When he looked up, he was annoyed to see that the muscular first mate was looking at him in amusement.

"It's not funny," said Jon. "I'm serious... I've seen what frostbite can do."

Tom's green-blue eyes creased at the corners as he grinned wide at Jon.

"Here, mate, let me see. It can't be that bad," he said, reaching for Jon's gloves. Peeling them off the shivering man's hands, he frowned; Jon's fingers were bone white from cold. Tom pulled him closer, lifted up the bottom edge of his thick sweater, and shoved one of Jon's hands against the warm skin of his side.

Jon let out a low moan and quickly tucked his other hand against Tom's flank; it always amazed him how incredibly warm the big man was. During the last few weeks, as the weather got progressively colder, the crew began to resemble moving piles of fur. Not so with Tom; it was only when the deck was consistently covered in ice that the first mate grudgingly put on a pair of boots. Even now, Tom went around bareheaded in the cold, the smoke from his cheroot adding to the constant halo of steam from his warm breath.

When Jon's hands touched Tom's skin, the first mate hissed through his teeth from the shock; chuckling, he put a big, gloved hand around the back of Jon's neck.

"Listen, love. Why dont'cha warm up here a spot," said Tom, his voice low and fond. "Ye won't lose yer fingers, Jon. Not on my watch, see?"

Jon nodded and leaned into the bigger man, thankful for his presence; he was glad that it was finally so effortlessly comfortable between the two of them.

~

Six Weeks Ago

"I'm very sorry you feel that way, Tom," said the captain with a frown. "I had assumed that we would be sharing my quarters."

Tom rubbed the side of his thumb against his stubbled jaw. With ocean-coloured eyes wide and seemingly focused on nothing, unable or unwilling to meet the captain's glare, he flared his nostrils slightly and shook his head.

"And why the fuck would ye think I'd just leap into yer fuckin' bed like a lust-wet strumpet, all big eyes and heart full of forgiveness, Da?" said Tom, his deep, gravelly voice taking on the edge of anger. "I'll be yer first mate, but I won't be sharin' yer bloody bed. Not now. Not yet."

Tom's eyes flicked to the captain's face for a moment, unmistakable pain in his gaze, before looking away again.

Jon let out a nervous sigh and ran his fingers through his dark-brown curls; his hair hung loose past his bare shoulders, and it tickled the back of his neck as he fidgeted with it. In dismay, he watched Tom bend slowly to pick up his sack of belongings, slinging it over his shoulder as he turned to leave.

Jon had assumed, like the captain, that the three of them would be sharing the large stateroom, and it was to these quarters that he had brought Tom's belongings when they had set off earlier.

The day had been incredibly busy, seeming light-hearted and hopeful to Jon. However, as the sun dipped below the horizon on this first day of their journey, when it came time to retire for the night, Tom had looked almost horrified at the prospect of sharing a bed with the captain.

As he stepped towards the door, Tom looked over his shoulder at Jon, his brow creased and eyes serious, before he let himself out into the salt-tinged night air, the door banging shut behind him.

At the creak of the bed, Jon turned to see that the captain had sat down on the edge of it, his eyes closed and fingers pinched over the bridge of his nose. Without looking up, Baltsaros held out his hand, and Jon crossed the room to press himself into the older man's embrace.

"Stubborn as a mule," muttered Baltsaros, shaking his head.

Jon looked down at the man leaning against his side and nodded; he brought his hands up to stroke the captain's shoulders and thought to himself for a moment before answering.

"I don't blame him, you know," Jon said softly. Beneath his hands, he felt the captain stiffen slightly. "You said yourself that you didn't think Tom would forgive you right away. And you were right. So... be patient."

Baltsaros looked up at him, his brown eyes almost black in the sombre lighting. Jon could feel weariness and anger in the captain as the man shook his head.

"I'm disappointed too, if it makes you feel any better," Jon murmured. He leaned down and pressed his lips to Baltsaros's high forehead; after a heartbeat, Jon pulled back, paused, and smiled before skimming his mouth over the older man's lips, hoping to turn the captain's mind away from Tom's unexpected rejection.

The captain let out a low growl and reached up to cup the back of Jon's head, deepening the kiss. When Jon started tugging at Baltsaros's loose shirt, the captain let out a sigh.

"Yes, patience," he agreed when he pulled away from Jon. The captain's hand closed tight over Jon's forearm, his stark face going still and cold as he stared up at him.

"Don't go to him," said Baltsaros slowly. "Don't seek out Tom by yourself."

Jon straightened and blinked at the captain, disconcerted by the older man's words. They were spoken as a command, the tone unmistakable.

"I mean it, Jon," warned the captain. "As long as Tom won't come to me willingly, you're not to go see him. I... won't have it."

The soft spark of passion that had begun to take hold of Jon sputtered and expired, and he pushed away Baltsaros's hand when it came up to pull him in for another kiss.

"The hells I won't," he said angrily, taking a step back. "During the day, as captain you can order me around all you want... but this? Baltsaros, you're being absurd." He watched Baltsaros's eyes go flat, devoid of emotion.

The way that the captain could suddenly seem so completely inhuman was unsettling, and it always triggered the ghost of something primordial within Jon, buried deep in his genetic makeup: the instinct to flee from a predator.

Run.

As he shook his head to dispel the feeling of unease that had slid into his veins like ice water, Jon held up his hand.

"Listen to me. Tom is angry at *you*... not me," he said, trying to keep the resentment out of his voice. "Do you think that forbidding me to spend any time with him will make Tom any more amenable to you?"

Jon frowned when Baltsaros dropped his eyes, a slow exhale rounding the man's shoulders. When the captain looked back up, the younger man was amazed by the fury in Baltsaros's gaze.

Without a word, Baltsaros stood, tucking his shirt back into the waistband of his black pants. He moved to open the chest at the foot of the bed and pulled out a blanket before walking towards the door. Looking back at Jon, Baltsaros finally spoke.

"If I stay here, I will *hurt* you," said the older man, his words deliberate. He turned his head towards the exit. "And... I'd rather not." Jon heard Baltsaros take another deep breath. "I will be above if you need me, but I do hope you won't."

With those words Baltsaros stepped out, closing the door quietly behind him and leaving Jon alone in the dark of the stateroom.

~

PRESENT DAY

When his hands were finally warm, Jon gratefully accepted Tom's big gloves in exchange for his frozen ones. The first mate slipped on Jon's gloves and curled his hands into fists.

"I'll have these warmed up for ye in no time, ducky," said Tom, his pink lips curled into a crooked grin. The first mate then reached behind him to pull the long knife out of its sheath, and he quickly sliced through the knot Jon had been trying to loosen. When Jon exclaimed in surprise, Tom just lifted one shoulder up in a shrug.

"We have plenty of rope, ye daft boy," he said. "Now get to work haulin' this to Cook or he'll make ye eat last." Tom reached out and pulled him forward again to press his forehead to Jon's before taking off at a brisk pace down the frozen deck, whistling a jaunty tune as he went.

Jon looked around. Seeing the eyes of a few of the deckhands on him, he coloured slightly. It was never going to be easy being seen as the captain and first mate's cabin boy, regardless of what his actual role was on the ship.

When a gangly, tow-headed deckhand they had picked up during their stop at the *Jewel* sniggered, Jon scowled at him and picked up the crate.

He had to do something about the teasing; it was blatant and getting out of hand. However, it wouldn't do to let Baltsaros or Tom know just how much it was bothering him. Both had a penchant for violence and an overprotectiveness of Jon that almost guaranteed excessive punishment for anyone involved.

~

Six Weeks Ago

Jon woke up when the sun's rays came through the stained glass at the back of the captain's quarters. As he opened his eyes slowly, he reached for Baltsaros and frowned when his hand encountered nothing but the cool sheet next to him. Jon lifted his head; the stateroom was empty. The previous night's drama came back to him in a rush, and he groaned. After turning over onto his back, Jon rubbed the sleep-sand from his eyes with the heels of his hands. What was he going to do?

Tom would be furious if he knew that Baltsaros had forbidden him from spending any time alone with the first mate, and the captain would be equally livid if Jon disobeyed him. The last place he wanted to be caught was between the demanding captain and his hot-tempered first mate. It was a shitty position to be in, and Jon desired nothing more than a quick resolution.

Sure, but... then what? he thought nervously.

After slipping off the soft bed, Jon paused to look at himself in the mirror above the teak dresser. Sleep had not come easily to him, and it showed in his face. He pressed at the bags under his eyes and frowned to himself; tilting his head up to the light, he scratched his chin and realized that he was also in dire need of a shave.

Abovedeck a short while later, Jon was astounded to see Tom and Baltsaros working companionably side by side as the morning checklist was run through. Munching on Cook's good sourdough and drinking a steaming cup of black coffee as he hung back, Jon watched the two men discuss the replacement of the starboard lines running up the mizzenmast. He could almost believe that the night's arguments had never happened. However, as he stepped up to them, it was obvious that not all had been forgiven.

Baltsaros's eyes were tired and aloof when he looked down at him, and Jon noticed immediately that Tom was purposefully keeping a set distance between him and the captain. When he got closer, Jon caught the smell of stale sweat and whiskey emanating from the bigger man; evidently Tom's first night aboard had been equally restless.

Achingly uncomfortable, Jon put his cup down and chose to address the air between the men rather than make eye contact.

"Cook says that someone has been nicking more than their ration of rum," he said blandly, scratching at his jaw. "He has an idea who it is—"

"Who?" asked Baltsaros, his voice harsh.

Jon winced. It didn't bode well for the man accused; the captain was just looking for something to sink his anger into. Before he had a chance to reply, Baltsaros held up a hand.

"Forget it. I'll go see to it myself," said the captain, turning his head towards the galley. "Tom, you stay here. Jon, go find something else to do." Jon clenched his jaw and stood his ground, ignoring the captain. Baltsaros looked back, and Jon finally met his gaze. Dark eyes wide at the expression on Jon's face, the older man stayed a moment longer before taking the steps down from the quarterdeck two at a time.

Tom chuckled.

"I never thought I'd live to see the day that ye'd stare down the cap'n, love," said the big man, his roguish face creased in a wide grin.

Jon sighed and scratched at his cheek.

"Yeah, well, obviously things change," he replied faintly. Rubbing hard at his neck, Jon shook his head. He started when Tom's hand cupped his chin and turned his head.

"Do ye have fleas, lad?" asked Tom with a laugh. "Will ye stop bloody scratchin'? Yer makin' me itch."

Wary of the captain's return, Jon's eyes darted to the stairs as he pulled his face out of Tom's callused hand.

"I just need to shave," he said, stroking his hand slowly over the hollow of his cheek. Over the course of the past year, Jon's beard had finally filled in, and he found it a constant annoyance.

"Then... shave," said Tom. His eyes had narrowed when Jon had pulled out of his grasp, and he crossed his arms across his broad chest. His gaze flicked towards the stairs and back to Jon. "What's stoppin' ye? Hm?"

"Kat used to do it for me. Since then, it's been either the captain or Cook," said Jon. He cringed when Tom suddenly let out a surprised laugh.

"Aw shit, ducky. Yer a grown bloody man," said Tom, his eyes shining with amusement. "Please tell me ye know how to shave yerself."

His face hot, Jon touched the sparse patch on his right cheek where one of his attempts had landed him a scar, and he chuckled ruefully.

"I haven't gotten the hang of it. I know, I know. Stupid, right?" he said, hoping he wasn't as red-faced as he felt.

With another glance at the staircase, Tom grabbed Jon's arm in a vice-like grip and pulled the slighter man down the steps.

Jon quickly tried to free himself, but Tom was built like an ox and just as strong; in the end, feeling like a child, he let himself be dragged belowdeck by the first mate.

Nervous as they passed the galley doors, though the captain was nowhere in sight, Jon followed Tom to a tiny storage room next to where the coal was kept.

He blinked and looked around. The room was no more than a large broom closet, but it looked like someone had been living there for some time. There was a thick mat on the floor to one side with a bright blue blanket pulled over it. Against the far wall was a rough, hand-carved shelf that held a few books. Atop a small crate sat a silver pitcher and a cup, as well as a delicate, little wooden box with an inlaid pattern on the cover. Jon frowned and looked at Tom.

"What is this?" asked Jon, confused. The room smelled faintly of the big man despite the open porthole: whiskey, tobacco smoke, and a scent that was Tom's own.

Tom shrugged, his wide frame almost comically large in the tiny room.

"Where do ye think I go when Da kicks me out of his bed, lovey?" he asked, pulling down a wooden bowl from another shelf set high above the foot of the bed. Tom eyed Jon. "Ye don't think yer the first reason I've been left in the cold, do ye?"

Jon's eyes widened. He shook his head after a beat even though truthfully it hadn't occurred to him. He felt weirdly betrayed by the information.

Tom set down the bowl next to the pitcher and poured a little of the water into it. Using the long knife at his belt, he shaved off a few flakes from the block of dark soap he held in one scarred hand and proceeded to churn the mixture together with a short-bristled, round brush. In no time the bowl was filled with thick, milky-white, sandalwood-scented suds.

"Sit," Tom said, pointing to the floor.

Jon looked down, furrowing his brow. His mind was a mess. Was this considered "seeking out Tom", he wondered; and, if so, what would he say if Baltsaros found out? Sure, he had stood up to the captain earlier, but...

"Hells, Jon... do ye want me to show ye or not?" asked Tom with a scowl.

With a startled nod, Jon sank to the hard wooden floor. A moment later, Tom sat behind Jon and pulled him back against his chest, his legs bracketing the smaller man's.

Instantly, Jon's heart started to crash against his ribs. Tom laughed low, and Jon felt the first mate's voice rumble against his back.

"Listen... I know he forbade ye from seein' me, lovey. I ain't stupid, and I've been with the captain long enough to know what he's like," said Tom softly, depositing the bowl in Jon's lap. "But I didn't come back aboard just to please Da."

Tom held up a mirror in front of Jon's face, and he could see the first mate's green-blue eyes beside his own blue-grey ones.

I came for you too.

Jon blinked and looked down. He gestured weakly to Tom's room.

"He didn't throw out your belongings. He kept your room," he said, his voice strangely hoarse. It was hard to breathe. Jon looked back up and saw that Tom was still staring at him in the mirror. The first mate nodded stiffly.

"Aye, lad. That he did," said Tom, finally looking away. "That he did."

∽

PRESENT DAY

After hauling the crate belowdecks, Jon finally managed to wrestle it through the doors of the galley. He looked up and smiled.

Behind the thick, stained wooden countertop stood Baltsaros with a long knife in one hand. Stripped to the waist in the humid heat of the kitchen, the captain held a large fish flat against the cutting block as he looked solemnly down at it.

Jon laughed and tugged his borrowed gloves off, draping them over the set of bars

Cook used to dry his towels on. After unwinding the scarf from his neck, Jon shrugged out of his thick cloak and left both in a pile in front of the hot coal stove.

"You'll never get the scales off if you hold it that way," he said, approaching the captain from behind. He passed his arms through Baltsaros's and shifted the man's hand to the left. "And you should be using a dull knife to scrape, not something so sharp... You know Cook is going to kill you for getting scales everywhere. How you've lived aboard a ship for so long without learning how to properly scale and debone fish is beyond me." Jon chuckled and shook his head. "Especially you... You who can prepare quail eggs six different ways and make vegetable stew taste like it was a gift from the gods."

Baltsaros turned his head with his stark brows high, a twist of amusement on his graceful lips. The beard he had grown over the past month was lightly streaked with grey, and Jon found it an attractive contrast to the captain's smooth, tanned skin.

"Do you want to make supper, Jon?" asked the man with the knife, his northern accent lending sibilance to his words. "Or will you let me work in peace?" At the last, Baltsaros smiled wide, his teeth sharp and white.

Jon moved his hands to the captain's chest, stroking down the thatch of curling hair to the waist of Baltsaros's black leather pants. Pressing himself up hard against the older man, Jon slipped his fingers below the wide waistband.

"What if I said neither?" he grinned and ducked his head to bite the captain's shoulder.

~

Six Weeks Ago

Jon was amazed when Tom started to show him how to shave in earnest. It hadn't been a ploy to get him alone to seduce him, and Jon was both relieved and disappointed. Shrugging away his misgivings and swallowing his pride, he paid close attention to Tom's hands as he slid the long blade along the curves of Jon's jaw.

It was strangely exciting to be letting a man who once plotted against him handle a sharp knife against his skin. But, if for nothing else, Tom's warmth felt good around him. While Tom had an easy physicality about him, Jon still felt a little odd sitting in another man's embrace, and he was glad that the first mate made no big deal about it. Tom was simply, and very patiently, teaching Jon how to shave. That's all it was.

And that's all that Baltsaros needs to know, he thought.

As if reading his mind, Tom wicked away the last of the shaving suds with his blade and then leaned down to bite down softly on Jon's shoulder, his tongue coming out to taste the flesh between his teeth.

With a gasp, Jon closed his eyes. His skin broke out in prickles, and he felt lightheaded, unable to move, drowning in the sudden torrent of *want* that poured over him. The reality of the situation broke through to him a second later, and he pulled away, up onto his knees, the wooden bowl tipping and suds smearing over the planks in his rush to flee. Jon scrambled to his feet and leaned into the door, his fingers clutching the brass handle.

"I... can't. I'm sorry, Tom." Jon felt his heart crashing, and the rush of white noise was loud in his ears. "Just... please. Ok? Shit, I don't even know what to say, but—" he stammered as he fumbled the door open. His breath hitched at the look of misery that flitted over Tom's face before the first mate's expression settled into one of exasperation. "Tom, we've got to do this right. Or else..." Jon frowned and shook his head. "I'm sorry." He turned his head away from the man on the floor and staggered into the hallway.

Walking blindly for a few steps, Jon crashed into the stairs and grunted as he caught himself. He glanced up and saw Cook looking at him curiously from the galley doorway. Jon gritted his teeth into the semblance of a smile and coughed out a small, embarrassed laugh before clutching the handrail to pull himself up the steep stairs.

~

Present Day

As Jon kissed his way across the captain's broad shoulders, fingers working at the laces of his leather pants, he heard the sound of someone clearing his throat. Startled, Jon turned his head and saw that Cook was standing next to the crate of vegetables he had just hauled in, embarrassment plain on his craggy face.

"Should I find somewhere else to be?" asked Cook, pulling his woollen sailor's tuque off and rubbing his bald head.

"Mmmmyes, I should think so," said the captain softly, pulling away from Jon and dunking his hands in the soapy water of the basin. "I will send someone for you when the galley is free."

Turning around to face Jon as Cook left and slid the door closed behind him, Baltsaros smiled his sharp-toothed smile and pulled Jon's hands back to the waistband of his leather pants.

"Continue," said the captain and leaned back against the edge of the counter. A low, pleased growl came from deep in his chest as Jon leaned in to kiss him, his fingers deftly pulling apart Baltsaros's laces.

BALTSAROS

Six Weeks Ago

Baltsaros returned above deck once the man who had been stealing rum was thrown in the brig, the captain's mood not much improved by the task. Clenching and releasing his fists as he walked up the narrow stairs, Baltsaros felt hot frustration like a fire burning deep in his belly.

Tom had *never* refused him; it was completely ludicrous. And, Jon...

Baltsaros glanced up as he emerged from below and saw that neither his first mate nor Jon were on the quarterdeck where he had left them. Jealousy reared up, clawing hard at him, and he clenched his jaw. He would be damned if Tom thought he could get away with touching Jon if he couldn't bring himself to submit to the captain.

As he tried to swallow down his ire, Baltsaros made for the door to his quarters instead of mounting the steps; he needed to get a hold of himself. His anger was getting out of control.

The captain pulled open the door and stepped into the relative darkness of the large stateroom. The addition of the stained-glass windows had definitely improved the disparity of light on entering, but it still took a moment for his eyes to adjust. As he made his way to the long mahogany table in the middle of the room, Baltsaros heard a noise and turned his head.

There were dark shapes moving on the bed.

Suspicion sharpened his anger, a howling tempest that churned inside him: *Tom and Jon.*

As he approached, barely able to breathe for the fury that choked him, the captain saw with relief that Jon was alone. When the young man sat up and turned to him, his eyes wide with worry, Baltsaros felt his anger shudder and go still inside him. There was a deep ridge etched between Jon's dark brows, and his face was drawn.

"Please," was all that he said.

With a deep sigh, the captain climbed onto the bed and took Jon into his arms, curling around the young man's slighter frame to bury his face in the back of Jon's neck. How could he refuse this solemn, dark-haired creature who looked at him with such love?

Shifting in Baltsaros's grasp after a few minutes, Jon's fingers tightened over the captain's hand, tugging it down to press it against the soft mound at the front of his pants.

Chuckling softly at the unexpected invitation, Baltsaros obliged and slid his hand up and then under the thin material to cup the soft warmth beneath. At his touch, Jon's cock began to stiffen, and Baltsaros pressed a smile against his nape. With a quiet, needy sound, Jon moved his hips back so that he was snug against the captain.

"I know you think I'm being absurd," Baltsaros murmured, "but I'm just frustrated."

Jon let out another soft noise, and his fingers stroked down the captain's muscular arm.

As he kissed Jon's neck slowly, Baltsaros closed his eyes and rubbed the ball of his thumb over the head of the younger man's cock, sighing in pleasure when he felt Jon tremble against him.

"You have to understand, my love," he said gently. "It never once occurred to me that this would happen."

At his words Jon pulled away slightly, twisting onto his back to look over at Baltsaros with a frown.

"What? That Tom might have spent enough time away from you to realize that he wants to be more than just your punching bag?" asked Jon. The words, though blunt, were spoken in earnest.

Baltsaros's hand, which had stopped moving, resumed stroking Jon gently, his gracefully curved cock sliding slowly within his grasp. The captain pondered for a moment and nodded, his lips pressed together in a rueful smile.

"Something like that," he answered, looking down to watch his hand moving below the sun-bleached fabric of Jon's pants. "I thought after our time at the *Jewel* things would be... normal. Though, to be fair, I don't really know what 'normal' would be. I don't yet know what's required to reach an equilibrium."

He glanced up at Jon's face and saw that he was being watched with curious eyes.

"What did you say to him?" asked Jon. His cheeks were infused with a flush, and his breathing had quickened.

Baltsaros frowned.

"When? At the *Jewel*?" he asked, and Jon nodded.

"Well... I said that I was sorry, and I called him my tomcat. Then I said that I wanted him to come *home* with me," answered Baltsaros with a smile. He remembered how his heart had begun to race when Tom had finally stepped into his arms, the big man's scarred back warm against his hands, his scent so familiar...

"And what did he reply?" asked Jon; eyes closed, he licked his bottom lip before grazing it with his teeth. He had begun to move his hips in an achingly lithe roll, matching the speed of Baltsaros's hand.

Baltsaros laughed loud, and Jon looked up at him, confused.

"He said, and I'm quoting word for word, 'If you ever whip me again, I'll cut your bloody cock off'," chuckled the captain.

"Here I thought it was something heartfelt," grinned Jon.

Baltsaros shook his head in amusement and leaned in to kiss him. With surprise, he noticed that Jon was freshly shaved and smelled of sandalwood soap; smiling, Baltsaros moved his lips slowly over the smooth skin of Jon's jaw as he changed his grip on his cock, moving faster. Jon closed his eyes again and moaned softly. Baltsaros could tell it wouldn't take long before he was panting and straining against him.

"Oh... it was heartfelt, that I know," murmured the captain. He closed his eyes, falling into the rhythm of his hand. Jon was right. Patience. Patience with Tom... and an open mind with Jon. He would work at it. But that could wait until later.

Baltsaros opened his eyes and pulled his hand away from Jon's cock.

"On your knees now, my love," he said and began to work the laces loose on his own pants.

~

PRESENT DAY

Jon slid his hand down the front of Baltsaros's leather pants, and the captain inhaled sharply at the icy touch. Chuckling, he pulled back from the kiss and frowned.

"Gods, your hands are frozen," he said, curling his own around Jon to pull him closer.

Jon grinned crookedly, his face impish as he stroked the captain's cock with one hand while tugging down the black leather with the other.

"You should have felt them before Tom warmed them," Jon said, leaning forward again to begin kissing down the side of Baltsaros's neck. "But my mouth is very warm, that I can promise you."

At the mention of Tom, Baltsaros felt a residual jealous twinge. His feelings about the two young men being alone together he kept buried deep, but he knew there would always be a tiny flame of resentment that flared up, no matter what. Closing his eyes as Jon slid his warm tongue over one nipple, teeth gentle yet firm on the sensitive flesh, he tried to make himself relax.

As if reading the captain's mind, Jon laughed as he sank to his knees on the galley floor.

"You're a controlling, possessive asshole, and that's never going to change, is it?" Jon said before licking a wide stripe up under Baltsaros's testicles to the base of his cock, his tongue flat and velvet-rough.

Baltsaros stroked Jon's long dark curls out of his face and solemnly shook his head. While watching the boys "play" together was something he rather enjoyed, the thought of them doing anything without his presence was still something he was learning to deal with.

～

FIVE WEEKS AGO

Leaning over the quarterdeck railing, the captain watched Tom reach out to touch Jon's cheek and nod with a smile. Baltsaros frowned but didn't move from his spot.

Patience. Understanding, he thought to himself.

However, when Jon's face immediately swivelled to glance up at Baltsaros with a guilty look, something *twisted* in his gut, and he turned away.

It had been a week since they had set sail, and Tom had yet to make any attempt at reconciliation. Working closely with the big man again was immensely satisfying; but, though the two fell quickly into the easy, practiced rhythm that made them the perfect team, gone was the steady underlying current of desire that had always been there before. In its place was... nothing.

Not nothing. Aloofness.

Baltsaros turned again to look below and saw that Jon had gone. Scanning the deck, the captain saw Tom standing on the port gunwale, one brawny arm curled through the ratlines. The first mate watched the captain with the coldly appraising look that the older man had come to abhor. Why did Tom think he could judge him so?

Then, as the captain was about to look away, the burly pirate dropped his eyes, raising them almost immediately with a small yet unmistakably coy grin on his face. It was gone in an instant when Tom jumped down and made his way towards the bow of the ship, but Baltsaros didn't doubt what he had seen. Watching his first mate walk away, the captain wondered what it meant.

For the rest of the day, Baltsaros kept an eye on Tom, curious to see if the muscular young man would again break from this strange, detached version of himself. The captain was finally rewarded with another brief, sly smile right before they parted for the evening meal.

Tom had always chosen to eat with the rest of the men rather than share the captain's table and, upon his return, he had resumed the custom. Afterwards, the first mate was almost always found sitting on the quarterdeck bench, eyes narrowed into the wind with a black cheroot between his lips as he manned the helm. It was this habit that the captain was counting on.

When Baltsaros and Jon finished eating that evening, the captain excused himself and left Jon reading one of the many new books they had brought aboard. As he made his way up one of the staircases leading to the quarterdeck, a mug of dark ale in each hand, Baltsaros was relieved to see that Tom was in his usual spot.

"It will start getting cooler soon," he said by way of greeting.

Tom turned his head; his brow furrowed and his blue-green eyes became suspicious slits in his sun-darkened face as he stared at Baltsaros. He worked the cheroot in the corner of his mouth for a moment before letting out a short grunt with a small dip of his head. Encouraged, the captain took another few steps and held out one of the mugs. After staring at it silently for a moment, the first mate finally accepted it with another nod.

"Thanks," Tom mumbled, gaze shifting back over the water.

Baltsaros sat down on the other end of the bench and leaned back on the painted boards. As the two men sat in silence, the sky slowly deepened to the true black of night above them.

Sipping his beer, Baltsaros studied Tom's profile. The man had a high forehead and a shapely brow that creased so often in amusement or consternation that Baltsaros could see faint lines there despite Tom's relatively young age. Though he knew Tom's nose had been broken a few times, it remained largely straight and seemed almost too aristocratic for his roguish looks. Below that were full lips that were often quirked into a smile, making Tom appear both sensual and boyish—a dangerous combination. It was a handsome face, with its scars and scratchy dark-blond stubble, and one that the captain had sorely missed.

"What else can I say?" Baltsaros murmured. "What can I do to make things better for you?" When there was no reaction from Tom, the captain thought he had not heard him, and he leaned forward with the intention of repeating himself.

Tom turned his head slowly and lifted his shoulder in a small shrug, his eyes focused on nothing.

"Tom, talk to me," said Baltsaros, reaching out to touch the first mate's shoulder briefly. When Tom didn't move away, the captain slid closer to him on the bench.

After taking a last drag from his cheroot, Tom flicked it overboard, and his eyes followed the orange spark as it arced through the darkness.

"When have ye ever cared about what I had to say, Baltsaros?" he asked, turning his gaze back to the captain.

Baltsaros frowned. Tom had been calling him "Da" for so long that it was startling to hear his name fall from the first mate's lips.

"I've always listened to you," said Baltsaros slowly, confused. It was true—

whenever there were decisions to be made aboard the ship, the first mate's opinions were invaluable.

Tom huffed out a small, sardonic laugh; as he looked down at the mug clasped loosely between his knees, the first mate shook his head.

"I don't mean the bloody fucking ship, ye fucking idiot," said Tom, looking up with a wry grin. "I mean... about..." The first mate sighed, his brow deeply lined. Tom lifted the beer to his lips and drained the contents in a few swallows. After depositing the empty mug on the deck next to his feet, he wiped his lips and turned his eyes to Baltsaros again, a distraught look on his face.

Baltsaros put his own cup down on the bench beside him and stared hard at Tom.

"I thought you enjoyed our arrangement," he said, sitting back.

Tom laughed and nodded his head.

"No, no, Da. I do... It's just... Why did ye set me aside so easily?" he asked, his eyes going quickly from sad to aloof as he looked back out over the water.

"This isn't about me whipping you," said the captain; it was a statement.

Tom's lip curled in disgust, and he shook his head.

"That's just the bloody icin' on the fuckin' cake," he said, his deep voice just a low rumble in his broad chest.

With a sigh, the captain reached out and curled his hand around the back of Tom's head, the short dirty-blond hair soft against Baltsaros's palm.

At the touch, Tom closed his eyes.

"I thought I made it clear when we came for you that I'm sorry for everything that happened, Tom. Putting you aside for Jon the way I did was an unfortunate mistake, one that I would like you to forgive me for," said Baltsaros, making his voice gentle. "I was like a child with a new toy. I understand that now. It was cruel beyond cruel, and you paid dearly for my whims."

Baltsaros stroked his hand down Tom's neck, his thumb sliding along the side of the first mate's jaw. Tom kept his eyes closed, the muscles of his strong jaw moving fluidly under his deeply tanned skin. The captain watched Tom swallow, the crease between his eyebrows deepening.

Yes, he was terribly fond of this young man.

When Tom opened his eyes to look at the captain, Baltsaros leaned forward and brought his mouth hard against the first mate's. Tom went rigid with surprise but kissed back, a rough-edged embrace that awoke the desire in Baltsaros. He pulled Tom closer to deepen the kiss; there were things that Baltsaros craved that he could not inflict on Jon, and finally the drought was over.

With one hand he quickly reached down to undo the belt at Tom's waist, and when the man tried to push him away, Baltsaros pulled back and backhanded him. Tom grunted with the impact of the captain's strike and lifted his hand to his face, his eyes unreadable in the dark of the quarterdeck. Baltsaros chuckled, his lust sharpening. With a low growl the captain pulled Tom from the bench and, caught off guard, he landed hard on the wooden boards. Tom tried to sit up, but the captain hit him hard again. Baltsaros dropped to his knees between Tom's legs and continued to work loose the fastenings of his pants.

"Stop," said Tom, his voice harsh. He shoved at Baltsaros's hands again, and the older man felt a moment of doubt.

"Don't play, Tom," he said, a frown on his face. He pulled open the first mate's pants, and when he started tugging them down, the captain realized that Tom had stopped struggling. Glancing up, he saw that Tom had turned his head and closed his eyes.

"No, Da. If ye do this, ye'll be forcin' me," said the big man beneath him, turning his furious ocean eyes on the captain. "I'm sayin' no."

The captain sat back on his heels. In disbelief he watched Tom pull his pants together and sit up slowly, breathing hard.

This was no act.

Once he'd staggered to his feet, Baltsaros balled his fists but resisted the urge to lash out at his first mate. He turned and, without a backwards glance, the captain left Tom alone in the dark.

Startled, Jon looked up when Baltsaros threw the door open to his quarters. He got to his feet quickly and crossed the room, his dark brows low over his storm-grey eyes when the captain leaned hard against the edge of the table.

"What happened?" asked Jon, placing a worried hand on Baltsaros's shoulder.

With eyes closed, the captain shook his head. He was at a loss.

Jon's fingers tightened on him.

"Tom?" asked Jon, his voice low. At Baltsaros's nod, he dropped his hand.

He looked up and saw that Jon was staring at him, apprehension clear in his eyes.

"What did you do to Tom, Baltsaros?" asked Jon, softly. Accusingly.

The captain sighed and straightened. It seemed that he had no choice; fate was forcing his hand.

"Go to him," Baltsaros said gently. The words stuck in his throat like bitter bile, but he made himself calmly place a steady hand on Jon's arm. "Go to him, and see if you can't make some sense of this. Go to him, and help me *fix this*."

Worry and suspicion flashed across Jon's face. After pulling away from Baltsaros, he just stared at the captain for a moment before turning to leave.

Alone in his quarters, Baltsaros glared down at his bruised fist wondering whether he would ever know calm again.

~

PRESENT DAY

The captain turned his head with an annoyed growl when he heard the galley door slide open behind him, but when he saw who it was, his lips curled into a pleased smile.

"Now, now... what's goin' on in here?" asked the first mate, stamping snow from his big boots and chuckling. Tom came around the counter and looked down; he put a large, scarred hand on Jon's head and softly stroked the young man's glossy dark hair.

Jon made a small noise, and the vibrations felt good on Baltsaros's cock.

The captain let out a soft groan, turning to watch Jon take in more of his length before he drew back to work his tongue against the underside of its head again.

Tom's hand curled around Baltsaros's neck, and when he looked up, the big man brought him in for a long, slow kiss.

Too soon, Tom broke away, and Baltsaros was dismayed to see the seriousness on the first mate's face.

"I'm sorry, Da... but yer needed above deck," said Tom, eyes down to watch Baltsaros's cock, shiny with spit, emerge from Jon's open mouth.

The kneeling young man looked up, worried.

The captain frowned and rubbed his beard. Another setback?

"Snow squalls, Malik called them," continued the first mate, ruffling Jon's hair. Tom looked up at Baltsaros, his cheeks ruddy from the cold wind. "The rest of what that bloody shipwright said was bloody fuckin' gibberish, but the gist is he needs ye to look at the ship. I ain't understandin' half of what he says... so..." Tom brought up his hands in a sheepish gesture.

"Can't this wait?" asked Baltsaros, though he could feel himself getting soft. The ship always came first.

Tom shook his head and put a hand over his nose. The tip of it had been icy against the captain's cheek, and Baltsaros realized that, for once, the first mate was actually cold. The captain sighed.

"All right," he said and started tucking himself back into his pants. He closed his eyes briefly, forcing himself to say words he didn't want to say. "Why don't you and Jon go warm up? There is no reason why we all have to suffer the weather. Go on. I will join you when I can."

Tom helped Jon up as the captain pulled his shirt on over his head. Baltsaros couldn't help but wonder at how protective and gentle Tom was towards Jon; even for the short journey to the captain's quarters, the first mate carefully draped the woollen cloak around the smaller man to make sure he wasn't cold.

Frowning to himself, Baltsaros watched them leave, trying to turn his mind from bitter thoughts to the dangers of sailing a ship through icy, winter seas.

TOM

> *"Not I, nor anyone else can travel that road for you.*
> *You must travel it by yourself.*
> *It is not far. It is within reach.*
> *Perhaps you have been on it since you were born, and did not know.*
> *Perhaps it is everywhere on water and land."*

—WALT WHITMAN, LEAVES OF GRASS

PRESENT DAY

Tom watched Jon pull the woollen scarf off his face and reached out to help when he saw that the end of it was caught underneath the edge of the thick cloak. Grinning, Jon shook his head, letting himself be unwound by Tom.

"I can undress myself, you know," the dark-haired young man pointed out ruefully even though he obliged and raised his chin when Tom lifted the cloak up and off of him.

Tom let out a short grunt and nodded. Turning to hang their wet outer clothes on the nails he had set into the wall for that purpose, he felt a small twinge of embarrassment for how much he doted on Jon. It was more than a little ridiculous, but he couldn't help himself.

He rubbed his thumb along the edge of his stubbled jaw and glanced back at Jon; when he saw that he was smiling at him, his blue-grey eyes fond, Tom grinned wide. It always amazed him that Jon had forgiven him for everything... Tom would have killed him had their positions been reversed.

Jon cocked his head to the side, his eyes growing dark suddenly as the tip of his tongue came out to touch his top lip. His hair was mussed; a few long curls had escaped the thong at his neck, and they followed the curve of Jon's jaw as he studied Tom.

"Come here," he said, beckoning.

Instantly Tom's heart rate accelerated, and he quickly moved forward to obey. When he brought big hands up to Jon's slender waist, he felt—as always—a little shy and wondered briefly if that would ever pass; he didn't really want it to.

Jon leaned forward to brush his lips softly against Tom's, and the first mate closed his eyes with a sigh, his breathing a little ragged. Would Jon be kind or cruel to him today? Tom tightened his hold on the smaller man, savouring the anticipation and thanking whatever gods there were for gifting him with this passionate, unpredictable creature who was able to take him apart with equal measures of pleasure and pain.

~

Five Weeks Ago

Pressing his fingers lightly to the bruises on his cheek, Tom winced. Baltsaros had a wicked backhanded strike that always made the world explode into bright colours when he hit him, and he did so often. Normally, it didn't bother him but... tonight...

He tongued the place where his teeth had sliced the inside of his lip and sighed as he leaned back against the bunched up pillows. Bumping his head lightly against the wooden boards, Tom closed his eyes.

Fucking Baltsaros. Actually... that was the point. Why *wasn't* he fucking Baltsaros?

He lifted the flask to his lips and grimaced when the rum burned the cut. After swallowing down the sweet, fiery liquid, he touched his cheek again. His mind was a worse mess than his face, that was for bloody fucking sure.

When he heard soft footfalls outside his door, he tensed, thinking it was the captain come to finish the job. However, he realized that there was a note of hesitation to the steps and, as far as Tom knew, Baltsaros had never had a moment's hesitation in his life.

Tom waited and smiled when the knock finally came, soft and timid; there was no one else on the ship it could be.

"Who the fuck is it?" he yelled, trying to mask the sudden excitement that had him smiling despite the pain in his face. When he saw the shadow under the door start to move away uncertainly, he swore under his breath.

Gods be fuckin' damned, Jon, he thought, shaking his head. *Grow a bloody pair.*

"Come in or get gone," he said loudly, flipping the corner of the blanket over to cover himself when the door opened a crack in response.

"Tom? It's me..." said the slight dark-haired man, peering around the wooden door. He was starkly outlined by the brighter corridor behind him; all Tom could see was the curve of Jon's shoulder and his head surrounded by a nimbus of curled wisps that caught the light. "Can I come in?"

Tom chuckled.

"What part of *come in* did ye not understand, lad?" he said, smiling. He saw Jon's shoulder lift slightly and knew that the serious young man would have a deep wrinkle between his brows. Tom reached up and shifted the dented cover on the lantern to make the space a little brighter as Jon stepped into the tiny room, closing the door behind him quietly.

After standing a little awkwardly next to the thin mattress where Tom was sprawled, Jon finally decided simply to sink down into a crouch. Looking worried, he licked his lips and swallowed before speaking.

"What did the captain do?" Jon asked, his eyes taking in the bruising down the right side of Tom's face. "Are you ok?"

Tom took another swig of rum and hissed in pain. He looked at the door.

"Does he know yer here, lovey?" Tom asked quietly; his heart was a quick thing knocking against his ribs, and it was making him a little lightheaded.

"He sent me," replied Jon, his storm-blue eyes wide. "Tom, what did he do? It had to have been something really shitty for him to send me to you. I automatically assumed that he beat you bloody..." He made a small noise and looked away quickly when he finally noticed that Tom was very obviously naked, covered only by the edge of the blanket.

Tom smiled; Jon was amusingly uptight. Making as if to stretch his shoulders, the first mate shifted under the coverlet a little to expose more of his inner thigh and grinned as Jon's eyes tracked the motion only to dart away again almost immediately. However, when Tom saw the way that the young man's lips parted after a slow swallow, he let out a hitched breath; he was falling prey to his own teasing. Quickly, he moved his hand over the bulge in the blanket ands rumpled the material to camouflage his sudden, unexpected arousal. The room felt very hot.

Tom lifted the flask again, and he took a deep swallow, his mouth now numb to the sting. He cleared his throat to try to cut the tension with words.

"Uh... aye, Da came up to see me above. Said some more about bein' sorry. And then... he bloody kisses me," Tom said, frowning.

Jon turned to Tom, confusion and concern on his fine-boned face.

"That wasn't what you wanted?" he asked.

"Oh, that was fine, lad. He just never does," Tom replied, realizing immediately by the way Jon blinked in surprise that the same wasn't true for him. As he swallowed against the sudden tightness in his chest, Tom went back to leaning his head against the wooden wall and stared up at the wavering shadows cast on the low ceiling. "Aye, that was fine. Nice, even. It was when he tried for more, the randy bastard." Rubbing a hand across his mouth, he scowled. "Somethin' just, don't know"—Tom gestured to his head vaguely, not able to put into words the feelings that had washed over him—"and, I said 'no'."

At a soft sound, Tom turned his head and saw that Jon had settled down more comfortably, legs crossed in front of him as he leaned forward, listening intently to Tom. The lantern threw exactly half of the young man's features into total darkness.

"And how did he react?" asked Jon, folding his fists under his chin.

Tom grinned crookedly; the right side of his face felt tight and swollen.

"The bugger actually stopped," he said, shaking his head in disbelief.

Lying on his back on the quarterdeck planks with Baltsaros kneeling between his legs, Tom had felt almost like a spectator when he heard himself tell the captain to stop. Even though his cock had been rock hard and raring to go, he had repeated his refusal, staring in amazement when the captain simply turned and left him.

"I was under the impression that you enjoyed being forced into compromising positions," said Jon quietly, a tiny reflection of the flame in his eyes. "What changed? Why did you say no?"

Why? Tom rubbed a hand over his lips again.

Why indeed.

❧

PRESENT DAY

Murmured against the side of Tom's jaw, Jon's words made the breath hitch in the big man's chest.

"Since you're so goddamn thick that you had to come interrupt the captain and me, I think you *owe* me something in return, don't you think?" purred Jon. "You need a lesson in manners, Tom, and I think you'll take your punishment in the form of my cock in your ass."

Tom licked his lips and nodded, wincing slightly when Jon's sharp teeth nipped his earlobe hard. He shivered as the other man's hands slid up along his ribs, Jon's touch confident as he held Tom hard against his body.

"You're going to take your clothes off and lean over the table. Spread your legs, chest down. Do it," said Jon with a sneer, pushing him away.

Tom almost grinned, but the trick to nurturing Jon's sadistic side was not to appear too eager, something that was difficult considering how much he enjoyed Jon's inventiveness.

Tom reached between his shoulders and drew the thick sweater he wore up over his head, discarding it on the floor before quickly undoing his belt and long trousers. After kicking off the big boots he hated wearing, Tom stepped out of his pants and stood naked in front of Jon for a moment, his hand covering his cock not out of modesty but in an attempt to hide his growing excitement.

Down boy, he thought.

"What are you staring at?" asked Jon, his voice low and harsh. However, as Tom moved to obey, he caught the dark-haired man's appreciative glance and allowed himself a hidden smile as he turned his head away.

He leaned over the mahogany table, spreading his legs just as he was ordered and lowered his torso down to the cold wood. Jon hadn't specified where he wanted his hands, so Tom just clutched the sides of the table, his body taut with anticipation. The edge of the table was a hard line below his hipbones; Tom would no doubt be bruised by being driven against it... and he looked forward to it keenly.

~

Five Weeks Ago

Tom went to take another sip from the flask and found it empty. Swallowing, regardless, just to wet his mouth, he realized he was stalling on answering Jon. The slender young man sat staring at him patiently, a soft worry in his eyes.

"I... don't fuckin' know, love. I don't fuckin' know," Tom muttered. "Be a dove and get the bottle? The little one." He pointed to the small crate holding the pitcher of water.

Jon leaned over and reached for it, fumbling at the sides of the crate until he realized that the front of it opened on leather hinges. Inside were two bottles of rum in stoppered earthenware jugs and one small bottle of good whiskey in a narrow, green bottle; Jon held the last out to Tom.

"Will ye join me... and come a wee bit closer?" asked Tom hopefully, taking the bottle from Jon.

After a moment's hesitation, Jon crawled onto the hard mattress and sat hunched beside Tom.

"That's not what I meant, ducky..." grinned Tom, pulling his knife out from under the blanket to slide the point around the wax at the top of the bottle. "Listen, love: If Da asked ye to come see me, dont'cha think he might be all right with us touchin' a tad? Can't ye see how much I'm hurtin'?" Tom chuckled and pulled the cork out with his teeth.

Jon turned his head and smiled crookedly before easing himself back against Tom's outstretched arm. However, as soon as his shoulders touched Tom's warm skin, the timidity left Jon, and he leaned against the bigger man's side with his head on Tom's wide shoulder. Tom's heart beat double a few times before settling down into a rapid rhythm; as he took a sip of the smooth whiskey, he wondered if Jon knew how nervous he actually felt. He passed the bottle to Jon, the only thing from the *Jewel* he had brought with him.

"I think you're scared," said Jon, just holding the green glass bottle in his hand for a moment.

Tom started, a little dismayed at how transparent he was. He licked the taste of whiskey from his top lip.

"Nah, I ain't scared of much, lad," he replied, closing his eyes.

. . .

When he had finally washed ashore after being swept overboard by the storm, Tom had spent a week just lying in a spare bed at the *Jewel*, recovering from the extreme dehydration he had suffered from. He had nearly died from exposure; fighting to stay afloat, he had held onto the barrel for dear life even though his arms had trembled and his brain had gone numb from exhaustion.

Once he was able to leave the bed on his own, the first thing Tom had done was steal a large batch of sleeping powder.

The man who found Tom collapsed on the floor realized right away what had happened and managed to empty his stomach with a tube.

Afterwards, Tom had been watched more carefully.

Fresia, whom Tom had always been friendly with, had looked at him sternly and said that she couldn't understand why, after fighting to survive, he was trying to take the coward's way out.

A coward.

That's exactly how he felt.

It was agonizing to be forced to endure Jon's presence from a distance for fear of driving the captain to extremes. A bad idea. Bloody stupid. Tom never wanted to face Baltsaros's cold wrath again. Ever. He was stupid for even having Jon in his room right now, regardless of what the captain had said. He blinked—maybe it was a bloody test. Tom scrubbed his hand over the top of his head, trying to block out his worries. Jon broke through his thoughts a moment later.

"See, I thought you were angry. That's certainly how you've been playing it— wounded pride and all that—but fear is the only thing that makes sense for why you're acting this way," mused Jon, rocking his head against Tom's arm.

Tom opened his eyes and sighed.

"Ye think I'm actin' the fool, love?" he asked, taking the bottle back from Jon. "I ain't scared of him. Not the way you're thinkin'."

Jon shrugged.

"Listen, ducky. Before the captain came along, every bastard who wanted to put his cock in me, did. No choice," Tom swallowed some whiskey and shook his head. "Same with beatin' me. I kept fightin' them but just sorta got numb. When Da bought me for a few coins, I was in a real bad way. I almost fuckin' killed the bastard the first time he laid a hand on me, but he was just fixin' me up. I kept waitin' for him to make me his bed boy and it just kept on not happenin'. After the shite with Abetha, well... I just crawled into his bed and sucked his cock. He got bloody rough with me..." Chuckling, Tom smiled at the memory. "And I fuckin' loved it. He's got this *way*... Came so hard I saw stars. Ye know, he's the only soul I ever went to for it. The only one."

The edges of his mind were starting to get blurry from drink, and he was tired, so very tired of thinking and talking about the fucking captain. He felt around for the cork and pushed it back into the neck of the bottle before wedging the whiskey between mattress and wall. Looping his arm around Jon, he pulled them further down on the bed to lie face-to-face.

Jon looked at him with a rueful smile.

"What do you call *this*, then?" he asked, sliding his hand around Tom's waist.

Tom closed his eyes and let out a soft sigh.

"This... this ain't what's good for anyone, that's what it is," he said with a frown. "I'm thinkin' it was a fuckin' mistake to come back. I'm thinkin' maybe ye should leave me to my bloody proble—"

Tom's ears were filled with a rush of white noise, his pulse jumping, as Jon's warm mouth touched his. With a groan, he opened his lips and pressed hard into the kiss.

~

Present Day

When he finished tying Tom's ankles to the base of the table legs, Jon smacked the back of his thigh with a bare hand.

"Arms behind you," said Jon, standing.

Obediently, Tom placed his arms behind him and winced as Jon tied his wrists together tightly. The room was warm from the pot-bellied stove that Malik and Baltsaros had installed as part of the Devil's Isles modifications, but Jon's hands felt cool against his skin as they moved to trace the tattooed lines that curled and twined over his left side. Tom let out a low groan as Jon slid his fingers lower, stroking down the furrow of his ass. Breathless with anticipation, Tom closed his eyes as Jon poured something cool on him, fingers pushing into him quickly to get him ready. The penetration was perfunctory, done without any gentleness; Tom didn't expect any. That would come later.

Tom let out a grunt when Jon's cock breached him, sliding deep inside him in one motion. He opened his eyes and craned his neck, glancing back at Jon when the man remained motionless. Confused, Tom watched Jon smile and lean over to pluck one of Baltsaros's good white candles out of the heavy wrought iron holder. The motion caused him to push into Tom, and the big man exhaled slowly. He placed his head back down on the table and closed his eyes, ready for anything Jon could dish out.

"You told me once that you weren't afraid of much. How about fire?" asked Jon.

Tom heard the unmistakable sound of a match being struck against the side of the table and felt the first twinge of real fear. His heart beat fast and hard wondering what Jon intended; when it came to finding new ways to abuse him, Jon was creative. He grunted again as the hard cock in his ass pulled back, only to plunge into him once more.

"Let's see if I can make you beg..." said Jon, and Tom gasped when the first drops of burning hot wax hit his skin.

~

Tom rubbed his face sleepily and took another deep swallow of rum. Bleary-eyed, he reached up and pulled the cheroot out from behind his ear to tuck it into the corner of his mouth.

"Matches, bloody matches…" he muttered, patting at the pocket sewn into his rolled trousers. When he thought he had found one, he tried pulling it out, but it snagged on the material and went flying off into the dark. Tom blinked and fumbled again in the pocket. When it was obvious that there wasn't another match, he scowled and tried to stick the slim cigar back behind his ear.

"Don't need no fuckin' match any—*Cock and bloody balls!*" he yelled as the cheroot dropped to the deck, rolling off into the dark to join the wayward match. With a string of low, muttered curses, Tom squinted and saw that his dicing partner had fallen asleep against the stack of crates; the man was snoring, mouth open and stinking.

Rubbing his eyes again, Tom fought his own desire for sleep. He had to stay away from his room for fear that Jon would come find him again. With a groan, he leaned his head against the rain barrel.

Jon. Passionate and gentle. Jon with his boundless hope that the three of them would find some kind of arrangement.

"Bloody fucking naïve fucking Jon," slurred Tom, shaking his head. The boy had been so soft in his hands, warm, willing. Tom had finally sent him on his way after regretfully breaking from the kiss. How could he explain to Jon that he was a coward? That he was terrified of being set aside again by the captain. That the reason he had been so late coming aboard that first day was because he had decided not to come at all rather than face Baltsaros and Jon.

~

Standing on the deck of the Sainte-Marie, Tom clutched his bag. He had spent the night tossing and turning, almost sick with unease, before boarding the small passenger schooner bound for the midlands.

The previous afternoon spent with the captain and Jon at the *Jewel* had been almost perfect; enough so that he had fooled himself briefly into thinking that everything was back to normal.

When the first twinges of doubt had struck him as he lay next to the two men, his body cooling, he wondered how it could ever be normal when Jon was involved. His desire for the dark-haired young man was like a slow-burning fire in his veins; Baltsaros would never put up with it. Jon would remain a constant threat, one that would have Tom beaten and banished again eventually.

And… he just couldn't live with being ousted from the captain's side again. There was no one else in the world that Tom respected or loved more; Baltsaros was his life. He knew that it was almost blind devotion, but he didn't care. For all that the man was a blatant sadist, no one else had shown him trust or friendship like the captain had;

and, in the rare moments of gentleness between them, Tom had thought maybe even love. That fool's notion had been blown to bits the moment he saw the way that Baltsaros looked at Jon.

Jaw clenched, Tom turned his eyes away from the painfully familiar mizzenmast that could be seen just past the harbour wall. *Baal's Heart*, the only true home he had ever known.

No, he would go to the midlands and find work, maybe as an apprentice blacksmith or a personal guard for a small lord... nowhere near open water. Captain Baltsaros would never find him, and Tom would eventually forget and grow numb; his constant dreams of a dark-haired sylph with Jon's eyes and gentle hands would fade away.

He would become nothing.

Tom closed his eyes, trying to push away the ache that was growing inside him, making his chest tight.

Fuck it.

When the schooner's first mate cried out to push away from the dock, Tom let out a long sigh before jumping down from the ship. As he made his way along the floating dock, Tom whistled loud to hail one of the small boats that ferried those to the bigger ships just outside the harbour, apprehension like a heavy cloak around his broad shoulders.

~

"Well, well... lookee, Dan! What d'we 'ave 'ere, aye?" growled a voice nearby.

Tom pulled his eyelids apart, blinking slowly at the approaching shapes. Licking his lips, he was dismayed to see that his drunkenness had reached the level where images were overlapping. When he closed one eye, Tom saw that instead of four men swaying up the deck towards him, there were two. He scratched his jaw, trying to coax recognition out of his brain. All he could remember was that the two were part of the new batch brought aboard after the massacre on Madierus.

Tom hiccupped a laugh when the memory coalesced: *Dan.* They were both called Dan. Big Dan and Little Dan. Both were trouble.

Big Dan, who rivalled Tom in size, walked slowly up to him and kicked the sole of his bare foot. Tom grunted; he wasn't in the mood for any foolery. When he tried to haul himself to standing, the world spun on a different axis, and he found himself down on the planks, the boards smooth and worn beneath his palms. There was raucous laughter from above, and Tom wiped at the corner of his mouth before turning his head with a scowl.

"Ye know what I 'ear about this 'un, Dan?" asked the bigger of the two. The smaller man kept silent, and Tom recalled that he was a mute. It made him wonder if his name was Dan after all or if the big brute had just named him such as a lark. Tom shoved himself to sitting and shook his head hard, trying to clear it enough so he could stand.

"I 'ear that Tom 'ere is a regular cock'ound. Aye. I 'ear 'e likes to take big fat todgers in 'is little pink man-pussy," drawled Big Dan, an ugly smile on his weatherworn face. "I 'ear 'e fuckin' *loves* it. Mebbe if I fuck 'im in that sweet little ass cunt of 'is, 'e'll think twice about makin' me swab the bloody fuckin' deck again... What do ye think, Dan? Do ye think maybe 'e'll come warm our cocks at night like 'e does the captain's?"

The man's hands had gone down to his belt, and Tom could see that he was unbuckling it. Anger crashed through him followed fast by a cold finger of fear when he realized he was probably too drunk to fight Big Dan off.

"Aye, 'elp me 'old 'im down, Dan," growled the big one, and the two men fell on Tom. He tried to shove them away, but Big Dan landed a blow to his temple, and he was overcome quickly as he lay there stunned. Tom was soon on his stomach on the boards, growling like a trapped animal, as his pants were yanked down past his ass.

Not again, thought Tom, breathing through clenched teeth, his chest crushed to the deck by the man sitting on his back.

There was a strangled gurgle, and Tom felt something hot and wet hit his shoulder.

"Tom is mine, lads," said the captain in a soft voice as the man above him slumped over and collapsed like a sack of potatoes on the decking next to the first mate's head. Tom opened his eyes and watched as Little Dan's pupils went slack, dark bubbles of blood popping and spattering along the deep cut in his neck. Confusion was immediately replaced with astounded relief, and Tom lifted himself up on his hands and knees, swaying slightly. He heard a loud thump and turned his head, hauling his pants up with one hand. There was a splash and then a gentle long-fingered hand helped him up to his feet.

Baltsaros had saved him again. Saved him and claimed him, just as he had so long ago. Tom's chest hurt, and his eyes burned.

Letting himself collapse in the captain's arms, Tom buried his face in the man's shoulder. He smelled Baltsaros's scent—the subtle musk of him, cologne, clean skin, ocean air. Tom clutched at him, gathering handfuls of the captain's loose white shirt at his back,

"Da, I'm sorry. I'm sorry... gods, I'm sorry..." he sighed over and over against the captain.

"Tom, you're completely inebriated. What are you apologizing for? Everything will be all right. Can you stand? Here... hold onto this for a moment please," said Baltsaros, leaning him against the big rain barrel. Tom swiped at his eyes and steadied himself as he watched the older man drag Little Dan across the deck. Leaving a wide, red streak behind him, the captain then lifted the dead man up and over the gunwale.

A graceful smile widened the captain's curved lips when he turned back to Tom, his hands bloody as he reached out to take the big man's arm.

"There's no need for apologies, my tomcat. You're *mine*... Which means you're mine to protect. Do you understand me? Gods you stink—how much have you had to drink? No wonder you get yourself into such trouble," muttered the captain, shaking his head. "Now, are you listening to me, you stubborn thing? Jon told me you were scared, and I think I know why. Tom, there's no justification for your fears. It's really very simple: I want you by my side... I *need* you with me. How can I get that through your thick skull, boy?" He reached out and touched Tom's face, thumb sliding along his sore cheek. "*I am the one who's sorry.*"

Need. Tom looked away as his heart stumbled and his breath was torn from him. With that simple word, his doubts sank along with the dead men overboard. The captain *needed* him.

"Aye, Da. If ye'll still have me after all my foolishness," he replied with an awkward grin.

There was no mistaking the fondness in Baltsaros's dark eyes as he smiled back at his first mate. With a nod, Tom looped his arm around the captain's neck for support and let himself be led to the stateroom below the quarterdeck.

As he ducked through the doorway, Tom groaned softly. Through the haze of alcohol, he began to realize just how hard Big Dan had hit him. He felt a stickiness on his jaw and neck that wasn't drying and figured it was probably his own blood. There was a rustle in the darkened room.

"Baltsaros?" came Jon's voice, confused and hoarse from sleep.

"Jon, can you please light some candles? And get my surgical kit please," said the captain as he helped Tom to cross the room.

Tom squinted as a match was struck. Jon, standing naked next to the bed, leaned over the table to light the candles at its centre. Turning to look at Tom, his shadow-blue eyes widened.

"Tom! Oh gods, are you ok? What happened?" asked Jon, reaching out to help Baltsaros lay him down on the bed. The dark-haired young man's brows were pinched together in worry for a moment, his hand gentle on Tom's chest before he went to fetch Baltsaros's surgical tools.

"I'm ok, lad. Just got into a fight, aye?" Tom said as he glanced at Baltsaros; the captain nodded once in understanding. "Fucker beat me when I was down on my luck at dice... Me, three sheets to the bloody fuckin' wind." Tom grinned when Jon frowned and clucked his tongue once; there was no need to tell him what had nearly happened. As the captain said: everything was going to be all right.

"Ach, my bloody face," he complained when Jon leaned over him to start dabbing at the wound at his brow. Tom saw the captain smile wanly as he threaded the needle with catgut. "Why does everyone hit me in the *face*? Ain't I ugly enough?"

~

Present Day

While it was bitterly cold outside, the two men in the stateroom glistened with sweat. Tom, his arms bound behind him and his ankles tied to the legs of the table, grunted and hissed as another stream of hot wax landed on his bare skin. Jon groaned in response; he loved the way Tom's muscles tightened over his cock with the sudden pain. He thrust himself into Tom's body a few times, his hands sliding over the tattooed skin of the bound man's side.

The candlelight made Tom's skin pure gold, and Jon thought it was beautiful.

The door banged open behind them, and Jon turned his head. The captain stepped in amidst a swirl of snowflakes and quickly shut the door against the wind.

His cheeks were red with the cold, and the collar of his greatcoat was pulled high over his ears. He yanked his gloves off, sighing happily from the heat in the room, and nodded at Jon to continue.

Jon turned back to Tom and spilled some more burning wax on him, moving within his body. With the captain's eyes on him, Jon felt his pleasure mount quickly, and soon he was pounding into Tom, a harsh growl bursting out of his chest as he pulled his cock out to rain his seed down on the bound man's back.

Breath heaving fast in his chest, Jon began untwisting the hempen ropes that were binding Tom. He looked curiously at the captain. Baltsaros's face had darkened with lust at the display; he loved to watch the boys "play", as he put it. However, he made no move to join them as he usually did.

Tom straightened and flexed his wrists, his head cocked curiously at Baltsaros.

"What is it, Da?" he asked, still using the ridiculous title though the two were no longer related through marriage.

Baltsaros smiled wide.

"I thought you boys would like to know that we've arrived within sight of the Devil's Isles," he said.

Jon and Tom looked at each other in excitement. It had taken nearly two months to reach them; finally it was the time to see what it was they were up against.

PART TWO

CHAPTER I
THE SPIRES

Jon shivered and squinted against the snowflakes that stuck to his eyelashes and whirled around like maddened, ghostly flies over the quarterdeck. Against his side, the captain was a solid presence as he peered through his binoculars at the looming mountain range ahead. Tom let out a long, low whistle that the wind attempted to snatch away. Leaning forward against the railing, the grinning first mate turned to look over his shoulder, his sea-green eyes wide with amazement.

"Bloody hells, Da," he chuckled. "Have ye brought us to our doom?"

Jon felt, rather than heard, the captain's bark of laughter as he lowered the short, custom-made, double spyglass. Curious, Jon took the binoculars from Baltsaros's hand and held them up to his own eyes.

What he beheld was mind boggling. Monstrous. Nothing Malik and Nathaniel had described nor what was written in any of Baltsaros's books could have prepared Jon for the overwhelming reality of the Devil's Isles. Out of a frozen, pale-grey sea sprouted colossal black spires, like clawed fingers or fangs that reached up into the snow-washed sky. There were seven of them, arranged in a slight outward curve, that jutted from the impassable mountain range that split the world in half from the northern isles to the frozen, uninhabitable wasteland to the south. Only through the relatively narrow gap between the third and fourth spires could a ship theoretically pass and *only* during the warmest weeks in this barren, snow-blasted land; at least that's what it said on the mouldering text that Nathaniel the cartographer had found. It still remained to be seen if *Baal's Heart* had made it in time and could navigate it at all. To Jon, it seemed like a frozen impasse ahead.

The Devil's Isles, the captain had explained, were formed from the same stone that the rest of the western mountain range was composed of. He theorized that there had been a softer stone between the veins of hard black granite and that, over the ages, the elements had worn it away to leave behind the hooked spires that clawed up from the frozen sea. Though Baltsaros's explanation made sense, it did nothing to still the nagging Jon's nagging belief that nothing natural could have created something so terrifying.

At a thump and loud creak, Jon started. His heart beat double for the moment it took to remind himself that it was only floating chunks of ice hitting the reinforced hull of the ship. They had lowered Malik's "bumpers" over the side of the prow the previous day when they began to encounter more substantial pieces of ice floating in the cold sea. Attached to the iron-and-wood struts that caged the hull, the bumpers were packets of leather-wrapped straw sewn onto a large net that swathed the entire front of the ship. The shipwright had been confident that they would be enough to deflect the ice long enough to make it through the gap. However, when the snow had started piling up at the bow earlier that day, he had started to worry that the weight would be too much and that the ship would start to be pulled nose-down into the icy water.

Jon had to smile; all it had required was that the snow be scooped overboard, something that Tom could very well have handled on his own. Instead, he had begged off, claiming ignorance before coming to interrupt Jon and the captain in the galley. Tom caught his eye then and, as if reading Jon's thoughts, the first mate winked with a sly grin.

Jon wrinkled his brow at the first mate. Had it been latent jealousy or simple desire to get out of the cold? No matter how much time Jon spent with Tom, he still had trouble reading the bigger man's honest intentions.

Tom slid away from the railing and pressed himself to the captain's other side as the three of them stood on the frozen deck, watching the approach of the looming spires.

~

With his hands clamped tight over his ears, Jon groaned. Even with Tom's heavy arms around him, no matter what he did, he couldn't block out the screams.

The evening after the Devil's Isles first came into view, the snow had finally stopped, and an eerie calm had fallen as *Baal's Heart* sailed towards the spires in the pitch dark. The submerged chunks of ice had increased in number and size, and Baltsaros had contemplated anchoring for the night out of safety; however, the wind had died down, and Malik had cautioned against it, pointing out that to be motionless could mean getting trapped in the ice. In the end, the captain had put himself, Tom, and Calum on short shifts overnight.

As Baltsaros was just settling into bed beside him, intending to take the second shift, a loud screech had filled the cabin, turning Jon's blood to ice. Heart lurching in his chest, Jon had sat up, wide-eyed and blind in the dark.

"What the hells was that?" Dry-mouthed, the words had come out as a mere croak, and he had flinched when Baltsaros's hand came up to touch his back.

Moments later a second scream had rent the air, and Jon's heart had stuttered again, beating hard against his ribs. The sound was ghastly, inhuman. Terrified, Jon had choked when the door to the cabin was thrown open, and a big shape shambled in. When Tom's deep voice had called out, Jon's nervous laugh had been shrill from relief.

As he had lit the candles, the first mate had explained that they were encountering yet bigger pieces of ice and that these were scraping slowly along the sides of the ship; the sound, reverberating through the *Heart*'s hull, was amplified. As if eager to lend credence to Tom's words, another long scream had echoed through the darkness. Even the stalwart first mate had blanched at the sound.

"Aye gods, that's a sound right outta the black hells, ain't it?" Tom had laughed, his eyes dark in the dim light.

Tom was no longer laughing.

The screeching had picked up in frequency, and soon it sounded like a chorus of men, women, and children were being continuously tortured to death outside the ship. No one would be getting any sleep that night.

Gritting his teeth, Jon tried to shake the images out of his head; he had worked a long time in the dungeons, and the sounds of the ice squealing against the sides of the ship were triggering images of torture that he had thought were long buried.

Tom pulled him against his warm chest, a big scarred hand around the back of Jon's neck.

"It's just ice, lovey," he kept murmuring against Jon's hair. Jon nodded, and squeezed his eyes shut tighter when there was a particularly jarring shriek.

"Do ye want to go back out?" asked Tom softly. Outside, the noises weren't nearly as loud. However, the air was a bone-numbing cold; even with the braziers burning hot on the quarterdeck, no one could stay outdoors for very long.

Jon pulled away and rubbed his face. His jaw was sore from clenching it.

"Yeah. Maybe for a bit. I'll be all right, I swear," he said. Both the captain and first mate were taking him very seriously, but Jon felt deeply ashamed of his reaction. It was just ice against the hull, but the noise brought back memories of the nightmares he used to have: the black water, the ship full of blood, the tortured dead crawling over its sides.

Shuddering, Jon grabbed for the thick sweater he always wore under his cloak and pulled it on over his head. Tom watched him for a moment, his eyes narrow with worry, before sliding off the bed to fetch their outer clothes.

When Jon stepped out the door, he let out a sharp gasp; the chill in the air made his breath burn like white fire in his lungs, and the inside of his nose crackled with ice. It was a terrifyingly bitter cold. After lifting his scarf over his face, he took the steps up to the quarterdeck two at a time, followed by Tom. He was exhausted and shaking with cold, but at least out here the sounds no longer sounded like screams—they'd been transformed back into icebergs scraping the ship's sides.

Standing by one of the braziers was the captain, his hands out over the crackling fire to warm them. Jon knew that Baltsaros hated having so much open flame on the ship, but they had no choice at this point; frostbite and death were the alternatives. With a glance towards the bow, Jon could see at least ten other bright spots of fire where men were huddled. They were like a floating island of light in a blackened sea.

When Jon joined the captain, he was bracketed by Tom's warmth on the other side; the first mate pulled out one of his small cigars and bent low to light it on a flaming brand.

"Still can't sleep, Jon?" asked the captain, his voice gentle. He'd started wearing a thick sailor's tuque low over his forehead, and with the big collar of his coat pulled high, his face was barely visible.

Jon shook his head and held his hands over the flames, trying to stay warm. Tom slung an arm around him and leaned into Jon's side as he passed his cheroot to the captain.

"We'll be through by mid-morning by my calculations," said the captain, taking in a lungful of the pungent smoke. "Then we can all sleep."

~

At dawn, the sun rose up behind *Baal's Heart*, a pale, sickly thing in the bone-white sky. Sitting swathed in blankets on the hard bench, Jon felt like every muscle in his body was screaming, and his head felt strange and numb, like he was only half-awake; the night had been so very long.

"Get up," said Baltsaros, grabbing a handful of the younger man's cloak. "Jon, get up."

Jon blinked slowly, moving his eyes from the low, flickering flames that burned in the big bronze bowl. He looked at the captain in confusion.

"Jon, you have to get up and move around. You're going to freeze just sitting there," growled the older man, stamping his feet on the deck. "Get up. Get up now."

So cold.

"I'm ok," replied Jon, his voice faint. "I'll be fine. Just let me stay by the fire." He turned back to the flames. The flames would keep him warm.

"Gods be damned, Jon," said the captain, yanking hard on his cloak. "You have to get back inside."

Jon gasped and tumbled off the bench, landing hard on one knee. He barely felt it.

"Don't make me go back inside, Baltsaros. I'm half insane from the sound... I don't think my nerves could take it. Please. I'll stay here with Tom," mumbled Jon, turning his head. The big man was nowhere to be seen. Had he fallen asleep on the bench? He couldn't remember Tom leaving his side.

"Tom is taking care of something. You have to listen to me, Jon. You have to stand up. Can you stand up for me?" The captain reached down to grasp Jon's arm, and he let himself be hauled upright. Groaning, Jon stood shakily on feet that felt like blocks of ice.

"Stamp your feet," ordered Baltsaros. "Get your blood flowing."

Jon felt like crying but obeyed. His feet began to burn and itch as he stamped the feeling back into his toes. When he heard a splash, he turned in time to see Tom pushing a body over the side of the ship; the cold was starting to claim victims.

"How many?" gasped Jon, looking up at the captain.

Baltsaros's eyes were in deep shadow as he looked over the ice-covered deck, his mouth hidden behind the high collar of his greatcoat.

"At least four," muttered the captain. "And there are sure to be more." Baltsaros's gloved hands were fists at his sides, and Jon could tell that the older man was trying to master his temper. The captain had put his men's lives in peril; he had made them victims of circumstances he couldn't control. One glance at the spires showed Jon that the captain's prediction of a mid-morning pass through them had proved ambitious. Sometime in the night, the wind had died almost completely; limp sails and a constant push against the floating ice meant that they were moving at a snail's pace. Tucking his hands under his arms, Jon tried not to panic. It could be *days* before they made it through, if at all.

Maybe Katherine had been right. Maybe this expedition had been built on madness.

~

"I can't believe we're really going," laughed Jon, dipping his finger in the dark foam at the top of a second mug of Maya's stout beer.

Baltsaros, stripped to the waist and, leaning back in his chair in the shaded patio of the *Grog Blossom*, curled his lips into a wide grin.

Chuckling again at the youthful excitement that infused the captain's eyes, Jon shook his head.

"You're insane, you know that, right?" he smiled and lifted his mug to his lips.

"Jon, there's nothing holding me here. Abetha's going to run things fine. I have confidence in her," replied the captain, resting his own beer against his thigh as he peered out over the water. The turquoise lagoon was alive with activity as jolly boats made their way to *Baal's Heart*, loading her up with supplies for the coming journey. "I've been making the same rounds, year after bloody year... It's time for a change."

Eyebrows raised at the captain's use of profanity, Jon studied Baltsaros's profile. There was excitement for adventure there, yes. However, Jon knew that the older man was also impatient to set off to find Tom; a dangerous journey that required the first mate's extensive skills was the perfect excuse to track him down.

Frowning, Jon tapped on the tabletop thoughtfully. The tropical blooms that surrounded the tavern were fragrant, and the sea air was a warm, salty kiss on his skin. Though he too was anxious to start the search for Tom, a dangerous journey through icy waters was so far from Jon's current reality that it seemed vaguely ludicrous. He thought of the recurring dream he'd been having:

When Baltsaros turned to look at Jon, his eyes were serious.

"Are you ok?" asked the captain.

Jon looked down and saw that he was rubbing at the scar on his chest; a finger's width to the left, and the knife would have claimed his heart. He dropped his hand to the table.

"I... dream about the Devil's Isles. About them and Tom," he confessed. "All the time."

The captain's eyes narrowed, and he nodded.

"I know, Jon. You sometimes yell out in your sleep," murmured Baltsaros. He leaned forward in his seat and wrapped his long, sun-darkened fingers around Jon's wrist. "When you were gravely injured, you carried on about them." The captain's thumb stroked the thin knife scar along the inside of Jon's forearm, the one that symbolized the oath between them.

Baltsaros's sudden smile was wide, and his teeth looked sharp and white in his tanned face.

"Something is telling you to go there," said the captain, leaning back again and taking a long pull from his mug of beer. "Maybe I *am* a little superstitious after all."

⁓

It was nearing twilight when at last the ship was within half a league of the looming black spires. At this distance, the Devil's Isles took up the entire sky; they seemed infinite, their tops lost in the hazy winter clouds high above. Though the temperature had risen a few degrees, the crew was in bad shape, listlessly going about dumping heavy snow and ice overboard. Strangely, the icebergs had spaced out again, and the squealing screams had become less frequent.

Jon was sprawled out on the bed, wedged against the captain's side, when he heard the first shouts. He lifted his head, groggy after finally catching almost an hour's sleep in nearly thirty-six. When there was no further sound, Jon lay back down on the feather mattress.

Nauseous with exhaustion, he jerked awake a few moments later when there was another shout; this time he recognized Tom's voice. He turned to the captain and saw that the older man was blinking slowly in confusion in the wan light.

"What now?" muttered the captain, groaning as he pushed himself up. Baltsaros placed a hand on Jon's shoulder when he tried to sit. The captain shook his head. "Sleep, Jon. I'll go see what's amiss."

Exhausted and only too happy to oblige, Jon closed his eyes, letting the warm darkness claim him once more.

Baltsaros stood outside the door to his quarters and stared curiously at the scene before him. A thin fog had risen up over the sides of the *Heart*, and it reflected the lantern light in a misty, white cloud around the whole ship. There was a strange quality to all the natural sounds of the ship; a drip of water from the prow sounded loud and close, as if falling down a deep well next to the captain. The creak of the boards beneath his feet sounded oddly muted. Voices seemed muffled and disembodied. Peering into the fog, Baltsaros tried to make out where Tom was.

As he walked slowly forward, the captain stepped to the side when two men grappling at each other nearly collided with him. With a deep frown, Baltsaros increased his pace, dismayed to see another fight taking place along the deck through the thickening mist. Finally, he heard Tom's voice raised in a shout, and the familiar, bulky silhouette of the first mate came into sight at the starboard gunwale. The big man had one hand extended as he leaned out over the frigid, ice-strewn water.

"Tom! What is going on?" yelled Baltsaros, reaching for Tom's belt to pull him back.

With a grunt, Tom stepped down, and the captain saw that the first mate's nostrils were flared and his lips were tight with anger. Or worry? Looking into Tom's wide sea-green eyes, Baltsaros was amazed to see fear there.

"What is going on?" he repeated, quieter this time. Tom started, as if breaking out of a trance and shook his head slowly. Turning to look back over the water, he simply pointed.

"Just... look," replied Tom.

The captain peered over the side of the ship and was confused by what he saw there. Three men were standing on ice floes next to the ship, and Calum was among them. Next to Baltsaros, Tom yelled out again.

"Calum, ye bloody fool, come back to the fuckin' tub, mate! There ain't nothin' out there for ye to go to!" Tom's deep voice boomed out over the cracked ice, and Calum turned to look at him.

"Aye, lad, Marg'ry is waitin' fer me! Can't ye see her? Can't ye see my beauty?" yelled Calum. Turning back to the ice and mists, he waved an arm over his head. "I'm-a comin', my love!"

"Who in the bloody hells is Margaery, Da?" asked Tom softly, his face slack with incomprehension as he looked at Baltsaros.

The captain frowned over the water, unease settling over him like a greasy second skin.

"Margaery was the name of Calum's wife," he replied, tightening his grip on the metal cleat as he leaned further over the gunwale. Out of the corner of his eye, he saw Tom peer over the side again.

"But, Da... She's been dead for nigh forty years... Ain't she?"

CHAPTER 2

THE MIST

om blinked slowly, staring at the captain for a moment before he frowned over the gunwale again.

"He's seein' bloody ghosts?" he asked, incredulous. Nothing in his life had ever made him hold with the notion of ghosts; it was superstitious hogwash as far as he was concerned. However, Old Calum was seeing *something* out there on the ice and, whatever it was, it was going to end up killing him.

As Tom and the captain watched, one of the other men stepped further and fell into the frigid water when the ice floe beneath him tipped under his weight. Without so much as a shout, the sailor slipped into the black water and was dragged down by the weight of his furs. The sheets of floating ice drifted, and the space between them disappeared.

Tom let out a surprised grunt. Though he didn't really give a shit about the pirate's chilling death in the frozen sea—the man was a complete bloody picaroon—Tom was rather fond of Calum. He had to do something to get the old codger back on board before he shared the same fate.

An idea struck him.

"Holy hells, Calum! Ye old dog!" he yelled out over the ice. The older man turned his head at the sound of Tom's voice, but he didn't stop inching forward on the cold, slippery surface. The first mate could see that Calum was getting dangerously close to the edge, and he clenched his fists in frustration as he continued. "Ye never told me yer woman had such gorgeous tits! Lookee here! Margaery has some fine lookin' knockers!" Tom's gravelly baritone carried easily across the distance; he took a hopeful breath when he saw the old man stop and turn again to peer up at them.

The captain furrowed his brow and nodded, urging Tom to continue.

Helplessly, Tom shrugged. He was at a loss for what else to say. He had no idea what the woman had looked like; for all he knew, she'd been as flat as a board. Leaning further out, he bellowed at Calum, hoping the old man was loopy enough to fall for his bluff.

"Aye! Calum! Ye wouldn't mind me touchin' the missus, would ye? Eh, Calum? Just want to get my fingers wet… ooh boy! She's a fine lookin' slut, and she's moanin' for my cock, mate! Lookee here!"

From where he was standing, Tom saw instantly that his words had the desired effect. The old man's face twisted into a mask of fury, and he turned back towards the ship.

"He won't be able to get back aboard," muttered the captain. "The ice is too far from the side now… We're drifting. How did he get down there to begin with?"

Face bleak, Tom pointed to the Jacob's ladder that had been lowered over the side. In the distance, the second man fell through the ice, and the first mate shook his head in disbelief. Why had everyone suddenly gone mad?

Tom glanced around him and frowned at some men grappling on the deck. It looked like two of them were trying to pin down a third so they could bugger him, and the smaller man was bleating like a sheep. A complete madhouse.

Rope. I need rope, he thought.

With a low growl, Tom jumped down from the crate and levelled a kick at one of the men. Tom's boot caught the man in the jaw, and the big northman went down like a wet rag on the snow-strewn deck. After scrambling to his feet, the other took off at a run, ricocheting off the forward mast before disappearing into the thick mist. The man on the ground stared up at him, his eyes devoid of intelligence and, with another pathetic bleat, he crawled away on all fours. Tom watched him go, a sick feeling in the pit of his stomach, as he took up a length of rope. Chewing the corner of his mouth nervously, he shook his head again; this was beyond comprehension. He turned back to the gunwale and saw that the captain was staring at his palm, his stark brow low over his dark eyes.

The fear that kept trying to break through to Tom finally slid its cold fingers into his veins as he watched the captain blink and shake his head as though groggy from drink.

Not the bloody captain.

"Da! What the fuck is goin' on? Please don't fuckin' crawl out onto the ice. So help me gods, I'll tie ye to the bloody mast if I need to," he pleaded as he coiled the rope around in his hand, one end now a slipknot.

Baltsaros just rubbed his fingers together and pursed his lips, lost in thought.

Tom clenched his jaw and looked away, hoping that he could get Calum aboard before the captain fell prey to whatever stoked the madness around them.

Leaning over the side of the ship, Tom anchored his weight by wedging his calf between the gunwale and the ratlines that ran down from the rigging. Calum was nearly at the edge of the ice closest to the ship, and Tom grunted as he threw out the rope, trying to snag it around the old man. On the second try he was successful, and he braced himself against the side of the ship; the old man's boots dipped into the icy water as he fell and was dragged forward. Tom let out a growl and hauled on the rope hard, the muscles straining in his brawny arms as he began to quickly hoist Calum into the air.

"Da! Da, wake the fuck up and grab him, will ye?" he shouted, gripping the rope tightly in his gloved hands. The sound of his voice roused the captain, and Baltsaros leaned over to pull Calum up over the edge. When the old sailor landed with a thump on the frozen boards, his eyes were roaming sightlessly; it was as if all intelligence had fled in the face of insanity.

Tom pressed his lips together—the situation was beginning to overwhelm him. He glanced at the man that he had always relied on and was utterly stricken with how dazed the captain looked.

"Da... Da, please," he groaned, fear beginning to unravel him. Clutching the captain's arm, he tried to shake Baltsaros from his stupor. The older man stroked his hand along the gunwale and squinted at his palm again, ignoring Tom completely.

"It's a spore. Not a mist. A spore. There must be some mould on the rocks... The warmer weather thawing... releasing a spore. Causing visions... Though, I wonder whether the men indoors are as affected. Hm," murmured Baltsaros, talking to himself. "I must conduct experiments."

Tom's breath stuck in his throat as he listened to the man he loved start muttering to himself in his native tongue, completely oblivious to the first mate clinging to his arm. There was a shout from the stern, and Tom turned to peer through the haze. He couldn't see anything for a moment and then...

No.

Tom's heart began a swift staccato rhythm that stole the breath from his lungs. He narrowed his eyes, hands dropping from the captain's arm as he gaped at the spectre in the mists. The balding head, the sloped shoulders... the cruel eyes and crueller hands. The man would smell of lavender but, when Tom's face was forced against his crotch, all he ever smelled was stale piss.

Tom shook his head to clear it, and the ghost was gone from sight for a moment. He looked around and saw that the captain had disappeared. He let out a low moan of terror.

No... No, gods, please no, no, no...

The man of Tom's nightmares strode again from the mists, the long whip curled in his hand as he sneered at Tom.

His master.

The man who had broken him over and over again from the time he was just a boy of seven.

Tom shook his head, tripping backwards and landing with a harsh grunt on his ass. The split end of the whip slithered across the deck like a leather snake, hungry for Tom's skin, and he cried out.

"I *killed* ye, ye bloody bastard. I fuckin' killed ye... lords in hell, go back to yer grave!" Tom choked over the words in his panic to get away as he crawled backwards on his hands.

Something. Something the captain said. Spores. The air filled with the poison of dreams.

Tom's master licked his lips and bared his yellowish fangs before taking another step towards him. Closing his eyes, Tom forced himself to think. The man was dead; Tom had slit his throat as the cocksucker lay sleeping in his bed, hot blood spraying into Tom's face and puddling in the sheets as the man's body twitched and then finally stilled. There were no ghosts. It was something wrong with the air. The men were sucking in madness with every breath; he had to make himself believe it.

When Tom opened his eyes, the ghost stood before him, his whip at the ready and thirsty for his blood. Against all the instincts that screamed at him to flee, Tom reached out a shaking hand to touch the man... and his fingers passed through nothing. He let out a short laugh, his body trembling in relief.

"Nothin' but air and mists that cause visions," he muttered to himself. "Nothin' to piss meself over. C'mon, Tommy boy..."

Tom pushed himself to his feet and, fighting the urge to run, he forced himself to walk right through the man with the whip.

~

Jon blinked sleepily up at the shadow that stood by the bed and smiled.

"Is everything ok?" he asked, holding up his hand. The captain's fingers closed around Jon's wrist, and he sighed when Baltsaros nodded. "Oh good. I was worried that yet another thing had gone wrong. Come back to bed?"

The older man stood still, his grasp tightening around Jon's arm as he murmured something; Jon felt a tingle of fear at the incomprehensible words.

"Baltsaros?"

Gasping as he was wrenched from the bed, Jon pushed against the captain, confused. Baltsaros's grip was like an iron shackle as he forced Jon face down on the long table. There were more foreign words, muttered as if spoken only to himself, before the captain addressed Jon with a chilling voice devoid of emotion.

"I must conduct an experiment. I will infect you with these spores; you must tell me exactly what you feel," said Baltsaros. "Then, I will look inside you."

Jon panted as he struggled, panic rising in him. He was still sluggish from sleep and unable to turn himself around, but when he felt the hemp rope loop around his arm, Jon started to buck against the captain in earnest.

However, the older man just reached down and almost leisurely pressed his thumb hard into the nerve cluster behind Jon's ear. With a low, pained gasp, Jon stopped moving and let himself be tied. There had to be some explanation for the captain's erratic behaviour.

"Please... Baltsaros... What are you doing? What's happening—" Jon grunted as his head hit the table.

"Quiet now. I need to concentrate," muttered the captain, releasing his hold on Jon's hair.

With growing horror, Jon watched as Baltsaros pulled out his surgical kit and held a sharp blade up to the light of the candle.

~

After he'd hefted Calum over his shoulder with a grunt, Tom walked towards the trap door leading belowdecks. As he leaned down to pull it open, he paused and frowned, remembering the way the captain's hand had come away from the railing covered in a pale powder.

Spores.

Tom had no bloody clue what the hells "spores" were, but when he looked down at his arms, he saw that he too was covered in a dusting of powder. He patted hard at his sweater, sending the dust flying, and did the same with the insensate Calum before he descended the narrow stairs.

Thankfully, because the shrieking of the icebergs had ceased, most of the crew had retreated to their bunks early to catch some much-needed shut-eye. They blinked groggily at Tom when he burst through the door carrying Old Calum. The first mate's eyes skimmed over the room, quickly counting the humped shapes in the long row of bunks. Nodding, he let out a satisfied grunt; there couldn't be more than eight souls left above, and it didn't seem like any of the men in their bunks were suffering from the effects of the mist. He dumped Calum onto his bed and turned to the rest of them, raising his hand to point at them.

"Yer to bloody well *stay put* if ye know what's good for ye. Any dog who touches that goddamn door, I'll measure for his chains, savvy?" he growled, jabbing his finger in the direction of the exit. Without another word, he turned and left the bunkroom. As an afterthought, he put his back against the stack of heavy crates outside the galley and pushed them in front of the bunkroom door.

Gritting his teeth, Tom pulled the neck of his sweater up over his nose and mouth and debated climbing the stairs to the upper deck once more. His decision was made for him when, a moment later, he heard a scream laced with pain and fear split the air.

Jon.

~

Baltsaros muttered distractedly to himself in his northern tongue. His big hand was wrapped around the back of Jon's neck, holding him down as he planned his cuts systematically. Coughing against the pressure in his throat, Jon's head throbbed and he licked his lips, grimacing at the grainy bitterness of the powder Baltsaros had smeared on his face. Fear squeezed his heart hard as the man above him took up the sharp blade, and he whimpered, no longer sure that it was the captain holding him down... He felt the hot breath of a devil against his skin and saw the barbed shadow of crooked horns cast upon the wall.

Jon filled his lungs to let out a terrified scream as Baltsaros's knife slid stinging along his flesh; the captain was going to tear him into pieces and eat his heart.

~

Tom growled and pulled Baltsaros away just as he was adjusting the knife in his hand to deepen the cut. After flinging the captain to the floor, the first mate let out a strangled sob and kicked him hard in the ribs, hoping the older man would stay down. In despair, he watched the captain sit up slowly; Baltsaros's dark eyes were wide and staring, his teeth bared in a fierce grimace. It was the face of utter madness.

"Please, Da, please stay down," begged Tom, pulling his glove off and balling his fist hard. His lungs burned from the harsh breaths that heaved past his clenched teeth.

Baltsaros let out a low chuckle and sprang at Tom, his hands reaching for the bigger man's neck. Tom let out another breathless whimper, and he smashed his fist hard into the captain's face, his knuckles registering the crack of cartilage against them. Tears coursed down Tom's cheeks as he pulled his hand back to punch Baltsaros again and once more, blood pouring from the older man's face as he went limp on the thick, handwoven rug.

With an agonized cry, Tom fell to his knees next to the man who had tamed and freed him, who had claimed Tom as his own, and he pressed his forehead to Baltsaros's shoulder.

After a few shaky breaths, he heard Jon's keening moan as he lay tied to the table, and Tom shook himself, realizing that he had to work fast before the captain came to. He stood in a daze, fumbling for the rest of the hemp rope as Jon's terrified blue eyes watched him.

"It's ok, Jon... Hush, hush, pet, I'm comin'," he murmured as he bound the captain's wrists together. In misery, he made the loops tight, not sparing Baltsaros any gentleness in case the man woke up a maddened animal once more. Brow deeply furrowed, Tom's chest ached as he stroked the side of Baltsaros's face.

"Oh, Da... forgive me," he whispered. "Gods, let this be over."

When he staggered to his feet again, Tom quickly undid the ropes binding Jon to the long table. He saw that the cut was superficial, but before he had a chance to find something to staunch the trickle of blood, Jon backed away from him with a low moan. The dark-haired, naked young man stared openly at Tom, eyes round and scared and without a trace of recognition. When the first mate reached for him, Jon cringed from Tom's touch.

Tom let out a long sigh; the adrenaline that had kept him going was starting to ebb, leaving him exhausted and brittle. The ship was adrift, and part of the crew had gone mad; he could only hope that they were being carried away from danger. He felt there was nothing else he could do until the captain awoke and was clearheaded again. Tom was at a complete loss as he pulled Jon to his chest, wrapping his thick arms around him when he began to struggle.

"Hush, lovey. Hush, it'll be ok, Jon. Stop your fightin', it's just me. Old Tom's goin' to make things better..." he murmured into the other man's hair as Jon began to sag against him. "That's it, pet. Hush now."

He wondered what waking nightmares were burning in the clever young man's brain as he drew Jon onto the bed with him, holding him tight and burying his face against his sweat-damp neck.

Tom's rough, scarred hands stroked Jon's smooth skin until the trembling stopped, and he closed his eyes, humming a soft nursery song that he barely remembered from a life stolen from him so long ago.

CHAPTER 3

PAST THE SHORES OF LUNACY

Baltsaros woke slowly, the left side of his face a throbbing web of pain, nose burning and so swollen he could barely breathe out of it. For a moment he couldn't tell where he was and why he couldn't move his arms. After he'd flexed his fingers a few times, he came to the conclusion that his hands were tied behind him, and the rough, crusty surface beneath his cheek was the rug in his quarters. Blinking slowly, Baltsaros took a few deep breaths, grimacing at the dull ache in his ribs, and tried to make sense of his situation.

Calum on the ice. Tom yelling. A strange scent in the air... The captain closed his eyes and saw again the pale yellow powder clinging to the fingers of his glove. He remembered his desire to check whether the spores had affected Jon, asleep behind closed doors.

A knife?

Suddenly an image of Jon, tied down on the table and bleeding, flooded his mind. His own hand held a knife. Baltsaros's eyes flew open.

Jon.

He let out a grunt as he tried to lift his head from the blood-soaked rug, his heart beating a swift rhythm as his mind tried to put the memory back together.

Where is Jon? It was a small, mewling, panicky thought. With dread he let his mind touch the possibility that he had ended Jon's life while under the hallucinogenic influence of the spores. A hoarse moan escaped his lips at the sudden sharp twist in his gut, far more agonizing than the pain he felt in his face.

From across the room he heard a rustle and felt the thump of something landing on the floor reverberate through his cheek. He thought he smelled tobacco; the captain closed his eyes with a sigh.

"Da! Shit... Tell me yer back to yerself." Tom's warm hand closed over the captain's shoulder.

Baltsaros frowned and nodded.

"Yes, Tom. I'm all right," he said, his voice strangely nasal. "Where's Jon? Please tell me I didn't kill him." He grunted in pain as the ropes binding his wrists were quickly cut; blood rushed back into his hands, and he rolled over onto his back, his face coming away from the rug with a sticky pull.

"He's fine, Da. Ye put a knife to him, but I stopped ye," said Tom, on his knees next to the captain. The first mate's hand closed gently on his wrist; moving up to squeeze at Baltsaros's palm, Tom's touch helped relieve the itching and tingling.

With the numb fingertips of his other hand pressed to his nose, Baltsaros winced.

"I think you broke my nose," Baltsaros said, gingerly prodding at the swollen bridge; he couldn't immediately tell if it needed to be rebroken to set straight or if he actually even cared.

With brows deeply furrowed, Tom pressed his lips together and nodded. His face was an almost comical mask of worry as his gorgeous eyes took in the damage his fists had wrought.

"I'm sorry, Da," the big man whispered, shamefaced, and Baltsaros let out a hoarse laugh, groaning again at the pain in his ribs. "I... might'a kicked ye in the side too," Tom added quietly, though this time the corner of his mouth quirked into a rueful grin.

Baltsaros squeezed Tom's hand and chuckled, curling his arm around the first mate's side.

"Help me up, you savage brute," he grinned, but when the muscular first mate hauled him quickly to his feet, the captain let out a sharp gasp. Baltsaros rested against Tom for a moment, dizzy from loss of blood and from being tied up for so long.

The ship... The spires. The only thing immediately important to him right now was making sure that Jon was all right; his questions could wait.

The captain pulled away from Tom and took the few steps to the bed, leaning across it with a frown. Jon slept, sprawled on his stomach with a crude bandage covering the left side of his back. Baltsaros saw immediately that there was no blood seeping through and let out a relieved sigh. The damage seemed minimal.

Jon's eyes were sunken, and his skin was pale, but he was breathing easily. As he stroked his fingers gently along the curve of the young man's face, Baltsaros glanced at Tom. When he saw the affection in his first mate's eyes as he looked down at Jon, Baltsaros had to accept a somewhat bitter truth: Tom would always protect Jon, no matter what, even from the captain himself. Gritting his teeth, Baltsaros pushed away the resentment and let that fact sink in. There was nowhere safer in the world for Jon than in the protection of his fierce tomcat, and he should be happy about that. After all, the first mate had just saved Jon from becoming a simple puzzle of flesh and bone at the captain's hands.

"I never thanked you for saving Jon's life the first time," he said, thinking of the storm that had nearly robbed him of so much.

Tom looked both pleased and embarrassed; dropping his blue-green eyes to his hands, the big man's shoulder came up in a tiny shrug.

"Just doin' what's right, Da," Tom muttered.

Baltsaros turned back to the dark-haired young man on the bed and smiled softly.

Just over a year ago, Baltsaros would have laughed to hear Tom say he was doing something simply because it was right—even now, he had expected his first mate to claim it had simply been his job to protect the captain's interests.

"Jon is special," murmured Baltsaros, watching the younger man's back rise and fall in the easy rhythm of sleep.

Tom grunted in gruff agreement and walked to the little cast-iron stove. When Tom opened the grate and poked at the fire within, Baltsaros thought they had reached the limit of the stoic man's comfort with such talk. He blinked in surprise when he heard Tom's deep voice break the silence a moment later.

"He sees the good in me, Da, plain as day. That's somethin' worth fightin' for. Maybe even dyin' for." His words sounded strangely choked.

When the captain turned to his first mate with curiosity, he was amazed to see that Tom's brow was low over eyes that shone with moisture, his jaw clenched and shoulders hunched as he stared into the fire. The night had taken its toll on Tom, and Baltsaros suddenly realized that the first mate was barely keeping it together.

"Tom, come here," he murmured.

Tom's lips worked together as he swallowed; he sniffed hard and passed a brawny arm across his face before lurching to his feet. When Tom leaned into the captain's arms with a sigh, Baltsaros felt a shudder run through him.

"You did good, Tom. You did very good. It's all right," he said, smiling against the younger man's hair. "Tell me everything, from the beginning. We'll figure things out from there."

~

The demon wielded the sharp knife, intent on taking Jon's heart from him. Jon couldn't move, couldn't see the monster's eyes. He could only feel its hot breath on his neck. Fear made him cry out... and a huge, tawny cat with crackling green-blue eyes let out a deep growl, pouncing on the devil's back. Confused, Jon saw that the devil was actually the black lion that often walked beside him in dreams. He screamed out at the cat as its claws made bright red streaks in the giant lion's fur. It didn't matter, he wanted to say. His heart was his own to give...

~

Jon tasted the residue of sleeping powder and rubbed his face against the soft, dark sheets of the bed. His back was a dull ache, and he thought he could smell the captain's healing salve. Groggy and confused, he lifted his head and saw that the room was empty. Something pulled at his back as he sat up slowly, and seeing the bandage

331

when he glanced over his shoulder, Jon realized that he was wounded. Try as he might, he couldn't remember what had happened.

There was a thump from above, and he heard the first mate's booming laugh. For a moment, Jon had a strange memory of Tom's voice gentle in his ear, soothing away a terrible fear... and then it was gone, caught up in the eddies that swept away pieces of a dream laced with terror and darkness. Running his hand through his tangled hair, Jon realized that, for the first time in weeks, he couldn't see the fire burning in the pot-bellied stove across the room. Yet the room was warm.

He slid off the bed and walked to the closest porthole. In amazement, he saw that the sky was a bright blue and no ice could be seen in the water.

How long have I been asleep? he thought with alarm.

He looked around for a shirt to wear and put on the first one he found. Quickly pulling on his pants and boots, Jon then reached for his woollen cloak and threw it over his head before he opened the door. When the bracing, cold wind he was expecting did not immediately assail him, Jon's heart began to beat faster in excitement. While there was still a brisk chill in the air, it was far from the bone-numbing cold of the past few weeks. He could hear voices above on the quarterdeck as he stepped out the door, and when he looked up, he saw that the sails were bulging and straining with a strong wind.

Jon climbed the wooden steps, smiling as the captain and his first mate turned to look at him. Both men were holding metal cups in their hands, and Jon could smell coffee. Tom sat at the bench, one booted foot on the felloe of the ship's wheel, and Baltsaros stood to his side, long strands of his hair whipping loose around his head as he smiled at Jon. As Jon squinted into the crisp wind, tears were whisked from the corners of his eyes by strong gusts. The Devil's Isles, the colossal spires that had taken up nearly the entire sky the previous day, were now just pale grey fingers rising up in the fog-shrouded distance.

In a daze, Jon looked at the captain.

"Have I been asleep for days?" he asked.

"No, my love. Only one night's sleep... " Baltsaros laughed and shook his head.

Jon frowned; though largely hidden by the captain's beard, the mottled hues of new bruises showed along one side of his face. Under his eyes were dark, yellowish shadows, and his nose was red and swollen. The captain looked like he had been in a fight.

Before Jon could ask what had happened, the captain started describing the night's terror and mayhem that, in his exhaustion, Jon had missed entirely. He stood breathing quickly, aghast at the stories of spectres and shocked by the deaths that had taken the crew whilst in the throes of some potent reaction to a mould in the air. Thankfully, most of the sailors had been spared; owing to Tom's quick thinking, those out of the mist had remained unaffected, and Calum had recovered swiftly once he'd been locked in the bunkroom with the others.

Nine men had been lost that night; it was a hard blow to a crew already diminished in number by the brutal cold but not an insurmountable obstacle to their survival.

However, none of what Baltsaros told him answered the two questions at the forefront of his mind.

"Wait, how did we get this far with no one manning the helm?" asked Jon, accepting Baltsaros's cup to take a sip of black coffee. "Why didn't we run aground?"

Tom's stubbled cheeks dimpled in a wide grin, his teeth slightly crooked but white in his handsome face.

"Malik," said the first mate, laughing. "The bloody fool thought he was in a navy battle. It's a bloody boon the squiffy bastard managed not to bilge us on the rocks! Sailed us straight past the devil's pointy cocks, and then the wind picked up... Blew us straight an' true all night. Malik's sleepin' off a night's holy terror, but I'm plannin' on pourin' my share o' rum down his bloody throat tonight." Tom's blue-green eyes twinkled in merriment, but Jon could see how deeply relieved the first mate was. He had to smile when he imagined the surly shipwright wresting the ship away from the imminent threat of a sea battle with phantoms.

Turning his eyes to the captain, Jon felt his heart thrum quickly for a moment in his chest, and he frowned. Though he didn't know why, his second question was suddenly hard to voice. When he moved his shoulder under his cloak, he felt the pull of the bandage and the ache of the wound again. Jon cleared his throat and made himself speak.

"Why am I wounded?" he asked quietly and felt an odd pain in his chest at the way the captain's eyes lost focus at his words.

"Ye fell on some ice, lad," replied Tom. "Sliced yourself up bad, but I fixed ye up smartly."

Jon tensed and looked at the first mate. On the big man's face was the same bland openness Jon had seen when Tom had lied to him about being in a drunken fight while playing dice—a fight that in no way explained the fact that Tom's belt had been undone, nor why there had been a long rip along the side seam of his pants. Jon's eyes flicked back to the captain's, and he pressed his lips together when he saw that Baltsaros was staring at Tom with a strange expression.

A lie to protect the captain.

A shiver took Jon and he swallowed, turning to look at the horizon.

Float above it, don't think...

When he looked back again, Baltsaros was gazing at him with solemn fondness.

It didn't matter, he thought reluctantly; if Tom was lying for the captain, then it must be important.

Forcing himself to smile, he gestured to his face.

"Don't tell me you fell on the ice too?" he asked the captain playfully.

～

With eyes narrowed at the setting sun, Baltsaros took a swallow of rum and passed the flask to the young man leaning against his side. It was amazing how much warmer it was on this side of the spires. Something about the mountain range must be altering the climate on this side, causing the weather to be milder. Nature was ingenious in its many forms.

He could see a few stars already sparkling where the sky was a deepening indigo, and he thought about how curious it was that, even though they had come so far, the same twinkling lights looked down on them. The firmament that held them in place must be further away than what was assumed, he mused to himself. Or maybe, like the sun and the moon, they were free agents, gliding through the sky in some intricate pattern.

"You're mumbling to yourself," said Jon, looking up at him with amused grey eyes, "which wouldn't be so bad except I can't understand a word of what you're saying."

Baltsaros laughed and nodded, accepting the flask again.

"I'm sorry, I think in my native tongue; it seems a natural progression that I'd think out loud in the same fashion."

He frowned as something occurred to him.

"Jon, do you want to learn to speak it?" he asked quietly, turning his eyes to the brazier that burned nearby. Maybe if Jon had been able to communicate with him while in his trance, the young man wouldn't have faced vivisection at the captain's hands. Baltsaros felt the corner of his mouth twitch as he shunted aside a scenario where Tom hadn't been there to use his fists.

"I'd like that, yes," said Jon, and he lifted his hand to twine his fingers in the captain's hair. The touch was confident and possessive and when Baltsaros turned to look at Jon, the breath caught in his throat at the fierce desire obvious in his eyes.

Smiling slowly, Baltsaros leaned forward to capture Jon's lips in a light kiss and let out a low growl of pleasure when the younger man moved his hand to the captain's neck to pull him closer.

Baltsaros nudged Jon's lips open, breathing him in as their tongues shared space, and he moved his hand beneath the blanket to place his palm against the firm warmth of Jon's cock through his pants.

Pulling his head back, he furrowed his brow at Jon.

"What did I do?" he asked, amused and charmed by how Jon's pupils became deep pools at Baltsaros's touch.

Jon's tongue touched his bottom lip before he answered. Moving against Baltsaros's hand, he sighed.

"Whatever it is that you and Tom are keeping from me... it has to do with how much I mean to you," he said, shifting so that Baltsaros's hand had space to slip between fabric and flesh. He let out an exhale that ended on a chuckle when the captain's chilled fingers closed over the head of his cock. "Fuck, that's cold. I can't wait for warmer weather," laughed Jon. Leaning back against the captain's arm, he let out a small groan as Baltsaros started to move his hand.

The captain watched Jon closely, intrigued that the boy knew there was more to the story yet seemed content not to pursue the matter. What Jon had spoken was the truth—the omission was fundamentally tied to how very much the young man meant to him. Baltsaros would have been thrown into torment if he had achieved the savagery of relieving Jon of his viscera, and he felt like an utter failure when he thought of the promise he had made.

Jon knew there was something monstrous about Baltsaros, but it was Tom who was intimately acquainted with the captain's particular predilection; the first mate had jumped in to protect him as always, and for that, Baltsaros was glad. As much as Jon wanted to know everything, there were things about the captain's compulsions that were best left concealed. The best course of action was not letting Jon know just how *easily* he would have killed him. Yes, Tom had been right to step in with his lies. There was no need to alienate Jon with the truth.

His thumb slipped smoothly over the head of Jon's cock, wet with the young man's arousal, and Baltsaros let out a slow breath. Turning his mind to the gorgeous brute asleep below them in their quarters, he realized that it had been a while since he'd been entirely alone with Jon. Shifting on the bench, he pulled on the laces holding the front of his leather pants together and dug his thumb beneath them to free the hard cock that had hugged the curve of his thigh. As he stroked himself with the same rhythm that he used on Jon, he smiled.

"I know it's cold, my love, but could I entreat you to remove these?" he said lightly and plucked at the fabric of Jon's long pants. He watched Jon turn to him with cheeks flushed by lust. "There's nothing in the world I want more right now than to have you splayed over my lap, full of my cock," he explained with a grin. When his words were met with a breathy moan, the captain leaned to help Jon remove the offending clothing.

CHAPTER 4
AN EDUCATION

The roots of education are bitter, but the fruit is sweet.

— ARISTOTLE

Jon groaned as Tom pulled away, Jon's spit-wet cock bucking up once in protest before settling down on his flat belly. The first mate then moved forward to press soft lips to his chest again, kissing along slowly and pausing to tease his velvet-rough tongue over Jon's sensitive nipples.

Shaking his head, Jon clenched his jaw in frustration.

"I was almost right," he complained in a hoarse voice as his heart thundered against his ribs.

Tom stopped his kissing and raised his eyes, quirking an eyebrow up at the man behind Jon.

"No, Jon. Almost right does not cut it, I'm afraid. Start again. What is the word for 'ship'? Tom... continue," said Baltsaros, his voice rife with amusement.

They had been at this for nearly an hour. Jon groaned and put his head back, leaning against the side of the captain's neck as Tom resumed teasing him with his tongue. Eyes closed, he took a deep breath and searched his exhausted brain for the right word.

Agreeing to this was a mistake.

～

"I can't do this. I just... argh!" growled Jon, pushing away the board and charcoal he was using to keep track of the vocabulary he was learning. "I don't understand how in the hells I'm supposed to learn another language like this. It's fucking frustrating, and I'm seriously getting sick and fucking tired of your condescending—"

"Jon," Baltsaros warned.

Rubbing his hand over his eyes, Jon let out a slow sigh. Counting to five in his head before he spoke, he forced his tense shoulders down.

"I'm sorry. It's just... all muddling around in my brain. I think this might have been a mistake. Maybe I'm just not cut out to learn another language," he said, wincing at how peevish he sounded. When he heard the first mate's chuckle from the doorway, he scowled. "Don't you start on me too... How many languages do *you* know?" He'd been amazed to learn that Baltsaros was fluent in five and conversant in a handful of others; Jon hadn't even known that many languages existed.

Tom walked up to the table where Jon sat and pressed his knuckles down on the wood. With the warming weather, the first mate had gone back to being barefoot. However, as there was still a deep chill in the air, Tom had taken to wearing a simple linen shirt when out of doors. It hung open at the neck as he leaned forward, and Jon could see the curling, dark-blond hair covering his muscular chest and the swirling lines of his tattoos meandering over the left side of his body.

"I can speak three and swear in six," grinned the first mate, pulling the splinter of wood out from between his teeth and winking.

"I'm not sure the mangled Common you speak passes for a language," laughed Baltsaros, his dark eyes crinkling at the corners.

Tom glowered at the captain in mock offence for a moment, but his pink lips curled up in a smile. He turned back to Jon and pulled the board closer, peering down at the scribbled words on its surface.

"Maybe what ye need is a little motivation, aye, lad?" grinned Tom, a sparkle of mischief in his ocean eyes.

~

Jon flicked through the jumble of words in his head. Five correct words in a row had Tom move down to tease and lick along the inside of his thighs; ten correct meant the first mate would start to work on Jon's cock with slow strokes of his hand and a soft tongue; fifteen words, and he would swallow down Jon's length... Twenty, and Jon would finally get relief. Any mistakes and Tom would stop what he was doing and go back to the beginning.

Shivering as Baltsaros's hands caressed his neck and chest, Jon let out another soft, needy sound; on top of Tom's gentle fondling, the captain's hard cock was buried deep inside Jon as he sat back with his thighs spread over the captain's lap. In near despair, he opened his eyes and watched Tom grin against the side of his shaft, his tongue leaving wet trails along the taut skin but never quite touching the head.

Seeing the hopelessness on Jon's face, the first mate chuckled and pulled his mouth away for a moment, the scratchy stubble of his cheek scraping at sensitive flesh; Jon gasped.

"It's like the word for 'build'," murmured the big man, his gorgeous sea-green eyes amused.

"Tom, stop cheating!" laughed Baltsaros, reaching forward to swat at the first mate's head.

The movement caused the captain's cock to move inside Jon, and he let out a whimper. However, the first mate's prompting was enough to jog his memory, and he blurted out the correct word. When Tom's hot mouth closed over his cockhead, the groan that burst out of Jon's chest was equal parts relief and bliss. When his shaft began to slide deep down Tom's throat, Jon furrowed his brow and turned his head, burrowing his face against the captain's neck, his mouth open in a slow pant.

"Almost there, Jon," said the captain, a smile in his voice. "I must admit I was skeptical, but Tom was right about motivation. Now come on... just five more. You're doing so well. And Tom... let's have no more cheating, shall we?" Baltsaros's hands scratched soft lines over his chest, and Jon arched his back slightly with a moan.

The next three words were relatively simple, but the fourth gave him pause. Tom's tongue slid smoothly along the base of Jon's cockhead, a firm yet teasing touch, before he opened his mouth again to take in his whole length. It was frustrating how perceptive the first mate was when it came to bringing Jon close; every time Jon started to skirt the edge of climax, the big man quickly pulled away with a smile.

It occurred to Jon then, as he was desperately seeking the word for "cat" (*why in hells would I ever need to say "cat"?*), that this was probably a novel experience for the first mate, as he was normally on the receiving end of such torture. It was no wonder Tom kept chuckling every time he brought Jon to a panting mess.

Jon blurted out the word when it rose out of the tangle in his mind and let out a long sigh, bringing his hand forward to push his fingers through Tom's short, dirty-blond hair. One more. However, when Baltsaros murmured the next word, Jon's eyes opened in dismay.

"Heart?" he gasped, lifting his head. "You haven't even taught me that one yet!"

Tom frowned, his lips brushing the tip of Jon's cock softly as he looked at the captain.

"Aye, Da. That ain't fair to the lad, dont'cha think?" he said, his deep voice sending vibrations through Jon's cock.

Jon felt the captain move behind him, and Baltsaros's long fingers tapped against his breast, right over where his heart was skittering like a hunted rabbit.

"Close your eyes, Jon," murmured the captain, his mouth touching the rim of the younger man's ear. "You've heard the word from my lips before. Just think."

Jon felt dizzy. The fingers thrumming against his chest opened a strange pit in his belly. Panic. Struggle. A knife. Jon let out a sharp gasp and trembled as Tom's warm, wet mouth enveloped his cock once more. A devil with a knife to carve out his heart. A sharp pain... darkness... then Jon sighed in relief as the strange thoughts were eclipsed by the answer.

"*Haeken*," he said, opening his eyes with a smile. "*Min haeken* is what you call me when you're feeling particularly sentimental. It means 'my heart', doesn't it?"

When Baltsaros let out a low chuckle, Jon grinned wide and let his head fall back again on the captain's wide shoulder. Shutting his eyes, he expected the first mate simply to finish the job he started. However, Baltsaros's arm quickly came around Jon's waist, and he was hauled up and pushed forwards onto hands and knees and entered again so that he could be fucked slowly from behind. Groaning softly, Jon fell thankfully into the shallow rhythm that the captain liked to use on him to make him cum from within.

Tom sat back a moment just watching the two with an amused look on his face as his rough hand squeezed and pulled at his own cock. Then, with an impish grin, the muscular first mate pushed under Jon headfirst to continue using his mouth while Baltsaros's thick cock thrust into the dark-haired young man.

Jon let out a deep moan; it was a feverish, exquisite feeling, and he let himself ride on the wave of it, panting and moving his hips wantonly as both men worked at him. When he lowered himself to his elbows to rest against Tom's hard stomach, he felt the first mate's cock touch his lips. With a pulse of desire, he quickly opened his mouth and sucked softly at the head of it, working along the flared edge of the glans and dipping the tip of his tongue into the salty slit while Tom's hand stroked the shaft, his hard fist bumping up against Jon's wet lips.

Beneath him, Tom let out a low moan and shifted his head back so that Jon's cock slid more easily between his lips. A moment later, the first mate's big hands came up to hold Jon's waist as the three of them moved slowly together.

Jon was the first to cry out; having been brought to the edge so many times already, he was nearly feverish with his mounting pleasure when Baltsaros quickened his pace. He pulled his mouth away from Tom with a sob as he came hard. The pleasure crashed through him, making his body pulse in a hot, sweet wave that wrung mindless gasps and moans from him. Pressing his forehead against the man beneath him as he rocked his pelvis, Jon whimpered as the first mate's lips and tongue milked his cock, and Baltsaros's thrusts stroked the throbbing, sensitive spot inside him.

Eyes closed, he panted against Tom's hip for a few seconds, his lips spreading into a wide grin as he tried to catch his breath. When he was able to lift his head, Jon took Tom into his mouth again, and the first mate released him with a gasp. Tom's fingers tightened around his waist as Jon forced his jaw wide around the first mate's cock, taking in as much as he could before working at a fast rhythm.

It seemed like only a few moments before Tom went rigid beneath him, a strangled cry heralding the yolky, bitter cum that pulsed hot over Jon's tongue. Jon groaned around the cock in his mouth, swallowing down quickly as Baltsaros began to pound into him, his sharp growl loud over Tom's panting as the captain shuddered with climax.

. . .

With his head comfortably against Tom's shoulder, Jon slid one finger across the broad, sculpted chest and flicked his nail against the silver ring in Tom's nipple. Tom let out a soft grunt and moved his fingers sleepily in Jon's hair. The lines that circled around Tom's nipple and fanned out down his left side were decorated with a multitude of dots, but it was to one particular cluster near the base of his ribcage that Jon's fingers were drawn to. He lifted his head slowly. The man who had tattooed the first mate had claimed that they were a representation of the Devil's Isles, and there they were: seven dots, spaced evenly except for the gap through which *Baal's Heart* had passed. Jon frowned.

"Funny. These curling lines mean something now, don't they?" he said softly. Tom made no answer except to twitch slightly in his sleep at Jon's touch.

Baltsaros leaned over and placed his own fingers on the first mate's tattooed side. Lips pressed together, he nodded slowly.

"We could interpret them to mean the mists, yes," he conceded, shifting his dark-brown eyes to Jon.

Jon touched a little swirl that vaguely resembled a figure. He was convinced that was exactly what the lines represented. He slid his fingers further up, along the path that the ship was taking. There, right below Tom's pectoral was something that looked vaguely like a flower made of triangles. It was surrounded by a square and bordered on one side by squiggles that reminded him of a jagged shoreline. He tapped gently on this design.

"I wonder what we're going to find here," he whispered, putting his head back down and staring across at the captain.

Baltsaros's sharp teeth shone white in his wide grin as he stretched himself out next to Tom.

"Adventure? Profit?" he said, lowering his head to the pillow and moving his shoulder in a shrug. "A new language for you to learn?" The last was said with a soft chuckle, and Jon wrinkled his nose at the captain.

"You're funny," he muttered. "You do realize now every time I think of the word 'cat', an image of Tom's mouth around my cock is going to come to mind."

Baltsaros smiled wider and pulled Jon's fingers to his lips to kiss the tips softly before closing his eyes.

When Baltsaros began breathing the slow rhythm of slumber, Jon lifted his head and stared at the collection of dots and swirls again. Right next to the jagged flower pattern, there was something that made Jon's skin prickle in foreboding.

Though he couldn't be sure, and it might have been a trick of the light, the hatched lines brought only one thing to mind: bones.

~

Jon turned the little handle on the pulley wheel, hauling in the thin line that held a struggling fish on the other end. Grunting as he pulled up on the flexible pole, Jon strained with one foot against the gunwale to pull in his catch.

"Tha's it! Now ye don' give 'im too much slack, lest ye let the bugger free now!" yelled Old Calum while he watched Jon fight to bring the fish closer to the ship. The old man's eyes were narrow against the midday brightness, and he chuckled to himself as Jon cursed and strained against the side of the ship. A few moments later, the silver fish popped out of the water, its smooth muscular sides flashing in the sun with its frenzy as Jon reeled it higher and higher. Calum slid off the crate and held a hand up as Jon brought the wriggling fish over the deck, deftly grabbing it beneath its jaw and through its gill with a practiced motion. Jon sagged against the gunwale, panting hard as he watched the old man pull the hook from the fish's mouth and stun it motionless against the side of the crate. With a grunt wrought of old age, Calum lowered himself to his knees to quickly gut the fish before throwing it into the bucket with the others.

Jon wiped his arm across his brow and smiled. He was happy to have found something that made him so useful to the crew; for once he was happy to have grown up in a poor fishing town where even the son of a lawman knew how to jig for cod. With a glance at the bucket, he nodded to himself and pulled in more of the line before wrapping it around the pole and securing it against the side of the ship.

"I think that's enough, don't you?" he asked Calum with a wide grin.

The old man's face crinkled into a smile of his own, his pink tongue visible through the gap of his missing tooth.

"Aye, lad. These'll be proper eats for th' crew. Now help an ol' man on 'is feet like a good boy?" Calum said, lifting a hand up to Jon.

The younger man tried not to let his smile slip as he helped his fighting teacher up. Old Calum could still pin Jon in a few seconds, but being in the cold for so long had not done any good to his aged knees. Seeing the look on Jon's face, Calum chuffed out a laugh.

"Don' ye be lookin' at me like that, yun' Jon," growled the old fighter. "I'm far from bein' dead an' buried yet." However, Calum's face went sober for a moment, and Jon wondered if he was thinking about his venture out onto the treacherous ice.

"Jon!" He turned his head aft at the booming call and saw that Tom was leaning over the quarterdeck railing, motioning at him with a hand. The old man had taken up the bucket full of fish to bring to Cook, so Jon waved and jogged towards the stern, climbing up the black and red steps to join the first mate. Tom's brow was furrowed over his ocean eyes as he ran his thumb along the edge of his jaw, lips moving as he chewed at the bottom one. When Jon came to his side, Tom handed him the binoculars and cocked his chin slightly portside.

"Tell me," he murmured. "What do ye make of this, love?"

Jon put the binoculars to his eyes and trained them to where Tom had pointed. For a few moments he saw nothing. However as he made a second pass, Jon saw a distant, dark shape floating in the water. He pulled the double-spyglass away from his face and rubbed at his eyes before lifting them again.

"It... looks like a ship?" he said and frowned. "With two hulls and only one mast.

I'm... not sure." Jon passed the binoculars back to Tom, and the first mate looked through them again, letting out a short grunt.

"Ye think it's a boat? I ain't never seen a boat like it, but I guess we're in new waters, aye, ducky? What d'ye think? Do we try to make like we're long lost friends or do we take the first plunder in this gods-forsaken sea?" chuckled Tom, putting the binoculars down and plucking the cheroot out from behind his ear. After pushing it into the corner of his mouth and cupping his hand to shield the match against the wind, Tom looked up at Jon curiously and puffed on the cigar to get it lit.

Jon shook his head. The one thing that had never sat easily with him was the utter ruthlessness Tom had in regard to plunder and pillage; as far as the first mate was concerned, anyone who was stupid enough to stray into their path was fair game. However, when Jon stared back at Tom, he thought he was witnessing a small crack in that cold-blooded facade as the first mate honestly seemed to be asking his opinion. He allowed himself a small smile and shrugged his shoulders.

"You know me," Jon said, taking up the binoculars again. "I'm less of a kill-first, ask-later kind of guy than you are."

Tom chuckled and slung an arm around Jon's waist, pulling the narrow cigar away from his lips to breathe out a plume of acrid, blue-grey smoke as his hand stroked up along Jon's ribs.

"Aye, lad," Tom agreed, leaning companionably against him as Jon swept the binoculars over the distant ship again with a worried look on his face. "That ye are... and that ain't a bad thing."

CHAPTER 5

SACRIFICES AND SCARS

*The ancients recommended us to sacrifice to the Graces, but Milton sacrificed to the
Devil.*

— VOLTAIRE

Though the strange ship was swift, the pirates had an overwhelming
advantage in firepower. When *Baal's Heart* had succeeded in getting within
range of the fleeing vessel, Captain Baltsaros had ordered his gunners to send
a shot across the other ship's bow.

Jon had been hugely relieved when the men aboard had had the good sense to
surrender.

With the other vessel tethered to *Baal's Heart*, the three strangers now stood on the
pirate ship's deck staring around in outrage as their boat was ransacked.

Standing next to the captain, Jon forced himself not to cringe when the hot glare of
the biggest of the three raked over him. He met the stranger's eyes with what he
hoped was a stony expression.

Owing to the resemblance between them, he assumed they were kin; the three
men were tall and bronze-skinned with crinkly, wiry, white hair that was worn in
long, matted locks down their backs and almond eyes that were bright blue like the
waters of Madierus. They were, like the crew of *Baal's Heart*, bare chested in the warm
midday sun, and Jon stared curiously at the rings of raised scars that circled the necks
of the two older men and continued down their backs in parallel lines. That the
youngest of the three had none made Jon think that it was probably part of some
coming-of-age ritual.

His eyes flicked up to the captain, and he gritted his teeth when he saw the admiration on Baltsaros's chiselled face as he looked at the willowy youth. The strangers had an exotic beauty but none more so than the fierce boy who glared a challenge back at the captain. Jon turned his head and met Tom's eyes. The big man was chewing the side of his thumb with a thoughtful expression on his face as he stared back at Jon. When Tom raised his eyebrows and crossed his arms across his broad chest, Jon could see the muscles work in the first mate's jaw as his lips twitched down with painfully obvious dismay; Tom was equally unimpressed with the captain's interest in the young man.

"They're just fuckin' fishermen, Cap'n!" shouted one of the pirates from where he clung to the shrouds of the foreign vessel. "There's nothin' 'ere of any worth. Do we scuttle 'er?"

Before Baltsaros had a chance to answer, Nathaniel, who had asked if he could help with the search aboard, piped up.

"I beg to differ," he yelled with a laugh. There was a tube under one arm as he held aloft something that sparkled. After someone leaned over to help him climb the rope ladder, Nathaniel crossed over to where the captain stood and handed him what looked like a water-filled glass globe mounted in a bronze base. In the water floated a wide silver cylinder with etchings on it. "If I'm right, this is some kind of compass, Captain. I'd like a chance to study it to see what the symbols mean."

Baltsaros tilted the base, and the cylinder rotated to stay level in the water. Lips curled into a smile, he nodded.

"What is this?" the captain asked, accepting the leather tube from Nathaniel.

The cartographer narrowed his hazel eyes and tilted his head, his forefinger tapping below his lips.

"They're maps, but I can't figure out what of," he said with a shrug. "Maybe stars? Shall I leave them in your quarters, Captain?"

Baltsaros handed the maps back to Nathaniel, shaking his head.

"No. Take some time with them. There's no rush. Come to me when you find something," he said and walked to the side of the ship where the strange boat was tethered.

"If there's nothing, leave it," he said to the men waiting aboard. "We'll stay here overnight. I'll decide what to do with the boat come morning."

A towheaded, gangly youth with a scar nodded once and called to his shipmates to abandon the fishing boat.

When Baltsaros turned back to the captives, his eyes narrowed. So far the men had not spoken to each other in anything other than a strange, guttural language, and Jon knew it would make interrogating them difficult. Coming to stand next to Jon again, the captain crossed his arms and looked at him appraisingly.

"If I were to keep one of them in the cage in my quarters, which one do you think I would have the most success with? I want to learn something useful from them," he said, his voice low. It still remained to be seen if the captives understood them.

Jon wanted to point out that hauling the men from their boat was probably not the best foundation for trust but instead turned his eyes back to the strangers.

Of the three, the oldest man honestly seemed like the best choice to him. While the other two glared at the pirates in defiance, the third's eyes kept straying to parts of the ship, distinct appreciation on his deeply lined face. There were two rows of raised scars around his neck, and Jon thought it could mean that he was someone of higher standing. Although, he admitted to himself, the extra markings could as easily be a simple indication of advanced age.

"The grandfather. I think you have a similarity of tastes that could be useful in gaining his trust," he murmured. *And you're far less likely to try to fuck him*, he added silently. His eyes slid to Tom for a second and saw that the first mate's lips were pressed together in a tight line.

Baltsaros frowned slightly, his head tilting.

"Not the young one? Wouldn't he be easier to break?" the captain asked, his eyes locked on Jon's. The younger man could feel suspicion colouring the captain's tone, and Jon shook his head.

"Too headstrong. Too proud. I feel like the old man has seen his share of heartache and loss... and I'm betting that the young one is his grandson. If you can't reason with him based on logic, you could always use the threat of harm to his grandson." Jon felt a little ill as he spoke.

He sincerely hoped that the old man was reasonable.

~

Smiling graciously at the old man in the cage, Baltsaros pulled up a chair. He then reached for the beaten metal cup and filled it with cold water, taking a sip of it in front of the old man before holding it out to him. The white-haired fisherman waited a moment, his eyes wary, but he reached out for the cup.

The captain sat down in the chair and watched curiously as the man quickly drank down the water and held out the cup for more. The stranger was well muscled and smooth skinned despite his age, and his eyes were lively with intelligence. The raised scars that circled the older man's neck were long healed, and the captain guessed that they were part of some ritual to mark lifetime milestones. He was interested to know how they had been created.

The most interesting thing was that, though he was wearing nothing but a pair of sun-bleached, loose white pants rolled at the knees, the old fisherman had a gold bracelet with intricate, knotted designs halfway up his forearm.

Baltsaros pointed to it, and the old man's eyes narrowed in suspicion.

"It's beautiful," said the captain, his words genuine. He wondered how a fisherman had come to have something so valuable. Frowning, he realized that perhaps on this side of the mountains, gold was not considered treasure. That would certainly make trade interesting... especially on their return trip.

When the captain made no move to confiscate the bracelet, the old man let out a short grunt and nodded his head.

"Do you understand my speech?" Baltsaros asked the man, surprised, and watched the clear blue eyes that regarded him thoughtfully. After a long pause, the old man pressed his lips together and then let out a slow sigh.

"Yes," admitted the man in the cage. "Some." After another pause, the corners of his mouth quirked up. "Most."

Relieved, the captain reached forward to fill the man's cup again.

"Welcome to my ship," he smiled, sitting back. "My name is Baltsaros."

~

Jon realized that he had tied the knot wrong a third time and huffed out an exasperated breath. As he pulled the rope to wiggle loose the other end, he furrowed his brow. He was distracted and tense. The captain had spent all afternoon locked away in his quarters with the stranger, and the only instructions he had given anyone were that he was to be left alone and that the other men be locked in the brig but treated kindly.

Jon had obediently seen to the men's supper, which they had refused, unsurprisingly, and had left the plates within reach if they changed their minds. Now he was wandering around aimlessly in the dark, making a mess of rigging that hadn't needed retying to begin with, trying to keep his mind off the fact that he would be bunking down with Tom tonight.

At least Baltsaros's not bedding the boy, he thought angrily to himself, trying once again to loop the rope around in the right configuration. His supper of fish and root vegetables sat heavy in his stomach as he finally managed to tie a proper midshipman's hitch. Letting his eyes stray to the quarterdeck, he could see the cherry from Tom's cheroot where the first mate was sitting behind the ship's wheel. Jon thought for a moment about joining him but felt like he would be intruding; the first mate was probably enjoying his solitude. Besides, he would be seeing a lot of Tom shortly. Jon licked his lips and swallowed, turning away.

As he walked towards the bow, Jon decided to make another circuit of the ship before finding a place to wait for Tom to invite him into the closet that served as his personal quarters.

He let out a slow breath through his nose and tried to ignore the tightness in his chest. Jon had spent time alone with Tom before—many times, in fact, since the reconciliation between the captain and his first mate. Just... never overnight. But that wasn't what was fuelling his anxiety.

Yes, it is.

Frowning, Jon nudged a coil of rope out of the way with the toe of his boot as he made his way along the side of the ship. He knew he shouldn't feel so annoyed about the fact that he had been barred from the captain's bed for the night—what Baltsaros was doing was important for the success of their expedition—but it was the first time it had happened, and it stung a little. Laughing a little bitterly under his breath, he thought about how he and Tom were like orphans tonight.

He stopped and looked out over the water, the sky black and sparkling with stars above him. As he rubbed a hand over his face, he grudgingly let himself admit that he was nervous about spending the whole night alone with Tom. It was stupid. After all, most nights he fell asleep against the big man's warm chest or... at least on nights when Tom wasn't in the hammock nearby.

Jon sighed and climbed a crate, loosening his belt so that he could relieve himself over the gunwale. The hammock... As Tom had stood that day with the awl, making holes for the thick metal hooks that would hold the colourful hammock in place, he had explained that he sometimes felt crowded in the bed with Baltsaros and Jon and just liked the option of sleeping alone. Jon had seen the lie immediately for what it was: diplomacy. He had a feeling that, given the chance, Tom would hold him close every night. Instead, the first mate chose to distance himself so as not to interfere with the captain's affection for Jon. A sacrifice.

He didn't want to think about why that made him ache, or why, when the three of them were together, he often went out of his way not to do anything with Tom that could be construed as tenderness or deeper devotion; he never kissed the first mate in the captain's presence. In fact, it was rare that they kissed at all...

Holding the taut rope above his head, Jon could faintly hear his stream hitting the dark water below. As he was mulling over his complicated feelings for the first mate, he heard a soft step behind him. Startled, he turned his head; Jon had chosen a spot between the hanging lanterns for privacy and so initially saw nothing in the dark. After tucking himself back into his pants, he jumped down from the crate and frowned.

"Who's there?" he asked, squinting into the gloom. When he heard a chuckle, Jon clenched his jaw; stepping out from behind the stacked crates, followed by two of his cronies, was Anslaw. The gangly, blond youth grinned wide at Jon, the knife scar on his cheek stretching grotesquely.

"Oh, it's just me, cabin boy," drawled the young man. "Takin' a stroll with me mates." The mates in question were two others that had come aboard with Anslaw during their stopover at the *Jewel*. It was these three that were responsible for the majority of the teasing and cutting remarks about Jon being nothing but a bedwarmer for the captain and first mate.

"My name is Jon, and I would thank you to remember that," said Jon through clenched teeth. He was in no mood for their nonsense tonight and made to pass them to head back towards the stern. However, Anslaw's hand shot out and blocked Jon's way before he had a chance.

"Aww, *cabin boy*. Are ye sad because yer daddy's too busy to 'ave 'is tallywhacker sucked?" sniggered the gawky deckhand, the other two laughing along with him.

Jon's heart sank. The boys reeked of something that reminded him of *char*, probably some drug they had brought aboard with them when they joined the crew.

"What's goin' on here, lads?" said Tom's gravelly voice from the darkness beyond. The first mate walked towards the group with a dangerous expression on his face.

While Jon was relieved to see him, he couldn't help but feel his reputation would not be improved by the first mate coming to his aid.

"I've got this, Tom," he muttered, balling his fists.

"Aye, we was just talkin', mate," said Anslaw, his dark eyes round as he looked at Tom. "And Jon 'ere threatened to tell ye and the cap'n we was thieves unless we let 'im suck our cocks."

The lie was spoken with such little credibility that no one in their right mind would have believed it; adding to the ridiculousness of the claim was the fact that one of the boys had collapsed in tears of laughter at Anslaw's accusation.

The corded muscles of Tom's neck stood out as he tensed, his blue-green eyes staring hard at the grinning deckhand. The first mate took a step forward, but Jon put a restraining hand against his chest before Tom could show Anslaw just how badly he had misjudged the effect his slander would have on the brawny pirate.

"I said I've got this," Jon repeated, and without a pause, he simply pivoted on the ball of his foot to let the momentum carry all of his weight behind the fist that connected with the smirking deckhand's jaw. The force of it was enough to snap Anslaw's head back; the tall, blond deckhand tried to catch his balance but fell to the deck, his head smacking down on the smooth wood with a loud thump.

Behind him, Tom let out a surprised chuckle.

Fist smarting and teeth bared in a fierce grimace, Jon stood above Anslaw, just daring the younger man to stand up. There must have been something in Jon's eyes that gave the bullying deckhand pause; Anslaw just sat up slowly and wiped his wrist over the blood leaking from the corner of his mouth, making no move to retaliate. Jon stared at him a moment longer before he turned on his heel.

"C'mon," he muttered to Tom as he walked away. With another laugh, the first mate followed Jon as he made his way to the trapdoor that led to the decks below.

~

Baltsaros chuckled and nodded, raising his cup of wine to Polas again. The old man grinned wide and lifted his own cup.

"Your health," said the man in his native language, and Baltsaros repeated after him.

The root of the language Polas and his kin spoke was not so far from Baltsaros's northern tongue. The main difference lay in the way the words were pronounced; otherwise, the sentence structure, use of neutral nouns, and lack of indefinite articles were the same. However, the captain's quick mind simply worked to file away the subtle variations as he was not yet ready to string together a sentence on his own, and the wine was doing nothing to help matters. He smiled. After spending so much time in the company of two who were over a decade his junior, it was a nice contrast to interact with someone older than he.

"Should we not let your son and grandson out of the brig?" asked Baltsaros, lifting his brows.

Polas shook his head then took a long swallow of wine before answering.

"They have, ah… hot heads. Jail makes them cool for now, yes?" said the old man, setting his cup down on the table. "Good for now," he repeated with a smile.

Baltsaros inclined his head. It was true—the men in the brig were no worse off than his own crew; the brig was comfortable enough accommodations, and Jon would make sure that the two were fed and warm. He grinned back at the man across the table from him, pleased that he had found a source of information in this new world. His lively yet stilted conversation with Polas was working to keep his mind off the fact that Tom and Jon were cloistered away together for the night, far from his watchful eyes. Swallowing his concern along with another mouthful of wine, Baltsaros began to question the old fisherman about the lands to the west.

~

Jon flexed his fist, the knuckles red and swollen from where they had met with Anslaw's lantern jaw.

"Did ye see the look on his face when ye clocked him?" chuckled Tom, holding out a rag with a chunk of ice wrapped in it. "I don't know who was more surprised… him or me."

Jon accepted the ice pack and winced as he placed it on his hand; he now understood why Tom's knuckles were so scarred. Watching Tom pull the linen shirt up over his head and wad it into a ball to throw in the corner, Jon began to feel the anxiety begin to creep back under his skin. When Tom unknotted his belt and began to pull his pants down, Jon turned his back.

"Jon?" asked Tom. "What's wrong, love?"

Shaking his head, Jon had no idea how to answer. His heart was hammering in his chest and his mouth had gone dry. The room was too small… it was too intimate.

"Don't tell me yer scared of my cock all of a sudden, ducky…" When his words failed to garner a response from Jon, Tom reached out and touched his shoulder.

Jon barely kept himself from flinching and let out a shuddery breath.

"Aye… oh Jon, hush, lad," muttered Tom, forcefully turning the smaller man around. When Jon saw that the bigger man had kept his pants on after all, he let out a shaky laugh.

"What in hells is the matter, love?" murmured Tom, his gorgeous eyes wide with worry.

Jon stared back at him, trying to find his voice. He watched with dismay as Tom eyes went flinty to cover the hurt that had flashed quickly across his handsome face.

"Ye don't have to sleep here if ye really don't want to," said Tom and dropped his hands. "I just thought—"

"I feel like this is… dangerous." Jon's whisper was hoarse.

Tom's brow creased and his head shook slowly.

"Ye've fucked and abused me every which way yer fine, perverse brain could cook up… and ye think *this* is dangerous, love? And, 'sides, he's the one who put us out in the cold, Jon," he muttered, reaching for Jon again. He plucked the ice pack from his fingers and dropped it. After he'd pulled him towards the low sleeping pad on the floor, Tom slid his hands beneath Jon's shirt and drew it up.

With eyes closed, Jon let himself be undressed, first his shirt and then his boots and pants. Standing naked in the tiny, lantern-lit room, Jon shivered slightly.

He sensed Tom's nearness a second before the first mate stepped forward to take him in his powerful arms, his furry chest warm and soft against Jon's skin, and his smell comforting and arousing at once. The achingly tiny shift of the big man's naked pelvis against his brought a breathless thrill that ran through Jon's skin like crackling fire and made him whimper at the sheer sensuality of being held this way by Tom.

The first mate let out a laugh, the sound just a low rumble.

"Aye, love," he said softly. "Dangerous. Ye had the right word after all."

Jon opened his eyes and looked at Tom in torment.

"There are... words I want to say to you," he breathed.

Tom's brow creased deep, and he let out a soft groan as if he were in pain; Jon could feel the rapid thrum of the big heart that beat beneath the brawn and scars of Tom's broad chest.

"Don't, Jon," said Tom quickly, his voice sounding ragged and weak. "Hush."

He reached for the lantern and turned the cover so that the light from the flame was blocked. After pulling Jon down on the bed, Tom fumbled for him in the dark with gentle hands that shook.

Jon let out a low moan as Tom covered his face with impossibly soft kisses before finally meeting his lips with breathless passion.

The kiss was endless, staggering. It was as if a dam had broken between the men as they strained against each other on the hard mattress. They were raw with desire and truths unsaid, both wanting to draw the moment out as long as they could, knowing that it might be a very long time before they had a chance to shed their skins and press their scarred hearts together again.

CHAPTER 6

DANGER AHEAD

Tom lay on his back and watched as the subtle grey of dawn filtered into his room from the porthole above his bed, his fingers stroking through Jon's long dark-brown curls. The serious young man from the midland isles sighed in his sleep and started snoring lightly, his head tucked beneath Tom's chin, body sprawled on top of the first mate's.

Tom smiled. Jon felt small in his arms, and he liked that. He liked a lot of things about Jon. Closing his eyes, Tom could feel a delicious ache in his cock, and for once it wasn't from some clever abuse.

No... he had fucked Jon.

Tom frowned. "Fucking" was far too crass a word for what had happened between them: Jon coaxing Tom on top of him, his thighs slick with sweat around the first mate's muscled waist, mouths locked together as Tom moved slowly within Jon... so very, achingly slow until Tom couldn't hold back, the two cresting the wave of climax as one, their muffled cries intertwined as they clutched at each other in the dark. His heart had beat so fucking hard...

Tom breathed slowly, trying to keep his erection down so not to wake the man sleeping on top of him. Grinning suddenly, he wondered if Jon realized he had never been on the giving end of sport with a man before. Plenty of women, sure, but he'd never been invited, or allowed, to put his cock in another man.

Despite the lack of sleep, Tom felt good. He pulled the coverlet up over Jon's shoulder and tilted his head to lean his cheek against the soft, dark hair that slid like silk through his rough fingers.

Mine, he thought and mulled over that idea for only a few seconds before another word replaced it.

No. *His.*

Sick to death of the fears and fools' desires that were rattling around in his head, Tom closed his eyes and sighed. The beast inside the captain would eventually try for Jon again, and Tom would have to protect him from it. However, letting himself even think about a permanent solution was just... impossible.

Dangerous.

As if summoned by Tom's covetous thoughts, the door swung open, and Baltsaros stepped in. Tom tensed and, flooded by hot guilt, he almost pushed Jon away. He watched the captain's eyes sweep over the tiny room, Baltsaros's jaw clenched tight at the sight of them entwined.

"Get up, Tom," growled the captain as he turned to leave. "I need you. We have a situation."

Tom let out his breath at the sound of Baltsaros's boots receding in the distance, and he carefully eased himself out from under Jon, pausing to ruffle the lad's hair and pull the blanket up high to cover him. He'd see to it that Jon would be left to sleep... and tan the hide of any who disturbed him.

Scratching his chest, he looked around for his clothes. Brain fuzzy from a night of little rest, Tom pulled the wrinkled linen shirt over his head and left the room while still tying up his belt. With a last look behind him, he closed the door and hurried down the corridor to the stairs.

Above deck, Tom heard the commotion before he saw it. Jogging towards stern, he realized that the shouting was coming from the captain's quarters. The door was ajar and when Tom let himself in, his eyebrows raised at the scene before him.

The three strangers were pointing and yelling at the captain who was holding his hands out to his sides, motioning for them to sit. When Baltsaros looked to Tom as he entered, his face was a mask of restrained anger.

Tom scowled at the fishermen and cleared his throat before letting out a bellow.

"Will ye bloody calm yer shit? Hells, a man can't fuckin' think with this racket!" His loud voice startled the group into silence, and the three of them turned as one to look at the first mate standing in the doorway. Despite the captain's ban on him smoking in their quarters, he pushed a cheroot into the corner of his mouth and lit it; his hands were shaking from fatigue, and he needed a little pick-me-up.

As he walked to the captain's side, he glared at the strangers.

"What the fuck is goin' on, Da?" he grunted. "Who let them out of their cages?" He turned to Baltsaros and was startled to see the captain looking haggard and far older than he normally did.

"I did, Tom. They're to be our guests, and for longer than I had intended," murmured Baltsaros, barely meeting Tom's eye before he turned his face back to the three men who stood in simmering silence. "Someone stole a crate full of supplies and left with their boat sometime in the night. I want you to find out who is missing while I try to mend relations here... and Tom? I can barely stand the smell of you. Please take a minute to clean up before you come back."

Tom bit back a retort, instead ducking his head in acknowledgement and leaving the captain to deal with the furious strangers. As he made his way to the crew bunkroom, he sniffed at his shirt.

<hr>

Jon blinked sleepily and turned onto his back, confused for a moment by his surroundings. When the events from the previous night came back in a rush, Jon grinned wide, his fingers sliding down to tug at the crinkly hair above his cock. Tom's body had trembled so hard as he had buried his thick shaft deep inside him, and Jon had realized in shock that it was a new experience for the lusty first mate. It made him happy that he had decided to share his body with the big man in the moment of heat; the memory brought a warmth to his skin, and he smiled softly.

His bladder full, Jon soon sat up and looked around for a chamber pot. After he'd finished using the one he had found in the corner, his eyes were drawn to the little wooden box he'd noticed before. Jon picked it up from the crate and rubbed his thumb over the inlaid wood design. He'd never seen anything quite like it. The craftsmanship was exquisite; it was simple yet beautiful, and the wood felt like soft satin under his fingertips.

As he sat down cross-legged on the mattress, Jon furrowed his brow and looked at the box in his hands. He was invading Tom's privacy by touching what had to be a prized possession, but he couldn't stop himself. He wanted to put the box back—he really did—but, instead, he watched his fingers flip up the small bronze catch and lift the lid slowly.

At first Jon was puzzled by the contents. There were only two things nestled against the ruby-red silk lining. The first looked like a fragment of a thin steel circlet, the edges of which were sharp and shinier than the rest of the metal, like it had been forcefully cut apart. The second item was a piece of yellowed parchment folded in half at the bottom of the box. Carefully, Jon lifted out the document and opened it. When he saw what it was, his eyes went wide: it was a bill of sale addressed to Captain Baltsaros for one slave... Tom.

Suddenly he understood what the broken circlet was. Taking up the fragment in his fingers, he looked along the edge until he found a stamp in the metal that matched the symbol on the document. This was a piece of Tom's slave collar, obviously cut off of him by Baltsaros when the first mate was brought aboard.

Jon's eyes brimmed with hot tears, and he tried to blink them away before they fell. In his hands, he held the concrete evidence of Tom's decade of slavery, and it suddenly made the big man's past painfully real to him. Pressing the collar to his lips, Jon thought he could sense the fear and pain of a little boy ripped away from his life to suffer years of cruelty at the hands of his master.

No... that first collar would have been much, much smaller to fit his young neck, and it would have needed to be replaced multiple times when it got too tight as Tom grew to the thick-muscled man he was today.

He quickly fumbled the paper and piece of metal back into the box, closing it before he was overwhelmed. How did Tom live with the memories?

After placing the wooden box back carefully on the crate, Jon curled up on his side on the mattress. Running alongside the guilt he still felt about what he had done to Tom and Baltsaros's relationship was the worry that he could be doing even more damage.

With the blanket over him and fisted in his hands, he closed his eyes and breathed in Tom's smell, trying to slow his speeding heart.

~

When Tom returned to the stateroom, the mood was slightly less strained. The men were seated, digging into bowls of Cook's spiced, yellow porridge as they conversed in low voices.

Straightening his shoulders, Tom hoped that his quick, open-air scrub was enough to mollify Baltsaros as he made his way to the captain's side. It was still cool outside but, seeing as the other men were bare chested, he had finally discarded the stained linen shirt.

A big part of him didn't understand why the captain was bothering with placating the white-haired savages; why not just toss them overboard and forget about their damn queer boat?

Clearing his throat, Tom pressed his knuckles to the table and leaned hard on them.

"Ok. We're missin' three," he reported, annoyed that the captain's eyes slid quickly away from his again.

It's yer own damn fault, Da. If ye weren't so fuckin' ornery about yer bloody fuckin' possessions, maybe ye wouldn't be so fuckin' sore that I fucked yer—Tom's inner monologue stopped when he realized that maybe Baltsaros knew *exactly* what had happened between him and Jon. Maybe he had somehow smelled it on him or could see the truth in Tom's eyes. Maybe he was furious and would toss Tom aside again. Fear scrabbled through the cracks in the first mate's heart, and his mouth went dry. As Tom stilled his sudden, guilt-fuelled panic, he tried to ignore the old fisherman staring openly at him.

"Tom?" asked Baltsaros, frowning at his first mate.

Tom huffed out a small breath. The captain's eyes were locked on his, but, thankfully, all the first mate could see was a man who had not had enough sleep, who was worried about peace aboard his ship, and who *needed* him. In the corner of his vision, Tom could see the white-haired stranger still staring at him, and he rolled his shoulder slightly at the uncomfortable attention.

"Uh... well, Da, it's the fuckin' pack of brats ye picked up when ye came for me," he explained. "See, Jon knocked one of them on his arse last night—"

"Is Jon all right?" asked Baltsaros, alarmed.

Tom barked out a laugh and nodded, running the tops of fingers against the stubble on his cheek.

"I think ye'd have been proud, Da," he said with a slow smile. The image of Jon's fist connecting with the deckhand's jaw was one that would stick with him a long time—as would the image of Jon's head thrown back, mouth open in a soft groan, as Tom moved above him. Tom felt heat in his cheeks, and he let out a small cough to cover his momentary lapse. "Er—Anslaw and the other two cocksuckers never went back to their bunks last night. Cook says he was up late playin' cards an' would'a seen them boys take the crate of supplies. I'm guessin' they waited until past midnight before sneakin' away, the bloody bilge rats... *And will ye quit bloody starin' at me, ye fuckin' savage!*" The last was addressed to the stranger whose eyes hadn't ceased boring into Tom.

The old man blinked at Tom slowly, apparently undaunted by his anger. Instead, he pointed to the first mate's chest.

"Now where have you get these, boy?" he said, his blue eyes narrow as he looked at Tom.

The first mate glanced down at his chest and frowned.

"Why is that any of yer bloody business?" Tom growled back, staring hard at the old man. No one called him "boy".

"Tom," murmured Baltsaros, and the first mate shot the captain a peeved look; none of this was helping his mood. Tom wished he were back in his room with Jon in his arms.

Turning to the white-haired fisherman, the captain raised his stark brow.

"Polas, what do Tom's tattoos mean to you?"

~

Tom let out a small groan as he sunk down to his haunches and pulled up the coverlet so he could slide in behind Jon. The sleeping man woke with a start and then sighed as Tom's arm came around his waist.

"Hey," whispered Jon, pushing back against the bigger man so that they fit together like spoons.

Tom pressed his face against the back of Jon's neck and let out a small, pleased noise from deep in his chest. Despite how tired he was, his cock had begun to get stiff at Jon's movements, and now it was a growing, hardening ridge between them.

Fuck it.

"I want ye again," he said simply, and pushed his hips forward, testing. When Jon shifted back again and nodded quickly, Tom felt nearly breathless with the lust that shook him.

~

After a sorely needed bath, Jon pulled open the door to the captain's quarters and peered inside. Baltsaros raised his head at the sound and looked over at Jon.

"Come in. It's ok," said the older man, putting aside his book.

Jon frowned and stepped inside, raking his fingers through his still-wet hair.

"What's ok?" he asked warily, eyeing the captain.

Baltsaros laughed and held out his hand. Jon hesitated a moment longer before dropping his shoulders and approaching the captain. Looking up at Jon, Baltsaros shook his head slowly.

"Listen to me, Jon," said the captain, lifting Jon's palm to his lips. "It's *ok*. I won't have you and Tom acting like you're sneaking around behind my back. We've gone over this; I can deal with this *fascination* you have for Tom. I have been fair to you, have I not?" Baltsaros's dark-brown eyes searched Jon's, and the younger man pressed his lips together and nodded. "Tom's fond of you, and he'll keep you safe when I'm not able to—What is it?" The captain furrowed his brow at Jon.

Jon shifted his weight to the other foot and lifted his chin slightly. The captain *was* trying; the fact that Tom and he had remained unmolested for the duration of the morning was testimony to that. But how far was Baltsaros willing to share Jon? Were he and Tom wrong in their assumption that the captain would zealously guard Jon's affections for his own? With a long sigh, Jon realized it was time to put that theory to the test.

"Baltsaros, what if I told you that Tom meant a great deal to me?" he asked quietly, moving his hand out of the captain's grasp to rest it against the older man's cheek. Baltsaros's eyes closed momentarily, and he leaned into Jon's touch, looking wearier than he had ever seen him.

"I expect that he does," muttered Baltsaros, raising his gaze again to Jon's. The older man's big hand covered Jon's hand, the palm smooth and dry over his sore knuckles. "Jon..." Baltsaros's brow creased but smoothed out almost immediately.

Jon tilted his head and frowned at the captain. It was his turn to ask the question.

"What is it?" he asked softly.

The captain let out a slow breath and pulled his face away from Jon's hand.

"I don't want to hear the word 'love' from your lips regarding Tom, but I fear that's the direction this conversation is going," sighed Baltsaros with a bitter smile. "You are my redemption, Jon. You are my soul. You are the hope that I never knew I needed. If that means that I have to share your heart..." The captain's shoulder came up in a small shrug. "So be it. Just don't leave my side, promise me that."

Jon let out a low sound, quickly moving forward to press his lips against the captain's as Baltsaros's hands came up around him. Breaking the kiss a moment later, Jon looked hard at the captain.

"I won't leave your side," he smiled, his fingers twining in the captain's hair. "I promise." The relief he felt completely overshadowed the niggling doubt in his head at the rash promise.

Baltsaros's face creased into a pleased smile, and he nodded once before growing serious again.

"Good. Now... in the next few days, spend as much time with Tom as you can," he said, his brow furrowed. "You both will have to get everything out of your systems before we make land."

Jon frowned, confused.

Baltsaros rubbed a big, sun-darkened hand over his mouth, stroking down on his white-streaked beard. "Go wake Tom and bring him here. I have to explain a few things."

~

Tom sat straddling the chair, his arms folded across the top and his head down against them as he swore softly under his breath.

Baltsaros felt for the big man, knowing that this was possibly the worst thing he had ever asked of him.

He turned to Jon who sagged back in his own chair, staring up at the captain.

Earlier, he'd sent Tom away when Polas launched into his stilted explanation of the first mate's tattoos. As soon as the old man described them as slave tattoos, Baltsaros had been glad he had dismissed the first mate. Now he was unkindly forcing Tom to adopt the role that he swore he would never be in again. He frowned at Tom.

"Polas said that the only way we could pass within the city walls without drawing attention is with a slave. I'm sorry, Tom, but you're going to have to come to terms with this. It's just an act... It's not like you're going to have to bow and scrape to me, and I will do everything in my power to keep you from facing any abuse."

Tom grunted against his forearm and raised his sea-green eyes to Baltsaros's.

"Fine," he muttered, his jaw tight and brows creased.

Though surly, Tom's answer would have to do. The captain nodded, and then let out a short sigh.

"Now, the other problem is this: where we are going, it is illegal for a man to lie with another," he said slowly, looking between Tom and Jon. "Punishable by death."

Tom lifted his head and let out a short laugh with no humour. Next to him, Jon just gaped at the captain with horror plain on his face.

Baltsaros lifted his hand.

"When Polas assumed you were my son, Tom, I told him the truth, and he was, I'm sorry to say, absolutely horrified. However, he admitted that different cultures had the right to different customs. I may have exaggerated somewhat when I told him that in our lands it was normal for men to lie together, but it was necessary for him not to see our arrangement as an aberration," explained Baltsaros, running his finger along the edge of his cup. At the time he had felt nothing but a shocked sort of curiosity at the discovery that they were in a realm of strict moral values that made his uncle Romas' faith look like a bunch of idol-worshiping whoremongers.

Jon's strained voice broke the silence.

"Why do we have to go to this city at all?"

Baltsaros lifted his eyes.

"The city is rich... There's gold inlaid in the very streets themselves. Perhaps we can set up trade once I figure out how to counteract the effects of the spores," he replied with a smile. "Polas speaks of other wonders. They have harnessed lightning... I want to see this with my own eyes." It was *nearly* the whole truth.

The captain thought that Jon and Tom needn't concern themselves with his primary motivation: the deep fascination with a city that was governed by gods who demanded constant human sacrifice. In Baltsaros's esteem, the streets were coloured by something far richer than mere gold.

CHAPTER 7
PAIN

The only antidote to mental suffering is physical pain.

— KARL MARX

Jon watched the tall, white-haired young man approach the captain to say a few words, Oren's head tilting gracefully as he gestured out to the water with a slender arm. However, when Calum walked up a moment later holding something in his hands, the captain turned his attention towards the old pirate. Oren stood uncertainly for a long minute, staring at the captain's back and shifting his weight slowly from one foot to the other, before turning to walk away.

"That's it. Go bat yer eyes at someone else, ye little cunt," growled Tom under his breath, leaning over the quarterdeck railing next to Jon. The first mate had a deep scowl on his face as he plucked the toothpick from the corner of his mouth, his blue-green eyes trained on Polas's grandson as the young man wandered towards the bow.

Jaw clenched, Jon turned around, leaning back with his elbows resting on the glossy black railing.

"You don't think Baltsaros would actually fuck him, do you?" he asked, frowning up at the flag snapping in the brisk wind; the black lion danced, its mouth stretched wide in a silent roar.

Tom let out a short laugh.

"I didn't think Da would fuck *you*, lovey," said the first mate, leaning to bump his shoulder against Jon's.

Jon's frown deepened into a scowl; Tom's words did nothing to allay his concern.

When Tom glanced over a moment later, his eyes softened. With a sigh, the burly first mate reached over and tugged at Jon so he would slide over. Tom's hard body pressed him back against the railing.

"Listen... as much as he likes to use what's hangin' between his legs, Da's not given to thinkin' with his tarse, lad," said Tom gently, his deep voice a low rumble. "Can ye imagine the shit storm we'd have if he stole that little cunt's cherry? Nah... I just don't like that skinny, white-haired fishmonger sniffin' around Da like a bitch in heat is all. Matter o' principle."

Watching Tom's face as he spoke, Jon had to smile. Tom was, at times, still intimidating; cheerfully brash and bluff, the first mate was almost aggressively masculine. Everything about him screamed of dominant, dangerous virility—from his swaggering gait and his hard, scarred fists to his unrepentant abuse of intoxicants and taste for brutal violence. Yet, less than an hour ago, those grinning pink lips had been wrapped around Jon's cock as Tom knelt submissively in front of him in the stateroom, hands tied behind him as he opened his throat to the abuse Jon inflicted on him. Reconciling the two images of Tom had become easier with time, but it still made Jon a little dizzy. He lifted a hand to Tom's cheek, the dark-blond stubble sharp against his palm, and watched the first mate's eyes grow dark. Jon suddenly felt flush with desire for the big man again.

"Would you like me to take over so you two can do that somewhere a little more private?" asked the captain as he walked up the stairs. "I know that our guests' views on sex are primitive, but there is no need to push it in their faces. A little tact would not go amiss, hm?"

Jon turned his head to look at Baltsaros, still feeling residual guilt about all the attention he'd been paying to Tom despite the captain's assurances.

Baltsaros's dark eyes locked on his, showing no hint of what was going on in his mind. However, when Tom pulled Jon's hand to his lips to slide his fingers into his mouth, Baltsaros's nostrils flared slightly and his lips twitched. The captain reached for Tom, quickly snagging his fingers in the first mate's short hair and yanking him away from Jon, a frighteningly cold expression on his stark features.

"Tom, that's quite enough," growled Baltsaros, tightening his fist and causing the first mate to wince as his head was pulled back.

Jon couldn't keep himself from smiling. Months ago, had he seen the same display, he would have been slightly worried for the first mate; however, he'd long ago learned to recognize what the two men considered foreplay.

Baltsaros dropped his hand and, after a pointed look at the first mate, descended the staircase quickly. Tom took a few steps to follow and paused, a somewhat sheepish expression on his face as he narrowed his eyes at Jon.

"Come and get me if there's anythin', lad," he said gruffly before turning to jog down the stairs.

Jon let out a slow breath and sat down on the bench behind the ship's wheel, feeling abandoned. He ran his hands through his hair and tried hard to stifle the jealous feelings that arose in him every time the captain and Tom excluded him. It wasn't fair of him and he knew it. It would just take a while longer for his brain to stop throwing scenarios at him where the first mate and Baltsaros decided they didn't need a third wheel anymore and dropped Jon off at the nearest uninhabited spit of land to fend for himself. Grinning at that scenario, Jon imagined himself trying to catch something to eat using only the knife at his belt. The image was preposterous, and he smirked, leaning forward to correct the ship's wheel when it turned slightly off course. A moment later he fancied he could hear the smack of something hard against flesh, and he frowned, licking his lips before tightening his jaw. Despite the exclusion, the thought of Tom being "punished" sent a surge through him, and he shifted on the bench, his face hot.

It hadn't always been like that.

~

Jon stood staring at Tom, a sick feeling in the pit of his stomach. The first mate knelt with his thighs spread for balance, his big arms bound tightly behind his neck by a length of red hempen rope, his muscles bulging and straining. Jon remembered how the captain had tied him up with the same rope and beat him with a slim rod before pleasuring himself. Jon had been in pain; the captain had pushed him to his very limits. However, in the end, it had been a revelation—something staggering and utterly freeing.

But this? This was shocking in its brutality.

Tom's head hung below his shoulders as he panted, his chest and back covered with a crisscross of red lines, some weeping blood down over his tawny skin, long wet streaks that followed the curves of his muscles. Slowly the first mate looked up, his eyes red and wet; he licked the cut on his top lip and let out a shaky breath. Without warning, Baltsaros lashed out and backhanded the first mate hard, a loud grunt bursting out of Tom as his head whipped to the side.

"Fuck... Baltsaros stop it," gasped Jon, reaching out for the older man's arm. The captain, eyes wild, turned to Jon. Baltsaros was breathing hard, and his bare, sweat-soaked chest heaved. He looked confused for a moment, as if surprised to see Jon there, and pulled his arm away.

Swallowing, Jon shook his head.

"Please. He's had enough..." he said, praying that Baltsaros could hear him through the savagery that had turned him into something cold and heartless. He only hoped that he wasn't too late and Tom wasn't badly hurt.

Jon started when Tom let out a hoarse laugh, and he frowned. The first mate's face was creased in a gory grin as he shook his head, his breath coming in short gasps between his clenched teeth.

Baltsaros's hand closed softly over Jon's shoulder, and he turned the younger man towards him. The captain's expression had softened; he looked at Jon with a touch of amusement in his dark eyes and a slight curl of his lip.

"Jon, it's ok," he murmured, his fingers squeezing him gently.

Jon frowned and looked back at the first mate. In amazement, he watched Tom press his lips together and dip his head once in agreement. However, his eyes spoke louder than his nod when Jon realized then that the big man's pupils were wide with desire and not fear.

Jon's chest constricted and he felt weak with confusion. How could anyone *like* this, let alone Tom of all people? Jon thought back to the night a few weeks ago when Baltsaros half-carried the first mate into his quarters, Tom's face bleeding from a deep cut and his pants strangely ripped. Had that been... play? Gritting his teeth, Jon shook his head again.

"I just... don't understand," he said quietly. He liked it well enough when he had Tom on his knees and the first mate let him get a little rough; but, that wasn't anything like this. This was pure abuse.

Baltsaros let out a slow sigh, his palm warm against Jon's shoulder before he let his hand drop.

"It's complicated," he murmured. However, after only a moment, the captain's face creased into a smile, and he pressed his fingers against Jon's back.

"Go kneel in front of him, Jon," coaxed Baltsaros, his voice amused. "Please. Trust me."

Jon's brows pinched over his eyes a moment, suspicious of the captain's motives; but, he wanted to trust the man. Watching Baltsaros take his place behind Tom, Jon let out a slow sigh and sank to his knees in front of the first mate.

Tom looked curiously at him, and Jon felt a little pain in his chest at the bruise blooming over the man's stubbled cheek. He lifted a hand to it and felt the heat against his palm.

"I can probably make him stop," he murmured to Tom. The big man's brows furrowed over his gorgeous eyes, and he gave a little shake of his head.

"Jon, unfasten Tom's trousers and pull his cock out," ordered the captain. Jon licked his lips and quickly did as he was told, eager to bring Tom at least some pleasure in all of this.

What he discovered confounded him even more. Once freed, Tom's erection was a rock hard curve pointing upwards, the head of it bobbing with his breathing. In amazement he saw precum glisten at the tip, beading over to run down the dusky-rose head, and past where someone long ago had cruelly cut away the loose covering of his foreskin. Slowly, Jon reached for Tom, his fingers brushing the hot shaft. It was only then that Tom spoke.

"Da, if he touches me, I'm like to cum," he gasped, closing his eyes.

"No you won't, Tom," said the captain, his voice cold and quiet. "If you do, you won't for a week."

Something about the exchange triggered a soft pulse of lust inside Jon, and he felt curiosity begin to eclipse his doubts. Jon lifted his eyes and saw that Baltsaros had picked up the thin flexible rod again; the captain bent it between his hands. As he placed his palm against Tom's chest, Jon decided to test something.

"The captain's going to hit you again," he said softly. Eyes flicking up to

Baltsaros's, he saw the older man smile. Beneath Jon's palm, Tom's heart began to beat faster.

When the rod cracked against the first mate's left buttock, Jon felt Tom's grunt through his hand, the thumping of the great organ beneath his ribs racing at a hard gallop. After Tom sucked in a quick, pained breath, he exhaled with an unmistakable groan of pleasure. There was suddenly no doubt in Jon's mind that Tom was enjoying every minute of this. In response to that realization, his own cock was hardening against the inside of his thigh. That was when Jon decided to leave the "why" for later and concentrate on the "how".

Jon leaned forward to brush his lips over Tom's and felt the man's heart stutter against his palm. The switch came down hard again, twice this time, with a deep grunt from the captain as he put more force into it.

Tom let out a sharp cry and ducked his head under Jon's jaw to bury it against his neck, the first mate's breath hot against his skin. With his fingers curled around Tom's shaft, Jon let his hand slide over the turgid flesh softly, careful to avoid the sensitive flared edges of its head; there was teasing and then there was torture of not being allowed any release for days. As he shifted his other hand to slide through the soft hair at Tom's nape, Jon locked eyes with the captain.

Baltsaros's face was flushed, his lip curled into a slight sneer as he stared back at Jon. He felt a rush of adrenaline as he realized what the captain wanted from him.

"Hit him again," Jon said. "And don't hold back this time."

Against his neck, Tom let out a long, muffled groan.

～

"The wind is good today," said an accented voice.

Jon started and frowned, quickly turning his head. Oren stood on the top step looking out at the water with one hand on the railing. With a scowl at the lithe, white-haired youth, Jon got to his feet.

"You're not supposed to be up here," he said, gesturing to the main deck. "You need permission before you can climb those stairs."

Brow furrowing over his limpid blue eyes, Oren looked at Jon but didn't reply. With an annoyed sigh, Jon took a step towards the young fisherman, intending to herd him back down the stairs. It galled Jon that he had to look up to address him; Oren stood at least a hand's width taller than he did.

"Please," urged Jon. "Go back down. It's not for you to be up here."

Oren frowned at him, lifting a shoulder in a slow shrug.

"I was looking for Baltsaros," he replied, his Common sharply flavoured with the accent of his people.

Baltsaros. Where does he get off not calling him Captain? thought Jon peevishly. There was nothing overtly unlikable about the young man. Any of his transgressions could be chalked up to misunderstandings and a difference of culture, but still...

"*The captain* is otherwise occupied with the first mate. I'll tell him you were looking for him," replied Jon, crossing his arms over his chest. At that moment, an unmistakable groan of pleasure could be heard from the quarters beneath them, and Jon clenched his jaw.

Oren's blond eyebrows lifted, and his cheeks took on a subtle blush. Blue eyes flicking to the planks beneath their feet, Oren pressed his lips together and glanced again at Jon.

"I... will wait. Below, as you say," said the young man softly. Jon nodded, and watched Oren descend the stairs; he didn't like the way that the young man's breathing had quickened at the sound of Baltsaros and Tom at play.

~

Sitting cross-legged beside Tom, Jon dabbed a little more salve onto the first mate's back. Next to him, the captain was sprawled out on his stomach, deeply asleep and completely oblivious. Still reeling slightly from the part he had played in Tom's punishment, if that's what it really had been, Jon chewed the inside of his cheek as he tried to soothe the damage done to the first mate's skin. His hand still stung from how hard he had clutched the leather belt wrapped around the first mate's big neck as Jon had savagely fucked him from behind, and the memory made him feel a little ill. However, Tom just let out a pleased sigh, his muscles soft and relaxed beneath Jon's gentle touch.

"Ye 'member the first time ye did this for me?" murmured Tom blissfully, his cheek pressed against his bicep as he looked up at Jon with a smile.

Jon smiled a little thinly; he had applied salve to the first mate's back when Tom had been whipped to unconsciousness by the captain.

"I'm not likely to forget that," he said, shaking his head.

Tom frowned at the look on Jon's face.

"What's eatin' at ye, love? Ye look like ye've been chewin' lemons."

Jon pressed the stopper back over the squat earthenware jar and shrugged before stretching out next to the first mate with his fingers curled around Tom's forearm.

"I just don't understand how you get off on being so... mistreated," he whispered. "And I don't like that I liked... doing those things to you." He slid his fingers gently over Tom's skin, the dark-blond hair on his arm soft against his fingertips. "Didn't you get abused enough when you were a slave?"

A slight crease appeared between Tom's brows, and he closed his eyes, lying motionless for a while. For a moment, Jon thought he had gone to sleep but, after a long sigh, his deep voice broke the long silence.

"It's like this. When ye have no choice, ye can either let it claim ye, or ye can claim it as yer own. The beatin's tore a good lot outta me, lad. But the pain... well, the pain, it helps to fix me back up. I dunno, love. Maybe I been knocked about and taken so many beatin's after fuckin' that my daft brain's got the two o' them mixed up?" Tom laughed softly and opened his eyes, the irises dark like deep, still seawater. "Now since I'm my own man, I get to choose who lays into me, see? It's my *choice*. No one else's. If some bloody asshole tries it with me, and he ain't got my say-so, he's like to die by my fuckin' hands. Right? But the captain, and *you*, ye silly worried thing... it's like heaven's come callin' full o' angels to suck my cock," grinned Tom, wrinkling his nose in amusement at Jon.

Nodding slowly, Jon tried to process the information.

"The captain once told me that you were broken, and that you knew it, and that it was ok," murmured Jon, pushing himself up onto his elbows to look down at the first mate. "And that you were better at coping with it than he or I would ever be."

"Da said that?" asked Tom, a smile creasing his cheek. When Jon nodded again, the first mate chuckled. "Well, fuck me." Placing his big, scarred hand over Jon's, Tom's face slowly went serious.

"Ye once said ye'd kiss me better after a beatin'," murmured Tom. "Can I hold ye to that, love?"

~

As he squinted into the distance with one hand on the spoked wheel, Jon grinned wide at the memory. How times had changed.

From below he thought he could hear the low, repetitive sound of Tom begging. It took a lot to get the first mate to break down, and Jon wondered with a pang of apprehension whether it meant the captain was working through some internal conflict about the fisherman's grandson. Pushing the petty worry away, Jon leaned back on the bench and sighed.

Warm in the sun, Jon closed his eyes and waited. He knew that after the captain was through with him, Tom would seek him out, and that thought alone was enough to put a soft smile back on Jon's face.

CHAPTER 8
A SNAKE IN THE BED

Baltsaros passed a rag behind his neck, wiping away the sweat that ran down between his shoulder blades. When the cloth came away black, the captain realized that he was just as filthy as the others. The three men stood in the small room that housed the trundlehead below the drum of the capstan, covered in grease and grime and bleary-eyed from exhaustion. Smiling tiredly at Malik and Polas, the captain leaned against the wall with a groan; if he were to sit down on one of the crates, Baltsaros truly believed he would not be able to get up again.

It had been a long night. Since the crew's numbers had dwindled, it was all hands on deck merely to keep the ship running, and many small repairs had fallen by the wayside. The previous day, Baltsaros had decided to drop anchor to take care of some much-needed repairs before continuing on. However, as if to make the captain's concerns manifest, the mechanism that allowed the capstan to turn had seized halfway through lowering the anchor, leaving them in a precarious position. They could neither stop from drifting nor could they flee if they found themselves in danger. While the double-headed design was advantageous for the extra-long cables required to anchor in the deep waters that *Baal's Heart* found herself in yearly, the failure of the aged mechanism had been a constant worry; the captain had known it was bound to break down sooner or later, and he was glad it had given out when they were not in any danger.

Thankfully, with Malik's and the old fisherman's help, they had been able to take the whole apart and, rather than just realign the drums, they had meticulously cleaned every piece of it before putting it back together. It had taken almost the entire night but, in Baltsaros's opinion, it had been time well spent. Once again, Polas had proved himself to be a worthy ally; a lifetime at sea had given the old man hard muscles and a deep well of patience, as well as the humour to make a long night of labour go a little faster.

After scrubbing his hand tiredly over his eyes, Baltsaros nodded to the old man and watched him leave the room with Malik close behind. Yes, Polas had proved his worth; Baltsaros was considering asking the old man if he wished to stay on as part of the crew. Once the captain had wiped the rag one last time over the tarnished copper that bound the wood of the trundlehead, he reached up to bang on the boards above his head and stepped back. As he watched the cable begin to wind itself around the drum, Baltsaros thought about the other two strangers.

Unlike Polas, his son Migri was simply a drain on the ship's resources; despite being tall and strong, the big fisherman was more interested in dicing or drinking with the less savoury individuals that lived and worked aboard the pirate ship than doing anything helpful. Baltsaros couldn't wait to be rid of the laggard. Migri was both lazy and dangerous, a bad combination that had landed him in the brig twice in less than a week.

With his arms crossed, Baltsaros kept his eyes on the spooling cable as the drum rotated to the sound of boots above his head. After it had wound all the way, saltwater dripping into the narrow gutter that encircled the mechanism, Baltsaros heard the men stop and turn around. Once more the drum began to rotate but now in the other direction to finally lower the anchor to the seabed.

Satisfied with the repairs, Baltsaros picked up his discarded shirt and ducked through the small door. After a quick stop in the galley to pick up one of the edible red-skinned fruits they had found on one of the small, uninhabited islands they continuously passed, the captain then made his way wearily up the stairs. Once up on deck, he waved a hand in thanks to the men who had roused themselves before dawn to work the capstan. When he noticed the willowy, white-haired youth standing apart, Baltsaros clenched his jaw, staring back at Oren for a moment before turning to his quarters.

On quietly entering the stateroom, Baltsaros's tense frown left his face at the sight of Tom sleeping with Jon clutched to him like a child's toy. It was getting easier for the captain to see the two boys together like this; they offered each other the solace that Baltsaros just wasn't capable of, and their relationship was a much-needed bridge for the gap that had always existed, unbeknownst to him, between Tom and himself. He had decided that he simply needed both of them to feel whole; it worked to soothe his possessiveness somewhat.

After pouring a little water into the shallow basin, Baltsaros quickly wiped his face, staring at his own shadowy eyes in the glass mirror that hung on the wall.

The grandson has to go, he thought.

His mind's eye painted him a picture of the white-haired youth with his unblemished golden skin, and long, lithe muscles. Oren's bright blue eyes seemed to follow Baltsaros everywhere, and it was beginning to make him feel restive. He was fully aware that bedding the boy was a fool's wish, but there wasn't a doubt in his mind that the fisherman's grandson would come to him willingly. Baltsaros scrubbed at the grease on his shoulder with a sigh and wondered how long Oren had known he preferred the company of men and whether he had attempted anything on his own despite the terribly restrictive society he was part of. The boy would probably be a virgin.

Jon had been a virgin, and it had been a heady thing to experience.

With the cloth pressed to his eyes, Baltsaros stood still for a moment, remembering that strange day at the *Jewel* when Jon had forced a promise of fidelity out of him. That promise had changed, of course, to include Tom, but the captain knew he couldn't kid himself into thinking that an indiscretion with the beautiful stranger would go well with either of the young men. Besides, there was the respect for Polas to think of.

Baltsaros dumped the rag into the basin and, longing for a bath, he padded quietly to the bed. As soon as he placed a warm hand on Tom's broad shoulder, he felt the first mate tense as he woke up, Tom's blue-green eyes blinking up at the captain with concern.

"What's the matter, Da?" asked Tom quietly, his voice hoarse from sleep.

"Can you take over? I am dead on my feet, and I need someone to split the men into work groups early before they start to wander off. I want all the repairs done by this evening, if possible. We'll leave for the mainland at first light tomorrow morning," murmured the captain, smiling as the muscular first mate untangled himself from Jon and got to his feet, naked and gorgeous.

When Tom saw the look in Baltsaros's eye, he did something that still tended to take the captain by surprise. Instead of his usual slightly surly "Yes, Da", the first mate reached out and curled his hand around the back of the captain's neck, pulling the older man in for a quick kiss before nodding and looking around for a pair of pants to wear. His eyebrows high in astonishment at the affectionate gesture, Baltsaros smiled at Tom and shook his head in amusement.

As he crawled into bed behind Jon once Tom was gone, the captain frowned, hoping that this new gentleness infecting Tom did nothing to diminish the cold brutality that he so depended on in the first mate.

~

Jon peeled the banana and took a bite, chewing with a smile. The fruit wasn't quite ripe, but it had been months since the last time he'd had one, and it tasted wonderful to him. Craning his neck, he squinted up at Tom, balanced barefoot on one of the yardarms to replace a pulley that had become stuck. After pulling the line out of the old one, Tom whistled at Jon before dropping it. Jon caught it and, taking another bite of banana, he tossed the broken brass-and-wood pulley onto the deck below where it joined three others. At the furious pace they were working, the minor repairs would definitely be done before sundown.

While he watched Tom climb down the shrouds, Jon finished his fruit and tossed the peel overboard, wiping his hand on the side of his trousers before jumping down from his crate. With the pulleys replaced, he and Tom were to tackle rehousing the starboard carronade together. The big gun's wheel had rusted solid, making it impossible to aim, but Tom thought he could get it working with enough oil. The problem was that the elevation thread was also thick with rust and getting the whole thing loose was going to be a hassle. It was worth a try though. Jon tried not to think about the fact that it was the gun that had burst free of its moorings and crushed a man to death the night Tom had been swept overboard.

As he stood braced against the side of the gun watching Tom try to wiggle the base of it back and forth, Jon caught a glimpse of Oren walking towards the stern. When the young fisherman glanced around him quickly, Jon straightened, his eyes narrowed.

What are you up to? he thought, wary of the youth's suspicious behaviour.

"Bloody hells! Will ye keep yer hip on the gods-damned bloody gun, love? D'ye think I'm doin' this for my bloody health?" panted Tom, smacking the back of Jon's calf as he knelt with his shoulder against the wooden pedestal. The big man grinned up at Jon. "Keep yer fuckin' mind on the job, and I'll give ye somethin' to smile about after, aye? Now heave, mate!"

Oren momentarily forgotten, Jon put his back to the side of the big gun and pushed back as hard as he could, his thoughts on what Tom might have in mind once the work was completed.

~

Baltsaros sighed as the warm body behind him moved closer, Jon's hand stroking slowly down his flank and coming to rest on his hip. Smiling, the captain pushed back against him; though he was half-asleep and sore from the night's work, there was nothing better than waking up to Jon's touch. The younger man behind him moved slightly, going up on one elbow to begin kissing the side of Baltsaros's neck and over his shoulder, fingers tracing meaningless patterns over the captain's naked thigh.

"Mmm," murmured Baltsaros, tilting his head with his eyes closed. "That's nice." The hand on his thigh moved lower, nails scratching softly as they came back up again. The sensation was incredibly pleasing, and the captain let out another soft moan. His cock, half-hard already from sleep-arousal, lengthened along the curve of his pelvis, and he rocked backwards a little to free it and bring it into Jon's grasp. Behind him, the boy let out a small sound, and his fingers stilled momentarily.

That should have been the first indication that all was not what it seemed.

However, Baltsaros just arched his back sleepily against the young man, pulling Jon's hand down to where the captain's cock lay waiting for warm fingers to close over it. After wrapping his own hand around Jon's fist, he moved his hips to fuck his cock through their grasp, sighing again with pleasure as the head brushed against Jon's palm. Groaning as his hunger began to mount quickly, Baltsaros was gratified to feel Jon's cock hard against him. He let go of the hand on his length and reached back to touch the young man moving slowly against him, to pull Jon closer... and opened his eyes in confusion when the hip his hand encountered was slimmer, far slimmer, than Jon's. Baltsaros turned his head quickly and frowned up into the sly blue eyes of the fisherman's grandson.

For a moment he was shocked into inaction; the boy's hand continued stroking along his hard shaft, but Baltsaros's mind finally registered the unpracticed way Oren held the captain, and how the younger man smelled absolutely nothing like Jon did.

The captain opened his mouth to tell Oren to remove himself but instead found himself kissing him, his fingers tangling in the long white dreadlocks as he continued to move in Oren's grasp. Heart beating a dizzying rhythm, Baltsaros turned onto his back and reached for Oren, crushing him against his body, a low growl in his chest. It was completely absurd to take such a risk, but his lust was a crazed thing that would not release him. When the long-limbed fisherman moved against him hesitantly, pushing his cock against Baltsaros's pelvis, soft little whimpers of need came from his graceful throat. With another growl, this time fierce, the captain tugged Oren's head back and leaned up to bite hard into the side of his neck.

"Fuckin' bloody hells!" yelled Tom, and Oren pulled quickly back in shock, a guilty expression on his face.

Baltsaros just closed his eyes slowly and lay panting, disappointment and annoyance warring with the self-reproach he felt.

Stupid.

Oren quickly climbed off the captain, and Baltsaros could hear him scrabbling about for his trousers before the door slammed shut.

"Have ye lost yer bloody mind, Da?" asked Tom, his gravelly voice low and furious. "I just finished tellin' Jon that ye'd never be so fuckin' stupid as to put yer cock in that little piece o' shit, and here ye are, about to heave the bloody cunt down and give him a good, deep ploughin'..." Baltsaros opened his eyes and watched as the first mate continued his tirade, pacing back and forth across the thick rugs. When Tom put one of his slim, black cigars between his lips and lit it, Baltsaros just frowned and said nothing.

The first mate stopped and turned to Baltsaros, his blue-green eyes narrow with anger as he pointed at the captain.

"There's somethin' bloody *wrong* with ye, Da. Ye can't keep just replacin' folks when some little slut shakes his hips at ye," spat the first mate. "And not to fuckin' bloody mention that yer the one who said we'd all be dancin' the hempen jig for stickin' our cocks in mates instead of skirts—"

"That's enough, Tom," warned Baltsaros sitting up, his eyes on burly young man. He rubbed a hand over his face, feeling suddenly twice his age and so very tired. With a sigh, he tilted his head at Tom.

"You're not going to tell Jon," the captain said softly.

Tom's brows pinched together as he chewed on the end of his narrow cigar, his big arms crossed over his chest. However, after a moment he shook his head once.

"Good," said Baltsaros, stretching his sore shoulders as he stood slowly. "That

370

little 'slut' as you so aptly called him stole into my bed... not unlike the way someone else I know did."

Tom blinked and then looked down at the floor, pulling the cheroot from his mouth and wiping his lips with the back of his hand. When he looked back up, there was a wry grin on his face; the first mate chuckled softly and shook his head.

"Ye were half-asleep," recalled Tom. "And ye weren't about to pull away once I got my hands on ye." Tom smiled a little wider with the memory, but he quickly sobered and frowned again at the captain.

"I know. Not an excuse," agreed Baltsaros, walking up to the first mate. He felt ridiculous for letting himself be chastised by Tom, but he needed his full cooperation in the days to come; making a show of contrition to mollify the first mate was something he could do. "I'll keep my hands to myself," he continued, and reached up to cup the back of Tom's head, the younger man's short hair slightly coarse against his rough fingers. "I promise."

Tom's eyes softened slightly at the gentle touch, and the big man let out a slow sigh. After pulling the cheroot from his mouth and stubbing it out quickly in the empty cup on the table, Tom closed his eyes and leaned his cheek against Baltsaros's wrist.

"If I find him in here again, Da, I'll cut the bloody balls off o' him myself," swore Tom softly.

Baltsaros smiled. Still ruthless after all.

~

Jon looked up from the crate he was tying when the door to the captain's quarters banged shut. In disbelief, he watched the young fisherman hurry away, a hand hastily working the fastenings at the front of his pants. Bitter bile rose up in his throat, and Jon clenched his jaw in anger, dropping the rope to the deck as he stood. A tightness in his chest made it hard to breathe as he tried to make sense of what he had just seen. Then, he saw the door open again and Tom step out, the first mate scanning the deck until he found Jon. Brows furrowed, Tom shook his head slowly.

Don't worry, said the first mate's eyes, and Jon swallowed, wanting to believe him. With lips pressed together, he nodded and started walking towards Tom. However, before he got halfway there, he spotted Oren sitting on the gunwale, his blue eyes trained on Jon as he made his way sternward. Jon wanted to avert his gaze but found that he couldn't as he watched the golden-skinned sylph's face split into a slow, wicked smile.

CHAPTER 9

THE METTLE OF A MAN

Truth, like gold, is to be obtained not by its growth, but by washing away from it all that is not gold.

— LEO TOLSTOY

Jon flattened his hand on the tabletop and stared down at it, jaw tight with anger.

"Tell me again why I can't come with you?" he asked, his voice quiet and furious.

"Because it's dangerous," said Baltsaros and Tom, speaking as one.

Jon raised his eyes to the first mate; at least Tom looked a little shamefaced as he lifted his shoulders.

"What am I to do, then?" Jon said, turning his eyes to the captain.

"You'll do what you normally do, and obey Calum as you would me. He'll take over while we're gone," replied Baltsaros softly, frowning down at Jon.

Staring up at the older man, Jon breathed quickly through his nose.

"You really have no idea how insulting it is to have the both of you acting like nursemaids," Jon growled. "I'm not a wilting flower, for fuck's sake. I can hold my own! I didn't come all this fucking way to just sit in the ship while you two go gallivanting off to gods-know-where."

Tom's face had creased into an amused grin as Jon spoke, but Baltsaros's eyes had grown darker.

"My decision is final, Jon. This is only the first trip into the city. I need Tom with me, not only because I know I can count on him not to lose his head, but because he's acting the part of my slave," the captain said in a low voice. Leaning forward with his knuckles pressed to the mahogany table, Baltsaros stared hard at him for a moment.

Jon watched the captain's expression begin to soften, some humour returning to his chiselled face.

"No, you're not a wilting flower, Jon. I'm honestly concerned with the safety of the whole crew—that's why we're anchoring so far from the harbour. I am going on the word of a man whose boat was stolen out from under him by my crew and, as much as I like the old man, I have no idea if anything he says is true. Polas is not even from the city; his people just do business in the fish markets. It's a different culture, Jon; one that is extremely wary of strangers. There are new rules to follow... harsh rules, from what I understand." The captain rounded the table and reached out to stroke Jon's dark curls back. "Patience, Jon. All right?"

Jon almost flinched at the touch, unable to forget the sly smile that had spread over Oren's elfin face. Instead he forced himself to close his eyes and lean into the captain's hand like he normally would.

As if I didn't know what you were up to, he thought bitterly. The previous day had been spent watching Oren as the young man made his way around the ship. Twice, the tall fisherman had approached the captain, both times his body language that of a fawning sycophant as he hung on Baltsaros's every word. It was enough to make a man sick. When the captain had quickly sent the boy away with a few harsh words, Jon had been childishly pleased; perhaps he had been imagining things. However, as Oren made his way belowdecks, Jon had raised his eyes and seen the captain's gaze following the willowy youth. When Baltsaros noticed Jon watching him, the older man's face had gone still, wiped of expression, before the captain had turned and walked away.

Jon opened his eyes and pulled away from Baltsaros's hand.

"Why are *they* still here?" he asked, looking up at the captain. He didn't want to say the boy's name.

Baltsaros narrowed his eyes at Jon, and he felt sure that his suspicions were grounded in *something*; it galled him that the first mate was once again covering for the captain.

They deserve each other, Jon thought, looking over at Tom. The big man's brow was furrowed in concern, his sea-green eyes on Jon's.

"I asked Polas to join the crew this morning," replied Baltsaros, dropping his hand. "He's mulling it over and will give me his answer before long. Migri and Oren are staying on until they can find a replacement boat or some other suitable accommodation." With a tilt of his head, he lifted his hand again, this time to Jon's cheek. "Don't worry, I want both of them off my ship," he said softly.

The words did nothing to appease Jon. They only showed that Baltsaros was aware that he had concerns, but Jon nodded anyway and bent his lips into a smile. The captain, satisfied with his response, smiled back and leaned in to kiss him quickly.

"I have things to take care of before we leave," said Baltsaros, straightening. "Tom, be ready to go in an hour."

Tom watched the captain depart then turned back to Jon, the same anxious expression on his face as before.

Jon folded his arms on the tabletop and rested his chin on his wrist, staring back at Tom.

"You hate lying to me," murmured Jon. "Yet, you fucking do it anyway." He watched something flit across the big man's features, the first mate still frustratingly unreadable when he wanted to be.

"Not my secrets to tell, love," said Tom softly. "I ain't really lyin'… " The hard muscles in Tom's jaw moved under his short stubble as his eyes lost a little focus. "Like Da said: patience. Have a little patience and… I'll straighten him out for ye."

Tom sounded distracted, as if he was thinking of something else. With a sigh, the first mate leaned back in his chair and rubbed at the tattoos on his skin.

"A fuckin' slave again," Tom muttered, and Jon realized that the first mate was feeling some strain about revisiting the role. He remembered the slave collar in Tom's room and felt a sharp twinge; with shame, Jon realized that his jealousy was the furthest thing from the first mate's mind. Tom needed to be fitted for a new collar today. It seemed that some customs were strangely universal. Watching Tom touch the marks on his skin, Jon felt almost sick with the thought of how that would affect the normally fearless first mate.

Abandoning his petty grievances for the moment, Jon slid out of his chair, padding around to Tom to put his arms around the big man's shoulders from behind. With a sigh, he laid his cheek down on the first mate's short, dirty-blond hair.

"The other day Polas told me that your tattoos aren't *slave* tattoos per se," murmured Jon, his hands stroking the marked skin, fingertips skimming over the slightly raised lines as he spoke. "They're tattoos that belong to a nomadic people, a warrior people, strong and proud."

When Tom remained silent, Jon decided to push on with the tale.

"See… about a hundred or so years ago, there was a great war between tribes, one that lasted for nearly a generation. One tribe stood out in bravery and strength of heart, and they were completely unbeatable. But, the other tribes banded together and got help from powerful warlocks from this 'golden city'. To the lords of the city, they had promised the spoils of war: the women and children.

"In the end the strong were almost completely destroyed by the weak. Afraid for the fate of the tribe, the elders sent the women and children away in secret, scattering them like seeds to the wind, before the lords of the golden city could enslave them. Each child was given a tattoo that would show them the path back to their homeland so that they could one day find their way back… if the golden city fell. But, the lords of the city had many allies, and lots of the children were caught and brought back as slaves. The practice of tattooing their children continued… The 'marked' slaves, as they're called now, are the most valuable slaves because of their great strength and fortitude. They're also said to be fiercely loyal." Jon decided to leave out the part about skinning the slaves and tanning their decorated hides for souvenirs; Tom was worried enough as it was.

The first mate sat quietly for a moment and then let out a short grunt.

"Nice story," he said, his deep voice a low rumble against Jon's fingers. "Doesn't explain why I got them though." Tom lifted a hand and stroked his thumb along the inside of Jon's arm, a touch that brought out goosebumps on his skin.

"You said you got them from an old man, didn't you?" asked Jon as he straightened, an idea forming in his head. Tom nodded, and Jon continued. "Did he have tattoos himself?"

Tom looked up, his brow deeply creased in confusion. After a moment his eyebrows rose.

"Are ye sayin' ye think the ol' codger was one of them kids? He *did* have a mess o' lines like the ones he did me. Shit, and he was really fuckin' old." Tom's eyes were wide as he shifted to see Jon better.

"Maybe he saw something in you that reminded him of the warriors he was descended from: fierce and proud," said Jon with a grin. He thought it was *possible* that the old man was one of the children from the story—how he had wound up in the southern peninsula was a complete mystery, but where else would he have gotten the tattoos? However, Jon knew that even if he *was* a child of these nomadic warriors, the old man probably tattooed people for money and not out of some bestowment of honour; the little lie didn't hurt if it soothed Tom's worry somewhat.

Jon almost laughed out loud at his hypocrisy.

~

Tom closed his eyes tight, remembering all too well the half-dozen times that he had been fitted for a collar. Granted, this time it was different; no one was holding him down nor was he tied up. Plus, Malik had been kind enough to put something between the metal and Tom's neck while he clamped the rivets and fastened the collar so it couldn't be taken off except by metal shears. The last time he'd had a collar put on, Tom had been so bruised that he hadn't been able to swallow for nearly a day.

The metal felt cold against his skin when Malik removed the rag, and Tom licked his lips and shivered. When his mouth filled with the thin spit of nausea, he quickly stood and spat over the side of the ship, knuckles white as he clung to the metal cleat, his breath heaving through clenched teeth.

"Hey, big guy, you going to be ok?" asked the dark-haired shipwright, putting a hand lightly on Tom's shoulder.

Tom let out a short grunt and nodded his head quickly, closing his eyes again as he listened to Malik put his tools away. However, the first mate stayed pressed up against the side of the ship for another few minutes until the dizziness passed completely.

Half an hour later, outfitted in just a pair of shortened pants belted at the calf, Tom climbed down the rope ladder after the captain and settled between the oars of the small rowboat they were using to get to land. Though he had bragged to Jon about his proficiency in languages, Tom was still running through a few key phrases—"Yes,

Master" being the one that stuck most in his craw—and feeling a little nervous as he fiddled with the metal band around his neck.

Polas and Baltsaros had explained that no one of any means went about Ereme'ia Balor, the "golden city" of Jon's story, without at least one slave. Since the captain wanted to fit in and be granted access to numerous establishments, the presence of a slave in his company was necessary; that Tom bore the tattoos of a highly valued one would only work to their advantage. With Polas's help, they had concocted a credible backstory about being travellers from somewhere the old fisherman, now a full member of the crew, called the Badlands. When Baltsaros had originally asked why they couldn't just speak the truth about being from the other side of the black mountain range, Polas had made the same strange sign across his chest that he made every time they mentioned their origins: an up-and-down movement of his fingers that touched spots on both shoulders and his sternum.

Tom smiled to himself, remembering the way the man had almost shat himself the first time they had explained where they were really from. Legends told here about the Devil's Isles were far more elaborate than back home, including stories of giant eels that could steal a man's soul by kissing him while in the guise of beautiful fish-bottomed women. Why anyone would want to kiss some tart with a tail was beyond him, but it had made for some pretty interesting listening. The part that had made the old fisherman the most nervous though was that, supposedly, a man could not cross through the Devil's Isles—or the Gods' Claws as they were called on this side of the mountain range—with his soul intact. Anyone caught sailing out of there was immediately deemed a ghost or a *duppy* and had their boats burned, and any men aboard were tossed into the sea.

So the Badlands it was. Baltsaros's northern accent could just pass for a rich Badlander, as long as he remembered to use the correct words. Both languages were similar and, while that was handy when it came to learning it quickly, it was becoming a pain in the ass to remember which one was the right word. Tom hoped he wasn't called on to speak too much. Still, despite all of his misgivings, he was pretty damn curious about this golden city, especially the "warlocks" that Jon had spoken of in the story.

As he curled his hands around the oars, Tom looked up and scanned the side of the ship for Jon. When he found him standing up on the gunwale with one arm through the shrouds and a deeply worried look on his face, the first mate chuckled a little and winked.

Be good, he thought. *Be safe.* Tom hoped he would be back real soon to coax some smiles out of the serious young man.

~

Feeling like a country bumpkin, Tom tried not to stare up, mouth agape, at the colossal doors that led to the walled city. He had never seen anything like them and had no idea what to expect when they finally made their way inside. Soon, he hoped.

Weapons were allowed within Ereme'ia Balor, but visitors had to pay a tax for the "privilege" of wearing them on their persons, so Baltsaros and he were standing in a long line waiting for admittance.

Chafing a little at the long wait, Tom glanced around at the folks milling slowly around them. Standing amongst a pretty normal-looking bunch of peasant-types were a few of the tall, white-haired fisherfolk. Interestingly enough, none of them seemed to be sporting the double-ring of scars that Polas had, and Tom wondered if the old man wasn't telling them something.

Tom scratched his nose and quickly ducked his head to avoid meeting the eyes of a fat man wearing blue silks; Tom was a slave, and slaves didn't have the *right* to look at anyone directly, he kept reminding himself. He gritted his teeth, his fists clenching and unclenching at his sides.

"Tom, you look like you're about to break something," murmured Baltsaros. "Or someone."

Tom let out a slow breath and nodded; straightening his shoulders, he glanced up at the captain.

Baltsaros was wearing a long black tunic, belted at the waist with a red sash. Tom recognized it as something he wore often when at home in Madierus, but the embroidery had been picked out of the hem. The captain's hair was tied back and braided in a long queue down his back, and his beard was oiled and tamed into a neat spade shape. Around one bicep, the older man wore what looked like a braided length of black leather, which Tom knew was just an oiled piece of black sailcloth. To finish the outfit, the captain wore a steel cuff over one wrist that had been stamped by Malik with the same symbol found on Tom's slave collar: the silhouette of a lion's head. It was a quickly cobbled-together outfit, but Polas thought it would pass muster.

The line inched along, and Tom nearly groaned from impatience. It seemed to him like the men at the gate were purposefully doing everything at a snail's pace. As he let his eyes wander again, Tom found himself staring once more in the direction of the fat man in blue, but this time, he looked curiously at the slaves standing with him.

Like Tom, the tall dark-haired man was tattooed. It was a slightly different configuration of dots and swirls from his own but definitely done in the same style. The other slave was a slight blonde woman, pretty enough to look at but with such a forlorn expression in her bright blue eyes that Tom had to look away.

As he glanced around himself, he met the eyes of another muscular, tattooed slave. The man's head was shaved on both sides, the short hair in the middle sticking up like a brush, and he had two silver rings in one nostril. The slave looked incredibly fierce because of it, and when the man nodded solemnly to Tom, the first mate was quick to return the gesture. Maybe the slaves here were better treated than he had been; this marked one certainly looked well fed, and he held his head high. However, when the other turned away, Tom saw that the man's back bore layers upon layers of scars just like his own.

With his heart beating a swift rhythm from the sight of the lash marks, Tom shuffled closer to the captain, embarrassed by the weakness that made him wish to bury his face against the older man.

Sensing Tom's discomfort, Baltsaros stared at him, his eyes a clear golden-brown in the bright morning sun.

"Stay a pace behind me, stop fidgeting, and stop looking around you like you want to start a fight. You were a slave long enough, start acting like one," said Baltsaros in a low, harsh whisper.

Tom clenched his jaw and looked down, nodding.

"Aye, Da," he murmured. Even at the best of times, Tom had made a lousy slave... but the captain was right; he was behaving foolishly. There was gold to be had here and maybe something even more valuable. He had to get a hold of himself. After all, it was just a bit of play-acting.

Following slowly along behind the captain, always a pace behind like a good little slave, Tom wondered if the city had taverns and whether they served beer on this side of the mountains. It had been far too long since he'd held a nice foamy dark beer in his hand. When he found himself grinning at the thought, Tom quickly sobered, letting out a frustrated huff of breath.

He doubted very much that slaves were given pints of beer to enjoy.

~

Jon sat cross-legged on the planks, eating his lunch off of a metal plate. It was a gruel mash that Cook had flavoured with some nuts and berries they had found on a little spit of an island. Though it was far from inedible, Jon couldn't wait to eat something that wasn't gruel or fish; he hoped that while the captain and first mate were out scouting about the city, they had the presence of mind to pick up a few supplies. As he scraped at his plate with his wooden spoon, Jon narrowed his eyes at the man below who was pacing from one side of the ship to the other.

"What do you make of him?" he asked, looking up at Calum, who was lounging back on the quarterdeck bench.

The old man blinked at Jon in confusion a few times, and he passed a gnarled brown hand over his face before he squinted down at the main deck.

"Ye mean Migri, lad?" replied Calum, frowning down at Jon. When Jon nodded, licking his spoon, the old man shrugged. "Well, 'e ain't much fer words, that's fer bloody sure. Mean as a pinched badger. Broke Timmy's nose last night, ye hear? Over a claim o' bad dice. Big lout was loaded t' th' gunwalls. Took three o' 'em to haul 'im off t' the pokey."

Jon nodded again. That was the third time that the big fisherman had landed himself a night in the brig. The crew was on strict orders to leave the three strangers unmolested, but Jon knew that, left to their own devices, the pirates would have cut Migri to pieces and tossed him overboard by now. Watching the beefy, golden-skinned man cross the width of the boat again, Jon was reminded of a wild boar he had seen at a fair once. It had paced back and forth in its tiny cage the whole time the fair was in town, half-mad with the need to escape. Watching Migri made Jon just as tense.

After scanning the deck for the son and not seeing him, Jon looked back up at Calum.

"What about Oren?" he asked, the name bitter on his tongue.

Calum's mouth turned down at the corners as he thought, his dark eyes narrowed to the midday sun.

"Tha' boy better watch 'imself," muttered Calum after a long silence. " 'E's got trouble in 'is soul, like 'is ol' man. Do 'imself a favour if 'e were t' look up more to 'is grand-da. There's some fine mettle in Polas. A shame 'is kin's such trash."

Jon had to agree. He found it odd that a man so level headed and affable could have spawned such an unlikeable character like Migri... and grand-sired such an ass-kissing, little twat. Jon grinned softly to himself; life with pirates had done wonders to his vocabulary.

With a sigh, he turned to look back across the water to the jungle through which Baltsaros and Tom had disappeared a few hours earlier.

"Don' worry, lad," chuckled Old Calum. "Them's been up t' worse. Tom'll see 'em home safe. 'E always does."

Frowning, he wondered if Calum was wrong—at least this time. Jon hoped that Baltsaros had the sense to realize that what he asked of Tom would be completely traumatizing for a lesser man. As it was, Jon had never seen Tom look so unnerved as he had earlier, his pallor noticeable even under his deep tan.

After placing the plate down beside himself on the wooden planks, Jon drew up his knees and wrapped his arms around them, resigned to wait for their return come nightfall.

CHAPTER 10
FEAR AND BLOOD

Fear is pain arising from the anticipation of evil.

— ARISTOTLE

Beneath Baltsaros's boots the cobblestones were smooth and even, and the street was well maintained. To his left, he could see what looked like swampy farmland within the city walls with a handful of slaves bent over or kneeling in the water among tall, green shoots. To his right there was a series of paddocks holding horses of various breeds, some of which he did not recognize. Behind them were other enclosed areas, and Baltsaros could see slaves feeding cattle and goats beyond. In a little field next to the fences, the captain spotted children working between rows of what looked like potato plants; all of them wore the thin metal collars of slaves.

Brow furrowed, Baltsaros picked up his pace slightly, trusting Tom to follow. In the distance, at what would probably be the end of the arrow-straight thoroughfare, was a stepped pyramid. Far off to the right and left of the squat structure were two more and, when Baltsaros looked back towards the city walls on either side, he saw yet another pair. Five pyramids arranged in a circle within the city walls; Tom's triangles-within-a-square tattoo made more sense now. Narrowing his eyes at the stone pyramid ahead, Baltsaros wondered what they were for.

The throng of people became thicker as they approached a large paved space that held a thriving marketplace. To avoid being jostled, the captain moved to the side of the street and stopped to watch the crowd pass by. Tom, on alert as always, stood at his side with his head ducked, eyes shrewdly scanning everyone who came near. Baltsaros turned and watched the first mate' hand lift slowly to his ear as he looked for the cheroot he usually had perched there. Finding none and obviously remembering why, Tom let out a rapid string of curses under his breath. The first mate clenched his jaw, rounded his shoulders, and let out a long slow exhale. Baltsaros pressed his lips together and looked back towards the market. Tom wasn't holding up as well as the captain had hoped. It definitely didn't help that the big man was probably beginning to feel the withdrawal from the mild narcotic that was found in the slim black cigars he habitually smoked. It was probably good that they not stay in town for long... at least not today.

Chin raised, and with a haughty expression on his chiselled features, the captain pushed his way back into the crowd, shadowed by the first mate. At first glance, the wares that were for sale were not much different than those that sold on the other side of the black mountain range. However, upon closer inspection, there were items that were baffling to Baltsaros. Turning a small earthenware bowl in his hands, he frowned at the corked hole in its side. Was it a serving vessel of some sort?

"Da, take a look at this," murmured Tom, pointing to a big cast-iron pot.

Baltsaros frowned, confused by the first mate's interest in the normal-looking pot. He then saw the manufacturer's mark: a double anvil with a circle around it. There was no mistaking it—the cast-iron pot had been made in the mainlands, not far from the mining and smelting town where he had found Tom.

Curious, the captain went from stand to stand, his eyes picking out familiar items at each one: watered silks from the southern peninsula, pottery from the midland isles, even an elk-bone throwing game from his own homeland in the north. Obviously, trade was flourishing with the east, but how?

Lifting a small silk scarf with a smile, he caught the merchant's attention.

"How much for this?" he asked in the foreign tongue.

The merchant grinned wide, showing off gold eyeteeth.

"Half a *dokscha*!" said the man. "Very cheap for something so beautiful!"

Baltsaros made as if to look for flaws in the brown- and copper-dyed fabric, curling his lip in a doubtful sneer.

The merchant, seeing the captain's hesitation, let out a pained sigh.

"The price does not please you? It is such exquisite work! An unusual colour! Straight from the silk makers of Jalon T'sek!" exclaimed the man, his eyes wide and guileless. "But... for a discerning man like yourself, I suppose I could part with it for four *rukscha*. No less or my family will starve. Please!"

Baltsaros continued to bargain with the seller until they agreed on one fifth of a *dokscha* or two *rukscha*—the equivalent of ten pieces of silver. In the southern peninsula where it had been made, not in this Jalon T'sek that the man claimed, the scarf would fetch a price of three or four pieces of silver and no more. It was exorbitant.

Polas had explained that gold was plentiful but hard metals scarce; the conversion rate was one steel *dokscha* to three standard gold pieces or forty-eight silver. Not having any of these steel coins—Polas's meagre, hidden stash having been stolen along with his boat—Baltsaros had had Tom beat some gold coins with a hammer to obscure the stamps on them.

The merchant stared down at the damaged gold coin in his palm for a long time before he looked back up at Baltsaros, his brown eyes narrowed in suspicion.

"Where did you say you were from, stranger? I don't recognize your accent," said the man, all pretence of camaraderie dropped.

Baltsaros tensed; *stranger* was synonymous with *intruder* here. Letting his lips curl into a sheepish smile, the captain touched the medallion on his chest, a trinket he knew would mean absolutely nothing to the merchant.

"I *was* worried my accent would give me away," he said, tapping the little silver disc. "I'm from the Otak clan. I needed to get away from the heat for a while, so I decided to visit your beautiful city!" Baltsaros grinned wider when the salesman nodded, his eyes on the medallion. The man, not wanting to seem ignorant, made as if to suddenly recognize it. According to Polas, the well-known clan rarely ventured beyond their walled compound in the Badlands and, while they did have a sigil, very few would have seen it firsthand.

"Of course!" said the man. "I hear that the Badlands are most oppressive this time of year! How silly of me to not notice the Otak clan's sigil! It must also be so nice for you to be around civilized folk for a change." The last was said with a wry grin and a laugh, a friendly gibe about the far-off Badlands. Polas said that the citizens of Ereme'ia Balor—or Balorians as they called themselves—viewed anyone from outside the city as uncultured. The old man was proving to be an invaluable source of information though it made Baltsaros wonder again whether Polas was more than just the simple fisherman that he claimed to be.

Chuckling at the merchant's words, Baltsaros accepted his change of a single *rukscha* and bid the man farewell. After fingering the slim, oval piece of bronze thoughtfully, he tucked it into the pouch at his waist. At this rate he would be a poor man before long. He would ask Polas later whether he would raise suspicions if he tried to trade broken steel swords.

Across the square, Baltsaros could see a number of food stalls. Curious to see what they served and feeling peckish, the captain and first mate slowly made their way over to where a man was selling what looked like meat and vegetables on long skewers.

"It must cost you a fortune to feed that brute," said the tall, dark-haired merchant good-naturedly as he handed over two skewers to Baltsaros.

The captain was momentarily confused until he realized that the man meant Tom. Instantly he wondered if he had made a blunder by buying his "slave" some food from the market. Laughing in response, Baltsaros nodded to the man before he turned away. Glancing around quickly, the captain tried to see whether slaves ate near their masters or if there was some other convention he was meant to follow.

It was hard to discern which slaves belonged to the patrons and which to the merchants; everywhere Baltsaros looked, he saw slave collars. Finally deciding that it seemed safe enough just to share his food, the captain handed over one of the sticks of meat over to Tom who accepted it gratefully; the first mate's face was set in serious lines, and Baltsaros couldn't remember ever seeing Tom so anxious.

"It'll be ok," he murmured to Tom in Common. "You'll feel better when you've eaten." It was everything he could do not to place a reassuring hand on the young man's shoulder.

Tom nodded as he chewed, his green-blue eyes darting around him.

"So many fuckin' slaves, Da. Seems like too many, don't it?" asked Tom in a low voice, wiping his lips with the back of his hand.

It was true; Baltsaros had never seen such a high number of slaves in one place before. Looking around him, he calculated that there were probably four or five slaves for every free man. It was bizarre... Why were there so many, and how were they being kept from rebelling in force? What were they used for? Most seemed to be simply following their masters around the square, arms laden down with purchases. Some were obviously bed slaves; a tall man in a scarlet tunic walked by with two nearly naked slave girls trailing behind him, their high breasts painted or tattooed with flowers that matched the embroidery on their master's clothing. Others seemed to act as bodyguards; Baltsaros could see marked slaves that walked behind their masters holding tall spears, the powerful young men all sporting interestingly shorn hair with their fierce eyes often ringed with black. Some slaves, employed by the merchants, did nothing but stand around or package purchased goods.

"Status symbols," guessed Baltsaros, taking another bite of the savoury meat. When the captain turned his eyes to a pair of marked slaves waiting for their master to finish a transaction, he saw that one of them was staring intently at Tom's tattoos. In dismay he watched the man nudge his companion and point his chin at the first mate, tilting his head to murmur something to the other. Belatedly, it occurred to the captain why Tom's tattoos would stand out.

"Put a hand over your ribs," he whispered quickly to Tom, catching the big man's eye. Frowning, the first mate crossed his right arm across his ribs, his big hand obscuring the tattoos that swirled down his ribcage... the ones that showed the path home past the Devil's Isles.

~

Jon peered at the maps that Nathaniel had unrolled on the crate, confused by all the dots and lines that joined everything.

"See, I knew they were maps, but I wasn't sure what of," said the middle-aged cartographer, using a cup to hold down the edge of the curling paper. "I was thinking stars at first, but it didn't explain why everything was superimposed on what looks like a shoreline. Polas here was kind enough to educate me." Nathaniel smiled wide, showing the slight gap between his front teeth. "It's like a calendar and a map at the same time. It shows the fisherfolk where they're supposed to be fishing on each day of the month according to a complicated set of rituals. It's absolutely fascinating."

Holding down the other edge of the map, Jon nodded and furrowed his brow.

"These dots are... rituals?" he asked uncertainly.

Polas nodded and placed a calloused finger on one of the dots, slowly tracing one of the thin lines to the next dot over.

"Yes. This is, ah... blessing of *soft*. If it is well received, we go along this path. If it is not, we go to this," said the old man, tapping another dot. "This is the blessing of *hard*."

"Blessing?" asked Jon, confused by what Polas meant by soft and hard.

The old man nodded again and moved his finger, tapping dot after dot.

"Light, dark, young, old, one, two, barren, virgin..." he listed.

"Wait, what? Virgin?" asked Jon, looking at Polas in confusion. "What do you mean by virgin? What are we talking about here? *People*?" Something about this "blessing" business was filling Jon with a feeling of extreme dread.

"Yes, people. Well... slaves," agreed Polas with frown. "They are blessed, and if gods are happy, then is good. If not, more blessings until they are."

Jon's mouth was dry. Nathaniel was staring down at the map, jotting something down on a piece of paper, lost in thought. Obviously, the man had not come to the same realization that Jon had.

"Polas... by *blessing*... do you mean *sacrifice*?" he asked quietly. When the old man stared at him blankly, Jon realized he didn't understand the word.

Nathaniel looked up with his forehead creased and hazel eyes on Polas.

"Do these people die?" asked Jon quietly.

"Yes," said the old fisherman with a bitter laugh. "With much blood for the gods."

~

After moving quickly away from the tattooed slaves, Baltsaros and Tom made their way out of the marketplace and back onto the main thoroughfare. They ducked behind a small structure, and Baltsaros rubbed the silk scarf in the dirt to dull the colours to an almost uniform tan. He then draped it over the first mate's shoulder and under his arm, turning it into a sling; the fake injury would work to hide the map of the spires on Tom's rib cage.

From this close, the big man smelled of nervous sweat, and it *pulled* at something inside Baltsaros. As they stood hidden from view, the captain placed a hand over Tom's heart, dismayed by how fast it was going. Tom leaned into his touch and let out a shuddery sigh.

"I'm sorry, Da. There's just so many," whispered Tom. "I'll be ok. I just need to stop..." The first mate shook his head, his sea-green eyes unfocused. "Did ye see their backs? Da, if somethin' happens to ye... an' I'm here..." A shiver ran through Tom's body, his heart racing beneath Baltsaros's palm.

"Listen to me, Tom. Nothing will happen to me. To us. Nothing, do you understand me?" murmured the captain, reaching up to touch Tom's cheek, a brief, soft caress before he adjusted the sling and stepped back. "Now... get a hold of yourself." Without warning, he smacked Tom across the cheek he had cupped tenderly only a moment earlier.

Tom's head snapped to the side with a grunt. When he turned back to the captain, the first mate's eyes crackled with blue-green fire.

"That's better," said Baltsaros with a nod.

With a soft chuckle, Tom knuckled the red mark on his face and nodded back.

"All right. I'm ok. I've got yer back, Da," said the first mate, straightening his shoulders. "Head on the prize... Let's find out where the gold's at an' get the fuck outta here, aye?"

Baltsaros's eyes turned to the closest pyramid.

"Yes," he said quietly. "Gold."

~

Head aching and reeling with the knowledge that they were dealing with a civilization, if it could even be called one, that relied on the death of dozens of people a week just to plan their activities, Jon made his way numbly down the stairs. Not only was fishing dictated by human sacrifice, but harvest, beer-making...

Laundry days for fuck's sake! he thought angrily, pulling open the door to his quarters. The most distressing part of all this was that the captain *knew* about the blood rituals and hadn't said anything to anyone.

There was a soft noise and Jon's head turned. Standing next to the open chest at the foot of the bed was Oren. The boy was frozen in place, a guilty flush on his face.

"What the *fuck* are you doing?" growled Jon, balling his fists. "Get the fuck away from there!"

Recovering quickly from his surprise, Oren straightened and smiled coyly.

"Oh, I thought I leave something in here the other day," said the tall youth, his clear blue eyes narrowed at Jon. "When I was *with* your captain."

There was no doubt in Jon's mind what the young fisherman meant when he had sneered the word. Before he had a chance to warn Oren that he was in no mood to be fucked with, the younger man continued.

"Oh, yes. Your captain, he did me. Did me hard and good," cooed the willowy youth. "He says I was like a perfect one."

With a strangled cry Jon leapt forward, intent on grabbing Oren. The young fisherman darted backwards with a laugh, evading Jon's grasp.

He couldn't understand why Oren was purposefully baiting him like this, but he was suddenly past all caring; the anxiety and anger of the past few days gave life to a crazed demon that took over Jon's body. When he lashed out to hit Oren, and the fisherman tried to jump backwards again, Jon let out a dark laugh as the youth's head hit the wall behind him. Oren was trapped, and his blue eyes widened with that realization. Hands up in supplication, the tall young man shook his head at Jon.

"It's... ah... it's joke," said Oren, his Common failing him as his predicament began to infuse real fear into him.

Jon's fists connected with the younger man's abdomen, first the right, then the left, doubling Oren over in a pained gasp. Fingers snarling in the fisherman's long white dreadlocks, Jon dragged the other forward and kneed him solidly in the face.

Oren collapsed on the floor with a groan, curling into a ball. Jon could hear him whining softly in his native tongue, the only word that he understood being "please".

"Shut it," yelled Jon, his chest heaving and eyes burning. "Shut the fuck up, you little shit. You think the captain would want *you?* Do you? I will break your godsdamned hands if you ever fucking touch him. Did you touch him? *Did you?*" He delivered a hard kick to the boy's side, eliciting a satisfying grunt. Kicking Oren again, Jon smiled. He was glad that he was wearing boots.

"I think I changed my mind," Jon said, his voice a low growl. "I want you to beg. Come on, boy... beg for your life."

Below him, Oren began to sob.

~

The open square that fronted the stepped pyramid was empty save for a few slaves that carried bundles on their heads as they made their way to one of the side streets. Baltsaros stood looking up at the stone structure for a long time, his arms crossed over his chest.

With interest, the captain saw that the pyramid, wider than it was tall, had gutters running down its steps that disappeared under the flat stones at the base of it. When he leaned down to peer thoughtfully at one of the gutters, he could see that it was stained dark brown; in fact, everywhere the paving stones met across the square, there was a thick, dried residue. He spied holes placed in the ground at regular intervals, and a fascinating picture began forming in Baltsaros's head.

"It reeks like the bloody pit o' hells, Da," said Tom nervously, his nose wrinkled. "What the fuck is this place?"

"I'm not sure," lied Baltsaros, looking around. It didn't seem like any sacrifices would be performed today, unless they happened after dark. Dusk was falling, and it was a shame that they had to leave so soon.

"I don't like this," muttered Tom, rubbing his thumb against the side of his jaw. "Not one bloody bit."

With a nod and a sigh, Baltsaros motioned for Tom to follow him. They would come back tomorrow; tonight he would ask Polas more about the sacrifices, specifically about when they normally happened.

As the captain and first mate made their way slowly back towards the main gate, Baltsaros was surprised to see that not many were walking in the same direction as they were.

"Ye'd think the street would be packed with folks leavin'," said Tom, echoing the captain's misgivings.

When they reached the gate, the reason was instantly apparent for the lack of foot traffic: the giant doors were closed and barred.

"Excuse me," Baltsaros said, stepping over to one of the guards. "Why is the gate closed?"

The tall man looked the captain up and down before answering, his mouth hidden behind a black cloth.

"Curfew."

After thanking the guard for the curt answer, Baltsaros turned to Tom. The first mate was staring at him with a distraught look in his eyes; the sight of such weakness in the big man brought about a strange twist of worry in his own gut.

"What d'he say, Da?" asked Tom quietly, his jaw tight and nostrils slightly flared.

"The gate's shut for the night, Tom," replied Baltsaros, wishing he could put his arms around the big man to reassure him; the tremors that shook Tom at the captain's words were noticeable even from a distance in the failing light. "Come, my boy. Let's find somewhere to sleep, shall we?"

~

Jon was about to kick Oren in the side again when he was pulled backwards by hard hands. With a yelp, Jon landed solidly against the corner of the heavy table and fell to his knees on the rug. Before he had a chance to bring a hand up, a big fist connected with his jaw, and his world exploded in a flash of light and pain. The whimper he let out was followed by a retch when his mouth filled with blood; opening his eyes in confusion, Jon saw that Migri stood above him, his face distorted in fury.

"My son," said the big fisherman, pointing a thick-knuckled finger at Jon. "My son!" repeated Migri with a shout when Jon made no reply. The man's Common was extremely poor; Jon knew that he couldn't communicate beyond a few simple words here and there. However, he quickly realized that even if he could explain the situation, it wouldn't make the slightest difference to Oren's father. All he cared about was that someone was attacking his son.

Oren spoke rapidly to his father as he slowly got to his feet. With some fatalistic satisfaction, Jon saw that the younger man's face was a mess of bruises, and his nose was a swollen, squashed-looking thing that leaked blood down Oren's chin. At least if he was going to die at the hands of Migri, he had done some permanent damage to the son. Served the little bastard right.

Gods, who am I becoming? he thought in alarm.

Body singing with the buzz of adrenaline, Jon crouched low trying to gauge whether he'd be able to take down Migri with a leg-sweep and grapple. It could be a thoroughly pointless endeavour; even if he managed to get the upper hand on Migri, it would leave him open to retaliation by Oren. Gritting his teeth, Jon tried desperately to come up with a plan of attack.

"Oi there," said Calum from the open doorway. "Let th' boy alone." The old pirate limped into the room, his eyes darting from Migri to Jon with his face set in serious lines. After staring hard at Jon for a moment, Calum motioned with a gnarled hand for him to stay down.

"It's my fault," said Jon between clenched teeth. "I should have kept my head."

"Should'a, would'a... lad," said Calum, holding his hands up as he approached the big fisherman. "Migri. Stop now... peace, aye? D'ye understand that? *Peace*? C'mon, let's all be takin' a breath o' fresh air, aye, mates? Get yer hot heads out in th' open t' work things out—" Before Calum could finish, Migri stepped forward with a roar and smashed his fist into the old man's nose with an audible crack.

Even before he dropped to the ground, Jon somehow knew that Calum was dead.

With a hoarse sob, Jon sprang to his feet, his hand darting to the knife he kept at his belt. In an instant he was on Migri, knocking the bigger man to the ground and straddling him as bucked and struggled. In an almost dreamlike state, Jon watched his hand come down, strange and slow, and drive the knife point-first into the fisherman's eye; there was little resistance when it sunk into Migri's brain right down to the hilt.

Jon went numb as the body beneath him twitched twice and went still. There was a loud keening noise in his ears, and he blinked slowly trying to clear his head.

Calum is dead.

The room spun and darkened. Jon stared at the blood on the hand still wrapped around the handle of the knife.

Calum is dead and it's my fault.

The keening had stopped, and Jon looked around in confusion. After getting to his feet shakily, he walked over to the basin. It would be ok. It would be all right. Maybe Calum wasn't dead. Maybe he hadn't just killed a man. Maybe he was asleep in his bed, safe against Baltsaros or Tom's side. He leaned over the basin and vomited, the bile burning the shallow cut in his mouth. Maybe if he closed his eyes, everything would go back to normal, but he gagged again, remembering the way the blade slid into the man's brain like a hot knife into butter.

Breathing deeply, Jon pulled himself away from the basin, wiping his mouth on his wrist. The front of his pants was wet where he had pissed himself.

Calum is dead and this isn't a dream. And, oh gods, I killed him.

Jon walked unsteadily to the crumpled form of the old sailor and sank to his knees on the rug. The motion caused him to realize that he was in extreme pain; his ribs throbbed with his heartbeat and screamed with every breath. He wouldn't be surprised if one or more were broken. With a shaky hand, he touched Calum's neck, searching for a pulse. However, the way that the old man stared sightlessly at the ceiling was enough to kill any hope of finding one.

When he heard someone approach, Jon froze, instinctively knowing who it was. With his heart redoubling its already frantic pace, he raised his eyes and met the wide, wet stare of the man standing above him.

With a shudder, Jon held out a hand to Polas, the word "please" on his lips.

CHAPTER 11

A WILLING SLAVE

Tom followed the captain in the direction of an inn that someone had been kind enough to point out to them. Eyes on his feet, the first mate breathed in time to his walking: one inhale for every three steps, one exhale for every four. His jaw was clenched so tight that his back teeth had started aching, but he couldn't relax. The collar felt like a noose around his neck, like it was tightening, but there would be no reprieve tonight since he'd have to sleep with the fucking thing on.

Stumbling against Baltsaros when the man stopped suddenly at the door of the inn, Tom clutched at the captain to steady himself and let out a pained grunt when his hand was grabbed and twisted. Wrist bent at sharp angle, Tom looked up at Baltsaros, his chest so tight he could barely breathe.

"Watch where you're going and don't touch me," Baltsaros hissed quietly. "People are looking at you. Say 'Apologies, Master'."

"Apologies... Master," repeated Tom in the Balorian tongue, the words like broken glass in his mouth. He shuddered and almost let out a groan when the captain released him.

I need a bloody drink.

Baltsaros's dark eyes held his a moment longer, not a shred of sympathy on his chiselled face, before turning to open the door. Miserable, Tom passed through the doorway behind the captain with his head held low.

The room they walked into was brightly lit and the hewn boards smooth and clean under Tom's bare feet. All around him, the first mate could hear the sounds of talking and laughing, but he didn't dare raise his eyes. The last thing Tom wanted to see were free men enjoying themselves. The big man swallowed back his ire and just stood quietly by Baltsaros's side, chewing on the inside of his cheek while the captain waited to speak to the proprietor.

It was as if, by putting on the collar and stepping into this gods-blasted world of slavers, Tom was taken back to the hells that five years with the captain had finally started erasing from his soul. All the anger, frustration, pain and fear... yes, fear, was creeping back under his skin like stinging poison, but here he could not spit in his master's eye. He couldn't crack his fist against any slave-lover who stared at him. No... He had to play the part of the obedient slave, and it was making him physically ill.

Not *once* in the decade he had served as a hard labourer in the mines, as an unwilling bed slave for anyone who could pay, or as a bare-knuckle fighter in the pits, had Tom bowed or scraped to any man. They had beaten him senseless over and over, but the only thing that had kept him going was his refusal to submit willingly. He had fought them every step of the way, and he had never broken.

No—that was just the lie he kept telling himself.

Tom felt nauseous.

It was a whip—a thick, black leather bullwhip—that had finally made him beg and weep. His flesh had been torn over and over into gory ribbons. He remembered the way his master had cracked the whip beside him, pausing, laughing, taking his time like he was courting a lover; Tom had been kept on edge, never sure when it would slice into him, and it had become the living fear that poisoned him still. Sometimes, he had been tied up for days, the smell of his festering wounds ripe in his nose.

Tom licked his lips and swayed slightly, remembering the way he had screamed until his voice was no more.

"Is your slave ill?" asked a man from somewhere close by.

Tom slowly glanced up, frowning.

Eyes down ye fuckin' worthless piece of shit, so help me gods, I'll cut yer cock off at the root, said his master, standing over him, pants undone.

He blinked the memory away.

"I don't want him contaminating the other slaves in the barn if he's sick," continued the fat man with the curly beard and dirty apron. The proprietor stared at the first mate with a worried look on his ruddy face, and Tom quickly looked back down again, glaring at the floor between his feet.

"The barn?" asked Baltsaros. Tom could hear a smile in the older man's voice, and he could see the captain's look of polite confusion in his mind's eye.

"Yes, sir, we have a sturdy barn out back where we keep the slaves for the night. They're all chained apart so there won't be any damage to your goods. Though with this fella... Well, he looks like he could take a lick and not be worse for wear, hey?" said the fat man with a chuckle. "Do you fight him in the ring ever? I'd put good money..." The man's voice droned on cheerfully.

Tom's head spun.

Sleepin' in the barn chained to the wall like a dog surrounded by slaves chained to the fuckin' wall like bloody dogs...

"I'm afraid I have to insist that he stay in my room," said the captain, cutting off the proprietor as the man started quoting prices for slave accommodation.

Tom closed his eyes.

"That's... an unusual request," said the man slowly. "I assure you, sir, your chattel will remain unmolested if that's what you're worried about. My personal guarantee."

Tom balled his fists and held his tongue.

"It is a question of the quality of my sleep," replied the captain, his tone amicably apologetic yet firm. "I rest better with him in the room. I hope you understand. It is by no means a slight to your establishment; I am simply accustomed to having him watch over me while I sleep. I hope this won't be a problem? He is fiercely loyal, I assure you."

Tom heard the sound of money clinking and let out a slow, quiet breath. Spared. Saved. But not free yet.

After the captain made arrangements for some food to be sent to the room, he beckoned for Tom to follow him. They went up the narrow staircase and down one side of a long hallway to a wooden door marked with a symbol that Tom didn't recognize. Following Baltsaros into the room, he looked around. A narrow bed, a wooden chair next to a low shelf mounted on the far wall, and a chamber pot in the corner.

Shitty accommodations, but at least they were away from prying eyes. He pulled off the makeshift sling, flexing his arm as he watched Baltsaros walk over to sit down on the edge of the bed. The captain looked hard at him, his face set in serious lines.

Now that they were alone, Tom felt a little better. It was just an act, after all. Just a stupid piece of metal around his neck. Jaw clenched tight, Tom rubbed the back of his head; when his fingers made contact with the slave collar, he felt his skin crawl.

With a grunt, Tom dropped down to his knees and put his knuckles to the floor; straightening his legs behind him, he began doing quick press-ups.

"What are you doing?" asked the captain.

"What does it look like I'm bloody doin'?" replied Tom curtly. The exercise felt good; his muscles were stiff from tension, and he was full of nervous energy. He wanted a drink or a smoke, but he figured this would have to do.

"Tom, I'm sorry," said Baltsaros quietly.

The words stopped the first mate in mid-lift, and he looked up at the captain. Baltsaros was staring at him with a thoughtful look on his face, his stark brows low over his eyes, hooding them in shadow.

Tom frowned and nodded, looking back at the floor between his hands as he continued his press-ups with a grunt. *Sorry...*

"I didn't know it would be so hard on you," said the captain matter-of-factly.

Tom felt a flash of anger and let himself up on his knees, glaring at Baltsaros in disbelief.

"What fuckin' part of 'I don't fuckin' want to do it' did ye not understand, Da?" asked the first mate, shaking his head. He stared wide-eyed at the captain a moment longer; the older man was silent and expressionless, a sun-darkened hand slowly stroking his greying beard.

Tom fell back on his ass to start doing some sit-ups, the boards hard against the knobs of his spine. Baltsaros was the smartest person he knew, yet he blew Tom away with how frustratingly bloody *clueless* he was at times. Breathing deep as he felt his stomach muscles begin to burn, Tom closed his eyes and worked on clearing his mind.

There was a knock at the door, and Tom heard the captain get up from the bed to cross the room. When Baltsaros kicked softly at the first mate's shin a moment later, Tom opened his eyes and saw that the older man was holding a plate with two trenchers in one hand and an earthenware mug in the other.

"I'm not hungry," Tom lied, sitting up.

"Now you're acting like a fool, Tom," said the captain with a small smile as he sank down gracefully to the floor next to him.

When his stomach growled in response to the sight of food, Tom jutted out his bottom jaw and accepted the trencher from the captain with a scowl. The hard loaf of bread was hollowed and filled with some meaty stew; it smelled absolutely bloody delicious.

"Here," said the captain, handing the mug to Tom. "Have it all. It's yours."

Tom let out a derisive snort and took a deep swallow of the dark beer.

"Ye are, are ye?" he asked, taking a big bite of the bread and stew. "Yer *sorry?*"

Though his eyes were narrowed at the captain, Tom's anger and frustration had begun to dissolve as the food and beer worked their magic on him. He sighed and shook his head.

"Hells... Listen... This is just doin' some really shitty things to my head. Can't think straight. Rememberin' things," he explained, gesturing with his mug as he chewed a savoury mouthful. After washing it down with some more beer, Tom licked the side of the bread to catch a drop of gravy before it fell. "Somethin' about this place gives me the bloody willies. I got ants in my skin. This ain't helpin'." Tom flicked a nail against the side of the collar. "Keep yer bloody sorrys to yerself."

The captain remained strangely quiet as he sat cross-legged beside Tom, his dark eyes just watching the first mate as he ate.

"Aint'cha eatin', Da?" asked Tom, licking his fingers when he had finished his trencher. The captain looked down at the bread in his hand and broke it in two, careful not to spill any of the stew that was soaked into it. After handing one half to Tom, Baltsaros took a bite out of his.

Tom frowned. Maybe this place was doing weird things to the both of them.

"Why're we even here, Da?" he asked quietly. "Why'd we come? I mean... adventure is grand, gold is better, but is that really why?"

Baltsaros blinked slowly, chewing the last of his meal carefully.

"I need to be here," said the captain after he had swallowed, his eyes losing focus for a moment as he stared off across the room. The older man's brow creased again, and he lifted his hand to brush the crumbs out of his moustache before turning his eyes back to the first mate. "Jon's dreams, your tattoo, the similarity of the language to my mother tongue." Baltsaros accepted the mug from Tom and took a small sip before handing it back. "I'm not normally given to fanciful thoughts, but doesn't it seem like too much of a coincidence?"

The words poured a cold trickle of dread down Tom's back, but before he could think of an answer, Baltsaros waved away the question and rose to his feet.

"It's not important. Ignore me, Tom," muttered the captain, looking down at the first mate with a frown. "There's something else we need to take care of."

Curious, the first mate watched the captain stride quickly to the door to pull the lock and, after a moment's hesitation, drag the chair over to wedge it under the latched handle.

Baltsaros then crossed the room back to the bed where he sank down and folded his hands in his lap. For a few heartbeats, the captain just stared back at Tom, his face unreadable.

Then he spoke in a soft voice.

"Slave, stand and strip," said Baltsaros.

The words were like a stinging slap. Frowning at the captain, Tom shook his head slowly.

"Da, that ain't fuckin' funny," he said.

Baltsaros tilted his head slightly and raised an eyebrow.

"You're wearing a slave collar, aren't you? So stand and strip, *slave*," repeated the captain, his voice now a low growl.

"I said that's not funny," growled Tom back. However, somewhere buried in his annoyance was a soft pulse of lust, and he felt disgusted at himself.

"I fail to understand how this differs from what I normally ask of you, Tom," murmured Baltsaros. The older man's eyes were dark chips of glass in his stark face. "You *are* my slave, are you not?"

"No... what?" asked Tom in growing alarm. What in the hells was the matter with the captain?

"Call me Master," sneered Baltsaros. "Now strip. Your body is mine, *slave*. Do as you're told."

The words... a familiar command... twisted. Tom felt dirty and betrayed.

"Don't call me that," snarled Tom. "An' I sure as shit ain't callin' you 'Master'."

At this, Baltsaros's expression shifted, the cold glare replaced instantly with curiosity.

"Because I am *not* your master?" asked the captain softly, raising his eyebrows. Baltsaros's bowed lips quirked up at the corners in something that was not quite a smile.

Tom let out a short grunt in reply, eyes fierce as he stared up at the older man.

"Yet you call me 'Da', and I am no more your father than I am your master."

"That's different," was all that Tom could think of saying.

"Tom, come closer," said Baltsaros with a sigh.

The first mate looked at his captain suspiciously before climbing to his feet. He took a step forward and crossed his arms over his chest, not understanding what in the hells was expected of him.

Sure he called Baltsaros "Da" but... He cleared his throat and shook his head.

"Listen, I call ye that because yer good to me. It started as a lark to get under

Abetha's skin, aye, but... yer..." Tom closed his mouth, crushing his lips together tight as he breathed quickly through his nose. This was harder to explain than he had expected. "Ye mean... uh... to me—bloody hells, Baltsaros... there's no higher word I can think of... so yer my Da. And... since ye've never minded..."

He looked desperately at Baltsaros; he knew it was a ridiculous thing to call the man he'd been fucking for years. It sounded more than a little perverted but, really, who cared?

"Tom... you'd do *anything* for me, wouldn't you? Even pose as a slave though it's obviously hurting you to do so?" asked Baltsaros softly. "Come closer and kneel."

Tom stepped forward and went down on one knee and then the other. Baltsaros reached out a hand and touched his hair, the captain's hand then sliding down the side of Tom's face. With a sigh, the big man leaned into the touch and frowned. The new gentleness that Jon had brought out in Baltsaros pricked at the scar tissue in his heart, but he clung to it like a man drowning.

"Aye, Da," said the first mate with a small nod. "Ye know I would."

"Then, how are you *not* my slave, if you obey me so?" asked Baltsaros, stroking his thumb along Tom's cheek. "Why, when I set you free, did you decide to pledge your body and soul to my happiness? You bind yourself to me... Tom, I need you, but *why do you need me?*"

Tom's eyes had closed slowly with the captain's caress, but at the renewed slave talk, he stared up in dismay at the man he loved. The captain sat quietly with his warm hand against Tom's face, a deep crease marking his smooth brow. The first mate let out a slow breath and placed his hands on Baltsaros's thighs, lowering his forehead down to the man's knee. He lay there just breathing quietly as Baltsaros's fingers tickled gently through the hair at his nape.

Even in the early days when Tom was no more than a miserable bastard with fresh scars, a limp, and something to prove, he had stayed. He had obeyed. He had watched the captain and learned that he was beholden to a man like no other. The iron fist that Baltsaros led with was tucked into a satin glove lined with the softest fur. Men looked up to the captain; they praised his fairness and feared his anger. They emulated his grace, refinement, and unshakeable self-confidence; they bowed their heads in loyalty and vied for his attention.

Then, when Tom had stolen into the captain's bed of his own volition, he had discovered that the man expertly mixed pain and pleasure in a way that had left him stunned and breathless.

From that day forward, Tom was simply Baltsaros's.

"Ye don't need to ask me that," Tom murmured against the captain's leg. Baltsaros's fingers paused in their tickling caress for a moment, one soft finger tracing the edge of the metal collar that bound him before sliding beneath it, pulling the metal tight against Tom's throat. Suddenly, it was like the captain was touching a raw wound inside him, and he felt himself shudder. Fear and anger bloomed. *Humiliation.*

The touch was possessive, and it felt more cruel than anything Baltsaros had ever done to him.

"Don't..." choked Tom. *Stop touching it.* The hand didn't move, and Tom balled his fists to either side of the captain's thighs.

"I've never thought of you as a lesser man for submitting to me, Tom," said Baltsaros, tugging harder on the collar.

Tom groaned softly, his eyes clenched tight. His heart hammered, and he felt a trickle of sweat make its way down his spine. Despite himself, Tom realized he was getting aroused, and it confused him. Why was Baltsaros doing this to him?

"It pleases me to no end that you indulge and actually *enjoy* my predilection for violence. The problem is that it never occurred to me that I failed in freeing you completely. I left the job unfinished," continued the captain almost conversationally.

Tom opened his eyes and watched as Baltsaros pushed aside the hem of his tunic, long fingers deftly undoing the laces at his groin.

"This," said the older man, slipping a second finger between metal and skin, "is not a cage. Nor is it a sentence. You have nothing to fear from it." The captain yanked Tom's head up using the collar, Baltsaros's face oddly serene as he freed his cock from the confines of his leather pants.

"Ye want my pride? Ye want to strip me of that?" breathed Tom hoarsely, his eyes on the captain's hand stroking the thick, veined shaft. Baltsaros's hold on the slave collar felt obscene, but it did nothing to slow the desire that had begun to unfurl inside him.

"I already have your pride, Tom," asserted the captain, staring down at the younger man. "Look at you. I have you by the throat, but you can pull away from me at any time. I've never forced you to do anything. Everything you do is freely offered. Tom, do you *know* what this collar symbolizes?" Baltsaros tugged softly at the metal tight around Tom's throat with a smile. "This is your trust in me."

Tom opened his mouth to deny it but shut it a second later, mute with bewilderment. Testing Baltsaros's words, the first mate pulled back out of the captain's grasp easily and sat back on his heels, his head spinning. Baltsaros's hand had stopped moving over his length, and he laughed at the expression on Tom's face.

"You laid your head and heart at my feet, my gorgeous brute, and I broke your trust. But here you are, wearing your trust for me, plain as day," murmured Baltsaros, his dark eyes fond as he watched Tom.

"Trust?" said Tom softly, one hand turning the metal around his neck. His thoughts touched briefly on the day he had been lashed to the mast. It felt like a lifetime ago. "Aye, Da, I trust ye."

"All right then, so trust me, listen to my words," replied the older man. "You are mine, and you are free..." He motioned for Tom to stand.

"*Slave*, stand and strip," said the captain again, his face serious.

This time, however, the words carried less sting. *Trust.* Tom narrowed his eyes at the captain and then let out a quiet laugh.

He could scarcely believe it. In the middle of this godsforsaken slavers' city, surrounded by men who would see them dead for sharing a little spit and cum, the captain was unambiguously inviting him to play... using the collar and some meaningless words as props. It was ridiculous, and it was freeing.

"Ye mean to break me?" asked Tom playfully, testing the waters. "*Master?*" No, not yet meaningless; the word still felt sharp on his tongue, but he understood what Baltsaros intended now. It was time to give new meaning to the words he'd carried for so long like burns etched into his heart, time to make them mean something positive, like the deep trust that he knew existed between the two of them. Hells, it was worth a shot.

"I mean to have your hide if you don't obey me," sneered Baltsaros as he leaned back on the bed on one elbow, his hand sliding once more along the half-hard cock jutting from his unlaced pants.

Eyes following his master's hand, Tom nodded and unbuttoned his trousers, a *willing* slave.

And he grinned.

~

Baltsaros looked down at Tom, sleeping on his side on the hard floor next to the bed. Their union had been quick, satisfying, and completely necessary. The captain only hoped that it had been enough to reassure the stubborn first mate and dull some of the negative associations he had. The whip would be a harder one, but, in time, Baltsaros thought he could cure Tom entirely of those fears. He needed the first mate to be his normal, capable, ruthless self.

Until Jon manages to make the both of us soft, he mused with a frown.

Lying flat on the narrow bed, Baltsaros stared up at the ceiling, thinking of his own past. How strange that the three of them, all essentially orphans, had wound up on the same path. Not only that, but Tom, Jon, and he himself had suffered one type of abuse or another for a long period of their lives. Closing his eyes, Baltsaros wondered if their scars would ever totally disappear and whether there was a physical aspect of them somewhere hidden inside their bodies that would match up if pressed together. It was one of those thoughts that often drifted through his head in the last minutes before he fell asleep. Absurd thoughts.

At the sound of a loud commotion in the hallway, Baltsaros sat up, tense and fully awake. He looked over and saw that the first mate had risen into a crouch, his eyes trained on the door.

"*Fire!*"

Boots thundered by their room, and Baltsaros quickly pulled on his own before lacing himself up. Tom stood with his back against the wall next to the door; he slowly opened it a crack and peered out. There were more calls of fire, and some angry yells as more men ran down the narrow hallway.

"Do you smell smoke?" asked Baltsaros quietly, tying the sash around his waist.

Tom frowned, nodding his head as he kept his eyes on the corridor. A moment later, the big man let out a startled grunt and pulled away from the door as a figure burst in. In seconds, Tom had the intruder down on the floor, one hand wrapped in the man's cloak, the other balled in a fist above his head.

"Tom! It's me, you idiot."

"Jon?" Tom dropped his hand and blinked in surprise.

Jon pulled the bunched fabric out from Tom's fist and tried to sit up, pushing back on the stunned man's chest.

"C'mon. Let's get out of here," said Jon, brushing himself off as he stood assisted by a grinning Tom. "We've only got about ten minutes before the guard at the side gate changes, and the next one's not amenable to bribes."

"You started a fire as a diversion?" asked Baltsaros, confused. The younger man nodded.

"I needed the cover to get you out," explained Jon quietly.

"That-a boy, Jonny!" said the first mate, playfully punching him on the shoulder.

However, when Jon pulled the hood away from his face, the captain felt a burst of fury erupt in his chest. The young man's jaw was mottled with fresh bruising, and his eyes were red-rimmed.

"Something's happened," said Jon in a faint voice, his eyes sliding away from Baltsaros's with an expression the captain couldn't read. "I'll explain on the way. Let's go."

Baltsaros and Tom shared a look before they took off after the young man in the cloak, the same apprehension mirrored on their faces. Unfortunately, in their hurry to follow Jon through the panicking crowd, the men missed the figure that watched them closely, clear blue eyes narrowed in keen interest.

CHAPTER 12
WEAKNESS

Baltsaros stared down for a long time at the two bodies lying on the deck. Both men had been placed on pieces of unbleached sailcloth, waiting only for the shrouds to be sewn shut. Jon knew that the decision to give Migri a proper sea burial wouldn't be a popular one, but he didn't care. He was responsible for the man's death.

"I screwed up, and it cost Calum his life," he said softly. In death, Calum looked small and shrunken, the fire and good humour of life leached out of him by one well-placed punch. "If I had kept my temper. Shit—" Jon looked down at his feet and rubbed his forehead, unable to finish. He could hear Tom's low curses as the first mate paced back and forth behind him. Baltsaros had long ago warned him that rash actions had deadly consequences. If only he had stepped back. Taken a breath. If only...

The captain knelt slowly and touched the old man's face. Turning it to the side, Baltsaros let out a sigh and shook his head; it was obvious even to Jon that the bridge of Calum's nose had been forced into his skull.

"At least he probably didn't feel it," said Baltsaros, standing up. "What an absurd way to die. That punch was pure chance; Migri's a drunk, not a skilled fighter." The captain's face was devoid of expression, but Jon thought he could detect sadness in the way Baltsaros's eyes swept over the corpse of the old man again. The captain put his hand against Jon's back; it felt gentle and warm through his thin shirt.

"Stop beating yourself up over this," the older man said softly. "What's done is done. I, for one, am incredibly thankful that Calum was there. Had he not stepped in, Migri would have undoubtedly hurt you further. Now," Baltsaros turned to him, his dark eyes on Jon's. "How long has Oren been gone?"

Jon furrowed his brow. The past few hours felt surreal, like a waking nightmare.

"Two, three hours. Maybe more. I... I don't know if he took off right after—" *...after I sank a blade into his father...* "After everything," he continued, his voice hoarse. "The ship's been scoured, and men went out to the jungle to look. No trace of him."

Baltsaros's lips worked against each other, a curse unspoken, and he nodded.

"Why the *fuck* hasn't 'e been chucked off the side like the piece o' shit 'e is!" growled Tom, jabbing a finger towards the fisherman's body. The first mate's shoulders were high, and he rocked forward on the balls of his feet, fury and anguish barely contained. Tom's eyes were wide and red-rimmed as he rubbed his nose, the muscles twitching in his strong jaw.

"I *killed* him, Tom. I killed him for trying to stop me from beating the shit out of his son," said Jon in anguish. "This is so fucked up. I just... with Polas—" Jon pressed the back of his hand against his lips, holding back the sob that was threatening to erupt from him.

"Aye. Where is that sack o' shit? I'll cut 'im down like I'm gonna cut down tha' bloody l'il fawnin' twat when I find 'im so 'elp me fuckin' gods," choked Tom, his agitation further roughening his accent.

The captain placed a calming hand on Tom's shoulder, leaning in to say something quietly to the first mate; Tom pressed his lips hard together and nodded stiffly in response, sniffing once and wiping at his nose again before turning to walk away.

Baltsaros's eyes were gentle when he looked back at Jon.

"Where is Polas?"

~

Baltsaros stood next to Jon in his quarters, watching the old fisherman through the bars of the cage. Polas lay on the narrow cot, fast asleep.

"You locked him in here after he attacked you?" asked Baltsaros frowning as he turned to look at the young man beside him. Jon's face was drawn and pale, and he held onto his biceps as he stared forward. "Jon?"

Blinking quickly, Jon turned his head to the captain; Baltsaros could see that Jon was in pain by the way he winced as he took a deep breath.

"What? No, he's not locked in," said Jon, and he pulled on the door to demonstrate; it swung open silently on oiled hinges. "He just wanted a place to... mourn. Alone. I guess. I gave him some sleeping powder. I hope that's all right? I didn't know where else to put him."

With a nod, Baltsaros reached out for Jon's arm and pulled him back towards the bed so they would not disturb the old man.

"I was sure he was going to kill me, Baltsaros. He was crying. But... he just lifted me up and hugged me. I killed his son, and he was comforting *me*," said Jon, shaking his head in a dazed way. He lifted his arms up obligingly when Baltsaros pulled up on his shirt, breathing out a soft groan as he did so.

The captain let out a sound of dismay as he saw the damage to Jon's side. Over his ribs, like a dark splash of paint, was a large contusion. Pressing on the area brought

399

out a pained gasp from Jon, but Baltsaros thought only one rib might be fractured, with a few more badly bruised.

"Did he say anything at all?" asked the captain, referring to Polas. Jon turned his head back towards the cage, his face grey-tinged with pain and exhaustion.

Jon's brows came together over his stormy eyes.

"He said something about not being able to save Migri after all and that I shouldn't feel bad about doing the work of the gods," said Jon, wincing when Baltsaros touched the bruise on his jaw.

"Are you hurt anywhere else?" The captain pulled back his hand and turned to the armoire to get some salve and something to wrap around Jon to protect his ribs. With Migri dead, Oren missing, and Polas seeking no vengeance, his immediate concern was making sure that Jon was all right.

"No. I don't think so, no," said the dark-haired young man quietly. "Baltsaros, it *is* my fault. I just lost it. The thought of Oren *insinuating* himself into your arms..."

Baltsaros's eyes widened as he watched Jon blink back tears and turn to him, his pale face taut with sudden anger.

"Gods, tell me there is no truth to his claims," breathed Jon.

Head tilted in thought, the captain unrolled the wide piece of silk in his hands; would the truth serve him, or was he better off with a lie?

"Yes, and no," he replied, deciding on a partial truth. "I didn't seduce the boy, Jon. He came to me while I was sleeping and, thinking it was you, I kissed him. That was all. I sent him on his way once I realized the mistake. Now, hold your arms away from your sides so I can bind your ribs."

Though Jon moved to obey, Baltsaros didn't like the way that the sombre young man stared at him. He frowned and passed the stiff silk around Jon's ribs, his hands smoothing the material as he went.

"That's not the whole truth," whispered Jon, watching Baltsaros closely. "What aren't you telling me?"

The captain paused. Anger flashed through him, swiftly followed by a finger of unease. He resumed wrapping Jon in silence.

"What is the *whole* truth?" Jon asked, reaching up to stop Baltsaros's hand. "Tell me all of it for once in your damned life."

After pulling his fingers out of Jon's grasp so he could fasten the bandage, the captain straightened. The younger man stood looking at him quietly, waiting for him to answer.

It was infuriating. It was unnerving. It was also fascinating.

"How do you know I'm not telling you the whole truth, Jon?" he asked, pulling the stopper out of the small jar of salve.

Jon let out a short, bitter laugh.

"When have you ever?" said Jon. "No, that's not it. Call it a gut feeling. Call it the fact that Tom isn't as skilled a liar when he's covering for you. But you know what? Never mind. I don't even care about the substance of the lie. As sick as it makes me to think of you and that... that—no, the thing I care about is why you feel the need to lie to me at all. Do you think so little of me?"

Gods be damned, Jon. Baltsaros felt uncomfortably like he was being cornered. But... why *was* he lying? What would happen if he started telling Jon the truth? The *whole* truth, as Jon had put it. Would Baltsaros lose him?

It occurred to him then that he would lose Jon regardless if he continued to lie; the boy was starting to see through him more easily. It would only get worse with time.

The captain nodded to himself then cleared his throat.

"Weakness," Baltsaros said finally. He reached out to dab some salve on Jon's face. When he saw that Jon was blinking at him in mute confusion, he continued while smearing the ointment gently over Jon's jaw. "Weakness is the answer you're looking for. And I would thank you not to accuse me of disinterest." He frowned when he saw the tired skepticism in Jon's eyes. "Oren snuck into my bed. I was sure he was you. When I realized he wasn't, it was my intention to push him away; but the truth is, Jon, that I didn't. You have Tom to thank for the interruption. I'm honestly not sure how far it would have gone otherwise."

The truth.

Jon's face had pulled away from Baltsaros's hand as he spoke, blue-grey eyes wide with chagrin.

"It is weakness in that I didn't even try to control myself. It is weakness in that I am affected by your opinion of me. You matter very much to me, Jon, and I didn't want to lose you for a stupid mistake," the captain said softly. Leaning his hip on the edge of the table, he watched Jon curiously.

Jon stared at Baltsaros for a moment, his hands coming up to test the stiff material that bound him from nipple to navel before he turned away, shaking his head. When he looked back at the captain, his eyes were glassy.

"Maybe if I had known that, Oren's words would have meant less to me," whispered Jon.

Baltsaros almost groaned as he reached for the young man. Jon let himself be pulled forward, and he leaned into the captain with a slow exhale, his body tense with obvious pain.

"Oren was out to make trouble; it's as simple as that. He had no business being in our room and had I been the one to find him, he would have spent the night in the brig with my boot print decorating his backside," Baltsaros laughed bitterly as he gently stroked Jon's back. "Be angry at me for betraying your trust, but my honesty, or lack thereof, is not the cause of anyone's death. Not today. Put that out of your mind. Yes, Calum is dead. It is a sad thing indeed. I was rather fond of the old man; it's in great part because of him that I am who I am today. However, his death was an accident, and your reaction, involuntary. That is what I believe."

Baltsaros closed his eyes, remembering the muscular, dark-skinned man who had befriended the frail orphan that he had been. As always, there was no rhyme or reason to death. The thought made him frown again, his chest tight as he put his cheek against Jon's hair.

"Do you realize that you're lucky to be alive?" he whispered, tightening his fingers in the dark curls that hung past Jon's shoulders. "You mean so much to me."

Jon raised his head, his face wet with tears but his eyes serious.

"Do you really think it's a weakness to be affected by me?" he asked, his voice barely audible.

Baltsaros nodded.

"It *is* a weakness. A weakness that might one day be my undoing." The captain leaned forward to brush his lips over Jon's and was gratified when Jon sighed into the gentle, brief kiss. "I left you here to keep you safe and, by doing that, nearly lost you. You'll come with Tom and me when we go back tomorrow."

"We're going back?"

"Yes. If for nothing else, I'd like to see if we can find Oren. There's no telling what sort of trouble he could cause for us on the loose," said the captain, stroking Jon's uninjured cheek. Some of the colour had come back into Jon's face, an easing of his tension, but Baltsaros knew that he needed something to kill the pain and some uninterrupted sleep.

"Thank you for telling me the truth," said Jon, closing his eyes to Baltsaros's caress.

"Truth, Jon, is what you will get from me from now on. I promise. Ask me anything and I will tell you... but only ask me questions you want to know the answers to."

~

Despite the throbbing in his side and the way his jaw clicked sometimes when he moved it, Jon felt a tug deep inside him at Baltsaros's touch. The warm hand moved down his cheek to his neck where the captain's long fingers tickled the sensitive skin at his nape. At Baltsaros's words about truth, Jon had opened his eyes. The captain's starkly chiselled face was soft with emotion, and his dark-brown eyes looked at Jon as if he were a sacred object and not just a weary, beaten young man with too much pain in his soul.

Heart pounding high and swift in his throat, Jon realized that he believed Baltsaros. The man would tell him the truth.

The thought frightened him suddenly.

Sagging against the table when Baltsaros pulled away, Jon watched the captain mix up some sleeping powder with something he'd given Tom after one of his many fights with the rougher denizens of the *Heart*. Jon accepted the cup and peered into it curiously.

"It will lessen your pain," explained Baltsaros with a grim smile. "Sleeping on broken ribs is not a pleasant experience. I will lock the cage door on the off chance that Polas has a change of heart when he wakes up, but I'll leave a note explaining. If I know the old man, he will understand my reticence to have him loose given the circumstances. Now, drink."

Jon lifted the cup to his lips and drank down the bitter potion in a few swallows.

Yes, sleep; hopefully dreamless. Baltsaros took the cup and helped him onto the low bed before covering him with the dark-red blanket. Almost nauseous from fatigue as the last of his adrenaline left him, Jon closed his eyes.

～

Jon walked down a long marble hallway. The stone felt ice cold on his bare feet. To his left was the giant, black lion; to his right, the tawny wildcat. The two bracketed him like guards, and he was glad for their presence. At the far end of the corridor was a set of red and gold doors, the shape of a human heart burned into the painted and gilded wood. There was danger on the other side, Jon could feel it. Breathless, agonizing suffering.

But not for him.

In terror he watched the golden snakes slither from beneath the door and rear up to quickly bind the legs of his companions with their muscular, sinuous bodies, pulling the lion and cat down to the ground. Jon cried out as the snakes reared back and bit, working to bleed his protectors dry...

～

Jon jerked awake and let out a grunt as the motion caused his ribs to twinge. He felt disoriented and hot, and he pushed the blankets away. The spot next to him was empty, but he could hear Tom's snoring close by. As he eased himself up carefully, Jon looked around the darkened room. The door of the empty cage was ajar, and Polas was not in the room. Jon rose to his feet and felt around for the shirt hanging from the back of the chair nearest the bed. After pulling it on slowly, he approached the hammock that hung in the corner of the room.

Tom was passed out in a drunken sleep, his broad chest rising and falling slowly in the light of the moon. Jon reached out to place his hand on the first mate's warm skin, and he furrowed his brow, noticing that the man still wore his metal collar. Tom would have to keep up the ruse of being a slave for at least one more day. He hoped that when they had accomplished whatever it was the captain had set out to do, Tom would not have any new scars, emotional or otherwise. The first mate frowned and muttered something under his breath, turning his head away from Jon.

"Don't touch," mumbled Tom and let out a long, shuddering breath.

At first, Jon thought the first mate was talking to him, but when he said a few more unintelligible words, it was obvious he was still fast asleep. With a pang of sorrow, Jon wondered whom Tom was talking to in his dream. The captain? His former master? Someone who had abused him? With a sigh, Jon pulled the thin sheet over Tom's body, pressing down softly on the big man's shoulder before turning to go.

Outside, it was quiet, not a soul to be seen. Jon knew that if he were to walk from stern to bow, he might find a sailor here or there, passed out atop gunnysacks or slumped against a crate. After weeks of frigid weather, the warm summer nights drew the men outdoors; it was a welcome reprieve from the stuffy bunkrooms.

With a pang, Jon realized at that moment just how much he missed Katherine. While he was friendly with much of the crew, Jon had yet to spark up a close friendship like he'd had with the wisecracking pirate. Many a night like this, he and Katherine had sat, thick as thieves, passing a bottle back and forth just enjoying each other's company in the warm night breeze. He wondered if he would ever see her again.

He heard muffled voices from above and turned to look up at the quarterdeck. Side by side on the bench behind the ship's wheel sat Baltsaros and Polas talking quietly. Jon watched them for a moment, loath to disturb the two men. He had decided to return to bed when he heard the captain's voice call to him.

"Jon, come up."

He climbed the staircase, a little nervous to be in the old fisherman's presence again. However, when he reached the top, Polas just smiled at him sadly. No, the old man did not harbour any bad feelings about his son's death. In fact, to Jon's keen senses, it seemed as though Polas was glad that something was over.

After lurching tiredly to his feet, the old fisherman patted Jon on the shoulder before he bid the captain and him goodnight.

"How are your ribs?" asked Baltsaros, watching Polas descend the stairs.

Jon put a hand to his side.

"Sore as hells. But I'll live," he said with a small smile. "Why are you still awake?"

The captain's brows pinched together, and he looked down at his hands, his lips parted in a slow exhale.

"I could not sleep, Jon," said Baltsaros softly. "I tried, briefly. But I find my mind unable to rest. Polas woke up, and we came up here not to disturb you or Tom." He raised his head, and Jon was alarmed to see that Baltsaros wore an expression he had never seen on the man before. The captain looked lost. "What have I done by bringing us here, Jon?"

Jon felt a sliver of fear pierce his heart at the captain's uncertainty; it was disturbing to see the man's confidence shaken. However, before he could answer Baltsaros, the moment had passed, and the crack in the captain's mask closed.

"Ah... listen to me. Tonight is a dark night, isn't it?" chuckled Baltsaros, reaching for Jon. "Come here, I have to take off that silk. You need to breathe deep for a while or else you'll wind up with congested lungs."

Jon held up his shirt while the captain swiftly unwound the silk from his ribs. His side hurt when he breathed, but the painkillers in his system dulled the ache. The breeze was cooler up on the quarterdeck, and he could hear it rustling the leaves of the trees on shore. Turning to watch the dark jungle, he wondered what dangers lay beyond for them on the morrow.

When Baltsaros's hands glided softly up his back, Jon let out a startled gasp. The captain moved close behind him, his chest pressed to Jon's back, arms wrapped gently around him.

I'm honestly not sure how far it would have gone otherwise.

Baltsaros's words had hurt, but not as much as he had feared. Jon's own weakness was that he forgave the man, again and again. He ran his fingers along the captain's strong forearm as Baltsaros pressed his lips to Jon's neck. There was a question he wanted to ask.

...only ask me questions you want to know the answers to.

Jon closed his eyes. He would ask it one day, but he feared that he already knew the answer. The captain was fond of him... but love?

Baltsaros murmured something against his skin.

"*Min haeken,*" whispered the older man, sliding his hands down to the waistband of Jon's pants and pulling apart the knot on his belt. "I don't want to hurt you when I take you, but take you I shall."

Jon shivered at Baltsaros's words. The captain's hand was cool when it slid into his pants to cup him softly. Already his cock was a throbbing thing, lengthening and hardening in Baltsaros's deft fingers. Was this also a weakness? Jon was virtually the captain's slave when it came to his body; in the midst of pain, sorrow, and fear was this burning, compulsive desire. It seared through Jon like a cleansing fire. He groaned, heedless of the pain in his ribs as he leaned forward to grasp the ship's wheel and push himself back against the captain.

Quickly, the captain tugged down the waist of Jon's trousers, exposing him completely in the dark of the quarterdeck. The hand around his cock tightened, stroking him quickly and firmly as the captain freed his own hard length from the confines of his pants. Jon felt the heavy organ rub up against the furrow of his ass, warm and hard against him. He heard the captain spit into his palm, and Jon's side ached as he panted with his need.

"Baltsaros," he whimpered when the older man pulled back. The head of the captain's cock pressed against him, pushing slowly into his body. Saliva was a poor substitute for oil, but it was enough. He would be sore later, but he needed to feel something other than the terrible guilt and fear that had hounded him all day. With a low moan, Jon gripped the wooden spokes of the wheel as Baltsaros's cock opened him up, and he shuddered when he was filled, the captain's pelvis tight against his buttocks.

Baltsaros began fucking him with short, quick thrusts, his hand stroking Jon's cock in time with his movements. Though his ribs twinged in pain with every jolt, Jon was soon sobbing his breath out, Baltsaros's cock hurtling him towards climax with every fast plunge. With a low grunt Baltsaros quickened his pace suddenly, and Jon let out a soft, ragged cry, letting himself go over as the captain spilled his seed inside him. Jon's orgasm was a sweet, aching, breathless thing that made his heart beat light and fast in his chest. His knees felt weak, but he held onto the wheel and tried to catch his breath as the captain rested his forehead against his back.

After a long, panting moment, the captain slipped wetly out of him, and Jon felt Baltsaros's seed slide down his thigh. With a small, pained groan, he turned and pushed himself into Baltsaros's arms. Warm hands slid gently down his sides as

Baltsaros leaned his head against Jon's, his body a comforting, solid presence in the dark.

"Come, my love," murmured the captain, pulling up Jon's pants to cover him. "I think I can finally sleep."

Jon nodded wearily against Baltsaros's neck and let himself be led to the safety and warmth of their shared quarters, trying desperately to keep thoughts of their future at bay.

CHAPTER 13

ONCE MORE UNTO THE BREACH

Jon winced as he pulled the shirt over his head, his ribs tender to the touch. Tom sat sideways in the hammock, one foot kicking slowly to make it rock, as he watched Jon dress.

"Well?" Jon asked when he was done, holding his arms out. Jon was outfitted similarly to Baltsaros, in tunic and sash, in an attempt to mimic the dress style of the Badlanders.

"I think ye look lovely," said Tom with a grin. "Really lovely. Now come give us a kiss." The burly first mate pushed himself up out of the hammock and reached for Jon, his usual bluff cheer having been restored by the catharsis of a late-night brawl. Amazed as always by Tom's ability to shrug off hardship, Jon kissed the bruise on the first mate's jaw with a soft smile.

"That ain't a kiss, lovey," laughed Tom, and the man bit at the corner of Jon's mouth before kissing him hard. Jon closed his eyes and opened to the kiss, shifting in Tom's grasp so that their hip bones touched. When the big man started kissing down the side of his neck, Jon's hands slid around Tom's back, his palms flat against the scar-layered skin. Tom let out a low growl and tightened his hold on Jon; but, with a gasp at the sharp pain in his side, Jon pulled back.

"Careful of my ribs," he complained, letting his hands drop to Tom's waist. The first mate nodded as he gathered up handfuls of Jon's shirt to avoid his ribs altogether and leaned forward again to recapture Jon's lips.

With a soft laugh, Baltsaros walked over to them and pressed himself against Jon from behind, ducking his head to kiss the back of his neck. Tom pulled away from Jon and grinned over his shoulder, his ocean eyes both amused and dark with desire.

"While I would love to see where this leads, we need to get going soon. I want to avoid another lengthy delay at the gate," murmured Baltsaros. "Finish up whatever it is you need to do in here, and meet me up top in a few minutes." Nudging his pelvis against Jon before turning away, the captain picked up the curved sword from the table and left the room.

Jon stepped back from Tom and tugged on the hem of his shirt to smooth it out. His earlier excitement at visiting Ereme'ia Balor had been eclipsed by the tragedy of Calum's death, but they needed to go, and quickly. Polas had told them that the city was the first place Oren would run to. Though the old man thought it more likely that his grandson would simply be hiding out and licking his wounds, they had to assess the damage the young fisherman may have caused in telling anyone about the ship from beyond the spires. It was for this reason that *Baal's Heart* would sail out to the safety of open water without them, returning two days hence to rendezvous at the same spot where they were currently anchored.

Jon felt a flutter of dread in his stomach, and he breathed deep, trying to clamp down on it before it became something worse.

Tom frowned at the look on Jon's face.

"It'll be all right, my dove," said the first mate as he untied his belt and passed it over to Jon. After Jon fastened it around his own narrow hips, Tom's knife sat in the small of his back, so he turned the belt to wear the knife more comfortably at his side. Since Tom was a slave, he couldn't carry weapons unless he was registered specifically as a bodyguard—something that required wading through bureaucracy to obtain stamps and signatures—so Jon had offered to wear it instead.

His fingers closed over the bone handle, and he pulled the blade out. It was longer than his own and sharp on both edges. As Jon rubbed his thumb over the notches in the handle, he remembered thinking that he would never have a chance to ask Tom about them.

"What do these mean?" he asked, tilting the handle towards Tom. "How many men you've killed?" It didn't seem far-fetched. There were over two-dozen notches in the yellowed bone.

Tom chuckled and looked down, his hand rubbing the back of his head. When he glanced back up, his blue-green eyes were sheepish.

"Aye. With that blade," he said with a wry grin. "Completely daft. Don't know why I'm keepin' track."

Jon felt a chill and wondered if he would ever feel so callous about death. The thought made him feel a little ill. Migri had *twitched* beneath him as the blade entered his brain. Jon licked his lips and swallowed back his unease.

Tom stared at him for a few heartbeats, his brow wrinkling at the effect his words had on Jon.

"Shit... sorry. Look at me bein' a heartless bastard," said Tom quietly.

Jon forced himself to laugh, and he shook his head.

"Don't worry about me. I'll get used to it," Jon said with a rueful twist of his lips. "I'm becoming more and more like you every day."

"Don't ye ever say that, lad," Tom growled, quickly reaching out to grab Jon by the shoulders. "Don't ye *ever* become like me! Yer good, Jon. Ye are. If any of us has a chance of escapin' the pits o' hell, it's *you*. Keep bein' good... for me. Aye?"

Jon felt his chest tighten from the urgency in the first mate's voice and leaned in to press his lips to Tom's in a brief kiss.

"I'm changing..." he whispered, pulling back to look sorrowfully into Tom's worried eyes. "What I did to Oren—Tom, I feel like I'm being consumed by all these *base* desires. I have to learn to embrace the violence or else I'm going to get lost in it."

The muscles in Tom's jaw worked for a second before he replied in a choked voice.

"Ye don't need to embrace it... I'll be yer sword, lad, and I'll be yer shield. The blood's already on my hands—don't dirty yers for hells' sake! I'll keep ye safe or die tryin', I swear to ye."

The exchange was so earnest that Jon didn't know whether to cry or to laugh at the raw pathos of it. Instead, he grabbed Tom's wrist and turned it, leaning down to kiss the tanned skin of the first mate's forearm before placing the blade against it. Tom watched, curious.

"I did this with Baltsaros before the battle at Madierus. I want to do it with you now. Before anything else goes wrong," Jon said in a rush, pressing the edge of the knife hard enough to make a cut; the big man didn't even flinch as the blade drew blood.

～

Jon had explained to him about the pledge before, when Tom had noticed that a new scar on Baltsaros's arm matched Jon's. It was a ritual, Jon had said, a mingling of blood to pledge loyalty to one another. At the time Tom's guts had twisted painfully in jealousy over something that bound Jon and the captain so tightly together; he had hidden his feelings and tried to accept the fact that the relationship he had with Jon was simply on a different scale than the one Jon shared with Baltsaros.

Tom's heart beat fast and light in his chest as Jon pressed their bleeding forearms together.

There are... words I want to say to you, Jon had said to him not so long ago as they lay entwined on the mattress in Tom's tiny room.

Fairy-tale words. Words for maidens and knights. Words for those without stones in their hearts. Sacred words.

Tom had stopped Jon from saying them for fear that it would bring down the wrath of the captain on the both of them. He realised he was no longer afraid.

"I love you," said Tom, speaking slowly. He knew they weren't the words to the ritual, but these were far more important. He frowned at Jon. It hurt to say them; his chest felt like it was on fire. Jon's eyes were wide and blue like dusk as he stared at Tom. Tom tried to slow his breathing and clutched at Jon, the blood warm between them. "I love you," he repeated.

For a moment he thought he had made a mistake; Jon stood motionless, silent. Tom was confused and felt his face start to burn. Then everything righted itself, and his heart started beating again when Jon pulled him in for a fierce kiss.

"I love you too, you big idiot," said Jon with a smile. "I've loved you a long time, it feels like." His fingers were cool against the back of Tom's neck, confident and strong. Jon was the one person who could understand the feeling of relief that coursed through Tom; the sombre young man who touched him tenderly had also been devoid of love for most of his life.

Tom's tears had long ago dried up inside him, but he thought he might just start to cry if he didn't say something. He cleared his throat and kissed Jon's temple, forcing his lips to curl into an easy smile.

"Now, just because I love ye, don't think it means ye get out of doin' grunt work," he said gruffly. Jon laughed, and Tom squeezed him softly, careful not to hurt his ribs, before pulling away. He had to get a hold of himself. There would be time to explore this later; at least he hoped so. The thought sobered him. "Now, let's shake a leg, aye?"

Jon nodded quickly and walked to the armoire, gathering some strips of cloth and the small pot of salve to attend to their wounds.

Tom waved off the bandages.

"Nah, leave it, lad," he said with a smile. "It's only a scratch. Who'd bother to bandage a slave—" He grinned wider; he'd just come up with a great idea.

~

Jon watched Baltsaros peer curiously at the bandage around Tom's ribs, his eyebrows raised.

"Elegant solution, Tom," said the captain with a smile. The bandage neatly covered up the fact that Tom originated from the other side of the Devil's Isles.

Tom chuckled.

"Aye. I ain't walkin' around with my arm done up again," grinned Tom. "Just tell any who asks that ye stabbed me for bein' smart with ye."

Jon watched the exchange quietly. He was still reeling from Tom's words and the staggering realization that he had probably never spoken them before. At least not out loud. He watched Tom grin and throw a length of rope over his shoulder as he joked with Baltsaros, and Jon wondered what had happened between the captain and the first mate in the city. Gone was the fear and uncertainty that had plagued the first mate the previous day, and Tom even made a wisecrack about Baltsaros being his master as he settled down between the oars to row them to shore. He was back to his normal, aggressively cheerful self.

No. Not quite.

Jon knew Tom was a changed man from the brute who had kidnapped and knocked him senseless almost a year and a half earlier. The sadness that had come to the surface had left its mark on Tom; but, now that he had confessed his feelings, Jon thought he could see a new sort of confidence flowing through the first mate.

When he'd felt Tom's slight tremble, Jon had also felt his relief and understood immediately that the first mate was trying to get himself under control. Now watching with a smile as Tom rowed, Jon realized that this was the first time he was getting a real sense of what went on behind Tom's gruff exterior.

Tom's eyes were fond when he turned to look at Jon, and the first mate winked, grinning wide as he pulled the oars. Unlike his love for the captain, what Jon felt for Tom was rough-edged, almost painful. Oddly protective.

When Baltsaros placed a hand on his shoulder, Jon turned, noting with dismay that though the captain smiled, it was a little thin-lipped.

"You two will have to stop grinning at each other like newlyweds," said Baltsaros, his dark eyes narrow. "Tom's a slave and you're my nephew. Act accordingly."

With so many slaves, the Balorians had no need for things like squires or valets, and the Badlanders supposedly eschewed such things anyway; Jon needed to play a different part. Neither Tom nor Baltsaros would even consider letting him be a slave for fear of him getting separated. So, since Jon looked nothing like Baltsaros, the captain thought that "nephew" would be the best fit. Polas had felt that the family connection would also seem less suspicious when it came to two men sharing a room.

The thing that worried Jon the most was that the old man had strongly advised against departing from the norm if they did have to remain in Ereme'ia Balor overnight should there be another unexpected curfew, and the captain had agreed; the first mate would stay in the barn with the rest of the slaves. Jon hoped it wouldn't come to that and that they would find Oren quickly. Though Tom had shrugged it off when it had been decided that he sleep apart, Jon thought it would be a strain on him.

Jon turned his head to watch the *Heart* recede in the distance, the crew already weighing anchor. It was unfortunate that they could not bring Polas with them; the man would have been a welcome help. However, after hearing his story that morning, it was obvious why that would not be possible.

~

Jon blinked at the old man.

"You were the headman of your tribe?" he said in amazement. Polas looked up at Jon and smiled his craggy smile.

"Yes. Headman. So hard to believe?" asked the old fisherman. Polas turned his bright blue eyes to Baltsaros who tilted his head thoughtfully.

"I had thought as much," confessed the captain. "At least someone with a much higher standing than you led us to believe."

"I am sorry," said Polas, turning the intricate knot-work bracelet over in his hands, the gold glinting in the morning sun. "It was necessary. I think? But I am sorry."

The man explained that over the years, his son Migri had found his way, over and over again, to a jail cell. Not a good man to begin with, the death of Oren's mother had killed the last of Migri's restraint, and the burly fisherman had descended into a spiral of self-destruction fuelled by drink and gambling. Migri's behaviour and Polas's refusal to give up on him had begun chipping away steadily at the tribe's esteem.

Then, after Migri had wounded the son of a lord, he was put behind bars for the last time. As the fisherfolk were considered barely above the status of slave, his life was proclaimed forfeit, and he would receive, as Polas put it, a "blessing" that would feed the gods and help the Balorians to stay on the sacred path.

By this, Jon knew that the old man meant a blood sacrifice that would dictate anything from that year's harvest to whether or not it was prudent to bake bread in the middle of the week.

However, the night before the sacrifice was meant to take place, Polas and Oren had incapacitated the guards and freed Migri. By that act alone, had they been caught, Polas and his grandson would have been sacrificed alongside Migri. They left the golden city via the same gate that Jon had used the previous night and fled for the water where their catamaran waited for them.

"It was a matter of time before gods took Migri," said Polas sadly. "But he was a bad man. Oren is good. You need to find him. Make sure he is safe; make sure you are safe. If you bring him back, and he is not welcome on your ship, we leave." Polas glanced at Jon before holding the bracelet out to the captain. "Take this. Show to my people and they will help."

Baltsaros frowned at the gold bangle.

"They will help even though you stole the gods' offering?" he asked quietly.

Jon frowned and turned his eyes to Tom; there was something in the captain's manner that spoke of profound curiosity, and it troubled him.

The first mate leaned back in his chair, cleaning his nails with his knife as he listened. He affected an air of indifference, but the way his eyes were trained on the captain instead of on Polas was enough for Jon to suspect that the first mate was also concerned about something.

"Yes. They will help. They have no love of the blessings. No love of the slavery. Pah... these blood gods. We are kin to the old gods. Please... my people, they will help," repeated Polas and closed Baltsaros's fingers over the bracelet with a nod.

~

After the trek through the jungle and the wait at the front gates, Tom could barely keep the grin off his face when he saw Jon take in the first view of Ereme'ia Balor. Though he himself had goggled like a fool the previous day, he couldn't help but be amused by the way Jon's head turned every which way. Tom worried that he'd get a cramp from all of his gawking.

On Polas's advice, they made their way to a second, permanent marketplace located between the dense buildings of the city-proper. Called the *madina*, this market was not in a square but crawled its way through the belly of the city like a narrow, winding maze. Behind buildings and in alleyways, the business that took place there was somewhat less scrupulous than that of the open market. If Oren was in the city, the denizens of the *madina* would know... for a price.

As Tom looked around curiously, he caught the eye of a woman in a red sarong who stood in a doorway, beckoning to passers-by. She was tall and dark-haired, and the flimsy material barely covered her. Before he was able to stop himself, Tom grinned. When he was rewarded with a coy smile in return, he realized that life in the *madina* was probably a little less cut-and-dry when it came to what slaves could and couldn't do. The thought heartened him a tad, and he winked at the woman as they passed her.

When he could smell fish, Tom knew they were close to the fish market that Polas had said was run by an old friend. This was where they would begin their search. However, before he turned down the alleyway to follow Jon and Baltsaros, Tom noticed a cloaked figure watching him from the other side of the narrow street. Bright-blue eyes stared hard at him for a moment before the slight figure turned away and was lost in the crowd. It wasn't Oren; that much was clear. The figure wearing the purple cloak wasn't nearly as tall as the young fisherman.

After a thought, Tom decided to keep the stranger's behaviour to himself, at least for the time being. They had more important things to take care of, and there was no need to bother the captain about his concerns when they might turn out to be shite. However, as they made their way to the small fish market at the edge of the *madina*, Tom kept his eyes on the crowd.

CHAPTER 14
A BLESSÈD RITUAL

The sprawling, covered marketplace was overwhelming. The sights, the smells... Jon had never been anywhere like it. Some of the alleyways and streets were wide enough to walk four abreast even with stalls lining each side. Others were so narrow that they had to walk single file. And the people! There were so many people swarming the *madina* that Jon started to feel a little nauseous from the constant movement of the crowd. As much as his general discomfort around people had decreased over his time aboard the *Heart*, the teeming *madina* was threatening to send him into a panic. Finally, Jon resorted to watching Baltsaros's boots as he walked, his head down in an attempt to insulate himself a little against the throngs of people around him.

Before long, Baltsaros turned down a relatively empty alleyway, and Tom increased his step to match Jon's, bumping him gently on the shoulder when he caught up. Jon lifted his eyes and saw that Tom looked worried. Thinking that the first mate was concerned for him, Jon shook his head.

"Don't worry, I'll be fine," he said with a strained smile. "Once we get out of this crowd, anyway."

Tom's brows dipped in confusion, and Jon realized that the first mate's mind was on something else; he frowned.

"What is it?" he asked as a cold finger of unease slipped beneath his skin.

Something had the big man on high alert. Tom's eyes darted to the side, narrow with suspicion.

"I think we're bein' followed," he said quietly, turning back to Jon. "There's a bloke in a hood that's been dartin' in an' out of sight. A purple cloak... ye seen him?"

Jon waited until a group of men passed them before answering.

"I've been too busy trying to keep sane with all these people around," he murmured. "Are you sure? It's awfully crowded."

Tom's lips pressed together, a crease appearing between his brows as he nodded.

"Aye. Blue eyes is all I seen of him other than the cloak," Tom replied. He lifted a hand and squeezed Jon's shoulder quickly. "Listen, love… if I ask for it, give me my knife and run like hell. I don't want ye to ask any bloody questions… Just get outta here. Savvy?"

Jon swallowed, his heart thumping quickly in his chest. After a second he nodded. Tom had better instincts than he did; he had to trust that the first mate knew what he was doing.

"Shouldn't you tell the captain?" he asked, turning his eyes to Baltsaros. The tall man was peering at the stalls as they made their way towards the wharf, looking for the symbol that Polas said would mark the one belonging to a friend.

Tom shook his head.

"Nay—not yet, lad. Don't need another bloody thing to bother Da. I'll keep my eyes out. Ye lemme know if ye see him. Listen, it's naught to worry about yet, Jon. I'm just bein' careful, aye?" The first mate smiled reassuringly then slowed his step, trailing once more behind Jon and the captain.

With a frown, Jon kept his head up, eyes moving over the crowd. While he saw no one matching the description of the man following them, Jon noticed something odd: despite the brilliant silks that were on sale all around them, the Balorians all seemed to favour sombre clothing. Something about the dark colours bothered him… it was funereal.

After a bit of backtracking when they had reached the water with no sign of the symbol, Jon spotted the stylized seashell on a sign above a tiny stall. There were thick boards that made up a long table to one side of the stall, and it was here that they found the man they had been looking for. Bare-chested, the stocky fisherman was covered up to the elbow in blood as he methodically gutted and chopped fish from a large bucket at his side. Baltsaros stopped in front of the stall, and the man looked up; Jon could see that one of his eyes was milky white. The man's name was Ertos, and he was kin and close friend to the old fisherman. When folks had begun turning against Polas as headman, Ertos had stayed a staunch supporter. His eyes widened at the sight of Polas's golden cuff on Baltsaros's wrist, and he nodded curtly before asking a question.

Jon listened to the captain and the fishmonger exchange words; though the language was similar to the northern tongue that Baltsaros spoke, Jon could not understand more than a few words.

"What are they saying?" he asked Tom quietly, leaning towards him.

Tom laughed softly.

"Ah, Jon… do ye need another lesson? Hm?" joked the first mate; Tom's eyes twinkled in merriment as he smiled at Jon.

Jon's cheeks burned and Tom's grin widened.

"They're talkin' fish, but not about *fish*, if ye know what I mean. Da says there's a special little white fish he's lookin' for. The big white-haired bastard thinks he's seen him. Spot o' good luck that, I think? Maybe we'll be beddin' down in the bushes, waitin' for the *Heart* to come back instead of lurkin' about in this fucked up place, aye, mate?"

They soon made their way to the part of the city where most of the fisherfolk lived, following the lead that Ertos had given them. There was a possibility that Oren had sought out a cousin of his.

When they turned yet another corner, Jon saw furtive movement from the corner of his eye. Turning to look at the alleyway, he saw nothing. However, a moment later, he spotted a figure in a burgundy cloak ducking into what looked like a bakery.

"Tom," he murmured. "I think I just saw the man you noticed earlier."

The first mate's expression turned dark, and he moved closer to Jon, protective and alert.

"Aye... There he is," said Tom, and Jon saw the figure keeping up with them across the wide street. He curled his fingers around the bone handle of the blade in his belt. Then the cloaked stranger quickly turned up a narrow side street, and Jon caught a glimpse of crystal-blue eyes in a pale face. He frowned.

"Fuckin' hells, I'm not likin' the attention," spat Tom. "Next time I see the bastard, I'm goin' to grab him."

"Her," corrected Jon.

Tom's eyes widened.

"Ye sure, love?" asked the first mate, and Jon nodded.

Jon wanted to let Baltsaros know about the woman following them, but the captain had stopped ahead and stood looking up at a small wooden building. When Jon and Tom caught up, Baltsaros curved his lips into a genteel smile and smoothed down the front of his tunic as he began quickly climbing the steps.

"All right. Let's see if luck is on our side."

~

Two hours later, Jon was thoroughly sick of searching for the brat. The first lead had turned out to be nothing; Oren's cousin hadn't seen him in some time and had no answers for them. However, a neighbour had sworn up and down that she had seen Oren at the open-air market that morning. That had proved to be fruitless too, and now Jon's feet ached from circling back through town a third time.

Over the shouts of the stall keepers hawking their wares, he heard bells ringing in the distance and turned towards the sound. Suddenly the *madina* was eerily quiet. Glancing around him, he saw that the other market-goers had all stopped to face in the same direction: towards the big stepped temple that rose above the city. Jon felt a prickle of fear.

416

"Now what in bloody hells..." murmured Tom, looking at the crowd. His jaw jutted out as he scanned the marketplace, blue-green eyes searching for any sign of danger.

"Come on. Let's go," said the captain, passing between Tom and Jon.

Jon glanced back at the fishmonger and saw that the man was hastily closing up shop. By the looks of it, the entire city was making its way towards the pyramid.

~

Heedless of the how it looked, Tom put an arm across Jon's back, pulling him close so that he wouldn't be jostled by the crowd. Baltsaros was ahead of them, getting further away as he lengthened his strides. Tom frowned at the captain's back, uneasy about how eager Baltsaros was acting. While searching for Oren was ultimately the reason for being back in the city, Tom was beginning to suspect that it was far less important than what had drawn Baltsaros here in the first place, something that the first mate was finally starting to piece together.

The captain's first priority was to himself, and Tom knew that there was one compulsion that Baltsaros rarely ever tried to curb.

The first mate looked over at Jon who was once again staring down at his feet as the crowd grew more dense; Tom had hoped that the strange influence that Jon was able to exert on the captain would have made Baltsaros a little less... *hungry*.

With a small curse, Tom set his teeth together grimly and pulled Jon along after the captain, wondering bitterly why he wasn't leading the two of them away to safety instead.

The crowd slowly spilled out from the narrow street into the large square that they had investigated the previous day. Looking around, Tom saw that on the lower steps of the pyramid, men juggled red balls while a woman played a stringed instrument about the size of a fiddle.

Now that it was filled with people, the square no longer reeked of death, and for that, Tom was glad. He wanted to get closer to the captain, but Baltsaros was halfway across the square, and Tom did not want to leave Jon's side nor did he want to drag him further into the crowd. Instead, he crossed his arms over his broad chest and stood there glowering, hoping that they were not about to witness what he thought they would. Thankfully, the stranger tailing them hadn't made another appearance.

When two more musicians joined the first a few moments later, Tom started to doubt his suspicions about the reason behind the gathering. The mood in the square was one of merrymaking, with people laughing and mingling as they ate spicy, brittle cakes wrapped in banana leaves. Finding himself beginning to relax, Tom saw that Jon had raised his head and now looked around him curiously.

"What's going on? What is this?" asked Jon, his blue eyes wide.

The woman standing next to them peered at the dark-haired young man suspiciously, and Tom frowned. He manoeuvred himself to stand in front of Jon and leaned in to whisper.

"If yer gonna speak Common, keep yer voice down, Jon. Ye don't sound right to them."

While in the city, Baltsaros and Tom conversed in the captain's mother tongue, knowing that it was close enough to Balorian and to the harsher dialect that the fishing tribes spoke that they could pass it off as a Badlands variant. Though Common *was* spoken freely in the city, the accent in Ereme'ia Balor had nothing like the flat-sounding vowels that marked Jon's midland origins. Tom kept his own voice down to a bare whisper when he spoke to Jon for the same reason.

Jon pressed his lips together and nodded stiffly, a deep comma between his brows. When he spoke next, Tom could barely believe his ears.

"How do you think they get wares from our side of the mountain range?" asked Jon. He spoke Common still, but with the guttural accent of the fisherfolk. It was absolutely flawless, and Tom stared at Jon for a moment, his face slack with surprise.

"How did you..." he started.

Jon's face creased into a smile, his unease forgotten for a moment because of Tom's reaction. He shrugged his shoulders and pushed a stray curl away from his face.

"I might not have a talent for languages, but I seem to have a gift for mimicry," said Jon, managing to look both sheepish and proud. "I can do ye too if ye'd like, lovey."

The last was a perfect replica of Tom's rough mainland accent; the first mate let out a surprised bark of laughter. It was simply amazing. Tom grinned like a fool.

"Can ye do anyone?" he asked, thinking of the outrageous accent Old Calum spoke with that put his own to shame. Then he remembered the man was dead and sobered.

Jon shrugged again.

"Maybe? I used to do it when I was a little kid. I had no friends, so I just pretended to be different people and acted out all the parts. I... I think I just picked up accents from the soldiers and servants. We had folk from all over the place," replied Jon, switching back to Polas's guttural accent.

"Well, it's a mighty fine talent, lad," said Tom with a soft smile. He thought it was a crying shame that the boy had been so utterly friendless; even Tom had had friends among the other slaves. He was almost overwhelmed by his desire to touch Jon, just skin to skin, fingertips to the clean-shaven curve of his strong jaw for a single moment to reassure him. However, he held back. There were too many eyes on them. "Ye know... I used to sound like my ma. Upper crust. Sometimes I think the reason Abetha was so scared o' me when I came back to her was that I sounded like a bloody peasant. What'cha think?"

Jon stared at him, his face drawn and stormy eyes locked on Tom's. After a second, he looked away, blinking quickly. As he rubbed a hand over his face, Jon sighed and then let out a low chuckle. When he glanced back up at Tom, Jon had a wry grin on his face.

"How pathetic are we?" he asked, the corners of his eyes crinkling.

"Bloody fucking miserable bastards," said the first mate with a wide smile.

Tom started when a loud cheer went up in the crowd nearby. He raised his head to get a better look.

Standing in a cleared area were two muscular slaves holding a long spear between them. At first glance, Tom couldn't figure out what they were doing; however, when the smaller of the two let out a loud cry, twisting the spear out of the other's hands, the crowd roared again. Tom could see money changing hands, and he grinned. It was obviously some contest, a feat of strength. A way to earn a few coins...

"Jon, I want ye to enter me," he said, cocking his head towards the cleared space where two more men now stood, holding the spear between them.

Jon tilted his head and watched the men fighting to gain control of the spear. After the short struggle was over and the bets collected, Jon nodded slowly.

"Aren't you afraid of drawing attention to us?" he asked quietly.

"Naw—them's that take up with this sort of sport ain't the kind to go lookin' too close at the details. What'cha say, love? I can blow off a little steam and make some coin at the same time."

When Jon turned to Tom, his blue eyes held a note of amusement in them.

"You sure you can win?" he asked, his tone a challenge.

Tom chewed on the side of his thumb for a moment. It seemed easy enough; he certainly had both the strength and the balance to pull it off. He nodded.

Jon narrowed his eyes in response, reaching out to squeeze Tom's bicep and prod his shoulder. The touch was both rough and strangely impersonal, and it took Tom a second to understand what it meant.

The master was sizing up his slave to see if he was fit to participate.

A thrill ran through Tom, and he held his breath for a moment, fascinated by the sudden shift in Jon. Mimicry indeed; it bordered on sorcery. He'd seen glimpses of it in their play before, when Jon took on his coldly dominant role, but this felt utterly genuine. There was nothing in the sombre young man's eyes except professional concern for his chattel... Then Jon winked, and the illusion was shattered. Tom suddenly wished that they were somewhere that he could fall to his knees and have Jon transform himself into that indifferent creature again.

"Stop staring at me and get to it," said Jon as he pointed. "I'd like to make some good money off of you before the sun goes down. Plus," he added quietly, tugging at the bandage around Tom's ribs to make sure it was secure, "if we have to stay here instead of looking for Oren, we might as well unwind and have a little fun, right?"

Tom blinked at Jon before grinning wide.

"As you wish, *Master*." The word was getting easier to utter every time.

~

Jon tried to rein in his anxiety as he bantered with the two men who were running the impromptu competition. The rules were simple: two men had to stand with the toes of one foot touching while they tried to twist and wrench a staff or spear out of the other man's grasp. The first one to have both hands off the spear was the loser.

As he looked over at Tom, Jon could see that first mate was bouncing on the balls of his feet, eager to begin. Jon smiled and shook his head, taking a bite of the spiced bread he held in his hand. There were two more bouts before Tom's turn, and Jon watched the men struggle for control of the long staff, finding himself getting caught up in the action.

Jon realized that his earlier reservations about being in the city were starting to fade, and somewhere in the back of his mind, there was a small voice murmuring words of worry.

As he had told Tom earlier, Jon knew he was changing. It was taking less and less effort to shrug off things, and he feared that he had no control over it. Despite Tom's pleas that he stay "good", Jon suspected that he would continue to shed morals the longer he stayed aboard *Baal's Heart;* he felt it was inevitable.

Jon took another bite and chewed thoughtfully; was he having a crisis of self or going through a metamorphosis? Why was he worried? It's not as if he had particularly liked the pale, weak thing that had scurried about Portsmouth doing Reginald's bidding. A sad, pathetic little worm working underground, he had been. Friendless and ignorant of the heady, addictive thing that love had turned out to be. He watched Tom flexing his large, scarred hands in preparation for his bout, and he smiled.

The first mate's short dirty-blond hair stuck up in a few places, and his thick stubble was at least half a week old; Jon thought he could make out a streak of dirt on the big man's cheek, and he laughed softly to himself. Overall, Tom looked rumpled and unkempt, and utterly gorgeous in the bright morning sun with his sun-bronzed skin and easy grin. The sparkle in Tom's sea-green eyes gave him a mischievous, dangerous air, and Jon thought again about how the man *was* most assuredly dangerous, in more ways than he was prepared to think about. Standing bare-chested, the brawny first mate made most of the other contestants look small in comparison, yet this ruthless brute often curled against Jon like a tame wildcat, his kisses ardent and tender. It made his chest ache just looking him.

A hand closed over Jon's shoulder, and he glanced up. The captain peered curiously at Tom as the first mate walked forward to take his place opposite a great, swarthy bear of a man.

"What's going on, nephew?" asked Baltsaros, his brows high.

Jon smiled blandly. *Nephew.*

"Just making a little money, *uncle,*" he replied.

Baltsaros's eyes widened at Jon's assumed accent, but he didn't comment. Instead, he turned to focus on the two men in the ring.

Tom and the dark-haired brute placed their hands on the spear as the crowd counted down. When the cheer went up, Jon saw Tom's muscles bulge as he struggled to pull the spear out of the other man's hands.

"They're a little mismatched, aren't they?" murmured Baltsaros.

Jon frowned; Tom's opponent stood a few finger widths taller than the first mate, and his shoulders bulged with great corded muscles under the dark hair that covered his torso. Jon felt a momentary pang of worry.

When Baltsaros saw the look on Jon's face, he laughed and pointed at Tom.

"No, I meant the other way," he grinned. "Watch." As he spoke, the first mate let out a grunt and pulled while twisting away. As easy as taking a sweet from a child, the spear was plucked from his opponent's grasp.

The crowd roared.

Jon let out a cry and pumped a fist into the air. He was, he suddenly realized, thoroughly enjoying himself.

Tom's lips spread in a cheeky grin, and he spread his arms to take a quick bow, twirling the spear lazily in one hand as he straightened and stood waiting for the next man to step forward.

Beside Jon, Baltsaros collected the winnings: a handful of *doksha* and a few ingots of gold. The captain smiled at him, the strange preoccupied look that he'd worn all morning replaced by amusement that mirrored Jon's own.

The captain shouted something, and the crowd cheered; Jon saw Tom dip his head at Baltsaros before stepping forward to hold out the spear to the tall blond man who was to be his next opponent.

"What did you say?" asked Jon.

"I doubled the wager," said Baltsaros, and his lips curled into a pleased grin. "Now let's hope that Tom's up for the challenge."

～

Tom won three more bouts before the bells sounded again a half hour later. Jon and Baltsaros stepped quickly to the side as the crowd went quiet and hurried to put away the makeshift seats and stalls. Tom, his torso slick with sweat, frowned in confusion as he walked up to Jon and Baltsaros.

"Good job, Tom," said the captain, placing a hand on the first mate's shoulder. "Though I think that last one almost had you beat."

Tom scowled, but Jon could see that he was pleased with the captain's compliment.

"Do you think the bells mean that whatever this was is over?" asked Jon quietly.

The question was answered for him a moment later when a great drum boomed, a giant heart beating over the square. In confusion, Jon heard soft weeping around him, and he realized with dread that the mood of the crowd had become permeated with fear and something *savage*; a corrupt, electrifying tension like a howling storm stoppered in a bottle. Dismayed, Jon looked up at the temple and saw that there were men standing on the wide platform, sharpening knives.

A blessing for you, a blessing for me, a blessing for slave, a blessing for free.

Jon's heart took a swift plunge, and he turned to the first mate.

Tom's eyes had narrowed as he stared hard at the captain. The glare was accusatory.

"Da," he said angrily. "This ain't right. Let's get the bloody hells out of here. Ye don't have to fuckin' do this. I'll find ye a place to hunt later, Da. Promise. But just... please, Da. Jon ain't gonna want to see *this*, and I ain't so keen meself. Please, Da."

Jon barely followed what was being said, so great was his shock at the change that had taken place in the captain when the drum started beating. The man's eyes glittered with a frantic excitement that made Jon's blood run cold.

"We don't have a choice now," said Baltsaros dismissively. The captain took a few steps into the crowd, and Tom reached out for his arm to pull him back. When Baltsaros swung around to Tom with his teeth bared, Jon recoiled in fear.

"I *need* to see it, Tom," growled the cold thing that wore the captain's face, and he turned back towards the temple, his eyes like shards of glass.

Jon's breath hitched in his chest at the confusion and terror that welled up in him, and he let out a startled cry when a horn blast rent the air.

The crowd went completely silent, and a man's voice rose up above them.

Clutching at Tom's arm, Jon whispered hoarsely.

"What is he saying? Translate. Now."

The muscles in Tom's jaw bulged, and his nostrils flared as he stared down at Jon.

"I can try to get ye out of here, love," Tom said, his eyes sorrowful.

Jon shook his head.

Tom's lips pressed together, and he nodded once. Quietly, the first mate started to translate, his voice a low rumble in Jon's ear:

"...the gods are wise... good. The gods call on blood. Call on ye to feed them so the crops can grow and the sun come up in the sky. Let the blessin's commence..."

Jon's stomach took a tumble when he saw that there was a line of people that stretched along one side of the huge square and up the near side of the temple; there had to be over a hundred of them. In horror, he watched the first sacrifice take her place at the top of the temple. Strapped onto a device that reclined, the woman let out a shriek as the two men above worked on her. When the pallet was righted, Jon pressed the back of his hand to his lips. The woman had been stripped. Even from this distance he could see that the woman's chest heaved in terror as she strained against the restraints.

"...with this blood we ask the gods..."

The man to either side of the woman made swift cuts to her inner thighs and down the inside of her forearms. A rivulet of red ran down the channels on either side of the device she was strapped to.

"...to bless the house of the... uh... *something*... lord for his comin' child..."

The woman's struggles grew weaker and finally stopped. Her blood was joined by that of a second sacrifice's as he was strapped to another reclining stretcher and hastily cut.

"...to bless the weddin' of the son and daughter of..."

The blood oozed down the open gutters that ran down the sides of the temple. Jon watched in horrified silence as a third and then a fourth were strapped and cut, the previous sacrifices pushed aside to tumble down the far side of the pyramid. He couldn't look away.

"...to bless the—"

"Stop it, Tom. Enough. I've heard enough. Oh gods, I've heard enough," choked Jon. He put out a hand to steady himself against the first mate.

There was a low gurgling sound, and suddenly, from the small holes that nestled between the paving stones of the square, founts of blood erupted high into the air, falling down warm and sticky on the crowd.

In the middle of it stood the captain, his face a mask of serenity as the blood rained down upon him.

CHAPTER 15
BLOOD SICKNESS

Jon felt dazed as he stood waiting for his turn to rinse off in the river, his skin coated and tight with dried blood. He knew he would be sick without the iron hold he had on his mind.

Float above it.

The water downriver was red as he stepped down the bank and waded up to his knees. Next to him, the captain scrubbed his arms and face, scooping up handfuls of the cool water nonchalantly as if performing his morning ablutions.

Jon splashed further in and sank down to his chest, eyes lowered.

It's just blood. You've washed blood off before, he thought.

Not the blood of a hundred men and women... whispered a small voice inside him; Jon felt it should have been a scream.

Unnerved, he reached down to the riverbed and brought up a handful of coarse sand. As he rubbed it against his skin, he watched the red drift down current. It was a strange sort of detached hysteria that he felt, his pulse quick and feathery light as he methodically cleansed himself.

John lifted his head to look for Tom. The first mate stood on the riverbank with the other slaves, waiting until the free folk were finished before taking their turns. Feeling Jon's gaze on him, Tom turned to look at him, his lips pressed together and nostrils flared. The blood on the big man's face made a striking contrast with the brilliant blue-green of his eyes; Jon thought the first mate looked a little pale beneath the gore.

Tom's eyes slid to the captain, and Jon read a deep worry coming off the first mate in waves.

What have you not been telling me? he thought.

Jon took a deep breath. After lowering his face to the water, he ducked beneath the surface to rinse his hair as best he could. When he emerged, the captain reached out a hand to help him up. Water dripped from Baltsaros's beard as he smiled at Jon, and Jon smiled wanly back, accepting the help. Lurching to his feet with pink-tinged river water streaming from his clothes, Jon finally understood why everyone in the city wore dark colours.

Silently following Baltsaros up the sandy bank, Jon saw that most citizens rushed away after cleaning up. The festive mood from earlier had been replaced by one that Jon read as equal parts relief, shame, and fear. He noticed that the Balorians carefully avoided looking at a woman who was on her knees in the river, crying brokenly.

How do they live with themselves?

Jon's mind touched briefly on the horror he had just witnessed, and he shivered despite the warmth of the late afternoon sun. In contrast, Baltsaros looked more relaxed than Jon had seen him in a long time. The man seemed refreshed, the tiredness that had lined his face washed away by lifeblood falling like warm rain.

Jon turned to watch Tom take his turn in the bloody river. The first mate quickly ducked underwater to rinse off and made short work of the blood on his arms and chest. Jon wondered how many times Tom had cleaned blood from his skin. A hundred times? A thousand? How many times before someone started washing away parts of their soul in the process? When he looked down at his hands, Jon saw that he still had blood under his fingernails and wondered about the state of his own soul; already the disgust and shock were starting to recede.

He lifted his eyes to the captain's.

"This," he said in a low voice, gesturing to the temple behind them, "it means something to you, doesn't it?"

Baltsaros frowned and tilted his head. For a moment Jon thought the captain was going to evade the question or lie.

"Yes... and no," replied Baltsaros slowly. "I know nothing of their gods."

"What of your gods?" asked Jon. "Do they demand blood as well?"

The captain laughed.

"I have no gods, Jon. God is a word men use to hide the truth of their desires," the older man said, turning to watch Tom climb out of the river. "I have no such need. What is a god to you? A rule maker? A judge? A parent? Behind every god there is the very mortal hand of man, trust me."

"Then why, Baltsaros? Why do I feel like what just happened resonates very deeply with you?" whispered Jon.

"It does, lad," said Tom, his eyes locked on Baltsaros. "And yer goin' to tell him every last bit, Da, so help me. But this ain't the place for it, aye? Let's get gone. We need a place to eat and bed down so we can get lookin' again tomorrow mornin'." Tom's irritation and disappointment were obvious; Jon saw the first mate's jaw muscles twitch under his dark-blond stubble as he stared hard at the captain.

Baltsaros nodded and squeezed the water from the braid hanging over his shoulder as Jon stepped back into his boots, retying Tom's belt around his hips. Though the hot sun was quickly drying their clothes, Jon was cold; the thought of a warm meal hurried his strides. It also took his mind off the taste of blood in his mouth.

~

The trio made their way back to the city centre, skirting the edges of the *madina*, and Tom was glad for the nearly empty streets as he followed Baltsaros. Quietly trudging by his side, Jon kept his head down, seemingly lost in thought. There was a soft curve to his shoulders that projected a deep weariness, and Tom frowned in concern for the sensitive young man; he had witnessed the shock and horror that had filled Jon's eyes when the sacrifices had begun, and it had made him sick with fury. Chewing on the inside of his cheek as he followed the captain down streets hazy with the falling dusk, he wondered what would happen when Baltsaros came clean to Jon about his obsession. Would it be the end of everything?

Tom glanced again at the tall, elegant man at his side and remembered his own feelings upon the discovery of the captain's grisly hobby.

~

Tom grinned wide at the woman in Baltsaros's arms, his fingers quickly undoing the buttons that held the flap up at the front of his pants, and wondered again whether the captain did this with all of his lovers. Sharing a woman with another was something that Tom had never considered before and, despite his preference for men, the thought of it made him horny as hell.

The captain let out a low chuckle and then a soft hiss when the pretty young whore bit his nipple with a smile. As her tongue licked a wet trail across Baltsaros's furry chest, Tom could see the woman's hand working quickly below the waist of the captain's pants. Tom's heart thudded in his chest, and he crawled forward, intent on freeing the captain's cock.

"What are you doing?" asked the woman, pulling her hand away in dismay when Tom reached out to untie the captain's laces. The first mate hesitated and looked up at Baltsaros.

The captain's eyes narrowed, and he stared at the whore with a blank expression that Tom knew hid a very dangerous temper.

"Continue," nodded Baltsaros without shifting his eyes from the woman.

Moving quickly to obey, the first mate pulled the leather laces apart and eased his fingers into the opening. The captain's cock spilled out into his hand, and Tom let out a pleased sigh before ducking his head to pull it into his mouth. He moaned softly around the cock between his lips, the simple act of putting his mouth to the captain making his own erection bob up eagerly. He tongued it slowly for a moment, savouring the feel and taste of the wide, smooth head before opening his jaw to take Baltsaros deeper.

The captain let out a low growl of pleasure, and his hand cupped the back of Tom's head, pushing him further. Baltsaros liked being rough with him, and it drove Tom wild to be used by a man who knew exactly how to control pain and pleasure to suit his needs; it was freedom like no other to give himself over completely to the captain.

Above him, the woman let out a sharp sound of disgust. Tom closed his eyes and ignored her, the edges of his mind blurring as his awareness narrowed down to the movement of his tongue and lips. Baltsaros's long fingers slid down around his nape and squeezed, exerting a painful pressure. Tom obeyed without pause, relaxing his throat and rationing his breath until his lips reached the base of Baltsaros's cock.

Tom's shaft throbbed, wrapped tight in his hard fist as he pulled back and slid the captain's thick cock back down the cradle of his tongue. Right here and now, his mouth's sole purpose was for fucking... for pleasing Baltsaros. The thought made him ache; a warm drop slid from the head of his cock down over his knuckles.

"That's sickening," hissed the woman. "You should be branded and your dicks torn o—" There was a squeak, and Tom lifted his eyes, startled. He saw that Baltsaros had wrapped his hand around the woman's neck, her face contorted with shock and fear as she began to struggle.

Tom pulled quickly out of the way. Sitting on his heels, his cock in hand, Tom watched with morbid curiosity as Baltsaros simply suffocated the woman to the point of unconsciousness and lay her back on the bed as if this were a common occurrence. The captain then rose up on his knees and slid the long hunting knife from its sheath by the bed. With the point of the blade hovering over the woman's heart, Baltsaros murmured something under his breath.

The blade sank so easily into her chest.

Tom blinked slowly. It was perplexing and slightly worrying; though the captain was certainly ruthless and had a deeply sadistic side to him, Tom hadn't seen him do something so... inhuman before. In a daze, he watched the captain pull the knife out to place his hand on the heart's blood that rose out of the wound in a thick, dark puddle; Baltsaros licked his dripping red fingers and smiled at him.

Somewhere in the back of Tom's mind was the thought that he should be more concerned about the captain's actions, but there was something so primal, fierce, and alive in the man's eyes that Tom felt nothing but awe. Maybe the *char* had something to do with it, but before his eyes, the captain had become a gorgeous, bloody, fallen god. Tom trembled.

Baltsaros spat into the palm of his hand, and he stroked the rigid, thick cock jutting from the opening in his pants, the smile fading from his face as he stared at Tom with eyes dark with lust.

With a growl, Baltsaros shoved him hard so that he fell back on the bed. The older man was on him in an instant, his teeth sharp and lips sticky and hot against Tom's throat as he quickly pushed his spit-and-blood covered cock deep inside him in one brutal thrust. Tom grunted from the pain, both in his neck and ass, and brought his hands up to the captain's waist to hold on as he was fucked hard and quick. His own cock sat heavy against his stomach, each stroke of Baltsaros's wide head inside him firing nerves that sent waves of pleasure to his groin. Tom let out a sharp cry as the captain bit him savagely, his thrusts vicious and jarring. It was almost too much for a moment, almost overwhelming, but then the adrenaline crested inside him and Tom let go, falling into the bliss of surrender.

~

That was the first time he'd seen Baltsaros sacrifice someone. The next time it had happened, it had taken a different form; the captain had pulled the young man's heart from his body to take a bite of it, but the result had been the same: Tom was fucked into oblivion. Initially, Tom had begun to find himself getting hard at the mere suggestion of a "hunt" as Baltsaros called it, but over time he'd started to grow concerned about the captain's state of mind.

It was an obsession, and a deeply disturbing one at that.

Tom didn't believe in sorcery, but the way that the blood renewed Baltsaros was something that worried him. It spoke of a dark power that Tom had no wish to be part of.

Glancing over at Jon, he wondered whether their shaky, three-part arrangement would survive the truth of Baltsaros's compulsion. He scratched the back of his head, turning the metal collar as he thought. If it did spell the end, would he be made to choose? The thought sobered him, and he drifted closer to Jon's side as they walked towards the brightly lit inn.

Tom reached out and let his knuckles graze Jon's arm, a hidden touch just to ground him for the span of a heartbeat. Maybe Jon would turn a blind eye. Maybe they'd continue to live in denial that they both loved a fucking monster.

Jon smiled at the brief caress, and Tom felt his chest get tight.

Love was a bloody, fucking headache.

428

CHAPTER 16

LAID BARE

The tongue like a sharp knife... Kills without drawing blood.

—BUDDHA

Jon watched money change hands as Baltsaros secured a spot in the slave quarters for Tom. The first mate would be given adequate food (an extra charge for Tom's bulk) and a comfortable place to sleep (chained to the wall, atop bedding that was changed weekly). Jon was furious, and fanning his anger was guilt; he had knowingly used slave-forged pots made from slave-mined ores in the past and had thought nothing of it. "Slave" had once held almost no meaning for Jon, and he had felt only a vague sense of pity over the plight of the faceless and nameless toiling away in the mainlands. Now, having had spent the day wandering through a city literally steeped in the blood of generations of slaves, Jon felt ill. How anyone could treat another human being with so little regard was utterly... shameful. Deplorable. It was everything he could do not to openly glare at the innkeeper and his casual cruelty. Jon tugged down on the edge of his tunic, fingers purposefully brushing the handle of the long knife and shifted his gaze from the inn's proprietor to the first mate.

Despite Tom's assurance that he would be fine sleeping with the other slaves, Jon could feel that the big man was anxious. He stood stock-still as the transaction took place, staring off over Jon's shoulder, his expression a little lost. Then, as Baltsaros discussed a last few details with the tall man behind the bar, Tom leaned towards Jon and muttered something that made his heart skip.

"If... ye need me," said the first mate, his eyes purposefully flicking to the captain, "run and find me. I'll keep ye safe, love."

Jon's reply caught in his throat. What in the hells did Tom mean? He thought he picked up on something unexpected in the man's tone and tried to focus on the emotion before Tom buried it.

Baltsaros caught the end of Tom's words and frowned at him. There was anger there, a sense of betrayal... Then it was gone, and the captain's eyes softened.

"He'll be fine, Tom," said Baltsaros quietly with the hint of a smile.

"He better be," Tom growled in response. There it was again: fear. This time Jon was sure of it. Tom was more than just anxious over sleeping locked away from him and the captain; he was *afraid*. But what of?

The innkeeper looked between the captain and the first mate with a bored sort of curiosity. Baltsaros nodded to the man, and Tom was led away, turning his ocean eyes to Jon again before he left the room.

Find me.

Jon was dismayed to learn that the captain had arranged for them to eat their meal in the main room. Almost nauseous from the constant crowd and distraught over Tom's words, Jon sank down onto the hard wooden bench and stared despondently at the bowl of fish stew in front of him. He breathed slowly through his nose, hoping the spicy smell of the dish would whet his appetite.

Jon was impatient to be alone with Baltsaros; he wanted to be somewhere where the only voices he could hear were theirs, and the desire for privacy was almost overwhelming. Jon was weary in mind and body; the search for Oren was fruitless, Tom's fear was ominous, Calum's death was senseless, Baltsaros's nonchalance over human sacrifice was... Well, he didn't even know. Didn't want to think about it. With a sigh, Jon lifted the bowl to his lips and took a sip of broth, barely registering the taste.

The captain dug into his own meal with gusto, dipping hunks of bread into the fish stew and drinking deep from the mug of malty brown beer. He peered curiously at the silent Jon as he ate, and when he had finished his stew, Baltsaros wiped the corner of his mouth with the heel of his hand. With a nod towards the door, the captain finally spoke.

"The woman who's been following us just made an appearance," said Baltsaros quietly. "But don't turn around; she's already gone."

Jon stared at Baltsaros a moment.

"How did you know there was a woman following us?" he asked, astonished.

The captain grinned wide before taking another bite of bread, chewing it thoroughly and swallowing before answering.

"Do you think that I am such an old man that my eyesight is feeble? I would wager that she's watching us on behalf of someone, but I cannot tell whether there is any malice in it. For the moment, I am content just to let her be; to confront her might put something into motion prematurely. Besides, I am curious to see whether she will approach us on her own." Baltsaros tore off another chunk of bread and held it out to Jon, his eyes amused. "You know, I did *somehow* manage to stay alive before you and

Tom decided that shielding me from pertinent information was in my best interest," laughed Baltsaros, his smile creasing his sun-darkened face.

Despite everything, Jon felt a little tension go out of his shoulders at the captain's good-natured chiding. He took the bread and followed the older man's lead, dipping it into his stew.

"I wanted to tell you," he said with a shrug. "Tom thought it was a bad idea."

"Tom is overprotective," replied the captain, some of the humour leaving his eyes. A touch of weariness returned to his face a moment later, and he looked down. In one large hand he held an eating knife, and he tightened his fist around it, knuckles whitening. Baltsaros's face went blank as he stared at the blade, motionless.

Unnerved, Jon put down his bread and watched the captain. When the older man finally lifted his head, his pupils were wide in his dark eyes, trapping Jon in an unblinking gaze that was menacing, self-possessed, and cold.

Run and find me.

"Tom is worried that I am going to kill you," said Baltsaros slowly.

He wanted to laugh, the words were so absurd. However, Jon's mouth went dry as he stared back at the creature of ice who looked at him through Baltsaros's eyes. He licked his lips.

"Why... would he think that?" whispered Jon. Something chuckled inside him. *Foolish boy*, it crooned. The scar on his back twinged as Jon hunched his shoulders. He remembered dreams of blood, of terror, of a black night, of Tom's strong arms, and the captain bleeding on the rug. Dreams? He realized that Baltsaros watched him closely, and he shivered as the captain smiled, his brown eyes once more warm and amused.

"Because I came very close once already," said Baltsaros, and he speared a thick chunk of fish from Jon's bowl on the end of his knife.

Jon stared at the fish and felt the bench beneath him sway as if he were at sea.

～

Sitting cross-legged against the rough-hewn wall, Tom stared down into his bowl. With a sigh, he sopped up the last of the stew with the hard heel of black bread, softening it lest he pull loose his teeth trying to gnaw the end of it.

The back building was little more than a long structure with four walls and a roof, each slave separated from the other by a low stack of wood that acted as a divider. The floor was earthen and covered in old straw that was infested with all manner of vermin. As he ate the rest of his supper, Tom noticed a tiny, fawn-coloured mouse watching him from under a clump of dirty straw, and he smiled. After working loose a crumb of bread, he reached forward slowly and held out his offering with a steady hand. Bit by bit, the tiny mouse came forward, its eyes black and shiny, its nose quivering.

"That's it, mate," he murmured to it. "Ol' Tom won't hurt ye. Come and get it; ye know you want it."

When the mouse finally stood on its hind legs and reached hesitantly for the crumb, Tom held his breath. He felt its little claws touch his skin briefly before the mouse plucked the bread from between his fingers. Without a backwards glance, the mouse scurried away and disappeared beneath the straw. Tom laughed.

"Without a bloody bit o' thanks..." Tom grinned wide and leaned back against the wall, the chain hooked to his collar clinking with the motion.

"If you're so full that you're up for sharing your meal, I'd prefer you share with me, friend," said a deep voice to Tom's left.

Startled, the first mate turned his head and saw a young man about his age looking at him over the low woodpile with an amused smile. The man's skin was the same deep walnut that Calum's had been, but his pupils were a surprising pale-amber colour. For a moment, Tom wondered if the man could see, so strange were his eyes.

"Tom," he said, gruffly by way of greeting.

The stranger grinned and tilted his head slightly in acknowledgment.

"So I gathered. I'm called Jarrod," he replied, placing a hand on his chest.

Tom noticed right away that the slave was missing a few fingers. He looked at Jarrod's other hand and saw that it too was short at least one digit.

Jarrod's eyes followed his gaze, and he let out a short laugh.

"I've got an unfortunate habit of running away," said the young man, holding up his hands for Tom to see. Despite his cheeky grin, Tom saw a man who was only a few fingers shy of losing hope. The slave was incredibly skinny, his ribs outlined clearly under his dark skin. Tom looked down at the bread in his hand.

"Here," he said, tossing it to Jarrod. The slave caught the heel of bread and set to work at it right away.

Curious, Jarrod looked up at Tom.

"*You* look to be intact," he said, chewing the stale bread and wiggling the stumps of his fingers. He gestured at Tom. "You marked ones sure get the lion's share when it comes to food, don't you? Look at the size of you! I don't see how you don't just break your master like a twig. Is he good to you?"

Jarrod seemed friendly enough, and Tom had nothing but time on his hands; the company was a welcome distraction from the worry he felt at being so far from Baltsaros and Jon. He smiled and shook his head.

"A real bloody tyrant," he replied and shifted in place so Jarrod could see the scars on his back. Jarrod whistled appreciatively.

They sat in silence for a few minutes while they finished eating. Then Tom had an idea.

"What say ye to a game o' dice?" he asked, reaching for the pouch sewn into the side of his trousers. He pulled out two carved-bone dice and held them up. For a second he wondered whether it was a gaffe to suggest the game, realizing suddenly that maybe they didn't have dice this side of the black mountain range. However, Jarrod's face split into a wide grin at the suggestion.

"Sure, my friend," said the young slave, rubbing his palms together. "What shall we wager? Imaginary wealth? Make-believe women? Our eternal souls... Ohh, wait... I know! The morning meal! What say you?"

Tom laughed and nodded, crawling as far as his chain would let him. When Jarrod pulled a rolled cigarette from a pocket in his rust-coloured vest, Tom's eyebrows lifted. Though the physical withdrawal was still gnawing at him, it was the simple, comforting act of smoking that he missed the most.

"Can I get ye to share that with me, mate?" he asked with a grin.

Jarrod chuckled.

"I'll roll you for it..."

~

Jon sat on the edge of the bed and rubbed his face.

"I honestly don't know how much I want to hear," he said quietly. He looked up at the captain standing in the centre of the room, his arms crossed. "Nothing I hear from you today will endear you to me, will it?"

Baltsaros shook his head slowly but then lifted a shoulder in a slow shrug.

"It's the last of it, Jon. The very last of it, I promise," said the older man. "No more secrets between us."

Jon laughed and pinched the bridge of his nose.

"Do you even hear yourself? How many times have you said what you were telling me was the last secret?" he asked. "Does it occur to you that maybe you've burned me out? That I no longer care whether what you spout is truth or lie?"

Baltsaros's lips pressed together.

"If that were true, you wouldn't have begged off the end of your meal and forced us to take to our room early, Jon."

After taking a deep breath, Jon wiped his palms on the knees of his pants and sat up.

"I'm sorry. You just confessed to trying to kill me. How else was I supposed to react?" he asked, annoyed.

Baltsaros stared hard at him, and Jon's eyes widened as the silence dragged on. Though the captain's face was set in stony lines, it was glaringly obvious to Jon that Baltsaros was conflicted about what he wanted to tell him. That alone made his heart beat a little faster.

"Just... tell me," he said gently. For a split second he saw something in Baltsaros's eyes that gave him pause. The captain was confused; Jon blinked and Baltsaros was younger, much younger, and afraid—keenly human.

Then the vision was gone, replaced by the self-possessed stare of a man in control.

"I kill people," said Baltsaros with a grim smile.

Jon frowned.

"That's not news to me," he said. "I've seen you kill, what... dozens of people now?"

The captain shook his head.

"No, Jon," said Baltsaros, stepping forward and going down on one knee in front of him. "I *enjoy* killing people. It gives me great pleasure. It gives me power."

"Power?" Jon searched Baltsaros's eyes as the older man looked up at him.

"Blood gives me power, Jon," Baltsaros's hands curled around Jon's forearms, fingers digging painfully into his muscles. "It... speaks to something inside me and grants me strength. It grants me peace." There was an odd cast to the man's eyes; Jon thought he could see desperation in Baltsaros's face, and it clashed with his words.

The blood on the captain's shirt, the heart in the icebox, the whore in the brothel that fateful day. Hands that had held him down and pressed the blade into his skin. The man that has no heart taking the hearts of others.

Baltsaros, what have you done? he thought weakly.

Run and find me. Run and find me. Run.

Jon felt dizzy, the two images of the captain overlapping: one charming and gentle, the other a blood-thirsty murderer. He let out a slow breath, his pulse thrumming in his ears. The monster holding his arms stared at him while the seconds ticked by.

Baltsaros was crazy.

Tom knew it and had hid the captain's insanity from him. Jon had to get away, now. Before it was too late. Before Baltsaros finished the job he had started the night they passed the spires. Before he went crazy himself. He had to go. Had to.

Jon didn't move. He simply closed his eyes.

The captain loosened his grip on Jon's arms, and his fingers stroked Jon's skin softly. He turned Jon's forearms in his hands and laughed quietly. Jon let out a small gasp as the captain ran a fingertip along the fresh knife wound.

"I'm not crazy, Jon," whispered Baltsaros. The captain touched the healed scar on the inside of Jon's other forearm, the one that had been made in a tiny room above a tavern half a world away. "You believe in blood magic too, after all."

Jon's eyes snapped open, and he growled at Baltsaros.

"Don't you *dare* equate the pact we made with your damned perversions." He yanked his arms out of Baltsaros's grasp and pulled himself backwards on the bed.

You are a liar too, Jon, said a little voice inside him. The voice of his innocence.

What have I lied about? he thought miserably.

You've always known the truth.

His head swimming, Jon watched Baltsaros stagger to his feet. The older man balled his hands at his sides, his eyes crackling with cold fire as he glared down at Jon; and then, as if a light went out, the captain's posture turned to defeat, and Baltsaros let out a low sound.

"Jon," said the captain in a strange voice as he sat down slowly on the edge of the bed, "when I thought I had killed you, it was as if I had killed hope itself... I couldn't bear it. I would never do anything to harm you. Never."

Jon closed his eyes tight and leaned his head back on the wall; he didn't need his gift to know that the captain was speaking the truth.

"I know," he murmured. The craziest part of it all was the glowing feeling the captain's words gave him.

Baltsaros's hand touched his calf, warm through his thin pants, and Jon shifted his leg away.

"Then what is it?" asked Baltsaros.

Frowning, Jon sat up. He looked at the captain, his eyes wide with chagrin.

"What about the others?" he hissed. "You're a murderer, Baltsaros. What about all the innocent people you *murdered?*"

The captain's graceful lips worked against each other for a second, the lines of his face taut and his eyes flinty.

"Innocent? Were they innocents, Jon?" asked Baltsaros finally. He sounded angry.

"They were guilty of what, then? The whore at the *Rose Garden*... tell me, what had she done except be born into poverty and sold into a life of prostitution? Or the one at the *Jewel?* Do you only kill whores? Is that some kind of sick shame for your total lack of self-restraint when it comes to shoving your cock into any willing hole?" Though Jon wanted to yell, he kept his voice down to a seething growl.

"They were degenerates who held ignorant beliefs, Jon. Little lives that would only serve to pollute others."

"Oh? And who told you that you could act like a god and take lives at a fucking whim just because you disagree with them? And... oh gods, we ate her heart, didn't we?" *...the heart in the icebox...* Jon's mind finally addressed the horror of it, and he pressed his hand to his mouth.

Liar. You knew.

He felt nauseous over the truth of his complicity.

Baltsaros watched him warily.

"You had *no right* to make me a party to your murdering ways," Jon said when his nausea began to recede. "You're sick."

When the captain made no response other than to continue staring at him with that same strange expression, Jon clenched his teeth with a frustrated groan and raked his hands through his hair. Death, death, and more death. Tom's knife with its grisly tally, Baltsaros's penchant for outright murder. There was a scream buried deep in his chest, trying to claw its way out. He buried his face in his palms, pressing against his eyes so hard he saw starbursts in the dark.

The bed shifted, the cords creaking as Baltsaros moved closer. When the captain's hand settled gently on his head, Jon cringed. Baltsaros's fingers stroked him slowly.

"I... wish I had words to make it better for you," said the captain in a small voice. He trailed his fingers down the side of Jon's throat, raising goosebumps as his touch always did. "There's nothing left of my lies. You know all of my secrets. You know *me,* Jon, more than anyone alive."

"Tom knows you better," Jon muttered against his hands. "He's the one who cleans up your messes and pretends like all is right with you." Baltsaros's warm palm slid across his shoulders, the captain's fingers caressing him softly.

Jon lifted his face and looked at the man on the bed next to him.

Baltsaros had a pensive expression on his chiselled face, his eyes far away.

. . .

"The first time it happened, I was seventeen years old. We had stopped at a port town, and my men had scattered among the four brothels there. I myself hadn't yet..." Baltsaros frowned and then laughed a little sheepishly. He looked over at Jon with a shrug. "Other than the few times I was put to, ah... servicing my uncle, there had been but a few kisses here and there, and some naïve fondling in the dark. I was, for all intents and purposes, a virgin." As he spoke, Baltsaros reached for Jon's hand and turned it palm up against his knee, tracing the lines there with the tips of his fingers.

There was something in Baltsaros's manner that automatically put Jon at ease, and he found himself wondering whether it was an act. However, despite his misgivings, he could feel himself being lulled into complacency by the captain. He was tired of fighting.

"She wasn't much older than me, pretty in a painted sort of way. After the act, which was largely forgettable despite it being my first time, she confessed that she had been afraid of being paired with one of the "animals". I had no idea what she meant at first so I pushed her to explain. She said that men like Calum and Peter, my former first mate, were so dark-skinned because they were less than human," Baltsaros laughed grimly. "I was instantly angry, but a coldness descended upon me, moving my hand to my sword. I knew what I had to do. I made her beg for her life before I cut into her like an animal for slaughter. I made a terrible mess, Jon."

Jon watched the captain's eyes grow distant again, his fingers ceasing in their motion. Through the crack in Baltsaros's walls, Jon could see a man who was searching for answers.

"But... why did you *kill* her?" asked Jon despite his horror and folded his fingers over Baltsaros's. "Make me understand."

Baltsaros pressed his lips together and shook his head once.

"Jon... You can't understand. If you ever come close, I think I would never forgive myself for killing the innocence in you..." The words were spoken in a rush, and there was a catch in Baltsaros's voice. In wonder, he watched the captain lean forward until his head touched Jon's thigh. Jon let out a slow breath, confused and concerned. He threaded his fingers through the captain's hair as the man curled up on his side on the narrow bed, resting in Jon's lap with his eyes closed.

"I killed her because she angered me. I killed her because I felt she deserved it. I killed her because something *told* me to. The reason is always so clear at the moment when my blade meets skin. When my hands are red and my tongue tastes the rich copper flow. I feel powerful. My thoughts clear... It's as if I can finally *see*. But the reason? I kill because I am a killer, my love. It's that simple. But... seeing that fact reflected in your eyes? It confuses me. It wounds me, Jon."

There it was. The captain's truth laid bare.

Jon pulled on Baltsaros's shoulder until the man turned, staring up at him with troubled eyes.

When he placed his palm against the captain's broad chest, Jon felt the regular, strong beat of the heart within and closed his eyes. Baltsaros was wrong; there was one more thing he needed to know.

"Do you love me?" asked Jon quietly.

...only ask me questions you want to know the answers to...

When the silence stretched on, Jon opened his eyes and looked down at the captain. Baltsaros looked weary, and he pulled Jon's hand to his mouth to kiss his knuckles softly.

"No, Jon. I don't."

CHAPTER 17

BROKEN BODIES AND SOULS

Baltsaros watched Jon's eyes lose focus. He could almost feel the confusion and hurt that ran through him, so plain were the emotions on the younger man's face. When the captain tried to press Jon's hand to his lips again, Jon pulled it slowly out of his grasp, shaking his head a little. Baltsaros almost groaned out loud, frustration spiking his blood and making him want to lash out, when what he really *needed* was to hold Jon close. It was important that Jon understand him, how he had been foolish in his hopes for the future, and how the knife wound on Jon's back was testament to that naïveté.

Now there was no way of telling Jon the rest of it without first addressing this futile question of love.

There was a knock at the door: three hard blows against the wood.

Startled, Baltsaros sat up, his hand reaching immediately for the dagger at his waist. He slipped off the bed and strode quickly across the room, casting a look over his shoulder at Jon who sat motionless as if in a trance. Baltsaros pressed his lips together; everything he was, everything he believed in, was cast into doubt by the look in those stormy grey-blue eyes. He clenched his jaw with annoyance at the interruption; damn Jon for his ill-timed question.

"Yes?" he asked, opening the door a crack. The innkeeper, a scowl on his face, stood on the other side.

"You have to come with me," said the man.

The captain frowned.

"Is there a problem?" Baltsaros's hand tightened around the dagger's handle.

The man on the other side of the door looked past Baltsaros's shoulder, his eyes narrowed in suspicion.

"What's wrong with him?" asked the tall man, pushing the door open.

The captain stepped back, resisting the urge to sink the point of his dagger into the crook of the man's neck; he felt strange and tense, off balance. As he straightened his shoulders, he took a calming breath. His eyes went to the bed where Jon still sat in a daze. It was as if he had not even registered the intrusion.

"He's had a spell. It's none of your concern," Baltsaros said curtly. He turned back to the innkeeper and made a show of sliding his blade back into its sheath. "Now what do you want?"

"It's your slave," said the man. "He tried to burn down my inn." When the innkeeper looked at the captain, Baltsaros realized he was sporting a fresh bruise just visible above his wiry black beard.

Gods be damned Tom, what have you done? The rejuvenating effects of the blood sacrifice had all but faded, and Baltsaros felt brittle.

"What happened to Tom?" Jon's voice was hoarse, and he sounded lost; Baltsaros wondered if he could be counted on to keep up the charade in this state.

"Nephew, stay here and get some rest," he said slowly. "You're unwell. I will be back as soon as I can."

Jon stared at him, a deep furrow between his dark brows. The worry in Jon's eyes loosened something in Baltsaros's chest, and his own concern for Tom reared up inside him, its intensity taking him by surprise.

"No... I'm coming with you," said Jon, pushing himself off the bed. The captain stared hard at him for a moment, but he knew there was nothing he could say that would change Jon's mind now. Not when Tom was involved. With a sigh, he nodded to Jon and then motioned for the innkeeper to lead the way.

"This had better be worth my time," growled Baltsaros at the man, following him out of the room. "I had your express assurance that my slave would be secure in this back building of yours."

They went down the back steps two at a time.

"He was smoking with another slave," said the man gravely, looking over his shoulder at Baltsaros. When he saw the puzzlement on the captain's face, the innkeeper threw up his hands in exasperation. "It is absolutely forbidden to smoke in the slave quarters! I said as much... I know I did. There is dry straw on the ground; what would happen if the building went up in flames? It is connected to my inn!" The bearded man gesticulated angrily as he went on with his rant, leading Baltsaros and Jon down a dark, narrow corridor. "Worse, he attacked two of my own slaves when we tried to restrain him! I don't know how you do things in the Badlands, but this is Balor, gods bless! He is a complete savage and should be put down. One of my slaves has a broken nose; the other, a broken arm. I even caught a fist to the face when pulling them apart! I've dealt with the other slave, but since yours is *marked*... and you seem to be a man of standing and, ah... means... I thought perhaps a little minted steel could remedy some of the situation"—the innkeeper shot a shrewd look at Baltsaros before continuing down yet another short staircase —"and you could handle the punishment of your own slave. We did subdue him, however..."

Baltsaros's jaw tightened as they went through a low doorway into a room that appeared to be used for the sole purpose of detaining or punishing slaves.

Tom lay curled on his side, chained ankle and wrist to a metal ring in the stone floor. When the men stepped closer, the first mate slowly lifted his head. Before Baltsaros could stop himself, a low sound escaped from his open lips from the sight of the damage wrought.

One of Tom's eyes was swollen completely shut, and blood ran freely down the side of his face from a deep cut on his scalp. His lip was split on one side, and a string of blood and saliva hung from the torn edge. His one eye stared angrily at Baltsaros; the captain ground his teeth and took a step towards his tomcat, horrified. Outraged. No matter what the cheeky mainlander had done, Tom was *his* to punish. That someone had taken it upon themselves to lay hands on Tom sickened Baltsaros.

You weren't there to protect him.

Baltsaros's heart hammered against his ribs, raw anger burning through his chest making it hard to breathe.

Tom was his responsibility. Baltsaros had let him down, and the beautiful, broken young man who had given him his loyalty and love had suffered for it. The captain pushed away the strange, terrible guilt that shook him and opened his mouth to chastise the innkeeper for his treatment of Tom when Jon stepped forward and spoke up.

Jon's voice was cold, his words flavoured with the sibilance of Baltsaros's own northern accent.

"How *dare* you? Who gave you the right to damage my property?" growled Jon. Baltsaros's eyebrows shot up, and Tom's one good eye widened in surprise. "I should have you whipped like a bloody cur for presuming you had authority to exact *any* sort of punishment on my chattel without my leave... *you piece of shit.*"

When the innkeeper started to respond angrily about the possible fire, Jon cut him off with a motion of his hand and an icy glare.

"Unchain him *now*, you worthless pig. I had hoped to fight him in the cages tomorrow, but you have robbed me of that with your mishandling of the situation. If... so help me gods, *if* my best fighter is permanently damaged, you can sure as hells expect me to come seeking payment." Jon stood a few inches shorter than the lanky innkeeper, but the haughty fury he projected had the other shrinking back in dismay.

"But what about *my* men? What about the damages your beast caused? I use those slaves to keep out the rabble—" stammered the man; his anger had a weakened edge to it.

Baring his teeth, Jon took another step forward, and Tom's long blade came out of its sheath slowly as he stalked the innkeeper. *"Unchain him, or I will flay the skin from your bones."* Jon's words were a low, deadly hiss, and in the wan, flickering torchlight, his lips seemed to curve into a bloodthirsty smile.

Stunned, Baltsaros watched the innkeeper fumble at his belt for the keys. The man tossed them at Jon, his eyes darting to Baltsaros's and back again.

"Take him and leave. I don't want to see you here again. Just go." Though he sounded irate, the innkeeper was pale, and the vein in his neck jumped visibly under his skin.

Jon quickly unlocked the shackles binding Tom and helped him to stand. Baltsaros saw that Jon took in a sharp breath when the big man leaned against him for a second, his ribs still obviously painful to the touch, but to his credit Jon's expression never changed from one of imperious outrage. Baltsaros's own fury and sharp guilt had sputtered to nothing over the astonishment at Jon's acting.

Without sparing a glance at the innkeeper, Jon turned and left the room. Baltsaros placed a reassuring hand against Tom's lower back, the first mate's skin warm against his palm, and gently pushed him to follow Jon.

Once they were outside and far away from the door of the inn, the summer night warm and scented with night blooms, Jon finally broke character. He turned, and Baltsaros saw that his eyes were full of pain as he took in Tom's injuries.

"Are you ok?" he asked in a hushed voice.

In contrast, Tom's face had creased into a gory smile. Wincing as he touched the cut on his lips with the tips of his fingers, Tom let out an amused chuckle.

"Jon, that was bloody brilliant," said the first mate, accepting Baltsaros's handkerchief. He dabbed at his mouth with it then pressed the white square of cloth to the cut on his scalp. "That cocksucker nearly shat himself when ye pulled out the ol' knife. I take back all the things I ever said about ye bein' soft, lad." Tom shook his head, his one blue-green eye narrowing in mischief as he looked up at Baltsaros. "Jon put ye to shame, Da. Shit, I got stiff jus' hearin' 'im talk like he was a right scourge."

Baltsaros smiled wryly. Despite the beating he took, Tom seemed no worse for the incident. The captain knew there would be no hard feelings there. Jon, on the other hand... The younger man's eyes were closed off to him, his shoulders high and tense when he finally met Baltsaros's gaze. Quashing his dismay, the captain let his features soften as he looked at Jon.

"He was certainly something," he said warmly. Jon had not only saved Tom from further molestation, but he had also kept their coin purse full. They were now short of lodging for the night, but that was a minor thing. They could try to find beds in the *madina*. "Thank you, Jon, that was very well done."

"Yes, that was quite the display," said a woman's voice. Out from the darkness at the side of the road emerged a hooded figure. Baltsaros's hand went to his sword, and out of the corner of his eye, he saw Tom take a step to place himself between the shadowy figure and Jon.

Gloved hands reached up to pull back the burgundy hood, revealing a woman about the same age as Tom and Jon. Her large, limpid blue eyes were set wide over a snub nose, and they narrowed in amusement as she looked at the three of them.

"Oh, you won't be needing that," she said, gesturing to Baltsaros's sword, her cupid's-bow lips quirking into a small smile. "I assure you that I am nothing if not friendly."

Baltsaros loosened his grip on the pommel but did not move his hand away. The woman's smile widened at his suspicion, and she shook her head, her springy, orange curls brushing her cheeks with the motion.

"So distrustful! I know who you are, Captain Baltsaros, and I give you my word that I mean you no harm. Not to you or your associates," laughed the woman. Her gaze slipped back to Tom, and Baltsaros frowned as she took a step towards the first mate. Tom looked down at her with a slow grin; however, Baltsaros knew that the potential for immediate violence lay behind his impish smile.

She placed a gloved finger on Tom's chest and ran the tip of it downwards, over the first mate's hard stomach.

"My, my... You're a big boy, aren't you?" she said in a husky voice.

To Baltsaros's complete surprise, Tom flushed visibly. The muscles in the first mate's neck twitched as he shifted his weight slightly, and the woman's lips parted in a low chuckle at his discomfiture, her teeth white and even in a smile that could only be called predatory.

Jon's face had darkened to a scowl, his upper lip curled in distaste.

Interesting. Baltsaros wondered what Jon's gift was telling him about the woman before them.

"See... I know that Jon is not your nephew," continued the woman, her eyes on Tom, "and this gorgeous creature here, despite obviously having *been* a slave, is certainly not one now." The woman winked at Tom before turning and tilting her face up to Baltsaros.

The captain cocked his head, both curious and wary. The woman exuded a brazen self-confidence that she wielded like both sword and shield; Baltsaros wondered what truths lived behind that hard exterior.

"You know who we are," he said with a smile as he ducked his head in a shallow bow. "However, you have us at a distinct disadvantage."

"Charming, well-spoken, handsome. I like you, Captain Baltsaros," said the woman with another bright smile. Once again, the captain noticed that it didn't reach her eyes. "Tonight, I am but a simple messenger, here to invite the three of you to the emperor's palace. He has taken an interest in you and would like to offer you a place to stay while visiting our golden city."

Baltsaros looked at Tom and Jon and saw that the latter was slowly shaking his head, his face drawn. Tom seemed equally leery, but Baltsaros knew the first mate would follow his lead.

"What if we refuse?" asked Baltsaros.

The woman laughed and snapped her fingers.

"Now why would you refuse? I took you for an intelligent man, Captain. The emperor, gods bless him, does not extend such invitations every day."

They were quickly surrounded by tall, muscular slaves, each armed with a spear.

Tom let out a low string of curses, his scarred fists white-knuckled at his sides. Baltsaros knew that the first mate was more wounded than he let on, and with Jon's injured ribs, they didn't stand a chance against so many.

With a graceful smile, Baltsaros extended his hands in a gesture of supplication.

"My dear, I was simply asking a question," he chided her. "There's no need to force the issue. We would be pleased to accept the invitation." In truth, he was extremely curious about the man who ruled Ereme'ia Balor through fear and blood. Polas had called him a "collector of broken bodies and souls", and Baltsaros had a keen interest in finding out what that meant. Maybe this man was what he needed...

The young woman's lips curled in amusement.

"In that case, *my dear*, we can be on our way. The emperor is anxious to make your acquaintance," she said. She tilted her head, her blue eyes wide as she regarded the captain. "I wonder what he'll make of you... I have a feeling that you and he share some common... interests."

Baltsaros smiled wider, his eyes crinkling at the corners.

"And what role do you play when you're not a 'simple messenger'?" he asked, keeping his tone light.

"Why, I'm the emperor's spymaster, of course," she said with crooked grin, staring at him a moment longer. "You can call me Ceara."

The slight woman pulled the hood back up to cover her hair and turned to lead them up the wide street towards the brightly lit pyramid that rose up above the city centre.

CHAPTER 18
FATHER OF THE RITE OF BLOOD

Each player must accept the cards life deals him or her: but once they are in hand, he or she alone must decide how to play the cards in order to win the game.

— VOLTAIRE

Flanked by armed slaves, the pirates followed the woman closely as she led them down one street and then another. Jon walked next to Tom, the big man's quiet presence a comfort. Though Jon desperately wanted to reach for him, he couldn't. Not in this world of slave and master. Not where a man was barred from offering succour to another man. Instead he kept his head down and trudged along, doing everything he could to keep his mind from returning to that terrible, hopeless moment in the inn.

The street was dark, lit only by firelight that spilled from doors and windows open to the cool night breeze. He could hear voices raised in laughter, anger; a child's cry rang out once and then went silent as a woman began singing quietly. Down one street, the scent of spices mixed with the salty sea air. Then the wind shifted as they crossed an open square, and Jon could faintly smell animal dung. He turned his head and saw that there was a series of pastures far off to their left; humped shapes dotted the fields, and Jon heard the lowing of a cow as they passed by.

Despite the terrors of the day, the city felt peaceful around him, the citizens safe in their homes. The night was quiet and pleasant; he could almost forget where they were.

Almost.

When they passed a post with a set of shackles bolted into its side, Jon looked quickly away in disgust. Next to him, Tom let out a low curse at the sight of the whipping post. This was what Jon could not understand about the captain's fascination with Ereme'ia Balor. Pushing aside the horror of human sacrifice, Jon couldn't believe that Baltsaros was so blind to the human suffering around him. Baltsaros had freed Tom. He cultivated freedom and equality aboard his ship... Yet it didn't seem to bother the captain that the blood feeding the "gods" came from the vast leagues of enslaved. That he didn't seem to care disturbed Jon.

He *didn't* care, did he? Jon was once again in the room, Baltsaros staring up at him with eyes dark and unreadable.

No, Jon. I— Jon felt the hollowness inside him again and shook his head, trying to force the memory away.

—I don't. On the edge of a precipice and pushed over, no one to catch him as he fell... He stumbled slightly, and Tom's arm shot out to steady him. The first mate's hand rested on his shoulder a moment, concern lining his bruised and bloody face.

"I'm ok," said Jon quietly. He had to be. What other choice was there? Nothing had changed... everything had changed.

Tom nodded, dropping his arm.

No, Jon. I don't.

Had he *really* expected a different answer?

This was Baltsaros... The man had no heart. And yet, when Baltsaros had frozen in reaction to seeing Tom beaten and bloody on the stone floor, Jon had seen nothing but pain and fury through the cracks in the captain's mask. It was then that Jon had jumped in, afraid that if he let Baltsaros speak, more blood would end up pooling on the cold ground. The captain was fiercely protective of his first mate... But was it love? It certainly seemed like it.

No, Jon. I don't.

Jon's pain was slowly evaporating, disappearing into the fissures of his growing anger. After everything, was he still an interloper? A pathetic third wheel that dragged behind Baltsaros and Tom as they lied, cheated, and murdered gleefully together? He knew it was a petty thought—especially when he met Tom's eye again and saw that the first mate's forehead was creased in worry—but he preferred anger to the aching dejection that soured his stomach. Fuck Baltsaros. Fuck Tom.

Being loveless and alone had not hurt nearly as much. Jon hitched his shoulders higher and glared at Baltsaros's back.

When they turned yet another corner, the pyramid loomed up high above them, lit on every tier with blazing white light. After walking through the darkened city for so long, Jon's eyes watered from the sight. As he lifted a hand to partially shield his vision, Jon tried to see how the effect was accomplished, but he could not see any flickering of flames.

"Bloody hell," muttered Tom from behind his own raised hand.

They followed the woman past a pair of marked slaves standing guard outside red and gold double doors.

Jon frowned. There was something extremely familiar about the doors that made his heart beat a little faster as they passed through them. He tried to shake away the feeling of unease, telling himself that he had probably seen other doors like this in the city. It didn't explain, however, why his palms felt damp as his eyes slid over the carved silhouettes of snakes that decorated the walls to either side.

When they came to a stop in a vestibule that was lit by the same brilliance as the exterior, Jon rubbed his eyes, peering around him at the bewildering white globes that shone bright.

"Phosphorus?" asked the captain, his features alive with curiosity.

The woman lowered her hood again and chuckled, shaking her head.

"Something much more interesting," she said with a wry grin. "I assure you."

Jon scowled at her. He didn't trust the spymaster in the least; his senses screamed at him that she was thoroughly duplicitous, someone capable of sinking to great depths to advance herself and her cause. When she turned her clear blue eyes to Jon, she smirked at the look on his face.

"You don't like me very much, do you, Jon?" Ceara asked, arching a shapely brow at him.

"You haven't exactly given me much cause," he replied tersely.

Her girlish laughter echoed in the small stone room, and she made a shooing motion with her hands. At once the slaves bowed and filed out of the room. The moment they were gone, the woman's smile disappeared, and her expression became serious, almost fearful.

"I don't have much time to explain, but listen to me carefully," she said quickly in a hushed voice, her gloved hands clasped together nervously as she looked up at each of them in turn. "You will have to keep playing your roles... for the time being. Do nothing to make him suspect you are anything but what you claim to be."

Jon blinked, remembering something she had said.

"You said 'I know who you are', not 'we'," he said slowly.

"I did, didn't I? Such a perceptive boy," she said, a touch of wry humour returning to her face. "Yes, our Most Exalted Emperor knows you come from beyond the Gods' Claws, as they are known here. However, I have kept the other truths from him. It's... for the best."

As she spoke, she pulled a small earthenware bowl with a cork in its side from an alcove in the stone wall. She motioned to Tom.

"Give me your hand," she said. "Quickly."

"The hells I will," growled Tom, crossing his arms.

"Tom," warned the captain, his brows low over eyes flinty and black. The first mate shot a dark look at Baltsaros but extended his hand, a scowl on his damaged face. Ceara pulled a needle-thin dagger from her sleeve and jabbed it quickly into the meat of Tom's thumb. The first mate flinched but didn't take his hand back, watching with wary curiosity as she turned his hand over the bowl and let the drops of blood flow into the vessel.

"We don't have much time before he sends someone looking for us, and this is the only place where we can speak privately," she explained. "I'm sorry about the cut, but the emperor demands a personal blood sacrifice from those who seek audience with him." When she was satisfied that enough blood had fallen, she dropped the first mate's hand and reached for Jon's.

Jon narrowed his eyes at her, bracing himself against the prick of the blade.

"What will keep you from holding the truth of who we are like a knife over us?" Jon asked. "Why should we trust you?"

Ceara lifted her gaze, and again he was struck with the impression that she was thoroughly unscrupulous; however, there was real fear in her wide, sky-blue eyes and that disturbed him even more.

"Because I'm going to help you get out of here alive," she said, holding his stare a breath longer before frowning down at his bleeding thumb.

Jon's heart froze in his chest, skipping over itself in dread. Mouth dry, he watched numbly as she squeezed another drop from his hand and then reached for the captain's.

"Why would you help us, Ceara?" asked Baltsaros quietly, watching her pierce his skin with her knife.

"Because you're going to take me with you when you go," she replied. She straightened her shoulders and stared a challenge at the captain, her face pale and lips pressed together in a grim line.

In the stark light of the small room, the captain's angular profile was a series of planes and shadows as he looked down at the woman holding his hand. Two predators: one fierce, the other devious.

After a moment Baltsaros nodded.

"If you truly think we are in danger, we shall do as you say, Ceara," he murmured, "though I do not like being a piece in a game that I am not familiar with."

She pulled away and smiled tightly.

"The game of survival is one that we should all know..." She turned and held the earthenware bowl over a golden urn to one side of the doors. "Do what I say, and we will survive. I give you my word."

Jon felt an icy touch of foreboding. What was her word worth?

After she pulled the cork out of the side of the small bowl, she let the mingled blood within it drip into the urn. A moment later, the gilded doors parted soundlessly.

"Please follow me," said the slight woman brightly, her veneer restored. She turned on her heel and led the way through the open doors.

~

Tom sucked on the ball of his thumb as he followed the others down a long corridor towards a raised, curtained platform in the distance. Beneath his feet, the stone was surprisingly warm, and he was glad for it. He'd lost quite a bit of blood in the fight with the innkeeper's bodyguards and felt cold and a little weak. Losing another few drops of it just to get through a bloody door hadn't helped any, he was sure. At least here it wasn't as bright as it had been in the other room; he was having problems focusing the one eye he could open and had felt nearly blinded by the glowing orbs. Touching the cut on his scalp gingerly, Tom wondered if there wasn't something a little wrong with his head; when the bigger of the two slaves had started in on him with hands the size of hams, Tom had seen some crazy flashes of light. The captain would know... though who could guess when they would next be alone.

He looked curiously at the woman leading them. His gut told him she was a real piece of work and probably a hellcat in the sack. He scratched his chest, remembering how her gloved finger had snaked its way down, following the line of hair to his belly. He grinned to himself, imagining her tiny, gloved hand wrapped around his thick cock.

"What are you smiling about?" asked Jon softly, a bewildered look on his wan face. "Aren't you the slightest bit worried that we're being led to our deaths?"

Tom smiled wider.

"Naw," he said. "Horny, maybe..." He shook his head when Jon's eyes widened in disbelief. How to explain to him that danger always made him feel a little randy? Now that they were no longer tip-toeing around the bloody back alleys like some cloak-and-dagger amateurs and finally facing some real fucking danger, he felt excited.

"Listen, love. There ain't nothin' to worry about yet. Don't be afraid of what ye don't know; that's a bloody waste of time. I'm thinkin' the little lady's puttin' on a bit of a show, aye? Don't tell me ye ain't seen it. A snake that one—" He frowned when he saw Jon's face go a shade whiter. "What's the matter?"

"A snake... The doors..." whispered Jon. "I had a dream where you and Baltsaros were attacked by snakes. You were a wild cat and he was a giant lion, and—"

"We were what? Was there fuckin'? Shit I'd love to see—"

"No! Tom, what the hell is the matter with you?" hissed Jon. They were quickly approaching the platform.

"It was a bloody dream, ducky," said Tom, shrugging. "Not a fuckin' prophesy."

Jon's face fell, the muscles working in his jaw as he looked hard at Tom.

That's it, lad, he thought. *Pissed is better than afraid.*

However, Jon's talk of dreams had unnerved him too. He didn't normally put any stock in dreams—ten long, bloody years of his own had been false visions of freedom —but this was Jon, and Jon had seen them coming to this land long before Tom's tattoos had healed.

There was a sudden blast of horns, and the red and gold curtains parted. Beyond them was a series of low couches on the carpeted platform with colourful floor cushions strewn haphazardly between them. The air was redolent with incense, and it reminded Tom of the church he once attended with his mother. Gods and prophecies... he didn't like either of them one bit.

In the middle of the platform was a couch larger and more elaborate than the rest. Reclined on it was a dark-haired man wearing loose, sand-coloured robes. At their approach, he sat up and looked down at them over the bridge of his hooked nose, his head tilted back arrogantly. He had blue eyes that bulged slightly in his sallow face, and his mouth was small and mean over a weak chin that bore the dark shadow of a beard; Tom thought he looked a little like a rat or a weasel and struggled to keep the sneer from his face.

Look at the good little slave I am.

The redhead stopped with a low bow and then turned to address the men with a smug smile.

"Please bow before the Pillar of the Gods, the Master of Sacred Blessings, Father of the Rite of Blood, our Most Exalted Leader... Emperor Ah'puch," she said with a flourish.

For a moment the pirates stood motionless. Jon looked dazed and a little frightened, and the captain stared at the man on the couch with a blank expression; Tom was almost certain that Baltsaros's brain had simply dismissed the request that he bow and was instead storing away all his little observations about the man. He himself had no desire to bow or scrape, but he was damn sure that if no one did, it would probably look bad for the three of them.

After taking a small step forward, Tom bowed low with a hand on his chest, the same way he'd done it as a child when his family had visited the king and queen. Following Tom's cue, Jon quickly bowed also. The captain took a moment longer, but when it finally occurred to him to show a little respect, Baltsaros ducked into a graceful bow that put both his and Jon's to shame.

"You may rise," said the emperor in a nasally voice.

Tom lifted his eyes and straightened, watching the man shift himself off the couch and stand using the aid of a gilded walking staff.

"Welcome to Ereme'ia Balor, Captain Baltsaros!" said the emperor with a small smile. "It was so good of you to accept Our invitation!" The man approached the captain and held out his hand. Tom was confused for a moment until he realized that the emperor meant for Baltsaros to kiss his ring. Laughter threatened to bubble out of him at the thought of the captain kissing someone's ring; he rubbed a hand over his face to hide his smile, glancing sidelong at Jon as he lowered his head.

Jon's expression was the same distracted, lost look that he'd been wearing since leaving the inn. Tom grazed his teeth along the cut on his lip, wondering what was going through his mind. One moment Jon could sound like the evilest bastard this side of the black hells, the next he was a frail wisp with eyes that showed the depths of his soul. Tom wished he understood Jon better, but it didn't change the fact that he truly loved all versions him.

Tom quietly clicked his tongue once to get Jon's attention. Face bleak, Jon turned, and Tom sighed, wishing he could take away some of his anxiety; with a tiny smile, he slowly tapped the fresh cut on the inside of his arm.

I have your back.

With his eyes on Tom's forearm, Jon's lips curled in a humourless grin as he thumbed his own thin scar. When he glanced back up at Tom, all the big man could see was despair.

What does it matter?

Tom shifted his gaze to the others and saw that Baltsaros and Ah'puch were exchanging pleasantries, ignoring the rest of them. He turned his eyes back to Jon but saw that the serious young man had resorted to staring at his feet.

This was going extremely well so far.

Tom shifted his weight, realizing just how tired and sore he was. As a slave, he would never be offered a seat, and he wondered how long they would be made to socialize with the rat-like emperor. As he looked around, Tom caught the spymaster's eye. The woman stared blatantly at him, and he found himself returning her coy smile. Certainly not meek, this one.

"Why don't we have a seat and get to know one another?" asked Ah'puch, motioning to the couches and cushions around them. "We would love to hear stories from your lands."

"I was led to believe that those coming from beyond the spires were assumed to be ghosts," said Baltsaros, seating himself slowly with a smile.

"Suspicious nonsense… But an utterly necessary ruse," replied the emperor with a conspiratorial grin. The man sat himself down on his gilded couch and pointed to Tom as if he were an object.

"Does he understand what we're saying?" he asked.

Tom stared blankly forward, feigning ignorance.

"No. What value is there in teaching a slave another language?" laughed Baltsaros. "But unfortunately," he said, switching to Common, "neither does my nephew."

"That is a shame," said the emperor with a moue. He tapped the side of his jaw. "We find Common tedious to speak. Never mind."

The captain glanced over at Jon, who still had not taken a seat. Astonished, Tom saw a flicker of something on the captain's face that he had rarely, if ever, seen. It looked suspiciously like shame.

"My nephew is unwell," said Baltsaros. "He should get some rest. Can he be shown to a room where he can sleep? When Ceara extended your gracious invitation, it was quite late, and the walk has exhausted Jon."

"Of course!" said the emperor, motioning to his spymaster. "Ceara, would you be so kind? You can also take the slave to the slave quarters—" Ah'puch turned back to Baltsaros. "If you don't mind, of course?" When the captain shook his head, the emperor smiled. "Also… please return with some more wine, Ceara, if you may? We are in for a late night."

Turning back to Baltsaros, the emperor dismissed the lot of them.

CHAPTER 19

DESPERATE MEASURES

Desperation is the raw material of drastic change. Only those who can leave behind everything they have ever believed in can hope to escape.

— WILLIAM S. BURROUGHS

Tom peered around the bathhouse and whistled quietly to himself in amazement. After being dropped off at the slave quarters by Ceara, he had asked the burly slave master whether he might get cleaned up. This is where he had been brought to.

From where he stood at the entrance, he could see that there were various pools of water spaced out between thick, intricately carved pillars. Steam rose from some but not others, and he grinned; it meant that both hot and cool waters were available to the bathers, and that was bloody fantastic. He shook his head. If this was the slaves' bath, he wondered what the emperor's looked like.

He took a step forward, the sandstone under his feet heated like the rest of the palace, and saw that along one wall was a vast scene picked out in small stones. It depicted a multitude of scantily clad men and women frolicking in dance. Or at least it looked like dance; amused, Tom squinted at a pair of "dancers" and took another step to get a better look just as loud voices erupted on his left.

Tom swivelled quickly, all of his senses focused on possible danger, and let out a frustrated sigh. *Almost* all of his senses; he still couldn't see out of one fucking eye, and the lack of depth perception was starting to get to him. The room was dimly lit, and it took him a few seconds to see the figures at the far side. Two men and a woman stood next to a row of stone benches, and at first glance it looked like a friendly argument between three slaves. However, when the woman kept shaking her head and stepping back as the two tall slaves stalked forward like cats cornering a mouse, Tom realized something felt bloody wrong. Tom scratched his cheek, wondering whether he should step in, when one man gave the young woman a quick shove that landed her hard on the bench. The other man barked an ugly laugh, and Tom's instincts took over.

The woman let out a small whimper; Tom could see that one of the men had his hand on her shoulder holding her down, while the other yanked up the hem of her dress, the bulge at the front of his loose linen pants evidence of his intent.

"Aye, mates," Tom called out as he approached the group.

At the sound of Tom's voice, the two men started and looked up, frowning at him as he came to a stop on the other side of the bench.

"What do ye think yer doin', mates?" he said with a friendly grin. He felt naked without his blade nestled in its usual spot at his lower back. Without it, he'd have to use his fists, and he was damn sore from his earlier fight.

"None of your business... *mate*," sneered the man holding the woman's dress up. He was tall and muscular with a thin face and hair that stuck up over a peaked forehead. Tom pegged him as the top dog, the one he needed to rattle. The slave's dark eyes narrowed at Tom with suspicion.

"Well, ye see... I was about to take a bath, and I can't be doin' any sort o' relaxin' with this sort of foolery goin' on," Tom said slowly, staring hard at the slave. "She'll be all screamin' and cryin' and carryin' on... puttin' off my bloody *requiescence*, if ye know what I mean? But! ye say. But! Oh... I know what yer about to say, matey: *they always get quiet after a few dozen thrusts*, aye? Well I ain't got that sort o' patience." Maintaining eye contact, Tom leaned slightly forward and crossed his arms across his broad chest. Flexing his shoulders, he curled his lip at the man in front of him. "So ye'd best be off, peaceful-like... What d'ye say, mate?" He saw from the corner of his eye that the other hadn't yet moved, and it seemed he wouldn't until his companion decided what he made of Tom.

Across the bench, Tom and the slave stared at each other, unblinking. He was beginning to think that maybe he would actually have to fight the fuckers, when the man restraining the slave woman slowly pulled his hand away from her shoulder.

"Laz, look at his tattoo," said the shorter man in a strangled voice. "He's the one that broke Saban's arm at the Stone Inn tonight."

Tom chuckled.

"So ye heard?" he said, smiling wide again. News certainly travelled fast in Balor.

The thin-faced slave blinked, an edge of uncertainty creeping into his expression. He glanced down at Tom's chest.

"It's true then," said Laz, looking back up at Tom. His voice was strangely hushed. When the slave released the woman's dress, she quickly pulled away, covering herself.

Tom glanced at her, and she stared back at him fearfully, her green eyes wide. She probably wondered if he meant to take her himself.

"Shoo," he murmured. "Run away little mouse." If there was one thing that Tom could not stomach, it was rape. "Hells, of course it's bloody true, and I'll break yer fuckin' arm too if ye don't stay out of my fuckin' way..." he growled, narrowing his good eye at Laz as the young woman fled.

The slave shook his head, hands up in supplication.

"No, *friend*," said the man gently. "I meant... that you're kin from across the mountains."

"You know that it's heresy to even think that," said Ceara, stepping into the light. "Now leave us, or I will make damn sure your names are in the drawing for the next round of blessings..."

Laz blanched and dipped his head quickly, crashing backwards into his companion in his haste to leave the room.

Tom watched the two men leave.

"Fuckin' dogs. Ye'd think they'd respect their own... but it ain't never like that, aye love? What's to keep 'em from preyin' on the weaker?" he asked with a frown.

Ceara lifted her hand, waving his question away.

"Despite what I generally lead them to believe, I have little influence over their discipline," she said. "My job is information, not punishment."

Tom shrugged. Life was a mess of shitty things; he wasn't out to save the world.

Turning his head, he looked longingly at the water, hoping whatever it was that she wanted wouldn't take up the rest of the bloody night. He ached everywhere, and the warm bath called to him.

"Don't let me keep you from it," said the woman with a wry twist of her lips.

Tom didn't need any coaxing. His hands went to the laces holding the front of his pants together, and he quickly loosened them.

"Ye here to give me a bath then?" he asked with a cheeky grin. He let his trousers drop. The woman's eyes stroked down his body, her eyebrows lifting as she took in his nudity. Her cheeks reddened noticeably, and she quickly raised her eyes back to his, her smile coy.

"Ah... no. I came to talk to you about getting us to your ship," she said softly.

Tom nodded and crouched next to one of the steaming baths. He dipped his hand into the water and found it to be so hot that it nearly burned. It was perfect. He slowly eased himself into the bath and let out a low, pleased groan as the hot water enveloped his aching skin. It was just the thing he needed.

"So... talk," he said, closing his eye as he leaned back against the marble edge. "I'm listenin'." He heard her soft step as she moved closer.

"The emperor is being gracious to you for now, but I don't see it lasting. He'll eventually separate the three of you, and I'm not sure what he'll do with your captain, but he's the real interest here. Ah'puch will put you to work in the mines or the leather pits, and you'll eventually wind up as a sacrifice, I have no doubt of that. With Jon... It might be execution for something petty if he can't find a use for him," she murmured.

At the mention of Jon, Tom opened his eye, his heart thrumming hard against his ribs.

"But he's safe for now?" he asked.

The woman nodded.

"Safe for now, yes. Perfectly safe... and I can *keep* him safe as long as you can convince him of something," she said. She knelt down at the edge of the bath next to Tom. He watched curiously as she took off her glove and put her hand into the water; cupping her fingers, she scooped some up to trickle it over his shoulder.

Tom frowned, but it felt great. Sensual. When she did it again and let her fingers trail along his collarbone, he felt himself stir.

"Why don't ye convince him yerself?" he asked gruffly. Her fingertips brushed the side of his face, her skin hot from the steaming water, and he closed his eye again, just letting her touch him. He breathed slowly, the motion sending delicious eddies against his sensitive, submerged cock.

"He doesn't like me," she replied, a smile in her voice. Her lips were so close to his ear that he felt her breath against him.

"Mmm...kay?" muttered Tom. "What do ye want me to tell 'im?"

"Just this: when the accusation comes, he has to say he was *forced*. It's extremely important for my plan to work," whispered Ceara, her mouth brushing the rim of his ear.

Tom flared his nostrils, concentrating on her words. Forced?

"Sure," he agreed. He didn't trust her, but what choice did he have? "He was forced. Got it." He shifted slightly in the hot water and turned to look at her. "Now can ye do somethin' for me, doll?"

Ceara smiled coyly, her cheeks a pretty pink.

"Of course," she said huskily. "Anything you want..." She slowly stroked one fingertip down the side of his neck, and he reached up to take her hand.

"Can ye go get Jon for me? See that we have some privacy, aye?" he said with a grin. "There's a good girl."

She looked confused for a moment and pulled her hand away. When she grasped Tom's meaning, her face fell slightly, but she quickly hid her disappointment with a smirk.

"And if I don't?" she asked, getting to her feet. Tom looked up at her and forced the corners of his mouth down, shrugging.

"I've been told that sleepin' abovedecks in the rain isn't *so* bad when ye don't have a bunk to call yer own," he drawled, watching his bruised hand flex below the water. "At least ye get to feel at one with nature... savvy?" He looked up at her and gave her a sudden, wide smile.

Ceara rolled her eyes at him.

"Yes, fine. Savvy," she muttered.

"Aw lovey, yer a fine-lookin' woman, it's not that," Tom said apologetically. "All jokin' aside, if it ain't the captain, or it ain't Jon..." He shrugged again. "There just ain't anyone else."

~

Jon jerked awake, hands out to push away the dark form that loomed above him.

"Ouch," said a woman's voice. A moment later, the room lightened as the emperor's spymaster tapped the globe on the wall.

"Oh, it's you," said Jon, annoyed. "What do you want?" He stretched his shoulders and winced as the movement twinged his ribs. He hadn't meant to fall asleep, but the bed was unbelievably soft and the room dark.

"I've been sent to fetch you," said Ceara with an ironic smile.

"By whom?" asked Jon, rubbing his eyes.

"By the big tattooed bastard that you've got wrapped around your finger," she said, turning to leave. "Come on... before he threatens to not only give me no place to sleep aboard your ship but forces me to swab the decks too."

Jon slid off the bed and padded quickly across the room to follow her. Before they turned down the corridor, she gave a short laugh.

"Wait... he's the first mate, isn't he?" she said, looking up at him with wide, blue eyes. "Come now... If we're going to trust each other, I should know more about you."

Grudgingly, Jon nodded his head.

"Yes... Tom's the first mate," he replied.

"Interesting," replied Ceara, a curious frown narrowing her eyes. "And what does that make you? The shipwright? The taskmaster? What *is* your role aboard?"

Jon suddenly had the feeling that she wasn't as ignorant as she was making herself out to be—the too-quick response, the flicker of satisfaction that had passed over her face. It was as if she was just confirming facts that she already knew. Jon's tired brain didn't know what to make of it.

"Me? I'm nothing," he said faintly.

Ceara stared at him a moment longer and then nodded once, turning to lead him down the hall without another word.

~

Jon pulled his shirt off, dumping it onto the ground before working loose his belt. He glanced to the side where Ceara stood watching, and he felt himself redden.

"Are you sure we won't be caught?" he asked, his brow furrowed.

"Yes," she said simply.

He felt too tired and too soul-weary to do anything but believe her. His senses told him she was telling the truth, though he was beginning to question just how reliable those senses were these days.

Tom beckoned to him from the water, and Jon hopped on one foot, taking off his boots and pulling down his trousers while trying to ignore the fact that Ceara had not yet left. Was she planning on watching them?

Jon wondered if he even cared.

He let himself down into the pool with a gasp; the water was hot and, though it was a shock to his system, it felt good. He walked forward, propelling himself with his arms until he reached Tom sitting on the submerged ledge. Exhausted and so sick of feeling the dull ache in his chest, he sagged gratefully against the big man; Tom let out soft sound and curled his arms around Jon. He closed his eyes tight, pressing his face against Tom's neck for a few breaths. This was good. This was right where he was meant to be.

When he looked up, he saw that the woman was watching them with a look of distaste on her face. She quickly smoothed her expression, but Jon shook his head.

"Let me give you some advice: never, ever let Baltsaros catch you looking at him like that. Ever," he said softly. "Now... please?" He motioned with his head towards the door.

Ceara, with a slightly mystified look, nodded slowly and left silently.

Jon's hands slid over Tom's slick back as he pushed himself against him, and he felt the first mate kiss the side of his head.

"Ah... So he told ye..." murmured Tom.

Jon nodded with his jaw clenched tight. All the outrage and betrayal he'd felt at Tom's silence and possible complicity over Baltsaros's murders had fallen to the wayside following the captain's rejection of him. However, with the big man's words, he felt a resurgence of bitter anger. He hooked his fingers around the edge of the metal collar Tom wore, causing him to let out a quiet grunt. The sight of the slave collar digging into the first mate's skin gave him a sense of satisfaction. He pressed his lips to the side of Tom's face and shuddered, his eyes squeezed shut.

"I am so *fucking angry* at you for keeping Baltsaros's secrets," he growled against Tom's stubbled skin, crushing his nose into the hollow of the big man's cheek. Baring his teeth, Jon pushed his forehead against Tom, his whole body tense. He wanted to tear into him, hurt him, *punish* him. He wanted to gather all of his anger, fear, and pain and bury it into Tom like a lance. He slipped another finger beneath the collar, and this time when Tom made a sound, it was a strangled little gasp.

"Not my secrets," whispered Tom, his voice hoarse. When Jon pulled back, he saw that the big man's face was turning red. For a second he felt sorry, ashamed of what he was doing to Tom. The first mate was bruised and battered, one of his eyes only able to open in the barest of slits. However, when Tom's thighs squeezed Jon's hips, his legs wrapping around him to pull him closer, the thick, hard cock that touched Jon's belly blew all of his doubts away.

"You are never to keep anything from me again, Tom," he whispered, yanking on the collar. "Never again." He ground his own half-soft cock against Tom's groin, suddenly filled with an aching *need*. He grimaced, fury and desire throbbing in his gut. "Never... Say it."

"Never," choked Tom, his brow furrowed. The big man kept his hands loose around Jon's ribs, gentle despite the fact that Jon was slowly strangling him.

"Say it again," growled Jon.

"Ne... ver," came Tom's response, a little weaker.

With a low, malicious laugh, Jon pulled the collar just a little tighter, gratified when he felt Tom's hands twitch ever so slightly. Just as it seemed like the big man was about to lose consciousness, Jon finally pulled his fingers out from under the collar.

Tom coughed and took in a big lungful of air, his eyes watering.

"Never," he croaked.

Jon grabbed Tom's jaw hard in his fingers, not caring about the bruises and the cuts.

"And why is that?" he asked softly.

"Because I'm yers, love," breathed Tom, his hands sliding around to grab Jon's buttocks to pull him even tighter against him.

Jon thought he would shake himself to pieces from the frantic desire that tightened his muscles and put a low growl deep in his chest. Yes, Tom was his. He wanted to mark him, carve his name in Tom's skin. With a moan he tilted Tom's face back and spat into his open mouth. Tom blinked in surprise, but the sound he let out was rough with lust. He dug his fingers into Jon's buttocks, and Jon let out a strangled cry; mashing his lips against Tom's, he savaged him with a brutal kiss.

Breaking away, Jon panted and took his cock in hand, stroking himself quickly. Again he looped a finger around the back of Tom's collar, yanking it tight against Tom's throat. He spat again, and Tom licked the saliva from his lips, a fervent glaze in his eyes as he panted against the constricting metal ring.

"I'm going to fuck you, you godsdamned bastard. I'm going to bury my cock in you and fuck you hard... you lying *asshole*," Jon's words were part growl, part sob, and he bent his knees, fumbling with desperate fingers between Tom's legs until he found his opening. "I don't care how much you like licking the captain's boots. You will never betray me again. Not for *anything*." This time his voice broke. His love for the big brute was a vivid, pulsing thing in his chest. He needed Tom so much—for his strength, his loyalty, his fierceness, his submission... cock in hand, he pushed the head of it into Tom, almost frantic. Jabbing himself hard into the big man, Jon let out a sharp cry. Water was a poor lubricant, but after a only few slowly-deepening thrusts, Jon's whole length slid tight into him. He leaned into Tom with every plunge, one hand curled around the bigger man's back, the other slowly cutting off his air supply.

"I want to feel you cum. Make yourself cum," he snarled. Forgiveness was couched in the permission for release; he was learning a new language after all. Leaning forward, he growled against Tom's lips. "Do it. Now."

Despite the fact that every breath Tom took whistled as he choked against Jon's hold, he obediently took his thick, curved cock in hand and quickly stroked himself. With a moan, Jon slowed his thrusts, realizing belatedly that he wasn't going to last long enough. However, as he skirted the edge, each push into Tom's body a panting breath closer to culmination, he felt the big man finally go rigid against him, his voice just a low, strangled hiss as his body jerked with the force of his orgasm. Jon released the big man's collar and grunted as he let himself go, the sound echoing against the stone walls of the bath house as his cock pumped and throbbed inside Tom. With a desperate cry, he brought his mouth to Tom's as the very last of his pleasure ebbed sweet and deep inside him, sharing his breath to replace that which he'd taken.

. . .

Tom's hands came up slowly, painting soft caresses on Jon's skin. His chest heaved with each laboured breath, and he pulled away from Jon with a hoarse chuckle.

"Holy shit," he wheezed with a grin. "Bloody fuckin' hells, Jon."

Jon shifted his hips so that his softening cock slipped out of Tom, and he groaned, feeling chafed. He wrapped his arms around Tom's back and pressed his lips to the dark red line that circled the first mate's neck right above the metal collar. He felt a little ill from exhaustion and from the heat of the water, and his ribs ached with every breath, but he didn't want to move. He wanted to sink beneath Tom's skin and hide there, forget his fears and pain and curl up in the first mate's solid warmth. He clenched his eyelids shut.

"Tell me you're mine again," he whispered. "I need to hear it."

Tom's hands ceased in their movement, and Jon could see the frown on his face painted against his eyelids by memory.

"I'm yers, Jon," said Tom slowly. His hands closed over Jon's shoulders, and he gently pushed him back.

"What's wrong?" asked the first mate, his voice low and gravelly. Tom's ocean eyes darted over Jon's features, worry plain on his face. "What happened?"

Jon shrugged.

"I asked Baltsaros if he loved me," he said quietly.

The surprised laugh that burst out of Tom was the last reaction he had expected.

CHAPTER 20
THE MENAGERIE

Tom was incredulous.

"Ye can't have figured Da would answer different," he asked, shaking his head. When Jon's grey eyes slid away from his, Tom realized that the sombre young man still held onto some innocent notion that Baltsaros was something that he wasn't. He squeezed Jon's shoulder. Fucking Baltsaros... what a bloody time for the captain to start telling the whole truth. "Why don't ye be glad that he's tryin' to be honest with ye? That's a bloody miracle, aye?"

Jon turned to look at Tom again, a scowl on his face.

"Yes. But where in hells does that leave me? Tom... I don't even know what to think anymore. He's insane. He kills people and gets off on it. The most fucked up part is that, despite that fact, I'm sitting here wondering how I can make him love me. It's sick. He's a fucking murderer, and I feel like it's something *I've* done that keeps him from loving me." Jon pulled out of Tom's grasp with a sigh and took a step back in the warm water.

"Aye, that's a fucking path ye don't want to go down, love," said Tom quietly. "Ye ain't done a bloody thing. Trust me. He's just... well, yeah, he's a black-hearted madman when it comes down to it; but he does love ye in his own way, lad. Ye gotta believe me. Just because he doesn't *think* he does..." He rubbed a hand over his face, not knowing what to say. "Hells, ye know what? It's all shite, but would ye rather he'd lied to ye?"

Jon shook his head; he was starting to seem less lost, but Tom knew that look. It was important to make him understand that it wasn't the words that mattered; Tom could see something in the way Baltsaros's eyes constantly turned to Jon, the way he touched him all the time, the care he took with the meals he prepared for the two of them. It was enough to make Tom cold with envy from time to time, but it was evidence that the captain felt more than he let on...

"Do you think that he loves you?" asked Jon.

Grimacing, Tom scratched the back of his neck where a thin welt had come up. Sometimes Jon was so frustratingly naïve that he wanted to shake him. Why was this so important to him? Tom clenched his jaw rhythmically as he thought.

"He needs me. And sometimes I think, aye, maybe he even loves me, lad. But with the captain... it's complicated," he finally muttered. "Listen, he's told ye he can't live without ye, aye?"

Jon nodded.

"Well, he ain't never said the same to me—" Tom waved away Jon's soft sound of dismay. It was honestly a sore spot with him, but how could he make Jon believe him if he couldn't believe his own damn words? "That he ain't said it, don't mean it ain't a fact. He's a bloody, stubborn tyrant who knows shite about being a decent, bloody person without makin' all that cares about him bloody insane." Tom smiled a little sadly. "I get what I can from Da, and fuck the rest. This fuckin' *word* between us... 'love'. Hells, some people just don't know how to make the word work for 'em. Da's one of them.

"Jon, I love ye more than I can say, but I think ye might be a damn fool when it comes to the cap'n. If ye can see past his murderin' ways, just... Look at his doin's with you... Don't wait for his words, lad."

Some of the tension that held Jon shoulders high had leached out while Tom struggled to explain himself, and he nodded slowly at the end of it.

"Do you think he will change ever?" asked Jon, his blue-grey eyes shrewd.

Tom lifted his shoulders.

"Maybe? Hells, years go by without a single 'sorry' from the bastard and, since ye been around, I heard it more times than I can count on one hand. That's somethin'," mused Tom with a crooked grin.

"Maybe you're right. It just... hurts," replied Jon.

With a sigh, Tom nodded.

"I know, love."

The heat of the water was starting to get to Tom, and he lurched to his feet, intent on getting out. He was about to comment that just being with Baltsaros was a recipe for pain, when he saw Jon's eyes drop to his abdomen and his nose wrinkle slightly.

Tom glanced down and saw that his seed had become a gluey mess that stuck to his chest and belly hair in pale clumps.

Tom let out groan and pulled at the mess.

"Fuckin' hells..." he muttered. When he looked up, he saw that Jon was smiling again, dispelling some of the gravity caused by their words a moment earlier.

"It's not bloody funny," scowled Tom, hamming it up slightly to further lighten the mood. He pointed to the line of fine, dark hair on Jon's belly that rose above the water. "And ye can wipe the bloody smirk off yer face, lad. It's not like ye came out clean..."

~

Tom stroked Jon's hair while he sat deep in thought. They had moved to a different pool after cleaning up, and Jon snoozed against Tom's chest in water that was warm like a soft kiss against their skin.

Jon wasn't stupid, and he was no longer the wide-eyed innocent that Tom had accosted at the *Rose Garden.* However, the way that Jon's face turned so bleak when he spoke of Baltsaros... Tom frowned, shifting slightly to press his cheek against Jon's soft curls. It was never going to be easy for him to accept what the captain was.

And what is he? he thought to himself. Was he truly loyal to a madman, as he had called him earlier? He closed his eyes. Before Jon, it had never been this complicated, but Tom wondered if that had been wrong. Perhaps he should have been questioning all along. Jon's hand twitched slightly against his side in his sleep, and Tom pressed his lips together and frowned.

He was furious that Baltsaros had purposefully hurt Jon. Would one more little lie have been so fucking hard? However, Tom *was* happy that he would no longer have to keep secrets from Jon to protect the captain. It was all out in the open, and maybe, just maybe, now that Jon had taken a good look into the belly of the beast, he knew a way of... bloody fixing things. The last few days had made Tom realize that things with Baltsaros were worse and far stranger than he had assumed.

Jon had done something to the captain to make him capable of being sorry; could Jon's influence make Baltsaros whole?

Then there were the woman's strange instructions. What did she mean by Jon having to say he was *forced*? Neither of them liked the sound of it.

Tom was tired of pushing his weary brain through convoluted thoughts; he needed to get some sleep. Just as he was thinking of waking Jon up, he heard the soft footfall of someone approaching.

"It's only me," murmured Ceara. "I have to get you two back to where you belong. There's only so long I can maintain the ruse that there's an interrogation taking place in here."

Jon blinked sleepily when Tom shook him, and he sat up looking disoriented. Tom helped Jon out of the water, and they dried off while the spymaster looked on impatiently.

"Is... uh... the captain back?" asked Jon groggily as he handed her the bath sheet back and moved to get dressed.

Ceara shook her head.

"No, he and Ah'puch have called for another jug of wine. There's no telling how long they'll be," she said. She lowered her eyes for a moment, a crease appearing between her brows before she looked up again. "Do you trust me now? I took a big risk letting you two in here together."

Tom couldn't help but wonder how much of her earnest expression was complete pig shit. He nodded anyway, though Jon shot him a sidelong glance. At least Jon wasn't fooled.

"Aye, lass. Ye've proved ye can be useful. Now when d'ye plan on tellin' us the rest of it?" he asked, lacing up his pants. "We've got our own woes to deal with, lovey. Can't be holed up here. We'll take ye with us, but it's gotta be soon."

Ceara smiled a little wanly.

"Yes, I understand that you're anxious to rejoin your crew, but I know for a fact that they won't be back to fetch you for another day, so we still have plenty of time. I can't tell you more than what I've already said," she shifted her blue eyes to Jon. "You're on board with this?"

The lines next to Jon's mouth deepened as his jaw worked.

"I don't like agreeing to something without knowing what it is," he said quietly, fixing her with a steely glare.

Ceara's smile had an edge to it as she stared back at him.

"I'm sorry you feel that way, Jon," she said. "But what choice do you have?"

～

Baltsaros suppressed a sigh, maintaining his air of interest despite the fact that Ah'puch's idea of an intellectual discussion was an hours-long, detailed, egotistical, and mostly one-sided account of everything wonderful that had happened since he took the throne. If even half of what he related was true, then Baltsaros would have been sitting in the presence of an innovative and exceptional man. It was not the case.

The captain was disappointed. The emperor of Ereme'ia Balor had turned out to be a strutting little cockalorum who had not, as of yet, provided any insight at all into the mysteries of sacrifice or of the blood rituals that literally kept the golden city running. Baltsaros had expected a man who understood the power of holding life and death in one's palm, a compelling sovereign who ruled with an iron fist, and a stimulating match for the captain's intellect... someone with answers. He had instead found a man so wrapped up in himself and his so-called accomplishments that he had little room for what he called the "day-to-day bloodletting" that went on at the hands of his warlocks. Ah'puch was nothing but a figurehead it seemed, and one that was grasping and desperate for the admiration he felt he was owed. The man had no respect for the life-giving ichor that flowed down the sides of his temples, and it was utterly frustrating.

After lifting the golden cup to his lips again in a mimicry of imbibing his wine, Baltsaros smiled as the man launched into yet another account of some lord that grovelled at the emperor's feet only to be shown great mercy and understanding. The captain was wondering if he could claim great exhaustion and retire for the night when his eyes strayed to the lights that hung over the raised platform where they were comfortably seated. Narrowing his gaze, he tried again to see whether there was any movement inside the globes. There was no hiss or smell of gas, and he was completely baffled as to how the light was created. Forgetting himself, Baltsaros spoke up, interrupting the emperor.

"What makes the illumination so bright?" he asked. He turned his eyes to Ah'puch and saw that, though the man looked a tiny bit annoyed at the interruption, having his magical lamps noticed and admired was enough to forgive the captain's rudeness.

"Ah! What is your guess?" asked Ah'puch with a smile, looking down his hawk nose at Baltsaros.

Stifling his irritation, Baltsaros smiled blandly and shrugged.

"It is a complete mystery to me," he said graciously, and then he blinked, remembering something Polas had said. "Wait, perhaps not... Is it harnessed lightning?" He sat up a little straighter, wondering if he was in fact looking at the product of somehow trapping the electricity of lightning within glass.

Taking another sip of his wine, Ah'puch looked almost coyly at Baltsaros over his cup, pleased to have yet another reason to show off.

"Not quite lightning, no. We fabricate electricity here, and it is channelled through the building on copper wires to filaments inside these blown glass bulbs. It is extremely complicated; I'm quite sure that I would lose you in all the details," said the emperor, smirking. "Suffice it to say that We are very proud of this invention."

Baltsaros felt a tiny buzz of excitement.

"You fabricate it? Can I see?" he asked. Before the emperor had a chance to turn him down, Baltsaros smiled graciously and bowed his head in reverence. "I would be so honoured to bask in Your Excellency's ingenuity." When he looked back up, the emperor was nearly preening with delight over Baltsaros's words.

"Yes, yes. We shall show you tomorrow," said Ah'puch with a generous smile, and Baltsaros gritted his teeth; so much for a change of venue. He tried to rein in his irritation, and taking a big swallow of wine, braced himself for another long-winded account of the emperor's accomplishments. However, the captain was surprised when the man changed the subject.

"The young man you travel with, your... *nephew*. Tell me about him," said the emperor, his eyes locked on Baltsaros's.

A touch of apprehension suddenly soured the wine in Baltsaros's mouth. He frowned. There was no mistaking the emperor's inference. Ah'puch knew *something* about his relationship with Jon, but Baltsaros decided to play it safe and feign ignorance.

"He is my sister's son by marriage," Baltsaros lied smoothly. "He works aboard as my advisor helping me to secure honest deals with dishonest men. He is particularly adept at detecting lies and foul intentions." He thought that perhaps if he spoke of Jon's gift, the emperor would be more inclined to share his secrets.

Ah'puch sat up and peered closely at Baltsaros.

"What do you mean? How does he do this?" asked the emperor, looking intrigued. "What is involved?"

"There's nothing mystical about it," replied the captain. "He is just extremely good at reading body language. Far more than any other I've seen. Sometimes it seems like he senses or detects the emotions of others even before they feel them themselves."

A drastic change had taken place in the emperor's demeanour at the captain's words. The man was wide-eyed and interested; gone was his haughty, half-lidded, self-important slouch. Baltsaros smiled, curious at the dramatic shift.

"I'm a keen study in the realm of the human psyche," said Ah'puch with a broad, toothy smile, discarding the royal "We" for the first time in their conversation. "Is he aware of what cues he is seeing? Can he explain to you how he comes to his conclusions?"

Baltsaros shook his head and held out his cup for more wine. This time, Ah'puch poured it from his own hand, and when the captain sat back in his couch, he smiled behind his glass.

Another evening of conversation, and he would have the man eating out of his hand.

"Jon can't explain, no. It's unfortunate, as I would love to better understand what he sees," he said sadly.

"Perhaps you're asking the wrong questions," replied Ah'puch with a raised eyebrow.

Baltsaros felt a sharp spike of anger at the man's suggestion and nearly sneered at him.

"I don't think so," he answered quietly instead. With a thin smile, he leaned towards the man across from him. "Why? What questions would *you* ask, if I may?"

The emperor had obviously missed the captain's reaction; he furrowed his brow and tapped a finger once against his bottom lip in thought.

"Perhaps it isn't the questions that are wrong, but the way you are asking them..." he said thoughtfully.

"What do you mean?" asked Baltsaros.

"Have you tried to force his brain to answer? Have you tried to hypnotize him?"

Baltsaros's brows rose slowly.

"Ah, you haven't. I can see that," responded the emperor with a smug grin. "Would you like to see what my own experiments in the mind have yielded?"

Four levels beneath the main floor were the palace dungeons. At least that's what they had been before the emperor had them converted into his own private laboratory. As they walked through the thick wooden door, Baltsaros was immediately assailed by a series of overlapping smells. Some he recognized, like urine, camphor oil, and valerian root. Others were not so familiar. There was something that smelled of the flowering plant he knew as monkshood, but it was subtly different. Same with the waxy, green scent that he associated with the aloe plant, and the tang of the snow-in-summer bush. Close, but not identical.

His nostrils flared as he turned his head like a hound scenting the air. It was everything he could do not to delve into the herbs and toxins that were neatly arranged on shelves along the back wall.

"Impressive," he murmured.

The emperor smiled and spread out his hands, making a show of looking humble.

"Alas, I am but an amateur. These are only the very basic of ingredients. But that is not what I wanted to show you." The emperor made his way across the dark room and hit a switch. A long corridor was illuminated, each of the dozen cells on either side fronted by gilded metal bars that gleamed in the stark light. Frowning, Baltsaros walked slowly to the first cage. Within it, blinking sleepily, was a man of about his own age. He was curled up on a mound of blankets in one corner, having eschewed the narrow cot bolted to the wall. When the man noticed Baltsaros staring at him, he opened his mouth wide, baring his teeth. A low growl emerged from his throat. Fascinated, Baltsaros took a step closer. The noise coming from the man became higher pitched at his approach.

"What is wrong with him?" he asked the emperor.

Ah'puch looked pleased with himself.

"He thinks he's a house cat," replied the emperor, grinning conspiratorially.

"*You* did this to him?" When the emperor nodded slowly, Baltsaros frowned and looked back at the cage. The man had retreated against the wall, his back rounded like that of a cat, his face in a tense rictus of fear. A small tongue flick... and still that low growling noise. It was mesmerizing.

"Does he understand us?" he asked quietly.

"Not anymore," said Ah'puch. "Not in this state. If I set up my apparatus and put the right drugs in his system, I can coax him through hypnotism back to a level of, ah... human-ness, as it were, where he can understand speech. Otherwise he just cleans himself and shits in that sandbox," the emperor said with obvious amusement.

Baltsaros nodded slowly, his mind stumbling over itself in waves of fascination, excitement, and a delicious sense of horror. He turned his head to look down the corridor at the other eleven cages; he could hear the inhabitants beginning to stir.

"Would you like to meet the rest of my menagerie, Captain Baltsaros?" asked the emperor, leaning forward on his golden cane, his eyes sparkling with enthusiasm.

"Yes. Yes, I would very much like that."

A few hours later, his mind reeling from the possibilities shown to him by the emperor, Baltsaros followed the weary slave to the chamber he had been given to sleep in. Before the woman turned to go, he touched her arm. The slave girl jumped at the contact, looking warily at him a moment before touching the strap on her simple dress.

"Do you want me to stay?" she said in accented Balorian, her meaning obvious.

"No, my dear," responded Baltsaros with a tight smile. "But thank you for the offer.

I simply would like to know where the other man I came with is sleeping. Is it nearby?"

The slave woman nodded and pointed to a door across the hallway. A brief, timid smile lit up her face.

"Your slave was very kind to me, sir," she said quietly. Her eyes darted to the side, obviously feeling reckless for speaking up. Before Baltsaros could respond, she sketched a quick bow and scurried down the corridor.

Surprised, the captain watched her leave, wondering what the woman meant. Random acts of kindness weren't in Tom's usual repertoire. He just hoped that whatever he was up to, the first mate didn't catch some foolish disease. The thought kindled a strange feeling in the pit of his stomach, and the captain frowned. Jealousy? Over Tom? Baltsaros shook his head to clear it. He was more tired than he realised.

After waiting another minute in the dark to make sure no one was watching, he crossed the hallway to the door the slave had pointed to. He pulled up on the latch and let himself into the room silently. Though it was nearly morning, Baltsaros wanted to curl up with Jon for just a few minutes before they had to be apart for another long day; he needed to ground himself.

As the captain navigated the small room in the dark, he put out a hand and found the bed at the far side. As soon as he put a knee up onto it, he heard Jon stir in his sleep. Careful not to startle the young man, he lay down slowly behind him and put an arm around his waist, pushing aside Jon's hair with the other hand so he could press his lips against the back of his neck. He felt Jon wake up, and he smiled before touching his tongue softly to the sleep-warm skin of his nape.

In dismay, Baltsaros felt Jon go rigid against him.

"No," said Jon, his voice hoarse. He pushed at Baltsaros's hand and moved away from him. Baltsaros frowned.

"Jon..." he whispered, skimming his fingers over his young lover's shoulder and tracing them down the defined muscles of his bicep and forearm, looking to link his hand with Jon's.

"No," repeated Jon a little louder. Baltsaros wondered for a second if Jon was actually awake and was aware of what he was saying, but when Jon continued after a few heartbeats, his voice was calm in the inky darkness.

"I'm not interested in sharing my bed or my body with you, Baltsaros," continued Jon. "Not here, not now."

The captain sat up slowly, just breathing deeply for a moment. He should have been angry, but he wasn't for once. There was something in Jon's tone that spoke of great pain... pain that *he* had put there.

No. He felt something akin to shame.

"Sleep, Jon," he said quietly. "I will see you in the morning."

When Jon didn't reply, Baltsaros slid off the bed and made his way out of the room.

. . .

Standing at the window of his own accommodations, facing the new dawn, he felt even more determined to go ahead with his plan.

The captain looked down at the blood on his hands that only he could see, blood that never washed away, and he closed his eyes, reaching for the calm that was ever further with every passing day. He'd found something better than the magic of blood sacrifice to make him whole:

If Ah'puch could put an animal in the body and mind of a man, could he not just as easily take the beast out of Baltsaros?

CHAPTER 21
A LOYAL MAN

Jon watched the light move across the ceiling as he lay on his back, hands behind his head. Sleep had eluded him once the captain had left, and he had spent the early morning just drifting, lost in thought.

He was alone for once, and it felt odd. It wasn't often that he got to lie in bed without Tom coming to seek him out. Though the big man's companionship was never quite smothering per se, it was almost constant. Jon smiled softly; sometimes the first mate reminded him a little of Brutus. The thought instantly sobered Jon; he didn't like thinking about the small, jewel-like island of Madierus. The good memories only served to cause him more pain.

Jon closed his eyes and curled onto his side, the sound of his slow breathing the only thing he could hear. After a moment, he opened them and looked at the pillow in front of him, a soft divot to one side of it where the captain had laid his head a few hours earlier. Jon wondered if he pressed his face into the soft silk, would he smell the sweet almond oil that Baltsaros used in his beard? Or the subtle, musky cologne that always reminded Jon of the first time the captain had touched him?

He stretched out his hand and patted the pillow flat, erasing the evidence of the man's presence. With a sigh, he stretched out on his belly, taking up the entire width of the bed, his arm cradled against his side to take the pressure off his ribs. Tom was right: he *was* a fool. When Baltsaros had pressed against him earlier in the cool dark of the bedchamber, his body had crackled with electricity; when the man had gone, he had been filled with a deep aching want that reached his very bones. It had taken everything for him not to call out to Baltsaros before he left to say that he had changed his mind. As the captain had quietly shut the door, Jon's chest had constricted, and he had buried his face in the covers to muffle his quick, pained breath. Pushing Baltsaros away had left him feeling hollow.

Right in the midst of a dangerous, desperate situation was not the time to have a crisis of the heart.

It felt foolish.

It also felt like the most important thing in the world.

With his eyes closed once more, he tried to steer his mind away from the downward spin it took every time he thought of the way Baltsaros's lips had brushed his skin so softly.

~

Baltsaros stood next to Ah'puch, watching what it took to create electricity. Behind the stepped pyramid that the emperor used as his palace was a large spoked wheel, not unlike the capstan of a ship. Turning it round and round at a constant, never-ending pace was an army of slaves. During the ten minutes Baltsaros stood there, mesmerized and disturbed by the sight, two men had fallen, collapsing from exhaustion. Instead of stopping to help their fallen mates, the slaves turning the wheel just stared forward with hollow eyes as they stepped over them. Slave drivers with long metal rods quickly looped the ropes at the end of them around the feet of the insensate men. The slaves were dragged out from under the machine as two new men were brought in. It was unending. It was utterly wasteful.

"Can't the wheel be turned by other means?" asked the captain, looking askance at the emperor.

Ah'puch, his eyes red-rimmed from little sleep and too much wine, twitched his upper lip into a small disdainful sneer as he shook his head.

"Why bother? Animals are too costly. Setting up a water wheel to turn it would require too much effort. With wind, it is too unpredictable. These"—he pointed to the slaves—"are plentiful. Cheap. Easy to replace."

Another slave fell, a woman this time, and was hauled out by her arm. The man with the staff bent low over the woman's body and, even from where Baltsaros stood, he could see the slave driver shake his head. A brawny brute in a harness was called forward to carry the woman's corpse away, and the captain grimaced. The casual cruelty to so many left a bad taste in his mouth.

Baltsaros decided right then that he would kill the emperor once he was through with him.

"Come! You must taste this coffee..."

Baltsaros curved his lips into a courteous smile and nodded, following the self-important little man off the balcony and back into the large sitting room. He was irritable this morning; not enough sleep and Jon's rejection made every attempt to seem gracious that much harder. Worse, the emperor wasn't interested in speaking about his "subjects" in the laboratory, nor was he forthcoming with any information about how they managed trade with the east. Despite seeing the creation of electricity in action, the morning had proven to be an exercise in patience.

With a quiet sigh, he let his eyes roam while the emperor directed a slave to place a tray of coffee on the low table between the cushioned *récamier* couches. Gold was everywhere, from the thick rods that held up curtains and tapestries to the very thread that wove those fabrics. There was an entire life's fortune just in the little statue of a bear-like creature that sat upon a pedestal near the captain's knee.

Baltsaros looked again at the two large slaves who stood to either side of the door, eyes trained on nothing. Tattoos swirled and meandered down their left sides, and Baltsaros felt an oddly anxious pang as the markings brought Tom to mind.

"My slave... when can I have him back?" asked Baltsaros with another courtly smile.

"I assure you that you do not need him while you're here, Captain. He's in good hands," smiled Ah'puch as he poured coffee into two golden mugs. "If you're worried about his physical conditioning, I would be happy to put him to work. We have many—"

"That won't be necessary," replied Baltsaros, accepting a cup, "as we unfortunately don't plan on staying very long."

"Of course," replied the emperor glibly. "It will be a shame to see you go."

Anyone watching the conversation would have thought that the two men were friends, and not captor and captive.

Baltsaros smiled blandly. He would continue to charm the emperor and feed into his need for intellectual legitimacy; as much as he hated the thought of such an inferior meddling with his mind, he had to persuade the man to take him back to the laboratory where he would pry loose the beast from within him. Then, he would kill Ah'puch... with his bare hands if he could.

Baltsaros brought the cup to his lips, hiding his look of sudden apprehension. *Would* he be able to kill when the procedure was done? He took a sip of the bitter coffee, swallowing it down along with his trepidation. It was his *obsession* that he wanted to remove, not his ability.

While the emperor chattered away about copper wires, slaves, and the expense of maintaining such a lavish palace, Baltsaros let his mind go back to the night where he had made the decision to travel beyond the spires.

~

Jon lay trembling on the pillow. His face was flushed with fever as his body tried to fight the infection that had taken root within the wound that Reginald had given him. As Jon moaned and tossed his head, Baltsaros clutched his hand, wishing that he could do something to help him. Nothing was working; not a single one of his medicines had effected even the slightest change in his condition.

Baltsaros was going to lose Jon.

All the suffering inflicted upon him in his life didn't even come close to the pain he felt at that single, horrifying realization. Each breath squeezed past a throat choked with emotion into lungs that burned and was exhaled between teeth clenched in

470

helplessness. This wasn't rage. This wasn't anger. This was anguish, pure and overwhelming.

With a soft groan, he pressed his lips to the weak pulse in Jon's wrist.

The chain of events leading up to this moment was entirely his fault. He'd chastised Jon for rash reactions when his was the most rash of all. Burning the castle... what kind of man did that?

He was no man at all. He was inside the barrel again, staring into the frigid black, and the beast with evil in its heart stared back at him, a smug smile on its face.

Suddenly Jon twitched, the breath rattling in his pierced lung... and then he was silent.

With a low sound, Baltsaros fumbled at Jon's neck, desperate to find any sign of life. His hands shook, fingers sliding down Jon's chest to the edge of the sucking knife wound he had covered in waxed linen, searching for his heartbeat.

There was none.

In that moment, Baltsaros was lost.

He bowed his head, mind numb.

"Anything," he whispered, kissing the clammy hand he clutched. "I will give up anything." He closed his eyes tight against the raw hopelessness he felt.

"I will give up anything for you." Prayers to gods he didn't believe in.

He let a long, slow exhale and pressed his face to Jon's shoulder.

At Baltsaros's touch, Jon jerked on the bed. He took in a strangled gasp of air and coughed a few times before letting out a hoarse moan. Astounded, Baltsaros quickly grabbed the cloth in the bowl of water by the bed, pressing it to Jon's lips to get moisture to his mouth.

"Balt... saros," wheezed Jon. "Baltsaros."

"Don't speak, Jon," said the captain, brow furrowed. His mind reeled. Hope. A second chance. He would redouble the medication. He would cure Jon.

"Devil's Isles..." whispered the younger man, his eyelids fluttering open though his eyes roamed from side to side as if he still dreamed. "Your... heart!" Jon's hand scrabbled over the captain's arm, his touch insistent. "Baltsaros, Tom and I found your heart! I know where it is. We have to go. Promise me..."

~

Baltsaros frowned. Someone had spoken to him. He blinked.

"I said, are you all right, Captain?" asked the emperor. Baltsaros looked up at the man, his heart thudding against his ribs at the memory.

You are my everything. I will give up anything for you.

He saw movement out of the corner of his eye and looked over Ah'puch's shoulder to the young man standing hesitantly at the door.

"Yes, I will be," Baltsaros said quietly.

~

Jon stared back at Baltsaros, struck motionless by what he read in the man's expression. The captain looked relieved and determined, proud and fiercely possessive as his dark eyes held Jon's, but the thing that made Jon's breath catch in his throat was the naked *want* he saw... Want that came from the soul. He frowned, and it was gone when Baltsaros turned away to smile at the emperor.

He took a few steps into the room, feeling dazed. He wondered belatedly if there was some sort of protocol he was supposed to follow on entering an emperor's presence, but the man swivelled in his seat and grinned wide at him, gesturing.

"Don't be shy, Jon," said Ah'puch in heavily accented Common. "Come. Join us for coffee. Your uncle was telling me last night that you have an exceptional gift. I would love to hear of it from your lips."

Jon glanced at Baltsaros in surprise. It wasn't like the captain to volunteer that kind of information; he wondered what it had been bartered for. However, Baltsaros's expression was a strange one and offered him no explanation. With a tight smile, he took one of the straight-backed chairs and accepted a cup of coffee from the sallow, dark-haired emperor. With another quick look at the captain, Jon wondered what had been said.

"What can I tell you about it?" he said softly, adopting Baltsaros's northern accent.

The questions that the emperor asked were straightforward. How had he learned to read people? How did he use it?

As Jon gave the man a faltering, semi-truthful account of his talent, his eyes kept turning to Baltsaros. The captain's face was pale, and he had dark smudges under his eyes. Jon wondered if Baltsaros had slept at all. Refusing to allow himself to feel bad about any part he played in that, he forced himself to adopt a cold look when he met the captain's eye again. However, what he was rewarded with was completely unexpected, and it sent a trickle of unease down his spine. The captain's lids had lowered quickly to stare down at the coffee in his hands, but not before Jon caught a look rife with pain. When Baltsaros looked up again a moment later, his expression was resolute. Pulse skipping along rapidly, Jon stumbled over his words and apologized to the emperor.

His brain on fire, Jon wished Tom were at his side to offer insight, strength... anything. He'd just had the distinct impression that the captain was planning something crazy.

~

Tom paced. Back and forth he went across the roughly cobbled square of the atrium. Though sleep had quickly found him on his narrow cot, he had woken at the crack of dawn with the other slaves. Unlike them, he had no work to take part in and thus was left to pace impatiently like a wildcat trapped in a cage, waiting to be summoned by Baltsaros or Jon. His lip was already on the mend, surprisingly not made worse by Jon's fervent kisses, and he could open his eye completely. He was sure that he wasn't pretty to look at, but at least he was not as sore as he had assumed he would be.

When he turned to make another trip through the sparse greenery, Tom was surprised to see Ceara watching him with an amused expression.

"Bored?" she asked.

He grunted in reply and stopped, crossing his arms.

"I need to see the captain," he said. "I don't feel right not bein' able to keep an eye on him or Jon."

Ceara shook her head at him then tilted it to appraise him.

"You're loyal man, I'll give you that much," she said. "Tom, they're fine. Trust me. But, if the emperor says you're to stay here, you stay here. The slave driver who overlooks this place is also a loyal man."

She took a few steps forward until she was close enough to touch him. Looking up into his eyes, she smiled.

"Can I get you anything?" she asked, her cheek dimpling.

"My blade," he replied with a wry grin. "And a smoke... and a bottle of somethin' that'll warm my belly."

"I can't give you your knife, but I'll see what I can do about the other two," Ceara replied blithely, but Tom heard a distinct "no" in her answer and scowled.

"Don't ye play games with me, love. Ye'll find that I ain't the cuddly kitten ye obviously take me for."

The spymaster's smile faded at the danger in Tom's eyes, and she took a deep breath as if steeling herself. He understood why a second later.

"Tom... What if I told you that I may only be able to get Jon and you out?" she said slowly.

Before he could stop himself, he had backed her against one of the wide pillars surrounding the atrium, his hand around her slender throat. When her head hit the stone, her fingers came up, trying to pry him off of her. Ceara's sky-blue eyes were wide and scared.

"No," he growled. Already his mind was putting together a simple plan to break his way out of the slave quarters and find the captain and Jon. He had seen at least a half-dozen items along the corridors of the palace that would do for a weapon in a pinch. "No!" he repeated. "Ye fuckin' said we'd all make it out if we listened to ye, ye cunt." He brought his mouth close to hers and felt her shaky breath on his lips. "I can squeeze the bloody life out of ye here and now..."

"Tom, no..." she gasped, digging at his hand with her nails. "Let—let me explain!" The woman stopped struggling all at once. "Please."

Tom loosened his grip slightly and curled his lip into a sneer.

"Talk," he grunted.

"The emperor is not a stupid man, despite how he seems. He's cautious. He's moved up his plan to incarcerate the captain—" she wheezed.

"What do ye bloody mean *incarcerate?* That wasn't part o' the bleedin' plan was it?"

"Yes... yes, it was. I was hoping to get the captain and Jon to the dungeons where I could spirit them out... but he's also now taken an active interest in Jon. I'm not sure how that will affect things. My whole plan relied on him waiting until tomorrow... and now I'm not sure he will. He knows something. Has something. I don't know, Tom. I haven't been able to find out anything—" she stammered.

"Try harder," spat Tom, squeezing her neck again.

The redhead let out a rasping breath and pulled on his hand.

"Please, Tom," she coughed. "Maybe—probably get Jon out... but not Baltsaros—"

With a roar he threw her down onto the ground and stood over her, fists balled at his sides.

"You fuckin' planned this... Yer a lyin' bloody cunt," he growled. "Ye never cared if it was us three or jus' the one ye thought would be dumb enough to think with 'is cock. All ye cared about was gettin' yerself a free ride out o' here, aye?" He wasn't Jon; he had no idea if the woman was lying, but he was furious. He was also on the verge of panic.

The woman held up a hand.

"It's ok, Mikon," she said in a tense voice. "I merely fell. This slave was just helping me up."

Tom's head swivelled quickly, and he saw that the big, bald bastard who kept the slaves in line stood at one of the doors. His blood ran cold instantly, crushing out the fire in his anger when he saw that the man held a big, coiled, shiny, black bullwhip in his huge hands. Time stood still for a moment, Tom's pulse loud in his ears.

Then he reached down slowly and curled his hand around the fallen woman's wrist, helping her up gently. His eyes remained locked on the slave driver.

"Thank you," murmured Ceara, dusting off her dark-grey dress.

Mikon wasn't fooled. Tom could see that. Despite the fact that the man made no move, Tom was certain that his flesh would feel the bloodthirsty kiss of that whip once the spymaster left.

"Take me with ye," he said urgently in a soft voice as he leaned closer to Ceara. "I don't care what bloody excuse ye use, but I'm comin' with ye. Now."

Ceara fixed him with a skeptical look. Then, with a slight pursing of her lips, she looked away, and for a moment Tom wasn't sure whether or not she'd feed him to the dogs.

As she began walking away, she beckoned at him to follow.

"Are you coming or not? I told you the emperor wanted to see you," she said impatiently.

Tom glanced again at the big man with the whip and stepped quickly to follow Ceara out of the atrium and into the corridor that linked the slave quarters to the main pyramid.

"Thank you," he said gruffly.

"Just keep your hands off of me and your godsdamned mouth shut," she muttered as she widened her strides. "So help me if we get caught and bled for a blessing, it'll be your fucking fault."

Without another word, Tom followed the slight woman into the heart of the emperor's palace.

CHAPTER 22

PARLEY

om balled his fists and hit the big burlap sack filled with rice again, trying to work loose some of the nervous energy that burned through his muscles, making him jittery.

Before pushing him into the storage closet, Ceara had said that she would find a way of getting him to the captain and Jon, but it felt like hours since she had left him there. Tom gritted his teeth and bunched his shoulders, giving the burlap sack a quick double jab with the left and right fist at around waist height. If the sack were a man, the damn scoundrel would be pissing blood tonight. Tom let out a grim chuckle, enjoying the stinging pain that warmed his knuckles.

The door opened behind him suddenly, and he spun around. A woman walked into the small storage room and froze, eyes wide. For a second, the two of them stared at each other. Tom's mind started clicking rapidly through ways of subduing the woman when she spoke up.

"What are you doing in here?" she asked in a hushed voice. The woman quickly turned and closed the door behind her.

Tom narrowed his eyes; she looked familiar. He lowered his fists slowly but stayed poised for a strike if she so much as hinted that she was looking to yell.

When Tom didn't answer her, she gave him a shy smile.

"You saved me," she said softly. "In the bathhouse?" Her round cheeks dimpled, but she sobered almost immediately.

Tom nodded slowly, relieved. An ally.

"Aye lass, I remember ye now," he said. "Be a good girl, and stay clear of those mates. They seem a peck o' trouble."

She smiled again, fidgeting under his scrutiny.

"I just wanted to thank you," she said, her hands clutched in front of her. "It was... nice of you to step in like that."

When Tom's noncommittal grunt put another brief dimple in her cheek, he returned the smile.

"Why are you in the dry goods pantry?" she repeated, her green eyes wide with curiosity.

"I'm waitin' for someone," he replied with a shrug. When she continued to stare at him in bewilderment, an idea popped into his head, and he grinned wider.

The woman flinched when he reached out and took her narrow shoulders gently in his big, scarred hands.

"Listen, lovey. If ye'd like to thank me, ye can take me to my captain, real quiet-like. Can ye do that, darlin'? Have ye seen him? He's a tall fella with a beard and a face ye wouldn'a forget," he said hopefully.

The woman nodded quickly.

"Yes. He's with the emperor right now. Him and the other man. I was just sent to get some dried figs... I have to go back right away. But if you stay here, I can return in not very long and take you to the room your captain is staying in," she said, looking nervous. "Is that all right? That's all I can do."

"Aye, lass. That'll do." It would have to.

He watched her pick up a small, wooden box from one of the lower shelves, eyeing him sidelong with a flush to her cheek.

"Are they right?" she asked quietly. "Are you really from the other side of the Gods' Claws?"

When Tom nodded, she clutched the box of figs to her chest tightly with one hand. With the other, she tapped out the same warding sign that Polas had used.

Tom chuckled.

"I ain't a bloody ghost or monster, if that's what yer thinking, lass. I'm just a man like any other." He frowned, realizing that it probably wasn't the best thing to say to her. "What's yer name, love?"

"Bettie," she said shyly, and ducked her head. She quickly turned to go. "I'll be back soon."

"It's Tom," he said, "and thank ye, Bettie. Truly."

～

Jon walked slowly next to the captain, so ill at ease that he was nauseous. They'd been dismissed by the emperor so that he could conduct some state business, but they had been told not to leave the palace. Though it had been couched in gracious terms, Jon had clearly caught the message: if they tried to leave, what little freedom they were afforded would be taken away. They really were prisoners; Ceara hadn't been lying about that.

He glanced at the captain as they were led to the floor where their sleeping chambers were located. Baltsaros had been nearly silent for the remainder of the morning, answering Ah'puch's questions with one- or two-word answers. It was unlike the man to be so terse when decorum was called for, and it fed into Jon's worry that the captain was planning on doing something reckless. When they reached Baltsaros's room, Jon hesitated for only a moment before following him in.

To his utter surprise, he saw that Tom was in the room, sitting cross-legged in the middle of the wide bed with a bright smile on his face.

"Bloody hells, is it good to see ye," said Tom, pushing himself off the mattress. He closed the distance quickly and looped an arm around each of their necks, pulling them in for a swift hug. The move hurt Jon's side, but he pressed his forehead to the bigger man's scratchy cheek, ridiculously happy to see him.

"I'm amazed they let you in here," said Baltsaros, drawing back after a moment. His dark eyes darted over the first mate's face, searching for any new injuries; Jon could see through the captain's worry that he was deeply relieved to see him.

Tom rubbed at the back of his neck, his brow wrinkling as he looked up at the captain, his green-blue eyes amused.

"Yeah... I ain't actually got leave to be here, Da," said Tom grinning. His face went dead serious in the next instant. "Listen, we have to get the hells out of this bloody place. Now. The redhead says there's plans to jail ye. I figure we can get—"

"We're not leaving, Tom," interrupted Baltsaros.

The silence that followed the captain's words was heavy, and Jon slowly closed his eyes. He felt Tom tense before the first mate dropped his arm from around his waist.

"What the fuckin' hells does that mean?" Tom's voice was rough-edged with anger.

"There is something I require here," replied the captain.

"Bloody hells, Da."

"No, Tom, I need this."

"Are ye fuckin' off yer nut, man? He's gonna put ye behind bars. We have to go!"

"There is something I need to do."

A deep tiredness washed over Jon.

He opened his eyes.

"Let him stay here. I'll come with you, Tom. Leave Baltsaros to his fucking blood rituals and insanity," he said softly. He felt defeated. The captain's dark eyes met his, but Jon couldn't read the man's expression. Didn't care to. "Just you and me, Tom. We'll get out of here. We can get one of those little catamarans and sail out together. We'll be free. Stop thinking you owe him anything..."

He looked over at Tom. The first mate's forehead was deeply creased, and his eyes flicked between the captain and Jon. Tom swallowed and then licked his bottom lip as he started to shake his head slowly.

"No. Don't you fuckin' do that to me," Tom said hoarsely, the desperation plain in his voice. "Please, Jon. Ye can't ask me to choose."

Listening to Tom plead just made him more weary.

"You know what? Stay here... Fuck you. Stay here with your pain and your lies and your godsdamned twisted loyalty," said Jon evenly. His heart felt heavy in his chest, but his eyes were dry. He didn't even sound angry despite his words. Jon looked at Baltsaros. "I can't keep forgiving you. Stay here... Get your sick fill of murder because that seems to be all that you care about. Otherwise we wouldn't—"

"*I haven't killed anyone*," said Baltsaros, his voice tight and quiet.

Jon couldn't believe his ears. What did the captain gain by lying now?

"That's bullshit, and you know it," he spat.

"Da?" said Tom. The first mate stared openly at Baltsaros.

The captain's lip twitched, and his jaw was tight as he breathed slowly. Jon realized that the man was struggling with something. A ripple of pain crossed Baltsaros's features before they smoothed out again.

Jon frowned.

"You're lying," he said, but he didn't feel as certain as a few heartbeats earlier.

"No, Jon. It's the truth," Baltsaros said, barely above a whisper. "I haven't killed anyone since I nearly lost you to Reginald."

Tom finally found his voice.

"Ye haven't killed *anyone*? No huntin'?" he asked slowly, his disbelief obvious.

The captain glanced at the first mate and shook his head.

"The only death by my hand since then was to save you, Tom."

Jon's eyes widened, and he looked in alarm at the first mate.

"Tom? What is he talking about?" he asked, but Tom lifted a hand.

"Hang on," said the first mate, his eyes fixed on the captain.

Jon watched his expression shift from skepticism, astonishment, and then once again to confusion.

"That's gotta be a bloody lie, Da. Ain't it been..." Tom looked down at his fingers, counting out on them. "...four months... nearly five since...?"

"Yes."

Jon's heart began to pound in his chest. He felt strange, every sense focused so intently on the words that were being said without really understanding what was taking place.

Tom glanced at Jon, pointing to the captain.

"Is he tellin' the truth, lad?" asked Tom, his ocean eyes wide.

Yes, whispered the tiny voice inside of him. Jon swallowed and nodded; the captain seemed utterly genuine.

Tom looked completely bewildered.

"Then... why? *Why the bloody hells are we here*, Da? If yer not lookin' for a bloodbath... why did ye drag us here?"

Baltsaros let out a slow sigh, his expression wary as he looked between Jon and Tom.

"Because I made a promise to Jon," he said finally.

Jon shook his head.

"I don't remember a promise," he said.

When Baltsaros's eyes met his, the depth of emotion he could see in them startled Jon.

"I never told you... You *died*, Jon. You died from your wounds, and there was nothing I could do about it. You died as a direct result of my actions. I may as well have murdered you myself," Baltsaros murmured. He stepped closer to Jon and reached out. Jon held himself still as the captain's outstretched fingers rested on the twisted scar beneath his shirt, and he shivered at the touch. "It was my fault. I realized it in the terrible moment when I thought I had lost you. So I made a promise to you: I would give up anything for you. Then you woke up, Jon. You lived."

Jon's mouth was dry; he was dizzy from the captain's words. He knew that his survival had been a close thing, but not *how* close.

"But... I don't understand. I thought you lied to us so you could take part in these human sacrifices. Feed into this blood magic you said gave you strength," Jon said helplessly. "Aren't we here because you want to learn... Because you wanted more... ugh. I don't understand. Earlier I could have sworn that you were going to fall in with the emperor... That you were set on doing away with the last bit of good in you somehow..."

Baltsaros laughed in surprise, and his hand moved from Jon's chest to his face. He stroked the ball of his thumb over the younger man's cheek.

"No, Jon. Quite the opposite," he said. His smile dropped a moment later, and he looked to Tom; the first mate frowned at him, suspicion plain on his battered face. "The discovery of a culture steeped in blood sacrifices was serendipitous. The very thing that could feed my fetish without me getting my hands dirty! Of course I needed to come here, but I came here to learn about *myself*. To see if I could trigger the same results that have always calmed my soul. To drench myself so thoroughly in the rituals that I might begin to understand the workings of this obsession. To find answers. *To find a cure so that I could keep my promise.*"

"But, Da... it's been months and ye ain't killed. If that ain't a bloody sign that yer fine to keep on that path..." Tom gestured, looking confused.

"The incident at the Devil's Isles makes it very clear that I am not fine, Tom," Baltsaros said tiredly, his chiselled face pale.

Tom nodded, and he passed a hand over his face, his eyes vague.

Jon was startled when the first mate suddenly stepped forward and grabbed Baltsaros's shirt, yanking him away from Jon. It took him a second to realize that Tom was furious.

"Why the *fuck* didn'cha say a bloody thing? Holy black hells, Da! Why the bloody secrets, ye daft fuckin' bastard?" he growled, shaking the captain.

Baltsaros wrapped his hands around Tom's wrists, but he made no move to pull out of the first mate's grasp.

"There was no way of presenting my intentions without divulging the truth of my past actions to Jon," replied the captain, his eyes flicking momentarily to Jon's. "I wanted to avoid that at all costs."

Tom shook him again, his rough fists white-knuckled.

"Then why the fuck wouldn't ye come to *me*? Ye godsdamned fuckin' arse... why in the bloody hells wouldn't ye let *me* in on yer fuckin' plans? Ain't I the one who keeps all yer bloody secrets? All this fuckin' time I thought ye was gettin' worse, and now ye tell me that ye been *curbin' yer appetite*? Why the *fuck* did ye let me worry ye were losin' yer bloody mind?"

"Tom, keep your voice down," said Baltsaros gently. "I had no idea you were worried."

"Why wouldn't I be? Gods, yer fuckin' thick, I swear to bloody damnation!" Tom said, incredulous.

"Stop. Just... Stop," said Jon, placing a hand on Tom's shoulder. "Please."

Tom's jaw jutted forward, and he reluctantly loosened his grip on the captain's shirt, but Jon could tell that the first mate's anger had run its course.

Jon shook his head at Baltsaros.

"You realize that in the span of a day I went from learning that you're a blood-obsessed maniac to finding out that you're also a man who is desperately seeking out a cure for his madness," Jon said. "If the latter is true..." He let out a slow exhale, sifting through his feelings. "It's a lot to take in."

The captain nodded mutely.

Jon tilted his head and searched Baltsaros's face for signs that the man was holding something back; what he saw was strength, hope, and determination... and a deep fondness that the captain was unable, for whatever reason, to call love.

"So what is your plan?" he asked finally with a sigh.

Baltsaros smiled.

~

Tom shadowboxed while Jon and the captain discussed the emperor's twisted hobby. The plan was to use Ah'puch's methods to somehow cure Baltsaros of his own grisly obsession. To Tom, it sounded completely crazy. He couldn't understand why flashing lights and mere words could cause someone to think they were a dog, but what did he know? Who cared as long as this wizardry killed the beast in Baltsaros? He smiled to himself and glanced at Jon; maybe everything was going to be all right.

Tom had felt sick to his stomach for a few minutes when he thought that he'd have to choose between Jon and Baltsaros; he'd die a happy man if he never had to feel that way again. He shifted his weight and bounced on the balls of his feet before neatly breaking the nose of his imaginary foe.

"What if he jails you like Ceara says he will?" asked Jon. He sat at the far corner of the bed, picking at the embroidery on the coverlet while Baltsaros leaned back against the bed frame, feet crossed at the ankles.

"I think I could persuade him not to, Jon. The man's not as clever as he thinks he is. I'm sure I can come up with a reason for why he and I should join forces," said the captain with a thin smile. "What if Ceara's warning was a ruse? Has that woman done *anything* so far to let you believe that she's trustworthy? Has she taken any real risks?"

When Jon glanced at him, Tom winked. He was still annoyed that the captain had kept things from him, so he felt no burning need to tell him about the bathhouse. A shadow of a smile crossed Jon's face before he turned back to Baltsaros.

"She brought Tom to the storage room when she could have just as easily left him in the slave quarters," said Jon with a shrug, neatly leaving out the fact that he and Tom had spent time together.

"Yes, but she left him there for quite a while, and we have no idea where she is now," Baltsaros pointed out.

"Aye, that's true," said Tom. "But she was sayin' that the emperor has something he ain't sharin' with her. I'm no bleedin' mind reader, but she seemed like she was real scared."

"Yes. Which brings me back to my original question: what do we do if he throws you in a cell, Baltsaros?" asked Jon.

"I don't know," replied the captain. He glanced at Tom. "I'm sure you two can come up with a plan. Just promise me one thing: don't die trying to save me."

Tom dropped his fists, the pit in his stomach having opened again at the captain's words.

Seeing Tom's expression, Baltsaros smiled wider.

"I'm hoping, of course, that it doesn't come to that. Believe me when I say that I want to get out of this unscathed as much as you do," laughed the captain, waving a hand in the air. The corners of his eyes creased in merriment. "Tom, come here. Stop looking at me like that." Baltsaros beckoned to him.

Tom chewed the corner of his lip.

Fuck it.

He took a step towards the bed. With a sigh Tom climbed up onto it and crawled across the mattress on all fours like a cat. He sank down onto his belly and pressed his face against the captain's thigh. After a moment, Tom felt the captain's fingers trace the bruises that Jon's rough handling had left around his neck.

"Is this your handiwork?" asked the captain quietly. Jon made no reply, but Tom heard Baltsaros chuckle a second later. "Don't look so guilty. But tell me, did you abuse my first mate before or after you refused my company last night?" There was a distinct smile in the captain's voice.

Jon let out a short laugh, tinged with bitterness.

Baltsaros's fingers begin to draw patterns, and Tom knew that he was following the tattoos that curled and meandered across his skin. It was a soothing touch; he let out a small contented sound.

"I am very sorry for the way I've completely mishandled this. In an attempt to lessen the damage I could do, I seem to have made matters worse," murmured the captain. "You both make me want to be a better man, and that puts me at a loss. I find myself... troubled. I'm sorry that I didn't grant you the trust that you both deserve. I'm sorry I have such a difficult time asking for help."

Tom smiled to himself. So many apologies. The man really was changing. Tom raised his head slowly, propping himself up on his elbows to glance over his shoulder, curious to see Jon's reaction.

Jon remained at the end of the bed, a pensive look on his face as he continued to fiddle with the blanket. After a moment, he lifted his blue eyes and regarded Baltsaros in his quiet, serious way.

"See, this is what comes from believing that what we have together is a weakness. If you understood that it was in fact a strength, we wouldn't be sitting here at odds." Jon's lips quirked into a wan smile before he let out a long sigh. "Yea gods, I was certain this was the last straw. You certainly test the promise I made to you time and time again. I feel crazy, absolutely crazy. Maybe I should have Ah'puch take a look in my mind too while we're here." He chuckled, shaking his head. "What do you think?"

"I think you should come here, Jon," said Baltsaros.

Jon blinked.

The captain's fingers touched Tom's shoulder again, and he turned.

"Why don't you coax Jon to come closer?" asked the older man with a small smile.

Tom was skeptical, but he was also tired of the distrust and miscommunication that seemed destined to forever plague them, so he shrugged inwardly and moved to obey.

When Tom pulled himself up onto his knees, Jon watched him dubiously as he moved towards him.

"I don't think this is the time," Jon said. However, he made no attempt to stop Tom when he lowered his mouth to the hand that Jon had curled limply in his lap.

Tom kissed one knuckle, and then another, opening his lips so that his teeth grazed Jon's skin as he moved to a third. Above him, Jon let out a huff of breath and Tom smiled. He pushed the tip of his tongue into the crevice between two fingers and was rewarded with another soft sound. Using nothing but his tongue, teeth, and chin, he gently turned Jon's hand over and kissed the centre of his palm. In response, Jon's other hand came up to rest on the back of Tom's head. Tom brushed his lips along the heel of Jon's open hand and pressed tongued kisses to wrist, forearm, and into the sensitive crease at the crook of his elbow. When he glanced up, he saw that Jon's eyes were half-lidded, the irises dark as dusk as he watched Tom seduce him slowly.

Tom smiled cheekily before ducking his head to push his face against Jon's abdomen. He knew he wasn't skilled at finding the right words to make things better; but if there was one thing that he *was* good at, it was this. Jon let himself be pushed back on the bed, his head at the edge of it, and cleared his throat as he watched Tom lift up the hem of his tunic to expose his stomach. Tom smiled and kissed the soft, dark hair below Jon's navel.

"What if someone comes in?" asked Jon in a breathless voice.

The bed creaked behind Tom, and the first mate looked up after licking a slow stripe along the line of Jon's pelvis. Baltsaros walked to the side of the bed, and stared down at Jon for a moment before he leaned forward and placed his hands to either side of the younger man's head, his expression strange.

"At this moment, the only thing I care about is that I don't lose you," said the captain quietly. "If love is strength, then let's have no more talk of leaving. I need your strength more than ever." His dark eyes were wide with emotion when they lifted to meet Tom's. "Both of yours."

Tom's chest felt tight; Baltsaros had never sounded this earnest before. Tom stroked his thumbs softly along Jon's skin and felt him shiver slightly.

"Aye, Da," he said gruffly. "Ye know ye have mine."

"I don't know what will happen. I'm in no way sure that my plan will work," said the captain, looking back down at Jon. "It may very well be for naught... But if I am to be dragged away in chains, please let me spend this stolen time here with you. Put away your doubts. Find the good in me so that I might hold onto it a little longer."

~

Jon stared wide-eyed into the captain's fierce gaze. He doubted the story of the promise; if Baltsaros didn't believe in a higher power, he had no reason to hold true to a vow made to a man deaf to his words. However, that didn't change the fact that the captain was willing to put his mind into the hands of a lunatic to try to cure himself. No, it had little to do with a promise, realized Jon. His pulse sounded loud in his ears in the silence as the captain waited for his answer. No... This was Baltsaros simply and honestly wanting to change himself so that they could be together. If that wasn't love...

Jon nodded once.

Baltsaros let out a little breathless sigh. There was a flush to his face as he leaned down again and pressed his lips tenderly to Jon's. It was awkward at first to kiss Baltsaros back, their mouths reversed, jaws working in opposite ways. However, when he brought his hands up to clutch at him, he felt the captain's pulse racing against his palms, and he no longer cared. He strained up from the bed, deepening the kiss, fingers locked behind Baltsaros's neck. He felt Tom's rough stubble scrape against his stomach before the big man's lips opened over his skin. He gasped. Tom's hand stroked down his side and down between his legs, cupping him warmly through the fabric. The touch was gentle, delicious, confident, and Jon felt himself react to it.

He released Baltsaros, shoving him up and away.

"Tom," Jon said, feeling utterly reckless. "Go push something heavy against the door."

"Aye, aye," replied the first mate.

When Jon raised his head, he saw that Tom was grinning at him.

The burly pirate lifted himself up on hands and knees and slid off the bed; he put his back to the heavy stone table nearest to the door and began to slide it across the floor.

Jon turned over onto his stomach, going up onto his knees quickly to back up. Baltsaros stood and watched as Jon straightened and did away with the sash around his waist, tugging the tunic up over his head with a wince. When the captain made to approach, Jon held up a hand.

"No," he said.

Baltsaros's expression darkened at the command, but Jon repeated himself, tempering the word with a smile.

"Not yet," he added.

Brows high, the captain crossed his arms over his broad chest, but he stayed where he was.

Tom finished sliding the table in front of the door, and when Jon beckoned to him, the first mate obeyed quickly, climbing up onto the bed in front of him. Eyes locked on Baltsaros, Jon undid his pants quickly and pulled his cock out. Without any ceremony, he grabbed the back of Tom's head and forced him forward. The first mate pressed his face against him willingly, his mouth opening over Jon's half-hard cock to quickly suck in its length.

Jon grunted from the sudden, eager contact, rocking back on his knees as Tom's hot mouth enveloped him. He closed his eyes, giving into the sensation for a moment before sparing a look at the captain.

Baltsaros had a smirk on his face, obviously amused by Jon's reaction.

When Tom's hand came up to fondle the soft sack between his legs, Jon let out a shuddering sigh. Maintaining the air of detached dominance he was trying to effect was nearly impossible given Tom's talented fingers and tongue. With a groan, he bucked his hips, his head down as he watched his wet shaft slide out of Tom's open mouth before the first mate swallowed it back down again.

Jon started when Baltsaros's hand touched his back, and he blinked at the captain.

"I told you not to move," he said, his words ending on a gasp as Tom's tongue dipped into the slit at the head of his cock.

The captain smiled darkly, and he lifted his other hand to run his fingers over Jon's nipple, pinching the bud of sensitive skin between thumb and forefinger.

"Yes, you did," said Baltsaros. He lowered his mouth to Jon's but stopped a hair's breadth away. "But I'm not in the mood for games."

He pinched harder, and Jon's groan of pain opened his lips to Baltsaros. He whimpered into the kiss, surrendering to the captain. His hands left Tom's head, and he scrabbled at Baltsaros's chest, wanting to pull the shirt off of him. The older man broke the kiss and laughed, ridding himself of the tunic swiftly as Jon took care of the laces at the front of his pants.

Tom let Jon's cock slide all the way out of his mouth, and he looked up at Jon for a moment, his lips red and wet. Jon watched as the first mate moved to use his mouth on the captain's exposed cock, his hand shifting from Jon's sack to stroke along his length instead. As Tom gorged himself on the older man's cock, Baltsaros let out a small growl and captured Jon's mouth again, savaging him with a kiss that brought out a keen edge to his desire. When Tom's lips and tongue reclaimed him, Jon felt the heat and hardness of the captain's cock against his own. With a moan, he pulled away from the kiss and saw that Tom held both shafts tight in one hand; the first mate licked and sucked at their cockheads, working his lips over both with a soft moan.

Jon could barely breathe, the ache in his side sharp as he strained to pull in air. Despite the pain, however, he found himself getting close as Tom stroked their shafts as one. He could feel Baltsaros's wet cock slipping against his; it made the heat in his loins swell and tightened the skin between his legs.

He pressed his face against the captain's neck and sobbed out his mounting passion; another stroke… yet another. Closer. He would soon spill. Baltsaros wrapped his arms around Jon's shoulders, one hand tight against the back of his neck, holding him firmly as he growled deep in his chest. Jon felt the captain's heart race against his chest, his fingers clutching at him almost painfully. With a gasp Baltsaros's body trembled, and Tom let out a small sound.

Jon closed his eyes tight; Tom's mouth was suddenly wetter, more slick, the captain's cum spread back over his own cock… and he fell headlong into his own orgasm, every liquid pulse forcing a helpless sound from his throat.

Shaking, Jon pressed breathless kisses to Baltsaros's neck when his groin stopped throbbing out its exquisite release.

Tom's soft licks were nearly too much for his spent cock, and he let out a shuddering sigh. Blindly, he reached out for the first mate and was rewarded with a soft nuzzle against his palm.

When Baltsaros released him, Jon let himself fall back on the bed, his thighs trembling. Baltsaros tugged his pants back over his hips; the captain's face was serene as he looked down at Jon, his lips slowly bowing in a fond smile.

Baltsaros turned to Tom and stroked his cheek, turning his hands to claws to scratch down the kneeling first mate's back. The sound that came out of Tom's broad chest was a low grumble of pleasure, and Jon could see that the big man's hand moved beneath the material of his shortened trousers.

There was a scraping sound. Startled, the three looked up to see a section of the wall come open.

Tom let out a frustrated noise when he saw the figure emerge.

"Cock and bloody balls, sweet cheeks. Could ye have waited another fuckin' five minutes?"

However, his face fell to stark seriousness a moment later at Ceara's words.

"The guards are coming."

CHAPTER 23

THE END OF THE ACT

I assess the power of a will by how much resistance, pain, torture it endures and knows how to turn to its advantage.

— FRIEDRICH NIETZSCHE

Baltsaros glanced at the door behind him and frowned as he fastened his pants.

"How much time do we have?" he asked.

"Minutes. Enough that you can follow me through here so we can be away," replied the woman in the burgundy cloak.

"Captain, let's go. We can find a different cure," Jon said quickly. "I'm sure there's some other method..."

Tom turned to Baltsaros; the first mate's blue-green eyes were hopeful.

Jon was right. His salvation could not possibly exist solely within this bloodstained citadel. They could leave here and sail from rumour to hearsay until they found something that calmed his soul. He could rely on Tom to protect Jon... Baltsaros clenched his jaw, his eyes on the two young men on the bed. Yes, and hunger would steadily chip away at his resolve until he was unable to deny himself any longer. Murders would follow. He would lose Jon, and he was not as sure as he once was whether Tom would stay by his side. Here and now, *this* was in his grasp. He had to take a chance. The captain shook his head and tensed at the disappointed look on Jon's face. However, Jon set his jaw a second later and nodded once. Tom followed suit.

"Why are the guards coming? What does he know?" he asked, turning to Ceara. Something akin to disappointment clouded her limpid, blue eyes when she realized he wasn't moving to follow her.

486

"I'm... not sure," said the women with twist of her lips.

A quick glance at Jon told him that she was lying; Jon's face was pinched in an expression of disgust as he stared at her, shaking his head slowly as if in disbelief.

Ceara glared at Jon.

"Listen, do you want to stick around here to find out? You won't be in any danger at all if you come with me *right now*. We don't have time to discuss this," she said, her voice tight and quiet.

"I simply don't trust you," the captain replied. "Jon thinks you're lying to us, and I trust his instincts implicitly. We are not leaving yet; there is business I have with the emperor that has yet to be addressed. Tom, go move the table."

"Aye, Da," said the first mate with a grim nod.

"What?" coughed the woman. "You've got *business* with the emperor? You cannot be fucking serious. I have a way for all four of us to get *out*. Right now. I've already wasted enough time trying to track down this big fucking lout."

Tom snorted in amusement as he slid the heavy table away from the wooden door.

The petite woman took a deep breath and stepped towards Baltsaros, putting her hands together in supplication as she changed tact.

"Captain. Listen to me. You're a man of reason. We can be away and hide in the city until *Baal's Heart* returns tomorrow. There is nothing for you here, and every second spent debating this is another step towards imprisonment," she pleaded.

"Aren't we already prisoners?" asked Baltsaros, brows high. "Despite not letting us leave the palace, Ah'puch has been nothing but courteous. As far as I can tell, he is simply curious about us. What is the impetus behind this sudden threat of further incarceration?" There was something incredibly odd about the woman's whole demeanour.

Ceara blinked twice, and her lips curved up into a weak smile, no doubt preparing another lie.

"What aren't you telling us, Ceara?" pressed Baltsaros, his voice cold. He could hear sounds coming from down the hallway.

"I wish you had come with me... It's too late now," she said hurriedly, glancing at the door. "I lied to you. He knows. He knows everything, but I will *fix this*. I promise I will prove my worth, Captain. Trust me. But no matter what, say nothing of my help; *he must not suspect me*." Her eyes were utterly guileless, and he doubted she could fake her sudden ghostly pallor.

Baltsaros held the woman's gaze a moment longer. He nodded as the door behind him opened; even a dubious ally was better than none at all.

Smoothly shifting his expression to one of outrage, he turned to the men who spilled into the room.

"What is the meaning of this?" he asked in Balorian, straightening to his full height. Though he was a tall man, the two marked slaves at the fore looked down at him.

"We're to take you to the emperor," one of them replied. "No delay. Come with us."

"And this gives you permission to simply walk into my room?" asked Baltsaros angrily. "Have you forgotten yourself... *slave*? Is this any way to treat a guest of the emperor?"

The guard stared back at him blankly, rendered momentarily uncertain by the captain's words. Behind him, another man spoke up.

"What is he doing in here?" asked a thin-faced slave, pointing to Tom.

"He is in my charge," answered Ceara, stepping forward. "The emperor asked to see the slave too, did he not?"

The man's eyes widened, startled by the spymaster's presence.

"Yes. But... Emperor Ah'puch only now just asked for—" he stammered.

"Do you not think that I know everything that goes on within these walls, slave?" sneered Ceara. "Do you not think that I have the power to anticipate Our Most Exalted Emperor's every wish?" The woman gave a throaty little laugh, her smile wicked. "Or perhaps Our Most Exalted Emperor sent me here to make sure that you performed your duties as quickly as He demanded... Tell me: have you done anything to make Him suspect you of colluding with these men?"

Baltsaros nearly chuckled at how quickly the spymaster was able to completely take apart a man twice her size. The slave was nearly shaking with terror; he would not bring up Tom's odd presence in the bedchamber. It had been neatly done. The captain looked curiously at the woman in the burgundy cloak. Her loyalty was unproven and her motives suspect, but he couldn't help but think that she would make a valuable addition to his crew... if they made it back to the *Heart*.

Maintaining his act of indignation, he motioned impatiently for the guards to lead them to Ah'puch.

~

Jon grunted when the guard hit the back of his knees with his spear. The slave growled a word that Jon didn't understand, but its meaning was clear: *kneel*. Hastily, he got down on his knees. Tom and Baltsaros followed suit to either side of him.

The room they had been brought to was yet another study in excess. Every narrow, fluted column was gilded, and every elaborate cornice glittered with gems. Small, burnished pedestals lined the walls, each holding the solid gold bust of a man. Above them, the ceiling was painted with a detailed scene of satyrs and nymphs playing by a river surrounded in lush greenery. To each side of the thick, colourful rugs on which they kneeled were tiered fountains that trickled melodiously.

Dominating the room was an enormous dais at its centre. It was modelled to look like a miniature of the palace, but each step of this pyramid was inlaid with different coloured gems that formed floral and arabesque patterns. At its apex sat an ornate throne and, unlike the rest of the gilded furnishings, it was painted blood red. It was from this grisly seat that the Emperor Ah'puch looked down upon them. Ceara stood at his side with her hands clasped in front and head down. Dread became a cold finger caressing the length of Jon's spine.

"The time for pretending has come to an end," said the emperor in accented

Common, his thin lips quirked in a disgusted sneer. "Our warlocks counselled against bringing forth the accusations against you until the end of this moon phase. However, We feel that even letting you roam free in Our palace risks polluting Our subjects and slaves with your degenerate sins."

"What are we accused of?" asked the captain.

Ah'puch motioned, and the slave behind Baltsaros kicked him hard in the kidneys. Jon flinched as the man fell forwards onto his hands and knees with a pained grunt.

"Do not speak until We have given you leave," scolded the emperor from his lofty seat. He glanced at the arm of his throne and fiddled with something for a moment.

Behind Jon, the doors opened, and he heard a small, choked sob. He turned and watched two marked slaves drag a limp figure past him. When they reached the base of the dais, the men threw their charge to the ground, and the figure remained prone, hands over his head.

"Kneel," barked the emperor.

Immediately, the young man on the floor scrabbled to his knees. It took Jon a moment to recognize Oren with his hair shorn and face bloodied. The slender fisherman shook as if palsied, and little whimpers escaped his swollen lips.

Jon felt ill; Oren's whole body was a mass of bruises, large burn blisters, and lacerations. Though Jon's own fists and boots had caused some of the damage, it was obvious that the boy had been brutally tortured. Tears made a clear path through the blood on Oren's face as he stared at Jon; he was terrified.

There was a rustle, and a group of masked figures entered the throne room; they walked slowly in single file to the base of the pyramid and turned to face the accused. The eight were draped in heavy red cloaks, and the masks they wore were fashioned to look like horned animal skulls.

"Oren, son of Migri, kin to the Dogfish clan, you are here to give testimony before the Council of the Eight, the Lords of the Knife. May your words match the truth in your blood," the cloaked figures said as one.

Their sepulchral voices made the tiny hairs on the back of Jon's neck stand up. He glanced quickly to his right and saw that the captain had resumed kneeling and stared curiously at the eerie figures. Tom, on the other hand, just looked unimpressed.

Jon turned back to Oren; the young fisherman had closed his eyes and in his terror had begun to rock back and forth.

One of the cloaked figures stepped forward holding a little corked vessel in his hands. Even from this distance, Jon could see that the man's fingernails were crusted with something dark. Without any warning, the man grabbed Oren's arm and sliced his wrist quickly with a small, curved blade. Oren gave a strangled cry as blood poured into the little bowl. When the warlock was satisfied, he turned back to the pyramid and lifted the sacrifice above his head. He intoned a few words, *blood* being the only one of which Jon understood.

Oren resumed his rocking as he clutched his arm to his chest.

"Speak, boy," said the emperor, leaning forward in his throne.

As if jabbed by a red-hot poker, Oren let out a sharp gasp; he began to speak in

Balorian, the words fast and so slurred that Jon understood none of it. However, his mouth went dry when he heard Tom's quiet "fuck".

"He's lying," growled Baltsaros. This time, the slave hit him hard in the head with the butt of his spear; the captain went down in a slump and didn't move again.

With a roar, Tom sprang to his feet and grabbed the guard before anyone could react. The sound of the man's neck snapping rang out in the throne room, and Jon let out a startled yell as the guard fell on top of him; in shock, Jon pushed the dying, gurgling slave away and crawled backwards on his knees. He watched in helpless dismay as four guards wrestled Tom to the ground.

At the foot of the dais, Oren wailed like a wounded animal, a puddle of piss at his knees.

"Enough!" roared Ah'puch. The emperor had risen and glared down at them from his lofty throne. From behind Jon came a low groan from Tom. The emperor pointed to his warlock. "What do the gods say?"

The cloaked figure raised the bowl to his lips. When it came away, the man's mouth was red. From between his gory lips hissed a single word, one that Jon understood: *death*.

Jon held out his hand in a panic, as if the gesture alone could halt the confusion and horror unfolding before him.

"Stop! Wait! What did he say?" he yelled, pointing at Oren. "What are we accused of?" He heard a step behind him and ducked as the spear came down. It missed his head but cracked against his shoulder, and he gasped in pain.

"We're fucked, lad," groaned Tom.

The next warlock took his taste of the sacrifice and repeated the verdict.

Jon suddenly remembered Ceara's words. He stumbled to his feet, his hands clutched in front of him.

"I was forced!" he shouted. "Please! I was forced!" His voice broke in his rush to get the words out, and he cried out as the slave hit him across the back with the spear.

"Forced?" rasped the figure with the bowl. The warlock sounded startled, and Jon felt a whisper of hope. He nodded frantically, hoping to the black hells that he wasn't damning them further.

The cloaked warlocks glanced at one another, the sentencing interrupted for the moment. Oren sobbed and gibbered as he lay curled up on the polished floor.

Ah'puch descended a few steps, and he pointed to Jon with his walking stick.

"Take his blood," said the man, but Jon could see that his words had softened the emperor's expression; there was sympathy there. What had Jon just admitted to? He hastily extended his arm when the figure with the blade approached and did no more than wince when a shallow cut was made.

The warlock smelled of fire and blood, and his skull mask was terrifying.

However, when Jon looked into his eyes, what he saw there surprised him. This was just an ordinary man, no demon: a little weary, skeptical... fearful. The masked man averted his gaze quickly, and Jon frowned. His mind spun in confusion and frustration at not knowing what was going on, but the edge had been taken off his panic by the very mortal unease in the warlock's eyes.

After the cloaked figure lifted the sacrificial vessel to his lips, he looked up at the emperor and nodded. Ah'puch's dark brows pinched together over his hooked nose as he stared hard at Jon for several seconds. Finally, he spoke.

"Ceara, since this is now a matter for the gods, please escort Jon back to his room. There's nothing else to be done for now. Guards, bring the captain to my laboratory," Ah'puch paused, his eyes on the first mate. Tom spat a bloody gob on the beautiful carpet and stared brazenly back at the emperor. "You were once a slave, were you not? Shall we make that permanent? What do you think? Yes?" The man on the dais chuckled as Tom started to struggle anew. "Mikon... Give him fifty lashes at daybreak tomorrow. Let's see if we can break this brute and turn him into something useful."

Part of Jon was glad that he was pulled away before he could see the look on Tom's face. He needed to think, to plan a way out of this mess. The panic he knew would beset the first mate at the threat of the whip would only serve to fuel his own abject terror; fear in those fearless blue-green eyes would derail any hope of keeping himself from falling completely to pieces.

Jon pulled his arm out of the spymaster's grasp and stepped away once they had reached his room.

"What did I just confess to?" he said hoarsely. "What was I *forced* to do?" He asked only to confirm his suspicions.

Ceara reached up and undid the hidden clasp on her cloak, letting it fall to the floor behind her. She looked fragile without its bulk. Slowly, she sat on the edge of the bed and looked around her.

"You might not know the language, but you're not stupid, Jon," she said finally. "You know perfectly well that you just admitted that the captain forced himself on you."

Jon's lip curled up in distaste, but he nodded.

"Sit, Jon," said Ceara gently. "I'll tell you why."

The last thing he wanted to do was sit, but he sank down on the mattress a moment later, suddenly exhausted and overwhelmed by the enormity of the situation.

Ceara appraised him with her wide blue eyes, and the cupid's bow of her mouth curved into a small, sombre smile before she began to speak in a low voice.

"Two days ago, some of my men found Oren wounded and completely incoherent, wandering in the *madina*," she said. She looked down at her hands and frowned. One shoulder came up in a little shrug a second later, and the lines around her mouth deepened. "Well... at least, at the *time*, nothing he was saying made any sense to me. Stories of a vessel from beyond the Gods' Claws..." She glanced up at him, her eyes wide. "Jon, you have to understand that even *suggesting* men can cross through there with their lives intact is heresy. To say that there are living men on the other side of that mountain range..." A crease appeared in her smooth brow as she searched his eyes. "Do you have the concept of purgatory in your lands? Where souls wait to get weighed before being sent to the gods or banished to the underworld forever?" When Jon nodded, she continued.

"The black mountain range is the wall that keeps the spirits locked in purgatory, and the Gods' Claws are the gate... That's what is taught. So you can understand why I didn't believe his rantings. I thought he was so wounded that it had enfeebled him somehow; no one in their right mind would speak blasphemy the way he was. If men could escape purgatory..." She shook her head and sat silent for several seconds before resuming with a sigh. "So... I handed Oren over to Emperor Ah'puch," she confessed.

Ceara twisted her fingers together and looked back down again. Jon's gut churned at the memory of the captain's description of Ah'puch's "patients".

"The emperor has a way with the mysteries of the mind. I thought he could study Oren." Another one-shouldered shrug; she glanced up, her features smooth. "It was a little over two hours later that I heard reports from my spies about a strange ship anchored not far away and strange men in the jungle. I began to have... doubts. I know there is no truth behind the stories of the black mountains."

As she talked, the woman kept shifting between a calm coldness born of duty and the appearance of heartfelt regret.

"Why do you know this as a fact?" he asked.

Ceara huffed out a tiny, bitter laugh.

"If you were the emperor, do you think *you* could conduct secret trades without the help of your spymaster?" she asked with a sardonic lift of one eyebrow. "Who do you think makes certain that the citizens of Ereme'ia Balor are none the wiser?"

Jon let this sink in for a moment; he ran a hand through his curls.

"Why then?" he asked, nonplussed and more than a little angry. "Why do you want to leave if you're so fucking cozy with the emperor? Nothing you've said so far makes me want to trust you. You gave what you thought was a—what did you call him? Enfeebled? You gave an *enfeebled* boy to a bloodthirsty sadist... to *study*."

She nodded.

"I'm not asking for forgiveness nor am I trying to justify my actions to you. I'm not even asking you to trust *me*, only to trust my honest, desperate desire to get us out," she said softly. "Let me finish before you judge me completely."

Jon chewed on the inside of his cheek. As far as he could tell, she was being completely honest with him.

"All right. What happened after you got your *doubts*?"

"I went to see whether I could coax more information out of Oren... only to find that the emperor had done it for me using his, ah, methods. However, along with the details of your ship, Oren also let slip that the captain, you, and Tom were lovers," she said. A delicate grimace creased her brow. "Because of this, you three were to be captured immediately and put to death as per the law. However, I stepped in and bribed the Counsel of Eight to dissuade Ah'puch from doing anything before the end of this moon phase; I was trying to buy some time.

"I quickly made my way alone to the inn, intent on approaching the captain, but

492

then you arrived with your fire and your daring rescue and seriously fucked things up for me. I thought I had lost my chance... I wanted to follow you back to the ship, but I couldn't. I've suspected for a long time that Ah'puch has me watched; he doesn't even trust his own spymaster. However, I did manage to keep the truth of your escape hidden from him so that guards weren't sent out to your ship. Imagine my surprise when the three of you came waltzing back in yesterday morning," Ceara laughed, shaking her head. "And you might have thought you were fooling people with your little act, but I was receiving a constant stream of reports about the three strangers in the *madina*. So, I decided to follow you myself until I could find a safe place to talk.

"Before I had a chance to, the emperor, pismire that he is, sent guards to bring you in; he wanted to keep an eye on you despite the warlocks' dire predictions. I intercepted them and took charge, knowing that if I brought you in myself, it would provide us with a chance to speak privately, however brief.

"My plan was simple: when you and the captain were thrown in the dungeons, I would bribe the guards to get you out. And, by you saying you were forced by the captain to submit to his perversions, the emperor would have no choice but to allow for a stay of execution, giving me ample time to get us away. The laws take this sort of thing very seriously; an oracle has to be consulted for the—"

"What about Tom?" Jon asked impatiently.

"Oh, I can get Tom out of the slave quarters any time I want," she replied with a small, dismissive wave of her hand. "No one guards the slaves. The guards *are* slaves, Jon. Anyway, my plan completely backfired when the emperor took a shining to both you and the captain. For different reasons, of course. Instead of a neat escape from the dungeons, I found myself faced with the task of freeing Baltsaros from the laboratory, an area of the palace that I have a hard time accessing. I told Tom that I could get you both out, but perhaps not the captain. He was, needless to say, not very happy with me."

With his mind reeling, Jon could do nothing but stare at the woman. While he didn't doubt her story, he was sickened by the irreverence with which she discussed their plight.

"...though I have to say that I'm not very happy with any of this either. You know, that escape I had planned for the four of us earlier? It cost me every last *rukscha* I had," Ceara said peevishly. "Now I have no clue what to do. What in demons' blood compelled the captain to want to stay here? What in hells is this 'business' with the emperor anyway?"

Jon leaned forward, ignoring her question.

"Why wait until now to tell us all of this?" he growled. "Why all the secrecy, the lies, the running around with cryptic messages?" Jon was exasperated, furious. At that moment he truly believed that he would slit the throat of the next person who lied to him.

"Simple," said Ceara with another little flick of her wrist. "I thought if you knew I was the reason behind your arrests, you would refuse to take me with you."

Despite the glibness of her answer, something in the woman's eyes kept Jon from throttling her right then and there out of sheer frustration; he had seen despair and more than a little fear for just an instant. It was enough to make him set his teeth together and take a slow breath to garner his calm before he spoke again. She looked at Jon curiously as he moved closer, his eyes fixed on her.

"I asked you something earlier and you didn't answer. Will you answer me now?" he asked softly. "*Why do you want to escape so badly?*"

The petite spymaster turned her head, staring off at the blue sky outside the narrow window set high in the stone wall. After a moment she let out a slow exhale and nodded to herself. She glanced at Jon but averted her eyes again quickly as she lifted her hands to the high neck of her dress and began to undo the tiny buttons. When the fabric parted, Jon's breath caught in his throat. Beneath the dress, the woman's pale skin was covered in a gruesome maze of twisted scars. Feeling ill, he hastily reached out and stopped her from undoing any more buttons; he had seen enough.

There was a subtle tic in her jaw as she turned, chin held high, and forced herself to meet his gaze again. When she spoke, her voice was defiant.

"Why do I want to leave? Let's just say that the mind is not the only thing that sadistic asshole likes to experiment with."

CHAPTER 24
LAYERS AND LEAVINGS

One, two, they're coming for you;
Three, four, always wanting for more;
Five, six, seven, the red hands, they beckon;
Eight, nine, ten, slaughtered now, feast on men.

— NORTHERN CHILDREN'S RHYME

Consciousness touched Baltsaros's mind like cold fingers slipping through layers of gauzy cloth. He groaned and turned his head, wincing as the swollen bruise on the back of his scalp touched the hard surface beneath him. His first attempt to open his eyes was painful; bright light seared his vision, and he closed his lids quickly. Tears beaded on his lashes and shimmered in his sight for a moment when he tried again. He blinked quickly and saw that right above him were four of the electric illumination globes. He went to shield his face from the harsh light but couldn't move; at wrists, ankles and shoulders, he was strapped down to a table.

"Ah, there you are," said a voice from somewhere to his left.

Baltsaros licked his lips, his tongue barely moist enough to make a difference.

"Where am I?" he croaked. The details were fuzzy. He could remember a farce of a trial, but nothing else.

"In my laboratory," said the man again. The emperor.

Baltsaros rested his eyes again. He was having a hard time concentrating. Suddenly the red-tinged, semi-dark he had retreated to flashed with starbursts, and his stomach roiled in protest. With a choked gasp he opened his eyes again. The lump at the back of his head now made sense.

"I'm concussed," he whispered, trying again with a leather-dry tongue to grant his lips some mobility. His throat stuck on a swallow.

The emperor leaned over Baltsaros for a moment, blocking the light. The captain was grateful for the short respite from the blistering brightness.

"What was that?" asked the man.

It was as if he was registering the man's words on a delay, the meanings lost momentarily in a haze, and it added to his confusion. Not able to see Ah'puch's features, only a dark shadow, the captain frowned and tried to force his thoughts into some order.

"A... brain injury," he said, the words a mere croak. His eyes felt gritty in their sockets as he blinked slowly.

"Ah, is that what you call it? *Concussed?*" asked Ah'puch. Baltsaros thought he could sense the man's dark eyes on his. Nausea rose like a tide within him.

"Sick," he whispered, and Ah'puch shook his head slowly. Baltsaros heard the man click his tongue once against his teeth.

"You're not going to be sick. I've given you a g------," said the man. Baltsaros didn't recognize the word.

An antiemetic? he thought fuzzily. He groaned when the emperor walked away; the lights began burning into him once more.

"How long...?" he rasped, crushing his eyelids together against the onslaught.

"Mm... only about two hours," said the emperor. "But you've woken up to ask me the same questions three times now." The man gave a little chuckle then began to hum softly to himself.

Baltsaros could hear a strange buzzing sound and water running. Slowly, he lifted his head, and his heart stuttered at the sight that greeted him. He was naked, and from his chest, arms, and legs trailed long, stiff ribbons of narrow, white cloth. They were adhered to his skin somehow, and their loose ends fell below the edge of the table to where Baltsaros could not see. He flexed his arms, trying to move, but the straps holding him down were secure.

The emperor stood with his back to him, doing something over a burnished golden counter. When the man heard Baltsaros grunt as he tested his bonds, he turned with a frown. In his hands was what looked to Baltsaros like a glass syringe, but the hollow needle at the end was crude and overlarge; it was nothing like the fine work that the steel craftsmen managed in the north.

It will hurt.

"This won't hurt a bit," said Ah'puch, and curled his thin lips into an eager smile. "Just relax. Don't worry! You're not going anywhere... You and I have a lot of work to accomplish, Captain."

When the thick needle stabbed into his skin, Baltsaros was silent despite the pain. It was only a moment later when the contents of the needle boiled through his veins did he lose control of his voice.

～

Tom shifted uncomfortably on the hard-packed earth, unable to move more than an inch or so in either direction because of the shortness of the chain. He thumbed the corner of his lip where another fist had opened up the healing cut, and he winced. Thankfully, the beating he had taken was largely just to subdue him. He had a feeling that Laz had pulled his punches on purpose even though Tom had robbed him of his sport earlier.

Must be the tattooed-kin thing, he thought to himself. *That's a bloody laugh.*

Another shift, and he extended his legs out in front of himself. He rubbed his heel on the ground to mark the limit of his reach should anyone approach. It would be quick work to get his ankles around someone's neck and twist; he'd done it before. However, if there was more than one, he was fucked... That is, if he didn't strangle himself on his collar in the process of breaking the neck of the first man.

Tom let out a frustrated growl and rubbed his eyes. No, he had to stay alive. The fear of the whip was slowly seeping through the cracks in his resolve, and he found himself thinking stupid, selfish thoughts. It didn't matter if he was to be whipped bloody, crying out like a suckling babe for his momma's teats while his legs turned to water. He couldn't do anything rash; who would rescue Jon and the captain if he died?

"Fuck you," he muttered to his frightened, chicken-shit guts.

"Fine, I'll leave you be then."

Tom looked up, startled. The figure before him lowered her hood as she crouched down in front of him. Right within his reach. He'd been so caught up in his own fucking panic that he'd let down his guard. *Sloppy. Stupid. Pathetic.*

"The fuck do ye want?" he grunted, scowling at Ceara. "Come 'ere to gloat? Poke me with a stick? Sit on my cock?"

"Hush, you idiotic brute," said the spymaster with a wry smile. "I'm going to get you out of here."

From beneath her cloak, she produced a key; she quickly rose to free him from his chain.

He pulled himself away from the wall and stood a little shakily. Between the beatings and the missed meals, Tom was feeling a mite unsteady on his feet.

"All right, big boy," said Ceara covering her hair once again with the hood. "Follow me, stick close, and for gods' blessings, don't say anything to anyone. Understood?"

Tom nodded.

Silently, he followed her through the back corridors of the slave quarters, past the baths and the atrium, up some stairs and through a number of doors that branched off to other hallways. As they walked, they passed a number of slaves, both servants and guards, none of whom bore them any mind. After a few minutes, Tom felt thoroughly lost even though he'd never had trouble in the twisty warrens of the mines he'd slaved in as a lad. As they ascended another set of stairs only to go down a level a moment later, Tom realized the interior of the palace had been built without rhyme or reason. He frowned; maybe that was the point? How could you easily take over the structure if you got lost five minutes after you stepped through the door?

Suddenly, they stopped at a bare piece of wall. Tom frowned and looked askance at the petite woman at his side. She peered at the wall for a few more seconds, then tapped out a pattern on the sandstone bricks. Instantly, the wall parted on a seam, and he smelled fresh air. The spymaster glanced around quickly and then gestured. Tom followed her through the hidden door.

He looked around him in confusion. They were outside.

"Where's the captain and Jon?" he asked.

Ceara turned to him, her blue eyes narrowed.

"They're still in the palace," she whispered.

Dread squeezed at his chest, and he tensed.

"Yer gonna go get them, aye?" he asked, staring hard at her.

"No," she replied.

He heard a shuffle of footfalls to his right and spun to face the sound. Out of the darkness emerged two veiled and helmeted guards. They were heading straight for him.

～

Baltsaros slowly realized that the sound he was hearing was the emperor talking.

"...find it interesting to see where the languages diverged when my ancestors crossed the mountains during the *year of the thousand snows*. See, what you're asking for right now is called *water* here. See how it's ever so subtly different? This sort of thing absolutely fascinates—" Ah'puch's face wavered into view, and Baltsaros's head swung to the side as the emperor slapped his cheek. "Are you still with me? Pay attention! I'm sure this sort of thing fascinates you just as much as it does me.

"Take your name for instance. Baltsaros. Baal-tsaros. Baal... like your ship, the root of your name. You northerners have the word "Baal" to mean God, correct? Well... *a* god, yes? We have the god *Bal* here! In fact, He is what our golden city is named after: *the eater of hearts*. The name comes from the same root! You and I, Captain, are kin. From a long, long, long time ago. Hang on, this will pinch a bit..."

The captain's entire body jerked against the restraints as another thick needle pushed some chemical into his blood. For a moment all went dark, and noises echoed as if he were in a tunnel. There was a sudden iron taste in his mouth, and he gasped for air as the cold trickled through him. He panted and twisted with agony for a moment, convinced the pain was unending, his mind worn down to a raw, blistered nub. Then, the spasms stopped and were replaced by a strange floating sensation. He couldn't see out of his left eye, but he felt... nice. Part of his mind told him he had just suffered a seizure, maybe even a stroke, but strangely he didn't care.

"Oh, that's better," crooned the emperor. The man's face lacked dimension with only one of Baltsaros's eyes working for the moment. "That's nice. I like to see my subjects happy. Look at that smile! Here, let me help you with the drool..."

The captain's face was entirely numb, but his head moved as the man patted at him with a cloth.

"Where was I? Oh yes... So, you see, the Balorian doctrines—these "blessings" and the nonsense about purgatory—are only a few generations old, twisted from previous beliefs for the single purpose of keeping a population ignorant and the men in charge very, very rich. There are walled cities, just like this one, dotting the entire continent. At the head of each is a man, like myself, who is responsible for maintaining the bloodletting, the slavery, the superstitions, and the intense xenophobia," said the emperor, flapping his hand in haughty disinterest. Baltsaros realized that he must have passed out again; the man's monologue seemed to have jumped topics quickly. "See, all these walled cities share a common problem: a lack of mineable ores and metals. That's where my great-grandfather comes in. He was the first one to create an antidote for the m------ that affects the Gods' Claws—"

"Spores," whispered Baltsaros. The word sounded wrong. Muffled. Inside out. A laugh threatened to bubble out of him, unbidden.

What a helpful child! said his grandmother. *What a sweet boy!* The monsters ate her up in one bite. Little Baltsaros closed his eyes.

Red hands, red feet, sharpened teeth, and fists that beat.

"Spores?" repeated the emperor from a lifetime away. Baltsaros's mind drifted closer to hear him. "All right. *Spores.* Yes, my great-grandfather found a way past the Claws into your lands. Understand that there was not much of a taboo then, just reports of hallucinations and whatnot. Imagine what the people of your lands thought when they saw the shiny yellow metal that he brought with him! That was the beginning of trade. Ereme'ia Balor began to prosper *immensely* because of your metals. Our gold fetches a high price in your lands. The taboo of the Gods' Claws was expanded on afterwards just to hide the trade from the other cities..."

The emperor's voice droned on and on. The light was replaced by darkness at one point. Baltsaros remembered someone he had lost and began to weep because he couldn't think of his name. The boy with black curls. The boy with eyes like a storm. The boy with scars on his back. The boy with eyes like the ocean. One boy or two? ...dreams?

He jerked awake, the four lights above his head bright as the noonday sun. In his mouth was something he couldn't spit out. There were straps on his face. He could see out of both eyes now, but could no longer move his head. His jaw ached like he had clenched it tight enough to break his teeth. The spots where the ribbons of stiff cloth stuck to his skin burned and throbbed. He could no longer remember his name, and that bothered him. For a moment.

He closed his eyes. Red. Red like the hands that took him from his mother's arms. Red like the feet that kicked his father's corpse. A wicked knife made a weeping, red smile on his mother's chest. Sharpened teeth tearing into the heartmeat *one, two, they're coming for you; three, four, always wanting for more; five, six, seven, the red hands, they beckon; eight, nine, ten, slaughtered now, feast on men.*

"- - - -," said Ah'puch. "- - - -, - - - -"

The man's hands were cold on Baltsaros's cock. Something slipped slowly into him, widening, opening him up. It was an unwelcome pleasure that fought tooth and nail with an alien, surrendering sensation, almost itchy in its intensity. Gloriously strange and suddenly breathless.

Tom would like this, he thought. *But who is Tom?*

The pleasure was forgotten a moment later when the machine behind Baltsaros began to buzz again.

"...man of your intelligence. It is sad to destroy such a mind..."

[...]

"...fucking repugnant f----- deviant sex..."

[...]

"...root of the evil inside you..."

When the buzzing reached its crescendo, Baltsaros could hear a shrieking noise. He looked around to try to figure out what it was. The body on the shiny table below him jerked and trembled as the machine belched its eye-blistering sparks. The bearded man's eyes bulged, red and black and full of rage. Baltsaros was free of rage now. Gone, gone, gone. No more need for the constant, iron control. No more worrying about Jon.

Jon?

Jon!

~

Tom's hands came up in tight fists, and his muscles bunched to attack when one of the guards raised his arm, palm out in a calming gesture.

"Whoa there, buddy," said a familiar voice. "Peace, friend."

Frowning, Tom hesitated. It took him nearly a second to recognize the amber-coloured eyes that narrowed at him in amusement over the black cloth. In amazement, he let himself relax a little bit.

"Jarrod?" he said, uncertainly.

The man who had been his neighbour in the Stone Inn's slave quarters pulled away the veil with his truncated fingers and smiled wide.

"The one and fucking only," said Jarrod with a little flourish of his maimed hand.

"Of course you two know each other," said Ceara with a short laugh. "The two most problematic slaves in Balor's recent history; why wouldn't you know each other?"

"I thought they'd done ye in!" said Tom with a grin. He had watched the guards at the inn pull Jarrod down the hallway, sure that the oft-runaway slave would finally meet his end before the night was over.

"Naw," said the dark-skinned man, with a cocky smile. "They beat me some, but when you started fighting them, they just dumped me in a side room. Didn't take much to get out of there."

Tom laughed. He'd liked the brash slave from the get-go and was glad that he'd made it out in one piece. Then something occurred to him.

"But... how are ye...?" Tom frowned and looked over at the spymaster.

Ceara had a smirk on her face.

Jarrod laughed.

"Ceara's one of the good guys, Tom. She's been helping escaped slaves for years now. Keeps us safe. Finds us places to live. Does what she can to free more of our kin. In return, we're her ears and eyes," he explained. "And sometimes, we dress up and take away some big fucker who's bound to eat all the food in my house." Jarrod's smile faded at the look on Tom's face when the first mate realised that the captain and Jon hadn't yet been mentioned.

Tom swung around to glare at Ceara. Last time he'd held her neck between his callused fingers, it had felt like a bird's: thin and all a-tremble with a skittering pulse. He didn't kill women often... didn't like it; the two women he'd had killed to get Jon behind bars in Portsmouth sometimes came to him in his dreams. But he'd kill Ceara if he had to.

"Where're Jon and Baltsaros?" he growled.

"I told you," she said, her clear-blue eyes wide. "They're still inside. Listen to me... I can't get to your captain. He's with the emperor right now. I can get to Jon, but I gave him some sleeping powders, and he'll be out until morning."

"Why... the fuck... did ye...?" Tom took a step towards the spymaster, his tone menacing. He needed to get back in. Had to figure out a way of getting them back to the *Heart* and sailing out of this bloody, fucking, loony town.

"He started to freak out when I told him that he had to stay put for now," she said.

"And why did ye tell him that?" he rumbled; anger and worry were fighting for space in his chest, and all he wanted to do was hit something. He clenched his fists harder, the skin taut over his knuckles.

Ceara took a small step back but lifted her chin.

"Tom, please, this is the way it's going to have to work," she said. Her voice was a little unsteady. "If I take Jon out... understand that Ah'puch will *kill Baltsaros*. He will, Tom. I know the man. He's petty, and he hates to lose. You, he cares almost nothing about. He has zero dealings with the slaves. The captain's sword and dagger are more than enough to bribe the folks I need to. But Jon... He's taken an interest in Jon. Instead of sending him to the dungeons, he's letting him stay unfettered in the palace. That is something. *We can work with that something.* We will need to get you to the *madina*. I've arranged it so that you'll stay with Jarrod. But Jon needs to stay here. For now. Do you understand me?"

Tom swallowed and let his shoulders fall. He nodded, defeated and deflated and terribly weary. The woman was talking sense, wasn't she? To get everyone out in one piece was the goal...

"What is the emperor doing to Da?" he asked quietly.

A few heartbeats ticked by as she stared at him with an expression steeped in dread.

"Tell me, Tom," she whispered. "Is your captain a strong man?"

CHAPTER 25

THE SACRIFICIAL LAMB

reaction formation • *n.* *psychoanalysis* the tendency of a repressed wish or feeling to be expressed at a conscious level in a contrasting form.

Jon pulled on the cord to let more water flow from the tub above; it was cool and felt good on his sweaty skin. The sound of the falling water echoed on the glossy tiles of the small bathhouse he had been brought to, and he wondered briefly who else used these guest facilities. Did the men in cloaks and animal horns strip down naked in these stalls to wash the blood off? Did they have loved ones to go home to once the slaughter was over? This morning, Jon was the only one there, and he was thankful for that.

He had awoken before dawn, gasping and choking for breath as he frantically struggled with the covers. The guard who had been tasked to watch over him as he slept had stared at Jon impassively as he fought his way out of bed and collapsed panting on the floor, soaked in the cold sweat of terror. It had taken him a few moments to remember where he was and why he felt so frantic.

He had been hounded by nightmares all night. Unable to fully wake, Jon had been plunged over and over into blood-slickened dreams full of demons and pitfalls, held in thrall by the sleeping draught Ceara had given him. All he could remember now was a dream of a giant, skinned lion running him down, its eyes like burning coals. The tawny wildcat had called to him from far away, unable to reach him before sharp claws pierced him through.

As he pressed his forehead to the cool, wet wall, Jon let out a slow sigh. He grimaced as the spymaster's words snaked through his mind, poisoning him slowly.

~

"Flirt with him," she said, her sky-blue eyes earnest.

Jon stared at her, deeply confused and more than a little alarmed.

"Isn't that why we're...?" he asked.

Ceara grimaced slightly and looked away.

"I know, I know. I don't pretend to understand it." When she turned back to Jon, she frowned at his expression. "Listen, I'm not asking you to fuck him, ok? Just... I don't know. Compliment him. Show him your... Fuck, I don't even know how this works for men. Show him your muscles?"

Jon let out a helpless laugh; he couldn't believe what he was hearing. Ceara glared at him and stood. She began to pace in front of him, her gloved hands rubbing and twisting over each other.

"Jon, I don't know what else to say," said the woman. "He has... tastes. But, be subtle! Be charming. I know you can act; I watched you play the master at the blessings ceremony. Just do this! Jon, think of it this way: the less time he spends with your captain, the higher the chance we have of getting your captain out alive. You understand?"

Jon let her words sink in.

"I'm to seduce the emperor, but not let him think I am seducing him," he said faintly. "What do you take me for? I have no... skills at this." He pressed his lips together tight and thought about the teasing, coy creature he could become when the mood struck him; but that was for Baltsaros and Tom. He... couldn't with a complete stranger. Especially one that he wanted to see die a painful death by his own sacrificial blades.

But it seemed he would have to. The thought of it made him nauseous.

"And Tom?" he asked quietly. "What will become of him? Can you save him before he gets whipped?" He remembered the way that the stolid first mate had begged when the captain's long black whip had whistled through the air.

"Yes. I'll have him out before dawn, Jon. I promise you," she said with a resolute nod. "He'll be safe. This will all be over soon if everything goes as planned. I know, I know, I don't have a great track record so far, but this time I have your help. Right?"

Jon clenched his jaw and stared at her before dipping his chin a little.

~

Jon followed the slave guards to a large open terrace at the rear of the great pyramid. Colourful pillows and throws were scattered on the sandstone, and a large, triangular piece of pale-rose silk was stretched out overhead to create an area of shade. It was beneath this canopy that the emperor was stretched out on his side on a mound of bright cushions. Before him on a low table were dishes filled with various fruits and a graceful decanter with a pale-yellow liquid in it. Jon took a deep breath and stepped forward, his head lowered meekly.

"Jon!" said the emperor cheerfully. "Come! Come closer. Sit with me. Thank you for joining me for breakfast." The man said it like Jon had been given the choice.

Jon took another few steps and sank down onto a thick mauve cushion with golden tassels; he watched a bead of water slip down the side of a green apple and waited for Ah'puch to continue, his shoulders up and tense.

"The clothes are all right?" asked the emperor.

Jon looked down at the outfit he had been given. The soft, grey silk tunic and flowing trousers were mere whispers against his skin, barely felt.

Not too forward, not too fawning, he thought to himself.

"Yes. Thank you," he murmured, glancing up shyly at the emperor for a moment before looking down at his hands. "I... have never been given silks to wear before, Your Excellency." Jon knew that the best lies were built on the foundation of the truth.

He risked another look at the man across the low table, this time without raising his head. He knew his lashes would shadow his eyes and that he looked absolutely guileless; the important thing was to make sure that the emperor saw no artifice in Jon. He launched into his prepared words.

"I want... to thank you," he said, letting his voice waver a little. "For–for freeing me." He blinked his eyes rapidly to give the impression that he was tearful before looking back down again. In reality, he was fighting the urge to leap forward and snatch the knife from the wooden board to sink it into the emperor's neck to the hilt. He allowed himself a hidden smile at the thought and then frowned. Maybe the reason he had been so hysterical over Migri's death wasn't that he had killed a man, but because it had been strangely *satisfying* to feel the knife slip into him. His heart knocked hard twice before settling into a fast rhythm, and his mouth tasted sour. Since the emperor hadn't invited him to partake in any food or beverage yet, he simply sat with his fists clenched in his lap, waiting.

"Are you all right?" purred the emperor softly. "You seem distraught."

Jon nodded quickly and brought a hand up to his eyes to rub at them.

"I'm sorry, Your Excellency," he whispered. "It has been a terrible time for me. I can hardly believe it to be over." He heard the emperor shift on his bed of cushions with a soft sigh. "If only you knew..." He let his words trail off and wrapped his arms around himself.

"Jon, look at me," said Ah'puch. When Jon raised his eyes again, the man smiled kindly at him. "Please, have some wine. It will make you feel better."

The emperor motioned, and a fluted glass was filled with wine and held out to Jon by a petite slave woman. He reached for it, his eagerness completely sincere. He drank down the small glass quickly and placed it back on the little table where it was immediately refilled by the emperor himself.

"Do you wish to speak of it? I will not judge your words. We are but two men speaking, but I may be able to help you further. I could try to give you ways of dealing with your trauma. Can you trust me with your story, Jon?" said Ah'puch as he sat up and held out a plate of fruit. Jon chose a plum and turned it in his hands, contemplating its glossy, nearly black skin for a moment before answering.

"Yes. I guess I can speak of it," he said, and lifted his eyes to the emperor again, smiling shyly. "I... trust you." *To die by my hands,* he decided grimly. He took a bite of the plum and chewed it thoughtfully before continuing.

"He... *they*... kept me in a cage," he started. When the emperor nodded in encouragement, Jon looked away, as if in shame. "The captain tied me up," he continued, thinking of the red hempen rope. "They both made me... do things." Jon began to feel both uncomfortable and weirdly excited; he couldn't have faked the blush that infused his cheeks if he'd tried. Jon licked a little plum juice off his fingers, knowing that the emperor's eyes were on him. It was done as though innocently, but when Jon looked at Ah'puch, he saw that both his words and actions were having the desired effect.

"What *kind* of things?" asked the emperor as his dark eyes widened eagerly.

Ah, there it is, he thought to himself. *Ceara was right about him.*

He waited a moment, letting the silence drag a little, and bit the corner of his lip before responding.

"He..." Jon swallowed, his discomfort only partially an act. "He liked to make me... make me... *beg...*"

"Beg?" The emperor's voice had taken on a breathy quality, and he leaned forward slightly. "Beg for what?"

~

Tom pulled the thin comforter over his head and let out a little pathetic groan. His mouth still tasted of the plum-flavoured rice liquor that he and Jarrod had drunk until the wee hours of the morning, and his skull felt like it was too small for his throbbing brain. The slave with the missing digits had proven to be a surprisingly adept drinking partner, given that Tom outweighed him by at least seven stone.

And a hell of a gambler.

Tom rubbed his face and scowled at the memory of losing his favourite dagger. His stomach gave a rumble of hunger; maybe there was more of the spicy goat stew from the night before.

Just as he was contemplating sitting up, he heard a soft noise. Tom pushed the covers away and reached for his knife. When his fingers closed on nothing, he swore under his breath.

"Relax," said a familiar voice. "It's just me."

Tom raised himself onto his elbows and grimaced at the spymaster. She was perched on the windowsill with an amused look on her freckled face.

"Yer a sneaky little thing. I'll give ye that much. What the fuck do ye want?" he asked groggily. As he sat up fully, his vision swam with dark shapes. He swallowed against the nausea that had reared up inside him at the motion.

"It's nearly noon, Tom. I came to see you off to your ship," said Ceara. She slid off the windowsill and threw something dark at his head. Tom grunted with surprise and caught it with one hand. When he opened the cloth sack, he saw that it was filled with clothing.

"I don't know if any of it will fit," admitted Ceara as she stepped closer to him. "But you need to cover up those tattoos to get through town. You're a free man now; congratulations."

Tom snorted in derision and began pawing through the sack. The first shirt he found turned out to be too tight over his shoulders and biceps and the second, too tight across his chest. He scowled in annoyance and was ready to toss the sack at Ceara in frustration when he pulled out a loose black tunic with sleeves long enough to cover his arms. He yanked it over his head and it fit, but only just. Next, he found a pair of thin, dark-blue trousers that seemed to be the right size. He glanced up at Ceara as he lowered his sweat-soiled pants and grinned at the blush that infused her cheeks before she rolled her eyes and looked away.

He folded the sleeves up over his tanned forearms and tucked the hem into his pants before tying on his leather belt. Then, Tom held out his arms.

"Well?" he asked.

Ceara turned to him. From the look on her face, Tom gathered that the clothes suited him. The petite woman stared at him for a moment, and then her face closed down into the slightly haughty expression she normally wore. She clucked her tongue at him and reached for the shirt.

"The purpose was to conceal your markings, you dolt. Not to walk around with your tits hanging out," she sighed. Tom frowned and looked down at himself. The shirt was undone nearly to his navel. "Listen, you can go about like a half-naked savage on your own time but—" She tweaked his nipple mischievously as she quickly buttoned him up to the throat; the teasing touch caught him unawares, and he let out a short, startled laugh. "—in Balor, free men tend to dress a little more conservatively. *Savvy?*"

Tom grinned even wider at her use of mainlander slang. Part of him hoped that they wouldn't be forced to kill the gutsy Ceara; he could her see getting along with the rough louts aboard the *Heart*. Maybe the captain would—

His face fell, and he snatched one of her small hands in his.

She blinked up at him, surprised.

"How's Da?" he asked quietly. Baltsaros was stronger than anyone he knew, and his mind was like a blade of folded steel, but from what Ceara had told him, the emperor was very good at breaking strong men. When the woman shook her head in response, he let out a slow exhale. He hated being so fucking powerless.

"I don't know. I wish I could give you news, but I have no way of getting to him, and the men who guard the laboratory are profoundly loyal to the emperor. I'm sorry, Tom," she said, squeezing his fingers.

He dropped her hand with a sigh. He just had to trust that the captain was able to withstand whatever was being done to him.

"And Jon?" he asked, hopeful.

Ceara reached up and draped a dark-grey silk scarf around Tom's neck to hide the slave collar until he could get it removed. Her forehead creased at his question.

"Jon... is... fine. He's actually doing better than I'd hoped," she said with a tight smile. "He's going to have Ah'puch eating out of his palm, literally, if he keeps it up. Hells, if I didn't know it was an act, I would swear to the heavens that the boy is really looking to be bedded by the emperor."

"What?" growled Tom, confused. "What the fuck do ye got him doin'?"

Startled, Ceara backed away from him quickly, and Tom reached out and grabbed her cloak, twisting the fabric in his fist.

"Shit! He's buying us some time. Ok?" she exclaimed as she pulled on her cloak. "Tom, I swear to Bal... You've got to stop thinking that I'm the bad guy."

As Ceara explained the plan to him, Tom sat down on the edge of the bed slowly. His nausea had returned, and the image of Jon and Ah'puch together was like cold seawater in his veins.

"He hasn't *touched* Jon, has he?" he asked in a bleak voice when she was done. He could feel his pulse in his clenched fists. Thoughts of that slimy, hooked-nose bilge rat putting his hands on Jon coursed through his mind. He imagined Jon trembling in a corner, his clothing ripped and his limp cock exposed while the emperor stroked his own tiny, twisted shaft and laughed. Tom tasted bile in the back of his throat.

"I don't think so," said Ceara, her expression softening at the look on his face. "Tom, honey, it's the only way. The faster you can get to your ship, the safer everyone will be. I will come up with a plan on my end. It can work."

"Then what the fuck are we waitin' for?" growled Tom as he lurched to his feet. He had to get back to the *Heart*. Polas was sure to have an idea.

"No... I see that look," she frowned, placing a hand on his arm. "You have to stay on board until *I* come up with something. You can't just barge into Balor with men and weapons and think you can rescue the captain and Jon. You don't have enough manpower."

He scowled at her for a moment and then he blinked as something occurred to him.

Tom smiled.

"Actually... I think we do."

508

CHAPTER 26
LEARNING TO SPEAK

Lust is to the other passions what the nervous fluid is to life; it supports them all, lends strength to them all ambition, cruelty, avarice, revenge, are all founded on lust.

— MARQUIS DE SADE

Jon peered at the open book on the low table. On each page was a beautifully rendered illustration depicting the life of a god the Balorians worshipped. One page showed a tall, blue-skinned, three-headed man with what looked like a giant axe over one shoulder; the next showed a hunched, leathery demon with a lolling red tongue and fangs edged in gold.

The emperor tapped the image.

"There he is," he said. Ah'puch was so close to Jon that the man's breath tickled his neck as he leaned over. "That's Bal. *The eater of hearts.*"

At the base of the image, Jon saw that there was a jumble of red hearts; the paint was so shiny and thick there that it seemed the page itself bled. He held his breath as the emperor touched his shoulder. Ah'puch smelled like flowers, a sickly sweet scent that made Jon a little nauseous. However, he forced himself to keep still as the emperor pressed his chest to Jon's back with the pretence of getting a better look at the god's image. Jon swallowed and nodded.

"I see! That is very interesting," he said in a bland, friendly tone that belied his utter loathing for the man. After a moment he frowned; he wasn't going to keep the emperor's interest with empty pleasantries. It was only a matter of time before the man tired of showing him knickknacks and retired to the dungeons to continue carrying out his "work" on Baltsaros. Jon stared at the god Bal atop his gory mound of hearts and had an idea.

"He tried to cut my heart out," he said quietly. He felt Ah'puch tense. A gentle hand closed over Jon's shoulder.

"The captain?" asked the emperor.

Jon pulled away slowly and climbed to his feet. He took a step back, nodding as he looked at the ground. When he lifted his eyes, he saw that Ah'puch was staring up at him with a strange expression. The emperor was trying to look sympathetic, his brow wrinkled and mouth turned down at the corners, but Jon's gift read only morbid curiosity and a sense of validation. A black tide of emotion rose up quickly in Jon, and he nearly stumbled when he stepped back again. In painting a picture of the captain as a depraved sadist who only kept Jon as a bed slave, he wound the truth and fiction together tightly to make his words credible; but, as he forced himself not to think of the real captain, locked away and suffering beneath the palace pyramid, he found himself getting confused. Reality was leaching away, and the truth of the past was undermined slowly by his clever lies and the constant anxiety that plagued him. Jon was adapting to the strained situation too readily, his brain finding ways to blur the edges of the worry and abandonment he felt. How long would it take before he believed his own words?

He grimaced at the emperor.

"Yes... the captain," said Jon. He lifted the hem of his tunic, at first thinking just to pull it up high enough to show the evidence, but instead, he slid the thin, grey silk shirt up over his head. Emperor Ah'puch let out a small noise and rose quickly to his feet with the help of his cane, his eyes on Jon's chest. Jon looked down at the twisted scar that Reginald had given him. Fingering the slightly raised flesh, he blinked sadly at the emperor.

"He nearly killed me," Jon said. He turned to show the matching scar that Baltsaros's knife had left a few weeks earlier. "And then he tried again."

"You poor boy," breathed the emperor. "You poor, poor boy."

When he turned back and saw that the man's eyes had focused lower on his body, Jon looked down and was suddenly made extremely aware of just how thin the silk pants were. Without the tunic covering him to mid-thigh, Jon could see the bulge of his cock through the material. He felt appallingly exposed. Heat flushed his face.

You can use this.

With a disgusted little shudder, Jon glanced back up.

"I... I need to sit," he said in a choked voice, passing a hand over his eyes. "I don't feel so well."

"Of course!" exclaimed Ah'puch and stepped forward hurriedly. He grabbed Jon's arm before he "fainted" and helped him onto the low settee. The emperor then filled a beautiful glass goblet with water for Jon.

Jon accepted the glass with a meek, thankful smile. He took a small sip and sighed.

"I'm sorry, Your Excellency," he said. "I don't know what's wrong with me." He tried not to cringe when the emperor's hand slid around his back.

"It's perfectly understandable," said Ah'puch. His fingers squeezed Jon's side, and the younger man winced. "You've been through so much." The emperor's other hand patted his knee kindly; the sweet, cloying smell of the man's perfume made Jon's head swim. "Maybe it would help to talk more about it?"

"Maybe..." said Jon uncertainly. Up until this point he had only skimmed the topic, not going into detail but giving the emperor choice tidbits to keep him hungry. Ah'puch, in turn, had taken every opportunity to ply Jon for more overt descriptions of the acts he had been "subjected" to.

He took another sip of water but pretended to choke on it this time, making sure to spill some from the goblet as he coughed. A cold splash landed squarely in his crotch, and Jon heard the emperor's quick intake of breath. He looked down and felt a blush sear his face again. For one long second, he thought he had completely overdone it. The water had rendered the pale grey silk almost translucent, and the thin material clung to him like a second skin. He might as well have just taken his pants off for all the cover the wet silk afforded him; Jon hadn't meant to be so *blatant*, but it was too late for that. The best he could do was to appear as if he hadn't noticed that his cock was on display. He coughed again belatedly and looked around the room, only too aware of the emperor's eyes on him.

"I know. You spoke about Captain Baltsaros tying you up... Tell me about that," murmured the emperor. "It will help you to talk. Trust me."

"I... guess so," Jon conceded, his jaw tense.

Ah'puch's eyes flicked down to Jon's wet crotch, and he nodded eagerly.

"The captain has a chest full of... objects," Jon started awkwardly. "Things that he likes to use on me. When I've been bad. You know, when something gets broken or I misbehave; Baltsaros has a terrible temper," he explained. The emperor nodded again in encouragement, his fingers stroking Jon's thigh lightly.

"There was one time when I was clumsy and knocked over the captain's coffee as I was reaching for something," Jon said, leaving out the part where he had done it on purpose. He'd wanted to provoke Baltsaros into some anger-fuelled play, and the captain had known it too. Jon had to keep himself from smiling at the memory, and then realized that his hands were shaking. That, at least, wasn't an act.

Baltsaros. Don't think.

He licked his lips and continued.

"He made me get on my knees on the floor, and he took a rope and tied my hands behind my head. But not just at the wrists... The rope was all the way up my arms and around my throat. Then he... He told me to spread my legs, and he tied rope around the top of my thighs and— You're sure you want to hear this?" he asked, narrowing his eyes at Ah'puch. "I thought this was unlawful. Forbidden. Isn't my talking about it just as wrong as the act?" He knew that pointing out the hypocrisy would allow the emperor to justify it somehow.

"You can speak of it to me, Jon. This is a safe environment. Your tormentor is in a cage, and you have nothing to worry about from him," said the emperor calmly. However, when he squeezed Jon's leg, Jon saw that Ah'puch's forehead was shiny with sweat. "I am but an ear to listen to you. It will cleanse you to speak of these things. Go on. He tied rope...?"

"Around my thighs. I could feel it against my... um... buttocks. I was so scared of what he would do that I was shaking. I couldn't move my arms or look around to see what he was doing because of the rope around my neck. And then... Then he put a blindfold on me," Jon said in a low voice.

He swallowed thickly at the memory. The blindfold was never easy for him to accept, but in the end, he always found a sort of peace in the dark. Ah'puch didn't need to know this.

"I heard him walk away and open the chest, but I didn't know what to think. Baltsaros likes to hit me with a bamboo switch or a bundle of leather strips tied to a handle. They both hurt in their own way, but when I heard him opening the drawers to his armoire too, I got even more scared." The emperor's fingers tightened on Jon's leg. The man's breathing sounded a little faster. Jon didn't dare look at him. Instead, he concentrated on the abstract tapestry on the opposite wall.

"What was it, Jon?" asked Ah'puch quietly.

"At first I didn't know. He... the captain... pushed me down on the rug so that I was on my chest and knees. Then, something cold touched me... it touched me right on my —" He fumbled for the right word. "—my *opening*." Jon's breath hitched in his throat, and he coloured, his heart hammering his ribs. In dismay, he felt himself stir and closed his eyes. "It was something hard and smooth that the captain had oiled. He *pushed* it, and it slid inside me. I couldn't fight it, I couldn't move. The thing was thick and it *hurt* me," whispered Jon. He was caught up in the memory. The captain had fucked him slowly with the wooden phallus to let Jon get used to the girth of it, but the stretch hadn't been the bad sort of pain. No, it had made Jon's cock rock hard and had coaxed needy little pants and moans out from between his open lips.

"He fucked me with it, pushed it deep into me, and he laughed." In truth, it had been Tom who had laughed when he had walked in and seen Jon tied up. The captain had said something in his mother tongue, and Tom had replied, his voice husky. A moment later, Jon had felt Baltsaros secure the phallus somehow using ropes stretched across his ass before doing something with the bindings around his ankles.

Jon clenched his fists against the burgundy brocade of the low divan and let out a shuddery breath.

~

He blinked as the blindfold was removed, and Baltsaros lifted Jon back up onto his knees with a smile. His large hand closed over Jon's stiff cock, and he leaned forward to brush his lips to Jon's in a brief kiss before gesturing to Tom.

Jon watched as the first mate quickly rid himself of his pants and positioned himself on the floor where Baltsaros pointed, broadside to Jon. The muscles in Tom's wide shoulders rippled as he supported himself on fists and knees and waited.

The captain took his place behind Tom, cock in hand, and rubbed it into the furrow of the first mate's ass. Jon watched the shiny, purplish head peep out above Tom's ass as it slid between his cheeks, and he was held rapt and aroused by the sight.

The captain narrowed his eyes at Jon, and the corner of his lip curled up in an amused smirk. With one hand, Baltsaros pushed between Tom's shoulders, and the big man obediently let himself down onto his elbows. Tom looked up at Jon, the excitement and desire yawning dark in his pupils before he closed his eyes.

"Knocking things over on purpose is a crude way of getting me to do what you want. You can't just act out to force my hand. You have to learn to speak your thoughts and desires, my love," murmured the captain. "As your punishment, you get to watch me fuck Tom. Maybe it will teach you a thing or two. How do you like that?"

Jon pinched his brows together and shook his head. This isn't at all what he had expected. How was he supposed to do anything while he was tied up? However, the disappointment did nothing to slow his pulse as he watched Baltsaros oil his cock slowly and plunge it deep into the first mate with a soft grunt. Tom's lips parted with a low moan, and Jon felt his cock tense and bob up in response. Baltsaros fucked Tom with a few quick thrusts, and then he stopped.

Jon could see the first mate move eagerly up against the captain, wanting more. However, Baltsaros kept his eyes on Jon and just smiled. A moment later, Tom let out a pathetic little sound.

"Fuck, Da. Please. Please, Da. Fuck me," gasped Tom. Jon's heart leaped with the first mate's shameless words. Baltsaros slapped Tom's ass before sliding his length back into him a few times. Jon saw that Tom's cock swung heavy and hard between his legs, but he knew that the first mate wouldn't touch it unless the captain gave him leave.

"Tell me what you want, Tom," purred Baltsaros with another wicked smile. He pulled himself out to slide his length up along the furrow of the first mate's ass again. Tom's lids lifted slowly and his forehead creased. With his eyes on Jon, he began to speak as Baltsaros waited.

"I want ye to fuck me, Da. I wanna feel yer thick cock fuckin' me deep," Tom gasped. "I want ye to drive yer cock into my ass, Da. Please, Da. I want yer cock... please, Da."

The words made Jon's groin ache, and his ass throbbed over the phallus lodged inside him. However, when Jon squirmed slightly in discomfort, he noticed that while the wooden cock was held inside him by one rope, the rope around his ankle pulled it out a little. He experimented by moving his hips forward and was rewarded with a shallow plunge. He gasped at the feeling.

"More, Tom," he whispered. "Say more..."

~

"He wanted me to say 'I want you to fuck me hard, Daddy' while he watched me play with myself," breathed Jon, paraphrasing Tom. "And 'I want you to cum in my ass'..."

"And did you?" The emperor was almost panting.

Jon closed his eyes and leaned his head back on the couch. He realized he could do absolutely nothing about the fact that his cock was getting hard from telling the story. He gritted his teeth and took a few shallow breaths. The room was too hot and the emperor too close. He was getting shamefully aroused. He wanted to stop. To leave.

No, you don't. You want him to touch you.

However, when the emperor's fingers crawled up his thigh and tentatively traced the length of his cock a heartbeat later, lingering over the flared edge of its sensitive head, Jon hesitated only a second before pushing himself off the couch.

His mind raced.

Say something, he thought. He blinked rapidly.

"I'm sorry," he groaned. "I'm sorry!" He covered his cock with both hands and took a few steps backwards, frantic to get out.

He turned quickly and without a backwards glance raced out of the room.

Startled, Jon looked up when he heard something strange. He saw the handle of the door slowly move in the dim light, and his breath left him. The emperor had followed him to his room.

I'm going to have to fuck him.

His pulse spun out of control, and he pushed himself off the bed, fumbling for the light globe. He prodded at it with shaking hands, and the room darkened. A few quick steps brought him to the door where he waited with the gold statuette of a fawn clutched in his hands. A dark shape slid into the room, and Jon swung at it. He didn't care about the ruse he was supposed to keep up. There was no way he was actually going to submit to the emperor. The dark figure grabbed his wrists, and he let out a frustrated sound as the gold fawn dropped to the floor. In terror, Jon struggled to get free.

"Whoa, whoa there," rumbled Tom's distinct voice. "Jon, it's Tom. It's me, lovey. Quit yer fightin'!"

Jon went limp from shock and relief, and his wrists were freed. A moment later, the light came on, and he saw Tom, dressed in long-clothes and boots, standing by the bed. With a wry grin on his roguish face, the first mate held out his arms.

"Tom!" Jon nearly tackled the first mate in his desire to bury himself in the big man's embrace. Tom smelled like tobacco and sea air.

However, Jon quickly pulled away.

"Three days," he said in a hoarse, furious whisper. "Three long fucking days, Tom. Where the hells have you been?" Not waiting for him to answer, Jon took handfuls of the first mate's shirt and began to tug it off of him. Startled, Tom laughed and lifted his arms. Jon attacked him again when his shirt was off and sank his teeth into the first mate's shoulder. Tom let out a pained gasp, but his hands tightened around Jon's waist.

"I missed you," Jon growled. "I was worried about you. I have been going fucking crazy here by myself. Where have you been?"

"*Baal's Heart* mostly. Here and there. But, this is the first time I could get myself snuck in here, lad. Swear to fuckin' gods," said Tom, submitting to Jon's bites with little grunts.

Jon scowled at him and fumbled at the fastenings at the front of Tom's pants. He had them undone in a few seconds and then pulled Tom's pants halfway down his thighs. The first mate's cock hung limp against the coarse, dark-blond curls.

"On your hands and knees," choked Jon, pushing Tom back on to the bed. "I want to fuck you. I want my cock inside you *now*." His lips were salty from Tom's skin. All the pent up arousal from earlier churned wildly inside him; he felt desperate and brittle. Out of control.

With his eyes narrowed with understanding, Tom reached up and threaded his fingers through Jon's hair, pulling his head down until their lips met. All at once the tension left Jon like a flame going out, and he sagged against Tom, melting into the kiss.

"I'm sorry," whispered Jon against Tom's jaw, the first mate's stubble sharp against his lips. "I've had a rough few days. You're right; it can wait. I'm sorry." He pulled back and stared at Tom, wide-eyed. "What are we going to do?"

"We're goin' to take everythin' one step at a bloody time, love," laughed Tom. "First, we'll work on this." Tom's hand slipped between skin and silk to take Jon in a firm grip. "I didn't mean to stop ye just now... I only wanted a kiss first cuz I bloody missed ye too." With a grin, Tom ducked his head to nuzzle Jon's cock through the thin fabric, his breath hot and moist.

Jon let out a slow sigh; it felt incredibly good. Tom tugged down the waist of Jon's pants and licked him slowly from root to tip, his callused hand holding Jon's cock upright. Over and over his rough-velvet tongue stroked him. Then, Tom's lips pushed back his foreskin gently so that he could lick the underside Jon's cockhead and up over the taut skin before sucking him down into the wet tunnel of his mouth. Jon groaned, twisting his fingers in Tom's hair. Tom's instincts were good; Jon had been too wound up before. This was better. However, now that he was calmer, Jon realized that the first mate's hands trembled slightly. It occurred to him then that Tom was being thorough and slow because he was trying to control an overwhelming sense of relief. Closing his eyes, Jon smiled though his chest felt so constricted that it was several seconds before he could take a clear breath.

Soon Jon arched his back with a groan, sweat running down between his shoulder blades, his hands locked behind Tom's head to hold him in place as he fucked his mouth slowly, savouring every languid, deep thrust. Tom made small, hungry noises, his throat open and willing as he clutched at Jon's hips to pull him in. He trembled, softly panting as his lust unfurled its tendrils inside him.

When he let go, Tom didn't need any coaxing to get up onto his hands and knees. Jon spat on Tom, thumbing the thin saliva into him before spitting again, this time into his hand to stroke his cock with. When he pushed himself into Tom's body, it was with a low moan of pleasure, and he moved slowly for a few strokes, letting Tom's passion catch up as the first mate jerked the thick cock between his legs.

Jon fell forward with one arm locked around Tom's neck, the other around his torso, and his forehead pressed to the scars and tattoos on the first mate's back as he slid his length into Tom's heat. He brought himself close twice, three times, four... stopping each time on the very brink to rest shaking and panting against Tom. Jon could feel the first mate's heart beating hard and fast, his tanned skin slick as he also held himself back. Finally, even the slightest movement became too much, and Jon pushed himself up off Tom to pound quickly into him, his hands tight around the first mate's narrow hips. With a strangled cry, Jon spilled over, his cock throbbing as the hot, liquid current crackled through him, and he shuddered, blind and deaf to anything but his fevered, breathless climax.

~

Tom breathed slowly, his fingertips stroking down Jon's back gently as the young man lay against his chest. It felt like forever since they had lain together like this. Tom was exhausted. Sated. But he couldn't let himself drift off like he wanted to. There was still so much to do. For the moment, however, this was what he needed, and therefore this is where he would stay... at least for another hour. He stared off into the blackness, deep in thought. The unknown state of the captain was like a raw, open wound hidden beneath the thinnest bandage. He knew it was there, but he didn't want to look at it. Tom had to trust that Baltsaros was strong enough to withstand the torture, if that's what it was.

Or still alive.

With a grimace, Tom turned his mind to another of his worries.

"Has he touched ye?" he rumbled softly.

He felt Jon tense, and it took him a long moment to reply.

"Yes," was the quiet response in the darkness.

Tom furrowed his brow and rubbed his thumb along the curve of his jaw, trying to push away the ache in his chest and the sharp sting of guilt over leaving Jon at the hands of a twisted pervert.

"It's ok, Tom," whispered Jon, lifting his head.

Tom could only see the outline of Jon against the pale sandstone walls and was thankful that he couldn't see the soft pain in Jon's eyes that he could hear plain as day in his voice. Tom's big hand cupped the back of Jon's head, and he grunted in reply. What was done was done; getting misty over it wasn't going to solve anything. He clenched his jaw.

"Aye, it'll be ok once my blade cuts that mongrel cocksucker's balls off tomorrow, lad. Not before," he growled. He felt Jon move and saw his silhouette shake its head. Confused, he opened his mouth to speak, but Jon leaned forward to press a kiss to his lips.

"No," said Jon in a strangely sanguine tone, smiling against Tom's mouth. "His balls are mine."

CHAPTER 27
COMING ABOUT

The god opened Its eyes before dawn. It could smell the living creatures around It—a meaty richness that coated Its nose and tongue—and hear them scurrying in their cages. The god was hungry. Flaring Its nostrils, It raised Its head, scenting the air and searching for the one that ruled this degrading little prison.

The man who had sent bolts of lightning into the god's head.

The tiny, disgusting mortal who had strapped It down and caused It pain.

The gaoler with the golden key.

The god couldn't see, smell, or hear Its tormentor. Curling Its claws into fists in Its lap, the god sat still on Its cot and waited.

~

Jon stared down at his hands.

"I'm sorry, Your Excellency," he whispered. "My time with the captain... it's made me"—he glanced up and licked his bottom lip nervously—"*corrupt*. I'm sorry for yesterday." He quickly looked back down again and let out a little uncomfortable huff of breath.

As if I was the one who tried to cop a fucking feel, he thought in disgust. He twisted his fingers together as he waited to see how the emperor would take his words. When Ah'puch's hand closed on his bicep, Jon only barely kept himself from cringing; Tom's touch was still fresh in his mind, and Jon instantly felt sullied by the unwanted contact. However, he curled his lips into a soft, graceful smile and peered up at Ah'puch through his dark lashes.

"It's all right, Jon," said the emperor, charmed. His thumb stroked Jon's skin gently. "Talking will help. Even if there are, ah... steps backwards, in time you will heal."

Next, he'll be asking me to demonstrate what the captain did to me.

Jon wanted to pull away, but he couldn't think of a way to do it without making it seem like he was trying to escape. He shifted slightly; the dagger strapped to his calf felt conspicuous even though it was well concealed by the loose grey pants.

Eyeing the overlarge guards that bracketed the door to the audience chamber, Jon nipped at the inside of his lip in worry. The emperor was never truly alone, and there was no way he could take the two slaves by himself. He thought about what Tom had said before leaving that morning.

~

"Who watches over the slaves?" asked Tom, his voice rumbling against Jon's ear. Jon frowned.

"Guards, taskmasters... but they're all slaves, really. Yeah, I'm beginning to understand why the sacrifices have to be so frequent and gruesome. Fear is the only way that a system like this could work. Otherwise, it would be nothing for the slaves just to up and take over. They outnumber free men something like five to one." Jon felt Tom nod. He could see the outline of the chair across the room and realized it was getting lighter.

"Aye, loyalty ain't about worryin' over yer own skin," murmured Tom. "Ye can't whip someone into wantin' to save yer life. Trust me on that one." The big man laughed and then let out a quiet groan. "Shit, I have to go, lovey."

Jon closed his eyes and let out a small sigh before rolling off Tom. He watched quietly as the first mate sat up and stretched his shoulders with another soft groan. Scratching his stomach, Tom peered around blearily, and Jon smiled.

"Don't forget that you were wearing a shirt," he said teasingly, trying to ignore the fact that he was getting increasingly anxious about the coming day.

Tom let out a chuckle and stood. In the hazy light of breaking dawn, all Jon could see on the first mate's broad back were the twisting black curls that decorated his skin; the raised ridges of his layered scars were hidden in the penumbral gloom, and the illusion brought a lump to his throat. He pressed his lips together and sat up.

"There has to be a better way," he whispered, the earlier comment about the whip and loyalty finally sinking in.

The first mate stopped groping around the foot of the bed looking for his clothes and glanced up at Jon. Though it was too dark to see his expression, Jon knew that there would be deep lines in Tom's forehead and that his ocean eyes would be narrowed in determination ghosted by the slightest hint of sorrow. It was an expression Jon knew well.

"Aye, love," said Tom, resuming the search. When he found the black shirt, he pulled it on before reaching out to swat Jon playfully on the side of the head. "But I don't see *you* comin' up with a plan, hm? Ye'll jus' have'ta put up with ol' Tom's crazy schemes to get our asses out of here." Tom pinched Jon's cheek and then patted it with a laugh.

Jon pushed himself up onto his knees and slid his arms around the first mate.

Tom sobered.

"I just can't sit around doin' nothin' and waitin' to take the safe road, Jon," muttered Tom against his hair. "I have'ta save him."

~

"Jon?" The emperor's voice snapped him back to the present.

Jon quickly put a smile on his face and nodded.

"Sorry," he said. "I'm just a little tired." He glanced around the room, looking for ways to get the emperor alone. It had sounded like something so easy to accomplish when Tom and he had talked. His eyes went back to the silent pair of guards at the door.

The guards are slaves.

He had an idea.

"How do you keep your slaves from rising up against you?" Jon asked shyly. He stood and took a step towards the door, peering up at the men there.

"They know that they are part of the gods' cycle and that if they are obedient, they will be granted freedom in the next life," replied Ah'puch.

"But not before you carve them up alive, right?" said Jon, the picture of innocence. Though he hadn't been sure earlier that the guards could understand him, he was now. The man on the left had curled his lip into the tiniest sneer at Jon's words.

"Ah... well... We generally only perform blessings on the disobedient. Their blood goes to feed the gods, and their souls are bound to serve them for all eternity," said the emperor.

"Oh, I see," nodded Jon. "And you give rewards to those who are loyal to you? I only ask because we had a similar slave system in my lands, and I'm trying to figure out where we went wrong."

"Wrong?"

"Yes, well, my da was the lord of a grand castle," explained Jon. "We had many, many slaves, and we too had gods to keep them in line... but one day, the slaves rebelled anyway. There were so many of them and so few of us that it was over in just a few hours! I'm wondering if we had rewarded them more whether it would have caused them to be more loyal. We only barely got out with our lives! It was a massacre." The guard's eyes flicked to Jon's for a moment, and the man frowned at him before looking away.

Good, I have your attention.

"Can free men become slaves here?" asked Jon. He glanced at the emperor. Ah'puch's dark brows were low over his eyes.

"Yes, they can," replied the emperor slowly.

"But slaves can never, ever become free men, no matter how loyal they are?" asked

Jon, his eyes wide and guileless. "Is it because of blood? No, wait, that would make no sense. I think I'm getting it wrong... Does the blood of the condemned-but-born-free and the blood of a slave feed the gods in the same way?"

"Ye-s? I don't understand this line of questioning, Jon," said the emperor, his face suspicious.

"I'm sorry," Jon said in a rush. "It just seems to me that if the gods don't care about who gives them blood, what is keeping the slaves from just sacrificing the free men to them? I think that was the logic behind the uprising in my lands. Or not. I'm not sure. But whatever it was, it certainly worked." The guard's eyes met Jon's again, his brows high. Jon knew he wasn't feeding them anything they hadn't thought of before, but the story of a successful coup was sure to spark something among the slaves. "All it really took was a few slaves to—"

The emperor said a few words loudly over Jon, and the two guards bowed before leaving the room.

Success.

"Slaves and their gossip," smiled Ah'puch apologetically when the younger man turned to look at him. "Not that I think any of mine would try the same, but..." The man chuckled and shook his head. He sobered a moment later. "Jon, I'm sorry about the massacre. How insensitive of me."

Jon needed a way of getting to the knife without alerting the emperor. He had to take him by surprise. There was no way of telling how far the guards had gone; Jon was only one man and not terribly skilled with a knife. He took a few steps towards one of the couches.

"Yes, it was terrible," Jon said, sitting down. He thought to put one ankle over his knee but decided against it in case the knife showed through the silk when he moved. "Awful." Besides, he needed the emperor closer.

"What happened to your father?" said the emperor softly.

Jon remembered the way that the blades had slid through Reginald's neck, splashing him with hot blood.

"He was beheaded," he murmured, rubbing his face with his eyes closed. After a moment, the couch sank down next to him, and Jon's nose was filled with the emperor's flowery perfume.

If I lean forward, I should be able to get the blade, he thought to himself and let out a shuddering breath as if he were on the verge of tears. When Ah'puch's gentle hand stroked across his back, Jon bent at the waist, and his fingers slid down the inside of his calf. *Perfect.*

"Who murdered him?" asked the emperor in a kind voice.

Jon lifted up the cuff of his pant leg and touched the leather sheath strapped there.

"Captain Baltsaros," said Jon distractedly, grimacing in concentration. *Only a little more...*

The emperor's hand ceased its soft caress.

"The evils this man has done to you!" growled Ah'puch. "I will make him pay for all of them."

Jon frowned, and he stopped pulling the blade free, startled by a sudden thought. He dropped his pant leg and straightened, staring wide-eyed at the emperor.

"I would like to see this," he said quietly. "I would like to... help you." He knew that the jagged emotion in his voice could be mistaken for passion born of anger. The barest hint of suspicion flickered across the emperor's face, but when Jon curled his hand around the man's thigh, Ah'puch's pupils expanded and his lips parted in a sigh.

"Please, Your Excellency?" asked Jon urgently, squeezing the man's leg gently. It was a hell of a risk—he was being way too forward—but it was worth a shot. Maybe he didn't need to force Ah'puch to take him to Baltsaros at knifepoint. There would be less opportunity for error this way.

His heart thrummed hard a moment later when Emperor Ah'puch closed his own hand over Jon's.

"Of course, Jon," said the man in a husky voice. "It would be my pleasure."

~

Tom grunted as the chain tugged him forward, and he stepped nimbly over the exposed root that had tripped up his fellow "slave".

"Watch yer bloody feet, Harris," he growled, and yanked on the chain that bound the line of men together from slave collar to slave collar.

"Yessir," coughed the tall, rangy pirate and resumed walking, this time lifting his feet high so that he didn't stumble over anything.

Ceara caught Tom's eye and scowled; she was afraid there might be spies not her own in the jungle. Tom ducked his head and continued to shuffle forward like the captured slave he was supposed to be.

In under an hour they found themselves at the gate to Ereme'ia Balor. Instead of waiting like the rest of the bloody fools who lined up to get into the city, they were ushered in immediately thanks to Ceara. As he trudged forward, Tom lifted a hand to his head and stroked his bare scalp slowly with his palm. The disguise was simply a precaution as no one really paid attention to slaves, but it made him a little nervous regardless to be re-entering the city without the cover of night. He scratched at his shorn head and thought how much it felt like dried sharkskin, rough even to his callused fingers.

"Stop that," murmured the woman who walked by his side. "You're going to make a mess."

Tom quickly lowered his hand and saw that his fingers had rubbed away some of the dark oil they had smeared on his scalp to match the deep tan he had everywhere else.

"Sorry," he muttered. He was keyed up and jittery, and that wasn't going to do a lick of good for anyone. He straightened his shoulders and stared ahead, thinking only of how good it would feel to squeeze the life out of that scrawny, ridiculous little man that held the captain captive.

Jon stared in horror at the man that paced in front of the bars. The captain's hair was loose, and it hung matted and dirty over his shoulders. His beard was wild; chunks looked to have been torn out of it, and the skin on his face and chest was raw and blistered in patches. The worst thing, however, was how utterly filthy he was. Baltsaros despised being dirty, but this creature trudging back and forth was absolutely covered in dried blood and dirt. From the finger marks in the filth, it seemed like Baltsaros had smeared it on himself.

Baltsaros's head swung around like a wooden doll's, and the captain fixed him with a wide stare. Jon struggled to take a breath as the world narrowed down to a tunnel in front of him. There was no recognition in the man's bloodshot eyes.

"What have you done to him?" whispered Jon. Ah'puch's arm brushed his, and Jon almost shuddered in revulsion.

"Meet the god Bal," chuckled the emperor with a little flourish of his hand. Ah'puch was completely oblivious to Jon's distress.

The man... The *thing* in the cage growled and resumed its pacing, the wide shoulders tense and muscles twitching jerkily.

"It's a little rough yet, I know, I know," said the emperor walking away. Jon could hear him fiddling with something, but he couldn't tear his eyes away from the captain. "But this is after only what... six sessions? Imagine what he'll be like after a few more!" The man's laugh was high and nasal. "Let me just get him restrained, and then I'd like you to use your talents to see what you can tell me about him. I'm curious to know what you see when I ask him questions." There was a clinking of metal behind him. Jon kept his eyes on the thing in the cage; there was a sick, hopeless feeling in his stomach. It was like a waking nightmare.

"Do you know what the most ridiculous thing I learned was? The captain actually believed he was doing these awful, demeaning, perverted things to you out of *love*! How depraved is that?" chuckled Ah'puch.

All Jon could hear was a rush of white noise as his pulse sped up. He staggered a step backwards, his mouth dry.

"What?" he breathed. "What did you say?"

~

Ceara pointed to Tom and the pirates.

"These lot are to be put to the mines," she said dismissively. "The big one here is about as strong as they come. Put him in a harness, and he'll be pulling out twice the load of your usual. Don't say I never do anything nice for you, Loma. I could have given him to the stonemasons."

The big slave with the eye patch nodded with a grunt and stared hard at Tom. The first mate focused on nothing and just waited with his head low. Ceara had said that Loma was a real ball-breaker with his slaves but that he didn't dole out the whip as often as the other slave masters, and for that he was glad. Just the sidelong glance at the glossy brown whip curled at the big man's side was enough to send a trickle of ice into Tom's veins. He flared his nostrils and clenched his fists tighter.

"Harness," grumbled Loma, and he motioned with a long, hairy arm bulging with misshapen muscle.

For an instant, Ceara's crystalline blue eyes met Tom's, wide with fear or excitement, and then she was gone in a swirl of purple fabric.

Tom lifted his arms obediently as he was fitted with a half-harness, the kind that went from one shoulder to the ribs opposite. He'd worn one like it during his time as a slave in the mines. Closing his eyes as the buckles were tightened over his chest, he thought about how he'd been made to wear the same harness day in and day out. His skin had been thickly callused from where it rubbed him while he hauled iron-rich rock and from how, when Tom was down on his knees, the master's hands tugged hard on the straps. When Baltsaros had bought him, the buckles had been so rusted that he'd had to cut it off of him along with his slave collar.

Tom clenched his jaw and took a deep breath, thinking of what Ceara had told him.

In trying to find every available scrap of iron buried in the ore-scant rock beneath the city, the miners had dug tunnels that reached under the pyramid that Ah'puch used as his palace. Sometime during their excavations, the old bricked-up corpse-chute from the converted dungeons had been breached, and it was to this tunnel that Tom was to go to while the others secured the route back out again. There was no telling what condition the captain would be in, and Tom would need every bit of help he could get if he had to carry the man out of the mines.

Finally, the man adjusting the harness stepped back when he was done and pointed wordlessly to the entrance to the mine. With a surly nod, Tom walked towards the dark tunnel. After only a few steps he paused and pictured the map that Ceara had drawn for him. With a quick jerk of his head, he made his way down the right-hand fork, Harris and the others trailing behind him.

~

Dazed, Jon blinked and saw that the emperor was looking into the cage where Baltsaros continued to pace. Ah'puch was admiring his *work*.

"He thinks... or at least he *thought* he loved you," Ah'puch replied. "He kept saying it. Maybe he thought I was you... the dark hair and blue eyes, hm? He kept saying 'I'm sorry, Jon' and 'I do love you' over and over again. *Pathetic*. What kind of monster is so sick in his mind that he thinks that he's in love with his victims? So *sick*. And all those things he did to you! Dis*gusting*."

The captain looked again at Jon and let out a small, feral noise before he started to speak in a language Jon didn't recognize. Jon could barely think. He *hurt*.

The long, gentle fingers that liked to stroke Jon's cheek were now curled into hooked claws. The dark eyes that used to narrow in fondness at Jon were now wide and staring. The graceful lips that could stretch into a pleased smile or press fervid kisses to Jon's skin were now twisted into a bestial snarl. This was the *real* Baltsaros. This was the beast that lived inside the man Jon loved.

"See, he's not actually saying anything," said Ah'puch. "I just gave him the *suggestion* that he was the god Bal, and his damaged psyche did the rest. It's not a real language, just a series of sounds strung together, listen..."

Jon turned to the emperor, his heart thundering. He took a step towards the man.

"It's utter nonsense. Fascinating. And the only thing he's eaten in three days has been raw meat. I wonder what would happen if—"

The emperor looked down at the knife sticking out of his chest in confusion. He dropped the manacles he held and grasped at Jon's hand clenched around the wooden handle. Ah'puch scrabbled at it with a gasp, but Jon just stared him down, motionless.

"Jon?" Ah'puch said, sounding bewildered. "Guards..." The word was just a whisper that trailed off when he remembered that they were alone.

Jon pulled the blade out, and it made a sucking sound. Immediately, blood welled up with a slight froth as Ah'puch let out a pained gasp. With a grunt, Jon stabbed the emperor again.

And again.

And again.

~

Tom closed his eyes and pictured the map in his mind again. Ceara had assured him that it was up to date. So far the woman had been right. However, a moment later, Tom turned down what was supposed to be a rarely used side tunnel and emerged into a brightly lit room. In dismay, he saw that there was a slave driver seated at a small table eating soup from a wooden bowl.

"What the hells are you doing here?" grunted the man as he stood up. His thick fingers lifted the whip from the hook on his belt. "There ain't supposed to be work done in this end until the next blessing cycle! Get back to your post!"

At the sight of the whip, Tom froze. A cold icicle of dread speared his guts and spurned his heart to gallop high and fast in this throat. All thought left him as his eyes watched the tip of the whip trail through the dust as the man held it looped in his fist.

"Did you hear me?" bellowed the fat man with the whip. "Are you deaf, boy?"

Tom was alone. The other pirates had split up to begin either incapacitating or recruiting the slaves in the tunnels. He took an unsteady step backwards, all his senses screaming at him to bolt.

Think.

He blinked and took another step back. The room was new. He could see the walls were freshly dug. If this used to be the old tunnel, then the entrance to the laboratory would be just beyond this room. He had to move forward, which meant getting past the slave driver.

Tom lifted his hands in a gesture of supplication.

"Listen. I don't want no trouble," he said quietly. "I'll get back to my post, but I need to be goin' *that* way." He pointed past the man.

"The hells you are," growled the big man with the whip. The slave driver hefted the handle and let the coil drop to the ground.

The first sting wouldn't be so bad. Nor would the second. But his world would shatter and his mind would be tossed into the black pits of hell as he begged and pleaded. He let out a low sound and took another step back.

Coward, he thought. *I'm a bloody coward.*

It's just a thing, said the captain reassuringly. *You're not a coward, but you are foolish at times, my tomcat. Why fear an object? An object has no power on its own. It's a man who wields it, and when have you ever been afraid of a man?*

Tom's brows pinched over his nose, confused. He fell to his knee with his arm up to protect his face as the first lash came down. A whimper burst from between his lips, and he quailed as the whip came down again. It cut into his forearm as it looped around, and Tom let out a cry.

He was almost blind with fear, crazy with it, and hearing voices in the dark that weren't there.

Crazy is better than afraid, no? laughed the captain. *Come, you're better than this. Be my fearless tomcat. I need you. Jon needs you.*

Tom blinked, realizing that the whip was still around his arm. He looked up at the slave driver wielding it and saw the *man*, not the object. This wasn't his Master. This was a tired-looking, overweight, middle-aged slave that had snuck off on his own to have a bite to eat, probably worried about being caught. There was soup on his stained, brown tunic, and his body sagged with flaccid muscle.

He was faintly ridiculous.

Then, Tom noticed that the whip the man held wasn't tightly woven and well-kept at all; the leather was coming apart in places, and it had a few kinks in it where it had obviously been repaired.

It too was faintly ridiculous.

Tom began to laugh. He threw back his head and laughed loudly, not caring who heard him. The ridiculous slave driver goggled at him, his face twisted into a fearful expression at Tom's reaction.

Baltsaros was right. He wasn't afraid of any man, and this thing, this flimsy weapon held no power over him. He looped his fist around the whip and pulled as he got to his feet. Blood dripped down his forearm where the whip had sliced into him, but the cut was superficial. It would heal and life would go on. Tom grinned wide as he tugged the whip again. This time it came out of the man's hands, and the slave driver took a few shuffling steps backwards before hitting the wall behind him. He put his hands up.

"Aye... There we go," said Tom. "That's what I like to see."

"Don't kill me," stammered the slave driver.

"Now, see... I'm gonna let ye go," smiled Tom, curling the whip into a few big loops. "I got better places to be, aye? But I can't have ye hootin' and hollerin' about me, savvy? So what am I goin' to do?"

He let a few seconds go by in silence. The slave driver stared wide-eyed at him.

"C'mon. Guess," grinned Tom.

"You're... going to... knock me out?" said the man hesitantly.

"Bingo!" replied Tom, and he hit the man as hard as he could with the heavy whip handle clenched in his fist. The slave driver thudded to the ground like a sack of wet potatoes, and Tom nodded to himself.

"That's a good boy," he grinned. "Sleep, matey. I hope they won't skin ye in the mornin'... Ye didn't seem like such a bad fella after all, aye?"

He turned and made his way down the tunnel, whistling to himself as he passed his arm through the loop of the whip and settled it comfortably on his shoulder.

CHAPTER 28
RED HANDS

The god stopped Its pacing to watch the young one kill the gaoler. Blood arced up into the air and landed in drops at the god's feet. It was glorious, this sacrifice. Watching the wolf pup pierce the man with his shining tooth made the god smile, and It wrapped Its claws around the bars to get a better look... at the boy with eyes like a storm at sea. Jon.

Jon? Where was Tom?

The god blinked Its eyes and chased the poisonous, painful thoughts away.

The god waited.

Jon's chest burned, and he dropped the gory dagger. Taking in great lungfuls of air, he struggled to get his breathing under control. The man beneath him stared sightlessly, his face frozen in a rictus of pain and terror. The pool of blood spread out, soaking into Jon's pant legs, and the wet silk stuck to him uncomfortably. With a grimace, Jon planted a hand in the middle of the dead emperor's chest to push himself to his feet.

Frowning down at the corpse, he realized that he felt no horror over killing Ah'puch. As his heart rate slowed, Jon took stock of his feelings. His anger had drained away, and he felt... justified. Jon wiped his hands on his pants. No, he would not be crying or pissing himself over this death.

Or maybe over any death again? he wondered.

Jon shook his head. No, maybe not, but he wasn't about to become a depraved killer just because he ended some asshole's life. He blinked slowly at the dead man and then spat in his face before finally walking away.

There was complete pandemonium in the cages. In the one closest, the man inside shrieked and howled like a monkey as he hung from ropes strung across the space. In another, a tiny, frail-looking woman rammed her head against the bars repeatedly. Blood leaked down her face but she was unrelenting. Jon grimaced. Putting them out of their misery might be the kindest course of action since the emperor couldn't cure them now. For all he knew, they could be past helping anyway.

But... What about Baltsaros?

He clenched his jaw and made himself turn to the captain's cage. The first sharp pangs of regret made themselves known at the sight of the man beyond the bars. By killing Ah'puch, Jon had condemned Baltsaros to live out his life as the monster he'd always tried to hide.

The captain stood with his hands curled around the bars, his eyes wide as he stared at the blood on Jon's clothes. A smile sliced open the ratty, wild beard, and Baltsaros licked his lips. He pointed to Jon as he began to speak the guttural language he had spoken before.

Jon's eyes blurred. The emperor had awoken the beast inside Baltsaros and destroyed any good that had been there. This was the creature that had hidden behind all of the captain's easy smiles; this was the coldness in Baltsaros's eyes. This was the thing that had pushed Baltsaros to kill and kill again. It was the monster that had tried to murder him in the mists. Jon breathed quickly through his clenched teeth.

"You killed him," Jon whispered hoarsely. The captain's incomprehensible words continued to hiss and growl in the air between them without pause. "Ah'puch might have been the one to let you loose, but you were the one who killed Baltsaros in the end. I think you've been slowly killing him for a long time now, haven't you? You've been biding your time, waiting for your chance..." Jon's voice broke and he took a step forward.

"What *are* you?" he spat, his anger sparking briefly, but the thing behind the bars didn't reply. Instead, it continued speaking, one finger pointed at him. Jon sank down to the stone floor; he felt weak as the adrenaline left his system. Tom would be here soon, if he made it through the mines. What would he make of this?

It didn't make any sense. This couldn't be a god. There were no gods. That's what Baltsaros had said. Jon rubbed his face; the cacophony of the other prisoners was beginning to give him a headache. Nothing made sense.

Then the emperor's words came back to him, and he frowned.

"Wait... Why would you be speaking a made-up language?" he asked. "When you attacked me that night, you were speaking your native tongue, weren't you? Why the nonsense now?"

Jon narrowed his eyes at the captain. Something felt strangely *off* now that he thought of it. Before, when he had caught glimpses of what Baltsaros's charming mask covered, he'd felt a sort of primal fear. This creature in front of him now didn't scare him. It was like a pale version of the darkness that lived inside the captain.

"I don't think you are what you think you are," he said slowly, an idea forming in his head. "I think you have this deep-seated belief that you're truly *evil*, whatever that is. When I saw it in your eyes, I think that I felt fear because *you* felt it. I think you've always been terrified of what you believe yourself to be. Now that you're 'transformed' into a monster, you're not afraid anymore, are you? In fact, you *should* be relieved. Happy, even, because you can finally just give in to it. But... Why do I still sense conflict when I look at you?

"This compulsion, this murdering spree you've been on for gods know how many years. Where does it stem from? What triggered it? Ah'puch said something that I almost missed. He said you had a damaged psyche. I don't know what *psyche* means, but I'm guessing it has to do with your mind. I've called you damaged in the past, and you really are, aren't you?" As Jon spoke, the captain's voice got quieter until he finally fell silent. The man stared at him, expressionless.

"What could have happened to you to make you honestly believe that you're a monster? And it wasn't the time you were dumped overboard in a barrel by your uncle. I think it happened when you were younger. Much younger," murmured Jon. He had a sudden thought. "Baltsaros... *how did your parents die?*"

Jon climbed to his feet as the silence stretched on. The man behind bars watched him, his dark eyes wary.

"You never told me," explained Jon. He took a step towards the bars and saw a flicker of apprehension cross the captain's face. "Tell me. I know you can understand me. How did they die?"

He was rewarded by another long stretch of silence. Then the captain spoke two words in his native tongue that Jon recognized.

Red hands?

"What does that mean? Red hands... Your red hands? My red hands? I don't understand," said Jon softly. Slowly, tentatively, he reached his own hand out. The captain's eyes widened as Jon's fingers touched the older man's hand gently. Instantly, Baltsaros recoiled with an angry growl. Jon watched in dismay as the captain began to pace anew, muttering to himself quietly.

A grinding noise startled Jon, and he spun on his heel. From a small metal door at the end of the row of cages emerged a familiar figure. Jon felt relief crash over him.

"Tom!"

The first mate straightened and looked around, his eyes wide at the sight of the cages and their crazed occupants. He stepped forward, barefoot and filthy from his time in the mines. When he reached Jon, he cupped the back of his head and pressed their foreheads together quickly.

"Thank the gods," breathed Jon.

"Thank the gods my arse, lad," smirked Tom. "It was a piece o' cake."

Jon's eyes slid from Tom's narrow, tufted strip of hair to his black-ringed eyes and down past the harness, the tattered whip, and blood on his arm; he raised his eyebrows, curious.

"Where's Da?" asked Tom, looking past Jon. When Jon pointed to the raving madman in the cell, the first mate paled visibly.

"Bloody hells, what the fuck is wrong with him?" choked Tom. He curled his fists over the bars. "Da?"

The man inside the cage stopped his pacing and turned to look at the first mate. Jon let out a slow breath. There was recognition there. Brief, but he had seen it.

"We have'ta get him out of there. What the fuck is wrong with him?" growled Tom. "Where's the bloody key?" Tom's knuckles whitened.

"It's probably on Ah'puch," replied Jon.

Tom's head swung around.

"Where is that fuckin' cunt?" snarled Tom. When Jon pointed to the open space beyond the row of cages, the first mate's face went momentarily slack with surprise. With eyes narrowed, he looked at Jon.

"Yes, it was me," replied Jon to Tom's unvoiced question.

The big man squeezed Jon's shoulder before walking towards the body.

"I'm not sure it's a good idea to let him out just yet," said Jon, watching the captain. The man had resumed his pacing, but now he threw glances at both Jon and Tom. Jon could see confusion like cracks in his eyes. "He's not himself."

"That's for fuckin' sure," said Tom, returning to Jon's side. There was a golden key in the first mate's bloody hand. Jon stared at it a moment.

"Tom, do the words *red hands* mean anything to you?" he asked. Tom turned to him, and shook his head.

"Nay, love. He spoke 'em?" Tom frowned at the captain.

"Yes. I asked him how his parents died, and that was his answer. Do you know the story?"

Tom shook his head again. His shoulder was warm against Jon's.

"No. He never said. I never asked," admitted Tom. "Why?"

Jon quickly told Tom about what Ah'puch had said.

"If he's a bloody god, then I'm the king o' the world, love," scoffed Tom.

"No, he's not an *actual* god. Ah'puch just made him believe he was one, or at least what Ah'puch thought a god was like... all mixed up with the guilt that Baltsaros has over something."

"Da? Guilt?" The first mate peered at the captain.

Baltsaros had stopped pacing and simply stood motionless in the centre of the cage. Jon tilted his head at the captain and thought hard.

"What if something terrible happened to him when he was really young. Something that he thought was his fault and left a scar so deep and so horrible that, somewhere inside, he began to think of himself as a truly evil person. Not consciously, I mean... Hells, maybe he doesn't really remember it."

Jon watched Tom mull over his words.

"Ye think Da's been killin' because he thinks he's *evil?*" asked Tom. The first mate slowly rubbed the stubble on the side of his head with his palm, a deep comma of confusion between his brows.

"Yeah. Because he thinks he has to for some reason. I've seen it in the dungeons— men who thought it was ultimately in their nature to kill. But the people the captain's been killing... They've all shown some kind of prejudice or hate, right?"

Tom thought a moment and nodded.

"It's like he was having some sort of fucked-up, good-versus-evil war in his head and the emperor tipped him over into... this. This has to be just some kind of reaction to being told that he's an evil, heart-eating god. There's just enough behind the legend that it fits with Baltsaros's past somehow. Ah'puch worked with that." Jon decided not to give voice to his conflicted feelings about the peculiar string of coincidences that seemed to follow them... if that's what they were. The alternative was just too strange to think about. He watched the captain for a moment, letting his clever brain sort through theories.

"See, now he's off the hook for his past behaviour," Jon finally continued. "Ah'puch granted him permission to be the evil thing he always feared he would be. So he's retreated into this... *performance*. I think, at least partially, to free himself of the guilt he feels over almost killing me."

Baltsaros let out a small, strangled noise and sank down to his knees.

Jon nodded, his heart beating quickly. He was definitely getting somewhere.

"He'd stopped murdering, and he'd truly begun to pull away from this notion that he was a monster... and then he nearly killed me. It must have been quite a blow."

Tom slipped the golden key into the lock and turned it. With an anxious look at Jon, the first mate pulled the door open. The captain didn't move; his eyes were red.

"He thinks," Jon said, stepping into the cage, "that if he admits to having feelings, having weaknesses, the monster inside him will get out and destroy everything he holds dear."

Baltsaros moaned softly. He flinched when Tom placed his hands on his shoulders, but his eyes closed, and he leaned into the first mate's touch.

"But that makes absolutely no sense, Baltsaros," said Jon. "You *know* that. How can you protect something you care about without acknowledging that you care about it to begin with? Think about it."

"Why would I try to kill something I love?" came the whispered reply. Baltsaros opened his eyes and stared at Jon. One tear spilled from the corner of his eye, tracking a path over his cheekbone and into his beard. A tremor shook him, and Tom sank down to his knees, folding his arms around the captain. Baltsaros took a hoarse breath, clenching and unclenching his fists in his lap. "What kind of monster would do that?"

"No monster at all," replied Jon. His throat felt tight as he crouched in front of the captain. "What about all the others? You're not the only person who attacked someone that night. People killed, Baltsaros, and it wasn't because they were monsters."

"What about... the others? Before..." rasped the captain.

"Yes, you are guilty of murdering people," said Jon with a nod. "There's no way around that, but you'd no more kill Tom or me than you would take your own life. So, instead of trying to find secret, crazy ways of 'purging' this so-called monster inside you, you're going to help me find out what started it to begin with."

"But I... don't..." Baltsaros sounded lost, afraid, helpless. Jon caught a flash of the boy he had seen before.

It gave him hope.

There was a thundering at the door. Tom was up on his feet in an instant. Jon stood and glanced at the entrance. The emperor's absence had probably been noticed; he also hoped the ruckus at the door wasn't because the pirates had been captured in the mines.

"Shit," Tom muttered. "Looks like we're outta bloody time. Can ye walk, Da? Or are ye gonna make me carry ye?"

"I can walk," said Baltsaros, his voice stronger. However, when he stood, he stumbled forward, and Tom had to catch him before he fell.

"The fuck you can," grunted Tom. He grabbed the captain's wrist and bent his knee, preparing to lift him over his shoulder, when the captain stopped him.

"Wait, no, I'll be ok," said Baltsaros with a short huff of breath, nearly a laugh. "The day I let you carry me out of somewhere..." He shook his head. "We need to find the antidote to the spores first. It's there." Baltsaros pointed to the long row of shelves above the burnished worktable. "Somewhere."

Tom stepped up to the shelves and peered at the gleaming bottles. The pounding on the door doubled, and Jon thought he could hear shouting. He wondered whether someone else in the emperor's employ had the key.

"Da, which one?" asked the first mate, his ocean eyes wide. "I can't fuckin' read half o' these."

"Ah'puch showed it to me. When he was... *working*. He liked to talk. Brag," Baltsaros said. He coughed into his fist, and Jon saw another tremor go through him. "It's a bluish-white powder." The captain shuffled to the wall full of bottles and began to search with the first mate.

Jon walked over to the emperor's corpse and grabbed the dagger. The patients in the cages had begun screaming and crowing all over again in agitation, and he could barely think. He heard Tom let out a long string of curses as bottle after bottle crashed to the floor.

"Come on, we have to go," Jon said urgently. The corner of the door was denting out. There was no way that the hinges would hold much longer.

"Is this it?" yelled Tom over the ear-splitting noise. Jon watched the door shake in its frame and held the dagger out in front of him. They were out of time. Then something caught his sleeve, and he spun. Tom pulled at his arm again with a glance at Baltsaros, and Jon helped the first mate support the captain as they ran to the corpse-chute. The woman who'd been bashing her head against the bars was unconscious or dead in a pool of blood, having finally succumbed to her self-inflicted injuries. He caught a glimpse of a figure at the back of the cage and stopped in surprise.

"Oren?" he yelled.

The boy lifted his head, a dazed look on his face.

"Jon! We ain't got time, lad," shouted Tom. He grabbed the metal door and lifted it. Baltsaros ducked through the low opening.

Jon nearly tripped in his hurry to get the key, and when he turned it in the lock to Oren's cage, the willowy youth staggered to his feet.

"Jon…" growled Tom. His muscles bulged from holding the heavy door up. Jon grabbed Oren's arm and half dragged the younger man out of the cage before pushing him to follow Tom. He slipped into the narrow space behind Oren and slid down the chute, half landing on the young fisherman at the bottom. He quickly got out of the way as the door above clanged shut. Tom slid down the incline and landed with a grunt.

Jon and Oren helped Baltsaros to his feet, and the three of them made their way down the rock-hewn tunnel with Tom following close behind. When they reached a juncture, Tom stopped and put his back to the wooden beam that reinforced the tunnel ceiling.

Tom let out a roar, and the tendons in his neck stood out in stark relief as he pushed as hard as he could. There was a crackle and then a high squealing noise. Finally, with a spray of rock dust, the beam shifted. After a few more heaves, Tom managed to push it over. He leapt forward as it collapsed across the tunnel entrance followed by a shower of loose rocks and a few large boulders.

"That should slow 'em down at least," said Tom. He took off at a slow lope and squinted down the tunnel, motioning for the others to follow a moment later. Behind them came the noise of the metal door slamming, and Jon hurried Baltsaros forward. Tom led them down one tunnel and then another, the passages twisting and sometimes doubling back on themselves until Jon was convinced they were lost. Tom stopped again at the entrance to yet another side tunnel and pressed his back to the wall before glancing into the space beyond. It was pitch dark.

"All right, quick as ye can, after me," he rumbled. "The exit's not far, but since we ain't seen Harris or the boys yet, we can't be sure it's clear. Someone's broken the lantern so watch yer feet, lads."

Jon nodded quickly and looked at the captain. Baltsaros's skin had taken on a greyish tinge, and his eyes were half-closed.

"Baltsaros?" he said, adjusting the man's arm on his shoulder. "Stay with me."

"I'll always stay with you, Jon," whispered the captain. "Always. I promise. Always."

Jon was suddenly short of breath from Baltsaros's words even though it was obvious that the man was starting to lose his senses again.

"Shit, don't do this to me now," gasped Jon with a half-laugh over the helpless tears that rose in his eyes. "I love you. We'll get you out of here, and then we'll have all the time in the world for promises. Just put your weight on me. One foot in front of the other. Come on now."

Tom shoved Oren roughly out of the way and took Baltsaros's other arm. The skinny, bruised young man stood uncertainly, blinking his large blue eyes slowly for a moment before he turned and ran quickly up the tunnel. Jon thought he had simply fled until he heard a quiet, "Come, come, it's safe," from the dark. With the help of Tom, he manoeuvred Baltsaros into the tunnel, the two of them supporting the captain almost entirely. Jon felt Baltsaros's head loll on his shoulder, and he ground his teeth in frustration.

Up ahead, they could hear the sound of fighting. Jon and Tom slowed down, nearly crashing into Oren in the dark.

"What's happening?" whispered Jon. He couldn't see Oren's face, but he saw the faint silhouette shake its head.

"I can't be knowing," replied Oren quietly. "I go look. You stay." The youth took off at a quick step, barely visible in the dark.

A few seconds later, they heard Oren cry out, and Jon assumed the worst. However, when the boy let out a relieved laugh, he frowned. Jon tensed as a tall shape came up the passageway towards them. A match flared in the dark. Polas smiled at them, and the tears in his eyes glittered in the light of the flame.

Tom gave a whoop of laughter.

"Bloody fuckin' cocksuckin' bloody hells am I fuckin' glad to see yer fuckin' face!" he exclaimed.

Polas's smile widened, and he reached out to pat Tom's shoulder.

"Come, come. We will get you through here. Come. I see the captain? He is injured? We will carry him. I have so much thanks for my grandson. So much. So many?" said Polas with a laugh as he led them down the tunnel towards the light. "I lose my speaking, I am so glad!"

When they emerged into a wide main tunnel, Jon saw a group of fisherfolk assembled. Each held a double-pronged spear in one hand and a net in the other.

"What's happening? How are you here?" asked Jon. He let the captain down onto the tunnel floor gently, and Baltsaros slumped over. Tom knelt at his side and lifted a waterskin to his lips. Jon watched the captain take a few sips and sighed in relief.

"A revolution, Jon," said Polas, his face creasing in another wide grin. "A beautiful revolution. And it is to you and Tom that it is thanks."

CHAPTER 29
BROKEN GOD, WOUNDED BEAST

J on sat cross-legged on the captain's wide bed watching Baltsaros sleep. Gone was the straggly, dirty beard; Tom had very carefully shaved the captain before he left to help Polas and the marked slaves take out the last of the resistance. Without his beard, Baltsaros suddenly looked like a stranger... older for the deep lines to each side of his mouth; frail, even. Jon frowned and reached out to move a loose strand of hair away from Baltsaros's face. The captain was covered in sweat, and the hair stuck to his forehead; at Jon's touch, Baltsaros let out a small moan and a shiver as his body fought the damage done to it.

The boom of the cannon startled Jon, and Baltsaros's eyes flew open, sightless, before closing again. They were anchored in the mouth of the harbour outside of Ereme'ia Balor, and the *Heart's* guns were being used in aid of the rebellion. Jon wondered how long it would be before the last of the lords and slavers of the city finally gave up or were defeated.

Without opening his eyes, Baltsaros murmured a word.

"Water."

It was the first thing he'd said since he was carried aboard the previous evening.

Jon slid off the bed quickly and went to the icebox to get cold water for the captain. When he turned back to the bed, Baltsaros was up on one elbow, his red-rimmed eyes on Jon. Jon sat on the edge of the bed and handed over the metal cup, unsettled by the way the captain's hand shook.

"What's happening?" rasped Baltsaros after he had taken a slow swallow.

Jon quickly brought the captain up to speed as he sat taking tiny sips of water.

. . .

Shortly after the guards had been dismissed from Ah'puch's chambers, they began to spread Jon's story of the successful slave rebellion. It didn't take long before the news made its way out of the palace, at which point Tom and the pirates had already set off towards the mines. After leaving Tom with the slave drivers, Ceara learned about the rumour from her spies. Seeing her chance to create a distraction to help with the captain's rescue, she had sent word to Jarrod and the bevy of escaped slaves in the sprawling *madina* to spread the story ever farther. On hearing the rumour, Ertos the fishmonger had sent a runner to *Baal's Heart* to tell Polas that the slaves were being whipped into a frenzy by stories of a rebellion; one that grew more and more outlandish with every retelling. Polas had taken a few of Baltsaros's men with him to Balor by jolly boat to lend support. He had arrived at the mines only moments before Oren had come running out of the dark into his arms, leading the three men to safety.

Baltsaros listened quietly as Jon talked, his dark eyes slightly unfocused. When Jon had finished, the captain narrowed his gaze at him.

"Why?" he asked softly.

"Why what?" replied Jon, confused. "Why were the fisherfolk so quick to help the rebellion? Why had the slaves rebelled so easily?"

"Why do you love me?" asked Baltsaros.

Jon frowned and wondered if the captain had heard anything he had said. When he didn't reply right away, Baltsaros's fingers closed around his forearm and squeezed hard. Jon winced but didn't move.

"Why? Jon... why?" repeated the captain, searching his face.

Jon's first impulse was to blurt "I don't know", but the crazed, desperate look in Baltsaros's eyes demanded more. He took a deep breath.

"Because, despite everything, despite all the shit you've put me through, despite the fact that I've wanted to kill you myself more than once... I still find solace in you. A place where I belong. You gave me the gift of freedom, and I took it willingly, and I just as willingly bound myself to you," Jon said and let out a small, pained sound as Baltsaros's fingers tightened on him. "But... I love the man you are and hate the monster. Or do I? See... This is the problem. My feelings, my thoughts get all fucking tangled when I'm with you. Part of me just wants to follow you blindly to the ends of the world. The other would see me far, far away where you couldn't hurt me anymore. Because that's what you do, Baltsaros. You *hurt* me. Over and over again. And you do the same to Tom." Jon was getting angry. He wrenched his arm out of Baltsaros's grasp and stood, staring down at the older man.

Baltsaros's expression had shifted to sadness. There was a tic in his cheek as he looked up at Jon, but his eyes were clear.

"Find the man," murmured Baltsaros, "and you'll help me defeat the monster. But... Jon, do you truly love the man?"

Jon looked hard at Baltsaros. His handsome, chiselled features framed brown eyes wide with rare emotion. His broad, muscular shoulders, sun-dark despite his sickly pallor, were stooped as he waited for Jon's answer. His long-fingered hands that could be gentle or cruel lay limp in his lap. He was a man defeated, but as Jon watched, Baltsaros's face creased into a wan smile though he seemed a shadow of his usual self.

"You're being cruel in your silence, Jon," he said. "You've already followed me to the ends of the world, but you didn't do it blindly. You succeeded in stripping me of lies I didn't even know I had... Did you also want my blood?" Baltsaros lifted his arm, showing Jon the scabbed wounds left behind by the emperor. "You can have it. You can have everything I am. I give it all to you."

Jon let out a small sigh.

"Of course I love the man. Didn't I just say that?" he smiled sadly. He sat back down on the bed and took the cup from Baltsaros; Jon set it on the floor. "I don't want your blood. I've had quite enough of that this past week. All I want, Baltsaros, is to leave this place. I want long days of sunshine and hard, satisfying work aboard the ship, *our* ship, without feeling the need to look over my shoulder all the time. I want, at the end of those days, when my muscles are sore and I'm filled with simple happiness, to fall into your arms and have you show me how to be yours all over again." The words poured out of Jon as if a dam in him had broken. He felt a desperate hope. "I want you to be sane and whole. I want to spend my nights with you and Tom, playing and fucking and loving until I'm sore all over again. And then I want to fall asleep, and dream stupidly happy dreams, bothered by nothing more frightening than Tom's snoring."

Baltsaros laughed and reached for Jon. He let himself be pulled down and stretched himself out carefully beside the captain, mindful of his wounds. He lay there quietly while Baltsaros trailed his fingers over his cheek and down to his shoulder and back again, the touch as soft as a whisper.

"We can do that, Jon," said the captain after a time. "I promise."

Jon nodded and closed his eyes.

~

A metallic clinking pulled Baltsaros from sleep. He opened his eyes and saw that the room had darkened. He had slept the entire day away. Or... had he? His memory felt full of holes, and time was unfolding strangely. He hoped that the damage to his brain wasn't permanent. There was another clink and then a crash followed by a muttered string of curses. Tom bent over to pick up the fallen plate and saw the captain's eyes on him.

"Oh. Sorry, Da. Didn't mean to wake ye," said the first mate, placing the golden plate on top of a precarious stack of dishes. The long mahogany table was piled with riches: golden cups, statuettes, and platters sat amongst chests filled with jewellery that glittered even in the muted light of the captain's quarters. "I was just pickin' out the things I thought ye'd like. Ye know... for yer fancy meals and, ah... things." The first mate held a heavily ornamented spoon aloft, the smile on his rugged face enthusiastic.

"I take it that the rebellion went well?" asked Baltsaros with a wry grin. He tried to sit up, but halfway there he gasped with the pain that erupted in his groin. Tom was at his side in an instant, pushing him back down. Jon was nowhere to be seen.

"Hang on, Da. Lemme get ye some painkillers," said the big man, his eyes worried. Baltsaros shook his head.

"Not yet," he said. "My head is clear right now. I want it to stay that way, at least for a little while." He gingerly touched the thick bandages that swathed him from hip to mid-thigh and hid the worst of the damage done to him. Hopefully, he'd retain the use of his cock once the burns healed. He grimaced. To hells with his cock; he was lucky to be alive.

"You sure took your bloody time rescuing me," he said good-naturedly and smiled wide at the look of chagrin on Tom's face.

"I'm sorry, Da," mumbled Tom, stooping to crawl onto the bed.

Baltsaros sobered as he watched Tom sit at his side, his blue-green eyes narrowed with misery.

"Thank you, Tom. Truly. I owe you my life," said the captain. He reached for the first mate's hand and realized, as he did so, that though he often held or touched Jon's hands out of simple affection, he had never really done so with Tom. The brawny young man looked away, and Baltsaros thought he detected a flush in his face.

Curious, Baltsaros turned Tom's hand over in his. The back of the first mate's hand was covered in a smattering of small scars—old burns and wounds acquired from his life of servitude and from working aboard the old pirate ship. His knuckles were crisscrossed with raised, white lines where the skin had split and healed over and over from his penchant of using his fists to get his point across. Even now they were red, and on the first two there were fresh scabs. The third knuckle had a squashed look to it, and Baltsaros remembered when the first mate had broken it in a fight the first year he was aboard. They were hands that he knew almost as well as his own. He rubbed his thumb softly over the scarred skin before lifting Tom's hand to his mouth. He kissed Tom's battered knuckles gently, one by one, before turning the man's hand over in his to press his lips to the deeply lined palm. When he looked up, Tom was staring at him, a glimmer of wetness in his eyes.

The sight made Baltsaros hurt.

"I'm sorry, Tom," he whispered. "You've put up with too much."

Tom made a small noise deep in his chest and lifted his shoulder up in a shrug.

"No. Listen to me," growled Baltsaros. "I am sorry. I've never told you enough how thankful I am that you came into my life—"

"Or ever," interrupted Tom with a twisted grin. He closed his callused fingers over Baltsaros's and squeezed softly. "Save yer godsdamned words, old man. I ain't a soft thing that needs to be coddled, aye?" However, the tears that threatened to spill from Tom's eyes belied his words. The first mate dashed them away with his wrist and clenched his jaw.

Baltsaros lay there holding Tom's hand and closed his eyes.

"When Jon wanted to leave, just you and him together, how long were you tempted?" he said. He felt Tom tense and he smiled.

"Not a godsdamned bloody second, Da," said the first mate. It was a lie, Baltsaros was sure of it, but he liked the answer regardless.

～

Tom found the ingredients that Baltsaros had jotted down the last time he was conscious. *Aloe, turmeric, yellow dock, powdered ephemroot mould, calendula, qaphberries...* Tom took out the small jars one by one and placed them on the table along with the mortar and pestle. Some of the ingredients were powders; others were just leaves kept in clear alcohol or oil. Mashed together in the right proportions and cured quickly over fire in the metal tablet mould, they would make a powerful medicine to fight the infection that had taken root in Baltsaros.

Jon's face was drawn as he looked down at all the ingredients.

"You sure this is everything?" he asked, his brow furrowed.

Tom read over the list again and nodded.

"How are we supposed to know if these are the right ones? He hasn't been the most lucid. I barely understood half of what he said earlier," said Jon, glancing up at him.

Tom grimaced. It was true. Baltsaros's waking periods had become shorter and shorter over the past few days and were often punctuated by strange turns in the conversation and periods of delirium.

"What else can we do?" Tom said quietly. He stroked the side of his jaw, the stubble sharp against his palm.

Jon stared at him; his blue-grey eyes were bleak.

"What if I mix it wrong?" he said.

Tom looked away as he put the thin black cigar between his lips and started rooting around in a drawer for a match. He was sick with worry over Baltsaros, but Jon didn't need to know that.

"Ye'll mix it the way ye mix it, and it'll all work out in the end, lovey," he said, keeping his tone cheerful. "Da's got the luck of the black devil himself. Don'tcha worry one bit." He struck the match against the corner of the armoire and put the flame to the end of the slim cheroot. Thick smoke filled his lungs as he puffed on it, and he felt the welcoming tingle of the mild narcotic make his head feel momentarily light.

Tom turned back to Jon and saw with relief that he had squared his shoulders and set his jaw with a nod.

"Okay," said Jon, "tell me again what to do."

Tom pulled out a chair and turned it around so he could straddle it and rest his arms across the backrest. He read out Baltsaros's instructions, one step at a time, and watched Jon grind the ingredients together. Tom felt like a coward making Jon do the work, but he just couldn't do it himself. What if he killed the captain? He would never be able to live with himself.

When Jon finished mixing everything together and pressed the resulting greenish paste into the mould, Tom struck another match and held it beneath the piece of tin;

539

he kept the flame close until it burned the tip of his fingers, and he dropped the match to the tabletop with a curse.

The two of them stared at each other in silence for a moment, and then Jon's lips quirked up into a slight smile.

"All right," he said. "Let's see if we can't get Baltsaros back to the healthy, black-hearted scourge of the seven seas we all know and love, shall we?"

Tom was surprised by his involuntary bark of laughter; trust Jon to suddenly turn a tense situation on its head. With a smile on his face, he lurched to his feet to grab some water as Jon popped the cooling tablets onto a plate.

~

The god awoke in the dark, Its prey mere feet away. It could smell them. The two entwined on the bed. It made him sick.

Wait. Sick?

The god... The beast? The beast sat up despite the pain. Pain is mortal. Pain is nothing. Gods don't feel pain.

Wait. Beast or god?

The world tilted on an angle as he tried to stand. He fell on one knee.

Pain.

Pain.

PAIN.

Baltsaros dry-heaved on hands and knees. His mouth was sour. His head pounded. He blinked in the dark, trying to make out his surroundings. With a trembling hand he reached up and touched the black shapes in front of him. Bars. Cold, flattened iron.

It took him a few seconds to realize that he was in the cage in his quarters.

The captain groped for the narrow cot and pulled himself back onto it.

Not a god. Not a beast. Just a man. A very weak, sick man.

His brain burned.

He tried to remember what he had done to get himself locked in the cage, but he came up empty. How much time had passed since he had been rescued from the menagerie of the mentally abused? He touched his chest and his fingers came away sticky with salve. The electrodes had burned into him, again and again. The lights. Bright.

Pain.

Pain.

Pain.

When the warm hand reached through the bars and stroked his hair back from his face softly, Baltsaros realized he was weeping brokenly.

"Hush, Da. Hush," rumbled Tom.

A second hand reached through and clasped his shoulder.

"It'll be all right," whispered Jon.

Baltsaros closed his eyes and drifted off, the pain chased away by the touch of two souls that would watch after his own.

CHAPTER 30
THE LAST SACRIFICE

Baltsaros ran across the ice. His tears froze on his cheeks. He was furious. They would pay. All of them. His skinny legs were a blur. He was fast! Fast like the lion on his family crest. His breath heaved in his bony chest. They would pay. Pay for being so... being so mean! Baltsaros tripped over a chunk of ice and went sprawling. He let out a cry and pulled himself up, wrapping his thin arms around his knee and rocking as he sobbed. There was blood on the ice. He had torn open his knee. He had ripped his pants. Mother would be furious about the pants. He sat and wept like a baby. It wasn't fair! Then he saw the men on the ice. Strangers. Red hands. Red feet.

~

The captain jerked awake, his strangled yell like a distant memory to his ears, and he blinked rapidly a few times to clear the strange vision. The portal above his head was a circle of cloudless blue, and he could hear men shouting outside. He waited until his heartbeat slowed a little before sitting up. After a moment, he smiled. That was no fighting; it was just the simple sounds of the rough men working aboard *Baal's Heart*. From the way that the boat gently rocked beneath him and the water softly slapped the hull, he knew they were still anchored.

Baltsaros grimaced, hauling himself to his feet with one hand hooked into the flat iron bars to hold his weight as he shuffled forward like an old man. Standing over the piss pot, he gingerly eased down the thick, clean, white bandages at his groin. He peered at himself with a sigh; his skin was a mess of burns and contusions. Wincing, Baltsaros pulled his cock out, handling it as lightly as possible as he pointed it over the earthenware pot. When his stream came, the captain gritted his teeth against the searing pain. Ah'puch had really done his best to "cure" him of his sexual deviancy.

With a muttered curse, he shook himself and pulled the bandages back over his damaged skin. Ah'puch would pay.

Ah'puch is dead, he reminded himself.

Yes, your wolf cub is turning out to be quite the little killer, said the beast, looking at him with burning eyes. *Just like you wanted him to be. Like I wanted him to be. What fun we will have together when I take his mind like I've taken yours.*

"Shut up!" snarled Baltsaros, lashing out at the air.

"Da?"

Baltsaros started and turned around. Tom stood in the doorway to their quarters with a worried expression. All that remained of the damage done to his face was the healing cut on his lip and a little yellow-greenish hue in the corner of one eye.

How long had he been sleeping?

"Sorry," muttered Baltsaros, easing himself slowly back down on the cot. "I'm all right. I'll be all right."

"Who were you talking to?" asked Tom as he stepped towards the cage on silent feet. In his hand, he held a plate of food; Baltsaros could see that there were two pieces of battered fish and a scoop of Cook's spicy vegetable stew. His stomach rumbled.

"No one. Is that for me?" asked Baltsaros with a smile.

The big man nodded slowly, his eyes narrowed in skepticism. However, he unlocked the cage door and handed the plate to the captain, pulling up a chair a moment later to keep Baltsaros company while he ate.

"So yer feelin' better?" asked Tom. Gone was the black kohl around his eyes that he had worn at the captain's rescue, but the strip of short hair that stuck up from his shorn scalp remained... as did one other thing. Baltsaros ignored Tom's question and pointed.

"Why are you still wearing *that*?" he asked.

Tom's fingers touched the slave collar, and Baltsaros could swear that the first mate's face reddened a little. Tom looked away and then up to the ceiling where there was the creak of someone walking above them on the quarterdeck. He shrugged, and his lips parted in a coy, almost sheepish grin.

"Ah. I see," laughed Baltsaros, shaking his head. Pangs of jealousy should have had no place in the deep well of gratitude he felt towards his boys for rescuing him, but there they were. Something of his thoughts must have shown on his face because Tom's eyes went wide, and he pushed himself off the chair and down on his knees in front of the captain.

"Yer gettin' better, Da. There's no more infection. Jon did ye up good. Ye'll be back to slappin' me around in no time," said the first mate, his voice gruff and full of forced cheer.

Baltsaros nodded with a sigh and, after an idle thought, pulled a piece of the tender fish apart with his fingers, holding it in front of Tom's lips. He smiled at the surprised grin on the young brute's face; Tom opened his mouth and took the fish obediently. After he had swallowed, and without prompting, he licked Baltsaros's fingers clean. So many possibilities that they hadn't yet explored in this capacity.

The captain let out a sharp cry and nearly dropped the plate.

"Da? Bloody hells, Da? What's the matter?" asked Tom. His hands steadied Baltsaros, fear making deep pools of his pupils as he stared at him helplessly.

Baltsaros began to laugh. He curled one hand around the tender mound in his groin, the one that had begun to harden at the touch of Tom's warm tongue against the whorls of his fingertips. The pain had startled him more than anything, and the sheer relief made him laugh even harder. Tom watched him in total confusion as the captain laughed himself to tears in front of him.

"Da, yer scarin' me," said Tom. True enough, there was a hint of fear in his voice.

Baltsaros waved his hand, tears streaming down his face as he tried to get himself under control. He couldn't remember the last time he'd laughed so hard.

Tom lurched to his feet and bellowed in the direction of the stateroom door.

"Jon! Get yer ass in here. Da's having some kind o' turn. Jon!"

Baltsaros grabbed Tom's hand and shook his head, the laughter crushing his insides and making him gasp for air.

There was the thunder of boots on the stairs outside, and Jon appeared at the door, his blue-grey eyes wide with fear.

Finally, Baltsaros could breathe again. He rubbed at his face, still chuckling.

"It's ok. It's fine. I'm fine. It's just that it seems that my recovery is going… better than expected," he smiled, looking up at Jon and Tom. "I'm sorry. I didn't mean to worry you. It's just that part of me is rather eager to get behind the wheel, so to speak."

Tom looked unconvinced, but Jon nodded slowly.

"Da's never laughed like that before," said the first mate quietly, his voice like velvet-covered gravel.

"No. I wouldn't think so," replied Jon, his eyes on the captain.

Baltsaros sobered at the expression on his young face. It was a knowing look; Jon understood something that he himself had yet to grasp. It made him angry all of a sudden. And then very sad. His chest hurt. Emotions punched through walls as thin as paper. He groped around looking for his sense of self and found that the well of peace that he depended on was empty. So much confusion mixed up with pain and… relief?

"I think you're going to find that the captain's going to surprise the ever-loving hells out of us in days to come, Tom. And not necessarily in a bad way."

Jon smiled reassuringly at the captain. Baltsaros's eyes went flinty as he appraised him like he was a morsel of food or a small rodent trapped in his claws. Then the warmth returned to the captain's face, and the older man smiled back with a small nod. Watching the naked emotions flit across Baltsaros's face like ripples in a clear lake was startling and worrisome. He wondered if the captain could recover on his own or if he needed something that neither Jon nor Tom could provide. Baltsaros glanced down at his plate and resumed eating with a slightly lost look in his eyes.

Abetha, said a small voice inside him.

It made sense. She had helped Baltsaros find answers about himself before; maybe she could do it again.

"We should get him to your mother," he said quietly to Tom. "She might be able to offer some insight."

A deep furrow appeared in the first mate's brow, and he scratched at the short stubble of his jaw.

Jon almost laughed at the fear he saw there.

"She's your mother. Not the black devil," he scolded Tom, bumping his shoulder.

"Indeed, Tom. Your mother has been a boon to me in the past. Jon's suggestion is sound," agreed the captain, setting down his spoon. He passed his plate to Jon, his eyes clear again. Baltsaros's mercurial moods were disconcerting, but at least he seemed happy enough to defer to Jon's judgment until he had recovered.

Jon frowned. There was something else that needed to be resolved.

"We need an interim captain until you're well again," he said to Baltsaros. He watched anger and resignation battle for dominance in the captain's eyes. "You know that's a fact."

"What? You don't want a madman at the helm?" grinned Baltsaros, instantly full of good humour again. "Yes. You're right, Jon. Tom, you will replace me—"

"Nay, Da," grunted Tom, crossing his arms over his bare chest. "No fuckin' way. Ye know I like to make the crew hop, but I ain't the one who makes the bloody orders. No."

"Then, who?" grimaced Jon. "Calum's dead. Polas is staying here to help rebuild the city. Shit, I wish Katherine were here; she could have..." he trailed off when he saw Tom's lips stretch into a wide, playful smile. Baltsaros was staring at him with a shrewd look. Jon blanched when he realized what they were thinking, and he shook his head. "What, *me*? You've got to be kidding. Who the hell is going to listen to *me*?"

"Jon. Tom listens to you. If Tom listens to you, the crew will listen to you. Besides, what have you been doing for the last two weeks?"

Jon sat down slowly on the chair Tom had pulled out, his heart in his throat.

~

Polas walked with long strides, surveying the damage. At his side, Jon stepped over the cobblestones torn up by the ship's guns. Everywhere they went, there were men and women wandering around in a daze with white bands of sun-virgin skin around their necks where metal collars used to sit. Many of them held the cut collars in their hands, the steel in them the only valuable things they owned. The blacksmiths in town were offering to melt down the collars to mint new *dokschas* in return for a small fee; Jon wondered if their current economy would survive the upheaval.

Reading the worry on his face, Polas laughed softly.

"With big changes come bad things. But I think the good will come soon," said the white-haired man sagely. He had reclaimed the role of headman shortly after helping to free the captain. The part he played in the slave emancipation had raised him in the esteem of his people, and he now held his head high as he walked. "This is not the first big change. It's not the last. The world is very old, and she has the seeing of many things before."

Jon nodded, looking up at the damaged pyramid they had arrived at. The interior had been gutted, and all valuables had been stripped away. The other four pyramids were in a similar state, but this one had held the motherload, the majority of it now safely secured in the *Heart's* holds.

"What are you going to do now?" he asked the old fisherman.

Polas smiled wide, his face creasing in easy amusement.

"I am not of the knowing. That is up to the gods. The older gods. The gods before the filthy blessings. We fishermen will fish free. The barbarian tribes will come back. A city stays or falls, and we hope new things will taste of good instead of tears," said Polas. He turned at the sound of a woman's voice raised in distress, and Jon followed his gaze. The woman cried out again. A man had snatched the collar from her hands, her only wealth. Seconds later an ex–palace guard tackled the fleeing thief to the ground, and the collar was returned. Polas chuckled and pointed. "See? Good. Maybe for more than an eye blink, eh?"

Jon smiled tightly. Ereme'ia Balor had existed on the backs of slavery and bloodshed for so long; how could it be kept from returning to its former state? His eyes slid to the top of the pyramid, an idea forming in his head.

"How many so far know that the emperor is dead?" he asked. They had kept the information secret for fear of adding to the chaos that had followed the slaves' rebellion.

The old man turned to him, his bright-blue eyes curious. He thought for a moment before answering.

"Ten. No more."

Jon nodded.

"Polas, send a runner to fetch Tom. I'm going to need him for this. Have him meet me at the top of this pyramid in, uh... half an hour," he said, setting off at a brisk pace.

"Where will you go?" called Polas after him.

"Me? I have a date with the dungeons," replied Jon with a tight smile.

An hour later, Jon stood atop the pyramid, clothed in robes of deepest purple and wearing the emperor's massive, gilded crown. His ears keened in protest following the ringing of the great bell, and he felt a little ill looking down at the hundreds assembled below; steeling himself, he held his back straight and stared down at the crowd through his mask. In the midst of all the fallout, the only ones who had turned up at the square were the curious or those who desperately wanted some kind of order to return. Hopefully, it was enough. He thumped his walking stick a few times, mimicking the emperor's behaviour.

He searched the almost-silent crowd and quickly found Ceara. The woman nodded once when she met his eye; the players for this performance were in place. He glanced at Tom who crouched beside him. The big man grinned and winked. *Now or never.*

"You traitors!" bellowed Jon, pointing his staff at the assembly. He could do the emperor's accent; he just hoped no one would find it so unusual that the man would give his "sermon" in Common. However, he was gratified when the crowd recoiled in reaction to his words. Some started weeping. More than a few fell to their knees. "You have defied the gods! You, who were born into slavery, who were pressed into service of the gods... Your blood is their payment for our lives, for our health, for our crops! Do you think that the gods will stand for this? Do you think they will allow you to shirk your *gods-given duties*?" He let his voice take on the edge of hysteria, spittle flecking his lips. The eight warlocks stood in a line to his side. They lifted their hands and began to chant at Jon's glanced signal. "You will pay with your blood! All of you! The gods will take you!" he shrieked at the citizens of Balor. He stalked back and forth, warming to his subject. He railed at the crowd, gesticulating wildly, stalling until the sun dipped below the tree line to shroud the city in the gloom of dusk. By the time he gave the nod to Tom, half of those below were sobbing and screaming for forgiveness.

Tom ran below, heading for the great spoked wheel of the electricity generator at the rear of the palace. Jon eyed the men in red cloaks, chanting in unison. The front of their robes bulged awkwardly but that couldn't be helped. Jon had been firm about this part of the plan: no more death.

Suddenly, all the lights of the pyramid went on at once, an eye-watering, sensory explosion. The crowd wailed in surprise, but Ceara's network of spies at the edge of it had silently put up barriers to keep anyone from escaping. Jon worried that if he didn't end this performance soon, those assembled below would start to trample each other in panic, and the square would turn into a complete bloodbath.

Jon lifted his arms into the air and let out a terrifying roar that would leave his throat sore for days. The warlocks let their chanting reach a crescendo of ululations before falling utterly silent; the Lords of the Knife were well schooled in theatrics. The crowd hushed into silence as everyone atop the pyramid ceased moving. The light globes began to flicker as the first mate had Harris and the boys slow their turning of the generator. Jon lowered his arms, letting them fall limply to his sides. Using his own accent for once, he began to speak as if in a trance.

"My sons and daughters," he said, "you have freed me. The age of tyranny is over! I am free as you are! Gone are the false gods of the false emperor." He stood quietly and waited. The crowd started to murmur, confused.

"Who are you?" yelled someone. Jon thought he recognized Jarrod's booming baritone.

He pulled the crown off of his head and set it on the ground.

"Have you forgotten me? My sons and daughters?" he said sadly. "I am Lakkim. Your father. The father of this land." Polas and Jon had narrowed it down to the god of agriculture since Lakkim presented a nice counter to the claims that only blood could grow crops. Despite understanding the need for the act, the old headman had seemed slightly scandalized by the idea of using what he considered a true god, an old god, in this ruse. However, he agreed that Lakkim probably wouldn't mind, if it meant the end of the false gods.

"Lakkim?"

Jon could hear the people murmuring to each other, memories refreshed by Ceara's men scattered among the crowd. Though he now knew that she had helped slaves all these years, countermanding the emperor rather than working for him, he still didn't quite trust her; however, she was playing her part well this evening. Soon the crowd started shouting things on their own, no longer in need of prompting. The warlock closest translated quietly for him when needed.

"Lakkim! Who trapped you?"

"Lakkim! I remember you!"

"Will you punish these evil men?"

Jon held out his arms, and silence fell over the crowd again.

"The man you see before you, the flesh in which I stand, trapped me in servitude while he forced his false gods upon you. For this he will die, and I will depart to the sky to watch over you. Together we can rid the land of the evil this man has done! These agents of evil... These *warlocks* as they call themselves, they have no power over you! They took your blood to feed false gods. I will take theirs and give you something better!" Jon shouted the last and the globes returned to full brightness.

Each of the warlocks raised their sharp daggers one by one, and one by one they plunged them into the bladders filled with cow's blood attached to their abdomens. Blood poured out from their "wounds" and into the tracks made for that gory purpose down the front of the pyramid.

The crowd shuffled quietly below, uncertain how this differed from the usual ceremonies they'd been forced to attend. There was a gurgling noise in the square and when the last of the warlocks fell "dead" at Jon's feet, a great, warm gush exploded out of the holes set in the paving stones. However, instead of blood, it was clean water pumped in from the river and through the heated pipes that ran through the palace floors. Polas and his men had made the switch earlier, using swim bladders from the gigantic bowfin that they routinely caught to bridge the two systems. The cow's blood drained below the palace and into the soil; hopefully the last blood sacrifice this land would see for a long time.

The people below stared up at Jon in a daze, soaked to the skin. He could see a few smiles here and there and more than a few skeptical looks. He needed to drive his point home. He heard a grunt and saw that Tom had hauled the emperor's corpse to the top of the stairs, hidden behind the tall screen. They had laid the body atop some heating vents to make it warm again. However, the emperor's skin was grey from lack of blood and his face had a sunken look. Ah'puch was starting to go gassy and bloat; Jon hoped no one would notice. He grimaced at the first mate before turning back to the crowd.

"Listen to me, my sons and daughters! My time here is nearly done. Take my laws to heart and your lives will be filled with joy: Never again shall blood rain down on you! Never again shall man bow his head in slavery to another man! Never again shall false gods rule over you!" he shouted, his voice growing hoarse. Then for good measure, even though he saw Tom shake his head from the corner of his eye, "Never again will man be persecuted for lying with man... nor woman with woman." He heard Tom snort in amusement. Even as he said it, it sounded foolish, but Jon felt it was right to add that "law". It was only fair. Besides, if they were ever to return to these lands, he sure as hells didn't want to wind up on the wrong side of the law again. The murmuring from below grew louder. He could hear that a few arguments had broken out, but as Polas had said, everything would work itself out for better or for worse; Jon was just helping it along.

He looked at the warlocks lying at his feet, their eyes on him. Each man had been promised a reduced sentence in the dungeons if they worked to uphold "Lakkim's" laws. Polas's men would make sure they kept to their end of the bargain; it was lucky for them that their identities as warlocks were known only by a select few; otherwise, Jon might have been forced to have them killed. Tom hadn't agreed with him on letting them loose, but Jon saw no reason for more bloodshed. It was the end of an era.

It was also the end of his performance.

He let out another throat-searing roar that rendered the crowd silent. Then he pretended to convulse and shake, tearing at his clothing as though possessed by a demon.

"No! No!" he yelled in the emperor's accent. "You cannot take my slaves away! You cannot take my city! I have fooled them for so long! They believe in my false gods! I will lock you away, you—" He let out a burbling scream, laying it on thick so there was no doubt in anyone's minds that he was fighting with a higher power. Then, he yelled out in his own voice:

"You have led your people astray for too long! You will die, and I will be free!" Jon tossed up his cloak and fell back just as Tom heaved the emperor's body over the edge. The dead man rolled like a ragdoll down the stepped slope of the pyramid, bouncing into the air, his dark purple robes flapping. Jon heard the commotion below, but he didn't look over the edge. Instead, he gestured for the former warlocks to follow Tom down the stairs and into the ravaged palace.

Jon was exhausted, both mentally and physically. Ceara would make sure that the crowd was incensed enough that they would tear the emperor's body to pieces. Jon had no wish to see it happen. At the foot of the stairs, they were met by Polas and his men. Oren stood with them, his expression unreadable as he stared off to the side. Jon knew that the young fisherman would never forgive him for killing his father, and Oren was uncomfortable with the fact that Jon had saved his life. He just ignored the young man. Some things were better left alone. Polas clasped Jon's arm, his smile like a proud father's.

"Did good, you did. Loads. I'll be seeing more happiness, I think," said the old man. "You're a good man, Jon."

Jon let out a tired chuckle and nodded, clasping the man's arm in return before he turned away and walked to Tom.

The big man wrapped his brawny arms around him and hugged him close, the heat of his skin soothing to Jon's tired body.

"C'mon, lad," said the first mate softly against the side of his neck. Jon felt the little hairs at the back of his neck stir with Tom's warm breath and he sighed into the embrace. "Let's go home."

~

Jon looked between Tom and Baltsaros. Captain? Him?

"Listen, love: if ye can pretend to be an emperor and a god, ye sure as hells can pretend to be a lowly boat captain," said Tom with a chuckle.

"Lowly?" smirked the captain, a spark of his old self in the curl of his lips.

Jon shook his head.

"I don't know. *Captain Jon* doesn't sound very impressive," he laughed. The idea had merit though. He could see himself shouldering part of the responsibility with Baltsaros's counselling and Tom's fists. Not quite a figurehead... and it would be temporary.

"Aye, but *Captain Jon, The Black Brigand* is a great fuckin' pirate name," grinned Tom, squeezing his shoulder.

Jon blinked.

"All right, but let's make it simple. I had a great-great-uncle or something who was a pirate; did I ever tell you that? *Captain Black.* If I'm going to follow in his footsteps, I might as well take his name, aye, matey?" he said with a jaunty tilt of an imaginary hat.

There was a girlish laugh from the open door, and he turned, startled. Ceara, in a pair of tight leather pants and a high-necked, sleeveless black shirt, stood leaning against the wooden frame with a bag at her feet.

"Captain Black? It does have a nice ring," she smiled.

"Well, lookee here," drawled Tom, a mischievous sparkle in his green-blue eyes. "It's the new chambermaid! Go get in t'yer skirts, wench. That ain't no sort of uniform."

Ceara looked uncertain for the span of a heartbeat before she realized that Tom was joking. She smiled at him, but there was a brittle edge to it. Jon knew that beneath her sass and easy confidence, there was a damaged girl who knew only too well how to put her back to the wall to defend herself. He wondered how long it would take before Tom would realize that too. Jon thought about the twisted red scars that covered her from neck to waist and what Tom's reaction might be when he saw them. A little jealous flame licked at his heart, but he nearly laughed out loud as he shoved the worry away. Tom was his. His and Baltsaros's and no one else's. Jon smiled at the collar around the first mate's neck; Tom knew it.

"All right, then... *Captain Black,*" she said with a tiny bow. "I'll do what I can to spread words of your newfound bravery and appetite for cruelty around the crew. It's the least I can do."

Jon dropped his smile and walked quickly up to her, his face set in deadly seriousness as he stood almost touching her. He looked down into her crystal-blue gaze and could see the tiny tremor in her eyelids.

"I don't trust you," he said, soft like silk against steel. "Not yet. So I will be watching you, Ceara, and gods help you if I so much as hear a single whispered word to make me doubt your loyalty, you'll find the truth in those *rumours* you just offered to spread. *Do I make myself clear?*"

Ceara's eyes widened even more, and he saw real fear in them. She quickly nodded her head, and he stepped back, letting his expression settle into a grim smile. One look at Tom and his slack jaw nearly broke Jon's act.

C'mon, Jon... an act? Do you still think you're acting? whispered the little voice inside him with an evil chuckle. Jon blinked and turned his eyes to the captain. The steely, cold creature stared at him from behind the captain's dark-brown eyes. Jon scratched the back of his head and turned away to hide the shiver of unease that took him.

He straightened his shoulders, his eyes settling on the map on the far wall. Nathaniel had been adding to it as the *Heart* made its way along the coast during the two days Polas had kept the ship out of harm's way, waiting for their return. He squinted at it.

"I guess as captain, my first act is to decide what in hells we're going to do until the passage opens up again at the Devil's Isles, right? We've got months to wait before we can start making our way back again," he said with a sigh. "Any suggestions?"

"What do you mean months?" asked Ceara with a twist of her cupid's-bow lips. She approached the map with her head tilted, her confidence having recovered from Jon's threat.

"We can only get through the spires once the weather has grown warm enough that the ice has melted. Otherwise, we will be trapped there," said Jon.

Ceara let out a small laugh and shook her head.

"Think, gentlemen: what kind of trade could we *possibly* maintain with such a limited window of opportunity? And trade, as you have surely seen, has been quite good," she said, sliding her fingers up the drawing of the impassable mountains. She stopped and tapped a point northeast of where they were located. "No, trade with your lands to the east would have surely been tedious and unprofitable were it not for a very, very well-kept secret."

"Spit it out, woman," frowned Jon, made impatient by her gilded showmanship.

"A deep fissure in the mountain, twisted and fraught with dead ends called simply *The Rift*," Ceara said with a smile. "And you just so happen to have taken aboard the one person who knows exactly how to get through it."

"Who's that?" grunted Tom, a comma of skepticism etched in his brow.

At this, Jon burst out laughing. He clapped the first mate on the shoulder hard, and gave Ceara and genuine smile.

"She means her, you lunkhead," he said affectionately, his mood much improved by the sudden possibility of a swift journey home.

Ceara looked relieved by his reaction, and he felt a little easier about her. What would she gain to win if she led them astray? No, she had to be telling the truth.

Jon ran a hand through his curls and walked to the door.

"Tom, make sure everyone's ready to leave. I want the last of the men on board and the supplies stowed by the time the sun comes up tomorrow morning. Any who dawdles gets left behind. Go. Now," he said. Tom was out the door and shouting orders in moments. Jon turned. "Ceara, you'll be staying in the smaller of the two bunkrooms. Go put your sack on your bunk and report to Cook. Don't think this is going to be a pleasure ride just because you can get us through some crack in the mountains."

"Yes, Captain," she said in all seriousness and picked up her sack before following Tom out.

When they'd gone, Jon walked to the cage where Baltsaros sat quietly on his cot, staring at him with amusement. Jon sat down next to him with a wry grin.

"How's that?" Jon asked him. Baltsaros nodded, his fingers coming up to curl comfortingly around the back of his neck. Jon leaned into Baltsaros and pressed his forehead against the older man's cheek, letting out a sigh when Baltsaros wrapped his other arm around his shoulders.

"You'll do fine, Jon," murmured Baltsaros. "I'm proud of you." A tremor shook the captain, and he tightened his hold on Jon with a laugh. "Seems we've changed places, you and I."

Jon pulled away with a soft smile before leaning in to brush his lips softly against the captain's.

"It's only temporary," he chided Baltsaros. "We'll be back under the swinging lanterns of the *Blossom* in no time, a glass of Maya's good brown beer in front of us, and the night air fragrant and warm. This will all seem like a dream, a bad dream. Just think of your carved bed and crisp sheets and the three of us falling asleep to the sound of waves breaking on the white sandy beaches below."

Jon frowned. Baltsaros's eyes had gone glassy and he'd turned away; Jon knew that he was no longer listening to him. He reached for Baltsaros's cheek to turn his head, but when Jon touched him, the captain cringed. There was no recognition in the dark eyes that widened at him, but Jon pulled Baltsaros against him regardless with a desperate whimper fighting for release deep in his chest.

"I'll get us there," he whispered into the trembling man's hair. "I will."

After a moment, Jon released Baltsaros and stood. Baltsaros looked lost and confused as Jon left the cage and locked the door behind him. After taking up Baltsaros's long coat to shield him against the slight chill in the night air, Captain Black left the stateroom. As his step crossed the threshold, he left behind his weaknesses and doubts, finally setting aside the boy to become the man he had to be.

~

END OF BOOK II

EPILOGUE

Jon smiled as Tom let out a soft groan, muffled by the red silk of his gag. The first mate was kneeling on the bed, thighs wide and pelvis forward, with his wrists secured tightly to his ankles behind him. This had the effect of bowing his back in such a way that his ribs were starkly outlined, and the thick tendons in his neck stuck out as he held up his head, blue-green eyes fixed on Jon. He trembled from the strain of keeping the uncomfortable pose, but Jon had told him if he let himself sink down onto his calves, he would be denied release again.

With a pleased sigh, Jon leaned forward to lick another slow line down Tom's chest before closing his lips over a nipple to worry the bud with his teeth. Despite how the first mate's muscles bulged and strained against his bindings, he didn't struggle. Jutting from the thatch of dark-blond hair at his groin was the reason why; Tom's cock was a thick, hard, upward curve that jumped up every time Jon bit down harder.

This was the first mate's idea of a good time.

Jon chuckled against Tom's skin, almost lazily stroking his hands down the big man's sides to grasp his muscular buttocks before biting him again. This time he took the metal ring between his teeth and tugged on it. In response, Tom's cock grazed Jon's bare stomach and left behind a slick streak. Jon grinned and sat back on his own heels, grasping his cock in one hand to rub it against the head of Tom's. The first mate let out another low sound, closing his eyes as he thrust his hips further forward. Jon obliged him for a moment; taking the wide head in one hand, he thumbed along the underside, teasing Tom as he stroked his own cock. They'd been at this for the better part of an hour.

"Do you want it?" asked Jon with a wolfish grin.

Tom nodded quickly, a plea in his eyes. Jon reached for his jaw and tugged down the gag.

"Let me hear you say it," said Jon softly. His fingers stroked along the edge of the slave collar Tom wore. The first mate's skin was hot and wet to the touch, and his pulse thumped against the tips of Jon's fingers.

"I want yer cock," rasped Tom. Another drop of arousal slipped from the slit of his cockhead and perched there for a moment, shiny and clear, before sliding down along the thick vein and over the smaller metal circlet that he wore tight around the root of his cock. "Please, Jon. I want ye to fuck me. Hard. Please. I'll do anythin' ye want. Just... please."

Jon patted Tom's cheek lightly with a smile and looked up. The captain's tanned face was creased in amusement as he lounged behind Tom on the bed stroking his own cock and watching Jon taunt the big man. At Jon's nod, Baltsaros sat up and moved forward to quickly free Tom's wrists. Jon watched the captain narrow his eyes in concentration as he undid the knots.

Jon smiled softly. The captain's body had healed, but his mind had taken longer. For the past week, however, Baltsaros's eyes had been clear and his strange turns had all but vanished. That the captain felt "sane" enough to participate in some slightly rougher play with him and Tom gave Jon hope that things would soon return to normal.

Whatever that is, he thought.

He turned back to Tom and saw that the first mate was looking at him with pupils blown out from lust and *char*, completely oblivious and lost in the moment. He was absolutely gorgeous like this, willing to do almost anything for the sake of pleasing him... a living plaything, but so much more.

Someone to cherish.

Jon widened his grin and ducked his head to cover Tom's lips with his own, nudging them open to begin kissing him slow and deep. When Tom's arms finally came free of the rope, he curled them around Jon's waist and surrendered to the embrace, his chest rumbling with small growls of pleasure. Then Tom tensed suddenly against Jon, breathing a gasp into the kiss. Curious, Jon slid his hand down Tom's hard stomach, past his cock and sensitive sack, to discover that the captain had slid two fingers into the first mate. Baltsaros let out a slow breath when he felt Jon's tentative touch, and leaned over Tom's shoulder to press his lips to Jon's cheek.

Jon broke the kiss to share breath with Baltsaros for a moment. Smiling against his lips, he slid his own finger next to the captain's and into Tom. The first mate trembled between them as they fucked him using their fingers, opening him up, their hands slick with oil. Soon Tom's normally gruff voice broke on a whimper as he begged.

"Please, Jon... Da. For love's sake," said the first mate. "I've been good, aye?"

Jon laughed, breathless and wild with desire, and he shared a look with Baltsaros. It was tempting to make the first mate wait longer, just to hear how desperate he could sound, but instead he grabbed the back of Tom's head and kissed him again.

"Yes, you've been a good lad, Tom," murmured the captain. His long-fingered hand stroked up Jon's arm, the touch gentle. "How would you like to take the both of us? Hm? Would that make you happy?"

Tom pulled away from Jon, his eyes glazed and fervid, lips parted on a slow pant.

"Oh... fuck yes, Da."

Jon's heart pounded, and his cock throbbed in his hand as he watched Tom straddle Baltsaros and then lay back against the man's chest, bracing himself on his heels. The captain cushioned the big man's weight with one hand, moving to push his thick cockhead against Tom's puckered opening with the other. Jon licked his lips, an involuntary moan expelled with a hitched breath at the sight of Baltsaros's cock stretching Tom open and sliding deep into him. Tom let out a shallow grunt and closed his big fist over his own length. Jon watched hungrily as the captain fucked the first mate slowly for a few thrusts.

He felt suddenly uncertain, wondering if Baltsaros had been serious about what he had offered. It didn't seem possible. He might hurt Tom. With a crease between his brows, he climbed back up on the bed and stroked himself, unsure about how to approach. Tom's eyes were closed, but when Jon made no further move, the first mate lifted his head and frowned at him. Tom held out his hand.

"Come," he said with a smile that faltered into a grimace of pleasure as Baltsaros's cock thrust deep again. "You can't hurt me, lovey."

Jon nodded weakly. Dizzy and excited, and a touch nervous, he found a place for his legs, straddling the captain, and leaned forwards over Tom. The first mate's legs hooked over Jon's hips as he stroked the head of his cock over the captain's thrusting length and then eased in slowly when the man paused. He pushed hard, and Tom's eyes closed once more. It was tight, almost too much. When Tom let out a pained breath, Jon stopped, but the first mate just chuckled a shaky laugh.

"Don't ye dare stop, Jon. Don't ye stop..." Tom groaned and let his head fall back over Baltsaros's shoulder. Jon's fervour took over. He plunged his cock into Tom's heat, sliding tight against the captain's length. It was glorious, and he found himself teetering on the edge of climax quickly. He paused, eyes closed and so sensitive that he was almost in pain. For a moment Jon just held back, waited, and relished the feeling of the captain's cock sliding against his before resuming. However, it wasn't long before he couldn't stop himself from spilling over, the swell of pleasure breaking out into molten waves of intensity that tore the voice from his throat and left him breathless and weak. When the liquid pulses that rocked him slowed, then stopped, he leaned his head against Tom's furry chest and eased out slowly, wincing as he did so.

Tom let out a grunt of surprise a moment later when Jon moved over to begin working his mouth over Tom's cock. The first mate buried his shaking hands in Jon's dark curls as Jon gagged trying to take all of Tom in. Jon swallowed and tried again, keenly wanting to reward Tom. He relaxed his throat, shifted his position, and lapped at the head of Tom's cock before sliding it back into his throat.

With Baltsaros thrusting into him from below and Jon gorging himself on his cock, Tom soon started breathing through clenched teeth with a low, rumbling moan that Jon knew meant he was close. Jon curled his fingers around the base of Tom's cock and tightened his lips, spit running down the sides of the big man's shaft and over Jon's fingers.

Suddenly Baltsaros let out a low growl, fucking Tom faster with his arms tight around the first mate's chest, the muscles taut and twitching as his body rocked beneath him, caught in the feverish, frantic surge of orgasm. Then, with a strangled cry, Tom finally let himself cum, his bitter seed gushing over Jon's tongue as his body shuddered and hands clutched at him before falling limp to his sides.

Jon almost laughed with giddiness. With a grin he came forward to press kisses to Tom's sweat-slick skin when the captain rolled the first mate gently to his side and began murmuring soft praises.

"Good boy."

~

Jon woke a few hours later, curled against Tom's side. Tom slept soundly, his broad chest rising and falling with every deep breath. On his other side, the bed was empty. Jon frowned and sat up. The early morning light streamed in through the curtains and painted the room in a hazy, golden hue. After climbing out of the huge four-poster bed, Jon padded quietly to the front room to see where Baltsaros was. He still didn't trust the man out of his sight. Not after everything that had happened. When he saw that this room too was empty, a finger of worry stole into his heart. Then he saw the note. He picked it up from the big desk and peered at it.

> *J & T,*
> *All hands needed to stock up and ready the ship. We leave tomorrow at noon. Meet me below when you wake.*
>
> *— B.*

Jon pulled the thick velvet curtain aside and squinted at the beach. Sure enough, there was a bustle of activity. He could see a jolly boat making its way to the ship with a load of supplies. Confused, he turned back to the desk. There he spotted a letter written in the spiky alphabet of the northerners. He snatched it up and ran back to the bed, shaking Tom from his slumber.

Tom rubbed his face blearily, blinking around him in confusion with eyes tinged in red before he scowled in annoyance.

"What?" he rumbled.

Jon shoved the letter into his hand.

"The captain is down at the ship, getting her ready to leave tomorrow," he said, his heart skipping in his chest. "Does this have anything to do with it?"

556

After swiping at his face again, Tom focused on the letter. A deep crease formed in his forehead, and when he looked back up at him, Jon saw deep concern.

"Aye, lad," said Tom quietly. "Seems we're headed north. Far north."

BEY DECKARD

Fated

Blood and Redemption
Baal's Heart III

PROLOGUE

The beginning is the most important part of the work.

— PLATO

The slave breathed through his mouth slowly, nose not yet numb to the fresh pile of excrement someone had deposited right in front of him earlier. Naked except for the slave collar and harness that never came off, his whole body ached from the uncomfortable position he was in. The ground was cold and slimy under his knees, and his back throbbed from the way he was bent forward, neck and wrists secured in the wooden stocks. He shifted slightly and winced as his movements caused a sharp lance of pain through his bowels. Someone had penetrated him with something the previous day. Probably a branch, judging by how rough it had been. He'd been blind with agony.

Now it was mostly a constant, dull ache, but he dreaded the thought of taking a shit.

The slave opened his eyes and was relieved to see that the little town square was almost empty. That was good. When the men from the mining town were on their own, they mostly left him alone; the abuse came when there were a few of them together, and it was always worse when they had been drinking. The slave figured he'd been pissed on by every man in town. And probably every dog. He winced at the thought. His own bladder was full, but he held it even though eventually he'd be kneeling in his own piss puddle again.

With another painful shift, the slave closed his eyes. He wished that they'd just killed him when they found him covered in his master's blood.

. . .

Blinking slowly, the slave raised his head at the sound of someone approaching on the wooden planks that served as walkways in the town square. He must have fallen asleep again. It was amazing what someone could suffer through and still get some bloody sleep. He eyed the men approaching as he licked rainwater off his lips.

The one on the left, the one who had put him in the stocks nearly a week earlier, was his master's brother-in-law Lester. He didn't recognize the other.

The stranger was tall, and as he walked with long strides, the hard soles of his black leather boots thudded loudly on the warped, wet wood. As they got closer, the slave could see that the man wore a greatcoat that covered him from chin to ankle, and atop his head was a wide black hat with a curved brim. The only hint of colour he saw was a bright-red silk scarf that peeped above the coat's collar when the stranger turned his head to speak to Lester. The men stopped next to the slave, and as he craned his head up to see the two of them, the rain blurred his vision somewhat. Or, he thought, maybe it was the lack of food finally getting to him.

Squinting, the slave silently studied the stranger. He was a middle-aged man with a tanned, angular face, a fine, thin nose, and an upper lip that was bowed like a gull's wings. He had a foreign look to him that was confirmed by the strange accent he spoke with after he had circled the slave a few times.

"He's damaged," the man said quietly, "on top of being obviously half-starved and subjected to the elements."

"What of it?" growled Lester. "I ain't lowerin' the price, if that's what yer after, Captain. Yer gettin' him fer a song as it is. He's as strong as a bloody bull, I can guarantee at least that."

"Regardless of what you get for him, you're making a profit," pointed out the tall man, a wrinkle appearing on his smooth brow. "You told me you were going to have him put down."

"Three silver. Take it or bloody leave it," muttered Lester.

The slave made himself look directly into the stranger's dark, deep-set eyes and was surprised by what he saw there. No disgust, no scorn, and nothing resembling pity. Just quiet self-possession. The tall man's eyes widened slightly after a moment.

"I will give you four if you arrange for his transport to my ship," said the stranger as he turned away and lifted a small, red velvet pouch from his coat pocket.

Lester swore under his breath. After a few seconds he nodded.

"Fine. But, I'm bloody done with this devil. He's yer trouble now," he growled and accepted the coins. Lester handed the keys over to the stranger and turned to go arrange for a wagon.

The slave ground his teeth together. He had just been sold for less than the price of a barrel of beer. He scowled at the stranger in the coat. The man was probably a pervert. The slave had seen his kind before. All perfumed and proper and dainty manners until they had him chained to the bed. His heart jumped quick in his chest as he prepared to bolt as soon as the stocks were open. However, the tall man stared at him a moment longer, a small smile playing over his lips.

"There is nowhere to run," he said softly. "It would be a miracle if you could even get to your feet on your own."

The slave bared his teeth and clenched his hands into hard fists.

The stranger chuckled and slipped the key into the lock. The mechanism clicked.

With a roar, the slave forced himself up and ran, his legs pure fire as he tried to make his escape. However, he got no further than a half-dozen paces before something cool and strong curled around his neck and jerked him backwards. He landed on his back in the thick mud and began to writhe, trying to regain the breath that had been knocked from him. The stranger stooped over the slave, pulling free the whip from around his neck.

"Impressive," was all the man said before relieving the slave of consciousness with the weighted whip handle.

The slave awoke to find himself lying on worn boards in a small jail cell. Painfully, he got to his knees and looked around. The room where the cell was housed was entirely made of wood. There were odd, little round windows on one side that showed grey sky beyond. As the slave was contemplating the strange room with the curved wooden wall, the floor beneath him moved, and he was momentarily unbalanced, falling forward onto his hands. Beneath his palms, the planks were worn smooth, and there was an unmistakable bloodstain that darkened the wood in a broad, uneven shape. He frowned and pushed himself back up again. A ship. What's more, the stranger had said *his* ship. What could a ship's captain want with him?

The slave reached forward and used the bars to haul himself slowly to his feet. The pain in his ass throbbed with every heartbeat, and he wondered if he was permanently damaged. When the ship rocked again, the slave shifted his weight with the motion and felt a grin crease his face. Despite his discomfort, he felt a little excited. He'd never been on a boat before. Not even a small one.

The door opened and three men descended the steps into the small room. The captain had shed his greatcoat and stood wearing a loose blood-red shirt cinched tight over his torso by a glossy black vest covered in raised shapes.

Brocade. Just like the cushions in father's study.

The slave shook his head hard to rid himself of the prim little voice in his head. It had been a long time since last he heard it speak, and it brought with it a deep ache in his chest.

"Is he mad?" asked a deep voice.

The slave looked up. The man to the captain's right had the darkest skin he had ever seen. He stood with his arms crossed over his chest as he appraised him, his black eyes narrowed. The hair that fell from his scalp was corded into long, thin, matted braids that were several shades lighter than the gaunt face they framed. When the man turned to look at the captain, the slave saw that there were carved beads chased with silver that hung on a few of his locks.

Mad?

"No, Peter. Just ill-used, I think," said the captain. He then said something in a tongue the slave didn't understand, and the men with him nodded.

"I'm going to unlock this door. Again, there is nowhere to run to, and I doubt you can swim," said the captain to the slave; his dark eyes had the same amused glint they'd held before as he reached forward and placed a key in the lock.

As soon as it had turned, the slave pushed open the door and rushed forward. Hands grabbed at him, but he fought free, landing at least a few solid punches before he was able to break for the stairs. Up he ran, then out onto the deck of a large ship. He didn't slow. Men stopped what they were doing to stare at him, naked and wild and running for his life. When he reached the front of the ship, he saw that that captain had spoken the truth. They were in the middle of the harbour; the only way to shore was to swim. Then he would be free.

The slave looked behind him and saw that they would be on him in a few seconds. Without another thought, he stepped up onto the side of the ship and jumped overboard.

Instantly, he knew he was in trouble—he couldn't keep afloat. Thrashing his arms around and kicking wildly in a panic, the slave tried to keep his head above water, but again and again he sank below the surface, choking and spluttering. Finally he was lost in a murky, green world, his lungs burning as he fought to find the way back up... But which way was up? He felt the edges of his mind get blurry.

A hand closed over the slave's wrist, and another circled his waist. He struggled weakly in the man's grasp, but he was barely holding onto consciousness. Then something tightened over his chest, and he was quickly hauled up and out of the water. He swung in midair, rising slowly as he coughed out the water in his lungs. Beneath him, he thought he could see the dark-skinned man swimming in place.

When at last he reached the side of the ship, he was grabbed by his harness and dumped onto the deck like a bloody fish. Before he could turn to get to his knees, the captain planted a boot in the middle of his chest and held him down while the others put shackles on his wrists. The man was laughing and shaking his head.

The slave would kill this bloody captain, just like he had his last master. Then who would be fucking laughing?

The slave sat in his little cage, his arms wrapped around his knees with his eyes half-closed. He'd been brought to this new prison the previous day, an iron cage bolted into the side of the captain's quarters. He could tell it was new; the iron smelled freshly forged, and the well-worn wood of the floor and wall was brightly scored in places. A cage built especially for him. Seemed like he was to be kept as an object for sport after all.

Though the slave had drunk down the whole pitcher of water, he couldn't bring himself to touch the food he had been given. He was terrified of what would happen if he did. That morning, he had finally sat down on the pot to take a shit, and he had gone faint from the pain of it. When he made himself look, there was nearly as much blood as stool. The pain continued to twist inside him with every movement.

Despite his injuries, he'd made the best of his time. The slave had worked free one of the metal rings on the small barrel inside the cage and had bent it in his hands until the metal gave and snapped. Then, he'd folded the piece over itself again and stomped it flat beneath his heel. The new edge of the metal had cut into him, and his foot still bled, but he thought it had been worth the effort. Though the weapon wasn't particularly sharp, with enough desperate force it would pass easily between a man's ribs.

Desperation was all he had left.

The door to the room opened, and the captain walked in, the thump of his boots on wood muffled once he reached the thick carpet in front of the cage.

"Will you try to run again, I wonder?" asked the captain softly with a twist of his lips. His dark eyes were once again creased in amusement.

The slave didn't respond. He just pushed himself up onto one knee and bowed his head slightly, as if in deference. He would attack the man as soon as the door was open.

The captain unlocked the cage, but instead of stepping into it like the slave had expected, he took a step back. The slave frowned. It would be harder to stab a man who was on his guard. However, he got to his feet with a grunt and, weak from pain and lack of food, he took an unsteady step forward.

The captain's eyes darted to the slave's hand, spotting the makeshift blade.

"Ah, so you're going to kill me? Is that it?" said the older man with a smile.

The slave growled at him and tightened his fist on the folded metal, preparing to slash out with it with his next step.

"I admire your tenacity. Any other man in your position, with the extent of your injuries and malnourishment, would have given up by now. I have to say that I am amazed you're able to stand at all," said the captain.

With a quick step forward, the slave lashed out, but the captain moved gracefully out of the way with a small laugh. Frustrated, he lurched forward again, but once more the man avoided his blade. He held it out, hand shaking with the effort of keeping his arm up. Teeth clenched, he steeled himself to try once more before he collapsed, but then the captain took a half step forward so that the folded metal rested against his breast.

"You don't have the strength, Tom," said the man in a gentle voice.

Tom?

There was rushing noise that blocked everything out for a few heartbeats, but when the blade fell from his nerveless fingers, he heard it bounce from the carpet to the wooden planks. The slave let himself fall slowly to his knees, his mouth dry and his heart slamming against his ribs. He stared up at the captain in agony.

"That's what it says on your papers," said the captain with a tilt of his head. "Your name is Tom."

CHAPTER 1
CAPTAIN BLACK

And when the day arrives, I'll become the sky, and I'll become the sea, and the sea will come to kiss me, for I am going home. Nothing can stop me now.

— TRENT REZNOR

WEEK ONE

Captain Black stood on the quarterdeck, arms crossed over his chest, surveying the noisy crowd below. Over half of those assembled were crew hopefuls, and he was glad for their presence. The *Heart's* numbers had dropped dangerously low on the journey to Ereme'ia Balor, and they desperately needed to replenish their crew if they were going to make the journey home. Scanning the crowd, Jon was happy to see a few of the tall, bronze-skinned fisherfolk. Having them come on account would most likely be a great help, as they were already sailors. If they were anything at all like the hardworking Polas, it would take a minimum of effort to get them integrated into the crew.

Already thinking like a captain, thought Jon with a smile.

On top of the aspiring pirates, they had also taken on a number of passengers. Anxious to leave these lands and memories behind, some of these ex-citizens and slaves of Balor would travel all the way to Madierus to help repopulate the island. A life of peace and freedom under a fair ruler was understandably appealing after the horrors that they had been subjected to.

"Shit," murmured Tom at his side.

Jon frowned and followed the first mate's line of sight. Near the back of the crowd stood a number of burly men sporting the same winding black tattoos as Tom. One of them had his arm in a sling.

"That's the fucker whose arm I broke," grumbled the first mate.

Jon looked over at Tom. He lounged almost indolently forward over the black and red railing, forearms crossed and elbows resting on the painted wood as he watched the group of men. However, Jon knew that the first mate was anything but relaxed. Tom's green-blue eyes were narrowed in suspicion, and the lines of his jaw were tense. From one large, callused hand dangled the glossy, brown loops of a whip, and Tom's knuckles whitened as he shifted his grip; the first mate had carefully repaired, oiled, and rebraided his trophy from the mines, and he'd learned quickly how to use it.

"You think they're here to make trouble?" asked Jon quietly. He glanced again at the ex-slaves and frowned.

"Let's bloody hope they're not," said Tom grimly.

Jon nodded. If there was anything they could do without, it was more trouble. With a sigh, he turned his eyes back to the current crew of *Baal's Heart* and tried not to cringe at what he saw there. Save for Cook and two or three others, the pirates stared up at Jon with expressions ranging from disbelief to unveiled contempt as they muttered amongst themselves. They weren't happy that Baltsaros's "cabin boy" was now their captain, and Jon didn't blame them. Normally, the crew elected a captain, but these weren't normal circumstances.

"Shall we get this over with?" asked Jon, dropping his hands to the railing.

Tom nodded and headed to the staircase.

"We will be taking on twenty-five men and women as crew. No more, no less," shouted Jon, leaning forward to stare down at the assembly. "Those who have experience as sailors or have relevant skills will be chosen first. Understand that you will be leaving your old life behind you. Slave or master, you are all equals under these sails. If you take issue with that fact, do not even think of joining my crew—"

"Fackin' 'ell, this ain't yer bloody crew!" yelled someone from below. Jon couldn't tell who it was, but Tom's whip picked out the man for him a heartbeat later; following a loud crack, a line of red appeared on the grizzled pirate's cheek a finger's width from his eye. With a howl, the man clutched at his face, blood leaking from between his fingers as he fell back into the crowd.

"The next fucker who opens his bloody mouth will lose his bloody eye," growled Tom from his place on the stairs. He stared at the crowd as he coiled the whip in his hands. "When the fuckin' captain is speakin', ye bloody well listen. That goes for all of ye, Jack Tar and landlubber alike. I don't care who the fuck ye think ye are!"

"I will speak to you all individually before asking you to make your mark," continued Jon as if there had been no interruption. "Aboard my ship"—he looked pointedly at the scowling pirates—"there will be *zero* tolerance for treachery or rabble-rousing. If you can't obey the simple articles we have, leave immediately. This will be the only warning I will give." He locked eyes with each known troublemaker in turn, waiting for them to begrudge him a nod before moving on to the next. The crowd

568

grew so quiet and tense that all he could hear was the water chuckling against the hull. Ceara, standing up on a crate near the back, gave him a quick thumbs-up of encouragement when he spotted her. He furrowed his brow and nodded after a heartbeat, turning his eyes back to the men and women below. He clenched his teeth hard but then let out a sigh.

Ceara. A snake among jackals.

This should be interesting.

He straightened and clapped his hands hard together once, though he already held the rapt attention of all aboard.

"Good. Now that *that* is out of the way, it's time to get acquainted," Jon smiled warmly. "Welcome to *Baal's Heart*!" He gestured to Nathaniel who stood at the base of the steps holding a sheaf of pages tacked to a small board—the middle-aged mapmaker had been chosen for this task due to the quality of his penmanship. "Those who are passengers, please line up in an orderly fashion so Nathaniel can get your details. Don't expect this to be a pleasure cruise, however. You will all be assigned duties for the duration of the trip."

A few of the passengers, obviously ex-citizens, looked dismayed by the news.

"What about them who can pay?" piped up a very short, portly man in maroon silks. In his arms, he held a lumpy bundle. Jon frowned. Passengers weren't the same as crew and thus wouldn't share in the plunder, should there be any; the "no prey, no pay" model wouldn't benefit them. As such it was potential for glaring inequality between rich passengers who could pay for others to do their chores and those who had nothing but the clothes on their back. He rubbed the collar of his coat between thumb and forefinger as he thought.

What would Baltsaros do? he wondered. However, it was doubtful that asking Baltsaros would accomplish anything. The captain's mental state had deteriorated further since they had put him in the cage, but neither Tom nor Jon thought letting him out was a good idea. Not with that happened the other night.

~

Jon stared at the ceiling above the bed, sleepless with worry. The moon was so bright that it shone through the stained-glass windows and made pale patterns on the smooth boards overhead. With his brain churning in the relentless grind of worry, Jon's eyes tracked the ghostly shapes as they slid back and forth across the ceiling with the ship's gentle rocking. Though he couldn't hear his footfalls, the occasional creak of wood told him that Tom was above on the quarterdeck, probably pacing as he smoked. Tom's bluff, dismissive confidence in regard to Baltsaros's recovery didn't fool Jon for a second; the first mate was just as stressed as he was about the captain's injuries.

Jon rubbed his face, bleary and tense, and looked over at the man lying beside him on the bed. He was startled to see that he was awake. Tiny pinpricks of light were reflected in Baltsaros's dark eyes as he watched Jon silently.

"I'm sorry, did I wake you?" whispered Jon.

A deep crease appeared between Baltsaros's brows. After a moment, he shook his head slowly.

"Are you in pain?" Jon said, turning onto his side. Another headshake. "Thirsty? No?" He sighed and reached out to check the man's forehead for fever. He felt powerless and frustrated in the face of Baltsaros's suffering.

At his touch, Baltsaros's brow smoothed out, and he reached up to place his fingers against the back of Jon's hand.

Jon smiled at the contact, but his heart sank at the dry heat that burned beneath his palm—he was getting worse. "We'll get home to Madierus as soon as we can... I'm sure Abetha will be able to help you somehow."

"Yes. It will be all right," Baltsaros rasped, encircling Jon's wrist with his long fingers.

Jon nodded quickly, made suddenly uneasy by the glittering gaze of the sick man. It was as if the only signs of life in his face were the coal-black eyes that watched him without expression. Baltsaros pulled Jon's hand away from his forehead and pressed a soft kiss to the inside of his wrist before letting go. His lips were hot and parched, and Jon felt another pang of concern.

"Come here," whispered Baltsaros. "I want to hold you in my arms. It will make me feel better like nothing else can."

Something felt... *off*. However, Jon brushed aside the feeling and moved closer to him, placing his head on the man's shoulder. Gingerly, he curled his arm around Baltsaros's waist, bracing himself and trying not to put too much weight on the man beneath him. The position would quickly get uncomfortable, but he didn't want to hurt him. A little sacrifice.

Baltsaros's fingers came up to stroke his cheek, his jaw, down the bridge of his nose; when his fingertips brushed Jon's bottom lip, Jon let out a little sigh.

"You're such a soft creature," murmured Baltsaros.

Jon frowned, none too happy to be called "soft". He was not the weak thing he had once been. However, he forced himself to let the words run off of him like droplets down a duck's glossy back. It was meant as a compliment, a way for Baltsaros to say how much he liked touching Jon. Nothing more. It should make him happy.

Then why do I feel like running?

The thought had barely touched his mind before Baltsaros's hand closed over his mouth, his thumb and forefinger painfully pinching Jon's nose shut as he rolled over on top of him. He froze for half an instant before he tried to push the man off, but Baltsaros wrapped his other hand around Jon's throat and *squeezed*. Panic flooded Jon's brain as he fought to free himself. For a man who was so wounded, Baltsaros bore down distressingly hard on Jon as he crushed his windpipe, slowly robbing him of breath. Nothing Jon did shifted his iron grip—not his nails clawing into flesh nor his feet battering at Baltsaros's shins as he struggled desperately. It was like Baltsaros was made of senseless clay. A deadly golem.

"*Min haeken,*" murmured Baltsaros. "Stop struggling. Give in, my soft little thing.

Give up. Hush now, Jon. It will only be a moment longer. Give in. That's it, my love... You don't need to suffer life any longer. Let me take this pain from you. I will never be able to hurt you again... Trust me, Jon. Trust me..." His voice continued to coo and whisper in Jon's ear as he fought for his life. His vision swam with amorphous shapes that fled down a narrowing tunnel of darkness. With his last surge of strength, Jon reached up and beat against the headboard with his fist, nerveless to the carved figures that dug into his knuckles with every strike.

There was a strange, warm feeling in Jon's chest, and the world went crazy with bright colours right before the blackness overtook him.

Jon gasped, clawing at his throat with one hand while the other pushed at the figure above him. The cool air seared his lungs, and he felt tears run down the sides of his face as he fought to free himself.

"Jon! Jon, it's me," said the man straddling his waist as he grabbed Jon's hand.

"Tom? Wha—" Jon was momentarily overcome by a coughing fit.

Tom quickly helped Jon to sit up, his brow wrinkled in concern. The first mate then lurched to his feet and splashed some water into a cup, returning with it to the bed where Jon sat.

After taking a few sips, Jon tried again.

"What happened? My fucking throat..." he said hoarsely. "Where's Baltsaros? He tried to kill me."

"Aye. Bloody good thing I heard ye bangin', lad," said Tom, glancing at the cage across the room. In it, Jon could see a figure huddled on the narrow cot, rocking slowly. The first mate's fingers touched his neck softly, and Jon turned to look at Tom. The big man was trying to hide his fear, but Jon could almost see it like a cold mist in the air between them.

"This'll hurt ye for a bit, but he ain't done ye real harm," said Tom in a choked voice as he delicately prodded at Jon's bruised throat. With a sudden realization that the first mate had breathed life back into him, Jon hiccupped a sob and leaned forward until his forehead rested against Tom's collarbone. He closed his eyes. The first mate's arms came around him, and he both heard and felt Tom's long, shuddering sigh.

"What are we goin' to do, love?"

"I don't know. I just... don't know."

~

"All personal wealth will be stored in my quarters until we reach our destination," Jon said to the crowd of passengers. There was a surge of voices raised in dismay, but Jon held up his hands, pushing back the tide of objections. "It is not optional. You will simply have to suffer through a taste of equality while aboard."

"Equally poor!" someone shouted.

Jon shook his head with a laugh.

"As far as I am concerned, the lot of you are getting free passage; you will have somewhere to sleep, and we shall feed you. If that is poverty, then maybe you should reassess your decision to sail with us." He smiled. "The discussion is *closed*. We sail in three hours. Stay or go; it is up to you. I don't care. However, you will not sail with full purses."

Jon turned away, his heart beating nervously against his ribs. *Show no fear*. He took a deep breath and tried to relax into the role.

"You mates," he shouted at those who wished to join the crew, "line up smartly against the gunwale, if you will. Tom will get to you in a moment." He watched the men and women move to obey him. Some lined up quickly, desperate to show how eager they were to become pirates. Others walked almost nonchalantly to the side of the ship, believing that eagerness wouldn't work in their favour, and Jon smiled at the ridiculous display of indifference. However, when he saw Ceara jump down from her crate and join the hopefuls, he felt a lick of disquiet again. He had agreed to take Ah'puch's ex-spymaster as far as the southern peninsula as a passenger. There had been no talk of her joining the crew.

With a frown, he looked away. Despite all the help she had given them, Jon knew that she was loyal to one person and one person alone: herself. They needed her, and it worried him that their lives depended on someone he couldn't trust.

We'll cross that bridge when we get to it, I suppose, he thought, rubbing his hand across his forehead. After a thought, he turned to the first mate.

"Tom," he said quietly, "can you assign a taskmaster to watch over the passengers? Someone you trust. I don't want any shenanigans, got it?"

"Aye, Cap'n," said the first mate with a grin. The husky sound of Tom's voice and the way his sea-green eyes twinkled mischievously at Jon brought a hot flush to his face. The first mate was getting a kick out of Jon being captain. No doubt the minute the two of them were alone, Tom would show him a different version of the fealty Jon was looking for in the crew. The thought made his cheeks even warmer, and he let out a slightly awkward laugh.

"Stop thinking about your cock, Tom, and see to my orders like a good boy, hm?" he said, trying to sound playful.

Tom's eyes darkened, and his grin widened as he scratched his chest.

"It ain't *my* cock I was thinkin' about," said the first mate with a wink. However, he quickly went down the rest of the steps and started yelling orders at the crew along with a rolling, abuse-laden stream of curses. Jon smiled wide.

It was good to be home.

CHAPTER 2
SKELETONS IN THE CLOSET

Tom let out a grunt as he lifted the heavy coil of rope onto his shoulder. With all the added bodies, they needed to free up space so that everyone had somewhere to sleep—those sleeping abovedeck for the time being would only be able to do so as long as the weather held out. That morning Tom thought he could smell rain on the horizon, so had pressganged some muscle into helping him clear out the starboard bunkroom.

For as long as he had been on board, it had been used as a storage room, and that made it a big, tedious job. The room was piled high with all number of ship's supplies: spare rope, barrels that badly needed to see a cooper for repair, piles of old sailcloth, crates full of odds and ends.

He dumped the rope outside the door for one of the others to take and turned back to grab a pair of boards leaning against one of the bunks. With a surprised huff of breath, he skipped a step back and dropped the boards when he saw what lay behind them. Chuckling sheepishly when he realized what it was, Tom scratched the back of his neck and leaned forward to take a closer look at the larger-than-life wooden skeleton that lay on the sagging bunk mattress.

"Well, hello there, matey," he said with a grin. "Yer a gruesome fella, aint'cha?" He reached out to wipe some of the thick dust off its skull. The skeleton's mouth was open in a soundless scream, and its body was bound with a rusted length of chain. Most of the paint had worn off the old ship's figurehead—leaving it a stained and mottled thing of mismatched wood—but the carving itself was incredibly lifelike.

Bloody deathlike is more like it, thought Tom in amusement. He wondered who had made it and whether it had once graced the front of *Baal's Heart*. Maybe it was just plunder from another ship? He gave it a soft pat on the clavicle.

"If ye sit tight like a good skelly, maybe I'll bring ye out to see the light o' day an' fix ye up with the best view on the ol' tub. Aye? Hm? All right then," laughed Tom, taking up the wooden boards again.

When the light dimmed behind him, Tom turned quickly. Standing in the doorway was the big tattooed fucker that he'd fought at the inn, Saban. The ex-slave had his arm in a sling, which made him about as useful as teats on a nun for most of the work that needed to be done. Worse was the fact that Saban had neither his numbers nor letters; they'd only taken him on because he'd had experience working on a boat before he'd turned bouncer.

He will be useful; bones knit in time, Jon had said.

Aye, but what about grudges?

Tom eyed Saban warily. Even with his busted arm, the Balorian ex-slave was a match for the first mate if it came to violence; at the inn, it had been Saban's sledgehammer fist that had downed Tom like a sack of wet meat in the end.

"Peace, friend," said Saban quietly. His baritone was as smooth as river rocks compared to Tom's gravel. "I did not come aboard for revenge."

"Friend, aye?" muttered Tom with a sidelong glance at the taller man as he walked past him. After handing off the boards, he turned and appraised Saban. "What d'ye want then, mate? I'm busy." There was something about the way the other man stood —emanating a quiet, self-possessed power despite his injury—that made Tom's pulse tick up a notch. He felt strangely intimidated.

And just a wee bit horny. With an inward chuckle, Tom crossed his arms and tried to shoo away the stray thought that had him wondering what it would be like to have that hard, smooth body bent over his.

"I had never seen a slave stand up and fight the way you did," said Saban with a soft smile. "There is such fire in you. Even if in reality you had not been a slave for some time, I can't imagine that your head bowed as swiftly as ours to a master."

Tom grunted and dipped his chin slightly, made uncomfortable by the praise. He leaned down to pick up a big bundle of what seemed to be old clothes and threw it out the door.

Saban watched Tom silently as he worked. After a few moments the ex-slave spoke again.

"I wanted to thank you personally... and pledge brotherhood to you for what you did for us," said the broad-shouldered Balorian.

"Didn't do nothin', mate," growled Tom. He glanced up and met Saban's eyes; they shifted between green and brown in the rays of late-day sunshine that spilled into the dusty room. Saban stared back at Tom, his expression of calm confidence unchanged. With a sigh, Tom scrubbed a hand over his shorn hair and lifted the other shoulder in a shrug. "Listen... Honest to fuckin' gods, Saban, I didn't do nothin'. Was all a bloody coincidence. I only had the mates spreadin' tales of mutiny in the mines to cause confusion... never meant to start up a bloody rebellion. I had no idea Jon was also

574

spreadin' rumours and that the redheaded bitch would spread 'em further. We weren't out to save anyone but the captain, understand? I ain't no hero. Go find some other mate to be yer brother, aye?"

Saban just smiled wider and nodded solemnly before turning to leave. Tom had a feeling that his words had little effect.

"Why do you have *such* a hard time accepting thanks or praise when, as soon as you're in your cups, you make everyone keenly aware of just how much of an important man you are?" said a nearby voice, full of amusement.

Tom grimaced and turned his head to the woman sitting cross-legged on a dusty bunk. The way she managed to appear as if out of thin air made him feel embarrassingly uneasy.

"What do *you* want?" he mumbled, gathering up an armload of sailcloth.

"He is quite the handsome one, isn't he?" Ceara said. "With that smooth, dark skin and those gorgeous eyes of his. I wonder how tall he is." The slight woman tapped her bottom lip, a little wrinkle appearing between her brows.

"Don't know. Didn't notice," grumbled Tom, almost tripping on a loose board as he turned away. "Now get yer skinny ass gone if ye don't have somethin' of bloody use to me."

"Don't be so tetchy, sweetheart. This 'redheaded bitch' was simply sent here to tell you that Captain Black wants you in his quarters," said Ceara with an amused twitch of her lips as she stood. As she passed him, Ceara gave Tom a quick little pat on the backside and was gone.

Tom clenched his jaw and balled his fists, taking a few slow breaths to tamp down his annoyance.

Tetchy indeed.

Tom ducked through the door of the captain's quarters and saw that Baltsaros was out of his cage. The older man sat at one end of the long mahogany table, a bowl and mirror in front of him as he shaved carefully with a sharp blade. Jon sat at the opposite end, poring over a map he held stretched out between his hands. As Tom strode into the room, he saw that Jon had a long, unsheathed knife across his knees. The young captain wasn't taking any chances with Baltsaros, and Tom was glad for it.

The first mate leaned his discovery up against the back wall and stood back, admiring it.

"What in hells is that?" said Jon, looking up, his blue eyes wide.

"It's the old figurehead for the ship," said Baltsaros quietly as he stared at the wooden skeleton. There was a deep crease in his forehead. "Where did you find it?"

"It was in the bunkroom we're clearin'," Tom replied with a frown. Though Baltsaros had sounded annoyed, he just nodded, smiled, and resumed shaving.

"Why is it so... grotesque? I thought that the ship was called *God's Hammer* not *Hell's Minion*," said Jon, grinning.

Tom chuckled and reached out to mime pinching the skeleton on its cheek.

"Don't let Jonny-boy here make fun of ye, matey," he said in kind voice. "I think yer just fine." Tom turned to look at Baltsaros and saw that he was staring hard at him with eyes like pitch. In the blink of an eye, his sharp-planed face creased into an amused grin. However, when Baltsaros looked back down at the mirror he held, his expression went dark once more.

Tom straightened his shoulders and tried to ignore the pulse of worry that suddenly soured his stomach. He hated Baltsaros's constantly shifting moods. The captain he had worked and fought with was lost somewhere in this strange husk of a man. Tom wanted nothing more than to shake the bloody hells out of him until his senses came back, but he knew that it was a fool's thought. It felt like the separation was driving him mad; it was bloody depressing that the last time he and the captain had even touched was when Tom had had to wrench a knife from Baltsaros's hand a few days earlier.

"I have to go see Nathaniel. This map needs to be updated with the one from Polas's ship," said Jon. He had his eyes on Baltsaros as he spoke, a tense expression on his youthful face.

Tom knew that Jon was even more sensitive to the chaos that whirled through the captain like a maelstrom. It made him furious that Baltsaros had put them through all of this. At least when he had been killing folks and eating bits of them, he had been in control of himself the rest of the time. And what was this bullshit jealousy he was feeling over the fact that Baltsaros had tried to kill Jon numerous times now but hadn't *once* tried to kill him? What kind of stupid did you have to be to—

"Tom?" Jon's voice cut into Tom's thoughts, and he looked up. "Can I leave you here with him?"

"Aye," replied Tom, pulling out a chair for himself. The first mate was tense. Unhappy. Bloody miserable even. He smiled wide at Jon. "Dont'cha worry, love."

Jon's eyes narrowed, and he pressed his lips together. Tom knew he wasn't fooled for one second. When Jon came around the table and put his arms around Tom for a quick embrace, he murmured in his ear:

"We'll make this right. Don't *you* worry."

Tom let out a slow sigh, nodding again, but grinned in surprise when Jon took his earlobe between his teeth and bit softly. Jon's breath was warm against the side of Tom's neck for a moment longer, and then he was gone.

Tom let his smile fall.

"What's the matter?" asked Baltsaros, patting his starkly planed face with a soft cloth. His eyes were clear again, his mind once more his own.

But for how long?

Tom just scowled at the man's question and shook his head.

"What is it?" pressed the older man, a note of concern in his voice.

Tom scrubbed a hand over his face, closed his eyes, and took a deep breath.

"Tired of jerkin' off," he finally muttered. He risked a glance at Baltsaros and hunched his shoulders in embarrassment and annoyance at the man's grin.

"Feeling neglected?" asked Baltsaros, laughing.

"It's not funny," mumbled Tom, balling his fists under the table. He heard the captain sigh and then the muffled scraping sound of chair legs against the wool carpet. He stared down at the tabletop as Baltsaros came around and put his hands gently on his shoulders.

"You're right. I'm sorry, my tomcat. It's not funny," said Baltsaros quietly. "Has Jon not been...?" His words sounded odd, as though he was forcing himself to say them.

"Not with you sittin' there half-mad in yer fuckin' cage. It ain't right..." growled Tom, his jaw tense. He closed his eyes and chewed on the inside of his cheek. Baltsaros's fingers had tightened their hold, and the first mate could feel a faint tremor in the man's hands. "It's more'n that, Da," he said softly. "Not just the fuckin'... I... just miss... *you*. I bloody want ye to get well, ye know?" Tom looked over his shoulder at Baltsaros; the older man's eyes were vague as he stared off to the side.

Tom frowned, but just as he was about to speak up again, even though he could barely breathe for the tightness in his chest, Baltsaros suddenly dropped his hands and took a step back. The tall man's chiselled face contorted in anger as he stared at Tom.

"Who are you? How did you get on my ship?" growled Baltsaros in his native tongue.

Suddenly, all the worry and horror of the past few weeks came to a head inside Tom; fury crashed through him as he lurched to his feet, and he grabbed Baltsaros's collar in one callused fist, yanking him forward roughly.

"Ye know who I bloody am," he said hoarsely, catching Baltsaros's wrist in his other hand when he began to struggle. "Ye know ye did this to yer fuckin' self, aye? This is yer godsdamned fault, Da. We could'a left—me, you, an' Jon—but *no*... Ye had to go an' get yer bloody head scrambled, didnt'cha? And ye did it without a single, fucking, bloody thought about what would happen to—" Tom's voice broke and he couldn't finish the words.

Without a thought about what would happen to me if I lost you.

Blood sang in his ears as his heart battered his ribcage, and he tightened his grip. When he saw Baltsaros's eyes widen in fear, Tom let out a low groan.

Da didn't fear.

"*Why are you afraid?*" Tom shouted into his face, made angrier by the fact that Baltsaros flinched. "Just stop it. Please fuckin' stop it, Da! Please... Come back to me."

The captain's brows came down in confusion over eyes that couldn't see Tom for who he was. It was bloody hopeless.

Panting through clenched teeth, Tom dragged Baltsaros across the room and threw him into the cage. He slammed the door shut and, without a backwards glance, stalked out of the room.

A deckhand ran up to him with a bucket and brush, obviously intending to ask him something. Tom's hard fist connected with the young man's jaw, knocking him senseless with one blow. Blind to the shocked faces around him, the first mate simply stepped over the prone body and walked away.

~

Baltsaros looked up when he heard a soft sound from across the room.

"You," he breathed in dismay. "How did you get back on board?"

The other didn't reply.

"You came here to gloat, didn't you?" said Baltsaros, sneering as he got to his feet. He held onto the bars, his knuckles whitening. "I should have cut you into tiny pieces instead of just sinking you in that barrel. *I should have cut your fucking heart out.*" He pressed his forehead to the bars, angered by the silence.

"I wanted you to *suffer*. I wanted you to *feel* yourself dying slowly. I don't know how you managed to escape, but you're not getting this ship back, Romas. You'll have to kill me first," he growled.

"Baltsaros?"

He turned his head. Jon's dark eyebrows were pinched over his storm-grey eyes as he stared at him.

"Are you ok?" asked Jon, approaching the cage.

Baltsaros glanced back at his uncle, but the light had shifted, and he saw that the man had somehow hidden himself in the skeletal figurehead. *I'll be watching you,* he thought.

Twisting his features into what he felt was a pleasant smile, Baltsaros turned to Jon.

"Yes, Jon. I'm perfectly fine," he replied.

CHAPTER 3

HOPE AGAINST ALL HOPE

Hope is the pillar that holds up the world. Hope is the dream of a waking man.

— PLINY THE ELDER

WEEK THREE

Jon washed his hands and face with cold water from the ewer and sighed when he looked at himself in the mirror. He was scruffy and his curls were a wild scribble around his head from being whipped up by strong winds. He looked more like a madman than a captain. He frowned at the thought and turned to the cage bolted into the side of the large stateroom.

Baltsaros was asleep and, though he was covered in a warm blanket, his bare feet dangled off the end of the cot. With a small smile, Jon walked over and reached through the bars to tug the blanket into place; it was getting cooler the further north they went, and he hoped that it wouldn't get as cold as the first pass through the black mountain range had been or else they would run short on fuel for the potbellied stoves and braziers.

Ceara should have warned me.

He frowned and looked over at the great map at the back of the room. He was starting to have his doubts as to whether the ex-spymaster really knew as much as she claimed she did. She was frustratingly vague on details about their destination, claiming that she was keeping that information to herself because she felt it was her only leverage. She had depended on such tactics in the emperor's court, and Jon had tried—with little success—to get it through her thick skull that he wasn't the type to just throw someone overboard when they outlived some bit of usefulness. He just hoped she knew what she was doing.

Jon extinguished the candle before tugging his shirt up over his head. Instantly, the skin of his chest prickled, and his nipples turned into hard little sensitive points. Once he'd kicked off his boots, he undid his pants and stepped out of them, leaving his clothes on the floor to crawl onto the low, wide bed. The sheets were chilly against Jon's bare skin, and he shivered as he burrowed further under the covers.

As he closed his eyes, he wondered whether Tom would stay out all night yet again.

~

Tom bounced on the balls of his feet and brought his fists up. Wrapped around his hands were thick strips of unbleached hempen cloth, bloody now for the damage he had wrought.

"C'mon, poppet," he taunted his opponent. "Ye said ye would down me in less than three punches. What are we up to now, mate?" Grinning lopsidedly because of the swelling on the right side of his face, Tom danced around the man, jabbing at the air playfully. Laz had hit him perhaps a dozen times, each strike an explosion of pain that pumped sweet adrenaline into his system. He was high as a kite and everything was fucking grand.

It was almost enough to take his mind off things.

Laz threw a punch at his face, and Tom ducked with a low laugh at the last second, catching the ex-slave with a hard blow to the kidney as he fell past the first mate. The tall man crashed to the boards with a groan of pain; breath whistling past swollen lips, he panted for a moment before climbing unsteadily to his feet. The small crowd shouted and laughed their encouragement as Tom hopped back when Laz lunged for him. Unfortunately, Tom wasn't quick enough this time and was barrelled back into a crate by the lanky ex-slave. His head hit the edge of it, and the pain momentarily stunned him. White-hot stars flashed in his vision as his heart raced, and he fought against the faintness that loomed. With a growl, he shook his head, sending drops of blood and sweat into the audience and tried to free himself from Laz's bear hug, toppling both of them over onto the deck where they began grappling at each other, each trying to gain the upper hand. With Laz on top of him, Tom managed to loop his legs around the other man's waist and he squeezed, but Laz reared back and head-butted him hard in the nose. Overwhelmed with pain, Tom nearly went limp, but he forced himself to wrap his arms around the taller man's neck and hook his ankles together. He hung onto the ex-slave with all his might as Laz bucked like a trapped badger. Tom crushed his thighs together, letting out a pained grunt when he was punched in the ear. Tom felt the bloom of excruciating pain, but it didn't matter... He knew he had won; he was simply stronger than the ex-slave. He tightened his hold on

580

Laz's neck, slowly cutting off his air and blood supply while his legs squeezed the breath out of him.

"Give up, matey," panted Tom. "Yer bloody beat."

Laz wheezed in his ear, the blows to Tom's head getting weaker and weaker with every punch. Finally the lanky Balorian let out a strangled groan and strained hard against Tom before he finally went still. Tom loosened his grip and pushed the insensate man off of him, staggering painfully to his feet. His ears were ringing. He spat a bloody gob onto the deck and looked around.

"All righty, who's next?" he slurred. When no one stepped forward, he lurched a step and pointed at a husky, dark-haired man he only vaguely recognized. "You. C'mon."

However, the man just shook his head and quickly turned to go. As the crowd began to trickle awkwardly away—a couple men dragging Laz behind them—Tom swayed slightly as he glared. Harris clapped him on the shoulder.

"Tom, ye beat the shit outta four lads t'night. I think ye can call it a night... Save some for 'nother day?" said the bearded pirate. " 'Sides, yer lookin' a little cockeyed, matey. Why don't ye git yerself t' bed?"

With a scowl, Tom pulled away from Harris.

"Fuck off," he growled.

Harris shook his head before he too left.

Alone in the dim, golden nimbus cast by the lantern, Tom lowered himself down onto a squat crate with a groan and looked at his hands. His fists throbbed tight against the strips of material, and he let out a long, frustrated sigh. He knew he had one more fight in him. Tom needed that last bit of violence so that when he staggered back to his little room belowdeck, he would be asleep before he closed his eyes.

At the soft sound of footfalls, Tom lifted his head. Saban stared down at him, his hazel eyes wide with sympathy. Without a word, the big Balorian sank down in front of Tom and slowly began unwinding his bindings one-handed. The first mate just watched him, too surprised to react.

Saban's long fingers easily took apart the bloody hemp cloth, and he let out a low whistle at the first mate's bruised and bloody knuckles. Then he started on Tom's other hand. When he spoke, his voice was low and gentle.

"Who are you really fighting?"

Tom frowned. He lifted his freed hand to his nose to gingerly wiggle the bridge of it. It hurt but didn't seem to be broken. Eyes closed, he leaned his aching head back against the mast.

"No one," he muttered.

"Then, what are you trying to prove?"

"Why the fuck d'ye care?" Tom grunted. He cracked his eyes open and met Saban's oddly soulful gaze. The big ex-slave had the same kind of good looks that were carved onto statues of gods and princes. The only thing that marred his beauty was a pale scar that ran down one dusky cheek and puckered up the corner of his lip slightly. It wasn't even ugly. It just gave him a sort of wistful grin. Saban pulled away the last of the bindings, and Tom winced as the material stuck to the drying blood on his split knuckles. He grimaced and flexed his fist.

"Why shouldn't I?" asked Saban, smiling as he reached up to grab Tom's chin and tilt his head in the lantern light. Saban's dark brows came down slowly as he appraised the damage.

"That bad, aye?" said Tom with a chuckle, but both the words and laugh came out sounding stiff. His pulse was stuttering; the Balorian's fingers had been so gentle on his hands, and as they slid along his jaw, Tom felt a small ache in his chest that had absolutely nothing to do with his wounds.

"Nah, I've seen you take worse," said Saban, the corners of his eyes crinkling in amusement.

Tom let himself be pulled forward slightly so that the ex-slave could take a look at his ear. Saban cupped the side of his head softly and peered at the wound there. He was so close that Tom could see that he had a tiny mole at the corner of one eye.

Without thinking, he turned his head to press his lips to the other man's in an open-mouthed kiss. However, Tom felt Saban immediately stiffen, and the first mate felt a heart-stopping flood of embarrassment as he was pushed back. With a fiery flush burning his face, Tom tried to get to his feet. However, Saban held onto his wrist, his brown-green eyes unreadable.

"Listen," choked Tom, "I didn't mean to... I thought ye..."

"It's all right," Saban replied after a moment. "Really. It's all right. Just... a misunderstanding. It's fine. Really." He released Tom's arm and stood, brushing off his knees.

Tom looked down and rubbed his face.

What the hells was I thinking?

Saban sat down on the crate next to him, his shoulder almost touching Tom's.

"Tom, you smell like you've been drinking all day, and you look like you've barely slept. Plus, you're probably punch-drunk from those last few blows. You were reacting to my kindness... nothing more," said Saban in his velvety baritone. "Forget it happened. I already have."

Tom clenched his teeth, ignoring the pain in his jaw.

"It was stupid," he muttered. His mind skittered away from the thought of Jon.

It didn't really happen. Not really.

He turned and stared into the inky darkness off the port side, breathing deep to clear his mind. After a thought, he dug a finger into his mouth and pushed at a back tooth to see if it was loose. When Tom spared a glance at Saban, he saw that he was staring off in the other direction; the first mate furrowed his brow, confused.

"Why are ye bein' nice if ye aren't lookin' to..." Tom trailed off awkwardly.

Saban turned, his eyes wide.

"Is that the only reason you think I'd be kind to you? No, I have no desire for men as lovers; but I am kind to those I desire in *friendship*," said the man with a smile. "And you are nearly impossible to befriend, you know that? Every single one of my attempts has been rebuffed in one way or another."

582

Tom grunted and spat pink onto the worn wood between his feet, mulling over Saban's words. It was true. The broad-shouldered Balorian had approached him a few more times since the day in the bunkroom, and Tom had sent him away each time with terse words, made uncomfortable by what he had thought were advances of a more carnal nature. He felt like a bloody idiot.

"Aye. Sorry," he finally said, nodding to himself. Tom pushed himself to standing without looking again at Saban. "Talk to me again when I ain't half-dead. I'll have... friendlier words for ye next time."

He walked away, but when he reached the trap door to belowdecks, he decided not to descend to his room after all. The tiny space had seen far too much of him lately. It had seen too many nights of his self-pity.

No, he needed Jon.

~

Jon lay awake, restive and worried. Baltsaros had cried out in his sleep like he did most nights since his rescue, and he had startled Jon from his slumber. Alone in the cold stateroom, Jon wondered where the first mate was. Was he fighting? Drinking? Passed out and at the mercy of some unsavoury characters? Ever since Tom had finally confessed to Jon that two men had nearly molested him when he was too drunk to defend himself, he found himself thinking a lot about the big man's safety.

I can take care of myself, Tom had said with a surly scowl.

"But you didn't," whispered Jon into the dark. "The captain had to save you."

Jon threw back the blanket, but just as he was about to get out of bed to go find the wayward first mate, the door to the captain's quarters opened and shut quietly. A shadow crossed the room on silent feet.

"Tom?" he whispered.

"Aye," replied the first mate.

Jon moved over and turned onto his side, waiting for Tom to join him. When the mattress sank down under Tom's bulk, Jon pulled the blanket up over the both of them. The first mate stank of whiskey and blood.

"Are you ok?" asked Jon in a hushed voice. Tom remained silent, and Jon frowned, feeling out with a blind hand for the man next to him. He encountered Tom's warm skin and felt him let out a slow exhale.

"I'm a bloody fool," muttered Tom. "Yer gonna hate this... but I have to tell you. I kissed someone, Jon."

Jon's hand froze and his mouth went dry. He thought about Ceara with her flame-red ringlets, sapphire eyes, and cupid's-bow lips.

"Oh?" he said faintly.

Tom's hand closed over his and squeezed.

"I'm tellin' ye because I want ye to know there ain't no secrets I'll keep from ye. And I know ye'd wanna know. And I swear to fuckin' gods that it won't happen again, love," replied the big man. Jon felt the rumble of Tom's voice through his fingertips. "It was a mistake. A misunderstandin'... honest."

Jon licked his lips and swallowed; he was irritated and hurt, but Tom had told him and that counted for something. He had to trust.

"Ok," he whispered. He must have sounded skeptical because Tom let out a low sound that was part groan, part sigh, and he pulled Jon onto him.

"It was bloody stupid of me," said Tom, curling his rough fingers around the back of Jon's neck when he settled against his shoulder. "I'm sorry. Really, really, fuckin' sorry."

Jon nodded and ran his hand softly over the first mate's furry chest. Putting the kiss out of his mind, he instead concentrated on the fact that he was really glad Tom was there with him. Though the weeks at sea had gone by in a blur, Tom's absences had been strongly felt. The first mate always claimed that he slept belowdecks so that he didn't wake Jon up when he came in late, but it was blatantly obvious that Tom was having a hard time facing Baltsaros and had turned to drink and violence to drown out his feelings. Because of that, they hadn't spent nearly enough time together; Jon was sick of sleeping alone, and something had to be done about it.

With that in mind, he slid his hand slowly down Tom's stomach, but the first mate grabbed his wrist to stop him.

"Jon," breathed Tom. However, he didn't resist when Jon pulled his wrist free and brushed his fingers lightly over Tom's soft cock. "What if he wakes?" The first mate's voice was hoarse. "Stop it."

"So he wakes up. What of it?" replied Jon. Tom began to harden under Jon's fingers, and he traced the flared edge of his cockhead with a fingertip. The first mate sighed, but Jon couldn't tell if it was from pleasure or frustration. "*I* had to listen to you two fuck before, remember? I'm sure he'll live through it."

"Not what I mean..." muttered Tom.

"Then what is it?" Jon turned his wrist so he could encircle Tom's cock with his hand. He squeezed and felt the first mate's throbbing pulse against his palm.

Tom tensed and let out a soft groan.

"Hells, he might be lucid enough to join us—if he's up for it. Or, if he isn't, he might not even know what's going on," Jon pointed out.

Tom shifted slightly beneath him.

"What?"

"Don't talk about Da like that," replied Tom tersely.

"Like what?"

"With bloody disrespect."

Jon's forehead wrinkled.

"You think that acknowledging Baltsaros's mental state is some sort of disrespect? You can't even stand being in the same room as him most of the time. Don't you feel that *that* is disrespect?" asked Jon, incredulous. The big man stayed silent. "It's the reality, Tom, and you're going to have to face it and quit being so fucking touchy." Jon pulled his hand away. "He needs you. *I* need you."

"Love, he ain't even sure who the fuck I am half the time," murmured Tom. Another long pause. "What if he never gets better?"

"Then he never gets better. But I very much doubt that," said Jon with a sigh.

"I'm just so... bloody pissed at him," said Tom.

"I know." Jon tilted his head up to kiss Tom's jaw. He tasted blood on his lips.

"And I'm pissed that I'm pissed, ye understand?"

"Yes, I do," whispered Jon. He reached for Tom's cock again and began to stroke it slowly. However, it was obvious from the way it stayed only half-hard that the first mate might be too drunk or tired for anything more to happen.

"And I just fuckin' *hurt*. All the time." The first mate's voice was faint.

"I know," repeated Jon. And he did. There was a raw wound inside of him that bled every time he let himself think about Baltsaros. It took everything he had to cover it up. They had to make it to Madierus. He had to believe that Abetha could somehow help. So... He had to go on. And so did Tom.

"No more fighting," said Jon to fill up the silence.

"What? None?" Tom sounded so dismayed that Jon finally smiled.

"How are we going to sail this ship when you beat up all my sailors?" Jon laughed softly.

"How 'bout I beat them only a little?" Jon could tell Tom was grinning, and suddenly, in the midst of all the pain, everything was all right again.

~

Tom winced as Jon kissed down his ribs, sore from the pummelling he had taken. However, when Jon's hot breath touched his cock, Tom forgot all about his woes. He put a hand on Jon's soft curls and closed his eyes as the dark-haired young man brushed his lips over the head of his cock. Despite how tired and anxious he was, he felt suddenly as hard as a bloody rock and, when Jon's wet tongue lapped over his glans and stopped to tease into his slit, he couldn't hold back the groan that burst from him.

"That's more like it," said Jon, chuckling.

Tom thought of the pathetic one-handed sessions in his sad little room and shut his eyes, pushing down on Jon's head to coax him to continue. He let out a shuddering sigh as Jon closed his lips over him and sucked softly, his velvet-rough tongue stroking the underside of his cockhead. Shifting his hips slowly, Tom surprised himself with a little, needy moan. He hadn't cum in a few days; he wasn't sure how long he'd last. As if reading his mind, Jon took his mouth away, though his fist remained tight around the root of Tom's cock.

"Tell me when you're close," whispered Jon.

"Mmhm," said Tom, then let out a sharp exhale when Jon's hot mouth covered him again.

Alternating between bathing Tom's cockhead with his soft, wet tongue and deep-throating his thick length until Tom thought he could feel Jon's lips touch his groin,

Jon brought him quickly to the point where he was moaning with every breath. His cock was slippery with Jon's saliva, and spit ran down to where his skin was tight over his tender balls. He quickly put out a hand to stop Jon when he felt a hint of the sweet, exquisite pulse start deep inside him.

"Close," he gasped, using all of his self-control not to spill right there and then.

Jon released him, and Tom frowned as he tried to slow his breathing; his cock bobbed up from his belly as he panted softly, and the keen edge of his passion slowly dulled as he waited for Jon to continue. It felt like forever before Jon moved again, but when he did, it wasn't to resume sucking Tom's cock. Jon crawled up and over Tom's body until he was straddling the first mate's chest.

"I'm going to fuck your mouth, and you're not to touch yourself," warned Jon. Tom grinned wide in surprise. He'd been expecting a quick suck and fuck, but it seemed Jon was in the mood for something better. He opened his mouth obediently when the cock touched his lips, but when Jon's hands slid under his head to hold it up, Tom was barely given a chance to take in a breath before Jon pushed his length into him, bumping the back of his throat.

Tom choked and tears sprang to his eyes, but Jon pulled back before he gagged.

"That's a good boy," murmured Jon. Tom's heart pounded in his ears as he let out a small groan around the cock in his mouth. It leaked salty precum onto his tongue, and Tom felt his own still-hard erection stir against him, aching for contact. "I can't decide what I'd like more," said Jon almost conversationally. "Do I cum down your throat or do I fuck your ass instead?"

Tom's brow wrinkled and he made another soft sound. When Jon talked about fucking, it always drove him crazy. With his cock so hard he thought the skin would split, he felt utterly frantic with need. Tom was dying to touch himself, but instead he reached up to grab Jon's hips to pull him forward again; relaxing his throat, he lost himself in the feeling of Jon's cock sliding between his lips in short, trembling little thrusts. Jon soon began to let out shuddering breaths, but he stopped suddenly with a low moan. After climbing awkwardly off Tom, Jon lay down next to him and pulled at his arm.

"I want you on top of me," whispered Jon. "Come here."

Tom immediately moved to obey. Straddling Jon's narrow hips, he reached back, grasped Jon's spit-wet cock in his fist, and positioned the head of it against his pucker. Jon's hand closed over Tom's cock as the first mate eased himself down into the stretch, taking in all of Jon's length as he settled.

"Fuck that feels good," Jon said, his voice a little shaky. "Tom, you're not to cum. Not until I say so."

Tom nodded and began to move—forward to fuck his own length through Jon's fist, and back to slide the cock deeper inside him. He was covered in sweat despite the chilly room, and it ran cool down his chest. The sky had started to lighten outside the portholes, and Tom realized he could make out Jon's face. Mouth open and eyes closed tight, the young captain's head was flung back as Tom rode him slowly. Seeing Jon's naked abandon almost tipped him over the edge; Tom had to fight for a moment to control himself.

Thankfully, Jon opened his eyes with a quiet, raw sound right then.

"Cum for me," he said. He curled his other hand around Tom's balls and stroked him faster. The first mate didn't need any more prompting.

Pleasure uncoiled quickly inside him, and he let out a low growl a heartbeat later at the heady, almost agonizing release, thick cum erupting from his sensitive cock and onto Jon's chest and belly. Each breathless pulse sent another jet, and he panted and grunted with the force of his orgasm. Beneath him, Jon bucked up, his eyes clenched tight again, teeth bared as he came deep inside Tom, his hands squeezing the first mate's cock almost painfully as he rode out the ecstasy that thundered through him. Then, with a last shuddering sigh, Jon went still, his chest heaving and skin slick.

Tom chuckled and wiped the sweat from his eyes, his mind hazy and vague from glorious relief. Jon's blissful grin made him feel softly emotional, and he leaned down to kiss him lightly.

"Thank you," murmured Jon. "I needed that."

"Aye," said Tom happily. He was wonderfully sated and really fucking exhausted. Everything actually felt all right for once. Tomorrow was a new day, and he would face it with a new hope.

However, sleep's siren call had him in its clutches and pulled at him like a jealous mistress. With a grimace he lifted himself off Jon and leaned over the side of the bed to grab Jon's discarded shirt to use as a makeshift cloth to clean up. When he sat back up, he was startled to meet Baltsaros's silent gaze across the room. The older man stared openly at him, and Tom clenched his jaw, his heart sinking and his good mood all but forgotten.

A deep wrinkle appeared on Baltsaros's brow. He turned away and pulled the blanket over his shoulder, but Tom hadn't missed the glimmer of wetness in those dark eyes.

He frowned and turned back to Jon, wiping at his chest with the wrinkled shirt.

"You ok?" asked Jon, his blue eyes only half-open.

"Sure, love," muttered Tom and forced a smile. "Just bloody tired is all."

When he finally settled down next to Jon a few minutes later, he curled his arm around the slighter man's waist and pressed his face against the side of his neck. Hope. Hope and trust. That's what Jon was to him. He just had to hold on to him and everything would be all right. It had to be.

CHAPTER 4
MENDING CRACKS

Tom whistled cheerfully as he carefully carved another sliver from the peg he was making. The top bolt in one of the foremast's horn cleats had rusted in two, and he hadn't been able to find another one in the ship's stores. Instead, he was whittling a small piece of hardwood into what he hoped would be a fair replacement. He turned the cleat so the holes met up and tried to push the peg through. It was still too wide, so he shaved another small piece off.

"You seem to be in a good mood this morning," said Saban as he walked up. The ex-slave held a little pot of warmed tar in his big hand. Tom nodded in greeting. He watched Saban kneel down and pour a little of the tar onto an exposed rope wedged between the worn boards to shore up the weatherproofing.

He *was* in a good mood; the previous night's fucking had been followed up with a little head in the empty galley that morning, and he felt like a new man. Tom couldn't wait to get Jon behind closed doors again so he could repay the favour. He grinned and resumed shaping his wooden bolt as Saban worked next to him. He appreciated the Balorian's quiet company; Tom had been worried whether friendship had meant a whole lot of jawing, but Saban seemed to be happy with silence. The first mate found his calm nature oddly comforting. Something about the big man reminded him of Beard—a sort of gentle giant until the hells broke loose, and he became a godsdamned, living battering ram.

Tom pushed the peg into the hole again and was happy when it was a tight fit. He worked it into the hole as far as he could with his hand before he turned his long knife around and started hammering at it with the bone handle. Slowly but surely, the makeshift bolt sank into the mast.

When he heard a sharp intake of breath, he turned and saw that Saban was curled forward, his torso trembling. Slowly the man lifted his head, and Tom was astonished by the change that had taken over him. Saban's normally dusky face had gone ashen, and his eyes bulged.

"What is it?" asked Tom, confused.

Saban licked his lips and blinked rapidly. Panting, he rocked slightly as he held his broken arm against his chest. Tom frowned; it looked like he was on the verge of collapse. He got to his knees and put a hand on the ex-slave's shoulder.

"Saban?"

"It's ok. I just knocked my arm," Saban replied hoarsely, but the skin beneath Tom's palm was covered in sweat and gooseflesh.

The first mate felt a pang of alarm; Saban should have been well on the mend by now. He gently pushed the man's hand away from his arm and pulled aside the material of the sling. What he saw beneath made him grimace. About halfway up Saban's forearm, the skin was swollen and purplish around a prominent bump.

"Fuck, I'm sorry, mate," said Tom, looking up into Saban's pain-reddened eyes.

Saban let out a short laugh.

"No, you're not. You broke it fair and square," he replied faintly. "It'll be fine. Just give me a minute."

"It ain't healin' right," muttered Tom. He touched Saban's arm gently and was dismayed by how hot it was. He'd seen bad breaks before; this one wasn't getting better on its own. The ends of the bones weren't aligned properly, and the arm had no protection. He just hoped…

"Come on, mate," he said, bracing Saban under his good arm with his shoulder.

Saban let out a groan as he got to his feet, and he leaned heavily on Tom a moment, obviously feeling faint.

"Where are we going?" he mumbled. Sweat was beaded on his upper lip.

"To see Da."

～

Baltsaros peered across the room. It was a godsdamned sculpture. Just wood. There was no sign of his uncle because his *uncle couldn't possibly be on the ship*. He tried to focus on that fact and make it stick. Not his uncle. Just a carving. When Jon had caught him talking to the screaming skeleton again, he had asked Baltsaros if he wanted it taken away. He had said no, wanting to use it to help train his mind.

Romas is dead. You stuffed him in a barrel weighed down with cannonballs and threw him into the deepest waters you could find.

Even if his fanatical uncle *had* managed to escape the barrel, he would have died from divers' disease at that depth. Romas had been fat and old, and the water frigid—three factors that always seemed to contribute to deep-water fatalities. Baltsaros figured the man's odds of survival would have been slim.

Scratching at his jaw, he was startled to feel the thick stubble there; time was still passing strangely. Wearily, he sat back down on the cot and looked over at the books piled up on the small barrel he used as a side table. Those he had read when he was younger he could still remember, but the ones he had read in the past year were gone from memory. Same with his recent diaries—it was as if a stranger had penned them. Baltsaros was utterly frustrated. At times he felt a glimmer, a mere hint of what was there before, but his mind seemed full of holes. Just that morning he had woken up thinking that Tom was dead but couldn't remember why he would have thought that.

He picked up one of the leather-bound books with his family crest embossed on the cover and flipped back to an entry that said simply in his own elegant handwriting:

Bad storm. Eight men lost. Tom?

All following entries after it were the usual observations about weather patterns, the ship, the crew—here and there something about Jon specifically—but nothing about Tom until the very end where he had noted that the first mate had come back. That was it. The next book was spotty in its records; Jon had said that the weather had turned so cold that the ink had frozen in the inkwells, and he had been unable to write. Again, the memories were there somewhere in his mind. He could feel them. He just had to find them.

The door to the stateroom opened and in came Tom supporting a tall, dark-skinned man who had one arm in a sling. The stranger had tattoos down one side of his body, and Baltsaros frowned.

The same as... Tom's? he thought in confusion. Sure enough, the first mate's torso was also covered in markings. When had that happened?

Tom fixed him with a steady, narrow-eyed appraisal as he helped the man to sit.

"I'm all right, Tom," he said quietly, lifting his chin a little. He couldn't remember the last time he had seen the first mate.

Not true, whispered the throaty little voice inside him, and his mind was flooded with an image of Tom straddling Jon across the room, his body moving in a sinuous, smooth motion as he rode the panting, straining, dark-haired man on the bed. He remembered the way the sweat on the first mate's muscled thighs had caught the early-morning light. Baltsaros felt a soft pulse of emotion, and it wasn't particularly pleasant. He ground his teeth together and stood, reaching for the bars.

Tom came across the room and stood outside the cage. His brows were low, shadowing his eyes so they were dark like the ocean's depths. His sun-bronzed skin bore new marks—healing bruises and new shiny scars—and the creases in his face were more prominent. His tomcat seemed older and more serious. Staring at him silently, Tom rubbed his thumb along the side of his jaw; it was a tic that Baltsaros knew so well.

All of a sudden, a memory bobbed to the surface of his fog-shrouded mind. Tom tied to the mast as the captain's whip kissed his back. At first there was no context to the fragment, but as Tom watched him warily through the bars, a portion of the last year's events spread through Baltsaros like blood in water. It was faint and felt almost like it had been lived by another man, but it was there.

"Da?"

Tom's gravelly voice touched a raw nerve inside him, and he closed his eyes, breathing slowly while he tried to piece himself hastily back together. Tom needed him. Baltsaros had to force his damaged mind to find the old channels of familiarity, the ones that Ah'puch's machine had tried to obliterate. A man lost in his own brain, he had to dive into open wounds and strange waters to find his way through the burnt labyrinth. He opened his eyes gave a little smile.

"Apologies, Tom," he said softly. "What do you need?"

Tom looked a touch relieved at his words, his broad shoulders lowering slightly from their tense upward slant. He pulled the iron key from somewhere in his shortened trousers and jammed it into the lock.

"This mate's Saban," he replied as he yanked open the cage door. "His arm's busted. Weeks past, now. Still ain't healin' right. Can ye take a look at it?"

Baltsaros nodded and stepped past Tom.

"Saban, can I see your arm please?" he asked gently. The tall stranger looked up at him with a pained expression. Suspicion clouded his dark eyes, and he glanced over at Tom.

"You keep your father in a cell?" asked the man in accented but fluent Common.

Baltsaros lifted his eyes and met Tom's.

The first mate paused for only a second before his face creased in a smile.

"He's a bloody, fuckin' lunatic," said the burly pirate, crossing his arms. "But, he's been settin' bones since before ye were whelped, mate. Trust him."

Baltsaros stared at him, aghast at being called a lunatic. He'd have the first mate over a barrel and ploughed with no relief for the sheer impertinence of his words. Then he blinked at the first mate's widening grin, Tom's words coming back to him through the haze: *I just miss you.*

Indeed.

He quickly lowered his gaze to the wounded man to try to intercept the jumble of emotions that rushed to batter at his impaired brain. But it was good. Something deep inside him felt a little more familiar.

With careful hands, Baltsaros quickly divested Saban of his sling and laid his arm on the table. It was a compound fracture—closed thankfully. The last thing the man needed was an infection settling into his wound. He prodded gently along its edge while Tom did something behind him. It was somewhat hard to tell with the swelling, but it felt like an oblique break with only slight luxation. It was relatively good news for the future of the man's arm as it would most likely lay straight if Baltsaros was successful in setting it. A tight splint would be enough to hold it. The bad news was that the bones had had plenty of time to knit together and the length of the raw edges pressed together would mean rebreaking it was going to be more difficult. The first mate handed Saban a mug full of rum and pulled up a chair to watch Baltsaros.

"So?" asked Tom. He sounded strangely invested, and it made Baltsaros wonder if there was something between the two young men. Did Jon know?

He pushed a little harder along the edge of the break and heard Saban try to hold back a grunt of pain.

"Son, you better down that rum and more," he said kindly, looking up into the man's eyes. They were a blend of greens and browns, a beautiful complement to his dusky-skinned, aristocratic face. "I don't understand why no one reset your arm—"

"I was a slave, sir," replied the man, his deep voice slightly hoarse. "My master, that dog-fucking imbecile, decided that teaching me a lesson was more important. How he thought I was going to serve him properly after that..." Saban shook his head and took another deep swallow of dark rum.

"It's over, mate," growled Tom. "He's rottin' in the pits of the black hells."

Yes, definitely something between them, judging by the first mate's vitriol.

"I have to rebreak your arm. Do you understand?" Baltsaros said. "It's going to hurt. But it's the only way. I'll do my best to set it straight, and then it should mend properly."

Saban nodded quickly, his face greyish.

"Tom, I need you to get a few things and then help him onto the floor. You're going to have to hold him down and keep him from jerking away."

Tom stood and left the room quickly to get a leather belt, some wood, and some strips of cotton or silk.

Baltsaros watched Saban down the rest of the rum, and he went to go get the bottle. As he sat down and refilled Saban's mug, pouring himself a small measure in the process, he realized something. This was the first time he could remember being free without Jon or Tom's presence. At least, he *thought* so. Smiling thinly to himself, he drank down a little rum and studied Saban. Tall, undoubtedly strong, handsome, and there was obvious, keen intelligence in his hazel eyes.

"You're not his father," said Saban, wincing as he sat back more comfortably.

Baltsaros shook his head with another smile.

"And I would say, judging by how quickly he hopped to obey you, that he's used to following your orders," continued the ex-slave.

This time Baltsaros chuckled.

"Yes, he is. Though not always well, he does obey me."

"So *you* are the captain that he went to rescue, not Captain Black." Saban looked at him curiously.

"You're very observant. Your intelligence, I take it, was entirely wasted in your previous duties?" Baltsaros asked.

"Entirely," agreed Saban, his smile rueful. There was an interesting, quiet power to the man that Baltsaros found soothing.

"Well, once you're healed, I'll try to find something to use your skills on," he replied. He touched a spilled drop of rum with his forefinger and traced a circle on the tabletop with it. "However," he said, choosing his words carefully, "whatever your *arrangement* is, I want you to understand that Tom belongs to me. And to Jon. Don't have any aspirations of coming between us."

Saban raised his brows.

"Tom is a friend. Nothing more," said the tall Balorian softly.

"Tom's not one for friends," replied the captain with a frown.

Saban shrugged and then leaned towards him, a thoughtful expression on his face.

"Sir, are you genuinely suffering from some malady of the mind?" he asked. The question, though off-putting, was spoken without a trace of prejudice.

"Yes," admitted Baltsaros. "Temporary, I'm sure."

"I think I am beginning to understand why Tom fights now. He's worried for you." Saban's face was slightly flushed with drink, but he seemed far from inebriated. "What form does it take?" he asked with interest.

Baltsaros thought for few seconds before answering.

"Loss of memory, but not all memory—only from the last year or so," he said. "I have, ah... turns where I am not myself during which time have no control over my violent actions nor do I have any subsequent recollection. Why? Do you know of such things?"

"My father suffered from something we call *dementia*," said Saban quietly. He said the word in Balorian, but it was similar to one they used in the north to describe those who had lost their mental faculties. "I took care of him and was able to affect positive changes in him. Perhaps, as repayment for treating me, you'd let me try some of the same things with you that helped to ease my father's mind."

"I'm afraid my actions are probably not on the same level as your father's," replied Baltsaros, intrigued. "What makes you think you can help me?"

"He killed my mother."

A long silence passed between them. Saban's eyes shifted from brown to green with a subtle movement of his head, and Baltsaros was reminded of the deep, ancient forests of the mainlands. Calm. Still.

Finally, he nodded.

~

Tom walked into the room and put his armful down on the table. Without a word, he quickly helped Saban down onto the thick, hand-knotted silk rug while Baltsaros picked through the pile of wood pieces. The older man chose three narrow slats that Tom had pilfered from Nathaniel's map-framing supplies and placed them next to a length of garnet-coloured silk that Baltsaros probably recognized as an old shirt of his. The first mate grinned reassuringly at the big Balorian.

"All righty, mate," he said, holding up the leather belt. "You're goin' to bite down on this. It's gonna hurt, but yer a big boy, and I think ye'll be fine," Tom told Saban, placing the belt between his teeth. He'd had enough bones set to know that it wasn't as painful as you'd think; fear and expectation were the worst parts. "I'm gonna kneel on yer shoulder a bit so ye don't jerk, but try not to move, savvy? I have no bloody problem knockin' ye out with a punch, ducky."

Saban chuckled with the leather belt clenched between his teeth and nodded once.

Tom glanced up at Baltsaros and saw that the older man's deep-brown eyes were on him. He didn't look like he was about to launch into his bloodthirsty god bit, nor did he look vague and scared. No, Da looked confident, thankful... and fond. Tom ducked his head and adjusted his hold on Saban's shoulder to hide the heat that rose in his face.

"Ok," said Baltsaros quietly, placing one hand under the Balorian's wrist and the other on his upper forearm. "Take a deep breath."

CHAPTER 5

THE BURDEN OF TRUST

Tom took a step back and rolled his shoulder, pushing into sore muscles with his fingers as he craned his head to the side. A whole morning spent sanding and carving was starting to wear on him. Maybe it was time to call it quits. He squinted at the ship's figurehead, lashed for the moment to the mast, and nodded to himself. It was starting to look pretty decent. Once he was done fixing it up, he'd paint it; black for the contours, red for the eyes... But they had no white paint. That part would have to wait until they made port somewhere.

"Not bad," said a deep voice.

Tom turned to Saban with a smile. Over the course of the last week, a real friendship had begun to grow between the two of them, and he was bloody glad for it. Saban seemed to know exactly when Tom needed him to keep his mouth shut and when he needed some good-natured ribbing. In return, Tom had found himself confiding in the man. They were just little things, but it surprised him that he felt he could trust Saban at all with his words. There was such a deep well of understanding and patience in those hazel eyes.

Tom realized he was staring and looked back at the wooden skeleton with a shrug.

"Ahh, mate. I ain't got Da's skills, that's for bloody sure. But... aye... not bad."

"I think it'll make a fine addition to the ship," said Saban.

Tom nodded and leaned down to pick up his knife. Jarrod had given the bone-handled dagger back to him as a parting gift before they had set sail; the cheeky, stub-fingered young man had claimed that he had too many knives anyway, but Tom had seen the gesture for what it was. He smiled and tested the edge. It was dulled from use.

595

"Can I have the key?"

Tom nodded distractedly, digging around in the deep pouch sewn into his trousers for the iron key. He stood and handed it over to the big Balorian. Saban had definitely proven his worth when it came to Baltsaros; he had been spending all his free time with the captain, doing gods knew what, but it was definitely helping Baltsaros to regain control of himself.

"Tell Da that we're gettin' close to the mountain range. He might be up t' seein' it with his own eyes, aye?" said Tom, sliding the knife into its sheath at his belt. "Take advantage of the good weather an' all too." Though the wind still brought with it a chill, the sun shone bright in a cloudless sky.

Saban nodded with a smile and turned to go. Tom watched him walk away, admiring the hard muscles of his shoulders and calves. He couldn't wait until the Balorian's arm healed completely; Saban had promised to show him a new way of fighting, and Tom was looking forward to it.

He pocketed the good bits that were left of the sandpaper, lest they be blown overboard, and made his way to the trapdoor. As he descended the narrow stairs quickly, Tom was assailed by the smell of burnt hair, and he wrinkled his nose, scouting around for the cause. After a second, a loud popping noise came from the biggest of the bunkrooms followed by a long string of curses. Tom frowned and walked to the room. Fingers wrapped around the handle of his knife, he pushed the door open slowly. Smoke drifted out of the crack, an acrid smudge that immediately coated his throat and caused him to choke.

"What in bloody hells is goin' on in here?" he growled when his coughing subsided, peering into the gloom.

Nathaniel waved his arms through the smoke with an embarrassed grin, and Tom saw that Malik was stooped next to one of the small electricity generators they had taken from Ereme'ia Balor. When the dark-haired shipwright looked up, Tom saw that he was missing his eyebrows. The first mate barked out a laugh and stepped into the room.

"We are trying to enter a new age of technology," said Nathaniel, coughing. "But we can't get the blasted thing to work. Uh, careful where you step!"

Tom stopped and saw that the ground was littered with broken glass.

"What in Bal's name is that stench?" Ceara peered into the room, her hand over her mouth and nose. "Please tell me you're not cooking dog in here."

Next to her was the small, mousy slave girl from the emperor's palace, Bettie. Tom furrowed his brow. Maybe *mousy* wasn't the right word, at least not anymore. The time spent in the sun and wind had transformed the young woman somewhat. She had some colour in her cheeks, and her hair looked a mite more bronze than the dull brown it had been. She looked... nicer. Happier.

"Oh no!" said Bettie and stepped forward, nimbly avoiding the broken glass. She went down on her knees next to Malik and reached for the machine.

"Miss, you'd better not... touch..." said Nathaniel quickly but trailed off in amazement as Bettie confidently flipped a few toggles and turned a small knob.

"There. You had the levels all wrong for these! No wonder you've been blowing bulbs," she said with a nod. Tom almost laughed at the looks on the men's faces, but then he realized he probably looked just as astonished. He grinned.

Bettie glanced around, suddenly aware of all the eyes on her. Colour rose in her face like pink blooms. She definitely blushed pretty.

"How did you? What..." started Malik, wiping at the smoke stains on his face. He pointed quickly at the middle-aged cartographer. "Turn the crank."

Nathaniel immediately started winding the leather-covered handle at the back of the machine, and the shipwright lifted a nervous hand up to his eyes, the other arm shielding Bettie.

The bulb on the floor next to Malik started to glow and Tom took a step back, but when a few seconds went by with nothing exploding, he let out an amazed chuckle.

"Well, I'll be damned!" said the surly, dark-haired Malik. He cracked a smile and turned to the young woman next to him. Tom couldn't help but notice how his eyes widened at Bettie. Malik opened his mouth to speak, but nothing came out.

"I am Nathaniel," broke in the cartographer after a second of awkward silence. "Nate, if you'd like. This is Malik. I don't believe we've had the pleasure of your acquaintance." Nathaniel's eyes were creased at the corners as he sketched a bow to the kneeling ex-slave girl. Tom smiled and joined Ceara at the door.

"Huh, I knew that she handled changing the bulbs, but I had no idea how much she had picked up from the engineers. Interesting," murmured Ceara. "You know, I assumed that those two were... together."

Tom shrugged. So had he. However, the way both men looked at Bettie as she used Nathaniel's chalk to sketch out something about the machine on the floor spoke volumes.

Should be interesting.

He figured that the machine was in good hands and turned to go. If they managed to get the generator working via wind power and bulbs placed around the front of the ship, the long pass through the rift in the mountains wouldn't be so fucking gloomy.

"Tom," Ceara said, grasping his arm.

He stopped and frowned at the redheaded woman.

"What d'ye want, wench?"

Ceara's lip curved in amusement at what had become almost a term of endearment.

"I think we have a problem on board," she said quietly, her expression sobering as she lead him away from the door. "I think someone's been... ah... taking liberties with some of the female passengers. No one wants to talk about it, but I overheard something distressing this morning." Ceara's wide blue eyes searched his. He knew that she was having a hard time acclimatising to this new life. Gaining the trust of some of the ex-slaves was proving to be difficult; not everyone believed that she had been helping in their cause while spying for the emperor. For someone who had built her life on filching information, Tom was sure that it was a bit of a hit to the ol' self-esteem to have to rely on her own ears for the inside scoop.

"Why the fuck are ye tellin' me, love?" he asked. "The captain's the one who deals with the—"

"I'm not sure I want to bring it to Jon just yet. Bal knows, he seems to have enough on his plate at the moment. Plus, well... I have no idea who it is."

Tom's mind went immediately to Laz. After all, the man was a known rapist. However, the first mate had personally promised Laz that if he got any ideas about continuing his behaviour, Tom would tie one end of a rope to the ex-slave's cock and the other end to a cannonball and let fly. Laz had turned white as milk before assuring him that he was a changed man. But maybe it was a case of a badger not being able to change its stripes. What could he do? Threaten him again?

"Fuck," muttered Tom. "Can't ye just tell them girls to—" He saw the warning in Ceara's eyes and cut his words short. "Fine. I'll bloody look into it. But ye gotta give me more 'n that, dove."

"I think it's one of the rich passengers. The girl mentioned *dokschas* in exchange for her silence," said the petite woman, her gloved hand plucking at the high collar of her dress.

"Ah! See, now ye might be mistakin'. Might be a case of ol' fashion whorin'. Ain't nothin' wrong with that," he pointed out, hopeful for a quick resolution.

"Tom, she was crying."

He pressed his lips together and scratched the back of his head. He nodded.

"Ye keepin' safe?" he asked gruffly after a thought.

Ceara did nothing more than twist her wrist and a small dagger appeared in her hand. With a dark smile, the knife disappeared and she turned to go.

"I'll let you know if I hear or see anything else," she said over her shoulder as she walked away.

Tom grinned, not knowing whether he'd feel sorry for or envious of the man who could make the fiery woman's heart go pitter-patter.

~

Jon flipped through the sketches Ceara had handed over. They all showed the same thing: the black mountain range.

"I don't see it," he finally said, looking up at her.

"I didn't expect you to," she said with a smile. The sun had brought out more freckles on her snub nose, making her seem younger. Jon realized he had no idea how old she actually was. Ceara winked at him and plucked the drawings from his hand. She rifled through them, sorting them.

"See this mark here?" she asked, pointing to a small smear in the corner.

Jon nodded.

"This is one," she said. Then she held up the next drawing. "This... is two."

Sure enough, there were two small smears.

"Place one and two on top of each other and hold them up to the light... What do you see?" she handed over the sheets of paper.

Jon frowned and lifted them up. There, in the middle of the drawing, where the lines met up, was a symbol. It looked familiar. He reached down next to him for the water-filled compass they had taken from Polas's boat. Sure enough, on the silver cylinder floating inside, was the same symbol on one end. He glanced up and saw that Ceara was watching him with obvious amusement.

"Well, you're no dummy, that's for sure," she said, flashing a white-toothed smile. She gave him two more sheets, one with three smudges and the other with four. Jon aligned them and held them up to the sun. There, in the midst of all the lines, was another symbol. He grinned. The symbol matched one of the ones on the brass ring around the compass's base.

"That's really clever!" he said with a laugh. "Did you design this?"

"I did."

Jon turned the globe in his hands and looked at the four feet that held up the device.

"So, if this part of the base points towards the rising sun... That's what this sun symbol means, right? I'm guessing we will know the correct path when these two symbols line up. Am I getting that right?"

Ceara simply nodded and turned towards the mountain range looming in the distance. Her fiery ringlets danced in the cool wind.

Jon put the sheets of paper down on the bench and weighted them down with the ocean compass.

"Why did you finally decide to give me these, Ceara?"

The ex-spymaster said nothing for a long moment. When she turned back, her eyes were wide and scared. Jon frowned.

"Trust for trust. You'll trust me if I trust you, right?" Ceara said softly, her lips barely moving. He was still angry with her for kissing Tom, but he could see she had completely dropped her guard; it was naked fear he was staring at. He instinctively reached for her shoulder.

When she flinched at his touch, he nearly pulled his hand away, but she quickly grabbed it and curled her fingers over his with a little squeeze.

"What is it?" he asked.

She laughed a little shakily, and he felt her tremble. He frowned and pulled her into his arms, her tiny frame held rigid for a moment before she sagged against him.

"I... may have exaggerated a little when I said that I knew there was no truth to the stories of what lies beyond the mountains," she whispered.

"Ceara, don't be foolish. There is no truth," he said, rubbing her back slowly in a way that he hoped soothed her.

"A lifetime of belief is hard to give up," she replied, her voice muffled by his greatcoat.

"Trust me," he said with a grim smile. "There are no monsters on the other side." *The only true monster I know is right here with us.* He felt Ceara nod against him and take a slow breath. He closed his eyes briefly and tightened his jaw. Why was he always the one offering solace these days?

When Ceara pulled away, her eyes were red-rimmed but dry. She quickly straightened her cloak and brushed her hair out of her face, squaring her shoulders. The walls were back up. However, when she smiled a little sheepishly, he realized that she had given him a tiny window to see through.

Trust for trust.

Jon thought back to the way she had bared herself to him before, showing him the secret scars beneath her clothes.

"Sorry," she muttered, her cheeks rosy. "Moment of weakness. But... Thank you."

"Thank *you* for trusting me with these," Jon said, gesturing to the coded drawings.

Ceara nodded again.

"Listen, I am sorry that I've been... terse with you," he continued. "Why don't we start over? Ok? Show me I can trust you, Ceara."

"I can try," she said, her cheeks dimpling with a grin.

"And... I'm willing to forgive you and Tom. But I don't want it to happen again."

Ceara's eyebrows shot up; immediately, Jon felt stupid for bringing it up.

"Tom... and I?"

"Yeah," he said, his face hot. However, he frowned when she continued to look at him in confusion. "The kiss?" he prompted, but he was rewarded with a slow shake of her head.

"I have no idea what in the name of Bal and his unholy minions you are talking about, Jon Black," she said.

"You don't?" he asked faintly, but it was blatantly obvious to him that she was telling the truth.

She shook her head again.

"But... Who else could it be?" Jon said in dismay.

Ceara shrugged.

"Shouldn't that be a question for Tom?"

Jon let out a humourless laugh and ran a hand over the tangled mess of his curls.

"I suppose it is. I just thought asking him would sound... peevish. I'm trying to be less sensitive, I guess," he said.

"And you just figured it *had* to be me?"

When he nodded, Ceara surprised him by punching him in the shoulder. He recoiled with a sharp cry and then laughed, rubbing what would undoubtedly turn into a bruise. For such a slight woman, she packed one hell of a wallop. He wondered what Katherine would make of her.

The ex-spymaster smiled serenely and sat down on the bench, arranging her skirts as she gazed up at him with wide, limpid blue eyes. When she hadn't said anything after a few moments, he scowled at her.

"What?" he asked, suspicious.

"I may be wrong," said Ceara lightly as she crossed one knee over the other, "but it seems to me like you're a man who needs to get a few things off his chest; don't take this the wrong way, but you look like shit, Jon. If you like... If you can *trust* me, I can be the person to listen to you. I can offer my advice, if you want it. And, I promise not to breathe a word of anything you say to me. I swear on my life."

Jon felt a small swell of gratitude that was quickly shredded into lace by doubt, and he turned away to look again at the looming mountains they were approaching. It *was* tempting to tell Ceara everything. Just to have someone to talk to. He could tell her about his persistent lack of confidence when it came to his relationship with Baltsaros and Tom. How he felt like he was holding them to ridiculous values that they didn't believe in... but that he had no idea how to change that about himself. About how deeply, yet differently, he felt for both men. About his strange dreams. About his fears and doubts over Baltsaros's recovery.

About Baltsaros's bloody appetites and penchant for outright murder? whispered the little voice inside him.

No. Never about that, he thought. Jon just couldn't trust her with that information, and far too much of what he could say otherwise was tainted by those secrets.

He turned back to her.

"You *are* wrong, Ceara. I'm fine," he said with a wan smile. But when she narrowed her eyes at him, he felt an impatient spark of anger quickly turn to flame and he glowered at her, suddenly sick to death of having his fortitude questioned. "I just don't need you meddling into my affairs. Now get out of my sight."

Ceara gaped at him for a half second before her features reclaimed their usual expression of artful scorn. She stood and shook her head.

"I'm going to give you one piece of advice, sweetheart," she said, tugging her cloak around her as she started down the quarterdeck stairs. "Stop being such a godsdamned prick. It doesn't suit you."

CHAPTER 6
MEASURE FOR MEASURE

Eye for eye, tooth for tooth, hand for hand, foot for foot...

— KING JAMES BIBLE, EXODUS 21:24

Tom had briefly considered using Bettie as bait to find out who the molester in their midst was. However, planning the ridiculous ploy had worsened his hangover, so he had decided to take a good measure of hair-of-the-dog to remedy the situation.

He belched and put down the mug, wiping his mouth with the back of his hand and feeling on the edge of squiffy. He wasn't a spy. Meeting problems head-on had always been his strong suit. Hells, his underhanded attempt at landing Jon in the Portsmouth jail had nearly cost him everything, hadn't it? No, this dog's breakfast didn't warrant fucking tippy-toeing around like some cloaked weasel.

Tom slid off the crate, grabbed the lantern, and headed to the trapdoor.

On reaching the smaller of the bunkrooms, the one designated for women passengers, Tom pushed the door open with such force that it banged hard against the wall. There was a small, surprised shriek, and several women sat up and goggled at him in the dark. It was well past midnight, but he figured that meant they were all in one place.

Tom lifted the lantern high so he could see all their faces.

"I'm gonna ask ye ladies a question, and I bloody expect to be answered," he growled. "Who's the scoundrel been doin' some unwanted rootin' of yer cunts for pay?"

The room was utterly silent. A few of the women shared looks. Others simply stared at him in sleepy confusion. Tom frowned, realizing that perhaps his meaning has been lost. He hung the lantern on the hook next to the door, and speaking in what he thought was pretty decent Balorian while thrusting his finger into the hole made by the thumb and forefinger of the other hand, he repeated himself.

"Who's been fuckin' ye and givin' ye coin to quiet yer tongues?"

This time he figured everyone got his meaning; a few of the women smirked at the rude gesture, and he let himself grin a little. When no one responded after a few moments, Tom let out a frustrated sigh.

"Listen, lassies, ol' Tom is just tryin' to do right by ye," he implored. "I don't want anyone on this ol' tub gettin' done to 'em what's them don't ask for, savvy? Tell me, an' I'll see yer troubles gone." He figured the man had probably threatened that more pain would come to them through his mates should any of them squawk, but he didn't have time for this shite.

Tom pulled his long dagger out from the sheath nestled in his lower back and held it up. Eyes widened nervously at the sight.

"I'll just keep askin' the same fuckin' question, loveys. Every time I get no reply, someone's gettin' a haircut," he growled. It was a ridiculous threat, but he hoped at least one of them was vain enough to care about it. He scowled, looking around for someone fitting. To his right was a woman who looked like she had either been moneyed or a well-kept slave; her dark braid hung thick and glossy over her shoulder. "Let's start with *you*, darlin'."

Immediately the woman sat up straight in bed.

"You wouldn't *dare* lay a hand on me!" she spat. She glared down at him from her bunk like he was nothing but a turd, even lifting her nose a little to get away from the stench.

Tom sighed. Aye... rich.

"You can't just come in here... It's the middle of the night!" she continued, stoking her affront. "And you certainly can't threaten us into talking about such a... such a... *sensitive* matter!"

"S'all right, Samma. I am wanting to see the fat pig pay," said a small voice to Tom's left.

He peered into the gloom and saw a sandy-haired woman sitting in one of the lower bunks. She swung her legs over the side of the bed and leaned forward into the light, looking up at him with tired eyes. The woman had the faded remains of a bruise on one side of her face, and her coarse nightgown did nothing to hide how pathetically thin she was.

"He is named Punga," she said with obvious loathing. "I am of the hoping your sharp blade will be of cutting off more than his hair."

He grinned.

Pleased with himself, Tom made his way back to the night air above, happy to have taken care of at least half of that little problem. Ceara'd be off his back now.

He rubbed a hand over the top of his head, brow furrowed in thought as he made his way to the gunwale to drain his bladder before heading to bed. He felt like it was a good thing that he had done. Something to be proud about. Taking coin for a little bit of sport was nothing to look sideways at, but when it came to not wanting the sport to begin with? Tom shook his head as he stuffed his cock back in his pants and then thumped back down onto the planks. Memories of a small room and a creaking, stinking bed came back to him. Worse even was when you weren't the one taking the coin… just sold off as a warm hole. With a sigh, Tom reached down and grabbed the lantern, thinking again about how much he would love to see his master's brother-in-law pay for what he did. It had been Lester's idea, after all, to make money off Tom on nights when he wasn't fighting in the cages. The fat bastard was probably still laughing as he collected money off the back of some other poor sod.

Yeah, he was glad that Punga would be stopped.

Tom extinguished the lantern, suddenly feeling lower than he had in days. The thought of curling up with Jon was nice, but what he really needed, really ached for right then was the man who had freed him from the black hells with a few bits of silver.

~

Baltsaros heard the door open and lifted his head. In the centre of the long table, the candle was drowning itself slowly in wax, and in its dim light he saw Tom enter the room. Jon snored quietly in the low, wide bed, oblivious to the first mate's return. Baltsaros placed his head back on the pillow and watched as Tom made his way towards the bed. However, after staring down at Jon for what felt like a long time, the burly pirate turned around and made his way to the cage on silent feet. The first mate peered down at him and Baltsaros decided to keep pretending sleep—the last thing he wanted was a late night exchange that could turn ugly because of his cracked mind. Tom waited a moment longer and then grabbed the back of one of the chairs to drag it closer to the cage.

With a deep sigh, Tom settled back in the seat and crossed his arms, obviously having decided to watch over Baltsaros's sleep. However, almost immediately the first mate's head began to nod. After a few minutes the candle finally expired, and the resulting puff of smoke drifted pale in the moonlight. Baltsaros smiled; he could barely make out Tom sprawled backwards in the wooden chair, sound asleep with his arms dangling to either side.

The first mate would be sore in the morning; Baltsaros knew from first-hand experience what spending the night in those chairs felt like.

~

Captain Baltsaros cleared the maps and books off the long table and stepped quickly to help Peter heave the unconscious slave onto the mahogany surface.

"Shit," gasped the first mate. "He's a heavy one, isn't he?"

The captain nodded distractedly and turned to the armoire to get his surgical tools.

"Turn him onto his stomach, please," he said, picking out a few jars of salve and a small bottle of refined oil before grabbing the small box containing his scalpels, forceps, and needles. "And tie his wrists to the center legs. There's no telling how long the laudanum will last."

"Aye, aye, Captain," said his first mate with a nod. "I'm amazed you got him to take it at all."

Baltsaros shrugged, depositing the items on the table as he watched Peter bind Tom. To be honest, he was somewhat amazed too. He'd fully expected to have to wrestle the burly slave to the ground to rid him of his pathetic little weapon and then force-feed him the sedative; the boy was completely wild, and the captain needed to take a close look at his injuries. However, when Baltsaros had spoken his name, it was as if he had thrown seawater onto flame. Tom had gone limp and wide-eyed, collapsing in front of him in an almost catatonic state. It had been nothing then to hold a cup of water laced heavily with laudanum to his lips.

Baltsaros wondered how long it had been since the boy had heard his given name.

"Sweet mother of lords, will you look at this?" murmured Peter. "What have you brought aboard?"

Reaching out, the captain touched young man's back. The dive into the harbour the previous day had relieved the slave of his patina of mud and filth, and Baltsaros could clearly see that what he had mistaken for clumped dirt was flesh marred by layers and layers of healed whip marks—a horrifying landscape of punishment that started at his shoulders and tapered off below his buttocks. In addition, the skin beneath the captain's palm was hot; a fever seemed to have set in.

"I don't know yet," he confessed. He tapped the leather harness. "Here, help me get this off of him."

It was immediately obvious that they would have to cut the harness off; the buckles were rusted shut and caked thick with grime. Thankfully, the leather was rotted and came apart easily with the use of sharp blades. When the harness fell away, it left behind thick calluses and fainter scars beneath it.

"I've seen overworked beasts with marks like this... never a man," said the first mate, his dark eyes wide. He reached out and touched the dark ridges on the boy's back.

Baltsaros stroked the stubble of his cheek, wondering what his silver had purchased.

When he had been told of a rebellious slave killing his masters, his interest had been piqued. It wasn't often that one heard such things; the mainland mining towns that still used slave labour had been doing it for generations and had slavery down to an art. That a man had not only escaped but had also managed to get past the guards and into his master's very bedroom was impressive indeed. Then, when it had been mentioned that the slave was being sold off for pocket change, the captain had decided to take a look.

On arriving at the town square, he had been dismayed by what he had found. Naked and filthy, a young man, barely out of boyhood, knelt bleeding in the mud with his head and wrists secured in the stocks. The scene was utterly pathetic, but the captain had no desire to nurse a beaten, cringing creature back to health. Baltsaros had almost turned to leave right then, but the slave had lifted his head and met his gaze with eyes the same colour as the water off the white beaches of Madierus. The captain had expected to see defeat, fear, and despondency, but all he saw was determination and a fierce will. Those eyes are what had moved his hand to his purse.

The captain looked up at Peter and smiled at the first mate.

"Leave us," he said.

"Aye, Captain," replied Peter, his eyes darting to the slave boy lying face down on the long table. "I'll be above if you need me. Just shout."

Baltsaros watched him leave and waited until the door was closed before he looked down at Tom again. The boy was impressively muscled, and Baltsaros recalled what the man who sold him had said: Tom had worked in the mines hauling stone before he had been put in the cage to fight for money. The man had also said something about having to keep Tom separate from other slaves due to a penchant for violence. The captain placed a hand on the boy's warm calf, the muscle hard and defined against his palm. Then, with a grunt of effort, he forced the boy's legs apart as far as he could and set to work.

After carefully washing his hands, Baltsaros poured a little white alcohol on them before he reached for the thick oil he liked to use as lubricant. When he'd first inspected the slave in the stocks, he had noticed dried blood along the inside of his thighs; he suspected he knew why by the way the boy's walk was slightly crouched as if movement caused him pain.

Baltsaros rubbed the boy's anus with oil and gently slipped two fingers inside him. Sure enough, there was an object lodged in the lining of his rectum. Feeling around its edges, he thought he could grab it with the narrowest set of forceps.

Moments later, when he held the long, bloody splinter of wood in his palm, Baltsaros felt the first honest swell of anger over the boy's treatment.

With Tom drugged anew and sleeping easily on his side in the cage, Baltsaros leaned across the table and stared hard at his first mate.

"Take Calum and Wraith with you into town as soon as the sun sets. Find me the man I spoke to earlier today; he goes by the name of Lester. Bring him to me, and make sure no one sees you. Do you understand?" he said quietly.

Peter's eyes took on a guarded cast, but he nodded without hesitation.

"It will be done, Captain."

Baltsaros smiled again as Tom shifted in his sleep on the uncomfortable chair. Lester had lasted nearly four hours before he had succumbed to his injuries, the least of which was caused by a long splinter of rough wood. Afterwards, Baltsaros had pulled a chair up to the cage, exactly where Tom now slumbered, and had spent the night watching over the boy, too fired up from blood to sleep and full of ideas on how to win the young slave's trust.

The memory suddenly made him sit back slowly against the bars and furrow his brow. He had never told Tom about what had happened that night; it had never occurred to him to do so, and Baltsaros wondered why that was. Would telling Tom that he had killed the man for what he had done have changed the timbre of their relationship from the beginning? Sorrow coloured his thoughts, and he sighed softly to himself. Why had it taken over five years and another feverish, ill-used boy in his cage to show him Tom's true worth?

He rubbed at his chest as if he could make the tight ache disappear. With Saban's help he had begun to get himself under control, but it was a far cry from the iron hold he'd had on his emotions before. They now soared and churned inside him at every moment, his pulse skipping like a drunken madman as it tried to keep up with the tumult that drove the sleep from his mind and plunged him into a torrent of self-doubt and fear. Even when he seemed like his old self, it was a sham; he couldn't find the well of peace that had always cooled the fury in the past.

However, the semblance of control was better than naught.

Tom muttered in his sleep, something crass and nearly unintelligible. With a soft chuckle, Baltsaros stood and put his hand on the lock, intent on getting the big brute back to bed so he wouldn't be in a sour mood in the morning; when Baltsaros realized what he was doing, he pulled his hand away from the lock, staring at it in dismay, and took a step back.

It was the last thing he needed to remember, given his predicament.

CHAPTER 7
THE RIFT

Tom whistled a little shanty he had learned from Calum as he made his way down from the main topgallant mast. They'd been beating to windward all morning and had finally arrived at the mouth of what Ceara called simply "The Rift". According to the ex-spymaster, the strong headwind that moaned through the slit in the mountain range would change direction with the setting of the sun—something about cooling air and warmer waters beyond the narrow fjord that would shift the wind eastward. To Tom it sounded a little hogwashy, but it was true that he'd seen it happen in other places, only not as violent a turnabout as the woman claimed this one to be. For the moment, however, they were anchored as they prepared for the journey through.

Tom peered around below him as he climbed down and saw that Malik and Bettie were still fiddling with the rack of bulbs they had mounted on the bowsprit. He was glad that they'd brought the outlandish things aboard; with bright lights shining before them, they would easily be able to navigate through the forked channels.

Forked like a dozen devils' wicked tongues.

Looking up at the towering black cliffs to each side of the *Heart*, he could barely see the birds that were wheeling high above the ship. There was no mist here to shroud the stupefying size of the mountains they'd sail through, and Tom had never felt so *small* in his entire life. He'd been studying the diagrams that Ceara had brought with her because he would be at the helm tonight, and it honestly made him more than a little bloody nervous; if he missed a quick course change, it could mean anything from being becalmed in a blind alley to being dashed against submerged rocks. A dubious fucking honour indeed.

He jumped down and landed easily on the deck. That was later though. He had to look into his little side project first.

Taking the portside stairs two at a time, Tom pulled the blade from his belt before he reached the low door to the brig. He pushed it open and went down the last few steps into the pitch darkness beyond. There was a muffled groan straight ahead, and Tom grinned. Reaching up, he scraped his knife against the wall until it encountered brass. He then flipped the latch on the blacked-out porthole cover and swung it open, letting a little light and air into the dank, stuffy room.

"There, lovey. Ain't that a little better? Awww... Who's the fucker who let ye stew in the black all night, aye?" he laughed, walking towards the bars set into the back of the small room. Hanging upside-down from one of the beams above was a fat little man, stripped naked and trussed up like a pig; the lass had wanted to see the *pig* pay, after all.

Tom unlocked the door and stepped in, prodding with his knife at the fat that bulged out between the hempen ropes. With a squeal, the man writhed, trying to get away from the sharp blade, but Tom just chuckled to himself and kept poking at him until the man swung back and forth, turning in a slow circle. The stench of urine was ripe in the room, and Tom noted with some amusement that the wood was wet below the man's head.

"Gah, ye stink, Punga," he said, sneering. "How d'ye like pissin' on yer own face? Ye like that?"

The fat, little rich man just let out a low, pathetic moan behind the gag Tom had put on him.

"Now are ye gonna finger yer mates to me and make godsdamned sure they ain't gonna stand so much as in the same breeze as them girls, or do ye wanna spend another night down here, pissin' up yer nose?" he asked, pushing Punga again with his knife.

With another squeak, the fat man nodded quickly, his bulging red eyes pleading with Tom.

The first mate smiled and began sawing at the rope above. Just before it gave, he kicked the hanging man in the shoulder so he wouldn't land on his head. With a frown Tom wondered why he bothered sparing Punga the bruised skull when no one else had done the same for him.

~

Jon stared hard at the four men lined up on the deck and then glanced over at Tom. The first mate sat on the gunwale fishing pieces of conserved pear out of a jar with his knife, slurping them down and licking his fingers as he watched Jon pace back and forth. They had less than an hour before the sun went down; meting out punishment was the last thing Jon wanted to do. Irritated, he walked past the men again.

He glanced up at the quarterdeck and saw that Ceara also watched him, her blue eyes unreadable with the sun behind her. This was the first real discipline he'd had to dish out since taking on the title of captain. He felt like everyone was judging him. Eyes closed, he squeezed the bridge of his nose and thought for a few seconds.

"All right," he said, straightening his shoulders. He glared at Punga. "You're the ringleader and the one responsible," he said. "Ten lashes and a fortnight in the brig. The rest of you lose your bunks for a week just for agreeing to intimidate other passengers." His eyes darted to Tom and saw that the first mate's eyebrows were high. He looked skeptical.

Were ten lashes not enough? Should he have said twenty? Jon gritted his teeth. What was the proper punishment for this sort of thing? He wished Tom hadn't put him on the spot like this.

"Ten lashes? You mean you will have me whipped? For seeking out a little companionship? She was a slave, Captain. They're used to this sort of thing!" blurted out the fat man. He clutched at Jon's arm.

Jon pulled his arm away and took a step back. On Punga's face was a look of pure incomprehension. The fact that there was not a shred of remorse or even understanding of what he was being punished for finally pushed Jon's mood over into true anger. He balled his fists and, resisting the urge to shout, began to speak in a low, furious voice.

"Not only did you *disobey* my direct command to give up all personal wealth during your time aboard, but you *assaulted* a fellow passen—"

"Assaulted?" spluttered Punga. "Listen, I don't know about that. A little misunderstanding. Heh heh. For certain! But... that your beast had me hung upside down in the dark like a fucking slave. Isn't that punishment enough? Lords of Summer, you can't expect to have women on board your ship without knowing they'll provoke the appetites of..."

Jon's blood felt hotter, and his mouth tasted sour as he listened to the shit pouring out of Punga's mouth.

Degenerates who held ignorant beliefs, Jon. Little lives that would only serve to pollute others. Baltsaros's words.

"Tom. Throw him overboard," he growled. "I don't have room for trash on my ship."

Punga's eyes bulged with terror, and he took a step back, his mouth opening and closing like a dying fish's. Jon's gaze darted to Tom; he saw that the first mate stared at him with deep creases in his forehead and ocean eyes narrowed in concern.

Oh for fuck's sake, Tom, he thought in annoyance and locked eyes with him.

Do it.

With a tight nod that spoke volumes about his disapproval, Tom grabbed the man by his tunic and bent his knees. The first mate grunted as he hoisted the struggling little fat man and tossed him over the gunwale. Punga let out a strangled yell as he flew headfirst over the edge into the dark water below with a loud splash.

Jon turned to the other men to ask if there was anyone else dissatisfied with their punishment when a scream rent the air. Heart in his throat, he jumped to the side of the ship and looked over. When he saw the great, slimy black shapes churning the water red where Punga had been a moment earlier, the blood froze in his veins.

More screams and yells erupted as passengers and crew alike witnessed the creatures writhing in their feeding frenzy. Tom's hand on his shoulder broke Jon from his horrified trance, and he looked up at the first mate. He was sure that the shock on the big man's face was mirrored by his own.

"Weigh anchor. Now. The current should be enough... Now, go do it," he said hurriedly, but something stopped Tom before he took a step—a shower of small rocks clattered to the deck from above, and they both looked up in time to see a large chunk come loose from the cliff wall and crash into the water only feet from the boat. Jon realized that the creatures weren't their only problem.

Face bleak, he looked around; it was complete chaos along the deck as men and women ran around with nowhere to go, the sounds of their panic echoing and amplified by the high cliff walls to either side. As he watched, another piece of the cliffside broke free and slid into the water. Jon realized he had to get them quiet, but he remembered Ceara's fear about the myths of the mountains. There would be no pacifying them now. He turned back to Tom.

"Belay that last order. Get everyone below, Tom. Lock them in the bunkrooms. Place good, strong men with them," he yelled above the growing din. "We need to get this panic under control!"

"What the fuck are they?" shouted Tom, his face grim.

"Sharks? Sea serpents? I don't want to find out. But we have to shut everyone up or they'll bring down the mountain on our heads. Anyone panicking goes below, no exception."

Tom nodded quickly and turned to go, but before he could, Jon grabbed his arm.

"I meant to pull him back on board. I swear to gods, Tom, I didn't mean for him to die."

Tom's eyes softened, and he gave Jon's hand a quick squeeze before he pulled away to start rounding up passengers.

Jon watched him go, unsettled by the blatant doubt he had seen flash over the first mate's face.

≈

It took nearly a quarter hour to get the frightened Balorians secured away belowdecks. Once he was pretty sure there would be no more bloody excitement, Tom sent a few men to stand by the capstan; the wind had shifted, and the ship strained to be on its way. As he mounted the steps to the quarterdeck, he kept his eyes on Jon. The serious young man was looking over the charts at the bench; he would be helping the first mate to navigate the narrow channels once they were on their way.

Tom gave Jon a faint smile as he took his place behind the ship's wheel. Pitching the bastard overboard wasn't what was bothering him; the man's life or death hadn't concerned him in the least... though being ripped apart by those *things* sure made for a good tale to tell. No, it was the way that Jon's voice had taken on the same cold, precise tones that so often fell from Baltsaros's lips. Even his accent had changed a little. Tom shook his head and tightened his hands on the handles without a word.

"You're worried about me," said Jon softly.

Frowning, the first mate nodded, keeping his eyes forward.

"Don't be worried about me, Tom," said the young captain.

Chewing the inside of his cheek for a second, Tom nodded again.

"We ready?" he asked gruffly. He looked over at Jon and saw that he was staring at him with an odd expression on his face.

"I'm not turning into him," said Jon. "If that's what you're worried about."

Tom shrugged and turned the wheel a little back and forth, impatient to get going.

"Ye bloody sounded just like him, Jon."

When Jon reached for him, he wasn't expecting the sudden, sharp pain in his scalp as his fingers snarled a wicked handful of Tom's hair and tugged his head back. Jon brought his face close, his storm-grey eyes furious.

"You wanted me to be captain, so I am being captain. It is not easy for me, but I am fucking doing it the only way I know how," Jon growled through clenched teeth. "If you don't like it, you can go fuck yourself. And... What makes you think you can go behind my back and string up passengers without my say-so?"

Tom opened his mouth to speak, but Jon's hand tightened its hold, and he let out a pained grunt instead.

"The issue should have been brought to me first. Me. The *captain*. Isn't that how it works on this fucking ship? No. Instead you go around terrorizing people and then suddenly come dump the problem in my lap with no warning, putting me on the godsdamned spot to figure out what sort of punishment fits the crime. I had no idea what to say... Shit, how do you think that makes me look in front of the crew? Half of them still see me as some kind of fucking bed warmer for you and Baltsaros."

Jon gave Tom's head a little shake, and he winced.

"You need to work *with* me, Tom. Not against me. Godsdammit, you know Punga could have sat, not *hung*, in the brig for another day or two, and we could have taken care of things *together*. And, for hell's sake, you ass, of *course* I was going to pull him out of the water. I saw that look on your face, Tom. I'm not a godsdamned killer. I've killed three men now, and I'm pretty damned sure it's not going to become a hobby. I don't want to see you doubt me like that again. *Understand?*" He let go of Tom and stood glaring him.

Tom rubbed the back of his head.

"Yes, Cap'n," he said sedately with a small nod. Then Tom let the grin he'd been holding back curve his lips and cocked his head. "Feel better?"

Jon's face creased into a sheepish smile, and he chuckled, nodding.

"Much," he confessed. "Gods, I am not cut out for this shit."

Tom shook his head.

"Naw, love. I think yer doin' just fine. Yer bloody right, ye know. I should stop worryin' about you so much, and I should'a come to ye the second that red-haired witch came to see me."

"Ceara came to you?" Jon heaved a sigh and raked both his hands through his mess of curls. "Argh! Fuck. Ok. I'll take care of her too. If she's trying to win me over, she sure as hells is taking the wrong path. I can't stand the idea that people would take things like this into their own hands rather than bother me. Bother me, for fuck's sake. I know I'm stressed as fuck, but bloody hells, how else am I going to learn?"

Tom grinned wider at Jon's increased use of profanity.

Jon furrowed his brow and leaned forward, his blue eyes dark in the dying sunlight as he studied Tom for a long moment. When he finally spoke, his voice was low and intimate.

"What? You think this is amusing? Just so you know, if you get us through these mountains in one piece, I plan on using you so thoroughly that the only words left to you will be *please* and *more*."

The first mate blinked, taken by a sudden pulse of heat when his heart kicked up in surprise. He laughed and Jon smiled back a little wolfishly.

"Aye, aye, sir," Tom said and eagerly grabbed the ship's wheel again.

With men positioned at the bow and along both sides of the ship, holding oars and long boat hooks to push away from the rocks should they get too close, Jon hollered down the orders to wind the capstan so they could be off. As soon as the anchor lifted from the seabed, the *Heart* moved forward, driven by the strong wind and current.

Hands tight on the wheel's handles, Tom took a deep breath and said a stupid little prayer under his voice, hoping for the best. As they passed between the black cliffs, it felt like being entombed. The high walls to either side of the ship blocked out most of the sky, leaving only a narrow, dark-blue ribbon above them. The lights at the front of the ship, though shining brighter than any lantern could have, seemed swallowed by the dark; Tom could see next to nothing.

Beneath his feet, the ship barely moved, so still was the water they sailed through. However, he could almost feel the pull of the strong undercurrent, as they were pushed further and further into a silent world hedged in by the massive cliffs. Next to him, Jon shuffled through a few pages, seemingly unaffected by the oppressive gloom around them.

"I wish there was a better sense of scale," Jon muttered to himself as he held a diagram up to the lantern he'd placed on the bench.

"What's Ceara say?" asked Tom.

"Hasn't actually been through this before. Just knows about it... or at least knew where all these maps were kept. Gah... What in hells does this one even mean?" Jon furrowed his brow and peered closer at the page in his hand.

Tom shrugged and tried to brush off his jitters. When he looked to the side, at first he saw absolutely nothing, but when something glittered and his eyes quickly refocused, he realized the walls were a lot bloody closer than he'd assumed. He squinted at the shimmer and was startled when he realized they were eyes: thousands of little, shining eyes watching him silently from nooks and crannies in the mountainside. Even though he knew they were birds or small, harmless critters, they gave him the heebie-jeebies.

"Port! Port!"

Tom easily heard the call from the bow before it was relayed back to the quarterdeck, the night was so quiet around them.

"That's the first fork," said Jon, holding up a page. "About thirty degrees before we can straighten out again."

Nodding, Tom spun the wheel while the men pulled the braces to turn the yards slightly. The ship reacted quickly, like she too was in a hurry to be out of the narrow passes.

"Good. Ok, we go back starboard for a while after this. Then there is a section where—hang on..." Jon flipped through some more drawings. "Yeah. There's a section where it'll be a really tight squeeze. The ships coming through here are not as wide as *Baal's Heart*, but we should make it."

Tom tightened his jaw at the use of the word *should* but just gave another curt nod, staring off into the black hells. It would take them the entire night to get through the rift in the mountain range. If he made an error and they found themselves still between the walls at sunup when the wind would die out, it would mean having to spend the entire next day anchored in the squeeze, waiting until the wind turned their way again.

Narrowing his eyes, Tom gritted his teeth and prepared for the next turn. There was no fucking way they were going to spend a whole day trapped in the black mountains.

Nearly ten hours later, dead on his feet and shoulders aching from what felt like a thousand turns of the ship's wheel, Tom watched the grey skies lighten over the water with a smile. They had made it through the rift without a single mishap and, bugger it all, it actually felt a little like a letdown. All night, the crew had acted as a tight unit, helping him to get through the winding forks easily. Even Ceara had been a help deciphering the maps in the end and had made sure deckhands brought Jon and him a little grub and drink to brighten the gloom somewhat.

With a yawn that threatened to dislocate his jaw, Tom scratched at his chest and looked over at Jon who sat drinking a mug of warmed, sweet wine.

"Piece o' cake," said the first mate with a grin.

Jon nodded and smiled tiredly.

"Piece of cake," he agreed.

Tom felt a few cool drops pepper his face and squinted at the clouds. It was a light drizzle for now, but it looked like the sky would open up and they'd get soaked. As if to confirm his suspicions, lightning flashed bright right then.

He called out for the men to pack up the bulbs and stow the electricity machines belowdeck before they got too wet. Then Harris could take over, and he and Jon could finally go rest their weary heads. Tom sank to his knees in front of the bench and placed his hands on Jon's thighs, smiling up at the tired young captain.

Jon let out a soft sigh and reached for Tom; his palm, heated from the mug, was warm against the first mate's cheek.

"I know I keep saying it, but I *need* you," Jon murmured with a small frown. "But, I don't need your fucking worry. I need *guidance*. I need you by my side... Just like you were this whole night."

"Aye, love," rumbled Tom. "I'm here now."

～

Never leave my side again. Words spoken by Baltsaros a million years earlier when hope had been a new and shining thing. Jon suddenly felt old. He closed his eyes for a moment, burying his thoughts. When he opened them again, he saw that Tom was just watching him quietly, his blue-green eyes somewhat sleepy and red-rimmed... completely guileless. Jon stroked Tom's rain-wet cheek with his thumb and then trailed his fingertips along a scar that followed the line of his brow bone and bisected his sandy-blond eyebrow. He'd never asked where Tom had gotten the scar but thought he was probably better off not knowing. Jon had stopped asking about the marks that ran the length of Tom's body when he realized that most of them came with a story of abuse that soured his stomach. The fact that they were always delivered with a wry smirk and a show of indifference made Jon feel even worse. The things that Tom had been through... He couldn't even imagine it.

"What's the sad look, love?" asked Tom, moving his hands up Jon's thighs to clasp him around the waist.

The big man stared up at him, and Jon thought again just how remarkable it was that Tom was *his*. His to share, of course, but still. He shook his head and smiled, taking hold of the first mate's head to pull him up for a kiss.

However, the moment was shattered when Ceara came running up the stairs, a look of worry on her freckled face. Tom scowled at the interruption, pulling away from Jon.

"Bloody hells, what the fuck is it now?"

CHAPTER 8
THE DEVIL YOU KNOW

Baltsaros woke with a groan, blinking away dreams he didn't understand. The light was dim, and the floor beneath him rocked as if the waves were chopped up by a strong wind. Shakily, he got to his feet and looked out of the porthole. The sky was dark with ominous clouds, and the glass was speckled with rain or seawater.

Baltsaros glanced around the empty room and frowned; he was thirsty but his cup was empty. Curling his hands around the cold iron bars, he stared at the icebox for a long moment. There was a pitcher of water in there. Cold water to soothe his parched throat. Baltsaros sighed and looked at the door to the stateroom. He'd promised himself he wouldn't but...

His fingers found the small catch, and he pressed down on it while pushing up on the other corner of the lock where there was a second, tiny button. There was a click, and the door swung easily on its oiled hinges. Having orchestrated his own mutiny, Baltsaros had thought it wise to put something into the design of the cage should he find himself made the occupant. He was, at least for the moment, thankful his memory of the lock's fail-safe had returned.

Baltsaros slipped out of the cage and quickly opened the icebox, pouring himself a cup of cold water. He was on his second glass when suddenly he was pitched against the table by an especially jarring wave. The metal cup fell from his hand, and it bounced to the floor, rolling away. Unbalanced, he grasped the sides of the table.

Have to get back to the cage, he thought. The cold water sat strangely in his gut, making him a little nauseous. There was a low laugh and Baltsaros looked up. Ah'puch grinned at him from the shadows, the handle of Jon's knife sticking out from his chest.

Oh gods, not now.

"You're dead," choked Baltsaros, his fingers curled into claws on the wood as he leaned forward over the table. "Go back to the black hells!"

"Do you really think that soft little creature you keep in your bed could have killed me? Do you really think that?" laughed the emperor. His face was pale as the moon, drained of blood. Blood that was now on Jon's hands.

"Oh... Of course he could, don't be stupid," hissed the beast as he stepped out from the dark. "When we're done with him, he won't be able to stop killing and killing and killing again. You'll have ruined him, Baltsaros. Doesn't innocence taste good?"

"No," he whispered. He had to find Jon. Protect him somehow. Warn him. Baltsaros felt hot bile in his throat and nearly gagged.

"Well, what are you going to do then?" asked the beast with a rasping chuckle. It wrapped its hand around the dagger in Ah'puch's chest and yanked on it. Fresh blood poured down the man's shirt and over the carpet. The floor yawed beneath Baltsaros's feet, and he clung to the table like a man drowning.

"Oh ho... But you'll have to get to him before I do," said the beast and licked the blood from the knife with its long tongue. *Hungry.* The emperor looked on with a crazed, gory smile.

"Oh my, We think that may be a good idea," agreed Ah'puch. "We think you need to get to Jon. To kill him. Kill him, Baltsaros. *Kill him* before he kills you."

No. No, that's not right, thought Baltsaros; his hand scrabbled over the surface of the table, closing over the dagger that lay there. *No. I need to kill Jon before I destroy who he is.*

Yes, that was much better.

Baltsaros stumbled across the empty room and grasped the door. He opened it a crack and looked beyond. When he saw that there was no one close by, he left quickly.

The deck rocked beneath his feet, but Baltsaros had regained his footing. Shivering from the cold wind and rain, he peered up the stairs and thought he saw the silhouette of two men on the quarterdeck. If Tom was up there, sinking a dagger into Jon would prove to be difficult. He would simply have to kill them both... But something was nagging at him.

He felt nauseous again and blinked rainwater out of his eyes.

What am I doing? He looked at the dagger in his hand. In the murky light, he could see that rain was washing away the blood on it. Blood from where? His hands were covered in it.

Out of the corner of his eye, he saw movement, but when he turned, he saw it was only a swaying, dark lantern. A second later, lightning crackled across the sky and was reflected in the four panes of glass of the lantern. *Four lights.* Baltsaros moaned and stepped backwards, his mind closing in on itself. Escape. He needed to escape.

"No more," he whimpered. "I can't take any more pain. Please."

Four lights above his head, the cold metal table beneath his body.

In a panic, he turned and ran, pushing men out of his way.

Have to get belowdecks, he thought. *Have to get away from... Ah'puch? Romas?*

The fact that he did not know terrified him.

He reached the trapdoor and hauled it open, stumbling down the narrow, steep stairs into the dark passageway below. He turned and in another flash of lightning saw *it*. The machine.

Pain.

Pain.

Pain.

Electricity like hot knives burning into his skin, into his brain. Chasing him like a beast in his own mind, pulling shriek after shriek from him as it worked to rob him of all coherent thought and destroy his body. The nausea crested in Baltsaros again, and he retched, staggering backwards in the dark. He had to get away.

Cries. Darkness. More lightning. Blood.

He waved the dagger in front of him, trying to fend off the monsters real or imagined that crowded him into a corner. His back against the wall, Baltsaros howled his pain.

"I don't want to kill!" he shouted. "Please don't make me do it!"

Red hands, red feet, sharpened teeth, and fists that beat. How they laughed...

Like an egg cracking and spilling its yolk, Baltsaros's mind suddenly let free the memories it had kept locked away for so long. With a low moan, he felt himself collapse, the dagger clattering to the floor as the truth of his past came back to him.

~

Tom held his hand out to stop anyone from coming forward. He glanced over at Jon and saw that he had gone down on one knee to examine Baltsaros. They'd followed Ceara down and discovered the captain muttering to himself and waving a bloody dagger as he paced frantically back and forth in the galley. Then, with a cry that chilled Tom's blood, the fight had gone out of the older man, and he had fallen down in a heap.

Baltsaros sat staring at his hands, oblivious to the crowd that had formed around him.

"Get the fuck out of here, ye cunts!" Tom yelled. "And close the bloody door!"

In embarrassed silence, the crew filed quickly out of the room, leaving Jon and Tom with the stricken man. Everyone would now know the damnable truth of Baltsaros's condition. Jon rose slowly to his feet and put his hand on Tom's shoulder.

"I'll keep everyone away," said Jon. "And I'll get the Balorians abovedeck to see with their own eyes that we haven't sailed into the afterworld." He chuckled, but there was no humour in it. "I have captain-y things to do."

"What about Da?" asked Tom.

"I think the less people the better. And... well... He doesn't trust himself around me. I'm starting to realize that he probably never has," said Jon a little sadly with a shrug. "Just... I don't know... Watch him. He trusts you, Tom." He squeezed Tom's shoulder and furrowed his brow. "Or... Do you think you can't handle him? Do you need me to send Saban down?"

Tom shook his head.

"Naw, love. Yer right. I'll be fine with Da. I'll get him back to his cage as soon as I can."

Jon nodded tiredly, and Tom watched him go, closing the door behind him.

Looking down at Baltsaros, he saw that there was more blood on the man than before. With a frown, he swiped a few of Cook's clean towels and sank down cross-legged in front of the captain. He started tearing the white cloth into strips as Baltsaros watched him quietly.

"It's my blood, isn't it?" he asked.

"Aye, it's yer fuckin' blood, ye daft bugger," grunted Tom. "Where the fuck did ye get the knife, Da? Who let you out of the cage?"

Baltsaros smiled, but it didn't reach his eyes.

"I let myself out. That cage was meant to hold others, not me. As for the knife? I... think someone may have left it on the table. I honestly can't tell you."

Tom reached for Baltsaros's arm and turned it. There were slices along the inside of it, right over the scar that he had made with Jon. With a shake of his head, the first mate set to work bandaging up the mess as best as he could; thankfully, it didn't look like stitches were needed. He glanced up and saw that Baltsaros's dark eyes were on him, but there was no hint of insanity in them. Just sadness.

"Da, what happened?" he asked gently as he tucked in the edge of the towel.

Baltsaros took his arm back and smiled appreciatively at Tom's handiwork.

"You've got skilled hands," said Baltsaros. He then leaned back against the wall and rubbed his face, like a man weary beyond words.

Tom picked the dagger up off the floor and stared at it. He recognized it as the dagger he had given Jon. Noticing something on the handle, he frowned; there were three notches carved into the wood, one of them fresh.

Bloody hells, Jon, he thought, the small knot in his gut tightening. *And ye wonder why I worry...*

Wrinkling his brow, he looked back up at Baltsaros, but he had closed his eyes and seemed lost in thought. As Tom waited for him to break the silence, he took up a piece of towel and began to wipe the blade clean.

~

Baltsaros opened his eyes and saw that the room had lightened. It looked like the rainstorm had passed and had been replaced by a weak afternoon sun shining through the portholes. When he shifted, his arm throbbed and he grimaced. For once, he could clearly remember everything that had happened.

Sitting on the floor with his back against the freestanding counter was Tom, turning something over in his hands as he whistled low to himself. When he felt Baltsaros watching him, Tom looked up, the amusement in his green-blue eyes barely hiding his concern.

"Ye fell asleep," accused the first mate with a cheeky grin. It looked forced.

Baltsaros smiled.

"I'm sorry I fell asleep on you, Tom."

"Look," said the first mate, holding up the turnip he had been carving. "It's a cock."

Baltsaros laughed and shook his head. Sure enough, the turnip looked like a very squat, erect penis, complete with a suggestion of testicles at its base. It was utterly ludicrous, but so comfortingly Tom. The first mate smiled wide, looking a little more relaxed. However, when he put the turnip down, his face grew serious. On hands and knees, he approached Baltsaros and settled closer.

With a groan, Baltsaros pulled himself away from the wall to stretch his shoulders. However, despite being sore from sleeping against the wall, seated on the hard floor of the galley, he felt more rested than he had for the past month. It was good.

"How long was I out?" he asked.

" 'Bout an hour or so," replied the first mate. "D'ye feel like talkin' to me now?"

Baltsaros shook his head slowly.

"I don't know," he admitted. "I've remembered something, but it's a little too... raw to talk about. I'm not even letting myself think about it too much for fear that I'll be spun into another episode like the one that landed me here to make a complete spectacle of myself in front of the crew." It was the truth. Even letting himself brush the edges of these new memories brought a sense of deep dread unlike anything he had ever felt. The memory was back, but he could not yet use it.

"Though, I think I understand the danger facing Jon now," he continued. Tom's brows pinched together in concern, and Baltsaros watched the first mate's eyes grow wary.

"Jon was right. I've been holding on to a... belief that I am naturally morally corrupt. A killer by accident of birth," he said slowly. The words felt odd to say. "Something *evil* as he put it."

Tom snorted, but Baltsaros shook his head.

"I'm being serious, Tom. I... know now where it stems from."

"Is it about *red hands*?" the burly pirate asked quietly.

Baltsaros winced and took a deep breath, looking away. Too much pain.

"Sorry, Da," said Tom, reaching out to clasp his uninjured arm.

Baltsaros sighed at the warmth of his touch and placed his hand over Tom's rough one, patting it.

"However, Jon was obviously wrong in his assurance that I would not try to kill him again," Baltsaros continued. He couldn't remember trying to suffocate Jon, but the bruises around the younger man's neck had haunted him for days. "Seems I keep trying for him because, for some reason, my subconscious has decided that killing Jon is preferable to killing his innocence."

"Subconss...?" Tom's frown deepened.

"Ah... There's no word for it in Common, I'm afraid. In the north we use it to mean the part of us that brings us dreams. Thoughts hidden from ourselves that speak truths. Understand?"

620

"Aye," mumbled Tom. "So, we're to continue keepin' ye from killin' Jon? Ye know, the lad's not near as innocent as yer damn head thinks he is, Da." The first mate looked exhausted as he pulled his hand away to scrub at his face.

"Yes, I'm aware. I'm trying to keep that in mind," said Baltsaros. He frowned at Tom as the first mate blinked his reddened eyes, knuckling the corner of one as he sighed softly. "What's wrong with you? You look like you've been up all night."

Tom let out a laugh and clapped his hands to his knees, leaning forward with a weak grin.

"Aye, that I have. Bloody dog-tired. Shall we get ye back to yer cage so I can get some shut-eye? Oh hells…" Tom's forehead creased as he climbed to his feet and helped Baltsaros to stand. "Keepin' ye in there ain't gonna work, is it?"

Baltsaros shook his head with a smile.

"I'm afraid not," he replied. "But I'm sure you and Jon can come up with something to keep this 'daft bugger' from killing anyone or cutting himself up again."

Tom winced, and Baltsaros reached out to smack his cheek playfully.

"But, you ever call me *daft* again, or any variation thereof, I will dedicate myself to reacquainting you with the definition of *obedience*. Have I made myself clear?"

With a wry grin, Tom ducked his chin.

"Aye, Da," he replied. "Gods, I've missed ye."

Baltsaros chuckled. There was still a long road to recovery ahead, but he felt something he hadn't felt in a long time: hope.

CHAPTER 9

NO REST FOR THE WICKED

The voyage of discovery is not in seeking new landscapes but in having new eyes.

— MARCEL PROUST

Tom squinted in disbelief at the tiny catches on the iron lock and shook his head.

"Yer fuckin' tellin' me that I sat like a bloody dog in this godsdamned thing for six bloody months—"

"Five," Baltsaros corrected him.

"Five bloody months and I could'a let myself out at any time?" He looked over at the bed where Jon was busy with Baltsaros. Since they couldn't keep him in the cage any longer, and Punga's cronies occupied the brig, Jon had suggested that they just tie Baltsaros up; the captain had laughed and offered up his wrists with an amused twist of his lips.

Tom grinned at the look of concentration on Jon's face and let out an exaggerated sigh.

"Fuckin' hells, lovey," he chided, walking up to the bed. "When are ye gonna learn how to tie a bloody half-decent knot?"

"Hey, it's not that bad," said Jon, but when he went to tighten the knot he had made, it fell apart. "Ok. Maybe it is. What did I do wrong?"

Baltsaros smiled patiently and settled back more comfortably on the bed; he almost seemed like his old self.

"Here, let me." Tom took the tangled hempen rope from Jon and climbed up onto the soft mattress. Doubling the length over in his hands, he quickly wove a clove hitch on a bight around Baltsaros's wrist, careful to avoid the bandaged cuts. As Tom reached for his other arm, he saw that Baltsaros watched him closely.

Tom started to feel strangely shy with the man's dark eyes on him, and he realized it had been a long time since he and the captain had been so close; it was almost overwhelmingly intimate. Fumbling the rope, he dropped the loose end on the older man's chest.

"Sorry," he mumbled, keeping his eyes on his task.

"Don't tell me that you're suddenly unable to knot a rope too?" said Baltsaros, clearly amused.

Tom just scowled, but he'd been bound so often by the man that tying him up in return felt absolutely foreign. It was making his fingers clumsy.

It was also making him bloody horny; by the time Tom had finished tying up Baltsaros's arms, his pulse was thrumming in his ears, and he felt hot and tense.

When he glanced up, he saw that Baltsaros looked subtly amused. There was something else in his gaze too: lust. Then, when Baltsaros let out a small noise and shifted slightly, closing his eyes, Tom looked over in surprise and saw that Jon had lifted up the bound man's shirt and was stroking down the line of his pelvis with his fingertips, teasing at the waistband of his pants. Trust Jon to grasp the mood of the captain before he did.

As he watched, Jon leaned forward and kissed Baltsaros's hip bone, eliciting another quiet sound from the man. But, when Jon raised his blue-grey eyes to Tom's, he looked a tad unsure, as if he were waiting for the first mate to do something.

"Tom? Come here." Baltsaros's voice was quiet, and Tom turned to look at him. All exhaustion was gone from his system and his cock, already primed from embarrassed arousal, started pressing against the material of his pants. However, Tom faltered a moment with an exaggerated grin built on nerves; he hadn't felt this awkward since that first time.

~

Tom paced the dark corridor. His ire had brought him right to the captain's chambers but had sputtered out somewhat, leaving him unable to open the door. As he made another pass in front of the rooms, Tom shook his head and muttered to himself as he rubbed a hand over his shaggy, dirty-blond hair.

"Fuckin' Abetha and her fuckin' bloody uppity fuckin'..." he said, trying to rekindle the outrage that had brought him to Baltsaros's door in the dead of night. He swivelled on his heel to come back about and, fists clenched, he bowed his head and rested it against the dark wood of the door.

It was the way Abetha always *looked* at him, like he was the scum of the world. The way she constantly corrected his speech. And what about the utter and total lack of remorse over his ten fucking years as a slave? She was his bloody *mother*, the cold cunt. That they—her and his yellow-belly of a father—had given up on him after so little effort. Shit, all those long nights... poor little boy crying and praying himself to sleep... just wanting to go *home*.

Tom let out a slow breath, the anger in his belly growing.

And then, since his father had stretched his own neck like the bloody coward he was, the fucking captain had married his "poor", widowed mother. That was a fucking laugh. Tom pressed his palms to the wood and smiled a bitter smile. Well, that wasn't going so shit hot, was it? Tom had bloody made sure of it. The little birds that whispered into Abetha's ear about the captain's conquests and appetites had been costly, but it was working. Baltsaros now slept alone.

Lying in bed earlier, restless and brimming with rancorous feelings, Tom had thought about how, if he beguiled his way into the captain's bed and won him over with lust, the sham of a marriage would be over.

Then why couldn't he bring himself to open the door?

After pushing away from it, he resumed pacing. He had never seduced someone before. Had never wanted to. Sex held almost zero appeal for him.

But, there *had* been those dreams. Tom stroked the hollow of his stubbled cheek as he glanced at the door. Nothing concrete, nothing too specific. Baltsaros's long legs coming towards him... the way the black leather hugged the muscles of his thighs and the bulge between them. The hint of a wicked, dark smile. Tom was only ever partially clothed in the dreams and when the captain's large hands reached for him, he felt *good*. Good enough that he would often wake with a mess to deal with. The thought made him grin a little. The captain *was* an attractive man—that was a fact. Tall, muscular, and broad-shouldered, he was like a handsome storybook hero come to life. Except this hero's dark eyes sometimes betrayed the cold savagery he was capable of, even if his lips lied with their graceful smile. And yet... There were the incredible kindnesses he had bestowed on Tom: saving him, fixing him up, making him whole again, and giving him purpose.

Straightening his shoulders, Tom decided that if he didn't do it now, he'd never be able to.

The door opened quietly on its hinges, and Tom made his way across the darkened room and through the second door within. Beyond, he could make out the large four-poster bed and hear Baltsaros breathing deep in slumber. Tom tugged his shirt up and over his head, pausing to undo and kick off his pants before he circled to the side of the bed, his heart hammering. Quiet as a snake, he slipped under the cool covers and heard the captain stir in his sleep. Slowly, Tom reached for him. When his hand encountered bare skin, he nearly pulled away. He hadn't expected the captain to sleep naked.

That makes it easier, don't it? he thought. He slid further down the mattress and under the sheets, moving closer. The captain was on his side facing him, and it took Tom no time to find his cock. When he lifted the soft thing and sucked gently it into his mouth, he felt Baltsaros start awake. Doubt flared up in Tom for a heart-stopping second; what if the captain rejected him? He had only heard from others that Baltsaros liked men as well as women... But what if they were wrong? However, when the captain's hand found the back of Tom's head and didn't pause before pressing into him harder with a groan, he relaxed a little; he knew there was no mistaking him for a woman.

As the heavy organ in his mouth began to stiffen against his tongue, he tightened his lips near the root of it. When he reached up to grab the captain's hip, the man's skin was soft and sleep-warm against Tom's hand. Eyes closed, Tom thought he could do this. It wasn't so bad. The captain smelled clean yet musky, and the way his fingers stroked his head and neck felt... nice. Still, he wondered how long it would take to get him off.

Baltsaros's cock was big but, Tom thought with a sardonic, inward smile, nothing he couldn't handle. He started moving with more purpose, letting the muscles of his throat relax so he could take in more of the hard length. What he got in response was a deep groan, and he pulled himself closer, wrapping his arm around the captain's waist as the man thrust himself against Tom. Soon, between the cock in his mouth and the smothering blankets, Tom started to feel a little lightheaded. He stretched his arm up to push aside the covers but was startled when the captain suddenly grabbed him by the hair and pulled his head back. Tom clutched at Baltsaros's hand, but the captain wouldn't release him. The blanket was lifted away.

"What are you doing in my bed, Tom?" asked Baltsaros, staring down at him, his features barely visible in the gloom of the bedchamber. However, there was a smile in his voice. "And sucking me off with such consummate skill, I might add..."

Before Tom could reply, Baltsaros rolled over on top of him and, straddling his neck, he forced his cock back into Tom's mouth and further down his throat for a few thrusts. This wasn't turning out the way Tom had planned. Nausea began to rise in his gut; he felt the tiniest flutter of panic at being trapped but kept himself from biting down.

What a fucking stupid bloody idea, he thought, realizing that he'd have to shove the captain off and scupper whatever good will that had grown between them. *Forget being part of the bloody crew now.* Tom knew he had lost the upper hand. He couldn't stomach the thought of slaving under another man again, and this was no different, not a fucking bit different from any other time.

Then, all of a sudden, it was.

With a small moan, the captain pulled his cock from Tom's mouth and crawled backwards, pushing Tom's thighs apart and covering his body with his own. Burying his face in the side of Tom's neck, he bit gently and then brushed his lips softly against his skin. Tom closed his eyes and frowned at the resulting shiver.

"Ah, you gorgeous brute..." murmured Baltsaros, his voice a warm purr in Tom's ear. "You have no idea how ridiculously tempting you are, do you?" He chuckled and closed his hand loosely around Tom's throat. Using his thumb, he pushed Tom's jaw up, opening his neck to more bites... harder this time. "I don't normally fuck my crew —business should never bunk with pleasure—but I cannot lie and say that I haven't thought about you naked and willing in my bed." The captain kissed the rim of his ear, making the hair on Tom's neck prickle before he moved his tongue to the soft area below it. "Often, I must confess."

Tom let out a shaky exhale. The words and the focused attention to sensitive skin made him feel really strange. Like in his dreams.

Shivering again in the captain's grasp, he furrowed his brow and brought his hands up to clasp Baltsaros's waist. With surprise, Tom realized he was getting hard against the older man's belly.

Baltsaros's teeth closed on his neck again, this time with some real pain, but it felt good. Experimentally, Tom let out a shy little noise to show the captain he was enjoying himself, and Baltsaros laughed huskily against the side of his neck before biting again with more force. When it sent a jolt of pleasure straight to his groin, Tom groaned and shifted his hips slightly, eager for some friction on his stiff cock.

The captain pulled back, going up on one elbow to scrutinise him for a moment.

"What I do?" Tom asked warily, eyes narrowed. Suddenly nervous and exposed, he thought about ending whatever this was and telling the captain to piss off and go fuck some other wretched thing. Tom would then go drink himself sick on his mother's too-sweet wine and try to find his own way off this fucking island. However, when the older man stroked back Tom's hair and then slid his thumb along the side of his neck, he felt his breath catch in his throat.

With a little tilt of his head, the captain shifted his hand and pressed his thumb hard into the spot right below the corner of Tom's jaw. The pain was sharp and immediate, and Tom let out a grunt of surprise, but the pressure stopped only a few moments later. Baltsaros ducked his head to lick at the area instead; his tongue felt soft against his skin and left cool traces behind.

A helpless whimper escaped Tom's lips at the sensation, and he tightened his hold on the captain. His cock was a fucking iron bar trapped between them.

"Didn't that hurt?" asked Baltsaros.

Hurt? Tom blinked. Yes... but... He just shook his head, not trusting himself to explain what he was feeling.

"Interesting," mused Baltsaros.

Closing his eyes, Tom felt confused and slightly embarrassed by his body's reaction. However, when Baltsaros found Tom's nipple and pinched it hard, the noise that came from deep in his chest sounded raw, needy. Then the captain bit at it with sharp teeth, and Tom couldn't help but let out a full-throated groan of pleasure.

"You like that?" asked the captain.

Tom's nipple throbbed. Eyes still tightly closed, he nodded quickly, trembling.

"I want to hear you say it." Baltsaros's voice was quiet, confident.

Startled, Tom opened his eyes. *Say it?* He felt a rush of heat in his face. When the captain lifted himself off Tom a moment later and reached down past his cock to grab his balls in a long-fingered hand, Tom's heart began to race.

"Say it, Tom," purred the captain. Tom let out another hitched breath and then a low moan as Baltsaros squeezed his sack, sending more pain and pleasure coursing through him.

626

How could he say it? The pain became intense, and he nearly yelled out. He had spent the last decade being forced to do things against his will; he wasn't about to submit to something he didn't want to do.

But that's it, isn't it? The realization made him groan, shaking him with more than the physical agony inflicted on him. The fucking truth was that he *wanted* to do it.

"Yes," he finally choked out. "Aye. Yes." The pressure on his balls decreased for half a heartbeat before Baltsaros squeezed again.

"Yes, what?"

Tom bucked up from the bed, his eyes clenched tight and heart like a crazed animal trying to burst from his chest.

"Yes!" he cried out. "Yes, I like it!"

"There we go," chuckled Baltsaros, easing up on his brutal hold. "Just like that. That wasn't so bad, was it?" Tom panted and strained up against the captain as the older man began to stroke his cock slowly with a sure hand. He was lost in the sensation. Tom had never felt this sort of desire before; it was overwhelming.

"Yes, you're perfectly exquisite. A handsome tomcat just begging for a firm hand to tame you, hm?" murmured the captain. "Oh, my boy, I think we will have a lot of fun, you and I."

～

Tom stretched himself out next to Baltsaros as the captain closed his eyes and let out a soft sigh; Jon had undone the laces of his black pants and was kissing his way across newly exposed skin.

The first mate couldn't help but notice how much Baltsaros had aged since he had first rescued him; the creases at the corners of his eyes were now deeply etched and the lines next to his mouth more pronounced. It was to the former that Tom bestowed his first light kiss as he leaned over, the skin soft and thin against his lips. Baltsaros sighed, submitting to the gentle treatment, and Tom smiled wider. Older, but no less handsome. He moved further down, kissing the man's sharp cheekbone, and then continued along the curve of his strong jaw. Baltsaros's stubble was rough on his lips, and Tom let his tongue slide over the short bristles as he pressed his kisses into his skin. When he made his way to Baltsaros's neck, he smiled again; Baltsaros lifted his chin, leaning into him with a low, pleased growl, his pulse strong and fast against Tom's mouth.

When Jon made a small noise and Baltsaros's breath hitched in his chest, Tom pulled away and looked over. The dark-haired young man held Baltsaros's hard cock in his hand, but his brow was knotted as he stared at it, motionless. It was obvious why—though healed, Baltsaros's length was crisscrossed in shiny, taut pink scars from the abuse he had suffered.

"Shit, Da," said Tom, scowling.

"Does it hurt?" asked Jon quietly.

Baltsaros's laugh rang out, startling the first mate.

"No. No... not really. But, Jon, even if it did," Baltsaros replied with a grin, "I'd never forgive you if you stopped." He lifted his torso a little, looping his bound wrists up over Tom's head to pull him back down again.

"I was enjoying that," murmured Baltsaros, his face serious and dark gaze locked on Tom. "Kiss me again."

Tom felt a tightness in his ribs that spread up his sides and crept up his neck as he stared back. Heart thudding in his chest, he leaned in and pressed his lips to the corner of Baltsaros's mouth. He was startled when Baltsaros turned his head and captured Tom's mouth fully.

All timidity left Tom as he opened his mouth to the kiss; breathing into it, he curled his hands under Baltsaros's head, the long strands of his hair snagging on his rough fingers in his fervour to deepen the kiss. Baltsaros groaned into his mouth and Tom quested out with his tongue; finding his eagerness matched, he let out a small sound of his own. They didn't often kiss this way, and it made him feel both wanted and desperate for more at once. However, when Baltsaros tensed, he quickly pulled back, breathless. Tom saw that he had an almost pained expression on his face and turned to see that Jon was slowly running his tongue along the scarred skin of his cock.

Baltsaros let out a shaky breath.

"The scarring makes me more sensitive than I'm used to," he said with a tight smile. "Pair that with the fact that I haven't ejaculated in a very long time. Ahh..." Baltsaros closed his eyes, his body trembling. Panting a few short breaths, he lifted his head and looked past Tom to where Jon had begun to slide his hand along his shaft while his mouth worked the head of his cock. "Well, I'm afraid it won't take much."

"That's fine, Da," said Tom with a grin and shifted his hand so he could run a thumb along the older man's cheek. "Just relax and let Jon make ye cum. Then, we're all gonna sleep right here like old times, and in the mornin' we'll do it again. If yer up to it."

Baltsaros let out a chuckle that ended on a low, needy gasp. In reply, he just nodded his head.

Tom leaned in to kiss him again, slowly and deeply until the body beneath him shuddered. When Baltsaros came, he turned his head to cry out, but his arms held Tom against him, possessive and thankful.

Tom lay on his side watching Baltsaros sleep. Jon was passed out, curled up against the older man's other side, completely dead to the world. Blearily, the first mate rubbed his face. He hadn't slept in a long time, but he couldn't let himself doze off now. He didn't want to wake to find Baltsaros strangling Jon in his sleep, no matter how sane the captain had seemed earlier. He reached out and touched the back of Baltsaros's hand, testing to make sure that the binds were not too tight. Tom figured he'd lie there just a little while longer, until he couldn't keep his eyes open anymore, and then would ask Saban to watch over them while they slept. That or he and Jon could take turns. Tom let out a yawn that creaked his jaw and turned onto his back. After sliding a hand beneath the waistband of his pants, he scratched lazily at his balls and pinched the loose skin of his limp cock; even his pecker was too exhausted to perk up. Stroking it softly, he wondered whether trying to wake it up was worth it.

There was a rapid knock at the door, and he sat up with a groan, annoyed at the disturbance. He quickly draped a small throw over Baltsaros and Jon and padded to the door. When he opened it quietly, he was surprised to see one of the younger deckhands, flushed and wide-eyed with excitement on the other side.

"Ship," panted the boy. "Ship off port bow. Two sails, but all-a bristlin' with guns like a bleedin' hell's warship and flyin' the cross n' crown. They seen us, sir. Comin' right for us, almighty."

Tom clenched his jaw in frustration; it didn't look like he'd get rest any time soon.

"Aye," he grumbled. "Go feed the bloody chase guns. And the portside sixteeners. Run like a devil's after ye, lad. I'll be deckside in a jiff."

He turned back and saw that Jon watched him sleepily from the bed, a worried expression on his face.

"What is it?" he asked, his voice hoarse.

"Just our fuckin' luck, ducky," growled Tom. "It's the royal bloody navy."

CHAPTER 10
PLUNDER

Through his binoculars, Jon watched the ship—what Tom had called a *ketch*—coming towards them. He lowered the double spyglass and looked over at Tom. The first mate stood with him at the bow, glowering like a storm cloud as he chewed on the end of his slender cigar.

"We can't come about?" he asked with a frown.

Tom shook his head and then passed his hand over his eyes tiredly.

"Nay," said the first mate. "Fuckers'll be on us before we can run. If they catch the same wind, we're beat for sure. They're smaller and faster than us, love."

Jon's heart felt like it was lodged in his throat.

"So your solution is that we face them head-on?" he replied. "I thought we were outgunned."

"Aye, that we are," said Tom with a scowl but didn't offer anything else. When he saw Jon's bleak stare, his green-blue eyes narrowed coolly at him.

"Ye got a better fuckin' plan, Jon?" he growled, smoke trickling from his nostrils.

"No! I don't! You know I don't have a fucking clue about sea battles. I've never been in one, only read about them."

"Then keep yer bloody mouth shut n' leave me to it."

Jon stared at the first mate, offended and hurt at once. He felt completely useless, and Tom was being unnecessarily harsh. His stomach churned as he wondered for the hundredth time why they had made him captain if he was just going to be a puppet.

"It's almost sundown," he said. "Isn't there some kind of gentleman's agreement about not fighting after dark?"

Tom just laughed harshly and turned away.

"Brace round portside, ye lazy bastards. Put yer bleedin' backs into it and haul, lads!" he bellowed to the men pulling at the rigging.

Jon threw up his hands.

"Fine," he said a little angrily. "I'll stay out of your fucking way. I'm sure there's something I can do elsewhere."

Without a backwards glance, he made his way sternward, weaving through the bustling crew as they prepared for the coming battle. As he avoided a pair of men playfully swinging cutlasses at each other, he shook his head. He couldn't understand why the hells anyone was laughing or joking. Were they so eager to wind up at the bottom of the sea? Jon might not have that much experience, but it didn't take a genius to see that the odds were definitely not in their favour. On top of the fact that they were no match for the heavily armed ketch, the Devil's Isles modifications still encumbered the *Heart*, making her unwieldy. The navy couldn't have picked a worse time.

Why in the hells are they out here anyway?

Jon yanked open the door and then ducked quickly as something came flying towards his head. The golden tureen bounced against the wooden frame and landed with a clang on the wooden planks. Wild-eyed and dishevelled, Baltsaros paced at one end of the long table while Saban stood slightly crouched at the other.

"What in hells is going on?" asked Jon, frowning at the dented dish that rocked a few more times slowly on its side. When he and Tom had left Saban to watch over Baltsaros earlier, the man had been asleep still. From the looks of it, he had been wrong in assuming that the worst of the captain's episodes were over. It was hard to believe that the lunatic across the room was the same man who had laughed and kissed him in breathless thanks less than an hour earlier.

"I don't know what set him off this time," said Saban, his deep voice quiet. "I was just sitting here, and suddenly he started shouting about being attacked."

Baltsaros muttered to himself, shaking his head like a dog with ear ticks before he turned around to dig through the armoire.

"Well, he got that right," replied Jon, watching the captain. "By Tom's estimates, the navy will be on us shortly after sunset."

Saban blinked.

"That's... soon. Isn't there anything we can do to evade them?" asked the Balorian. "What should I be doing?"

Jon knew that Saban was anxious to show his worth as a sailor; the broken arm, though mending well, was a source of frustration for the ex-slave.

"Tom's got everything under control. Supposedly. We're to keep barrelling towards them like fools and then rake them with cannon and pistol fire as we swing back into the—Watch out!" Jon pulled Saban to the side as Baltsaros lunged at them with one of his small surgical knives. Saban quickly grabbed Baltsaros's arm and twisted his wrist. The older man panted, letting out a small grunt of pain as Saban wrenched it further around, and Jon reached out and grabbed the knife before it dropped to the carpet. He held it in front of Baltsaros's face, his heart breaking at the utter madness that seemed to crackle around the man like a lightning storm.

"Saban, go into the third drawer of the armoire and look for a blue velvet bag full of a yellowish powder. And get the rope from the bed," said Jon soberly.

"What are you planning on doing?"

"We're going to sedate him, and if we make it out of this alive, we're going to *keep* him sedated until we get to Madierus."

Jon mounted the quarterdeck stairs and approached Tom. The first mate leaned forward against the wheel, his eyes focused on the ketch coming towards them in the grey murk of dusk. They'd soon be in firing range of the naval vessel. Jon felt almost high from lack of sleep and fear, like it was all happening to someone else. He could see the flurry of activity below as the men rolled and heaped cannonballs and grenadoes on the deck while others loaded rifles and pistols.

"Sorry I bit yer head off before," said Tom quietly after a moment. "Just fuckin' tired and pissed is all. After all we been through, it don't seem fair for us to be holed through by the bloody navy." He lifted a flask to his lips and took a long pull before passing it over to Jon.

Jon accepted it with a nod.

"S'ok," he said, taking a small sip of the rum before handing it back. "You know what you're doing."

"What I'd like to know is why the fuck they're out here at all," spat Tom. "We're in the middle of bloody nowhere! What sorta fuckin' business do the king's bilge rats have all the fuckin' way out here?"

Jon blinked. *Business.*

Jon's pulse sped up, and he grabbed Tom by the shoulders, pressing a hard kiss to the first mate's lips.

"Don't let anyone ever say you don't have a way with words," he said with an excited grin.

Tom stared at him like he had gone completely insane.

"*Business*, Tom," laughed Jon. "Business! Gods, I hope I'm right. Really... It's the only thing that makes sense!"

"What in hells are ye yammerin' about?"

"I don't think they're going to fire on us," said Jon quickly. "Why would they be out here? No one comes out this far because there is no way through the mountains. Or, that anyone *knows* of, right? What if it's the king who's been in business with Ah'puch?"

Tom's ocean eyes widened, and Jon could see that the wheels were turning.

"Aye... No one'd think of attackin' the navy for a belly full o' gold. Shit, Jon... Bloody hells, ye could be right." The first mate frowned and looked out over the preparations below.

An idea took hold of Jon.

"How many men to sail the ketch? Minimum, I mean."

Tom thought a moment, his brow creased. He shrugged a shoulder.

"Ten. What are ye thinkin'?"

"What if we didn't fire on them... but *took* the ship instead? Pretend that we're the ship they're meant to meet with and wait until they're close enough to use grapple hooks to board her?" asked Jon.

"Why in hells for?"

"So we can use it to send Baltsaros to Madierus while we go drop some of our passengers off at the southern peninsula," he replied. "He's really not good, Tom." Jon told him what had taken place belowdecks with Saban.

Pain flashed across the first mate's face before he turned away, craning his head to look up at Baltsaros's family shield flying on the ship's flag.

"Well... I just hope you're bloody right," muttered the big man. He nodded to himself. "With the sun at our backs, they might'n have made out our colours. Take the helm, lovey. I'll get us sorted in two flicks of a lamb's tail." Tom made for the stairs, shouting over his shoulder. "And if ye got a juju, kiss it and ask it for some luck. I think we're bloody owed some."

Jon smiled broadly, feeling completely exposed as he held the lantern over his head and waved at the navy ketch. However, his gamble that the king was using the navy to do his dirty work had paid off. Instead of firing on them as they came into range, the smaller ship had simply swivelled its main mast and swung about in the wind so that the *Heart* would come up beside her.

"Ahoy!" he yelled out over the darkened waters that separated the two ships. "Ahoy there!"

"Ahoy!" came the reply after a moment. "Where's Captain Roki? What is this ship?" The man's voice had a reedy quality to it, and his tone was suspicious. Jon imagined he could hear the hammers being pulled back on muskets pointed at his head.

"The captain's sick!" he shouted back, accenting his Common with the slight rasping sounds and cadence of Balorian. "I am the first mate!" He didn't have to convince the man, just stall long enough that the strong swimmers who had dived overboard made it to the other ship. They would climb aboard and begin picking off the crew so that the grapple hooks would find their marks and not be cut loose.

The other man was silent for a long time. When he finally yelled back, Jon almost groaned.

"What is the name of Roki's daughter?"

Jon's nerves were shot. He was going to get them all killed.

"I'm sorry? Please again? I did not hear you!" he shouted helplessly across the water, exaggerating his accent further. When the man repeated his question, Jon tilted his head. He could barely see the ship's captain, but there was something in his voice. *Something like a man lying.*

"Are you forgetful? Roki has no daughter!" he hollered. There was another long pause during which Jon worried over whether he had blown it.

"All right, all right! Same deal as before then? I'll send my men over as soo—Hey!"

Jon watched the man's lantern bounce off the side of the ship before splashing into the water below. Next to Jon, Harris spun his grapple hook in a wide circle before letting it fly with a grunt, and a moment later there was an audible thud of metal against wood as it landed aboard the ketch. When Harris hauled on the line and found resistance, he let out a little whoop. Quickly, the others followed suit and began the task of hauling the two ships together. Grinning wide, Tom jogged up with the captain's long scimitar in his belt.

"Let's go get us some navy scum, boys!"

~

Tom clung to the shrouds for a second, judging the distance. The sea was calm so the ships were tight and cosy, and Tom doubted anyone would wind up in the drink this time. Above them, the sky had cleared and the gibbous moon shone bright.

Bloody nice night for some plunder. He grinned to himself as he leapt across and landed nimbly to the other ship's deck. Two men grappled at each other near him, and he had to step backwards to avoid them.

"Scotty! Aft!" he barked. "Rémi and Harris! Below... See what we got here." He heard a grunt behind him and turned quickly to see a naval officer collapse with a gushing bloody hole in his throat. Tom smiled up at the tall, white-haired man holding the fishing spear—Tuli or Tuvi, he could never tell the twins apart—and ducked his head in thanks before moving on to see what they were up against.

The ketch had been shored up and modified to hold what seemed like twice the number of guns than she was meant to. The crew quarters, always tiny on a ship this size, must have been reduced even more, making Tom feel almost sorry for the men who had to live in such cramped quarters. He snarled and leapt forward, swinging his sword to take the hand off a man who had stepped out of the dark pointing a pistol. *Almost* sorry. The naval officer let out a shriek, and his flintlock bounced to the boards, letting off its shot with a deafening bang. The upside to the diminished crew quarters, Tom knew, was a diminished crew. He figured they numbered no more than twenty. This would be duck soup for the pirates.

Tom let out a yell when fire suddenly exploded in his face. Blinded, he lashed out with his sword, trying to cut his assailant in two. A boot kicked him in the ribs and he grunted, swinging around. All he could make out were bright blooms in the blackness, and his eyes streamed and smarted. However, when the boot hit his side again, he lunged and caught the man around the waist. The move sent the both of them flying, and they glanced off the mast, landing on the wooden planks where Tom used his weight to pin the man beneath him. His hand closed on his attacker's throat, and he squeezed hard, pawing at his eyes with his free hand. When his vision cleared a little, he saw that the gasping, struggling man's face was growing dark.

"Ye bloody hit me in the head with a lantern?" he growled, still blinking rapidly. The man's eyes bulged, and he scratched hard at Tom's hand as he tried to free

634

himself. With a frown, Tom reached behind him for his long dagger and released the man's throat only to slit it a second later.

Jon looked away with his jaw clenched tight when Tom reported that all the naval officers had been killed and tossed overboard. It was hard to tell what was going through his mind, but to his credit, he didn't object. Tom had reasoned that they couldn't take navy men on as prisoners and that leaving them in a dinghy just meant they would die slow deaths; even by sail, it would take over two weeks to get to the closest island. Tom had heard stories of men surviving a long time aboard rowboats far from shore, but they'd mostly been stories about cannibalism. A quick, clean death was better.

"What did you find on board?" asked Jon after a moment, obviously eager to get off the subject of the men's fates.

Tom grinned wide.

"Nothin' as shiny or gold as what we already have, but lovely things all the same," he replied and handed Jon an inventory of the plunder. The hold of the ketch had been chock-full of silks, steel and iron pots, spices, and swords. However, none of those things were as valuable as the barrels of wine and beer that Tom had ordered brought aboard the *Heart*. That was treasure indeed.

With treasure in mind, Tom dug into the pouch in his trousers and pulled out something else he had found while rooting through the ketch's hold. Feeling a little silly, he handed it to Jon.

Jon looked curiously at the piece of blue silk, his brow furrowed.

"What is it?"

Tom laughed and rubbed a hand over his mouth, lifting his shoulders in a shrug.

"It's just a scarf. I thought it'd look nice at yer collar," muttered Tom, embarrassed. The wisp of blue had reminded him of Jon's eyes so he had pocketed it. "Ye don't have to wear it. Forget it." He reached for the scarf, but Jon pulled back and smiled.

"Thank you. It's just unexpected, that's all. It's beautiful, Tom. Really."

Tom scratched the back of his neck and nodded, his face hot.

Jon watched him for a moment before holding out the piece of silk.

"Actually," he said with a smirk. "Can you put it on me? You know how I am with knots."

Tom took the soft piece of grey-blue silk and looped it around the back of Jon's neck, carefully tying it over itself like a cravat in the front and tucking the loose ends beneath Jon's black shirt. After giving him a quick, chaste kiss on the cheek, Tom stepped back and smiled sheepishly.

"There. Ye look like a right lord," he said. Jon's seal-brown curls framed his face and continued in a tumble over his shoulders, nearly as dark as his shirt. The scarf that peeped out from the open collar really did bring out the blue in his eyes, and Tom was glad that he had given it to him.

"*Sweet* is definitely not the word I would have chosen to describe you when we met," laughed Jon, fingering the silk at his throat.

Tom scowled, but really it was just an act.

"Who d'ye want to send with Da?" he asked before Jon had the chance to say something completely ridiculous.

"Saban definitely. And Ceara—I want to be rid of her. Pick ten men to go with them, but make sure not to gut us too much. The ketch has superior guns. They won't need our best men."

Tom nodded.

"Of course, Captain," he said with small smile.

"We'll part ways at daybreak," continued Jon, running a hand through his curls. "Shit, I am starting to forget what sleep feels like. You know what? I'm going to admit defeat right now and just crawl into bed."

With a laugh, Tom grabbed Jon's arm and pulled him towards the door.

"Ye'll do no such thing, lovey," he said. "We just pulled off a pretty bit o' piracy. Let's go open one of them barrels and have a drink or five with the lads. Show 'em the captain's proud of 'em, aye?"

Sighing as Tom led them out of their quarters, Jon nodded tiredly but didn't resist.

CHAPTER 11
STRAIGHT AND NARROW

The jealous are troublesome to others, but a torment to themselves.

— WILLIAM PENN

Jon laughed until he got a stitch in his side and tears rolled down his cheeks. The story wasn't even that funny—just something stupid about a near-sighted man mistaking a horse for his wife—but Jon was so exhausted and near-drunk that he couldn't stop himself long enough to take a breath.

Then a pair of warm lips touched the side of his neck, and his laughter turned into a gasp. Tom's deep voice spoke softly in his ear.

"If there was a good bloody time to take a powder, here's yer chance." The first mate's breath tickled the little hairs at his nape, and Jon shivered when Tom's mouth brushed the rim of his ear. He was struck with an almost overwhelming urge to be alone with Tom.

Wiping his eyes, he rose quickly from his crate and ducked through the crowd, following the first mate through the dark. When they reached the door of the stateroom, Jon grabbed Tom's wrist and turned him, backing him against the wood so he could kiss him hard. The big man moaned softly when Jon's hand closed over the bulge in his pants, but he pulled away from the kiss with a laugh.

"I thought ye were tired, lad?" asked Tom with a wide grin.

"Mmmhmm. I am," replied Jon with a little squeeze that made the first mate wince. "But I want to fuck you first. Then we sleep like the dead. Sound good? Fuck, that sounds good to me."

Tom just nodded, eyes crinkling at the corners as he cupped Jon's face in his big, scarred hands.

"What ye say t' gettin' indoors before ye have me on my knees fer all t' see, love?"

Jon grinned and stepped back, releasing the first mate so he could open the door to their quarters. He dragged Tom inside and, walking a little unsteadily, propelled him towards the bed with one hand while he worked on the opening of his trousers with the other. After turning around so he could sit against the box holding the feather mattress, he pulled his cock out of his pants and began to stroke it.

"Down," he gestured impatiently. "Get down. I want your lips around my cock."

Without a word, Tom dropped to his knees and grabbed Jon's hips, opening his mouth to take in his length quickly. The first mate's tongue flicked underneath the sensitive head, working its way along the edge of the foreskin as Jon squeezed his shaft.

"Take it deep," he murmured after a moment, moving his hand away. "And look at me while you do it."

He stroked Tom's hair almost distractedly, looking down into his gorgeous blue-green eyes as he gorged himself on Jon's cock, his lips brushing the thatch of curly dark hair at the root of it. Tom's mouth felt so great on him; he wrapped his hands around the back of the first mate's head to keep him in place while he shifted his hips a little. It always amazed him how well Tom could do this. In the same position, he was usually forcing himself to relax, tears in his eyes and just waiting for that moment where he could finally surrender to it. Tom, on the other hand, could deep-throat him without a hint of a struggle, submitting willingly to Jon's sometimes cruel treatment.

The thought of Tom struggling sent a strong surge into his cock, and he pulled back with a groan, rubbing the head of it against the first mate's lips.

When a floorboard squeaked, Jon's heart stuttered and he looked towards the sound, startled.

Across the darkened room stood Saban looking incredibly embarrassed.

"I am so very sorry. I came in here earlier to check in on Baltsaros and fell asleep at the table. I was just trying to leave so you didn't see me. I am so, so sorry. I didn't mean to interrupt. I had perhaps too much to drink. I should be going to my bunk," stammered Saban.

Jon stared at him. Normally he'd be in an agony of shame, but something about the man's words conflicted with the way he held himself. Almost like he'd been standing there for a while.

Feeling reckless with the wine singing in his blood, Jon smiled wide at Saban.

"Did you want to join in?" he asked, his tone less teasing than he had intended. It was only as he said it that he realized that the idea actually appealed to him. A lot. Maybe he was getting over his archaic, prudish ways? "You can if you want. Why don't you come here?"

Tom's head swung around, and he looked up at Jon with a wrinkle between his brows.

"No. No, thank you," replied Saban in a choked voice. "I'm not... ah... uh..."

Jon had never seen the big Balorian so flustered before.

When he glanced down at the first mate again, he saw that he was shaking his head slowly. Jon frowned and stroked the side of Tom's face. There was something in Tom's expression that stilled his fingers. His fevered high beginning to ebb, Jon looked from Tom to Saban.

"Oh." Understanding dawned on Jon when he met the tall man's hazel eyes.

Guilt.

It was stupidly obvious. Why hadn't he seen it before? Jon's anger bubbled up, coupled with the deep feeling of betrayal he hadn't yet been able to shake over Tom's indiscretion. The two men were so often together... and Saban was so arresting with his handsome face and his broad-shouldered, sculpted body. Why *wouldn't* Tom want to kiss him?

He let out a small, harsh laugh and shook his head, letting his gaze drop to Tom; the muscles in the first mate's jaw bulged and he shrugged. Feeling like a fool, Jon clenched fists and shut his eyes before he made anything worse. The door of the stateroom opened and closed a moment later as Saban left.

When Tom came up to sit next to him on the bed, Jon heaved a sigh and leaned against his muscled shoulder. Why was he still filled with bitterness about a stupid kiss—something Tom had confessed to and apologized for? It was such a small thing.

"I'm sorry," Jon said faintly. "Ceara was right. I should have asked you who it was you kissed. If I had known, I would have never suggested... with Saban... Agh!" He scrubbed a hand over his face, growing angrier with himself. "I'm sorry I'm such a godsdamned immature *child*. Why can't I just get over this... this *stupid* blinkered way of thinking? Why does my stupid heart feel like it's going to break just thinking about you with someone else? I don't even know why I tried to get Saban to... What was I thinking? I'm not like you. I would have just regretted it." He was weary beyond reason, brittle and bordering on hysterical. Jon knew he would start to laugh any second, and then he would cry.

"Ahh, Jonny... love," rumbled Tom, wrapping his arm around Jon's back. With his other hand he patted Jon's chest, right over his heart. "Ye do all of yer thinkin' with this... and not so much with *this*." The first mate rested his hand on Jon's flaccid cock. "It ain't a bad thing. Just a thing."

Jon chuckled softly at Tom's logic.

"Yer laughin', but if ye change or not, I don't rightly care. As long as yer happy, I'm happy. Aye?" said Tom, fondling Jon's cock teasingly. "I'll suck almost any's cock ye order me to, but only when yer there and only if ye *really* want me to."

"Well... I'll keep that in mind," Jon replied with a soft smile and then let out a little groan, moving Tom's hand away. "I've completely fucked up for tonight, and all I want to do is sleep and forget everything. Can we do that? Is that ok?" He peered across the room to where Baltsaros slumbered on in his drugged sleep.

Tom just nodded and set to work ridding himself of his pants before sliding naked beneath the covers; lying on his back, he watched Jon undress. When Jon joined Tom, he lay on his stomach, half on the first mate. Tom curled his arms around him, and they lay there entwined, skin against skin, soft and warm. It was both comforting and sensual; when Tom stroked down his back and cupped his buttock and squeezed, Jon gave a sigh of pleasure. He was debating trying to rekindle the earlier mood when Tom's gravelly voice woke against his ear.

"Wouldn't have worked anyways," said the first mate. "Saban's as straight as a bloody pin."

Jon frowned.

"I'm not so sure about that," he replied, thinking again about what it was that had bothered him about the man's stance. "He was facing away from the door, not trying to get out. I think he was watching us and just him shifting his weight caused the board to squeak." Tom's hand stopped in its caress, and Jon suddenly wished he hadn't said anything. However, when the first mate began snoring quietly a few moments later, Jon wondered if Tom had heard him at all.

Bleary from too little sleep, Tom leaned against the rigging and supervised the exchange of supplies. They had decided that half of the gold would go to Madierus with the ketch, while the lion's share of foodstuffs would come with them. Baltsaros was already safely aboard and sleeping peacefully in the tiny captain's quarters and once they were done loading and unloading, they would part ways.

In the wan light of dawn, Tom caught himself staring at Saban again as the big man stretched up to grab a bundle, and he looked away. He thought about what Jon had said about Saban watching them. Jon had to be mistaken. But if he wasn't... Tom turned to watch the tall Balorian lift another sack over his shoulder. When he saw Tom's eyes him, Saban looked embarrassed before averting his gaze. The first mate took another drag from his cigar just to have something to distract him from the nervousness squeezing his guts to jelly.

Truth was, the thought of being made to service Saban had wildly excited him. However, his knowledge of the man's tastes had just made the whole thing bloody uncomfortable, and he'd been glad that nothing had happened. But... If Jon was right about Saban...

Tom blew out a plume of smoke and sent the stub of his cigar flying over the gunwale. That line of thinking was pure rubbish, and he'd better get his head on straight; Saban was his mate and that was that.

Jaw clenched tight, Tom jumped to the deck to help the boys haul up a particularly unwieldy bundle. Damn Jon. In just a few words, he had turned Saban from a safe fantasy to a... what? A possibility? Damn Jon to *hells* for planting the seed in his head. Shit, he figured that Jon would fly right off the handle even *knowing* that he sometimes jacked off thinking about the handsome Balorian.

When Tom leaned over the side to grab the last of the grapple hooks that had held the boats together, his eyes met Saban's again. Instead of looking away this time, a tiny wrinkle appeared on the man's brow, and he pressed his lips together. Tom stared into that green-brown gaze for a moment before nodding.

"Safe journey," he muttered. When Saban nodded back, Tom turned on his heel, anxious to get back to Jon. He was glad the big Balorian was leaving; it meant he wouldn't have to go out of his way to avoid him.

CHAPTER 12
WELL KEPT

Good things come to those who wait.

— ENGLISH PROVERB

Jon stretched out, his tendons popping as he let out a long groan. When he rubbed his eyes and sat up, he was dismayed to see that the light outside was far too bright for it to be daybreak. He slid off the bed in alarm when he noticed the empty cage and began digging through the pile of clothes on the floor, looking for a pair of pants. The door opened as he was jumping on one leg, trying to pull up a pair of half-inside-out trousers. Glaring at Tom, he grabbed the side of the table as he tried to untangle the pant leg.

"Is he gone? Lords of the black hells, please tell me he is not gone," he growled, dreading the answer.

Tom looked surprised and stopped in his tracks, a steaming cup of coffee in each hand. It was obvious by his expression that Baltsaros was indeed on his way to Madierus.

"Shit, Tom... *Why didn't you wake me up?*" He stopped wrestling with the pants and stood half-naked, clutching the material to his hip.

Creases appeared on the first mate's forehead, and he slowly put the mugs down on the table.

"Tried," he replied. "Ye said to leave ye."

What Jon felt was panic, and it crushed his lungs. He'd missed Baltsaros's departure.

"He was drugged, lad. Wouldn'a mattered. Not like he'd notice if ye was there or not."

642

"That's not what matters, you idiot. Fuck..." Jon let the pants fall and wrapped his arms around himself. "You should have tried *harder*. Tom, what if I never see him again? The least you could have done is given me a chance to say goodbye! How long have we been sailing? Can we come about to catch up with them?"

Tom shook his head.

"The sun's past the yardarm," he replied. "Hours gone, love."

"Fuck fuck fuck fuck!"

"Two n' a bit weeks to the peninsula, five more south to Madierus. We'll see Da in two months. What are ye goin' on about?" said the first mate, taking Jon's shoulders in his hands.

"What if we get attacked? What if there's another big storm? What if they sink?" Jon whispered.

With a little shake of his head, Tom furrowed his brow at him.

"Listen," said the first mate quietly. "If I knew ye'd be this sore, I would'a tried harder to wake ye. But yer talking bloody nonsense. Aint'cha tired of worrying yer damned head over things ye got no control over? Jon, if ye die, how're you gonna feel bad about not sayin' what I figure is a useless goodbye to Da? Ye'll be dead. Now, there's all manner of ways Da could perish outside our reach, ye know that right? Aye, they could sink. Or they could get to Madierus all dandy and throw bloody *soirees* every single fuckin' night, and Da could choke on a bloody fish bone and die right before we make shore."

Jon frowned at him.

"That's not making me feel any better."

"Ye made the right choice... *We* made the right choice. Da wasn't gettin' any better with our half-arsed doctorin'. We were bloody shooting into the brown on our own, and ye were right to strike sails and send him off. He'll get to help faster; it ain't healthy for a man to be sleepin' on the toxy powder fer two months, love." Tom sighed and squeezed Jon's shoulders. "I'm just sayin' ye gotta stop worryin'... Whatever happens, happens, and there's no point in thinkin' of future tears now. Aye?"

Jon shrugged. He wished he could be as jaded as Tom was to the possibility of tragedy. Then he realized something and smiled a little.

"We always seem to be telling the other not to worry," he pointed out.

With a twist of his lips, Tom rubbed the side of his thumb against his dark-blond stubble.

"Aye. Too much worryin' on board," he grinned. "Worryin' ain't good for a man's soul."

Jon tilted his head at Tom.

"I don't know why, but it surprises me that you believe in souls, given your complete disregard for anything sacred," he said.

"Who says I'm disregardin'?" replied Tom. His ocean eyes narrowed in amusement as he slid his hands down over Jon's naked hips before dropping down to his knees and nuzzling against his soft cock.

"I've got a burnin' need to kneel and pray right now."

Jon laughed and pushed Tom's head away.

"You and Baltsaros," he chided. "You can't solve everything with sex."

The big man just shook off Jon's hand and licked delicately at his cock before looking up at him wide-eyed.

"I can try," he said, smiling. He face grew serious, and he leaned forward to bathe Jon's stiffening cock with his tongue softly, tugging gently at his foreskin using only his lips. He glanced up again. "Jon, do ye remember the last time we weren't interrupted or too tired to fuck? When was the last time ye had me on my knees for a good ploughin'? Yer cock balls-deep in my hole, fuckin' me hard and rough..."

Jon let out a huff of breath at Tom's words, his brow pinched. He felt almost bad thinking about it, but the fact that Baltsaros was not there felt a little... *freeing*. His cock bobbed higher with every rapid pulse of his heart, fed by the look in Tom's eyes.

"Aye, that's better," breathed Tom before curling his hand around Jon's shaft to suck the head of it between his lips. He bobbed his head a few times, his tongue running along the bottom of Jon's cockhead every time he pulled back.

Jon closed his eyes and took Tom's head between his hands, giving in to the sensation. When Tom brought up his other hand to cup and fondle his balls gently, Jon gave a soft sound and tightened his hold, plunging his length faster into the hot, wet tunnel of Tom's mouth. His knees started to feel a bit weak as he was brought closer by the first mate's skilled tongue and hands, and he slowed his pace, holding Tom and his eagerness back. He felt a trickle of sweat run down his chest and was panting when he finally pushed Tom away roughly.

"On the bed," he said, pointing.

Tom rose to his feet a little unsteadily and dropped his pants before climbing onto the bed. He quickly got onto his hands and knees and looked over his shoulder, waiting for Jon.

"Spread your knees more," said Jon. "The way I like."

Without a word, Tom lay his head down on the bed before he widened his legs further.

Jon loved seeing Tom this way, completely exposed. It brought out urges in him that other positions didn't. He felt little to no tenderness... only a desire to feel the mouth of Tom's pucker open over the head of his cock before he shoved his whole length roughly into his oiled hole. He grabbed the bottle they kept handy and poured a little of the pale oil into his palm. Stroking himself, he watched Tom's cock sway in time with the big man's breathing for a moment before he tipped the slender bottle above Tom's furry crack and let a slow trickle out. Tom's sphincter contracted when the cold oil touched it, and Jon reached out to smear it, sliding a finger into him. The hot, slick walls hugged him up to his knuckle and, hand on his own cock, Jon searched and quickly found Tom's sweet spot to begin rubbing it in a slow circle.

Muffled by the bed, Tom's low whimper made Jon smile.

"You like that?" he asked, his oiled finger stroking the dimpled little nut inside Tom. When Tom didn't answer, he pulled his finger out and delivered a hard slap to the back of the first mate's thigh.

The groan that came from Tom had nothing but pleasure in it, and Jon laughed to himself over the strange conundrum of how he was supposed to punish someone who enjoyed being punished a little too much. He slipped his finger back inside Tom and continued to jerk himself slowly, watching the first mate's cock drip a clear string onto the coverlet. He had an idea.

"You'd love to touch your cock, wouldn't you?" he murmured. "Or have me touch it?"

"Aye," came the reply.

"Well... You can forget about that," he said with a smirk. Tom stopped pushing back against Jon and stayed still. "No one is touching your cock today. At all. That's your punishment for not waking me up."

Tom lifted his head and twisted to the side, staring at Jon with his face flushed.

"That's damn cruel," he said, obviously not believing him.

Jon stopped fingering him and dealt him a few stinging slaps before thumbing him open to continue the slow tease. His own cock was throbbing in his fist, the length of it slick with more than just oil.

"Yes, it is," agreed Jon. "But that's the way it's going to be."

With a deep furrow in his brow, Tom thought.

"Please?" he said after a moment.

"You can say please a thousand times, and I won't relent. Not this time."

"Ye can't be bloody serio—"

"Keep talking, and I'll make it tomorrow too," growled Jon.

When Tom turned his head away with a small sound, Jon stroked his reddened ass cheek and slid his thumb over the slick, sensitive opening.

"Just think about how good it'll feel when you *do* cum," he murmured, pushing a finger back inside Tom. The first mate moved against Jon, and he let out an appreciative noise.

"Yeah, it'll feel really nice when I let that fat cock of yours spill," continued Jon, exciting himself even more. His cock was leaking over his knuckles, and he moved closer to rub it against Tom's ass. He pulled his finger to the side, stretching Tom open a little and let out a slow breath at the sight. Experimentally, he began to push his cockhead against Tom's hole without moving his finger away and groaned when the edge of his glans squeezed passed the constricted entrance.

Tom made a faint sound, something that sounded a little pained, but he didn't move away. Instead, he shifted his hips eagerly, inviting Jon to slide his cock deeper.

Jon's breathing was hoarse as he pushed harder, so tight against the finger shoved inside Tom.

"Fuck!" He squeezed the base of his cock quickly to stop himself but let out a strangled groan as he realized he was too late and going to cum right then and there. Jon shifted his hands quickly to Tom's hips and pounded into the first mate, crying out and then grunting with the force of his release as he came hard inside Tom.

~

Tom let out his own cry with Jon's orgasm. When he was told he wasn't going be allowed to cum, Tom's first honest reaction had been annoyance. However, he had stifled it and forced himself to concentrate on what Jon was doing to him instead; in the end, the rush he felt at Jon's climax filled him with an intense pleasure and when they collapsed together, he breathed as hard as if he had cum too. Jon pulled out with a small gasp, and Tom lay there a moment, groggy and oddly happy with himself. So he wasn't going to cum... It wasn't the end of the world. After all, Baltsaros had made him wait numerous times before. Jon was just normally a little kinder. It was an interesting change, but he wasn't convinced that Jon would actually go through with his promise.

Tom shrugged to himself and turned over onto his back, watching Jon as the slight, dark-haired man made his way across the room to clean up at the basin. When Jon came back and handed him a cup of water, Tom accepted it with a small smile and sat up to down it in two gulps, very aware of the tenderness of his slowly softening cock and the dull aching need in his balls. However, as Tom waited for Jon to say that he had changed his mind, Jon walked over to the cupboard, pulled out a fresh pair of pants and a shirt, and began to get dressed. Tom folded his hands behind his head and leaned back against the headboard with a resigned smirk.

Bastard, he thought fondly.

When Jon saw him watching, he smiled. This time he definitely looked proud of himself.

"Lordin' yer satisfaction over me, lad?" Tom asked, eyebrows high.

Jon's smile widened before he turned to grab the shirt from the back of the chair.

Though hard work aboard the ship had changed Jon's body, packing sleek muscle onto his slight frame, he still retained his slender, lithe youthfulness. In the shifting light, the damp cherub curls, though nearly black and not gold, did nothing to squelch that image of unsullied boyhood. However, the illusion was shattered when Jon tilted his head and Tom saw the dark stubble of his cheeks; even more so when Jon reached for him with a bold hand to pinch his nipple and then pet the fur of his chest like he was a dog.

"Aw, poor Tommy-boy. You'll keep," Jon assured him. "Get some sleep now if you want, but I need you up by mid afternoon. We still have that issue with those assholes in the brig. I want to make sure they're not going to try to take some kind of revenge over their mate's death. We need to put our heads together and come up with something to keep this sort of thing from happening. We have two weeks aboard with these... Tom, you're not listening to me, are you?"

Tom shrugged a little. He looked down at his cock; it had visibly plumped up a bit and lay straight and half-hard on his belly.

"Is it because I said 'put our heads together'?" said Jon, grinning.

Tom grinned back.

"You're incorrigible," said Jon, rolling his eyes before he made his way to the door. "Mid afternoon! Be up!"

Tom watched Jon leave and let his smile drop, wondering how he would get any sleep at all without taking care of his cock or without letting his thoughts wander to the worries over Baltsaros's journey that hung like black clouds at back of his mind.

CHAPTER 13
FORTUNE'S TELLING

Fate leads him who follows it, and drags him who resist.

— PLUTARCH

Jon stared up at the *Jewel*. It looked like the marble finish had cracked on the east side of the building and was being repaired; he could see crumbling red brick between the posts of the scaffolding. As Jon watched, a pallet was hoisted up a wooden crane powered by three long-eared donkeys and lowered to the roof of the second floor.

"I wonder what happened?" he mused.

The first mate finished tying the rowboat's mooring line to the bollard and straightened, putting his hands on his hips.

"Old buildin'," he said with a shrug. "Cheap materials."

Jon nodded and followed Tom off the floating dock and up the path leading to the brothel. He remembered how awestruck he had been the first time he had seen it and laughed a little at himself. After everything he had witnessed in the past months, the *Jewel* just looked a little dingy. It was nothing but a red brick building fronted by an elaborate façade to make it look like a fairy-tale castle. Even the "guards" at the front didn't look as grand as they once had to him; as they passed between the huge doors, Jon saw that the uniform of the man closest to him had been patched, and there were sweat marks under his arms.

Curling his lip in distaste, he mentioned it to Tom after the first mate had ordered something at the bar.

"Look at you, mister fancy world traveller," said Tom, sliding a small glass towards Jon. He chuckled. "All snooty and lookin' down yer nose..."

Jon made a face at him, then peered at the murky green liquid suspiciously. Despite how vile it looked, he lifted it up and touched the rim of the glass to the first mate's before he brought it to his lips. His nose told him only a split-second before he tasted it that the liquid would burn, and burn it did. It tasted like nothing he had ever had before; pungent and rotten, it seared his throat all the way down and set fire to his chest. Jon choked and coughed, tears streaming down his face as Tom downed his and smiled serenely. When he could swallow without gagging again, Jon wiped his face and glared at the first mate.

"What in the black hells was that?" he rasped.

"It's called *Dragon's Milk*," laughed Tom, collecting Jon's glass. "And don't ask me how it's made... Ye don't wanna know, love. Another?"

"Ugh. No. Never," Jon said with a grimace and watched Tom pour himself another shot before tossing it back without so much as a lip-twitch. His tongue felt burned, and his mouth tasted like stagnant harbour water. "You think you're so tough, drinking fucking poison. Hey... Wait... Don't tell me you made me drink that shit because I haven't let you touch your cock in three days."

Tom grinned wide and lifted his hand palm up. *What can I say?*

"What if I make it four?"

"Ye wouldn't..."

"Try me, big guy," Jon said, smiling. It had become a new facet of their play, one that he knew they both enjoyed. While Tom claimed that it was honest-to-gods, horrible punishment for him, it didn't explain why he was going along with it so willingly. It's not like Jon had anything to keep Tom from jerking off anytime that he so wished. He just... obeyed.

Tom capped the bottle of Dragon's Milk and passed it back to the man behind the bar, asking a few questions in a language Jon didn't recognize. With a nod of his head, Tom turned back to Jon with a frown.

"Can I leave ye here, lovey?" he asked. "Got somethin' I'd like to take care of. Be back before ye miss me, aye?"

Tom winked and slapped some coins down on the glossy wood before making his way around the side of the bar and through the door there.

When the bartender pointed to a clean, empty glass with a raised eyebrow, Jon asked for something to wash the horrible taste from his mouth. With a smile, the man pulled a pint of pale beer and set it in front of Jon with a flourish before pouring himself a small glass of amber liquid and picking up the book he had set down on their arrival.

"Cheers," said Jon, but the man didn't hear him. Turning, Jon leaned back against the bar and looked around while he sipped his beer. It was the slowest period of the day, Tom had explained. It was post-breakfast so the late- or overnight clients had left with their "pipes cleaned", as Tom had put it, but it was too early for the afternoon crowd. Theoretically, the only reason they were there was to kill some time; they had dropped off their passengers earlier that morning and were only waiting for some supplies and mail to be loaded onto the *Heart* before they made their way south to Madierus.

Across the room, a pretty girl in an almost see-through purple dress smiled at him, and Jon smiled back. He knew that she might only be interested in him for the gold in his purse, but a small part of Jon hoped it was because he cut a pretty dashing figure.

The first mate had tamed Jon's hair into a tight, braided queue that had made his scalp ache at first until some of his ringlets had worked themselves loose, and during the three-week trip to the southern peninsula, the beard he was trying to grow had filled in enough that he no longer had patchy parts. It was barely more than thick, black stubble, but he thought it made him look slightly dangerous, which he liked. His pants were new, bought the previous day up the coast at a small town that specialised in textiles. They were black and made of a heavy, soft material that clung to him like a second skin. His loose white shirt was freshly bleached, and at his neck he wore Tom's gift; he knew that the blue silk made his eyes seem a brighter hue. He had even polished his boots to a shine that morning. Tom had laughed and called him a strutting peacock when he saw him all dressed up, but the approval and admiration in his gorgeous eyes had made Jon's cheeks hot.

Grinning to himself, Jon glanced again at the prostitute in purple and took a swallow of beer. As he lounged against the bar trying to recreate the sort of charming disinterest that Baltsaros seemed to so effortlessly project, he was startled when something hard whacked the side of his leg.

"Buy me a beer and I'll read your fortune," croaked a tiny old woman with a cane and an ill-fitting wig.

"Um. Ok?" replied Jon. A little flustered, he began digging around for some coins. When the beer had been poured, he carried it to a small table for the woman. However, when Jon turned to go back to the bar, she hooked his arm with the crook of her cane and pointed to the seat across from her.

"Oh. No… That's all right," he said kindly. "You can have the beer. It's on me. No need for fortunes or anything. I don't believe in that sort of thing."

"Then whatever I have to say won't make any difference, and you can just laugh to yourself over the foolishness of an old woman," she said with a smile that showed off her lack of teeth. However, there was something in her rheumy eyes that made Jon feel a little guilty about not being more charitable, so he let out a silent sigh and sank down into the hard-backed seat, wishing he had brought his beer with him. To go get it now just seemed rude at this point.

The woman pushed her beer towards Jon with a tilt of her head.

"Go on, son," she said in a voice as weathered as her skin. "I don't much like the taste of it."

"Then… Why did you want me to buy it for you?" he asked, perplexed, but the woman was busy shuffling some dog-eared cards in front of her and didn't reply. With a frown, he picked up the pint glass and took a long swallow, watching as she took forever to move the cards around the table with no rhyme or reason. He wondered what the hells was taking Tom so long.

Finally, when the cards were arranged in a crooked semicircle, the old woman sat back in her chair and peered at Jon.

"Well. Go on," she coaxed, waving a gnarled finger at him. "Pick."

Jon furrowed his brow and looked down at the mess of cards. When he glanced up at the old lady, she was watching him so closely that his skin prickled in discomfort.

"How many?" he asked and then cleared his throat because his voice sounded odd. "How do I choose?"

"Doesn't matter!" said the woman, laughing. "You don't believe in this anyway, do you, son?"

With an impatient sigh, Jon reached out and held his hand over the cards, intent on just selecting a few at random quickly so he could get it over with. He tapped three and sat back.

The old woman put her crooked finger on each of the cards, pushing them away from the rest before sweeping the pile to the side. Slowly, she turned over the three cards.

"Ahhhhhhh..." she said, nodding her head. "Yes, yes. I see." When she didn't offer anything else, Jon felt himself growing annoyed.

"So? What do you see?"

"Don't rush an old woman, Jon," she scolded him. "Drink your beer like a good boy."

Jon felt a cold flood of unease.

"How do you know my name?" he asked quietly.

The woman squinted at him shrewdly.

"Do I? Aren't you all johns? This is a whorehouse, isn't it?" she said and cackled like it was the best joke she'd ever told.

He laughed along with her a little hesitantly; there was something about her that made him think she was not nearly as batty as she made herself out to be. Jon started to wonder if Tom had put him up to this.

"The Moon," said the old lady, pushing the card towards Jon. On the card was a picture of a boy with a moon for a face sitting in a pool of water. He had one eye opened, and the other closed, and in his hand he held a crayfish. "The Moon represents dreams and intuition. The inner self. This little crawdad here is all the strange things that can crawl up out of the pool of the mind. One eye open for visions. One eye closed for dreams. Do you have strange dreams, Jon?"

Jon swallowed, mesmerised by the movement of her finger over the worn card. There could be no mistaking her use of his name this time. He could hear his pulse like muffled drumbeat in his ears, and he nodded slowly as he thought of his dreams that often seemed weighted with portent.

"The Tapestry..." said the woman, sliding the next card towards Jon. On it was a blue, three-sided tapestry with three yellow stars in the middle, a clawed animal holding each corner. *A three-sided tapestry.* Just like the one in his daydream the day they had come for Tom.

Then, to his alarm, he realized that the three animals were a thickly maned lion, a large cat, and a wolf. Mouth dry, Jon looked up at the old seer in alarm. The wild cat and lion from his dreams—Tom and Baltsaros.

"This has to be a joke," he whispered. "Tom set you up to this, didn't he?" He had told Tom about the dreams, but there was no way that Tom knew about Jon's family crest—the one that was woven into the moth-eaten cloth that used to hang above the small breakfast table in his castle home. *A wolf.*

The old woman sucked on the corner of her toothless mouth for a moment before continuing.

"The Tapestry represents the warp of Fate and weft of Time working to weave together different aspects of your life to create a strong bond. The three corners are birth, life, and death—there cannot be one without the other two. But see here? There is a tear on one side... one that will have to be mended. Once you do, you will stop looking at your feet and realize that looking to the stars is a better means of finding your way. But, is this a joke? Could be. Could be that this tapestry here is just to keep you from the cold. What do I know? But three... oh three. *Three* is a magic number. Did you know that, Jon?"

The woman grinned to herself and pushed back on the ratty wig perched atop her head.

Jon blinked and was startled when he found himself staring at a stunningly beautiful young woman smiling like an imp at him from across the table. Her eyes were a soft, warm brown framed by dark gold lashes, and they crinkled at Jon in amusement as he stared agape at her. Her full, rosy lips made a playful pout, and she swept her thick, autumn-honey hair back over her shoulder.

"Shall I continue?" she asked with a wink.

Though Jon didn't answer, she slid the next card towards him. This one looked older and smaller than the rest, like it had come from a different set of cards altogether. The only thing on it was a blue whirlpool, crudely drawn. The young woman's finger circled the painted water as she spoke. Jon's vision began to swim, and he clutched at the table to keep from slipping out of his chair.

"The Whirlpool. Swirling and dragging all towards it, pulling everything closer and closer, round and round. You are the epicentre. Events in your life, often unrelated, coming together *just so*. Tell me, Jon... Are there things in your life you cannot explain? Do fluke and fortuity court you like lovers?

The question sent a chill down his back, and Jon started to feel nauseous. The Devil's Isles and Tom's tattoos. The blood rituals and Baltsaros's desires. So many other little coincidences that seemed to follow Jon wherever he went. He couldn't pull his eyes away from the woman's finger stroking the flaking paint around the black abyss of the whirlpool's centre. He felt as if he were falling headfirst into it.

"Jon?" A hand clasped his shoulder, and he started, breaking out of his trance. Tom smiled down at him. "There ye are."

Jon swallowed and stared up at Tom, speechless. The first mate frowned, and there was a touch of worry in the lines of his face.

"Now, Granny, have ye been fillin' the boy's head with yer bloody foolishness?" he asked with a shake of his head.

When Jon turned to the woman across the table, he saw that she was once again a toothless old woman with skin like long-crumpled paper and eyes that were clouded and heavy-lidded with age.

Beaming up at Tom, the woman flapped a hand like a gnarled claw at him.

"Oh, Tommy, my love," she said with a fond sigh. "Were I a century younger, I would put you over my knee for such impudence... But we all know you would like that far too much! Ha!" The old woman chortled to herself, rocking back in her chair. The wig slipped further, showing more of her patchy, wisp-covered scalp.

Tom chuckled.

"Oh yer still a great beauty, darlin'," said the first mate with a waggish smile, "with men singin' songs of your loveliness from shore to shore!"

"Hush now, you silly thing. We both know that no matter how buxom or lovely I once was, you'd have never given me the time of day if there was a bonny lad in the room!"

Jon's heart had slowed a little, but he felt dazed as he watched the exchange.

Tom just laughed with the old woman before grabbing Jon's arm.

"Up, lad," he said, pulling Jon out of his chair. "Quick as wink! We gotta be runnin'... There's an escape to be made! So long, Granny. May ye bloody outlive us all."

"Escape from what?" asked Jon as he spared a glance back at the old woman. Her smile was sly and eyes canny as she watched them depart.

When he looked over at Tom, he saw that the first mate had an old jute bag slung over his shoulder. Jon thought he heard the clink of bottles within.

"Well," replied the big man, opening the door for Jon, "some might take exception to me takin' a few things. Figure it's only fair considerin' I never collected the last of my wages..." He grinned wide and headed down the path at a brisk pace with Jon following.

Jon waited until Tom was settled between the oars before pushing the dinghy away from the dock. He was confused and nervous about what had just happened. It felt like he had just woken from a dream and couldn't remember all the details.

Tom watched him as he rowed.

"I gotta say, love, it was a damn sight eerie seein' ye starin' at the empty table, still as a statue an' bug-eyed like ye were seein' visions."

Jon started.

"What do you mean *empty*? There weren't any cards? Oh *fuck*," he breathed, feeling lightheaded.

Tom burst out laughing.

"Ye can be a damned gullible fool, love," he said, shaking his head at Jon. "No, Jon. I was just takin' the piss outta ye. Lords tell me, ye didn't take any of that ol' biddy's nonsense serious, did ye?"

"She said some very... relevant things. I don't know." Jon fiddled with his shirt cuff, embarrassed. "Enough that I thought you'd put her up to it."

"Me? Naw. Listen, she's just some ol' tramp lady who's been swindlin' folks out of coin since back in the days when the *Jewel* was just a four-room hump shack. They just keep 'er around for the tourists, mainly," replied Tom. Sweat beaded on his sun-bronzed brow from the exertion of pulling the oars. "I got no bloody idea how she makes any coin, seein' as she never charges for a 'bad' readin'."

Jon stared at Tom, wondering if he was just teasing him again.

"What? Didn't ye give her any money?" asked the first mate with a smirk.

"No... I didn't."

"Oh," replied Tom, sobering a little. It had obviously just dawned on him that Jon was honestly rattled. He glanced over his shoulder at the *Heart*, anchored just outside the narrow, manmade harbour. When he turned back to Jon, he smiled reassuringly. "It ain't anythin'. Trust me. Forget what she said."

Nodding, Jon tried to brush off the feeling of dread that had taken hold of him. She was obviously good at reading body language, and Jon could very well have led the woman's whole performance, feeding her information just by his reaction to her words. He was reminded of the far-travellers that came to the maidens' faire every spring and the way that they would prey on easy marks; he had witnessed with his own eyes how an old man with tarot cards had fished and obtained cues from the woman he was doing the reading for. It must have been the same with the old woman at the *Jewel*.

"What's on my family crest?" he asked Tom.

The first mate flashed a white smile as he put away the oars and then stood to grab the line dangling from the *Heart*.

"Easy," replied Tom with a wink. "A wee mouse with dewy eyes holdin' a lovely little flower, all precious and fuckin' innocent like."

Laughing, Jon stood.

"Fine!" he said, throwing up his hands. "I'm a gullible twit."

His anxiety over the strange card reading began to retreat even further into distance as he helped the first mate prepare to hoist the dinghy up the side of the pirate ship.

CHAPTER 14
AT LONG LAST

release • *n.* relief or deliverance from sorrow, suffering, or trouble.

Once the supplies were stowed and they were on their way, Tom dragged Jon to their quarters and emptied the contents of the bag onto the bed. He grinned at the look on Jon's face and climbed onto the mattress to sit against the headboard, pleased with himself.

Tom had been pissed as hells when the new manager had denied his request for his final wages. Not that he really needed the money, seeing as he was a rich man with a king's ransom of gold, but it was the *principle* of the thing. However, instead of punching the fucker—as was his first instinct—Tom simply walked away and swiped a set of keys from the holder in the hallway on his way out. After a visit to one of the liquor closets, he'd ducked into his favourite of the specialty playrooms to grab a few items.

On the bed lay the spoils of his plunder.

Jon grabbed the four bottles of whiskey and lined them up on the table before picking up the flogger with a raised eyebrow at Tom.

"We have one of these."

The first mate shrugged with a smile.

"This one's better. And ye can never have too many!"

With a little laugh, Jon set it down next to the shackles Tom had also taken. He then picked up a leather box and shook it with a jingle before undoing the little clasp on one side. His eyes darted to Tom's in bewildered surprise.

"What are these?" he asked, holding up a smooth metal ring.

Tom scratched at his jaw and grinned wider. He knew that the box contained more metal rings of different sizes as well as a few leather ones.

"Cock rings."

Jon stared at the ring in his hand, his brow furrowed in confusion.

"How do they work?" he asked after a moment.

"Ye know when Da ties your cock up tight? Right behind yer balls...?"

Understanding dawned on Jon's face, and he reddened a little, nodding. He dropped the ring back into the box and frowned.

"There's one with a bunch of little bells on it in here."

Tom laughed, sliding one hand into his trousers. He was already too hard to put one of the rings on, but that was ok. He used the tips of his fingers to softly tease the head of his cock.

"I just grabbed the box. Fucked if I know," he said. He almost regretted not taking one of the leather masks fitted with a wide O at the mouth. Watching Jon blush as he looked through the sex paraphernalia was both amusing and more than a little arousing.

Jon put aside the rings and picked up a small wooden box. When he saw the sticks of *char* in it, he just chuckled and shook his head. The last thing on the bed he lifted with a smirk on his face.

"Sort of big, isn't it?" he said, turning the smooth wooden phallus around in his hands.

Tom squeezed his cock and gave him a crooked smile. Jon glanced at the first mate's crotch, only just registering that he was playing with himself without permission.

"Aren't you afraid I'm just going to leave you high and dry again? Hm?" asked Jon with a little head tilt.

Moving his hand down to his aching balls, Tom dipped his chin and sobered.

"Aye. But I don't really care, love."

Jon stared at him for a long moment.

"Take off your pants," he said.

Tom sat up and quickly rid himself of his trousers. His cock jerked by itself as he shifted up on his knees, and he wrapped his hand around the base of it with a smile. However, Jon shook his head when Tom reached for him.

"Hands off your cock, Tom," said Jon, his blue-grey eyes amused. His expression darkened as he watched Tom. "Lie on your back, hands behind your head."

After he lay down, Tom closed his eyes and waited. After a moment, he thought he heard the soft sounds of Jon undressing. Jon joined him on the bed, and Tom let out a small sigh as his cool palm stroked him from stomach to thigh, avoiding his cock altogether. While it was frustrating, it did feel nice, and when Jon leaned down to kiss the curve of his pelvis, Tom groaned quietly in encouragement. Jon's beard scratched softly against his belly, and Tom opened his eyes to watch, shifting his hips eagerly.

"Bring your knees up," murmured Jon against his skin.

Tom did as he was told, opening his legs and pulling his knees up to bare himself. Jon cupped Tom's sack and squeezed, tugging it playfully. Tom crushed his eyes shut;

while it looked like his cock wasn't going to get any love, Jon *did* know how to treat his balls.

However, he gave a little grunt of surprise when something cold touched him a moment later. Tom lifted his head and saw that Jon had the large wooden cock in his hands, a serious expression on his face. Tom licked his lips and took a deep breath; he'd stolen the overlarge dildo on a lark, not really expecting to have it used on him.

To be honest, he really wasn't sure how he felt about it. He put his head back on the pillow and stared at the boards above.

Without a word, Jon rubbed the fake cock over Tom's hole as he poured oil on him and then began fingering him to get him ready. Tom knew he could say no. Jon would stop and then maybe they'd just fuck normal-like instead, but Tom's cock was rock hard, and he had to admit to himself that he was actually excited about being fucked by something so big. Jon's fingers stopped moving, and Tom raised his head again.

Looking at Jon, he saw that the dark-eyed lust had been replaced with a question.

Is this ok?

In response, Tom grinned—embarrassed that Jon had picked up on his nervousness—and nodded. He lay back again, hands cradling his head and closed his eyes, breathing deep to relax himself.

Jon began working on him carefully and slowly. His finger was joined by a second, and he added more oil as he slid them in and out of Tom with teasing strokes of his prostate. Almost all his jitters gone about the big dildo, Tom moved his hips in time to Jon's finger fucking. It felt so good. He pulled his hands out from under his head to curl them behind his knees, holding onto his legs to give Jon better access to his ass. Jon laughed softly, slipping his fingers out to knead Tom's balls for a moment. Then the head of the dildo touched him again and Tom tensed.

Jon paused, just squeezing at Tom's sack before stroking behind his balls and along his inner thighs gently until Tom had taken another deep breath or two. There was no hurry in his caress; it dawned on Tom then that Jon would take all the time in the world if he needed it.

Tom clenched his teeth against the tightness in his lungs and forced himself to breathe deep again. Though Jon didn't know the extent of the abuse he had suffered—and never would, if Tom had his way—the way he was so attentive reinforced one thing over and over to Tom: no matter how much pain Jon could inflict, he would never *hurt* him.

Jon pushing the wooden phallus against his puckered opening brought Tom out of his reverie, and he made a small, slightly shaky sound. Jon's hand stroked the back of his thigh, his palm now warm and slippery with oil. The pressure increased and Tom felt himself begin to open up. He winced as the stretch bordered on painful for a moment, but it was more out of nerves than any real discomfort.

"Fuck, Tom," breathed Jon. "I am so *fucking* hard right now... watching this... doing this to you. I never thought..."

Tom let out a groan at Jon's words, his arousal rekindling again as he realized that the wooden cock sliding into his ass was not going to be the uncomfortable challenge that he had assumed it would be. Since the thing didn't actually have a head, being smooth and widening only slightly near the base, he knew he could take it.

Tom heard Jon take a shuddering breath and, hearing the rapid sound of skin on skin, came to the conclusion that Jon was jerking himself off as he fucked Tom's ass with the dildo. Tom's cock twitched against his stomach in response, almost painfully stiff and so sensitive that when he breathed and it moved against his belly hair, it sent little jolts of pleasure through him.

He lifted his head to look at Jon and saw that he was flushed; his eyes had taken on the glazed, rapt look of profound arousal as he stroked himself quickly. Then Jon began pulling the phallus almost all the way out and pushing it back in, slick and hard into Tom's body.

"Oh gods," murmured Jon. "I think I'm going to cum just looking at you."

Tom arched his head back on the pillow, his breath short and his heart thundering. He let out a gasp a moment later when the dildo left his ass and he heard Jon's strangled cry as he sent a jet of cum right against Tom's throbbing pucker. A second volley followed and then Jon pushed his slick cock inside Tom, fucking him quick and hard with a few deep thrusts as he rode out the tail of his climax.

Tom felt frantic and desperately aroused when Jon pulled out with a satisfied growl.

"Wow, sorry..." he said, panting. "I meant to draw that out more but..." He let out a breathless laugh. "Well, I guess it was a little too much for me."

It was hard not to feel disappointed. Jon obviously meant for him to "keep" another night. Tom started to lower his legs, but Jon stopped him with a hand, shaking his head as he caught his breath.

"I didn't mean I was done with you," he said with a smirk.

The first mate watched as Jon uncorked the little bottle of oil and poured some into his palm. He then stroked over Tom's asshole and into him, taking up the dildo a second later to begin working it into him again.

Tom was getting to the point where he was getting tense and frustrated, and if Jon wasn't going to let him touch his fucking cock, he'd rather just end their play right there. He was about to tell Jon exactly that when the smooth tip of the dildo prodded right into his prostate and sent a distinct burst of pleasure through him. A little startled at the sensation, Tom let out a soft sound.

Eyes closed, Tom furrowed his brow as Jon began to thrust the wooden cock quick and shallow into him, deliberately rubbing it over and over again at the sensitive point. It started off as a small, albeit pleasurable thing, but then he began gasping as an insistent, heady feeling began building inside him, like a bubble swelling with every pass of the dildo.

Tom whimpered. It was nearly intangible and sweetly agonizing at once—a growing pressure spreading warmth through his groin that would recede a little and elude him as the wooden cock moved away. He was only just aware of Jon whispers of encouragement as he began to moan louder and louder.

Drenched in sweat, Tom dug his fingers into the backs of his own thighs almost painfully. He was nearly there. So close. He was almost beside himself. *So. Fucking. Close.* It was insanity.

Then, deep inside him, the bubble finally burst and unleashed a rushing, wild tide that tore through his body. What came from his throat was nothing short of a yell; Tom arched his back and shuddered as his cock jerked, sending a thick jet of cum onto his chest. Powerful and violent, the waves surging inside him didn't crash to the shore; one would swell up only to be taken over by another and another, sharpening the intensity of the torrent that shook him. He was completely unable to stop the sounds pouring from him as he came harder than he ever had before. All at once, it was too much.

"Out," he gasped. "Out. Please *out out, out.*"

Jon pulled the wooden phallus out of him, and Tom turned to his side, curling into a ball as the pulsing, pounding surf finally began to recede. Hand around the base of his cock, clutching at himself so he didn't shake to pieces, Tom realized that his face was covered in tears and he was bawling his eyes out.

Jon curled up behind Tom and put his arm around him, murmuring soft things against his neck as he shuddered and wept. He didn't even know why he was crying... just that he was, and it felt like his heart was both breaking and flying at the same time.

"Sorry," he said and began to laugh, but a tremor shook him just then, and he went back to sobbing like a babe.

"It's ok," whispered Jon. "Don't be sorry. It's all right. I'd never judge you for crying, Tom. I love you. Cry as long as you need to. I'm right here. It's ok."

Tom cried until his tears dried up and then lay quiet on the pillow, just thinking. It was the second time something like this had happened to him, though it hadn't been *quite* so intense last time. He thought about the night that he snuck into Baltsaros's bed and how the captain had held onto him as he was beset by an inexplicable swell of emotion. Tom buried his face in the wet pillow, trying not to set off another bout of tears. A little embarrassed, he tightened his hand around Jon's, sighing when Jon kissed the nape of his neck.

"Five more bloody weeks," he muttered, thinking about much he missed Baltsaros.

"Yes, five weeks," replied Jon, with a small bite to his shoulder. "It'll go by fast. I'll make sure of it." His body was soft and warm against Tom's back, and when he nestled closer, Tom smiled.

"Aye, I can believe ye will, love," he said, wincing as the shift made him aware that he was a little sore. Moving his arm to get more comfortable, he encountered a cooling puddle on the pillow and grimaced. "Jon, we made a mess." Between their cum and the copious amounts of oil Jon had used, the sheets were completely soiled.

"Mmhmm," came the sleepy reply. "We'll clean up later."

Tom chuckled, sliding the wet pillow out from under his head and pushing it off the bed. He thought about the piles of discarded clothes on the floor and the dirty dishes they'd left on the table that morning. Baltsaros would be appalled at the pigsty they'd turned his cabin into.

Jon's mind must have followed the same path because he nuzzled against the back of Tom's neck with a little sigh.

"Like y'said... five weeks. S'nuff time... clean. Hm?" mumbled Jon.

Even though it was only barely past midday, Tom felt Jon twitch against him as he fell asleep. The first mate was also completely exhausted, like he had just fought a brutal fight and won. He closed his eyes and sleep claimed him almost immediately.

CHAPTER 15
HOME, SWEET HOME

With a grunt, Jon pulled on the rope, helping to haul the buntline as the men above worked to quickly furl the sails and tie them.

"Heave!" he yelled. "Heave, lads!"

When the sails were finally secured, he stepped back and smiled up at Tom. The first mate climbed down the rigging quickly and jumped to the deck next to Jon. He could almost feel the excitement radiating off the big man as they watched the hidden lagoon of Madierus get closer. They had made exceptional time; the trip had taken them only four weeks thanks to an unusually strong late-summer wind. The crew was exhausted, but their supplies had lasted well, and nothing unusual had happened during the journey south. Tuli clapped Jon on the shoulder, and he turned.

"It is beautiful!" exclaimed the tall ex-fisherman, his bright blue eyes wide. "Is there a... magic we should create for the arriving?"

Jon laughed and shook his head. No matter how many times he had reassured the newest members of the crew, they still had a hard time accepting that there were no set rituals to follow aboard. He didn't blame them; a lifetime of following a strict regimen of rites and sacrifices wasn't something so easily shrugged off. He smiled to himself as the lanky, white-haired man wandered away to the capstan. The men from the fishing clans were probably the worst, but superstition seemed to run rampant in sailors as a rule, no matter where they hailed from. As if to emphasise this fact, Jon saw one of the older northerners kiss a medallion he wore around his neck as he watched the harbour come into view.

"We bloody made it," murmured Tom.

Nodding, Jon saw that the land bridge they had concocted to keep invaders from entering the harbour had been shored up. It looked less like a bunch of floating bundles and more like a permanent addition. As the *Heart* approached, a man ran along the narrow strip of land and bent low to fiddle with something on a small boulder. A piece of the land bridge began to swing outward, and Jon saw that there were men on the other side pulling on a rope.

The man at the edge of the manmade strip of land pulled off his hat and began to wave it at the ship. When a woman's voice drifted over the water, Jon felt his face stretch into a wide smile and the fever of excitement he'd been keeping at bay finally took hold. He ran to the side of the ship and skipped up onto the gunwale to hang off the shrouds and yell back at Katherine, waving like a complete fool.

"Ahoy!" he laughed, giddy at seeing his friend.

"Ahoy yourself!" cried Katherine with a whoop, and she began running back along the land bridge to meet them at the beach.

Once they were past the opening, Tom glanced over at Jon, his brow wrinkled and his blue-green eyes wide. He'd never seen the first mate look so nervous before, and it resonated inside him.

Baltsaros.

Were they coming home to a madman?

Jaw clenched tight, Jon looked back over the clear turquoise water to the white beach and saw a group of people waiting for them in the shade of the almond trees.

"Ye got this?" asked Tom, his face tense.

Jon frowned.

"What? Why? Where are you going? We can't lower the boats yet, we haven't—"

"Don't need one," replied the first mate, and he took off at sprint without waiting for Jon's response. In amazement, Jon watched the big man clamber nimbly up the bowsprit and then dive headfirst off the front of the ship. Jon jogged to the bow and peered over the gunwale.

"Impatient ass," he said, smiling to himself as he watched Tom swim away from them. Glancing around, he saw that the crew's eyes were on him. He scowled.

"Well, what the fuck are we waiting for? Let's get that anchor down so we can get our asses to the beach. I don't know about you, but I'd like to feel a little sand underfoot!" he yelled.

A loud cheer went up and Jon grinned wide.

~

Tom turned his head to the side and sucked in a lungful of air as he propelled himself forward with long strokes, cutting through the water easily. The water was cooler than his skin, but not by much, and it stretched in front of him—a bright, clear blue against a sandy bottom dotted here and there with dark smudges that could be rocks or fish.

Tom was a powerful swimmer; he'd made sure of that after the long-ago blunder of jumping off the ship without knowing how to stay afloat. He'd been out further than this before, way past the mouth of the lagoon, especially in those early days when swimming had been a form of escape. Anything to get away from the fury that baked his bones every time he bore witness to his mother's scorn. Getting so worked up about it was stupid, he knew. But if she had done anything... *any* bloody thing at all to make him feel welcome, then she wouldn't be the one bearing the brunt of his bitterness for what had been done to him.

He took another deep breath and was startled when his hand hit sand. Tom stopped and reached down, steadying himself and letting his legs drop so he could kneel in the long, shallow stretch of water. Scanning the beach, he saw with dismay that there was no sign of Baltsaros. Kat nodded at him when their eyes met, and his little sister beamed at him with Jon's giant mutt panting at her side, but there was only a coldly appraising look from the woman who had given birth to him. He shook some water off as he staggered to his feet, surprised by the depth of anger that spiked him.

Forcing an impudent grin onto his face, he walked through the thigh-deep water and up onto the hot sand, stopping short of the shade.

"Well, well... Ain't this the poorest piss of a welcomin' party?" he said with a wink, avoiding his mother's gaze. "A man comes back from the bloody dead and not a mug o' beer on the lot of ye!" Kat rolled her eyes and the dog came padding towards him. He patted its gigantic, furry head and then smiled at his sister.

Tom got down on one knee and held out his arms to Eloise. The little girl had grown at least a hand since he'd last seen her.

"Come 'ere, my wee love," he said with honest warmth. His sister smiled shyly at him. "Aww... C'mon my poppet." This time she approached him and submitted to a rough hug with a little giggle. "Wait 'til ye see what I got for ye," he whispered to her, thinking of the golden tiara he had found among the golden loot from Balor. He squeezed her thin arms and pecked a kiss on her cheek before standing.

Brushing sand off his wet knees, he looked up and met his mother's eyes. They widened at him.

"Where the fuck is he?" he asked, his words barely a growl.

"He's in his tower," Abetha said after a moment, her pale hands clutched in front of her. How in hells a woman living on a tropical island remained so bloody white was beyond him. For some reason it made him even angrier.

Without a word he pushed past her and headed up the crumbling steps that led to the cobbled street above. The stones burned the soles of his feet when he got to the top, and he took off at a quick jog that would get him to the castle in no time. He had intended to wait for Jon, but between Baltsaros's absence and the presence of his mother, he felt on edge. Tom just needed to see... with his own eyes...

One breath for every three beats of his bare feet on the narrow road brought him to the castle gate in only a few minutes. He went past the koi pond and down the covered, arched walkway to a set of wooden doors that led to the tower stairs. Taking them two at a time, he made his way to the second floor and down the little hallway. Tom was surprised to see Saban seated in a chair right outside Baltsaros's bedchamber with a book of children's fairy tales open in his lap.

Saban looked up, startled. A slow smile spread across his face, and he quickly rose to his feet.

"Tom! You made it!" said the big man, clapping Tom on the shoulder. For a moment, it was like old times as he threw an arm around Saban's neck to slap his back in greeting; but, when Saban's big hand touched his side, the awkwardness came back in a rush, and Tom took a clumsy step back. Saban's eyes narrowed, looking both puzzled and a little crestfallen at his reaction.

Scratching the side of his thumb against his stubble, Tom glanced down at the book in Saban's hand. It was only then that he remembered that the ex-slave had only begun to learn his letters when they parted.

"When did you arrive?"

"Just now," Tom replied. "Wait… Didn'tcha hear we were spotted?"

Saban shook his head.

"No. I've been on watch all morning and came straight here from my quarters downstairs," he replied.

"Ah. Have they got ye in the old closet of a servant's room then?"

"Yes," replied Saban with a laugh. "I don't mind. Really. I'm close to Baltsaros in case he wants me."

Jealousy suddenly flared up in Tom like a hooded green snake at the thought of the handsome ex-slave in Baltsaros's bed, and he clenched his fists. Saban shook his head at Tom's reaction.

"I'm a glorified nurse. Nothing else. Relax," he assured him, and Tom let out a grunt, feeling both foolish and anxious. He was getting as bad as Jon. As Tom forced his shoulders down, he stared at the big wooden door behind Saban with a scowl.

"Really, Tom, I get it," said Saban softly. "He told me about what happened with Jon and what you went through. We… actually talked about it a whole lot."

"Yer not makin' me a whole lot happier 'bout it," muttered Tom, not thrilled to have his past aired like dirty laundry.

"And I told you… I'm not like *that*."

Tom turned to Saban and met his hazel eyes; he couldn't help but think of what Jon had said. However, all he saw before him was a man who was trying to comfort him and who was honestly glad to see him. He reached out to clasp Saban's forearm again.

"Sorry," he grumbled. "Four weeks can take the wind out of a mate's sails." He turned back to the door. "He ain't privy to us arrivin' then?"

"No. Like I said, I've been here all morning. So has he. He rarely leaves his quarters. Abetha and I have been trying to keep his days stress free. I'm sure she didn't tell us of your arrival because she wanted to make sure both you and Jon were aboard and alive first. Jon *is* here, right?"

"Aye," replied the first mate and took a step towards the door. "I need to see Da."

"That might not be a good idea." Saban's hand closed over his shoulder, but Tom shrugged it off. Keeping Baltsaros from excitement… It made bloody sense. But he didn't care.

Tom reached behind him and pulled the long knife out of his sheath. He looked at Saban with a menacing smile.

"I bloody need to see Da," he repeated. "Don't make me slit yer fuckin' throat, lad."

A flash of something crossed the big Balorian's face. Tom had seen it before... a second before he had been knocked senseless by Saban at the inn. He braced himself, dagger tight in his scarred fist, but Saban just smiled with a shake of his head and lifted his hands in supplication before stepping away from the door.

Tom yanked it open.

For a moment he was surprised by how bright the room was. He didn't know what he had been expecting... a darkened sickroom? His da stretched out in bed? Maybe tied to the posts with some heavy chains. Instead, what he was greeted with was a rather startled-looking Baltsaros who glanced up at him from behind a messy desk, a book in one hand and a quill in the other.

"Tom!"

The first mate quickly shut the door as Baltsaros rose to his feet, his eyes wide. For a second, all he could do was stare. The captain looked well. His hair was much shorter, falling only just past his cheekbones, and the dark circles under his eyes had vanished. Baltsaros looked younger, refreshed; he stepped out from behind his desk and smiled.

"Of course they wouldn't want to tell me," he said, shaking his head ruefully. "Welcome to my life. Do you have any idea what it's like to be nursed back to health by a brute with the strength of three men and a woman with a mind like a hedge maze?"

Tom stood rooted to the spot. He realized that he was clenching his teeth and took a quick breath through his nostrils.

"It's not the most pleasant thing in the world, though they do mean well, I suppose," laughed Baltsaros. He motioned to the plush, wing-backed chair. "Sit! Please."

After weeks of nervous anticipation, this was not what Tom had expected. Half of him was giddy with relief at finding the captain not only alive but also with both oars in the water, and the other half was weirdly reluctant to move from his place near the doorway. He wanted to press himself into Baltsaros's embrace, but the man's how-do-you-do had only stretched to offering him a comfortable fucking seat.

"I love ye and bloody missed ye, Da," he blurted out, all of his rehearsed words flying from his mind in favour of bluntness.

Baltsaros froze. He tilted his head, his dark-brown eyes on Tom's. All the first mate could see at first was confusion.

What am I doing? he thought in dismay. *Jon is right... I'm a stupid hasty fool. There's a time for everything and now's the wrong fucking time.*

However, Baltsaros took him in his arms a moment later with an audible sigh.

Tom sagged against the captain and buried his face in his collar. Baltsaros smelled like the imported eastern perfume he liked to wear—sandalwood, cardamom, woodsmoke—and his own soft musk beneath that. *This* was home. Tom's hands scrabbled over Baltsaros's back for a better hold, pressing them together. His heart thundered in his ears, and he felt like a hundred thousand miles were peeled from his past.

Baltsaros let out a small, hoarse laugh.

"You're crushing me, my tomcat," he said with an exaggerated wheeze.

Tom didn't care. He tightened his grasp like he was holding on to a rope above a bottomless pit. When Baltsaros held him tighter and he pressed his cheek to Tom's hair, the first mate ground his teeth together. Tom knew they had made the right choice to send the older man away, made obvious by his apparent recovery. But...

"I also fuckin' hate ye a little," he growled against Baltsaros's pale linen shirt.

Da's long fingers stroked the short hair at his nape, and Tom let out a heavy breath.

"Is it strange that I'm glad for both?" asked Baltsaros after a moment, his touch soothing.

Tom laughed. Before it became awkward, he pulled away. Tom scrubbed at his face and then sniffed a few times to get a hold of himself. He curled his lip.

"Well... I'm glad yer alive," he said, forgoing the offered chair and straddling the cushioned stool in front of it instead. He looked around at the familiar surroundings before bowing his head and rubbing both hands over his cropped hair. When he looked up again, he saw that Baltsaros had leaned back against the big desk and crossed his arms.

"Where's Jon?" asked the captain.

"He'll be here soon enough, Da," replied Tom with a crooked grin. "Can ye blame me fer wantin' ye to meself for a titch?"

Baltsaros chuckled and the crows' feet at the corners of his eyes deepened. He pointed to the cut-crystal glass decanter of something honey coloured, and Tom nodded, feeling a little nostalgic about this tradition of sharing a drink in the captain's sitting room. After pouring a few fingers into two tumblers, Baltsaros handed one to Tom and walked past him to sit in the comfortable chair he had earlier offered. Tom turned the ottoman around, the wooden legs scraping on the marble floor, and faced the captain. He lifted his glass.

"Strong winds and merciful fuckin' seas," said the first mate soberly.

Baltsaros raised his own drink and repeated the time-honoured toast of sailors before touching his glass to Tom's.

After downing the liquor, Tom held the glass out to Baltsaros with a wide grin.

With an amused shake of his head, the older man poured another liberal measure of the fine rum and watched the first mate knock it back with a smile.

Tom frowned and looked at the wide-open leaded-glass window. He could hear the clop of horse hoofs on the cobblestones. Jon would want to come see them but—and it made Tom feel like an asshole even thinking it—after nearly seven weeks, he needed to be far away from Jon's bleeding heart.

When he glanced at Baltsaros, he saw that he was being watched with an almost pained expression, and he felt a lance of worry spear him. He eyed Baltsaros warily.

"Get that look off your face, Tom," said Baltsaros reproachfully before taking a small sip from his tumbler. "I was just thinking to myself that I missed you very much."

Nodding, Tom scratched his neck. Though they touched him, the words sounded weird coming from Baltsaros.

The silence that followed was uncomfortable, and Tom realized he'd gotten used to Jon's constant need to talk everything out. He smiled to himself.

"Ye had no troubles?" he asked after a moment.

Baltsaros shook his head and leaned forward to fill Tom's glass again.

"We ran into a squall a week into our trip, but the ketch handles storms better than the *Heart*. We got blown off course but not by much, and we didn't lose anyone. Ceara has proven herself to be quite the competent sailor. I'm glad you and Jon decided to send her with me."

Tom just nodded, thinking about how she had been sent away by Jon to rid themselves of her.

"I have to say that I was not very happy when I awoke aboard the *Saber*. However, when I finally came to my senses, I understood why you did it."

"Saber?"

Baltsaros chuckled.

"*Black's Saber*. Not my idea. The boys named it after Jon," he replied. "I'm sure he'll be thrilled about that. I had to name my own ship after myself."

Baltsaros turned his head and his eyes went slightly vague for a moment.

"You should go," he said abruptly. "I feel... not... well."

"Ye seem fine," said Tom, alarmed.

"Am I fine? I don't think so. My memory is still spotty... When things do come back to me, it's as when circulation comes back to a numb limb. Saying that it's unpleasant is an understatement."

Baltsaros turned back to Tom and smiled sadly.

"See, the day I named *Baal's Heart*... It was the day we lost you. I just remembered that now. I also now remember not understanding why Jon was so broken-hearted over your death," he said, turning the crystal tumbler in his hands. There was a deep crease between his brows, and Tom was dismayed by the tremor he saw go through him. "I'm not happy about being reminded how foolish I was in that regard. Not realizing your worth was the most idiotic thing I've ever done. Argh!"

Baltsaros lurched to his feet and startled Tom by throwing the glass against the wall. It shattered and sent shards flying. The door opened and Saban poked his head around.

"Everything all right?"

"It's ok, Saban," said Tom, standing up.

"You should go, Tom," growled Baltsaros.

"I'm stayin' put. It's bloody time I muck in. Saban, mate, go to Jon. Don't tell 'im that Da's off his nut, but let 'im know that I'm takin' the night, aye?"

Saban's eyes darted between Tom and Baltsaros, and he slowly nodded. Before Saban turned to leave, Tom grabbed his arm.

"Jon'll be sore, but tell 'im not to fret. Savvy?"

With another nod, the big Balorian left and closed the door quietly behind him. Tom slid the bolt home so they wouldn't be disturbed.

"You have no idea what this is like," whispered Baltsaros behind him. "Tom, I am better and I am worse. Just when I think I can control myself, I remember things and it drives away everything but these... *feelings*. There's a maelstrom in my head."

"Use me," said Tom, turning.

Baltsaros's eyes went flinty for second before they widened in something that looked like fear.

"I can't."

"Use me, Da," repeated the first mate, taking a step closer. Baltsaros's nostrils quivered and he reached for Tom's shoulders, digging his fingers in painfully.

"I *can't*," breathed Baltsaros. "I can't control it. I can't take the chance."

"Bloody quit yer 'can't' bullshit, Da. Yer not a bloody coward and yer not a weak man, for hells' sake. *Use me.* I can take it. We'll get ye sorted out... Are ye still havin' turns as a madman?"

Baltsaros shook his head once.

"Not often," he replied softly.

"All righty," said the first mate with a grim smile, "if all ye are is pissed, then take it out on my hide, old man."

"Tom," warned Baltsaros.

"Don't tell me ye've gone all soft on me, ye daft fucker."

Baltsaros bared his teeth and pushed Tom away. The first mate fell back against the corner of the desk and landed hard on the floor. One of his hands came down on a piece of broken glass and when he lifted it, he saw it was bleeding. He slowly got to his feet, his eyes on Baltsaros. With a growl, he lunged forward at a crouch and barrelled into the taller man at waist height, sending them both crashing against the footstool and onto the carpeted marble floor. Baltsaros let out an enraged yell as he flipped Tom over onto his back and punched him square in the jaw.

Pain exploded in Tom's face, but he just bucked up hard and dislodged Baltsaros, grabbing him by the shirt to shove him headfirst into the wall. He climbed again to his feet, breathing hard and ready for more, and watched Baltsaros pull himself to standing by using the arm of the wide, wingback chair.

Glaring at Tom, his chest heaving, Baltsaros took a step forward. There was a bloody handprint on his linen shirt, and his hair had fallen over his eyes; he looked furious... and, to Tom's relief, just the tiniest bit amused. Tom didn't normally fight back so hard.

"I'm stronger 'n ye, Da. And ye've obviously been sittin' on yer arse too godsdamned long," taunted the first mate with a wry grin. He brought up his fists. This was exactly opposite of what Abetha and Saban would want, but he didn't care. Tom wanted to see if he could spark some kind of reaction out of the captain that wasn't immediately overshadowed by that bloody fear he kept seeing.

When Baltsaros came at him with a roar, Tom was ready for him.

Jon stepped out of the jolly boat, and as he turned around to grab the rope from Harris, he heard a thundering clatter behind him. Before he had a chance to react, something slammed into him, and he fell back on the sun-bleached boards, nearly rolling off the edge of it as he fought to free himself.

"Brutus!" he shouted with a laugh, pushing the mastiff's muzzle away from his face. "Stop it! Ouch... ouch! Watch it! Hey, buddy, yes I missed you too. Agghh! Stop it!"

He was trying to wiggle out from under the overexcited dog when there came a shrill whistle. Right away, Brutus stopped trying to lick the skin from Jon's face and jumped off, trotting back down the pier. Jon sat up, wiping dog slobber off with the hem of his black tunic. He could see Eloise dancing around the giant mastiff on the beach, and he grinned to himself. When Jon turned, he was startled to see that some of the passengers on the jolly boat were staring at him in shock.

"My dog," he said by way of explanation. Though from the looks of it, Brutus was more than happy to obey Eloise better than he had ever obeyed Jon. Maybe it was time to stop thinking of him as *his* dog. But Brutus was really the only link left of his old life; the dog had been his constant companion and only real source of happiness for a time. Jon let out a sigh and got to his feet.

As he was helping people out of the boat, Katherine approached with a broad smile on her tanned face.

"Jon."

"Katherine," he replied with a grin. When she continued just to stare at him, he frowned.

"What?"

"Jon... I don't know if you know this... but there's some sort of terrible growth on your face," she said, pointing to his chin with a smirk.

In mock indignation, Jon stroked his short, well-groomed beard.

"You're just jealous because you can't grow one."

Katherine barked out a single harsh laugh and shook her head at him.

"No, I'm just amazed because I didn't think you could grow one, kiddo."

Then Jon noticed something and laughed.

"What in the black hells? Lords, that thing is going to give me nightmares."

Katherine lifted her arm and appraised the hook that was attached to her stump. It was shaped out of dull grey metal, scored and dinged in places, and looked like it had been repurposed from something used to torture people with.

"Sexy, ain't it?" she said with a wink.

"Oh yeah. I'm getting hard just lookin' at it," he drawled.

Katherine blinked at him before grinning wide again. She pulled Jon into a quick, firm hug.

"Missed you, cabin boy."

"Missed you too," he replied. "And it's *captain*. Show some bloody respect."

"So I heard. How's that treating you?"

"Pretty great, actually. How's the farming life?"

Katherine made a tragic face and tugged on her braid.

"Not cut out for it," she said. "Fucking hate it. And"—Katherine glanced around—"Maya is driving me up the fucking wall, Jon. Not cut out for happy home life either, it seems."

Jon handed her a bag that she could sling over her shoulder, and he picked up a sack of his and Tom's clothes.

"What are you going to do, then?" he asked, as they began to walk down the pier.

"Ask for my spot back on the crew," replied Katherine with a little shrug.

"Like that's going to happen. Kat… You've got a hook for a hand. You're going to be as useful as tits on a nun, as Tom would say. How are you going to hoist a rope? Or load a pistol?" he said teasingly. But when he saw her smile fade some, he bumped his shoulder against hers. "Hey… I was kidding. We'll figure it out. I'm sure Baltsaros will find a place for you."

"What? Not you, *Captain* Black?" Kat grinned at Jon and jammed her rather squashed-looking straw hat back on her head.

"Well. No. When Baltsaros is back to health, he'll want his ship back." Not *if*… when. Jon had to believe he'd recover.

The sun shone down bright, and Jon shaded his eyes to glance back at the ragtag group that was following them. Madierus had gained eleven new citizens, soon to be twelve since one of the women was heavily pregnant. They were mostly ex-slaves and poor folk. The rich passengers had all disembarked at the southern peninsula. He turned back to Katherine.

"First thing we need to do is get these folks settled. I'm going to need your help with that." When Katherine nodded, he continued. "We picked up some tents and cots on the way here so we'd have temporary shelter for them at the very least. However, we're going to have to build at least three more structures, I believe, to accommodate everyone."

"Four."

"Ok, four. We also bought some basic materials and brought back window glass. It's all coming in on the next jolly boat. See Hitch for the full inventory. I also need for someone to show our new immigrants around and get them acquainted with laws and customs here. Most speak decent enough Common, and the ones that don't are still able to make their needs known. Talk to Nathaniel, and he'll give you the passenger manifest," said Jon. He stepped onto the sand and let out a little sigh at the soft heat between his toes. "Another thing—I'd like everyone to be made welcome, so I figure we should have some sort of welcoming celebration. Tom says it'll be the full moon in three days, so we'll hold it then. These folks are a little on the superstitious side, so it doesn't hurt to have the party made more meaningful by the moon. Or something. Just feels right. Though, skip using the word "blessing" or any permutation of that. And definitely no human sacrifice."

He chuckled to himself but saw that Katherine just stared at him wide-eyed.

"I'm not going to get into all the details, but the place we went to was wholly driven by human sacri—"

"Yeah, we heard," said Katherine, waving his explanation away.

Jon frowned. She seemed amazed at something.

"Kat? What is it then? Why are you looking at me like that?"

"It's just... You're different, Jon," she replied. Grinning away the seriousness after a pause, she leaned back to appraise him with a glint in her eye. "I got it! Your balls finally dropped!"

"Oh, fuck you!" He laughed and punched her playfully in the shoulder. Then he took a deep breath and straightened his spine.

"Come on," he said. "We're keeping the queen waiting."

~

Tom grunted and struggled hard against his bonds as he lay facedown on the mattress with his arms tied behind his back and his pants down around his knees. Baltsaros had finally managed to pin him, and, using the silk curtains that had been torn from the bed in their struggles, he had trussed Tom up tight.

With an aching jaw and his ribs sore from the fight, Tom breathed heavily through bared teeth as the adrenaline coursed through him, lighting his blood and giving him that dizzying high he always chased after. Growling, he tried to twist his arms apart but was rewarded with another hard crack of the riding crop to the back of his thigh. Tom clenched his jaw against the pain that lanced through him, setting his skin on fire.

Baltsaros chuckled and struck Tom again, this time across his ass, and the first mate let out a sharp gasp. A few more cutting blows, and Tom finally cried out, eyes shut tight and face pressed against the bloodstained sheet. Bracing himself, he waited for Baltsaros to hit him again.

"Please," he choked when nothing happened. "Da, please?"

"Please what, Tom? Please hit you again? Please *stop* hitting you? Or please fuck you?" laughed Baltsaros, stroking the tender flesh of Tom's backside with the crop. "You don't even know, do you?"

Tom moaned and turned his head. His cock was so bloody hard beneath him. Getting fucked *did* sound good to him... but...

"That's what I find so absolutely fascinating about you," said Baltsaros as he ran the tip of the crop along Tom's crack before striking him again across his thighs, forcing another strangled cry out of him. "And so marvellous. It's all mixed up in your head... You get lost in this, and then I find you, don't I? At the very edges of your pain, I pull you back."

The switch came down again, slicing into the back of Tom's biceps this time, and he yelled out.

"Please, Da," he said, panting.

"That very first night. Right in this bed... I spent a long time wondering why I didn't turn you away," murmured Baltsaros, placing his cool hand on Tom's burning thigh. "But then I asked you to join me again the next night. And the next. I was stupid not to realize that you *meant* something to me."

This time, Baltsaros slapped him with his bare hand. Less painful. More personal. Possessive. Tom's breath whistled from his lungs, and his senses were screaming at him.

"Please, Da," he whispered.

Laughing, Baltsaros slid his arm under Tom's hips and helped him to kneel so that he was presented, ass up. A few more slaps tore a soft sob out of Tom, and then there was pause where he could hear Baltsaros fumbling with his clothing.

Tom groaned loud as Baltsaros's cock breached him. Thick and hard, Baltsaros pounded into him without mercy, his big hands locked around Tom's hips to drive himself deep. The first mate began to grunt in time to the relentless fucking, the noises forced out of him by the brutal thrusts.

The loud slapping of Baltsaros's thighs against him was a frenzied thing, and each slam into his body coupled pain and pleasure in Tom. Panting, he closed his eyes tight as he felt the sweet warmth grow. Then Baltsaros growled and buried his cock to the hilt inside him; Tom's hands came free, and he realized that Baltsaros had cut his bonds. He quickly went up on one fist as the man resumed fucking him at a frenetic pace and began to stroke himself with the other hand, his torn palm stinging from the friction. His balls were tight, and every time Baltsaros's big cock opened him up, he came closer to spilling. He cried out softly, skirting the edge again, swollen and needy.

In response, Baltsaros leaned into his thrusts, letting out a long groan, and Tom couldn't hold back anymore. He let out a loud grunt and came hard, each pulse a deep burst of pleasure that radiated through him and left him shaking, weak, and empty in the end.

In a daze, he collapsed flat on the bed when Baltsaros finally released him, his pulse loud in his ears and a warm, buzzing feeling in his limbs.

"That wasn't prudent," muttered Baltsaros as he settled next to Tom.

"Mm? Fuck off."

Baltsaros let out a surprised laugh and kissed Tom's shoulder.

"I said it wasn't prudent. I didn't say I didn't enjoy it, Tom," he pointed out. "That being said… I feel… good. Normal." His fingers traced the welts on Tom's backside, and the first mate let out a huff of breath. "How did you know I wasn't going to really hurt you?"

Frowning, Tom lifted his head and looked over at Baltsaros.

"Didn't. But what's a bit o' my blood when it gives ye peace, Da?"

"Ah."

Tom grinned and then winced at the pain in his face.

"You know you're crazy?" Baltsaros said fondly.

"Naw," said the first mate and moved so that he could lie on his side with his head in Baltsaros's lap. The captain stroked his fingertips along the line of Tom's jaw and then skimmed the rim of his ear. It tickled, but Tom liked this new aspect of

Baltsaros... where he was softer after fucking. Before Jon, there had only been a handful of times where Baltsaros was so... Tom frowned and searched for a fitting word.

Kind? Could a dyed-in-the-wool killer—if that's what the man still was—be kind?

He reached up and touched the bruise on his da's jaw gently and made a face.

"Sorry."

Baltsaros caught Tom's hand in his and when he saw the cut on his palm, he kissed it quickly and looked away. He blinked rapidly, but not before the first mate saw the glimmer of wetness in his eyes. Tom pulled his hand away, unnerved by the captain's reaction.

When he noticed Tom's scrutiny, Baltsaros swiped at his eyes tiredly and let out a long exhale.

"See? I'm not all right," he said with an apologetic smile. "According to Abetha, I should be talking all these emotions out and finding out what triggers them. She thinks it's healthy and crucial to my recovery. I think she's foolish, but then again, I've been stuck here as a virtual prisoner. It makes me irrational, I'm afraid. Besides, you don't want to hear what I have to say."

"Who says?" asked Tom, wrinkling his brow.

"You've never been one for talk," said Baltsaros. He then shook his head. "Sometimes I think... well, that things were simpler before..."

Before Jon.

The words hung unspoken in the air.

Tom curled down the corners of his mouth and shook his head.

"Simpler ain't better."

Baltsaros laughed and nodded a few times, stroking Tom's short hair.

"True," he murmured.

Tom closed his eyes, giving in to the soft caresses. It was a nice complement to his aches elsewhere. He thought of something.

"I sent Saban to keep the lad away... but... Should I go fetch him?" Tom looked up at Baltsaros, not knowing whether he would be disappointed if the man said yes. However, Baltsaros shook his head after a thought.

"No. Not yet. Stay with me tonight. Jon can keep until morning."

Tom closed his eyes again and smirked at Baltsaros's choice of words. It was true, though. Jon would be ticked off, sure, but he was leagues away from the boy who had made mountains out of every fucking molehill. He'd get over it. Tom let out a little happy groan when Baltsaros's fingers slid down his neck, scratching softly at his chest before pinching his pierced nipple.

"I'm glad you're here, my tomcat."

"Mmm," he agreed, arching a stretch of his back as if he were really a giant cat. "Do that 'gain but harder."

Baltsaros chuckled and obliged.

CHAPTER 16
TROUBLE IN PARADISE

Jon stared at Saban, letting the words sink in. The tall ex-slave regarded him quietly, sympathy in his green-brown eyes.

"He doesn't want to see me," Jon said tersely.

Saban's shapely brows pinched together.

"I don't think it has to do with *want*, Captain."

"No, I get it. Tom and Baltsaros are going to hole up for the night and call for me in the morning like a bloody servant," snapped Jon. But, when Saban opened his mouth to reply, Jon lifted a hand to stop him.

"I'm sorry," he said with a sigh and let his shoulders slump. "You're just the messenger. Don't mind me." Jon massaged his temples, eyes closed, and tried not to feel the anger by telling himself that it wasn't betrayal. If Tom thought he should stay away, he probably had a very good reason. The first mate's instincts were good, and the truth of the matter was that he had known Baltsaros for far longer than Jon had. It just stung. He looked up and saw that Abetha watched him with guarded eyes. There was compassion there and warmth... and bitterness. At first he thought the last was aimed at him, but as he stared at her, she swallowed, lifting her chin a little, and he understood.

"Thank you, Saban. Let me know if anything changes?" he said awkwardly, still feeling a little uncomfortable speaking to the ex-slave after what had happened. Saban just nodded slowly.

Jon took a step towards the queen, and Abetha raised an eyebrow at him.

"Both of us left in the lurch, hm?" he smiled sympathetically. He then tilted his head at her. "Your Majesty, why do you let Tom believe you care so little? Why not let him into your pain? He has no idea..."

Abetha's eyes turned cold, and as her nostrils flared slightly, Jon realized that he'd crossed a line in assuming that he could speak to her as a friend—especially about something so personal.

Drawing herself up, the icy queen averted her gaze and focused on a spot over his shoulder.

"I had Cook make up some beefsteak pies with stuffed quail and greens. We dine in an hour. I'll have Pesha show you to your room," she said in reserved tones.

"No, thank you, Your Majesty," he replied politely. Baltsaros was right about the pigheadedness of mother and son. Suddenly his exile didn't seem so cutting, compared to the river of tears he saw behind the stately queen's luminous eyes. "I'll pop down to the *Grog Blossom* and catch up with old friends. If you'll excuse me, that is."

Abetha just gave a prim little nod and turned, dismissing them. Jon felt bad for a moment, wondering if he should stay after all and keep company with the sad queen during the meal. However, Saban gave him a quiet, reassuring smile.

"Go see your friends, Jon," he said, eschewing Jon's title for the first time. "The queen and I have things to discuss anyway."

Jon realized then that Saban was also aware of the queen's feelings, and he pressed his lips together with a nod. Though there was still jealousy in his heart over what had happened with Tom, he knew he was indebted to Saban.

"Thank you," he replied, putting extra warmth in his voice. "You're a good man. I'm glad for your presence."

At Saban's skeptical brow lift, Jon let out a genuine laugh.

"Ok... mostly glad," he admitted. "I'm working on it, but we are allies. I promise you that. Maybe friends one day." He put out his hand and when Saban took it, Jon shook it with a heartfelt squeeze, truly believing his words.

Jon pushed open the doors of the *Blossom* and smiled wide when he saw that it looked exactly as it had when he left. The place was full, and he had to push his way through a group of deckhands to get to the bar. Standing on a stool with her back to him, Maya was lighting one of the coloured lanterns against the growing dusk.

"I heard that the beer here was pretty good," he said loudly.

Maya started and turned around, shaking the burning taper in her hand.

"Gods and goddesses! Jon!" she exclaimed, jumping down. She quickly ducked beneath the bar and hugged him tight with a soft little laugh. Then she pulled back and stared up him, clucking her tongue. "Just look at you. You were comely before, but I'd have to call you downright handsome now. I love the beard! You look so dashing!" Her big blue eyes crinkled at him fondly.

"Oh, babe, don't tell him that. Now he'll want to keep that god-awful face fungus," laughed Katherine, appearing with two mugs of ale in her good hand. Jon took one and downed half of it in a way that would make Tom proud.

Maya snapped her fingers and pointed at someone in the crowd. A young, gangly lad with bright-orange hair nodded and passed under the bar, taking his place at the pumps.

"Send a pitcher out back," she told him. "And have Wenz bring us three trenchers of chowder when it's ready."

Jon let himself be led to the patio where Maya good-naturedly ousted a pair of carpenters to free up one of the tables for them. He sat down and looked out over the water where the *Heart* was still being unloaded.

"Wasn't expecting you here until tomorrow at the earliest, Jon," said Maya reaching for his arm. "What happened?"

Jon wrinkled his nose as he stared down into his near-empty mug and shook his head.

"He just wasn't ready to see me," he replied. "It's ok though. I'm not sore. I waited nearly two months to see him. Another night is not going to kill me."

"Where's Tom?" asked Katherine.

"Where do you think?" he replied with a short laugh.

"Ah. Poor honey," said Maya with a little pat to his bare forearm.

Jon looked up and saw that both of them were staring at him with pity. Instead of making him angry though, it just made him feel sheepish, and he shrugged, chuckling to himself.

"I'm a big boy," he said and drank down the rest of his beer just as the ginger youth set down a pitcher and third mug in front of them. Jon smiled. "Like I said: I'll live. Stop staring at me like that." He poured himself another beer and served Maya and Katherine.

"So! Tell me everything that's happened while I've been gone," he said after another deep swallow.

The chowder was good, but he barely tasted it. He'd had too much to drink and his senses were a bit hazy. It was pitch-dark beyond the tavern, but if Jon leaned forward in his seat, he could just see the lights of the castle nestled against the mountainside.

During the *Heart's* trip to the southern peninsula, Madierus had known a strange outbreak of something that had claimed three lives. However, four babies had been born, so Katherine had quipped that it hadn't been all bad. They'd also seen a drier summer than usual, which explained the ex-pirate's frustration at being a farmer. Jon had laughed and teased her about it, but that had led to a bickering fight between the two women that had seen Maya storm off in the end, claiming that she needed to take a look at the stores in the cellar. Katherine had just shaken her head and poured another round of drinks before launching into a tirade of what felt like every single argument the married couple had had since his departure.

Finally, Katherine's ranting wound down, and she let out a long sigh.

"Well... How is everything with you?" she asked, peering at Jon.

"S'ok," he slurred a little with a shrug.

"I mean... like, *everything*?" Katherine said with an exaggeratedly shrewd look. The tall woman was definitely as drunk as Jon, and he smiled at her expression.

"You mean between me n' Tom?" he replied, taking another sip.

"Yeah. You know I don't get it. Fucker's not good enough for you."

"That's not true," he said with a scowl.

"Oh, s'everything is rainbows and fucking kittens with you two?"

After another long look at the castle, Jon heaved a sigh of his own.

"No," he admitted. "Not really."

Jon grinned at the newly painted figurehead. He was impressed. Tom had cut out the rotten parts of the skull's jaw and replaced them with new pieces of wood that he had carved to match. His addition had altered the skeleton to make it look like it was laughing manically instead of screaming. To Jon, it was an improvement. Tom had also removed the rusted chains so that he could paint the whole thing. It now just looked like it was clutching its bony chest instead of being bound.

"I think you should leave the chains off," said Jon, squinting. "I've got an idea. Why not paint a heart in red between the fingers here? Would certainly hold with the name of the ship, right?"

The first mate's brow wrinkled, and he nodded slowly.

"Aye," he agreed. "Just hopin' Da won't take offense at the fact that the skelly looks barmy, seein' as if it's *Baal's* heart, then..."

With a laugh, Jon nodded, but it was fitting. The ship had always had a madman at the helm... The thought sobered him. He watched Tom take up the red paint and begin to trace out the shape of a heart between the figurehead's bony fingers. However, he smiled to himself again as the first mate's tongue poked out of the corner of his mouth with his concentration. Jon stepped forward and slowly stroked Tom from shoulder to hip. In response, Tom let out a little growly sound and ceased his painting.

"Do ye want me to join ye somewheres, love?" asked the first mate.

"Yes," replied Jon, reaching around to grab the bulge at the front of Tom's shortened pants.

"Is it gonna be like last time?"

Jon stopped fondling the first mate.

"What does that mean?"

"Ye've been—" said Tom a little hesitantly, "—soft a lot. Just wanted to know if that's what yer gonna be like."

Jon pulled away and frowned.

"I have not. What are you talking about?"

Tom turned to him and smiled crookedly.

"No... Not yer pecker, lovey. Just the way ye've *been*."

Jon thought about the last few times Tom and he had been together. Shared passions, slow build-up, breathless afterwards and sated. He stared at the first mate.

"This is because I don't feel the need to beat the shit out of you every time we fuck?" he said, incredulous. "I'm sorry that bothers you so much."

Tom's jaw worked for a second, and Jon was sure he was going to say something, but instead he turned and went back to his painting.

"I just need to be in the right frame of mind," Jon said. "We talked about it."

Tom let out a grunt with a little nod, but he didn't turn again.

"I can't be like that all the time," continued Jon.

This time Tom didn't reply.

"If that's what you really want though, I suppose I could try to..." Jon said faintly.

Turning to face him, the first mate looked exasperated.

"All I needed was a bloody *yes* or *no*, Jon," Tom replied. "Just wanted to fuckin' know if I was gonna be coddled or cocked hard. That's it. *Yes* or *no*. We'd fuck all the same... Just wantin' to know."

"Tom... If I'm not doing it for you, I'm sorry. Shit, I wouldn't mind it if you took the lead sometimes, but I haven't complained, have I?" Jon pointed out. "If you just told me what you wanted, then maybe I could—"

His fists balled, Tom stared at Jon.

"*Yes* or bloody *no*. That was it, Jon. Stop yer fuckin' yammerin'. I don't rightly care."

"You obviously do," whispered Jon, dismayed by the first mate's reaction.

Tom narrowed his blue-green eyes at Jon for a moment and then resumed his work on the figurehead like Jon wasn't standing there.

The first mate was right. Jon hadn't been very commanding with Tom, and he couldn't remember the last time they'd done anything but just fuck and fall asleep together. He realized that he had misunderstood just how much violence was a part of Tom's make-up; he had assumed—wrongly, it seemed—that Tom was happy for the reprieve from Baltsaros's sadism. The taciturn first mate didn't exactly make his needs known. In fact, Tom rarely wanted to talk about anything; it was more than a little frustrating.

After watching him for a couple of minutes, Jon spoke up.

"Yes," he ventured quietly.

Tom side-eyed him.

"Yes, it was going to be like last time."

After capping the pot of red paint, Tom then dropped his paintbrush in the jar of turpentine and started towards their quarters without a word.

However, the exchange had soured Jon's mood, and he no longer felt particularly into it, knowing the first mate's dissatisfaction. But, that was part of the problem: was Tom really dissatisfied or was Jon just projecting his own biases? It was so hard to tell. If he asked, Tom would shrug and say that Jon was putting words in his mouth and that just because he mentioned something, didn't mean that there was more to it than that.

Confused and a little tense, Jon followed Tom anyway.

～

Katherine banged on the table, laughing as Jon finished giving a not too explicit account of some of the problems Tom and he had faced in the long weeks alone with each other.

"Sounds like the honeymoon is over!" she chortled. The ex-pirate then rocked back in her chair and beer slopped over the edge of her glass as she tried to take a drink from it.

Maya, having rejoined them, glared at her wife.

"Jon... Those *are* valid complaints," said Maya, taking away Katherine's mug of beer.

"Hey!"

"For all that you dislike Tom, you two are pretty similar in some respects," said the pretty tavern owner, her blue eyes snapping at Katherine.

The pirate blinked slowly at her wife in confusion.

"Wha? What I do?"

Jon stood unsteadily, realizing that he'd set off another round of bickering, and decided to call it a night.

"Forget I said anything," he mumbled. "Going home... Ha! *Home*. Fuckin' home? As if that's home." He held tight to the side of the table to stop himself from swaying.

"Jon, you should probably stay here. The little room upstairs is empty."

Screwing up his eyes at Maya, Jon shook his head. His vision was a little doubled, but it wasn't too bad. Sleeping in that bed upstairs would only remind him of the night he had spent with Baltsaros there, and he was already feeling like a sad sack.

"Nah. I'm good," Jon said, patting her shoulder. "See ya tomorrow, Maya. Have good night, hm? And Kat?" He grinned drunkenly.

"Yeah?"

"Fuck you."

Jon barely registered the walk home except for getting turned around after taking a piss against a fan palm. It had taken him a few minutes to realize he was going downhill instead of up, and he had nearly fallen down onto the beach when he tried to correct his course. After staggering up the long walkway, he steered way clear of the fishpond in case he tripped and fell in, and then he quietly opened the side door.

With a mumbled curse, Jon stopped at the foot of the stairs. He couldn't go up to Baltsaros's room; he wasn't wanted.

Don't be such a bloody baby. Jon scowled at the first mate's voice in his head.

Leaning against the stone wall, he peered down the dark corridor. In his haste to get away from the castle, he'd neglected to find out where his own room was. Where was he going to sleep? Then he recalled seeing a sitting room somewhere nearby and started to make his way down the hallway, his hand trailing over the stones to steady himself; Jon figured he could sleep on a chair if he found one.

However, when he reached the room, Jon realized that Abetha would probably have his hide if he dirtied any of her chairs; he didn't want to chance it. Jon turned when he heard a noise behind him and smiled when he saw it was just Brutus.

"Hey, boy," he whispered. "Come to spend a li'l time with me?" The big dog sat down on his haunches and tilted his blocky head at Jon, a glimmer of slobber on his jowls. Jon took a step towards Brutus and knocked his leg against a small stool. With a pained, muted groan, he rubbed his shin. When he turned to replace the dainty piece of furniture, he saw glass doors and remembered that this room led out to a small terrace with *chaises longues* and parasols.

"Good 'nuff, eh, Brutus?" he said with a wry grin.

After he'd stretched out on one of the wicker couches, Jon looked up at the twinkling stars and sighed. At least he wouldn't freeze—the night was balmy. Brutus turned around three times, settling down on the ground next to the chair, and Jon put a hand on the dog's head just like old times. He closed his eyes and shifted on the hard surface until he was as comfortable as he'd get. Before long, the sounds of the surf and the whistling frogs lulled him to sleep.

~

Jon stared up at the sky. There were pale-green lights that danced in the deep blue-black expanse, painting a path across it. His feet were cold and when he looked down, he saw snow. At first he thought he was on the deck of the Heart, *but the silhouette of sails were actually mountains, and the snow beneath his feet covered frozen soil, not boards. He took a step forward, glancing up at the night sky again. This time he could see stars. They blazed like electric lanterns above his head. There was a keening behind him, and he saw that the black lion held the back of the tawny wildcat's neck in its teeth. With fascination he watched the lion mount the cat, thrusting quickly as blood ran from where its fangs had punctured skin. Jon found himself getting aroused. When he walked forward to join them, Jon realized he was on a path between two large mounds, and that he was freezing. His bare foot touched ice, and he looked down to see that there was a frozen whirlpool in front of him. In the center was a heart carved out of ice. It began to beat, and Jon felt a pressure in his chest. He looked down and saw that his chest was made of clear ice and that there was no heart within. He called out to the animals, to his protectors, but they were too involved in their mating to pay attention to him. Across the whirlpool, a boy with a moon for a face had one eye open and one eye closed. He smiled at Jon.*

"Are you awake, Jon? Or are you sleeping?"

~

Jon blinked awake and stared up at the man standing over him. Saban smiled, the scar at the corner of his mouth dimpling.

"Are you awake, Jon?" asked the big man in his smooth baritone.

Jon licked his lips and squinted. The sun was just coming over the trees, and for a moment he had no idea where he was. His head felt like there was a cannonball in it, and his mouth was pasty and foul. Jon knuckled his eyes and then swallowed against the nausea that assailed him when he sat up. A shiver went through him, and he wrapped his arms around himself, realizing that he was slightly damp from sleeping out of doors. Only broken pieces of the previous night came back to him, and Jon hoped he hadn't made a complete fool of himself.

"Late night?" asked Saban, looking amused. In one hand he held a cup, and when Jon's brain finally registered the smell of coffee, he pointed to it.

"Mine?"

Saban nodded, handing the mug over to Jon, and watched him down some of the bitter black liquid.

As it hit his stomach, it churned; Jon quickly pulled the cup away from his lips and clenched his jaw. Salty saliva pooled in his mouth as he sat with his eyes shut, fighting against the urge to be sick.

"Do you want me to bring you some bread?" asked Saban. When Jon shook his head, Saban added: "It's fresh baked and will sop up some of that alcohol you still have floating around in your guts."

"Ok. Yes," whispered Jon.

He cracked an eye when the turmoil subdued somewhat in his belly and looked around. Brutus was nowhere to be seen. He had probably gone back to his mistress's side once Jon passed out in sodden slumber. The dew sparkled on the short spring grass, and Jon shivered again, wishing he had asked Saban for a blanket.

The broad-shouldered Balorian returned a few minutes later with a small basket containing half a loaf of dark bread. After handing it to Jon with an amused grin, he dragged one of the smaller wicker chairs closer and sat down, legs stretched out in front of him.

"Another beautiful day in paradise," rumbled the big man as he closed his eyes and turned to face the warm rays of sun. "If you had told me one day that I not only would be a free man, but one who lived on an island such as this, I would never have believed it. I would have probably told you that you were a prime candidate for a sacrifice, spreading such preposterous tales."

Jon nodded as he chewed slowly. The bread was unbelievably good. He waited a few moments after swallowing to make sure that it wasn't going to come right back up and took another bite. Saban turned his hazel eyes again to Jon and watched him silently.

"I was wondering... Do I owe you an apology, Jon?" Saban asked in a soft voice.

With a frown, Jon tore another piece off the loaf and ate it. Tom had been very clear that it had been he that had kissed Saban, not the other way around, and that Saban had pushed him away immediately. Jon thought about the Balorian watching Tom pleasure him in the dark of the captain's quarters, and he felt himself redden, both from the embarrassment of being seen and from the stupidity he had uttered.

"I feel like I owe *you* one," he admitted, meeting Saban's eyes.

With a chuckle, the big man shook his head.

"No apologies then. A new page."

Jon returned the friendly smile and then nodded. After a few more mouthfuls of bread, he gestured to the nearly empty basket.

"You were right. My stomach is better, thank you. I need more coffee, but it looks like I'm going to live," he said. Though his head was pounding, the warming sun was drying his clothes and he was beginning to feel more human.

"Good," said Saban. He stood and took the basket from Jon. "Because the captain wants to see you."

Jon's heart dropped off a cliff at the words and his pulse felt light and airy. Dizzy, he laughed to himself and rubbed at his face with numb hands.

"Shit," Jon muttered.

He rose to his feet unsteadily and mumbled a thanks to Saban before turning to leave.

The ex-slave touched his shoulder, and he looked up.

"Don't look so worried, Jon," said Saban with a quiet smile. "He spoke often about you with warmth. I'm sure that hasn't changed."

After smoothing back his wet hair and tugging down his fresh tunic, Jon opened the door to Baltsaros's rooms. When he saw the upturned furniture and blood on the floor of the empty sitting room, he felt worry lick his heart. He crossed the space in a few quick strides and yanked open the door to the bedchamber, afraid of what might be on the other side.

In the large room beyond, chairs had been tipped over—one of them missing a leg —and it looked like a chunk of plaster from the wall had exploded on the rucked-up carpet. The big four-poster bed was in shambles; the coloured silk hangings were torn, half of them on the floor, and there were big bloodstains on the sheets. However, sitting serenely in the midst of the disaster was Baltsaros, reading a bound book and drinking from a delicate, pale-blue porcelain cup. Next to him, face down and only half-covered with the sheet was Tom, fast asleep with one brawny, tattooed arm dangling over the side of the bed. There were two heavy tomes open on his broad back. It seemed that the first mate was being used as a makeshift bookstand by Baltsaros.

The scene was so preposterous in its domestic tranquility in comparison to the surrounding destruction that Jon let out a laugh. Tom twitched and shifted slightly in his sleep, and Jon saw that his muscled buttocks were striped with fresh welts that continued down the back of his legs.

When Jon took another step into the room, Baltsaros hastily put down his coffee and got out of bed. Wearing only a blood-red silk dressing gown, Baltsaros crushed Jon into his embrace. With a startled laugh, Jon hugged the tall man back and then smiled up at him when he pulled away.

"I have *missed* you, my love," said Baltsaros, giving Jon's shoulders a hard squeeze.

682

Obviously not enough to see me right away, said the bitter little voice in Jon's head. He felt his smile slip a notch, but he pressed himself back against Baltsaros and closed his eyes.

"Missed you too," he mumbled. The robe was slippery-soft against him as he cleaved to Baltsaros's strong body a moment longer. When they finally broke the embrace, Baltsaros's eyes searched Jon's face, his eyebrows high.

"You look sick, Jon. Are you all right?"

Jon knew that he was probably pale, and just then a tiny tremor went through him. The second cup of coffee was sitting badly in his gut, and he felt weak and shaky.

"Had drinks with Kat and Maya last night," he admitted, wiping at the sheen of perspiration on his forehead. "Many, *many* drinks."

Gaze narrowed in amusement, Baltsaros shook his head. He reached for the hem of Jon's tunic to pull it up, and Jon automatically lifted his arms to let himself be undressed. Baltsaros's eyes were clear, and he seemed self-assured. Jon felt his hope swell; maybe things would be better now.

"What happened to the room?" he asked, glancing around. Jon shivered when a warm breeze came in through the window, and he realized just how awful he felt.

"Tom was helping me work through something," Baltsaros replied, dropping the shirt next to an upended table.

When Baltsaros reached for Jon's belt, Jon stopped him.

"I feel like shit," he whispered.

With a chuckle, Baltsaros moved Jon's hand away and resumed.

"I'm not expecting anything," he replied with a soft smile.

Baltsaros's expression was serious but tender as he undid Jon's belt. His light-brown hair had been cut shorter; it concealed his eyes as he leaned forward and Jon could see how threaded it was with white. When Baltsaros saw him watching, the graceful curve of his lips spread into a grin and he tilted his head. Despite his throbbing headache and the green nausea that kept sloshing through him, Jon found himself grinning back shyly and wished again that he hadn't gone to excess the evening before. His pants fell to the floor, and when Baltsaros moved to hold him again, Jon let out a nervous little laugh. It had been nearly two months since they'd really had a moment like this—three, if Jon counted the trip from the other side of the black mountain range while Baltsaros struggled so hard with the effects of his ordeal. Held confidently in strong arms, a steady heartbeat against his skin... Hells, if the floor had been rocking gently beneath his feet, Jon would have thought himself back aboard the *Heart* before all of the madness had started. But was it truly over? Not if the state of the bedchamber was anything to go by.

Baltsaros's voice broke through his thoughts.

"Tom said that you've been doing a praiseworthy job, and that I should consider making you quartermaster once we set sail again."

Jon pulled back and frowned up at Baltsaros.

"He did?"

Nodding, Baltsaros touched Jon's cheek, his warm brown eyes on his beard. Jon could tell he approved of it.

"I had the impression that I was beginning to annoy the fuck out of him," said Jon, turning his eyes to the slumbering first mate.

Baltsaros laughed and led Jon towards the bed.

"Yes. Maybe a little," he said as he took the books off Tom's back to pile them on the bedside table. "But he also sounds more deeply devoted to you than ever."

Jon climbed onto the mattress, looking askance at all the bloody handprints on the white sheets as he crawled in next to Tom. Baltsaros undid his robe to let it fall from his shoulders before he gathered it up and draped it at the foot of the bed. In addition to the healed burn marks from the electrodes on his torso, there were bruises and scratches that he had obviously sustained during his tussle with the first mate.

"He does?" asked Jon.

"Tom?" replied Baltsaros as he slid under the covers and settled next to Jon. "Of course he does. Your need for constant reassurance hasn't changed, I see." Despite the teasing words, Baltsaros's tone was fond.

At the sound of his name, Tom turned over and threw his arm around Jon's waist, dragging him closer so that the first mate's mostly limp cock nuzzled up warm between his cheeks.

"Mmm?" Tom burrowed his face into Jon's shoulder and promptly fell back to sleep.

Baltsaros stretched to his full length with a quiet groan and turned to smile at Jon.

"And, before you ask: No, I am not 'cured'. I'm still unable to gather my thoughts at times, and when it comes to regulating my reactions, I'm still doing poorly. However, Abetha believes that the worst is over and I truly, honestly think that you are in no danger from me. As long as we keep things... sedate. Now," Baltsaros reached out and stroked Jon's curls, "why don't you try to sleep. You'll feel better. We have all the time in the world to talk."

Tom's heat felt good against his back, and when Baltsaros moved closer to him, Jon curled his arm around his hip, let out a long sigh, and closed his eyes.

CHAPTER 17

BLOOD AND PROMISES

Happiness or satisfaction consists only in the enjoyment of those objects which are by nature suited to our several particular appetites, passions, and affections.

—JOSEPH BUTLER

Baltsaros watched his boys sleeping entwined on the soft feather mattress and smiled to himself. After tightening the sash around his waist, he smoothed the tunic over his hips and left the bedchamber. The door closed silently behind him, and Baltsaros looked around at the shambles that his sitting room had been turned into. With a crooked grin, he stooped to put right the ottoman; Tom had been correct to provoke him the previous day. Instead of being launched into lunacy by the fight, Baltsaros had been *right there* the whole time, in control and aroused and... happy. As he picked up the stack of letters that had been swept to the floor, he frowned in thought.

His adult life had mostly been one of contentment—a calm, clear sea of satisfied self-possession, marred only occasionally by ripples of annoyance. Those sources of irritation had, for the most part, been easily dispatched, thus returning his mood to a placid, mirror finish. However, Jon had somehow managed to dip into deeper waters to stir up the emotions that rested like silt at the bottom. What had surfaced had changed him. Like happiness. Baltsaros could truly say that having both Tom and Jon in his life made him *happy*.

Unfortunately, the chain reaction catalyzed by Jon had made Baltsaros rather susceptible to the emperor's device. It had churned up everything that Baltsaros was, leaving only turbulence and ruin behind.

Baltsaros pressed his lips together and straightened. Normally, the thought of his torture brought with it sharp, hot spikes of anger that he fought to control. However, as he stood still in the early morning light, waiting for the fury to overwhelm him, he found that he was able to address it with some detachment, thanks—at least in part, he figured—to the rough play with Tom.

Am I just suppressing my anger? he wondered as his heart rate slowed and his good humour returned.

With eyes narrowed at the bloodstained rug, he wondered whether Abetha was right about how to approach the repercussions of his ordeal. His ex-wife was convinced that having iron control over his emotions was deleterious to his recovery. That to feel *less* would somehow continue to cripple him.

His mind on the interesting conundrum, Baltsaros left the room and started down the stairs. Before Jon, there had been satisfaction. Contentment. Peace. If suppressing his emotions would bring him back to that, would that be so bad? He'd be giving up the happiness he had found, but he'd also be losing the simmering rage that constantly set his blood to boiling over the smallest things. He'd no longer be robbed of coherent thought as he was torn apart by furious emotion.

Brow furrowed, he turned down the corridor and headed towards the rear of the castle. Maybe keeping his emotions buried *was* best for him. Who was to say which path was right when it all felt so labyrinthine? He passed through the big glass doors and into the topiary garden. The late-morning sun was hot, and Baltsaros ducked beneath one of the orange trees that shaded the garden. Reaching up, he quickly found a ripe fruit and then sat down with it on the marble bench.

Smirking, he wondered if it were even possible to keep his feelings bottled up given that he would never let Jon go. He also had to admit to himself that he didn't *want* to give up what he was feeling for the boys, whatever it was. But did that spell a life of constantly shifting waters for him?

Baltsaros let the orange peels fall between his bare feet and breathed in the sweet, tangy smell. As he chewed on a juicy slice, he mulled over his dilemma and waited for Abetha to join him with a mug of coffee in each hand, just as she had most mornings since his arrival.

~

Jon cracked an eye open and saw that Baltsaros had gone. His bladder was full, and he was groggy and sweaty, but his hangover seemed to have peaked, and he felt better for sleeping. Judging by the slant of the sun outside the leaded-glass windows, it was past noon. When he tried to lift the first mate's arm away, Tom moved against him and let out a little rumbled growl.

"Where d'ye think yer goin'?"

"I'm overheating and I have to pee," complained Jon, giving the burly man's arm another shove. "Get yer bleedin' carcass off o' me."

Tom laughed low at Jon's imitation and released him with a dramatic sigh.

Jon slid off the bed and made his way to the small door that led to the water closet beyond. When he was done, he walked back into the bedchamber and saw that Tom sat on the edge of the bed with a pained look on his face. Jon raised his eyebrows. In addition to the tattoos, the first mate's chest sported fresh, mottled bruising, and he winced as he prodded at his ribs.

"Fucker knows how to land a punch," he muttered when he saw Jon watching him. There was a painful-looking cut on one of his cheeks, and he let out a low grunt as he flexed his hands. The knuckles of his right hand were torn up.

Jon smiled at him.

"Was it worth it?" he asked as Tom tried to peer over one big shoulder to see the damage on his back.

Tom laughed and nodded, his green-blue eyes amused. However, when he went to push himself up, he grimaced and stood slightly hunched. Forehead creased, he looked sheepishly at Jon and held out his hand. There was a bloody, jagged slice across his palm.

"Can ye take a look at this, love?" asked the big man. "Think there's glass in there. I'd be obliged if ye got it out."

Jon grinned wider and teasingly clucked his tongue before taking Tom's hand in his to see if he could find the sliver.

After squeezing lemon over what Abetha had called *harira*, Jon stirred the thick soup and ate a spoonful of the chickpeas and chicken. It was delicious and savory, and the meat was extremely tender. Across the table, Tom dunked a piece of flatbread into his bowl with his bandaged hand, a frown on his battered face. Abetha watched the first mate for a moment, her nose slightly lifted, and turned her attention back to Jon. Her eyes, so like Tom's, regarded him coolly for a moment.

"No, I'm sorry, Jon," she finally answered him. "Baltsaros won't be joining us. He has decided to take the noon meal in his rooms. He was unduly stressed by your arrival, and we believe that a quiet afternoon to himself is what is needed."

Jon's eyes widened and he glanced at Tom. The first mate's scowl had deepened as he attacked his soup with more bread.

The moment they had sat down, Abetha had coldly upbraided Tom for his lack of shirt—something that Jon could sort of understand; they were eating in a lavish dining room, and that *did* call for a slight bit of decorum. In return, Tom had just curled his lip and had basically turned into a sulky child with shoulders high and eyes focused on the table in front of him. The queen had then proceeded to belittle the first mate every chance she got—using polite terms of course—but Jon couldn't ignore the rancour that poured from her. It made no sense, given the deep well of pain that he saw in her. Or did it? She had pulled the same sort of thing with Baltsaros, hadn't she?

Jon spooned up more soup and tried to come up with something to say that would diffuse the tension a little. Maybe he could find some common ground to get the two of them talking. However, Tom pushed his bowl away and locked eyes with his mother before Jon had a chance.

"Ye mean *you* think a quiet day is the right fuckin' way, aye?" he growled. "Ye meddlin' old cunt. Ye can't bloody keep Da from me, ye know."

The queen's eyebrows shot up and bright spots appeared on her pale cheeks.

"The language on you... And when will you desist in calling him that? Do you know how *sick* that makes you sound?" she shot back in venomous tones. "No, Thomas. Baltsaros was in on the decision."

Jon's senses told him that she was telling the truth and felt a small pang of disappointment. Baltsaros had taken a different route back to his tower, and they'd missed him by mere minutes; it would have been nice to confirm for a fact what the queen was saying.

She ripped off a tiny piece of bread and chewed it slowly before continuing in a low voice.

"You and Jon can work out whatever arrangement suits you concerning your sleeping quarters; I have no desire to know more about that." Abetha flared her nostrils and shook her head. "However, you will *not* go to Baltsaros whenever you feel like it."

"Like hells, I won't," spat Tom, lurching to his feet.

"Thomas, I swear that if you take a step near that tower, I'll have you put under lock and key."

Jon's eyes went to Saban, and he saw that he was shaking his head slowly at Tom.

The first mate pointed at Abetha, his bright eyes snapping with fury.

"Ye'd like that, ye bloody witch. Lockin' up yer son like an animal? I hope ye choke on this crap." Tom backhanded the bowl of *harira* and sent it flying to the floor. He turned to go but not before meeting Jon's eyes. The creases deepened further on his forehead, and Jon saw something like confusion cross his rugged face before he stormed off. Surprisingly, he went in the opposite direction from Baltsaros's rooms.

Abetha pushed her chair back.

"Please excuse me," she said in a faint voice and left.

Saban let out a long sigh and scraped the bottom of his bowl, spooning up the last of his soup with a grimace.

"Well... That was awkward," he muttered after he'd swallowed. "I have half a mind to put the both of them in a small room and not let them out until they resolve whatever it is that makes them so awful to each other. However, it would probably end in murder."

"Whose?" asked Jon with a smile.

"That, I am not sure of," replied Saban, grinning as he tore off another piece of flatbread to mop up any remaining liquid in his bowl.

Jon glanced down the corridor where Tom had disappeared.

"The weirdest thing is that I think he's actually going to obey his mother," he said with a headshake. "But I wonder where he went."

"Easy. What does our laconic first mate do when he's pissed off? He drinks or he gets into a fight, or both," said Saban, shrugging. He stood up. "Shall we go see if he's already ripping into some poor fool at Maya's?"

Jon nodded and pushed away from the table, following the taller man out of the dining room.

~

Baltsaros sat in the comfortable chair in his study with his feet up on the cushioned stool as he watched the maid scrub the bloodstain on the rug. On his knee was the copy of *Standard Parables* that he was translating into Common—an activity suggested by Abetha—but the monotonous task had turned into an irritation. All the passages seemed insufferably bromidic to him suddenly, and he found himself skimming and unable to give a shit about any of it.

With head tilted, he narrowed his eyes at the young woman on the floor. She was not yet twenty, he guessed, and had a pleasing figure that ran to plump. As she worked on her knees, he was given an excellent view of her heart-shaped backside straining against the stiff, dark material of her uniform. He let his lips curl into a hungry smile. She was pretty and probably would not mind it if he took liberties with her.

Hands folded in his lap, Baltsaros imagined himself standing up and closing the distance before falling to his knees behind the girl. Then he thought about pulling up the maid's skirt, freeing his cock, and taking her quickly and roughly from behind. He pictured her cheeks and neck going pink as he'd labour over her like a beast, with no tenderness or mercy to his thrusts.

Maybe she would even enjoy it.

Baltsaros cupped his hand over his hardened length.

Ok. Good, he thought.

She would then have to say something to trigger him. It was always deep ignorance that made the bloodlust sing in his ears, so he imagined her making some sort of crass, small-minded comment about the relationship with his boys. Baltsaros watched her working for another long moment before leaning his head back against the chair with his eyes closed.

He thought about flipping her over forcefully, his knife cutting away the material of her uniform to bare her breasts as she lay supine beneath him. Baltsaros's breath became a touch laboured as he imagined her eyes bugging out in fright, her rosebud lips squashing beneath his palm against the hardness of her teeth... The vibrations of her terrified scream would be felt in the small bones of his hand.

Baltsaros squeezed his cock gently through his pants and let out a slow sigh. He'd taken Tom twice in rapid succession the day before and once more upon waking. Though the semi-serious brawl between them had granted him the lustiness and recuperative powers of a much younger man, he was a touch tender. Regardless, his erection throbbed hard and willing against his fingers at his little fantasy.

He took a deep breath and imagined that, as the maid struggled, he would press the tip of the knife against her soft skin and then push it in so slowly that he could feel the beat of her heart shiver the blade as it slid home. Jaw clenched, Baltsaros thought about the blood that would well up almost black, but that would taste so rich and *red*.

"Sir?"

Baltsaros opened his eyes. The young maid was less pretty than the one that still lay beneath him in his mind. Her cheeks were flushed with embarrassment, but he didn't care that she was witness to his blatant arousal.

"Yes?"

"That's the best I can do for now," she nearly whispered, her eyes darting down to the hand in his lap.

Baltsaros looked past her to the rug. It would have to be replaced.

He thought for a moment about asking her questions to unearth any slight bigotry she had. It would be just a test to see whether he could keep from killing so as to honour his promise. Otherwise, he would have to start hiding his hunts from both Jon and Tom; Baltsaros knew the first mate was no longer his ally in that regard.

"Thank you, my dear," he said instead and dismissed her. After she had gone, Baltsaros leaned back again in his chair and thought some more about blood and promises.

On the way to the *Grog Blossom*, Saban brought Jon up to speed on a number of things. The first made him pause in his tracks and stare at the Balorian in disbelief for a moment. Ceara had been given the repainted *Saber* and had set sail on a mission for Baltsaros. She had been sent to strike a deal with the masters of the mainland iron holdings and the silk producers of the southern peninsula in regard to continued trade with Ereme'ia Balor. She was also to spread rumours of a navy ketch seen sinking off the midland isles during a bad storm. The rationale behind this was to keep the king from sending an armada to the rift; if the ketch had simply sunk due to bad weather and dumb luck, there was no burning need for retaliation.

Jon agreed that it made sense, but he wondered what would happen when Ah'puch's ship missed the next rendezvous. Would the navy simply give up and turn around, or were the citizens of Balor going to get an unpleasant visit? Saban pointed out that the latter was highly doubtful, as they almost certainly had no map to get through the winding mountain pass.

As Saban talked about Ceara, Jon kept glancing at him. The way he spoke of her made him think that there was more there but before he could ask, Saban switched to Baltsaros and his "treatments".

On their arrival, the deposed captain of the *Heart* had had one of his crazed spells that had resulted in him barricading himself in his rooms. When they'd finally been able to get to Baltsaros, he had been covered in his own blood but calm. After that he had just gone along almost meekly with whatever Abetha came up with: quiet walks, something called *meditation*, and a cocktail of medicines to lessen the opiate addiction he had developed from being drugged so often on the trip back from Balor.

"So, all these things helped?" Jon asked as they walked side by side down the steep, cobbled road.

690

Saban nodded slowly, his eyes on the cobbled road ahead of them.

"I've also been helping out with the mind-strengthening activities that worked with my father," the big man said, then frowned. "Though if you want the honest truth, I think that his recovery was beginning to stagnate."

"Meaning, you think that Tom's presence helps?" asked Jon.

"And yours," said Saban with a glance at Jon. His green-brown eyes were warm. "It seemed that he was just going through the motions after a while. Baltsaros cares for the two of you very much; your arrival has reminded him of that. I think it's a good thing. Maybe. Though who really knows what goes on in that man's mind? Maybe he opted for seclusion today because it really was too much for him all at once."

"Or he could be testing himself to see what the effects of our arrival have had on him," offered Jon.

"You know him better than I do," replied Saban with a shrug.

"And Tom knows him the best," affirmed Jon. "You know, Tom stalking off like a wounded panther might have nothing to do with him obeying Abetha. If the captain decided he needed space, and I do believe the queen was speaking the truth, then Tom would be the first to give him that. I think."

Saban's face creased into a soft smile.

"I think you might be right."

"Saban, I know how much you like Tom," said Jon to the man at his side as they neared the *Blossom*. Saban stopped walking and turned to stare at Jon, his hazel eyes wary. Jon chewed the inside of his cheek and tried set aside his jealousy; the look on Saban's face had just confirmed his suspicions.

"I just meant that I can count on you to help me help Tom, right?" Jon asked lightly with a friendly smile that hoped hid his discomfort.

"Of course, Jon," came the quiet reply. "I promise to do whatever is in my power."

Jon nodded up at Saban and then pushed the tavern door open.

CHAPTER 18

THE WRONG PEG

om watched the bottle bob in the water in front of him, lost in thought. He was kneeling in the shallow surf with the warm water up to his chest as he scooped up handfuls of fine sand from the bottom. Occasionally, little schools of transparent fish with black eyes would surround him, and he would try to catch them, but they always eluded his grasp. The salt in the water stung his wounded palm, but he knew he would heal all the faster for it. Tom grabbed the bottle, pulled the cork, and took a deep swallow of the rum within. His eyes caught movement below the surface, and he recorked the bottle, setting it to floating again as he watched the crab make its sideways journey towards deeper water.

"Tom?"

At the sound of Jon's voice, Tom smiled to himself. He turned around and saw him standing at the shoreline, accompanied by Saban.

"What are you doing?" asked Jon, shielding his eyes against the glare that came off the water.

"Thinkin'," replied the first mate. He plucked the bottle from the water again. "Drinkin'."

"Kat gave me your message," said Jon. "It said you'd gone for a swim."

"Didn't get to swimmin'," replied Tom, licking saltwater and rum from his lips. He'd intended to swim out past the land bridge but instead had found himself dawdling in the shallows. While waiting for Jon to find him—lords knew, the lad was predictable and would come running the minute he could—he had forced himself to really *think* about his anger. Not to drown it completely in liquor or violence for once. Not to shove it into a dark corner until it grew like a poison in his blood.

The truth was that all the evil bitterness he had inside him was over something *already done*. It was over the actions of family that he hadn't even known when he *was*

692

there—hells, he'd called Polly the wet nurse "ma" when he was a wee tyke. This hatred of a woman whom he had never really known was bloody stupid, and it shamed him that it had taken seeing the look on Jon's face earlier to finally realize he was acting like a crybaby over milk that had been spilled a long fucking time ago.

He had to stop hating the family who had lost him and concentrate on the family who had found him.

Jon watched him for a few seconds, a concerned look on his handsome face, and Tom felt his cheeks dimple in a broad, saucy grin.

"Drop yer shorts an' come for a dip? Water's lovely," he said, swishing his hand beneath the crystal-clear surface. Then he lifted his dripping fist and pointed to Saban. "Yer welcome to join, fella."

The tall Balorian grinned and started to strip. If there was one thing that being a slave taught a man, it was how to be unashamed of nakedness. Jon on the other hand... He stood with his hands on his belt, but from the look on his face, he was going to need a little more coaxing.

"C'mon, lovey. Don't be such a fuckin' prude," chided Tom with a laugh. " 'Sides, Saban's already seen yer damn cock. What's the bloody harm?"

Even from this distance he saw the colour rise in Jon's face, and he wondered if reminding him of that night was a mistake. However, Jon just pressed his lips together with a tight nod before pulling his tunic over his head to drop it and his shortened, black linen pants to the white sand. The sight of the ugly, twisted scar on Jon's chest always made Tom feel guilty for not being there for him when the shit went down with his crazy, bloodthirsty step-da. He sighed and turned to watch Saban enter the water.

As Saban walk towards him, Tom admired the well-defined, flat muscles of his stomach and the alluring V of his pelvis. Then, more than a little astonished, Tom saw that the man's cock, cut like his own, sported a shiny silver ring at its head. He squinted, trying to tell where it went in and where it came out. When he glanced up, he saw that the Balorian looked amused at the scrutiny.

Jon splashed through the shallow water quickly, passing Saban, and sank down onto his knees next to Tom with a small smile. Jon took the bottle of rum from him.

Tom watched Jon take two long swallows, his Adam's apple working below the trim black beard, before handing it to Saban who had crouched nearby in the warm water.

"I thought you'd be drunk as a skunk or brawling by now," said Jon, his dark brows high.

Tom just shook his head.

"But, what are you going to do about your mother?"

"Don't bloody care," replied Tom. He scrunched up his eyes in the direction of the castle and lifted his shoulders. "She ain't my ma. Just some old queen. Never really knew 'er. Not sure why I should be dinin' at a queen's table, anyway. No place fer the like o' me. Her little boy, the one who got nicked in the middle o' the night?" Tom scowled and shook his head. "He's dead. Gone. So who the fuck cares whose bloody fault it was?" He felt an unexpected lump form in his throat and took the bottle from Saban to take another few swallows. It was good rum, nice and dark with molasses sweetness to it, and it worked well at washing away some of his bitterness. Or so he told himself.

"Tom, I'm not sure that's the best—" Jon started.

"It'll do for now," growled Tom. He let out a slow breath and then smiled at Jon. "Just... Lemme work on it, lad."

There was a deep crease between Jon's brows; he was obviously skeptical, but he dipped his chin in a small nod. The sunlight glinting off the water made bright ripples over his skin as a small wave passed. Jon's nipples were puckered, and Tom watched a drop make its way down his chest to fall from one of them. With a growl, Tom reached for Jon and pulled him in close; he weighed next to nothing in the water. With a nervous laugh, Jon pushed at Tom with a look at Saban, but Tom wouldn't let him go.

When Jon felt Tom's growing erection against him, his eyes widened a touch.

"Oh."

Tom laughed and quested forward to capture Jon's lips with his own in a brief but heated kiss before releasing him. What was it about water that always made him so horny?

When he glanced over his shoulder, he saw Saban turn his head away quickly, and Tom felt his pulse kick up a notch.

Just as he was about to kiss Jon again, Saban let out a yell, and Tom turned in time to see the big man rise quickly to his feet and fall backwards with a big splash. Saban flailed for a second and regained his footing as he backed into deeper water. He looked like he was in some amount of pain.

"I think something bit my... uh," said Saban, wincing.

Tom burst out laughing.

"That bit o' shine on the end of that long cock o' yers is like to have made an ol' robber crab greedy, mate," he said. "Are ye bleedin'?"

Saban hunched his shoulders and peered down into the clear water, inspecting himself.

"Want me to take a closer look, lad?" asked Tom, grinning. "It'd be my pleasure."

Jon smirked and splashed water at the first mate.

"I... think it's fine. Mostly took me by surprise. Are you sure there's nothing that could have bit me?" grimaced Saban.

"Could be a peckerfish lookin' for a mate," joked Tom. "Though their bite's a fair bit toxic. If that's the case, me and Jon can take turns suckin' the poison out."

This time Saban let out a bark of laughter, and he sent a volley of water at Tom's head.

Tom yelled and dove forward to duck into water that came up to his shoulders. He wiped seawater out of his eyes and Jon laughed. The mood had gone to playful, and he was damn glad for it.

"Bring the bottle here, love," he beckoned to Jon. "An' come wrap those skinny legs o' yers around me." Jon gave him a mock scowl and drank some rum, but with nothing more than a quick, backwards glance at Saban, he came closer and hooked his legs around the first mate's hips. Tom let out a little growl of pleasure and grasped the moons of Jon's ass, leaning forward to plant a kiss on the corner of Jon's mouth. When he pulled back, he saw that Jon's blue eyes had gone dark with lust. Tom moved one of his hands so that he could stroke a fingertip over Jon's pucker softly. Jon started, his sphincter contracting at Tom's touch.

"Tom…" he warned.

Tom grinned, his heart hammering and cock getting harder with every beat. He glanced over at Saban. The Balorian raised a quizzical eyebrow, but there was something in his face that said he knew exactly what Tom was about.

"He can't see," he murmured close to Jon. "I could push ye down and fill ye right up with my cock, and he wouldn't see." He tested Jon's opening with his finger, feeling Jon's pulse as he breached it slowly. "That is… if ye weren't as tight as a vestal bloody virgin."

Jon flushed dark at Tom's words and surprised him by suddenly shoving him backwards, sending Tom over the ledge of the seabed so that he had to tread water.

Tom laughed and ducked below the surface, swimming along the sandy bottom until he reached Jon. He turned over onto his back and could see a wavy version of Jon looking down at him, framed by a sky of purest blue. He noticed that the lad's cock was as stiff as his, and as Tom surfaced, he made a point of stroking it with his fingers. Jon scowled at him, but between the rum and the water, and the gorgeous bloody sunshine, there didn't seem to be much real reproach. Tom picked the bottle out of the water and drank some more.

"Saban!" He flipped the corked bottle into the air, and the tall man caught it easily. Tom swam closer, wishing he could think of a way to… *something*. He was starting to feel reckless.

Saban took a sip of rum, looking a little nervous. He met Tom's eyes but turned away almost immediately.

Tom felt Jon's hands on him, and he smiled as he was pulled backwards and dunked in the water again. He popped up, shaking salt water from his face and then sent a wave over Jon's head. Saban let out a yell as Jon barrelled backwards into him. To Tom's amazement, the big man picked Jon up out of the water and sent him flying over his shoulder.

The first mate grinned wide at Saban.

Soon it was an epic battle to drown the other as the three splashed and wrestled in the chest-deep water. They all laughed breathlessly as alliances forged and changed on a dime. However, this was innocent play only on the surface, and the tension in the air was so thick it seemed to gain real weight. Tom's body felt tight and sensitive to every touch—wet skin sliding over wet skin to ostensibly throw the other when, in reality, hands had begun to wander. The first mate let out a little, barely voiced groan when Jon's fingers encircled his stiff cock for a quick squeeze before pushing him below the surface. A moment later a hand too big to be Jon's touched his ass and lingered. Tom was panting, but it had little to do with boys' horseplay.

He moved into deeper water with a grin, crazy lust painting a wonderful and terribly bloody stupid idea in his head.

"Catch me if ye can, ye bloody landlubbers!" He laughed and turned, swimming out with broad strokes towards the *Heart* anchored not far away. When he heard splashing behind him, he glanced over his shoulder and saw that the others were gaining on him. He made himself go even faster, strong arms propelling him forward through the cooler deep water until he got to the ship. He reached up and grabbed hold of the bottom rung of the Jacob's ladder, climbing quickly. When he got to the top, he felt the rope ladder jerk and saw that Saban was hot on his trail. After jumping down to the deck, Tom started jogging sternward.

He knew he was being feckless, but he was so horny he could barely contain himself. Two sets of thudding footfalls behind him meant that Jon had made it, so Tom slowed his pace. Grinning like a loon, he wrenched open the door to the captain's quarters and let himself into the cool shade. Tom's eyes adjusted in moments, and he turned when the others entered the stateroom. The tension had turned into a high keening noise just beyond hearing, and Tom felt as if he would burst from it.

He grabbed Jon by the arm, dragging him roughly to the table. Breathing heavily, Jon stared at Tom, looking unsure but just as excited as he was. Brow furrowed, Jon licked his lips then let out a small moan as Tom pressed his pelvis against him, drawing him in for a kiss. Cock to cock, they strained against each other, Jon's mouth tasting of rum and seawater. When Tom broke away, he took a handful of Jon's dripping black curls.

"I want you," he murmured, leaning in to press another kiss to Jon's open lips. "Right now. Right here."

Jon's eyes darted to where Saban stood frozen to the spot. Tom could feel Jon's heartbeat against his chest; it sped as fast as his own in the few seconds that it took for him to make up his mind. When Jon looked again at Tom, he nodded once.

With a pleased growl, Tom butted himself harder against Jon, his cock wet and almost hurting as he kissed him deep. Then he stepped back and forced Jon to turn around and lean over the table, his chest to the cold, hard wood. Hand on the back of Jon's neck, he cast about for something to use as lubrication and spotted the small bottle of oil on the armoire.

Tom contemplated Saban who continued to stare mutely at them; the muscles twitched in his strong jaw as he met Tom's gaze.

"Tom... This isn't going to... I am not..." whispered Saban, letting his eyes drop to Tom's stiff cock. However, his arousal was blatant in the dark, veiny staff that curved up proud from a nest of crinkled black hair.

"Be a love and get me that?" said Tom, pointing to the oil.

Saban's eyes widened, but he went quickly to fetch it, his long cock bobbing with his strides. When he handed the little bottle to Tom, he held onto the first mate's hand for the span of a breath, and his eyes were so tragic that Tom felt a small pain erupt deep in his chest. Saban shook his head. There was a war going on in the big man that

Tom didn't envy one bit… one that he realized wouldn't be solved in one sunny afternoon in a darkened stateroom.

"Tom, I can't…" Saban whispered, watching Tom smear oil on his cock and push some into Jon.

"But ye wanna watch, don't ye?" murmured Tom, his heart pounding; Jon's body quivered, and he let out a soft groan as Tom's finger quested deeper into him. "No harm in watchin', mate."

Saban didn't reply, but his eyes stayed locked on Tom's oiled finger slowly fucking Jon's tight hole.

Tom swallowed hard, watching the bead of perspiration making its way down the Balorian's neck. He was fucking gorgeous and so obviously turned-on by what he was seeing that it made Tom's cock throb hard in his fist. Eyes on Saban, Tom pulled his finger out of Jon and placed his cockhead against the greased opening. As slow as he could, he pushed himself into Jon's slick heat and gasped both at the feeling and at the way Saban's brow furrowed as if in deep pain, his mouth open in a soft pant. However, Saban stumbled backwards a moment later and was gone before Tom could say anything.

Tom reined in his disappointment and pressed his lips together, turning away to concentrate on what he was doing to Jon instead. Hands on Jon's hips, he fucked him with slow strokes and let out a soft sound when Jon began pushing back against him. Fucking Jon was a glorious bloody thing; he responded with such enthusiasm and with all these gorgeous little needy noises. Tom knew for sure that Jon was stiff and drooling clear drops onto the carpet below, needing nothing more than a cock in his ass. It always fucking amazed him.

Eyes closed and cheek pressed against the mahogany, Jon began to whimper in time to Tom's thrusts.

"Ye like that, love? Ye feel so good," murmured Tom.

Jon's groan had a desperate edge to it, and Tom began to pound into him, driving himself quickly to the edge. Jon cried out and tensed with a shudder, his ass almost too tight on Tom's shaft for a second. Tom closed his eyes with a growl and let himself go, every cum-slippery thrust pulling a grunt out of him as he rode out his climax, his jerking cock buried deep in Jon. Finally, he slowed and then stopped, leaning forward over Jon to place his forehead against his shoulder as he panted. He rested there a moment, catching his breath, until his softening cock slid out of Jon's body. Jon let out a little gasp and Tom pressed his lips to Jon's sweat-covered back.

When Tom could stand again, Jon pushed himself off the tabletop and turned, looking a little dazed. He shoved back his damp tangle of curls and rubbed his face.

Saban was nowhere to be seen. Tom figured he probably wasn't even on the ship anymore.

"Tom… What were you trying to pull with Saban?" Jon said quietly. He didn't look happy.

Tom groaned and ran a hand over the top of his head, his eyes lowered to the rug beneath his feet. Jon had said yes, hadn't he?

In the heat of the bloody moment.

After a few breaths, he looked up and saw that Jon was watching him, his grey-blue eyes cautious.

"Ye sore at me, lad?" Tom asked with a grimace.

Jon responded with a shrug and came forward to wrap his arms around Tom, burying his face in the crook of the first mate's neck.

"Yeah. Maybe a little," came the mumbled reply.

With a deep frown, Tom stroked down the curve of Jon's spine as he stared out the open door at the blue sky beyond, feeling like a bloody arse. Now that it was over, fucking around with Saban seemed like such an idiotic thing to do. What had he been thinking?

"I'm sorry," he rumbled, feeling ashamed.

"S'ok," sighed Jon. "Forget about it."

Tom knew that Jon was more hurt than he was letting on; he didn't even want to touch on what the captain would say when he found out that he had tried to add a third without his permission. One thing was for certain: he had to get Saban out of his head for good. Nothing right would come of it. He was thoroughly disgusted with himself for letting an idea get him all fired up.

As he led Jon to the bed, he tried to come up with a way to fix things. Jon curled up quietly against his shoulder and draped one leg over Tom's thighs. The breeze that came in from the windows felt nice, and though Jon was lying directly on some rather tender ribs, Tom didn't want him to move.

When Tom was very young, he had stolen one of his mother's scented silk handkerchiefs—a small square of royal blue—because he had been obsessed by the colour and the softness of it. He'd kept it hidden in his room, a cherished secret that he would rub between his fingers or against his face as he lay in his little bed. It had been so damned pretty. Then, one day, he noticed that the silk was getting worn in places, and he'd somehow managed to get it dirty. There was even a little blood on it from a cut on his finger.

He had *ruined* it.

That horrible realization was the closest thing he could think of for how weighted his heart felt when he thought of what had just happened... Well, what had *nearly* happened with Saban.

"I'm sorry," he said again, whispering the word into Jon's hair.

"Tom, I want to let this *go*... But you can't do that again," said Jon slowly after a few breaths. He played gently with Tom's nipple ring. "I don't want either of us to."

"Aye," murmured Tom. "Don't bloody know why I was thinkin' with my fuckin' cock. Ain't like me. I love ye, Jon. Never again."

Jon nodded against him, and Tom felt a little better.

"You're not the only one to blame, remember?" said Jon. "You know, you and I haven't exactly been doing very well. I think it's ok to admit that."

Tom grunted in agreement. It was true. With the captain's malady, something had broken between them.

"We been tryin' to plug a hole with the wrong-shaped peg," muttered the first mate.

Jon laughed.

"Well, that's one way of putting it."

"Mm." Tom smiled then winced a little as Jon shifted against his bruises. "Da's better. He'll be back behind the wheel before too long... keep us both in fuckin' line, aye?"

Jon just chuckled in response and kissed the side of Tom's neck.

Tom tightened his hold on Jon and shut his eyes.

As he felt slumber creep up to him like a cat on silent, furred feet, Tom thought about the look in Saban's eyes that had been so at odds with his impressive erection, and a memory filtered through that image. It was one of Jon lying in the washtub when he first came aboard.

Unaware that Tom had returned to fetch the captain for something, Jon's face had been twisted in the heat of desire as he jerked off slowly in the warm bath water. Tom had stood, transfixed and breathlessly hard, watching the dripping pink head of the boy's cock emerge from the water, the pads of Jon's fingers teasing at its plump crown before it submerged again with the motion of his hips.

It had been a maddeningly gorgeous sight, one that conflicted with all the rancour and betrayal he had felt over the captain's ridiculous mooning about over the pale, skittery whelp. Once more, Jon's cock had broken the surface, and Tom had nearly let escape a groan as Jon's fingers squeezed and pulled at the taut flesh. Tom's hand had gone to his own straining erection, squeezing hard when Jon let out a soft cry as he covered his jerking cock to catch his seed in the washcloth he held in the other hand. However, when the boy's face had fallen a moment later, Tom's hand had stilled and he had taken a quick, silent step back through the door.

He stroked his fingers sleepily through Jon's hair, remembering how he had felt sudden shame at witnessing such an unguarded moment. Tom had been oddly torn between laughing off his own discomfort and going back into the room to take Jon in his arms to soothe away the same tormented look that had been on Saban's face before he had fled.

Tom's folly had probably cost him the friendship.

He hoped not.

CHAPTER 19
A THIRD BOND

Jon started awake when he heard a thump. Lifting his head, he squinted at the open door. The wind had died down while Tom and he had slept; despite the wide-open portholes, the room was like an oven. When he peeled himself away from Tom's side, Jon felt a little nauseous from the heat. The first mate groaned, rolling over on the sweat-soaked sheets just as Baltsaros ducked into the room with a wry grin on his face.

"You do know that there's a room at the castle for each of you to use, don't you?" he said, chuckling.

Jon blinked slowly, trying to get his cooked brain to work. When he pushed himself to standing, his legs felt weak.

"Yeah... So I hear," he muttered. His head spun.

"How'd ye find us?" asked the first mate in a hoarse voice.

"I didn't think you'd be wandering around town naked," Baltsaros replied, holding up the clothing they'd abandoned on the beach.

"Ah. Right," Jon said and took his tunic and shortened pants with a crooked smile. Teetering on one leg to get dressed, he watched the first mate get out of bed, scratching himself as he blinked sleepily.

"I thought ye needed an afternoon to yerself?" Tom mumbled as he accepted his pants from Baltsaros.

"I thought I did," admitted the captain, hooking his thumbs into the red sash around his waist. "Then I found myself unable to stop thinking about the two of you and said *scupper that*... So I flew the coop."

Baltsaros's white smile was wide in his tanned face, and his dark eyes crinkled at the corners; Jon thought he looked happier than he'd seen him in a long time.

Wrinkling his nose, the captain looked around.

"Yea gods, I leave you alone for a few weeks, and you manage to make my quarters smell like a barn." He scratched at something that had spilled on the table, curling his lip in disgust.

Jon glanced at Tom and grinned.

~

Baltsaros watched Tom deftly peel a mango then cut thick slices away from the fibrous pit as juice ran down his arm. Jon accepted a piece with a grin and offered the plate of cheeses to the first mate. Tom chose some hard-rind cheddar from the midlands and held it between his teeth while he poured himself and Jon some more of the strong black coffee from the golden ewer at the centre of the table. They were completely in sync with each other, and it made Baltsaros smile.

"Saban told me about Ceara," Jon said, munching on some toasted currant bread. "You really trust her? What happens if she decides to just go to the navy and collect the bounty on our heads?"

The captain shook his head.

"She won't. What motivates Ceara isn't money, Jon. It's power and knowledge. I've put her in a position where she has both, and I think it will be enough to keep her loyal. Besides, I told her that if she crosses me, I will have Saban flayed alive in front of her," he said and bit into a ripe *gessal*. The fruit's sweet skin was a nice complement to the tart flesh inside, and he chewed it slowly to savour the taste.

Jon's eyes widened.

"I was kidding," Baltsaros laughed. "Jon, relax."

"Wait... Why Saban?" asked Tom with a frown.

"Didn't he tell you?" asked the captain, surprised. "The two of them were married a few weeks ago."

Tom and Jon glanced at each other, and Baltsaros felt something kindle deep in his chest at the looks on their faces. Tom's green-blue eyes were the first to turn back to the captain, and Baltsaros didn't like the bland expression in them. The fact that Jon stared down at his plate before meeting his eyes made it worse. It seemed that the boys were hiding something from him.

"Excuse me," said Jon, getting to his feet. "I need to use the facilities."

Baltsaros watched him go, tapping his bottom lip with the side of his finger.

"Tom... Do I want to know?" he asked finally. He turned to the first mate and saw that Tom's gaze was trained on nothing. The big man's forehead wrinkled as he rubbed the coarse dark-blond stubble of his jaw. After a few seconds, he focused on the captain, grimaced, and shook his head.

"You instigated?"

The first mate gave a terse nod but then frowned and shook his head.

The possessive spark took flame, and Baltsaros felt heat course through him. How dare Saban think he could—

"Was Jon's idea," Tom broke in gruffly. "At least the first time."

The *first* time? Baltsaros took a deep breath and closed his eyes. He was incredulous, angry, curious, and jealous at once. The emotions simmered just below the surface, fighting to break through.

Calm yourself.

"Is it likely to happen again?" asked Baltsaros, trying to keep emotion from his voice. He looked again at the big man across the table.

A firm headshake.

"You are certain?"

This time it was a tiny scowl followed by a nod.

The captain tilted his head and stared hard at Tom. The first mate stared back, unblinking.

"Ok," Baltsaros said... and simply let go of his anger.

It almost startled him how easily he did it. Just like dropping a pebble over the side of a ship, it faded from sight as it sank beneath deep waters. Oddly, he didn't *feel* less. It was just tempered with something he was only beginning to understand: trust.

Tom's eyes widened for a brief instant, suspicion flaring only to be extinguished by astonishment. When Baltsaros gave a reassuring nod to show he was serious, the first mate's face creased into a relieved grin. After he ate another piece of mango off the end of his knife, Tom chuckled.

"Yer a changed man, Da."

Baltsaros smiled and turned his head when he felt the breeze on his cheek; scented with fruit, flowers, and the tang of the sea, it cooled the skin at the open collar of his shirt. The sky was cloudless, and the palm fronds swished over the sound of the surf below. A perfect day.

After a moment, Baltsaros thought of something and narrowed his eyes at Tom.

"What did you do to the figurehead on the *Heart*?" he said, changing the subject. "It looks completely insane. I hope to hells that's not some kind of commentary on my mental acuity."

Tom began to laugh.

As they waited for Jon to join them again, Baltsaros leaned back in his chair and crossed his arms as Tom began to describe the fight aboard the *Sabre*. The first mate's hair was a little too short for his liking, and the bruising on his face had started to go an unattractive shade of olive, but his ocean eyes were lively and the way the light caught them caused Baltsaros to ache a little. In a good way.

"You're beautiful," he murmured.

Tom choked on his words, his hands stopping in mid-gesticulation.

"You're beautiful, Tom," the captain repeated, "but... so much more than that. I am a very lucky man to have found you... I am incredibly thankful for everything you've done for me."

"Da, stop—" growled Tom, hunching his shoulders.

"Son, I just want you know how *much* you mean to me. You make me very happy. *Do you understand me?*"

The first mate quickly looked down to stare at the table, blinking fast; Baltsaros could see the play of muscle in his jaw.

"Tom?" asked the captain, leaning forward.

Tom nodded slowly. When he glanced up, there was a shimmer to his eyes.

"Aye, Da," he said in a hoarse voice. "I understand."

Baltsaros rose to his feet and rounded the table to sit in Jon's departed chair.

"I need you to do something for me."

"Always, Da. Anythin'," swore Tom.

The captain reached out and curled his hand behind Tom's big neck, watching the tropical ocean hues of his eyes shift as they widened slightly. Slowly Baltsaros leaned in to kiss Tom's full lips and tasted mango when he bit down softly on the lower one. Baltsaros's pulse skittered and went wild as he gently investigated Tom's mouth. Dipping his tongue between Tom's open lips to taste more sweetness, he wrapped his other hand around him to deepen the kiss. When Baltsaros finally pulled away, Tom's eyes stayed closed for a moment. Looking a little flushed when he opened them, Tom's gaze darted over the captain's face.

"I don't know why it took me so long to realize you were such an incredible kisser," said Baltsaros. "And that you needed a bit of tenderness once in a while."

Tom chuckled and looked down at his hands, his face reddening further.

"Now *that*," laughed the captain, squeezing the back of Tom's neck, "is a blush worthy of Jon."

"Oh bugger off, ye ol' fiend," said Tom with a grin. Then his forehead creased in confusion as he appraised Baltsaros. "That's what ye needed me to do for ye?"

"No. Give me your knife."

Baltsaros ignored the flash of concern that passed over the first mate's features as he handed over the long, bone-handled dagger. Knowing that he'd probably have to treat the two of them for infection afterwards, he pressed the blade to his forearm and mirrored the healed scar he'd made with Jon on the other arm. Tom watched him with a deep comma between his sandy brows and let out a small grunt when Baltsaros took his thickly muscled arm in hand.

There were no words spoken between them as Baltsaros sliced into Tom's skin, nor were there any when they pressed their bleeding forearms together. They weren't needed. Tom bent forward and placed his forehead against the captain's shoulder with a long sigh, and Baltsaros pressed his cheek to Tom's cropped hair, wrapping his free arm around his broad, scarred back.

~

Jon washed his hands slowly and carefully. Aware that he was stalling, he wiped his fingers on the square of white cloth that hung above the pitcher and basin and straightened his sweat-stained black tunic. Wishing that there was a mirror in the little alcove where he stood, Jon smoothed back his hair and took a few calming breaths. Every time he thought about what had happened with Saban, Jon's pulse sped, and he felt a pit open in his stomach.

Mouth a little dry, he rubbed his face hard to try to snap himself out of it. Baltsaros would no doubt be furious when he found out... That, or he would see it as an excuse to break his promise and try to add a fourth—or more—to their bed. Jon groaned inwardly as he made his way back down the hallway to the patio where they had been eating lunch. The problem was... Jon was confused. He'd been excited knowing he was being watched by Saban—incredibly, unbelievably, agonizingly turned-on. Then it had turned to deep shame and... fear? Anger? He realized that the only reason he wasn't incredibly pissed off at Tom was because Jon knew he had planted the idea in the first mate's head. It wasn't an excuse. It just wasn't, but he knew that Tom understood that too.

Jon just wanted to leave the whole fucking mess behind them and chalk up the morning to a lapse in judgment. With shoulders squared, he pushed open the glass door and stepped out into the bright sunshine.

When Jon saw Baltsaros and Tom in their quiet embrace, he stopped. More than a little uncertain, he stood just watching them for a moment. However, when the captain lifted his head and looked at him with nothing but open affection, Jon's jittering pulse began to slow. He stepped forward, and Tom turned to watch him approach. He nodded at Jon with an encouraging smile.

Everything will be all right.

It seemed that the first mate had decided to trust Baltsaros with what had occurred earlier, and there would be few or no repercussions. Something had... changed.

Jon noticed the blood on Tom's knife and their clasped arms and let out a small noise, realizing what it meant. There were no feelings of betrayal, no sense of exclusion. No... It was as if something had finally been fixed, a hole patched. The old woman's orphic words about mending the tapestry came back to him but he quashed the tiny trill of horror that rose up in him at the memory. While there were things in the world he didn't or couldn't understand, here was something before him that he *did*.

Their relationship would continue to grow, to change. There would always be pain, and they would be tested... Their triad had the shakiest of foundations, based as it was on mistrust, jealousy, and deception. But *ships* didn't need pillars pounded into the earth; no, they needed strong, protective hulls that could carry them over the ever-changing waves of an uncaring sea. With trust, hope... love—all things they had built *together*—they could weather anything.

Jon closed his eyes and folded himself into the three-sided embrace, no longer adrift.

CHAPTER 20

DIVINE TORTURE

Jon took a breath and as he let it out slowly, squeezed the trigger. The flintlock jumped in his hand, and the bottle on the pile of driftwood exploded in a shower of brown glass.

"That-a boy, Jonny!" whooped Katherine and lifted the flask of whiskey to her lips. "Now let's see if you can do that again."

With a wry headshake, Jon pulled the other pistol from the holster at his hip and pointed it, left-handed, at the beer bottle's twin. He moved the cock to full and fired. This time, the lead shot hit the bottle's thick bottom and sent it flying into the air.

"I never thought I'd see the day," said Katherine, grinning. "With a little more practice, I think I'll make a crack shot of you yet."

"Uh huh," smirked Jon. He was able to hit a target if it was both inanimate and close by. He doubted that he'd ever be a great marksman. He started to unbuckle the belts, but Katherine stopped him.

"Keep 'em," she said.

Jon looked at the beautiful pistols and shook his head.

"Kat... I couldn't—"

"You can and you shall," said Katherine, sobering. She lifted her hook to eye level and sighed. "They're a matched pair, kiddo. A lotta good they do me. Go on, keep 'em."

Smiling a little sadly, Jon slid them both back into the tooled leather belts.

"Ok fine, but let me give you something in return." Jon thought for a moment but couldn't come up with anything on the spot. "When I think of something suitable."

"I won't argue with that," said Katherine with a grin.

Jon looked at the sun. It was not yet midday. The item he had commissioned from the blacksmith wouldn't be ready until that afternoon, so he had time to kill.

"I'm hungry. You hungry? Want to check out that new place?"

Since their arrival, a pair of ambitious ex-Balorians had set up shop selling something they called *fish cutters*—pieces of battered fish in a salt bread roll—and Jon hadn't had the opportunity to try them yet. With a nod, Katherine wedged the flask at her belt and made towards the crumbling staircase that led to the cobbled road above.

The small structure had been quickly built from odds and ends and decorated with old fishing nets and glass buoys. It housed a stone fire pit with a cast-iron shelf above it. At the small counter leaned the proprietress, a slightly hunchbacked older woman wearing colourful silks. At their approach, she straightened and smiled wide.

"We are just having the fire lit! Come, come," she said, gesturing to the tiny eating area in front of the shack.

Jon and Katherine sat down on old crates to either side of a table made of a barrel and a few boards nailed together. Katherine looked at Jon in amusement and wrinkled her nose.

"You take me to the fanciest places," she teased.

Jon shrugged just as the woman came out the side of the shack and set down two mugs in front of them.

"First customers will always be having free drinks to start," said the woman happily. "Two cutters?"

"Yes, please," replied Jon.

"With pepper sauce?"

"Sure... Why not. Kat?" Katherine nodded, and the woman hollered in a dialect of Balorian that Jon couldn't understand. The woman's partner, a much younger man from the fisherfolk tribes, peered out from the ramshackle hut and yelled something back.

"Will be soon," said the proprietress and turned to greet some more customers who had just arrived.

Jon lifted his mug and took a swig. He recognized Maya's brown mild and sighed happily. If there was one thing that Katherine's wife excelled at, it was brewing beer. He wondered if she had ever thought of exporting some to the *Jewel*. With a frown, he remembered the strange conversation he'd had there with the old seer woman over a pint of beer.

"Kat... Do you believe in fate?"

Katherine devoured her fish cutter and ordered a second while Jon told her of the woman's fortune-telling. When he was done, she shook her head at him.

"You know how I hate to agree with Tom, but he's right, Jon. It's just total bullshit."

"Then why didn't she take my money?"

"Because she's a loony old bint? I don't know. It doesn't even make any sense," replied Katherine, shrugging. "Like the tapestry thing. So your family crest is a wolf and Baltsaros's a lion. Big fucking deal. Do you know how many families have the same? Hells, I think Maya's got one of each on hers. And Tom's crest isn't even a cat. I think it's some kind of fish. If this were some magical fucking card, don't you think there would have been a fish instead of a cat?"

"Well. The captain calls Tom his tomcat all the time..."

Katherine nearly choked on her beer and started laughing.

"He does? Hells, that is funny. I didn't realize they were into pet names. Hmm... I like 'kitten' for Tom. What do you think?"

"Kat, don't you say one word that I told you!" he said, aghast. "It's just that... Well, ever since I came aboard, I've had dreams about a black lion and a wildcat. I know that they represent Baltsaros and Tom..."

"And she made a card suddenly appear that fit?"

"Well..."

"I think maybe Tom just interrupted before she could fleece you."

"But... the moon boy. The way I see things."

"I'd hardly call a knack for body language 'visions', but that's just me."

"And the coincidences..."

"Pure bunk," insisted Katherine. "Listen... When you're looking for accidents of chance, you see them all around. Trust me."

Jon was about to point out that they predated his encounter with the woman, but Katherine narrowed her eyes at him.

"Speaking of trust... How's it going with the captain and Tom? You know I worry about you with those two."

"It's going well, actually. Really well. There's no need to worry about me. Baltsaros is leaps and bounds better than he was just a few weeks ago. Tom and I are still keeping a close eye on him just in case, but I really believe that he's almost recovered," Jon said, handing their plates over to the proprietress of the fish shack. "You know, you're wrong to despise Tom so much. He's not like what you think."

"So you keep saying. But I've known him longer than you. That boy is nothing but trouble with a troubled past."

"*You've* got a troubled past," Jon pointed out. Katherine didn't talk much about her life before she went pirate, but Jon knew she had been a prostitute from a young age in a brothel that catered to men with "exotic" tastes.

"Yeah well, I don't get off on being tortured. There's liking a little pain... and then there's Tom. He's unhinged."

"It's not torture. It's... I can't explain it, but it's ok."

"And you like torturing him? See, that's the thing that bothers me the most."

Jon laughed.

"It's *not* torture," he repeated. "And yes... I like it. And so does he. And so does Baltsaros. It just seems to work between the three of us. Trust *me*. I'm happy... Happier than I've ever been in my whole life."

"Fine. You know what's best!" Katherine chuckled and lifted her hands in defeat.

Jon averted his eyes from the dented hook. If only there were something that would serve her better. Looking skyward, he was startled to see that the sun was on the downswing; it was later than he thought. After brushing crumbs from his shirt, Jon stood and dropped some coins on the table.

"Thanks for eating with me," he said. "Now, I have to go pick up something from the blacksmith and head back to the castle. Do you want to meet on the beach for more target practice tomorrow morning? See if I can hit something a little more challenging?"

Katherine grinned and nodded before downing the rest of her beer.

Jon looked at the hoop of metal, testing the hinge. Doug folded his arms across his leather apron.

"I had to outsource the clasp to Tegan the jeweller because she's so much better at the small stuff than I am, but she promised me it would hold up to quite a bit of force," said the huge blacksmith and handed over a pair of small, silver keys.

Nodding, Jon opened and closed the clasp a few times.

"Perfect," he said with a smile. "It's exactly what I asked for. How much do I owe you?"

"Why don't you consider it a gift for giving me some ideas?" said Doug with a smile. The blacksmith scratched the back of his neck, and Jon saw that he had reddened slightly. "I'm thinking of making one that'll fit me. You know... for the missus."

With a laugh, Jon pressed a few coins on him anyway and thanked him again.

~

Tom glanced up when Jon came through the door and saw that he looked as chuffed as a dog with a bone, a cheeky smile stretching from ear to ear.

"Why are ye lookin' so pleased with yerself, lad?" the first mate asked with a grin. Baltsaros put down the book he'd been reading and raised his brows at Jon as the younger man crossed the room.

"I have a gift for you," replied Jon, reaching into the cloth pouch he carried. "Since we had to cut the last two off of you, I thought you might like something a little more lasting." He pulled out a silver circle of metal and handed it to Tom.

Tom's heart began to pound faster as he turned the slave collar over in his hands. It was fitted with a little hinge and what looked like a lockable clasp. It was lovely little bit of craftsmanship. He swallowed thickly; the air in the room had gotten thin.

"I had two keys made. One for me, one for Baltsaros," said Jon quietly. "Do you like it?"

Tom ground his teeth together and looked up. Jon's storm-grey eyes were on him, curious. Baltsaros had risen from his seat and looked on with the hint of a smile on his gracefully curved lips.

"Tom?" asked Jon, the tiniest touch of concern in his voice.

With a shiver of excitement, Tom licked his lips and tried to find his voice. How in hells could he explain what it meant to him that Jon had done this?

"Aye," he rasped finally. "Like nothin' else."

"Would you like us to put it on you?" Baltsaros reached out and accepted one of the little silver keys with a smile before stepping to Tom's side.

Instead of answering, Tom just slid off the small, cushioned stool and knelt on the carpet. He closed his eyes and waited.

Two sets of hands touched him, gentle and sure. The metal was cold around his neck, and he let out a shuddering sigh as it closed with a sharp *click*.

"Come," murmured Baltsaros, helping him to stand. "That's not the only metal I want you wearing." Jon tilted his head at the captain, but he nodded in understanding a moment later.

Tom was led to the bed, and when he lay back, the captain deftly undid his pants and lowered his trousers. Jon appeared with something in his hand. As the captain claimed Tom's mouth, Jon slipped something cool around Tom's hardening cock, snapping it closed carefully behind his balls. With a little moan, Tom recognized the cock ring. It was one that wasn't particularly tight to begin with but would get almost painful the longer he was kept hard. When Jon's hot mouth sucked in the head of his cock, Tom let out a groan.

Baltsaros pulled back.

"How long has it been?" The captain's fingers closed over Tom's nipple and pinched.

Tom closed his eyes with a sigh as Jon's hand gently stroked the inside of his thigh.

"Three days," he replied and gasped when Baltsaros squeezed his nipple harder.

"That's not a very long time. Jon, is that a long time?"

Jon chuckled and licked around the crown of Tom's cockhead.

"No. Not very long at all."

Tom let out a sound that could only be called a whimper. Yes, three days didn't sound like a lot unless your balls were aching day and night and you couldn't think of anything but cumming; since the incident with Saban, they'd begun to regularly take him to a state of hyper arousal to keep him there for long stretches of time without any relief.

It was divine torture.

Jon smiled as Tom let out a soft groan, muffled by the red silk of his gag. The first mate was kneeling on the bed, thighs wide and pelvis forward, with his wrists secured tightly to his ankles behind him. This had the effect of bowing his back in such a way that his ribs were starkly outlined and the thick tendons in his neck stuck out as he held up his head, blue-green eyes fixed on Jon. He trembled from the strain of keeping the uncomfortable pose, but Jon had told him if he let himself sink down onto his calves, he would be denied release again.

With a pleased sigh, Jon leaned forward to lick another slow line down Tom's chest before closing his lips over a nipple to worry the bud with his teeth. Despite how the first mate's muscles bulged and strained against his bindings, he didn't struggle. Jutting from the thatch of dark-blond hair at his groin was the reason why; Tom's cock was a thick, hard, upward curve that jumped up every time Jon bit down harder.

This was the first mate's idea of a good time.

Jon chuckled against Tom's skin, almost lazily stroking his hands down the big man's sides to grasp his muscular buttocks before biting him again. This time he took the metal ring between his teeth and tugged on it. In response, Tom's cock grazed Jon's bare stomach and left behind a slick streak. Jon grinned and sat back on his own heels, grasping his cock in one hand to rub it against the head of Tom's. The first mate let out another low sound, closing his eyes as he thrust his hips further forward. Jon obliged him for a moment; taking the wide head in one hand, he thumbed along the underside, teasing Tom as he stroked his own cock. They'd been at this for the better part of an hour.

"Do you want it?" asked Jon with a wolfish grin.

Tom nodded quickly, a plea in his eyes. Jon reached for his jaw and tugged down the gag.

"Let me hear you say it," said Jon softly. His fingers stroked along the edge of the slave collar Tom wore. The first mate's skin was hot and wet to the touch, and his pulse thumped against the tips of Jon's fingers.

"I want yer cock," rasped Tom. Another drop of arousal slipped from the slit of his cockhead and perched there for a moment, shiny and clear, before sliding down along the thick vein and over the smaller metal circlet that he wore tight around the root of his cock. "Please, Jon. I want ye to fuck me. Hard. Please. I'll do anythin' ye want. Just... please."

Jon patted Tom's cheek lightly with a smile and looked up. The captain's tanned face was creased in amusement as he lounged behind Tom on the bed stroking his own cock and watching Jon taunt the big man. At Jon's nod, Baltsaros sat up and moved forward to quickly free Tom's wrists. Jon watched the captain narrow his eyes in concentration as he undid the knots.

Jon smiled softly. For the past week, Baltsaros's eyes had been clear and his strange turns had all but vanished. That the captain felt "sane" enough to participate in some slightly rougher play with him and Tom gave Jon hope that things would soon return to normal.

Whatever that is, he thought.

He turned back to Tom and saw that the first mate was looking at him with pupils blown out from lust and *char*, completely oblivious and lost in the moment. He was absolutely gorgeous like this, willing to do almost anything for the sake of pleasing him... a living plaything, but so much more.

Someone to cherish.

Jon widened his grin and ducked his head to cover Tom's lips with his own, nudging them open to begin kissing him slow and deep. When Tom's arms finally came free of the rope, he curled them around Jon's waist and surrendered to the embrace, his chest rumbling with small growls of pleasure. Then Tom tensed suddenly against Jon, breathing a gasp into the kiss. Curious, Jon slid his hand down Tom's hard stomach, past his cock and sensitive sack, to discover that the captain had slid two fingers into the first mate. Baltsaros let out a slow breath when he felt Jon's tentative touch and leaned over Tom's shoulder to press his lips to Jon's cheek.

Jon broke the kiss to share breath with Baltsaros for a moment. Smiling against his lips, he slid his own finger next to the captain's and into Tom. The first mate trembled between them as they fucked him using their fingers, opening him up, their hands slick with oil. Soon Tom's normally gruff voice broke on a whimper as he begged.

"Please, Jon... Da. For love's sake," said the first mate. "I've been good, aye?"

Jon laughed, breathless and wild with desire, and he shared a look with Baltsaros. It was tempting to make the first mate wait longer, just to hear how desperate he could sound, but instead he grabbed the back of Tom's head and kissed him again.

"Yes, you've been a good lad, Tom," murmured the captain. His long-fingered hand stroked up Jon's arm, the touch gentle. "How would you like to take the both of us? Hm? Would that make you happy?"

Tom pulled away from Jon, his eyes glazed and fervid, lips parted on a slow pant.

"Oh... fuck yes, Da."

Jon's heart pounded, and his cock throbbed in his hand as he watched Tom straddle Baltsaros and then lay back against the man's chest, bracing himself on his heels. The captain cushioned the big man's weight with one hand, moving to push his thick cockhead against Tom's puckered opening with the other. Jon licked his lips, an involuntary moan expelled with a hitched breath at the sight of Baltsaros's cock stretching Tom open and sliding deep into him. Tom let out a shallow grunt and closed his big fist over his own length. Jon watched hungrily as the captain fucked the first mate slowly for a few thrusts.

With a crease between his brows, Jon climbed back up on the bed and stroked himself, unsure about how to approach. Tom's eyes were closed, but when Jon made no further move, the first mate lifted his head and frowned at him. Tom held out his hand.

"Come," he said with a smile that faltered into a grimace of pleasure as Baltsaros's cock thrust deep again. "You can't hurt me, lovey."

Jon nodded weakly. Dizzy and excited, and a touch nervous, he found a place for his legs, straddling the captain, and leaned forwards over Tom. The first mate's legs hooked over Jon's hips as he stroked the head of his cock over the captain's thrusting length and then eased in slowly when the man paused. He pushed hard, and Tom's eyes closed once more. It was tight, almost too much. When Tom let out a pained breath, Jon stopped, but the first mate just chuckled a shaky laugh.

"Don't ye dare stop, Jon. Don't ye stop..." Tom groaned and let his head fall back over Baltsaros's shoulder. Jon's fervour took over. He plunged his cock into Tom's ass, sliding tight against the captain's length. It was glorious, and he found himself teetering on the edge of climax quickly. He paused, eyes closed and so sensitive that he was almost in pain. For a moment Jon just held back, waited, and relished the feeling of the captain's cock sliding against his before resuming. However, it wasn't long before he couldn't stop himself from spilling over, the swell of pleasure breaking out into molten waves of intensity that tore the voice from his throat and left him breathless and weak. When the liquid pulses that rocked him slowed, then stopped, he leaned his head against Tom's furry chest and eased out slowly, wincing as he did so.

Tom let out a grunt of surprise a moment later when Jon moved over to begin working his mouth over Tom's cock. The first mate buried his shaking hands in Jon's dark curls as Jon gagged trying to take all of Tom in. Jon swallowed and tried again, keenly wanting to reward Tom. He relaxed his throat, shifted his position, and lapped at the head of Tom's cock before sliding it back into his throat.

With Baltsaros thrusting into him from below and Jon gorging himself on his cock, Tom soon started breathing through clenched teeth with a low, rumbling moan that Jon knew meant he was close. Jon curled his fingers around the base of Tom's cock and tightened his lips, spit running down the sides of the big man's shaft and over Jon's fingers.

Suddenly Baltsaros let out a low growl, fucking Tom faster with his arms tight around the first mate's chest, the muscles taut and twitching as his body rocked beneath him, caught in the feverish, frantic surge of orgasm. Then, with a strangled cry, Tom finally let himself cum, his bitter seed gushing over Jon's tongue as his body shuddered and hands clutched at him before falling limp to his sides.

Jon almost laughed with giddiness. With a grin he came forward to press kisses to Tom's sweat-slick skin when the captain rolled the first mate gently to his side and began murmuring soft praises.

"Good boy."

Jon woke a few hours later, curled against Tom's side. Tom slept soundly, his broad chest rising and falling with every deep breath. On his other side, the bed was empty. Jon frowned and sat up. The early-morning light streamed in through the curtains and painted the room in a hazy, golden hue. After climbing out of the huge four-poster bed, Jon padded quietly to the front room to see where Baltsaros was. When he saw that this room too was empty, a finger of worry stole into his heart. Then he saw the note. He picked it up from the big desk and peered at it.

J & T,

All hands needed to stock up and ready the ship. We leave tomorrow at noon. Meet me below when you wake.

— B.

Jon pulled the thick velvet curtain aside and squinted at the beach. Sure enough, there was a bustle of activity. He could see a jolly boat making its way to the ship with a load of supplies. Confused, he turned back to the desk. There he spotted a letter written in the spiky alphabet of the northerners. He snatched it up and ran back to the bed, shaking Tom from his slumber.

Tom rubbed his face blearily, blinking around him in confusion with eyes tinged in red before he scowled in annoyance.

"What?" he rumbled.

Jon shoved the letter into his hand.

"The captain is down at the ship, getting her ready to leave tomorrow," he said, his heart skipping in his chest. "Does this have anything to do with it?"

After swiping at his face again, Tom focused on the letter. A deep crease formed in his forehead, and when he looked back up at him, Jon saw deep concern.

"Aye, lad," said Tom quietly. "Seems we're headed north. Far north."

Tom sat up and read the letter out loud, translating as he went. Written by someone called Sister Iezabel, it described a barbarian raid that had destroyed a nearby settlement. The letter was addressed to Baltsaros, and the wording suggested that they had known each other for a long time. However, it was the first that Tom had heard of a friendship with some nun.

Jon sat down on the bed next to him looking worried.

"You mean where the captain's from?"

"Aye," muttered Tom. "Bloody hells, I hate fuckin' snow."

CHAPTER 21

FIRST BLOOD

*Monsters are real, and ghosts are real too. They live inside us, and sometimes,
they win.*

— STEPHEN KING

Captain Baltsaros pointed to the trapdoor, and the young deckhand made his
way belowdecks with the bag of supplies over his shoulder.

"I don't understand," Jon said. "That letter has to be months old. Why
are we going now? Isn't it a little after the fact?"

Tom was cleaning his nails with his knife while he lounged on the stairs. Though
he seemed concentrated on his task, he lifted his eyes to the captain's, an expression of
disapproval on his rugged face.

"Aye," said the first mate. "We only bloody just got here, Da. What is the fuckin'
rush? Are ye havin' a turn?"

"I'm fine. And the letter is at least a year old."

"Then why are we leaving *now*?" asked Jon, his eyes round in confusion.

Baltsaros reached out and clasped him on the shoulder with a smile before
directing another load of supplies. He then gestured to Jon and Tom and led them to
the captain's quarters.

"Sit," he said and pointed to the table, closing the door behind him. He walked to
the crate next to the empty fridge and pulled out two bottles of Maya's strong beer.
They were warm because that month's ice shipment had not come in yet, but he didn't
think the boys would mind too much. He felt his pulse get a little faster, and it felt like
there was a hand in his chest squeezing his heart. With a deep breath, he placed the
bottles in front them and sat down. Tom grabbed one bottle, untwisted the wire and

pulled the cork out with his teeth. He handed it to Jon and did the same for his own; the first mate's forehead wrinkled as he watched the captain mutely.

"What's going on?" whispered Jon.

Baltsaros took another long breath and steepled his fingers, staring at the space between them as he tried to gather his thoughts.

Just speak.

The captain closed his eyes and swallowed in the stillness.

With eyes shut, Baltsaros began to unwind the memories that sat coiled and cold in the space between his soul and heart. When he spoke, his voice was steady and calm.

"The place I was born is called Heaven's Gate, or *Sormaheine* in my native tongue. It is an ancient city built high on a steep mountain, protected from raids by barbarian tribes by a massive gate at its base. One day, in a fit of childish rage, I led monsters through the gate and then helped them to slaughter my family."

~

After escaping past the gate guards, Baltsaros ran across the ice, furious tears freezing on his cheeks. They would pay. *All of them.* His skinny legs were a blur and his breath heaved in his bony chest. It wasn't *fair* that he had to wait another year to apprentice. He'd been counting on his father's approval. He had been *so* sure of it that he had secretly spent his coins on an alchemist's vest. If he had to wait another year, the vest would be too small! It was a *waste*! Baltsaros had never been so angry before. He wanted to hurt someone.

Suddenly, he tripped over a chunk of ice and went sprawling. With a cry, he pulled himself to sitting and wrapped his thin arms around his knee; he rocked as he sobbed. There was blood on the ice. He had torn open his knee, and Mother would be furious about the rip in his pants. Weeping like a stupid baby, he didn't see the men until they were nearly upon him.

Baltsaros's stomach dropped, and he froze in terror when the leader pointed to him; the huge stranger's hand was bare despite the cold, and he could clearly see that the palm of it was blood red.

Blood ogres from the northern hill! The rhyming song about them was in his head as he stared slack-jawed at the fur-covered strangers.

One, two, they're coming for you...

Before Baltsaros had a chance to get to his feet, one of them grabbed him by the front of his parka and lifted him straight into the air. With a scream, he struggled and kicked in the man's hold; he tried to dig his nails into the stained fist, but it was as if it were made of stone.

Three, four, always wanting for more...

Baltsaros let out another shriek as he was tossed in the air. A second man caught him and turned him around; he whimpered when he saw the sharpened teeth. The man's breath was foul, and when he smiled wider, Baltsaros felt his bladder give out.

Five, six, seven, the red hands, they beckon...

Baltsaros was shaken roughly, and the laughing man who held him said a few words in a strange tongue to the others. The sound of their laughter surrounded Baltsaros. He began to cry harder.

Eight, nine, ten, slaughtered now, feast on men...

His school friend Kyrillosr had made fun of him when he had said they were real ogres like in the fairy tales. Kyr had told him that his father said they were just brutal barbarians from far, far in the north where there was no break from the cold in summer.

Saros, don't be stupid. People just call them ogres because they eat human flesh.

"Child of Sormaheine," growled the man holding him. He had horns on his leather helm, and around his shoulders he wore a great black musk-bear pelt; the reek of it was heavy in the air. "What are you doing so far away from home? Don't you know there are bad men who would do bad things to you?"

Baltsaros's sobs had turned to high wails, and his whole body heaved and trembled. He barely heard the words.

"What should we do with you, hm? Roast you over a fire and pick your bones clean? Or... Should we have a little fun with you first?" said the huge, grinning cannibal.

The men tied him to the saddle of a shaggy, four legged creature. Head hanging over the side of it, he thought that when it glanced back at him, it looked a little sad. Baltsaros's crying had stopped. He just felt numb like his heart or his mind had been frostbitten; he barely understood what was happening to him.

After a long, cold, bumpy ride he was taken into a tent and forced to drink something bitter. At first he was nauseous, and then it was like he was watching the world from one end of a paper tube. The blood ogres had stripped out of their furs. Baltsaros could see their red-stained feet and hands, and for some reason it made him laugh. Kyr had said it was something called *pigment*. Baltsaros had no idea what that was. Did it come off with water? Did they wear it for fashion, like his mother wore colour on her eyelids?

Baltsaros was hot. However, once he had wiggled out of his parka, he felt too light as if he would float away. The men laughed at him, and he scowled. He couldn't understand their words... and then he could. They were speaking of ransoming him. Or eating him.

But, it didn't matter. He was no longer afraid of them.

With a smile, Baltsaros sat down on the piled furs. Then he had an idea and pulled off his shirt to feel the softness against his skin. He squirmed and sighed. A man reached for him and pulled him up. Again the language was gibberish. He laughed and copied them. The giant men found it funny and gave him another bitter drink. His head began to spin again, and the next few hours were just moments that jumped faster and faster towards him:

Telling the leader of the ogres that he knew how to get them into the city.

A cold ride in the dark.

Stairs and great splashes of blood on the wall from the dead guard.

A woman crying for help.

A headless man.

An ogre grunting between the legs of another woman as she stared blankly at Baltsaros.

His father lying in a puddle of blood with his head caved in.

Then, his mother picked him up and for a moment, a tiny moment, he knew fear again as she ran with him in her arms. Blood was everywhere—in his mouth, in his hair. He whimpered when he saw that his hands were red like the ogres' hands. Then more red hands took him from his mother, and she fell, a great wound in her chest. A barbarian worked at her with a knife and pulled her heart from her chest. Had Baltsaros also taken a bite? Was he crying or laughing? Vomit on the ground. His grandmother dead. The neighbour's wife stripped naked and on her hands and knees, screaming as an ogre did something to her. Baltsaros shook his head when the flask was pressed to his lips, but a third time he was given the potion. Everything was jumbled in his head. The barbarians turned to true ogres, carving up the living. Stacks of bodies. His little sister found in the closet crying. A knife thrust into Baltsaros's hand. Laughter.

Do it, do it, do it! Were they chanting? Was he screaming? Excitement. Horror.

He stabbed Cassia so many times that she no longer looked like a person.

The night became grotesque tintype stills in black and white, and minutes were preserved as hours.

He remembered wondering why, when he'd had the knife clutched in his little fist, he had not stabbed one of the men instead of Cassia... And then there was nothing.

~

"I must have passed out from exhaustion or from shock, I don't know which," said the captain softly. His voice had not once wavered in his narrative. He'd already told the tale to Abetha, and this second time around was much easier. "Sister Iezabel found me under a bed. The citadel's guards had finally arrived on the scene some time earlier and had dispatched only a few of the attackers. Seems like most of the barbarians had abandoned their revelries and left with their *meat*. I don't know if they meant to leave me behind or if they had simply forgotten about me." He rubbed his forehead and closed his eyes. "It gets a little fuzzy after that," he said, sighing. "I remember that I was mute for the first six months I was in the orphanage. A year and a half later, shortly after my ninth birthday, my uncle came to get me, and you both know the rest."

"Bloody hells, Da," said Tom in a hoarse voice. Baltsaros opened his eyes and smiled wanly.

"That memory has been locked away for a long time."

The captain looked at Jon. The young man was staring at the table, pale with shock. When he raised his head, Baltsaros was alarmed by the fury in his eyes.

"What kind of monsters would do that to a *child?*" he choked out. Baltsaros glanced at Tom and they shared a long look. The first mate's face was drawn with sympathy, remembering his own monsters. For a moment no one spoke.

"Did they do anything else to you?" whispered Jon. Baltsaros frowned at him, trying to keep from feeling or thinking too much about that long, bloody night.

"There is a lot that I don't remember, and I am glad for it. I've only told you because it may shed some light on some of my behaviour... my buried guilt over what happened."

"How can you possibly think you're guilty for *any* of it? They drugged you!" Jon exclaimed.

"I was, as you pointed out, a child. What child could possibly understand the logistics of blame in that situation? I suppressed the memory, either on purpose or as a result of shock; I have no way of knowing. Since I never spoke of it to anyone, no one knew that it was me that distracted the guards, or that it was my hand that ended by sister's life, so no one helped me. They treated me like a victim without knowing that I blamed myself. It's like I've been harbouring a terrible secret—one that I wasn't even privy to myself until my mind recently vomited forth everything in luminous detail."

"But... You have to know now that you're not to blame!"

Baltsaros lifted his hand.

"I *do* know that, Jon. Trying to convince my psyche of that fact is specifically what I've been doing since the memory resurfaced," he said grimly. "And that is the *last* I would like to speak of it."

"That's not—"

"Jon. I am in control of myself, now more than ever. I may be a broken thing, but I understand *how* I am broken. I don't need to rehash the past," he reached out and covered Jon's hand with his.

"Why're we goin' north then, Da?" asked Tom in a quiet voice.

"Sister Iezabel, in all her letters, never once mentioned a word of what had happened to me. I think she feared reminding me would revive my trauma. Then about year back, when her letter arrived with the news of a barbarian attack, I honestly thought nothing of it. This morning, there was a new letter from her— nothing out of the usual with this one—but when I put it away with the rest, I saw the previous one and suddenly understood the significance of what she had written. Though we are too late to save those lost in that attack, Sister Iezabel's description of the barbarians closely matches that of the ones that took me as a child. I want to attempt to track them down."

"To what end?" asked Jon softly.

"To kill every last one of them."

CHAPTER 22
FATE'S FOOLS

J on held onto the ratlines with his eyes closed, happy to feel the sun and salt spray on his bare chest as the ship cut through the water at full speed. They had been at sea for nearly three weeks and with only one planned stop to resupply along the way, they would continue to sail day and night until they reached the northern continent. Jon was excited, worried, nervous... He breathed in deep the buffeting wind and let it out as a long sigh. He was trying to keep himself from overthinking things.

Deeply disturbed by the horror of the captain's story, Jon had felt nothing but a rousing thrill when Baltsaros had revealed his motives for going north. Jon's blood had sung at the words, as if they were nobly setting off for battle. It was only when the adrenaline had worn off that Jon wondered if retribution could ever be called *noble*.

He looked back at the straining sails. It would take them two more months to get to Sormaheine—*if* they weren't becalmed by a lack of wind like Captain Romas had. He jumped down from the gunwale and walked slowly sternward, trying to turn his mind away from heavy thoughts. If he let worry gnaw away at him this early in their journey, Jon would be a wreck by the time they landed at the northern coast.

Jon smiled to himself. No, for the moment the most he had to worry about was making sure that he lived up to his new position as quartermaster. Jon was still surprised and humbled that the crew had voted in agreement to the captain promoting him; times really had changed. Now he was the second only to Baltsaros, ranking even above Tom, and his job was to counterbalance all of the captain's orders —to keep him in check. It was a daunting honour; Jon didn't look forward to the time he had to veto something. He could just imagine the furious spark in the captain's eyes as he stared down at Jon, the beast forged inside his mind by blood and terror trying to convince him that Jon was a nuisance that needed to be removed. However, Baltsaros was confident that Jon was safe from him. Jon just had to trust that he was right about that.

Tom sat cross-legged on top of a large crate with a book open in his lap. His forehead was creased in concentration, and his lips moved ever so slightly as he read. It was a peculiar sight. Jon approached and grinned up at the first mate.

"You're reading."

Tom marked his spot with a finger and glanced over at Jon.

"Aye. What of it?" asked Tom with a frown.

"You're reading out in the open... I thought you revelled in your reputation as an uncultured lout."

Tom snorted in amusement.

"Ye know I don't give a rat's arse," he said. He lifted the book so Jon could see the cover. It was one of Baltsaros's surgery books. "Just doin' some thinkin' about the little project ye gave me."

Jon felt a touch of alarm.

"I didn't mean to do anything drastic. Nothing invasive... Just something simple."

With a chuckle, Tom nodded.

"Don't ye worry, Jonny-boy. I ain't goin' to be butcherin'... I think ye'll be happy with what I got planned."

"I hope so," said Jon with a grin and thumped the side of the crate with his fist. "Hey, I still need you to get that gun hoisted back into its moorings."

"Anythin' fer you, big brother."

Jon scowled and shook his head.

"Don't you start on that again unless you want to see how long it takes before your balls actually turn blue."

Tom just winked and looked back down at his book to continue reading.

Amused, Jon thought about the first mate's peculiar ideas about family as he went belowdecks to find something to eat.

~

Jon took his chair at the long table in the palace dining room and looked at those seated across from him. The captain was in quiet conversation with the queen, their heads tilted towards each other. Saban was conspicuously absent; the man had been so more often than not after that confusing day aboard the *Heart*. Jon's face felt hot at the memory of what Saban had been witness to.

Since being made so acutely aware of Saban's confusion, Jon had begun to ponder his own experiences and wondered why there had been so little inner struggle for him in comparison... Was he open like the captain in his preferences, or was he like Tom, who always said that he'd take "cock over cunt" if given the choice?

As if his thoughts had summoned the man, Jon raised his eyes at the sound of a cleared throat and was surprised to see the first mate in the doorway. Despite what Tom had said about not being suited for the queen's table, it seemed that he had finally decided to make a concession; it was obvious to Jon that the belted tunic Tom wore was a peace offering. Jon nodded at him with a tense smile, thinking that the first mate looked both nervous and a little hostile. This could go very badly if Abetha chose to be on the defensive.

"Thomas," said the queen quietly. "Please join us."

The crease between Tom's brows deepened, and Jon held his breath.

"*Tom*," corrected the first mate. For a moment it looked like the queen was going to retort with her usual vitriol, but then she just inclined her head graciously.

"Tom," she conceded and gestured to the empty chair next to Jon with a delicate, pale hand.

Jon hid his smile by wiping his mouth with the napkin from his lap.

Well... It's a start.

"Good for you," he said quietly when Tom had settled. The first mate just grunted noncommittally, but he squeezed back when Jon reached under the table and took his hand.

The conversation circled around trade; Ceara would be back soon, and the queen would be responsible for keeping track of everything. It still bewildered Jon that the captain felt confident enough about the ex-spymaster to give her such an important role. However, he had begun to realize that Baltsaros was much better at using people's skills than he was. Jon frowned and wondered if his overdeveloped sense of empathy kept him from seeing people as tools like Baltsaros did. Or maybe it was the captain's *under*developed sense that made him better at it?

The queen's voice interrupted his thoughts.

"It's peculiar, Jon. With that beard, you remind me of a young man I used to know."

Jon smiled politely.

"Yes?"

"His father was employed as my father's stableman," she continued after taking a sip of wine from her fluted glass. "Yes, there's something about the lines of your face. Richard was the same age as me... We grew up together."

A prickle went up the back of Jon's neck, and he swallowed his mouthful, staring at the queen.

"My father's name was Richard," he said softly. "He was also a stable master."

The queen's eyes widened a touch, but her lips slid into an indulgent curve.

"It *is* a common enough name," she pointed out. "Was your father from the midlands isles too?"

"No, Your Majesty," Jon replied; he heard a note of something approaching fear in his voice. "He was actually a mainlander. His father was a stable master somewhere in the northern area... near the lakes."

"How... amazing! What are the chances? That is exactly where my family hails from," laughed the queen. "Your father must be the Richard I knew!"

Jon could feel his pulse stuttering as he contemplated the incredible coincidence.

Do fluke and fortuity court you like lovers? He could almost hear the old woman laughing.

"No, it's impossible," he said, groping for a solid reason. "It can't be the same man... Reginald told me that my father had been expelled from the household he grew up in because he was caught in an indiscretion with the lord's daughter... Oh." As the words left his mouth, he saw bright spots appear in the queen's cheeks, and she dropped her eyes.

Tom barked out a laugh.

Aghast, Jon desperately tried to think of something else to say as Abetha started to push her chair back; Baltsaros quickly caught her hand and stopped her.

"Abetha, we were all young once," he said with a gracious smile devoid of any reproach. "No one at this table would judge you for a maiden's tryst." The queen stared at him for a long moment, her bright blue-green eyes unsure. Jon elbowed Tom to try to stop his chuckling, but all it did was make him laugh louder.

"Holy hells, Jon!" he whooped and slapped the tabletop. "We're bloody brothers!"

"You most certainly are *not!*" exclaimed the queen, drawing herself up. Her face was almost crimson, and Jon thought he could see a glimmer of embarrassed tears.

"Lookit you! Dickin' about with the help!" Tom said with a grin, but Jon caught something surprising. The first mate was amused, yes, but there was nothing malicious about his tone for once. In fact, he seemed almost impressed.

Abetha flared her nostrils and raised her chin a notch.

Tom held up his hands, his expression quickly falling serious.

"Naw, listen... Peace. Really. I'm just glad to see you've got blood runnin' through your veins like the rest of us." Tom's accent had shifted ever so slightly—an echo of what it must have been like when he was a boy. "I'm sorry. Please?"

The queen lips worked together for a moment.

"Ye know, if this bonny Richard of yers was half as good-lookin' as Jon here, ye didn't stand a bloody chance..." continued the first mate with the first friendly grin Jon had ever seen him give the queen.

Abetha's cheeks flushed even darker, and her neck was mottled; Jon was worried for a second that she would storm off, but instead she surprised him by smiling a little sheepishly.

"Yes. And he was as young and foolish as I was," she muttered, and Jon suddenly saw her as she had been then. Headstrong, somewhat brash, a little wild... Jon glanced at Tom; the apple did not fall far from the tree.

Abetha cleared her throat and stopped fiddling with the cloth napkin, her cool composure returning to her.

"Now, if we've finished discussing my lapse in judgment, I would like to get back to the business of trade, if you will?" said the queen.

Mother and son stared at each other for a few beats. Jon sensed something pass between them. The beginning of an understanding? Tom finally nodded and went back to his meal. However, Jon could see that his posture was much more relaxed.

"Yer thinkin' it's a hell of a coincidence 'bout yer da, aint'cha?" murmured Tom a few minutes later when he had finished his curried goat and couscous. "Mind's on the ol' fortune-teller again?"

Jon nodded slowly. He had just been replaying in his head the encounter with the old woman.

"Well, ye can stop," said the first mate. "It's not even—"

"Tom, I can't... Everything she said is true!" Jon exclaimed. Tom stared hard at him as though he were sizing him up; not for the first time, Jon wished he could read him better. At last a sly grin stretched Tom's lips, and he winked.

"All the bloody coincidences happened to me too, ye know," he said, reaching for his wine. "Hey, what if I'm the one who's causin' them, and yer just along for the ride?"

Jon blinked. It hadn't occurred to him. The first mate *had* been part of every twist of fate. Or... Had he? But then so had the captain. Jon scratched at his beard, feeling a little flustered.

Tom leaned closer and tapped his callused forefinger against the glossy pale wood. He narrowed his eyes.

"Ye know... Maybe when that witch was lookin' in her crystal ball—"

"They were cards."

"Fine. Cards. Maybe..." Tom moved even closer, his voice dipping to a hush. "Maybe she could see that fate..."

"See that fate what?" whispered Jon, his heart skipping.

"Maybe she could see that fate's chosen us special because we're brothers," said Tom with a little waggle of his eyebrows.

"What?" Jon couldn't help laughing at the impish look on the first mate's face. "Ok, it is *literally* impossible that we're brothers, given that I'm older than you. My father married my mother, and I came about less than a year later. He died four months after that."

"He could-a paid a wee visit to my ma and done 'er somewhere between then?"

"Oh, for fuck's sake, will you stop it?" said Jon with another laugh.

"Well. It's *like* we're brothers, aye? Seein' as our da's both dipped in the same waters?" Tom's grin had a coy edge to it.

"You worry me, you know that?"

~

Jon had just finished up changing the duty roster for the coming weeks—Baltsaros believed in altering it a bit every month to keep the men interested in their work—when Tom came up the stairs to sit next to him at the helm. The big man stretched his arms out with a groan and then took a thin cheroot out from behind his ear. As he lit it, he looked around with a peaceful expression on his face. Jon smiled. The first mate's cheek was smeared with something black, and he smelled of clean sweat and salt air.

"I sometimes find it hard to believe that you weren't born to this," Jon said.

Tom laughed and flicked away some ash from the end of his smoke as he contemplated Jon.

"Why d'ye say that?"

"You just seem so much more at home... happier? I don't know. It's like you were meant to be a pirate."

"Oh, I was a bloody piss-poor sailor for a long bloody while, love," said Tom, the slim cigar jammed in the corner of his mouth. "But if ye really want somethin', ye gotta work for it."

Jon nodded and watched the smoke curl from Tom's nostrils as he squinted into the distance.

They sat in silence, watching the sun set slowly to the west.

The pink sky was hung with small clouds that seemed blue in comparison. When Jon raised his eyes to the darkening canopy above, he saw a few bright stars.

Looking to the stars is a better means of finding your way...

"Do you think going north is foolish?" he asked, turning to Tom.

Tom thought for a moment. When he took a drag of his smoke, Jon could see his eyes were narrowed shrewdly.

"I tend to think most o' life is foolish, lovey," he muttered after a while with a little shrug. "But... If we can grant a little peace to Da by goin' on what I figure is a bloody wild goose chase—" He turned at the soft footfall on the quarterdeck staircase.

The captain looked down at the two of them.

"Wild goose chase, hm? Why don't you continue, Tom?"

The first mate looked a bit self-conscious and grimaced.

"I was gonna say that it was bloody worth it to me," he pointed out.

"It just makes me happy to hear you say it," replied the captain with a smile. He walked over to the side of the quarterdeck and leaned on the railing, watching the sky for a moment. "However, I do hope you're wrong."

CHAPTER 23
BAD LUCK

Jon watched Katherine lift the musket and rest the long barrel on her hook as she aimed at the target—a dummy made of an old leather coat stuffed with sailcloth on a frame of wood. The shot she fired went over the side of the ship, but she was definitely improving.

"Fucking hells," she growled. "I'm worse than you are. Talk about luck… Why couldn't the fucking cannonball take my other fucking arm?"

"I wish it hadn't taken your arm at all," said Jon with a sad smile. Katherine huffed out a little laugh and passed the musket over to Jon so that he could reload it.

"I used to be great marksman," she sighed. "The captain used to say that I was a better shot than Peter, and that man was well known for his skill with a pistol."

Jon made sure the wadding was tamped firmly and handed the musket back to Katherine.

"The captain's mentioned him before. What happened to him?"

Katherine poured the fine powder, pulled the hammer to full cock, aimed, and fired again. This time she had better results—the lead ball actually grazed the target. She shook her head in disgust and walked up to the dummy to lean the long gun against it, obviously done for the day.

"Peter?" she asked. "He was first mate when I joined the crew. Had been since the mutiny. When the captain brought Tom aboard, it never sat well with Peter. I overheard a few arguments, and it wasn't pretty. Then, when the captain and Tom started to, well… When things changed between them, Peter was *extremely* vocal about his disapproval. He had religion and was a bit of a holy joe—didn't stop him from sleeping with whores or slitting throats, mind you—but he took exception to what went on behind the captain's doors. He criticized the captain in front of the crew, and that was it."

"Baltsaros killed him," murmured Jon with a nod.

Katherine's dark brows rose up.

"Uh, no," she replied, sounding confused. "The captain can be cold-blooded, sure, but why would he kill Peter? No... He just gave him a fair amount of coin—enough to buy himself a ship should he like to—and we dropped him off at the next port."

"You saw this with your own eyes?" asked Jon.

"Jon, what are you on about?"

"Never mind," he replied, spying Tom coming towards them. The first mate held a bundle in his hands. Excited, Jon smiled.

Tom stopped before them and creased his forehead at Katherine after a quick glance at Jon.

"I only did it because Jon asked," he muttered and held out the lumpy sack to Katherine.

Her eyes widened, and she opened it awkwardly, pulling out what Tom had made for her.

Jon grinned wide. It wasn't pretty, but it was definitely an arm. It had a long leather tube with buckled straps on one end, a jointed elbow, and wooden forearm that ended in a lifelike carved hand. Jon could see a leather thong running along its side that disappeared into a hole in the wrist.

Katherine seemed not to understand what she was looking at, so Tom took it back and held it up.

"This," he said impatiently, squeezing the leather cuff, "fits over yer damn stump. It'll probably be needin' somethin' to pad it, but... Do ye need me to put it on ye, or do ye think ye can handle that yerself?"

Katherine hastily pulled up her sleeve and undid the buckles that held her hook in place. It thumped to the deck, and Jon had to avert his eyes, sickened slightly by the sight of her stump. When he heard Tom swearing under his breath, he chanced a look and saw that he was adjusting the prosthetic. Mute, Katherine just watched as Tom lifted her arm to tighten the straps. Her eyes were bright, and her expression was one of sheer amazement.

"All righty... See this?" Tom said, tapping a bolt on the outside of the hinged wooden elbow. "This'll tighten or loosen the joint here. Ye can keep it bent, or ye can keep it straight. Whatever yer little heart desires." The first mate crooked the elbow and twisted the bolt so that it stayed bent. Then he showed them that the wrist swivelled a few degrees. Finally, Katherine's grin widened in disbelief when he demonstrated that the fingers were jointed and that pulling the leather thong would curl them in.

Jon whistled under his breath.

"Tom, that is fantastic," he said. Tom's eyes flicked to him, and Jon could see that beneath his gruff, impatient demeanour, he seemed a little flustered.

"Uh... And ye'll have to hold the end of the cord with yer teeth for a sec—bloody sorry 'bout that, couldn't think of better—and so when ye push in this here"—he pointed to a metal clasp on the outside of the wrist—"it'll keep the grip locked in. So ye can hold... somethin'."

Blinking rapidly to try to dry the tears that rose in her eyes, Katherine let out a small, choked laugh and threw her good arm around Tom to pull him in for a tight hug.

Jon swiped at his own eyes, laughing at the look on Tom's face. The first mate looked startled, and there was a flush in his tanned face. He patted Katherine's back hesitantly a few times and glanced at Jon.

Bloody hells.

"Weren't my idea, love," Tom mumbled. "Was Jon that asked fer it."

Katherine pulled back, her dark eyes amused. Before the scowling first mate had a chance to step away, she pecked a quick kiss on his cheek.

"Thank you," she said, smiling. "Really. Thank you for putting so much thought into it. I didn't realize you were so talented. It's really amazing... I've never seen anything like it."

Tom grunted and looked down, scratching the back of his neck.

"You really outdid yourself," said Jon before turning to Katherine. "Seriously, I asked him for something simple. He designed it himself."

"All right!" growled the first mate, crossing his arms. "Enough already. So I'm the cock of the bloody walk. I get it." Despite his words, Jon had never seen him look so proud of himself.

"Come on, lads," said Katherine with a laugh. "Let's go see if I can hold a tankard of ale in this thing!"

She took off towards the hatch with a strut in her step that Jon hadn't seen in a while.

Finally letting his face settle into a cocky grin, Tom slung his arm over Jon's shoulder.

"Ye heard the wench," he said with a wink. "I got a mighty thirst."

~

Tom leaned back against Jon's legs, a mug of slightly warm beer in his hand. They had taken out one of the low brass braziers and formed a circle around it with crates and barrels to sit on. Tom sat cross-legged on the deck, gazing into the fire. Soon they would have to light braziers all the bloody time to keep from freezing; thankfully, this night only needed a little warming, and the fire was there mostly for cheer. According to Baltsaros, the north wasn't as brutally cold as the trip to the spires, but Tom would be happy if he never saw another fucking iceberg for the rest of his natural life.

He took another sip of beer and looked at Katherine sitting across the fire on the now-empty barrel of beer. She was holding a tankard awkwardly in her carved hand, but she was bloody holding it. Thinking about a jointed toy soldier he'd had as a boy, Tom saw how he could improve his design by making the wrist move in the other direction. When he lifted his eyes, he saw that Katherine was watching him. She held the mug a little higher and nodded to him with a tight-lipped smile. Hells, it looked like she was a little dewy in the eye region again. Tom just grinned and raised his own beer in salute. He had a feeling that they'd go back to razzing each other in the morning, but could be that a knife-edge would no longer be hidden in their taunts.

Bloody kind-hearted Jon, he thought with a smile.

"So the mate's talkin' nineteen t' the bloody dozen so's I can't understand a bloody word 'e's sayin'," laughed Harris, his face glowing in the firelight as he told his story. "Well, 'e's jus' pointin' to the bloody thing like 'e's wantin' it fer 'is own, but ev'ry time I ask t' see 'is bloody—"

"Shut it!" growled Tom, cutting Harris off. On alert, he held out his hand and sat up. He could have sworn he'd just heard something off port. Everyone was quiet as he listened hard. After a minute of not hearing anything further, Tom frowned. He looked across the fire at Baltsaros and saw that the man's hooded eyes were trained off in the same direction as the noise he'd heard. The captain turned back to him, concern etched on his face. Baltsaros rose to his feet and left the warm circle of light to peer off the port side.

"What is it?" whispered Jon.

"Thought I heard somethin' creak," Tom replied, getting to his knees. He'd had a fair bit to drink, and his balance was off as he lurched to his feet. He used Jon's shoulder to support himself. "Stay here, love. Could be nothin'." He patted Jon's shoulder before making his way through the dark to the captain's side.

"I heard it too," said Baltsaros quietly when Tom stepped up.

Tom squinted into the distance, night-blind from staring into the fire. It hardly mattered though; there was only the barest sliver of a moon left, and with the scattering of clouds above, the night was rendered almost pitch-black. A few minutes passed, and Tom was about to return to Jon's side when he caught sight of something darker than the sky around it. A second later, he heard another creak. There was a ship sailing less than a quarter league away from them.

"Cock and bloody fuckin' balls, where in the bloody hells did that come from?" he said, pointing. The captain followed the first mate's finger and leaned further over the gunwale, looking at the ship.

"It's completely dark," murmured Baltsaros. "Could be abandoned, just moving along in the same wind as us. You and I both have seen that happen in the past."

"Aye, and could be that they've snuck up on us," rumbled Tom. He had to hold onto a line of rigging to keep from swaying from drink. Great bloody time to run into trouble.

"I'm going up top to take a better look," said the captain. Tom nodded and followed him up the port staircase to the quarterdeck. Malik was behind the wheel, looking a little sleepy and bored in the lantern light.

"What's going on?" he asked with a yawn.

"We're being shadowed by a ship," replied the captain, taking his binoculars from the shipwright.

"What? Where?" asked Malik, glancing around.

"Port. Look between the shrouds and the last gun," said Tom, pointing.

Malik peered off into the night.

"I don't see anything."

"It's there," said the captain in a quiet voice. "Three masts. I'd say twice the size of us. Looks like a frigate." He passed the binoculars over to Tom.

Tom lifted them to his eyes and nodded. He could just make out the masts by starlight.

"Shit. If they ain't friendly, we're in a lick o' trouble, I'd say," he muttered.

"That's if it's not a ghost ship."

Tom was about to lower the binoculars when he saw a glint of light from the other ship. At first he took it to be a window-glass reflection of their own burning brazier, but when he saw the flicker again, he recognized it for what it was.

"*Guns!*" he roared. He grabbed the captain's arm to pull him away from the side and throw him to the deck. The double boom of cannons rang out only a breath before the ship shuddered and the air exploded in a shower of wood splinters. Below, the men yelled out in surprise. Tom didn't hear any shrieks of agony—that was a good sign. Buzzing adrenaline had wiped the alcohol out of his system; his mind was racing but clear. When he got up on one knee, he saw that a cannonball had taken out part of the railing that ringed the quarterdeck. Another volley could hit them at any moment. Tom glanced at the captain who had also risen to his knees. With a tight nod to his first mate, Baltsaros got to his feet and ran towards the wheel; Tom knew what to do. He skipped the stairs, jumping over the railing to land easily on the deck below.

"Douse the lights! Brace hard to port!" he shouted and then pointed to the metal fire pit as a few men sprinted quickly to extinguish lanterns. "Harris! Give a hand." Harris bent low with Tom, and they each grabbed a side of the brazier. The first mate gasped as the handle seared his flesh, but they both ran the few steps to the side of the ship to toss it overboard. They couldn't take a chance that the bucket of water they kept at the fire's side would be ample enough to put it out immediately, and the resulting smoke billowing above them was sure to catch what little moonlight there was.

Blowing on his smarting hand, Tom glanced up at the captain just as the lantern above him was extinguished. The last image he had of Baltsaros was of teeth bared and eyes wild, straining hard to port to turn the ship starboard. He hoped that with the lads hauling the yard round to match, they'd turn smartly. The wind wasn't blowing hard, but it just might be enough.

Where is Jon?

As the thought crossed his mind, he heard the double boom again, but this time with a slight pause and the hint of a whistling before the deck bucked beneath his feet. He heard the crunch of wood and a scream. Praying that they hadn't been hit badly, he jogged towards the sound of mayhem.

Please, brothers of the sea and lords of the light and devils of the underworld, if you let us survive this bloody mess, I will be a better man and never steal from a temple again, and I'm sorry for some of the folks I've killed...

When Tom reached the bow, he could see nothing but dark shapes. He smelled blood.

"What happened?" he growled, pushing his way through the crowd.

"There be a hole, sir," said someone to his right. Tom recognized Hitch's voice. "Next to th' capstan. Ye'll be mindin' yer step. What I be thinkin' were a chain-shot aimed t' cripple us took a mate's leg clear off, poor craiter, before holin' the deck."

"Holed right through, ye think?" Tom asked, falling to his knees to search for the edges of the jagged breach in the wooden planks. He could hear someone moaning softly and wondered who had lost his leg.

It can't be Jon. He forced himself to pay attention to Hitch.

"Canae rightly say, sir," said the scrappy pirate, crouching next to Tom, "but it be darker than th' black hells, be damned. No hearin' any water below, though, and no leanin' yet. Feck… It'd be the luck o' the gods if we be spared."

Tom pressed his ear to the boards and listened for the telltale gurgle and surging sound of a ship pierced through. He heard nothing and heaved a quiet sigh. However, as he lifted his head, he heard another double cannon blast.

All the men seemed to hold their breath in the heartbeats that followed. Then, off the port side, they heard a loud splash and then another. Tom heard a few whispered prayers and some relieved laughter. They might be out of range, but they were far from safe. He slapped Hitch on the back, gave permission for light belowdecks as long as the portholes had their blackers on, and turned his attention to the man groaning on the deck. As he crawled to the side, his hand came down in what could only be blood.

Please don't be Jon.

He reached out and felt for the man's leg. When he touched the sharp edges of bone, he moved his hand higher.

"Mate?" he asked, wondering if the man was conscious; he'd gone quiet. A moment later, a moving light shone up from the hole in the deck—which was thankfully smaller than what he had feared—and was relieved to see that the man wasn't Jon but one of the new deckhands from Ereme'ia Balor. He was pale and sweaty in the dim light, and his eyes wandered as if he had lost his senses. Tom squinted at the wound. What was left of the man's calf was a mess of shattered bone fragments and clumps of flesh. He was bleeding badly; there was a steady torrent of red pouring into the hole made by the chain-shot.

"Someone get Cook," he shouted, pulling off his belt so he could make a tourniquet. However, as the words left his mouth, the skinny Balorian's breath started hitching in his chest, and he stared at the first mate with wide eyes. Tom recognized the look; Cook was a decent surgeon, but the lad was past saving.

The dying man clutched at the first mate's hand, and Tom squeezed back reassuringly.

"I'm sorry, mate," said Tom, shaking his head. "Ye weren't a pirate long, but ye did yer job well. I remember ye, and I'll find out what words to say over ye from yer friends so that yer gods can find ye—the good ones, anyway. Make yer peace, but don't go scared, mate. I'm here with ye." Tom had no idea whether the young man could hear him or even understand him, but he felt like someone should witness his passing. The poor bugger had come from a world away, only to die a bloody, dark, and gruesome death. After a few more gasps, each more ragged than the last, his hand went limp in Tom's. The first mate closed the young man's eyes and stood just as Cook came running.

"He died well," said Tom, wiping his bloody hands on his trousers. "Now get him out o' the fuckin' way, and be prepared for more o' the same if we can't outrun the bloody scoundrels before the sun comes up."

Cook nodded and gestured for the kitchen boy to help him haul the body out of the way.

With a look to the east where the sun would be rising in a few hours, Tom ran through the dark to aft and took the steps two at a time. There was a faint glow from a covered lantern set on the wooden boards by the captain's feet, and Tom was glad to see Jon standing by his side.

"Bloody hells, Da," swore Tom, his heart finally beginning to slow. Jon turned and gave Tom a quick hug.

"Oh gods, I am glad you're ok," said Jon. The back of the slighter man's shirt was damp with what Tom assumed was nervous sweat.

"Damage report," murmured Baltsaros, his eyes on the blind darkness ahead of them.

"Not much. Near the bow, we got a hole big enough to swallow a barrel sideways but doesn't look like we're takin' on water. Got the boys lookin' into it. One man down... one o' them lads from Balor," Tom replied.

The captain just nodded. Lit from below by the lantern, his face was all angles and planes. He resembled nothing so much as a demon from a fairy tale.

"Who are they?" asked Jon. "That was no warning shot across the bow."

"Blasted if I know, love," said Tom, looking over his shoulder as if the ship were looming right there in the dark. "There's no tellin'. With a frigate that size... could be navy or could be pirates. All's I know is that they're bloody sneaks and yellow curs to be firin' at us from the dark."

"Like you wouldn't do the same, given the chance."

Tom frowned at Jon. To his amazement, Jon winked.

"All righty, lad. Yer right," he smirked. However, he quickly sobered when he heard a shout. When it turned out only to be an update on the state of the hull—intact, thank the gods—he took a deep, calming breath. *Baal's Heart* could weather this if they managed to get far enough from their attackers, but they had to assume that the other ship had turned as well.

"Do we tack back to port, Da?" he asked quietly. Changing their course would help them lose the tail; the frigate was faster than they were and every effort counted.

The captain frowned in thought.

"We'll wait a little while before resuming our original course. At least then if we do run into them again, we'll still be under cover of night. Keep the lights low or covered for now, Tom. I'll let you know when to have the men square sails."

"Aye, Da."

As his sweat cooled and the adrenaline left his system, he realized he was holding his hand curled into a claw. When he closed his fist, he understood why. He squatted next to the lantern and held his palm out to the light. Under the dried blood there was a blister in the shape of the brazier's handle raised on both the heel of his hand and across his fingers. Tom swore under his breath; it wasn't bad, but he'd be favouring the other hand. Not great if they were boarded and had to fight.

Tom heard Jon let out a shaky breath and glanced up. The lad rubbed his face, looking weary and pale in the wan light. When a shudder ran through his slight frame, Tom stood in alarm.

"Are ye ok, love?" he asked, curling his good hand around the back of Jon's neck. His hair was wet, and Tom's hand came away bloody. "Bloody hells, yer hurt!"

"Hurt?" asked Jon, his voice vague. "I'm just a little cold. Unh—" He teetered and collapsed against Tom. The first mate's pulse jumped and his guts twisted as Jon shivered. "I feel weird."

"What's wrong?" The captain's voice held a tinge of fear. Tom looked up and shook his head. Carefully, he examined Jon's neck and shoulders looking for a wound. When he found nothing, he slid his fingers along Jon's scalp.

"Why am I bleeding?" asked Jon, sounding a little scared. Tom's fingers came into contact with something small and hard sticking out of the back of Jon's head. "Ow! What is it?"

Tom frowned and felt around the edges of what he thought was a big splinter of wood embedded in Jon's scalp.

"Sliver o' wood, Jon. Ain't nothin'," he said lightly, dismayed by how much blood he felt in Jon's hair. Scalp wounds bled like the black devils; Tom didn't dare pull the splinter out. He lifted his eyes and met Baltsaros's.

"I'm gonna take him to Cook," he said quietly, knowing that the captain would want to stitch Jon up himself. However, the crew needed their captain, and Tom hoped that Baltsaros wouldn't let his fragile emotions get the better of him. He saw something cross the captain's stark face, but he just nodded quickly.

"Tell the men to square," said Baltsaros, his voice calm. "And return to me."

~

Jon held his breath as the needle poked into him again. He could feel the catgut pull his skin, and it made his nausea from blood loss worse; he was afraid he was going to be sick. However, he closed his eyes tighter and took a few quick breaths through his nose, waiting for the next stitch to be tied.

Cook's hands smelled of onions, but he was gentle as he worked on Jon's wound.

"You are lucky, my boy," said Cook with a smile in his voice. "Any deeper and you might not have made it."

"Thanks, but I'd rather not think about that," muttered Jon. He couldn't help but let out a pained sound as the needle pierced him again.

"You should, Jon," replied the ship's cook. Jon felt the tension of the thread break when the catgut was cut with a knife. "You should take the time to really think about the near misses."

"I'd rather not dwell on my mortality, if it's all the same to you," replied Jon as he sat up slowly. The back of his head throbbed and the room spun in a lazy circle. He swallowed hard.

"Not *dwell*," said the Cook, his midlander accent so similar to Jon's. "But *face* them. It makes life that much more precious to know how close to death you've been. This is the third time, isn't it?"

"Third?"

"Third time you've been close to death... Hey, you know three's a special number, right?"

Jon's head swam.

Three is a magic number. Did you know that, Jon?

He licked his lips and tried to find his voice.

"Did you just hear a woman laughing?" he whispered, blinking at Cook. The tall, bald man shook his head, a worried look on his homely face. When he lifted a hand to touch Jon's forehead, Jon noticed the tattooed ring of stars around the man's wrist. The sound of his pulse was like a deep drum in his ears. He slid off the counter and stood shakily for a moment.

"Thank you," he said hoarsely. "I have to get back to the captain."

"Are you sure, Jon? Why don't you have a lie down?"

Jon pressed his lips together and shook his head before stumbling out of the room.

Cook frowned at the door, looking a little concerned that Jon wouldn't make it up the stairs by himself. With a shake of his head, he took up his knife and needle to dump them in the cleaning basin. As he was washing the blood from his hands, he paused as if in deep thought.

"Oh, that's right... It was four times, not three," he muttered to himself with a nod. "Poor kid's got the worst luck."

CHAPTER 24
DEATH'S REAPER

We don't beat the reaper by living longer, we beat the reaper by living well and living fully.

— RANDY PAUSCH

Tom eyed Jon and rolled his cheroot slowly between thumb and finger before taking another deep drag on it. The lad was pale and bug-eyed like he'd seen a ghost, and he hugged himself so tight that his fingers dug into his biceps. Tom didn't like the way his knuckles were turning white.

"Go lie down, Jon," he said quietly. "Yer hurt, and we ain't in any pressin' danger. There ain't much ye can offer right now, 'cept give me cause to worry about ye. Go on now while ye can."

Jon's lips were in a straight, bloodless line, and he shook his head, strong jaw jutted slightly forward. However, he didn't offer any explanation; he just stood there with a half-crazed look in eyes gone to storm-grey in the lantern's meek glow. With a long sigh, Tom gave up. He turned and lifted the lid to the bench and dug around for the thick blanket they kept there. Jon let himself be bundled up and pushed down on the wooden seat. Tom was a little unnerved by the tremble he felt go through Jon's body.

"What is it, love?"

Jon's gaze darted away.

"I know you don't believe in fate, but—" Jon answered at long last.

"Bloody hells! Yer on about this again?" groaned Tom. Jon was going to drive him crazy with all this blasted talk of fate. He wished he'd never let Jon out of his sight at the *Jewel*.

734

"On about what?" asked Baltsaros, returning from the stern with binoculars in hand.

"Jonny-boy here got his fortunes told by an old witch, and now he's seein' chance like it were writ in celestial bloody stone," replied Tom.

The captain's eyes widened ever so slightly, and he looked hard at Jon.

"Why didn't you mention this before?"

"Because everyone's been telling me that I'm stupid for believing it, but... it's... there's just too much... coincidence," replied Jon in a small voice. "Too much she said was true."

"Did she give you a dark prophesy of some sort?" asked Baltsaros with a tilt of his head.

Jon's forehead furrowed as he thought, his black brows pinched together over distant eyes.

"Not... no, not really. It was more that she knew my mind."

"There was no instruction in her words? No hint of what's to come?"

"Oh bloody hells, Da. Don't encourage him. Ye can't bloody *believe* in this malarkey?" growled Tom. Astounded by the sincere curiosity he heard in Baltsaros's voice, he looked from the captain to Jon and back. They ignored him.

"No. Just that I was at the centre of forces... And that we needed to mend the tapestry, which we *did*—" replied Jon.

"Tapestry?" Tom asked, confused. He rubbed a hand over his cropped hair.

"Well, not an *actual* tapestry... Fuck, it sounds so stupid to say it out loud." Jon hitched the blanket higher over his shoulder, looking uncomfortable. "Baltsaros, what are your thoughts on fate?"

The first mate watched the captain's face grow still, his eyes just shadows in his face. After a short silence, he spoke.

"Do you remember the conversation about fate we once had?" he said softly to Jon. "It feels like an eternity has passed since we sat at my table, and I offered you a place aboard my ship. I said you were a man unhappy with the cards fate had dealt to him, and you literally sneered at my use of the word."

Jon's brows quirked up at the memory, and Tom winced. *Cards.* Like Jon needed any more fodder for his fixation. However, Jon just let out a hoarse little laugh and nodded.

"Honestly, I can't tell you what my thoughts are on fate, Jon. I find it a strange, untenable theory that we are all on predetermined paths towards a fixed point. I don't like the thought of it; it *chafes*. However, at times, my mind is unsettled by chance and consequence that seem too fortuitous... And I find myself turning the idea of fate around in my head like a well-worn river rock between fingers," confessed the captain. He glanced at Tom and smiled at the look on his face. "But, one thing that I know is that it's not healthy to drive oneself to distraction with concepts that are beyond the reach of logic." The captain's tone took on a teasing edge. "It doesn't hurt to have an open mind, however."

With a grimace, Tom shook his head. Jon stared off to the side, seemingly lost in thought, but he seemed less troubled by whatever it is that had set him off earlier.

"I don't hold with none o' that shite," Tom muttered.

"I know you don't, which means you're the voice of reason right now," said Baltsaros, grinning.

Tom wrinkled his nose and let out a plume of cigar smoke before putting out his hand for the binoculars.

"I'll go see if we shook the scourge from our wake," he said, made uncomfortable by this talk of fate. He looked over his shoulder. "Sun's peepin' up." The night had lost its true darkness, and Tom could just make out the damaged quarterdeck railing to his left. The captain pressed the double-spyglass into his hand, and Tom left the others at the helm to go peer about in the early-morning gloom. He could hear Baltsaros and Jon talking quietly behind him as he swept the barely visible horizon. A haze of fog that came off the water obscured the line between sky and sea.

Tom didn't like the idea of fate... or religion for that matter. Then he thought of the little prayer he had uttered earlier and smirked. Well, he obviously didn't like religion until it suited him. He made another sweep of the water and pulled the binoculars away from his eyes when he saw nothing. The problem he had with fate was that it hinted of *something*, be it force or spirit, which had made the decision to rob him of his boyhood. That somehow he had been predestined to grow up a damaged man with strange desires. He ground his teeth together.

Fuck fate—he froze when he spotted something in the fog. Pulse skipping a frantic beat, Tom lifted the binoculars again and saw the prow of a ship emerge from the fog like a knife.

"Da!" he yelled. "We got trouble!"

The approach angle of the other ship meant that they had tacked towards them recently. They had probably changed course once they were too long in coming up to the *Heart*; they'd soon be in cannon range again. Tom heard Baltsaros's orders followed by Katherine's fainter shouts as she relayed them to the crew. It was all hands on deck to ready for attack as they turned starboard.

Tom wondered for the hundredth time why they had never built an aft gun deck below the captain's quarters. At least then they could fire at their pursuers without showing their flank to the fuckers. Going broadside was near suicide.

He stared hard at the approaching frigate and tried to make out their flag. When he saw the long, fanged skull with crossed cutlasses, he swore under his breath and ran back to the captain.

"It's Kriegaard and his Hounds," he spat. "Where he got his fuckin' hands on a fuckin' frigate..."

"Ah... damn," said Baltsaros softly. "I was hoping he was dead."

Jon's blue-grey eyes were wide in his pale face.

"Who's Kriegaard, and why does he want to kill us?"

"A bit o' bad business there, love," muttered Tom, locking eyes with the captain. "A year or so before you came aboard."

With a shake of his head, Baltsaros grimaced as he turned the wheel hard to port.

"He was a… ah… well, sort of a partner for a while, you could say; at the very least, we had regular dealings with him. I thought he had cheated us on a job, and I lost three men in the resulting knife fight aboard the *Heart*," said the captain quickly, holding the wheel steady. Tom glanced at the frigate that loomed large as they swung starboard. "We won the fight. I had his ship sunk in front of him and then threw him and his men overboard. Turns out that I had been wrong about the swindle, which is why we came looking for you and your talent, Jon. I really hate being wrong."

Tom smirked.

"Ye were wrong too about Kriegaard's visit to Davy Jones, it seems."

"Yes, well. Obviously, they were resourceful… that or we're facing a crew of demons. That's all I need: more blasted demons."

"We're about to be killed, and you're making jokes?" The blanket had dropped from around Jon's shoulders. Tom almost laughed at the look on Jon's face.

"Who says we're to be killed, lad? Have ye so little faith in our wee ship's guns?" said Tom with a grin.

However, as if fate had decided to make Tom eat his words, Katherine came running up the stairs just then, stopping halfway to shout that one of the starboard guns was cracked. Tom's guts twisted; they'd been meaning to replace the old cannon for a while. Why didn't anyone notice until they were about to be blown to smithereens that the damn thing was cracked and useless?

"Bloody… Fuck!" growled Tom through clenched teeth, all humour drained and replaced by a bleak anger. Or was it fear? He grabbed the nearest object, a metal cup, and threw it as far as he could. "Everythin' on this fuckin' old tub of a… Fuck! Why does everythin' have to fuckin' fall apart at the last bloody fuckin' cocksuckin' godsdamned—"

He was startled when Baltsaros grabbed him and pulled him so close their noses almost touched. Over Baltsaros's shoulder, Tom saw that Jon held the wheel, deep lines of worry on his face. The captain's fingers were cool on the back of Tom's neck, and his thumbs bracketed the first mate's cheeks; the chaos inside him stilled as Tom stared wide-eyed into Baltsaros's dark, unblinking gaze.

"Hush," murmured Baltsaros, his lips barely moving. "Stop your foolishness, my tomcat. Won't have you scaring the boy, or I'll have you over my knee." The captain's lips stretched into a slow grin, and Tom let out a huff of breath ending on a chuckle.

"Sorry, Da," he replied, the black waves receding in the distance. He found that the brown eyes he stared into held nothing but unguarded affection… and complete trust. The captain's smile softened as Tom straightened his shoulders and let the fear drain away. He could do this… He always had.

"There. That's better. Keep your head. Now, go!" Baltsaros pressed his lips to Tom's in a hard kiss before releasing him.

"Aye, aye, Captain!" shouted Tom, stepping back and offering a cheeky salute. Oh, they would probably die, but he'd die knowing Baltsaros's heart, and that warmed him like nothing else.

He grabbed Jon's arm and pulled him in for a quick hug.

"C'mon, love," he rumbled. "We've got a ship to sink."

〜

Baltsaros kept an eye on the frigate, pleased to see that with the jibs let out, the *Heart* had made a lot of headway while turning. If there was one thing he loved about the old ship, it was that though she would never be great in a storm, she came about swiftly and handled like a dream in calm waters. Below him, the deck thrummed with activity as everyone made ready. The *Heart* had been in two battles under Romas and another two during Baltsaros's time as captain. The ship bore as many scars as he did. He smiled grimly. Was this the last one?

A fitting end to a turbulent history, he thought.

He heard the boom of one of the frigate's forward guns and watched as some chain-shot came spinning towards them, aimed high; the two half-balls connected by a length of chain was designed to take out masts and would cripple them if it hit true. However, it fell short of its mark and splashed into the sea. He heard Tom's bellow and felt the ship shudder with a twin thunderclap as they let loose with the two starboard 16-pounders, their only hope in reaching the other ship at this distance... A distance that was closing fast. A cheer went up when one of the cannonballs hit their mark. From this far away, it probably wouldn't punch through the deck, but it would bounce and wreak havoc as it made its way sternward. The captain hoped it would find flesh.

"Get some chain-shot in that beast's gullet, matey!" barked Tom above the shouts, pointing to one of the squat 8-pounders. As the *Heart* came broadside to the approaching ship, the cannon would be well placed to take down the foremast. The first mate turned and glanced back at the captain high on the quarterdeck. Baltsaros smiled and nodded once in approval.

"Let's give 'em all we got, lads!" roared the first mate, slapping the shoulder of the man next to him. With his earlier outburst quieted by Baltsaros's own sang-froid, Tom had recovered his usual mix of cockiness and equanimity in the face of danger. When he heard Tom let out a hearty laugh, Baltsaros chuckled to himself; he didn't doubt that the first mate's cock would be primed with lust from the excessive—and spectacularly diverting—addiction to adrenaline he suffered from.

The captain let out a slow breath and realized he was feeling more confident than he had any right to. They might fare badly in this, but it was no guarantee; the sea was a fickle mistress that could change the rules on them at a whim. He smiled; at least their speed was good.

Baltsaros corrected his course slightly, his hands tight on wooden handles worn with age. The one benefit of going broadside with the approaching ship was that they could fire all four guns at once.

Make that three guns, he corrected himself with a frown as he watched the other ship get closer.

Baltsaros scanned the deck quickly and saw that Jon was helping Katherine to preload muskets and pistols, including a few of the new blunderbusses they had found in the *Sabre*'s holds. Jon lifted his eyes and looked at Baltsaros. The boy was pale and wide-eyed, but there was a resolute set to his jaw and his shoulders were squared. The captain nodded to him.

Good luck, Jon.

Then the young man he had kidnapped turned and yelled the order to take arms. Baltsaros felt his chest ache and his throat constrict strangely, but there was a smile on his lips. Perhaps he had lied to Jon about something after all.

~

It was utter chaos as the dawn sky swirled with gun smoke, the air throbbing with cannon fire and the screams of the dying. A lucky shot had taken out the mainmast of the frigate, crippling her, but she had retaliated by punching holes in the side of the sleek corvette. *Baal's Heart* shuddered and creaked as she came about to try firing upon the other ship again.

Katherine reassured Jon that the hits to the hull had to be above water or else they would be listing by now, and Jon just nodded slowly, staring at the frigate with his heart pounding and throat dry. He could see part of the name painted on the side of it in big curling letters: *Reaper*. There had been something before that, but a cannonball had taken out most of the lettering when it had blasted through the hull.

D... Dead Reaper? Day Reaper? No... Day Reaper makes no sense.

"Jon?" Katherine smacked his shoulder, and he blinked, feeling dazed.

"What?"

"Give me a hand with these," she growled, pointing to the stack of grenadoes they were readying.

"A hand?" Jon's laugh had a hysterical edge to it as he looked at her wooden hand. They were all going to die.

He let out a yelp as Katherine grabbed him by the ear and twisted.

"Snap the fuck out of it, Jon!"

"I feel like I'm in a bad dream," he said, shoving her away. He rubbed his ear, wincing. The whole back of his head was throbbing. Jon turned his eyes back to the *Reaper*. It looked like they were turning to meet the frigate head-on. Orders were shouted; cannons belched fire, iron, and lead. Men cried out as pieces of them were torn away... It all came to Jon through a haze. Nothing felt quite real. The sea around the warring ships was full of floating debris, and Jon made himself stare at the arm that floated serenely between a barrel and a broken piece of wood. The wind shifted, and the grisly sight was obscured by grey, nostril-stinging smoke.

"I'm not made for this," he said. He glanced back at a sharp laugh from Katherine.

"No, you're not," she said with a kind smile and handed him one of the hollow iron spheres. She had a smear on one cheek, and escaped tendrils of dark hair played across her forehead, but her almond eyes were calm. "I don't think anyone is, Jon. You just have to grab whatever stones the gods granted you and try not to lose your fucking head. That's it. Now quit being a moon boy and fill those smokepots with shot."

Jon's hand stilled as he reached for the pouch of lead shot.

One eye open for visions. One eye closed for dreams.

"Moon boy?" he shouted over the salvo of cannon blast. He felt like he was going both crazy *and* deaf.

Katherine jammed the wooden fuse into the filled grenadoe held between her knees and nodded.

"Mooning about! Now get that filled and get ready to start lighting and tossing them as we come alongside that bitch!"

Jon felt the *Heart* lurch under his feet and swung around in time to see a second cannonball fly over the deck and bounce twice, leaving chewed up deck boards in its wake before blasting through the door to the captain's quarters.

"Fuck!" he yelled, scrambling to his feet. "Shouldn't we be raising the white flag now? Kat, why isn't the captain surrendering?"

"Ain't gonna happen, Jon," said Tom, clapping him hard in the centre of his back.

Jon spun and stared at the first mate. Tom had a cheroot wedged in the corner of his mouth, and his eyes were bright spots against his smoke-darkened face. There was a dripping line of red across one big pectoral, and the lower part of his right arm was dark with blood, but he was grinning.

"We're never going to win," stammered Jon, his guts turning to water. "Surely if we surrender..."

"They'll serve us tea an' bloody crumpets?" chuckled Tom grimly. "No. Ye never parlay when yer on the back foot, lovey."

Jon felt the boards beneath him shudder again. He thought he was going to be sick.

"I want ye to fire the smokepots quick as a wink and lob 'em over when we scrape by," said Tom with a glance at Baltsaros fighting with the wheel high on the quarterdeck. The first mate's expression faltered a moment, but he found his smile again as he looked at Jon. A big, rough hand squeezed Jon's shoulder. Though his lips were curved, there was deep sadness in Tom's ocean eyes.

"I bloody love ye, Jon," said the first mate.

Jon forced himself to laugh.

"Ok. Now you're *really* scaring me," he said. He'd meant it to sound bluff, but his voice sounded thin.

"Shit! Get down!" yelled Katherine, and Jon heard the belch of a cannon followed by a rapid *thwack thwack thwack* against the hull. More grapeshot. Not fired high enough to pass over top the gunwale nor hard enough to pierce through, thank the gods. Or so he thought until he turned and saw that Tom was staring down at a perfect, round hole in his side. Jon let out a devastated cry as it began to weep a thick fall of blood that followed the curve of Tom's hip and pooled along the waistband of his pants. Eyes wide, Tom clapped a hand over his wound.

"Fuck," he muttered to himself. "Bastards."

"Jon!" shouted Katherine. Jon turned in a daze and watched her pull in the leather cord to curl the fingers of her wooden hand around a burning brand. She held the cord in her teeth and jammed the clasp to keep the grasp in place before stooping to pick up one of the grenadoes. The wooden wick caught easily, and she awkwardly tossed the metal sphere left-handed. Jon blinked. The other ship was so close he thought he could reach over the side and touch it.

Tom let out a pained grunt beside him. He saw that the first mate held another grenadoe out. Things slowed to a crawl in his mind as he stared at the hollow iron ball filled with gunpowder and shot. Even terribly wounded, Tom held it together better than Jon did.

If you assume that you will die today, you drag death to you as a cold, unforgiving stranger. Instead, embrace death like an old friend, for you will fight side by side with her; and, if death decides to choose you as her champion, you may yet live to fight, and love, another day.

Jon blinked again. Suddenly the panic let go of his limbs, and he stooped to grab a smokepot of his own in one hand and a burning brand from the brazier in the other. Quickly, he lit both his and Tom's grenadoes and they threw them hard. Jon watched the arc of the two hand-bombs, Tom's flying a little lower than his, and smiled when they exploded on the deck of the *Reaper*.

A moment later, his world erupted in fire and splinters.

~

The four port cannons thundered one after the other. Baltsaros strained hard on the wheel, and men pulled at the braces to try to keep them from crashing into the *Reaper's* side as they passed so close. The captain could almost feel the cannonballs punching through the hull of the other ship in the deafening sound of wood cracking. Above the roar, Baltsaros could hear men screaming. It was chaos aboard the frigate as explosion after explosion rocked the massive, crippled ship… Yet she still did not sink.

He glanced down at his own deck. Barely visible through the rising haze of smoke, he saw that every man not working a rope was lobbing grenadoes and firing flintlocks.

Or dragging away the dead. There were red streaks of blood across the worn boards to where bodies were piled up. Just dead things pushed to the side so they wouldn't get in the way of the living. He frowned and looked away. A cold hand wrapped its fingers around his heart at what he had glimpsed in the stack of corpses.

A tattooed arm. A mop of dark curls.

Baltsaros realized he was breathing quickly through his nose. Frigid seawater flooded his veins, and he smelled the tang of blood. Nothing could make him take a closer look at the bodies thrown aside on the deck. Water shimmered in his eyes as his jaw clenched; his hands had turned to claws on the wheel.

Weak, hissed the beast over his shoulder. He felt the leathery skin graze his back, cold as death through his coat as the beast curled around him. Baltsaros ignored it. Baring his teeth in a rictus of effort, he kept his footing and twisted the wheel further to counter the swell of waves buffeting the *Heart*.

Lost, it taunted him.

"Shut up," growled the captain under his breath. He had to remain in control.

"It's nice to see you're planning on returning my ship to me, nephew," said another voice to his left.

"*My* ship," Baltsaros whispered to the ghost at his side. He felt the familiar flutters of madness clouding his mind, and he shook his head to clear his vision.

"Don't you want to look below again? See what your folly has caused you?" chuckled Romas, his fleshy face pale as milk in the corner of the captain's eye. "Ah. I see. You want to hide from the fact that you've killed those poor lost boys. Oh, how they loved you! But that's what happens to those who do... You know that now don't you, Saros? Your parents. Your grandparents. Poor little Cassia! The way you carved her up. *Tsk*. Even Ol' Calum's gone because of you. They all die in your wake. Just like those boys below."

"Stop," mumbled the captain; his eyes closed for a moment before he remembered where he was. The yard swung, and he yelled out in a strangled voice for more slack in the jib.

"They loved you, and now they're dead," sneered Romas, his words finding all the little, stinging cracks in Baltsaros's stone heart. "How many more will die following you and your foolish crusades?"

"You died too, you bastard," growled Baltsaros, keeping his gaze focused on the choppy water ahead of the bow. They would come about and fire again at the now-listing frigate. "You held no love for me, only some sense of twisted *duty*, and I certainly held no love for you."

"Then why did you get on your knees and open your mouth so eagerly to me?" Romas paced behind him. Baltsaros could hear the way that the dead man's waterlogged boots squished as he walked.

"Fuck you," he whispered, shoving the loathsome memory aside. "Get off my ship."

"You'll be coming to see me soon enough, Saros," said his uncle, wet hands on Baltsaros's shoulders. He could hear the beast's hissing laugh. "You've doomed your entire crew..."

Baltsaros barely heard the cheer when it went up. He glanced around him in a daze, the ghost of Captain Romas gone. At first he thought the sounds of jubilation came from the other ship and that they had been holed through, but more happy shouts broke out and his brain finally registered that they came from *Baal's Heart*. When he saw who mounted the steps, he leaned his weight against the wheel, weak with relief.

"They've surrendered, Captain," said Jon, smiling. There was a cut under one eye that would need seeing to, and he was absolutely filthy, but he seemed intact. Jon's grin slowly faded. "Baltsaros?"

With a dry lick of his lips, the captain nodded.

"Tom is...?" Baltsaros asked, voice tight in his throat.

"Tom managed to attract a stray shot, but he's being a bullheaded idiot and acting like it's no worse than a hangnail," said Jon with a shrug. "You know, the usual. Kat says that he got lucky, and it went straight through. He also somehow managed to burn his hand pretty badly. Cook's patched him up for now, but I'm sure you're going to want to take a look after Tom's satisfied that the other ship's not just going to cut and run."

A parched swallow and another nod. Baltsaros lurched away from the wheel.

"Good," he muttered. "Jon, take the helm for the moment please. I have something to attend to in my quarters. Thank you."

He left Jon staring at him and nearly stumbled down the stairs in his haste to get to the stateroom. When he was confronted with the destroyed door, he stepped over it, scraping his hands on the jagged wood that jutted from the frame.

He nearly didn't make it to the basin before his stomach emptied itself. Leaning over the porcelain bowl, he shut his eyes and made himself breathe slowly lest he throw up a second time. Baltsaros waited until his shaking had subsided somewhat before straightening, and he pulled a handkerchief out of his pocket to wipe at his lips.

Jon and Tom were alive. The ship had not sunk.

Disquieted by his body's reaction to those two facts, he threw the embroidered hemp square over the mess in the basin to clean up later and rooted around in the bottom of the armoire for the bottle of aged rum he kept there. Eschewing a glass, he turned to sit and noticed for the first time that the long mahogany table lay in pieces on the hand-knotted silk carpet. He glanced around and spotted a hole at the back of the room. After taking a swig of rum, he squatted and peered through the hole. It seemed a cannonball had come in through the door and had taken out both the table and one of the chairs before exiting through the far wall. He sighed and stroked the worn boards.

"I'm sorry," he whispered. "I've not been very kind to you, have I?" Romas was right. Everything he held dear got hurt, including the old ship. With a sigh, he straightened and dragged a chair through the rubble so he could sit on it with his feet up on another. The second swallow of rum brought with it a delicious warmth as it settled his belly. After a moment, he furrowed his brow and lifted a hand to his cheek. It was wet.

"Da?" Tom's voice was hushed in worry.

"Baltsaros, are you ok?" asked Jon, stepping over the mess as he followed the first mate across the room.

The captain grimaced a little and lifted the bottle to his lips again.

"I don't know," he said finally. He looked up into two sets of blue eyes—one dark, one bright—and smiled sadly.

Tom crouched next to him with a low painful sound, his hand shielding the bandages on his side. Baltsaros reached out and ran his thumb over Tom's bottom lip. The first mate opened his mouth and licked at the wide pad. It was a sweet display of submission, and it made the captain smile. However, the concern in Tom's upturned eyes hadn't broken at the touch. Jon's hand came down gently on his shoulder and stroked to the crook of his neck. Baltsaros closed his eyes and sighed at the caress.

"As soon as we deal with all of this mess, I want you both aboard a jolly boat—

Katherine too—and away from me. You can make it to the *Jewel* in less than three days from here and arrange passage back to Madierus. I've decided I won't be stopping at the southern peninsula to resupply; I'm sure there's enough in that bastard's hold to keep us in provisions for—"

"No," said Jon quietly. Baltsaros opened his eyes and looked up at the sombre young man.

"Jon, it's not up for discussion. I nearly led the two of you to your deaths before, and it looks like I'm doing it once again. I... just can't stomach the thought of it," he said wearily. Tom rubbed his stubbled cheek against Baltsaros's knuckles, and something twinged inside him at the thought of never seeing the clever, gorgeous brute again. He took a long pull from the bottle. Shouts came from outside the room as the pirates secured their prisoners. They would tether the ships together if the other one wasn't sinking.

"You don't get to make that decision," replied Jon, his fingers massaging the captain's shoulder softly. "I nearly lost my head out there today; I was absolutely terrified. Then something reminded me why I am here. This is my home, Baltsaros. *You* are my home. I've thought this many times, but *there is nowhere I would rather be*. It's here or nowhere. I think I'm speaking for the both of us."

Tom nodded mutely. Baltsaros could see the strain of his injury in the lines of the first mate's rugged face, but his eyes were wide and clear.

"I don't want to put you in danger," the captain said softly.

"Too late, old man," said Tom, smiling wide. He winced as he shifted his position slightly, and Baltsaros realized that he should really be seen to.

"Yeah, loving you is a real godsdamned hazard," Jon said, grinning. The cut beneath his eye had opened back up, and he bled freely.

Love.

Somewhere in the back of his mind, the beast chortled.

"You're going to follow a madman to your deaths," Baltsaros stated, but the rum had warmed his blood and he knew he had lost the argument.

"I'd rather die followin' a bleedin' madman than die a sad ol' bugger without ye," said Tom. "But"—he gasped in pain as he stood slowly—"please tell me ye'll hold onto yer senses long enough to stitch me up?"

Baltsaros laughed and nodded. He glanced around. They would need to use Cook's counter for a flat surface... if the galley had survived better than the stateroom.

"Oh, and, Da?"

The captain looked over at Tom. The first mate's face had gone grey, and Jon was holding him up. Barely.

"Yes?"

"Pass the rum?"

With a throaty chuckle, the captain passed the bottle over and helped Jon support Tom as they made their way out the destroyed door.

CHAPTER 25
DEAD MEN TELL NO TALES

The captain ran his hand along the banister as he made his way down the stairs, happy to see the crew busy with repairs. The results wouldn't be pretty, but hopefully the makeshift patches would hold until they made their way to a decent port where Malik could hire a few shipwrights to help finish the job. Baltsaros narrowed his eyes in thought. It definitely wouldn't hurt to careen her too so they could take a measure of the hull. The *Heart* hadn't been taken out of the water in years; there was no doubt that there was plenty to scrape from her bottom. Hells, maybe once they were shipshape, he would forget his foolish pursuit of vengeance. They could turn back south, and he would just try harder to embrace happiness and make himself learn to accept the peace that Jon and Tom had bought with blood and trust.

And love. Yes, he was a man loved, wasn't he?

The captain frowned at the men waiting for him on the deck. The four of them kneeled with their arms bound behind them, expressions ranging from outrage to terror. Kriegaard was on the far left, his one good eye watching Baltsaros warily as he stepped towards him. The northlander was almost as broad as he was tall, and though he was bald as a priest, a thick red beard fell halfway down his chest. Baltsaros could see the small bird skulls Kriegaard liked to braid into it and smiled; some things didn't change. When the captive pirate captain swivelled his head to watch him approach, Baltsaros saw that the dog-skull-with-cutlasses that flew aboard the *Death's Reaper* was embossed on his leather eye patch.

Baltsaros came to a stop in front of Kriegaard and stared hard at him. As he had told Jon, they had once been partners, often teaming up to take down the massive merchant galleons that came through the trade passage. However, when part of some treasure had come up missing, and Baltsaros had blamed Kriegaard, their partnership had ended.

Badly.

As it turned out, a week prior, half the valuables had been unloaded from the target ship in preparation for taking on some passengers midjourney—a change in cargo that had eluded the pirates' information source. No one, in the end, had been to blame.

"You tried to sink my ship," Baltsaros said softly.

Kriegaard laughed, the sound hollow.

"You sunk mine," growled the red-bearded pirate.

Baltsaros lifted his eyes to the frigate listing slightly to port off the bow. Kriegaard's previous ship had been a sloop of war, not that dissimilar to Baltsaros's corvette. It had sunk in only a few minutes.

"Where did you get your new one?" he asked. He was honestly curious.

"In a sea battle," replied the thickset captain. "Easy pickings."

Baltsaros's brows rose, and he turned to Jon.

"He's lying," said Jon with a small tilt of his head. In the bright sunlight, the swelling under his eye was mottled and ugly. Baltsaros had been as careful as he could with his stitching, but he knew Jon would always bear a scar. For that alone, Kriegaard would die.

"This again?" asked the bearded pirate, incredulous. "I'm not lying! You almost killed me over a mistake before. Don't you think you should—"

"Where did you get the ship?"

"Why in the hells do you care? But if you want the bleeding truth, I found it. All right?" huffed Kriegaard. "It was abandoned about a day's sail east from Sormaheine... along the rocky coast."

Baltsaros glanced at Jon who stood watching with deep creases between his dark brows. When he saw the captain's look, Jon pressed his lips together and nodded his head.

"That's better," said the captain, smiling.

"Now, will you let me and my men go? Let bygones be bygones? Come on, old friend," said Kriegaard, revealing a gold-capped front tooth as he grinned; the smile didn't touch his eyes. "For old times..."

"You tried to sink my ship," Baltsaros reiterated. "You *killed my men*. I should skin you alive for that." He placed a booted foot on Kriegaard's shoulder and shoved hard. The man landed on his side with a grunt, and as he squirmed on the floor trying to right himself, Baltsaros saw something around the pirate's wrist that strangled the breath from him. He stared at the jewelled cuff for a moment, then grabbed his sword. Pulse racing, he leaned over and severed the rope binding the man. He pulled Kriegaard's arm towards him, his fingers digging hard into the captive pirate's forearm.

"Where did you get this?" asked Baltsaros. The words were said very slowly, making absolutely sure that the man did not mishear him.

Kriegaard's eye went wide.

"It was on board the frigate," he replied. Perspiration beaded on his forehead, and his face grew red. "Really... It was just lying there. In a huge heap of treasure. Ow! Fucking hells, Saros!"

One glance at Jon showed the man was telling the truth; Baltsaros ignored the questioning look in Jon's eyes and turned back to his captive.

"Was there another one?" growled the captain. He twisted Kriegaard's wrist and was rewarded with a grunt of pain. "Was it a matched pair? Tell me."

"Why... Augh! Yes, godsdamnit!"

"Where is the other one now?"

"I don't know... Ow! Fuck!" howled Kriegaard. "I must have sold it with all the rest, you fucking lunatic!"

Baltsaros pulled hard on the man's wrist and twisted as he brought his curved sword down in a full swing. A shriek burst out of the bearded pirate as his arm was severed midforearm.

The captain stepped quickly back to avoid the arc of blood and stared down at what he held in his hands. There was nothing but stillness in Baltsaros for a moment, and then memories flooded through a breach caused by the sight of the big red jewel embedded in the bronze. He slid the bracelet off the limb and dropped the arm to the deck, barely registering Jon's nervous jump to avoid it.

In the background someone gibbered and wailed, but it was quiet in his mind.

"This was my father's," he said, turning the marriage band around in his hands. "See?" He lifted it up to the sun and pointed to the silhouette of a lion etched in the red spinel stone.

Jon nodded quickly, but his eyes returned to the man who bled and writhed on the deck. His face was pale behind the bruising.

"Oh, for..." Baltsaros muttered. He reached out and plucked one of the pistols from Jon's belt. He quickly cocked it to full, pointed it at Kriegaard's head, and fired. Baltsaros then handed the flintlock back to Jon and squeezed his shoulder gently. "Better?"

Jon stared at him in shock.

Such a soft touch.

"This was my father's," Baltsaros repeated with a frown. "My mother had a matching one."

Jon hesitantly accepted the bronze cuff and held it carefully as if it were the most precious of things. He was a little glassy-eyed and looked utterly confused.

"Oh, it's not worth anything to me, Jon. Maybe a little sentiment... But that's not what's important," the captain said, his excitement building. "My parents were wearing these marriage bands when they were killed... Don't you see: *these are trophies.* They have to be. Why else would they be kept in a set?" His mind reeled with theories and possibilities as he paced back and forth in front of his captives.

"You," he said, pointing to a dark-skinned man with a dirty bandana on his head. "Kriegaard said the ship was abandoned. For how long?" The man's eyes bugged, and he shook his head quickly.

"Sir, I don't know, sir," he stammered. He let out a long, burbling croak as

Baltsaros's sword opened his throat. The next captive over was much more keen to find immediate answers to the captain's questions.

"No more than a day, Captain!" offered the young man. He had long, messy blond hair and dark-green eyes that sat a tiny bit too close together over a hawk nose. The effect was that it gave him a slightly birdlike cast. He looked up at Baltsaros eagerly, and the captain could see his pulse in the vein throbbing on his otherwise smooth forehead.

"How do you know that?"

"Perishables ain't had time to rot. I found a half-eaten bone that weren't covered in flies," chirped the young pirate, gaining confidence. "If you pardon my opinion, I think it were left guarded by a man or two and them were taken unawares-like."

Baltsaros reached out and stroked the boy's hair out of his eyes. The young captive didn't flinch from the captain's touch, choosing instead to lean into it. Baltsaros caught Jon's frown in his peripheral.

"What's your name, son?" he asked, letting his lips bow up slightly.

"Sten, sir," replied the blond boy with an overly friendly smile. He was a canary trapped in a lion's claws, singing prettily in hopes of being let go.

"Well, Sten, you can tell me all about your theories," said the captain, his voice low and kind. "I'm interested."

Sten's eyes lit up, and he began to tell them about the burned and gutted villages they had encountered along the coast, about the signs of encampments that pointed to a roving band of barbarians, and about the giant musk bear tracks that were found all around the area where the ship was anchored. While he talked, Baltsaros gently smoothed back the boy's hair.

"So you think that the men guarding the ship went off to hunt the bear?" he asked quietly when Sten had finished speaking.

The blond boy nodded brightly, but his green eyes, despite being held wide in the semblance of innocence, were cagey.

"You're from the tiny islands near the mountain range in the north, are you not?" he asked Sten, guessing from his accent. The young pirate nodded again. "Do the children there sing songs about the blood ogres and their red hands?"

This time, Sten's smile held a touch of mockery. Baltsaros glanced over at Jon who was watching the exchange closely.

"You think them barbarians are the cannibals in the fairy-songs?" laughed Sten. He then winced as Baltsaros's fingers closed in a fist in his blond locks.

"I do. Now, since you've been so helpful, I will kill you swiftly and with little pain," said Baltsaros, baring his teeth as he raised his blade.

Sten went rigid in his grasp, his dark-green eyes so wide it was almost comical. Again, Baltsaros spared Jon a look and waited a moment.

"But—but I told you all I knows, Captain!" Sten stuttered, trying to pull his head free. "I can be more help to you. I swear it! I'll... I'll keep double watch... and watch you while you're sleeping. And... uh... and I'm a damned good cocksucker, sir. If you like that, I mean..." When he saw that his words had no effect on the captain, he tried to shift closer, licking his lips. "I'll show you. I'll suck your man's cock too, if it were to your like—"

Baltsaros's blade quickly severed his vocal chords, and there was an odd little warbling hiccup and a hiss before his neck was sliced far enough to end his life. At the moment of death, Sten had that startled, glazed look of stuffed birds with glass eyes. He let the boy fall to the boards and quickly dispatched the next man without a word.

Curious, he looked at Jon. His face was still pallid, but there was no recrimination in his eyes.

"Not angry at me?" asked Baltsaros.

Jon took a deep breath and glanced down at Sten's corpse.

"No," he said quietly as he watched two deckhands begin to drag the dead away.

Baltsaros approached Jon and reached down to tilt his head up.

"Why?" he asked with a smile.

"If we had spared his life and kept him aboard, he would have killed us in our sleep," replied Jon with the hint of a shrug. Then he curled his lip. "Or, if we had spared him to go free—" Jon rubbed at his mouth as if disgusted by the words he had to speak. "Baltsaros, that boy was a murderer and a rapist." The captain saw a shudder go through Jon's body, and he pulled him into a warm embrace. Jon's lips touched Baltsaros's neck as the older man buried his hands in his ebony curls.

"How do you know that, my clever boy?" he murmured, happy with the outcome of his demonstration.

"The way he talked about the corpses in the burned villages. The women... He got pleasure from seeing them... that way. What had been done to them. Baltsaros, I could *see* it in his words," said Jon, his warm breath rising to tickle Baltsaros's earlobe.

The captain nodded and held on tighter to Jon's slight frame.

"Did you believe me, my love, when I said that I was done killing the innocent?" he asked, resting his cheek on the crown of Jon's head.

"I think so," came the slow reply. A long pause. "If I had told you to spare that boy's life, would you have?"

"Yes," replied Baltsaros truthfully.

Jon pulled away to stare up into the captain's eyes, his expression serious.

"So I'm to be your moral compass?" he said after a few breaths. At the captain's nod, one corner of Jon's mouth quirked up momentarily, just a twitch. "And if I can't stop you?"

"That's what Tom is for," answered the captain, tugging gently on Jon's curls.

Jon's storm-grey eyes bore into Baltsaros a moment longer before he nodded once. He seemed sufficiently satisfied with the captain's answer.

Oh how you've changed, Baltsaros thought. But somehow, remarkably, Jon had retained much of his innocence; it had simply been altered a little to fit into the world he now lived. The captain wondered whether Jon realized that he had adapted without losing himself as he always feared.

Baltsaros stroked Jon's cheek with the ball of his thumb gently and returned his soft smile. Then he pulled away and looked down at his father's marriage band held tight by Jon.

"So you think the roving barbarians he described are the same bastards who destroyed your family?" asked Jon, handing it over.

"Oh, yes," breathed Baltsaros, his heart a steady thrum in his broad chest. He lifted the gem up to the sun again and stared at the etched lion. "We will find them, Jon. I can feel it."

~

Jon supervised the loading of valuables from the *Reaper* into their own hold. True to the captain's word, there would be more than enough to sustain them for the trip north, so no stop would have to be made. Malik was busy repairing the hull as best as he could with some help, but all told, the *Heart* had fared reasonably well in the battle. The few holes here and there had been patched, and they would just make do where furnishings had been destroyed. He thought of the broken table in the captain's quarters. They had propped the pieces up on crates, and Jon was sure that Baltsaros was suffering a little due to the disorder in his normally elegantly appointed quarters. He smiled.

After waving at Harris to let the man know that they were done and he could start placing the charges around the frigate, Jon busied himself by tidying some newly acquired rope and waited for his crewmates.

When everyone was back aboard, and he felt had done his duty, Jon stood in the dying light of day and watched the lit grenadoes arc through the sky and explode on the *Reaper*'s deck. Within minutes, there was a lively fire burning. Then, as the fire began licking the kegs of gunpowder, Jon turned and walked away. A thunderous blast was followed by a second and then a third; even from this distance, Jon could feel the heat at his back. Jaw clenched, he made his way aft to the captain's quarters and tried to push from his mind the image of Kriegaard's men locked in the belly of the frigate, doomed to share the fiery fate of the blood ogres' ship.

CHAPTER 26

TIED DOWN

Tom threw up his hands in frustration and lay back down on the bed as he was told, despite the fact that he thought Jon was being completely and totally fucking ridiculous.

"Bloody hells, Jon, I'm all right!" he groused. Being kept immobile was starting to make him downright tetchy.

"A metal ball went right through you. Don't act like it's nothing," said Jon, scowling as he dropped the cloth in the cooling bowl of water and deposited both on the sundered table.

"I've had worse, lad," said Tom, trying not to wince as he shifted to get more comfortable against the pillows propped up on the headboard. The wound had closed well, but it would take longer for his muscles to mend fully. He crossed his arms over his chest, and grey-blue eyes regarded him solemnly.

"How does that make *this* any better? You're still recovering, Tom. Stay the fuck in bed, or I will tie you to it," said Jon.

Tom let himself smile. It had been nearly three weeks since they had defeated that bilge rat Kriegaard, and he had seen very little in the way of action since then.

Jon saw the look on his face and shook his head.

"Don't be an idiot."

"Don't yerself, lovey. Shite... If Da says I'm fine, ain't that enough for ye? It's barely a flesh wound—no rot and pain's just fine. Ye don't need to be nursemaidin' me to bloody death, darlin'... I'm as right as rain," he laughed. "Bloody relax, Jon. Really. Yer scowl's gonna stick to ye."

With a sigh, Jon sat back down on the edge of the bed. He looked at his hands for a moment.

"I'm just... nervous," he said.

Tom sobered. They would be in Sormaheine in less than a week, and despite his assurances to Jon, Tom didn't know how well he would fare in a fight with bloody ogres. However, there was no point in worrying over it now. Could be they'd never find the bastards.

"Come 'ere," he said, crooking his finger at Jon. Jon hesitated for a second, but after a playful moue from Tom, he struck sails and gave in. He crawled further onto the bed and curled up against Tom's uninjured side.

Wrapping his arm around Jon's shoulder, Tom closed his eyes.

"Honestly, though, Jon…" he said quietly, trying to keep the smile out of his voice. "What's hurtin' me more than my bloody side are my balls. My hand to the gods."

Jon's laugh made Tom grin wider.

"You can't go more than a day without thinking of your cock, can you?"

Tom furrowed his brow and shook his head.

Another chuckle came from Jon, and to Tom's surprise, his fingers came skating over the first mate's stomach, featherlight. His fingertips skimmed the edge of the sheet that covered Tom from hip down before returning to tease at the fur line below his navel.

From weeks of doing nothing more than lying around, Tom felt as soft as milk pudding. He tensed his abdomen under Jon's touch a little, but it hurt like hells, so he let out a slow breath and willed himself to still and relax under the caress.

Tom had the same sort of pain when he tried to jerk off; he'd discovered that he couldn't keep from tensing right before he came, and it was driving him crazy. It wasn't the sort of pain he liked, and it stole the thunder right out of his pleasure every time. He felt like he hadn't had proper release since his injury.

As Jon's hand moved lower, Tom's abs tightened, almost of their own accord, and he grimaced again. Jon saw the look on his face and shook his head.

"Relax yourself completely," murmured Jon, sending little vibrations into Tom's cock as he scratched lightly at the sheet covering it. "Don't force it… Just let it happen."

"Mmm," said Tom with a smile, trying to hide his frustration. His cock throbbed as it swelled fuller, making the sheet dance under Jon's palm. He moved his hips a tad for more contact. However, the motion hurt, and he must have winced, because Jon noticed and took his hand away.

"I said relax, not 'hump my hand'," said Jon, laughing.

Tom opened his eyes and wrinkled his brow.

"Love, I'm hurtin' here," he pleaded. "Don't stop."

"I'm going to stop every time you try to move. I want you relaxed. Completely limp," replied Jon. His hand hovered over the sheet.

With a cheeky grin, Tom put his arms behind his head and sank further down into the cushions carefully, spreading his legs a little wider.

"Oh, I don't think ye want me completely *limp*, ducky," he said with a wink. "Where's the bloody fun in that?"

Tom heard Baltsaros's boots, and he turned his head. The pirate captain's cheeks were ruddy with the chill night air, and his ashen hair was windswept. Tom smiled serenely when Baltsaros's dark eyes homed in on the outline of his erection.

"Am I interrupting something?" he asked, pulling the scarf from around his neck.

Tom looked to Jon. It was amazing that the lad had the capacity to blush after everything they'd been through.

"I'm trying to help Tom with his ridiculous needs," said Jon, trying to sound annoyed as he rested his hand on Tom's hard length. "His bellyaching is driving me crazy."

"It has been bad as of late, hasn't it?" said Baltsaros with a smile as he rid himself of his coat. He slung it over the back of one of the undamaged chairs before taking a seat on the mattress by Tom's side. "Still having the muscle pain issue?"

"Yes, but nothing I'm doing helps, it seems. He just ruts against my hand and hurts himself, then complains when I stop even though he's going to curse and swear when he's cumming in agony."

"He's too worked up to be patient and then tenses because it gives him some amount of control over his orgasm. I don't think it's entirely voluntary though. I could be wrong. If we had any *char* left, I would suggest using that to help him relax, but since we don't, we'll have to rely on other means of providing Tom with some pain-free release..."

Tom's cock pushed at Jon's hand again as they continued discussing him. For some reason, he liked it when they talked about him as if he wasn't there. It didn't make him feel invisible... No, it was more like he was a cherished belonging that they took great pains to care for. He closed his eyes again and breathed deep through his nose, startling when Baltsaros's mouth touched the rim of his ear.

"Lie down flat, Tom," said the captain, his voice soft.

Tom winced as he wriggled down further on the bed, but he made it onto his back and let out another slow breath. Despite all the kidding around, he really was trying to do what he was told and relax every muscle in his body.

Jon's hand touched his cock, and Tom concentrated on keeping still; he let out a little humming sound of pleasure as Jon squeezed and stroked him through the sheet. However, it wasn't long before he strained up and sent pain knifing through his side again. Jon's hand stilled.

"Fucking hells," griped Tom. The captain's fingers slipped under his jaw and turned his head. Baltsaros's eyes were an opaque black, and he stared silently at Tom for a moment.

"If you can't be still on your own, I will force you to be still," he said softly. Baltsaros stood and walked to the foot of the bed to begin rummaging through the chest there. When he came back, he held a bundle of black rope in one hand.

"I was waiting for a special occasion," said Baltsaros as he placed the items on the bed. "But I suppose now is as good a time as any."

Tom felt a tingle of apprehension as he heard the undercurrent of the captain's words: they were close to their goal... How many special occasions did they have left to them with their fate unknown? With jaw clenched, Tom tried to settle his mind as he watched Baltsaros tug his shirt over his head. The sight of the captain's broad, furry chest made him grin however, and he threw his dark thoughts overboard.

Baltsaros sat back down next to Tom and showed him the rope. It was thinner than the red hemp one that Baltsaros normally used, and it had different texture to it.

"Silk. Strong and beautiful... I think you'll appreciate how it warms to the touch, almost like it's a living thing. Feel how soft it is." Baltsaros slowly swept the rope up Tom's chest and teased his nipples with the bundle. Tom let out an appreciative sigh as he felt his nipples harden, and Jon gave his cock a little squeeze. A moment later the sheet was folded back, exposing him to the cool air, and he shivered as two sets of hands stroked the length of his body slowly. He licked his lips and shut his eyes, letting himself float with the sensation. He was almost deliriously excited, and his heartbeat was a quick, hushed tempo in his ears.

Then, with extreme care, Jon helped Baltsaros to bind him.

Tom had always found it a mesmerising process. Baltsaros would first stroke the area he wished to cover softly with his palm or the pads of his fingers, as if to wake the skin and prepare it to take the rope. After he was satisfied with the placement, he would twist a knot and double back the length to begin anew. Sometimes, when Baltsaros was at his most cruel, he would place the knots directly over painful pressure spots. Other times, he would weave and wind the ropes around Tom in complex patterns, seemingly satisfied with just the aesthetic effect. He was usually bound in ways that exposed him entirely to Baltsaros's desires and for some reason that always calmed him completely. His rebellious soul, the true pain he rarely let surface, the memories that burned like a poison in his heart—all of it fell away when Baltsaros stripped him of control. It was like losing the fight but winning the battle; it was defeat and love and courage and *need*... Tom felt himself relax into it.

Binding was always done very quietly—the captain's voice only breaking the silence now and then to coax Tom into position or to soothe him into submission— but this time Baltsaros murmured of the past to Jon as he tied knots and slid the soft black rope over the first mate's sensitive skin.

∼

Baltsaros wiped a hand across his mouth and winced when his knuckles came away bloodied. Tom crouched, panting and sweaty, against the back wall, green fire in his eyes. It seemed that they had arrived at an impasse; submission didn't come easily to the ex-slave.

"Need I remind you that you came to *me*?" Baltsaros said, keeping his voice even.

"Aye," growled Tom. "But I ain't bloody doin' *that*." His hands were balled into fists, and every muscle in his naked body was tense. He looked furious... and terrified.

Baltsaros had had the younger man pinned against the wall, trembling and whimpering in conflicted pleasure as the captain alternated between choking and biting him. He'd been growling his own desires, driven mad by the ex-slave's rock hard erection against his own as he pressed himself against him. It had been going so well... until he forced Tom to face the wall and began to slide his cock against the younger man's ass.

Then the hells had completely broken loose.

Tom had effortlessly pulled out of the captain's grasp with a choked shout—his strength completely dwarfing Baltsaros's—and lashed out, leaving him reeling from a blow to the jaw.

Nostrils flared and eyes wide like a cornered cat, Tom waited for Baltsaros to retaliate. However, when the captain raised his hands and took a step back, Tom's brow creased in confusion.

"I'm not looking to harm you, Tom," Baltsaros said gently.

"Bullshite," spat Tom.

"You let me beat you, tear your flesh, make you bleed... Yet when I coax you to accept something that will bring you at least some measure of enjoyment, you run scared."

"Ain't scared." Tom's expression had gone sullen, but his eyes were guarded and closed off to the captain.

"Then submit to me."

"Listen, Captain... I'll suck yer fuckin' cock all nice, but yer never gonna stick it into me. Never," promised Tom. He straightened from his crouch, but his hands were still fisted, and he came no closer. Despite being free from his cage for well over half a year, Tom was still like a wild animal at times.

The thought gave Baltsaros an idea. He remembered the wild foal with the broken leg he had discovered in the woods behind the orphanage. Baltsaros had made it his goal to use the horse to practice his bone-setting and plastering skills. However, despite all of Baltsaros's best efforts, the wounded horse had reacted almost violently to his touch, hurting itself further. Sister Iezabel had witnessed his frustration and had suggested that he bind the creature up so it couldn't move. When Baltsaros did, he witnessed an incredible change in the foal as it was rendered completely immobile. At first, Baltsaros had wondered if it was frozen in terror, but when he saw that its breathing had slowed, and it looked at him with nothing but curiosity, he realized that binding the young horse had calmed it. It made some sense, given that was essentially what the nuns did by swaddling crying newborns.

Tom, however, was not a horse. It would have to be done with a little more consideration.

"Go on," he said to the naked young man. "I'm done with you. You're to spend the day helping the workers. I want this palace near finished before we set sail."

Before Tom stooped to retrieve his clothes, Baltsaros caught a glimmer of something in his eyes. He looked either bewildered or disappointed, but he couldn't be sure. It was frustrating being so inept at reading the emotions of others, and Baltsaros wished it were a skill he could learn. He feared it was simply beyond him; sometimes even the most blatant shifts of temperament managed to catch him completely by surprise. His relationship with the boy's mother was a good measure of that deficit.

He rubbed his sore jaw and turned away, deciding to give the youth some privacy and time to get himself back in hand. As he stepped through the outer door of his chambers, Baltsaros began to form a simple plan in his mind. First, he needed rope...

Two weeks later, Baltsaros stood supervising the final pieces of the arched walkway being put into place. The graceful, fluted columns had been designed to resemble the architecture of his homelands, but he wondered if that had been a mistake. When he looked at them, it was like something scratched around inside his head. Memories. Memories of...

"They're gonna put water in the fountain this afternoon," said Tom. "I think that's the last thing. Well, that and the bloody fish."

Baltsaros laughed and nodded, the strange tickle in his mind gone. He reached out and rested his hand on Tom's broad shoulder. Pleased that Tom didn't shy from his touch, he gave a gentle squeeze.

"You did well, Tom," he said, trying to ignore the prickling sensation radiating down from his nape caused by the contact. "Come have a drink with me? As a thank you?" He felt Tom's muscles tense under his palm at the words, and the burly young man looked at him apprehensively. Baltsaros hadn't pursued any sort of physical intimacy with Tom since the day he had taken a blow to the jaw—avoiding him altogether when he could—so he didn't blame him for being suspicious of his motives. However, after a moment, Tom bobbed his head and followed the captain to his tower.

When they stepped into Baltsaros's sitting room, Tom declined a seat with a gruff noise. Eyeing Tom thoughtfully, the captain handed him a cut-crystal tumbler of aged rum and watched as he mechanically lifted it to his lips. Baltsaros grinned wide as Tom's brows shot up. With a dazed expression, the ex-slave held up the rum to the light.

"That's bloody good, mate," breathed Tom, and he took another sip.

"I thought you'd like it," said Baltsaros. He settled back in his chair and put his feet up on the stool, crossing them at the ankle. "Feel free to have as much as you'd like."

The guarded look returned to Tom's eyes, but the captain left his expression neutral and looked away. Swirling his glass, he watched the dark amber liquid coat the inside of it. After a long stretch of silence, he heard Tom pour himself another measure of rum and sit down on a chair. At the creak of wood, Baltsaros lifted his head.

Tom's blue-green eyes regarded him shrewdly. He rubbed the side of his thumb along the line of his jaw slowly; Baltsaros could hear the scratch of his stubble.

"What are ye playin' at, Captain?" Tom asked finally, his voice a low rumble in his broad chest. "One day yer all grab-hands and wantin' to impale me on yer cock, the next yer treatin' me like I ain't nothin' but a bloody builder."

"I want you, Tom," said Baltsaros with a shrug. "And you're going to submit to me."

Tom barked out a humourless laugh before knocking back his rum in one motion. He reached down, and Baltsaros saw that he had placed the bottle of dark rum on the carpet between his feet. After sloshing more into his glass, he held up the bottle with a quirk of one sandy eyebrow. The captain shook his head.

"So it's that simple, aye?" said Tom after he'd downed more rum.

Baltsaros nodded and took a small sip.

"And if I say no?"

"That's your prerogative. However, judging by the way you're burning through my rum, I would say that you're conflicted about your own desires."

Tom looked nervous, and he let out another hoarse laugh. But were the nerves tempered by excitement?

You're nowhere near as skittish as a colt...

"What do *you* want, Tom?" asked Baltsaros, watching him closely.

A look of pain flashed over the young man's face.

"Want?" Tom scrubbed the top of his head. "Ye know... Yer the first bloody person to ask me that question in a long fuckin' time."

Baltsaros waited.

Tom frowned into his glass. The captain thought he could detect a flush in his cheeks, but whether from drink or from something deeper, he couldn't tell. He tilted his head and decided to take a different approach.

"*Tell* me what you want." It was a command.

Ocean eyes narrowed, Tom stared at a spot over Baltsaros's shoulder for a moment.

"I ain't got a bloody clue what I want," he confessed.

Baltsaros changed tactics again.

"If I asked you to strip naked for me, would you do it knowing that it pleases me?"

There was the slightest hesitation before a mumbled reply.

"Aye, Cap'n."

"Good. Now... Do you *want* to strip naked for me?"

Tom's eyes darted to Baltsaros's. The captain remembered how hard it had been for Tom to admit to desire that very first time. The ex-slave licked his lips once, and Baltsaros realized that Tom was perspiring. He was sure that if he put his hand to Tom's chest, he would feel the heart racing beneath the thick slabs of muscle.

"Yes." It was barely a whisper.

"Then do it."

Over the next half hour, he asked Tom questions. Each one was answered with a quiet *yes* until the boy was kneeling, his lips red and wet from having Baltsaros's cock so far down his throat that he had choked tears. However, not once had he tried to pull away. Not once had he refused. Baltsaros smiled down at Tom and wiped at his bruised cheek with this thumb. Tom closed his eyes, his swollen cock held firmly in one scarred fist as he leaned into the moment of gentleness.

"If I asked to fuck you, would you do it knowing that it would greatly please me?"

"Not that."

"Why not, if you give the rest to me?"

"Can't," mumbled Tom.

"Because you're afraid I'm going to hurt you?"

Tom's eyes snapped open, and he stared up at Baltsaros, his brow wrinkled.

"Ye can't hurt me," he replied.

"Then why are you afraid?"

Instead of a response, Tom just gave a little headshake.

"So this is the only thing you won't do for me?"

Tom thought for a moment.

"Aye, Cap'n."

Baltsaros smiled.

"Ok. Come with me," he said and walked to the door to his bedchamber. Tom followed obediently.

"On the bed," said the captain, pointing. He rid himself of the rest of his clothing as he watched Tom climb hesitantly onto the bed to kneel near the close edge. Then Baltsaros took up the bundle of red hempen rope that he had dyed and braided with his own hands, and Tom's eyes went wide at the sight.

"Now wait a bloody second, mate," he said, backing up as Baltsaros approached.

"Trust me, Tom," murmured Baltsaros. "Lie down on your stomach and put your arms behind you."

"Like hells I will," growled Tom, but he didn't move away. Baltsaros quickly grabbed him by the throat and brought his lips close to Tom's.

"What? Is this another thing you won't do for me?"

Tom grunted when Baltsaros curled his hand around his cock and squeezed hard. The captain then traced the edge of the flared head with this thumb, letting the nail drag on the hot skin. It was enough to pull a hoarse moan from the big man's trapped throat. His cock wept a slick trail across Baltsaros's palm.

"Trust me."

He stroked Tom a few times and then reached for his testicles. Tom's eyes closed and a deep V appeared between his brows as Baltsaros fondled him gently.

"Obey me," he said in a soft voice and released Tom.

The sound that came from the naked young brute was barely a whimper. He looked so tormented that Baltsaros feared that he wouldn't submit. However, Tom dropped his shoulders in defeat and threw himself down on the bed. As he turned his face away from Baltsaros, he clasped his hands behind his back.

Baltsaros pressed his lips tightly together as his eyes swept over the twisting map of scars that covered Tom from shoulder to below his buttocks. It was a testament to his inner strength that he had made it out of slavery alive. He crawled onto the bed and stroked Tom's back softly. The thick ridges of scar tissue were a living landscape under Baltsaros's hand, and he frowned to himself.

He needed to secure the ex-slave's absolute trust; it had become curiously important to him that he be the first man not to take Tom in rape.

To start, he simply wrapped the rope around Tom's wrists, not tying a knot just yet. Tom held himself rigid; Baltsaros could feel a tiny tremor go through his body as he looped another length of rope higher up his arms.

"You'll submit to me, Tom. Of your own free will."

Tom's noncommittal noise made Baltsaros shake his head. He reached between Tom's thighs, coaxing him to spread his legs so he could fondle his sack.

"Do you like that?"

Silence. He tightened his grip until he heard Tom's muffled cry.

"Do you like that?" he repeated a little louder.

Tom just nodded, and his back rose and fell with his rapid breathing.

Baltsaros then wove a few quick hitch knots to secure the loops in place and pulled, tightening the whole. Tom grunted, and Baltsaros realized how hard the first mate was trying to stay still and obey. Another slow stroke of Tom's sweat-damp skin was followed by a loop worked underneath Tom's chest to bind his arms in place.

Soon he had woven a net that extended from Tom's shoulders to his waist. It was tight but not enough to constrict Tom's lungs. In fact, as he worked, he noticed that Tom's breathing had slowed and he no longer held himself so stiffly.

However, when he moved down the bed to secure his ankles to the bedposts, Tom raised his head in alarm.

"What are ye doin'?" Tom's voice was strangled, and his cheeks were pink.

"I'm going to tie your legs open so that I have access to you without worrying that you're going to kick me in the head."

"Fuck you!" growled Tom, wresting his ankle out of Baltsaros's grasp.

The captain raised his hands in a gesture of surrender, hoping to calm Tom somewhat.

"I'm not taking anything from you that you won't freely give me," he said.

Tom dropped his head back down on the bed, and Baltsaros could hear a hissing sound as if Tom were breathing quickly through clenched teeth.

Brow furrowed, Baltsaros waited a moment.

"Tom? Do you trust me?"

"No. Fuck... yes? I don't bloody know, mate," grumbled Tom.

"What do you *want*?" Baltsaros reached again for Tom's ankle but just held it in his hand. "Tell me."

"To kick yer bloody teeth in," replied Tom, but he made no move to pull his leg away when Baltsaros slipped the rope around his ankle and bound it securely to the partially carved post.

"Really?" Baltsaros stroked his hand all the way up the back of Tom's thigh and then delivered a hard smack to his ass. "I don't think so."

Tom's breathing stilled for half a heartbeat, and Baltsaros smiled. He smacked him again, harder this time, and left his palm against the warming skin.

"That," whispered Tom raggedly against the coverlet.

"Hm?"

"I... I want *that*," replied Tom. Oh, what did it cost him to admit to these things?

"You want me to spank you?"

Nothing at first but then a stiff nod from Tom.

"Will you let me tie your other leg?"

Another nod and an audible sigh when Baltsaros pulled the rope tight and knotted it off. He slipped off the mattress and stood back to admire his work.

Tom lay in the center of the bed on his stomach, his arms bound to his torso, hands clasped above the cleft of his ass, and his legs spread wide. It was an impossibly delicious sight. He stroked his cock back to fullness, enjoying just looking at the immobilized young man on his bed.

"Where d'ye go?" asked Tom after a moment, lifting his head. When he saw that Baltsaros was touching himself, he let out a barely heard groan.

"Tell me what you want."

"Ye know that. Just said it, didnt'cha?"

"I just want to make absolutely sure," purred Baltsaros, taking a step closer regardless. There was a play of muscles in Tom's jaw and a deep frown before he let his head sink back down.

"I want ye to come lay yer bloody hands on me. Spank me if ye like... but make me *feel* somethin', Da."

Baltsaros nearly laughed with astonishment at being called "Da", but the gruff honesty of Tom's words merited a more composed reaction. He climbed up onto the bed again and began to strategically lay down strikes across the back of Tom's thighs and buttocks, making sure to cover the same areas again and again. Tom writhed against the bed, his groans getting louder the longer Baltsaros hit him. By the time the captain tired, Tom had almost dissolved into the mattress; there wasn't a shred of tension left in his body.

The captain stroked Tom's heated skin and let his fingers slide along Tom's softly furred cleft. Unfortunately, this had him go rigid once more, and Baltsaros stilled his hand. His brows rose in surprise when Tom shook his head.

"No... Don't stop," Tom said with a tight smile as he looked over his shoulder. "This is fuckin' stupid, but I wanna trust ye."

"Good," Baltsaros replied and moved his fingers lower, ghosting Tom's hole before he began a slow massage of the area between it and his testicles. The other hand he worked beneath Tom's body and found his cock hard and leaking. It was frankly astonishing how much pleasure Tom derived from pain.

"Don't!" gasped Tom, trying to move out of his grasp. "Too close."

Chuckling, Baltsaros just tightened his hold but didn't move his hand. The first night Tom had stolen into his bed, the boy had ejaculated almost as soon as he was touched. Tom would need to learn a little discipline, but for the moment the captain felt charmed that he could bring him so close so quickly. He brought the fingers of his other hand to his mouth and wet two of them. He gently worked them into Tom and his gasp brought more blood to Baltsaros's cock. As he began to steadily stroke his fingers over Tom's prostate, the sounds that came out of the bound man became shamelessly eager.

He closed his eyes, relishing the subtle movements of Tom's hips as he fucked him with his fingers. Tom let out a long, low moan and Baltsaros stopped and pulled away.

"Not yet. Soon, but not yet. I want to fuck you first," he murmured with a little smile. "You're going to let me fuck you now, aren't you?" He saw that Tom's face was completely flushed, and his brows were pinched together. Breath hitching in his throat, Tom licked his lips.

"Fuck," he croaked. "Gods."

Baltsaros left Tom on the bed to grab the bottle of oil off the nearby table.

"Yer a right bastard, ye know that?" Tom laughed breathlessly. "Ye've got me near beggin' for yer cock in my arse when I said ye'd never have me."

"I've been told I can be rather persuasive."

"Bloody hells," swore Tom as Baltsaros slid his oiled fingers back into his ass. He was panting like he had run a mile.

When Baltsaros had finished slicking his cock and began to rub the head of it slowly over Tom's puckered hole, Tom tensed again with a whimper. The captain stopped moving.

"No. No, don't fuckin' stop, ye bastard. Don't ye fuckin' stop," growled Tom through clenched teeth.

"You want this?" asked the captain, his own breathing a little uneven.

"Yes, fuck," snarled Tom.

Baltsaros pushed against Tom, not hard enough to penetrate, just to tease. Tom's buttocks flexed, and he let out a soft cry, shifting his hips. Smiling, Baltsaros realized that Tom was trying to move towards him, not away. Then, a string of choked, frustrated-sounding curses burst from Tom, followed by a harsh laugh.

"Fine. Ye bloody win, Da. *Fuck me.* Is that what yer waitin' to hear?" he said, twisting his head to look back at Baltsaros. "Just bloody fuck me. *Please.*" The captain was almost startled by the fervid, furious passion he saw in Tom's gorgeous eyes. He didn't hesitate or tease, but obeyed Tom immediately and slid himself deep, groaning when Tom's body yielded to him so easily.

~

"That's definitely not how I imagined it happening," murmured Jon. His heart was forcing a stutter in his breathing, and the blood pounded in his ears. Tom and Baltsaros shared a look before turning to Jon; they both looked a little amused.

"How so?" asked Baltsaros, sitting back on his heels. His hand strayed, as if of its own volition, to rest on Tom's thigh.

Jon scratched the back of his head and lifted one shoulder in a shrug.

"I... thought it would be more... I mean, I didn't think it would be so..." He stumbled over the words he wanted to say: *I thought it would be more like abuse.* Instead, the scene that Baltsaros had described surprised him with its warmth of mutual desire, acted out under a guise of unwilling submission to allow Tom to confront his own fears.

"So considerate?" said the captain, his stark brow held high. "What kind of a monster do you think I am?" The last was said a little playfully, and Jon felt his face get hot.

"Like I said, Tom is not a horse. However, he did need a little... ah... *gentle* breaking," said Baltsaros, looking over fondly at his first mate.

Tom smirked and rolled his eyes.

"Right, right... enough about what a fuckin' bleedin' heart Da is. My cock's feelin' slighted, Jon. I think ye might just be able to make it up by givin' it a kiss."

Jon glanced at Baltsaros and the captain gave him a little nod. Tom was trussed up on his back with his arms over his head and secured to a pin in the carved headboard. His chest was bound by a radiating pattern of knots that avoided the healing wound at his side, and one leg was straight with the ankle of the other leg tied to the knee. What Jon had realized as the captain wound the rope around Tom, sharing the origins of their relationship, was that when he had said he would *force* Tom to be still, it had little to do with how immobilised the first mate actually was. Tom could still move if he wanted to; it wasn't as if he was tied down to the mattress. It was just a symbol... a way for Tom to release control of his body. Jon smiled and leaned forward to place kisses on Tom's inner thigh between the lengths of rope.

The first mate remained completely still, held that way by nothing more than Baltsaros's will. When Jon licked gently at the root of his cock, Tom gave a muffled groan. Looking up, he saw that Baltsaros was kissing Tom with gentle passion. Jon let out a soft sigh... No, he was no longer jealous nor did he feel like an intruder. They had needed him to get to this point in their relationship; in a way, Jon was responsible for this.

It made him happy.

Opening his lips over Tom's cockhead, he closed his eyes, working his tongue in lazy circles and prodding the tip of it against the bundle of nerves beneath the smooth, swollen glans. Despite the low noises that seemed to sigh out of Tom with every slow breath, the captain stopped Jon every time Tom started to tense up. The first mate's cock throbbed taut and hard in Jon's mouth; the constant slow seep of precum was testament to how close he was to release, kept on the edge by his body's inability to remain limp. At one point, Jon heard Baltsaros whisper "breathe" and Tom let out what sounded like a sob. Jon reached up and rested his hand against the first mate's chest—just a reassuring touch as he worked his mouth faster over Tom's cock. The first mate's balls were huddled tight against his palm.

So close. Just fall into it, he thought. Tom exhaled a shuddering sigh. *You can do it.*

Then, Tom let out a startled-sounding cry and his cock bucked in Jon's mouth. As the first surge of cum hit the back of Jon's throat, Tom's moan grew louder as if he were pouring all the pent-up energy from keeping his muscles loose into his voice. Jon swallowed, milking Tom's cock quickly with the other hand. When Tom finally let out one last hoarse groan, his cock spent, Jon lifted his head. The first mate's eyes were closed, and he breathed jaggedly, but his lips were curled in a serene, blissed-out smile.

762

"That wasn't so hard, was it?" said Jon, grinning.

A soft *Mmm* was the only reply.

Jon turned in time to see Baltsaros's bleak look before his features composed themselves. Ever since the discovery of the bracelet, the captain's mood had been odd, and it made Jon worry about what would happen if they found no trace of the barbarian horde. Would he be able to let go?

Baltsaros gestured to Jon to help him untie Tom, and Jon set to work, praying to fate that whatever they found in Sormaheine would give the captain piece of mind.

At the expense of yours? asked a dark little voice in his head. With a frown, Jon pulled another knot loose and tried not to think of sacrifice.

CHAPTER 27

BROKEN THINGS

Do not be too hard, lest you be broken; do not be too soft, lest you be squeezed.

—ALI IBN ABI TALIB

Jon stared up at the rolling green hills to either side of the ship as they sailed slowly into the natural harbour. He'd been expecting snow, not short scrub grass dotted with black boulders and long-stemmed pink wildflowers blowing in the chilly breeze.

It was summertime in Sormaheine.

With a hand on the wheel, Jon watched the crew heave to in preparation for dropping anchor. When the mainsails and foresails were pulled in opposite positions to counter the drive of the wind, Jon lashed the wheel in place. A flock of gulls arrived to dive and whirl above the ship, crying their harsh calls to one another as they searched for something to eat. They were almost twice the size of gulls from the midland isles, and despite the overall bleakness of his time there, the sight treated him to some unexpected nostalgia about growing up in a port town.

A memory came to him, and he quickly searched the coast, curious to see who was watching the ship approach. High above on the hill to his left stood a young man tending a small herd of broad-antlered deer. With his arms crossed over his slim chest and his dark hair blowing in the wind, he could have been Jon that day on the hillside, looking down at the sleek pirate ship docking in the Portsmouth harbour.

He startled at a touch on his shoulder and looked over at the captain.

"Is something wrong?" Baltsaros asked, concern narrowing his dark-brown eyes; Jon could see the flecks of gold in them that only made an appearance when the sun was bright.

He shook his head with a wry smile.

"Nah. I was just remembering the first time I saw you," he replied.

"Oh?" Baltsaros's gaze softened in amusement. "At the brothel?"

"No, before. When I watched the ship come in. You know, I could swear that you looked straight up at me that day," said Jon. After his capture, knowing that he'd been the sole purpose for the pirate ship's stop in Portsmouth, he'd often wondered whether the captain had actually seen and recognized him that day. "Did you know it was me?"

Baltsaros's smooth brow crinkled.

"How would I know it was you? I didn't have a description of your appearance, only of your talents of observation." He finished wrapping up his binoculars and placed them in the leather sack he had been filling.

"Oh," Jon said. He pulled the neck of the dark-grey coat closed and shivered a little. Despite the dazzling sunshine and green hills, it felt barely above freezing. He frowned.

"What is it?" asked Baltsaros.

"It's just... I don't know how it is you knew of me." Jon glanced over at the captain. "It's not as if I was written about outside of Portsmouth... Was I?"

Baltsaros tilted his head; he looked startled.

"Tom never told you?" he asked.

"No," replied Jon. "He wouldn't give me a straight answer when I first came aboard, and it just sort of became unimportant." He laughed. "Fuck, bringing it up with him now would probably just get him teasing me about how it was fated because we're *brothers*. I know I'm seeing coincidences everywhere I look, but the fact that his mother knew my father... That one takes the cake."

"Jon," said Baltsaros with a smile. "Where do you think I got the information about you? Abetha knowing your father is no coincidence."

Jon's eyes widened.

"Wait, what? But the queen said it was," he said, confused.

"The queen also calls all of her maids Pesha because she can't be bothered to remember their names," replied Baltsaros, shaking his head. "Despite her efforts to appear sensitive to the needs of her servants, she is still the daughter of a lord who has been surrounded by these 'invisible' people her whole life. I'd be surprised if she even knew a single concrete detail about their private lives."

"And you do?"

"I listen," said the captain. He furrowed his brow at Jon. "A few months before I came looking for you, I was getting a horse saddled and overheard an interesting conversation between the old stable master and one of the grooms. It was about a boy who could see a lie in a man's words as easy as reading a book. Because of what happened with Kriegaard, it piqued my interest, so I asked a few questions.

"Jon, when Richard left, he kept correspondence with his father, Duncan—the old stable master that Abetha inherited from her father's estate. After your father's death, your mother wrote to Duncan to tell him of your birth. Because the old man liked hearing of you so much, they kept writing, and when your mother passed, her handmaiden kept it up, sending him news from time to time of your accomplishments and talents."

"Handmaiden?" Reeling from the news, Jon tried to think of who this handmaiden was. He could remember no one taking an avid interest in him.

Baltsaros frowned, thinking to himself.

"I believe she stayed on and became Lord Barton's cook," he said after a moment.

"Cook?" Jon asked numbly. The fat old woman with the checked apron was a far cry from what he imagined a handmaiden to look like. Cook... who had always kept little things on the side for Jon, like apples and the mince tarts he liked so much. He breathed out slowly, trying to curb his mind's breakneck speed as it pulled up his every memory of the old woman at once. It was true—out of everyone in Barton's employ, Cook had always been the kindest to him. Regret flooded through Jon for never taking the time to get to know her better before... before...

Jon sat down hard on the bench. He was nauseous.

Before she was killed in the fire.

"Shit," he whispered.

"Jon?"

Jon looked up at the captain; his throat was completely dry.

"You killed her."

"Me?" Baltsaros looked confused. He sat down next to Jon, but made no attempt to reach for him.

"In the fire. She burned alive. Oh gods..."

"No one was in the fire that night save Reginald, a handful of guards, and Lord Barton," replied the captain with a slow shake of his head.

Jon stared at the captain, his mind stumbling over itself; he wasn't lying.

"You didn't kill them all?"

"Why in the name of the gods would I kill them all? What purpose would that have served?" Baltsaros asked. "Don't you remember me telling you that my men emptied the servants' hall?"

"I thought you were lying," Jon said in a weak voice. "I was sure of it."

"As I recall you weren't exactly at your best that day," said the captain with the hint of a smile. "And on top of what was a harrowing, exhausting day, I woke you up in the middle of the night to dazzle you with a rather grisly display of devotion. It doesn't surprise me that you assumed I was lying."

Jon slowly stroked the hollow of his cheek, absorbing this new information.

"Though I have to say, what I *am* surprised about is that you didn't make more of it, if you thought I murdered all those people," continued Baltsaros. He reached out and touched Jon's arm, and Jon moved to curl his fingers into the captain's hand. His soul felt a little lighter.

"You know strange things happen to my head when I'm with you," Jon said softly.

"And I've given you cause to doubt me, time and time again," said Baltsaros with a small nod. He squeezed Jon's hand. "All I can think of saying is that I'm sorry."

Feeling foolish, relieved, and bewildered all at once, Jon blew out his cheeks and sat back. In silence, the two of them watched the jolly boat being lowered over the side.

Something occurred to Jon and he turned to Baltsaros.

"I have a grandfather?" he asked hopefully.

"I'm afraid you don't," replied the captain, a tiny comma between his brows. "He died weeks before we even left the island. Nothing tragic... just old age. But, I can show you where he's buried if you'd like."

"Yeah. I'd like that," he replied. "But... Why didn't you think to tell me about him before?"

"What would you gain from learning you had yet another dead relative?"

The question was asked so guilelessly that Jon had to laugh despite everything.

"You know, sometimes I think you're not even a real human being... just a close approximation," he mused. "When you ask me questions like that, I begin to really question why you care so much about this vendetta you have."

"Why *do* you care, Baltsaros?" asked Abetha, leaning towards him in the shade of the orange trees.

The captain looked away from the steady blue-green eyes that reminded him so much of Tom and watched a pair of goldfinches play a sort of aerial leapfrog through the branches of a nearby tree. The story of his childhood trauma was now laid out end to end and made real by telling it out loud; it no longer burrowed like a poisonous black worm in his brain and for the first time since he had recalled that blood-soaked day, Baltsaros felt like he could take a step back from the events. It amazed him how much and how little he felt about it.

"Baltsaros?" Abetha thought she could help him, but even with all of her intelligence and the mounds of books she devoured on the subject of the human mind, Baltsaros knew there was a limit to what she could do for him. Healing would have to come from within; in the meantime he would humour her and wait for his boys to return to him. He pinched the bridge of his nose and turned back to the queen.

"Why do I care? My family was murdered. I was mentally and perhaps physically tortured. I let down my city," he said tiredly. "I murdered my sibling..."

"Yes, but you and I both know that you only care about one of those things."

Baltsaros let out a small laugh. Perhaps he had underestimated the queen's ability to see into him.

"Which do you think it is?" he asked, sitting back on the stone bench.

"When I look at you, I don't see sadness. I don't see shame. I don't see horror. I see *anger*," Abetha said, her voice hardened by her words. "Because they made you weak, didn't they? And you don't like being weak."

"No," agreed Baltsaros, feeling the heat of his temper swell. "I don't like being weak."

"Why do I care?" said Baltsaros. "I could tell you that I want retribution for the wrongs done to my family and countrymen because a 'real human being' would want that, correct?"

Jon nodded, simultaneously fascinated and a little unnerved by the captain's complete candour. The mask had dropped, and Baltsaros's face was smooth and expressionless. He eyed Jon thoughtfully, studying his reaction to his words.

"I would be lying to you if I claimed those were my motivations, and I don't lie to you, Jon," said the captain. "No... I'm simply seeking redemption for the evils I have committed because of what was done to me. Those savages took something away from me that day and made me an accomplice to their depravity, then and during the life that I've led. I am done being a subordinate to this *canker* in my past. With their deaths, I take back what was stolen from me."

Baltsaros's dark eyes burned with emotion, and for one startling moment, Jon saw the man that lived within the beast. He blinked and the vision was gone, replaced by the charming smile Baltsaros wore to hide the broken things inside him. If anything, the captain looked a little rattled beneath his composed façade, and his hand trembled in Jon's.

"It's ok to be afraid," said Jon quietly, speaking to the lost soul within the broken man beside him.

"I'm not, Jon," replied Baltsaros, his voice a little curt.

Jon wanted to shake him, but instead he fisted a handful of the captain's coat and pulled him closer so he could put his arms around him. Baltsaros stiffened immediately from the abrupt contact but relaxed slowly as Jon's fingers threaded through his hair and tugged softly. The captain's lips found Jon's neck, and he breathed warm against his skin.

"It's ok to be scared," repeated Jon.

Baltsaros curled his arms around Jon, and he let out a long sigh as he hugged him tight.

Jon closed his eyes, praying that Baltsaros would find whatever it was that he was looking for and that it didn't cost them too much.

Tom mounted the stairs a little stiffly. The wound on his side was still raw-looking, both front and back, but he was already regaining muscle strength. However, it would be a while before he was completely healed. Baltsaros had voiced his concerns that he might have permanently lost some flexibility on that side, and he was still in some amount of pain, but he shrugged it off like he did most injuries. If fate was kind and he made it to old age, there would be plenty of time to complain then. The image of himself as a broken, crotchety old man made Tom smirk.

At the top of the quarterdeck staircase, he paused, dismayed by the fact that he was interrupting what looked like a quiet, private moment between Jon and the captain. On hearing Tom's tread, Jon lifted his head, and the first mate frowned at the worry in his storm-grey eyes. However, Jon simply nodded at him.

It's ok.

Tom stepped forward as the captain pulled away from Jon. He wondered what he had missed; Baltsaros's smile was a little strained.

"Da, there's folks linin' up on the beach," said the first mate. He looked over his shoulder. "Friend or foe, I can't tell." A few minutes prior, the usual fishermen and beggarly idlers that seemed to be universal fixtures at harbours the world over had been joined by a group of officials protected by men holding pikes.

"Most likely they're just being cautious," said the captain, standing up. He reached for the leather sack he'd been packing and motioned for the two of them to follow. "They saw us coming from a long way off. You know, it's the same feature that drew me to Madierus when I found it: a natural harbour with the backdrop of a high hill so that intruders could be seen at least two leagues away. It's nice not to be caught unawares."

Tom quirked an eyebrow at Jon behind the captain's back. Baltsaros sounded odd, and he was worried that it meant the captain was on his way off the deep end again. The look Jon gave Tom in return pulled at his heartstrings; he seemed so afraid. Tom wished he could shield him from his own fears.

However, he had no time to lend Jon a little courage by giving him a quick cuddle or a teasing word. The captain, having regained his composure, ushered them with a brisk step to the ladder so they could board the jolly boat. As Tom carefully sat down on one of the planks that made up the seating, he scowled at the crewmen at the oars. Baltsaros had forbidden Tom from rowing until he was completely healed, and it made him feel like a bloody milksop.

"Stop making that face, Tom," laughed the captain. "You'll be back to yourself soon enough."

"Aye, Da," Tom muttered. He clasped his hands loosely between his knees and watched the shore approach. While normally the promise of a brutal fight got him raring to go, Tom felt nothing but the dull ache in his side and a deep weariness. He realized that, for the first time in his life, he'd rather let someone else do the fighting.

~

Tom watched Baltsaros from the bed, legs crossed and elbows on his knees. He was still sore in a few places from a sparring-match-turned-fuck-session with the captain, and he tried not to wince as he shifted slightly. Across the room, Baltsaros was packing the cedar chest that contained the bulk of their clothing as well as a number of sundry personal items. When he saw the captain place a bundle of letters into the chest, Tom frowned.

"Why d'ye never tell me ye wrote to yer nun friend?" he asked.

Baltsaros gave Tom an amused look.

"I wouldn't count her as a friend, per se," he replied. "But why should you be privy to my correspondence? What, pray tell, could you possibly want with that information?"

Tom scratched at his stubble, slightly put out by the captain's teasing tone.

"I dunno. Just, dont'cha think it's somethin' ye could've mentioned? Like 'Hey, Tom, ye might not know this, but I been writin' to the woman who raised me, and oh, by the bloody way, I been also sendin' her a part o' my pay every year.' Aye?"

The captain smirked with a little headshake before he resumed his packing.

"Is it really that interesting? Do you want to know that I also hold correspondence with a number of others? Let's see... the management from the *Jewel*, certain merchants, the harbourmasters from the various ports we stop in every year, an ambassador from the lands to the east..."

"Yer not makin' yer bloody point, Da," replied Tom. "Ye've been writin' back to and fundin' yer homelands when I didn't even know ye had anyone there."

Baltsaros glanced over at Tom and an odd flicker of emotion passed over his face before he straightened.

"Speaking of mother figures..." He walked out of the room, and Tom could hear him pulling open drawers. A moment later he came back and held a small packet out to Tom.

"What's this, then?" asked the first mate. The only thing on the brown wrapping was his name written in a neat hand.

"Your mother gave it to me to give to you. She apologizes for not being able to see us off today but offered no excuse."

Brow creased, Tom turned the package over and pulled apart the twine holding it together. Inside was a piece of folded paper, and his mother's perfume drifted off of it, giving Tom an unexpected pang. It was made worse when, on unfolding the paper, something dropped in his lap. Astounded, Tom picked it up and looked at it. Though carefully mended in a few places and obviously washed and ironed, it was the royal-blue silk handkerchief that he had stolen from his mother as a child. For a moment, he couldn't swallow for the thick lump in his throat.

"What is that?" asked Baltsaros, curious.

Tom crushed the handkerchief in his palm and lifted one shoulder in a shrug.

"Nothin' important," he lied. That Abetha had kept and clearly cherished the little square of silk... He blinked a few times and was glad when the captain went back to filling the chest. He flattened the note against his knee and read it.

Tom,

Here is something that I hope will make you realize how very difficult it has been for me to face the emotions and memories I had to bury deep in the heartrending months following your abduction. Please accept it as a peace offering and understand that I desire nothing more than

Jaw clenched, Tom pushed himself off the bed, his vision a little blurred. Before the captain could ask him anything further, he shoved the note and the handkerchief into his trouser pocket and left the room quickly.

Bloody hells, he fumed, angry with himself for nearly breaking down over some sodding words. Walking fast with no destination in mind, Tom made his way through the palace and out through the garden exit, trying to get his heart to stop trying to squeeze itself to a pulp in his chest. After he turned past a shrub tortured into a wedge shape, he came to a stop suddenly at the sight of Saban sitting on one of the marble benches that seemed to litter the grounds like some form of infestation.

Startled by Tom's sudden appearance, Saban lurched to his feet. He wore a pair of dark-blue pants turned up at the calf and nothing else but a long, knotted strand of leather around his neck. From his time on the island, his already-dark skin had gone a deeper shade, and as he looked nervously at the first mate, Tom couldn't help but notice how the tan set off the green in his hazel eyes.

"Sorry, mate, I didn't mean to intrude," Tom said gruffly. They hadn't spoken a word since he'd fucked Jon in front of him.

"I was just leaving," replied Saban, looking away. He started to walk back towards the palace, but Tom grabbed his arm, wanting to try patching things up between them before he left. Baltsaros had mentioned Saban's request to join the crew of the *Sabre* in lieu of serving on the *Heart*; this was the last that they would see of each other for a long time, if ever. However, at Tom's touch, Saban swung around with a snarl and landed a punch to the first mate's solar plexus, knocking the wind out of him. As Tom struggled to breath, Saban stared at him, the savagery of his emotions distorting his handsome features.

"Don't you touch me!" he growled.

Tom coughed and managed to take in some air. He held his hand out, trying to shake off the pain.

"Fer bloody sakes, lad," he said hoarsely. "Why the fuck did ye hit me? I thought we were mates?"

"We're not. You're not very good at taking a hint, are you? I have no interest in continuing whatever the hells you think we were doing." There was no trace of the quiet self-assurance that normally radiated from the big man.

"Hey... Saban, yer overreacting, lovey," said Tom with a frown.

"How many times do I have to say it? We're not friends," said Saban, balling his hands into hard fists. "And stay the *fuck* away from me."

Tom started to get angry.

"What the fuck bit yer ass?" Saban took a step towards him, but Tom held his ground. "Listen, I'm fuckin' sorry 'bout what happened. Ok? But ye gotta admit that—"

"I don't have to admit to *anything*!" yelled Saban, jabbing at Tom's chest with his forefinger. "I told you! I am *not like you*. I don't like to fuck men. For Bal's sake... Get it through your thick skull! I am *nothing* like you, you fucking degenerate. In fact, you make me sick to my stomach." With the last of his words, he spat on the ground in front of Tom and said a few words that sounded like a curse in Balorian. Too dumbfounded by Saban's reaction to do anything but stare, he watched the big man stalk off angrily out of the garden.

A little while later, Baltsaros found Tom in the garden sitting on the stone bench Saban had vacated.

"There you are. I've been looking for you. It's time to leave," said the captain as he eyed the shrub that had been ripped from the ground. "Are you ok?"

"Aye," replied Tom, standing up. He curled his hands into fists so Baltsaros couldn't see his shredded palms.

"Are you sure?" asked Baltsaros.

Tom nodded.

"Let's get the fuck outta here, Da," he said with a forced smile. "I've had enough of this bloody depressin' place."

～

From his seat in the jolly boat, Tom watched the shore approach. As they neared the armed guards and the grim-faced looking bunch of officials, he groaned inwardly. He had the feeling that, seeing as Sormaheine was half-governed by a religious order, they'd have to play chaste, and he'd have to keep his hands off Jon. Burned him to no end what some folks thought was proper and not.

After rising to his feet with a small grimace of pain, Tom sighed and straightened his shoulders, hoping that whatever they found in Sormaheine, it didn't break things further.

CHAPTER 28

SORMAHEINE

Jon stood uncertainly on a beach made of round stones, trying to make out what was being said as Tom and the captain spoke rapidly with the delegation that had been sent to meet them. In front of a cadre of guards armed with tall bladed weapons, there were three men and two women dressed in tunics with geometric designs like the ones that Baltsaros sometimes wore. While they seemed friendly enough, so far the tenor of the exchange felt strained. With a silent sigh, Jon wished that he understood more than just the basics of the northern tongue; he let his eyes roam over the features of the strangers instead, hoping that he could pick up their intentions at the very least.

The Sormet, as the citizens were called, were very tall, men and women alike. They had the same sharp cheekbones and smooth, high forehead as the captain, as well as the slightly dusky cast to his skin. However, unlike the Balorian fisherfolk who all seemed to share the same hair and eye colour, the Sormet were as varied as any mid- or mainlander.

The woman at the centre of the group eyed Jon curiously as she spoke. She wore her silver hair pulled back tightly, making the planes of her face even more severe. It was impossible to tell how old she was; save for the silvered hair and the lines at the corner of her thin lips, she looked ageless.

Jon saw that others deferred to her, so he assumed that she was someone of authority. He chanced a polite smile at her and was startled when a friendly grin creased her face in return.

"Come now. Don't look so worried," she said to him in Common. "Baltsaros, I take it your young friend here doesn't understand us, otherwise he wouldn't look as if we were about to toss him to the bears."

Baltsaros laughed.

"No. Unfortunately Jon has had difficulty learning the language," he replied.

The woman's eyebrows rose and Jon saw a spark of indignity in her icy blue eyes.

"The failure of the student speaks to the failure of the teacher," she said in a disapproving voice.

To Jon's utter surprise, the captain's smile disappeared and he ducked his head slightly like a chastised schoolboy.

"Yes, ma'am," he said softly.

With a little nod, the woman turned back to Jon, the warmth restored to her expression.

"Now, I know of Tom from the captain's letters," she said, glancing over at Tom who looked like he was having trouble keeping a straight face. "A ruffian if there ever was one, but you look like a proper young man, Jon."

Jon realized he was unconsciously straightening his posture under the woman's scrutiny and just shrugged a little, not knowing exactly what a proper young man's response should be. When her eyes shifted down to where Jon was fiddling with a button on his coat, he shoved his hands into the deep pockets and offered a sheepish grin.

"Jon... Tom, this is Sister Iezabel," said Baltsaros, saving Jon from doing anything else that might make him seem completely inept. "Sister Iezabel, Jon and Tom are my" —there was the slightest hesitation before the captain finished with a smile—"life mates."

Almost choking from Baltsaros's choice of words, Jon nearly didn't take the nun's hand when she held it out with a cordial welcome. Then, as soon as she and the captain started up the beach towards a path visible between the great pines, Jon turned to Tom and saw that the first mate's expression hovered somewhere between amusement and awe.

Tom just shook his head slowly.

"I'm as gobsmacked as you, ducky," he said quietly.

When Tom began to grin, Jon had to look away or else the crazed laughter he was keeping in check would bubble to the surface, and he would completely lose it. Feeling a little dazed and absurdly overjoyed, Jon slung his arm through Tom's and followed the group with the armed guard taking up the rear.

~

Tom climbed up into the simple wagon and settled in next to Jon. They had walked only a short distance through the dark woods, but they were both covered in red welts from being feasted on by the black flies. Tom grimaced and rubbed the back of his arm.

Bloody hells.

He looked to the front of the open wagon as it started bumping up the crushed-stone road and saw that Baltsaros and the nun were deep in conversation. Sister Iezabel was nothing like he'd imagined. For starters, she was wearing pants. Tom couldn't remember ever seeing a nun wear pants. No, he'd been picturing the round-bottomed, kindly sort of nuns who wore black or grey habits and collected money for the poor at every temple in town—not this towering mast of a woman who shook hands like she meant business and stared down at him like he was a wee nipper with a dirty face. With a frown, he lifted his hand to his cheek and rubbed at it, wondering if he'd missed a spot when Baltsaros made him wash up earlier. Jon smirked at him, so he dropped his hand and twined fingers with him. Tom hated to admit it, but Sister Iezabel was one intimidating nun.

Tom winked to reassure Jon and turned again to study the woman who had managed to cow Baltsaros with a handful of words; that alone made him intensely curious. It was obvious that Tom would be expected to keep his language clean, and he was sure that the old broad probably wouldn't take kindly to a missed *please* or *thank you* either.

On the plus side, however, she hadn't looked the least bit put off by the captain's introduction. Apart from a slight widening of her eyes that spoke of surprise rather than shock, she had taken the news as nonchalantly as if Baltsaros had said they were his drinking buddies. Aye, she was like no nun he'd ever met.

Life mates. Tom gave a little headshake at that new development. Said out loud, the words sounded ridiculous. However, it was all that he could do to keep grinning like a gormless twit every time he thought about just how much he'd liked hearing them.

The lot of saplings that fashioned themselves guards and jogged along with the wagon on either side seemed like a bunch of amateurs by the way they held their pikes. Tom would be surprised if any of them had been in a real fight. The rest of the uppity-looking folk failing to hide their curious stares were a bunch of bureaucrats. Tom could smell it on them.

Jon bumped his shoulder, and he started, then craned his head back to see what had the lad's eyes so wide. Through a break in the trees, Tom saw a city perched atop a high mountain; all gleaming domes and pointed spires, Sormaheine looked like it was part of the heavens.

It was bloody beautiful.

Baltsaros caught Tom's eye and flashed his sharp teeth in a wide smile. It must have been a trick of the sunlight stuttering through the tall pines as they made their way towards the mountain, but Tom could have sworn that for a moment he had seen a dark, horned shadow rise up behind the captain. The first mate smiled back but squeezed Jon's hand until he felt the shiver of dread pass.

The only access to the lofty city of Sormaheine was through a single set of gates in each wall that ringed the mountain. Every time they stopped at one, a complicated series of passphrases and counters were shouted between one of the men on the wagon and the guards who stood atop the parapet. Baltsaros had made mention of only one wall when he had told the grisly story of his past, and Tom wondered whether those events from so long ago are what had prompted an increase in defenses.

As the horses pulled the wagon higher up the mountainside, Tom was surprised that there were no buildings to be seen in the spaces between the gates, only narrow tiered fields of the same scrub grass he'd noticed on their way into the harbour. Here and there were herds of animals being tended to, but the lean-tos and shacks of the poor that were usually relegated to the outer rings of a walled city were nowhere to be seen. It meant either the leaders of the city cared enough to protect their poor or the poor buggers had to live somewhere else. Something told him it was the former.

As they passed through the third and final gate, Tom found himself nodding along mutely as the captain and Sister Iezabel started to identify the buildings that rose up to either side of the well-paved road. The big building with the peaked roof and columns was a bank. The sprawling multistory one was one of the four academies in the city. What Tom took for a temple of some sort turned out to be a hospital, and the tall building with a domed roof that they passed a moment later was something called a *planetarium*. It was no wonder that stories out of the north always sounded so outlandish; Tom had never been in a city with so much bloody stone dedicated to learning. It made more sense to him now why Baltsaros had decided to gift the city with one of the emperor's electricity generators. It also shed some light as to why the captain was so damned learned—it had to be bloody hard to grow up in a place like Sormaheine and not pick up some wisdom just from walking down the street.

As they passed the hall of the alchemist's guild, Tom saw Baltsaros's jaw tighten and he remembered that being barred from joining it was what had him out so far from the city as a boy. The captain remained silent as they continued on, but the nun kept up a steady narrative of what had been built in the city since the captain's uncle had taken him away. When Tom glanced over at Jon, he chuckled at the look of concentrated awe on his face.

"Close yer mouth, lovey," he teased. "Ye look like yer tryin' to catch flies."

Jon blinked as though coming out of a trance and shook his head in amazement.

"Holy hells, Tom. This place... Just imagine how many books there must be here!" he said excitedly.

"I'll thank you to keep a civil tongue in your head, young man," warned the nun though she looked amused. "Don't make me rethink my impression of you." She pointed to a huge structure with four domes and a steep stone staircase leading up to a pair of massive doors. "That is the library, Jon. In it are upwards of forty thousand unique works in scroll, tablet, and bound book. You are very welcome to take advantage of it during your stay here."

"Thank you," Jon breathed.

Then Sister Iezabel turned her ice-blue gaze to the captain, and a few lines appeared on her high forehead as she stared at him.

"Why *are* you here, Baltsaros? After all these years, why have you come home?"

The captain's lips twitched into a humourless curve, and his dark eyes swept over the passing city.

"Home? Not *home*, Sister. This stopped being my home the moment I let those monsters through the gate," he said in a tight voice.

Sister Iezabel stared at him, blank incomprehension on her angular face.

"I will tell you all of it when we've settled in," said the captain, a crease between his brows. "Let's just say that I have a lot to atone for."

The nun accepted Baltsaros's words with a tiny nod. Though she seemed somewhat shaken, she regained her composure enough to continue pointing out details about the city. A few minutes later, they pulled up to a squat building fronted by a covered, arched walkway that Tom immediately recognized from the palace in Madierus. The sight of something so familiar in the midst of the strange city took the edge off of his apprehension, and he grinned at Sister Iezabel.

"Lords help me, but please let there be some grub waitin' for us at the end of the tour?" he said hopefully. He was quickly going from peckish to starved, and his stomach would soon be grumbling loud enough to drown out the details of any more damned buildings.

With a short laugh, the nun stood to disembark.

"Yes, Tom, in just a moment. We've arrived at our destination. You'll be staying in the men's wing of the cloister if that suits you? Yes?" At Baltsaros's nod, she smiled and then put her hand out to the strong-looking middle-aged man who had come up to the side of the wagon. The man, either her servant or something more (did nuns take vows of chastity here too?), peered at the new arrivals with shrewd black eyes before helping the woman descend; he couldn't put a finger on what it was, but the man's scrutiny made the first mate uncomfortable. He scowled at the servant and was unnerved when the man just stared back, his face blank, before turning away slowly to his task.

Bold fucker, he thought. There was definitely something vaguely repellent about the man.

Sister Iezabel stepped down to the paving stones, and when Tom saw the wince of pain, he remembered that despite her spry appearance, the woman had to be in her sixties at the very least. She saw him watching and twisted her lips into a smirk.

"Getting old is no fun," she said and surprised the first mate with a wink, something that immediately bolstered Tom's opinion of the woman, as did what followed. "I take it I should arrange for one room for the three of you to share? We'll have to push a few beds together, but it should do."

As the three of them followed the tall woman up the stairs to the cloister, the wagon continuing on its way with the others, Tom leaned close to Jon's ear.

"Never thought I'd say it, but if this is religion here, it ain't half bad," he murmured. "In fact, I may even be doin' a little prayin' once my belly's full... Do ye wanna hear my sins, Jon?" Jon laughed and playfully shoved Tom away. However, this caught the attention of Sister Iezabel, and when she levelled a disapproving look at the two of them, Tom and Jon both dropped their eyes and continued to tail along after her, meek as lambs.

Jon stood at the window, lost in thought as he watched the play of moonlight on the stark landscape beyond the city. After a simple yet filling meal, the captain and nun had excused themselves to discuss their unexpected arrival. Jon was glad that he wasn't asked to join them—he wouldn't want to be part of that exchange for all the gold in the world. Behind him on the makeshift bed made of three narrow cots, Tom lay on his back, snoring loudly. He'd partaken of the abbey beer brewed on the premises and, pronouncing it to be one of the best he'd ever tasted, Tom had proceeded to drink himself into a stupor with the monks who had made it cheering him on.

Jon looked over his shoulder and smiled at the sprawled-out first mate, thinking he should get to bed too; he wanted to get to the central library early. However, something was keeping him awake.

Returning to the bleak view, Jon's brows met over his eyes in a deep frown, trying to figure out what it was that was bothering him so much. He felt as if something were out of place, and his brain itched as he tried to reconcile his sense of confusion.

It's the lack of snow, he finally determined. Scratching at a bug bite on his neck, he squinted at the tundra beyond. It was all wrong. In his dreams of the north—the ones that left behind a strange sense of portent upon waking—there had been snow on the ground. He shook his head over the weird disappointment he felt. More than ever, Jon knew that he should admit to himself that everyone was right in mocking him for believing the old woman when she said he had some special sight.

Hells, it's not like she said anything like that outright, you idiot. He grimaced. She had merely put the idea in his head, and it was time to let it go once and for all. Besides, all of those dreams had felt ominous; he should be happy that he wasn't predicting their doom.

He turned his back to the window and made his way to the bed. Stripping down to his skin, Jon wondered how in the black hells he was going to get to sleep with Tom making so much noise. With a sigh, Jon began to shove Tom, trying to get him to roll onto his side so he could make a little room for himself and maybe even stop Tom's snoring. If Baltsaros joined them he'd have to find his own space on the bed, but Jon had little doubt that it would be morning before the captain returned.

CHAPTER 29

SICK

The night had been long and difficult, but ultimately had brought Baltsaros some unexpected peace. Sister Iezabel had surprised him with her tears at the end of his confession, and as he had held her gently in his arms, he had been made to understand that she was not crying for the lives that had been lost. No, her sadness was for the little boy who had been twisted and used for evil against his will; there was no recrimination there. The immediate relief he had felt over that realization had startled Baltsaros. Attended only by her somewhat taciturn manservant, they had spent the rest of the night together in quiet conversation, discussing everything—with certain omissions—that had happened to him since.

Then, in the morning, after sending Tom to supervise the transportation of the generator and seeing Jon off to the central library, Baltsaros had returned to their room with the intention of resting. However, as he had lain there, a thought had occurred to him that set his mind ablaze. Despite not having slept yet, he'd suddenly felt anything but tired.

The captain walked quickly down the echoing hallway, remembering his time there as a boy. The building that served as both orphanage and children's hospital was the north wing of the cloister, and he had often wandered into the other wings to escape the bedlam created by the two dozen or so rambunctious boys and girls that called the orphanage their home. As Baltsaros made his way to the cloister's modest library, he passed his favourite of the five small chapels that were placed throughout the sprawling building and smiled. He had spent what felt like hours contemplating the figures carved into the misericords by pagan craftsmen before taking up a knife and chisel himself to see if he could reproduce the fanciful creatures found there. They had sparked a creative urge in him, one that he had kept up over the years in his drawings and carvings.

Frowning, Baltsaros realized that he couldn't remember the last time he had *created* something. Had the emperor burned that out of him, or had he done that to himself? Disturbed by the thought, he turned his mind to the flipside of his desire to create.

Even more interesting to the boy he had been were the surgeries he had watched performed in the tiny operating theatre. Where carving had brought a steady calm, the sight of blood and bone had excited him like nothing before. Held in thrall by what was happening below, Baltsaros had desperately wanted to know what it felt like to run the wickedly sharp scalpel along unresisting flesh. However, the doctors were too smart to leave the tools of their trade lying around for curious boys to steal, so he'd had to content himself with helping the nurses change bandages and remove sutures in the hopes that one day he would be the one holding the scalpel. At night, he had read by candlelight anything he could get his hands on for as long as he could keep his eyes open. Medical books, surgery diagrams, old crumbling scrolls that held nuggets of wisdom alongside blatant quackery—they all had held a deep fascination for him.

Stepping over the library's threshold, Baltsaros wondered whether, had he become a doctor as he had wished, his desire for blood would have been quenched. More likely, training and experience in surgery would have elevated his penchant for murder to a grisly art form. The captain smirked at the morbid thoughts.

Perhaps the only reason you haven't put charcoal to paper lately is because you've been so damn busy, he mused. Busy recovering, busy discovering what truly mattered to him... busy trying to find peace. The last one made him pause. It was true; he was trying to find peace by waging war, but he had no choice. The anger would grow until it tore him apart, taking Tom and Jon with it.

So ready to die? asked the beast.

"I'd rather die than lose control of myself," he fired back at it, annoyed at the intrusion into his thoughts. "If I could cut you out of my head and survive, I would, but it seems that fate has given me another option."

He pulled down a few leather tubes, looking for the map that Sister Iezabel had mentioned. When he found it, he unrolled it on one of the tables and held down the corners with heavy books. Tracing his finger along the box ravine northeast of Sormaheine, he found the tiny village that the nun had mentioned in her letter. Then, he followed the river that started there and continued until it hit the sea. He tapped the spot. That was where Kriegaard had found the frigate loaded down with treasure. Back west along the coast, he came to the villages that had been beset by barbarians, prompting Romas's unsuccessful trip north years after the attack on Sormaheine that had put Baltsaros in the orphanage.

The captain slowly stroked his stubbled cheek, deep in thought. The impetus for Romas's actions had been of a religious matter, having heard that men and women were being forced into rituals venerating the old bloodthirsty pagan gods. Could these barbarians have been the same ones who had taken him as a boy?

If so...

He stared hard at the map, wishing he had more information to confirm his theory, but all he had were decades-old memories and a second-hand account of an attack that had happened over a year ago. He had to believe it was possible that the barbarians were close, returning time and time again to what they considered their favourite hunting grounds. There were so many small villages along the coast and up along the rivers that could easily be wiped out with none the wiser; the boy Sten's account had described exactly that. For a moment Baltsaros's anger blossomed bright. Sormaheine, bastion of civilization, had done nothing but put up walls to block out the threat. As far as he knew, no one from the city had spared a moment's thought about going after the bastards. He rolled the map up, crushing it slightly in his fist as he made his way out of the library.

~

Jon walked slowly through Sormaheine's colossal library, his mind reeling with the sheer amount of words that existed between these marble walls. It was absolutely incredible. He passed through a small room where visitors could sit in snug, green velvet armchairs and stepped into what had to be the central room of the building. From floor to ceiling were shelves that held bound books. It was a fortune in leather and paper, not to mention what they contained. Jon remembered how awed he had been over the captain's meagre collection aboard the *Heart* and again when he had gone to a real bookstore in one of the bigger port towns they had stopped at. This? This was a hundred times that feeling. A thousand.

Nearing one of the shelves hesitantly, Jon's heart sank a little when he spied the spiky writing of the northerners. If all of these books were written in their tongue, they were absolutely useless to him. He swallowed back the bitterness he felt over his mind's lack of flexibility. Where Baltsaros and even Tom could pick up a new language with what seemed like preternatural ease, Jon floundered miserably with even the simplest of words. With an ironic grin, he thought about how he'd always remember the Sormet word for *cat*; that one was burned into his brain, alongside the image of Tom kneeling between his thighs, lips and tongue teasing him mercilessly as he looked up at Jon with blue-green eyes narrowed in amusement. Jon felt his cheeks get a little hot, and his heart sped, but he knit his brows when a little faintness washed over him.

That's weird, he thought, breathing deeply through his nose. Despite how easily he blushed, he was no fainting damsel. When the feeling passed, Jon continued on his way, searching for someone who could tell him if there were books written in a language he could understand.

Distracted by the sight of a larger-than-life sculpture of a warrior in the next room, Jon didn't notice that he was scratching hard at the bites on the back of his neck.

An hour later, ensconced in the corner of a small room that held a treasure's worth of bound books and scrolls written in Common, Jon flipped happily through a selection of short biographies of the men who had ruled when the world had been split into numerous small kingdoms. It was fascinating.

When he tired of history, Jon looked for a volume of fairy tales to see if he could find the ones his mother used to tell him as a child. He could barely remember them, but one had featured a man who could fly with wings given to him by an ancient wizard, and another had been about a blue dragon that befriended the knight who tried to kill him. As he searched the titles on a low shelf, he came across a small, thin black book with no writing on the spine. Curious, he pulled it out and nearly dropped it in shock at what it contained. Then Jon glanced over his shoulder to see if anyone was watching and turned the page.

In what Jon immediately assumed were descriptions of torture techniques, naked men and women were bound in numerous poses with the details of their anatomy rendered in stark black-and-white illustrations.

However, by the third and fourth pages, he realized that—whether for titillation or instructional purposes—what he held was an explicit guide on sexual practices. Jon felt a drip of sweat make its way down behind his ear and into his collar, and he wiped at the moisture on his forehead. He felt hot and a little dizzy, the erotic illustrations obviously doing something to him. As he scratched at the back of his neck, he made a small noise at the picture on the next page. A woman with bare breasts looked like she was wearing some sort of belt with a fake phallus attached, and she was penetrating a man bound to a cross. In her hand, she held what looked like a small whip, and Jon breathed hard, wondering if she was alternating between fucking the man and—

"Did you find what you were looking for?"

Jon slammed the book shut and thrust it back between the other volumes. It didn't fit all the way, sticking on something, so he fished around in the gap and found a folded bit of parchment that he pocketed before wedging the book of nude pictures back into place. When he realized the boy was still standing there, just watching Jon flail, he turned and stood. Perspiring as he tugged his tunic lower to hide his erection, Jon licked his lips and cleared his throat before answer.

"Yes. I mean, no. Yes, I am looking, but no I haven't found it. Yet," he said, flustered.

The boy, a gawky teen with unfortunately large ears, peered at him curiously.

"Are you ok?" he asked, his limpid blue eyes concerned.

"Yes!" choked Jon, wondering why his heart was beating so fast. "Thank you. Really." It wasn't as if the boy had caught him doing anything wrong. If that book was here, it was meant to be, no? Jon wiped his sweaty palms on his thighs and watched the boy turn and leave him. A moment later, a shiver went through him, and he wished he had something warmer than his long-sleeved tunic to wear.

By the time Baltsaros arrived to claim him, Jon could barely lift his head from the table. His skin ached, and every tiny sound made him want to weep. Clutching to

Baltsaros, he felt himself lifted into the air, and he burrowed his face against the captain's coat, desperate to block out the light.

~

Baltsaros closed his eyes as he felt Jon's forehead. The boy was hot but not dangerously so.

"What the fuck's the matter with him?" asked Tom. The first mate was crouched near the head of the hospital cot, his hands clasped between his knees as he stared disconsolately at the wan, sweaty figure of Jon.

"It's just a small sickness that comes with the black fly bites. Nothing serious," said Baltsaros, checking the glands in Jon's neck. Jon's eyelids fluttered for a moment, and he pushed weakly at Baltsaros's hand. "It never once occurred to me. The Sormet have a natural immunity to the sickness."

"Shit," swore Tom. "I'm gonna get it too? I got bit."

Baltsaros glanced over at the first mate. Other than his bloodshot eyes and dark shadows beneath them—both results of overindulgence—Tom looked as hale and hearty as usual. However, there was a visible bite at the edge of his scalp, and he was scratching at a second one on his wrist.

"Stand up," the captain said, gesturing. Tom rose to his feet stiffly, still pained by the healing wound in his side, and the lines across his forehead deepened. Baltsaros took his temperature and felt his neck. "If you're not presenting any symptoms yet, I'd say that you won't get it. Not all strangers do." He turned back to Jon and frowned to himself. Jon being sick would mean they would have to postpone the hunt for the blood ogres until he was better. Even if the fly sickness was usually mild, there sometimes arose complications, and Baltsaros wanted to be there if that happened. He couldn't leave Jon without knowing he would recover completely.

Weak, hissed the beast, and Baltsaros curled his lip.

"This is more important!" he growled and started when Tom's warm hand closed over his forearm.

"Da?" The first mate looked concerned.

Baltsaros shook his head slowly.

"Sorry, Tom," he muttered. "I was just thinking to myself that Jon's health was more important than our search."

"But, he's gonna be all right... Right?"

Grinning at the big man's wide-eyed worry, Baltsaros patted Tom's cheek.

"He's going to be just fine. A little fever and some disorientation, but he should be right as rain in a couple of days," he replied. "I promise."

The first mate visibly relaxed, nodded, and went back to Jon's side.

With a resigned sigh, Baltsaros glanced around; Tom would need a chair if he was planning on holding vigil. Across the big room, he spotted Sister Iezabel's attendant and beckoned him over with a hand. However, the man just stared at him a few seconds longer, his expression unreadable, before he turned and left. The captain watched him go, unsettled by his reaction.

When Jon was lucid again, he would ask him what he thought of the man and see whether the malice he detected in those dark eyes was just his imagination.

~

His feet thudded on the packed snow, claws barely making a dent in the hard surface. Ahead of him the wild cat chased the black lion between high white mounds that sparkled in the moonlight. Their shadows were long, reaching back throughout time. Jon should have been cold, but he wasn't. His shaggy grey fur kept him warm. Above, the stars were so numerous that it seemed the firmament would crumble from being so pierced through. Jon stopped running after the other two and sat back on his haunches. When he lifted his nose to the sky, a mournful howl echoed through the stark landscape. They were going the wrong way! The lion had to chase the cat. Jon let out another cry. Cracks appeared beneath him and the world rumbled. He was going to fall! Jon struggled, trying to free himself from the thing that wrapped around him, confused by the sound of a child crying...

~

Jon jerked awake, tangled in the blankets and sweating profusely. He had no idea where he was. Light filtered in through windows set high in the walls, and he could see he was in a long hall filled with narrow beds. Breathing hard, he wiped his face and tried to remember how he got there. The library... faint memories of being uncomfortably warm. Or was it cold? There had been a cart. Baltsaros's greatcoat. He licked his cracked lips, bewildered by how parched he was, and sat up slowly. Near him, a skinny child lay crying in a bed, a woman in a white smock holding its hand. When Jon swung his legs over the side of the bed, the nurse looked up at him but said nothing when he got to his feet.

Have to tell Baltsaros... he thought and stopped, not knowing what it was that was so important. His head was muddled as he sat down in the empty chair beside the bed and started tugging on his clothes. Couldn't remember what it was, but he had to go. The nurse frowned at him and that was all.

[...]

When he remembered the parchment in his pocket, Jon flattened it out on the stone wall and peered at it. There were stars, patterns of stars, and here and there a word.

It must mean *something,* he thought, hunching his shoulders when the guards passed by again. He was in a building, but he didn't recognize where he was. A door opened and he saw the covered walkway with the fluted columns, and he smiled because it meant he was still in the palace. Had to get to Baltsaros. Tom too. They were going the wrong way.

Wrong way to what? he asked himself, doubt flooding his mind. He stumbled a little as he made his way to the walkway. Didn't matter. He just had to get to Baltsaros's tower and then everything would be ok.

~

Baltsaros looked up from his maps and stared at Tom for a moment, trying to make sense of his words.

"What the hells do you mean Jon is nowhere to be found?"

CHAPTER 30

LOST AND FOUND

J on winced and hugged himself tighter. He was freezing and whatever he lay on
was cold and lumpy, and it jostled to and fro. Cracking open one eye, he was
immediately confused by his surroundings. Stacked in front of his nose were a
half-dozen or so dirty sacks filled with something that smelled like earth. He
knuckled his eyes and blinked, the minute details of the burlap coming into sharp
focus in the crisp grey light. As he lifted his head and peered around, Jon realized that
he was on the back of a wagon travelling through the woods. His brain slowly
unfolded memories of being beset upon by children in the streets who emptied his
pockets and kicked him in the side when he wouldn't let go of the creased parchment
in his hand. Then there was a kindly old woman. And a... man?

Jon pulled himself to sitting and regretted it almost immediately when his head
spun and blackness threatened.

"Awake at last," said a deep voice. "Do not worry. I will have you back to your ship
soon."

"My ship?" Jon blinked slowly at the hooded man driving the wagon. He had huge
red hands and a black beard that took up most of his face.

"In your fever... You said that you wanted to see your captain," said the man in
accented Common. "You're from that ship that arrived? The *Heart of Baal*?"

"Oh gods. Wait no... The captain is in the city! Stop, I have to go back," Jon said,
alarmed. He held onto the side of the wagon as it swayed and shimmied over the
crushed-stone road.

"Well, you cannot go back to the city yourself, little man," said the wagon driver
with a furrowed brow. He scratched at the leather hood he wore and stared at Jon over
his shoulder for a few seconds. "Are you certain? I can still take you to your ship. It is
not far now. You can then figure out where you want to be from there—"

"I have to get back to the city!" insisted Jon, his heart thudding hard. He had to tell Baltsaros about his dream... about... how they were lost. He closed his eyes and let his head loll forward as another wave of dizziness overtook him.

"You were in the city and my mother-in-law found you on a street corner. That is certainly no place for the likes of you! Wandering by yourself in the market. Tsk. The street rats had already picked you clean," the man rumbled on cheerfully as the wagon made its way over the bumpy terrain. "If you still want to go back, I can take you when I'm done delivering these potatoes to the harbour warehouse. You need the passphrases to get through the gates."

"Please..." Jon rasped. "I don't feel so well."

"I can see that. You have the fever. It will pass. It is not serious," said the farmer with a firm nod. He clucked his tongue at the antlered animals pulling the wagon to speed them on before twisting again on the hard bench to look back at Jon.

Jon stared blearily at the man with the reins for a moment and then down at his hands. The parchment was twisted and sweat stained, and he could see that he had gotten ink on his fingers. *Think about the dream... about the stars...*

He unfolded the map in his lap as the curious farmer looked on. Jon had very nearly ruined it; the drawn stars were smeared and blurred. However, there was one word that remained legible, penned in the spiky writing of the Sormet.

"This..." he whispered, holding it up to the bearded man. "What constellation is this?"

The man reached for the star map, but when Jon wouldn't surrender it to him, he squinted hard. After a moment he said a word that made Jon's pulse race and his stomach drop.

"Cat," the man said in the northern tongue.

Out of all the words... the only northern word he knew well.

Follow the cat, Jon.

Without another thought, Jon rolled off the wagon, landing painfully on the hard-packed stone. However, before the man in the wagon could stop and grab him, Jon had picked himself up and darted into the deep woods at the side of the road.

Jon had mended the tapestry. He had to look up at the stars.

He had to find the cat.

~

Baltsaros pinched the bridge of his nose and forced himself to think.

"I said I was fuckin' sorry, Da," growled Tom. "I was gone for all o' five minutes. Did ye want me to just piss myself?"

"No. Of course not," said the captain softly. He wanted nothing more than to strike the first mate for leaving Jon alone, but Tom was not to blame, and the first mate was beside himself with worry and guilt.

"I just can't believe the nurse just let him walk out in his condition," said Katherine, shaking her head.

"They're understaffed. Overworked. It's a hospital for orphans and the poor. I can't put any blame on them." Despite his words, he was seething on the inside.

He pressed his knuckles hard on the mahogany and took a deep, calming breath. When the heat of his anger had died down a little, he ventured a look at Tom. He stood in the middle of the captain's quarters, his arms down at his sides and hands curled into hard-knuckled fists. Staring at Baltsaros in anguish, Tom bared his teeth and let out a frustrated sound.

"Da, what if he's hurt? Fuckin' hells. Fuckin' bloody godsdamned mother-whorin' hells," he groaned. "Bloody Jon…"

"You said that the guard is scouring the city?"

"Aye. Yer nun lady made 'em hop the second I seen he was gone," said Tom, looking like he would either start cursing again or break something.

More like Tom will break down in tears, thought the captain.

"Da, I came here as fast as I could. Thinkin' maybe he was tryin' to get home to the *Heart*."

Baltsaros sighed and rounded the patched-together table and pulled Tom to his chest.

"You did good, Tom. It's all right. We'll find him. Just let me grab my things, and we'll head back to the city," he said, resting his cheek on Tom's rough-shorn hair for a moment before he stepped back. "I'm sure he hasn't gotten very far."

Tom cleared his throat and straightened his shoulders with a little nod. Baltsaros was a little surprised when Katherine slung an arm around Tom's waist and offered him a quick hug and a few quiet words the captain couldn't make out. The sight brought a smile to his face. That Jon had managed to forge a path to friendship between the pirates was amazing; the two of them had been at loggerheads since day one. He shook his head and turned away. They *had* to find Jon.

As Baltsaros was closing the bag of warm clothes they'd need for the expedition, Hitch popped his head around the door.

"Cap'n, sir," said the scraggy pirate, tugging on his forelock. "There be a tater farmer 'ere says 'e seen yun' Jon."

"Oh, thank the bloody gods," breathed Tom loudly as he and Katherine followed Hitch out of the room with a quick step. Baltsaros slung the bag over his shoulder and made his way with them towards a dark-haired man standing nervously at the bow. Tuvi and Tuli loomed to either side of him, watching him suspiciously, and it was obvious that the man had come aboard with them. Baltsaros waved the twins off with a smile and stepped closer. Over the stranger's shoulder, the captain could see a wagon hitched to a pair of reindeer on the shore.

"You've seen my missing man?" he said, trying to keep the urgency out of his voice.

"Yes, sir," said the farmer, his mouth almost completely concealed by a bushy black beard. He held a hat or a hood in his hands, creasing the leather in his big, red-knuckled hands "My wife's mother found him passed out under the archways of the marketplace. Some street urchins had already turned his pockets, but he was holding onto some old star map like it was made of gold."

"Star map?"

"Yes, sir. He wouldn't let go of it. He was feverish with fly sickness and kept saying he had to speak to his captain. That's how I knew he arrived with your ship. I was coming this way anyway, so I loaded him onto my wagon but"—the man twisted the leather harder, and his black brows pinched together high in the middle of his forehead—"it was the damnedest thing... He asked about the little otter constellation and then just jumped off and ran into the forest! I'm sorry, but he was away before I could catch him. I looked in the woods for a while, sir. No trace of him. But I'm no woodsman, sir. I know fields..." The man seemed so wretched that Baltsaros put a hand on his big shoulder.

"You did well in coming to tell me," he said reassuringly. He glanced to the side and saw that Tom was already pulling together a search team of their best hunters. The first mate turned to the captain, his bright eyes full of fear but jaw set in determination.

We'll find him.

"Katherine, you are in charge. Send runners if there are new developments."

"Aye, Captain!"

Baltsaros turned back to the farmer.

"You'll show us where he jumped off?" he asked.

"Of course, sir," the man nodded, placing the mangled hood back over his wild hair.

Yes, gods... We'll find you, Jon, promised the captain and tried to ignore the malevolent laughter of the ghosts in his head.

~

Jon marched through the underbrush, his eyes narrowed against the prickly needles of the pines reaching for him from either side of the winding track. Though his arms were crossed over his chest and hands jammed into the opposite armpit, Jon was growing colder the longer he walked. Breath pluming with every step, he fought the urge to just find somewhere to hole up until it got warmer.

Warmer... Jon laughed to himself. He doubted that it got much above freezing this far north, especially as the sun went down. It just baffled him why there was no snow on the ground. It made no sense.

All of his dreams had shown him snow... He huffed and panted as he broke through between the trees, still unable to see past the branches above his head.

The constellation couldn't be just a coincidence. It *had* to mean something. Of all the creatures it could have been named after, it ended up being a *cat*. Like Tom. Like his dream. He had to find and follow it to get... to get...

Jon stamped his feet hard as he walked, forcing the feeling back into them.

What are ye lookin' for, Jon? There was a mocking quality to Tom's voice.

"You're going to laugh at me," murmured Jon through numb lips. "I'm tired of you teasing me for this." A root hidden beneath the thick, almost spongy blanket of rust-coloured pine needles nearly succeeded in tripping him. There *had* to be a way out of these woods. Then, when he could see the stars, he would follow the cat, just like in his dream. It would take him to... take him to... Baltsaros? No. Wait... Something that would *help* Baltsaros?

Puzzled, Jon paused almost midstride, trying to remember exactly what it was that the cat would bring him to, but came up blank. It had been so clear to him just a moment earlier. Would it bring him to the blood ogres? The thought made him resume his pace.

No, that can't be it, he thought with a frown. The wolf and the lion needed to follow the cat. But to what end? Up ahead in the dying light, there seemed to be a break in the trees, and he anxiously picked up his pace.

Dont'cha want my help? laughed the first mate.

"Not unless you can part the trees so I can see the *fucking sky!*" Jon shouted in tearful frustration as what he thought was a clearing turned out to be just a dense copse of white-barked trees. He slumped against one of the strange trees, his forehead pressed to the peeling bark, just breathing deep for a moment.

"What am I doing?" he muttered. It had all made absolute sense to him before: his dream, finding the map and constellation, striking out on his own... Jon closed his eyes and swallowed thickly.

Are ye ok, love? rumbled Tom.

"No," whispered Jon to the ghost in his head. "I'm not. I'm lost and I'm cold, and I swear to fucking gods that I am going as crazy as Baltsaros."

Why don't ye tell ol' Tom about it?

Jon pushed himself away from the tree trunk and peered around in the deepening gloom. After a moment, he slid down to the small hassock at the tree's base and pulled the calfskin map out from the neck of his shirt. He unrolled it, laid it across his knees, and then blew into his cupped hands.

"I'm looking for a fucking cat," he muttered, but it didn't make much sense anymore. Jon couldn't even remember which constellation was the cat. He should have stayed in the hospital.

Hospital? Jon covered his ears with his hands, the latter only slightly warmer than the former.

You're lookin' for me, love? We're lookin' for you...

"I wish you really were," mumbled Jon. "I should have stayed on that fucking cart. Then at least I would have made it to the *Heart*. Now you'll never know where to look. Tom, what have I done?"

When Tom didn't answer, Jon let out a shuddering sigh and wiped at his leaking nose with the edge of his sleeve.

Move or die, he thought grimly as he stood. His feet were nerveless blocks of ice, but he forced himself to start trudging forward again. Night was coming and it sure as hells wouldn't get warmer once the sun went down. If he had any chance at all in finding a way out of the woods, it wouldn't be by sitting and feeling sorry for himself.

Tom let loose with another stream of curses under his breath as he kept close to Rémi, stamping flat ferns and saplings with his big boots as he went. They'd been searching for nearly two hours in these godsforsaken fucking woods, following what the southlander pirate swore were Jon's tracks until, suddenly, they'd lost sight of them near a bunch of paper birches.

Baltsaros walked alongside him, his head swivelling from side to side as they made their way deeper into the woods.

"How are we supposed to hear Jon if you won't cease your endless profanity," admonished the captain quietly.

Tom glanced over at Baltsaros and clenched his jaw. The captain frowned at him from beneath his sailor's tuque but said nothing else. Behind them, trailing to either side, were a few more men that swore up and down to the blue heavens that they knew their way around a forest.

Bloody good it'll do us in the stone dark.

"Tom, you're doing it again."

With a scowl, Tom picked up his pace, overtaking Rémi. He could swear that they had passed this exact same spot twice now. If they were going in circles, he would personally tie the good-for-nothing southlander to the mast and whip him raw himself.

You're going the wrong way.

"Am I, Jon?" whispered Tom, his nerves obviously beginning to wear thin.

Glancing over his shoulder, Tom realized he was alone. However, he could hear the others nearby, so he stopped walking and rubbed his face as he waited for them to catch up. Jon was lost somewhere in these woods, and from what the farmer had said, he hadn't been wearing nearly enough clothes to be out in temperatures that were dropping the longer they searched.

They *had* to find him.

Tom stuck the black cheroot between his teeth before patting his pouch for a match, thinking about what Baltsaros had said when they set off. Jon was probably delirious with fever, which could be why he broke away from the farmer like a blasted madman, but it didn't explain where in the hells Jon had found a fucking star map.

Tom, really, you're going the wrong way.

"Completely barmy," he grumbled, but he couldn't shake the feeling that they were indeed heading in the wrong direction. Tom struck the match against the tree and lifted it to the slender cigar. As he puffed a few times against the flickering flame, something caught his eye off to the left. It was a glimmer... Tom squinted into the shadowed dusk and lifted the match above his head. There it was again. A light.

And then it blinked.

Tom's eyes widened when he saw the grey wolf emerge from between two ground-hugging spruces. It stood appraising him for a long moment, the flame reflected in its eyes. The same cold gust that played in the wolf's thick ruff sent the match's fire back against Tom's fingers, and he dropped it with a curse. The wolf, startled by the sudden motion, turned and darted back under the tree cover. When the trees swung with its passing, Tom saw something and his heart began to box a merry beat against his ribs —there were branches broken at man-height above where the wolf had gone. Hope rekindled, Tom set off after the wolf. At the sight of more freshly torn foliage just beyond the broken twigs and then an obvious boot print in a bed of moss, Tom stopped in his tracks.

"We're going the wrong bloody way!" he bellowed. "Follow me. I think I found where he went."

≈

Baltsaros sank down to his knees and reached for Jon, afraid of what he would discover. However, when a branch cracked loud beneath his boot, the younger man started awake. Jon looked blearily around, clearly disoriented. Tom let out a relieved laugh and squatted next to the captain.

"Jon?" murmured Baltsaros. Jon was lying on his side in a small depression at the base of a red pine, his arms tight around his torso and knees nearly to his chin. He uncurled himself with a pained expression and groaned softly.

"Fucking hells, am I glad to see you," Jon said in a hoarse voice and winced as Tom helped him all the way to sitting.

Baltsaros pulled the wool blanket he had brought out from his pack and quickly wrapped Jon up. He was shivering, but apart from a few scratches on his face, he seemed unharmed.

"Fuck, I'm cold," mumbled Jon, burrowing into the blanket. Tom curled around him from behind and buried his face in Jon's neck. From the way Jon's brow creased in chagrin at Tom's rough whispers, Baltsaros guessed that the first mate was scolding him.

"I'm sorry," said Jon. "I am so sorry." His blue-grey eyes lifted to the captain's, and Baltsaros forced a calm smile onto his face.

"We found you. That's all that counts, my love," he replied. "That's all that counts."

"I don't know what happened," Jon said quietly. "It's all muddled in my head. I woke up in a hospital, but I don't know why I was there. And then there was a man with a wagon. And... a map, but I lost it when I rolled down a hill. I walked and walked, but then I just couldn't anymore. I... I needed to sleep a little to regain my strength, and I was going to set out again." His confusion seemed to have a cleared completely. The captain guessed that the frigid temperatures had brought down Jon's fever enough to stop the delirium that had caused him to wander off to begin with.

"Well, I'm glad we found you before you slept too deeply," said Baltsaros. Tom lifted his head and frowned at the captain. The first mate gave a tiny headshake; there was no need to continue that train of thought.

"Ye had a fever, lovey," rumbled Tom. "Nothin' terrible, just a bit o' sickness. But, I'm the one who's bloody sorry. I went for a leak and left my post. Ye were gone when I—"

"Yes, you're all very, very sorry," said a new voice. "It's unexpectedly sweet coming from the lot of you, I must say."

Startled, Baltsaros looked up and saw a few men standing by a group of pines. In the faded light, he couldn't make them out clearly, but by the tongue spoken, they were obvious natives of Sormaheine.

"Who are you?" he asked, rising to his feet.

"Oh, you know who I am… But now I know who you *really* are," said one of the men, but Baltsaros barely heard his words because as the speaker stepped forward, the captain recognized the middle-aged attendant that served as Sister Iezabel's manservant.

Baltsaros then felt a conflicting mix of relief at seeing a would-be rescuer and confusion as his brain finally registered the malice in the man's tone. At a shout from Tom, the captain turned to see the first mate and Jon struggling with more men. Nearby, the body of Rémi lay in a mess of pine needles slicked with red, steam rising slowly from it in the deep cold. This was not a rescue.

Before Baltsaros had time to dodge the big man who grabbed at him, he felt something hard hit the back of his skull. The last thing he saw was Tom with his arm around Jon, his wrist bent at an impossible angle, as he tried to fight off their assailants with his long, bone-handled knife clutched in the other hand.

Then the world went black.

CHAPTER 31

THE DEAD

Whoever fights monsters should see to it that in the process he does not become a monster. And if you gaze long enough into an abyss, the abyss will gaze back into you.

— FRIEDRICH NIETZSCHE

Tom fingered the raised calluses on his chest, twisting his lips in disgust at how pale and sensitive the skin was beside them. How long had it been since his master had put that fucking harness on him? Now, it was gone, cut off by an oddly genteel pirate captain and his sour-faced first mate. The latter, a son-of-a-fucking-whore if there ever was one, had just thrown him back in the tiny cage in the captain's quarters with nary a word before he stormed off, leaving Tom in the bloody dark by himself.

With a sigh, he sat down gingerly, still sore from being abused and then doctored on, and wondered what in the black hells was expected of him. Three days aboard the bloody ship, and Tom had done almost nothing but sit in his gods-be-damned cage like a fucking animal. Hands curled to fists in his lap, he bared his teeth in a frustrated grimace and thought about the shard of pottery he had hidden beneath the thin mattress.

Soon.

It had taken most of the previous afternoon tossing the tied strips he'd made of his shirt at the jug on the table before the loop had caught the lip. A quick jerk had brought the jug down to the floor, but it had survived the fall, landing unharmed on the thick carpet below. Tom had had to strain through the bars to reach the jug and then dash it a few times against the wall of his prison to get it to break.

As luck of bloody fucking luck would have it, Peter had been on his way into the room when he heard the pottery break, and then all hells had broken loose of course, with the surly first mate cursing and hollering while he and two others had tackled Tom to the floor. He'd nearly broken his wrist trying to jam the jagged splinter of pottery under the bed while being pinned by the fuckers.

Tom rubbed his wrist with a scowl. Being forced to scrub the deck for three hours as punishment certainly hadn't helped his sprain or his mood. As he was debating whether he should try to get some sleep or do some more sit-ups, he saw something that made his heart falter and his hackles rise. There, on the little crate that served as a table within the small jail cell, was the shard he'd thought hidden away. Just sitting there, plain as fucking day. Tom blinked slowly at it, wondering what it meant. It seemed like a big *fuck you*—like they were laughing at him and his puny excuse for a weapon—and it sat there mocking him.

See how easily I found your sad little secret? See how I let you keep it?

Aye, it bloody reeked of that poncy fucker in the greatcoat with the peculiar fucking name. The one who stared at him with those pitchy eyes of his, lips all curled and pleased with how he thought he'd bested Tom.

Tom.

The ex-slave closed his eyes with a smile and rolled the name around in his mind before giving it breath.

"Tom," he murmured. It was the first thing that was truly his. Not *Thomas*. Nay, Thomas was a little boy dressed in silks and crying as the men—

"If you learn how to behave like a human being, you'll have much more than just a name, Tom," came the voice from the darkness.

Tom leapt to his feet, hands tight around the bars as the captain's words split the silence. Furious at having such a pathetic little private moment witnessed, he hunched his shoulders and let out a low growl at the man reclining on the bed across the room. When the captain chuckled and sat up, Tom thought he would break his jaw, his teeth were clenched so tight.

"Not tonight, then, I take it?" asked Baltsaros. He slipped off the bed and, dressed only in tight black leather trousers, padded barefoot across the rug to the front of the cage. The captain's hair was loose and a little dishevelled and made him look as if he had just now woken. It hung down past his powerful shoulders, a tress of it straying against the broad pectoral generously furred with dark hair. As the captain crossed his arms, Tom's eyes were drawn to the way the moonbeam from the porthole played on the sculpted, hard muscle of his forearm, sun-dark skin turned pale in the cold light.

Strong. He felt a flutter of dread as the captain continued to watch him silently. Though rigid with apprehension, Tom leaned harder into the bars and sneered at the man.

"Fuck ye lookin' at?" he growled.

"And so it can speak," said the captain, his tone playful.

Tom's fear turned again to fury at being mocked, and he lunged out quickly to grab his tormenter. However, the captain was too quick for him and simply stepped out of reach.

"You want to kill me. That much you've made blatantly clear, Tom," said Baltsaros with a little tilt of his head. The captain's accent gave his words a clipped quality that accentuated the aura of good breeding that he perpetuated with his manners and dress.

All it did was remind Tom of those who had given up on him; shoulders hitched up further, he let out another low animal noise as he watched the captain walk to an armoire. When Baltsaros returned to the cage, he held up a long, bone-handled knife in a leather sheath. Tom's pulse sped, and he felt the familiar cool surge of adrenaline tighten his loins in preparation for a fight. However, Baltsaros merely shook his head at Tom's desperate display.

"The day you prove to me that you are more than *that*," the captain said, pointing to the slave collar that Tom still wore, "is the day I will give you *this*." He unsheathed the knife and turned it for Tom to see. "Prove to me that you're worth as much as I think you are, Tom, and you'll know what freedom means again."

Tom breathed quickly through his nose, eyes on the fine blade, then hawked and spat at the captain.

Quick as a snake, the man jumped forward and punched Tom hard through the bars. Pain exploded in Tom's face as he felt his nose break and again when he fell back and landed hard on his sprained wrist. With another derisive laugh, the captain turned away, leaving Tom to lick his wounds.

~

The pain in his face and wrist had brought back old memories as he rose out of his stupor, but unlike his recollection, this time he could feel the bones grinding together as he tried to move in his restraints. Broken wrist for sure. Biting back a cry as he was jostled from behind, Tom turned his head and spat out the dust that coated his lips. It was dark, but he could make out candles flickering somewhere above him. Wherever he was, it reeked of age and mould... and death. He narrowed his eyes, focusing on a broken dust-and-cobweb-laden skull near his head, and saw another one lying right behind it. Judging by the roughness of the ground beneath him and what looked like a stone sarcophagus to his left, he was in some sort of crypt. It was only when he was nudged again that he realized that whoever was tied up with him was waking up.

"Jon? Da?" he whispered.

There was a weak moan behind him, and he tried to lift his head to see if Jon was all right, but all he did was twist his wrist further. It also felt like he had ripped something inside the healing wound at his side, and Tom felt nauseous from the pain.

"Jon?" he tried again.

"Huh fuck," coughed Jon, sounding muffled. "What...?" When he shifted against Tom, the first mate let out a pained grunt.

"Stop movin', Jon," he rasped. "Yer hurtin' me."

796

Instantly Jon stopped squirming and lay still.

"Where are we?"

"I don't fuckin' know, love," said Tom with a grimace. "Do ye see Da?"

"No." Jon's voice sounded small, like he was terrified.

"Don't worry, love," murmured the first mate. "We'll figure it out. Keep yer head."

However, when the fall of boots sounded loud on the stones a moment later, heralding the approach of a group of men, Tom began to feel his own panic. Their captors had hit the bottle hard; Tom's nose burned with the smell of rotgut when one of them bent low to peer at him with a malicious grin.

It was always worse when they had been drinking...

Baltsaros woke in a dimly lit room with hewn stone walls, his head throbbing in a nauseating tempo of agony. After licking his lips with a nearly dry tongue, he found he could barely swallow for the dust in his throat. Despite how disoriented he felt, it only took him a few seconds to place the smell of powdered bone and mildew that assailed his nose with every breath.

The catacombs.

Short of aboveground land to bury the dead, a sprawling necropolis undercut the mountaintop city of Sormaheine. Miles of narrow, sarcophagus-lined tunnels looped beneath the streets, sometimes doubling back on themselves—like a giant spiral maze fashioned to keep the spirits of the dead from ever finding their way to the surface. There were entrances to the catacombs all over the city, but Baltsaros knew one of them very well; the children of the orphanage would often sneak into the cloister's cellar and dare each other to climb through the trap door to the crypts below with nothing but a bit of pilfered candle to keep the ghosts at bay. Baltsaros, smaller and deemed strange by the other boys, had been forced down there alone many times, made to wander for hours until he found an alternate way out.

"Ah, you've returned to us," said a voice, and Baltsaros lifted his head to squint at the figure before him. It was the middle-aged man from the woods, the attendant that always seemed no further than Sister Iezabel's elbow, always at the ready with a steadying hand or a cup of the mulled wine the old nun liked to drink. There was no mistaking him. The man had been there with the captain and Sister Iezabel the whole long night they had spoken of times past; Baltsaros had memorized the slant of his dark eyes and the way his greying hair curled across his high forehead.

"What do you want from me?" asked the captain hoarsely.

"To the point. I do like that. I was told you were a man who understood the value of succinctness in the face of death," replied the man with a smile.

"I apologize if you think I've wronged you in some way," said Baltsaros, wishing he could touch the back of his head to assess the damage. However, his hands were useless to him as they were bound to the arms of an old wooden chair. "You and I don't know each other. I have no conflict with you, so I ask again: what do you want from me?"

"Oh, yes, we do know each other. Though you've only just become aware of my existence, I've known of yours for a very long time," said the man, his voice growing quieter. "A long fucking time."

As he gazed at the captain, his lip twitched up slightly in what looked like a nervous tic.

"Let me and my men go, and I will make you a rich man," said Baltsaros, working his fingers around the seam where the chair arm was joined.

"You want to pay me to let you go? No, Captain. You owe me *far* more than that, it seems," the man said, pushing his face close to Baltsaros's. His breath was rank, and the captain nearly gagged from it. Then, after his wide-eyed stare ended with a humourless chuckle, the man tutted and shook his head in disappointment.

He had to be mad.

Trying to keep his breathing steady, Baltsaros pressed back against the chair, testing the state of the wood, and was pleased when he heard a creak. Instantly his head was flung back when the man punched him, forcing his damaged skull against the hard surface with a painful rap and causing him to see bright lights behind his eyelids. The candlelit room shimmered strangely when he opened his eyes.

"None of that, now! You're my prisoner, and you'll die by my hands... you and the two you seem to hold so dear. That is, when we're finished with you of course. It's been a while since my men have had a little reward for loyalty, and they're not especially choosy as long as they each get a turn."

Baltsaros panted quickly against the rising faintness, disturbed by the sound of a struggle somewhere behind him. He heard Tom cry out in pain, followed by a surge of ugly laughter. Then, heart in his throat, Baltsaros heard Jon's whimper, and he gnashed his teeth in anguish. Tied as he was to the chair, he couldn't see behind him and trying to twist around brought with it another wave of cold nausea.

"You bastard," he growled. "Let them go."

"Or what? You're going to scowl me to death?" taunted the man as he pulled up another mouldy-looking chair to sit on. "You're right, you know," he continued quietly. "I'm a bastard... And now I know *you* are the reason why that is." He leaned forward in his seat with hands clasped together and stared again at Baltsaros with a curious blankness in his dark eyes.

"Growing up in an orphanage isn't easy. Something you're well acquainted with, I know. The teasing, the bullying... Lords, I'm sure they even made you come down here by yourself..."

Jon let out a low moan, and there was a string of curses from Tom that led to a thud and a grunt of pain. Baltsaros let out his own strangled yell when the man in front of him rose out of his chair and slapped him hard across the face.

"Pay attention to me when I'm talking to you. I'm *saying* that you and I are not that different," said his captor calmly and reclaimed his seat. "We *both* grew up in that godsforsaken fucking cloister, Captain. So I'm *also* acquainted with what it's like to be terribly scarred and bullied for it. The barbarians... the blood ogres... Those monsters took our families away from us. See, your family and my family were neighbours, and they killed my mother just as surely as they killed yours, except mine"—the man laughed a little jerkily; his hands twisting together, white-knuckled, were the only indication that he was struggling with extreme emotion—"mine took another nine months to die. They tell me she died screaming as they pulled out the baby those monsters put in her belly."

Baltsaros didn't need Jon to see from the man's vehemence where this tale was going. Behind him he heard Jon's voice again, muffled and in pain. He scratched at the chair arms, desperate to free himself.

"Do you have any idea how much fucking harder it is to grow up among those fucking brats when you're the son of a faceless rapist *monster*? Do you have any idea what that was like? But you... You were the boy that survived! Sure, they all whispered that you were cursed, or you did horrible, perverted things with them so they would let you go, but it couldn't possibly have been as bad as being the *get* of those bloody savages."

Nostrils flaring, the captain tried to chase from his mind the memories of those taunts; he remembered all too well those accusations. He was in agony, madness only a step away as he heard Jon whimper again.

"I started to help Sister Iezabel because she was kind, and because I knew she had been kind to you. Lords, you probably have no idea how happy she was when you sent that very first letter, do you? And it made me happy too. Here was another scarred, damaged boy... And he had escaped! Lords, and he was making something of himself... a true survivor. Gods, I wanted to be you, Baltsaros. Waiting each year for that single, dry, impersonal letter you sent Sister Iezabel out of some strange sense of duty... and all that coin! Do you know I travelled out to the midlands to see you? I had some notion of becoming part of your crew. Perhaps becoming friends because we shared our terrible beginnings. But you wouldn't even see me. No! That miserable animal you call a first mate... *He* turned me away. Said that you didn't need another land-grubbing sailor to dilute the ranks. And then I heard *stories* about you..."

Tom cursed again, and Baltsaros closed his eyes as the first mate began to beg, not for himself but for Jon.

You made this happen, snickered the beast from somewhere. It was too crowded in Baltsaros's head. He could hear Jon's cry of pain, and his whole body trembled from the sound of it.

"So I began to practice pillage and plunder on my own. Then, I found others who *understood* the power behind fear, like you do. And we started taking settlements, villages—small at first, then bigger. Oh... We've gotten very good, Baltsaros."

The words finally caught fire in the captain's brain and started burning through the threatening madness. He stared hard at the man, comprehension finally dawning on him.

"*You* are the barbarian raiders," Baltsaros said. His hands were claws on the chair's arms.

"Yes. But that's not what I'm—"

"You have been raping and destroying, emulating the blood ogre tribe."

"The blood ogres? The blood ogres are *nothing*, Baltsaros. *Nothing*. I was not much past twenty when we hunted them down and killed every last one of them. I was emulating *you*, you dim fuck! And then, during your sob session with that old cunt, I discovered that my idol, the man that I'd been striving to be all these years, is the *one who let those monsters into the city. You* are the reason I suffered all of those years. You. Do you have any idea how hard it was for me not to just slit your throat right then and there? No, I had to keep playing my part until I could get you alone. How fortuitous is it that Sister Iezabel sent me to help you, and that you and your men were as easy to track as musk bears crashing through the woods?" The man's chuckle was bitter, and though the fervour in his voice had grown, there was little rebuke in his expression. He remained an unremarkable man in his middle age with a solicitous smile and an almost kindly manner. It was as if he could not rid himself of the mask he wore day to day. However, the twitch in his lip returned as he leaned far forward again to peer almost curiously at the captain. "Baltsaros, *you* are the monster. By killing you, I redeem myself, don't I? Take back what you've stolen from me? Yes... I'm going to put an end to you and take your ship. We are very much alike, aren't we? Both dark-eyed northerners... Why I could even take your name, couldn't I? How many would realize before it's too late? Oh, I am so very thankful for whatever gods or devils it was that brought you to me... like fate itself blessed me to take your place..."

The captain's head spun, trying to put together the pieces.

Look behind you, said Romas with a truculent laugh. *Look what your stupid quest is doing to those dear boys of yours. Can't you hear Jon sobbing? Oh, Tom will never cry. He'll just take it, but you know what it'll do to him...*

Something clear and painful cut through Baltsaros, and he grasped at it, feeling like he was opening his eyes for the first time. Before Romas could say another word, Baltsaros simply dismissed him and narrowed his focus down to a needle's width.

"—finally found my own ship to get away from this—"

"The ship. The frigate... It was yours," Baltsaros whispered.

His captor sneered at him.

"Yes, and it was stolen from me. Along with—"

"All the treasure you stole from these crypts. My parents' wedding cuffs weren't trophies kept by the ogres, they were burial items taken by you and your *pathetic little band of savages.*"

The man's eyes bulged and he stood, taking a swift step backwards when the rotting wood of the chair finally gave way beneath Baltsaros's wrist. It was as if he was held in thrall by the captain's unblinking gaze and, complexion waxy, he gaped as Baltsaros quickly freed his other arm.

Baltsaros smiled grimly. Was it fate or uncaring gods or even fucking devils that forced him to use to his advantage the harrowing abuse taking place just paces away? The men were so distracted with their beastly sport that they didn't realize their leader was in trouble.

"Let me guess... You don't have enough men to sail that frigate, so you needed the riches of our dead to fund your cause of murder and mayhem. Oh, you *are* right, you know. We are both murderers, you and I," purred Baltsaros. He felt a little faint as he stood there, but the tremor that went through the snivelling traitor before him bolstered his step. "I wish I could honestly say I was sorry for your beginnings, but I am not. I don't care."

Baltsaros couldn't help but risk a glance back across the chamber. Jon's face was wet with furious tears as the man behind him grunted and thrust. Tom's eyes were closed.

The claws that had held the beast to the captain for so long could find no purchase in what that sight had unleashed within him, and the phantom howled as it was torn loose. This would end here and *now*. No more madness feeding on madness. Nothing but the future... and only if he managed to mend it after this night.

Time stopped as Baltsaros reached for the man who had captured them, twisting his head so violently that he felt his jaw dislocate before the crack of broken bone jolted his palms. The man, unnamed and rendered meaningless, fell in a heap. Quickly, Baltsaros dug into the corpse's belt to retrieve Tom's blade.

Startled into action by the captain's shout of rage, two men then set upon him as the others abandoned Jon and Tom on the dirty floor. The long knife, always kept razor sharp by the first mate, sliced through jugular and tendon, scraping against bone as the captain wielded it furiously. Tom, up onto his feet in a flash, looped his bound arms over the head of one of the attackers and bit deep into the side of the man's neck. Though it must have been agony on his broken wrist, he fought the man to the floor and finished him off with a knee to the back of the head, snapping his neck.

As Baltsaros took on a third and then a fourth, he saw Jon cut Tom's bindings. Then, freed from his own ropes, Jon set about hacking and slashing with a dagger taken from one of the dead men.

The captain let out a cry as the man he was fighting managed to cut his arm, but he retaliated and, changing his grip on the long knife, managed to sink the blade deep into his attacker's eye.

The triumphant bellow that burst from Jon nearly startled Baltsaros into dropping his weapon, and he turned in time to see him slice through his opponent's neck with a bright arc of blood. Eyes wide and crazed, Jon then jumped to the first mate's aid.

In less than a minute, it was over.

The three of them stood panting in the dusty mausoleum, surrounded by the bodies of their abductors and covered in blood. Tom held his wrist to his chest, and his face was pale beneath the streaks of dirt and gore. Even so, he cracked a grim smile at the captain who was putting pressure on the deep cut in his arm.

Jon looked dazed, his grey-blue eyes huge and lost. Apart from a dark bruise on one cheek, he seemed relatively unharmed.

"Did they hurt you?" Baltsaros asked softly, reaching for him. However, Jon shied away from the captain's touch like a skittish colt and wouldn't meet his eye.

"I'm fine," said Jon, his voice tight. "I'll... be fine. Just..." Jon wiped the back of his hand across his mouth and then looked around. He walked away from the captain and stood staring down at one of the bodies for a long time in silence. Tom leaned with a gasp against Baltsaros as the last of his strength ebbed. The captain looped his arm around the first mate's waist to support him and watched as Jon kicked the corpse as hard as he could in the side. When Jon turned back to the others, his face was blank of expression, but he wouldn't lift his eyes.

"Are we going after the blood ogres?" he asked.

"No. No, the blood ogres are dead," Baltsaros said, shaking his head. "The last one died here tonight."

Not seeming to care enough to ask why that was, Jon just nodded once. With a sigh, he ran a bloody hand through his curls and finally met the captain's gaze. His eyes were red-rimmed, but if there was pain there, it was locked away. Baltsaros thought he heard a ghostly chuckle from within.

"Then are you satisfied?" Jon asked. "Is there enough redemption in this for you?" It was an accusation.

The captain's guts twisted at the hollow sound of Jon's voice.

"Yes, Jon. We're done," Baltsaros replied. "We're going home."

CHAPTER 32

THE LIVING

After we found our way to the surface following our ordeal, we were tended to in the small hospital by Sister Iezabel's staff. My injuries were minor, but Tom suffered a bad break in his right wrist as well as some tearing in the healing wound in his side. He's still on the mend and not happy about it. While I think we managed to isolate the bones as best as possible, I'm afraid he'll lose some mobility when using his dominant hand.

As for Jon, I don't know the extent of the physical damage he sustained; he refused treatment, assuring me he was fine, and I chose not to press the issue. My general observations over the last month have led me to conclude that the physical trauma he suffered was minimal.

Sister Iezabel was devastated that she had failed to notice the monster in their midst. It seems that he was able to commit his barbarity undiscovered by first telling her of raids that had not yet happened then attacking the villages or settlements when Sister Iezabel sent him with relief funds and supplies. She blames herself for not seeing him for what he was, but I assured her that his disguise had fooled everyone.

When the man's quarters were searched, they found all the letters I had sent to Sister Iezabel along with never-sent missives penned by his hand and addressed to me. All of them described brutal acts that he thought we both could partake in, growing ever more cruel and sadistic with each consecutive letter. It seems his obsession was complete, and I was gleefully painted such a monster in his eyes that I felt strangely lacking in comparison upon reading the letters.

On top of his depraved ramblings, a cache of bones was found beneath a loose flagstone in his room. These grisly trophies seem to span as far back as his childhood—so clearly his appetite for murder was not, in fact, born of being spurned from my ship by Tom (or Peter?).

One thing I find most fascinating is that he didn't seem capable of reconciling his "positive" view of me with the "negative" truth of what I had done to cause the death of our families and his subsequent suffering at the hands of his fellow orphans. What makes a monster? A small, selfish part of me wishes I had not ended his life so quickly, for when I looked into his eyes, I saw a deformed reflection of myself.

I could have studied him.

However, I am honestly glad that I did dispatch him as I did. And, though I did indeed learn the man's name from Sister Iezabel, I won't give it form here. Let him be forgotten so that his legacy is nothing but dust.

This is the last I will touch on the subject.

After the startling and rather abrupt end to our purpose in Sormaheine, we left almost immediately, and I do not think that a return trip will be in our future. Though I will maintain my yearly letters to the good sister until her death, and a portion of my wealth will continue to make its way to the coffers of the cloister beyond that time, there is nothing left for me in the north. However, it was not—as Jon claims—all for nothing. What I took away from our time there was an understanding that I cannot find redemption through vengeance. When I was robbed of my chance to hunt down the men who abused me and that failed to wound me as I thought it would, I realized something:

My past is unimportant. It is what the future holds for me that will be my salvation—and that is the love of two broken creatures that I cherish more than life itself.

I truly believe that there is no cure for what causes my deficiency of emotion or my inability to empathize with my fellow man. I am simply what I am: a cultured monster. I have finally made peace with that fact. What I can and will do is stop putting my needs and desires at the forefront.

I have lost that privilege.

Instead, I will devote myself to making sure that my boys never suffer harm through my influence again. It is a worthy cause, and I can only hope that whatever damage I have caused so far will truly be forgiven in time.

After we set sail from Sormaheine, it troubled me deeply that Jon chose to sleep apart. My instinct was to pull him to me, but I held back and said nothing as he retired, alone, to Tom's tiny cupboard of a room belowdecks night after night.

Tom, on the other hand, acted like he always has: gruff and dismissive of his own abuse. It is an admirable quality in him, and though I recognize the selfishness of this, I was thankful for his ability to bury pain. I have no shame in admitting this now, but I desperately needed him to be there in the face of Jon's desertion. In return for his generous loyalty, I have started to frequently offer Tom tenderness in what we do, knowing that though he desires it from me, he would never ask on his own.

After all, I desire it too.

With Jon, things soon started to improve on the surface. I recognized that his friendship with Katherine gives him something that neither Tom nor I can, so I began to nurture it as much as possible. Then, one night, Jon crept into my quarters and slipped between the sheets without a word of explanation. That he stayed there all night, pressed to my side... I cannot amply describe the relief I felt.

We have not slept apart since.

However, all is not right with Jon. Not yet. Jon has always been prone to a solemnity bordering on the morose, and what happened to him in Sormaheine only served to worsen that predilection. Day by day, I see changes in him, some good, some bad, some simply... incomprehensible to me. While he is decidedly more confident about what he wants and does not, both in his work aboard the ship and in my quarters, he maintains this ridiculous guilt over our abduction. As far as I can understand it, he blames himself and his fixation on the tarot card reading for the capture and subsequent abuse he, and especially Tom, suffered. He believes that it was the reading of signs in everything that made us fall prey. I don't pretend to understand it, and I have tried to turn his mind away from such thoughts, but it is like a burr within him.

Fate may no longer be a topic of interest for Jon, but I have found myself mulling over what happened with a strangely indulgent mind. While he did not lead us to the blood ogres by following the stars (I am a little unclear about the link), Jon did lead us to their proxy, did he not? Simply put, I do not feel I can dismiss the fortuity of what happened so easily.

Now, despite all the strides made towards recovery, there is one change that frustrates me beyond reason at times:

I no longer have full access to Jon's body. He sleeps with me, lets me kiss him and stroke him to completion, but the moment I try for anything more, he rebuffs me—politely and respectfully done, but still a rejection. I understand that he needs to heal and that the best thing I can offer him is time and patience, but it distresses me that he no longer submits willingly. It is made worse by the fact that I know he lies with Tom in private. It is no secret kept, and they are not going behind my back, but it weighs heavily on me. Tom assures me that things will resume their course one day, and I have learned that trust is something worthy to uphold, so I bide my time and accept Tom's word. What choice do I have?

We will be arriving at the southern peninsula in a few days. The men are restless and the pleasures of the Jewel will provide them with ample divertissement in preparation for our long journey south to Madierus. I have planned to seek out the vile old woman who put such foolishness in Jon's head and—

"Da, will ye quit yer fuckin' scritch-scratchin' and come to bed?" groaned Tom from across the room.

Baltsaros looked up from his writing and saw that the candle had burned down quite a bit. The hour was later than he had thought, so wrapped up as he was in updating his neglected journal. He dropped his pen in the inkwell, and, leaving the leather-bound book open to dry, he stood with a crackling of tendons.

Tom lay on the bed on his stomach, one beefy forearm supporting his cheek while the other, still sporting a stiff bracing bandage around the wrist, rested on the mattress beside him. Other than the bandage, the first mate was completely naked. Beside him, dressed only in a pair of loose silk pants, Jon scowled at small book he held in one hand while his fingers idly played over Tom's back. The sight made Baltsaros chuckle, and Jon looked up from his book with a frown.

"What?"

"I like looking at the both of you together like this. Just... simple and comforting is all," he replied, ridding himself of his shirt.

Jon's expression softened, and he gave a tiny nod. When the captain finished unlacing the front of his pants and pulled them down, a crease appeared between Jon's dark brows, and he stared at Baltsaros a moment before shifting over.

"Put out the candle and come here," said Jon, gesturing to the space between him and the first mate.

Curious, Baltsaros snuffed the flame and crawled onto the low mattress, settling himself on his back between Tom and Jon. Though it was dark in the stateroom, the sky outside was clear; both star and moonlight made their way through the stained-glass windows above and cast the three of them in a ghostly light.

Tom rolled over onto his side and draped his bandaged arm across Baltsaros's chest as he moved closer. With a smile Jon clasped Tom's hand and bent down to press a kiss to the captain's lips. However, when Baltsaros lifted his hand to cup the back of Jon's head, Jon pulled away. Baltsaros furrowed his brow, questioning the way that Jon's eyes seemed to narrow at him, but the younger man just leaned in for another quick, almost chaste kiss before he undid the drawstring of his pants and pushed them away.

"Turn onto your side," said Jon, lying down beside Baltsaros.

The captain made to turn towards Jon, but when Jon shook his head, he realized that he had meant towards Tom. He turned over and saw Tom's grin stretch as they faced each other, and he found himself smiling back. Gently, he placed his hand on the first mate's warm side and felt the scar left behind by the stray shot that had holed him through. Slowly, he trailed his fingers up over Tom's ribs, turning the first mate's skin to gooseflesh, and settled his hand behind Tom's neck.

Tom's eyes closed at the touch, and he let out a low, appreciative noise.

Behind Baltsaros, Jon slowly stretched out with his chest to the captain's back and the knobs of his hips touching Baltsaros's buttocks.

He was astonished and intrigued when the younger man began to move against him—he registered the soft, crinkled hair at Jon's groin tickling the cleft of his buttocks only moments before he felt the firm push of Jon's cock getting hard.

Breath turned unsteady, he clasped the back of Tom's neck a little harder, wondering what Jon's intention was.

"Kiss him," whispered Jon in Baltsaros's ear, nudging his hips harder into him.

The captain frowned. His natural inclination was to refuse the softly spoken command, the third of which Jon had uttered in the last few minutes. He was all for indulging Jon's desire for a little control, but the hard cock butting against him suggested that he was aiming for more than what was reasonable.

Or *was* it unreasonable? It wasn't like Jon hadn't taken him before in the past. Once at the *Jewel*, and a second time when they first arrived in Madierus. When Tom's eyes opened and he watched the captain quietly, Baltsaros realized what it was that was bothering him about Jon's forwardness: he had never submitted to Jon in front of the first mate.

Does that matter?

"Kiss him," repeated Jon, his tone patient but firm.

Brow still creased, Baltsaros moved forward on the pillow and claimed Tom's mouth in a soft kiss. The first mate's lips were supple and warm against his for only a heartbeat before the small groan of pleasure from Tom turned Baltsaros's kiss greedy and he deepened it, his mouth wide to devour Tom's needy rumbles that urged him on. Eyes closed, he breathed into the heat of the kiss, fingers digging gently into Tom's scalp as he let out his own quiet moan. Already his cock was a thick hardness against his thigh, and he wanted to feel Tom against him. However, Jon held onto his hip, stopping him from shifting forward for contact.

He gasped in startled pain when Jon's teeth closed hard on his shoulder, and he pulled away from Tom, breathing hard. Jon slipped his arm around Baltsaros's waist and used his knee to push the captain's thighs forward a touch so that he would lay with his legs bent. He resisted for a moment, but then Jon bit him again, a little harder this time, and he relented.

Conflicted, Baltsaros let himself be moved so that Jon could rub the swollen head of his cock over the captain's sensitive opening.

Do I want this? Tom quested forward to kiss him again, and Baltsaros let the first mate's soft lips take his, passionate and slow. Jon shuddered behind him, his cock stroking over Baltsaros's pucker again, a little teasing push, then away, so slippery that the captain thought Jon must have slicked his cock with oil while he lay kissing Tom. Another pass of Jon's cockhead caused Baltsaros to push back, losing himself in the first mate's embrace, their mouths locked and tongues seeking. Yes, he did want this. If Jon needed to use him to reclaim the sense of control he had lost, so be it.

Jon finally stopped his slow tease, and he forced his cock into Baltsaros, slow and hard until his hips were flush against the captain.

When Baltsaros tensed and gave a small, pained grunt as Jon opened him up, Tom drew back, his eyes wide. His hand slid down from where it rested on Baltsaros's side to his hips. Understanding dawned on his face as he realized exactly what was happening. With a raw-sounding moan, he shifted close enough that their cocks touched and pulled the captain's leg up onto his thigh. Baltsaros's pulse soared, and he felt a surge of lust from the naked desire in Tom's eyes as the first mate held onto him while Jon fucked him slowly from behind.

Jon's teeth closed on skin again—there was no doubt in the captain's mind that he would be marked and sore, but it made him groan in encouragement. With panted grunts, Jon fucked into him faster, more frantic, and Tom and Jon's hands clawed lines of pain over his skin as he was savaged by the first mate's fevered kiss. Then Jon let out a strangled cry and buried his face into the back of the captain's neck as his thrusts went erratic, a few deep plunges followed by a series of shallow strokes that sent a sweet pulse into Baltsaros's core.

Lungs heaving, Jon lay still for only a moment before he pulled out of Baltsaros.

Hand on the captain's shoulder, he roughly turned him onto his back. Jon's eyes were dark as he leaned over him.

"It's Tom's turn now," he said quietly, his breathing ragged.

Baltsaros frowned, wondering if he had misheard.

"Jon?" said Tom. He sounded more confused than aroused.

"It's ok, Tom," said Jon, gaze locked on Baltsaros. There was power there. A challenge... and yet, affection. "He'll submit because I want him to and because he loves you. And... He loves me." He stroked the side of Baltsaros's face, lips barely moving as he spoke in a hush. "Baltsaros, I want to watch Tom take you."

Baltsaros winced and made a small sound in the back of his throat; he was so tense that a tremor went through him. He didn't know how to voice what he felt at Jon's words. Heart thundering and breathing made difficult, he hesitated only a moment longer before turning on his side. Baltsaros lay there, amazed at how easy it was to obey Jon. Without quite knowing why he did, Baltsaros realized that he completely trusted him.

"Tom, this isn't always. This is just right now," said Jon. "Just for me."

Eventually, there was a small grunt of assent from Tom, and he curled his warm body behind Baltsaros's. With a gentle hand, he carefully manoeuvred Baltsaros into a suitable position so he could penetrate him. Though he couldn't see Tom, the captain could tell how apprehensive he was.

The captain had to laugh.

"I'm not made of glass," he said, opening his eyes. Jon's cheek dimpled in the briefest of smiles.

Tom mumbled something against his skin; though he didn't catch what it was, it sounded like either a prayer or a curse.

Or, he thought with a smile, *it could be both.* However, his levity was broken a moment later when Tom's cockhead pushed hard against his opening and began to slide tight into his body.

~

Baltsaros let out a sudden sharp breath and his brow furrowed, eyes locked on Jon's. Tom had obviously found the nerve to do as he was asked and let out a soft grunt as he thrust his hips forward slowly against the captain.

A sound caught in Jon's throat, and he nodded quickly.

"That's it," he whispered. "Fuck him deep, Tom." Jon couldn't explain to himself why he needed to make them do this, only that it ate up some of the anger and shame that he was carrying around like lead in his belly. It was as if he needed to restore some of the power and control that had been ripped from him. He lifted himself up on one elbow to watch Tom and Baltsaros; the first mate's side glistened with sweat as he fucked the captain slowly with brows pinched together and eyes closed with his efforts.

Jon reached out and placed a hand on Tom's ass, coaxing him to move faster.

"This is for you, not for him," he said, and found that though he was sated, the sight of Tom ploughing into Baltsaros had his cock again at half-mast. "Gods, that's gorgeous. Don't hold back... Do you like fucking him? Do you like having your cock in his ass?"

Tom let out a small moan and fucked the captain harder, curling his arm around Baltsaros's chest possessively; though he didn't reply, he sighed a word.

"Da."

Jon touched himself, teasing the head of his cock as Tom worked himself closer using Baltsaros's body. He lay back down and saw that Baltsaros had closed his eyes.

"Don't... I want you looking at me," he said softly, kissing the older man's bottom lip. Baltsaros opened his eyes, and when Jon reached down to begin stroking the captain's cock, the hoarse groan that burst from him sounded raw. Baltsaros kept his eyes on Jon's, desire and devotion giving him an almost pained expression as he breathed heavily in time to Tom's thrusts.

Behind Baltsaros, the first mate's grunts began to be punctuated by broken, sobbing sighs, and Jon voiced a soft moan of his own.

"Don't hold back."

In response, Tom let out a growl, a deep, desperate thing that sounded like it was torn from his chest, and Baltsaros bucked hard against Jon as the first mate came inside him. Jon waited until Tom had stilled, panting loudly, before he pushed him away from the captain.

"Fuck..." panted Tom.

Jon shifted lower on the mattress and quickly took Baltsaros's cock nearly to the root into his mouth. It was only a matter of seconds before he swallowed down the captain's salty-bitter cum with Baltsaros's fingers twisting almost cruelly in his hair as he cried out in pleasure.

~

The captain cleaned up as best as he could, postponing a full bath until daylight, and returned to the bed. Tom was fast asleep, but Jon watched Baltsaros silently as he climbed around the first mate and between the sheets. He sighed at the feeling of Jon's naked skin against his as he gathered the younger man to him.

"Are you all right?" he asked quietly.

Jon laughed and nuzzled against the captain's neck.

"I was actually going to ask you the same thing," Jon replied. "And apologize if I was out of line."

"No apologies necessary," said Baltsaros with a smile. "That's not something I would like to repeat any time soon, but... I understood it." Baltsaros felt Jon tense at his word choice. He couldn't tell him that he had *enjoyed* it, because enjoyment had little to do with the complex and strangely tender emotions that the act had brought him. He stroked Jon's dark-brown curls, thinking about how to reword what he'd said when Jon spoke up.

"I'm hurt," he confessed.

For a moment, Baltsaros thought he was talking about physical pain, and he stopped his hand, startled.

"I'm hurt," repeated Jon, his voice a little rough with emotion. "I've been feeling so fucking *raw*, but I'm getting better." He sighed. "I also feel like I'm overreacting because, shit, that was nothing compared to what Tom and you have been through."

Baltsaros shook his head, tugging softly on Jon's hair.

"Rid yourself of those thoughts immediately, Jon. Take the time you need to heal and know that Tom and I will always be here for you."

"I know," whispered Jon. "And we'll live happily ever after..."

With a chuckle, Baltsaros nodded.

"Indeed we will."

The captain had thought for certain that Jon had fallen asleep as they lay entwined on the cool sheets. However, Jon lifted his head a few minutes later and peered thoughtfully at Baltsaros.

"I've been having dreams," he said, sounding hesitant. "The kind that feel, um, *important*."

Baltsaros's brows rose. It was the first time Jon had voiced anything of that nature since leaving Sormaheine.

"Oh?" he said, trying not to let his curiosity make him sound too eager lest he deter Jon from telling him of it.

Jon's forehead creased, and he turned his head away, thinking.

"Yeah. A few times a week... the same dream," he said.

"What happens in the dream?"

"We sail east," replied Jon.

"Ah," said Baltsaros. "Would you like to go east?"

With a little laugh, Jon lay his head back down, twining his fingers with the captain's.

"Maybe, but let's just spend a long, *long* fucking time doing nothing but sitting on the beach first, ok? Maybe build that shack you talked about?"

Baltsaros laughed and closed his eyes.

"That sounds perfect."

"Aye, it does," muttered Tom sleepily. "Now quit yer jawin' and let me get some bloody sleep."

Despite the annoyance in his voice, the first mate's hand crept over Baltsaros's hip, pulling himself closer, and the three remained that way, with tangled limbs and quiet hearts, as sleep finally lay claim to them.

~

END OF BOOK III

BEY DECKARD

Careened

Winter Solstice in Madierus
Baal's Heart III S

CHAPTER 1
THE PALACE

Without its legion of servants, the palace was eerily silent, and the slap of his bare feet on the marble tiles echoed as he searched the deserted rooms. A fortnight prior, Queen Abetha had taken Eloise and nearly her entire retinue with her on the voyage to Rampitoor, an island about a week's journey northeast, where they were to spend the holiday season with Lord and Lady Phakos, distant relations of hers.

Relations of his too, of course, but his mother had felt no need to extend the invitation. Not that he would have accepted anyway.

Tom scratched at the stubble along his jaw and peered through the archway. The room was empty, and no one was on the patio outside. He muttered a curse. Now, when it'd help to have a bloody servant to question, there was none to be found.

A quick movement caught his eye, and he looked up at the bright-green lizard clinging to the stones beside his head. It cocked its tiny head at him, and he smiled.

"Well, hello there, matey. Ye wouldn'a happen to see a bonny, black-haired fella pass this way?"

The lizard blinked at him; after a moment, it began to bob its head.

"Oh, ye did, did ye? And where might I find my lost love?" joked Tom. However, his guts had already told him where he'd find Jon. Again.

As if answering his question, the lizard skittered quickly across the white stones with their bright-blue inlays, going in the direction of Baltsaros's tower. Tom let out a long sigh and rubbed at his face again before following.

He soon reached the captain's old rooms and cracked the door open quietly, just as he'd done so long ago as an angry young man intent on secreting himself between his stepfather's sheets, and found the study empty. Bereft of furnishings, the room looked strange. Abandoned. The only things they had left behind were the rug in the study and the huge four-poster bed in the bedchamber. Tom toed the faded bloodstain in the middle of the rug... his blood. Smiling at the memory, he shook his head.

That was a good bloody fight.

Tom then straightened his shoulders and steeled himself for yet another dreary fucking discussion with Jon.

He pushed the door and it swung open on silent hinges. Just as he'd feared, it was dark as pitch beyond. However, it was obvious that the bed's occupant was awake; Tom heard a muffled sigh of frustration and the rustle of sheets. Carefully, he made his way to the window and tugged the curtain aside to let in some light.

Clothed only in a pair of old trousers bleached to a drab grey by sun and saltwater, Jon lay in the middle of the bed, one arm thrown over his eyes in protest to the intrusion.

"I been lookin' for ye, lovey," said Tom, sitting on the edge of the feather mattress.

"Well, you found me. Hooray," muttered Jon.

"Are ye feelin' ill?"

"No, I'm not feeling ill."

"Well, yer layin' abed, the sun well past the yardarm. Either yer ill or—"

"I'm fine. I just wanted some time by myself," said Jon, pulling his arm away to squint up at Tom. His blue-grey eyes were bloodshot, and Tom could smell old whiskey on him.

"Jon, it's a gorgeous bloody day out—"

"It's always gorgeous out."

"—and yer lyin' in here like a sad bloody bastard," Tom pointed out.

"I'm *fine*," growled Jon.

"If ye were fuckin' fine, I wouldn't fuckin' keep findin' ye in here, now would I?" The first mate let out a slow breath, trying to find his patience. "Jon... I'm just worryin' for ye, love. Can ye blame me?"

Jon closed his eyes and the creases between his brows deepened. Never a big man, the weight he had lost in the last few months had made him downright gaunt, and his face had become lined and drawn. Tom's heart squeezed in his chest, causing him to grit his teeth in frustration. It wasn't easy watching Jon go through this.

"No. I don't blame you. I'm sorry," Jon said, his voice barely above a whisper. "I'm just... I need..." He trailed off with a shrug.

"Why don't ye come with me to the *Blossom*, aye? Let's go devil Kat a bit and get ourselves good an' squiffy."

"Ugh, no. I really don't need to listen to her moan and complain again."

Tom chuckled. The women were besieged by some bit of matrimonial drama over how Maya had gotten herself in the family way. The fair barkeep had spread her legs for some mate while the crew was still at sea—something she and the missus had agreed on, seeing as they wanted a babe and couldn't manage without a pair of testicles—but Kat was sorely vexed that she'd been plum left out of the act. Worse, Maya was keeping the name of the prick-for-hire secret, for fear that Kat would blow a hole in the man's head should she confront him.

Some thought the babe would be born with a head of ginger curls, considering how much time Maya spent with her bar-boy Wenz. However, Tom had made a wager on the blacksmith being the father, since Doug and his wife Janie were so fond of bringing extra fillies into their stable, so to speak.

"Ok... well... Then let's go for a swim? We could go to them flat rocks out past the shipwrecks, and ye could get me on my hands and knees in the sun... Unless, of course, ye'd like to sit on my co—"

"I'm not in the mood."

"Yer never in the bloody mood!" protested Tom, his restraint finally starting to wear out.

"You'll just have to wait until *he* gets back, if you're in such a damn hurry to fuck." Jon turned away from Tom, effectively ending the conversation. Tom snorted in irritation.

Everything had seemed like it was going to be all right at first. *Baal's Heart* had made good time back to Madierus, and the three of them had set to work right away renovating the temporary builder's barracks into something they had called *Triskele Manor*—a place for them to live happily ever after together. A silly notion, but Tom had been powerfully optimistic when they first arrived back on the tiny tropical island they called home. Things between the captain, Jon, and himself had become a little odd, yes, with Jon sometimes forcing Baltsaros to submit to either Tom or himself, though *forcing* honestly wasn't the right word... more like Baltsaros was willingly paying penance for what had happened in Sormaheine, but then Jon started acting peculiar.

The first thing Tom had noticed was Jon's lack of appetite for anything he couldn't drink out of a bottle. It didn't concern him too much in the beginning, seeing as he himself was prone to overindulgence to chase away demons, but when it only grew worse over the course of a month, Tom began to worry.

Then there were Jon's vanishing acts. They'd be lying in bed, still sweat-slick and buzzing with contentment, when the lad would excuse himself to take a piss. Tom would wake an hour or two later with the spot next to him still empty, and he and Baltsaros would rouse themselves to go searching for their wayward companion. Most nights Jon would be at the *Blossom*, sitting alone on the back patio or sometimes on the pitch-dark beach below, eyes turned out to sea; initially, it took only a tiny bit of coaxing and the promise of a private cuddle with Tom to get him to return, but soon they found themselves giving up on their search when he couldn't be found at his normal haunts anymore. It was Tom who had discovered Jon's habit of sneaking into Baltsaros's old rooms at the palace.

It was just nights at the beginning, but Jon's disappearances began bleeding into days. On top of losing weight he couldn't afford to, he was often distracted or became easily angered when he wasn't completely lethargic and just going through the motions. Tom couldn't remember the last time he'd seen Jon truly smile.

Finally, about a fortnight earlier, Jon had stopped calling Baltsaros by name, referring to the captain only as *he* or *him*. Despite the fact that Baltsaros was a right blind bugger when it came to knowing what was going through Jon's head, he'd gained enough common sense to step back and let Tom handle it. The captain had sailed off with some of the crew to careen *Baal's Heart* in the shallower waters on the other side of the island. Scraping the old ship's bottom would take until tomorrow at the least. She had a thick coat of barnacles and molluscs on her futtocks slowing her down, and when they were done with her, *Baal's Heart* would be a faster ship for all the hard work—not good as new, but as good as she could be.

If only there were a way of doing the same sort of thing for Jon, like a careening of the soul, but so far Tom was having no luck bringing him out of his shell.

With a sigh, he reached for Jon, just hoping to pull him into his arms to comfort him, but Jon visibly flinched at his touch and pulled away further. Two things happened in Tom's head at that moment. The first was that he felt gravely hurt by the blatant rejection—enough that his breath caught in his throat, nearly choking him. The second was a knee-jerk reaction to that pain: he roughly yanked on Jon's arm to turn him back around, angry that Jon was overreacting to something that Tom had long ago learned to deal with. It was completely unfair of him, and Tom knew it, but he couldn't stop the bilge from spewing out.

"Stop actin' like yer arse was made of gilded porcelain," he growled, though he could feel tears threatening. "Yer not the first fuckin' man to be buggered without his say-so, ye know. Yer bein' a bloody coward—"

Fury flashed in Jon's blue eyes, the first spirited reaction Tom had seen in some time, and he sat up and grabbed Tom by the jaw, his teeth bared as he stared hard at the first mate.

"You tell me to 'get over it,' and so help me gods, I will never let you touch me again, you thick fucking bastard," growled Jon, so pissed off he was shaking.

Tom grabbed at Jon's wrist, but Jon surprised him with a head-butt straight to the nose. Pain exploded in Tom's head, followed by a fount of blood, but he grappled at Jon, trying to pin him down despite being barely able to see. Beneath him, Jon fought like a trapped rat, raking at him with dirty, ragged nails and biting any part of Tom that was within reach.

"I think you fucking *liked* it, you fucking masochist. You loved being held down by those fucking monsters and"—Jon's voice broke, and he gagged and coughed like he was going to be sick before resuming his struggles against Tom's bulk—"and getting ploughed by their filthy fucking cocks. Captain's been raping you for years... I bet you couldn't tell the fucking difference!" Jon's face was wet with tears as he whipped his head back and forth, letting out a low wail of frustration at being restrained. Tom pushed Jon down into the mattress, hands locked around his wrists, panting from exertion and heartbroken from the malice and raw torment pouring out of the stricken man. No longer angry or impatient, and aghast at himself for being either, Tom just held on as Jon began to shriek and buck his hips, trying to get free.

They'd often wrestled—mock fights, sometimes with a slight undercurrent of real anger—but nothing resembling *this*. There wasn't anything playful about Jon's desperate need to get away from him. For a second, Tom thought about letting him go, just letting Jon run off somewhere to lick his wounds, so he could try to reason with him again another day; but instead, he stretched his body out on top of Jon's and wrapped his arms around him, letting Jon pummel at his back with fists and elbows, his heels battering the backs of his legs. Burying his face in the side of Jon's neck, Tom just kissed him and murmured to him softly.

"I love ye. Jon, do ye hear me? Do you? I bloody love ye. I'm sorry for any shite I said just now. Wasn't thinkin'. I *am* a fuckin' bastard. Yer right. Yer bloody right. And yer breakin' my heart, Jon. I love ye. I love ye so much it scares me. Bloody hells, love. It *scares* me. Bein' without ye. I can't even think about it. Fuck, if I could, I'd take every hurt done to ye so ye didn't have to. If I could kill those fuckers again, I'd do it slower than hells. I just love ye so much, Jon. With all my bloody heart." Tom knew the tears in his eyes weren't solely from the hit to his nose, and he held onto Jon like his life depended on it.

Finally, Jon stopped trying to fight him, and when Tom rolled off, he didn't try to flee. Instead, Jon curled up against Tom and sobbed against his bare chest, his whole body shuddering so hard Tom could hear Jon's teeth clack together.

Wiping at his own eyes with the heel of his hand, Tom silently recited the names of all the knots he knew in alphabetical order, afraid he'd start bawling like a babe himself before too long: *becket bend, bight, blackwall hitch, boat knot, bowknot, bowline, chain knot and toggle, cat's-paw...*

"I'm suh-sorry, Tuh-Tom," stuttered Jon between hitched gulps of air when his sobs began to weaken. His fingers dug into Tom's skin and his breath was sour, but Tom wouldn't dream of complaining. He kissed Jon's forehead and then his cheekbone, Jon's tears salty on his lips.

"Aye, it's ok, love. It's ok. Hush hush. It's all right. Yer safe with me, love," rumbled Tom, reminded of the time he'd had to hold Jon like this as they made their passage through the Devil's Isles, Jon wounded and terrified, his brain on fire from the spores he'd inhaled.

"But... gods, Tom. It's not all right. It's never going to be all right," Jon said in a choked voice and started weeping a little harder again. "I dream of them. Every night. Every fucking night, they come for me. Every night, I have to feel them—Gods, *how do you do it?* How do you live with it?"

Tom closed his eyes, his heart beating too fast for a moment. How *did* he live with it?

"A day at a time, ducky," he replied. Too many faces to count, not including the ones he had never seen. Taken in the dark. Hurt. Made to submit. Over and over. But that was the past, and the past was over.

"You're a stronger man than I am," Jon whispered against Tom's neck.

Now Tom really *was* going to start bawling. He shook his head quickly.

"Don't know," Tom confessed in a hoarse voice. "Is it stronger to face it or stronger to bury it?" He cleared his throat, swallowed hard, and forced himself to breathe slower.

"I love you," Jon said softly. He drew his head back, and when Tom opened his eyes, he saw that Jon's face was blotchy from crying, but some of the desperation had lifted. At least for the moment. "I never want you to be scared."

Tom cracked a small smile, and he threaded his fingers through Jon's dark-brown mop of hair, long overdue for a washing but soft still against his callused skin.

"I was terrified the day ye really kissed me," he said. "The heavens in a fury, and the sea threatenin' to send us to our doom... You were the only thing I was scared of, lad."

Jon's eyes brimmed over with tears again for a moment, but he dashed them away and laughed.

"You know, I feel like that was the first time in my life that I'd taken matters into my own hands. Everything else just... I just let happen to me. Kissing you, you gorgeous bloody scoundrel, that was me choosing my fate."

"I'm a bloody scoundrel now, am I?" said Tom with a grin.

Chuckling softly, Jon nodded and then sniffed hard, his expression sobering. He rested his head back down so that his cheek rested on Tom's collarbone. Tom could feel Jon's breath warm against his throat.

"I'm sorry—no, let me finish," said Jon when Tom tried to interrupt him. "I'm sorry I haven't been able to just get over what happened. I wish I could. Gods, I wish it was as easy as taking it out on you and... *him*, and honestly, I thought it was working. I thought I was getting better, but maybe it's just that I was so busy that I didn't have time to really face what had happened. And then..." Jon shook his head. Tom thought he could feel Jon's heart thumping hard against him, but it might have been his own pulse battering his ribs. "Then there was less and less to do and less to occupy my mind. That's when the dreams started..."

"Mm," grunted Tom with a little nod, waiting for Jon to finish. Dreams were a real goddamn bitch. When Jon stayed silent, he tried prompting him. "What about Da? Yer feelin's soured on him, and he knows it. He's worried about ye."

"I know. I can't help it. I just need... Fuck, I keep wanting to say 'I need more time,' but what if it isn't that? You've given me loads of time, and it's not making things any better. And what do I do with my time? I drink until I can't see straight, and then I pass out. But when I wake up, my head is so fucking messed up, all I do is lie here and cry my eyes out until I pass out again. I barely have the energy to get out of bed, let alone pretend that I don't feel like I'm shrivelling up inside."

Tom could hear in Jon's voice that he had started crying again, and he heaved a gentle sigh, stroking Jon's back and wishing that he could do something. Anything to make things a little better for him.

"The worst... and why I haven't been able to look at hi—at Baltsaros in the eye is that he's in league with the men in my dreams."

"Yea gods, Jon," muttered Tom with a pained frown. "Never. He'd *never*."

"I know that. I do. I just need more—" Jon broke off, sounding frustrated.

"*Time*. Aye, lad. And time ye'll get. We'll find a way... But ye gotta do one thing for me," said Tom.

"What's that?"

"Keep talkin'," answered the first mate with a tiny shrug. "Talk to me. Talk to Da. Hells, talk to Kat. Gods know, she needs to get her head out of her arse and think about somethin' else than that damn baby. She's yer friend, aye? Keep talkin' and dont'cha bottle it up, love. Don't leave us all in the bloody dark until we're all in a fret over what's vexin' ye."

"Ok. I promise."

Tom smiled and gave Jon a squeeze. Disturbed by how thin Jon's skin felt and how knobby his spine was, Tom added a little growl to his next words: "And bloody eat somethin'!"

Jon let out a weak-sounding laugh, but he nodded.

"I'll try."

CHAPTER 2

THE GROG BLOSSOM

Jon sat up and wrapped his arms around himself. The dream had come back, even while he was sleeping safe in Tom's embrace. He looked around quickly but then scrubbed at his face in frustration when he realized what he'd been searching for: the bottle of whiskey. Jon knew it was under the bed, half-empty. He'd heard it roll under there when he'd had his fill—before he'd passed out and been awoken by Tom's searching him out.

Slowly, he lay back down and lifted Tom's beefy arm to drape it back over his waist; it sounded like the first mate muttered *thank you* in his sleep, but it could have as easily been something more crass.

Jon felt embarrassed over how he'd acted earlier. It was like there was a sickness in his head making him think he *should* feel embarrassed for not being able to get past what had happened to him in Sormaheine. But he didn't want to be lying in Tom's arms, deeply ashamed over the tears he'd wept... He wanted to heal, but he didn't know how.

Closing his eyes, Jon tried to clear away the tattered fragments of the dream that still clung to him and made him wish for the comfort of the whiskey bottle.

On his hands and knees in the cold, dusty crypt. The way the old bone fragments had dug into his palms. The smell of alcohol on the men's breath...

Don't think about it.

"Jon?" Tom mumbled. "Ye all right, love?"

Jon opened his eyes. "Yeah," he lied.

"Then... Will ye stop tryin' to crush my arm?" said the first mate quietly.

Looking down, Jon saw that he had both hands wrapped around the big man's forearm and the skin was red from where he'd been digging his fingers into it. He let go quickly.

"Sorry."

" 'Sall right, pet," said Tom, patting his hand. "No harm done. I'm made of tougher stuff."

"You are," Jon sighed.

The late-afternoon sun had just kissed the edge of the volcano's crater by the time Jon and Tom left the deserted palace. Passing the wide-bottomed flagon of whiskey between them, they made their way down the steep, cobbled road that turned into the main street of town. Near the coral-rock stairs leading down to the beach, they found Katherine lugging some boxes out of an old ramshackle shed. The one-armed pirate cursed when the boxes shifted in her grasp, and she tried to steady them with her wooden prosthetic before kicking the door of the shed closed.

"Need a hand?" asked the first mate with a chuckle. What he got in return was a look of pure contempt.

"Go shove a dick in that gaping cunt you call a mouth, you bilge-sucking cockhound," snapped Kat.

Tom's sandy brows shot up, and he blinked in astonishment, but to Jon's keen senses, the big man was nothing if not impressed by the profanity. With a grin, he held out his arms.

"Oh, hey, Jon," said Kat, noticing him. Despite her outburst, she happily handed over the boxes to Tom and then stretched her back with a grimace. "Fucking hells."

"Where d'ye want these, ye bleedin' trollop?" asked Tom sweetly.

"Around front," said Kat, pointing to the tavern next door, "but bring that big one right through to the patio, you scabby whore."

Tom nodded and hefted the boxes to the *Blossom* with the others following.

"What are those?" Jon asked.

"Yule decorations," grumbled Kat. "Maya wants them up by end of day."

"Yule?"

"You know. Winter Solstice. Bells and snowflakes and shit. Red and gold streamers. Didn't you have Yule back home?"

"We called it Winter Mass," said Jon with a nod. "Reginald wasn't big on holiday cheer. Thought it was too pagan. But, when I was little, my mom used to hang star garlands around the keep, and on the eve of Mass, I'd hang a stocking at the end of my bed. The next morning it was filled with gifts and sweets."

Kat smiled and thumped him on the shoulder before snatching the bottle of whiskey out of his hand. She helped herself to the last gulp, dumped the empty flagon on the shiny bar, and stopped to fish around in an open crate overfilled with packing hay. She found what she was looking for and lifted out a deep-red bottle with a thick black cap of sealing wax.

"Ah, there you are," she said. Then, as Tom bent over to drop the big box on the patio overlooking the bay, she reached over and filched the long knife from his belt.

"Bloody thief," growled the first mate but he wore an easy grin. "Get yer own damn knife."

"You call this itty bitty thing a knife?" said Kat, slicing quickly through the wax as she walked back to the bar. "Big man like you... I figured you'd have something a little, you know, more manly..."

Tom grabbed the red bottle out of her hand as soon as the wax fell free, and he tugged out the cork with his teeth. He took a big gulp from the bottle, swallowed, and then immediately began to cough. Wiping at his mouth with the back of his hand, he laughed, and Jon could see tears in his blue-green eyes. Tom held out the bottle to check the label and whistled.

"Hooboy. Pepper brandy? Where in the black hells did ye get a bottle of fuckin' pepper brandy?"

"Smuggler by the name of Galut."

"Shite... Ye know Galut? How is the old bastard?" said Tom, taking another swig from the bottle and following it up with more coughing. He offered the brandy to Jon, but Jon just shook his head quickly. If the first mate could down something as vile and caustic as Dragon's Milk without so much as an eye twitch, this pepper brandy would surely kill Jon.

Kat just rolled her eyes and took the bottle from Tom.

"C'mon, kiddo, it'll put hair on yer chest," she teased and then took a pull from the bottle. She let out a harsh breath and shuddered, licking her lips. "Damn, that's something, ain't it?" She handed the brandy back to Tom. "Galut? Galut's good. Got himself another wife. Tiny little thing with tits out to here." Kat held her hands far out in front of her with a crooked grin.

"What's that? His fifth?" laughed Tom. "Tell me she's older than the last one..."

Meanwhile, Jon slipped behind the bar to find himself a beer mug. As he straightened, he heard someone clear their throat, and he froze.

"What in the world is going on?" asked Maya. Though her voice was calm, there was an unmistakable edge to it. "When did it become self-serve here?" Jon cringed and turned, handing the mug to Maya.

"It's not like the place is packed, sweetie," said Kat, gesturing to the *Grog Blossom*'s empty main room with her wooden hand. She flinched when Maya took the pepper brandy out of her grasp and recorked it.

"Where are my decorations?" asked Maya, her big blue eyes remarkably steely. With a deft hand, she pulled a pint of brown from the open cask and set it down in front of Jon without looking at him.

"I was just getting to it, love. The lads came to lend a hand," replied Kat, her tone gentle. "See?" Her smile was full of teeth, but her expression was pleading.

Maya snorted, and then she turned to Jon as Kat and Tom hurriedly began prying open the bigger box.

"Wow," she said, not bothering to hide her surprise. "You look like shit."

"Thanks," he muttered. He scratched at his untidy beard and then shrugged. "I feel it."

"Well… Why don't you come by later? We're going to be serving some chicken pot pie. With green peas, just like you like it," she said. "You could use an extra helping, Jon. Two, even." She gave him a soft smile and squeezed his arm before heading back to the apartments at the rear of the tavern. "Now, if you'll excuse me, I have some more throwing up to do."

No one spoke a word for a few seconds. Then, when the coast was clear, Tom sniggered.

"Yer bloody whipped, aint'cha?" he said, smacking Kat on the arm. "What happened to *you* being the one sore about the big *fat* cock she took deep in her cunn—uufffhhh!" Tom doubled over, trying to catch his breath from the hard punch Kat had delivered to his diaphragm.

Kat clenched and unclenched her fist, shaking her head. She looked dazed, staring at the doorway where Maya had disappeared.

"One second I'm the one who's doing the yelling and then… It all got turned around… And I somehow wound up in the doghouse," she said faintly. "I… don't even know." A real smile slowly spread across her fine features, lighting up her warm brown eyes. "But… fuck… We're having a baby. Gods. *Me*… with a godsdamned baby."

"To godsdamned babies," wheezed Tom.

"To babies," agreed Kat with a laugh. She pulled the cork out of the bottle of brandy again and took a swig before passing it to Tom. Then the two pirates set about hanging garlands and pasting paper snowflakes on the driftwood walls of the tavern.

"I'll give you a hand," said Jon, setting down his mug. If for nothing else, helping out would give him something to occupy his mind with.

CHAPTER 3
TRISKELE MANOR

Jon heaved a long sigh, rocking his head back and forth on the pillow, Tom's dirty-blond hair clutched in one hand, the heel of the other pressed over his eyes. With a strangled groan, he pumped his hips a little, wanting Tom to pick up the pace. Obediently, Tom began to swallow down Jon's length a touch faster, his hot mouth a swirling, sucking, glorious embrace that took him fully to the root with every plunge.

The pleasure that had begun with soft touches and gentle caresses was swelling to a heady, throbbing, almost aching *need* with the first mate's skilful treatment of his cock; Jon sighed again deeply, honestly happy that he'd let Tom coax him into bed. Suddenly, Tom let Jon's cock slip out from between his lips, and Jon lifted his head with a sorrowful whimper. When he saw that Tom had just paused to lick his finger, he let out a shaky laugh. Tom's grin stretched wide, and he kept his eyes on Jon's as he slid his finger inside him, quickly finding the spot that drove Jon absolutely crazy.

"Fuck," Jon choked out and dropped his head back down on the pillow as Tom lowered his mouth over his length again, tongue slick and warm, lips tight. It was like his cock was being stroked from both sides, and the surge of ecstasy crested so quickly and violently that Jon's cry sounded surprised as he sent the first hot gush of cum down Tom's throat, his head held tight by Jon's grasping hands.

With a last quiet groan, he lay there, panting and sweaty as Tom lapped at his spent cock, cleaning him gently. When the first mate prodded at the sensitive opening of his glans, as if seeking to lick out any remaining drops of cum, Jon began to squirm and pushed Tom's head away.

"Enough!" he laughed and then stroked the side of Tom's sun-bronzed face, shaking his head. The first mate gazed at him, his blue-green eyes crinkled at the corners and mouth twisted in a wry grin.

Jon frowned, noticing for the first time the state of the big man's face.

"I know *this* is my fault," said Jon, gingerly touching Tom's sore nose. He then touched a healing cut on Tom's forehead before running his fingers along the strong, stubbled jaw to the greening bruise on his chin. "But what about these? My fault too?"

"Naw, lovey," rumbled Tom, but he ducked his head to kiss Jon's hip bone in an obvious attempt to hide his expression. "Just a little misunderstandin' with the boys..."

"You've been worried about me, so you got into a fight," murmured Jon, running his fingers through the first mate's straw-coloured hair.

Tom just mumbled something noncommittal against Jon's skin and shrugged.

"Come here," said Jon, and Tom crawled further up the bed, gladly burrowing into Jon's open embrace. "I'll get through this. Promise."

"Ye will." Tom's gravelly baritone had a skeptical edge, but before Jon could try to assuage him, the sound of the lookout's horn came in through the open window. When another two quick blasts followed it, signalling the approach of a friendly vessel, Tom sat up. Abetha and Eloise weren't expected for another three weeks, and *Black's Saber* had come and gone only a month ago, so there was only one ship it could be.

"Da's back?" asked Tom, his expression hopeful.

Jon slid off the bed and walked barefoot to the window facing the bay. *Baal's Heart* was just passing the land bridge, her sails already furled. He nodded, wishing he shared the first mate's enthusiasm. There had to be something Jon could do to stop this unrelenting descent into the colourless, suffocating depths of depression. Rubbing a hand over the top of his head, Jon watched the *Heart* approach and, repelled by how dirty his hair felt, decided that a bath would be a fine place to start.

~

Baltsaros walked through the front doors of *Triskele Manor* and threw his bags down in the vestibule.

Home—well, as much as anywhere on land could be, anyway. It was something he had built with his boys, and he was proud of it. For a moment he thought that no one was home, but when he heard Tom's familiar light footfall on the wooden staircase, he smiled.

"Yer back!" said the first mate, after eschewing the last bend of the staircase to simply jump down to the sand-scoured birch floor below. Shirtless, bruised, and wearing a cheeky grin, Tom was a welcome sight.

Baltsaros relished the little flutter he felt in his breast at the brawny young man's appearance, recognizing it for what it was: affection. He reached out and wrapped his hand around the back of Tom's neck to bring him in for a soft kiss, noting Jon's unmistakable scent on the first mate's lips. He pulled back and searched the wide, ocean-coloured eyes.

"Is he any better?" the captain asked quietly.

"Not sure," admitted Tom, his expression sobering. "Found him in yer old rooms again this morn."

"Ah." Baltsaros shook his head and looked up at the ceiling. "Where is he now?"

"Washin' up."

"Well, that's something, right?" replied the captain with a tight smile.

The first mate nodded. "So... How'd it go? Ye managed ok without me?"

"Better than I had hoped," said Baltsaros, crossing the room. He sat down in the big overstuffed chair that had once graced his study at the palace and began tugging off his high boots; quickly Tom sank to his haunches in front of the captain and took over from him, pulling off the boots with a grunt. "Found a few rotten boards in the process, but we replaced them without a problem. We also discovered that we've been dragging a piece of fishing net. Not sure when we picked that up—probably quite a while ago, judging from how enmeshed it was with the barnacles and growths we've accumulated since we last tipped the *Heart* for cleaning. All in all, however, it wasn't as taxing as all that." He looked down at his hand where he'd managed to slice his palm. "Though a touch dangerous, perhaps."

Tom smirked and kissed the shallow cut. "Could be yer out of practice," he teased.

A creak startled Baltsaros out of the moment just as he was considering showing Tom what he'd found in his chest aboard ship; he looked up to see Jon standing still as a statue at the foot of the stairs.

The young man's long, dark curls hung past his shoulder, still dripping from his bath. He'd trimmed his beard down until it was little more than stubble, and it did almost nothing to hide the gauntness of his cheeks. Baltsaros felt almost wounded by the sight of Jon's thin paleness—it was as if Jon had become a mere ghost of himself. The black hells were too good for the men who had caused him so much pain. When Baltsaros met Jon's eyes, he saw what he assumed was fear in their storm-grey depths, and suppressing his desire to shake some sense into him, Baltsaros only nodded in greeting.

"Welcome back," said Jon with forced warmth.

Baltsaros turned his gaze back to Tom with a sigh. The first mate smiled a little wanly.

"Thank you, Jon," said the captain, deeply dismayed by the lack of change.

What can I do to make you come back to me?

~

Tom dumped the captain's dirty clothes into a woven basket to be taken to the launderer the next day and gave the man's boots a quick one-over with a brush before setting them down neatly beside Jon's on the back porch. He eyed Jon, sitting on a low divan with a big book of maps open on his thighs, reading by lantern light.

"D'ye need anythin'?" he asked.

Jon just shook his head, flipped a page, and took a sip from the small flask of rum at his side. Tom nodded to himself while cursing under his breath at the lad's moroseness and jogged up the steps two at a time. At the top of the stairs, he pushed open the door to the washroom and sank down onto his knees next to the big copper tub where Baltsaros lay soaking in honey-scented water, head back and eyes closed. Without a word, he reached over the rim and fished in the warm water until he had the captain's limp cock in hand. Experimentally, he gave it a squeeze. Baltsaros's lips curled into a smile, and he gave a tiny nod, his eyes slipping open for only a moment before settling himself back down.

Tom stroked his fingers along the soft shaft, coaxing it to grow and harden in his grasp. Slowly, it filled his palm, and the thin foreskin stretched open to allow the swelling roundness of the captain's cockhead to emerge. Tom brushed his thumb over the glans, spreading out the slick drop of precum, distinct from the water surrounding it, and felt his own cock surge in response.

"Mmm, my tomcat," was all that Baltsaros said, obviously happy to let Tom do all the work. Tom stroked the thick, curved cock, increasing the speed of his squeezing grip until finally Baltsaros made a harsh noise in the back of his throat. The captain sat up and pushed Tom away, rising to his feet. Staring down at Tom, Baltsaros grimaced and let out a small grunt from between his clenched teeth. "Open up," he said, his voice rough.

Tom opened his mouth wide just as a volley of warm seed hit him in the face. It dripped down onto his tongue, but he kept himself from swallowing it until Baltsaros had squeezed out his last spurt and stood panting and empty. Carefully, the captain lowered himself into the water and lay back again with a contented sigh.

Tom wiped his hand over his face and tightened the other around the root of his own aching cock.

"What do we do about Jon?" asked the captain after a moment. He lifted his head, his dark eyes full of genuine sorrow. "Will we ever get him back?"

Settling down onto the floor cross-legged, Tom pulled his hand out of his pants and lifted his shoulders. It didn't look as if he'd get any relief today after all.

"Aye. He's just havin' a turn, Da. Earlier today, we were payin' a visit to the girls at the *Blossom*, doin' up the ol' place in Yule wreaths and baubles, and Jon lost a bit o' that look he's taken on lately. Smiled. Laughed. We told some tales... ye know, holiday stories. Seemed like his old self for a bit," said Tom, rubbing the side of his thumb along his jaw, pondering the idea that had come to him earlier. "I was thinkin'... what I were to surprise him? Do a little decoratin' of yer old rooms up at the palace and make it special-like. Give Jon a gift... Ye think he'd like it?"

Baltsaros tilted his head a tiny bit, his high forehead wrinkling as he appraised Tom. For a second, Tom couldn't tell whether the captain was pleased with the idea or not—Baltsaros's expression took on an odd cast for a second. But then he gave a nod and smiled.

"I think that's a fine idea, Tom. Maybe it'll cheer him up a little."

Tom grinned, happy with the plan coming together in his head. He could ask Maya for some of the decorations she wasn't using. Maybe get Jon the blue waistcoat that

Polly-Meg had sitting in the window of her little dressing shop. He was sure the old broad would trade it for the last share of his rum.

Aye. It was a mighty fine idea.

~

Jon sat up on the second-floor balcony, nursing his hangover with a cup of strong black coffee and watching Tom and the crew replace the sails on the *Heart*'s foremast. Though he couldn't hear what was being said, the way Tom barked and bellowed made him smile. The first mate was no doubt threatening the lot of them with a hanging or whipping should they make a misstep.

At a soft knock, Jon looked up. The captain stood at the entrance to their bedchamber, his knuckle still poised near the wooden doorjamb. His hair was neatly tied back with a leather thong, and he was shirtless, wearing only a pair of faded black linen pants turned up at the knee.

"May I join you?" asked Baltsaros with a restrained smile.

Jon just nodded and shifted over to make room for the captain on the wicker bench.

"Did you sleep well?" The captain and Tom had shared the huge bed, but Jon had retired to the room adjacent.

Nodding again, Jon took a small sip of coffee. After a moment he sighed.

"I don't blame you for anything," he said quietly. He glanced over at the captain, but Baltsaros's brow was furrowed, and his eyes were on the ship anchored in the bay. However, Jon's gift told him that all of the older man's senses were trained on him, anxious for his words. "Well, not *actively*. I just have to find a way of... turning my mind. I'm confident it'll happen, but it's just very hard for me at the moment when my dreams paint you in the worst light."

Baltsaros inclined his chin slightly, acknowledging Jon's words but not seeking to interrupt him. Jon drank some more coffee and, as a token of his desire to see things return to what could be considered *normal* between the two of them, held out the cup to the captain.

Baltsaros blinked in surprise and took the offering, turning his deep-brown eyes to Jon's. Wordlessly, he drank and handed the mug back.

"Thank you."

"You're welcome," said Jon, trying on a smile. The captain's expression mirrored his, and as Jon thought about the first time he'd kissed those curved lips, his own grin relaxed into something more natural. "Yeah, I promise everything will be ok. I'm working on it. Right now, I think what I need is a diversion... And I might have come up with an idea."

"What is it?"

"Well," Jon said, turning back to the ship. He could see Tom about halfway up the mast, gesturing to someone above him. His broad back was a deep golden-brown, distance effectively blurring the horrific scars that covered it. "Yesterday, we were putting up holiday decorations at the tavern with Kat. You should have seen Tom's face... He has so few good childhood memories, and Winter Mass... or Yule... or Winter Solstice, or whatever you call it, is obviously one of them. He talked about a tree with bright glass balls hanging in it and colourful candles and strings of beads hanging all around. It wasn't Abetha's doing—he says it was the servants who spoiled him—but even so... What if we did something like that? I've been neglecting the hells out of him lately, and I thought it might be nice, you know... to share in a celebration?"

Jon looked over at the captain and saw that Baltsaros was watching him with a guarded expression.

"Didn't you have some sort of winter holiday in Sormaheine?" he asked.

Baltsaros's eyes narrowed a touch, and Jon wondered whether asking him about his childhood was such a great idea, seeing as he spent most of it an orphan or worse, under Romas's care. However, the captain just smiled.

"Yes. We call it Winter Dark, or Corestmas. In fact, it's the most important holiday of the year. We celebrate it on the longest night of the year, a night lasting a full five days in Sormaheine," said Baltsaros, his expression distant. "It's about surviving through the darkness together..." He glanced at Jon, then looked back out across the bay, clearing his throat before he continued. "It was our tradition to light candles, sing, and exchange presents. I remember it fondly... It was lovely."

Moved by the subtle emotion in the captain's voice, Jon reached for his large, sun-darkened hand and clasped it in his own. The three of them were such broken things. They truly needed one another; Jon made a silent vow to Baltsaros and Tom that he'd find his strength again. Like Tom said: one day at a time.

The captain squeezed Jon's fingers gently as Jon told him about the sweet cheroots he would trade Malik his last share of rum for and about borrowing some glass balls from Maya so he could decorate a tree for Tom.

CHAPTER 4

HAPPY HOLIDAYS

Tom stepped back and squinted at his handiwork. He'd braided together some green twine and strung paper spirals from it. However, the spirals were just plain white and they hung sort of funny from the homespun garland tacked up on the wall. At least it was more festive than the other thing he'd tried; all around the room, he'd placed cuttings from a spiky bush that grew everywhere in the island, but they didn't smell much like the pine boughs they'd used to decorate his childhood home in the northern mainlands. Sucking on his teeth for a moment, he contemplated asking Maya again for some stars. He shook his head. It pissed him off that Maya'd been so fucking stingy with her baubles and paper snowflakes. He'd seen a whole slew of papery and sparkly things left over in the crate after they'd finished their decorating.

No matter... It still looked nice enough, he figured. He hammered another nail into the wall above the braided twine and draped a second handmade garland above the first.

"There," he said with a firm nod. "That'll do." He glanced around, feeling a little deflated at the state of his holiday decorations. The captain's old study was set up with some furniture he'd scavenged, but they were mismatched, and he had no idea whether he should go find some different ones or if Jon would even care. Tom gave a long sigh.

Poor Jon. Someone had already bought the pretty blue waistcoat out from under Tom, and since the old biddy couldn't even remember who had taken it, Tom had no way to get it back. Instead, Tom had traded the last of his rum for an old brass telescope and three bottles of pale rose wine that he thought Jon would like.

"Aye. That'll do," he mumbled again, shaking his head. He took another look at his slapdash decorations and left the room, trying not to let his disappointment get the best of him. It was the thought that counted, and Jon would see that... Surely, he would. Now, he just had to think of a way to get Jon up to the tower without making him suspicious. He really wanted it to be a surprise.

~

Jon stared miserably at the tiny tree in the pot, a few large colourful glass beads hanging from its droopy branches.

"I don't know," he said to Kat. "It doesn't look right."

"It's a tree with balls in it," argued the one-handed pirate peevishly. "What the hell else is it supposed to look like?"

"I don't know," Jon repeated. "Bigger? And the leaves are all wrong. Ugh... Why did I think this was a good idea? Tom's just going to take one look and bust a gut laughing."

"Well... What did you expect? We're on a tropical island. Pines and firs are a little scarce, you know?"

Jon knew Kat was doing her best to help, but Maya had been up half the night because of bad heartburn, and Kat hadn't slept much. Just as he was wondering if he should ask the pirate to climb up into the attic again to look for a bigger pot, Kat yawned and blinked at him, her eyes red.

"Yeah, ok," Jon said, resigned. "It'll do. It's fine, really. Thanks for your help."

"Any time, kiddo," Kat replied.

Maya emerged from the back with a tray of fine glasses between her hands. She was only a few months along in her pregnancy, but Jon thought she already seemed a little plumper. It suited her.

"Hello, Jon," she said, setting down the glasses. Kat swung herself over the bar to help Maya put them away on the shelves above. "What are you doing?"

"I had the stupid idea of trying to do something nice for Tom... I wanted to make a holiday tree like he had when he was little. Before he was—well, when he still living in the mainlands."

Maya nodded, looking at the sad little bush in the pot.

"I'm sure he'll love it," she said in her quiet voice.

Jon heaved a sigh. "I don't know. It's gone all wrong. I wanted to get him something special, a gift... But I went to see Malik, and he wouldn't trade me for those fucking cigars he won from Dakka at the *Jewel*. So now I have nothing to give him except for this stupid tree that's not even a tree. *Fuck*." He put his head down on his arms and closed his eyes, wanting to crawl away and lock himself up in the captain's old rooms. Maya's fingers ruffled his hair, and he heard a smile tinge her voice when she spoke.

"It will be just fine, Jon. I'll bet you a bottle of spiced rum that Tom will be thrilled that you're taking the time to make something for him. He's definitely one for heartfelt gestures. He's been missing you like crazy, and I daresay that your project's pulled you out of your slump a little."

Jon lifted his head and stared at Maya.

"When did you talk to Tom? I thought you didn't like him."

Maya's big blue eyes widened, and she let out a short, nervous-sounding laugh as she wiped at an invisible spot on the pristine bar with her rag.

"Well. I never said *that*. I said he was trouble. And... seeing what he did for my Kat... making her that hand. And... well"—Maya shrugged and turned to adjust the glasses that Kat was placing in already straight lines—"he seems like the sort who might like surprises. But that's only a guess. I don't know anything about him." Maya smiled awkwardly, wiped her hands on her apron, and perked up at the sound of a high-pitched whistle coming from the other room. "Oh! There's the kettle... I'll see you tonight, Jon."

Jon and Kat looked at each other.

"What's gotten into her?" asked Kat, her eyebrows high.

"She's keeping a secret," said Jon, looking down at the little tree he'd decorated, "and I have a feeling that I know what it's about."

"Yeah?"

"I think Tom's planning on surprising me with something," he muttered, shaking his head.

"Wait, but that's... *good*, no? Why the glum face?"

"Now I feel even shittier for not having anything nice to give him," confessed Jon.

They both stared at the silly little tree for a moment, not speaking. Then Jon frowned.

"Were we doing something later?" he asked.

"Not that I know of."

"What did Maya mean by, 'See you tonight'?"

"Who knows," replied Kat with a shrug. She looked over her shoulder at the door through which Maya had passed and snagged a bottle of the top-shelf whiskey. "Let's have a little drink and put our heads together and see what we can come up with for ol' Tommy-boy, hm?"

~

Tom looked up as the door opened. It was nearly noon, and he was getting anxious about the surprise for Jon. He'd wanted to return to take another crack at making it look all nice, but Baltsaros had sent him to supervise some of the repairs taking place on the old pirate ship, so he'd spent all morning refitting screws that no longer held and replacing hinges that were nearly rusted through.

"Jonny, my love," he said in greeting and was pleased with Jon's fond grin. He noted that Jon had a little more colour in his face and wondered what he'd been up to.

"Hey," replied Jon, his grey-blue eyes less bloodshot than Tom had seen in a while. "Are you busy?"

Shaking his head, Tom jumped to his feet.

"Not even a bit," he said and smiled wide. "In fact, I been lookin' for ye."

"Oh?" Jon's expression changed slightly, but Tom pressed on, hoping that Jon would keep to the plan he'd concocted in his head.

"Aye... I was wonderin' if ye'd like to take a walk," said the first mate.

"A walk?"

"Aye, a walk. With me."

"Where to?" asked Jon.

"I was thinkin' we'd go take a walk to the palace."

"To the... palace?" Jon's eyes were wide, and he seemed sort of caught off guard. "Why to the palace?"

"I left somethin' there when I came to find ye the other day."

Jon frowned at him, but after a moment his shoulders just sagged.

"Yeah. Ok. Sure."

Though he was a touch worried about Jon's reaction, Tom just grinned like nothing was amiss and motioned towards the door, inviting Jon to lead them out.

They were only just past the edge of town when they encountered Baltsaros walking down the cobbled road.

"Tom, Jon," said the captain with a little head bow. "Where are you off to?"

"To the palace," answered Jon, his voice sounding oddly tense. "Tom left something there."

"He did, did he?" said Baltsaros with a wry twist of his lips. "It's a nice day for a walk. May I join you?"

Tom furrowed his brow. He'd shared his plan to surprise Jon with the captain, but now Baltsaros was playing the innocent.

"If ye like, Da. But didn't ye have that... *thing* ye were supposed to take care of?" he said pointedly.

The captain just shrugged. "I took care of it," he replied. "Shall we?" Baltsaros turned to retrace his steps, not waiting for them to respond.

Jon's face was the picture of sorrow for a moment, and he raked his curls back out of his face, eyeing Tom nervously before following the captain up the hill.

Why in the bloody hells was everyone acting so damn peculiar?

~

Jon glanced to the side, brow furrowed, and watched the captain. Earlier, he'd given Baltsaros the little decorated tree and the bottle of pepper brandy he'd traded the rest of his share of rum for to hide in his old quarters in the palace. When they'd run into the captain coming down the hill a few minutes earlier, Jon had assumed that's where he'd been returning from. However, Baltsaros was acting as if he were none the wiser and had invited himself along to witness Tom's mirth over the silly tree.

Well, at least Tom will enjoy the brandy.

He sighed to himself, wishing he'd thrown out the tree. Maybe the brandy would have been just fine on its own... But there was nothing particularly festive about it—and he'd really been aiming for *festive*.

As they climbed higher towards the elegant palace, Jon had a sudden vision of his mother leaning towards him to tuck a curl behind his ear as he fished around for sweets in his stocking. Smiling sadly, he looked over at Tom, wondering if he had any such memories of his own mother, and noticed again just how nervous Tom looked. It was obvious that the first mate was fretting over the surprise he'd planned. Tom had no doubt set something up with Maya at the *Blossom* for that night—hence Maya's cryptic leave-taking—and Jon had planned on acting surprised... But the way that Tom kept peeking over at him made him wonder what else was going on. He seemed awfully anxious to get to the captain's old rooms.

Had Baltsaros told Tom about the tree and the gift?

Jon shot an accusing look at Baltsaros, but the older man just gave him a smile, his eyes unreadable. What motivation did he have for telling Tom about his plans? Unless, of course, Tom had found out some other way. Maya? Kat?

Tom and Jon climbed the stairs to the second floor, but the captain stayed behind, saying he'd wait for them. When they reached the big wooden door, Tom paused, his expression somewhere between hopeful and worried as he grasped the handle.

"So... Here's the thing: since ye've been so poorly as of late, I thought it a fine idea to do somethin' a little special for ye. To make ye smile. A surprise... but... well..." Tom paused and rubbed the top of his head, looking sheepish. "I might'a made a dog's breakfast of it, lovey. I hope ye don't think it too silly... It's not much..."

Before Jon could speak up, Tom pushed the door open.

The walls of the room beyond were strung with glittering garlands in gold and silver and decorated with sparkling stars; over the window hung a pretty red curtain covered in a pattern of snowflakes that was gathered back with a gold tassel to let the bright sunshine in; and all around the room, sitting on a cheerful green and white rug, the furniture was draped prettily with cloth-of-gold.

However, the most astounding thing in the room was that, up on a short, gilded column in the corner, was his silly, tiny, pathetic tree surrounded by all sorts of packages wrapped in colourful paper. Everything was so beautiful.

Dog's breakfast, my ass.

Trying to hold back the looming tears, he turned to Tom with a huge grin. However, from the look on the first mate's face, it seemed that the decorations were just as surprising to him.

"Wait, this wasn't you?"

"Hells no," breathed Tom. "Bloody fuckin' hells..."

"Happy holidays."

Startled, Jon turned to see the captain leaning against the doorjamb, looking rather pleased with himself. On his head, he had on a strange, pointed red hat; after a moment, when no one had spoken a word, he laughed a tad self-consciously and adjusted the hat.

"I'm supposed to be Father Winter," said Baltsaros, shrugging. He passed between them and sat himself in one of the chairs.

"Da, this was *you*?" asked Tom, his amazement making his voice hoarse.

"Only partially," admitted Baltsaros. "I took what you started with and just added my own touches. I just thought it would be nice to get into the spirit of things and surprise the two of you."

"Well, I'm bloody surprised, Da," said Tom, beaming. He turned to Jon. "He put my shitty decorations to shame, that's for bloody sure!" Understanding dawned on Tom's face and he scowled good-naturedly at Baltsaros. "Maya was bloody in on it. That's why she wouldn'a give me any more trinkets. Yer a sneaky fuckin' bastard..."

Jon couldn't stop smiling.

"Well... The tree was my doing," Jon admitted. To his utter amazement, Tom's eyes got a little glassy, and he gathered Jon into his arms, sniffing hard.

"I bloody love it, Jon," the big man murmured. "*Bloody* love it." Jon shut his eyes and clung onto Tom—Tom, comforting and strong, whose warmth permeated Jon's thin shirt as he held him tight.

Almost regretfully, Jon pulled away a moment later, but there was something important he wanted to do. He sank down to his knees in front of Baltsaros and slowly, hesitantly, rested his cheek against the soft black cotton of his pants. Jon could feel how tentative the captain's touch was when he rested his hand on Jon's back, and he smiled.

"Thank you." Jon meant it from the bottom of his heart. The captain had taken a silly idea and turned it into something filled with wonder. It was at times like these, when Baltsaros did something truly thoughtful, that Jon wondered whether he was so doomed after all. He lifted his head. Baltsaros watched him silently, but there was something, maybe a trick of the light... It seemed as though the captain's eyes were a little wet.

"Shall we open presents?" asked Baltsaros quietly.

Jon's face fell. "I... didn't get you anything," he confessed. He'd been so caught up in making Tom's day special that it hadn't even occurred to him to get something for the captain.

"Aye, me neither." Tom sounded crestfallen, but Baltsaros just smiled his toothy, white grin.

"Why would I need presents when I have the two of you?" asked the captain blithely. The lump in Jon's throat threatened to choke him, but Baltsaros just pointed to the presents, adjusting his hat with the other hand again. "Come on, we don't have all day. I want to see what you think of your gifts... Then we're all going to the *Grog Blossom* for a proper Winter Solstice party."

Jon and Tom exchanged a look, twin smiles on their faces.

~

Baltsaros grinned as Tom opened the little wooden box, the first mate's sandy brows meeting over his nose in confusion. Lying on a bed of black velvet was a device of the captain's own design. During his convalescence earlier that year, waiting for the *Heart* to return to Madierus, he'd had it made special for Tom out of a gold statue from the emperor's palace in Ereme'ia Balor. He'd brought it with them to Sormaheine, intending to use it as a fun divertissement on their trip, but it had fallen to the bottom of the chest, and he'd completely forgotten about it. It was only when he was rummaging through his belongings after the ship had been properly cleaned that he'd found it. Giving it to the first mate as a Corestmas present seemed like the perfect thing to do.

Tom lifted the gold device out of the box and looked up at Baltsaros for an explanation. Jon, wearing the blue silk waistcoat that the captain had traded for on Tom's behalf, peered over the first mate's shoulder, eyes wide.

"What is it?" asked Jon.

"A chastity cage," replied Baltsaros smugly. "Doug made it to my specifications to fit Tom exactly." He held out his hand, and Tom placed the cage on his palm, his blue-green eyes uncertain. Baltsaros showed how one of the four rings was hinged, meant to loop around the base of the testicles to hold the device in place, and then pointed to the round cap. "This goes over the head of your cock."

"And where the bloody hells does *that* go," asked Tom, pointing to the short catheter perforating the cap.

Baltsaros just gave him a grin, and the lines of Tom's face deepened for a moment as he stared back, seeming in shock. For a moment the captain wondered if he had made a poor choice, but when a lusty flush began burning in the young man's suntanned face, he laughed.

"You want to try it on?"

Nodding quickly, Tom began to tug on his belt, but Baltsaros lifted a hand to stop him.

"Not so hasty. I want Jon to open his present first," said the captain, turning to Jon. He pulled a small, flat box out of his vest and held it out to the dark-haired young man. "This is for you."

Jon accepted the gift with a nod and proceeded to open it carefully. However, when he found the box to be empty, his eyes darted to the captain's suspiciously.

"It's... empty," said Jon in a tight voice.

Baltsaros frowned and reached for the present. He made a show of looking inside and then smiled at Jon.

"I'm afraid you're mistaken. I see a few things in here..."

Jon shook his head slowly, his expression wary.

"What are you talking about?"

"Well," said Baltsaros, peering into the package. "Here is my strength to keep you safe, no matter the cost to myself." He tilted the box and pretended to move something aside with a finger. "Here is the understanding that I"—he chuckled softly—"don't always understand you... But see? I've put my willingness to learn right next to it. Here is my sorrow over what happened to you, and the wish that I could make it all better... But then *here* is all the time in the world you need to heal, along with my full patience to wait until you're ready. Here is my desire for you that will never fade, regardless of how long it takes before or even *if* your desire for me returns. Oh... And this is the best one right here. See this?" The captain just smiled at Jon's dazed expression. "This is my complete and utter devotion to both you and Tom and the hope that I still have the chance to prove myself you."

Jon swallowed audibly and lowered his eyes. Baltsaros had a feeling that the stricken young man was on the verge of tears, so he just closed the box up and tucked it into the pocket of Jon's waistcoat. He glanced over at Tom, and the first mate nodded slowly, looking completely stunned.

When Jon finally lifted his eyes, his smile was a touch shy, and Baltsaros knew his silly but meaningful gift was well received. It surprised him just how much that meant to him. He let out a small, relieved sigh.

"Now," Baltsaros said, perhaps a little too loudly in the hush, wanting to lighten the mood. "Shall I get Tom into his cage?"

Jon's grin got a little crooked, and his shoulder came up in a shrug, but when he shifted his gaze to Tom, he gave a simple nod.

CHAPTER 5

CAGED

Tom groaned, trying not to think about anything at all lest he wreck his cock in the confines of the golden cage. It had taken Da a few tries to get it on, since Tom's cock wouldn't behave at first, excited as he was, but when it was finally on and locked shut, it fit like a glove. A constricting, penetrating, frustrating glove.

He rocked forward on hands and knees, breathing heavily as Baltsaros's thick cock opened him up again. Beneath him, the white designs of the rug were darkened with the precum that seeped out of the tube that held his piss-slit wide. Tom grunted as the captain ploughed into him hard, his balls slapping against the base of his trapped cock and causing the little lock to make a quiet metallic chime at the end of every jarring plunge.

Jon caressed the side of his face, and Tom turned to press his lips into the proffered hand, squeezing his eyes shut. If Jon decided that he wanted to take part... Well, Tom didn't know what would happen. He was already dangerously aroused and in some amount of pain.

While he'd gotten both Jon and Baltsaros off the previous day, his own cock had gone untended, and between the repairs on the ship and setting up the decorations, he hadn't had the time to take care of his own needs—*and*, if the captain had his way, he'd be at least a day in the infernal device...

He whimpered as the captain fucked him deep, nuzzling Jon's hand and desperately reciting ship's knots in his head, hoping to ease the throbbing in his cock some. However, after the sound of rustling fabric, Jon turned Tom's head and began to rub the head of his cock on his lips.

"Fuck," Tom muttered and then groaned in mock objection as Jon pushed his length into his mouth. Truth be told, Tom was in heaven. He was already thinking about how he could wear the cage beneath his clothes. How Jon or Baltsaros could punish him by making him wear it until they decided it was time for him to cum. Reward him by taking it off... like his cock was truly no longer his own to command.

Tom let out a little growl around the shaft between his lips, warning his stiffening length to mind him, and sent another slow dribble down to the rug below. Jon held fast to him, fucking his mouth in shallow thrusts, the hint of precum on Tom's tongue. It had been far too long since the three of them had done anything like this.

Jon panted a few breaths and pulled his cock out of Tom's mouth, bending low to kiss him, his tongue desperately seeking contact. With one hand around the back of Tom's neck, the kiss slowly gentled until Jon drew back to fondle himself and watch the first mate.

Tom winced, his length trapped in the cruel rings, but he was happy, and he knew Jon could see it. Then Jon's expression grew heated and he rose up on his knees.

"I want Tom on his back," he said, and Baltsaros pulled his cock out of Tom's ass and gave him a good slap across one cheek.

"You heard Jon. Get on your back."

Quickly, Tom turned over, laying in the mess he'd leaked all over the carpet, and Jon lowered himself down on top of him, claiming his mouth in a fever as he rutted against him. Tom clung onto Jon, drowning equally in bliss and pain. Jon's hard length slid against his belly and then pushed at his trapped cock, causing Tom to wince and shiver. Then Jon rose up, spat into his hand, sank his cock into Tom with a groan, and began fucking him in a fury. However, after only a handful of thrusts, Jon faltered and Tom saw Baltsaros's hand on Jon's shoulder. He knew what the captain wanted to do, and he prayed that Baltsaros had the prudence to remember his promise.

Jon's dark brows met over his nose, his distress marked out in a deep V. But when the young man shook his head, it was as if to himself, and his words came out sounding choked but without scorn.

"What are you waiting for?"

Tom thought he heard the captain laugh, and Jon's gaze locked with Tom's, wide and scared. Tom curled his arms around Jon and kissed him again, trying to soothe away the fear as best as he could, and Jon responded with ardent passion.

A moment later, Jon cried out, a sound that was both pained and relieved, and Tom let out his own moan of encouragement, kissing Jon deep as Baltsaros began fucking him from behind, driving Jon's cock into Tom.

Face flushed and chest heaving, Jon drew back and smiled down at Tom.

"Just like old times?"

Tom grimaced. "Not quite," he said in a hoarse voice, only too aware that he was perilously close to losing his control and genuinely worried what would happen if he managed to actually cum while caged.

When Jon began to whimper in time to the captain's thrusts, Tom knew he was getting close—only a few more quick plunges and Jon's full-throated groan caused Tom to struggle and moan through his own weak proxy of orgasm, his pulsing cock sending out a gush of thick seed, but nowhere near the unfettered release he craved.

With a gasp, Baltsaros began fucking Jon harder, and he finally shuddered to a stop, panting through the throes of his climax.

The three of them relocated to the big bed in the other room, and Tom sprawled out comfortably against the pillows, puffing at the sweet cheroot that Jon had picked out for him. Next to him, Baltsaros and Jon spoke quietly, and though the topic was only about their plan to sail east through the green seas come spring, their conversation seemed to hold deeper meaning.

Or maybe it was all in Tom's head. He was cock-sore, dazed, and nowhere near sated, and all that he cared about was that the three of them were together.

After a moment he scowled, scratching his chest.

"Aye... Da, were ye hopin' to take all the credit for yerself, pilferin' our gifts the way ye did?" rumbled Tom.

The captain's smile flashed white.

"No. I just didn't want to see you two spending the last of your rum is all," admitted Baltsaros. "Not when I could get the gifts for you more cheaply... I'm owed quite a few favours." He'd done them one better, in fact, seeing as there was a full cask of rum sitting untapped in the other room, more than covering what they had ended up spending on gifts.

"Hey, speaking of rum, shouldn't we be heading to the *Blossom* soon?" asked Jon. He sat up and stretched, his black curls mussed and eyes sleepy.

Baltsaros shrugged.

"There's no rush. We have all the time in the world."

"We do, don't we?" replied Jon, tilting his head to appraise the captain. He smiled.

"That we do," murmured Baltsaros with a nod.

Tom cleared his throat and the two of them turned to him.

"Aye, we might have all the time in the bloody world, but if ye don't take this contraption off my todger sooner than later, ye might get to see me cry." Tom shifted painfully. "Jus' sayin'."

The captain patted his bare thighs as if searching for something.

"I seem to have misplaced the key," he said, his dark eyes amused.

Tom scowled and let a plume of smoke drift from his nose.

"That ain't funny... It's Li'l Tom's first time in his golden gibbet. Give the poor hurtin' thing a bloody break!"

"Little Tom?"

Jon began to laugh—an honest to goodness, real belly laugh, and that, thought Tom, was the best damn present of them all.

BOOKS BY BEY DECKARD

FOR AN UP-TO-DATE LIST OF TITLES, VISIT:

https://beydeckard.com/blog/buy-my-books/

MAX, THE SERIES

Max

Max, the Sequel

BAAL'S HEART SERIES

Caged: Love and Treachery on the High Seas

Sacrificed: Heart Beyond the Spires

Fated: Blood and Redemption

Careened: Winter Solstice in Madierus

F.I.S.T.S

Sarge

Murphy

F.I.S.T.S. Handbook For Individual Survival in Hostile Environments

THE ACTOR'S CIRCLE

The Complications of T

The Last Nights of The Frangipani Hotel

THE STONEWATCHERS

Kestrel's Talon

STANDALONE BOOKS

Better the Devil You Know

Exposed

Beauty and His Beast

The Blacksmith's Apprentice

SHORT STORIES

Don't Touch Me (UnCommon Bodies Anthology)

Rakka Surprise (UnCommon Lands Anthology)

About the Author

Artist, Writer, Dog Lover

Bey Deckard is the author of a number of novels including the *Baal's Heart books, Max, Beauty and His Beast,* and *Better the Devil You Know.*

Bey lives in Montréal, Canada where he spends most of his time writing, doing graphic work, painting portraits, speaking French, cooking tasty vegetarian eats, or watching more movies than is good for him. If you're the curious type, www.beydeckard.com is where you'll find art and free stories by Bey as well as information on his published works.

bey.deckard@gmail.com
Look for Deckard's Diablerie on Facebook

facebook.com/authorbeydeckard
twitter.com/BeyDeckard
instagram.com/beydeckard
goodreads.com/beydeckard
bookbub.com/authors/bey-deckard
pettingzoo.co/@Beybey